THE GOLDEN TREASURY

F. T. PALGRAVE

英诗金库

（修订版）

[英] F.T.帕尔格雷夫　原编
曹明伦　罗义蕴　陈朴　编注

-下-

卷五

1850—1910

289. 'I STROVE WITH NONE'

I strove with none, for none was worth my strife;
　Nature I loved and, next to Nature, Art;
I warmed both hands before the fire of life;
　It sinks, and I am ready to depart.

　　　　　　　　　　　　W. S. LANDOR.

289. "我从不与人斗"

兰多

我从不与人斗,因没啥值得我争斗;
我爱过自然,此外还爱过艺术;
我曾依偎生命之火,烘暖过这双手;
如今火快熄灭,我也准备离去。

曹明伦 译

编注 沃尔特·萨维奇·兰多(Walter Savage Landor,1775—1864),英国诗人及散文家,写有大量抒情诗、剧本和英雄史诗,散文作品有《想象的对话》(*Imaginary Conversations*,1824—1829)和《老树末果》(*The Last Fruit off an Old Tree*,1853)等。诗人早年个性张扬,爱挑战权威,为此先后从拉格比公学和牛津大学辍学;后命途多舛,长期流亡国外,七十五岁生日时写下这首四行诗。此诗最初见于《老树末果》一书,故此诗通常被命名为《哲人暮语》(Dying Speech of an Old Philosopher)。《英诗金库》编者评注这首诗时说:"也许像众多生性好斗者一样,兰多也认为自己是温和的化身。"

290. ROSE AYLMER

Ah what avails the sceptred race!
Ah what the form divine①!
What every virtue, every grace!
Rose Aylmer, all were thine.
Rose Aylmer, whom these wakeful eyes
　May weep, but never see,
A night of memories and of sighs②
　I consecrate to thee.

W. S. LANDOR.

---

① *the sceptred race ... the form divine*: *i. e.* neither kings nor gods have a monopoly of goodness or beauty.
② *memories*: 'sorrows.'

290. 罗斯·艾尔默[①]

兰多

啊,帝王有什么用!
　啊,神仙有啥了不起!
所有美德,所有魅力算什么!
　罗斯·艾尔默,这一切都属于你。
罗斯·艾尔默,这不眠的双眼　　　　　　　　5
　会哭泣,却再也见不到你,
一个充满回忆和叹息的夜
　我把它献给你。

姚奔　译

[①] 罗斯·艾尔默为诗人在威尔士结识的朋友。——译者

291. THE MAID'S LAMENT

I loved him not; and yet now he is gone
    I feel I am alone.
I checked him while he spoke; yet could he speak,
    Alas! I would not check.
For reasons not to love him once I sought,
    And wearied all my thought
To vex myself and him: I now would give
    My love, could he but live
Who lately lived for me, and, when he found
    'Twas vain, in holy ground
He hid his face amid the shades of death.
    I waste for him my breath
Who wasted his for me; but mine returns,
    And this lorn bosom burns[①]
With stifling heat, heaving it up in sleep,
    And waking me to weep
Tears that had melted his soft heart: for years
    Wept he as bitter tears.
Merciful God! such was his latest prayer,
    These may she never share!
Quieter is his breath, his breast more cold,
    Than daisies in the mould,

---

① *lorn*: 'deserted.' It is the past participle of the verb *leese* (= lose), which was in use till the end of the 17th century.

291. 一个少女的悲哀

兰多

我不爱他;可他现在离开我
　　我却感到寂寞。
他一讲话我就打岔;他要再能讲话,
　　哎呀,我决不会再堵他嘴巴。
我曾寻找不爱他的理由,
　　而我想得心烦意乱
自寻烦恼也折磨了他,现在我愿
　　献出我的爱情,只要他能再生。
他不久前还为我而活着,而当他发现
　　这原是一场空,在神圣的地下
死亡的阴影藏着他的面容。
　　我为他空费唇舌
他为我白把话说,而我总是顶撞他,
　　这颗被抛弃的心燃烧着
心头郁闷似火,在睡眠中内心犹在翻腾
　　我醒悟过来不禁泪如泉涌
泪水融化了他温柔的心,几年来
　　他也同样流下伤心的眼泪。
天哪!这就是他最后的祷告,
　　愿她永不分担这些烦恼!
他的呼吸寂静,他的胸口冰冷
　　胜似坟场上的雏菊。

  Where children spell, athwart the churchyard gate①,
   His name and life's brief date.
25   Pray for him, gentle souls, whoe'er you be,
   And, O, pray too for me!

            W. S. LANDOR.

---

① *athwart*: 'across,' *i.e.* looking over the gate.

孩子们在教堂墓地的门口张望,
　　拼读着他的名字和短暂的一生。
好心的人哪,为他祈祷吧,不管你们是谁,   *25*
　　啊,也请为我祈祷!

姚　奔　译

292. TO ROBERT BROWNING

There is delight in singing, tho' none hear
Beside the singer: and there is delight
In praising, tho' the praiser sit alone
And see the praised far off him, far above.
Shakespeare is not our poet, but the world's,
Therefore on him no speech! and brief for thee,
Browning! Since Chaucer was alive and hale,
No man hath walked along our roads with step
So active, so inquiring eye, or tongue
So varied in discourse. But warmer climes
Give brighter plumage, stronger wing: the breeze
Of Alpine heights thou playest with, borne on
Beyond Sorrento and Amalfi, where
The Siren waits thee, singing song for song.

W. S. LANDOR.

292. 致罗伯特·布朗宁①

兰多

以歌唱为乐,虽然没有人
在歌手身旁倾听;以赞美为乐
虽然赞美者孤独一人
望着被赞美的人离他很远,远在天上。
莎士比亚不属于我们,而是世界的诗人,　　　　　　5
所以对他无须饶舌!而对你却要评说,
布朗宁!自健旺而活力充沛的乔叟之后②
没人以如此矫健的步伐,如此探索的目光,
或如此丰富多彩的言谈,前进在我们的道路上。
但越是温暖的地方,羽毛长得越艳丽③,　　　　　10
翅膀越坚强;你戏耍的阿尔卑斯高峰的微风
越过索伦托和阿马尔菲
向远方劲吹,在那里
塞壬等待着你,唱着一支又一支歌④。

姚奔　译

---

① 关于罗伯特·布朗宁,参见第338首编注。诗人与布朗宁夫妇过从甚密,写此诗时,同住佛罗伦萨。——编注者
② 人们常把叙事诗作者与乔叟(1340?—1400)相比,乔叟确为叙事诗创作的泰斗,但布朗宁的诗隐晦,常用粗字,亦有深刻的心理分析,所以布诗当时是独树一帜,或者诗人这里专就布朗宁的素体叙事诗而言,说他可以和乔叟相比的,甚至两者兼而有之。——译者
③ 布朗宁中年时在意大利定居,直到一八一六年布朗宁夫人逝世后才返回英国。——译者
④ 索伦托和阿马尔菲是意大利的两个城市,前者位于那不勒斯湾,后者在那不勒斯湾下游的萨勒诺湾。塞壬,见第86首注,传说塞壬所住的卡普里岛,与上述西城相距甚近。——编注者

293. 'PROUD WORD YOU NEVER SPOKE'

Proud word you never spoke, but you will speak
   Four not exempt from pride some future day.
Resting on one white hand a warm wet cheek
   Over my open volume you will say,
     'This man loved *me*!' then rise and trip away.

W. S. LANDOR.

293. "你从不说骄傲的话"

兰多

你从不说骄傲的话,但有朝一日,
 你将会说出四个有骄傲意味的字眼。
一只皙白的手托着温暖而湿润的面颊,
 审视着我的一本打开的书,你将会说,
 "此人爱**我**!"于是你立起来轻快地离去。 *5*

姚奔 译

294. 'WELL I REMEMBER HOW YOU SMILED'

    Well I remember how you smiled
        To see me write your name upon
    The soft sea-sand ... '*O! what a child!*
        You think you're writing upon stone!'
    I have since written what no tide
        Shall ever wash away, what men
    Unborn shall read o'er ocean wide
        And find Ianthe's name again.

                                  W. S. LANDOR.

294. "我清楚记得你怎样面带微笑"

兰多

我清楚记得你怎样面带微笑
　　望着我在松软的海滩上
写下你的名字……"啊,真是个孩子!
　　你以为你是把字写在石头上!"
从那以后我曾写下海潮
　　冲洗不掉的字,未来的人们
将在广阔的海洋上读到它的字
　　并将重新发现伊安西的名字①。

姚奔　译

---

① 伊安西是一位姑娘的名字,兰多为她写过不少诗。——编注者

295. TO A WATERFOWL

    Whither, midst falling dew,
While glow the heavens with the last steps of day,
Far through their rosy depths, dost thou pursue
    Thy solitary way?

    Vainly the fowler's eye
Might mark thy distant flight to do thee wrong,
As, darkly seen against the crimson sky①,
    Thy figure floats along.

    Seek'st thou the plashy brink②
Of weedy lake, or marge of river wide,
Or where the rocking billows rise and sink
    On the chafed ocean side?

    There is a Power whose care
Teaches thy way along that pathless coast, —
The desert and illimitable air③, —
    Lone wandering, but not lost.

    All day thy wings have fanned,
At that far height, the cold thin atmosphere;

---

① *seen against*: in earlier editions 'painted on.'
② *plashy*: 'swampy,' derived from *plash*, 'a pool' or 'puddle,' a word found as late as Tennyson.
③ *desert*: an adjective, 'deserted,' 'lonely.'

295. 致水鸟

布莱恩特

在露水下降中
当天空随着白昼最后的脚步闪耀着红光,
穿过玫瑰色深邃的天空,你向远方何处
  寻找你寂寞的路?

  打鸟猎人的目光 5
会空怀恶意,追寻你遥远的行踪,
望红色天空一片朦胧
  当你的身影向前飘动。

  你是寻找多沼泽的湖畔
还是水面宽阔的河边, 10
或是汹涌起伏的巨浪,
  拍打冲击的海岸?

  一个神明将你保护
为你指引道路,沿着没有路径的海岸——
寂寞而又寥廓无边的天空—— 15
  孤独地飘泊却不迷途。

  你整天展翅飞翔,
在遥远的高空,寒冷稀薄的大气里;

Yet stoop not, weary, to the welcome land,
    Though the dark night is near.

And soon that toil shall end;
Soon shalt thou find a summer home and rest,
And scream among thy fellows; reeds shall bend,
    Soon, o'er thy sheltered nest.

Thou'rt gone, the abyss of heaven
Hath swallowed up thy form; yet on my heart
Deeply hath sunk the lesson thou hast given,
    And shall not soon depart.

He who, from zone to zone,
Guides through the boundless sky thy certain flight,
In the long way that I must tread alone,
    Will lead my steps aright.

W. C. BRYANT.

你疲倦了也不俯身飞向可喜的大地
　　　　纵然黑夜就在身旁。　　　　　　　　　　　20

　　辛苦的跋涉即将结束,
　　很快就将找到夏天的家园和休憩场所;
　　在同伴中你可啁啾鸣唱;芦苇即将躬身
　　　　守望着你隐蔽的鸟窝。

　　你已飞去了,无边的苍穹　　　　　　　　　25
　　吞噬了你的身影,然而在我心上
　　却深深地铭刻下你给我的教训,
　　　　而且不会很快消亡。

　　他,从一个地带到一个地带①
　　穿过无边的天空引导你飞行,　　　　　　　30
　　在漫长的道路上我必须孤独地跋涉
　　　　他将正确地指引我走上征程。

姚　奔　译

编注　威廉·卡伦·布莱恩特(William Cullen Bryant, 1794—1878),美国诗人及新闻记者,十九世纪美国浪漫主义诗歌的创始人。他的第一首长诗《死亡的冥想》是当时美国诗歌的最好作品。《致水鸟》描写地平线上一只孤零零的鸟,它使诗人感到万物都受神明保护,而神明的力量也会指引他的每一步伐。布莱恩特善写大自然,认为自然美使人向善。人们常把他与华兹华斯相比。

---

① "他"指前文提到的神明。——编注者

296. RONDEAU

    Jenny kissed me when we met,
    Jumping from the chair she sat in;
    Time, you thief, who love to get
        Sweets into your list, put that in①!
5   Say I'm weary, say I'm sad,
    Say that health and wealth have missed me,
    Say I'm growing old, but add,
        Jenny kiss'd me.

                          J. H. LEIGH HUNT.

---

① *to get Sweets into your list*: 'to record delights.' For Time, the Obliterator, to act as Recorder is a novel idea.

296. 珍妮吻了我

亨特

我们见面时珍妮吻了我,
　　她跳出了坐椅迎过来；
时间呵,你这窃贼就爱做
　　美事儿的记录,也记下那事来!
说我疲倦,说我沉郁,
　　说健康和财富漏掉了我,
说我在衰老,但要加一句:
　　珍妮吻了我。

鲍屡平　译

编注　詹姆斯·亨利·李·亨特(James Henry Leigh Hunt,1784—1859),十九世纪英国批评家和诗人,政治上较为激进,曾因著文讽刺未来的国王乔治四世坐牢二年。写有《里米尼的故事》等叙事长诗,抒情短诗《阿布·本·阿德罕姆》和《珍妮吻了我》流传也很广。

297. THE WAR SONG OF DINAS VAWR

The mountain sheep are sweeter,
  But the valley sheep are fatter;
We therefore deemed it meeter
  To carry off the latter.
We made an expedition;
  We met a host, and quelled it;
We forced a strong position,
  And killed the men who held it.

On Dyfed's richest valley,
  Where herds of kine were browsing,
We made a mighty sally
  To furnish our carousing.
Fierce warriors rushed to meet us;
  We met them, and o'erthrew them:
They struggled hard to beat us;
  But we conquered them, and slew them.

As we drove our prize at leisure,
  The king marched forth to catch us:
His rage surpassed all measure,
  But his people could not match us.
He fled to his hall-pillars;
  And, ere our force we led off,

297. 戴纳斯·弗尔的战歌

皮科克

山坡上的羊儿多柔顺,
　但山谷中的羊更肥壮;
因此我们觉得更好些——
　还是抢掉山谷中的羊。
我们作了一次远征; 　　　　　　　　　　　　　　*5*
　我们遇到了主人,把他杀死;
我们还干掉了坚守阵地的人,
　强攻下那个牢固的阵地。

在狄弗特最肥沃的峡谷里①,
　一群奶牛正吃着草儿青青, 　　　　　　　　*10*
为了我们在宴席上能酣畅痛饮,
　我们发动了一场猛烈的攻势。
凶猛的战士冲下来对付我们;
　我们迎上前去,把他们打翻;
他们拼命厮杀,要打垮我们; 　　　　　　　　*15*
　但我们赢了,送他们归了西天。

当我们悠闲地赶着战利品走远,
　国王率着人马,追上来抓我们;
他真是暴跳如雷,怒气冲天,
　但他的士兵可对付不了我们。 　　　　　　*20*
于是国王逃到了大厅柱子间;
　我们的人马还没有离开之前,

---

① 英国人称西南威尔士为狄弗特。——译者

>   Some sacked his house and cellars,
>   While others cut his head off.
>
> We there, in strife bewildering,
>   Spilt blood enough to swim in;
> We orphaned many children,
>   And widowed many women.
> The eagles and the ravens
>   We glutted with our foemen;
> The heroes and the cravens,
>   The spearmen and the bowmen.
>
> We brought away from battle,
>   And much their land bemoaned them,
> Two thousand head of cattle,
>   And the head of him who owned them:
> Ednyfed, King of Dyfed,
>   His head was borne before us;
> His wine and beasts supplied our feasts,
>   And his overthrow, our chorus.

T. L. PEACOCK.

一些人去把他的房子和地窖洗劫干净,
　　另一些人去把他的脑袋砍下。

在那里,我们杀得日月无光, 25
　　洒下的血呵,简直可以变成游泳池塘:
我们使许多孩子失去了爹娘,
　　我们使许多女人失去了男人。
我们让那些老鸦和秃鹰
　　啄食我们敌人的尸体—— 30
那些英雄们和懦夫们,
　　那些长矛手和弓箭手——啄得多肥。

他们的土地上一片啜泣,
　　我们一仗打下来,夺走了
足足有两千头牛羊, 35
　　还有那个拥有这些牛羊的头颅:
爱德尼弗德,狄弗特的国王①,
　　他的头挂在我们的前方,
他的美酒和牲口成了我们的酒席,
　　他的倒台呵,成了我们的合唱。 40

裘小龙　译

编注　托马斯·洛夫·皮科克(Thomas Love Peacock, 1785—1866),英国诗人兼小说家,其好诗大都出现在他的小说里。本诗即出自小说《爱尔芬的恶运》(*The Misfortunes of Elphin*, 1829)第六章。行吟诗人泰利辛在去亚瑟王宫廷的路上,停留在戴纳斯·弗尔的城堡里,所谓"了不起的英雄们"——一群强盗——款待了他,并唱了这支歌。

---

① 诗人杜撰的一个国王名。——译者

298. THREE MEN Of GOTHAM

Seamen three! What men be ye?
   Gotham's three wise men we be.
Whither in your bowl so free?
   To rake the moon from out the sea.
The bowl goes trim. The moon doth shine.
And our ballast is old wine.
And your ballast is old wine.

Who art thou, so fast adrift①?
   I am he they call Old Care.
Here on board we will thee lift.
   No: I may not enter there.
Wherefore so? 'Tis Jove's decree,
In a bowl Care may not be.
In a bowl Care may not be.

Fear ye not the waves that roll?
   No: in charmèd bowl we swim.
What the charm that floats the bowl?
   Water may not pass the brim.
The bowl goes trim. The moon doth shine.
And our ballast is old wine.
And your ballast is old wine.

T. L. PEACOCK.

---

① *so fast adrift*: *i.e.* being carried swiftly out to sea by the current.

298. 戈瑟姆的三个人

皮科克

三个水手！你们是什么人？
  我们是戈瑟姆的三个聪明人。
这样自由地乘着你们的大酒杯去哪里？
  去把那轮月亮从远远的海上捞起①。
酒杯漂漂亮亮。明月闪闪发光。   5
我们的压舱物是陈年佳酿。
你们的压舱物是陈年佳酿。

你是谁，在海面上这样飞快地飘？
  我是他们称为"古老的忧愁"的那个人。
在这酒杯里，我们要把你举得高高。   10
  不，这里我可不能随便踏进。
为什么这样？那是朱庇特的法律②，
在酒杯里"忧愁"没有容身之地。
在酒杯里"忧愁"没有容身之地。

难道你们不怕那翻腾的波浪？   15
  不，我们在充满魔力的杯中游得欢。
什么样的魔力使酒杯飘向远方？
  滔滔的海水可不会溢过杯边。
酒杯稳稳当当。明月闪闪发光，
我们的压舱物是陈年佳酿。   20
你们的压舱物是陈年佳酿。

裘小龙 译

---

① "捞月亮的人"，在英语中意即"笨蛋"。——译者
② 罗马神话中的主神名。——译者

编注 此诗根据一个古老的民间传说而写。戈瑟姆为英国诺丁汉郡南六英里的一个村子,村民以单纯出名。据说在约翰王的年代,每当国王传令官到此,村民们为不使君王来访,总是佯装做着一些令人发笑的蠢事,因此传下一首无出处的童谣:"戈瑟姆的三个聪明人/乘坐一只大酒杯出海;/要是那只酒杯再结实一些/我的歌儿也许会更长一些。"本诗选自皮科克《噩梦般的修道院》(*Nightmare Abbey*,1818)第六章,原诗无标题。

299. THE GRAVE OF LOVE

I dug, beneath the cypress shade,
    What well might seem an elfin's grave;
And every pledge in earth I laid①,
    That erst thy false affection gave.

I pressed them down the sod beneath;
    I placed one mossy stone above;
And twined the rose's fading wreath
    Around the sepulchre of love.

Frail as thy love, the flowers were dead,
    Ere yet the evening sun was set;
But years shall see the cypress spread,
    Immutable as my regret.

                        T. L. PEACOCK.

---

① *pledge*: 'gift made as a proof of affection.'

299. 爱情之墓

皮科克

在松柏的青影之下，我挖掘，
　　洞穴好似幽灵的坟冢；
我把每一个誓言埋进土里，
　　那是往昔你给我的虚幻的温情。

我把它们拍打在草皮下面，　　　　　　　　　　5
　　压块长着苔藓的石子；
捆扎玫瑰败落的花圈，
　　环绕着爱的墓地。

你的爱呀好脆弱，花也凋谢，
　　而夕阳尚未退去；　　　　　　　　　　　　10
岁月会看见松枝飘零，
　　如同我不变的叹息。

陈朴　译

编注　此诗原无标题，现标题为《金库》原编者所加。

300. A JACOBITE'S EPITAPH

To my true king I offered free from stain
Courage and faith; vain faith, and courage vain.
For him I threw lands, honours, wealth, away,
And one dear hope, that was more prized than they[①].
For him I languished in a foreign clime,
Grey-haired with sorrow in my manhood's prime;
Heard on Lavernia Scargill's whispering trees,
And pined by Arno for my lovelier Tees;
Beheld each night my home in fevered sleep,
Each morning started from the dream to weep;
Till God, who saw me tried too sorely, gave
The resting-place I asked, an early grave.
O thou, whom chance leads to this nameless stone,
From that proud country which was once mine own,
By those white cliffs I never more must see,
By that dear language which I spake like thee,
Forget all feuds, and shed one English tear
O'er English dust. A broken heart lies here.

LORD MACAULAY.

---

① *one dear hope*: presumably that of winning his mistress.

300. 杰克拜特的墓志铭①

麦考莱

为我真正的国王,我献出自己无瑕的
勇气和信念;然而信念和勇气何益?
为了国王,我抛弃名誉、财富,背井离乡,
丢掉了比这更多价值的真诚信念。
为了国王,我忍受着异国的陌生气候, 5
刚刚步入人生盛年便愁白了头。
在拉威涅尔山脊,我听见司各杰村庄飒飒作响的树叶②,
在亚诺河畔,我思念故乡愈发可爱的梯河流溢③;
酣睡时,我每夜看见我们的家园,
清晨,从梦中醒来我仍然热泪涟涟。 10
终于到了某天,上帝见我日子难过,
给我一个向往的安息之所,一座早夭之墓。
呵,你,命运将你引到这块无名的石碑,
离开了也曾属于自己的骄傲的国土,
永远不会再见那些白色的断崖, 15
永远听不着我和你亲切的谈吐,
忘却所有的恩怨,淌尽英国之泪呀,
落入英国的尘埃,一颗破碎之心在此安眠。

陈朴 译

---

① 杰克拜特,英王詹姆斯二世(1685年被迫退位)的拥护者,一个狂热的保皇党人,英王垮台后被迫流亡国外,客死异乡。诗人作为一个坚定的辉格党人(维新党人),满怀同情地写诗叹息,悲哀杰克拜特所忠于的是一个不值得追随的偶像。——译者
② 拉威涅尔(Lavernia),从意大利台伯高地延伸的亚平宁山脉。司各杰(Scargill),英国约克郡毗邻布鲁涅尔的一个小村庄,过五六英里地便为梯河。——译者
③ 亚诺河(Arno),在意大利中部。——译者

编注 托马斯·巴宾顿·麦考莱（Thomas Babington Macaulay，1800—1859），英国著名的历史学家、政论家与诗人，著有《英国史》（*History of England*）及《古罗马述事诗》（*Lays of Ancient Rome*）等，是描写风景的大师，诗风活泼有力。

301. THE BATTLE OF NASEBY

By Obadiah Bind-their-kings-in-chains-and-their-nobles-with-links-of-iron, serjeant in Ireton's regiment

Oh! wherefore come ye forth, in triumph from the North,
    With your hands, and your feet, and your raiment all red?
And wherefore doth your rout send forth a joyous shout[①]?
    And whence be the grapes of the wine-press which ye tread[②]?

5   Oh, evil was the root, and bitter was the fruit,
    And crimson was the juice of the vintage that we trod;
For we trampled on the throng of the haughty and the strong,
    Who sate in the high places, and slew the saints of God.

It was about the noon of a glorious day of June,
10   That we saw their banners dance and their cuirasses shine,
And the Man of Blood was there, with his long essenced hair,
    And Astley, and Sir Marmaduke, and Rupert of the Rhine.

---

① *rout*: 'band' as in No. 66, l. 61.
② *the wine-press*: a Hebrew metaphor which here amounts to 'Who are the men over whom you have triumphed?'

301. 纳什比之战①

麦考莱

爱尔登军团的中士奥伯迪,用铁链捆绑他们的国王和贵族

呵!你为什么前来,从北方凯旋而归,
　　红手套,红马靴,一身红装?
为什么你的伙伴发出一阵欢呼?
　　你们榨酒机的葡萄从何来②?

呵,罪恶是根,苦难是果,　　　　　　　　　　　　　　　　5
　　那腥红的是我们踩出的葡萄汁;
我们踏碎了傲慢而强大的敌兵,
　　他们居高而坐,谋杀过上帝的选民③。

那是六月里一个灿烂的正午,
　　我们看见他们的军旗起舞,　　　　　　　　　　　　　10
胸甲耀眼杀人成性的刽子手,披着长长的香发④
　　还有阿斯特利、马默杜克爵士和莱茵的鲁珀特⑤。

---

① 此诗写的是一六四五年六月十四日英国内战中的一场关键性战斗——纳什比（英格兰南部汉普敦郡）之战。此战以克伦威尔的军队得胜结束。第一节是一个英格兰的清教徒向胜利后的军队发问,以后为军士的回答。——译者
② 榨酒机本为希伯来比喻,指胜利的牺牲品,此处意为你们打败了什么人。——译者
③ 查理一世曾残杀过清教徒。——译者
④ 此处指查理一世,他用武力胁迫国会。当时流行的硬币与画像上,他披着长发。——译者
⑤ 阿斯特利（Sir Jacob Astley）当时领导皇家军队；马默杜克爵士（Sir Marmaduke）指挥骑兵左翼,正对克伦威尔铁甲军,在首次冲锋中便逃跑;鲁珀特（Rupert）是查理之姐伊丽莎的大儿子,此人是一个冲劲十足的骑兵统帅,纳什比之战时他领导皇家军队右翼。——译者

Like a servant of the Lord, with his Bible and his sword,
    The General rode along us to form us to the fight,
When a murmuring sound broke out, and swell'd into a shout,
    Among the godless horsemen upon the tyrant's right.

And hark! like the roar of the billows on the shore,
    The cry of battle rises along their charging line!
For God! for the Cause! for the Church! for the Laws!
    For Charles King of England, and Rupert of the Rhine!

The furious German comes, with his clarions and his drums,
    His bravoes of Alsatia, and pages of Whitehall;
They are bursting on our flanks. Grasp your pikes, close your ranks;
    For Rupert never comes but to conquer or to fall.

They are here! They rush on! We are broken! We are gone!
    Our left is borne before them like stubble on the blast.
O Lord, put forth thy might! O Lord, defend the right!
    Stand back to back, in God's name, and fight it to the last.

Stout Skippon hath a wound; the centre hath given ground;
    Hark! hark! — What means the trampling of horsemen on our rear?
Whose banner do I see, boys? 'Tis he, thank God! 'tis he, boys.
    Bear up another minute; brave Oliver is here.

就像上帝的臣仆,带着他的《圣经》和宝剑
　　总司令横马指挥我们出战①
在暴君的右侧一群邪恶的骑兵爆发出　　　　　　　　　　　15
　　一声低怨,即刻变成高声的呼喊。

呀! 如波涛拍击海岸的咆哮
　　厮杀的吼声震撼冲锋战线!
为了上帝! 为了事业! 为了教堂! 为了法律!
　　为了英王查理,还有莱茵的鲁珀特!　　　　　　　　20

疯狂的德国人来了,带着号角和战鼓,
　　阿尔萨蒂尔的亡命徒,白厅的皇家骑士②
他们突破了我们的侧翼,拿起枪集中你们的队伍;
　　因为鲁珀特为征服或死亡而出战。

他们来了,蜂拥而上! 我们的阵地被攻破! 我们开始溃散!　25
　　败兵倒在他们面前如爆炸后的残物。
哦! 上帝,显出你的威力! 呵,上帝,捍卫正义!
　　顶住吧,回去,以上帝的名义,战斗到最后一卒!

有人呼叫斯基庞负伤;中央阵地被敌人占领③:
　　听! 听! 为什么我们的后方响起了骑兵的声音?　　　30
我看见了谁的军旗,孩子们,是他,感谢上帝! 是他,孩子们。
　　再坚持片刻:勇敢的奥立弗已经来临④。

---

① 总司令指费尔克斯(Sir Thomas Fairfax, 1612—1671),战后五个月他被任命为总司令,任职至一六五〇年。——译者
② 阿尔萨蒂尔为伦敦东部一寺院,以白衣修士著名,该院具有收容犯罪等特权,常培育出亡命徒、流氓等。白厅是亨利八世的皇宫。——译者
③ 斯基庞(Philip Skippon),当时统率步兵。——译者
④ 奥立弗即克伦威尔,他在这次战斗中保留了一定的突击力量,关键时刻猛扑保皇军中央阵地。——译者

  Their heads all stooping low, their points all in a row,
    Like a whirlwind on the trees, like a deluge on the dykes,
35 Our cuirassiers have burst on the ranks of the Accurst,
    And at a shock have scattered the forest of his pikes.

  Fast, fast, the gallants ride, in some safe nook to hide
    Their coward heads, predestined to rot on Temple Bar:
  And he — he turns, he flies: — shame on those cruel eyes
40   That bore to look on torture, and dare not look on war.

  Ho! comrades, scour the plain; and, ere ye strip the slain,
    First give another stab to make your search secure,
  Then shake from sleeves and pockets their broad- pieces and lockets,
    The tokens of the wanton, the plunder of the poor.

45 Fools! your doublets shone with gold, and your hearts were gay and bold,
    When you kissed your lily hands to your lemans to-day[①];
  And to-morrow shall the fox, from her chambers in the rocks,
    Lead forth her tawny cubs to howl above the prey.

  Where be your tongues that late mocked at heaven and hell and fate,
50   And the fingers that once were so busy with your blades,
  Your perfum'd satin clothes, your catches and your oaths[②],
    Your stage-plays and your sonnets, your diamonds and your spades?

  Down, down, for ever down with the mitre and the crown,

---

① *lemans*: 'mistresses.'
② *catches*: see note to No. 282, l. 11.

他们低着头,瞄准点成一线,
　　如旋风刮树,似洪水决堤,
我们身着胸甲的勇士,突然扑向那些可憎的敌兵,　　　　　35
　　他们惊慌失措,长枪散落在密林。

快呵,快,勇士们策马狂奔,在那些安全的角落
　　躲藏着懦夫,他们的头颅注定在巴庙腐烂①。
而他转身落荒而逃——冷酷的眼中露出愧色,
　　他厌怕亲睹折磨,他不敢正视战争②。　　　　　　　　40

嗬,战友们,清扫战场,搬走死者,
　　为防万一,再补上一刀,
抖出袖里袋里的银钱和贴身宝盆③,
　　那是蛮横者的标志,取自穷人的掠夺。

傻瓜们! 今日你们吻着情人雪白的手臂,　　　　　　　45
　　你们盔甲金光闪闪,人人踌躇满志喜气洋洋;
明朝狐狸从她的岩窟里跑出,
　　领着幼狐大嚎大嚼地上的尸骨。

那不久前你曾嘲笑的天堂,地狱和命运的口舌在何处?
　　你那曾大力挥舞刀剑的双手在何处?　　　　　　　50
你那沁出香味的绸服,你的轮唱曲与誓言④,
　　你的剧本和十四行诗,你的方块黑桃游戏又在何处?

完了,完了,僧帽和王冠已被永远打倒,

---

① 巴庙是十八世纪末经常悬挂叛徒头颅之地。——译者
② 此处的"他"指皇帝查理。——译者
③ 挂在项链下暗藏纪念品的贵重金属盒。——译者
④ 参见282首注。——译者

　　　　With the Belial of the Court, and the Mammon of the Pope①;
55　　There is woe in Oxford Halls; there is wail in Durham's Stalls;
　　　　The Jesuit smites his bosom; the Bishop rends his cope②.

　　　　And She of the seven hills shall mourn her children's ills③,
　　　　And tremble when she thinks on the edge of England's sword;
　　　　And the Kings of earth in fear shall shudder when they hear
60　　What the hand of God hath wrought for the Houses and the Word.

　　　　　　　　　　　　　　　　　　　　　LORD MACAULAY.

---

① *Belial*: a Hebrew common noun meaning 'worthlesssness'; in the Hebrew idiom a 'son of Belial' means a worthless person, but from the word being printed with a capital it was taken as a proper noun and personified (*e.g.* by Milton) as a demon. *Mammon*: the Aramaic word for 'riches,' which in like manner was personified as the devil of covetousness.
② *cope*: this vestment, a kind of long cloak, is not peculiar to bishops.
③ *She of the seven hills*: the Church of Rome.

教堂的守护神和教皇的财富也被打倒①;
牛津大厅在悲哀,德汉姆牧师在恸哭②;　　　　　　　　　55
　　耶酥会会员在捶胸拍肚;主教撕破长长的斗篷。

罗马教堂为信徒们的痛苦而伤心,
　　想到英格兰的刀光剑影他不寒而栗;
地球上皇帝们提心吊胆,当他们听见
　　上帝一手创造的教堂和圣经成了这般模样。　　　　60

金敏　译

---

① 守护神原词为 Belial,希伯来语意为"无价值",此处作为专用名词,译为"守护神"。财富原词为亚拉姆语(Mammon),此处拟作魔鬼的贪婪解。——译者
② 纳什比之战后查理撤到牛津(1642 年 10 月),这是他唯一拥有之地。德汉姆是英国最富的教区,该地的牧师全部支持国王。——译者

302. BLACKMWORE MAIDENS

The primrwose in the sheäde do blow,
    The cowslip in the zun,
The thyme upon the down do grow,
    The clote where streams do run[①];
An' where do pretty maïdens grow
    An' blow, but where the tow'r
Do rise among the bricken tuns[②],
    In Blackmwore by the Stour?

If you could zee their comely gaït,
    An' pretty feäces' smiles,
A-trippèn on so light o' waïght,
    An' steppèn off the stiles;
A-gwaïn to church, as bells do swing
    An' ring within the tow'r,
You'd own the pretty maïdens' pleäce
    Is Blackmwore by the Stour.

If you vrom Wimborne took your road,
    To Stower or Paladore,
An' all the farmers' housen show'd[③]
    Their daeters at the door;

---

① *The clote*: 'the yellow water-lily.'
② *bricken tuns*: 'brick-built chimney-tops.'
③ *housen*: the plural 'houses' is earlier than this form, as it is used from the 14th century, 'housen' not being found till about 1550.

302. 布莱克默的姑娘

巴恩斯

浓荫中,樱草花正尽情怒放,
　　阳光下,一朵朵立金花千姿百态,
麝香草在绿坪上如火如荼地长着,
　　溪水里,黄睡莲是多么婀娜可爱;
哦哪里,哪里有美丽的姑娘们 　　　　　　　　　　5
　　含苞欲放,只有那尖塔高高翱翔
在砖垒成的烟囱帽中间的地方,
　　在布莱克默,在斯托尔河旁①?

要是你能看到她们优美步子,
　　还有那些动人的脸蛋上的笑颜, 　　　　　　　10
如此轻盈地走着,如此纤细的腰肢,
　　从靠着篱墙的梯子上走到下面;
接着又去了教堂,当大钟
　　在高高的塔内晃动、鸣响,
你得承认,美丽的姑娘们的故乡, 　　　　　　　15
　　在布莱克默,在斯托尔河旁。

如果你从威姆本起程行走②,
　　去斯陶尔,或去帕拉多尔③,
在路上所有的农家门口,
　　你都可以看到他们的女儿, 　　　　　　　　　20

---
① 斯托尔河是多赛特郡的一条河流。——译者
② 威姆本是一个小市镇名。——译者
③ 斯陶尔和帕拉多尔是距威姆本西南面大约二十里的两个村庄。——译者

You'd cry to bachelors at hwome —
'Here, come; 'ithin an hour
You'll vind ten maïdens to your mind,
In Blackmwore by the Stour.'

An' if you looked 'ithin their door,
To zee em in their pleäce,
A-doèn housework up avore
Their smilèn mother's feäce;
You'd cry — 'Why, if a man would wive
An' thrive, 'ithout a dow'r,
Then let en look en out a wife
In Blackmwore by the Stour.'

As I upon my road did pass
A school-house back in Maÿ①
There out upon the beäten grass
Wer maïdens at their plaÿ;
An' as the pretty souls did twile②
An' smile, I cried, 'The flow'r
O' beauty, then, is still in bud
In Blackmwore by the Stour.'

W BARNES.

---

① *back in Maÿ*: 'last May.'
② *twile*: 'toil.'

你会对呆在家中的单身汉高声叫喊——
　"这儿，来吧，不用一个时辰，
你能找到十个称心的美人，
　在布莱克默，在斯托尔河旁。"

如果你举目望进门的里面，
　在她们的房间里看到她们，
在她们微笑的母亲面前，
　做着种种家务，忙个不停；
你会喊——"嗨，如果谁想娶妻，
　日子过得红火，而不要一份嫁妆，
那么让他来这里找一个妻子，
　在布莱克默，在斯托尔河旁。"

去年的五月，我走在路上，
　经过一座学校的校舍，
那里，在踩倒的青草上，
　姑娘们在嬉戏欢歌；
因为可爱的心灵既要辛劳
　而又微笑，于是我喊声嘹亮，
"美的花朵，此刻还是含苞待放，
　在布莱克默，在斯托尔河旁。"

裘小龙　译

编注　威廉·巴恩斯（William Barnes，1801—1886），英国诗人，生于布莱克默山区，爱用方言写诗。这首赞美故乡姑娘的诗选自他的《朴实的歌谣》（*Hwomely Rhymes*，1859）。

303. THE WIFE A-LOST

Since I noo mwore do zee your feäce,
    Up steärs or down below,
I'll zit me in the lwonesome pleäce,
    Where flat-bough'd beech do grow;
Below the beeches' bough, my love,
    Where you did never come,
An' I don't look to meet ye now,
    As I do look at hwome.

Since you noo mwore be at my zide,
    In walks in zummer het,
I'll goo alwone where mist do ride,
    Droo trees a-drippèn wet;
Below the raïn-wet bough, my love,
    Where you did never come,
An' I don't grieve to miss ye now,
    As I do grieve at hwome.

Since now bezide my dinner-bwoard
    Your vaïce do never sound,
I'll eat the bit I can avword
    A-vield upon the ground;
Below the darksome bough, my love,
    Where you did never dine,
An' I don't grieve to miss ye now,
    As I at hwome do pine.

303. 悼亡妻

巴恩斯

既然我再也见不到你的脸,
　　无论是在楼下或是楼上,
我将端坐这个寂寒的地方,
　　这里,粗枝条的山毛榉树生长;
在山毛榉的枝头下,我的爱人,　　　　　　5
　　那是你从未到过的地方,
现在,我不会指望见到你的音容,
　　就像我在家里真切看见那样。

既然你再也不会在我的身旁,
　　在盛夏的炎热里一起漫步,　　　　　10
我将独自在浓雾弥漫中彷徨,
　　树木还在湿漉漉地滴水;
雨点打湿的枝头下,我的爱人,
　　那是你从未到过的地方,
现在,我不会因为想念你而悲恸,　　　　15
　　就像我在家里那样。

既然如今在我的餐桌旁
　　你的声音再也不会响起,
我将吃着这坎土地上
　　我所能买得起的任何东西;　　　　　20
在那黑魆魆的枝头下,我的爱人,
　　那是你从未用过餐的地方,
现在,我不会因为想念你而悲恸,
　　就像我在家里那样。

Since I do miss your vaïce an' feäce
    In praÿer at eventide,
I'll praÿ wi' oone sad vaïce vor greäce
    To goo where you do bide;
Above the tree an' bough, my love,
    Where you be gone avore,
An' be a-waïtèn vor me now,
    To come vor evermwore.

                                W. BARNES.

既然我想念你的声音,你的脸,   25
 在傍晚的祷告声里,
我要用悲伤的声音祈求恩典:
 能到你居住的那里去。
在树木和枝条上,我的爱人,
 那是你已先去的地方,   30
此刻,等待我的来临吧,
 我会永远来到你的身旁。

裘小龙 译

304. THE NAMELESS ONE

Roll forth, my song, like the rushing river,
    That sweeps along to the mighty sea;
God will inspire me while I deliver
    My soul of thee!

Tell thou the world, when my bones lie whitening
    Amid the last homes of youth and eld①,
That once there was one whose veins ran lightning
    No eye beheld.

Tell how his boyhood was one drear night-hour,
    How shone for him, through his griefs and gloom,
No star of all heaven sends to light our
    Path to the tomb.

Roll on, my song, and to after ages
    Tell how, disdaining all earth can give,
He would have taught men, from wisdom's pages,
    The way to live.

And tell how trampled, derided, hated,
    And worn by weakness, disease, and wrong,
He fled for shelter to God, who mated

---

① *eld*: an old word equivalent to 'age' in its various senses; it is now found only in poetry, and even there it savours of affectation.

304. 小人物

曼 根

唱起来吧,我的歌,像条奔腾的河,
    急匆匆涌向浩瀚大海;
老天鼓励着我呵,
    我倾泻着我的灵曲!

告诉你吧,世界,当我白骨成灰,   5
    在青春与老年最后的归宿之中,
他也曾才华烁烁,
    却无人识货。

告诉你吧,他的童年是怎样一个沉闷的夜晚,
    透过忧愁和悲痛,   10
天空中没有星星照耀,
    从未光顾过人生的旅途。

传播吧,我的歌,向着未来的世纪,
    宣告那尘世赋予的一切如何应该抛弃,
他本可以用明智的篇幅,指导人们   15
    怎样生活。

告诉人们,他备受凌辱,惨遭憎恨与愚弄,
    告诉人们,他如何变得苍老,由于虚弱、疾病和委屈,
他逃去寻求上帝庇护,上帝赐予他

20   His soul with song —

               With song which alway, sublime or vapid,
                   Flowed like a rill in the morning-beam,
               Perchance not deep, but intense and rapid —
                   A mountain stream.

25   Tell how this Nameless, condemned for years long
                   To herd with demons from hell beneath,
               Saw things that made him, with groans and tears, long
                   For even death.

               Go on to tell how, with genius wasted,
30   Betrayed in friendship, befooled in love,
               With spirit shipwrecked, and young hopes blasted,
                   He still, still strove;

               Till spent with toil, dreeing death for others[①],
                   And some whose hands should have wrought for him
35   (If children live not for sires and mothers),
                   His mind grew dim;

               And he fell far through that pit abysmal,
                   The gulf and grave of Maginn and Burns,
               And pawned his soul for the devil's dismal
40   Stock of returns[②];

[①] *dreeing*: 'enduring'; now seldom heard except in the phrase 'to dree one's own weird,' *i.e.* endure one's own fate.

[②] *returns*: 'payment' for his soul, *i.e.* the exhilaration or oblivion which drinking brought.

一阕安魂之曲——

　　总是高昂飘逸的歌呵，
　　　湍动如晨光中微笑的小河，
　　或许并不深邃，却热情急切——
　　　哦，山溪涨落。

　　告诉世人，这位小人物，多少年呀
　　　被判处与地狱恶魔为伍，
　　看见的丑事令他恶心流泪
　　　他甚至呻吟着期待死亡。

　　再向世人诉说吧，天才惨遭浪费，
　　　友谊无情背叛，爱情也被践踏，
　　而精神备受折磨，青春的希望破灭，
　　　他仍然，仍然拼命在挣扎；

　　直到苦役耗尽生命，为他人忍受死亡，
　　　为那些伸手的白食者做工，
　　（但愿孩子们不为祖先和母亲而活），
　　　他的才智变得多么暗淡；

　　呵，跌进无底悔恨的深渊，
　　　马奎与彭斯的阴曹地府①，
　　为了偿还魔鬼恶毒的回程期票②
　　　他将自己的灵魂押出。

---

① 马奎，即威廉·马奎（William Maginn，1793—1842），爱尔兰作家及报人，好狂饮唱诗，经常由于债务入狱；彭斯（参见第125首注），晚年沉溺于酒精，以至大部分密友都与他疏远。——译者
② 此处的回程期票意指使人忘却、飘然的酒。——译者

But yet redeemed it in days of darkness,
    And shapes and signs of the final wrath,
  when death, in hideous and ghastly starkness,
    Stood on his path.

And tell how now, amid wreck and sorrow,
    And want, and sickness, and houseless nights,
He bides in calmness the silent morrow,
    That no ray lights.

And lives he still, then? Yes! Old and hoary
    At thirty-nine from despair and woe,
He lives, enduring what future story
    Will never know.

Him grant a grave to, ye pitying noble,
    Deep in your bosoms; there let him dwell!
He, too, had tears for all souls in trouble
    Here, and in hell.

                        J.C. MANGAN.

来不及在黑暗的时光设法赎回
　　他满腔最后的疯狂愤怒,
但是死亡,终于悄然而可怕
　　赫然挡住他的道路。

控诉吧,如今,在毁灭与悲愤之中, 45
　　还有贫穷,疾苦,无家可归的黑夜相随,
默默地,他守住无言的次日
　　却没有一丝光缕。

那么,他是否活着?呵!衰老而苍白
　　经历了三十九个失意与忧患的岁月, 50
他还活着,强忍着去捱过将来
　　那永难为人知晓的故事。

你可悲的高贵者,赐给他一座坟墓,
　　在你们心灵深处:这便是他的安身之所!
呵,他,为所有受难的灵魂罄尽泪水, 55
　　在这里,在这苦境之狱。

陈朴　译

编注　詹姆斯·克拉伦斯·曼根(James Clarence Mangan,1803—1849),爱尔兰诗人,一生坎坷,长期生活在贫穷、疾病与失恋之中,颇愤世嫉俗。此诗写于一八四二年,发表于一八四九年,为诗人自传性质的代表诗作之一,被后人称为"可怕之诗"。

305. BRAHMA

If the red slayer think he slays,
    Or if the slain think he is slain,
They know not well the subtle ways
    I keep, and pass, and turn again.

Far or forgot to me is near;
    Shadow and sunlight are the same;
The vanished gods to me appear;
    And one to me are shame and fame.

They reckon ill who leave me out;
    When me they fly, I am the wings;
I am the doubter and the doubt,
    And I the hymn the Brahmin sings.

The strong gods pine for my abode,
    And pine in vain the sacred Seven;
But thou, meek lover of the good!
    Find me, and turn thy back on heaven.

R. W. EMERSON.

305. 梵天①

爱默生

如果残酷的杀戮者认为他在杀戮
　　或是被杀者觉得他是被害；
他们就都不清楚我是怎样
　　一保初衷,历经磨难,不死不降②。

遥远或被遗忘者近在我身旁,
　　阴影也就相同于阳光；
逝去的神祇为我显灵,
　　荣辱与毁誉在我都一样。

摒弃我者想错了主张,
　　当他们飞离我时,我是飞翔的翅膀,
我怀疑别人,又被别人怀疑,
　　我是梵天,为婆罗门所歌唱③。

威严的神灵要想占去我的地方,
　　七圣也盼之无望、黯然神伤④。
然而你,善良的温顺的恋人,
　　探寻到我在何方,然后你背对上苍。

朱　徽　译

---

① 梵天,亦称"大梵天",是印度教的创造神,近似于基督教中的上帝,他既无限,又无形,无处不在,无时不有,是世界万物(包括善恶)的创造者。——编注者
② 意为杀戮和被害同是梵天的意志,并无区别。这里第一节几乎是照引《薄伽梵歌》:"有人将此视为杀戮者,有人认为这是被杀戮,他们两者都浅薄无知。这既不是杀戮,也不是被杀。这既没有出生,也没有死去。"——译者
③ 婆罗门,印度四大阶级中最高一级。——编注者
④ 七圣,印度教中具有灵感的圣人,神的儿子,被认为是《吠陀经》的作者。这里还是引自《薄伽梵歌》:"诸多神明,伟哉圣人,都不知道我将来临。"——译者

编注 拉尔夫·沃尔多·爱默生（Ralph Waldo Emerson，1803—1882），美国重要诗人、散文作家、颇具创见的思想家，主张人能超越感觉和理性而直接认识真理的超验主义，提倡美国本身的民族文学，认为美的目的在于创造，诗人是美的君主，构成诗的不是韵律，而是由韵律所组成的主题与生气蓬勃的思想，他的诗文语言洗练、比喻生动、哲理性强且气势磅礴，被称为"爱默生式风格"。

306. TO EVA

O fair and stately maid, whose eyes
Were kindled in the upper skies
    At the same torch that lighted mine;
For so I must interpret still
Thy sweet dominion o'er my will,
    A sympathy divine.

Ah! let me blameless gaze upon
Features that seem at heart my own;
    Nor fear those watchful sentinels,
Who charm the more their glance forbids[①]
Chaste-glowing, underneath their lids,
    With fire that draws while it repels.

R. W. EMERSON.

[①] *the more*: this seems to be taken with both verbs, 'the more their glance forbids, the more they charm.'

306. 给伊娃

爱默生

啊,美丽端庄的姑娘,
你的明眸被点燃在高天之上;
　　同样是那只火炬把我的双眼照亮。
正因为如此,
我得把你征服我意志的柔情蜜意,　　　　　　5
　　看作是你抚慰我心灵的神圣力量。

啊,让我胸怀坦荡,
久久地凝视我心上的姑娘。
　　我也并不畏惧那些警觉的门岗:
闪闪的火焰摇曳,圣洁的光彩明亮　　　　　　10
他们的目光越要禁止圣洁在眼前闪光,
　　姑娘的形象就越具有神奇的力量。

朱徽　译

307. AND SHALL TRELAWNY DIE?

A good sword and a trusty hand!
　A merry heart and true!
King James's men shall understand
　What Cornish lads can do.

And have they fixed the where and when?
　And shall Trelawny die?
Here's twenty thousand Cornish men
　Will know the reason why!

Out spake their captain brave and bold,
　A merry wight was he:
'If London Tower were Michael's hold,
　We'll set Trelawny free!

'We'll cross the Tamar, land to land,
　The Severn is no stay, —
With "one and all," and hand in hand①,
　And who shall bid us nay?

'And when we come to London Wall,
　A pleasant sight to view,

---

① *With "one and all"*: *i.e.* with the cry, "one and all."

307. 难道特里劳尼非死不成?

霍克

一身好武艺,一只可靠的手!
　一颗欢乐而忠诚的心!
国王詹姆士的人马应该懂得
　康尼许的男儿能干惊天动地的事情①。

难道他们已经判定了时间和地点?
　难道特里劳尼非死不成?
这里有两万名康尼许人
　他们要把道理问个明白!

他们的队长勇敢地高声讲话,
　他是一个好样的汉子:
纵然伦敦塔像米切尔要塞一样坚固②,
　我们也要把特里劳尼救出牢门。

"我们要渡过塔马河,陆地联成一片③,
　赛芬也挡不住我们的脚步④
我们"万众一心",手拉着手,
　谁又能对我们说一声不?

"当我们来到伦敦塔的墙头,
　看到一幅令人好笑的景象,

---
① 人们通常称康沃尔人为康尼许人。——译者
② 康尼许人认为,康沃尔的米切尔山上的要塞是世界上最坚固的。——译者
③ 塔马河,德旺与康沃尔之间的河流。——译者
④ 赛芬,地名。——译者

>   Come forth! Come forth, ye cowards all,
>   Here's men as good as you.
>
> 'Trelawny he's in keep and hold,
>   Trelawny he may die; —
> But here's twenty thousand Cornish bold
>   Will know the reason why!'

R. S. HAWKER.

你们这群胆小鬼,出来啊,快出来,
　　这里的人们和你们一样高强。　　　　　　　　　　*20*

"特里劳尼被囚禁在牢房里,
　　特里劳尼也许会被杀害——
但这里有两万康尼许男儿
　　要把道理弄个明白。

裘小龙　译

编注　罗伯特·斯蒂芬·霍克(Robert Stephen Hawker,1803—1875),英国诗人,南部康沃尔郡牧师。此诗写的是詹姆士二世时代的事。特里劳尼是一名主教,因为拒读国王纵欲免罪令被关入伦敦塔(著名监狱)。他在康沃尔深得人心,几万名矿工和农民向伦敦进军来营救他,直到听到他获释的消息才回去。

308. THE SHANDON BELLS

With deep affection
And recollection,
I often think of
    Those Shandon bells,
Whose sounds so wild would,
In the days of childhood,
Fling round my cradle
    Their magic spells.
On this I ponder
Where'er I wander,
And thus grow fonder,
    Sweet Cork, of thee;
With thy bells of Shandon,
That sound so grand on
The pleasant waters
    Of the River Lee.
I've heard bells chiming
Full many a clime in,
Tolling sublime in
    Cathedral shrine,
While at a glibe rate[1]
Brass tongues would vibrate —

---

[1] *glibe*: this spelling of 'glib,' here demanded by the rime, is not recognised by the dictionaries.

308. 沙丹的钟声[①]

马奥尼

怀着深深的爱
和回忆,
我常常怀念
　　那沙丹的钟声,
它响得那么猛烈,　　　　　　　　　　5
以神秘的魅力,
敲在我的童年,
　　撞在摇篮旁边。
于是,我觉得
无论往何处流浪　　　　　　　　　　10
我愈加珍爱你,
　　那甜蜜的科克;
你有沙丹的钟声,
庄严地鸣响
在李河[②]　　　　　　　　　　　　15
　　快活的水上。
我听见钟声敲打
响彻在四方,
庄严的钟声
　　来自大教堂,　　　　　　　　　　20
尽管铜管乐声宏亮,
节奏十分流畅

[①] 沙丹,即爱尔兰南部城市科克市的圣·安妮·沙丹教堂。它是市内的主要建筑物,也是一座著名的教堂。——译者
[②] 李河,流过科克市的河流。——译者

But all their music
    Spoke naught like thine;
For memory, dwelling
On each proud swelling
Of thy belfrey knelling
    Its bold notes free,
Made the bells of Shandon
Sound far more grand on
The pleasant waters,
    Of the River Lee.
I've heard bells tolling
Old Adrian's Mole in,
Their thunder rolling
    From the Vatican,
And cymbals glorious
Swinging uproarious
In the gorgeous turrets
    Of Notre Dame[1];
But thy sounds were sweeter
Than the dome of Peter
Flings o'er the Tiber,
    Pealing solemnly; —
O! the bells of Shandon
Sound far more grand on
The pleasant waters
    Of the River Lee.

---

[1] *Notre Dame*: the Cathedral of Paris.

可所有的声响
　　　都不及你那样；
人们永远不会忘记　　　　　　　　　25
你的钟楼响起丧钟，
大胆而自在的起落，
　　　它清晰而自由，
把沙丹的钟声
奏得更加宏亮　　　　　　　　　　30
响彻在李河
　　　快活的水上。
我听见钟声就想起
古老的阿德里亚长廊①
从梵蒂冈传来　　　　　　　　　　35
　　　雷声滚滚，
还有灿烂金钹
在巴黎圣母院
辉煌的塔顶
　　　高声震荡；　　　　　　　　40
但你的声音更加甜美
赛过那回荡在台伯河上
圣彼得教堂②
　　　神圣的轰响——
呵！沙丹的钟声　　　　　　　　　45
遥远欢乐地响彻
在李河
　　　快活的水上。

---

① 阿德里亚长廊，哈德良大帝(Hadrain，117—138)之墓，在意大利罗马市内，后来迁到梵蒂冈附近，由一长廊把它与梵蒂冈连在一起。——译者
② 圣彼得教堂，与梵蒂冈毗邻，位于台伯河西。——译者

    There's a bell in Moscow,
50   While on tower and kiosk O[①]
    In Saint Sophia
      The Turkman gets[②];
    And loud in air
    Calls men to prayer
55   From the tapering summit
      Of tall minarets.
    Such empty phantom
    I freely grant them;
    But there is an anthem
60   More dear to me, —
    'Tis the bells of Shandon
    That sound so grand on
    The pleasant waters
      Of the River Lee.

        F. MAHONY (FATHER PROUT)

---

① *kiosk*: 'pavilion' or 'summer-house.'
② *Turkman*: a metrical necessity for 'Turk.'

莫斯科的那只大钟①
矗立在高塔与凉亭之中,呵　　　　　　　50
在圣苏菲亚寺院②
　　土耳其人也曾听见:
从巍巍高大的
清真寺顶端
传来天上的音响　　　　　　　　　　　55
　　呼唤人们去祈祷。
我坦率地承认
这是空幻的形象;
而一首赞美诗
　　我觉得更为宝贵——　　　　　　60
那是沙丹的钟声
遥远而壮丽地鸣响
在李河
　　快活的水上。

　　　　　　　　　　　　　　陈朴　译

编注　弗朗西斯·希尔维斯特·马奥尼(Francis Sylvester Mahony,1804—1866),即普劳特神父,爱尔兰诗人及批评家,原是爱尔兰教区牧师,由于酷爱文学而放弃教职。

---

① 亦称沙皇钟,高十九尺,直径超过二十尺,重一九二余吨,建于一七三五年。——译者
② 圣苏菲亚寺院(Saint Sophia),康斯坦丁堡有名的清真寺,最初修筑得像希腊教堂。——译者

309. 'I THOUGHT ONCE HOW THEOCRITUS HAD SUNG'

I thought once how Theocritus had sung
   Of the sweet years, the dear and wished-for years,
   Who each one in a gracious hand appears
To bear a gift for mortals, old or young:
And, as I mused it in his antique tongue,
   I saw, in gradual vision through my tears,
   The sweet, sad years, the melancholy years,
Those of my own life, who by turns had flung
A shadow across me. Straightway I was 'ware,
   So weeping, how a mystic Shape did move
Behind me, and drew me backward by the hair;
   And a voice said in mastery, while I strove, ...
'Guess now who holds thee?' — 'Death,' I said. But there,
   The silver answer rang, ... 'Not Death, but Love.'

E. B. BROWNING.

309. "我想起昔年那位希腊的诗人"

伊丽莎白·布朗宁

我想起昔年那位希腊的诗人①,
　　唱着流年的歌儿——可爱的流年,
　　渴望中的流年,一个个的宛然,
都手执着颁送给世人的礼品:
我沉吟着诗人的古调,我不禁　　　　　　　　　　5
　　泪眼发花了,于是我渐渐看见
　　那温柔凄切的流年,酸苦的流年,
我自己的流年,轮流掷着暗影,
掠过我的身边。马上我就哭起来,
　　我明知道有一个神秘的模样　　　　　　　　10
在背后揪住我的头发往后掇,
　　正在挣扎的当儿,我听见好像
一个厉声"谁掇着你,猜猜!"
　　"死,"我说。"不是死,是爱,"他讲。

闻一多　译

编注　伊丽莎白·巴雷特·布朗宁(Elizabeth Barrett Browning, 1806—1861),十九世纪英国著名女诗人,早年坠马致伤,长期卧病在床,与诗人罗伯特·布朗宁相爱成婚,客居意大利,写有反映社会生活的诗篇,代表作有《孩子们的哭声》《圭迪公寓的窗子》等。最著名的抒情诗集《葡萄牙的十四行诗》是赠给丈夫的感情真挚的爱情诗篇,诗句精练,才气横溢,是英诗中的精品。此为该集第一首,两个主题:期待中的"死亡"和向她突然袭击,跟死亡一样威猛的"爱情"。

---

① 此处指公元前三世纪的希腊田园抒情诗人狄奥克里特(Theocritus)。——编注者

310. 'WHAT CAN I GIVE THEE BACK, O LIBERAL'

What can I give thee back, O liberal
    And princely giver, who hast brought the gold
    And purple of thine heart, unstained, untold,
And laid them on the outside of the wall
For such as I to take or leave withal[1],
    In unexpected largesse? am I cold,
    Ungrateful, that for these most manifold
High gifts, I render nothing back at all?
Not so; not cold, — but very poor instead.
    Ask God who knows. For frequent tears have run
The colours from my life, and left so dead
    And pale a stuff, it were not fitly done
To give the same as pillow to thy head[2].
    Go farther! let it serve to trample on[3].

                              E. B. BROWNING.

---

[1] *withal*: this word ordinarily means 'likewise,' 'at the same time'; here it apparently means 'equally,' 'with free choice.'

[2] *the same*: see note to No. 238, l. 5.

[3] *it*: sc. my life.

310. "你那样慷慨豪爽的施主呀"

伊丽莎白·布朗宁

你那样慷慨豪爽的施主呀,你把
　　你心坎里金碧辉煌的宝藏
　　原封地掏出来,只往我墙外堆,
任凭像我这样的人去拣起,还是
把这罕见的舍施丢下;叫我拿什么　　　　　5
　　来作为你应得的报答?请不要
　　说我太冷漠、太寡恩,你那许多
重重叠叠的深情厚意,我却
没有一些儿回敬;不,并不是
　　冷漠无情,实在我太寒伧。你问　　　　　10
上帝就明白。那连绵的泪雨冲尽了
　　我生命的光彩,只剩一片死沉沉的
　　苍白,不配给你当偎依的枕头。
　　　走吧!尽把它踏在脚下,作垫石。

方平　译

编注　此为《葡萄牙的十四行诗》第八首。当女诗人的情人向她呈献爱情时,她已年近四十,半辈子的光阴都消磨在病床上,因此,她怀着绝望的心情恳求情人舍下自己:"走吧!"

311. 'YET LOVE, MERE, LOVE, IS BEAUTIFUL INDEED'

 Yet love, mere, love, is beautiful indeed
  And worthy of acceptation. Fire is bright,
  Let temple burn, or flax. An equal light[1]
 Leaps in the flame from cedar-plank or weed.
 And love is fire; and when I say at need[2]
  I love thee ... mark! ... *I love thee*! ... in thy sight
  I stand transfigured, glorified aright,
 With conscience of the new rays that proceed
 Out of my face toward thine. There's nothing low
  In love, when love the lowest: meanest creatures[3]
 Who love God, God accepts while loving so.
 And what I *feel*, across the inferior features
 Of what I *am*, doth flash itself, and show
  How that great work of Love enhances Nature's.

            E. B. BROWNING.

---

[1] *Let temple burn, or flax*: 'whether that which is burning be costly and sacred or cheap and common.'
[2] *at need*: 'at thy need,' 'in answer to thy urgings.'
[3] *when love the lowest*: 'even when offered by the lowest'; *love* is the verb, and it is rather awkwardly followed by its subject.

311. "不过只要是爱,是爱,就够你赞美"

伊丽莎白·布朗宁

不过只要是爱,是爱,就够你赞美,
　　值得你接受。你知道,爱就是火,
　　火总是光明的,不问焚着的是庙堂
　　或者柴堆——那栋梁还是荆榛在
　　燃烧,火焰里总跳得出同样的光辉。　　　　5
　　当我倾吐出:"我爱你!"在你的眼里,
　　那荣耀的瞬息,我成了一尊金身,
　　感觉着有一道新吐的皓光从我天庭
　　射向你脸上。是爱,就无所谓卑下,
　　即使这爱来自最微贱的:那微贱的生灵　　10
　　献爱给上帝,宽宏的上帝接受了它
　　又回赐给它爱。我那迸发的热情,
　　就像道光,通过我这陋质,昭示了
　　爱的大手笔怎样给造物润色。

方平　译

编注　此为《葡萄牙的十四行诗》第十首。被病魔折磨得奄奄一息的女诗人,被爱情彻底征服,爱情成为她创造奇迹的巨大精神力量。她从床上站起来了,走向生活,走向了新的天地。她于是满怀热情为爱情唱起了颂歌。

312. 'IF THOU MUST LOVE ME'

If thou must love me, let it be for naught
   Except for love's sake only. Do not say
     'I love her for her smile ... her look ... her way
Of speaking gently, ... for a trick of thought
That falls in well with mine, and certes brought
   A sense of pleasant ease on such a day' —
For these things in themselves, Belovéd, may
Be changed, or change for thee, — and love, so wrough,
May be unwrought so. Neither love me for
   Thine own dear pity's wiping my cheeks dry, —
A creature might forget to weep, who bore
   Thy comfort long, and lose thy love thereby!
But love me for love's sake, that evermore
   Thou mayst love on, through love's eternity.

                                            E. B. BROWNING.

312. "如果你一心要爱我"

伊丽莎白·布朗宁

如果你一心要爱我,那就别为了什么,
 只是为了爱才爱我。别这么讲:
  "我爱她,为了她的一笑,她的模样,
她柔语的声气;为了她这感触
正好合我的心意,那天里,的确   5
 给我带来满怀的喜悦和舒畅。"
  亲爱的,这些好处都不能持常,
会因你而变,而这样唱出的爱曲
也将这样哑寂。也别爱我因为你
 又怜又惜地给我揩干了泪腮,   10
一个人会忘了哭泣,当她久受你
 温柔的慰安——却因此失了你的爱。
爱我,请只是为了那爱的意念,
 那你就能继续地爱,爱我如深海。

方平 译

编注 此为《葡萄牙的十四行诗》第十四首。这是一首经常入选各种版本的著名十四行情诗,诗人写出了唯恐爱情得而复失的不安和疑虑。

313. 'HOW DO I LOVE THEE?'

How do I love thee? Let me count the ways.
   I love thee to the depth and breadth and height
   My soul can reach, when feeling out of sight
For the ends of Being and ideal Grace①.
I love thee to the level of every day's
   Most quiet need, by sun and candlelight.
   I love thee freely, as men strive for Right②;
I love thee purely, as they turn from Praise.
I love thee with the passion put to use
   In my old griefs, and with my childhood's faith.
I love thee with a love I seemed to lose
   With my lost saints, — I love thee with the breath,
Smiles, tears, of all my life! — and, if God choose,
   I shall but love thee better after death.

                              E. B. BROWNING.

---

① *feeling out of sight For the ends of Being*: 'groping into infinity to find the purpose of the Universe.'

② *freely, as men strive for Right*: the efforts of those who are working 'to make the crooked straight' are prompted by no outside compulsion, but are the service freely given at the dictates of their own hearts.

313. "我究竟怎样爱你?"

伊丽莎白·布朗宁

我究竟怎样爱你?让我细数端详。
 我爱你直到我灵魂所及的深度、
 广度和高度,我在视力不及之处
摸索着存在的极致和美的理想。
我爱你像最朴素的日常需要一样,
 就像不自觉地需要阳光和蜡烛。
 我自由地爱你,像人们选择正义之路,
我纯洁地爱你,像人们躲避称赞颂扬。
我爱你用的是我在昔日的悲痛里
 用过的那种激情,以及童年的忠诚。
我爱你用的爱,我本以为早已失去
 (与我失去的圣徒一同);我爱你用笑容①、
眼泪、呼吸和生命!只要上帝允许,
 在死后我爱你将只会更加深情。

飞白 译

编注 此诗在《葡萄牙的十四行诗》初版时序号为第 42 首,现为第 43 首。

---

① 诗人早年曾崇拜过基督教所宣扬的圣者,随着成长解事,圣者的形象也在心中淡漠。——编注者

314. A MUSICAL INSTRUMENT

What was he doing, the great god Pan,
    Down in the reeds by the river?
Spreading ruin and scattering ban,
    Splashing and paddling with hoofs of a goat,
    And breaking the golden lilies afloat
      With the dragon-fly on the river.

He tore out a reed, the great god Pan,
    From the deep cool bed of the river:
The limpid water turbidly ran,
    And the broken lilies a-dying lay,
    And the dragon-fly had fled away,
      Ere he brought it out of the river.

High on the shore sate the great god Pan,
    While turbidly flowed the river;
And hacked and hewed as a great god can,
    With his hard bleak steel at the patient reed[①],
    Till there was not a sign of a leaf indeed
      To prove it fresh from the river.

He cut it short, did the great god Pan
    (How tall it stood in the river!),

[①] *hard bleak steel*: from meaning 'exposed,' *bleak* is here apparently used to mean 'bare' or 'cold'.

314. 乐器

伊丽莎白·布朗宁

他在干什么,这伟大的潘神①?
　　沿河而下钻进芦苇。
他传播毁灭,撒下诅咒
　　山羊足跶跶溅起泥浆,
　　水面上,蜻蜓落翅的金百合　　　　　　　5
　　　也让他用羊蹄踏碎。

他剥开一根芦苇,这伟大的潘神,
　　在深澈冰冷的河谷:
清清河水哗哗流过,
　　残碎的百合奄奄一息,　　　　　　　　10
　　蜻蜓也慌忙逃避,
　　　他带芦苇离开了这一河清水。

潘神坐在高高的岸上
　　脚下奔腾着湍急的河流;
像一尊伟神,劈着,砍着,　　　　　　　　15
　　用他的利刃,为耐心的芦杆加工,
　　直到完全没有一轮新叶
　　　再也辨不出刚从河边采来。

伟大的潘神,他把芦苇削短,
　　(他站在河中多么伟岸!)　　　　　　　20

---

① 潘神,希腊神话中羊和牲畜之神,人身羊足,头上有角。他发明了一种乐器,即潘神箫或排箫,一组长度不同的芦管排列一起,构成不同音阶。——译者

Then drew the pith, like the heart of a man,
    Steadily from the outside ring,
And notched the poor dry empty thing
    In holes, as he sate by the river.

'This is the way,' laughed the great god Pan
    (Laughed while he sate by the river),
'The only way, since gods began
    To make sweet music, they could succeed[①].'
Then, dropping his mouth to a hole in the reed,
    He blew in power by the river.

Sweet, sweet, sweet, O Pan!
    Piercing sweet by the river!
Blinding sweet, O great god Pan!
    The sun on the hill forgot to die,
And the lilies revived, and the dragon-fly
    Came back to dream on the river.

Yet half a beast is the great god Pan
    To laugh as he sits by the river,
Making a poet out of a man:
    The true gods sigh for the cost and pain, —
For the reed which grows nevermore again
    As a reed with the reeds in the river.

                          E. B. BROWNING.

---

① *they could succeed*: sc. in which they [the gods] could succeed.

汲出芦汁,如取人心,
　　紧紧包好外壳
　　刻痕于空洞的菲薄
　　　　他坐在河边钻着笛眼。

"好了!"伟大的潘神笑着,　　　　　　　　　　25
　　（坐在河边大笑,)
"行了,只有当神真正造出
美妙的乐曲,他们才能满足。")①
他那嘴唇贴住芦萧,
　　使劲在河边吹响。　　　　　　　　　　　30

呵,潘神,美妙,美妙,真美妙,
　　河边飘出醉人的神曲!
伟大的潘神,迷人的美妙,
　　太阳忘记了归山,
　　蜻蜓飞回河上做起美梦,　　　　　　　　35
　　　垂死的百合花也已复苏。

你半人半兽的伟大潘神呵,
　　坐在河边纵情欢唱,
你把人造就成为诗人:
　　真神却为付出的代价和痛苦而叹息　　　40
　　——因为这根芦苇不会再次生长
　　如同小溪中别的芦苇一样。

陈朴　译

编注　此诗选自《最后的诗行》(*Last Poems*, 1862),发表时带有插图说明。

---

① 这里的意思是说,神创造了音乐(却没有乐器),只有造成了乐器,他们才能如意。——译者

315. THE SLAVE'S DREAM

Beside the ungathered rice he lay,
    His sickle in his hand;
His breast was bare, his matted hair
    Was buried in the sand.
Again, in the mist and shadow of sleep,
    He saw his Native Land.

Wide through the landscape of his dreams
    The lordly Niger flowed;
Beneath the palm-trees on the plain
    Once more a king he strode;
And heard the tinkling caravans
    Descend the mountain-road.

He saw once more his dark-eyed queen
    Among her children stand;
They clasped his neck, they kissed his cheeks,
    They held him by the hand! —
A tear burst from the sleeper's lids
    And fell into the sand.

And then at furious speed he rode
    Along the Niger's bank;

315. 奴隶的梦

朗费罗

他躺在未收割的稻禾旁,
　　镰刀握在他的手上;
缠结的头发埋入沙土,
　　赤裸着的是他的胸膛。
在睡梦的烟雾和阴影里
　　他又一次看见了故乡。

穿越他梦中广阔的天地,
　　威严的尼日尔河水奔流①;
在平原的棕榈树下,他又一次
　　像个国王,阔步行走;
听到了沙漠商队的驼铃
　　叮叮当当摇下山头。

又看见他那黑眼睛的王后
　　站立在她的孩子们中间;
他们搂紧他的脖子,抓住手,
　　不断地亲吻着他的脸!——
从他的睡眼里迸出一滴泪,
　　滚着滚着,落到沙土里面。

沿着威严的尼日尔河岸
　　他骑着马儿飞快地奔跑;

---

① 尼日尔河,非洲西部的河流,长达二千六百英里,为非洲三大河流之一。——编注者

His bridle-reins were golden chains,
　　And, with a martial clank,
At each leap he could feel his scabbard of steel
　　Smiting his stallion's flank.
Before him, like a blood-red flag,
　　The bright flamingoes flew;
From morn till night he followed their flight,
　　O'er plains where the tamarind grew①,
Till he saw the roofs of Caffre huts,
　　And the ocean rose to view.

At night he heard the lion roar,
　　And the hyena scream,
And the river-horse, as he crushed the reeds②
　　Beside some hidden stream;
And it passed, like a glorious roll of drums,
　　Through the triumph of his dream.

The forests, with their myriad tongues,
　　Shouted of liberty;
And the Blast of the Desert cried aloud,
　　With a voice so wild and free,
That he started in his sleep and smiled
　　At their tempestuous glee.

He did not feel the driver's whip,
　　Nor the burning heat of day;

---

① *tamarind*: a large tree, valuable for its hard wood and its fruit, the latter being used in medicine and in cookery as a relish.
② *the river-horse*: a literal translation of 'hippopotamus.'

手上的缰绳是黄金的链子,
　　每一次纵跳,他都感觉到
青钢的刀鞘敲打着马腹,
　　发出威严的铿锵声调。

成群的火鹤像鲜明的红旗
　　飞翔在他的前面;
他追随着,从清晨直到夜晚,
　　驰过罗望子树生长的平原,
直到他望见卡弗人茅舍的屋顶①,
　　海洋也闪进了他的眼帘。

夜里他听到狮子的咆哮,
　　听到鬣狗的悲鸣,
还听到河马,当他压碎芦苇
　　躺卧在隐僻的河滨;
河水淙淙过,像奏着欢乐的鼓
　　驰越他辉煌的梦境。

森林的千百条舌头
　　高声呼唤着自由;
沙漠里的阵阵狂飙
　　用粗野、豪放的腔调怒吼,
在梦中他被惊动,微笑着倾听
　　这一曲暴风雨般的合奏。

他不再感觉监工的鞭挞,
　　不再感觉烈日的炙烤;

---

① 卡弗人,南非洲的聪明而强壮的黑人民族。——译者

For Death had illumined the Land of Sleep,
   And his lifeless body lay
A worn-out fetter, that the soul
   Had broken and thrown away!

H. W. LONGFELLOW.

因为死亡照亮了睡乡,
　　他失却生命的躯壳躺倒,
像一副磨损的锁镣,
　　已经被灵魂突破、抛掉!

杨德豫　译

编注　亨利·沃兹沃思·朗费罗(Henry Wadsworth Longfellow,1807—1882),美国著名诗人。第一部诗集《夜吟》及第二部《歌谣及其他》曾在大西洋两岸风靡一时,其主要作品包括三首长篇叙事诗:《伊凡吉林》《海华沙之歌》和《迈尔斯·斯坦狄什的求婚》。他一生创作了大量的抒情诗、歌谣、叙事诗和诗剧,认为自己的使命是"以隽永的诗的形式创造出美国人共同的文化遗产,并在此过程中培育一代诗人"。此处所选之诗出自组诗《奴役篇》(包括《奴隶的梦》《奴隶的夜半歌声》《警告》等),预言被奴役的黑人终将像《旧约》中备受屈辱的力士参孙一样,"举起手臂,把这个国家制度的基础动摇"。

316. THE ARSENAL AT SPRINGFIELD

This is the Arsenal. From floor to ceiling,
    Like a huge organ, rise the burnished arms;
But from their silent pipes no anthem pealing
    Startles the villages with strange alarms.

Ah! what a sound will rise, how wild and dreary,
    When the death-angel touches those swift keys!
What loud lament and dismal Miserere①
    Will mingle with their awful symphonies!

I hear even now the infinite fierce chorus,
    The cries of agony, the endless groan,
Which, through the ages that have gone before us,
    In long reverberations reach our own.

On helm and harness rings the Saxon hammer,
    Through Cimbric forest roars the Norseman's song,
And loud, amid the universal clamour,
    O'er distant deserts sounds the Tartar gong.

I hear the Florentine, who from his palace

---

① *Miserere*: 'cry for mercy.'

316. 斯普林菲尔德的军械库①

朗费罗

这是军械库。从地板到天花板,
　满堆着闪亮的武器,像巨大的风琴;
但它们无声的管子里,没有鸣响
　异常恐怖的乐曲使乡邻震惊。

啊!那将是多么野蛮凄厉的声音呀,
　一旦死神将那敏捷的键盘触摸!
放声的悲痛和忧郁的"怜悯我们吧"②
　将渗和着那异常可怕的交响乐!

我现在还听到那极其凶残的大合唱,
　惨痛的呼喊,夹杂着无尽的呻吟;
经过以前的多少世纪,这声浪
　长期地回响着,自远古传到如今。

撒克逊人的铁锤在马鞍和盔甲上回响,
　古北欧人的歌声震撼着辛布里的森林③,
还有那鞑靼人的铜锣声震霄汉,
　在遍地的喧闹中响彻了沙漠无垠。

我听到佛罗伦萨人在皇宫幌动击锤,

---

① 美国有四个城市都叫斯普林菲尔德,此处所指的是马萨诸塞州的同名城市,内有建于一七九四年的国家军械库。——译者
② "怜悯我们吧",引自《圣经·诗篇》第五十一节。——译者
③ 辛布里是古北欧日耳曼族的一个部落,后侵入意大利半岛北部,于公元前一世纪被罗马征服。——译者

>
> Wheels out his battle-bell with dreadful din①,
> And Aztec priests upon their teocallis
>   Beat the wild war-drums made of setpent's skin;
>
> The tumult of each sacked and burning village;
>   The shout that every prayer for mercy drowns;
> The soldiers' revels in the midst of pillage;
>   The wail of famine in beleaguered towns;
>
> The bursting shell, the gateway wrenched asunder,
>   The rattling musketry, the clashing blade;
> And ever and anon, in tones of thunder,
>   The diapason of the cannonade②.
>
> Is it, O man, with such discordant noises,
>   With such accursed instruments as these,
> Thou drownest Nature's sweet and kindly voices,
>   And jarrest the celestial harmonies?
>
> Were half the power that fills the world with terror,
>   Were half the wealth bestowed on camps and courts,
> Given to redeem the human mind from error,
>   There were no need of arsenals or forts;
>
> The warrior's name would be a name abhorred!
>   And every nation that should lift again
> Its hand against a brother, on its forehead

---

① *Wheels out his battle-bell*: when a bell is rung, it revolves upon its upper part so as to describe almost a complete circle.
② *diapason*: see note to No. 63, l. 15.

使战斗的警钟发出可怕的鸣轰；
阿兹特克的僧人在锥形的古墨西哥庙堂内①
　　疯狂地擂起了蟒皮的战鼓隆隆。　　　　　　　　　　20

每个被劫掠和焚烧着的村庄的骚乱；
　　掩盖了乞求怜悯的祷告的喊叫；
士兵们在抢劫之中的纵情狂欢；
　　被围的市镇里饥民的哭泣与哀号；

那爆炸的炮弹，猛然砸开的通道；　　　　　　　　　　25
　　刀刃的交锋，步枪的砰砰射击声；
不时还有震耳的雷鸣喧嚣；
　　那是战炮轰击的全部音响历程。

人们啊，竟用这般不协调的噪音，
　　你们用这些受诅咒的乐器，　　　　　　　　　　　　30
来淹没大自然温柔甜美的万籁之声，
　　来冲击那天上笙箫的和谐仙曲！

只要用使世界充满恐惧的一半力量，
　　用赐给军营和宫庭的半数财产，
来拯救心灵，使人类迷途知返，　　　　　　　　　　　35
　　便不需军械库和碉堡逞凶恃强：

武士的称谓将成为可憎的名词！
　　任何国家再敢举手打击
一个弟兄，在它的前额将永世

---

① 阿兹特克，古代统治墨西哥的一支印地安人部落，于十六世纪初被墨西哥人征服。他们的庙宇建立在金字塔式的角锥形底座上。——译者

40   Would wear for evermore the curse of Cain!

    Down the dark future, through long generations,
        The echoing sounds grow fainter and then cease,
    And like a bell, with solemn, sweet vibrations,
        I hear once more the voice of Christ say, 'Peace!'

45   Peace! and no longer from its brazen portals
        The blast of War's great organ shakes the skies!
    But beautiful as songs of the immortals,
        The holy melodies of love arise.

                                      H. W. LONGFELLOW.

铭刻着上帝惩罚该隐的印记①！ 40

　　经过漫长的世代，在渺茫的未来，
　　　这喧嚣的回声将日趋微弱的终尽；
　　像洪钟般，带着庄严而悦耳的震颤，
　　　我又听到基督的声音说："和平！"

　　和平！再不让战争大风琴的呼啸 45
　　　穿过那厚厚的铜门震撼穹苍！
　　而是像神仙的歌声般无限美好，
　　　爱的圣洁的旋律将高高飘扬。

解楚兰　译

编注 此诗选自诗集《布吕赫钟楼及其他》(*The Belfry of Bruges and Other Poems*)，集中因收有《斯普林菲尔德的军械库》《桥》《努伦堡》和《布吕赫钟楼》等佳篇而受人称道。

---

① 《旧约·创世记》第四章：该隐是亚当和夏娃的长子，杀死了他的弟弟亚伯，因而受到耶和华的诅咒，使他耕耘而无所收获，漂泊而无家可归。耶和华在他的额上烙了字句以示惩罚。——译者

317. CHILDREN

Come to me, O ye children!
    For I hear you at your play,
And the questions that perplexed me
    Have vanished quite away.

Ye open the eastern windows,
    That look towards the sun,
Where thoughts are singing swallows,
    And the brooks of morning run.

In your hearts are the birds and the sunshine,
    In your thoughts the brooklet's flow;
But in mine is the wind of Autumn,
    And the first fall of the snow.

Ah! What would the world be to us
    If the children were no more?
We should dread the desert behind us
    Worse than the dark before.

What the leaves are to the forest,
    With light and air for food,
Ere their sweet and tender juices
    Have been hardened into wood,

That to the world are children;

317. 孩子们

朗费罗

到我这儿来呵,孩子们!
　我听见你们在嬉戏,
于是那些困扰我的疑问
　便都一股脑儿失去。

你们给打开东边的窗,　　　　　　　　　　5
　那窗子直对着太阳,
在那儿,思想是歌唱的燕子,
　早晨的溪水在流荡。

你们心里有鸟儿和阳光,
　小溪在你们思想里流过,　　　　　　　　10
但是,我的心里只有秋风,
　和雪絮的初次飘落。

呵,这世界会成了什么,
　假如我们没有儿童?
我们会留在后面一片荒漠,　　　　　　　　15
　比前面的幽暗更惊心。

有如树叶之于树林,
　以阳光和空气为食物,
直到它们甜蜜的汁液
　逐渐变成坚硬的树木。　　　　　　　　　20

儿童对世界正是这样;

Through them it feels the glow
Of a brighter and sunnier climate
Than reaches the trunks below.

Come to me, O ye children!
And whisper in my ear
What the birds and the winds are singing
In your sunny atmosphere.

For what are all our contrivings,
And the wisdom of our books,
When compared with your caresses,
And the gladness of your looks?

Ye are better than all the ballads
That ever were sung or said;
For ye are living poems,
And all the rest are dead.

H. W. LONGFELLOW.

通过他们,世界才感受
比下面树木所能接触的
　　更明亮、更美好的气候。

到我这儿来呵,孩子们!　　　　　　　　　　　25
　　附在我的耳边低语:
告诉我,鸟儿和风唱着什么
　　在你们煦和的大气里。

因为我们的追求算得什么?
　　书本的智慧有什么用?　　　　　　　　　30
它们怎比得你们的抚爱
　　和你们欢喜的面容?

你们胜过所有的民歌,
　　无论是说过的,唱过的;
因为你们是活的诗篇,　　　　　　　　　　　35
　　其余的诗都没有生气。

　　　　　　　　　　　　　　　查良铮　译

318. 'I DO NOT LOVE THEE!'

I do not love thee! — no! I do not love thee!
And yet when thou art absent I am sad;
   And envy even the bright blue sky above thee,
Whose quiet stars may see thee and be glad.

I do not love thee! — yet, I know not why,
Whate'er thou dost seems still well done, to me:
   And often in my solitude I sigh
That those I do love are not more like thee!

I do not love thee! — yet, when thou art gone,
I hate the sound (though those who speak be dear)
   Which breaks the lingering echo of the tone
Thy voice of music leaves upon my ear.

I do not love thee! — yet thy speaking eyes,
With their deep, bright, and most expressive blue,
   Between me and the midnight heaven arise,
Oftener than any eyes I ever knew.

I know I do not love thee! yet, alas!
Others will scarcely trust my candid heart;
   And oft I catch them smiling as they pass,
Because they see me gazing where thou art.

CAROLINE ELIZABETH SARAH NORTON

318. "我并不爱你"

诺顿

我并不爱你——不!我并不爱你!
但你不在时,我又伤心,
　甚至妒嫉你头上明朗的高空,
静谧的星星看你也那么高兴。

我并不爱你——不知其中有何奥秘, 5
依我看,你做什么事情都十分完美,
　我却时常在孤独中叹息,
我的爱人永远不会更像你!

我并不爱你——呵,当你离去,
我憎恶那声音(虽然那么甜蜜) 10
　它损坏心灵萦绕亲切的共鸣
你如音乐的话语回荡在我耳际。

我并不爱你——虽然你的眼睛那么传神,
清澈,明亮,最富表情的碧蓝,
　在我夜半的苍穹中升起 15
比我曾见过的所有眼睛更加频繁。

我明白我并不爱你!然而,哎!
人们不会相信我坦白的诚意;
　我时常瞥见他们从我身边走过,他们微笑,
因为他们正好看见我对你凝视。 20

陈朴 译

编注 卡罗琳·伊丽莎白·萨拉·诺顿(Caroline Elizabeth Sarah Norton,1808—1877),英国著名戏剧家及演说家谢里丹的孙女,颇有文才,所写小说、诗歌大都反映了自己不幸的婚姻生活,后有人以她为主人公写过小说。

319. RUBÁIYÁT OF OMAR KHAYYÁM OF NAISHÁPÚR

1

Awake! for Morning in the Bowl of Night
Has flung the Stone that puts the Stars to Flight:
   And Lo! the Hunter of the East has caught
The Sultan's Turret in a Noose of Light.

2

Dreaming when Dawn's Left Hand was in the Sky
I heard a Voice within the Tavern cry,
   'Awake, my Little ones, and fill the Cup
'Before Life's Liquor in its Cup be dry.'

3

And, as the Cock crew, those who stood before
The Tavern shouted — 'Open then the Door!
   'You know how little while we have to stay,
'And, once departed, may return no more.'

319. 奥马尔·哈亚姆之柔巴依集①

菲茨杰拉德

1

醒醒吧！清晨已在黑夜的碗中②
投进了石球，叫星星匆匆飞动：
　　看哪！那东方猎手的光明之索③
已把苏丹宫墙上的塔楼套中。

2

晨曦在天边微微露脸，我听见
梦中的酒店里有个声音呼喊：
　　"醒醒吧，我的孩子们，把杯斟满——
趁这杯中的生命之酒还没干。"

以上黄杲炘　译

3

四野正在鸡鸣，
人们在茅店之前叩问——
　　"开门罢！我们只得羁留片时，
一朝去后，怕就不再回程。"

郭沫若　译

---

① 奥马尔·哈亚姆(Omar Khayyám，1048？—1123？)，波斯天文学家、数学家兼诗人。柔巴依，突厥语系的一种古典抒情诗形式，名称源于阿拉伯语(意为四行诗)，十一世纪中期较为流行。奥马尔·哈亚姆作为诗人而享有盛名，他成功地运用了"柔巴依"诗体，全面地表现了对生活、人生、世界、宗教等方面的看法，经英国诗人爱德华·菲茨杰拉德的翻译(再创作)，奥马尔·哈亚姆确立了他在世界文学中的地位，菲茨杰拉德的《奥马尔·哈亚姆之柔巴依集》(又名《鲁拜集》)也成为英国文学史上的纪念碑之一。此为菲译第一版(七十五首)。——编注者
② 据伊斯兰教，天空为倒扣的碗。——编注者
③ 此处指太阳。——编注者

4

Now the New Year reviving old Desires,
The thoughtful Soul to Solitude retires,
    Where the WHITE HAND OF MOSES on the Bough
Puts out, and Jesus from the ground suspires.

5

Irám indeed is gone with all its Rose,
And Jamshýd's Sev'n-ring'd Cup where no one knows;
    But still the Vine her ancient Ruby yields,
And still a Garden by the Water blows.

6

And David's Lips are lock't; but in divine①
High-piping Péhleví, with 'Wine! Wine! Wine②!
    '*Red* Wine!' — the Nightingale cries to the Rose
That yellow Cheek of hers to incarnadine.

7

Come, fill the Cup, and in the Fire of Spring
The Winter Garment of Repentance fling:
    The Bird of Time has but a little way
To fly — and Lo! the Bird is on the Wing.

8

And look — a thousand Blossoms with the Day

---

① *David's Lips are lock't*: 'the Psalmist will sing no more.'
② *Péhleví*: or Pahlavi, here used of the language in which the Zendavesta is written, but more appropriately applied to the characters in which that language is transcribed.

4

新岁使旧时的愿望焕发生气①,
沉思的性灵退到孤寂中隐匿——
  摩西的素手缀满那里的枝头②,
耶稣在那里的地上发出叹息③。

5

伊兰园同它的玫瑰荡然无存④,
杰姆西王的七环杯湮没无闻⑤;
  但葡萄依然酿出古老的红酒,
有个傍水园子照旧花开缤纷。

6

大卫的双唇紧锁;但是夜莺啊⑥,
使血色涌上玫瑰萎黄的脸颊——
  她,操着神妙的佩雷维语尖叫⑦:
"来! 来呀! 来酒! 来红酒! 来红酒啊!"

7

来,把杯儿斟满;往春天的火里,
抛去你悔恨交加的隆冬外衣;
  时光之鸟只能飞短短的距离
看哪! 这鸟儿已经在振翅扑翼。

8

看哪! 千百朵花儿天亮时醒来,

---

① 新岁,这个新岁以春分为元旦。在波斯改用阴历后的长时期内,这一天仍是一个相传由杰姆西王规定的节日。——译者
② 语出《圣经·出埃及记》第四章第六节。据说这诗中指的是一种颇像藏红花的波斯花儿。——译者
③ 古代波斯人认为,耶稣起死回生的法力在他的呼吸之中。——译者
④ 伊兰园,波斯一古园名,为夏达德王所建。现已湮没于阿拉伯沙漠之中。——译者
⑤ 杰姆西王,传说中的波斯王;七环杯,灵杯,象征七天、七海、七行星等。——译者
⑥ 大卫,《圣经》中的古希伯来王,善歌。——译者
⑦ 佩雷维语,三世纪到七世纪期间通行于波斯的语言。——编注者

Woke — and a thousand scatter'd into Clay:
And this first Summer Month that brings the Rose
Shall take Jamshýd and Kaikobád away.

9

But come with old Khayyám, and leave the Lot
Of Kaikobád and Kaikhosrú forgot:
　Let Rustum lay about him as he will,
Or Hátim Tai cry Supper — heed them not.

10

With me along some Strip of Herbage strown①,
That just divides the desert from the sown,
　Where name of Slave and Sultán scarce is known,
And pity Sultán Máhmúd on his Throne.

11

Here with a Loaf of Bread beneath the Bough,
A Flask of Wine, a Book of Verse — and Thou
　Beside me singing in the Wilderness —
And Wilderness is Paradise enow.

12

'How sweet is mortal Sovranty!' — think some:
Others — 'How blest the Paradise to come!'
　Ah, take the Cash in hand and Waive the Rest,

---

① *strown*: cf. below, l. 298, 'Among the Guests Star-scatter'd on the Grass.' Some verb like 'lie' must be supplied before 'With me.'

千百朵花儿又飘零化作尘埃; 30
　就是这带来玫瑰的初夏月份
带着杰姆西、带着凯柯巴离开①。

9

但随我老哈亚姆来吧,凯柯巴
和凯霍斯鲁的命运别去记挂②;
　让鲁斯吐姆随意去横冲直撞③, 35
让哈蒂姆大呼开饭;你别管他④。

10

任哪片牧草地上,倚在我身边——
它,隔开了沙漠和下种的农田;
　在那儿,君奴之称已难得听见;
可怜,高踞宝座的马穆德苏丹⑤。 40

以上黄杲炘　译

11

树荫下放着一卷诗章,
一瓶葡萄美酒,一点干粮,
　有你在这荒原中傍我欢歌——
荒原呵,呵,便是天堂!

12

有人希图现世的光荣; 45
有人希图天国的来临;
　呵,且惜今日,浮名于我何有,

---

① 凯柯巴,古波斯国王。——译者
② 凯霍斯鲁,即波斯帝国创建者居鲁士(前598—前530)。他于公元前539年带军占领巴比伦城,灭新巴比伦王国。——译者
③ 鲁斯吐姆,传说中的英雄扎尔之子,以勇武著称。——编注者
④ 哈蒂姆,以东方式慷慨而著称的人物。——译者
⑤ 马穆德(Máhmúd, 971—1030),阿富汗加尼兹王朝国王,曾统治波斯部分地区。——编注者

Oh, the brave Music of a *distant* Drum①!

13

Look to the Rose that blows about us — 'Lo,
'Laughing,' she says, 'into the World I blow:
   'At once the silken Tassel of my Purse
'Tear, and its Treasure on the Garden throw②.'

14

The Worldly Hope men set their Hearts upon
Turns Ashes — or it prospers; and anon,
   Like Snow upon the Desert's dusty Face
Lighting a little Hour or two — is gone.

15

And those who husbanded the Golden Grain,
And those who flung it to the Winds like Rain,
   Alike to no such aureate Earth are turn'd
As, buried once, Men want dug up again.

16

Think, in this batter'd Caravanserai③
Whose Doorways are alternate Night and Day,
   How Sultán after Sultán with his Pomp
Abode his Hour or two, and went his way.

17

They say the Lion and the Lizard keep

---

① *of a* distant *Drum*: 'beaten outside a Palace,' to summon the soldiery. Death's summons need cause no anxiety while it is yet far off.
② *its Treasure*: 'the Rose's Golden Centre.'
③ *Caravanserai*: an inn in Eastern countries where caravans put up; in shape a quadrangular building with a large courtyard in the centre. Here it stands for the earth.

何有于远方鞳鞳的鼓音①。

以上 郭沫若 译

13

瞧我们身旁盛开的玫瑰。她说:
"看哪,我含笑来世上绽出花朵,
  转眼,我香囊的丝穗断裂破碎,
囊中的珍宝就在园子里撒落。"

14

人们所心向神往的世俗企求
变成了灰烬或烈火烹油,尔后,
  就像雪飘落灰封尘蒙的沙漠,
辉映了一时半刻便化为乌有。

15

辛勤耕耘的,种出了金穗玉粒,
挥霍奢靡的,在风中撒粮如雨;
  他们,都不会变成金色的沙泥——
一朝埋下,再不会被重新掘起。

16

你想,在这门前便有日夜交替,
已经凋敝破败的商队客栈里,
  一个个苏丹如何在荣华之中
守到他命定的时辰,就此别离。

17

人说杰姆西得意豪饮的宫廷②,

---

① 据说这首柔巴依是除《圣经》外最为英语国家人民熟知的四行诗。在我国,这首诗有多种译法,如:有人说;"人间的富贵甘甜如蜜!"/有人说:"未来的天堂才是福地!"/拿好这现钱,丢开其他的一切;/呵,管它远处鼓乐的美妙华丽!"(黄杲炘译)——编注者
② 此处指现在伊朗的波斯波利斯。该城又称塔赫特·伊·杰姆西,意为"杰姆西的御座",现仅存一些遗迹。——译者

The Courts where Jamshýd gloried and drank deep①:
And Bahrám, that great Hunter — the Wild Ass
Stamps o'er his Head, and he lies fast asleep.

18

I sometimes think that never blows so red
The Rose as where some buried Caesar bled;
That every Hyacinth the Garden wears
Dropt in its Lap from some once lovely Head.

19

And this delightful Herb whose tender Green
Fledges the River's Lip on which we lean —
Ah, lean upon it lightly! for who knows
From what once lovely Lip it springs unseen!

20

Ah, my Belovéd, fill the Cup that clears
TO-DAY of past Regrets and future Fears —
To-morrow? — Why, To-morrow I may be
Myself with Yesterday's Sev'n Thousand Years.

---

① *The Courts*: at Persepolis, which Jamshýd is credited with having built.

如今猛狮和蜥蝎在那里巡行；
　　野驴也在巴拉姆的头上跺脚①，
但这伟大猎手还是长眠不醒。

18

我怕最红的红不过
生在帝王喋血处的蔷薇；
　　园中朵朵玉簪儿怕是
从当年美人头上坠下来的②。

以上闻一多　译

19

草色喜人，毛羽般的新翠嫩绿
铺满江湑，这儿我们靠下身躯③；
　　啊，轻轻地靠下吧！谁知道从前，
多美的绛唇才把它暗中化育④。

20

啊，我亲爱的，斟满这今日之杯，
浇却那往日之悔和来日之畏；
　　明天哪！哎，到了明天连我自己
怕已归入昨天的七千年之内⑤。

以上黄杲炘　译

---

① 巴拉姆，波斯萨珊王朝(224—651)的一个君主，好色。此处的渔色之意用的是"猎"。——编注者
② 亦译为"有时我想：古来今往的玫瑰丛，/就数理过恺撒血肉处的最红——/朵朵招展的玉簪花儿，也都是/从春风一度的头上坠落园中"(黄杲炘译)。——编注者
③④ 江湑，绛唇，原文为 river-lip 和 lip，以表示两者之间存在着某种联系，为在译文中传达这种联系，特译为江湑(意为江边)及绛唇。——译者
⑤ 按诗人年代，波斯人以为地球年龄为七千岁，此处含有明日身死化为尘土之意。——编注者

21

Lo! some we loved, the loveliest and best
That Time and Fate of all their Vintage prest,
   Have drunk their Cup a Round or two before
And one by one crept silently to Rest.

22

And we, that now make merry in the Room
They left, and Summer dresses in new Bloom①,
   Ourselves must we beneath the Couch of Earth
Descend, ourselves to make a Couch — for whom?

23

Ah, make the most of what we yet may spend,
Before we too into the Dust descend;
   Dust into Dust, and under Dust, to lie,
Sans Wine, sans Song, sans Singer, and — sans End②!

24

Alike for those who for TO-DAY prepare,
And those that after a TO-MORROW stare,
   A Muezzín from the Tower of Darkness cries,
'Fools! your Reward is neither Here nor There!'

25

Why, all the Saints and Sages who discuss'd
Of the Two Worlds so learnedly, are thrust
   Like foolish Prophets forth; their Words to Scorn
Are scatter'd and their Mouths are stopt with Dust.

---

① *They left, and Summer dresses*: sc. which they left and which Summer dresses.

② *Sans*: before the time of Shakespeare this substitute for 'without' was 'used almost exclusively with substantives adopted from Old French, in collocations already formed in that language.'

21

往日的良朋,多少是貌美身强,
滚滚的时辰把他的葡萄压成酒浆,
　　他们只饮得一杯,或者两杯,
已次第进了那长眠的茔圹。

郭沫若　译

22

如今我们欣赏着新夏的花衫,
在前人留下的屋里作乐寻欢;
　　但我们也得躺在大地的床下——
让自己变作床铺给谁来长眠?

黄杲炘　译

23

呵,在我们未成尘土之先,
用尽千金尽可尽情沉湎;
　　尘土归尘,尘下陈人,
歌声酒滴——永远不能到九泉。

郭沫若　译

24

有些人为了今天而张罗奔忙,
有些人瞪着眼睛把明天盼望;
　　司祷从黑暗之塔向他们叫喊①:
"这儿和那里都没蠢人的报偿!"

黄杲炘　译

25

伊古以来的圣哲,
惯会说现世与天堂——
　　一朝口被尘封,自嘲莫解,
同那江湖的预言者一样。

郭沫若　译

---

① 司祷,清真寺塔楼上的呼叫者,每天在一定的时刻叫信徒们祈祷。——译者

26

Oh, come with old Khayyám, and leave the Wise
To talk; one thing is certain, that Life flies;
   One thing is certain, and the Rest is Lies;
The Flower that once has blown for ever dies.

27

Myself when young did eagerly frequent
Doctor and Saint, and heard great Argument
   About it and about: but evermore
Came out by the same Door as in I went.

28

With them the Seed of Wisdom did I sow,
And with my own hand labour'd it to grow:
   And this was all the Harvest that I reap'd —
'I came like Water, and like Wind I go.'

29

Into this Universe, and *why* not knowing,
Nor *whence*, like Water willy-nilly flowing:
   And out of it, as Wind along the Waste,
I know not *whither*, willy-nilly blowing.

30

What, without asking, hither hurried *whence*?
And, without asking, *whither* hurried hence!
   Another and another Cup to drown
The Memory of this Impertinence!

31

Up from Earth's Centre, through the Seventh Gate
I rose, and on the Throne of Saturn sate,

26

啊,跟我来吧!让聪明人去研讨;
但有一点无疑:此生像飞一样;
　　就这点无疑,其他的全是撒谎;
一度盛开的花朵它将永归灭亡。

27

年轻时,我也对那些学者圣人
热切地造访;谈生说死的宏论
　　也颇有所闻:但我出来时走的
无非还是进去时走的那道门。

以上黄杲炘　译

28

我也学播了智慧之种,
亲手培植它渐渐葱茏;
　　而今我所获得的收成——
只是"来如流水,逝如风"。

29

飘飘入世,如水之不得不流,
不知何故来,也不知来自何处;
　　飘飘出世,如风之不得不吹,
风过漠地又不知吹向何许。

30

请君莫问何处来,
请君莫问何处去!
　　浮此禁觞千万锺,
消沉那无常的记忆。

以上郭沫若　译

31

从这大地的中心我腾身而起,
飞过七天门坐上了土星宝椅①;

---

① 古希腊天文学家托勒密的天动说认为,围绕地球运转的第七圈是土星。——编注者

And many Knots unravel'd by the Road;
But not the Knot of Human Death and Fate.

32

There was a Door to which I found no Key:
There was a Veil past which I could not see:
   Some little Talk awhile of ME and THEE
There seem'd — and then no more of THEE and ME.

33

Then to the rolling Heav'n itself I cried,
Asking, 'What Lamp had Destiny to guide
   'Her little Children stumbling in the Dark?'
And — 'A blind Understanding!' Heav'n replied.

34

Then to this earthen Bowl did I adjourn
My Lip the secret Well of Life to learn:
   And Lip to Lip it murmur'd — 'While you live
'Drink! — for once dead you never shall return.'

35

I think the Vessel, that with fugitive
Articulation answer'd, once did live,
   And merry-make; and the cold Lip I kiss'd,
How many Kisses might it take — and give!

36

For in the Market-place, one Dusk of Day,
I watch'd the Potter thumping his wet Clay:
   And with its all obliterated Tongue
It murmur'd — 'Gently, Brother, gently, pray!

一路上解出过多少巧结难题，
但没解出人类生死命运之谜。

　　　　　　　　　　　　黄杲炘　译

32
此地是无钥之门；
此处是窥不透的帷幕；
　　有的在暂时地呼帝呼神——
少时间已不闻我我汝汝。

　　　　　　　　　　　　郭沫若　译

33
于是，我朝着回旋的苍天呼叫——
我问："命运用什么灯盏来引导
　　她那些黑暗中跌跌撞撞的孩子？"
"用一种盲目的悟性！"苍天答道。

34
于是我把嘴凑上陶瓷的酒碗，
把这生活的神秘之泉探一探；
　　碗口刚沾嘴就向我咕哝："活着，
就喝！因为一去世你再难回返。"

　　　　　　　　以上黄杲炘　译

35
幽幽对语的这个土瓶
是曾生在世间，曾经痛饮；
　　呵！我今亲着它的唇边，
不知它又曾授受了多少接吻！

　　　　　　　　　　　　郭沫若　译

36
因为有天黄昏，我在那个市集，
看那位陶工使劲地捣着湿泥；
　　那泥用早已失传的语言低叫：
"轻些，兄弟！请轻些，兄弟，求求你！"

37

Ah, fill the Cup: — what boots it to repeat
How Time is slipping underneath our Feet:
    Unborn TO-MORROW and dead YESTERDAY,
Why fret about them if TO-DAY be sweet!

38

One Moment in Annihilation's Waste,
One Moment, of the Well of Life to taste —
    The Stars are setting and the Caravan①
Starts for the Dawn of Nothing — Oh, make haste!

39

How long, how long, in infinite Pursuit
Of This and That endeavour and dispute?
    Better be merry with the fruitful Grape
Than sadden after none, or bitter, Fruit.

40

You know, my Friends, how long since in my House
For a new Marriage I did make Carouse:
    Divorced old barren Reason from my Bed,
And took the Daughter of the Vine to Spouse.

41

For 'IS' and 'IS-Not' though *with* Rule and Line,
And 'UP-AND-DOWN' *without*, I could define,
    I yet, in all I only cared to know,
Was never deep in anything but — Wine.

42

And lately, by the Tavern Door agape,

---

① *The Stars are setting:* presumably this means 'fading,' as the stars are rising and setting continuously throughout the twenty-four hours.

37

啊,把杯儿斟满;一遍遍地惊呼
"转瞬间时光已逝"又于事何补?
　　只要今天过得美,未生的明朝、
已死的昨天,为它们烦恼何苦!

38

寂灭的荒漠里作一片刻羁留;
片刻之中,把生命之泉尝一口——
　　斗转参横,瀚海中的旅行商队
向乌有之晨进发。啊,快喝个够!

39

对这对那所作的无穷尽追求
使人努力和争论了多久多久?
　　消愁解颐的葡萄酒一杯在手,
强似为苦果或空无所有担忧。

40

你知道,朋友,为了第二次婚礼,
我早就在家办过狂欢的酒席;
　　衰老不孕的理性我把她休去,
娶了葡萄的女儿做我的爱妻①。

41

我虽然靠绳墨判断是非正误,
能不凭它们来区别兴衰沉浮;
　　然而在我愿意了解的一切中,
除了酒我从未深究任何事物②。

以上黄杲炘　译

42

在日前,茅店之门未闭,

---

① 葡萄的女儿,喻葡萄酒。——译者
② 这里诗人是在拿他的学术活动开玩笑。——译者

Came stealing through the Dusk an Angel Shape
    Bearing a Vessel on his Shoulder; and
He bid me taste of it; and 'twas — the Grape!

43

The Grape that can with Logic absolute
The Two-and-Seventy jarring Sects confute:
    The subtle Alchemist that in a Trice
Life's leaden Metal Into Gold transmute①.

44

The mighty Máhmúd, the victorious Lord,
That all the misbelieving and black Horde
    Of Fears and Sorrows that infest the Soul
Scatters and slays with his enchanted Sword.

45

But leave the Wise to wrangle, and with me
The Quarrel of the Universe let be:
    And, in some corner of the Hubbub coucht,
Make Game of that which makes as much of Thee.

46

For in and out, above, about, below,
'Tis nothing but a Magic Shadow-show,
    Play'd in a Box whose Candle is the Sun,
Round which we Phantom Figures come and go.

47

And if the Wine you drink, the Lip you press,

---

① *transmute*: supply 'can' from l. 169.

黄昏之中来了一个安琪；
　肩着的一个土瓶，她叫我尝尝；
　土瓶里原来是——葡萄的酒浆！

43

葡萄酒呀，你是以绝对的逻辑
说破七十二宗的纷纭①：
　你是崇高的炼金术士
　瞬时间把生之铅矿点化成金。

以上郭沫若　译

44

这是伟大的马穆德，神武非凡②。
他呀，挥舞着法力无边的长剑，
　杀得那一帮信邪的黝黑贼冠——
　那骚扰灵魂的忧惧，纷纷逃窜。

45

但是，任那些贤哲去争争吵吵，
让天地之间的不和同我一道；
　在那喧嚣声中找个角落蹲下，
　把取笑你的也同样捉弄取笑。

46

进进出出，上上下下，前后回迂——
这个只是一出走马灯的戏剧；
　灯里的火便是太阳，在它周围
　是我们这些影像在来来去去。

47

如果说，你吻的唇和你喝的酒

---

① 据说，世界上有七十二种宗教，世界为他们所分割，其中包括伊斯兰教。——编注者
② 马穆德，参见本诗第10首注。此句字面上指马穆德对印度战争的这段历史。据记载，他曾多次侵犯印度，用掠夺来的财富把加兹尼改建为辉煌的城市。——译者

End in the Nothing all Things end in — Yes —
Then fancy while Thou art, Thou art but what
Thou shalt be — Nothing — Thou shalt not be less.

48

While the Rose blows along the River Brink,
With old Khayyám the Ruby Vintage drink:
And when the Angel with his darker Draught
Draws up to Thee — take that and do not shrink.

49

'Tis all a Chequer-board of Nights and Days[①]
Where Destiny with Men for Pieces plays:
Hither and thither moves, and mates, and slays,
And one by one back in the Closet lays.

50

The Ball no Question makes of Ayes and Noes[②],
But Right or Left as strikes the Player goes;
And He that toss'd Thee down into the Field,
He knows about it all — HE knows — HE knows!

51

The Moving Finger writes; and, having writ,
Moves on: nor all thy Piety nor Wit
Shall lure it back to cancel half a Line,
Nor all thy Tears wash out a Word of it.

52

And that inverted Bowl we call The Sky,
Whereunder crawling coop't we live and die,

---

① *a Chequer-board*: a chess-board was originally called a 'chequer.'
② *The Ball*: an allusion to the game of polo, which originated in the East.

都归于万物的结局:子虚乌有;
　　试想:如今健在的你只是未来
那乌有之你:到头来你还依旧。

48
趁如今河边的玫瑰盛开怒放,
随我老哈亚姆喝喝嫣红佳酿;
　　等那天使捧着他的浓酒敬你①——
你得接下它,可不要退缩惊慌。

以上黄杲炘　译

49
我们是可怜的一套象棋,
昼与夜便是一张棋局,
　　任"他"走东走西或擒或杀,
走罢后又一一收归匣里。

50
皮球呵也只有唯命是从,
一任那打球者到处抛弄;
　　就是"他"把你抛到地来,
一切的原由只有他懂——他懂!

51
指动字成,字成指动②;
任你如何至诚,如何机智,
　　难叫他收回成命消去半行,
任你眼泪流完也难洗掉一字。

以上郭沫若　译

52
那翻转的碗儿我们唤作天空,
下面是我们生死其中的樊笼;

---
① 这里指的是死亡天使阿兹雷尔(Azrael)。——编注者
② 把人生比作一本书,那么人的生活就犹如在书中写字。—　编注者

Lift not thy hands to *It* for help — for It
Rolls impotently on as Thou or I.

53
With Earth's first Clay They did the Last Man's knead,
And then of the Last Harvest sow'd the Seed:
   Yea, the first Morning of Creation wrote
What the Last Dawn of Reckoning shall read.

54
I tell Thee this — When, starting from the Goal,
Over the shoulders of the flaming Foal
   Of Heav'n Parwín and Mushtara they flung,
In my predestin'd Plot of Dust and Soul

55
The Vine had struck a Fibre; which about
If clings my Being — let the SKúfi flout;
   Of my Base Metal may be filed a Key①,
That shall unlock the Door he howls without.

56
And this I Know: whether the one True Light
Kindle to Love, or Wrath-consume me quite②,
   One glimpse of It within the Tavern caught
Better than in the Temple lost outright.

---

① *a Key*: sc. to the mysteries of man's origin, purpose, and ultimate end.
② *Wrath-consume*: a strange compound for 'consume in wrath.' The omission of 'is', in l. 224 is rather harsh.

别趴倒在地下举手向天求助——
它之无能为力也和你我相同。

黄杲炘　译

53

最初的泥丸捏成了最终的人形①，
最后的收成便是那最初的种子：
　　天地开辟时的老文章
写成了天地掩闭时的字句。

郭沫若　译

54

你听我说：从终点出发之时起，
他们就把帕尔温和穆希塔利②
　　抛过了喷火天驹的肩头，这时③，
在我命定是尘和魂的心田里④

55

葡萄树把须根扎下；如果同它
我把缘结下，任苏非们去笑话；
　　我这贱料也许可做钥匙一把——
能把门打开：他就在门外叫骂。

56

我知道：不管是真火点着情爱⑤，
还是天怒之火烧尽我的骨骸，
　　如能在酒店里把它看上一眼，
强似在圣堂神殿里踌躇徘徊。

---

① 据《圣经》，上帝按照自己的形象，用泥土捏成了人，又向他吹了口气，于是人就有了生命。——编注者
② 帕尔温即昴宿，穆希塔利即木星。——译者
③ 天驹喻太阳。此诗涉及星象学，诗人谙于此道，曾以此谋生。这三句意即，创世之初，我奥马尔的一切便命中注定了。——译者
④ 此处无标点，可与下面一首连起来读。——译者
⑤ "真火"指真主。——编注者

57

Oh, Thou, who didst with Pitfall and with Gin
Beset the Road I was to wander in,
    Thou wilt not with Predestination round
Enmesh me, and impute my Fall to Sin?

58

Oh, Thou, who Man of baser Earth didst make,
And who with Eden didst devise the Snake;
    For all the Sin wherewith the Face of Man
Is blacken'd, Man's Forgiveness give — and take[①]!

KÚZA-NÁMA

59

Listen again. One evening at the Close
Of Ramazán, ere the better Moon arose,
    In that old Potter's Shop I stood alone
With the clay Population round in Rows.

60

And, strange to tell, among that Earthen Lot
Some could articulate, white others not:
    And suddenly one more impatient cried —
'Who *is* the Potter, pray, and who the Pot?'

61

Then said another — 'Surely not in vain
'My Substance from the common Earth was ta'en,

[①] This tremendous line, with its last two words flinging on God's shoulders the responsibility for man's sins, is not in the original.

57

你呀,你在我彷徨流浪的路上,
布置下陷阱机关和美酒佳酿,
　　总不会撒下难逃的罪孽罗网,
再把堕落的恶名安在我头上?

以上黄杲炘　译

58

呵,你呀,你用劣土造人,
在乐园中你也造出恶蛇;
　　人的面目为一切的罪恶所污——
你请容赦人——你也受人容赦①!

郭沫若　译

陶壶篇

59

再听听。斋月将尽的一个傍夜②,
转缺为盈的月亮还没有露脸;
　　我独自站在那老陶工的店中③——
周围是一排一排的陶国成员。

60

说也奇怪,那一大堆陶器之中,
有的能发言,有的却非哑即聋;
　　忽然,一位急性子的发出叫喊:
"你说,谁算是陶器?谁算是陶工?"

61

另一个接着说道:"这不会徒劳——
从普通的泥中挑中我的材料,

---

① 此诗的反宗教思想达到了高潮。诗人毕竟还是一个名义上的穆斯林,此处的"你"已不再是中世纪波斯的伊斯兰真主,而是维多利亚时代英国的基督教上帝。——译者
② 斋月,伊斯兰教历的九月是信徒的封斋期。——编注者
③ 这里是把人和造人的人比作是陶器和陶工。——编注者

'That He who subtly wrought me into Shape
'Should stamp me back to common Earth again.'

62

245 Another said — 'Why, ne'er a peevish Boy,
'Would break the Bowl from which he drank in Joy;
'Shall He that *made* the Vessel in pure Love
'And Fancy, in an after Rage destroy!'

63

None answer'd this; but after Silence spake
250 A Vessel of a more ungainly Make:
'They sneer at me for leaning all awry;
'What! did the Hand then of the Potter shake?'

64

Said one — 'Folks of a surly Tapster tell,
'And daub his Visage with the Smoke of Hell;
255 'They talk of some strict Testing of us — Pish!
'He's a Good Fellow, and 'twill all be well.'

65

Then said another with a long-drawn Sigh,
'My Clay with long oblivion is gone dry:
'But, fill me with the old familiar Juice,
260 'Methinks I might recover by and by!'

66

So while the Vessels one by one were speaking,
One spied the little Crescent all were seeking:
And then they jogg'd each other, 'Brother, Brother!

他把我精巧地做成这模样后
　　竟然再把我踩成普通的泥淖。"

62

又一个说道:"从来没一个顽童
会砸碎他曾喝得开怀的陶盅;
　　出于喜爱而**做**的器皿不肯砸——
哪怕**他**以后怎么样怒气冲冲!"

63

这话谁也没搭腔;静了会之后,
有个形象丑陋的家伙开了口:
　　"他们笑话我,老说我歪歪扭扭——
怎么,那陶工的双手曾经发抖?"

64

一个道:"人们说起个凶狠的酒保①——
用地狱之烟把他的脸弄得够瞧;
　　他们说我们得经受严峻考验——
呸! 他是个好样的,事儿错不了。"

65

接着,另一个吐了声长长的嗐②:
　　"长期搁置干得我的泥块裂开;
　　但只要给我灌满熟稔的酒浆,
我想,我能够很快就恢复过来。"

66

坛坛罐罐们正这样纷纷发言,
它们期待的新月已给谁发现③;
　　这时它们你推我碰:"兄弟! 兄弟!

---

① 此处是酒坛们在说话,"酒保"指酒商。——编注者
② "另一个"指的是一个丢弃了过去的信仰,现又想恢复的人。——编注者
③ 伊斯兰教历九月(阴历)封斋后第二十九天黄昏时,如望见新月,第二天就开斋,否则便推迟一天。因此急于开斋的穆斯林等待新月的心情十分殷切。——译者

'Hark to the Porter's Shoulder-knot a-creaking!'

67

Ah, with the Grape my fading Life provide,
And wash my Body whence the Life has died,
    And in a Winding-sheet of Vine-leaf wrapt,
So bury me by some sweet Garden-side.

68

That ev'n my buried Ashes such a Snare
Of Perfume shall fling up into the Air,
    As not a True Believer passing by
But shall be overtaken unawere.

69

Indeed the Idols I have loved so long
Have done my Credit in Men's Eye much wrong:
    Have drown'd my Honour in a shallow Cup,
And sold my Reputation for a Song.

70

Indeed, indeed, Repentance oft before
I swore — but was I sober when I swore?
    And then and then came Spring, and Rose-in-hand
My thread-bare Penitence apieces tore.

71

And much as Wine has play'd the Infidel,
And robb'd me of my Robe of Honour — well,
    I often wonder what the Vintners buy
One-half so precious as the Goods they sell.

听听搬酒人吱吱作响的垫肩!"

以上黄杲炘　译

67

呵,我生将谢,请为我准备酒浆,
生命死后,请洗涤我的皮囊,
　　请把我埋葬在落叶之下,
间有游人来往的花园边上。

郭沫若　译

68

这样,我的遗体虽然已被埋葬,
还向空中撒一个芬芳的罗网,
　　使那一个个过往的虔诚信徒
都不知不觉地被它缠住绕上。

黄杲炘　译

69

诚哉,我爱了这么久的
偶像们把我的品行坏了:
　　把我的光荣溺在个浅杯之中,
把我的名闻换首歌儿卖了。

郭沫若　译

70

真的,我从前也常常起誓改悔——
不过,起誓的时候我可曾酒醉?
　　待到春风一吹,我又手拈玫瑰——
我陈旧的忏悔已被撕得粉碎。

黄杲炘　译

71

酒呀,你便是我的叛徒,
屡次把我"荣名的衣裳"剥去——
　　剥去吧,我不解卖酒之家,
何故要换取这半价的敝屣。

郭沫若　译

72

Alas, that Spring should vanish with the Rose!
That Youth's sweet-scented Manuscript should close!
   The Nightingale that in the Branches sang,
Ah, whence, and whither flown again, who knows!

73

Ah, Love! could thou and I with Fate conspire
To grasp this sorry Scheme of Things entire,
   Would not we shatter it to bits — and then
Re-mould it nearer to the Heart's Desire!

74

Ah, Moon of my Delight who know'st no wane,
The Moon of Heav'n is rising once again:
   How oft hereafter rising shall she look
Through this same Garden after me — in vain!

75

And when Thyself with shining Foot shall pass
Among the Guests Star-scatter'd on the Grass,
   And in thy joyous Errand reach the Spot
Where I made one — turn down an empty Glass!
        TAMAM SHUD.

E. FITZGERALD.

72

唉,可春天要同玫瑰一起消亡!
芬芳的青春手稿呀,也得合上!
  夜莺啊,曾在树枝间娇啼曼唱——
谁知道她来自哪里、去向何方!

黄杲炘　译

73

爱哟,你我若能和"他"勾通好了,
将这全体不幸的世界攫到,
  我们怕不要捣得它碎片纷纷,
好依着你我的心愿再持再造!

74

(那儿方升的皓月又来窥人了,
月哟,你今后又将)圆缺几遭;
  又几遭来这花园寻觅我们,
恐怕此中有一人再难寻到!

以上闻一多　译

75

啊,当你自己迈着雪亮的脚儿,
穿过那些星散在草地上的游客,
  欢乐地来到我曾坐过的地方——
啊,请把空空的酒杯倒个个儿!

黄杲炘　译

编注　爱德华·菲茨杰拉德(Edward Fitzgerald,1809—1883),英国作家、翻译家,以翻译波斯诗人奥马尔·哈亚姆的《柔巴依集》(《鲁拜集》)闻名。诗集译得自由,诗句洗练、自然,音调优美,被认为是诗人译诗的成功范例。初版时不受注意,后为罗塞蒂等诗人推崇,名声大震,成为英语诗史上的瑰宝,并促进了英国十九世纪"世纪末诗派"厌世气氛的形成。他还翻译过西班牙剧本和波斯寓言,晚年致力于希腊古典悲剧的改写工作。

320. THE CHAMBERED NAUTILUS

This is the ship of pearl, which, poets feign,
    Sails the unshadowed main, —
    The venturous bark that flings
On the sweet summer wind its purpled wings
In gulfs enchanted, where the siren sings,
    And coral reefs lie bare,
Where the cold sea-maids rise to sun their streaming hair.

Its webs of living gauze no more unfurl;
    Wrecked is the ship of pearl!
    And every chambered cell,
Where its dim dreaming life was wont to dwell,
As the frail tenant shaped his growing shell,
    Before thee lies revealed —
Its irised ceiling rent, its sunless crypt unsealed[①]!

Year after year beheld the silent toil
    That spread his lustrous coil;
    Still, as the spiral grew,

---

① *irised*: 'coloured like the rainbow.'

320. 带壳的鹦鹉螺①

霍姆斯

这是一艘美如珍珠的船,诗人们想象②
　　它在浩瀚明亮的大海里扬帆,——
　　冒险的小舟,它扑动着
紫红色的双翼,乘着温和可爱的夏风
在令人痴迷的海湾,海妖女轻舒歌喉③,　　　　　5
　　珊瑚礁裸露在水面,迎着太阳
冰冷的美人鱼爬上礁石,秀发随风飘散。

它再不能歙张那肉的薄膜如蹼翼一般,
　　美丽的珍珠船儿已经破残!
　　船上一个个幽闭的壳室　　　　　　　　　　10
是朦胧的梦中生命往常留连的温柔乡。
当脆弱的居上增造他那扩张的壳壁,
　　在你躺下舒展身躯之前——
黑暗的窨窟裂开缝隙,它让出彩虹色的天花板!

年复一年,注视着他用默默的辛劳　　　　　　　15
　　展现了那一种光辉的螺壳圈;
　　静静地,螺旋的年轮放大了,

---

① 鹦鹉螺,头足纲贝壳动物,表面灰白,有很多橙红或褐色波状横纹,内面具极美丽的珍珠光泽,由许多弧形隔板将内腔分为许多小室,随肉体生长而不断成形,故诗人有 chambered 之说。——译者
② "诗人们想象"及以下三行:以往的诗人都以为鹦鹉螺以带蹼的脊鳍为帆在海里游动,例如诗人蒲柏的《论人》第 178 首写道:学小鹦鹉螺航行海上,展开薄鳍迎接行船的风。——编注者
③ 海妖女(Siren),通译"塞壬",参见第 86 首注。——编注者

He left the past year's dwelling for the new,
Stole with soft step its shining archway through,
    Built up its idle door,
Stretched in his last-found home, and knew the old no more.

Thanks of the heavenly message brought by thee,
    Child of the wandering sea,
    Cast from her lap forlorn!
From thy dead lips a clearer note is born
Than ever Triton blew from wreathéd horn!
    While on mine ear it rings,
Through the deep caves of thought I hear a voice that sings: —

Build thee more stately mansions, O my soul,
    As the swift seasons roll!
    Leave thy low-vaulted past!
Let each new temple, nobler than the last,
Shut thee from heaven with a dome more vast,
    Till thou at length art free,
Leaving thine outgrown shell by life's unresting sea.

                OLIVER WENDELL HOLMES.

他从往年的住舍出走,留赠新的房客,
　　步履轻轻,偷偷溜出了辉煌的拱道,
　　　　堵住这所空居的大门
爬伸进他刚找到的府邸,从此忘却了旧寮。

多谢你把天上的消息向我传告,
　　你这被徘徊的大海从浪尖
　　　　抛出的孤独凄凉的孩子!
你麻木的嘴唇吹出的音乐之声
清嘹的音色胜过海神的花环号角①!
　　　　它响起在我的耳旁,
　　从我的心灵深处,我听见一个声音在唱:——

替自己建造更多雄伟的大厦吧,哦,我的灵魂,
　　　　既然时光飞逝不停!
　　丢开吧,你往昔生活其中的低拱顶!
让每一座新的神庙都比前一座高贵,
用更广袤的圆屋顶把天空和你隔分,
　　　　等到你最终获得自由的天地,
　　便把狭小的贝壳,扔在人生动荡的大海之滨!

　　　　　　　　　　　　　　　林骧华　译

编注　奥利弗·温德尔·霍姆斯(Oliver Wendell Holmes, 1809—1894),美国作家及诗人。著有长篇小说和诗集多种,代表作是《早餐桌上的霸王》(*The Autocrat of the Breakfast Table*),本诗即选自该书第四章。在诗中,诗人借用随着鹦鹉螺的生长螺壳随之增大一事来告诫读者不断去开辟新的、更广泛的生活。

---

① 语出华兹华斯,参见本书卷四第278首末行。——编注者

321. THE MEN OF OLD

I know not that the men of old
    Were better than men now,
Of heart more kind, of hand more bold,
    Of more ingenuous brow:
I heed not those who pine for force
    A ghost of Time to raise①,
As if they thus could check the course②
    Of these appointed days.

Still it is true, and over true,
    That I delight to close
This book of life self-wise and new③,
    And let my thoughts repose
On all that humble happiness,
    The world has since forgone④, —
The daylight of contentedness
    That on those faces shone!

With rights, tho' not too closely scanned,

---

① *pine for force A ghost of Time to raise*: 'wish they had it in their power to bring back the past.'
② *thus*: this must mean by the mere wishing; for obviously, if they could restore the past, they would be abolishing the present, as the two times could not run concurrently.
③ *self-wise*: 'wise in its own conceit.'
④ *forgone*: 'left alone,' 'relinquished.'

321. 咏古人

霍顿勋爵

我不知道,那些优秀的古人
    是否就强过我们几分,
有更善良的心,更勇敢的手
    前额比我们更坦率天真:
我没留心过那些人,渴望着力量   5
    想**抓住**时间消逝的幽魂①,
好像这样就能检点以往的时辰
    把历史的事业评论。

我的行为比这更真,切实可行,
    我乐于合上这部   10
自以为是的新的生活课本,
    让我的思想躺在
一切卑微的幸福上安眠,
    从此就放弃了这世界,——
使那种人脸颊生辉的、   15
    心满意足的黎明!

虽说有权细看,又不那么贴近

---

① 此处的"时间"以及下文的"道德""自然""希望"几个词,原文都以大写字母起首。另外,"如今"一词原文是斜体,译文都以粗体标出。——译者

>   Enjoyed, as far as known, —
>   With will by no reverse unmanned, —
>   With pulse of even tone, —
>   They from to-day and from to-night
>   Expected nothing more,
>   Than yesterday and yesternight
>   Had proffered them before.
>
>
>   To them was life a simple art
>   Of duties to be done,
>   A game where each man took his part,
>   A race where all must run;
>   A battle whose great scheme and scope
>   They little cared to know,
>   Content, as men at arms, to cope
>   Each with his fronting foe.
>
>
>   Man *now* his Virtue's diadem
>   Puts on and proudly wears,
>   Great thoughts, great feelings, came to them,
>   Like instincts, unawares;
>   Blending their souls' sublimest needs
>   With tasks of every day,
>   They went about their gravest deeds,
>   As noble boys at play. —
>
>
>   And what if Nature's fearful wound
>   They did not probe and bare,
>   For that their spirits never swooned[1]
>   To Watch the misery there, —
>   For that their love but flowed more fast,

---

[1] *For that*: it was on that account, *i.e.* because they made no attempt to expose or solve the mystery of evil.

赏心悦目,只须知晓几分,——
带着并不使人颠倒失态的意志
　　带着平稳语调的冲动,——　　　　　　20
从今天,从今夜,他们
　　就把这一些期等,
比昨天,比昨夜,先前
　　给他们的不多一丝半星。

生活,对于他们只是一种手段　　　　　　25
　　去承担应负的责任,
是一种游戏,每人都去加入,
　　是一场比赛,人人必须竞争;
是一场战斗,它的谋略和范畴
　　他们从来不去问津,　　　　　　　　30
像是武装的士兵,只满足于
　　各人所面对的敌人。

如今的人,带上**道德**的冠冕
　　骄傲地顶着它奉为至尊,
伟人的思想,伟大的感情,从内心产生　　35
　　全无意识,仿佛出自本能:
心灵至高无上的需求中
　　交织进每日每时的膺命,
去开创最庄严的业绩成就
　　本着高贵青年行事的本分。　　　　　40

要是尚未探索**自然**的可怕伤痕
　　没有去剥开过,那又该作何论?
正因为未曾见人世的悲苦
　　他们才免难于颠倒神魂,
情爱来去更快,博爱之心易存　　　　　　45

　　　　Their charities more free,
　　Not conscious what mere drops they cast
　　　　Into the evil sea.

　　A man's best things are nearest him,
　　　　Lie close about his feet,
　　It is the distant and the dim
　　　　That we are sick to greet①:
　　For flowers that grow our hands beneath
　　　　We struggle and aspire, —
　　Our hearts must die, except they breathe
　　　　The air of fresh Desire.

　　Yet, Brothers, who up Reason's hill
　　　　Advance with hopeful cheer, —
　　O! loiter not, those heights are chill,
　　　　As chill as they are clear;
　　And still restrain your haughty gaze,
　　　　The loftier that ye go,
　　Remembering distance leaves a haze
　　　　On all that lies below.

LORD HOUGHTON.

---

① *we are sick to greet*: the 'we' is emphatic, '*we* are longing to find.'

全由于他们涉世未深。
几时可曾顾及,将爱的水滴洒落
却被恶之海水悄然噬吞?

人的安乐,离他自己最近
　　一如他脚边躺着的纤尘,
只有我们才急于去逢迎,
　　那遥远而又模糊的事情:
在我们手底下盛开的鲜花
　　如果让我们去追寻去夺争,——
我们的心会死去,除非它们呼吸到
　　希望的空气,它是那样清新。

弟兄们,只有在理性的山峰攀登
　　才能一路前进,和着希望的呼声,——
哦,不要游闲踯躅,山巅是寒冷的
　　它寒冷而又清楚分明;
请收起对古人傲然的睥睨①,
　　你们脚踏在通向崇高的征程,
记住,远方总有一片朦胧的雾霭
　　把那一切目标遮隐。

林骧华　译

编注　霍顿勋爵(Lord Houghton),英国诗人。本名理查德·蒙克顿·米尔纳斯(Richard Monckton Milnes,1809—1885),国会议员,受封为男爵。本诗选自诗集《多年的诗》(*Poems of Many Years*)。

---

① 此句意为:别把古人看得比你低劣,因为年代久隔,你不可能了解他们是些什么样的人。——译者

322. THE MILLER'S DAUGHTER

It is the miller's daughter,
    And she is grown so dear, so dear,
That I would be the jewel
    That trembles at her ear:
For hid in ringlets day and night,
I'd touch her neck so warm and white.

And I would be the girdle
    About her dainty dainty waist,
And her heart would beat against me
    In sorrow and in rest:
And I should know if it beat right,
I'd clasp it round so close and tight.

And I would be the necklace,
    And all day long to fall and rise
Upon her balmy bosom[①],
    With her laughter or her sighs,
And I would lie so light, so light,
I scarce should be unclasp'd at night.

LORD ALFRED TENNYSON.

[①] *balmy*: this may mean either 'fragrant' or 'soothing.'

322. 磨坊主的女儿

丁尼生

那是磨坊主的女儿,
　她长得可真是漂亮;
我多想变成颗珠宝,
　挂在她耳垂下晃荡——
日夜在她的鬈发中隐藏,　　　　5
挨着她温暖洁白的颈项。

我多想变成根腰带,
　围着她美妙的细腰;
无论她忧愁或平静,
　让她的心贴着我跳;　　　　　10
要知道她的心跳得怎样,
我得紧紧地缠在她腰上。

我多想变成串项链,
　挂在她芬芳的胸前;
整天儿起伏个不停——　　　　　15
　随着她欢笑或悲叹;
我要轻轻巧巧地偎着她,
让她晚上也不把我解下。

黄杲炘　译

编注　丁尼生(Alfred Tennyson,1809—1892),英国著名诗人,继华兹华斯之后被封为"桂冠诗人",主要作品有《诗集》《悼念》、独白戏剧《莫德》、组诗《国王抒事诗》等,思想上较为保守,艺术上特别注重诗的音乐性,格律严谨,但有时流于雕琢。

323. ST. AGNES' EVE

Deep on the convent-roof the snows
    Are sparkling to the moon;
My breath to heaven like vapour goes;
    May my soul follow soon!
The shadows of the convent-towers
    Slant down the snowy sward①,
Still creeping with the creeping hours
    That lead me to my Lord;
Make Thou my spirit pure and clear
    As are the frosty skies,
Or this first snowdrop of the year
    That in my bosom lies.

As these white robes are soil'd and dark,
    To yonder shining ground;
As this pale taper's earthly spark,
    To yonder argent round②;
So shows my soul before the Lamb,
    My spirit before Thee;
So in mine earthly house I am,
    To that I hope to be.
Break up the heavens, O Lord! and far,
    Thro' all yon starlight keen,

---

① *the snowy sward*: 'the lawn covered with snow.'
② *yonder argent round*: sc. the silver moon.

323. 圣·安妮节的前夜

丁尼生

在修道院的屋顶上,深深的
　　积雪在明月下闪光;
我的呼吸像雾霭氤氲升向碧落;
　　愿我的灵魂快随着飞翔!
修道院的楼阁在银白色的　　　　　　　　5
　　草地上画出斜影,
它们静静地随推移的时间推移,
　　引导我向我主飞升:
主呵,使我的精神像崇高的
　　霜天一样澄澈明净,　　　　　　　　10
或像我胸前那初雪的
　　雪花一样皎洁无尘。

宛如受到玷污的白袍跟远处
　　光辉的地面相比一般;
又像这尘世苍白的烛花跟遥远的　　　　15
　　一轮银月相比一般;
这就是在基督面前我的灵魂,
　　在您面前我的精神;
这就是身在尘寰的我
　　跟我所想望的圣女的区分。　　　　　20
把天国的门打开吧,呵主!
　　把您的新娘,一颗闪烁的星,

Draw me, thy bride, a glittering star,
In raiment white and clean.

He lifts me to the golden doors;
The flashes come and go;
All heaven bursts her starry floors,
And strows her lights below①,
And deepens on and up! the gates
Roll back, and far within
For me the Heavenly Bridegroom waits,
To make me pure of sin.
The sabbaths of Eternity,
One sabbath deep and wide —
A light upon the shining sea —
The Bridegroom with his bride!

LORD ALFRED TENNYSON.

---

① *strows*: an archaic form of 'strews.'

穿着白净的衣裳,越过耀眼的星光,
　　远远地接引进您的灵境。

他把我升举向金色的大门, 25
　　一道道光芒忽闪忽亮;
整个天国的地面由星星铺成,
　　往下界撒播万千神光,
同时又深不可测!大门自动
　　后开,在那幽邃的深处, 30
天上的新郎在等待着我,
　　把我所蒙的罪涤除。
乐园中永恒的无数安息日呵,
　　这个安息日既深且广——
看哪,在灿烂辉煌的光海上—— 35
　　新郎和新娘是光中之光!

　　　　　　　　　　　倪庆饩　译

编注　本诗初版与二版时诗题均为"圣·安妮节",现标题为编者所加。圣·安妮(St. Agnes)是罗马的一个殉道者。十三岁时死于"罗马皇帝戴克里先的迫害",后来基督教教会规定一月二十一日为纪念她的节日。据说少女们在节日前夜通过规定的仪式可以见到未来丈夫的面影。诗中的修女因此从修道院的窗口中看到她"天上的新郎"。

324. SIR GALAHAD

My good blade carves the casques of men,
    My tough lance thrusteth sure,
My strength is as the strength of ten,
    Because my heart is pure.
The shattering trumpet shrilleth high,
    The hard brands shiver on the steel,
The splinter'd spear-shafts crack and fly,
    The horse and rider reel:
They reel, they roll in clanging lists,
    And when the tide of combat stands,
Perfume and flowers fall in showers,
    That lightly rain from ladies' hands.

How sweet are looks that ladies bend
    On whom their favours fall!
For them I battle till the end,
    To save from shame and thrall:
But all my heart is drawn above,
    My knees are bow'd in crypt and shrine:
I never felt the kiss of love,
    Nor maiden's hand in mine.
More bounteous aspects on me beam,
    Me mightier transports move and thrill;

324. 加拉海德爵士①

丁尼生

我的利剑劈开人的头盔,
　我的长矛刺得又狠又准,
我的力气跟十个人相当,
　因为我的心地真纯。
惊心动魄的号角在凄厉地吹, 5
　坚硬的宝剑在钢甲上震荡,
折断的枪柄喀嚓一声飞出手,
　骏马和骑士都昏头转向:
他们晕眩,在铿锵的比武场上翻滚,
　决斗的高潮一告结束, 10
一阵香水与鲜花轻盈地散落,
　纷纷来自女郎们的纤手。

多么甜美呵女郎们的秋波,
　送给她们敬佩的英豪!
因此我战斗到底,从不认输, 15
　为了荣誉,不屈不挠:
但是我整个的心向往着天国,
　我只向圣殿跪拜屈膝。
我没有接受过爱情的吻,
　也从未握过少女的柔荑, 20
神赐给我更为慷慨的福祉,
　更大的恩惠使我感动,

---

① 加拉海德爵士,朗斯洛特爵士与爱兰两人之子,为亚瑟王圆桌骑士中最纯洁最高尚的骑士。　编注者

So keep I fair thro' faith and prayer
A virgin heart in work and will.

When down the stormy crescent goes①,
A light before me swims,
Between dark stems the forest glows,
I hear a noise of hymns:
Then by some secret shrine I ride;
I hear a voice, but none are there;
The stalls are void, the doors are wide,
The tapers burning fair.
Fair gleams the snowy altar-cloth,
The silver vessels sparkle clean,
The shrill bell rings, the censer swings,
And solemn chaunts resound between.

Sometimes on lonely mountain-meres
I find a magic bark;
I leap on board; no helmsman steers:
I float till all is dark.
A gentle sound, an awful light!
Three angels bear the holy Grail:
With folded feet, in stoles of white②,
On sleeping wings they sail.
Ah, blessed vision! blood of God!
My spirit beats her mortal bars,
As down dark tides the glory slides,

---

① *the stormy crescent*: the moon on a stormy night.
② *stoles*: used here for 'long cloaks.'

所以由于信仰并且通过祈祷，
　　行动和意志上我都保持纯真。

一个风雨交加的夜晚，星沉月落， 25
　　一道光芒浮现在我眼前，
森林在漆黑的枝桠间发光，
　　赞美诗的歌声响起在我耳边：
我随后骑马走过一所隐秘的圣祠，
　　我听到人声，但不见人影， 30
所有的座位空空，所有的门扉洞开，
　　蜡烛燃点得透亮通明，
祭坛上雪白的帷幔生辉耀眼，
　　祭祀的银具光洁干净，
钟声嘹亮，香烟缭绕，庄严的 35
　　合唱在殿宇间共鸣。

有时我在孤寂的山间湖泊水面
　　发现有一叶魔舟。
我一跃而上，随舟飘流
　　直到日暮，并没有舵手； 40
忽然，轻轻一声，三位天使捧着
　　圣杯出现，放出威严的灵光①，
他们披着洁白的斗篷直盖到脚面，
　　双翼一动不动地滑翔。
呵！神圣的幻影！上帝的鲜血！ 45
　　我的灵魂像要从躯壳出动，
那光辉随漆黑的潮水一道流走，

---

① 圣杯据说是耶稣在最后的晚餐时所用，耶稣殉难时所流的血曾由亚力马太的约瑟接盛在这只杯子里，传到英国的格拉斯顿布里，后来便失踪了，只有心地纯洁的人才能找到它。尽管亚瑟王的圆桌骑士中有好几个人同时出发去找，最后惟有加拉海德一人寻获。——编注者

And star-like mingles with the stars.

When on my goodly charger borne
    Thro' dreaming towns I go,
The cock crows ere the Christmas morn,
    The streets are dumb with snow.
The tempest crackles on the leads,
    And, ringing, springs from brand and mail;
But o'er the dark a glory spreads,
    And gilds the driving hail.
I leave the plain, I climb the height;
    No branchy thicket shelter yields;
But blessed forms in whistling storms
    Fly o'er waste fens and windy fields.

A maiden knight — to me is given
    Such hope, I know not fear;
I yearn to breathe the airs of heaven
    That often meet me here.
I muse on joy that will not cease,
    Pure spaces clothed in living beams,
Pure lilies of eternal peace,
    Whose odours haunt my dreams;
And, stricken by an angel's hand,
    This mortal armour that I wear,
This weight and size, this heart and eyes,
    Are touch'd, are turn'd to finest air.

The clouds are broken in the sky,
    And thro' the mountain-walls
A rolling organ-harmony

融合在星斗中分辨不清。

当威武的坐骑载着我
　　穿过酣眠的城镇，　　　　　　　　　　　50
雄鸡在圣诞的凌晨啼鸣，
　　白皑皑的街道一片寂静。
暴风雪在铅皮屋顶上狂嚎，
　　把宝剑和铠甲刮得铿锵出声，
但是一道光明遍照黑暗，　　　　　　　　　55
　　给疾下的冰雹镀上黄金。
我离开平地，登上高山；
　　没有枝柯交错的树丛让我藏躲；
但在呼啸的暴风雪中，神圣的形影
　　在荒凉的沼泽和刮风的田野上飞过。　60

对我——一个初出茅庐的骑士，
　　赐予这样的希望，我无所畏缩；
我渴望呼吸到天国的气氛，
　　这儿我对它也常有感触。
我思念着不灭的光明所涵容的净界　　　　65
　　和那永远常在的欢欣。
象征永久和平的纯洁的百合，
　　它的馨香为我魂梦牵萦。
一位天使的手碰到了我穿戴的
　　人间的铠甲，我深受感动，　　　　　70
我的肉体，我的心灵和眼神
　　都向往着那最美好的灵境。

天上密布的浓云散开，一曲风琴
　　奏出的圣乐愈来愈悠扬，
透过屏障一般的山峦，　　　　　　　　　75

Swells up, and shakes and falls.
Then move the trees, the copses nod,
    Wings flutter, voices hover clear:
'O just and faithful knight of God!
    Ride on! the prize is near.'
So pass I hostel, hall, and grange;
    By bridge and ford, by park and pale,
All-arm'd I ride, whate'er betide
    Until I find the holy Grail.

LORD ALFRED TENNYSON.

在天地间忽高忽低地荡漾。
于是大树感动,灌林点头,
　　羽翼振拍,清晰的声音盘旋:
"呵,上帝的正直和忠诚的骑士!
　　大功即将告成,继续向前!"
因此我经过驿舍,厅堂和田庄,
　　越过园林和栅栏,桥梁和津渡,
全副武装,策马前进,不顾艰险,
　　不找到圣杯决不罢休。

倪庆饩　译

325. BREAK, BREAK, BREAK

Break, break, break,
   On thy cold grey stones, O Sea!
And I would that my tongue could utter
   The thoughts that arise in me.

O well for the fishermap's boy,
   That he shouts with his sister at play!
O well for the sailor lad,
   That he sings in his boat on the bay!

And the stately ships go on
   To their haven under the hill;
But O for the touch of a vanish'd hand,
   And the sound of a voice that is still!

Break, break, break,
   At the foot of thy crags, O Sea!
But the tender grace of a day that is dead
   will never come back to me.

LORD ALFRED TENNYSON.

325. 破碎，破碎，破碎

丁尼生

破碎，破碎，破碎，
　碎在你冰凉的石上，哦，海洋！
但愿我的舌尖能表露
　从我心底涌起的哀伤。

多快活啊，那渔家少年　　　　　　　　　　5
　正与妹妹嬉戏喧嚷！
多快活啊，那少年水手
　在海湾泛舟歌声飘荡！

还有雄壮的渔家船队
　正驶向山脚下的渔港；　　　　　　　　10
可我多想听听那沉寂的声音，
　多想握握那消逝的手掌。

破碎，破碎，破碎，
　碎在你乱石堆下，哦，海洋！
可昔日的温雅早已经逝去，　　　　　　　15
　一去不返，那美好时光。

　　　　　　　　　　　　　曹明伦　译

编注　此诗是丁尼生为悼念其亡友海拉姆（Arthur Hallam）而写的一首挽歌，最初发表于一八四二年。另参见本卷第333首编注。

326. THE BROOK

I come from haunts of coot and hern①,
    I make a sudden sally
And sparkle out among the fern,
    To bicker down a valley②.

By thirty hills I hurry down,
    Or slip between the ridges,
By twenty thorps, a little town③,
    And half a hundred bridges.

Till last by Philip's farm I flow
    To join the brimming river,
For men may come and men may go,
    But I go on for ever.

I chatter over stony ways,
    In little sharps and trebles,
I bubble into eddying bays,
    I babble on the pebbles.

---

① *hern*: another form of 'heron.'
② *bicker*: originally to fight or wrangle, it has later been used for any sound suggesting repeated blows, such as the rippling of a stream or the pattering of rain.
③ *thorps*: 'villages,' a word commonly found in place-names on the East Coast where Tennyson was born.

326. 小溪

丁尼生

我来自鹭鸶栖息之处,
　　我自平地冒出,
我闪烁于蕨薇之间,
　　我潺潺流下山谷。

我匆匆经过三十道坡,　　　　　　　　　5
　　在山脊之间滑过,
我流经二十村和一镇,
　　小桥五十多座。

我一直要流到菲力浦庄①,
　　去汇入江河浩荡,　　　　　　　　10
世上的人们有来有往,
　　而我却永向前方。

我在石路上潺潺而谈,
　　唱出高音串串,
我注入湾里的涡漩,　　　　　　　　　15
　　弹响卵石的琴弦。

---

① 菲力浦,丁尼生《小溪》原诗中爱说闲话的老农,是农庄上的佃户。——编注者

With many a curve my banks I fret
By many a field anol fallow,
And many a fairy foreland set
With willow-weed and mallow.

I chatter, chatter, as I flow
To join the brimming river,
For men may come and men may go,
But I go on for ever.

I wind about, and in and out,
With here a blossom sailing
And here and there a lusty trout,
And here and there a grayling,

And here and there a foamy flake
Upon me, as I travel
With many a silvery waterbreak①
Above the golden gravel,

And draw them all along, and flow
To join the brimming river,
For men may come and men may go,
But I go on for ever.

I steal by lawns and grassy plots,
I slide by hazel covers;
I move the sweet forget-me-nots
That grow for happy lovers.

---

① *waterbreak*: 'ripple.'

我冲刷得两岸曲曲折折，
　　蜿蜒穿越田野，
我遍植柳条和锦葵，
　　造成个神仙境界。

我喋喋不休，边流边唱，
　　去汇入江河浩荡，
世上的人们有来有往，
　　而我却永向前方。

我弯曲蜿蜒不停，时而
　　我带朵花儿航行，
这儿那儿，斑鳟出没，
　　银鳟泼刺一声。

这儿那儿，卷起一片浪花，
　　浩白有如雪花，
无数银色的涟漪呀，
　　笼罩着我的金沙。

我把它们全都带上，
　　去汇入江河浩荡，
世上的人们有来有往，
　　而我却永向前方。

我潜越林间空地草坪，
　　我滑过榛树之荫；
我摇着甜蜜的毋忘我花，
　　致意天下有情人。

I slip, I slide, I gloom, I glance①,
    Among my skimming swallows;
I make the netted sunbeam dance
    Against my sandy shallows.

I murmur under moon and stars
    In brambly wildernesses;
I linger by my shingly bars;
    I loiter round my cresses;

And out again I curve and flow
    To join the brimming river,
For men may come and men may go,
    But I go on for ever.

LORD ALFRED TENNYSON.

---

① *I gloom*, *I glance*: 'I look dull or bright.'

> 我在飞掠水面的燕子间
> 　　滑行着,明暗变幻;
> 我叫网格般的光影舞蹈
> 　　在我的清浅沙滩。
>
> 我在月光和星影下絮语,　　　　　　　　　45
> 　　在丛莽之间低吟;
> 我在我的卵石滩留连,
> 　　我环抱我的水芹;
>
> 但我重新转向了前方,
> 　　去汇入江河浩荡,　　　　　　　　　　50
> 世上的人们有来有往,
> 　　而我却永向前方。

飞白　译

编注　丁尼生的《小溪》原来是二百多行,以农村为背景,记叙一段失恋故事,故事中有十几节描写溪水的歌谣体小诗穿插其间。《金库》原编者将这十几节抽出专门组织成《小溪》一诗,一方面烘托农村的安静气氛,一方面又加强了物是人非的惆怅感。

327. 'AS THRO' THE LAND AT EVE WE WENT'

As thro' the land at eve we went,
    And pluck'd the ripen'd ears,
We fell out, my wife and I,
We fell out, I know not why,
    And kiss'd again with tears.

And blessings on the falling out
    That all the more endears,
When we fall out with those we love
    And kiss again with tears!

For when we came where lies the child
    We lost in other years,
There above the little grave,
O there above the little grave,
    We kiss'd again with tears.

LORD ALFRED TENNYSON.

327. "黄昏里,我们过麦地"

丁尼生

黄昏里,我们过麦地
　　采成熟的麦穗,
我们争吵了,妻跟我,
我们争吵了,我不知为什么,
　　然后又相吻,珠泪盈盈。　　　　　　　5

要是我们跟自己所爱的人
　　争吵,然后又含泪相吻,
这种争吵真该祝福,因为
　　它反使相爱的人更亲近。

当我们来到多年前　　　　　　　　　　10
　　我们失去的孩子长眠的地方,
就在那小小的坟茔上,
呵,就在那小小的坟茔上
　　我们又相吻,珠泪盈盈。

倪庆饩　译

编注　本诗选自长诗《公主》第三版(1950年版)。

328. 'THE SPLENDOUR FALLS ON CASTLE WALLS'

The splendour falls on castle walls
 And snowy summits old in story:
The long light shakes across the lakes,
 And the wild cataract leaps in glory.
Blow, bugle, blow, set the wild echoes flying,
Blow, bugle; answer, echoes, dying, dying, dying.

O hark, O hear! how thin and clear,
 And thinner, clearer, farther going!
O sweet and far from cliff and scar①
 The horns of Elfland faintly blowing!
Blow, let us hear the purple glens replying:
Blow, bugle; answer, echoes, dying, dying, dying.

O love, they die in yon rich sky,
 They faint on hill or field or river:
Our echoes roll from soul to soul,
 And grow for ever and for ever.
Blow, bugle, blow, set the wild echoes flying,
And answer, echoes, answer, dying, dying, dying.

LORD ALFRED TENNYSON.

---

① *scar*: a steep face of rock.

328. "辉煌的夕照映着城堡"

丁尼生

辉煌的夕照映着城堡,
  映着古老的雪峰之巅;
 长长的金光在湖面摇荡,
  野性的瀑布壮丽地飞溅。
吹吧,号角,吹吧,惊起那荒野的回声,   5
吹吧,号角;回声呼应,一声声轻了,更轻,更轻。

 听啊,听仔细!它微弱而清晰,
  越去越远却越明朗,
 啊,又远又甜,传自峭壁悬岩,
  精灵之国的号角在隐约吹响!   10
吹吧,让我们听那紫色的幽谷回应,
吹吧,号角;回声呼应,一声声轻了,更轻,更轻。

 爱人啊,回声在美丽的天边溶化,
  在山野、在河面熄灭、消散;
 咱俩的回声在心灵间应答,   15
  却不断增强,永远,永远。
吹吧,号角,吹吧,惊起那荒野的回声,
呼应吧,回声,呼应,一声声轻了,更轻,更轻。

飞 白 译

编注 此诗为长诗《公主》中的第三首抒情插曲。

329. 'TEARS, IDLE TEARS'

Tears, idle tears, I know not what they mean,
Tears from the depth of some divine despair
Rise in the heart, and gather to the eyes,
In looking on the happy Autumn-fields,
And thinking of the days that are no more.

Fresh as the first beam glittering on a sail,
That brings our friends up from the underworld①,
Sad as the last which reddens over one
That sinks with all we love below the verge;
So sad, so fresh, the days that are no more.

Ah, sad and strange as in dark summer dawns
The earliest pipe of half-awaken'd birds
To dying ears, when unto dying eyes
The casement slowly grows a glimmering square②;
So sad, so strange, the days that are no more.

Dear as remember'd kisses after death,
And sweet as those by hopeless fancy feign'd
On lips that are for others; deep as love,
Deep as first love, and wild with all regret;
O Death in Life, the days that are no more.

LORD ALFRED TENNYSON.

---

① *the underworld*: 'the antipodes.'
② *The casement slowly grows a glimmering square*: i. e. the outline of the window becomes visible as daylight appears.

329. "泪哟,泪哟"

丁尼生

泪哟,泪哟,我不知为何缘由,
从某个神圣的绝望之深渊涌出,
涌上我的心头,又盈聚在眼眶,
当我眺望金秋时节欢乐的原野,
当我想起那些一去不返的日子。   5

鲜艳得宛如清晨那第一道曙光
照亮从远方载友人归来的帆船,
矇眬得恍若傍晚最后一抹红霞
带着我们所爱的一切坠下天边;
鲜艳而矇眬,一去不返的日子。   10

哦,让人感到那么伤感而陌生,
犹如在黑沉沉的夏夜破晓之际,
弥留者听见半醒的鸟初试歌喉,
临终者看见熹微晨光爬上窗扉;
伤感而陌生,一去不返的日子。   15

亲切得就像死后记忆中的热吻,
甜蜜得如同在无望的幻想之中
偷偷地亲吻本不该亲吻的芳唇;
深奥得堪比犯热而惆怅的初恋;
一去不返的日子哟,生中之死。   20

曹明伦 译

编注 选自叙事长诗《公主》(*The Princess*,1847)。美国诗人爱伦·坡在其《诗歌原理》(The Poetic Principle,1850)一文中评说这首诗时,用了"最空灵、最高雅、最纯粹……最少世俗之气"等溢美之词。

330. 'O SWALLOW, SWALLOW, FLYING, FLYING SOUTH'

O Swallow, Swallow, flying, flying South,
Fly to her, and fall upon her gilded eaves,
And tell her, tell her what I tell to thee.

O tell her, Swallow, thou that knowest each,
That bright and fierce and fickle is the South,
And dark and true and tender is the North.

O Swallow, Swallow, if I could follow, and light
Upon her lattice, I would pipe and trill,
And cheep and twitter twenty million loves.

O were I thou that she might take me in,
And lay me on her bosom, and her heart
Would rock the snowy cradle till I died.

Why lingereth she to clothe her heart with love,
Delaying as the tender ash delays
To clothe herself, when all the woods are green?

O tell her, Swallow, that thy brood is flown:
Say to her, I do but wanton in the South,
But in the North long since my nest is made.

O tell her, brief is life but love is long,
And brief the sun of summer in the North,

330. "燕子呵,燕子,飞吧,飞向南方"

丁尼生

燕子呵,燕子,飞吧,飞向南方,
飞到她那儿,栖止在她涂金的屋檐上,
把我对你说的知心话跟她讲。

告诉她呵,燕子、南方和北方你都熟稔,
南方呵,开朗,热情,可是变幻无恒,   5
北方呵,抑郁,可是温柔,诚恳。

燕子呵,燕子,如果我能随你飞度关山,
栖息在她的画梁上,我就要曼语呢喃,
把那千重万重的相思情婉转歌唱。

我要是你呵,她也许放我进香闺,   10
让我靠在她雪白的胸口,她的心跳
摇我入睡,我却愿从此长眠也不悔。

为什么她还犹豫不让爱情打动她的心?
整个的树林披上了新装,翠色青青,
她好像那柔嫩的桦树迟延不定。   15

呵,告诉她,燕子,你的姊妹都已飞走,
对她说,我只是到南方游逛,在北方
我早筑好了巢,那才是我的归宿。

呵,告诉她,生命短,恩爱长,
北方夏天和煦的太阳,南方皎洁的   20

And brief the moon of beauty in the South.

O Swallow, flying from the golden woods,
Fly to her, and pipe and woo her, and make her mine,
And tell her, tell her, that I follow thee.

LORD ALFRED TENNYSON.

明月都不过是转瞬即逝的韶光。

　　燕子呵,从那秋色金黄的树林飞走吧,
飞到她身边,为她歌唱,向她倾诉,
告诉她,我会跟着你来,为了得到她的心。

倪庆饩　译

编注　选自长诗《公主》。

331. 'NOW SLEEPS THE CRIMSON PETAL'

Now sleeps the crimson petal, now the white
Nor waves the cypress in the palace walk;
Nor winks the gold fin in the porphyry font:
The fire-fly wakens: waken thou with me.

Now droops the milkwhite peacock like a ghost,
And like a ghost she glimmers on to me.

Now lies the Earth all Danaë to the stars[①],
And all thy heart lies open unto me.

Now slides the silent meteor on, and leaves
A shining furrow, as thy thoughts in me.

Now folds the lily all her sweetness up,
And slips into the bosom of the lake:
So fold thyself, my dearest, thou, and slip
Into my bosom and be lost in me.

LORD ALFRED TENNYSON.

---

① *lies ... all Danaë*: 'lies ready to be embraced.'

331. "时而是紫色的花瓣在沉睡"

丁尼生

时而是紫色的花瓣在沉睡,时而又是白色的,
宫庭径道上的柏树也不颤动了;
连紫岩泉中的金鳍也不再发亮①:
萤火虫醒了,你跟我同时醒了。

这会儿乳白色的孔雀像幽灵般沮丧, 5
也像幽灵般微弱地发光。

这会儿大地正期待群星的环抱②,
你的心花儿也会向我开放。

这会儿静寂的彗星掠过太空,留下
一道光辉的痕迹,正为你的关切深印在我的心坎。 10

这会儿百合花卷起她享有的芬芳,
轻盈地滑进了湖心里:
我最亲爱的,你也卷起你的身子,
投入我的胸怀,跟我融化在一起。

吴景荣 译

编注 本诗选自长诗《公主》,叙述王子对爱特公主的怀念。

---

① 紫岩,诗人们常用此词,泛指紫色光滑的石头,包括花岗石和大理石。——译者
② 根据希腊神话,达那厄(Danaë)系阿耳戈斯国王的女儿。神谕祭司告诉国王说,他会死在他未来的外孙手中,因此国王就把他的女儿囚禁在一座铜境里。可是宙斯化作一阵金雨接近了达那厄,这样她就怀胎生下名叫珀耳修斯的儿子。后来在一次竞技中,珀耳修斯果然误杀了他的外祖父。这个故事一般解释为创宇宙的神话:达那厄就是地球。——译者

332. 'COME DOWN, O MAID, FROM YONDER MOUNTAIN HEIGHT'

Come down, O maid, from yonder mountain height:
What pleasure lives in height (the Shepherd sang),
In height and cold, the splendour of the hills?
But cease to move so near the Heavens, and cease
To glide a sunbeam by the blasted Pine,
To sit a star upon the sparkling spire;
And come, for Love is of the valley, come,
For Love is of the valley, come thou down
And find him; by the happy threshold, he,
Or hand in hand with Plenty in the maize,
Or red with spirted purple of the vats,
Or foxlike in the vine; nor cares to walk
With Death and Morning on the silver horns[1],
Nor wilt thou snare him in the white ravine[2],
Nor find him dropt upon the firths of ice,
That huddling slant in furrow-cloven falls
To roll the torrent out of dusky doors:
But follow; let the torrent dance thee down
To find him in the valley; let the wild
Lean-headed Eagles yelp alone, and leave
The monstrous ledges there to slope, and spill
Their thousand wreaths of dangling water-smoke,

---

[1] *the silver horns*: 'the snowy mountain summits'.
[2] *the white ravine*: a crevasse in a glacier.

332. "下来吧,少女啊,从那儿山巅下来"

丁尼生

下来吧,少女啊,从那儿山巅下来:
什么人间乐趣逗留在高山(牧童唱),
在高山和严寒里,在峰峦起伏的壮伟景象里呢?
切莫太走近苍穹,不要
随着一缕阳光绕过那枯萎了的柏树 5
把一颗星星安放在冰峰;
来吧,因为爱属于人间溪谷的,来吧,
因为爱属于人间溪谷的,你下来
把他找到;他或在喜盈盈的门槛旁边,
或在玉米丛中与丰收携手同行, 10
或一身染红从桶桶果物沁出的紫汁,
或时隐时现在葡萄藤中;他不愿
在白雪皑皑的山巅同死神和晨曦漫步,
你也不会在冰川的裂口把他拦住,
也不会发现他掉到那冰柱和杂石堆里①, 15
在那挤成一团裂痕纵横的窄坡上
顺着激流从黑黝黝的冰川口倾泻下去;
而要追踪;让激流拥着你舞踏而下——
在人间溪谷里把他找到;让荒野的
窄头鹰独自嗥叫,离开 20
那儿可怕的峭壁往下滑,激起
蒙蒙水烟的千万种花环,

---

① 当冰川慢慢地沿着它的冰床滑下去时,就把掉在它表面的一切石头和杂物推走或冲到一边,因此冰川口狭窄地带总有许多碎片。如果冰床是个平面,那么冰川也是平的;如果冰床从上而下,就有相应的"冰瀑",充满着乱成一堆、裂痕纵横的冰柱。——译者

That like a broken purpose waste in air;
So waste not thou; but come; for all the vales
Await thee; azure pillars of the hearth①
Arise to thee; the children call, and I
Thy shepherd pipe, and sweet is every sound,
Sweeter thy voice, but every sound is sweet;
Myriads of rivulets hurrying thro' the lawn,
The moan of doves in immemorial elms,
And murmuring of innumerable bees.

                        LORD ALFRED TENNYSON.

---

① *azure pillars of the hearth*: *i.e.* columns of blue smoke from the fires lit for thy coming.

而这一切又嗒然若丧地消逝无踪:
你可不要消逝啊,而要下来,因为人间溪谷
期待着你;万家火焰的蔚蓝烟柱　　　　　　　　25
正向你升起;孩子们在呼唤,而我啊
你的牧童在歌唱,声音何等柔美,
千百万的小溪穿过草地奔驰,
邈古的榆树中鸽子正咕咕鸣叫,
数不尽的蜜蜂正在嗡嗡低语。　　　　　　　　30

吴景荣　译

333. 'RING OUT, WILD BELLS'

Ring out, wild bells, to the wild sky,
    The flying cloud, the frosty light:
    The year is dying in the night;
Ring out, wild bells, and let him die.

Ring out the old, ring in the new,
    Ring, happy bells, across the snow:
    The year is going, let him go;
Ring out the false, ring in the true.

Ring out the grief that saps the mind,
    For those that here we see no more;
    Ring out the feud of rich and poor,
Ring in redress to all mankind.

Ring out a slowly dying cause,
    And ancient forms of party strife;
    Ring in the nobler modes of life,
With sweeter manners, purer laws.

Ring out the want, the care, the sin,
    The faithless coldness of the times;
    Ring out, ring out my mournful rhymes,
But ring the fuller minstrel in.

Ring out false pride in place and blood,

333. "敲吧,乱钟"

丁尼生

敲吧,乱钟,向着寥廓的苍穹,
　　向着飞渡的云,向着冰冷的光:
　　旧岁逝去就在今宵;
敲吧,乱钟,就让它逝去吧。

送去旧的,迎来新的,　　　　　　　　　　　　5
　　让欢乐的钟声响彻这雪地:
　　旧岁就要离开了,让它离开吧,
送走伪的,迎来真的。

送走为那些已经谢世的人
　　而劳瘁心神的忧伤;　　　　　　　　　　10
　　送走贫富间的夙怨,
迎来全人类的仇解恨消。

送走垂亡的旧时道义,
　　和远古的、形形色色的党争:
　　迎来更为高贵的生活风尚,　　　　　　　15
有更和睦的礼貌和更纯真的法律。

送走今世的匮乏、烦恼、罪恶,
　　和那背信弃义的冷酷:
　　送走:送走我那哀伤的韵曲,
而迎来更为完熟的歌手。　　　　　　　　　20

送走达官贵人的虚妄自豪,

　　　　　The civic slander and the spite;
　　　　　　Ring in the love of truth and right,
　　　　　Ring in the common love of good.

　　　　　Ring out old shapes of foul disease;
　　　　　　Ring out the narrowing lust of gold;
　　　　　　Ring out the thousand wars of old,
　　　　　Ring in the thousand years of peace.

　　　　　Ring in the valiant man and free,
　　　　　　The larger heart, the kindlier hand;
　　　　　Ring out the darkness of the land,
　　　　　Ring in the Christ that is to be.

　　　　　　　　　　　　LORD ALFRED TENNYSON.

市井的谰言和一切私怨：
　迎来对真理和公正的热爱；
　迎来对良善普遍爱戴。

送走旧时代一切邪恶的病患，　　　　　　　　　　25
　送走窒息人心的利欲，
　送走古往今来不尽的战争；
　迎来千秋万代的和平。

迎来英勇的人，自由的人，
　更宽广的胸襟，更亲切的握手；　　　　　　　　30
　送走大地的昏黑，
　迎来即将降临的基督。

吴景荣　译

编注　此诗选自丁尼生为纪念亡友海拉姆所写的《悼念》（*In Memoriam*，诗题为拉丁文）。海拉姆是丁尼生的剑桥好友，又是他妹妹的未婚夫，不幸在二十二岁时死于维也纳。丁尼生长时期地思念他，并在海拉姆去世十七年以后写了《悼念》这首长诗。

334. 'COME INTO THE GARDEN'

Come into the garden, Maud,
    For the black bat, night, has flown,
Come into the garden, Maud,
    I am here at the gate alone;
And the woodbine spices are wafted abroad,
    And the musk of the roses blown.

For a breeze of morning moves,
    And the planet of Love is on high,
Beginning to faint in the light that she loves[1]
    On a bed of daffodil sky,
To faint in the light of the sun she loves,
    To faint in his light, and to die.

All night have the roses heard
    The flute, violin, bassoon;
All night has the casement jessamine stirr'd
    To the dancers dancing in tune;

---

[1] *the planet of Love*: Venus; see note to No. 187.

334. "走进花园吧"

丁尼生

走进花园吧,莫德,
  因为黑色的蝙蝠,黄昏,已经飞走。
走进花园吧,莫德,
  我只是一个人在门边站着。
忍冬的馨香四处洋溢,   5
  玫瑰的芬芳阵阵飘来。

晨风正微微吹起,
  可爱情的星还高悬空际①,
在水仙花的巨幕上②,
  她逐渐在她钟爱的光辉里变得暗淡, 10
在她钟爱的太阳光里变得暗淡,
  在他的光辉里变得暗淡,终于消逝。

玫瑰彻夜听到了③
  长笛声、提琴声、低音管声;
对着婆娑起舞的年轻男女,   15
  窗边茉莉彻夜在跳跃;

---

① 指金星,希腊神话中金星是爱情之神。本诗提到金星在阳光中逐渐消失,希腊神话中的太阳神是阿波罗。参见本书卷四第187首注。——编注者
② 朝阳东起,天空一派霞光,颜色如同水仙花一样金黄。——译者
③ 本诗多次提到"玫瑰""百合"。玫瑰是英国人最喜欢的花,诗人往往用以象征爱情或所爱的妇女。十八世纪的诗人彭斯便写下过著名的诗句"我的爱人像朵红红的玫瑰"(参见本书卷三第150首首行)。百合花一般是白色,喻洁白或纯洁。——译者

  Till a silence fell with the waking bird,
   And a hush with the setting moon.

  I said to the lily, 'There is but one
   With whom she has heart to be gay.
  When will the dancers leave her alone?
   She is weary of dance and play.'
  Now half to the setting moon are gone,
   And half to the rising day[①];
  Low on the sand and loud on the stone
   The last wheel echoes away.

  I said to the rose, 'The brief night goes
   In babble and revel and wine.
  O young lord-lover, what sighs are those,
   For one that will never be thine?
  But mine, but mine,' so I sware to the rose,
   'For ever and ever, mine.'

  And the soul of the rose went into my blood,
   As the music clash'd in the hall;
  And long by the garden lake I stood,
   For I heard your rivulet fall
  From the lake to the meadow and on to the wood,
   Our wood, that is dearer than all;

  From the meadow your walks have left so sweet
   That whenever a March-wind sighs
  He sets the jewel-print of your feet

---

① *the setting moon ... the rising day*: 'the west ... the east.'

跳到鸟醒声沉,
　　跳到月儿西落,静寂无音。

我对百合说:"只有一个人啊
　　她才有同他寻欢作乐的心情。
这些歌舞的公子们何时才不去惹她呢?
　　她已疲于歌舞和玩乐了。"
这时一些人已朝着月落的方向走,
　　一些人已向着日出的方向行,
沙土上车声沉细,石路上车声辘辘,
　　最后的回响也逐渐稀远了。

我对玫瑰说:"短暂的夜晚
　　在寻欢作乐中度过了。
年轻的多情公子呀,叹息什么,
　　是为了那个永不属于你的人儿吗?
可她是我的,我的,"我对玫瑰这样发誓说,
　　"永远,永远是我的。"

当所堂里音乐尾声锵然一响,
　　玫瑰的深情就沁到我的血液;
我久久停立在花园的湖滨,
　　因为我听到你家的小溪从湖那边流,
流到草地,再流到树林,
　　那是比一切都珍贵的呀!

你漫步过的草地也变得如此芬芳,
　　每当春风轻轻地吹起
它就把你那珍珠般足迹

In violets blue as your eyes,
To the woody hollows in which we meet
And the valleys of Paradise.

The slender acacia would not shake
    One long milk-bloom on the tree;
The white lake-blossom fell into the lake,
    As the pimpernel dozed on the lea;
But the rose was awake all night for your sake,
    Knowing your promise to me;
The lilies and roses were all awake,
    They sigh'd for the dawn and thee.

Queen rose of the rosebud garden of girls,
    Come hither, the dances are done,
In gloss of satin and glimmer of pearls,
    Queen lily and rose in one;
Shine out, little head, sunning over with curls,
    To the flowers, and be their sun.

There has fallen a splendid tear
    From the passion-flower at the gate.
She is coming, my dove, my dear;
    She is coming, my life, my fate;
The red rose cries, 'She is near, she is near;'
And the white rose weeps, 'She is late;'
The larkspur listens, 'I hear, I hear;'
And the lily whispers, 'I wait.'

She is coming, my own, my sweet;
    Were it ever so airy a tread,

镶嵌在如你碧绿眼睛一般的紫罗兰里;
溪水从草地流到我们晤面的茂林深处,
　　流到天堂的幽谷里。

纤细的刺槐树不会摇落　　　　　　　　　　45
　　树上一朵长长的乳白花朵;
草地上紫蘩蒌瞌睡时,
　　白色的湖花掉进湖里了;
可是玫瑰为了你彻夜不寐,
　　她知道你对我的盟诺;　　　　　　　　50
百合和玫瑰都是彻夜不寐,
　　他们盼望黎明和你而叹息。

少女满园的玫瑰花魁啊,
　　到这儿来吧,笙歌已撤,
百合和玫瑰花魁浑而为一了,　　　　　　　55
　　她们都有丝锦的光泽,都有珍珠的灿烂;
朝着那些花朵,作为她们的太阳,
　　照耀吧,小小的头儿,闪着阳光的卷发。

长在门边的西番莲,
　　掉下一颗晶莹的眼泪。　　　　　　　　60
她来了,我的小鸽子,我亲爱的人儿,
　　她来了,我的生命,我的主宰;
红玫瑰嚷着,"她快到了,她快到了";
　　白玫瑰呜咽着,"她晚了";
飞燕草聆听着,"我听到了,我听到了";　　　65
　　百合花低声说,"我等着。"

她来了,我的人儿,我甜蜜的人儿;
　　即令她步步轻移,

1393

My heart would hear her and beat,
    Were it earth in an earthy bed;
My dust would hear her and beat,
    Had I lain for a century dead;
Would start and tremble under her feet,
    And blossom in purple and red.

LORD ALFRED TENNYSON.

即令她足底下就是花坛的泥,
　　我的心也会听到她而跳动;
即令我已经死去一百年了,
　　化着尘土也会听见她而轻轻敲拍,
会在她的脚底下微跳颤动;
　　开着紫色、红色的花朵。

吴景荣　译

编注　本诗选自长诗《莫德》(*Maud*,1855)。在诗中,诗人以第三者的身份,抒发了自己不同时期的感情。由于大所堂主人的暗示,莫德家破人亡,后来他对主人的女儿发生了感情;尽管他赢得了爱,由于环境所迫,仍然不得不逃亡国外。结局是他的醒悟,决心为祖国服务。

335. 'IN LOVE'

In Love, if Love be Love, if Love be ours,
Faith and unfaith can ne'er be equal powers;
Unfaith in aught is want of faith in all.

It is the little rift within the lute,
That by and by will make the music mute,
And ever widening slowly silence all.

The little rift within the lover's lute,
Or little pitted speck in garner'd fruit[①],
That rotting inward slowly moulders all.

It is not worth the keeping: let it go:
But shall it? answer, darling, answer, no.
And trust me not at all or all in all.

LORD ALFRED TENNYSON.

---

① *pitted speck*: a spot lying in a hollow.

335. "在爱情里"

丁尼生

在爱情里,如果爱真是爱,如果爱属于我们的,
信和背信永不能均衡匹敌:
一事背信就是万事乏义。

就是那琵琶琴的小裂痕,
日子久了也会使乐曲哑然无音,　　　　　　　　5
裂痕逐渐扩大,最后一切归于沉寂。

情人的琵琶琴上小裂痕,
或是所储果物上的小小疵瑕,
让它侵蚀就逐渐糜烂一切。

值不得保存它了:抛掉它吧:　　　　　　　　　10
然而丢得下吗?回答吧,亲爱的,回答,不。
要么,根本不信任我,要么,完全信任我!

吴景荣　译

编注　此诗选自《亚瑟王之歌》(*Idylls of the King*,1859)中的《韦梵》(Vivien),据一八四五年托里斯·马洛里的法语编译而成。

337. A CHRISTMAS HYMN

It was the calm and silent night! —
    Seven hundred years and fifty-three
Had Rome been growing up to might,
    And now was Queen of land and sea!
No sound was heard of clashing wars;
    Peace brooded o'er the hushed domain;
Apollo, Pallas, Jove and Mars,
    Held undisturbed their ancient reign,
      In the solemn midnight
        Centuries ago!

'Twas in the calm and silent night!
    The senator of haughty Rome
Impatient urged his chariot's flight
    From lordly revel rolling home!
Triumphal arches gleaming swell
    His breast with thoughts of boundless sway;
What recked the Roman what befell[①]
    A paltry province far away,
      In the solemn midnight
        Centuries ago!

---

① *What recked the Roman*: 'what did the Romam care?'

337. 圣诞赞歌

多梅特

这是安宁而静谧的夜晚！——
　　经历了七百五十三年
罗马已爬上了强盛的峰巅①，
　　而如今却全是女王的江山！
耳边再也不闻冲突战端；　　　　　　　　　5
　　笼罩大地的沉寂，显示一派平安；
阿波罗，帕拉斯，朱庇特，玛尔斯②
　　诸神统治过古时王国，绝无骚乱，
　　　　在这神圣的午夜
　　　　千百年前！　　　　　　　　　　10

就在这安宁而静谧的夜晚！
　　罗马的元老，多么傲慢
骄躁地催赶着战车飞行，
　　从显贵的闹宴隆隆地回程！
凯旋拱门上，辉煌的气派闪现　　　　　15
　　他心中思忖着权力无边：
罗马人的关注，降福遥远
　　低等的省份恩泽绵延，
　　　　在这神圣的午夜
　　　　千百年前！　　　　　　　　　　20

---

① 传说罗马城的建造年份为公元前七五三年。至耶稣纪年，罗马已强盛无比。——译者
② 皆系罗马神话中的神名。——编注者

Within that province far away
    Went plodding home a weary boor;
A streak of light before him lay,
    Fall'n through a half-shut stable door
Across his path. He passed — for naught
    Told what was going on within;
How keen the stars! his only thought;
    The air how calm and cold and thin,
        In the solemn midnight
            Centuries ago!

O strange indifference! — low and high
    Drowsed over common joys and cares;
The earth was still — but knew not why;
    The world was listening — unawares;
How calm a moment may precede
    One that shall thrill the world for ever!
To that still moment none would heed,
    Man's doom was linked no more to sever
        In the solemn midnight
            Centuries ago!

It is the calm and solemn night!
    A thousand bells ring out, and throw
Their joyous peals abroad, and smite
    The darkness, charmed and holy now!
The night that erst no name had worn
    To it a happy name is given;
For in that stable lay new-born
    The peaceful Prince of Earth and Heaven,

在那远方的行省乡间
  农人归去的步履彳亍蹒跚:
前面地上透映着灯光一线,
  坚实的门扉半开半掩,
光亮照在脚前。他走了过去——
  门内事都与他毫不相干;
繁星真是迷人!他只思念
  空气多么宁馨,寒冷又淡恬,
    在这神圣的午夜
      千百年前!

哦,奇怪的一致!——人不分高贵卑贱
  在寻常的欢娱和操劳后都能昏睡:
大地滞静——但不知是为什么;
  世界在侧耳细听——带着麻木;
万籁俱寂的瞬息,它时时会引起
  激荡人世风云的时刻!
在那个悄然的时候,谁能想到
  人类的噩运从此维系不断
    在这神圣的午晚
      千百年前!

这是安宁而静谧的夜!
  成千座大钟在敲响,震散出
它们的欢快谐音,划破长空的
  黑暗,迷人而又神圣!
这夜晚,从未有过名称
  如今赋予它欢乐之名;
那坚实的门内诞生了新的生命,
  他是大地和天堂的和平王子,

In the solemn midnight
Centuries ago.

ALFRED DOMETT.

在这神圣的午夜
千百年前!

林骧华　译

编注　阿尔弗雷德·多梅特(Alfred Domett,1811—1887),英国诗人,曾在新西兰任职三十年,是诗人布朗宁的终身挚友,布朗宁在《谨慎》一诗中描绘过他的性格。多梅特的诗神奇厚重,时时透露出异域生活的影响。

338. 'THE YEAR 'S AT THE SPRING'

The year 's at the spring,
   And day 's at the morn;
     Morning 's at seven;
        The hill-side 's dew-pearled;
The lark 's on the wing;
   The snail 's on the thorn:
     God 's in his heaven —
       All 's right with the world!

R. BROWNING.

338. "一年恰逢春季"

罗伯特·布朗宁

一年恰逢春季,
　一天正在早晨;
　　早上七点钟整;
　　　山边沾着露珠;
云雀正在展翼;
　蜗牛趴在刺丛;
　　上帝安居天庭——
　　　世界正常有序!

杨苡　译

编注　罗伯特·布朗宁(Robert Browning,1812—1889),十九世纪英国名诗人,二十岁开始发表诗作,著有诗集《男男女女》《剧中人》及二千多行的长诗《指环与书》等,其诗作的主要成就是创造了无韵诗体的"戏剧独白"体裁,以《已故的公爵夫人》最有代表,一八四六年与女诗人伊丽莎白·巴雷特结婚,婚后迁居意大利,同情意大利的民族解放斗争。布朗宁的诗打破了传统的题材及形式范围,他用形象表达哲理的论述,如用独特的比喻,很多诗作艰涩难懂,语言遒劲有力,带有维多利亚时代流行的基督教伦理道德与乐观情绪,对英美现当代诗歌有相当影响。

本诗选自诗剧《皮帕走过了》(*Pippa Passes*),为该剧四首歌的第一首。该剧写一意大利纱厂女工在节日唱着歌走过街市,她的歌对一些人产生了不同的影响,但这些人物互不关联,也构不成任何情节。

339. 'GIVE HER BUT A LEAST EXCUSE TO LOVE ME'

Give her but a least excuse to love me!
    When — where —
How — can this arm establish her above me,
  If fortune fixed her as my lady there,
There already, to eternally reprove me?
    ('Hist!' — said Kate the queen;
But 'Oh' — cried the maiden, binding her tresses,
  ''Tis only a page that carols unseen,
'Crumbling your hounds their messes!')

Is she wronged? — To the rescue of her honour,
    My heart!
Is she poor? — What costs it to be styled a donor?
  Merely an earth to cleave, a sea to part[①].
But that fortune should have thrust all this upon her!
    ('Nay, list!' — bade Kate the queen;
And still cried the maiden, binding her tresses,
  ''Tis only a page that carols unseen,
'Fitting your hawks their jesses[②]!')

R. BROWNING.

---

① *an earth to cleave, a sea to part*: to make gifts to the woman one loves merely means toil on land or sea, which any one can render if he wishes, and which can never prove too hard.

② *jesses*: a jess was the strap by which a hawk was held.

339. "就给她一丁点的借口来爱我吧!"

罗伯特·布朗宁

就给她一丁点的借口来爱我吧!
　　何时——何方——
如何——这只手臂能置她于我之上,
　　如果时运已安排了她作我的妻房,
已经在那儿,没完没了地将我斥骂?　　　5
　　("嘘!"——凯特女皇说;
可是"哦"——侍女在嚷,编着她的发辫,
　　"不过是一个侍童无中生有地乱唱,
他正在用杂食喂着你那些猎犬!")

她受委屈了么?——挽救她的荣誉,　　　10
　　就凭我的心?
她贫穷么?——要称为施主得付多少代价?
　　也只是开山劈岭,破浪前进。
可那个时运早已将这一切交给她!
　　("不,听!"凯特女皇在吩咐;　　　15
侍女仍然在嚷,编着她的发辫,
　　"不过是一个侍童无中生有地乱唱,
他正在给你那些猎鹰把脚带系上!")

杨苡 译

编注 此诗为《皮帕走过了》的第二首歌。

340. THE LOST LEADER

    Just for a handful of silver he left us,
        Just for a riband to stick in his coat —
    Found the one gift of which fortune bereft us,
        Lost all the others she lets us devote①;
5   They, with the gold to give, doled him out silver,
        So much was theirs who so little allowed:
    How all our copper had gone for his service!
        Rags — were they purple, his heart had been proud!
    We that had loved him so, followed him, honoured him,
10   Lived in his mild and magnificent eye,
    Learned his great language caught his clear accents,
        Made him our pattern to live and to die!
    Shakespeare was of us, Milton was for us,
        Burns, Shelley, were with us, — they watch from their graves!
15   He alone breaks from the van and the freemen,
        He alone sinks to the rear and the slaves!

    We shall march prospering, — not thro' his presence;
        Songs may inspirit us, — not from his lyre;
    Deeds will be done, — while he boasts his quiescence,
20   Still bidding crouch whom the rest bade aspire:
    Blot out his name, then, record one lost soul more,
        One task more declined, one more foot path untrod,
    One more devils'-triumph and sorrow for angels,

---

① *she lets us devote*: sc. to the cause of Liberty.

340. 失去的领导者

罗伯特·布朗宁

就为了一把银子,他离开了我们,
 就为了一条绶带,好挂上衣襟的——
他得了一份礼,那是幸福剥夺了我们的,
 他失去了一切,那是幸福让我们去追寻的①;
他们,可以给金子,只把银子施舍给他,
 他们有那么多,答应给人的却么少:
我们的铜币由于他伺候人而全流去了!
 破衣——只要是紫袍,他也会穿上而觉骄傲!
我们,曾这样爱过他,跟过他,尊敬过他,
 在他那温和而庄严的目光下生活,
学过他卓越的语言,把握过他清晰的声音,
 把他当作我们的生和死的楷模!
莎士比亚是属于我们的,弥尔顿是为了我们的,
 彭斯、雪莱是跟我们在一起的——他们在坟墓里守望!
他独自从前驱和自由者队伍里逃跑,
 他单个退入落伍者和奴才的一帮!

我们将前进而繁昌——不经过他的面前;
 歌曲会鼓舞我们——不从他的七弦琴;
事业将成功——当他夸耀他的缄默、
 总教人卑屈(别人希望人奋发)的时辰:
那就抹去他名字,记下来:多了个失去的灵魂,
 多了件失败的工作,多了条未曾踏过的道路,
多了个魔鬼的胜利,天使的悲悯,

---

① 此处的一切,指我们的品质。——编注者

One wrong more to man, one more insult to God!
25 Life's night begins; let him never come back to us!
There would be doubt, hesitation, and pain,
Forced praise on our part — the glimmer of twilight,
Never glad confident morning again!
Best fight on well, for we taught him, — strike gallantly,
30 Menace our heart ere we master his own;
Then let him receive the new knowledge and wait us,
Pardoned in heaven, the first by the throne!

R. BROWNING.

多了个人类的错误,多了个对上帝的亵渎!
生命的黑夜开始了:让他永远别回来! 25
那儿将有疑惑,痛苦,和彷徨,
对我们这边的不得不赞美——只有微弱的曙色,
永远不再有可以信赖的欢愉的晨光!
最好是战斗,我们曾这样教他,——勇敢地战斗,
在我们征服他的心之前,可以恫吓我们的心, 30
然后让他接受新的知识并且等待我们①,
那在天上被饶恕的、先到上帝座旁的人!

屠岸 译

编注 此诗选自《铃铛和石榴》(*Bells and Pomegranates*,1845)一书第七首,诗中的"他"指华兹华斯(参见本书卷四第174首编注)。华兹华斯为"湖畔派"首领,年轻时同情法国资产阶级革命,后转而反对,甚至完全变成了一个顽固的保守党人,并接受政府俸金与封号。作为自由党人的布朗宁,尖锐地指责华兹华斯的变节行为,"失去的领导者"就是此意,不过,布朗宁还是佩服华兹华斯的诗才,甚至说华兹华斯死后将会被上帝首先宽恕。

---

① 此处的"新的知识",即上行所表示的和他斗争到底的决心。——编注者

341. HOME-THOUGHTS, FROM ABROAD

Oh, to be in England now that April's there,
And whoever wakes in England sees, some morning, unaware,
That the lowest boughs and the brushwood sheaf
Round the elm-tree bole are in tiny leaf①,
While the chaffinch sings on the orchard bough
　　In England — now!

And after April, when May follows,
And the whitethroat builds, and all the swallows!
Hark, where my blossomed pear-tree in the hedge
　　Leans to the field and scatters on the clover
Blossoms and dewdrops — at the bent spray's edge —
　　That's the wise thrush; he sings each song twice over,
Lest you should think he never could recapture
　　The first fine careless rapture!
And though the fields look rough with hoary dew,
All will be gay when noontide wakes anew
The buttercups, the little children's dower
— Far brighter than this gaudy melon-flower!

　　　　　　　　　　　　　　R. BROWNING.

---

① *bole*: 'trunk.'

341. 异域乡思

罗伯特·布朗宁

呵,在英格兰,眼下正是四月,
一早醒来,谁都看见,在英格兰,不知不觉,
最矮的灌木林和密集的小树丛
在榆树周围已是满目葱茏,
苍头燕雀在今日英格兰的果园枝头   5
 正一片啁啾!

 四月去了,五月循踪而至,
白喉雀筑巢,接着是所有的燕子!
听,在我围篱中鲜花盛开的梨树
 俯向田野并往三叶草上面   10
散花洒露的曲枝尖处,
 那是机灵的画眉;每首歌他都高唱两遍,
免得你以为他再不能重温
 第一次美妙绝伦而无忧无虑的欢腾!
虽然原野因白露而显得凄清,   15
一切都将喜气洋洋,当正午重又唤醒
金凤花,那小孩子们的嫁妆
远比这炫丽的甜瓜花灿烂辉煌!

张秋红 译

编注 此诗选自《铃铛和石榴》,为布朗宁最有名的短诗之一。写此诗时,他身在意大利,意大利的春天虽也春光明媚,但嫌过度了些,诗人怀念北方故国四五月的风景,回忆英国的草木,更神往于会唱歌的鸟儿。

342. HOME-THOUGHTS, FROM THE SEA

Nobly, nobly Cape Saint Vincent to the North-West died away;
Sunset ran, one glorious blood-red, reeking into Cadiz Bay;
Bluish mid the burning water, full in face Trafalgar lay;
In the dimmest North-East distance, dawned Gibraltar grand and grey;
'Here and here did England help me: how can I help England?' — say,
Whoso turns as I, this evening, turn to God to praise and pray,
While Jove's planet rises yonder, silent over Africa.

R. BROWNING.

342. 乡思,自海上[1]

罗伯特·布朗宁

巍峨的、巍峨的圣·文森特角渐渐在西北边消逝[2];
辉煌的血红色的日落迅速把加地斯海湾浸染[3];
在汹涌的海中迎面是青蓝色的特拉法加角[4];
宏伟的灰色的直布罗陀在东北方迷茫中出现[5];
"英国就在这里帮助过我:我如何为英国效劳?"
今晚谁都如我一样转身向上帝赞美祷告,
此时木星远远升起,默默地在非洲上空照耀。

杨苡 译

编注 此诗选自《铃铛和石榴》。

---

[1] 此诗写于西班牙西南海岸。——编注者
[2] 此句说的是一七九七年杰维斯率领十五艘战舰战胜西班牙二十七艘战舰的事情,为此胜利,杰维斯被封给圣·文森特伯爵的贵族称号。——编注者
[3] 一五八七年无敌舰队首领德雷克在此为迎接英格兰的入侵而烧毁舰只。——编注者
[4] 一八〇五年十月尼尔松(Nelson)在此打败了法、西联合舰队。——编注者
[5] 一七〇四年直布罗陀为英国占领,以后又进行过若干次成功的保卫战。——编注者

343. MISCONCEPTIONS

This is a spray the Bird clung to,
    Making it blossom with pleasure,
Ere the high tree-top she sprung to,
    Fit for her nest and her treasure.
       Oh, what a hope beyond measure
Was the poor spray's, which the flying feet hung to, —
So to be singled out, built in, and sung to!

This is a heart the Queen leant on,
    Thrilled in a minute erratic,
Ere the true bosom she bent on,
    Meet for love's regal dalmatic[①].
       Oh, what a fancy ecstatic
Was the poor heart's, ere the wanderer went on —
Love to be saved for it, proffered to, spent on!

R. BROWNING.

[①] *dalmatic*: a wide-sleeved, long, loose vestment with slit sides, worn by ecclesiastics on certain occasions and by kings at their coronations.

343. 误解

罗伯特·布朗宁

这里有一权小枝,鸟儿曾依恋,
　　枝头为此繁花怒放,
这原是在她跳到高高的树巅之前,
　　那里才适合筑她的窠,贮存她的宝藏。
　　啊,怎样的一个过分的奢望　　　　　　　　5
属于那可怜的小枝,由于被飞跃的小脚攀上,
就希望被挑选,在那里筑窠,并向它鸣唱!

这里有一颗心曾被女王思眷,
　　引起了一刹那的战栗,心荡神移,
这原是在她偎依在真正的胸膛之前①,　　　　10
　　那才适合爱情的帝王礼仪。
　　啊,怎样的一种梦幻痴迷
属于那可怜的心,在流浪者继续上路之前
那克制的,为它献身的,耗尽心力的爱恋!

　　　　　　　　　　　　　　　杨苡　译

编注 此诗选自《男男女女》(*Men and Women*)第二卷。

---

① "真正的胸膛"指她爱的人。——编注者

344. A WOMAN'S LAST WORD

Let 's contend no more, Love,
    Strive nor weep;
All be as before, Love,
    — Only sleep!

What so wild as words are?
    I and thou
In debate, as birds are,
    Hawk on bough!

See the creature stalking
    While we speak!
Hush and hide the talking,
    Cheek on cheek!

What so false as truth is,
    False to thee?
Where the serpent's tooth is,
    Shun the tree —

Where the apple reddens
    Never pry —
Lest we lose our Edens,
    Eve and I[1][2].

---

[1] L13 - 20: It is better not to know the truth than to lose my faith in you.
[2] *Eve and I*: 'I, just as Eve did.'

344. 一个女人最后的话

罗伯特・布朗宁

爱人,让我们别再争论,
  不要斗嘴,不要哭泣:
亲爱的,一如以往,
  只是睡眠安息!

有什么能像词儿那般狂野?　　　　　5
  你我两人
辩论时有如鸟儿
  如同枝头争吵的鹰雀!

我们交谈的时间
  看那家伙蹑手蹑脚!　　　　　10
轻声藏住我们的情话
  脸颊紧贴脸颊。

对你虚伪?
  还不如对真理虚伪。
毒蛇的恶牙在哪?　　　　　15
  隐匿在树后——

苹果虽已成熟,
  决不要去采摘——
否则如同夏娃
  我会失去伊甸。　　　　　20

> Be a god and hold me
> With a charm!
> Be a man and fold me
> With thine arm!
>
> Teach me, only teach, Love!
> As I ought
> I will speak thy speech, Love,
> Think thy thought —
>
> Meet, if thou require it,
> Both demands,
> Laying flesh and spirit
> In thy hands.
>
> That shall be to-morrow
> Not to-night:
> I must bury sorrow
> Out of sight:
>
> — Must a little weep, Love
> (Foolish me!)
> And so fall asleep, Love,
> Loved by thee.

R. BROWNING.

做个天神举起我吧,
　　用你神秘的魅力!
做个男子汉拥抱我吧,
　　用你的双臂!

教导我,亲爱的,　　　　　　　　　　25
　　正如我应受到的教育;
爱人,我会如同你那样说话,
　　我会如同你一般思索。

来吧,如果你需要
　　两者都可满足,　　　　　　　　30
我会把灵与肉全部献出
　　献到你的手中。

那该是明天
　　而不是今夜:
我应把一切忧愁埋藏　　　　　　　　35
　　使它永不出现:

还须流点眼泪呵,爱人,
　　(我有多么愚蠢!)
我们就同枕一席吧,我的爱人,
　　——让我拥有你的爱!　　　　　　40

陈朴　译

编注 此诗选自《男男女女》第一卷。

345. LIFE IN A LOVE

Escape me?
Never —
Beloved!
While I am I, and you are you,
    So long as the world contains us both,
    Me the loving and you the loath,
While the one eludes, must the other pursue.
My life is a fault at last, I fear:
    It seems too much like a fate, indeed!
    Though I do my best I shall scarce succeed.
But what if I fail of my purpose here?
It is but to keep the nervest a strain,
    To dry one's eyes and laugh at a fall,
And baffled, get up and begin again, —
    So the chace takes up one's life, that's all[①].
While, look but once from your farthest bound
    At me so deep in the dust and dark,
No sooner the old hope goes to ground[②]
    Than a new one, straight to the selfsame mark,
        I shape me —
Ever
Removed[③]!

                                        R. BROWNING.

---

① *chace*: an alternative, though now old-fashioned, spelling of 'chase.'
② *goes*: the original had 'drops.'
③ *Ever Removed*: 'and the new one in turn always retires before me.'

345. 终身的爱

罗伯特·布朗宁

逃避我?
不!——
亲爱的!
只要我是我,你是你,
　只要世界容纳了你我,
　我一往情深而你退却,
我就必须追求下去。
真害怕呵,我的生命到底是场错误:
　是的,它看来太像天命,
　竭尽全力,我仍难成功!
倘若,达不到目的又会如何?
只要保持紧张的神经,
　擦干泪水,对失败一笑了之,
摔了跟头,挣扎起来重新开头——
　呵,就让追求占据人的全部生活。
而你从远方盼顾
　瞧我深深陷入的尘世黑暗,
每当旧望逝去,新绪复萌
　我朝着自己的目标前进,
　　但是我注定——
　　永远
　　难成功!

陈朴 译

编注 此诗选自《男男女女》第一卷,诗题的意思是说对爱的追求贯穿人的生活的始终。

346. A GRAMMARIAN'S FUNERAL
Shortly after the Revival
of Learning in Europe

Let us begin and carry up this corpse,
    Singing together.
Leave we the common crofts, the vulgar thorpes①,
    Each in its tether
5 Sleeping safe on the bosom of the plain,
    Cared-for till cock-crow:
Look out if yonder be not day again
    Rimming the rock-row②!
That's the appropriate country; there, man's thought,
10   Rarer, intenser③,
Self-gathered for an outbreak, as it ought④,
    Chafes in the censer⑤.
Leave we the unlettered plain its herd and crop;
    Seek we sepulture
15 On a tall mountain, citied to the top,
    Crowded with culture!
All the peaks soar, but one the rest excels;
    Clouds overcome it;
No, yonder sparkle is the citadel's

---

① *crofts*: enclosed spaces; their *tether* is the enclosing walls or hedges.
② *Rimming the rock-row*: 'fringing with light the rocky summit of the mountain.'
③ *Rarer*: 'finer.'
④ *Self-gathered*: 'drawn from the workings of the spirit within,' not picked up from others.
⑤ *That's the appropriate country*, etc.: i.e. he ought to be buried in the mountains, for there thought grows hot in the brain.

346. 一位文法家的葬礼
（写在欧洲刚恢复好学之后）

罗伯特·布朗宁

让我们开始抬起这具死尸，
　　一起唱着歌。
我们离开普通的房舍，庸俗的村庄，
　　让它们各自在自己的范围
安睡于原野的胸怀，　　　　　　　　　5
　　等待着直到鸡鸣：
看一看远处是否又是白天
　　给山岭峰巅镶上了边！
那里是合适的土地；在那里，人的思想
　　更珍贵，更热烈，　　　　　　　10
自己集合起来要迸发，早该是
　　如同香炉里的怒火。
我们离开无文的原野上的牲畜庄稼；
　　我们寻找坟墓
在一座高山，筑城于山巅，　　　　　15
　　挤满了文化！
所有的山峰都高耸，但是有一座出众；
　　乌云把它压住；
不，远处有着环绕峰巅的

                    Circling its summit.
                Thither our path lies; wind we up the heights;
                    Wait ye the warning①?
                Our low life was the level's and the night's;
                    He's for the morning.
                Step to a tune, square chests, erect each head,
                    'Ware the beholders!
                This is our master, famous, calm, and dead,
                    Borne on our shoulders.

                Sleep, crop and herd! sleep, darkling thorpe and croft,
                    Safe from the weather!
                He, whom we convoy to his grave aloft,
                    Singing together,
                He was a man born with thy face and throat,
                    Lyric Apollo!
                Long he lived nameless; how should spring take note
                    Winter would follow?
                Till lo, the little touch, and youth was gone!
                    Cramped and diminished,
                Moaned he, 'New measures, other feet anon!
                    My dance is finished'?
                No, that's the world's way: (keep the mountain-side,
                    Make for the city!)
                He knew the signal, and stepped on with pride
                    Over men's pity;
                Left play for work, and grappled with the world②

---

① *the warning*: 'the word to start.'
② *grappled with the world*, etc.: 'forced his way into the seats of learning, which tried to resist his importunity.'

城堡的熠熠闪光。 20
我们的道路通向那里；我们盘旋而走向高处；
  你还在等着那信号？
我们卑微的生命在平地,在黑夜:
  他却是为了黎明。
齐步走,挺起胸,都要抬起头, 25
  当心那些旁观的人!
这是我们的大师,著名,安详,死了,
  抬起在我们的肩头上。

睡吧,牲畜和庄稼,房舍和村庄,
  别怕天气的变化! 30
他,我们把他送上高处的坟墓,
  一起唱着歌,
他是个生来有着你的脸和嗓子的人,
  抒情的阿波罗!
他默默无闻地活了很久:为什么春天就该注明 35
  冬天就要随之而来？
直到唉,轻轻地一触,青春就已一去不返!
  虾着腰,耸着肩,
他呻吟,"新的拍子,别的步子啦!
  我的舞算是已跳完？" 40
不,世界上的事本来就这样:(沿着山边走,
  直向着城堡!)
他懂得这信号,骄傲地踏着步子
  踩过了人们的怜悯；
放弃玩乐,埋头工作,牢牢地抓住 45

>   Bent on escaping:
> 'What's in the scroll,' quoth he,'thou keepest furled?
>   Show me their shaping,
> Theirs, who most studied man, the bard and sage, —
50   Give!' — So, he gowned him①,
> Straight got by heart that book to its last page:
>   Learned, we found him.
> Yea, but we found him bald too, eyes like lead,
>   Accents uncertain:
55 'Time to taste life,' another would have said,
>   'Up with the curtain!' —
> This man said rather, 'Actual life comes next?
>   Patience a moment!
> Grant I have mastered learning's crabbed text,
60   Still, there's the comment.
> Let me know all! Prate not of most or least,
>   Painful or easy!
> Even to the crumbs I'd fain eat up the feast,
>   Aye, nor feel queasy.'
65 Oh, such a life as he resolved to live,
>   When he had learned it,
> When he had gathered all books had to give!
>   Sooner, he spurned it②.
> Image the whole, then execute the parts —
70   Fancy the fabric
> Quite, ere you build, ere steel strike fire from quartz③,

---

① *he gowned him*: 'put on the scholar's garb.'
② *Sooner, he spurned it*: i.e. he thought it a contemptible thing to try and live a life of action before he had learned wisdom.
③ *ere steel strike fire from quartz*: i.e. before you begin to cut the marble for the building.

弯身想要逃跑的世界:
"书卷里面是什么,"他说,"你手里卷着的?
让我看看他们的作品,
他们的,那些最有学问的人,诗人和贤哲——
　　给我!"——他就这样自己穿上学者的长袍, 50
把那书卷从头到尾直接记进心里:
　　于是有了学问,我们发现他。
的确,我们也发现他秃了顶,眼光如铅,
　　声音发颤:
"时间考验生命,"别的人也许会说, 55
　　"把幕布升起!"——
这个人却宁愿说,"真正的生活不是还在后面?
　　且忍耐片刻!
就算我已经精通了学问的艰难文字,
　　却还有评注未读。 60
让我懂得一切!不要空谈最多或至少,
　　困难或容易!
即使是面包屑,我也乐意当筵席吃光,
　　唉,也不会感到恶心。"
哦,他决意过这样的生活, 65
　　一旦他学到了手,
一旦他收集到一切必要的书籍,
　　他迟早会把它统统唾弃。
设想了整体,然后逐步加以实现——
　　计划好建筑的 70
全部,在营造之前,在铜钎凿石迸出火花之前,

　　　　　Ere mortar dab brick!

　　　　　(Here's the town-gate reached; there's the marketplace
　　　　　　　Gaping before us.)
75　　　　Yea, this in him was the peculiar grace
　　　　　　　(Hearten our chorus!)
　　　　　That before living he'd learn how to live —
　　　　　　　No end to learning:
　　　　　Earn the means first — God surely will contrive
80　　　　　　Use for our earning.
　　　　　Others mistrust and say, 'But time escapes:
　　　　　　　Live now or never!'
　　　　　He said, 'What's time? leave Now for dogs and apes!
　　　　　　　Man has Forever.'
85　　　　Back to his book then; deeper drooped his head:
　　　　　　　Calculus racked him;
　　　　　Leaden before, his eyes grew dross of lead:
　　　　　　　Tussis attacked him①.
　　　　　'Now, master, take a little rest!' — not he!
90　　　　　　(Caution redoubled,
　　　　　Step two a-breast, the way winds narrowly!)
　　　　　　　Not a whit troubled,
　　　　　Back to his studies, fresher than at first,
　　　　　　　Fierce as a dragon
95　　　　He (soul-hydroptic with a sacred thirst②)
　　　　　　　Sucked at the flagon.
　　　　　Oh, if we draw a circle premature,

---

① *Tussis*: 'a cough.'
② *soul-hydroptic*: 'having an insatiable thirst in his soul'; an unquenchable thirst is one of the symptoms of dropsy.

  在灰浆抹上砖块之前!

（这里是到了村镇的大门；那里是市集
  在我们面前展现。）
是啊，这在他，是特殊的才能 75
  （让我们的合唱更有劲!）
在生活之前，他得学会怎么生活——
  无休无止地求学问：
首先要赚到钱——上帝肯定会设法
  使用我们赚的钱。 80
别的人不相信，说，"但是时间消逝了：
  要么现在生活，要么就决不!"
他说，"时间算什么？把现在留给狗和猴!
  人有的，是永恒。"
于是他回到书堆里：脑袋越垂越低； 85
  结石把他折磨；
本来如铅的眼睛，长出了铅的渣滓；
  咳嗽又袭击着他。
"现在，大师，休息一会儿吧!"——他可不行!
  （警告成倍而来， 90
两个两个并肩而行，道路盘旋着越来越窄!）
   没有一丁点儿烦恼，
他回进了书斋，比原来更加精神，
  凶猛得犹如一条龙
他（灵魂的水肿引起的神圣干渴） 95
  狂饮于一只大瓮。
啊，要是我们划一个早熟的圆圈，

	Heedless of far gain,
	Greedy for quick returns of profit, sure,
100	Bad is our bargain!
	Was it not great? did not he throw on God,

Heedless of far gain,
Greedy for quick returns of profit, sure,
    Bad is our bargain!
Was it not great? did not he throw on God,
    (He loves the burthen) —
God's task to make the heavenly period
    Perfect the earthen?
Did not he magnify the mind, show clear
    Just what it all meant?
He would not discount life, as fools do here[①],
    Paid by instalment.
He ventured neck or nothing — heaven's success
    Found, or earth's failure:
'Wilt thou trust death or not?' He answered 'Yes!
    Hence with life's pale lure!'
That low man seeks a little thing to do[②],
    Sees it and does it:
This high man, with a great thing to pursue,
    Dies ere he knows it.
That low man goes on adding one to one,
    His hundred's soon hit:
This high man, aiming at a million,
    Misses an unit.
That, has the world here — should he need the next
    Let the world mind him[③]!
This, throws himself on God, and unperplexed
    Seeking shall find him.

---

① *discount life*: 'sell the amount due to him in the future for a smaller sum paid down now'; he chose rather to wait for his reward till his work was ended than take it by instalments as he worked.
② *That low man*: 'the man of low ideals.'
③ The man who has made worldly success his aim has only the world to look to if he is ever possessed with spiritual longings.

不管将来之所得
贪心地想获得快速的利益,肯定,
  我们的买卖就会坏得不可收拾。 100
难道这不伟大?难道他没有扔向上帝
  (他热爱这重负)——
以上帝的任务,把天上的时代
  变得跟尘世一样完美,
难道他没有把头脑放大,清楚地显示 105
  这一切的含义?
他不愿意把生命打折扣,像这里的傻瓜一样,
  分期收取报酬。
他拿脖子去冒险,或者一无所有——天上的成功
  被发现,或者地上的失败: 110
"你相信不相信死?"他回答"信!
  因此才有生命的苍白诱饵!"
卑微的人找一些小事做做,
  找到了就动手:
这个高尚人的人要干伟大的事, 115
  却死在还未知晓之前。
卑微的人做了一事又一事,
  很快就有一百件。
这个高尚的人,却目标向着百万,
  而失去了一个单位。 120
那一个,眼前就是世界——如果他再有需要
  就让世界想着他!
这一个,把自己抛向上帝,毫不困难的
  寻觅就能把他找到。

So, with the throttling hands of death at strife,
    Ground he at grammar;
Still, thro' the rattle, parts of speech were rife:
    While he could stammer
He settled *Hoti's* business — let it be! —①
    Properly based *Oun* — ②
Gave us the doctrine of the enclitic *De*③,
    Dead from the waist down④.
Well, here's the platform, here's the proper place:
    Hail to your purlieus⑤,
All ye highfliers of the feathered race,
    Swallows and curlews!
Here's the top-peak; the multitude below
    Live, for they can, there:
This man decided not to Live but Know —
    Bury this man there?
Here — here's his place, where meteors shoot, clouds form,
    Lightnings are loosened,
Stars come and go! Let joy break with the storm,
    Peace let the dew send!
Lofty designs must close in like effects:
    Loftily lying,
Leave him — still loftier than the world suspects,
    Living and dying.

R. BROWNING.

---

① *Hoti*: ὅτι, a Greek particle, whose 'business' is more easily 'settled' than that of some others.
② *based Oun*: traced the primary meaning of the particle οὖν.
③ *the enclitic De*: an enclitic is a word which throws its accent on the preceding word, to which sometimes, as with — δε, it is joined.
④ *Dead*: 'though he was paralysed.'
⑤ *your purlieus*: 'your own haunts.'

因此,竭力以死亡的憋气的手,　　　　　　　　125
　　他自己学起了文法;
通过咕噜的喉音,各种词类仍然猖獗:
　　而他却只能结结巴巴。
他安排好"霍蒂"的事——让它去!——
　　恰当地为"翁"找到根据——　　　　　　130
给了我们活用的"德"的原则①,
　　腰部以下就已经死去。
是啊,这里就是讲台,这里就是恰当的地方:
　　欢呼你们的领地吧,
你们羽族的所有的高飞者啊,　　　　　　135
　　燕子和麻鹬!
这里就是峰巅,芸芸众生在下面
　　生活,因为他们只能在那里:
这个人决定不生活而去求学——
　　难道把这个人就在那里埋葬?　　　　　140
这里——这里才是他的地方,在这里,
　　流星飞驰,云朵形成,闪电怒放,
星星忽明忽灭!让欢乐与风暴并起,
　　让和平由露珠送往!
崇高的设想必需要以类似的效果结束:　　145
　　崇高地躺着吧,
让他——要比世界的猜想更为崇高地
　　在生生死死之中。

　　　　　　　　　　　　　　　王央乐　译

编注　本诗选自《男男女女》第二卷。

---

①　"霍蒂",希腊文的冠词;"翁",希腊文的前置词;"德",希腊文中可与前词相连的词。——译者

347. PORPHYRIA'S LOVER

The rain set early in to-night,
    The sullen wind was soon awake,
It tore the elm-tops down for spite,
    And did its worst to vex the lake:
        I listened with heart fit to break,
When glided in Porphyria; straight
    She shut the cold out and the storm,
And kneeled and made the cheerless grate
    Blaze up, and all the cottage warm;
        Which done, she rose, and from her form
Withdrew the dripping cloak and shawl,
    And laid her soiled gloves by, untied
Her hat and let the damp hair fall,
    And, last, she sat down by my side
        And called me. When no voice replied,
She put my arm about her waist,
    And made her smooth white shoulder bare,
And all her yellow hair displaced,
    And, stooping, made my cheek lie there,
        And spread o'er all her yellow hair,
Murmuring how she loved me — she
    Too weak, for all her heart's endeavour,
To set its struggling passion free
    From pride, and vainer ties dissever,
        And give herself to me for ever.
But passion sometimes would prevail,

347. 波菲里亚的情人

罗伯特·布朗宁

今夜的雨来得早,
　　阴冷的风不一会儿就起来,
强把榆树梢头往下拉,
　　更坏的是还要去惹恼湖沼:
　　我怀着要碎的心静听, 　　　　　　5
这时候波菲里亚悄然溜进;直截了当
　　就把寒冷的风暴关于门外。
她跪下把没精打采的炉栅
　　吹得火光熊熊,茅屋里暖意洋洋;
　　然后她站了起来,从身上　　　　10
脱下滴水的外衣和头巾,
　　弄脏的手套放一边,解下
帽子,让潮湿的头发披垂;
　　最后,她在我身边坐下
　　把我呼唤。因为没有声音回答, 　　15
她让我的胳膊围住她的腰,
　　裸露出滑腻莹洁的肩头,
拂开所有金黄的长发,
　　俯下身子,让我的脸颊在那里贴着,
　　又把她全部金黄的长发盖上, 　　20
喃喃地说着她多么爱我——她
　　太软弱,虽然竭尽心力
想把挣扎着的热情摆脱掉
　　骄傲,割断更为虚荣的纽带,
　　让她自己永远归我所有。 　　　　25
然而有时候激情会占上风,

Nor could to-night's gay feast restrain
A sudden thought of one so pale
For love of her, and all in vain
So, she was come through wind and rain
Be sure I looked up at her eyes
Happy and proud; at last I knew
Porphyria worshipped me; surprise
Made my heart swell, and still it grew
While I debated what to do.
That moment she was mine, mine, fair
Perfectly pure and good: I found
A thing to do, and all her hair
In one long yellow string I wound
Three times her little throat around,
And strangled her. No pain felt she;
I am quite sure she felt no pain.
As a shut bud that holds a bee,
I warily oped her lids: again
Laughed the blue eyes without a stain.
And I untightened next the tress
About her neck; her cheek once more
Blushed bright beneath my burning kiss:
I propped her head up as before,
Only, this time my shoulder bore
Her head, which droops upon it still:
The smiling rosy little head,
So glad it has its utmost will,
That all it scorned at once is fled,
And I, its love, am gained instead!
Porphyria's love: she guessed not how
Her darling one wish would be heard.

今夜的盛宴也难以抑止
为了爱情而如此苍白的她
　　突发的念头,什么也不能阻挡:
　　因此,她冒着风风雨雨而来, 　　　　　30
肯定我抬头看见她的眼睛,会
　　幸福而自豪;终于我明白了
波菲里亚崇拜我;惊讶
　　使我的心膨胀,一直膨胀着
　　当我盘算着该怎么办的时候。 　　　　35
这时刻,她是我的,是我的,漂亮
　　完美无缺地纯洁而善良;我找到了
一件事情可做,于是她的全部长发
　　被我编成了一根金黄的长绳,
　　在她纤细的脖颈上绕了三圈, 　　　　40
把她勒紧。她不觉得痛苦;
　　我完全肯定,痛苦她并不觉得。
如同闭合的花蕾抓住一只蜜蜂,
　　我小心谨慎地拨开她的眼睑:重新
　　又笑开了那湛蓝的眼睛,没有一点污迹。 　　45
接着我松开了绕住她脖颈的
　　发辫;她的双颊又一次
在我的热吻下红潮焕发:
　　我托起她的头像原来一样,
　　不过这一次是我的肩膀 　　　　　　　50
让它靠着,贴在那里一动不动。
　　这颗微笑的玫瑰色的小小头颅,
那么高兴实现了它最终的意愿,
　　它所蔑视的一切立即化为乌有,
　　而我,它所爱的,却被她得到了手! 　　55
波菲里亚的爱:她没有猜着
　　她所钟爱的人的愿望如何能够听到。

And thus we sit together now,
And all night long we have not stirred,
And yet God has not said a word!

R. BROWNING.

现在我们就这样坐在一起,
　　　漫长的整夜我们一动未动,
　　　然而上帝却没有说一句话!

王央乐　译

编注　本诗原是题为《疯人院的小房间》(Madhouse Cells)的两首短诗之一,后收进《铃铛与石榴》,为第三首,一八六三年才冠以现名。

348. RABBI BEN EZRA

1

Grow old along with me!
The best is yet to be,
The last of life, for which the first was made;
Our times are in His hand
Who saith 'A whole I planned,
Youth shows but half; trust God; see all, nor be afraid!'

2

Not that, amassing flowers[①],
Youth sighed 'Which rose make ours,
Which lily leave and then as best recall?'
Not that, admiring stars,
It yearned 'Nor Jove, nor Mars;
Mine be some figured flame which blends, transcends them all!'

3

Not for such hopes and fears
Annulling youth's brief years,
Do I remonstrate: folly wide the mark[②]!
Rather I prize the doubt
Low kinds exist without[③],

[①] *Not that*: 'Do I remonstrate' must be supplied from l. 15 below; so also in l. 10; 'I do not complain that youth hesitates in choice of its pleasures and has extravagant longings.'

[②] *folly wide the mark*: 'that is a foolish supposition, and far from the truth.'

[③] *the doubt Low kinds exist without*: for it is only the high mind that is troubled by dissatisfaction and the stirrings of divine discontent.

348. 拉比本·埃兹拉①

罗伯特·布朗宁

1

跟我一起老去！
最好的还在后面，
生命的最后，为了它才造成最初；
我们的时间是在他的手里，
他说："我设计的是整体， 5
青春不过显现其半；相信上帝：看到全部，不要畏惧！"

2

并非如此，收集着花朵，
青春叹道："哪朵玫瑰造就我们，
哪支百合离去了，最值得回忆？"
并非如此，仰慕着明星， 10
它在渴望"不当朱武，不当马斯②；
我要当具有形体的火焰，掺和进，超越过，它们全部！"

3

不是为了这种希望，这种担心
要取消青春的短暂岁月，
我是在规劝：这些目标又愚蠢又遥远！ 15
我宁可看重那种无忧无虑
过活的卑微的人，

---

① 本·埃兹拉(本名 Abraham Ibn Ezra，1092—1167)，生于托莱多，希伯莱诗人和拉比(犹太教牧师)，精通天文和数学。——译者
② "朱武"即罗马主神朱庇特(Jupiter)，"马斯"即罗马神话中的战神。——编注者

Finished and finite clods, untroubled by a spark.

4

Poor vaunt of life indeed,
　　Were man but formed to feed
On joy, to solely seek and find and feast:
　　Such feasting ended, then
　　As sure an end to men;
Irks care the crop-full bird? Frets doubt the maw-crammed beast①?

5

Rejoice we are allied
　　To That which doth provide
And not partake, effect and not receive!
　　A spark disturbs Our clod;
　　Nearer we hold of God②
Who gives, than of His tribes that take, I must believe.

6

Then, welcome each rebuff
　　That turns earth's smoothness rough,
Each sting that bids nor sit nor stand but go!
　　Be our joys three-parts pain!
　　Strive, and hold cheap the strain;
Learn, nor account the pang; dare, never grudge the throe!

7

For thence, — a paradox③
　　Which comforts while it mocks, —
Shall life succeed in that it seems to fail④:

---

① *Irks care the crop-full bird*, etc.: mere animals are troubled by no cares or doubts but how to get food.
② *hold of God*: 'are the vassals of God.'
③ *thence*: 'through the pangs it feels.'
④ *in that it seems to fail*: 'because of its apparent failure.'

完整的有限的皮囊,一颗火星难以打动。

4

　　的确是生命的可怜的夸口话,
　　要是人不过是生下来以快乐
为食物,仅仅是去觅来饱餐一顿;
　　饱餐一结束,于是
　　肯定就是人的结局:
饱食了的鸟还有疑虑? 果腹了的兽还会担忧?

5

　　多么高兴我们联合了
　　总是供应而不分享
总是生产而不收受的那一个!
　　一颗火星打扰了我们的皮囊;
　　我们依赖上帝更近,
他给予,而不从他的部族征收,我得相信。

6

　　然后,迎接每一次的挫折,
　　使大地的光滑变得粗糙;
每一次的刺痛,使你不能坐不能站只能往前走!
　　使我们的快乐四分之三是苦痛!
　　奋斗吧,把家世看得一钱不值;
学习吧,不要考虑苦楚;放胆吧,决不吝啬创伤!

7

从这里开始——一件怪事
　　它给人安慰又是讽刺—
生命才会在仿佛失败的当口得到成功:

                What I aspired to be,
                And was not, comforts me:
            A brute I might have been, but would not sink i' the scale.

                              8
                What is he but a brute
                Whose flesh hath soul to suit,
            Whose spirit works lest arms and legs want play①?
                To man, propose this test②—
                Thy body at its best,
            How far can that project thy soul on its lone way?

                              9
                yet gifts should prove their use③:
                I own the Past profuse
            Of power each side, perfection every turn:
                Eyes, ears took in their dole,
                Brain treasured up the whole;
            Should not the heart beat once 'How good to live and learn'?

                              10
                Not once beat 'Praise be Thine!
                I see the whole design,
            I, who saw power, see now Love perfect too:
                Perfect I call Thy plan:
                Thanks that I was a man!
            Maker, remake, complete, — I trust what Thou shalt do!'

                              11
                For pleasant is this flesh;
                Our soul in its rose-mesh

---

① *Whose spirit works*, etc.: 'whose mind serves merely to direct his muscles.'
② *this test*: i.e. the test of a man's real worth is whether his body is used to forward and feed the soul or vice versa.
③ *gifts*: i.e. the gifts of Nature.

我渴望成为那样

　　　然而却没有,反而安慰了我:

我也许会成为一个粗人,但是不会变得下贱。

8

　　　一个人的肉体要求灵魂来配合,

　　　　怎能不是一个粗人,

他的精神在作用,否则四肢就只想怠惰?

　　　给人,建议这个试验——

　　　　让你的肉体任其所为,

看你的肉体在孤独的路上还能够有多少作为。

9

　　　然而天赋应该证明其用处:

　　　　我每一边都有着

往昔的充沛力量,每一个关节都完整无缺:

　　　　眼睛耳朵接受着施舍,

　　　　头脑则把全部收藏;

难道心就不应该跳一跳:"活着学着有多么好?"

10

　　　而不是跳着说:"你的心该赞美!

　　　　我见到了全部的设想;

我,见过力量,现在看见爱也变得完美,

　　　　我说你的计划完美:

　　　　真感谢,我是一个人!

造物主,再造吧,完成吧——我信任你要做的一切!"

11

　　　因为这个肉体很快活;

　　　　我们的灵魂在玫瑰的网里

  Pulled ever to the earth, still yearns for rest:
   Would we some prize might hold
65   To match those manifold
  Possessions of the brute, — gain most, as we did best①!

12

  Let us not always say
   'Spite of this flesh to-day
  I strove, made head, gained ground upon the whole!'
70   As the bird wings and sings,
   Let us cry 'All good things
  Are ours, nor soul helps flesh more, now, than flesh helps soul!'

13

  Therefore I summon age
   To grant youth's heritage,
75   Life's struggle having so far reached its term:
   Thence shall I pass, approved
    A man, for ay removed
  From the developed brute; a God though in the germ.

14

  And I shall thereupon
80   Take rest, ere I be gone
  Once more on my adventure brave and new:
   Fearless and unperplexed,
    When I wage battle next,
  What weapons to select, what armour to indue.

---

  ① *those manifold Possessions of the brute*: what we call the lower animals are our superiors in speed, strength, agility, health, and instinct. Man, who works harder than they, should have some special gift to balance these advantages, viz. the power to control — not extinguish — his bodily desires, and so find 'rest.'

总是被拖到了地下,仍然渴望着歇息:
  也许我们可以抓到一些赏赉,
   跟粗人的各种所有   65
相比——我们干得越多,得到的也越多!

12

  让我们不要总是说
   "别管今天这肉体①,
我奋斗,努力向前,争取得到整体!"
   如同鸟在飞翔歌唱,   70
  让我们喊:"一切好事都归我们,
现在,别再让灵魂帮助肉体,或者肉体帮助灵魂!"

13

  因此我召来年岁,
   让它答应给青春财产,
一生的斗争终于达到了期限②: 75
   从此我将离去,赞成
   一个人,因为,唉,他离开
发展了的粗人;是一个上帝,虽然还在胚胎。

14

  然后我将要歇息,
   在我再一次去   80
从事勇敢的新的冒险之前:
   无所畏惧,毫不困惑地
   在随后发动的战斗中
选择什么样的武器,穿上什么样的甲胄。

15

  青春结束了,我要试试今后   85

---

① 基督教认为,肉体是不洁物,只是为了有助于灵魂的发展,肉体才是有意义的。——编注者
② 意为:我已经到了中年。——编注者

15

Youth ended, I shall try
My gain or loss thereby;
Leave the fire ashes, what survives is gold①:
And I shall weigh the same②,
Give life its praise or blame:
Young, all lay in dispute; I shall know, being old.

16

For note, when evening shuts,
A certain moment cuts
The deed off, calls the glory from the grey:
A whisper from the west
Shoots — 'Add this to the rest,
Take it and try its worth: here dies another day.'

17

So, still within this life,
Though lifted o'er its strife,
Let me discern, compare, pronounce at last,
'This rage was right i' the main,
That acquiescence vain:
The Future I may face now I have proved the Past.'

18

For more is not reserved
To man, with soul just nerved
To act to-morrow what he learns to-day:
Here, work enough to watch
The Master work, and catch

---

① *Leave the fire ashes, etc.*: *i.e.* though the fires of youth burn out, they serve to purify man's nature.
② *the same*: see note to No. 238, l. 5.

我是有所得还是有所失；
让火烧成灰烬，剩下来的就是黄金；
　　我要称称它的重量，
　　给生命以赞美或者斥责；
年轻时，一切都有争议；老了，我就什么都明悟。 90

16

　　请注意，黄昏来临时
　　到某一个时刻，就把
行动打断，从灰暗中召唤光荣：
　　西方来的一阵低语
　　说的是——"请把它加上其他， 95
接受它，试试它的价值：从这里又消逝了一天。"

17

　　因此，依然在这生命里，
　　尽管拔升于它的奋斗之上，
让我加以辨别，比较，最后说出
　　"这种愤慨基本正确， 100
　　那种默认纯属徒劳：
现在我要面临的未来，已经有过去作了证明。"

18

　　因为"更多"并未保留着
　　给人，让灵魂激动地
明天去实行他今天学到的一切： 105
　　这里，要有足够的工作
　　去观看大师的工作，获得

Hints of the proper craft, tricks of the tool's true play.

19

As it was better, youth
Should strive, through acts uncouth,
Toward making, than repose on aught found made;
So, better, age, exempt
From strife, should know, than tempt
Further. Thou waitedst age; wait death nor be afraid!

20

Enough now, if the Right
And Good and Infinite
Be named here, as thou callest thy hand thine own,
With knowledge absolute,
Subject to no dispute
From fools that crowded youth, nor let thee feel alone.

21

Be there, for once and all,
Severed great minds from small,
Announced to each his station in the Past!
Was I, the world arraigned,
Were they, my soul disdained,
Right? Let age speak the truth and give us peace at last!

22

Now, who shall arbitrate?
Ten men love what I hate,
Shun what I follow, slight what I receive;
Ten, who in ears and eyes
Match me; we all surmise,

恰当的工艺的启示,那真正工具的技巧。

19

  最好是,青春应该奋斗,
  通过笨拙的动作,
学会创造,然后在造成的任何事物上歇息;
  因此,最好,应该知道,
  把奋斗的年龄免除;然后继续
尝试。你等着年龄,等着死亡,也别害怕!

20

  现在够了,如果权利,
  善良,永恒,都在这里
提到,如同你说,你的手是属于你所有,
  这种绝对的知识;
  那么没有争议的问题,就会
来自挤满了青春的傻瓜,使你也不会感到孤单①。

21

  到那里,一下子地,区分
  伟大的头脑和渺小的头脑,
对每一个说出它在往昔的位置!
  不是我,被世界所指责;
  不是他们,被我的灵魂所蔑视,
对不对?让年岁说出真话,给我们最后的安宁!

22

  现在,谁会来仲裁?
  十个人所爱的,正是我所恨;
回避我所追随的,蔑视我所接受的;
  十个人,他们的眼睛耳朵
  比得上我:我们都在猜测,

---

① 此节大意为:如果我们在老年,就像认识到自己的双手一样认识到了正确和错误,善和恶,变化和永恒,那么,这足以使我们心满意足。——编注者

They, this thing, and I, that: whom shall my soul believe?

23

　　Not on the vulgar mass
　　Called 'work,' must sentence pass,
135　Things done, that took the eye and had the price;
　　O'er which, from level stand①,
　　The low world laid its hand,
　Found straightway to its mind, could value in a trice:

24

　　But all, the world's coarse thumb
140　　And finger failed to plumb,
　So passed in making up the main account;
　　All instincts immature,
　　All purposes unsure,
　That weighed not as his work, yet swelled the man's amount:

25

145　　Thoughts hardly to be packed
　　Into a narrow act,
　Fancies that broke through language and escaped;
　　All I could never be,
　　All, men ignored in me.
150　This, I was worth to God, whose wheel the pitcher shaped.

26

　　Aye, note that Potter's wheel,
　　That metaphor! and feel
　Why time spins fast, why passive lies our clay, —
　　Thou, to whom fools propound,
155　　When the wine makes its round,

---

① *from level stand*: 'standing themselves on the same level as the actor.'

他们,这件事;我,那件事:我的灵魂相信谁?
23
不要对庸俗的多数
谈"工作",那是白说话①;
事情做成了,就会让人看见,具有价值;
在这之上,从同样高度的地方
卑微的世界以它的手按上,
直触到它的头脑,一下子就估出了它的价值:
24
总而言之,世界的粗糙拇指
以及手指,都难以探测,
因而只得不作出主要的计算;
一切本能都不成熟,
一切目的都未肯定,
衡量的并非他的工作,然而却使人的数量膨胀:
25
思想几乎难以
装进狭窄的行动,
幻想冲破语言而出,就逃遁不见。
一切,我决不可能,
一切,人们在我身上视而不见。
这一点,我是值得为上帝所有,是他的轮子做成的大杯。
26
唉,注意那陶工的轮子,
那隐喻吧!感觉到
为什么时间转得那么快,我们的泥土那么软——
你,傻瓜们向你提议
在酒过一巡的时候,

---

① 意为:评价一个人,我们不要仅仅凭着他为世界做的"工作"这个标准。——编注者

'Since life fleets, all is change; the Past gone, seize to-day!'

27

Fool! All that is, at all
　　Lasts ever, past recall;
Earth changes, but thy soul and God stand sure:
　　What entered into thee,
　　That was, is, and shall be:
Time's wheel runs back or stops; Potter and clay endure.

28

　　He fixed thee mid this dance
　　Of plastic circumstance,
This Present, thou, forsooth, wouldst fain arrest:
　　Machinery just meant
　　To give thy soul its bent,
Try thee and turn thee forth, sufficiently impressed.

29

　　What though the earlier grooves
　　Which ran the laughing loves
Around thy base, no longer pause and press?
　　What though, about thy rim,
　　Skull-things in order grim
Grow out, in graver mood, obey the sterner stress?

30

　　Look not thou down but up!
　　To uses of a cup,
The festal board, lamp's flash and trumpet's peal,
　　The new wine's foaming flow,
　　The Master's lips aglow!
Thou, heaven's consummate cup, what needst thou with earth's wheel?

31

　　But I need, now as then,

"既然生命飞逝,一切都变;过去已经过去,抓住今天!"

27

笨蛋!这一切都是,根本

总是如此,想想过去;

大地变了,但是你的灵魂和上帝巍然不变:

进入你身体里的东西,

过去在,现在在,将来也在;

时间的轮子会倒转或停止;陶工和泥土却继续如此。

28

他在这场圆舞中

把你固定于可塑的环境,

这个现在,你,今后,再也难以捕捉:

机械不过意味着

以其怪癖给予你的灵魂,

考验你,把你旋转,足以使你印象深刻。

29

那有什么关系,尽管早年的刻刀

刻出那些嬉笑的可爱的人

围绕你的底座,不再忽停忽刻?

那有什么关系,尽管在你的杯沿,

有些难看的髑髅似的东西

生长而出,模样阴沉,服从着更为严酷的压力?

30

你不要往下看而要往上看!

一只杯子的用处,是在

喜庆的桌子,灯火的辉煌,喇叭的齐鸣;

新酒冒着泡沫注满,

大师的嘴唇红彤彤!

你,天上的尽善尽美的杯子,还需要地下的轮子干什么?

31

但是我需要,现在和今后,

>   Thee, God, who mouldest men;
> And since, not even while the whirl was worst,
>   Did I, — to the wheel of life
> 185   With shapes and colours rife,
> Bound dizzily, — mistake my end, to slake Thy thirst:
> 32
>   So, take and use Thy work①!
>   Amend what flaws may lurk,
> What strain o' the stuff, what warpings past the aim!
> 190   My times be in Thy hand!
>   Perfect the cup as planned!
> Let age approve of youth, and death complete the same!

R. BROWNING.

---

① *So*: 'therefore,' *i.e.* since I never mistook the object with which I, the cup, was formed.

你,塑造了人类的上帝;
而且既然,即使旋转越来越厉害,
　　而我——在生命的轮子上
　　以无数的形状和色彩
头昏目眩地绑着——却弄错了目的,而来为你解渴:

32

　　因此,拿过来,做你的工作!
　　修补可能隐藏着的裂痕,
材料的劳损,目标的偏离!
　　让我的时间掌握在你的手里!
　　完成预先设计的杯子!
让年岁赞许青春,让死亡使它圆满完成!

王央乐　译

349. PROSPICE

Fear death? — to feel the fog in my throat,
  The mist in my face,
When the snows begin, and the blasts denote
  I am nearing the place,
The power of the night, the press of the storm①,
  The post of the foe;
Where he stands, the Arch Fear in a visible form,
  Yet the strong man must go:
For the journey is done and the summit attained,
  And the barriers fall②,
Though a battle 's to fight ere the guerdon be gained,
  The reward of it all.
I was ever a fighter, so — one fight more,
  The best and the last!
I would hate that death bandaged my eyes, and forbore③,
  And bade me creep past.
No! let me taste the whole of it, fare like my peers
  The heroes of old,
Bear the brunt, in a minute pay glad life's arrears
  Of pain, darkness and cold.
For sudden the worst turns the best to the brave,
  The black minute 's at end,

---

① *The power of the night*, etc.: co-ordinate with 'the place.'
② *the barriers*: sc. at the end of the lists, by which the combatants were admitted.
③ *forbore*: 'refrained from putting forth all his terrors.'

349. 展望

罗伯特·布朗宁

害怕死亡吗？——只觉得喉头升起了浓雾，
　　轻雾笼罩着我的脸，
那时大雪飘扬，又是狂风骤起，
　　宣告我快要接近终点：
是黑夜的统治，是暴风雨的压迫，　　　　　　　　5
　　是敌人的岗位。
"大恐怖"赫然现身，挺立在前①；
　　然而强者决不后退。
旅途到了尽头，顶峰已攀登，
　　比武场的栅栏已放下②，　　　　　　　　　10
在取得酬偿之前，还有一场硬仗
　　必须对付，要去拼杀。
我从来是个战士，再打一仗吧——
　　最后的，也是最出色的一仗！
不甘心让死神绑住我双眼，威胁我：　　　　　　15
　　爬过去——趴倒在地上。
不！什么苦我都能受。
　　我要前行像我的战友：那古代英雄，
顶住那沉重的打击，把人生的余欠
　　一下子偿清·黑暗、寒冷、苦痛。　　　　　20
灾殃，在勇敢者面前，顿时变成幸福。
　　黑暗时刻的结束就在眼前，

---

① 此处的"大恐怖"即死亡。——编注者
② 指战士入场比武之前，先放下通道前的栅栏。——译者

And the elements' rage, the fiend-voices that rave,
    Shall dwindle, shall blend,
Shall change, shall become first a peace out of pain,
    Then a light, then thy breast,
O thou soul of my soul! I shall clasp thee again,
    And with God be the rest!

R. BROWNING.

那风啸雨吼,那鬼哭神号①,
　　渐渐远去,渐渐溶成一片,
渐渐在转变——平静首先把痛苦点化,
　　然后闪出光明,然后是你的胸房,
你,我灵魂的灵魂呀!我又将把你拥抱,
　　永远安息在那天堂。

方平　译

译注　一八六一年六月二十九日,布朗宁的爱妻,女诗人伊丽莎白·布朗宁不幸逝世。秋天,布朗宁写了这首悼念的诗。在诗中,诗人对生命作了哲理性的思考:死神并不可怕,死亡不是生命的终点和屈服,而是生命的最后的,也是最悲壮的一场战斗,随之而来的将是宁静和光明;他将重和爱妻见面,在爱妻的怀抱里获得永久的安息。诗篇表达了诗人恬淡的生死观,倾吐出诗人对亡妻的一片真挚深沉的感情。

---

① 中世纪传说,人将死之前,天上的精灵和地狱的魔鬼互相搏斗,争夺即将离开躯体的人的灵魂,因此有风啸雨吼、鬼哭神号之声。——译者

350. THE EXECUTION OF MONTROSE

1

Come hither, Evan Cameron!
    Come, stand beside my knee —
I hear the river roaring down
    Towards the wintry sea.
There 's shouting on the mountain-side,
    There 's war within the blast —
Old faces look upon me,
    Old forms go trooping past:
I hear the pibroch wailing①
    Amidst the din of fight,
And my dim spirit wakes again
    Upon the verge of night.

2

'Twas I that led the Highland host②
    Through wild Lochaber's snows,
What time the plaided clans came down
    To battle with Montrose.
I've told thee how the Southrons fell
    Beneath the broad claymore,
And how we smote the Campbell clan
    By Inverlochy's shore.

---

① *pibroch*: see note to No. 204, l. 1.
② *led*: 'acted as guide to.'

350. 蒙特罗斯之死

艾顿

1

到这里来,埃文·卡梅伦!
　　来,站在我膝旁——
我听见江水汹涌而下
　　直奔严冬的海洋。
呐喊声震山峦四野,　　　　　　　　　　5
　　号角声带来战争气氛——
老战友们凝视着我
　　老队伍列队通过:
我听见风笛哀声变奏
　　混杂着喊杀之声　　　　　　　　　　10
我朦胧的灵魂重又苏醒
　　在夜幕将临的时辰。

2

我曾引导高地的大军
　　通过大雪覆盖的洛哈伯①
身穿苏格兰裙的部族冲下来　　　　　　15
　　迎战蒙特罗斯。
我向你述说过苏格兰大刀如何杀得
　　那些南方佬人仰马翻,
我们如何在因弗罗希的岸边②
　　把坎贝尔族人杀得片甲无还。　　　　20

---

① 洛哈伯(Lochaber),英国因弗罗希郡南一山区。——编注者
② 一六四五年二月,蒙特罗斯在因弗罗希(Inverlochy)大败坎贝尔族首领阿盖尔。四月,他大掠敦提市。——编注者

I've told thee how we swept Dundee,
    And tamed the Lindsays' pride;
But never have I told thee yet
    How the great Marquis died.

3

A traitor sold him to his foes;
    O deed of deathless shame!
I charge thee, boy, if e'er thou meet
    With one of Assynt's name —
Be it upon the mountain's side,
    Or yet within the glen,
Stand he in martial gear alone,
    Or backed by arméd men —
Face him, as thou wouldst face the man
    Who wronged thy sire's renown;
Remember of what blood thou art,
    And strike the caitiff down!

4

They brought him to the Watergate,
    Hard bound with hempen span①,
As though they held a lion there,
    And not a fenceless man②.
They set him high upon a cart —
    The hangman rode below —
They drew his hands behind his back,
    And bared his noble brow.
Then, as a hound is slipped from leash,

---

① *hempen span*: a span in nautical language is a rope fastened at each end and drawn taut.
② *fenceless*: for 'defenceless.'

我向你述说过我们如何横扫敦提，
　　把高傲的林赛族人降服①；
但还未向你陈述过
　　伟大的侯爵如何亡故。

3

叛徒把他出卖给敌人； 25
　　啊，对这恶行永不饶恕！
我告诫你，孩子，倘若你遇见
　　任何一个姓阿辛特的匹夫——
不管他在高山之麓
　　还是深深的峡谷， 30
不管他一人全副武装
　　还是后有千军万夫——
向他迎战，就像你要
　　迎战污辱祖先英名的人；
别忘记你那高贵的血统， 35
　　把那卑鄙小人手刃！

4

他们把他带到水门②，
　　用麻绳来绑紧，
好似缚住一头雄狮，
　　而不是毫无防卫的人。 40
他们把他高高放在马车上——
　　刽子手在下面骑马而行——
他们把他双手反剪，
　　高贵的额头也无遮荫。
接着，就像挣脱链条的疯狗， 45

---

① 林赛族系法夫郡一个遵守盟约、拥护长老派的部族。——译者
② 水门，在苏格兰爱丁堡市内。——译者

They cheered the common throng,
And blew the note with yell and shout,
And bade him pass along.

5

It would have made a brave man's heart
Grow sad and sick that day,
To watch the keen malignant eyes
Bent down on that array.
There stood the Whig west-country lords
In balcony and bow,
There sat their gaunt and withered dames,
And their daughters all a-row.
And every open window
Was full as full might be
With black-robed Covenanting carles[①],
That goodly sport to see!

6

But when he came, though pale and wan,
He looked so great and high,
So noble was his manly front,
So calm his steadfast eye; —
The rabble rout forbore to shout,
And each man held his breath,
For well they knew the hero's soul
Was face to face with death.
And then a mournful shudder
Through all the people crept,
And some that came to scoff at him
Now turn'd aside and wept.

---

① *carles*: 'men of low birth.'

他们向百姓大众欢呼,
欢呼声夹杂着狂叫乱吼,
　　命令他向前疾走。

5

这景象使勇士的心肠
　　在那天也哀痛悲伤,
看到尖刻凶恶的目光
　　落到这个行列上。
辉格党两部的老爷们站在
　　阳台和弓形窗前,
那里坐着他们瘦削憔悴的夫人,
　　他们的女儿也并排站。
每扇开着的窗户前
　　都挤满男男女女
穿黑袍的护教盟约派的老百姓
　　来观看这场好把戏!

6

当他走过,脸色虽苍白,
　　但形象伟大崇高,
他英武的眉宇如此高贵
　　他坚定的目光如此镇静;——
嘈杂的人群也不再喧闹,
　　人人屏声静气,
他们明白英雄的灵魂
　　正在面对死神。
接着,一阵悲恸的战栗
　　传遍整个人群,
那些本想嘲笑他的人,
　　现在也掩面抽泣。

7

But onwards — always onwards,
　　In silence and in gloom,
The dreary pageant laboured,
　　Till it reached the house of doom.
Then first a woman's voice was heard
　　In jeer and laughter loud,
And an angry cry and a hiss arose
　　From the heart of the tossing crowd:
Then, as the Graeme looked upwards①,
　　He saw the ugly smile
Of him who sold his king for gold —
　　The master-fiend Argyle!

8

The Marquis gazed a moment,
　　And nothing did he say,
But the cheek of Argyle grew ghastly pale,
　　And he turned his eyes away.
The painted harlot by his side,
　　She shook through every limb,
For a roar like thunder swept the street,
　　And hands were clenched at him;
And a Saxon soldier cried aloud
　　'Back, coward, from thy place!

---

① *Graeme*: another spelling of 'Graham.'

7

向前进——一直向前进,
　　一片沉默,一片阴郁,
可怕的行列缓缓前进
　　直到杀人场区。
首先听见一个妇人的声音①
　　大声嘲笑大声讥讽,
接着一片怒吼和嘘声
　　出自人们的内心:
于是,格雷厄姆举头仰望②,
　　他看见那张丑恶的笑脸
是他为金币把国王出卖——
　　那个元凶阿盖尔!③

8

侯爵注视了片刻,
　　他并不开言,
阿盖尔双颊死般灰白,
　　于是他把目光移开。
他身旁油头粉面的娼妓④
　　浑身不住抖颤,
只因街头掠过惊雷般的怒吼,
　　千万个拳头向他攥紧;
于是一个萨克逊兵高叫
　　"胆小鬼从你站处滚开⑤!

---

① 在成千上万聚拢来的人中只有一个叫做哈丁顿的伯爵夫人嘲笑蒙特罗斯,她受到群众的指责。——编注者
② 格雷厄姆,指蒙特罗斯,因其原名为詹姆斯·格雷厄姆(James Graham)。——编注者
③ 查理国王于一六四六年五月向苏格兰军队投降。次年一月,苏格兰人把国王交给英国人,苏格兰人接受了四十万英镑作为赔偿,并郑重声明此两事毫无联系。——编注者
④ 指新婚的阿盖尔侯爵夫人。——译者
⑤ 阿盖尔不会打仗,当他的部队在因弗罗希被打败时,他在一艘船上观战。——译者

For seven long years thou hast not dared
  To look him in the face.'

9

Had I been there with sword in hand,
  And fifty Camerons by,
That day through high Dunedin's streets
  Had pealed the slogan-cry①.
Not all their troops of trampling horse,
  Nor might of mailéd men —
Not all the rebels in the south
  Had borne us backwards then!
Once more his foot on Highland heath
  Had trod as free as air,
Or I, and all who bore my name,
  Been laid around him there!

10

It might not be. They placed him next
  Within the solemn hall,
Where once the Scottish kings were throned
  Amidst their nobles all.
But there was dust of vulgar feet
  On that polluted floor,
And perjured traitors filled the place
  Where good men sate before.
With savage glee came Warristoun
  To read the murderous doom;
And then uprose the great Montrose

---

① *slogan-cry*: the Highland war-cry.

整整七年你就是不敢　　　　　　　　95
　　正面瞧他一眼。"
9
假如我当时在那里手持长剑，
　　身边还有五十名卡梅伦汉①，
那天在杜内丁的大街小巷②
　　就会响彻战斗的呐喊。　　　　　100
不论那大群奔腾的战马，
　　还是那威武的战士们——
也不论南方全部反叛之徒
　　都不能把我们打退一步！
他的双脚再次在高地的荒原上　　　105
　　飞一般地自由迈开，
要不我，还有其他同族的人，
　　就会战死在他的四周。
10
这都不可能。他们接着把他送进
　　那庄严的厅堂里头③　　　　　　110
这里往昔苏格兰君王高踞御座
　　围统着王公贵胄。
但那被玷污的地面
　　布满了庸人扬起的尘土
还有发假誓的叛徒充塞其间　　　　115
　　过去正人君子曾在此停留。
沃里斯顿欢天喜地跑来④
　　宣读死刑的判决；
于是伟大的蒙特罗斯起来

---

① 卡梅伦汉，苏格兰一部族的人。——译者
② 凯尔特人称爱丁堡为杜内丁(Dunedin)。——译者
③ 庄严的厅堂，指议会大厦。——译者
④ 沃里斯顿为一个长老会的人。——译者

In the middle of the room.

11

'Now, by my faith as belted knight[①],
    And by the name I bear,
And by the bright Saint Andrew's cross
    That waves above us there —
Yea, by a greater, mightier oath —
    And oh, that such should be! —
By that dark stream of royal blood
    That lies 'twixt you and me —
I have not sought in battle-field
    A wreath of such renown,
Nor dared I hope on my dying day
    To win the martyr's crown!

12

'There is a chamber far away
    Where sleep the good and brave,
But a better place ye have named for me
    Than by my father's grave.
For truth and right, 'gainst treason's might,
    This hand hath always striven,
And ye raise it up for a witness still
    In the eye of earth and heaven.
Then nail my head on yonder tower —
    Give every town a limb —
And God who made shall gather them:
    I go from you to Him!'

[①] *belted*: a belt formed part of the insignia of earls and knights.

站在大厅的中央。

11

"且听我说,我以佩绶带骑士的信仰
 也以我的姓名,
也以明智的圣安德鲁的十字架起誓
 它正在我们头顶上随风飘扬——
是的,也以一个更伟大更有力的誓言——
 啊,这些事竟然出现! ——
也以那殷红的高贵血液起誓
 它正流在你我身中——
我不曾在战场上争取过
 这样一个声誉的花环,
我也不敢企望在临终之前
 会赢得一顶烈士的冠冕!

12

"遥远的地方有座厅堂
 那里安息的人勇敢善良,
但你们给我预备了一处地方
 远远胜过我父亲的墓旁。
为了真理和正义,反对叛变的力量,
 我的双手曾战斗不息,
在苍天和大地的眼里。
 而你们却把它举起作为见证
就把我的脑袋钉在那边的塔上——
 把我的四肢分给每个城市——
造物主将会收集它们:①
 我离开你们走向上帝!"

---

① 收集它们,在他被处决前的夜里,蒙特罗斯在窗户上写下了八行诗,其中包含了这个思想。——译者

13

145 The morning dawned full darkly,
　　　The rain came flashing down,
　　And the jagged streak of the levin-bolt①
　　　Lit up the gloomy town;
　　The thunder crashed across the heaven,
150　　　The fatal hour was come;
　　Yet ay broke in with muffled beat
　　　The 'larum of the drum.
　　There was madness on the earth below,
　　　And anger in the sky,
155　　And young and old, and rich and poor,
　　　Came forth to see him die.

14

　　Ah, God! that ghastly gibbet!
　　　How dismal 'tis to see
　　The great tall spectral skeleton,
160　　　The ladder, and the tree!
　　Hark! hark! it is the clash of arms —
　　　The bells begin to toll —
　　'He is coming! he is coming!
　　　God's mercy on his soul!'
165　　One last long peal of thunder —
　　　The clouds are cleared away,
　　And the glorious sun once more looks down
　　　Amidst the dazzling day.

15

　　'He is coming! he is coming!'
170　　　Like a bridegroom from his room,
　　Came the hero from his prison

---

① *the levin-bolt*: 'the lightning.'

13

破晓的晨曦多么晦暗,   *145*
　　骤雨倾泻也迅猛,
火龙般飞舞的闪电
　　照亮整个阴森的城镇:
雷声轰隆响彻云霄,
　　最后的时刻已到;   *150*
阵阵低咽的敲击声
　　带来了战鼓的警号。
人间再次演凶暴
　　天庭正怒火燃烧。
不管老幼,不分贫富,   *155*
　　都来看他受难。

14

啊,上帝! 多恐怖的绞架!
　　看去多么使人惊吓
那高耸的幽灵似的木架,
　　那阶梯,那十字架!   *160*
听! 听! 那是刀枪相击的声音——
　　丧钟已经鸣响——
"他来了! 他来了!
　　愿上帝宽恕他的灵魂!"
霹雳一声最后的闷雷——   *165*
　　驱散了满天阴霾,
灿烂的太阳又普照
　　明媚耀眼的一天。

15

"他来了! 他来了!
　　像新郎走出新房,   *170*
英雄走出他的牢房

  To the scaffold and the doom.
 There was glory on his forhead,
  There was lustre in his eye,
175 And he never walked to battle
  More proudly than to die:
 There was colour in his visage,
  Though the cheeks of all were wan,
 And they marvelled as they saw him pass,
180 That great and goodly man!

16

 He mounted up the scaffold,
  And he turned him to the crowd;
 But they dared not trust the people,
  So he might not speak aloud.
185 But he looked upon the heavens,
  And they were clear and blue,
 And in the liquid ether
  The eye of God shone through!
 Yet a black and murky battlement[①]
190 Lay resting on the hill,
 As though the thunder slept within —
  All else was calm and still.

17

 The grim Geneva ministers
  With anxious scowl drew near,
195 As you have seen the ravens flock
  Around the dying deer.
 He would not deign them word nor sign,
  But alone he bent the knee;
 And veiled his face for Christ's dear grace

---

① *battlement*: *i.e.* a heavy thunder-cloud.

走向绞架和死亡。
他的前额闪着光辉,
　　他双眸炯炯有光,
他往年勇敢奔赴疆场　　　　　　　　　　*175*
　　比不上这次走向刑场;
尽管大众双颊苍白
　　他满脸充满红光,
他们惊奇地注视着他走过,
　　那位伟大英俊的好汉!　　　　　　　*180*

16
他迈步走上绞台,
　　他转身面对群众;
但他们多么害怕人民,
　　禁止他高声讲演。
但他抬头仰望苍天,　　　　　　　　　　*185*
　　晴空蔚蓝无云,
从高高的天空
　　太阳的光芒照射下来!
但是黑压压的乌云
　　雄踞在山岗之巅,　　　　　　　　　*190*
雷声就像隐藏在里边——
　　四周却一片寂静。

17
严峻的加尔文教牧师
　　紧锁双眉走来,
就像一群乌鸦围绕　　　　　　　　　　　*195*
　　一只垂死的野鹿。
他既不开言也无手势
　　只独自屈膝跪下;
在那十字架下面,

200   Beneath the gallows-tree.
           Then radiant and serene he rose,
               And cast his cloak away:
           For he had ta'en his latest look
               Of earth and sun and day

18

205   A beam of light fell o'er him,
               Like a glory round the shriven①,
           And he climbed the lofty ladder
               As it were the path to heaven.
           Then came a flash from out the cloud,
210   And a stunning thunder-roll;
           And no man dared to look aloft,
               For fear was on every soul.
           There was another heavy sound,
               A hush and then a groan;
215   And darkness swept across the sky —
               The work of death was done!

                                        W. E. AYTOUN.

---

① *the shrivern*: one who has made confession to a priest and received absolution.

掩面祈求基督宽恕　　　　　　　　　　200
　　于是他光辉宁静地起来
　　　把斗蓬丢开：
　　他最后看了一看
　　　大地、太阳和白天。

18

　　一柱光辉投落他身上，　　　　　　　　205
　　　像荣耀归于向神忏悔的人，
　　他走上高高的台阶
　　　就像走向天国之路。
　　突然乌云发出闪电，
　　　还有震耳的雷鸣；　　　　　　　　　210
　　没人敢抬头观望，
　　　人人心怀恐惧。
　　接着一声轰鸣，
　　　一片死寂，一声叹息；
　　黑暗又笼罩着天空——　　　　　　　　215
　　　大刑就此完毕！

刘玉麟　译

编注　威廉·埃德蒙斯顿·艾顿（William Edmondstoune Aytoun，1813—1865），曾任爱丁堡大学修辞学教授，与西奥多·马丁（Theodore Martin）一八八五年合写的民谣集《苏格兰骑士歌谣集》流传很广。

　　此诗所写的蒙特罗斯为原名为詹姆斯·格雷厄姆（James Graham），是第五代蒙特罗斯伯爵。一六五〇年，蒙特罗斯率部队进入苏格兰，由于船只失事，士兵大多遇难，所余少量人马则在罗斯郡的因弗夏隆被击溃。他孑然一身在萨瑟兰的荒野流浪，几乎饿死，最终落入阿辛特族的一个名叫麦克劳德的人手中，被递交给莱斯利将军。诗人说，这首民谣是"由一个当年曾追随蒙特罗斯的苏格兰高地人在基利克兰战役(1689)之前不久向他的孩子讲述的"。

351. TUBAL CAIN

Old Tubal Cain was a man of might
    In the days when Earth was young;
By the fierce red light of his furnace bright
    The strokes of his hammer rung;
And he lifted high his brawny hand
    On the iron glowing clear,
Till the sparks rushed out in scarlet showers,
    As he fashioned the sword and spear.
And he sang — 'Hurra for my handiwork!
    Hurra for the spear and sword!
Hurra for the hand that shall wield them well,
    For he shall be king and lord!'

To Tubal Cain came many a one,
    As he wrought by his roaring fire,
And each one prayed for a strong steel blade
    As the crown of his desire.
And he made them weapons sharp and strong,
    Till they shouted loud for glee,
And gave him gifts of pearl and gold,
    And spoils of the forest free.
And they sang — 'Hurra for Tubal Cain,
    Who hath given us strength anew!

351. 土八该隐

麦凯

老土八该隐是个强有力的人①
　　那时天地刚创造不久；
在他那殷红耀眼的打铁炉旁
　　他的铁锤叮当作响；
他高高抬起强壮的双臂　　　　　　　　　5
　　下面就是灼热的铁块
火花似红雨般四面迸射，
　　直到他锻打出矛和剑。
于是他高唱——"我的手艺多好哇！
　　那些长矛和宝剑多好哇！　　　　　10
那挥舞矛剑的人有多好哇，
　　因为他将称帝为王！"

许多人来求土八该隐
　　当他正在熊熊炉边工作，
人人都求他打一把锋利的钢剑　　　　　15
　　这就是每人的心愿。
于是他打造了坚利的武器
　　直到他们雀跃欢呼，
于是赠给他珠宝和黄金，
　　还有林中的野味。　　　　　　　　20
于是他们高唱——"土八该隐多好哇，
　　他给我们增添了力量！

---

① 土八该隐，见《圣经·创世记》第四章第二十二节，"洗拉又生了土八该隐，他是打造各种铜铁利器的"。——译者

        Hurra for the smith, hurra for the fire,
            And hurra for the metal true!'

25   But a sudden change came o'er his heart,
            Ere the setting of the sun,
        And Tubal Cain was filled with pain
            For the evil he had done;
        He saw that men, with rage and hate,
30   Made war upon their kind,
        That the land was red with the blood they shed
            In their lust for carnage, blind.
        And he said — 'Alas! that ever I made,
            Or that skill of mine should plan,
35   The spear and the sword for men whose joy
            Is to slay their fellow-man.'

        And for many a day old Tubal Cain
            Sat brooding o'er his woe;
        And his hand forbore to smite the ore,
40   And his furnace smouldered low.
        But he rose at last with a cheerful face,
            And a bright courageous eye,
        And bared his strong right arm for work,
            While the quick flames mounted high.
45   And he sang — 'Hurra for my handicraft!'
            And the red sparks lit the air;
        'Not alone for the blade was the bright steel made,'
            And he fashioned the first ploughshare.

        And men, taught wisdom from the past,
50   In friendship joined their hands,

铁匠多好哇,炉火多好哇,
　　　　铁家伙多好哇!"

但是他内心突然转变,　　　　　　　　　　25
　　太阳那时还未落山,
土八该隐内心充满痛苦
　　因为他干出了坏事;
他看到,人们在仇恨怒火中,
　　互相残杀同类,　　　　　　　　　　　30
以至大地被血染红,
　　由于盲目疯狂的大屠杀。
于是他说——"哎呀!我竟会做出,
　　我的手艺也竟会设计出
长矛和宝剑给那些人去使,　　　　　　　35
　　他们的快乐就是屠杀同胞。"

多少天来老土八该隐
　　为自己闯的祸而忧伤闷坐;
他的双手不再锻打铁矿石,
　　他的炉火也晦暗无光。　　　　　　　40
但他最后满脸欢喜立起身来,
　　还有一双炯炯有神的眼睛,
他又裸开那有力的右臂去打铁,
　　炉里的火焰往上窜。
于是他唱——"我的工夫多好哇!"　　　45
　　红色的火星照耀着天空;
"耀眼的钢条不仅锻打宝剑,"
　　他又打出了第一把犁头。

人类,接受了过去的教训,
　　在友谊之中携起手来,　　　　　　　50

Hung the sword in the hall, the spear on the wall,
    And ploughed the willing lands;
And sang — 'Hurra for Tubal Cain!
    Our stanch good friend is he;
And for the ploughshare and the plough
    To him our praise shall be.
But while oppression lifts its head,
    Or a tyrant would be lord,
Though we may thank him for the Plough,
    We'll not forget the Sword!'

C. MACKAY.

把剑高悬大厅,把矛挂在墙上,
　　用犁开垦那肥沃的大地;
他们高唱——"土八该隐多好哇!
　　他是我们忠实的好朋友;
因为他造出了犁头和犁具　　　　　　　　　55
　　我们要高声颂扬。
如果压迫又抬起它的头,
　　或者暴君又来发威,
虽然我们感谢他造了犁,
　　我们也不会忘记那宝剑!"　　　　　　60

刘玉麟　译

编注　查尔斯·麦凯(Charles Macay,1814—1889),曾任英格兰和苏格兰几家报纸的编辑,以写歌谣而闻名。他写的歌谣数量很多,最著名的是《民歌和抒情诗集》(*Ballads and Lyrical Poems*,1856)。

352. QUA CURSUM VENTUS

As ships, becalmed at eve, that lay
    With canvas drooping, side by side,
Two towers of sail at dawn of day
    Are scarce long leagues apart descried;

When fell the night, upsprung the breeze,
    And all the darkling hours they plied,
Nor dreamt but each the self-same seas
    By each was cleaving, side by side:

E'en so — but why the tale reveal
    Of those, whom year by year unchanged,
Brief absence joined anew to feel,
    Astounded, soul from soul estranged?

At dead of night their sails were filled,
    And onward each rejoicing steered —
Ah, neither blame, for neither willed,
    Or wist, what first with dawn appeared!

To veer, how vain! On, onward strain,
    Brave barks! In light, in darkness too,
Through winds and tides one compass guides —
    To that, and your own selves, be true.

But O blithe breeze! and O great seas,

352. 风吹船儿去何方

克劳

黄昏的时分,船儿停下了,
　　风帆已下垂,两船相并靠,
黎明一来临,风帆挂云霄,
　　相距并不远,两眼能看到;

夜晚降临了,和风吹起来, 5
　　黑暗的夜里,一路驶向前,
谁也没想到,同越一个海,
　　破浪向前进,两船肩并肩;

即使是这样——为何有人讲:
　　一年又一年,人们不曾变, 10
短暂离别后,再次相会见,
　　觉得好奇怪,隔膜生心间。

黑夜死沉沉,风儿鼓满帆,
　　两船喜洋洋,各自向前航——
谁也不责怪,谁也不企盼, 15
　　黎明一出现,又是啥风光!

转向已无望,努力向前闯,
　　勇敢的船儿!依仗罗盘针,
穿过风和浪,穿过影和光,
　　忠于罗盘针,忠于你的心。 20

欢快清风啊,浩瀚海洋啊,

Though ne'er, that earliest parting past,
On your wide plain they join again,
Together lead them home at last.

One port, methought, alike they sought,
One purpose hold where'er they fare, —
O bounding breeze, O rushing seas!
At last, at last, unite them there!

A. H. CLOUGH.

两只小船儿，当初离家乡，
　　　永不再相聚，漂泊汪洋上，
　　　请你领它俩，最终归故乡。

　　它俩正寻找，共同的港口，
　　　不管上哪儿，共同的目标——
　　　欢腾的风啊，汹涌的海啊！
　　　最后把它俩，团聚在一道！

袁可嘉　译

编注　阿瑟·休·克劳（Arthur Hugh Clough，1819—1861），英国诗人，曾任牛津大学奥利尔学院研究员。克劳一生不得意，很早就逝世了。在英国诗史上，他的诗是以其轻快的特点而留传后世的。主要作品有《迪普赛丘斯》(Dipsychus, 1850)和长诗《托帕-纳-维尤奥莱奇的茅屋》(Bothie of Tober-na-Vuolich, 1848)。本诗选自克劳与他人合著的诗集《阿姆巴伐利亚》(*Ambarvalia*)。

353. 'SAY NOT'

Say not, the struggle naught availeth,
    The labour and the wounds are vain,
The enemy faints not, nor faileth,
    And as things have been they remain.

If hopes were dupes, fears may be liars;
    It may be, in yon smoke concealed,
Your comrades chase e'en now the fliers,
    And, but for you, possess the field.

For while the tired waves, vainly breaking,
    Seem here no painful inch to gain,
Far back, through creeks, and inlets making,
    Comes silent, flooding in, the main.

And not by eastern windows only,
    When daylight comes, comes in the light,
In front, the sun climbs slow, how slowly,
    But westward, look, the land is bright.

                        A. H. CLOUGH.

353. "你可不要说"

克劳

你可不要说，斗争没成效，
　　辛劳和伤亡也都是枉然，
敌人没失败，敌人没昏倒，
　　他们像当初神气活现。

如希望是欺骗，那恐惧便撒谎；　　　　5
　　也许隐藏在烟幕的背后，
故友们正穷追逃敌不放，
　　为了你们把战场抢到手。

倦了的波浪，徒然地拍击，
　　不费力，似乎寸土不要，　　　　10
但由于小河小湾的开辟，
　　汪洋大海悄悄中涌到。

白昼一降临，光明也来到，
　　并不只是东窗透亮光，
太阳在前头，慢悠悠升高，　　　　15
　　但你瞧，西边大地已亮堂。

袁可嘉　译

编注　克劳留传后世的短诗微乎其微，这首诗选自一八六二年出版的《克劳诗选》(*Poems of Clough*)，是克劳最著名的抒情短诗，在英美传诵很广。全诗充满必胜的信心，是乐观主义的高歌。

354. 'WHERE LIES THE LAND TO WHICH THE SHIP WOULD GO?'

Where lies the land to which the ship would go?
Far, far ahead, is all her seamen know.
And where the land she travels from? Away,
Far, far behind, is all that they can say.

On sunny noons upon the deck's smooth face,
Linked arm in arm, how pleasant here to pace;
Or, o'er the stern reclining, watch below
The foaming wake far widening as we go.

On stormy nights when wild north-westers rave,
How proud a thing to fight with wind and wave!
The dripping sailor on the reeling mast
Exults to bear, and scorns to wish it past.

Where lies the land to which the ship would go?
Far, far ahead, is all her seamen know.
And where the land she travels from? Away,
Far, far behind, is all that they can say.

A. H. CLOUGH.

354. "这只船儿要驶向什么地方?"

克劳

这只船儿要驶向什么地方?
水手只知道要去远远天一方。
这只船儿又来自什么地方?
远远天一方,别的他们说不上。

光滑的甲板上,中午阳光亮堂堂,   *5*
臂挽着臂慢步走,心头多欢畅;
斜靠在船尾,俯视身后的波浪,
船儿向前开,浪花纷纷溅四厢。

狂风骤雨的夜晚,西北风怒号,
我们战风又斗浪,心中多自豪,   *10*
水手们湿淋淋,身子挂在危樯头,
乐于受点罪,不屑让风浪退走。

这只船儿要驶向什么地方?
水手只知道要去远远天一方。
这只船儿又来自什么地方?   *15*
远远天一方,别的他们说不上。

袁可嘉　译

编注　此诗选自《克劳诗选》,为克劳回忆一八五二年赴美国寻找工作的海上航程而写。

355. 'O MAY I JOIN THE CHOIR INVISIBLE'

Longum illud tempus, quum non ero, magis me movet, quam hoc exiguum. — CICERO, *ad Att.* xii. 18.

O may I join the choir invisible
Of those immortal dead who live again
In minds made better by their presence; live
In pulses stirred to generosity,
In deeds of daring rectitude, in scorn
For miserable aims that end with self,
In thoughts sublime that pierce the night like stars,
And with their mild persistence urge man's search
To vaster issues.
         So to live is heaven:
To make undying music in the world,
Breathing as beauteous order that controls①
With growing sway the growing life of man.
So we inherit that sweet purity
For which we struggled, failed, and agonized
With widening retrospect that bred despair.
Rebellious flesh that would not be subdued②,
A vicious parent shaming still its child
Poor anxious penitence, is quick dissolved;

---

① *Breathing as beauteous order that controls*: the breath of the singer acts as a harmonizing influence.
② *Rebellious flesh*: opposed to the 'truer self' of l. 21.

355. "噢！但愿我能加入那无形的合唱团"

乔治·艾略特

> 当我不再存在时，那漫长的未来岁月，
> 比起这短暂的现时，更加使我担忧。
> ——西塞罗《致阿提克斯的信札》(xii,18)

噢！但愿我能加入那无形的合唱团，
它是由那些永垂不朽的人所组编，
他们重活在被他们感化而变得更加善良的心里，
重活在那些曾经激发着慷慨行为的脉搏间，
重活在勇敢、正直的业绩里，   5
重活在藐视中——嘲笑那可耻的个人打算，
还活在那些崇高的思想里，像划破夜空的群星，
用它们柔和而坚韧的精神去督促人类
把更宏伟的问题寻探。
      因此，活着就是天堂：
在世上创造出不朽的乐章，   10
唱出美丽的和谐，以那澎湃的气势，
支配着人类生机的不断增长，
于是，我们继承着那甜蜜的纯洁，
为了它，我们战斗过、失败过、痛苦过，
因为广泛的回顾产生过悲观失望。   15
这叛逆的血肉之躯不愿受到约束，
像一个德行败坏的父亲让孩儿脸上无光①——
可怜、焦虑的忏悔——肉体却转眼消亡；

---

① 这里的"孩儿"指的是改邪归正的决心，肉体虽然产生忏悔，但又有反复，因此使"决心"蒙受羞辱。——译者

    Its discords, quenched by meeting harmonies,
    Die in the large and charitable air.
    And all our rarer, better, truer self,
    That sobbed religiously in yearning song,
    That watched to ease the burthen of the world,
    Laboriously tracing what must be①,
    And what may yet be better — saw within②
    A worthier image for the sanctuary,
    And shaped it forth before the multitude
    Divinely human, raising worship so
    To higher reverence more mixed with love —
    That better self shall live till human Time
    Shall fold its eyelids, and the human sky
    Be gathered like a scroll within the tomb
    Unread for ever.
         This is life to come,
    Which martyred men have made more glorious
    For us who strive to follow. May I reach
    That purest heaven, be to other souls
    The cup of strength in some great agony,
    Enkindle generous ardour, feed pure love,
    Beget the smiles that have no cruelty —
    Be the sweet presence of a good diffused,
    And in diffusion ever more intense.

---

① *Laboriously tracing*, etc.: *i.e.* distinguishing between necessary and curable evils, always an extraordinarily difficult problem and one on which no two people will agree.

② *saw*: the subject is 'That' (l. 23); 'truer self' (l. 21) is left without a verb till l. 30.

人间的不和谐淹没在迎接它们的乐音之中,
在广阔、仁爱的气氛中统统涤荡。 20
我们更珍贵更善良更真实的自身①,
曾在虔诚中哭泣,渴望中歌唱,
它等待着卸去尘世的重荷,
曾艰辛地探索着人类生活的必然,
探索着更加美好的事物——在心灵中见到 25
一座比教堂更加高贵的圣像,
并把它呈现在大众面前,
这神圣的凡人呀,把群众的崇拜
化为富有爱的更为崇高的敬仰——
那个更善良的自我将生活下去,直到时光 30
把眼皮阖上,直到人类的天空
像书卷放进灵墓
再也得不到观赏②。
　　　　　　这就是未来的生活,
英烈们将使它更加辉煌, 35
为了我们去效法模仿。但愿我们能到达
那纯洁天堂,给别人在巨大痛苦中
献上一杯增加力量的琼浆。
点燃慷慨的火,哺育纯洁的爱,
唤起那不带残酷的微笑—— 40
化为美德芬芳,
在扩散中会更加浓醇

---

① 指"灵魂"。——编注者
② 见《圣经·以赛亚书》第三十四章第四节,"天被卷起,好像书卷"。——译者

So shall I join the choir invisible
Whose music is the gladness of the world.

GEORGE ELIOT.

因此,我将加入那无形的合唱团,
它的音乐就是人间的欢畅。

李赋宁 译

编注 乔治·艾略特(George Eliot,1819—1880),即玛丽·安·艾文斯(Mary Ann Evans),后来的克罗斯夫人的笔名,英国最杰出的小说家之一。读书很广,对宗教和哲学有深刻的研究,对个人主义和自私自利进行尖锐的批判,极力提倡"心灵的宗教",劝谕人们向善。

356. AIRLY BEACON

Airly Beacon, Airly Beacon;
   Oh the pleasant sight to see
Shires and towns from Airly Beacon,
   While my love climbed up to me!

Airly Beacon, Airly Beacon;
   Oh the happy hours we lay
Deep in fern on Airly Beacon,
   Courting through the summer's day!

Airly Beacon, Airly Beacon,
   Oh the weary haunt for me,
All alone on Airly Beacon,
   With his baby on my knee!

C. KINGSLEY.

356. 爱丽·彼耿

金斯利

爱丽·彼耿,爱丽·彼耿,
　哦,那是多么美好的风光——
从爱丽·彼耿眺望州郡和市镇呵,
　而我的情郎正朝着我爬上山冈!

爱丽·彼耿,爱丽·彼耿,　　　　　　　　　5
　哦,那时光过得多么欢快——
我们俩躺在爱丽·彼耿的深草中,
　在夏天,从早到晚地谈情说爱!

爱丽·彼耿,爱丽·彼耿,
　哦,这个教我生厌的老地方,　　　　　　10
我孤零零地,在爱丽·彼耿,
　带着他留下的婴儿在我的膝上!

屠岸　译

编注 查尔斯·金斯利(Charles Kingsley, 1819—1875),英国小说家、诗人,担任过剑桥大学现代史教授。他是一个穷苦牧师,在思想上受卡莱尔影响很深,曾积极发起并参与十九世纪中期的基督教社会主义改革运动,但并不否定旧制度。他一生著述甚丰,小说《酵母》(Yeast)、《阿尔顿·洛克》(Alton Locke)、《希帕蒂亚》(Hypatia)、《向西方》(Westward Ho!),儿童小说《水孩儿》(The Water-Babies),诗体剧《圣徒的悲剧》(The Saint's Tragedy),长诗《安德鲁米达》(Andromeda),还有许多杂论。此诗写于一八四七年,一八五八年才在诗集《安德鲁米达及其他》(Andromeda and other Poems)中发表。诗中的爱丽·彼耿系一山名。

357. THE SANDS OF DEE

'O Mary, go and call the cattle home,
 And call the cattle home,
 And call the cattle home
 Across the sands of Dee';
The western wind was wild and dank with foam,
 And all alone went she.

The western tide crept up along the sand,
 And o'er and o'er the sand,
 And round and round the sand,
 As far as eye could see.
The rolling mist came down and hid the land:
 And never home came she.

'Oh! is it weed, or fish, or floating hair —
 A tress of golden hair,
 A drownéd maiden's hair
 Above the nets at sea?
Was never salmon yet that shone so fair
 Among the stakes on Dee.'

They rowed her in across the rolling foam,
 The cruel crawling foam

357. 迪河的沙丘

金斯利

"啊,玛丽,快去唤回牛群吧,
　　快去把牛群唤回来,
　　快去把牛群唤回来,
　　它们在迪河沙丘的那厢①;"
这时候西风正劲,水沫雨一般四处喷洒, 5
　　她却仍孤零零独自前往。

由西方涌来的浪潮沿着沙丘翻滚,
　　一次次涌上沙丘,
　　一次次冲刷着沙丘,
　　一眼望去茫茫无涯界。 10
忽然间滚滚浓雾自天降,将大地吞并:
　　她从此再也没回来。

"啊!那是水草,是鱼,还是漂浮的头发——
　　是一绺金色的发丝,
　　一个溺水的少女的发丝 15
在一排鱼网上飘移?
啊,在迪河边挂网的木桩间
　　还从没有一尾鲑鱼的光彩如此秀丽。

它们越过一层层滚滚巨浪,
　　那残暴的爬动的浪花, 20

---

① 迪河,指迪江在弗林特县和柴郡之间的一个河岔,宽处达六英里,愈下愈窄,渐至约两英里而已。——译者

The cruel hungry foam,
 To her grave beside the sea:
But still the boatmen hear her call the cattle home
 Across the sands of Dee.

C. KINGSLEY.

那残暴的饥饿的浪花,
把她搬运到了她海滨的坟头:
但是啊,船夫们却至今仍听到她的唤牛声
直飘过那边那迪河的沙丘。

黄雨石　译

编注　选自《阿尔顿·洛克》第二十六章。

358. ODE TO THE NORTH-EAST WIND

Welcome, wild North-easter!
　Shame it is to see
Odes to every zephyr;
　Ne'er a verse to thee.
Welcome, black North-easter!
　O'er the German foam;
O'er the Danish moorlands,
　From thy frozen home.
Tired we are of summer,
　Tired of gaudy glare,
Showers soft and steaming,
　Hot and breathless air.
Tired of listless dreaming,
　Through the lazy day:
Jovial wind of winter,
　Turn us out to play!
Sweep the golden reed-beds;
　Crisp the lazy dyke[①];
Hunger into madness
　Every plunging pike.
Fill the lake with wild-fowl;
　Fill the marsh with snipe;
While on dreary moorlands
　Lonely curlew pipe.

[①] *Crisp the lazy dyke*: 'make curling waves on the sluggish ditch.'

358. 东北风颂

金斯利

欢迎,狂烈的东北风!
　有件事真是可惜——
对和风总有诗歌颂;
　唯独没诗献给你。
欢迎,阴郁的东北风! 5
　你从冰封的故乡
吹掠过丹麦的荒原,
　飘过德国的海洋。
我们已厌倦了夏天、
　温和蒸腾的阵雨, 10
厌倦了炫目的阳光、
　又热又闷的空气。
已倦于用怠惰的梦
　把懒散日子打发;
快乐的冬风,把我们 15
　赶出家门去玩吧!
吹皱沟渠懒懒的水;
　扫过金色芦苇塘;
把急蹦乱跳的狗鱼
　一个个饿得发狂。 20
让沼泽布满沙雉;
　叫湖泊充满野鸟;
在那凄清的荒原上,
　有孤独的麻鹬啼叫。

    Through the black fir-forest
     Thunder harsh and dry,
    Shattering down the snow-flakes
     Off the curdled sky①.
    Hark! The brave North-easter!
     Breast-high lies the scent,
    On by holt and headland②,
     Over heath and bent③.
    Chime, ye dappled darlings,
     Through the sleet and snow,
    Who can over-ride you?
     Let the horses go!
    Chime, ye dappled darlings,
     Down the roaring blast;
    You shall see a fox die
     Ere an hour be past.
    Go! and rest to-morrow,
     Hunting in your dreams,
    While our skates are ringing
     O'er the frozen streams.
    Let the luscious South-wind
     Breathe in lovers' sighs,
    While the lazy gallants
     Bask in ladies' eyes.
    What does he but soften
     Heart alike and pen?

---

① *curdled*: to curdle is property used of rendering milk solid by means of rennet or other substances, here it is used of the sky as being a solid mass of stormclouds.
② *holt*: 'wood.'
③ *bent*: 'a bare, uncultivated field.'

打起你刺耳的干雷, 25
　　把黑黑枞林响遍,
　　震碎那凝冻的天空,
　　　　洒下雪花一片片。
听!好个东北来的风!
　　跟着扑鼻的嗅迹, 30
脚下踏着石南、荒草,
　　穿越小林和野地。
叫吧,可爱的花猎狗,
　　穿过冰雹和雪花;
有谁能追得上你们? 35
　　看我们松缰驰马!
叫吧,可爱的花猎狗,
　　冲进呼啸的风里;
一个钟点也用不了,
　　就能打一只狐狸。 40
冲吧,但明天给休息,
　　让你们梦中行猎;
而我们在冰封小溪上
　　响着叮当的冰鞋。
当甜美芬芳的南风 45
　　同恋人一起叹息,
让懒洋洋的多情郎
　　享受青睐的情意。
它能做什么——除了使
　　心儿和笔头变软? 50

'Tis the hard grey weather
   Breeds hard English men.
What's the soft South-wester?
   'Tis the ladies' breeze,
Bringing home their trueloves
   Out of all the seas:
But the black North-easter,
   Through the snow-storm hurled,
Drives our English hearts of oak
   Seaward round the world.
Come, as came our fathers,
   Heralded by thee,
Conquering from the eastward,
   Lords by land and sea.
Come; and strong within us
   Stir the Vikings' blood;
Bracing brain and sinew;
   Blow, thou wind of God!

C. KINGSLEY.

可灰濛濛的坏天气
　　　　能练出英国硬汉。
　　西南方吹来的和风，
　　　　属于小姐和太太——
　　它呀，把她们的爱人　　　　　　　　55
　　　　从四海送回家来。
　　但怒冲冲的东北风，
　　　　却在雪暴中冲杀，
　　催英国的船上的健儿
　　　　出海向世界进发。　　　　　　　60
　　来，像我们祖先那样①；
　　　　这些海陆的主宰
　　从东方胜利地推进——
　　　　你预告他们到来。
　　来，北欧海盗的血液②　　　　　　　65
　　　　在我们胸中沸腾，
　　激励着头脑和筋肉；
　　　　你吹吧，上帝的风！

黄杲炘　黄杲昶　译

编注 此诗作于一八五四年，和《安德鲁米达》一并出版。

---

① "我们祖先"指盎格鲁人。盎格鲁人在五世纪前生活在不列颠东北（今丹麦、荷兰一带），公元四四九年，侵入不列颠并定居下来，成为英国人的祖先。——译者
② "北欧海盗"指丹麦人，或称斯堪的纳维亚人。八世纪开始，他们从东面进攻英格兰沿海，并在那里建立基地，定居下来，成为英国人的一部分。——译者

1513

359. YOUNG AND OLD

When all the world is young, lad,
    And all the trees are green;
And every goose a swan, lad,
    And every lass a queen;
Then hey for boot and horse, lad,
    And round the world away;
Young blood must have its course, lad,
    And every dog his day.

When all the world is old, lad,
    And all the trees are brown;
And all the sport is stale, lad,
    And all the wheels run down;
Creep home, and take your place there,
    The spent and maimed among:
God grant you find one face there,
    You loved when all was young.

C. KINGSLEY.

359. 青年和老年

金斯利

当整个世界都还年轻,小伙子,
　　所有的树木郁郁青青;
每只野鸭都是天鹅,青年人,
　　每个姑娘都成了皇帝;
嘿,脚蹬好靴,跨上骏马,小伙子, 5
　　在世上尽情奔驰;
青春的血液总在血管沸腾,小伙子,
　　狗也有自己黄金的时期。

当整个世界变得苍老,小伙子,
　　所有的树木都会枯死; 10
所有的娱乐都没有生气,
　　所有的车轮滚下山去;
爬回家哟,在精疲力尽与伤残之中
　　在那里找到你的位置。
上帝赐与你一张俊秀的脸蛋, 15
　　你曾恋爱,而那时一切都还年轻。

陈朴　译

编注　此诗选自《水孩儿》第二章,标题系原编者所加。

360. O CAPTAIN! MY CAPTAIN!

O Captain! my Captain! our fearful trip is done,
The ship has weather'd every rack, the prize we sought is won[①],
The port is near, the bells I hear, the people all exulting,
While follow eyes the steady keel, the vessel grim and daring,
      But O heart! heart! heart!
        O the bleeding drops of red!
          Where on the deck my Captain lies,
            Fallen cold and dead.

O Captain! my Captain! rise up and hear the bells;
Rise up — for you the flag is flung — for you the bugle trills,
For you bouquets and ribbon'd wreaths — for you the shores a-crowding,
For you they call, the swaying mass, their eager faces turning;
      Here Captain! dear father!
        This arm beneath your head!
          It is some dream that on the deck
            You've fallen cold and dead.

My Captain does not answer, his lips are pale and still,
My father does not feel my arm, he has no pulse nor will;
The ship is anchor'd safe and sound, its voyage closed and done,
From fearful trip the victor ship comes in with object won;
      Exult, O shores, and ring, O bells!
        But I, with mournful tread,

---

   ① *rack*: 'storm-clouds, driven by the wind.'

360. 啊,船长,我的船长哟!

惠特曼

啊,船长,我的船长哟!我们可怕的航程已经终了,
我们的船渡过了每一个难关,我们追求的锦标已经得到,
港口就在前面,我已经听见钟声,听见了人们的欢呼,
千万只眼睛在望着我们的船,它坚定、威严而且勇敢;
  只是,啊,心哟!心哟!心哟!
   啊,鲜红的血滴,
    就在那甲板上,我的船长躺下了,
     他已浑身冰凉,停止了呼吸。

啊,船长,我的船长哟!起来听听这钟声,
起来吧——旌旗正为你招展——号角为你长鸣,
为你,人们准备了无数的花束和花环——为你,人群挤满了海岸,
为你,这晃动着的群众在欢呼,转动着他们殷切的脸面;
  这里,船长,亲爱的父亲哟!
   让你的头枕着我的手臂吧!
    在甲板上,这真是一场梦——
     你已经浑身冰凉,停止了呼吸。

我的船长不回答我的话,他的嘴唇惨白而僵硬,
我的父亲,感觉不到我的手臂,他已没有脉搏,也没有了生命,
我们的船已经安全地下锚了,它的航程已经终了,
从可怕的旅程归来,这胜利的船,目的已经达到;
  啊,欢呼吧,海岸,鸣响吧,钟声!
   只是我以悲痛的步履,

Walk the deck my Captain lies,
　Fallen cold and dead.

WALT WHITMAN.

漫步在甲板上,那里我的船长躺着,
他已浑身冰凉,停止了呼吸。

楚图南　译

编注　惠特曼(Walt Whitman,1819—1892),美国著名民主诗人。出生贫苦,十一岁辍学做工,一八四二年搞新闻工作,五十年代开始写诗。其代表作《草叶集》(Leaves of Grass)鲜明地反映了十九世纪的美国,表现了民主精神。他的诗朴素自然,热情奔放,内在节奏感很强,创造的诗歌自由体被称为"惠特曼体",对后世有很大影响。本诗写于一八六五年,为悼念林肯总统而作,首次出版于一八九一年版的《草叶集》。

361. 'PLAYING ON THE VIRGINALS'

Playing on the virginals,
    Who but I! Sae glad, sae free,
Smelling for all cordials①,
    The green mint and marjorie;
Set among the budding broom,
    Kingcup and daffodilly,
By my side I made him room:
    O love my Willie!

'Like me, love me, girl o' gowd,'
    Sang he to my nimble strain;
Sweet his ruddy lips o'erflowed
    Till my heartstrings rang again;
By the broom, the bonny broom,
    Kingcup and daffodilly,
In my heart I made him room:
    O love my Willie!

'Pipe and play, dear heart,' sang he,
    'I must go, yet pipe and play;
Soon I'll come and ask of thee
    For an answer yea or nay;'

---

① *for all cordials*: 'as the only cordial I took.'

361. "我安坐在一架钢琴边轻轻弹奏"

英格洛

我安坐在一架钢琴边轻轻弹奏①,
　　独自一人! 那样安闲,那样欢畅,
我虽曾饮下一杯又一杯舒心酒,
　　却压不住满身茉乔栾气味和薄荷香②。
金雀花、驴蹄草和黄色的水仙　　　　　　　　5
　　花儿,正在我身边盛开,
我腾出地方让他在我身边坐下来:
　　啊,我的威利,我的爱!

"喜欢我吧,爱我吧,我善良的姑娘,"
　　他和着我弹奏的轻快曲调歌唱;　　　　　10
从他红红的唇边溢出浓稠的蜜汁,
　　直到我的心弦又一次被拨响。
就在那金雀花前,在那可爱的金雀花、
　　驴蹄草和黄色的水仙花前,
我为他把我的心扉全然敞开:　　　　　　　15
　　啊,我的威利,我的爱!

"尽情弹奏吧,我的心上人儿,"他唱道,
　　"我得离开一会儿,可你只管弹奏;
我马上便回来正式向你提出请求,
　　求你回答我:是可还是否;"　　　　　　20

---

① 钢琴,原文为"the virginals",实为在十六、十七世纪流行的一种无腿方箱式的古琴,为现代钢琴(piano)的前身。——译者
② 茉乔栾,原文为 marjorie,估计即是茉乔栾(marjoram),一种烹调用的佐料。——译者

    And I waited till the flocks
        Panted in yon waters stilly,
    And the corn stood in the shocks;
        O love my Willie!

    I thought first when thou didst come
        I would wear the ring for thee,
    But the year told out its sum
        Ere again thou sat'st by me;
    Thou hadst naught to ask that day
        By kingcup and daffodilly;
    I said neither yea nor nay:
        O love my Willie!

JEAN INGELOW.

可是我一直等到羊群被关进了
　　远处河水边的羊圈,
地里的庄稼也全都运回谷场来,
　　啊,我的威利,我的爱!

我原想着你来的时候我将为你　　　　　　　　25
　　而戴上一只订婚的戒指,
但是,一年的最后几天也已经过去了,
　　你却从没有来过我身边一次;
那一天在那金雀花和水仙花前,
　　你什么问题也没有向我提出,　　　　　30
是可还是否,我始终也未曾讲明白:
　　啊,我的威利,我的爱!

黄雨石　译

编注　琼·英格洛(Jean Ingelow,1820—1897),英国女诗人,出过八部诗集,亦写小说和儿童读物。诗风细腻缠绵,擅写妇女心理。此诗选自一八六三年出版的《诗集》(*Poems*)所收的《磨坊的晚餐》(Supper at the Miu)一诗。

362. THE HIGH TIDE ON THE COAST OF LINCOLNSHIIRE(1571)

The old mayor climbed the belfry tower,
    The ringers ran by two, by three;
'Pull, if ye never pulled before;
    Good ringers, pull your best,' quoth he.
'Play uppe, play uppe, O Boston bells!
Ply all your changes, all your swells,
    Play uppe "The Brides of Enderby."'

Men say it was a stolen tyde —
    The Lord that sent it, He knows all;
But in myne ears doth still abide
    The message that the bells let fall:
And there was naught of strange, beside
The flight of mews and peewits pied
    By millions crouched on the old sea wall.

I sat and spun within the doore,
    My thread brake off, I raised myne eyes;
The level sun, like ruddy ore,
    Lay sinking in the barren skies[①];
And dark against day's golden death
She moved where Lindis wandereth,

---

① *barren*: presumably, 'cloudless.'

362. 林肯郡海岸边的海啸(一五七一)

英格洛

老市长爬上了高耸的钟楼①,
  敲钟人,三三两两一路奔忙;
"敲吧,哪怕你对敲钟全不在行;"
  好伙计他说,"也请使出你吃奶的力量。"
  "敲得响些,再响些,啊,波士顿的铜钟! 5
敲出你们能敲的各种调门,各种声响,
  大声奏出'安德比的新娘'。"②

人们说这是一次偷袭的海啸——
  是上帝的安排,他什么全都知底;
可是在我的耳边却至今仍嗡嗡震响着 10
  那钟声,和它所传播的信息:
那时候,似乎一切都完全正常,只除了
成百万只色彩斑驳的海鸥和野鸡,
  密麻麻聚在海边岩石上,又不时飞起。

我那时正坐在屋门里纺织, 15
  线头断了,我抬眼向门外张望;
在那无云的天空中,静静呆看
  那红宝石般的已下落的太阳;
背衬着光天化日下的金色的死亡,
我看到我儿子的年轻貌美的媳妇, 20

---

① 高耸的钟楼指波士顿圣博托夫教堂的漂亮的钟楼,在四周的平原上,相隔四十英里外都可清楚看到。——译者
② "安德比的新娘",从诗中已可看出,这是在遇有重大灾祸向村民告警时使用的一种曲牌。——译者

My sonne's faire wife, Elizabeth.

'Cusha! Cusha! Cusha!' calling①,
Ere the early dews were falling,
Farre away I heard her song,
   'Cusha! Cusha!' all along;
Where the reedy Lindis floweth,
   Floweth, floweth,
From the meads where melick groweth②
Faintly came her milking song.

'Cusha! Cusha! Cusha!' calling,
'For the dews will soone be falling;
Leave your meadow grasses mellow,
   Mellow, mellow;
Quit your cowslips, cowslips yellow;
Come uppe Whitefoot, come uppe Lightfoot,
Quit the stalks of parsley hollow,
   Hollow, hollow;
Come uppe Jetty, rise and follow,
   From the clovers lift your head;
Come uppe Whitefoot, come uppe Lightfoot,
Come uppe Jetty, rise and follow,
   Jetty, to the milking shed.'

If it be long, aye, long ago,
   When I beginne to think howe long,

---

① '*Cusha*': a cry to cattle, from 'cu' a form of 'cow' which was in use up to 1500.
② *melick*: (or 'melic') a kind of grass.

伊丽莎白,正在林迪斯河边奔忙。

"哞哞!哞哞!哞哞!"她连声叫唤,
这时还不到夜露降临时分,
从老远外传来她歌唱般的叫喊:
"哞哞!哞哞!"一直不停; 25
那边那长满芦苇的林迪斯河流着,
  流着,流着,
从那青草茂密的广阔的牧场那边,
隐隐约约传来她唤牛挤奶的歌声。

"哞哞!哞哞!哞哞!"她声声叫唤, 30
"马上便会有露水下来沾湿衣襟;
快离开牧场吧,尽管草儿是那么鲜嫩,
  鲜嫩,鲜嫩,
先丢下你们的九轮草,黄色的九轮草;
回来吧雪花蹄,回来吧飞毛腿, 35
别舍不得丢下那欧芹,松脆,空心,
  空心,空心;
回来吧,杰蒂,从嫩苜蓿上
 抬起头,跟着大家一起跑回来;
回来吧雪花蹄,回来吧飞毛腿, 40
回来吧,杰蒂,快跟着大家跑回来,
 杰蒂,快回到奶棚来挤奶。"

这事也许已过去很久了,啊,是很久,
 可我只要想起当时的那番情景,

Againe I hear the Lindis flow,
   Swift as an arrowe, sharp and strong;
And all the aire, it seemeth mee,
Bin full of floating bells (sayth shee)①,
That ring the tune of Enderby.

Alle fresh the level pasture lay,
   And not a shadowe mote be seene②,
Save where full fyve good miles away
   The steeple towered from out the greene;
And lo! the great bell farre and wide
Was heard in all the country side
That Saturday at eventide.

The swanherds where their sedges are
   Moved on in sunset's golden breath,
The shepherde lads I heard afarre,
   And my sonne's wife, Elizabeth;
Till floating o'er the grassy sea
Came downe that kyndly message free,
The 'Brides of Mavis Enderby.'

Then some looked uppe into the sky,
   And all along where Lindis flows
To where the goodly vessels lie,
   And where the lordly steeple shows.

---

① *Bin*: *bin* or *been* was always plural and, though archaic, may be used for 'are'; to use it for 'is', as here, and as it is used by Byron in *Don Juan*, is incorrect.

② *mote*: 'could'; an old verb expressing permission or possibility (= 'may'), or necessity (= 'must'). It is a present tense and improperly used as a past.

便马上又听到林迪斯河的流水声, 45
　　那水流像离弦箭一般的强劲;
我仿佛又听到满天飘飞着(她说)
　　那震耳欲聋的急骤的钟声,
和它奏出的安德比曲牌的凄惨声音。

平坦的牧场看上去一片清新, 50
　　哪里都看不见任何人影,
只除了在足有五哩以外的地方,
　　耸立在青绿草原上的那钟楼的尖顶;
可是瞧啊!就在那个星期六的黄昏,
整个那地区的农村,远远近近, 55
无人不曾听到那巨大的钟声。

牧鹅的孩子在金色的余晖下嬉游,
　　在那边那长满蓑衣草的地方;
远处,传来一些牧羊儿和我的
　　儿媳伊丽莎白欢声笑语的声浪; 60
一直到在那由青草铺成的海洋上,
到处响起了"马菲斯·安德比新娘,"
将令人心悸的消息四处播扬。

这时,有些人抬头看看天上,
　　一直沿着林迪斯河流向前张望, 65
那里停靠着一些整洁的木船,
　　那边那雄伟的钟楼仍清晰在望。

They sayde, 'And why should this thing be?
What danger lowers by land or sea?
They ring the tune of Enderby!

'For evil news from Mablethorpe,
   Of pyrate galleys warping down①;
For shippes ashore beyond the scorpe②,
   They have not spared to wake the towne
But while the west bin red to see,
And storms be none, and pyrates flee,
Why ring "The Brides of Enderby"?'

I looked without, and lo! my sonne
   Came riding downe with might and main:
He raised a shout as he drew on,
   Till all the welkin rang again③,
'Elizabeth! Elizabeth!'
(A sweeter woman ne'er drew breath
Than my sonne's wife, Elizabeth.)

'The olde sea wall(he cried)is downe,
   The rising tide comes on apace,
And boats adrift in yonder towne
   Go sailing uppe the market-place.'

---

① *warping down*: to warp a vessel is to drag it along by ropes fixed to the shore or to buoys, etc., and hauled in from the ship.
② *scorpe*: may be 'scarp,' the steep face of a hill.
③ *the welkin*: 'the sky.'

他们止不住问:"这倒是怎么回事?
是陆地还是海上出现了什么祸殃?
使他们敲起了'安德比的新娘'!" 70

"因为从马波索浦传来坏消息①,
　说几只海盗船正绞索沿江而上②;
他们洗劫了峭壁那边停靠的船只③,
　同时也没放过到市镇上去行抢。
可现在向西方看过去是一派红光④, 75
　决不能有风暴,海盗也已经全离港,
却为什么要敲奏'安德比的新娘'?"

我向门外望去,瞧啊,我的儿子
　骑着马正气急败坏向这边奔跑:
刚到屋前,他用全力发出一声叫喊, 80
　使得整个天空都为之动摇,
"伊丽莎白,伊丽莎白!"
(啊,世上还从未有一个活着的女人
更比我的儿媳伊丽莎白美好。)

"海边的岩石(他叫喊着)已眼看被淹没, 85
　越来越高的浪潮正急速扑上陆地,
在那边市镇下面停靠着的船只,
　现已都向上游的集市边驶去。"

---

① 马波索浦,在林肯郡的海岸边,在波士顿西北约三十英里处。——译者
② 绞索,意思是在岸上或什么重物上拴牢一根绳索的一头,然后在船上倒拉绳索的另一头使船只前进。——译者
③ 峭壁(scorpe),无法弄清英格洛小姐的这个词是什么意思,我所见到的任何字典都无此字。如果她的意思是峭壁(scarp),一座山的笔立的垂直面,在波士顿附近又根本没有山。——译者
④ 西方一派红光,一般都认为这是天气晴朗的预兆。——译者

1531

He shook as one that looks on death;
 'God save you, mother!' straight he saith;
'Where is my wife, Elizabeth?'

'Good sonne, where Lindis winds away,
 With her two bairns I marked her long;
And ere yon bells beganne to play
 Afar I heard her milking song.'
He looked across the grassy lea,
To right, to left, 'Ho Enderby!'
They rang 'The Brides of Enderby!'

With that he cried and beat his breast;
 For, lo! along the river's bed
A mighty eygre reared his crest①,
 And uppe the Lindis raging sped.
It swept with thunderous noises loud;
Shaped like a curling snow-white cloud,
Or like a demon in a shroud.

And rearing Lindis backward pressed
 Shook all her trembling bankes amaine;
Then madly at the eygre's breast
 Flung uppe her weltering walls again②.
Then bankes came downe with ruin and rout —
Then beaten foam flew round about —
Then all the mighty floods were out.

---

① *eygre*: a pseudo-archaic form of 'eagre' or 'eager,' a tidal wave, caused by the rushing of the water up a narrowing estuary, such as the Humber or the Severn.

② *her weltering walls*: i.e. her sodden banks.

他浑身发着抖,仿佛眼看便将死去:
"上帝保佑你,妈妈!"他开门见山地说, 90
"我的妻,伊丽莎白,她,她在哪里?"

"好儿子,她在林迪斯河流动的那边,
　我和她的两个孩子一直在把她张望:
在那钟声在草原上响开之前;
　还听到从远处传来她唤牛的声响。" 95
他举目望着那芳草连绵的牧场,
看看左边,再向右望望,"噢,安德比!"
那钟声仍在奏着"安德比的新娘"!

忽然间他连声喊叫,捶打着胸膛;
　因为,瞧啊! 沿着那整条河谷, 100
一个巨大的恶浪已高扬起头
　正向着林迪斯河的上游奔突冲撞。
它挟带着震耳欲聋的巨响;
像一团凶猛的翻滚着的白云,
或者像一个裹着尸衣的魔王。 105

这时举起前蹄的林迪斯河往后一蹲,
　使得两边河岸全跟着剧烈抖动;
然后那恶浪又疯狂地把胸膛高挺,
　再次向着两边的堤岸猛冲。
接着两边的河岸立即土崩瓦解—— 110
接着雪花一样的巨浪到处翻滚——
接着一场洪水已把大片的陆地鲸吞。

So farre, so fast the eygre drave,
   The heart had hardly time to beat,
Before a shallow seething wave
   Sobbed in the grasses at oure feet:
The feet had hardly time to flee
Before it brake against the knee,
And all the world was in the sea.

Upon the roofe we sate that night,
   The noise of bells went sweeping by;
I marked the lofty beacon light
   Stream from the church tower, red and high —
A lurid mark and dread to see;
And awesome bells they were to mee,
That in the dark rang 'Enderby.'

They rang the sailor lads to guide
   From roofe to roofe who fearless rowed;
And I — my sonne was at my side
   And yet the ruddy beacon glowed:
And yet he moaned beneath his breath,
'O come in life, or come in death!
O lost! my love, Elizabeth.'

And didst thou visit him no more?
   Thou didst, thou didst, my daughter deare;
The waters laid thee at his doore,
   Ere yet the early dawn was clear.
Thy pretty bairns in fast embrace,
The lifted sun shone on thy face,
Downe drifted to thy dwelling-place.

那恶浪是那样迅猛地直向前闯,
　　几乎不等你的心有时间再一次跳动,
汩汩冒泡的水头便已漫过牧场, 115
　　把我们脚下的青草一口咽光;
不等我们的脚再往前迈出一步,
水流便已经将我们的双膝捆绑,
转眼间,全世界已是一片汪洋。

我们只得通夜在屋顶上坐下, 120
　　耳边听见钟楼上的钟仍在不停地敲;
我看到半空中灯塔上的灯亮,
　　一派红光,从高处向四方照耀——
看着那光亮我总止不住阵阵心跳;
那钟声也让我感到火烧火燎, 125
那在黑暗中敲出的"安德比"曲调。

钟声是为给年轻的船夫指明方向,
　　他们无所畏惧地在屋顶之间划行;
而我——我儿子也待在我身旁,
　　却只呆呆看着灯塔上的红光。 130
他仍在那里呻吟着低声哭泣:
"回来吧,不论是死了还是活着!
啊,不见了,伊丽莎白,我心爱的妻。"

你从此再也不曾来看望过他吗?
　　你来过,你来过,我的好姑娘; 135
第二天的黎明还没有完全揭开纱幕,
　　河水便把你送到了他的门旁。
你的两个漂亮孩子使劲亲着你的脸,
刚升起的太阳照亮了你的面庞,
你已漂回到了你的住房门前。 140

That flow strewed wrecks about the grass,
That ebbe swept out the flocks to sea;
A fatal ebbe and flow, alas!
To manye more than myne and mee:
145   But each will mourn his own (she saith),
And sweeter woman ne'er drew breath
Than my sonne's wife, Elizabeth.

I shall never hear her more
By the reedy Lindis shore,
150   'Cusha! Cusha! Cusha!' calling,
Ere the early dews be falling;
I shall never hear her song,
'Cusha! Cusha!' all along
Where the sunny Lindis floweth,
155   Goeth, floweth;
From the meads where melick groweth,
When the water winding down,
Onward floweth to the town.

I shall never see her more
160   Where the reeds and rushes quiver,
        Shiver, quiver;
Stand beside the sobbing river,
Sobbing, throbbing, in its falling
To the sandy lonesome shore;

165   I shall never hear her calling,
'Leave your meadow grasses mellow,
        Mellow, mellow;
Quit your cowslips, cowslips yellow;

那次洪水在牧场上铺满了杂物和烂泥,
　　退潮时却把羊群全带进海里去;
天哪,多么可怕的一次涨潮和退潮,
　　受其灾害的何止我们家和你:
可是各人自有他自己说不出的悲伤(她说),   *145*
人世上还从没有过一个妇女,
能比得上伊丽莎白,我的儿媳。

我将再也听不到她的声音
在长满芦苇的林迪斯河滩上,
在露水还没降临之前,   *150*
　　"哞哞!哞哞!哞哞!"声声叫唤;
我将再也听不到她的歌唱:
　　"哞哞!哞哞!"从牧草茂密的牧场,
一直沿着在灿烂的阳光下流淌,
　　　流淌,流淌着的   *155*
林迪斯河飘扬,而那
河水却翻滚着蜿蜒而下,
直流过前面的市镇旁。

我将永远再见不到她
站立在长满芦苇,不停地呜咽,   *160*
　　呜咽,呜咽的
河边,看着河水
在呜咽中把泪水
撒在两旁干枯寂寞的河岸边。
我将永远再听不到她的唤牛声,   *165*
　　"快离开牧场吧,尽管草儿是那么鲜嫩,
　　　鲜嫩,鲜嫩,
先丢下你们的九轮草,黄色的九轮草;

Come uppe Whitefoot, come uppe Lightfoot;
Quit your pipes of parsley hollow,
    Hollow, hollow;
Come uppe Lightfoot, rise and follow;
    Lightfoot, Whitefoot,
From your clovers lift the head;
Come uppe Jetty, follow, follow,
Jetty, to the milking shed. '

                  JEAN INGELOW.

回来吧雪花蹄,回来吧飞毛腿,
别舍不得丢下那欧芹,松脆,空心, *170*
　　空心,空心,
回来吧,杰蒂,从嫩苜蓿上
　抬起头,跟着大家一起跑回来;
回来吧雪花蹄,回来吧飞毛腿,
回来吧,杰蒂,快跟着大家跑回来,
杰蒂,快回到奶棚来挤奶。" *175*

黄雨石　译

编注 英格洛出生于林肯郡的波士顿。一五七一年十月五日,当地发生了一次由风暴引起的可怕水灾,其时英格洛尚幼,但水灾给她的印象非常深刻,此诗即为描写这次水灾,选自一八六三年版《诗集》。

363. THE FORSAKEN MERMAN

Come, dear children, let us away;
   Down and away below!
Now my brothers call from the bay;
   Now the great winds shoreward blow;
   Now the salt tides seaward flow;
Now the wild white horses play,
Champ and chafe and toss in the spray.
Children dear, let us away!
   This way, this way!

Call her once before you go.
   Call once yet.
In a voice that she will know:
   'Margaret! Margaret!'
Children's voices should be dear
(Call once more) to a mother's ear:
Children's voices, wild with pain —
Surely she will come again.
Call her once and come away;
   This way, this way!
'Mother dear, we cannot stay.'
The wild white horses foam and fret.
   Margaret! Margaret!
Come, dear children, come away down!
   Call no more!
One last look at the white-walled town,

363. 被遗弃的人鱼

阿诺德

走吧,亲爱的孩子们,我们走吧,
 让我们回深海!
我的兄弟们正在海湾里召唤;
 烈风正在向岸上吹,
 咸潮正在往海里退, 5
雪白的马群正在嘶咬撒野,
在水花白沫中暴跳如雷。
亲爱的孩子们,跟我来,
 让我们回大海!

临走前再叫她一声, 10
 再唤她一回。
这声音,她应该认得清:
 "玛格蕾!玛格蕾!"
孩子的声音(再叫她一声)
在妈妈耳里怎能不亲? 15
孩子的声音,充满发狂的苦痛——
她怎能不回来?
再叫她一次就走吧,
 让我们回大海!
"亲爱的妈妈,我们不能在这儿呆。" 20
雪白的马群口吐白沫,暴跳如雷。
 玛格蕾!玛格蕾!
走吧,亲爱的孩子们,下海来!
 不要再叫了!
最后再看一眼小镇的白墙 25

And the little grey church on the windy shore.
　　　Then come down.
She will not come though you call all day.
　　　Come away, come away!

30　Children dear, was it yesterday
We heard the sweet bells over the bay?
In the caverns where we lay,
Through the surf and through the swell,
The far-off sound of a silver bell?
35　Sand-strewn caverns, cool and deep,
Where the winds are all asleep;
Where the spent lights quiver and gleam①;
Where the salt weed sways in the stream;
Where the sea-beasts ranged all round
40　Feed in the ooze of their pasture-ground;
Where the sea-snakes coil and twine,
Dry their mail and bask in the brine;
Where great whales come sailing by,
Sail and sail, with unshut eye,
45　Round the world for ever and ay?
When did music come this way?
Children dear, was it yesterday?

Children dear, was it yesterday
(Call yet once) that she went away?
50　Once she sate with you and me,
On a red gold throne in the heart of the sea,

---

① *the spent lights*: i. e. the sunlight had lost its force and radiance in penetrating to the recesses of the cavern.

和迎风的岸上灰色的小教堂,
　　　然后该走了。
哪怕你们喊一整天她也不回来。
　　　让我们回大海!

亲爱的孩子们,那莫非是昨天—— 30
我们听见甜的钟声荡漾在海湾?
当我们躺在岩洞之中,
透过浪声,透过涛声,
听到了遥远的银钟?
铺满细沙的岩洞凉爽而深邃, 35
那儿,四方的风全都在安睡;
那儿,光线减弱而变幻闪烁,
那儿,海草在水流中摇曳婆娑;
那儿,有海兽到处繁衍生息,
在海底牧场的软泥上觅食; 40
那儿,有海蛇缠绕盘旋,
在盐水里把一身铠甲晒干;
那儿,时而驶过几头巨鲸,
它们圆睁着不闭的眼睛,
绕着世界永远不停地航行—— 45
音乐传来之时,是哪一天?
亲爱的孩子们,那莫非是昨天?

亲爱的孩子们(再叫她一声)
她离去的那天——那莫非是昨天?
那天她和我们一同坐在海心, 50
坐在金红的宝座上,

And the youngest sate on her knee.
She comb'd its bright hair, and she tended it well.
When down swung the sound of the far-off bell.
55 She sigh'd, she look'd up through the clear green sea;
She said: 'I must go, for my kinsfolk pray
In the little grey church on the shore to-day.
'Twill be Easter-time in the world — ah me!
And I lose my poor soul, Merman, here with thee.'
60 I said: 'Go up, dear heart, through the waves!
Say thy prayer, and come back to the kind sea-caves.'
She smiled, she went up through the surf in the bay.
Children dear, was it yesterday?

Children dear, were we long alone?
65 'The sea grows stormy, the little ones moan.
Long prayers,' I said, 'in the world they say.
Come!' I said, and we rose through the surf in the bay.
We went up the beach, by the sandy down
Where the sea-stocks bloom, to the white-walled town[①].
70 Through the narrow paved streets, where all was still,
To the little grey church on the windy hill.
From the church came a murmur of folk at their prayers,
But we stood without in the cold blowing airs.
We climbed on the graves, on the stones, worn with rains,
75 And we gazed up the aisle through the small-leaded panes.
She sate by the pillar; we saw her clear:
'Margaret, hist! come quick, we are here.
Dear heart,' I said, 'we are long alone.
The sea grows stormy, the little ones moan.'

---

① *sea-stocks*: a plant with a purple flower.

她把最小的孩子抱在膝上,
抚爱着他,把他的金发梳光,
这时,从上方飘来了遥远的钟声。
她透过澄碧的海水仰望, 55
叹息着说:"我必须去,因为我的亲人们
今天在岸边灰色的小教堂里祈祷。
人间要过复活节了!哎!
而我在这儿,跟你——跟人鱼一道,会把我可怜的灵魂失掉。"
我说:"去吧,爱人,穿过碧波上升, 60
做了祷告,再转回亲切的岩洞。"
她微笑着,浮上了浪花拍岸的海湾。
亲爱的孩子们,那莫非是昨天?

 亲爱的孩子们,我们已单独过了多久?
我说:"大海起了风暴,孩子哀哭不休, 65
人间做的祷告怎么这样长!来吧!"
于是我带着孩子们浮上海湾激浪,
上了海滩,沿着香石竹花开放的沙丘,
我们来到那白墙的小镇。
石板铺的小巷里一片寂静, 70
我们来到迎风的坡上灰色的小教堂。
教堂里传出人们喃喃祈祷的声音,
但我们却留在外面的寒风中。
我们攀上墓园,坐在风雨剥蚀的墓石上,
隔着小窗的玻璃向教堂的侧廊凝望。 75
她就坐在廊柱旁,我们看得很清:
"玛格蕾,嘘!是我们!快出来吧,
爱人!"我说,"我们单独过了很久。
大海起了风暴,孩子们哀哭不休。"

But, ah, she gave me never a look,
For her eyes were sealed to the holy book!
Loud prays the priest; shut stands the door.
Come away, children, call no more!
Come away, come down, call no more!

  Down, down, down!
  Down to the depths of the sea!
She sits at her wheel in the humming town,
  Singing most joyfully.
Hark, what she sings: 'O joy, O joy,
For the humming street, and the child with its toy!
For the priest, and the bell, and the holy well —
  For the wheel where I spun,
  And the blessed light of the sun!'
And so she sings her fill,
  Singing most joyfully,
Till the shuttle falls from her hand,
  And the whizzing wheel stands still.
She steals to the window, and looks at the sand,
  And over the sand at the sea;
And her eyes are set in a stare;
  And anon there breaks a sigh,
And anon there drops a tear,
  From a sorrow-clouded eye,
And a heart sorrow-laden,
  A long, long sigh;
For the cold strange eyes of a little Mermaiden,
  And the gleam of her golden hair.

但她呀，一次也没有向我望，　　　　　　　　　80
　她的目光专注在圣书上！
牧师高声念着祷文，大门紧紧关着。
走吧，孩子们，不要再叫了！
下海吧，孩子们，不要再唤了！

　　　往下，往下，往下去！　　　　　　　　85
　　　潜入深深的海底！
她在喧闹的镇上，坐在纺车旁，
　唱得多么欢畅。
听呀，她在唱："欢乐呀欢乐，
属于喧闹的小巷，属于玩耍的孩子！　　　　　90
属于牧师、钟声和圣水泉，
　属于我纺纱的纺车，
　属于太阳神圣的光！"
她这样尽情地唱，
　唱得多么欢畅，　　　　　　　　　　　　95
直到纺锤从她手里落下，
　嗡嗡的纺车停止了转动。
她悄悄走近窗边眺望沙滩，
　又越过沙滩远望海中。
她的目光变成了凝视，　　　　　　　　　　100
　胸中发出一声叹息。
从她悲伤笼罩的眼里，
　从她悲伤压抑的心底，
不时落下一滴眼泪，
　不时发出一声叹息，那么深，那么长——　　105
为了小人鱼姑娘奇冷的眼睛
　和她金发的闪光。

  Come away, away children[①]!
  Come children, come down!
  The hoarse wind blows colder;
  Lights shine in the town.
  She will start from her slumber
   When gusts shake the door;
  She will hear the winds howling,
   Will hear the waves roar.
  We shall see, while above us
   The waves roar and whirl,
  A ceiling of amber,
   A pavement of pearl.
  Singing: 'Here came a mortal,
   But faithless was she!
  And alone dwell for ever
   The kings of the sea.'

  But, children, at midnight,
   When soft the winds blow,
  When clear falls the moonlight,
   When spring-tides are low[②];
  When sweet airs come seaward
   From heaths starred with broom,
  And high rocks throw mildly

---

① A change of metre occurs from this line to the end, anapæsts, which have appeared at intervals before, e. g. ll. 53 – 62, being substituted for the prevailing trochees of the earlier part, 'Come awáy', away chil'dren! Come chil'dren, come down'!' etc.

② *When spring-tides are low*: 'spring-tide' is the name given to the tides which occur each month shortly after the new and full moons; the flood tide is then unusually high, and the ebb unusually lows; at the two other quarters there is a 'neap-tide', when the water neither rises nor sinks to the usual level.

走吧,孩子们,走吧!
　　来,孩子们,潜到水下!
嘶哑的风越刮越冷,　　　　　　　　　　　　110
　　灯火已照亮了户户人家。
每当疾风摇撼窗门
　　她会突然从梦中惊醒,
她会听见狂风怒号,
　　她会听见滚滚涛声。　　　　　　　　　　115
而我们,当我们的上空
　　波浪汹涌翻卷,
我们会抬头看见
　　一层珍珠琥珀的天。
我们唱:"这儿来过一位凡女,'　　　　　　　120
　　可是她不守信义!
从此海王的家族
　　永远独居海底。"

但是,孩子们,每当子夜,
　　每当和风轻吹,　　　　　　　　　　　　125
每当月色明媚,
　　每当大潮尽退,
每当石南花和金雀花
　　向海上吹送阵阵甜香,
每当高耸的礁石　　　　　　　　　　　　　130

On the blanched sands a gloom;
Up the still, glistening beaches,
　Up the creeks we will hie,
Over banks of bright seaweed
　　The ebb-tide leaves dry.
We will gaze, from the sand-hills,
At the white, sleeping town;
At the church on the hill-side —
　And then come back down.
Singing: 'There dwells a loved one,
　But cruel is she!
She left lonely for ever
　The kings of the sea.'

M. ARNOLD.

把柔和的影子投在沙上，
　我们就匆匆升上海湾，
　　登上静静闪光的沙滩，
　　明亮的海草覆盖的岸
　　　退潮后露出了水面。　　　　　　　　　　135
　我们将从沙丘上凝望，
　　望那沉睡的白色的镇，
　　望那山坡上的教堂，
　　　然后又悄悄回到海中。
　我们唱："那儿住着亲爱的人儿，　　　　　140
　　可是她太冷酷！
　　她离开了海王的家族，
　　　使他们永远孤独。"

飞白　译

编注　马修·阿诺德（Matthew Arnold，1822—1888），英国诗人，著名文艺评论家。曾任牛津大学英诗讲座教授，名诗有《色希斯》《多佛尔滩》《吉普赛学者》《拉格比公学教堂》《夜莺》《被遗弃的人鱼》以及《邵莱布和罗斯托》等。阿诺德认为诗是诗人对于"生活的批判"，诗有道德意义和教育意义，因此诗必须严肃真实。阿诺德的诗是维多利亚时期诗人中人情味最浓者之一。

　　此诗取材于丹麦传说，用第一人称，是男人鱼（Merman）的独白。

364. THE SONG OF CALLICLES ON ETNA

    Through the black, rushing smoke-bursts,
        Thick breaks the red flame;
    All Etna heaves fiercely
        Her forest-clothed frame.

    Not here, O Apollo!
        Are haunts meet for thee.
    But, Where Helicon breaks down
        In cliff to the sea,

    Where the moon-silver'd inlets
        Send far their light voice
    Up the still vale of Thisbe,
        O speed, and rejoice!

    On the sward at the cliff-top
        Lie strewn the white flocks;
    On the cliff-side the pigeons
        Roost deep in the rocks.

364. 喀利克勒斯的埃特纳火山歌①

阿诺德

透过腾跃的滚滚黑烟,
　　映出火红的浓重烈焰;
整个埃特纳在剧烈地呼吸,
　　满山的森林都在震颤。

啊,别在这儿,阿波罗! 5
　　这不是您出没之地。
但在赫利孔断裂的地方②
　　有一堵石壁浸入海里,

那儿,月色如银的海湾
　　会把她们轻妙的声音 10
送进塞斯比的幽深山谷③,
　　啊,快吧,快带来欢欣!

在绝壁顶部的草地,
　　雪白的羊群到处躺卧;
在绝壁一侧的岩穴, 15
　　栖息着无数的野鸽。

---

① 喀利克勒斯是一个年轻的竖琴家,他不露面地在埃特纳山间弹奏竖琴,以宽慰悲怆绝望的哲学家恩培多克勒斯。埃特纳火山位于意大利西西里岛的东部。——译者
② 赫利孔山为希腊中东部之山脉,据说是阿波罗和缪斯居住的地方。——编注者
③ 塞斯比为赫利孔山南面一小城。——编注者

In the moonlight the shepherds,
    Soft lull'd by the rills,
Lie wrapt in their blankets,
    Asleep on the hills.

— What forms are these coming
    So white through the gloom?
What garments out-glistening
    The gold-flower'd broom?

What sweet-breathing presence
    Out-perfumes the thyme?
What voices enrapture
    The night's balmy prime? —

'Tis Apollo comes leading
    His choir, the Nine[①].
— The leader is fairest,
    But all are divine.

They are lost in the hollows!
    They stream up again!
What seeks on this mountain
    The glorified train? —

They bathe on this mountain,
    In the spring by their road;
Then on to Olympus,

---

① *the Nine*: *i.e.* the Muses.

牧羊人沐浴在月光下,
　　耳边响着小溪柔和的潺湲,
　　他们身上裹着布毯,
　　　沉沉酣睡在山峦。　　　　　　　　　　20

——是什么身影在移动
　　白晃晃地从暗处穿过?
　　是什么艳装竟然辉掩了
　　　盛开的金雀花朵?

是什么温馨的气息　　　　　　　　　　　25
　　赛过了麝香草的馥郁?
　　是什么甜润的乐音
　　　直让静谧的夜晚入迷?——

这是阿波罗领来了
　　他的合唱队,九位女神,　　　　　　　30
——为首的美貌无比,
　　其余个个优雅超群。

她们忽地消失进山谷,
　　立即又在眼前浮现!
　　这一队光彩夺目的女神　　　　　　　35
　　　为什么来到这座山?——

她们来到这座山上
　　顺路去山泉洗浴;
　　然后再往奥林匹斯山①,

---

① 奥林匹斯山,希腊神话中的众神之山。——编注者

Their endless abode①!

— Whose praise do they mention?
Of what is it told? —
What will be for ever;
What was from of old.

First hymn they the Father
Of all things; — and then,
The rest of immortals,
The action of men.
The day in his hotness,
The strife with the palm;
The night in her silence,
The stars in their calm.

M. ARNOLD.

---

① *endless*: 'immortal.'

到她们永恒的住地。　　　　　　　　　　40

　　——有谁被她们赞美？
　　　有什么在赞词里提起？——
　　是永恒不变的事物，
　　　亘古长存的真理。

　　第一支赞美歌献给　　　　　　　　　　　45
　　　她们的父亲，然后称颂①
　　永生的诸神，
　　　人类的行动，

　　酷暑炎热的白昼，
　　　赤手空拳的斗争，　　　　　　　　　　50
　　静寂无声的夜晚，
　　　安详自若的星辰。

蓝仁哲　译

编注 本诗是阿诺德诗剧《埃特纳山上的恩培多克勒》(*Empedocles on Etna*)的最后一部分(第 417—468 行)。恩培多克勒是公元前五世纪古希腊的哲学家、科学家和政治家，诗剧描写了他晚年的悲观和纵身跳入火山口的自杀局面。这部诗剧最早见于阿诺德一八五二年出版的第二部诗集。

---

① 她们的父亲，诸神之父宙斯。——译者

365. SHAKESPEARE

Others abide our question — Thou art free!
We ask and ask — Thou smilest and art still,
Out-topping knowledge! So some sovran hill[1]
Who to the stars uncrowns his majesty,
5 Planting his steadfast footsteps in the sea,
Making the heaven of heavens his dwelling-place,
Spares but the border, often, of his base[2]
To the foil'd searching of mortality;
And thou, whose head did stars and sunbeams know,
10 Self-school'd, self-scann'd, self-honour'd, self-secure,
Didst walk on earth unguess'd at. — Better so[3]!
All pains the immortal spirit must endure,
All weakness which impairs, all griefs which bow,
Find their sole voice in that victorious brow.

M. ARNOLD.

---

[1] *sovran*: see note to No. 62, l. 60.

[2] *Spares but the border*, etc.: as the tallest mountain is known only at its foot, so the loftiest intellects are unknown to the world except in trifling points.

[3] *unguess'd at*: few things in the history of literature are more remarkable than the indifference shown by his contemporaries to one whom subsequent ages have, not merely in the English-speaking world, regarded as the master-mind of all time. He made less money than a successful grocer might reasonably look for, and received less honour than would now be paid to a provincial alderman.

365. 莎士比亚

阿诺德

别人都受我们质疑。你却无忧无虑,
　　我们问了又问——你微笑而无言,
　　耸立在知识之巅。最高的山峦,
向星空展示着他的雄伟壮丽,
把脚跟扎在海底坚定不移,
　　而把九重天作为他的家园,
　　只留下云雾笼罩的山麓的边缘
让凡人去徒劳地探索不已;
而你,你熟悉群星,你了解阳光,
　　你自修,自审,自信,自己建树光荣,
你在世间无人识,这又何妨?
　　一切不朽者必须忍受的苦痛,
一切折磨人的弱点和辛酸,
在你轩昂的眉宇间找到了无双的表现。

飞白　译

366. A SUMMER NIGHT

In the deserted moon-blanch'd street
How lonely rings the echo of my feet!
Those windows, which I gaze at, frown,
Silent and white, unopening down,
Repellent as the world; — but see!
A break between the housetops shows
The moon, and, lost behind her, fading dim[1]
Into the dewy dark obscurity
Down at the far horizon's rim,
Doth a whole tract of heaven disclose,

And to my mind the thought
Is on a sudden brought
Of a past night, and a far different scene.
Headlands stood out into the moon-lit deep
As clearly as at noon;
The spring-tide's brimming flow
Heaved dazzlingly between;
Houses with long white sweep
Girdled the glistening bay;
Behind through the soft air,
The blue haze-cradled mountains spread away.
That night was far more fair —
But the same restless pacings to and fro,

---

[1] *lost* and *fading* qualify 'tract' (l. 10).

366. 夏夜

阿诺德

在月光照白的荒凉街道上,
我脚步的回声响得多么孤独!
　那些窗户,我看着,都蹙起额,
　默默然,白蒙蒙,没有向下拉开①,
　跟人世一样冷淡——可是瞧哪!
　屋檐之间的一片空隙,露出了
明月;隐没在她背后的,逐渐暗淡地
沉进雾霭朦胧的黑暗之中
　直到远处地平线边缘的,
　是展开的整整一片天。

　我的脑海里
　突然想起了
从前的一夜,完全不同的一番景色。
山岬凸现于月光照亮的深处,
　恰似正午那样清晰;
　春潮满涨的水流
　眩目地起伏其间;
　房舍排成洁白的漫长一溜
　围绕波光粼粼的海湾;
　后面,透过柔和的空间
兜着轻霭的蔚蓝群山向远处伸展。
　那一夜要美好得多——
　只是同样有不安地徘徊踱步,

---
① 指的是上下启闭的窗户。——译者

And the same vainly throbbing heart was there
And the same bright calm moon.

And the calm moonlight seems to say:
Hast thou then still the old unquiet breast,
Which never deadens into rest,
Nor ever feels the fiery glow
That whirls the spirit from itself away,
But fluctuates to and fro,
Never by passion quite possess'd,
And never quite benumb'd by the world's sway?
And I, I know not if to pray
Sill to be what I am, or yield, and be
Like all the other men I see.

For most men in a brazen prison live,
 Where in the sun's hot eye,
With heads bent o'er their toil, they languidly
Their lives to some unmeaning taskwork give,
Dreaming of nought beyond their prison-wall.
 And as, year after year,
Fresh products of their barren labour fall
 From their tired hands, and rest
 Never yet comes more near,
Gloom settles slowly down over their breast;
 And while they try to stem
The waves of mournful thought by which they are prest,
 Death in their prison reaches them,
Unfreed, having seen nothing, still unblest.

同样有心的徒然跳动，
   还有同样皎洁宁静的月亮。   25

  宁静的月光似乎在说：
你是否仍然有着从前的不安胸怀，
  从不麻木而停歇，
  也从不感觉到有烈火
把灵魂从胸中夹裹而去；   30
   而是前后地摇摆着
  从不被激情完全控制，
也从不被人世的倾向完全僵化？
  于是我，我不知道是所求
依旧保持故我，还是让步，变得   35
   跟我看见的其他人一样。

因为多数人生活在黄铜的狱中①，
   置身在太阳的火眼下
俯首做着苦工；他们有气无力地
把生命给了某些无意义的劳动，   40
从来不对狱墙之外有什么梦想。
   于是，年复一年
他们无效劳动的新鲜产物
  从他们疲劳的手里掉落，而休息
   则始终没有更加临近一点，   45
忧郁逐渐地笼罩了他们的心胸；
   正当他们企图抵挡
压抑着他们的悲哀的思潮之时，
   死亡却来到了他们的狱中，
未曾解脱，未曾见到什么，仍然灾难深重。 50

---

① 西人常用黄铜喻坚硬，这里有"铜墙铁壁"的意思。——编注者

And the rest, a few,
Escape their prison, and depart
On the wide Ocean of life anew.
There the freed prisoner, where'er his heart
   Listeth, will sail;
Nor doth he know how there prevail,
   Despotic on that sea,
Trade-winds which cross it from eternity.
Awhile he holds some false way, undebarr'd
   By thwarting signs, and braves
The freshening wind and blackening waves.
And then the tempest strikes him; and between
   The lightning-bursts is seen
   Only a driving wreck,
And the pale master on his spar-strewn deck
   With anguish'd face and flying hair
   Grasping the rudder hard,
Still bent to make some port he knows not where,
Still standing for some false impossible shore.
   And sterner comes the roar
Of sea and wind, and through the deepening gloom
Fainter and fainter wreck and helmsman loom,
And he too disappears, and comes no more.

   Is there no life, but these alone?
   Madman or slave, must man be one?

Plainness and clearness without shadow of stain!

而其余的人,很少数,
　　逃脱了牢狱,重新出发
　　走向辽阔的生活海洋。
在那里,自由了的囚徒,可以
　　随心所欲地航行,　　　　　　　　　　55
　　也不知道在那里有施虐着
　　海洋的暴君,
那恒古以来就刮着的贸易风①。
不一会儿他就航向错误的路,
　　没有任何阻碍的迹象,迎向　　　　　60
　　更加强烈的风,更加乌黑的浪。
后来风暴向他袭击;倏忽的
　　闪电之间,只见
　　一艘随波漂荡的破舟,
脸色苍白的船主在木板开裂的甲板上　　65
　　怒容满面,头发披散,
　　紧紧抓着舵柄,
仍然竭力想航向他不知道在哪儿的港口,
仍然坚持要到达某处不可能存在的岸边。
　　大海和狂风的怒吼　　　　　　　　70
越来越厉害,越加深沉的阴暗里
破舟和舵手时没时现,逐渐衰竭,
他也消失不见,再不出现②。

　　难道没有别的生活,除了这些?
　　疯子或者奴隶,人必须选择其一?　　75

朴素和纯净,没有污迹的暗影!

---

① 即信风。——编注者
② 据说此诗为阿诺德悼念其兄弟逝世而写。——编注者

    Clearness divine!
  Ye heavens, whose pure dark regions have no sign
  Of languor, though so calm, and though so great
  Are yet untroubled and unpassionate!
  Who, though so noble, share in the world's toil,
  And, though so task'd, keep free from dust and soil[①]!
  I will not say that your mild deeps retain
  A tinge, it may be, of their silent pain
  Who have long'd deeply once, and long'd in vain[②];
  But I will rather say that you remain
  A world above man's head, to let him see
  How boundless might his soul's horizons be,
  How vast, yet of what clear transparency!
  How it were good to live there, and breathe free
    How fair a lot to fill
    Is left to each man still!

W. ARNOLD.

[①] *task'd*: the ordinary meaning would be 'strained,' 'oppressed by the task imposed on it.'

[②] *their silent pain Who*: 'the silent pain of those who.'

上天神圣的纯净!
啊,你的纯洁的黑暗区域没有
衰竭的迹象,尽管那么宁静,尽管那么伟大,
仍然没有烦恼,没有脾气! 80
你,尽管那么高贵,却参与了人世的辛劳,
尽管如此奔波,却不染上污泥和尘土!
我不愿意说你那柔软的深处还留着
一点儿,也许是那些人的沉默的痛苦,
他们曾经一度深深地渴望,徒然地渴望; 85
但是我宁愿说,你仍然是
人的头顶上的一个世界,让他看看
他的灵魂的地平线多么无尽无头,
多么广阔,而又多么纯净而透明!
在那里生活有多么快活,而且呼吸自由, 90
  每个人依然有一个
  多么美好的命运可以满足!

王央乐 译

367. MORALITY

We cannot kindle when we will
    The fire which in the heart resides,
The spirit bloweth and is still,
    In mystery our soul abides;
        But tasks in hours of insight will'd
        Can be through hours of gloom fulfill'd.

With aching hands and bleeding feet
    We dig and heap, lay stone on stone;
We bear the burden and the heat
    Of the long day, and wish 'twere done.
        Not till the hours of light return
        All we have built do we discern.

Then, when the clouds are off the soul,
    When thou dost bask in Nature's eye,
Ask, how *she* view'd thy self-control,
    Thy struggling, task'd morality —
        Nature, whose free, light, cheerful air,
        Oft made thee, in thy gloom, despair.

And she, whose censure thou dost dread,
    Whose eye thou wast afraid to seek,
See, on her face a glow is spread,
    A strong emotion on her cheek!
        'Ah, child!' she cries, 'that strife divine,

367. 德行

阿诺德

我们的心中蕴藏着一团火焰,
　　但我们不能随意将它点燃。
精神呼着气,显得安宁静谧,
　　灵魂的所在笼罩着一片神秘。
　　　我们在省悟时刻决意干一番事业,　　　5
　　　但事业的实现得经过阴霾的岁月。

手感觉疼痛,脚流着鲜血,
　　我们挖泥,堆土,还把石头砌;
整日里冒着酷热,负重干活不息,
　　但愿我们的事业能付诸实现。　　　　　10
　　　待光明的时刻又降临人间,
　　　我们才能看见自己的成绩。

这时灵魂已没有云雾掩盖,
　　你可以接受大自然的青睐。
你问她对你的自我克制有何看法,　　　　 15
　　对你的奋斗的德行有何评价——
　　　大自然一片光明,多么自由、欢畅,
　　　你历尽阴霾岁月,怎不令你懊丧。

你害怕大自然对你的谴责,
　　你不敢正视大自然的眼睛。　　　　　 20
瞧呀,她脸上展现出灿烂的光芒,
　　面颊上洋溢着高昂的激情!
　　　她说:"孩子啊! 你那神圣的努力

Whence was it, for it is not mine?

'There is no effort *my* brow —
  I do not strive, I do not weep;
I rush with the swift spheres and glow
  In joy, and, when I will, I sleep!
    Yet that severe, that earnest air,
    I saw, I felt it once — but where?

'I knew not yet the gauge of time,
  Nor wore the manacles of space;
I felt it in some other clime!
  I saw it in some other place!
    'Twas when the heavenly house I trod
    And lay upon the breast of God.'

M. ARNOLD.

从何而来?它从不在我这里①。

"**我**额头上没有劳动的痕迹—— 25
　　我不用努力,我也不用哭泣。
　我随着寰宇奔驰,满心欢喜,
　　只要愿意,我就可以歇息!
　不过严肃的神情,认真的态度
　　我曾看见和接触过一次——但在何处? 30

"我当时还没套上时间的进程表,
　　也没戴上空间的铁镣铐;
　我是在另一境地亲身接触,
　　我是在另一处所亲眼看见。
　那是当我踏进了上天的楼宇, 35
　　当我躺卧在上帝的胸前。"

沙铭瑶　译

编注　选自诗集《埃特纳上的恩培多克勒及其他》。在此诗中,阿诺德歌颂了人类尽职尽责,艰苦劳作,奋斗不息的创造精神,尽管他也将这些归结于上帝的恩惠。

---

① 大自然是按照一定规律,机械地行事,而人类却具有创造性,因而大自然说"它从不在我这里"。——编注者

368. THE FUTURE

A wanderer is man from his birth.
    He was born in a ship
    On the breast of the river of Time;
    Brimming with wonder and joy
    He spreads out his arms to the light,
Rivets his gaze on the banks of the stream.

As what he sees is, so have his thoughts been.
    Whether he wakes
    Where the snowy mountainous pass,
    Echoing the screams of the eagles,
    Hems in its gorges the bed
    Of the new-born clear-flowing stream;
    Whether he first sees light
    Where the river in gleaming rings
    Sluggishly winds through the plain;
Whether in sound of the swallowing sea —
    As is the world on the banks,
    So is the mind of the man.

    Vainly does each as he glides
        Fable and dream
    Of the lands which the river of Time
    Had left ere he woke on its breast,
    Or shall reach when his eyes have been clos'd.
    Only the tract where he sails

368. 未来

阿诺德

人一生下来就是个流浪者。
　他诞生在船上，
在那时间的长河的怀抱里
心中充满了惊异和欢乐，
　他伸出双臂迎接光明，　　　　　　　　5
将他的眼光紧紧盯在河岸上。

他看见什么，他也就想些什么。
　不论他在那儿醒着，
　白雪皑皑的山上的关口，
　回响着老鹰的尖声呼叫，　　　　　　10
　用它的道道峡谷包围着
　新生的清清流水的河床；
　还是他第一次在那儿见到光明，
　河流荡漾着闪光的圆圈，
　缓缓地蜿蜒着流过平原：　　　　　　15
要不在吞没一切的大海的喧哗中——
　岸上的世界是什么模样，
　他心里也就是什么模样。

当他轻轻驶过的时候，
　关于那些土地的传说和梦想　　　　　20
都是白搭——时间的长河
在他醒来前就离开那儿了，
或在他眼睛闭上时才到达。
只有他航行的那个地区，

He wots of; only the thoughts,
Raised by the objects he passes, are his.

Who can see the green earth any more
As she was by the sources of Time?
Who imagines her fields as they lay
In the sunshine, unworn by the plough?
   Who thinks as they thought,
The tribes who then roam'd on her breast,
Her vigorous primitive sons?

   What girl
Now reads in her bosom as clear
As Rebekah read, when she sate
At eve by the palm-shaded well?
   Who guards in her breast
As deep, as pellucid a spring
Of feeling, as tranquil, as sure?

   What bard,
At the height of his vision, can deem
Of God, of the world, of the soul,
   With a plainness as near,
As flashing as Moses felt,
When he lay in the night by his flock
On the starlit Arabian waste?
   Can rise and obey

他才知道;只有他经过的 25
那些景物引起的思想,才属于他。

谁能再看看那绿色的大地,
紧挨在时间的源头旁边?
谁能想象到这大地上的田土,
躺在阳光下,还没有用犁头耕过? 30
 谁能有他们的想法,
那些在大地上流浪过的部落,
大地健壮而原始的儿子们?

 什么姑娘
现在在心中理解得像丽贝卡① 35
那样地清楚,当她黄昏时
坐在棕榈树荫下的水井边?
 谁在她怀抱里拥有着
同样一个深邃、透明、
平静、可靠的感情的源泉? 40

 什么歌手
能够在他那幻想的峰顶上,
评价上帝、世界和灵魂,
 用摩亚所感到的同样亲切②、
同样闪光的平易的语言, 45
当他夜间躺在他的羊群边,
在星光灿烂的阿拉伯荒原上?
 谁能够像他一样

---

① 丽贝卡,也译加百利,见《创世记》第二十四章;不过,在《圣经》的故事里,丽贝卡并没有坐在水井边,只是在井旁去打水。——译者
② 摩西,以色列人的先知和立法者,见《出埃及记》第三章。——译者

The beck of the Spirit like him?

50

This tract which the river of Time
Now flows through with us, is the plain.
Gone is the calm of its earlier shore.
Border'd by cities, and hoarse
With a thousand cries is its stream.

55

And we on its breast, our minds
Are confused as the cries which we hear,
Changing and shot as the sights which we see[①].

And we say that repose has fled
For ever the course of the river of Time.

60

That cities will crowd to its edge
In a blacker incessanter line;
That the din will be more on its banks,
Denser the trade on its stream,
Flatter the plain where it flows,

65

Fiercer the sun overhead.
That never will those on its breast
See an ennobling sight,
Drink of the feeling of quiet again.

But what was before us we know not,

70

And we know not what shall succeed.

Haply, the river of Time,
As it grows, as the towns on its marge
Fling their wavering lights

---

① *shot*: 'variegated.'

站起来听从圣灵的召唤？

  时间的长河同我们一道
流过的这个地区,是平原。
 它那早先的河岸的宁静消失了。
  与城市接界的、嘶哑地发出
  千百个喊声的,是它的流水。
  而我们在水上,我们的内心
  像我们听见的喊声一样混乱,
像我们看见的景象一样变化多端。

  因此我们说:安静已经
永远逃离了时间的长河的航道;
  一座座城市将拥挤到河边,
  变成一条更黑更连续的线;
  河岸上将有更多的喧闹声,
  河流上将有更稠密的交易,
  它流过的平原将更加平坦,
  头上的太阳将晒得更猛烈;
  而那些航行在河面上的人
  将再也看不到庄严的景物,
再也体会不到那种宁静的感觉。

  但我们以前的,我们不知道,
  将要发生的,我们也不知道。

  或许,这条时间的长河,
  随着它的壮大,随着河边的城市
  将它们闪烁的灯光投射到

On a wider, statelier stream —
May acquire, if not the calm
Of its early mountainous shore,
Yet a solemn peace of its own.

And the width of the waters, the hush
Of the grey expanse where he floats,
Freshening its current and spotted with foam
As it draws to the Ocean, may strike
Peace to the soul of the man on its breast;
As the pale waste widens around him —
As the banks fade dimmer away —
As the stars come out, and the night-wind
    Brings up the stream
Murmurs and scents of the infinite Sea.

M. ARNOLD.

一条更宽广、更雄伟的河水上——
　　　会获得它自己庄严的宁静。　　　　　　　　　75
　　如果不是它那早先的
　　　高山河岸的宁静的话。

　　而当它流向海洋的时候，
　　　那河面的广阔，他所航行的
　　灰白色河流的静寂无声，　　　　　　　　　　80
　　　它那精神饱满的、点缀着泡沫的流水，
　　可能使那个漂泊者的灵魂感受到平静；
　　　随着苍茫的大海在周围展开——
　　　随着河岸更加朦胧地后退——
　　　随着星星的出现和夜风　　　　　　　　　　85
　　　　带来的潮水的
　　哗哗声和那浩瀚无边的大海的气味。

邹　绛　译

编注　一般说来，阿诺德的诗都对生活取悲观态度，此诗亦是如此。面对空前扩张的生产，资本主义的迅速发展，诗人的内心是苦闷的，深切地缅怀逝去的一切，宣称"但我们以前的，我们不知道，将要发生的，我们也不知道"。只是到了诗末，才透出少许希望的气息。该诗选自诗集《埃特纳山上的恩培多克勒及其他》。

369. PHILOMELA

Hark! ah, the nightingale!
　　The tawny-throated!
Hark! from that moonlit cedar what a burst!
　　What triumph! hark — what pain!

O wanderer from a Grecian shore,
Still, after many years, in distant lands,
Still nourishing in thy bewilder'd brain
That wild, unquench'd, deep-sunken, old-world pain —
　　Say, will it never heal?

And can this fragrant lawn
　　With its cool trees, and night,
　　And the sweet, tranquil Thames,
　　And moonshine, and the dew,
To thy rack'd heart and brain
　　Afford no balm?

Dost thou to-night behold,
Here, through the moonlight on this English grass,
The unfriendly palace in the Thracian wild?
　　Dost thou again peruse
　　With hot cheeks and sear'd eyes
The too clear web, and thy dumb sister's shame?
　　Dost thou once more assay
　　Thy flight, and feel come over thee,

369. 夜莺

阿诺德

听呀！哦，夜莺！
　　颈前长黄毛的鸟儿！
听！从月色朦胧的雪松里，响起了多婉转的歌声！
　　多么悠扬！听——又是多么哀伤！

　你是从希腊的海岸飘泊来的， 5
可过了这么多年，在遥远的国土里，
你迷茫的小脑袋中依旧怀着
往日无法扑灭的、无比深沉的哀痛——
　　唉，难道你的创伤永远无法消融？

　难道这片芬芳的草地， 10
　　草地上凉爽的树丛，夜色，
还有风光旖旎、静静流着的泰晤士河，
　　以及月光和露珠，
都不能为你那颗破碎的心
　　带来一丝儿慰藉？ 15

　莫非你今夜在这里，
透过这片英国草地上的月光，
看到了色雷斯荒原上那座满怀敌意的宫殿？
　　莫非你又一次
　　　两颊发烧，欲哭无泪， 20
看到了那幅极其光洁的织物，和你那哑了的妹妹蒙受的耻辱
　　难道你企图再一次远走高飞，
　　　而且又一次感到在你身上，

    Poor fugitive, the feathery change
25   Once more, and once more seem to make resound
    With love and hate, triumph and agony,
    Lone Daulis, and the high Cephissian vale?
     Listen, Eugenia —
    How thick the bursts come crowding through the leaves!
30   Again — thou hearest?
     Eternal passion!
     Eternal pain!

             M. ARNOLD.

可怜的逃亡者,忽然长满了羽毛,
同时想再一次让自己嘹亮的歌声　　　　　　　　　25
怀着爱与恨,欢悦和哀痛,
响彻幽寂的多利斯和塞费色斯高山深谷①?
　听呀,欧吉妮亚——
从树叶缝里泻下一阵阵的鸣啭声多么激昂而深沉!
　你还听到了什么?　　　　　　　　　　　　　30
　永恒的激情!
　永恒的悲痛!

钱鸿嘉　译

编注　此诗为阿诺德的最佳抒情诗之一,多年来一直脍炙人口。此诗取材于希腊神话,详见本书卷一第34首注释。

---

① 多利斯,古希腊城市名。塞费色斯系一道河谷。——译者

370. REQUIESCAT[①]

Strew on her roses, roses,
   And never a spray of yew.
In quiet she reposes;
   Ah! would that I did too.

Her mirth the world required;
   She bathed it in smiles of glee.
But her heart was tired, tired,
   And now they let her be.

Her life was turning, turning,
   In mazes of heat and sound;
But for peace her soul was yearning,
   And now peace laps her round[②].

Her cabin'd, ample spirit,
   It flutter'd and fail'd for breath,
To-night it doth inherit
   The vasty hall of death.

M. ARNOLD.

---

① *Requiescat*: 'may she rest.'
② *laps*: 'wraps,' 'folds.' Cf. No. 34, l. 24.

370. 安灵曲

阿诺德

用玫瑰花、玫瑰花覆盖伊，
　　却决不要一枝紫杉！
她安静地卧着休息：
　　啊，愿我也能长眠！

世界曾需要她的欢笑； 5
　　她曾以欢欣的微笑浸润它。
但她的心是倦了、倦了，
　　现在他们就不打扰她。

她的生活本在转动，
　　转动于兴奋与喧嚣的迷境中。 10
但她的灵魂在渴求安宁，
　　而现在安宁将她包笼。

她受束缚的、丰富的精神，
　　它颤动，它不济——气息已荒。
今夜它确实继承 15
　　这宏大的死亡之堂。

鲍屡平　译

371. THE SCHOLAR GIPSY

'*There was very lately a lad in the University of Oxford, who was by his poverty forced to leave his studies there; and at last to join himself to a company of vagabond gipsies. Among these extravagant people, by the insinuating subtilty of his carriage, he quickly got so much of their love and esteem as that they discovered to him their mystery. After he had been a pretty while well exercised in the trade, there chanced to ride by a couple of scholars, who had formerly been of his acquaintance. They quickly spied out their old friend among the gipsies; and he gave them an account of the necessity which drove him to that kind of life, and told them that the people he went with were not such impostors as they were taken for, but that they had a traditional kind of learning among them, and could do wonders by the power of imagination, their fancy binding that of others: that himself had learned much of their art, and when he had compassed the whole secret, he intended, he said, to leave their company, and give the world an account of what he had learned.*'

—— GLANVIL'S *Vanity of Dogmatizing*, 1661.

  Go, for they call you, shepherd, from the hill!
  Go, shepherd, and untie the wattled cotes[①]!
   No longer leave thy wistful flock unfed,
   Nor let thy bawling fellows rack their throats[②],

---

① *wattled cotes*: 'sheds made of hurdles.'
② *rack*: 'strain,' with shouting to him to come.

371. 吉普赛学者

阿诺德

就在不久以前,牛津大学有一位青年,由于贫穷的缘故,不得不中辍学业,最后加入了一群流浪的吉普赛人。置身游荡的人群之中,他靠着自己机灵而又得体的举止,很快赢得了他们的爱戴和崇敬,他们甚至向他昭示了自己的奥秘。经过较长时间,这时他已熟悉他们的生活方式,他偶然遇到两位与他相识的学者,他们马上从吉普赛人中辨认出了自己的老朋友。他概述了驱使他投身那种生活的缘由,还告诉他们:他所追随的人群并非大家所认为的是一伙骗子,他们保存着一种传统的学问,能依靠想象创造奇迹,因为他们的想象可以融会别人的思维;他们的本领他已经学到不少。等他将全部奥秘完全掌握之后,他声称自己打算离开他们的队伍,把学会的艺术公诸于世。

——引自格兰威尔的著作《教条化的虚浮》(1661)①

去吧,牧童,他们在山上呼唤你!
去吧,牧童,打开篱笆的羊栏!
别让你的饥渴的羊群饿坏,
别让你的伙伴老在叫喊,

---

① 约瑟夫·格兰威尔(J. Glanvil,1636—1680),英国学者,曾就读于牛津大学埃克特和林肯学院,后来成为教会牧师和哲学家。《教条化的虚浮》又名《对见解的信心》,旨在为思想自由和实验主义的观点辩护。——译者

>   Nor the cropp'd grasses shoot another head①!
>   But when the fields are still,
>   And the tired men and dogs all gone to rest,
>   And only the white sheep are sometimes seen
>   Cross and recross the strips of moon-blanch'd green.
>   Come, shepherd, and again begin the quest!
>
>   Here, where the reaper was at work of late —
>   In this high field's dark corner, where he leaves
>   His coat, his basket, and his earthen cruse,
>   And in the sun all morning binds the sheaves,
>   Then here, at noon, comes back his stores to use —
>   Here will I sit and wait,
>   While to my ear from uplands far away
>   The bleating of the folded flocks is borne,
>   With distant cries of reapers in the corn —
>   All the live murmur of a summer's day.
>
>   Screen'd is this nook o'er the high, half-reap'd field,
>   And here till sun-down, shepherd, will I be!
>   Through the thick corn the scarlet poppies peep,
>   And round green roots and yellowing stalks I see
>   Pale blue convolvulus in tendrils creep;
>   And air-swept lindens yield
>   Their scent, and rustle down their perfumed showers
>   Of bloom on the bent grass where I am laid②,

---

① *shoot another head*: 'spring up again.'
② *bent grass*: termed also merely 'bent,' a rushlike grass with a stiff stem. The word in its secondary sense of a field where such grass grows appears in No. 358, l. 32.

不等啃过的草再长出来!　　　　　　　　5
　　但是当田野变得静寂,
疲乏的人畜都已睡稳,
　　只是偶尔看见白色的羊身
　　在镀上月色的绿地上徘徊,
这时来吧,牧童,再一次开始搜寻!　　　10

这儿,收割者不久前干过活计——
　　在这块高地的角落里,他留下
　　他的外衣、篮子和瓦罐,
整个上午他顶着日头束捆禾把,
　　到正午才回来取用自备的午餐——　　15
　　我就坐候在这里,
　　我的耳边传来远处高地
　　羊栏里羊群的咩咩叫唤,
　　收割人在麦田里的呼喊——
以及夏日里种种天籁之声。　　　　　　20

在这块半收地掩护着的角落,
　　我将躺下,变成牧童,直到日落西边!
　　茂密的麦田里钻出殷红的罂粟,
绿根黄杆的麦田周围,我看见
　　浅蓝的牵牛花上爬,攀着卷须;　　　25
　　摇曳的椴树枝喷发出
芬芳,馥郁的花朵纷纷飘散
　　在我躺卧的荒草地上,

  And bower me from the August sun with shade;
  And the eye travels down to Oxford's towers.

  And near me on the grass lies Glanvil's book —
   Come, let me read the oft-read tale again!
   The story of that Oxford scholar poor,
   Of shining parts and quick inventive brain,
    Who, tired of knocking at preferment's door,
     One summer morn forsook
   His friends, and went to learn the gipsy lore,
   And roam'd the world with that wild brotherhood,
   And came, as most men deem'd, to little good,
  But came to Oxford and his friends no more.

  But once, years after, in the country-lanes,
   Two scholars whom at college erst he knew[①]
   Met him, and of his way of life inquir'd.
   Whereat he answer'd, that the gipsy crew,
    His mates, had arts to rule as they desired
     The workings of men's brains;
   And they can bind them to what thoughts they will.
   'And I,' he said, 'the secret of their art,
   When fully learn'd, will to the world impart;
  But it needs heaven-sent moments for this skill!'

  This said, he left them, and return'd no more. —
  But rumours hung about the country-side

---

① *erst*: this word is often used in Spenser and Milton with the meaning 'a little while since,' but in this sense it is obsolete; with the meaning 'formerly,' which it has here, it is merely archaic.

浓荫遮住了八月的骄阳；
　　我极目远望，目光落在牛津塔尖。 　　　　30

我身旁的草地摆着格兰威尔的书本——
　　来吧，让我重温这常读的故事！
　　　它讲到一个牛津的穷学生，
　　具有过人的才华，聪颖的天资，
　　　他厌倦了叩启功名的门， 　　　　　　35
　　　　便在一个夏日的凌晨，
　　抛下朋友，去钻研吉普赛人的学问，
　　　同他们亲如手足，飘泊在世，
　　　照世人看来，没有多大出息，
　　也从此不见朋友，不回牛津。 　　　　　40

几年后的一天，在乡间的小路，
　　他在大学结识的两位学人
　　　遇见他，问起他的生活方式。
　　于是他说：那群吉普赛人，
　　　他的同伴，具有非凡的才智， 　　　　45
　　　　能随意左右人们的思路，
　　把别人拴死在他们的愿望上。
　　　他说："他们的艺术的奥秘，
　　　一旦充分掌握，我将公诸于世；
　　但要掌握这本领，需待天赐良机！" 　　50

说完便撇下他们，再不露面。
　　于是乡间流行种种传闻：

That the lost Scholar long was seen to stray,
Seen by rare glimpses, pensive and tongue-tied,
55   In hat of antique shape, and cloak of grey,
The same the gipsies wore.
Shepherds had met him on the Hurst in spring;
At some lone alehouse in the Berkshire moors,
On the warm ingle-bench, the smock-frock'd boors①
60   Had found him seated at their entering,

But, mid their drink and clatter, he would fly; —
And I myself seem half to know thy looks,
And put the shepherds, wanderer, on thy trace;
And boys who in lone wheatfields scare the rooks
65   I ask if thou hast pass'd their quiet place;
Or in my boat I lie
Moor'd to the cool bank in the summer heats,
Mid wide grass meadows which the sunshine fills,
And watch the warm green-muffled Cumner hills,
70   And wonder if thou haunt'st their shy retreats.

For most, I know, thou lov'st retired ground!
Thee, at the ferry, Oxford riders blithe,
Returning home on summer nights, have met
Crossing the stripling Thames at Bablock-hithe,
75   Trailing in the cool stream thy fingers wet,
As the punt's rope chops round②;
And leaning backward in a pensive dream,

---

① *ingle-bench*: 'seat nearest the fire'; see note to No. 270, l. 16.
② *chops*: 'suddenly shifts.'

有人瞥见失踪的学者飘泊四方,
消失在瞬间,一副沉郁缄默的神情,
　　头戴古式的帽子,身披灰色大氅,
　　和吉普赛人一模一样。
春天,牧童遇见他在赫尔斯特山岭①;
在伯克郡荒野的偏僻酒店,
　　身穿长衫的村民在进店的瞬间,
　　发现他坐在靠火炉的暖和长凳,

饮酒交谈之间,他却悄然溜走。
然而你的容貌我已大致熟谙,
　　于是派牧童寻找你的行迹;
僻静的麦田,有嬉赶白嘴鸦的少年,
　　我问他们,可曾见你打那儿过去。
　　我或许躺卧小舟
停靠在盛夏的阴凉河岸,
　　周围是广阔的草地,阳光耀眼,
　　远眺暖烘烘绿绒般的坎纳山峦②,
我捉摸:你可时常出没隐蔽的山间。

我知道,你最喜欢僻静的地面!
　　欢乐的牛津骑士夏夜回返,
　　在巴罗海斯渡口曾同你③
横渡生气盎然的泰晤士河面,
　　你任手指漂在凉爽的水里,
　　像小船系岸的摆动绳缆;
　　你背靠船舷,陷入沉思的梦幻,

---

① 赫尔斯特,位于牛津西南的一处山林。——译者
② 坎纳山峦,位于牛津以西约三英里的地方。——译者
③ 巴罗海斯渡口,泰晤士河上,坎纳山以外约三英里的地方。——译者

And fostering in thy lap a heap of flowers
Pluck'd in shy fields and distant Wychwood bowers,
80   And thine eyes resting on the moonlit stream!

And then they land, and thou art seen no more!
Maidens who from the distant hamlets come
To dance around the Fyfield elm in May,
Oft through the darkening fields have seen thee roam,
85   Or cross a stile into the public way.
Oft thou hast given them store
Of flowers — the frail-leaf'd, white anemone,
Dark bluebells drench'd with dews of summer eves,
And purple orchises with spotted leaves —
90   But none has words she can report of thee[1].

And, above Godstow Bridge, when hay-time 's here
In June, and many a scythe in sunshine flames,
Men who through those wide fields of breezy grass
Where black-wing'd swallows haunt the glttering Thames,
95   To bathe in the abandon'd lasher pass[2],
Have often pass'd thee near
Sitting upon the river bank o'ergrown;
Mark'd thine outlandish garb, thy figure spare,
Thy dark vague eyes, and soft abstracted air —
100   But, when they came from bathing, thou wert gone[3]!

At some lone homestead in the Cumner hills,

---

[1] *words she can report of thee*: i.e. none of the maidens could say she had heard him speak.

[2] *lasher*: 'pool below the weir,' a term mainly confined to the Thames.

[3] *wert*: see note to No. 241, l. 2.

1594

　　　　膝头上簇拥一堆鲜花，
　　　　采自幽静的田野和威奇伍德的山崖①，
　　　　你的目光凝望着月色笼罩的河面！　　　　　　　　　80

当他们抵岸，却不见你的踪影！
　　少女，从遥远的村庄前来
　　　参加五月在怀菲尔德的榆下舞蹈②，
　　常常见你在幽暗的田野徘徊，
　　　或者越过篱边走上大道，　　　　　　　　　　　　85
　　　　你总是馈送她们以采撷的
　　花朵——叶片易损的银莲花，
　　　深蓝色的风信子，结着夏晚露珠，
　　　以及紫色兰，叶片带着斑点纹路——
　　但是问起你，她们谁也无言对答。　　　　　　　　　90

在戈兹多桥头，到了晒干草的时间③——
　　六月，大镰刀在阳光下挥舞闪亮；
　　　割草人走过微风吹的宽阔草地——
　　那儿黑翅的群燕飞向泰晤士河上，
　　　到往日的堰塘里浴洗，　　　　　　　　　　　　　95
　　　　常常掠过你的身边，
　　你正坐在野草丛生的河岸，
　　　注意到你古怪的服装，消瘦的形影，
　　　你两眼迷离，一副超脱的神情——
　　等他们浴毕回转，你却早已走远！　　　　　　　　　100

　　在坎纳山中的某个僻静家宅，

---

① 威奇伍德，一片森林的名字，其边缘距牛津约十四英里。——译者
② 怀菲尔德，位于坎纳山之外，距牛津约八英里。——译者
③ 戈兹多桥，在泰晤士河上，位于牛津上游约三英里的地方。——译者

Where at her open door the housewife darns,
    Thou hast been seen, or hanging on a gate
    To watch the threshers in the mossy barns.
105   Children, who early range these slopes and late
        For cresses from the rills,
    Have known thee watching, all an April day①,
    The springing pastures and the feeding kine;
    And mark'd thee, when the stars come out and shine,
110   Through the long dewy grass move slow away.

    In autumn, on the skirts of Bagley-wood,
    Where most the gipsies by the turf-edged way
        Pitch their smoked tents, ant every bush you see
    With scarlet patches tagg'd and shreds of grey②,
115   Above the forest-ground call'd Thessaly③—
        The blackbird picking food
    Sees thee, nor stops his meal, nor fears at all!
    So often has he known thee past him stray
    Rapt, twirling in thy hand a wither'd spray,
120   And waiting for the spark from Heaven to fall.

    And once, in winter, on the causeway chill
    Where home through flooded fields foot-travellers go,
    Have I not pass'd thee on the wooden bridge
    Wrapt in thy cloak and battling with the snow
125   Thy face toward Hinksey and its wintry ridge?
        And thou hast climb'd the hill

---

① *watching*: altered to 'haunting' in 1869, and again to 'eyeing' in 1890.
② *tagg'd*: 'having bits of rags hanging on it.'
③ *Thessaly*: this does not appear to have been identified.

主妇坐在敞开的门边织补,
　　抬头见你在门外徘徊,
观望打谷人在长苔藓的谷仓忙碌。
　　儿童,一早去山坡打草,晚来　　　　　　　105
　　　从小溪采回水芹菜,
看见你整日整日地注视
　　兴旺的四月牧场和放牧的牛群;
　　当天幕上闪现出点点繁星,
你却踏着带露的草地缓缓离去。　　　　　　110

秋天,在巴格利森林周围①,
　　许多吉普赛人沿小径两边
　　　搭起一个个熏黑的帐蓬,
灰白的和猩红的颜色成块成团,
　　遍及塞萨利山林的灌丛——　　　　　　115
　　　一只正在啄食的画眉
看看你,继续进食毫无惧怕,
　　因为常常见你从它身旁过去,
　　手里专注地搓动一节凋萎的树枝,
静待着灵感的火花从天降下。　　　　　　120

有一次,在冬天的寒冷堤道,
　　行人穿过淹过的田地归家,
　　　我不正好在木桥上经过你身边——
你身披大氅,迎着漫天雪花,
　　面对欣克塞及其肃杀的群山②?　　　　125
　　　你终于爬上山巅,

---

① 巴格利森林,在通向阿宾顿的路上,离牛津约三英里。——译者
② 欣克塞,位于牛津与坎纳山之间,在大道的南面。——译者

And gain'd the white brow of the Cumner range;
　　Turn'd once to watch, while thick the snowflakes fall,
　　　The line of festal light in Christ-Church hall —
130　　Then sought thy straw in some sequester'd grange.

But what — I dream! Two hundred years are flown
　　Since first thy story ran through Oxford halls,
　　　And the grave Glanvil did the tale inscribe
　　That thou wert wander'd from the studious walls
135　　To learn strange arts, and join a gipsy tribe.
　　　And thou from earth art gone
　　Long since, and in some quiet churchyard laid!
　　　Some country nook, where o'er thy unknown grave
　　　Tall grasses and white flowering nettles wave —
140　　Under a dark red-fruited yew-tree's shade.

— No, no, thou hast not felt the lapse of hours!
　　For what wears out the life of mortal men?
　　　'Tis that from change to change their being rolls;
　　　'Tis that repeated shocks, again, again,
145　　　Exhaust the energy of strongest souls,
　　　　And numb the elastic powers.
　　Till having used our nerves with bliss and teen[①],
　　　And tired upon a thousand schemes our wit,
　　　To the just-pausing Genius we remit
150　　Our well-worn life, and are — what we have been!

Thou hast not lived, why should'st thou perish, so?
Thou hadst *one* aim, *one* business, *one* desire!

---

① *teen*: 'suffering'.

站在白雪皑皑的坎纳山脊；
　大雪纷飞，你犹回首翘望
　基督教堂映射出的欢乐灯光，
然后再到某个隐蔽的去处歇宿。　　　　　　　　　　130

我可在做梦！两百年已经过去，
　自从你的轶事响彻牛津的厅堂；
　严肃的格兰威尔十分认真
记下你的故事：你离开学府高墙
　去追随吉普赛人，学习神秘的学问。　　　　　　　135
　　然而你早已辞别人世，
躺进了某个静寂的教堂墓地
　或某个村野角落，在你无名的坟上，
　开白花的荨麻同野草争相竞长——
坟头的浆果紫杉，枝叶浓郁。　　　　　　　　　　140

——不，你不曾感到岁月的流逝！
是什么消磨掉世人的生命？
　是生活中无穷无尽的变化，
是层出不穷的震惊，
　最强壮的人也精疲力乏，　　　　　　　　　　　145
　　最富弹性的活力也麻木松弛。
直到喜怒哀乐折断我们的神经，
　明争暗斗耗尽我们的才智，
　我们甘愿向公正的精神主子
交出疲惫的生命，恢复自己的原形。　　　　　　　150

你不曾经历这些，怎么会逝去？
　你只有唯一的目标、事业和心愿；

    Else wert thou long since number'd with the dead①—
    Else hadst thou spent, like other men, thy fire!
155   The generations of thy peers are fled.
      And we ourselves shall go;
    But thou possessest an immortal lot,
     And we imagine thee exempt from age
     And living as thou liv'st on Glanvil's page,
160   Because thou hadst — what we, alas, have not!

    For early didst thou leave the world, with powers
     Fresh, undiverted to the world without,
      Firm to their mark, not spent on other things;
     Free from the sick fatigue, the languid doubt,
165   Which much to have tried, in much been baffled, brings.
      O life unlike to ours!
    Who fluctuate idly without term or scope,
     Of whom each strives, nor knows for what he strives,
     And each half lives a hundred different lives;
170   Who wait like thee, but not, like thee, in hope.

    Thou waitest for the spark from Heaven: and we,
     Light half-believers of our casual creeds,
      Who never deeply felt, nor clearly will'd,
     Whose insight never has borne fruit in deeds,
175   Whose vague resolves never have been fulfill'd;
      For whom each year we see
    Breeds new beginnings, disappointments new;
     Who hesitate and falter life away,
     And lose to-morrow the ground won to-day —

---

  ① *wert* : here subjunctive, 'wouldst be,' put for 'wouldst have been.'

否则你也早就加入了死者行列,
像世人那样,熄灭了你生命的火焰!
　你一代的万千生灵已经与世诀别,
　　我们也将一同归去。
然而,你保持着不朽的生机,
　在我们的想象里你超越了时代,
　　像在格兰威尔的书本中永生长在,
因为你具有的,正是我们缺少的东西!

由于早辞人间,你的青春活力
　没有耗费在人寰尘世,
有了坚定的目标,精力没有分散;
　免受了令人厌倦的辛劳和疑虑
　　带来的种种烦恼和难堪。
　　　啊,这与我们的生活迥异!
我们的生活道路坎坷,漫无目的,
　大家都在纷争,却不知为了什么,
　　扮演不同的角色,都在同样蹉跎,
　我们也在等待,但没有希望,不像你。

你等待天赐的灵感,而我们
　随遇而安,没有自己坚定的信念。
　　从没有深刻的感受,明确的决心,
我们的见解从未在行动中兑现,
　我们模糊的打算从未实行;
　　我们看见年复一年
带来新的开端,接着是新的失败;
　我们的岁月在犹豫中蹉跎虚掷,
　　今天取得阵地明天却又丧去。

155

160

165

170

175

                    Ah, do not we, wanderer, await it too?

                Yes! we await it, but it still delays,
                    And then we suffer! and amongst us one,
                        Who most has suffer'd, takes dejectedly
                    His seat upon the intellectual throne;
                        And all his store of sad experience he
                            Lays bare of wretched days;
                    Tells us his misery's birth and growth and signs,
                        And how the dying spark of hope was fed,
                        And how the breast was soothed, and how the head,
                    And all his hourly varied anodynes①.

                This for our wisest! and we others pine,
                    And wish the long unhappy dream would end,
                        And waive all claim to bliss, and try to bear②,
                    With close-lipp'd patience for our only friend,
                        Sad patience, too near neighbour to despair;
                            But none has hope like thine!
                    Thou through the fields and through the woods dost stray,
                        Roaming the country-side, a truant boy,
                        Nursing thy project in unclouded joy,
                    And every doubt long blown by time away.

                O born in days when wits were fresh and clear,
                    And life ran gaily as the sparkling Thames;
                        Before this strange disease of modern life,
                    With its sick hurry, its divided aims,

---

① *anodynes*: 'drugs to alleviate pain.'
② *to bear*: sc. to bear up.

噢,游荡者,我们不也在把灵感等待! 180

是的,我们在等待,但它迟迟不来,
　　我们忍受苦痛!我们之中唯有一个,
　　经受了最大折磨的人,不情愿地①
登上了知识界的宝座;
　　然后将他在不幸的年月里 185
　　　　蕴集的痛苦经历公开;
告诉我们他的可悲身世和阅历,
　　微弱的希望之光如何得以维系,
　　如何安静头脑,如何镇定心绪,
以及他时常感到的种种慰藉。 190

那是大智者!我们其余人望尘莫及,
　　唯愿漫长的恶梦早到尽头,
　　放弃对幸福的追求,努力容忍,
以紧闭双唇的耐性作为唯一朋友,
　　可悲的耐性,绝望的近邻, 195
　　　　但谁能像你那样具有希望!
尽管你流浪在田野和树林,
　　像一个逃学的孩童徘徊在乡下,
　　以爽朗的喜悦抚育着你的计划,
心中的疑虑却早被时间荡涤无存。 200

呵,你出生的岁月才智清明,
　　生命像闪光的泰晤士河向前流淌,
　　未识现代生活的奇疾怪状:
没有统一的目标,到处病态般的繁忙,

---

① 所指说法不一,一说指德国诗人歌德,一说指英国诗人丁尼生。——译者

        Its heads o'ertax'd, its palsied hearts, was rife —
            Fly hence, our contact fear!
        Still fly, plunge deeper in the bowering wood!
        Averse, as Dido did with gesture stern①
        From her false friend's approach in Hades turn,
        Wave us away, and keep thy solitude!

    Still nursing the unconquerable hope,
        Still clutching the inviolable shade,
            With a free onward impulse brushing through,
            By night, the silver'd branches of the glade —
        Far on the forest-skirts, where none pursue,
            On some mild pastoral slope
        Emerge, and resting on the moonlit pales,
        Freshen thy flowers, as in former years,
            With dew, or listen with enchanted ears,
        From the dark dingles, to the nightingales!

    But fly our paths, our feverish contact fly!
        For strong the infection of our mental strife,
            Which, though it gives no bliss, yet spoils for rest;
            And we should win thee from thy own fair life,
        Like us distracted, and like us unblest②!
            Soon, soon thy cheer would die,
        Thy hopes grow timorous, and unfix'd thy powers,

---

① *Averse*: 'turning away.'
② *Like us* etc.: sc. to become distracted like us.

令人心力交瘁,晕头转向。 *205*
　　因此去吧,别同我们接近!
远远离去,投入幽暗的树林!
像狄多在冥界毅然转身,
　　当她伪善的朋友朝她走近①,
去吧,隐居独处,远离我们! *210*

继续孕育那不可抑制的希望,
　　继续占据那不可侵犯的树荫,
让内心的情感自由迸喷:
晚间,泻下林间空地的月光如银——
　　在森林的边缘地带,那儿出没无人, *215*
　　或在某个芳草茵茵的山冈
露面,斜倚在月照的篱栏,
　　同往年那样,让露水滋润
你的花朵,如醉如痴地倾听
从幽暗深谷传来的夜莺的哀怨。 *220*

避开我们的路径,避免我们病狂的接触!
　　我们内心的混乱极易传染,
　　它不能造福,反为他人带来损害;
我们会夺走你生活中唯有的恬淡,
　　使你像我们一样陷入不幸和困惑。 *225*
　　不用多久,你的欢乐便会结束,
你的希望会变得拘谨,你的活力散失,

---

① 典出古罗马诗人维吉尔的史诗《埃涅阿斯纪》第六卷。狄多为迦太基的女王,伊尼亚斯(特洛亚的一个王子)在特洛亚被希腊联军攻陷之后,携老幼出走,在海上漂泊七年后抵达迦太基,受到女王狄多的盛情款待,并与女王相爱结婚。但由于神的旨意,伊尼亚斯必须弃狄多而到意大利重建国家,于是狄多自杀身亡。后来伊尼亚斯游历冥府,见到狄多的亡灵而招呼走近她时,她立即转身以背相对。——译者

And thy clear aims be cross and shifting made;
And then thy glad perennial youth would fade,
230   Fade, and grow old at last, and die like ours.

Then fly our greetings, fly our speech and smiles!
— As some grave Tyrian trader, from the sea,
Descried at sunrise an emerging prow
Lifting the cool-hair'd creepers stealthily,
235   The fringes of a southward-facing brow
Among the Aegean isles;
And saw the merry Grecian coaster come,
Freighted with amber grapes, and Chian wine,
Green bursting figs, and tunnies steep'd in brine;
240   And knew the intruders on his ancient home,

The young light-hearted masters of the waves;
And snatch'd his rudder, and shook out more sail,
And day and night held on indignantly
O'er the blue Midland Waters with the gale①,
245   Betwixt the Syrtes and soft Sicily,
To where the Atlantic raves
Outside the western straits, and unbent sails②
There, where down cloudy cliffs, through sheets of foam,

---

① *Midland*: a literal translation of 'Mediterranean.'
② *unbent sails*: 'lowered his sails.'

你的明确目标变得模糊,动摇不定,
　　然后你欢乐常在的青春就会凋零,
　　凋零,最后老态龙钟,像我们一样死去。　　　　　*230*

避免同我们招呼、谈话和微笑!
　　——像那庄重的蒂尔商人,当旭日初照①,
　　发现海面上出现了一艘船,
　　正悄悄把掀起的毛茸茸的水草
　　　覆上船南面的边沿,　　　　　　　　　　　　*235*
　　　　前面是爱琴海诸岛;
他看见这希腊海船轻快地行进,
满载希俄斯美酒,琥珀般的葡萄粒②,
鲜绿欲绽的无花果,盐腌的金枪鱼,
　　他知道这些是侵占他故土的敌人③,　　　　　　*240*

如今成了海上欢乐的年轻主人。
　　他掌稳船舵,扬起其余船帆,
　　不分昼夜,迎着大风大浪
　　愤然驶过蔚蓝的地中海面,
　　　从西西里港到西尔特港④,　　　　　　　　　*245*
　　　　直抵大西洋海域,
　　穿出直布罗陀海峡,然后放下船帆,
　　　在高耸的悬崖之下,从泡沫的海面,

---

① 蒂尔商人,即古腓尼基商人。蒂尔是腓尼基南部的一个海港城邦,在今之黎巴嫩。——译者
② 希俄斯岛在爱琴海上,离亚洲海岸仅五英里左右,岛上以盛产美酒闻名。——译者
③ 蒂尔城邦的腓尼基人是历史上最早的航海家。为发展商业,他们在非洲和西班牙西部海岸建立了不少殖民地。诗人在这里用希腊人喻英国的贸易和海上霸权,即抢夺了蒂尔人(喻吉普赛学者)昔日的海上优势的英国当代人。——编注者
④ 非洲北部的两个海港。——编注者

Shy traffickers, the dark Iberians come;
And on the beach undid his corded bales.

M. ARNOLD.

黝黑的伊比利亚商人怯生生地出现①,
将捆束的大包货物运上海边。

蓝仁哲　译

编注　本诗素材取自格兰威尔的著作《教条化的虚浮》(*The Vanity of Dogmatizing, or Confidence in Opinion*),书中谈到牛津大学的一位学生辍学,追随吉普赛人的轶事。诗人通过对这个故事的沉思冥想、吉普赛学者与世人相遇的各种想象情景以及劝其远避世人的忠告,寄托了对往昔岁月的向往和怀念之情,表达了诗人对自己所处的时代的愤懑和谴责。《吉普赛学者》是一首富于田园牧歌情调的抒情诗,诗中的吉普赛学者与其说是一位传说人物,不如说是一种生活方式的象征。

---

① 伊比利亚人,指西班牙半岛上的土著人。——译者

372. RUGBY CHAPEL

November, 1857

Coldly, sadly descends
The autumn evening! The field
Strewn with its dank yellow drifts
Of withered leaves, and the elms,
Fade into dimness apace,
Silent; — hardly a shout
From a few boys late at their play!
The lights come out in the street,
In the school-room windows; but cold,
Solemn, unlighted, austere,
Through the gathering darkness, arise
The chapel-walls, in whose bound
Thou, my father! art laid.

There thou dost lie, in the gloom
Of the autumn evening. But ah!
That word, *gloom*, to my mind
Brings thee back in the light
Of thy radiant vigour again!
In the gloom of November we pass'd
Days not of gloom at thy side;
Seasons impair'd not the ray

372. 拉格比公学的教堂
(一八五七年十一月)

阿诺德

冷冷地,凄清地降临了
秋天的夜晚!田野
积盖了一层阴湿发黄的
凋落叶片,榆树
淹进了沉沉的暮霭, 5
一片寂静——几乎不闻
儿童在晚间游戏的叫声!
街道上,教室的窗口
亮起了灯光;但清冷,
肃穆,无光,朴素, 10
透过渐渐暗黑的夜色,耸现出
教堂的墙壁,墙内
埋葬着您——我的父亲①。

您躺在那儿,陷进了
秋夜的**阴郁**。啊,可是, 15
"阴郁"这个词,却在我心上
唤回了您,再现了
您容光焕发的雄姿!
阴霾的十一月,在您身边
度过的却不是阴郁的日子; 20
时令掩不住

---

① 诗人的父亲托马斯·阿诺德博士曾任拉格比公学校长达十四年之久,逝世后埋葬在该校的教堂里。——译者

Of thine even cheerfulness clear.
Such thou wast! and I stand
In the autumn evening, and think
Of bygone autumns with thee.

Fifteen years have gone round
Since thou arosest to tread,
In the summer morning, the road
Of death, at a call unforeseen,
Sudden! For fifteen years,
We who till then in thy shade
Rested as under the boughs
Of a mighty oak, have endured
Sunshine and rain as we might,
Bare, unshaded, alone,
Lacking the shelter of thee!

O strong soul, by what shore
Tarriest thou now? For that force,
Surely, has not been left vain!
Somewhere, surely, afar,
In the sounding labour-house vast
Of being, is practised that strength,
Zealous, beneficent, firm!

Yes, in some far-shining sphere,
Conscious or not of the past,
Still thou performest the word
Of the Spirit in whom thou dost live —

您硬朗快活的光辉。
您总是那样!而今我站在
秋天的夜里,回忆
与您一起度过的那些秋日。

十五个年头已经过去①
自您猝然踏上,
在一个夏日的早晨,死亡之路,
响应了没有料到的召唤,
何其猝然!十五个年头,
我们,惯于在您的庇荫下
生活,像在一棵参天的橡树
的浓荫里,好容易
熬过了日晒雨淋,
没有遮掩,孤苦无依,
一旦失去了您的庇护!

啊,坚强的灵魂,如今
您系在彼岸的何处?您的力气,
一定没有虚掷!
在遥远的某个地方,
在某个宽敞嘈杂的工场,
正施展您那强大的力量,
满怀热忱,慈善,无限坚定!

是的,在某个光芒四射的地带,
无论意识不意识过去,
您生活在圣灵之中,
仍在执行圣灵的旨意——

---

① 阿诺德的父亲死于一八四二年六月十二日,本诗作于一八五七年秋。——译者

Prompt, unwearied, as here!
Still thou upraisest with zeal
The humble good from the ground,
Sternly repressest the bad!
Still, like a trumpet, dost rouse
Those who with half-open eyes
Tread the border-land dim
'Twixt vice and virtue; reviv'st,
Succourest! — this was thy work,
This was thy life upon earth.

What is the course of the life
Of mortal men on the earth? —
Most men eddy about
Here and there — eat and drink,
Chatter and love and hate,
Gather and squander, are raised
Aloft, are hurl'd in the dust,
Striving blindly, achieving
Nothing; and then they die —
Perish! and no one asks
Who or what they have been,
More than he asks what waves,
In the moonlit solitudes mild
Of the midmost Ocean, have swell'd,
Foam'd for a moment, and gone.

And there are some, whom a thirst
Ardent, unquenchable, fires,
Not with the crowd to be spent —
Not without aim to go round

果敢,不倦,一如在世间!
您仍在热情地扶持
低下弱小的良善, 50
严厉地压制邪恶!
像一只号角,仍在激励
那些半开半闭着眼
行走在昏暗的
善恶之间的界道的人们,振奋, 55
救助他们!! 这是您原来的工作,
这是您在世上的一生。

世上终归一死的人,
他们生命的历程是什么?——
他们大多数漂泊 60
无定——贪吃,好喝,
闲聊,喜爱,憎恨,
聚会,离散——时而被抛向
高处,时而被掷到地上;
盲目地纷争,到头来 65
一事无成;然后,他们死去——
消亡! 没有人会问
他们是谁,干过什么,
正像没有人会问,
在淡淡月色下孤寂的 70
海面中心,有什么波浪掀起,
溅出泡沫,然后消失无影。

然而也有人,燃烧着
热烈的难以平息的渴求,
不与芸芸众生为伍—— 75
即使在毫无意义的尘世,

In an eddy of purposeless dust,
Effort unmeaning and vain.
Ah yes, some of us strive
Not without action to die
Fruitless, but something to snatch
From dull oblivion, nor all
Glut the devouring grave!
We, we have chosen our path —
Path to a clear-purposed goal,
Path of advance! — but it leads
A long, steep journey, through sunk
Gorges, o'er mountains in snow!
Cheerful, with friends, we set forth —
Then, on the height, comes the storm!
Thunder crashes from rock
To rock, the cataracts reply;
Lightnings dazzle our eyes;
Roaring torrents have breach'd
The track — the stream-bed descends
In the place where the wayfarer once
Planted his footstep — the spray
Boils o'er its borders! aloft,
The unseen snow-beds dislodge
Their hanging ruin; — alas,
Havoc is made in our train!
Friends who set forth at our side
Falter, are lost in the storm!
We, we only, are left!
With frowning foreheads, with lips
Sternly compress'd, we strain on,
On — and at nightfall, at last,

徒劳无益,枉费心机,
也不是没有前进的目标。
噢,是的,我们之中有人奋斗,
并非没有行动,临死 80
一事无成,而是极力从湮没之中
攫取,并不甘愿
进入吞噬一切的坟墓!
我们,我们已选择自己的道路——
通向一个明确的目标, 85
一条前进的路!——但它引向
漫长、崎岖的途程,穿过断裂的
峡谷,越过白雪皑皑的高山!
我们欢乐地同朋友一道出发——
登上山顶,却遇到暴雨! 90
惊雷在山岩之间
震荡,迎来暴雨如泻;
闪电照得我们两眼昏眩;
轰鸣的洪流冲垮了
路道——河床塌陷,塌至 95
徒步的行人在往日里
踏步的地方——浪花
涌上河道两岸!高处,
看不见的雪基摇动
塌下覆盖的雪山;——哎呀, 100
这给我们带来了灾难!
我们身畔走着的朋友
站立不稳,栽入了雪坑!
我们,唯有我们,得以幸存!
带着深蹙的眉头,双唇 105
紧闭,我们艰难地前进,
前进——终于在日暮时分,

> Come to the end of our way,
> To the lonely inn 'mid the rocks;
> Where the gaunt and taciturn host
> Stands on the threshold, the wind
> Shaking his thin white hairs —
> Holds his lantern to scan
> Our storm-beat figures, and asks:
> Whom in our party we bring?
> Whom we have left in the snow?
>
> Sadly we anwer: We bring
> Only ourselves! we lost
> Sight of the rest in the storm!
> Hardly ourselves we fought through,
> Stripp'd, without friends, as we are!
> Friends, companions, and train
> The avalanche swept from our side.
>
> But thou would'st not *alone*
> Be saved, my father! *alone*
> Conquer and come to thy goal,
> Leaving the rest in the wild.
> We were weary, and we
> Fearful, and we, in our march,
> Fain to drop down and to die.
> Still thou turnedst, and still
> Beckonedst the trembler, and still
> Gavest the weary thy hand!
> If, in the paths of the world,
> Stones might have wounded thy feet,
> Toil or dejection have tried

抵达了我们行程的尽头,
岩石之间的一家孤独酒店;
憔悴沉默的店主人 110
站在门槛,清风
吹动他稀疏的白发——
他掌着灯笼一一细看
经受过暴风雨雪的人,问道:
我们带来了什么人? 115
有谁葬身于雪崩?

我们悲哀地答道:带来的
只有我们自己!暴风雪
使我们丧失了其余的人!
我们艰苦地跋涉, 120
失掉了朋友,只剩我们!
雪崩从我们身边夺走了
朋友,同伴,随行人。

但您绝不愿独自
得救,我们的父亲!**独自** 125
获胜,达到自己的目标,
而把别人遗弃在荒野。
我们疲惫不堪,我们
畏惧,我们在行程中
愿意随时倒下,死去。 130
您却会转过身,还要
招呼颤栗的人,还要向
疲惫者伸出您的手!
走在世间的坎坷小道,
假若石头砸伤了您的脚, 135
劳累或沮丧折磨了

Thy spirit, of that we saw
Nothing! to us thou wert still
Cheerful, and helpful, and firm.
140 Therefore to thee it was given
Many to save with thyself;
And, at the end of thy day,
O faithful shepherd! to come,
Bringing thy sheep in thy hand.

145 And through thee I believe
In the noble and great who are gone;
Pure souls honour'd and blest
By former ages, who else —
Such, so soulless, so poor,
150 Is the race of men whom I see —
Seem'd but a dream of the heart,
Seem'd but a cry of desire.
Yes! I believe that there lived
Others like thee in the past,
155 Not like the men of the crowd
Who all round me to-day
Bluster or cringe, and make life
Hideous, and arid, and vile;
But souls temper'd with fire,
160 Fervent, heroic, and good,
Helpers and friends of mankind.

Servants of God! — or sons
Shall I not call you? because
Not as servants ye knew
165 Your Father's innermost mind,

您的精神,我们会
毫无所知!我们见您总是
快活,坚定,乐于助人。
因此,您把救助 140
众人视为己任;
到您生命终结的一天,
啊,忠实的牧羊人!归来时,
牵回了您的羊群。

从您身上,我相信 145
逝去的那些高尚、伟大的人;
他们纯洁的心灵,受到
以往时代的崇敬,他们——
对于我所目睹的
没有灵魂、十分可悲的世人—— 150
仿佛只是心中向往的美梦,
仿佛只是内心渴求的呼喊。
是的!我相信曾经有过
像您这样的先辈,
不像而今在我周围的 155
熙熙攘攘的人群,
不是耀武扬威,便是卑躬屈膝,
使人生可憎,可厌,可鄙;
然而,经过烈火冶炼的人,
热情,英勇,真诚, 160
成了人类的扶助者和友人。

上帝的仆人!或者
该叫您上帝的儿子?因为
作为上帝的儿子,您才洞悉
天父的内心深处—— 165

His, who unwillingly sees
One of his little ones lost —
Yours is the praise, if mankind
Hath not as yet in its march
Fainted, and fallen, and died!

See! in the rocks of the world
Marches the host of mankind,
A feeble, wavering line!
Where are they tending? — A God
Marshall'd them, gave them their goal. —
Ah, but the way is so long!
Years they have been in the wild!
Sore thirst plagues them; the rocks,
Rising all round, overawe.
Factions divide them — their host
Threatens to break, to dissolve. —
Ah, keep, keep them combined!
Else, of the myriads who fill
That army, not one shall arrive!
Sole they shall stray; in the rocks
Labour for ever in vain[①],
Die one by one in the waste.

Then, in such hour of need
Of your fainting, dispirited race,
Ye, like angels, appear[②],
Radiant with ardour divine.

---

① *Labour*: altered to 'Stagger' in the 1890 edition.
② *Ye*: sc. the servants of God, l. 161.

他从心里不忍看见
自己宠爱的儿子殒去。
赞扬归于您,倘若人类
还没有在旅程中
昏厥,倒下,死去! 170

瞧! 在人间崎岖的路上
行走着成群结队的世人,
一支疲乏、稀拉的队伍!
他们正往何处?——某个神
集合了他们,指示了他们的目标—— 175
啊,但那路途何其遥远!
他们年年走在荒原!
饥渴折磨着他们;山岩,
四周兀立,令他们生畏。
内讧酿成不和——他们 180
面临着分崩、离散。
噢,维持,让他们维系在一起!
否则,无数人汇合的
大军里,谁也到达不了目标!
他们都将迷途;在岩石之间 185
永远徒劳无益,
一个一个地死在荒野。

当您的萎靡不振的同胞
迫切需要您的时候,
您像天使一般,显出 190
神圣而又炽烈的光采。

Beacons of hope, ye appear!
Languor is not in your heart,
Weakness is not in your word,
Weariness not on your brow.
Ye alight in our van! at your voice,
Panic, despair, flee away.
Ye move through the ranks, recall
The stragglers, refresh the outworn,
Praise, re-inspire the brave!
Order, courage, return.
Eyes rekindling, and prayers,
Follow your steps as ye go.
Ye fill up the gaps in our files,
Strengthen the wavering line,
Stablish, continue our march,
On, to the bound of the waste,
On, to the City of God!

M. ARNOLD.

您宛若希望的灯塔!
您的心中不存在消沉,
您的话语不缺乏力量,
您的眉梢不挂着倦意。 195
您出现在我们的前列!一声呼唤,
仓惶和绝望都逃得不见踪影。
您走在行列之间,剔除
扼杀者,振奋虚弱人,
赞扬、激励无畏的勇士! 200
于是,秩序和勇气得到复苏。
眼里闪着新生的目光,祈祷
紧紧跟随您的脚步。
您填补了我们队伍的裂缝,
加强了我们摇摆的行列, 205
稳定地继续向前迈进,
向前,朝着荒野的尽头,
向前,抵达上帝之城①。

蓝仁哲　译

编注 这首诗是诗人怀念父亲的诗作,也是对《爱丁堡评论》上刊载的一篇抑贬阿诺德博士的评论文章的回答。选自《新诗集》(*New Poems*,1867)。

---

① 指天堂。——译者

373. MIMNERMUS IN CHURCH

You promise heavens free from strife,
    Pure truth, and perfect change of will;
But sweet, sweet is this human life,
    So sweet, I fain would breathe it still;
Your chilly stars I can forgo,
This warm kind world is all I know.

You say there is no substance here,
    One great reality above:
Back from that void I shrink in fear,
    And childlike hide myself in love:
Show me what angels feel. Till then,
I cling, a mere weak man, to men.

You bid me lift my mean desires
    From faltering lips and fitful veins
To sexless souls, ideal quires[①],
    Unwearied voices, wordless strains:
My mind with fonder welcome owns
One dear dead friend's remembered tones.

Forsooth the present we must give
    To that which cannot pass away;
All beauteous things for which we live

[①] *quires*: for the spelling see note to No. 62, l. 115.

373. 明纳摩斯在教堂里

柯雷

你说天堂上没有争吵,
　　有纯正的真理,完美的志向;
但这人间是又美又好,
　　这样美,我愿永远活世上;
你的寒星我可以舍掉, 5
这温暖善良的世界我却要。

你说这世上是空空一片,
　　天上却有伟大的实在;
我却怕与空灵之界沾边,
　　隐身于爱中,像一个婴孩: 10
在了解天使的心情以前,
我这个弱者还依恋人间。

你要我把一切卑下的欲望,
　　从乖戾的脾性,颤抖的嘴唇,
升华为纯洁的心灵,完美的合唱, 15
　　天籁的曲调,不倦的声音;
我的心却以热烈的欢欣
珍藏着亡友个火的音韵。

诚然,为了永生的东西,
　　我们必须放弃现世; 20
我们生活中的一切美丽,

By laws of time and space decay.
But oh, the very reason why
I clasp them, is because they die.

W.J. CORY.

都将随时空规律而消逝。
但是哦,恰好因它们要衰亡,
我才抱住它们死不放。

袁可嘉　译

编注　威廉·约翰逊·柯雷(William Johnson Cory,1823—1892),曾任著名的伊登公学校长助理,是英国诗史上的"学者诗人"之一。

明纳摩斯为古希腊诗人,大约生活于公元前六三四至六〇〇年间。本诗表达了柯雷对教会的看法,是他炙人口的诗作,取自柯雷的诗集《爱奥利亚诗》(*Ionica*)。

374. HERACLITUS

They told me, Heraclitus, they told me you were dead,
They brought me bitter news to hear and bitter tears to shed.
I wept, as I remembered, how often you and I
Had tired the sun with talking and sent him down the sky.
And now that thou art lying, my dear old Carian guest,
A handful of grey ashes, long long ago at rest,
Still are thy pleasant voices, thy nightingales, awake;
For Death, he taketh all away, but them he cannot take.

W.J. CORY.

374. 赫拉克利图斯

柯雷

他们告诉我,赫拉克利图斯,他们告诉我你已身灭,
他们让我听到了悲痛的消息,流下了悲痛的泪滴。
我哭泣着,追忆我们常常在一起谈心,
谈得太阳也累了,在西天消隐。
如今你躺下了,卡利亚的老友,亲爱的, 5
一把青白的骨灰,永生永世地安息。
但你可爱的声音,你的夜莺,还在歌吟,
死神可以夺走一切,这个他却不行。

袁可嘉　译

编注 此诗原作者为卡利亚的卡利马朱斯(Callimachus,约于公元前240年去世)。原诗为六行,柯雷将其从希腊语译为英语。仅知道赫拉克利图斯为原作者的朋友。

375. AMATURUS[1]

Somewhere beneath the sun,
    These quivering heart-strings prove it,
Somewhere there must be one
    Made for this soul, to move it;
Some one that hides her sweetness
    From neighbours whom she slights,
Nor can attain completeness,
    Nor give her heart its rights;
Some one whom I could court
    With no great change of manner,
Still holding reason's fort,
    Though waving fancy's banner;
A lady, not so queenly
    As to disdain my hand,
Yet born to smile serenely
    Like those that rule the land;
Noble, but not too proud;
    With soft hair simply folded,
And bright face crescent-browed,
    And throat by Muses moulded;
And eyelids lightly falling
    On little glistening seas,
Deep-calm, when gales are brawling,
    Though stirred by every breeze:

---

[1] *Amaturus*: 'ready to fall in love.'

375. 爱之歌

柯雷

太阳下某个地方,
　这发颤的心弦将证明,
总有那么个姑娘,
　为感动它而生存;
她瞧不起的邻居前头, 5
　把自己的妩媚掩藏,
十全十美到不了手
　也不让心愿得偿;
这姑娘我可以追求,
　无须大改仪表, 10
把理性的堡垒坚守,
　虽得把幻想招摇;
这姑娘不自视太高,
　看不上我的追求,
天生会安详地微笑, 15
　就像一国的皇后;
她高贵而不骄逸,
　随便将柔发卷好,
眉如新月脸光洁,
　喉头是缪司塑造; 20
睫毛下垂轻又轻,
　眼是小海光闪耀,
狂风怒叫它若定,
　微风吹来它轻摇;

Swift voice, like flight of dove
    Through minster arches floating,
With sudden turns, when love
    Gets overnear to doting;
Keen lips, that shape soft sayings
    Like crystals of the snow,
With pretty half-betrayings
    Of things one may not know;
Fair hand, whose touches thrill,
    Like golden rod of wonder,
Which Hermes wields at will
    Spirit and flesh to sunder;
Light foot, to press the stirrup
    In fearlessness and glee,
Or dance, till finches chirrup,
    And stars sink to the sea.

Forth, Love, and find this maid,
    Wherever she be hidden:
Speak, Love, be not afraid,
    But plead as thou art bidden;
And say, that he who taught thee
    His yearning want and pain,
Too dearly, dearly bought thee
    To part with thee in vain.

W.J. CORY.

说话迅疾如鸽飞， 25
　　飞过教堂的拱门，
突然把身转过去，
　　当爱者做得太过分；
巧嘴说柔声细语，
　　就像雪珠般晶莹， 30
半吞半吐真有趣，
　　就是不让人知情；
素手一碰要销魂，
　　就像赫耳墨斯任意地①
挥舞神奇的金棍， 35
　　使灵魂与肉作分离；
双脚轻盈踢马镫，
　　快活，无畏又英勇，
或起舞，直至燕雀欢腾，
　　众星堕入大海中。 40

去吧，爱，去找她，
　　不管她藏在何处，
说吧，爱，别害怕，
　　就像教你的去劝诉；
告诉她，是他教了你 45
　　他的渴望和苦恼，
为你他费尽了心机，
　　再不能白白分离了。

袁可嘉　译

---

① 赫耳墨斯，希腊神话中众神的使者，亡灵的接引神，他手中的金棍是用来使人启闭眼用的。——译者

376. THE MARRIED LOVER

Why, having won her, do I woo?
Because her spirit's vestal grace
Provokes me always to pursue,
But, spirit-like, eludes embrace;
Because her womanhood is such
That, as on court-days subjects kiss①
The Queen's hand, yet so near a touch
Affirms no mean familiarness②;
Nay, rather marks more fair the height
Which can with safety so neglect
To dread, as lower ladies might,
That grace could meet with disrespect;
Thus she with happy favour feeds
Allegiance from a love so high
That thence no false conceit proceeds
Of difference bridged, or state put by;
Because, although in act and word
As lowly as a wife can be,
Her manners, when they call me lord,
Remind me 'tis by courtesy;
Not with her least consent of will,
Which would my proud affection hurt,

---

① *such That*: this sentence is completed by, 'she with happy favour feeds,' etc. (l. 13).
② *familiarness*: the substitute for 'familiarity.'

376. 婚后的情人

帕特摩

既已赢得她,为何还求爱?
　　因为她心灵的贞静、美好
总引得我把她追求,但是,
　　又像个精灵,总回避拥抱①;
因为她这女性任凭接近, 5
　　也总像女王在朝觐之日
伸手给她的臣民吻一吻——
　　却一点没有亲热的表示;
对,反更清楚地显出崇高,
　　凭这个,实在就无须害怕—— 10
不像位分较低的贵妇担心,
　　恩惠会得到不敬的报答。
这样,她用愉悦的恩典
　　从高尚的爱情中哺育忠诚——
这爱情没有妄自尊大, 15
　　以为差别已除、彼此平等;
因为,尽管作为一位妻子,
　　她言词和行动那样谦卑,
那尊我为一家之主的礼仪
　　却提醒我:"这是出于仁慧"; 20
倒不是她有丝毫这心思②——
　　那样会伤我自尊的感情,

---

① 与第二行呼应,是第五行中抽象女性的淑雅娟美特征,对之进行了人格化的描写。——编注者
② 意即:她并非有意显示她的敬从是出于礼貌,但我可以从她的举止中看出。——编注者

But by the noble style that still
    Imputes an unattain'd desert;
Because her gay and lofty brows,
    When all is won which hope can ask,
Reflect a light of hopeless snows
    That bright in virgin ether bask;
Because, though free of the outer court
    I am, this Temple keeps its shrine
Sacred to Heaven; because, in short,
    She's not and never can be mine.

C. PATMORE.

而是她有一种高贵气派——
这又归因于难得的品性；
因为她欢快的高高额头—— *25*
在希望赢得全部之后——
映出无望的雪光，这明亮的雪
正在贞洁的氛围中快乐悠悠。
因为，虽然我早不在外院，
这殿堂的神龛却已献天国； *30*
因为，归根结底的原因是——
她永远也不可能属于我。

黄杲炘　黄杲昶　译

编注 考文垂·科尔西·戴顿·帕特摩（Coventry Kersey Dighton Patmore，1823—1896）。英国诗人，曾在大英博物馆担任多年图书馆员，学识渊博，二十一岁时出版首卷《诗集》（*Poems*）著名长诗《家中的天使》(The Angel in the House，1854—1866)，详述人性爱和神性爱之间的关系，对后来的诗歌运动有一定影响。本篇选自该诗第二卷第十二歌。

377. THE TOYS

My little Son, who look'd from thoughtful eyes
And moved and spoke in quiet grown-up wise①,
Having my law the seventh time disobey'd,
    I struck him, and dismiss'd
    With hard words and unkiss'd,
His Mother, who was patient, being dead.
Then, fearing lest his grief should hinder sleep,
    I visited his bed,
    But found him slumbering deep,
With darken'd eyelids, and their lashes yet
    From his late sobbing wet.
    And I, with moan,
Kissing away his tears, left others of my own;
For, on a table drawn beside his head,
    He had put, within his reach,
A box of counters and a red-vein'd stone,
A piece of glass abraded by the beach②,
    And six or seven shells,
    A bottle with bluebells,
And two French copper coins, ranged there with careful art,
    To comfort his sad heart.
    So when that night I pray'd
    To God, I wept, and said:

---

① *wise*: 'manner,' seen in 'likewise,' 'otherwise.'
② *abraded*: 'worn.'

377. 玩具

帕特摩

我的小儿子,用若有所思的眼神观察着
说话做事变得从容老成,
由于第七次违犯我的规定,
 我打了他,让他走开,
 用粗暴的话骂他,也没吻他,   5
 他的妈妈,是个有耐心的人,去世了。
害怕他悲伤睡不着觉,
 我来到他的床前,
 却发现他已睡熟,
微黑的脸上,眼睫   10
 留下潮湿的泪迹。
  呵,我涌出一声叹息,
吻没他的泪痕,我却泪眼清清;
因为,在他头旁,一张小桌放在
 手能伸到的地方,上面他放有   15
一盒硬币,一颗赭红的大理石子,
海滩上打磨过的一片玻璃,
 六七个贝壳,
 装着箭兰风铃草的小瓶,
还有两枚法国铜币,全都小心地排着,   20
 都来安慰他受伤的心灵。
  呵,那晚,我在上帝面前祈祷,
  我哭着说:

    Ah, when at last we lie with trancéd breath,
      Not vexing Thee in death,
    And Thou rememberest of what toys
       We made our joys,
      How weakly understood
      Thy great commanded good,
      Then, fatherly not less
   Than I whom Thou hast moulded from the clay,
     Thou'lt leave Thy wrath, and say,
  'I will be sorry for their childishness.'

            C. PATMORE.

最终,我们会躺下昏昏睡去,
　　甚至死之中也不打搅天神, 25
　　你还记得那些玩具
　　　　曾使我们自己高兴,
　　你伟大支配的善呵,
　　我们对你理解多么浅薄,
　　你用泥土塑造了我 30
你对我仍怀有父亲之情,
　　你并没有大发雷霆,还说,
"我原谅他们的幼稚无知。"

　　　　　　　　　　陈朴　译

378. KEITH OF RAVELSTON

The murmur of the mourning ghost
That keeps the shadowy kine,
'Oh, Keith of Ravelston,
The sorrows of thy line!'

Ravelston, Ravelston,
The merry path that leads
Down the golden morning hill,
And thro' the silver meads;

Ravelston, Ravelston,
The stile beneath the tree,
The maid that kept her mother's kine,
The song that sang she!

She sang her song, she kept her kine,
She sat beneath the thorn,
When Andrew Keith of Ravelston
Rode thro' the Monday morn.

His henchmen sing, his hawk-bells ring,
His belted jewels shine!

378. 拉弗尔斯顿的基思

多贝尔

哀哀切切的鬼魂在咕哝——
　它牧着缥缈的母牛——
"呵,拉弗尔斯顿的基思呀①,
　你的家世叫人难受!"

拉弗尔斯顿,拉弗尔斯顿,
　那快活的小路通向
远处金色晨光中的山峦,
　穿过银灿灿的牧场。

拉弗尔斯顿,拉弗尔斯顿,
　梯磴就在那树荫下②,
姑娘在给她妈妈放母牛——
　她唱的那支曲子呀!

她唱着歌儿,她管着母牛,
　她坐在那株灌木下;
那是在星期一的早上,
　基思正骑马经过她。

随从们在唱,鹰铃儿在响,
　一身珠宝彩溢光流;

---

① 基思是拉弗尔斯顿地方的一位贵公子安德鲁·基思的姓。——编注者
② 梯磴,田野间为路人跨入栅栏、矮墙所设,一般有两级,牲畜不能过。——编注者

> Oh, Keith of Ravelston,
> The sorrows of thy line!
>
> Year after year, where Andrew came,
> Comes evening down the glade,
> And still there sits a moonshine ghost
> Where sat the sunshine maid.
>
> Her misty hair is faint and fair,
> She keeps the shadowy kine;
> Oh, Keith of Ravelston,
> The sorrows of thy line!
>
> I lay my hand upon the stile,
> The stile is lone and cold;
> The burnie that goes babbling by[1]
> Says naught that can be told.
>
> Yet, stranger! here, from year to year,
> She keeps her shadowy kine;
> Oh, Keith of Ravelston,
> The sorrows of thy line!
>
> Step out three steps, where Andrew stood —
> Why blanch thy cheeks for fear?
> The ancient stile is not alone.
> 'Tis not the burn I hear!
>
> She makes her immemorial moan,

---

[1] *burnie*: a Scottish diminutive of 'burn,' 'stream.'

呵,拉弗尔斯顿的基思呀,
　　你的家世叫人难受!   20

一年年,当夜晚来到林间,
　　在基思到过的那里,
在阳光下姑娘坐着的地方,
　　有个鬼魂默坐在月色里。

她朦胧的头发又淡又美,   25
　　她牧着缥缈的母牛;
呵,拉弗尔斯顿的基思呀,
　　你的家世叫人难受!

我把手放在那梯磴上,
　　感到它又冷又凄寂;   30
那边上潺潺流过的小溪
　　没透露出什么消息。

可陌生人!她年年就在这儿,
　　牧着缥缈的母牛;
呵,拉弗尔斯顿的基思呀,   35
　　你的家世叫人难受!

跨前三步,那里基思站过——
　　干吗吓得脸上变色?
往昔的梯磴不是这样孤寂,
　　这不是我听见的河!   40

她自古以来就一直悲叹,

She keeps her shadowy kine;
Oh, Keith of Ravelston,
The sorrows of thy line!

S. DOBELL.

她放着缥缈的母牛,
呵,拉弗尔斯顿的基思呀!
你的家世真叫人难受!

黄杲炘　黄杲昶　译

编注　西德尼·托普森·多贝尔(Sydney Thompson Dobell,1824—1874),兼有诗人和酒商两种身份,和亚历山大·史密斯同属"痉挛派"(Spasmodic School)诗人。处女作《罗马人》(The Roman,1850)颇为成功。主要诗集《战争岁月中的英国》(*England in Time of War*,1856),描写克里米亚战争。诗集中有一首题名为《新婚前夜》(A Nuptial Eve)的抒情诗,歌谣《拉弗尔斯顿的基思》就取自该诗,描写了一位少女如何在新婚前夜唱"一首朦胧而悲哀的古老歌谣",这歌谣唱的是"不知何时也不知何处"的故事,它给人一种迷惘沉重的悲凉感。

379. THE BLESSED DAMOZEL[①]

The blessèd damozel leaned out
  From the gold bar of Heaven;
Her eyes were deeper than the depth
  Of waters stilled at even;
She had three lilies in her hand,
  And the stars in her hair were seven.

Her robe, ungirt from clasp to hem,
  No wrought flowers did adorn,
But a white rose of Mary's gift,
  For service meetly worn;
Her hair that lay along her back
  Was yellow like ripe corn.

Herseemed she scarce had been a day[②]
  One of God's choristers;
The wonder was not yet quite gone
  From that still look of hers;
Albeit, to them she left, her day
  Had counted as ten years.

---

① *Damozel*: a young unmarried lady.
② *Herseemed*: an archaism for 'it seemed to her.'

379. 天上的小姐

但·加·罗塞蒂

从天堂里的黄金栏杆上,
　那福小姐探出身体①;
黄昏时分的静水潭虽深,
　却难同她眼睛相比;
她手中握着三支百合花,
　头发里有星星七粒。

她的长袍上下都没系上,
　也没精制的花装饰,
但玛丽亚赏一朵白玫瑰②——
　戴了做礼拜正合适;
她披散在肩头上的头发
　黄得像成熟的谷子。

在她看来,上帝的唱诗班
　她进去还没满一天;
在她凝神注视的眼光里,
　还留着点惊异之感;
然而,对于她离开的人们,
　时间已过去了十年。

---

① 诗人叹服美国诗人爱伦·坡的名诗《乌鸦》,曾表示本诗的写作与之有关:"我看到,描摹留于人世的男子相思之苦,坡已作绝唱。我因此反之,唱出天上被恋女子的眷念之情。"——译者
② 玛丽亚,即圣母马利亚。——译者

(To one, it is ten years of years.
　　... Yet now, and in this place
Surely she leaned o'er me — her hair
　　Fell all about my face ...
Nothing: the autumn fall of leaves.
　　The whole year sets apace.)

It was the rampart of God's house
　　That she was standing on;
By God built over the sheer depth
　　The which is Space begun;
So high, that looking downward thence
　　She scarce could see the sun.

It lies in Heaven, across the flood
　　Of ether, as a bridge.
Beneath, the tides of day and night
　　With flame and darkness ridge
The void, as low as where this earth
　　Spins like a fretful midge.

Heard hardly, some of her new friends
　　Amid their loving games
Spake evermore among themselves
　　Their virginal chaste names;
And the souls mounting up to God
　　Went by her like thin flames.

(对我呀,这是怎样的十年①……
　　可现在呢,在这地方,
她确实曾经俯身望着我——
　　头发全散在我脸上……
没什么,这是秋天的落叶。
　　倏忽间一整年时光。)

她的双脚踏着的,是一道
　　上帝宫殿外的护墙;
上帝造的这道墙在空间——
　　在无限深邃的地方;
那个高呀,从那里向下望,
　　她几乎看不见太阳。

它横在天堂里,像是桥梁
　　跨越着茫茫的天穹。
那下面,日夜之潮用火苗
　　和黑暗隔开了空濛②,
也在那低低的地方,地球
　　转得像烦躁的小虫。

她几乎没听见一些新朋友
　　做着心爱的游戏时,
一直在互相呼唤各人的
　　纯洁而贞静的名字——
那些灵魂像细长的火焰
　　从她身边升向上帝。

---

① 括号中为诗人想象中主人公恋人的自语。下同。——编注者
② 意即在人间划分出白昼与黑夜。——编注者

And still she bowed herself and stooped
   Out of the circling charm;
Until her bosom must have made
   The bar she leaned on warm,
And the lilies lay as if asleep
   Along her bended arm.

From the fixed place of Heaven she saw
   Time like a pulse shake fierce
Through all the worlds. Her gaze still strove
   Within the gulf to pierce
Its path; and now she spoke as when
   The stars sang in their spheres.

The sun was gone now; the curled moon
   Was like a little feather
Fluttering far down the gulf; and now
   She spoke through the still weather.
Her voice was like the voice the stars
   Had when they sang together.

(Ah sweet! Even now, in that bird's song,
   Strove not her accents there,
Fain to be hearkened? When those bells
   Possessed the mid-day air,
Strove not her steps to reach my side
   Down all the echoing stair?)

她虽然身处迷人的环境，
　　却弓着身子朝下望；
她久久凭倚的栏杆准已
　　温暖得像她的胸膛——
连百合花也像进了梦乡，
　　偎在她弯着的臂上。

她在巍然不动的天堂里，
　　只见脉一样的时光
把全宇宙猛烈震撼。　她呀，
　　在苍茫中把那小径凝望①；
眼下她在说话，像是星星②
　　在各自天域中歌唱。

太阳已经消失；一弯月亮
　　像条瘦嶙嶙的毛羽——
在一片茫茫中飘落下去；
　　静夜里透出话语——
她的声音像所有星星的
　　歌声全聚集在一起。

（甜哪！甚至现在，在鸟啼声中，
　　难道不是她的音韵努力
让我欣然入耳？　当那钟声
　　充满了中午的大气，
难道不是她的脚步努力向我走来
　　走下那回响的天梯？）

---

① 从天上看大地，下界混沌一片，因此说"苍茫"。——编注者
② 从《圣经·约伯记》第三十八章第七节"晨星一同歌唱"转发而成，下诗节中重复出现。——编注者

'I wish that he were come to me,
   For he will come,' she said.
'Have I not prayed in Heaven? — on earth,
   Lord, Lord, has he not prayed?
Are not two prayers a perfect strength?
   And shall I feel afraid?

'When round his head the aureole clings,
   And he is clothed in white,
I'll take his hand and go with him
   To the deep wells of light;
We will step down as to a stream,
   And bathe there in God's sight.

'We two will stand beside that shrine,
   Occult, withheld, untrod,
Whose lamps are stirred continually
   With prayer sent up to God;
And see our old prayers, granted, melt
   Each like a little cloud.

'We two will lie i' the shadow of
   That living mystic tree,
Within whose secret growth the Dove
   Is sometimes felt to be,
While every leaf that His plumes touch
   Saith His Name audibly.

"但愿他已来到我的身旁,
　　因为他愿来,"她说道。
"是我没在天上祷告?主啊,
　　是他没在下界祷告?
两人都祷不是最有效验?
　　难道我还得把心操?

"当他的头上围绕着光环,
　　当他穿着一身白衣,
我要拉着他的手带他去
　　深深的光明泉那里——
像走下小溪似的走下去
　　在主的注视下梳洗。

"我俩要站在那人迹罕到、
　　隐蔽难寻的神龛边——
龛前的灯火闪闪不断——
　　把祷告一起送上天庭;
我们往昔的祷词得到应验,
　　然后像小云朵一般消散。

"我俩要躺在那活灵灵的
　　神秘之树的树荫里,
有时在长着它的幽僻处,
　　能感到圣灵在那里①——
他毛羽触及的片片树叶
　　大声地念主的名字。

---

① 见《圣经·马太福音》第三章第十六节:耶稣受了洗,随即从水里上来。天突然为他开了,他就看见神的灵仿佛鸽子降下,落在他身上。圣灵既然以鸽子为形象,故有"他毛羽"之说。——译者

'And I myself will teach to him,
   I myself, lying so,
The songs I sing here; which his voice
   Shall pause in, hushed and slow,
And find some knowledgs at each pause,
   Or some new thing to know.'

(Alas! We two, we two, thou say'st!
   Yea, one wast thou with me
That once of old. But shall God lift
   To endless unity
The soul whose likeness with thy soul
   Was but its love for thee?)

'We two,' she said, 'will seek the groves
   Where the lady Mary is,
With her five handmaidens, whose names
   Are five sweet symphonies,
Cecily, Gertrude, Magdalen,
   Margaret and Rosalys.

'Circlewise sit they, with bound locks
   And foreheads garlanded;
Into the fine cloth white like flame
   Weaving the golden thread,
To fashion the birth-robes for them
   Who are just born, being dead.

'He shall fear, haply, and be dumb;

"躺着时,我要亲自教他
　　我在这儿唱的那首歌,
歌唱时,他的声音会慢慢
　　悄悄地,与我和应。
每一音步他都有所发现, 95
　　或了解到新的领域。"

(哎呀! 你说我们俩,我们俩!
　　是呵,一个就是从前
同我在一起的你,我的灵魂
　　同你的相像的一点 100
只是对你的爱,上帝会让
　　我俩的灵魂永相恋?)

她说,"我们俩要把玛丽亚
　　逗留的树丛寻觅;
她那五位侍女的名字呀①, 105
　　是五支甜美交响曲——
婕楚德、玛德琳、玛格丽特、
　　罗莎琳斯和希塞莉。

"她们束着头发、戴着花冠,
　　围成一圈坐在那边; 110
在白得像火焰的细布上,
　　她们织进金色的线,
为那些刚刚死而复生者
　　制作新生儿的衣衫。

"有时他会吓得说不出话, 115

---

① 说圣母有这五人侍从显然无依据。此处或许仅取发音和谐而已。——译者

    Then will I lay my cheek
     To his, and tell about our love,
      Not once abashed or weak:
    And the dear Mother will approve
     My pride, and let me speak.

    'Herself shall bring us, hand in hand,
     To Him round whom all souls
    Kneel, the clear-ranged unnumbered heads
     Bowed with their aureoles:
    And angels meeting us shall sing
     To their citherns and citoles.

    'There will I ask of Christ the Lord
     Thus much for him and me: —
     Only to live as once on earth
     With Love, — only to be,
    As then awhile, for ever now
     Together, I and he.'

    She gazed and listened and then said,
     Less sad of speech than mild, —
    'All this is when he comes.' She ceased.
     The light thrilled towards her, filled
    With angels in strong level flight.
     Her eyes prayed, and she smiled.

    (I saw her smile.) But soon their path

我就要把自己的脸
贴着他的，絮说我们的爱，
　　一点也不胆怯羞惭；
亲爱的圣母将让我说话，
　　并把我的得意称赞。 　　　　　　　　　*120*

"她会亲自带我们见上帝——
　　她挽着我们俩的手；
上帝四周齐齐地跪着灵魂——
　　低着无数带光环的头；
天使们会唱着歌迎接我们—— 　　　　　　*125*
　　还把古筝竖琴弹奏①。

"在那儿，我要为他也为我
　　向主基督这样请求：
只求像以往那样，怀着爱
　　再度活在世上，只求
像往时过个片刻，从今后 　　　　　　　　*130*
　　同他在此永远厮守。"

她凝望、谛听后，带着略含
　　哀愁的柔情轻声道——
"全是他来后的事。"她住口，
　　闪烁的光把她笼罩—— 　　　　　　　*135*
一群天使平稳地疾飞而去——
　　她眼在祈祷脸在笑。

（我看见她笑。）转眼天使已

---

① 前者形似吉他琴，以翻或金属等材料制成的弦弹拨；后者形似竖琴，有一共鸣板。——编注者

　　　　　　Was vague in distant spheres;
　　　　　And then she cast her arms along
　　　　　　The golden barriers,
　　　　　And laid her face between her hands,
　　　　　　And wept. (I heard her tears.)

　　　　　　　　　　　　　D. G. ROSSETTI.

隐约在遥远的天边；
　　这时,她猛地伸出了双臂
　　　靠着那金色的栏杆,
　　两只手蒙住脸哭泣起来。
　　（她哭的声音我听见。）

140

黄杲炘　黄杲昶　译

编注 但丁·加百利·罗塞蒂(Dante Gabriel Rossetti,1828—1882),诗人、画家,在这两类艺术中皆以自己的独特风格享有盛誉,与米勒、亨特等人组成"拉斐尔前派兄弟会",主要信条是:真正的艺术在于返朴归真,应着意追求拉斐尔开创新画风以前流行的那种自然风格。这首著名诗作《天上的小姐》,描写一登仙的少女眷念留在尘世的爱人。他还著有其他诗集,如《诗集》《民谣及十四行诗集》等。他的意象具体,韵律平稳均匀,很有节奏感,并且富有画意。

380. REST

O Earth, lie heavily upon her eyes;
    Seal her sweet eyes weary of watching, Earth;
    Lie close around her; leave no room for mirth
With its harsh laughter, nor for sound of sighs.
She hath no questions, she hath no replies,
    Hushed in and curtained with a blessèd dearth
    Of all that irked her from the hour of birth;
With stillness that is almost Paradise.
Darkness more clear than noon-day holdeth her,
    Silence more musical than any song;
Even her very heart has ceased to stir:
    Until the morning of Eternity
    Her rest shall not begin nor end, but be;
And when she wakes she will not think it long.

                                    C. G. ROSSETTI.

380. 安息

克·乔·罗塞蒂

大地呵，重重地压上她的双眸；
　掩上她倦于观察的温情的眼，大地呵；
　紧紧围住她；不留下一点欢喜的空地
使她发出刺耳的笑声，或悲伤的怨诉。
她不再提问，她也不再答复，　　　　　　5
　悄悄地安放进来，掩埋时没有祷告
　她生来就讨厌这些礼数。
周围安静得几乎同天堂一般。
比正午还清晰的黑暗把她占有，
　比任何歌声还要悦耳的寂静；　　　　　10
甚至她的那颗心也停止颤抖
　直到那个永恒的早晨
　她的安息无始无终，只是存在；
她醒来时也不会认为躺了很久。

赵 澧 译

编注 克里斯蒂娜·乔治娜·罗塞蒂（Christina Georgina Rossetti, 1830—1894），英国著名诗人但丁·罗塞蒂的妹妹，与其兄有同样的诗才，她的诗感情真挚，但不少带有神秘悲苦的色彩，她的理想是精神世界的纯粹与自我克制，属于拉斐尔前派诗人，代表作为《精怪集市及其他》(Goblin Market and Other Poem, 1862)。本诗集所选的几首诗皆出于该书。

381. SONG

When I am dead, my dearest,
   Sing no sad songs for me;
Plant thou no roses at my head,
   Nor shady cypress tree:
Be the green grass above me
   With showers and dewdrops wet;
And if thou wilt, remember,
   And if thou wilt, forget.

I shall not see the shadows,
   I shall not feel the rain;
I shall not hear the nightingale
   Sing on, as if in pain;
And dreaming through the twilight
   That doth not rise nor set,
Haply I may remember,
   And haply may forget.

C. G. ROSSETTI.

381. 歌

克·乔·罗塞蒂

当我死了，亲爱的，
　　不要为我唱哀曲，
也不必在墓前植玫瑰，
　　也无须柏树来荫覆；
由草儿青青长在头上　　　　　　　　5
　　承受着秋露和春雨；
要是你愿意，就记得，
　　要是你愿意，就忘去。

我将感觉不到雨露，
　　我将看不到荫影，　　　　　　　10
我将听不见夜莺
　　唱着像是哀吟的歌声。
在那幽冥中我入了梦，
　　那薄光不明也不灭；
也许，我还能记得，　　　　　　　　15
　　也许，我忘去了一切。

　　　　　　　　　　方平　译

382. REMEMBER

Remember me when I am gone away,
   Gone far away into the silent land;
   When you can no more hold me by the hand,
Nor I half turn to go yet turning stay.
Remember me when no more day by day
   You tell me of our future that you planned:
   Only remember me; you understand
It will be late to counsel then or pray.
Yet if you should forget me for a while
   And afterwards remember, do not grieve:
   For if the darkness and corruption leave
     A vestige of the thoughts that once I had,
Better by far you should forget and smile[①]
   Than that you should remember and be sad.

C. G. ROSSETTI.

---

① *Better by far*: *i.e.* I shall think it better, etc.

382. 记着我

克·乔·罗塞蒂

望你记着我,在我离去之后——
　远远地离去,进入寂静之国;
　那时你不能再把我的手紧握,
我也不能再犹疑着,欲去还留。
记着我,当你不能再无止无休　　　　　5
　对我描绘我俩未来的生活。
　只望你记着我,因为你也懂得:
那时已来不及再商量或祈求。
不过如果你暂时把我忘记,
　随后又重新记起,你别悲痛,　　　　10
　因为假如黑暗和腐朽之余
还留下我的思念的一点痕迹,
我情愿你忘记而面露笑容,
　也不愿你记住而愁容戚戚。

　　　　　　　　　　飞白　译

383. UP-HILL

Does the road wind up-hill all the way?
    Yes, to the very end.
Will the day's journey take the whole long day?
    From morn to night my friend.

But is there for the night a resting-place?
    A roof for when the slow dark hours begin.
May not the darkness hide it from my face?
    You cannot miss that inn.

Shall I meet other wayfarers at night?
    Those who have gone before.
Then must I knock, or call when just in sight?
    They will not keep you standing at that door.
Shall I find comfort, travel-sore and weak?
    Of labour you shall find the sum.
Will there be beds for me and all who seek?
    Yea, beds for all who come.

                        C. G. ROSSETTI.

383. 上山

克·乔·罗塞蒂

这条路曲曲弯弯通上山吗?
　　是的,通上顶端。
白日的旅行需要长长的一整天吗?
　　朋友,需要从早到晚。

但是那儿有夜宿的地方吗?　　　　　　　　　　5
　　当漫漫黑夜来临时你有屋檐。
黑夜可以藏住,不在我这儿露面吗?
　　你不会错过那所旅店。

我晚上会遇见别的行客吗?
　　会遇见那些先去的人们,　　　　　　　　10
我敲门呢,还是见面再打招呼?
　　他们不会让你在门外久困。

我能找到安慰,消除痛苦和疲惫吗?
　　你的辛劳会得到报酬,
那儿有床位给所有的寻求者吗?　　　　　　　15
　　是的,床位人人都有。

罗义蕴　译

384. SONG

Oh roses for the flush of youth,
   And laurel for the perfect prime;
But pluck an ivy branch for me
   Grown old before my time.

Oh violets for the grave of youth,
   And bay for those dead in their prime;
Give me the withered leaves I chose
   Before in the old time.

C. G. ROSSETTI.

384. 歌

克·乔·罗塞蒂

玫瑰献给精力充沛的青年,
　为卓越成就的盛年献上桂冠。
采一枝长春藤给我吧①,
　我的衰老已经提前。

啊紫罗兰献给青年的坟墓,
　月桂花献给死去的壮年;
我旧日挑选的枯叶,
　送给我作为对我的奉献。

罗义蕴　译

---

① 此处的"长春藤"是老年的象征。——译者

385. A BIRTHDAY

My heart is like a singing bird
    Whose nest is in a watered shoot[①];
My heart is like an appletree
    Whose boughs are bent with thickset fruit;
My heart is like a rainbow shell
    That paddles in a halcyon sea[②];
My heart is gladder than all these
    Because my love is come to me.

Raise me a dais of silk and down[③];
    Hang it with vair and purple dyes[④];
Carve it in doves, and pomegranates,
    And peacocks with a hundred eyes;
Work it in gold and silver grapes,
    In leaves, and silver fleurs-de-lys;
Because the birthday of my life
    Is come, my love is come to me.

                                      C. G. ROSSETTI.

---

① *a watered shoot*: the rocks fringing a waterfall.
② *halcyon*: 'calm.' Cf. No. 62, l. 68 and note.
③ *dais*: here used for 'a seat on a platform at the end of a hall'; more commonly it is the platform itself.
④ *vair*: a fine fur used for lining robes; the term is now used only in heraldry.

385. 生日

克·乔·罗塞蒂

我的心像一只歌唱的鸟,
　　它的巢在瀑布边的岩石间;
我的心像一株苹果树,
　　它枝条被稠密果实压弯;
我的心像一只彩虹色贝壳,
　　它在静海里拍水向前;
我的心比这些都更快乐,
　　因为我的爱来到了我身边。

为我丝绸羽绒衬垫的高台椅,
　　把皮毛和紫色的饰物挂上;
在椅背等处雕出鸽子和石榴,
　　还有具百翎眼的孔雀的形象;
再镶上金黄的、银白的葡萄,
　　树叶,以及银白的鸢尾;
因为我生命开始的纪念日
　　来到了,我的爱来与我相会。

鲍屡平　译

386. BARBARA

On the Sabbath-day,
Through the churchyard old and grey,
Over the crisp and yellow leaves, I held my rustling way;
And amid the words of mercy, fallng on my soul like balms,
'Mid the gorgeous storms of music — in the mellow organ-calms,
'Mid the upward-streaming prayers, and the rich and solemn psalms,
I stood careless, Barbara.

My heart was otherwhere
While the organ shook the air,
And the priest, with outspread hands, blessed the people with a prayer;
But, when rising to go homeward, with a mild and saint-like shine[①]
Gleamed a face of airy beauty with its heavenly eyes on mine —
Gleamed and vanished in a moment — O that face was surely thine
Out of heaven, Barbara!

O pallid, pallid face!
O earnest eyes of grace
When last I saw thee, dearest, it was in another place.
You came running forth to meet me with my love-gift on your wrist:
The flutter of a long white dress, then all was lost in mist —
A purple stain of agony was on the mouth I kissed,
That wild morning, Barbara.

---

① *when rising:* as it stands, this agrees with 'a face,' which is absurd; the poet meant it, of course, to agree with an unexpressed 'I.'

386. 巴巴拉

史密斯

安息日那一天,
　　穿过古老灰色的墓园,
我沙沙地走在那清脆的黄叶上面;
周围是甘油般滴在我心灵上的感恩声音,
周围是壮丽的乐音轰鸣——甘美的风琴, 5
周围是越来越高的祈祷和低沉庄严的赞歌声,
　　我漫不经心地站着,巴巴拉。

当风琴奏鸣时,
　　我的心在他处,
牧师用祈祷祝福人们,把双手伸出, 10
但在起身回家时,一股谦逊而圣洁的光
闪耀在奇幻而美丽的脸上,天使般的双眼把我凝望——
转瞬间一闪而过——呵这来自上天的脸庞
　　肯定属于你,巴巴拉!

苍白、苍白的脸呵! 15
　　恳切的赐人神恩的眼呵!
最爱的,上次我见你时,是在另一个地点。
你跑来迎我,手腕上带着我爱的赠礼:
白色长袍在迎风飘曳,然后　一切在雾里消失——
我吻过的嘴边带着痛苦的紫色痕迹①, 20
　　在那狂热的早晨,巴巴拉。

---

① 脸上没有血色,嘴唇发紫。——译者

> I searched, in my despair,
>> Sunny noon and midnight air;
> I could not drive away the thought that you were lingering there.
> O many and many a winter night I sat when you were gone,
> My worn face buried in my hands, beside the fire alone —
> Within the dripping churchyard, the rain plashing on your stone,
>> You were sleeping, Barbara.
>
> 'Mong angels, do you think
>> Of the precious golden link
> I clasped around your happy arm while sitting by yon brink[①]?
> Or when that night of gliding dance, of laughter and guitars,
> Was emptied of its music, and we watched, through latticed bars,
> The silent midnight heaven creeping o'er es with its stars.
>> Till the day broke, Barbara?
>
> In the years I've changed;
>> Wild and far my heart hath ranged,
> And many sins and errors now have been on me avenged;
> But to you I have been faithful, whatsoever good I lacked;
> I loved you, and above my life still hangs that love intact —
> Your love the trembling rainbow, I the reckless cataract —
>> Still I love you, Barbara.
>
> Yet, love, I am unblest;
>> With many doubts opprest,
> I wander like a desert wind, without a place of rest.
> Could I but win you for an hour from off that starry shore,

---

① *yon brink*: satisfied with the rime, the poet apparently did not think that the reader might reasonably ask, 'brink of what?'

我在失望中寻求，
　　在阳光灿烂的正午和夜半的时候；
我无法驱除你曾在这儿逗留过的念头。
呵你离去后我留在那儿的无数冬天的夜晚，　　　　　　25
我双手捂住憔悴的脸，独自守在炉边——
雨打上你的墓碑，在淅沥的墓园，
　　你在长眠，巴巴拉。

在天使们中间，你可曾想到
　　我们坐在那儿旁边　　　　　　　　　　　　　　30
我扣在你柔臂上的那根珍贵的金链条？
还有那充满舞步、笑声和吉他的良宵
已歌歇舞散，我们还透过格子栏杆远眺，
静静午夜的天空，头上群星闪耀，
　　直望到天已破晓，巴巴拉？　　　　　　　　　　35

这些年我发生了变化；
　　我的心放荡无羁、百无牵挂，
我犯了许多罪过，我受到了惩罚；
但我对你是忠实不渝，尽管我一无是处；
我爱你胜过生命，我的爱情始终如一——　　　　　40
你的爱是闪灼的彩虹，我的爱是无羁的瀑布——
　　我仍然爱你，巴巴拉。

可是，爱，我这不幸的人；
　　受到的怀疑无穷无尽，
我像沙漠的风一样彷徨，无处得到安宁。　　　　　45
如果我能从那繁星照射的岸边把你赢来片时，

The hunger of my soul were stilled, for Death hath told you more
Than the melancholy world doth know; things deeper than all lore
    You could teach me, Barbara.

50   In vain, in vain, in vain,
    You will never come again.
There droops upon the dreary hills a mournful fringe of rain;
The gloaming closes slowly round, loud winds are in the tree,
Round selfish shores for ever moans the hurt and wounded sea,
55   There is no rest upon the earth, peace is with Death and thee,
    Barbara!

A. SMITH.

我的灵魂就会得到满足,因为死神告诉你的,
比忧伤的世界知道的更多;你可以教我的事
　　比全部知识更要深刻,巴巴拉。

　　徒劳,徒劳,徒劳, 50
　　你决不会再来了。
一阵忧伤的雨在向荒凉的山间倾倒;
薄暮慢慢临近,狂风在林中吼叫,
受伤的海在自私的岸边号啕①,
大地上没有安息,和平和死神与你一道, 55
　　巴巴拉!

赵澧　译

编注　亚历山大·史密斯(Alexander Smith,1830—1867),早年当过图案设计师。处女长诗《生命的戏剧》(*A Life Drama*,1851)受到欢迎,乃离职担任爱丁堡大学秘书。翌年与多贝尔(见本卷第378首编注)合作出版《战争十四行诗集》(*Sonnets on the War*),从而赢得"痉挛派"之称。此派诗人的诗矫揉造作,言过其实,具有强烈的浮夸风格。

---

①　很难看出海岸的"自私"指的是什么,除非说它拒绝接受海水侵袭,因此海是"受伤的"。这里可以看出"痉挛派"重视声音胜于意义。——译者

387. OLD LOVE

'You must be very old, Sir Giles,'
    I said; he said: 'Yea, very old:'
Whereat the mournfullest of smiles
    Creased his dry skin with many a fold.

'They hammer'd out my basnet point[①]
    Into a round salade,' he said,
'The basnet being quite out of joint,
    Natheless the salade rasps my head.'

He gazed at the great fire awhile:
    'And you are getting old, Sir John;'
(He said this with that cunning smile
    That was most sad;) 'we both wear on.

'Knights come to court and look at me[②],
    With eyebrows up, except my lord[③],
And my dear lady, none I see
    That know the ways of my old sword.'

(My lady! at that word no pang

---

① *basnet*: (or basinet), a small light steel headpiece, somewhat globular in shape with a point over the forehead.
② *to court*: i.e. to the Duke's court.
③ *With eyebrows up*: i.e. in surprise to see the outward insignificance of the famous old warrior.

1682

387. 往日的爱情

莫里斯

"你年龄一定很大了吧,吉斯爵士,"
　　我说;他说:"是呀,是上了年纪。"
他脸上一露出最悲戚的微笑,
　　那干枯的皮肤就浮现皱纹丝丝。

"他们把我那带叉的护面盔,　　　　　　　　　　5
　　改成了无叉的护颈盔,"他说,
"带叉的护面盔弄得七零八碎,
　　无叉的护颈盔又叫我的头部挨戳。"

他凝视了一下熊熊的火焰,
　　"约翰爵士,你也逐渐变老,"　　　　　　　10
(说话时,他脸上泛起狡黠的微笑,
　　最悲戚的微笑;)"我们两人都在衰老。

"骑士们进入宫庭把我打量,
　　不禁都有些惊讶;除了君主,
和那位亲爱的夫人,我再也看不见　　　　　　15
　　那些深知我往日剑术的老相识。"

(哦,夫人! 一听到这话,没有痛楚

    Stopp'd all my blood.) 'But tell me, John,
   Is it quite true that pagans hang
    So thick about the east, that on

   'The eastern sea no Venice flag
    Can fly unpaid for?' 'True, 'I said,
   'And in such way the miscreants drag
    Christ's cross upon the ground, I dread

   'That Constantine must fall this year.'
    Within my heart: 'These things are small;
   This is not small, that things outwear[①]
    I thought were made for ever, yea, all,

   'All things go soon or late;' I said —
    I saw the duke in court next day;
   Just as before, his grand great head
    Above his gold robes dreaming lay,

   Only his face was paler; there
    I saw his duchess sit by him;
   And she — she was changed more; her hair
    Before my eyes that used to swim,

   And make me dizzy with great bliss
    Once, when I used to watch her sit —
   Her hair is bright still, yet it is

---

 ① *things outwear*: i.e. his own feelings.

能止住我浑身热血奔流。)"不过,
约翰,告诉我,那些异教徒①
　　可真已聚集东土? 20

在东方的海面上,威尼斯的旗帜,
　　不能毫无代价地飘扬?""是这样,"我说,
"正是这样,恶徒们
　　把基督的十字架拖倒在地上。

"恐怕康士坦丁堡今年非陷落不可。" 25
　　我内心深处却说:"这是些小事;
唯有我自己的感触才非同小可,
　　它关系到永远,也关系到众人的事。

"一切都要泯灭,不论早迟;"我说——
　　第二天我在宫廷里见到了公爵; 30
一如既往,在他金袍的上部,
　　是一颗酣睡的巨大的头颅。

只是他的脸色比平时更加苍白,
　　我看见公爵夫人坐在他身旁,
而她呢,哦,又有不少变化; 35
　　她的秀发过去常在我眼前飘荡。

有一次,当我把她的坐态端详——
　　那时,她使我神魂飘荡,
她的头发如今虽然依旧光亮,

① 异教徒指的是土耳其人。土耳其入侵希腊是十四世纪中叶,不久侵占了阿德利安那堡。一四五三年康士坦丁堡陷落,东罗马帝国复灭。八年以后,土耳其人又与威尼斯发生冲突,占领东部地区。诗人对年代有所混淆。——编注者

40 　　　　　　As though some dust were thrown on it.

　　　　　　Her eyes are shallower, as though
　　　　　　　　Some grey glass were behind; her brow
　　　　　　And cheeks the straining bones show through,
　　　　　　　　Are not so good for kissing now.

45 　　　　　　Her lips are drier now she is
　　　　　　　　A great duke's wife these many years,
　　　　　　They will not shudder with a kiss
　　　　　　　　As once they did, being moist with tears.

　　　　　　Also her hands have lost that way
50 　　　　　　　　Of clinging that they used to have;
　　　　　　They look'd quite easy, as they lay
　　　　　　　　Upon the silken cushions brave①

　　　　　　With broidery of the apples green
　　　　　　　　My Lord Duke bears upon his shield.
55 　　　　　　Her face, alas! that I have seen
　　　　　　　　Look fresher than an April field,

　　　　　　This is all gone now; gone also
　　　　　　　　Her tender walking; when she walks
　　　　　　She is most queenly I well know,
60 　　　　　　　　And she is fair still: — as the stalks

　　　　　　Of faded summer-lilies are,

---

　　① *brave*: 'handsome'; the apples embroidered on them formed part of the Duke's armorial bearings.

不过似乎尘灰已撒落在她的头上。 40

她的双眸已经暗淡,像有灰色的玻璃
　　镶嵌在里面;她的双颊和眉尖
已凭空出现隆起的骨骼,
　　如今亲起吻来已不惬意舒坦。

如今,她的双唇已经更加干枯, 45
　　(多年来她一直是位高贵的公爵夫人,)
她的双唇不会像过去,为了一个亲吻
　　而颤抖,哪怕被热泪浇淋。

她的双手也失去了
　　往昔握住物体的丰姿; 50
从前,放在那丝绒的坐垫上,
　　她的手显得优美闲适。

带着这绿苹果图案的织绣,
　　我的公爵老爷枕着他的坚盾。
啊!她的脸,我看见了的, 55
　　比四月的原野还要鲜艳清新。

如今,这一切已一去无踪;
　　连同她那娇憨的步伐;
她一起步总有一种我熟悉的王后威仪,
　　她依然美丽:宛如夏天的百合花 60

凋谢后的残茎枯枝。在这个春天,

  So is she grown now unto me
  This spring-time, when the flowers star
  The meadows, birds sing wonderfully.

65   I warrant once she used to cling
   About his neck, and kiss'd him so,
  And then his coming step would ring
   Joy-bells for her, — some time ago.

  Ah! sometimes like an idle dream
70   That hinders true life overmuch,
  Sometimes like a lost heaven, these seem[①]. —
   This love is not so hard to smutch[②].

         W. MORRIS.

[①] *these*: the incidents of his bygone love.
[②] *smutch*: 'stain'; connected with the earlier verb to 'smudge.'

她对我说来长得正是这样，
当繁花缀满草原，
百鸟迷人地歌唱。

我确信她一度曾经 65
勾住他的颈部和他这样亲吻，
于是，他的脚步声常在她的心扉
敲响欢乐的铃声——许久以前的柔情。

唉！有时这一切好似虚梦一场，
过分地妨碍了真实的人生； 70
有时又好像一个失去的天堂，
这样的爱呵难免会染上污痕。

黄新渠　辜正坤　译

编注　威廉·莫里斯（William Morris，1834—1896），英国诗人，政论家，画家。早期属于拉斐尔前派，崇尚中世纪文化和唯美主义，后来则积极投身于社会政治生活，成为著名的进步作家。

莫里斯的作品甚丰，主要诗作有长诗《伊阿宋的生死》《沃尔松族的西古尔德》《美好未来的追求者》、诗集《地上乐园》《社会主义者的诗歌》等。他早期的诗作充满幻想，修饰纤巧，而后期的诗风则纯真遒劲。

本书所选四首诗作均出自诗人的诗集《格温维纳尔的辩词和其他诗篇》(The Defence of Guenevere and Other Poems，1858)。本诗和其后二首诗据弗洛沙特（Froissart）的《编年史》(Chronicle)写成，叙述十四世纪的战争。第一首老约翰爵士来看他青年时代的老友古斯爵士。吉斯爵士住在公爵的官邸内，他在这里遇到了婚前曾爱过自己的公爵夫人。他发现他的心跳正常，还能安闲自若地评论时间的流逝在她身上以及他本身感情上发生的变化。

388. SHAMEFUL DEATH

There were four of us about that bed;
    The mass-priest knelt at the side,
I and his mother stood at the head
    Over his feet lay the bride;
We were quite sure that he was dead,
    Though his eyes were open wide.

He did not die in the night,
    He did not die in the day,
But in the morning twilight
    His spirit pass'd away,
When neither sun nor moon was bright,
    And the trees were merely grey.

He was not slain with the sword,
    Knight's axe, or the knightly spear,
Yet spoke he never a word
    After he came in here;
I cut away the cord
    From the neck of my brother dear.

He did not strike one blow,
    For the recreants came behind,
In a place where the hornbeams grow,
    A path right hard to find,
For the hornbeam boughs swing so,

388. 羞辱的死亡

莫里斯

我们四人环床而立,
　旁边跪着做弥撒的神父。
我和死者的母亲站在前头,
　而新娘在他的脚前站立。
尽管他还圆睁着两眼,　　　　　　　　　　5
　我们都很清楚:他已经死去。

他不是在黑夜中殒命,
　也不是在白昼去世,
是在朦胧的晨光之中
　他的灵魂终于消逝。　　　　　　　　　10
太阳和月亮都暗淡无光,
　树影婆娑,只是一片迷茫。

他不是死于刀剑之下,
　也不是在骑士的斧钺、长矛下捐躯,
自从他来到此地,　　　　　　　　　　　15
　还不曾吐露只言片语。
我于是用刀割断
　套在亲爱的兄弟颈上的吊索。

他并未击倒一个对手,
　因为懦夫们只能从他背后袭击,　　　　20
他遇难的地方长满了铁篱树,
　一条暗径就掩映在这树丛里,
当铁篱树的枝叶摇曳不定,

That the twilight makes it blind.

They lighted a great torch then,
  When his arms were pinion'd fast,
Sir John the knight of the Fen,
  Sir Guy of the Dolorous Blast,
With knights threescore and ten,
  Hung brave Lord Hugh at last.

I am threescore and ten,
  And my hair is all turn'd grey,
But I met Sir John of the Fen
  Long ago on a summer day,
And am glad to think of the moment when
  I took his life away.

I am threescore and ten,
  And my strength is mostly pass'd,
But long ago I and my men,
  When the sky was overcast,
And the smoke roll'd over the reeds of the fen,
  Slew Guy of the Dolorous Blast.

And now, knights all of you,
  I pray you pray for Sir Hugh,
A good knight and a true,
  And for Alice, his wife, pray too.

W. MORRIS.

晨昏里的小路就更难辨出踪迹。

于是他们点燃熊熊的火炬，　　　　　　　　　　25
　　并把他的双手捆个结实，
泽国的骑士约翰爵士，
　　和狂飚骑士盖伊爵士，
带领另外七十个骑士，
　　终于将勇敢的休勋爵吊死。　　　　　　　30

如今我已年愈古稀，
　　满头白发银丝，
多年前在一个夏天，
　　我遇见了约翰，这泽国骑士，
一想起那个时刻我就快乐无比，　　　　　　35
　　因为我那时叫他一命归西。

如今我已是年愈古稀，
　　再不像当年一样强壮有力。
但多年前我带领随从，
　　趁天空乌云密布，　　　　　　　　　　40
烟雾在沼泽的芦苇上升起，
　　我们杀死了狂飚骑士盖伊。

如今，我请求你们，所有的骑士，
　　为了休勋爵而求祈，
他真是个杰出的骑士；　　　　　　　　　　45
　　也为阿丽丝祈祷，她是他的爱妻。

　　　　　　　　　　　　黄新渠　辜正坤　译

编注 本诗中，诗人叙述了兄长休勋爵如何被敌人吊死，表达了自己的悲愤，还谈到了自己如何替兄报仇。

389. THE HAYSTACK IN THE FLOODS

Had she come all the way for this,
To part at last without a kiss?
Yea, had she borne the dirt and rain
That her own eyes might see him slain
Beside the haystack in the floods?

Along the dripping leafless woods,
The stirrup touching either shoe,
She rode astride as troopers do;
With kirtle kilted to her knee①,
To which the mud splash'd wretchedly;
And the wet dripp'd from every tree
Upon her head and heavy hair,
And on her eyelids broad and fair;
The tears and rain ran down her face.

By fits and starts they rode apace,
And very often was his place
Far off from her; he had to ride
Ahead, to see what might betide
When the roads cross'd; and sometimes, when
There rose a murmuring from his men
Had to turn back with promises;
Ah me! she had but little ease;

---

① *kirtle*: 'petticoat.'

389. 洪流中的干草堆

莫里斯

她是否曾老远地跑来
只为了最后这无吻的别离?
啊,她是否曾踏着泥泞,冒着急雨
只为了亲眼看见他在这洪流中
在干草堆旁被人杀死? 5

沿着这木叶脱尽,淌着雨水的树林,
她脚踩着马镫
像骑兵一样跃马奔腾。
她把衣裙卷在膝头上,
依然避不开飞溅的泥泞。 10
每棵树上都滴答着雨水
淋湿她的头顶,浸透她满头浓发,
滴在她又大又美的睫毛上,
眼泪和雨水顺着脸颊往下流倾。

他们间或策马飞奔, 15
他经常跑在她的前头,
好看看在交叉路口
会发生什么事情;
有时从他的士兵中传来一阵私语,
他就得勒马回身,重诺相许; 20
啊!她一刻也不能安宁
往往完全出于疑虑和恐惧而抽泣;

And often for pure doubt and dread
She sobb'd, made giddy in the head
By the swift riding; while, for cold,
Her slender fingers scarce could hold
The wet reins; yea, and scarcely, too,
She felt the foot within her shoe
Against the stirrup: all for this,
To part at last without a kiss
Beside the haystack in the floods.

For when they near'd that old soak'd hay,
They saw across the only way
That Judas, Godmar, and the three
Red running lions dismally
Grinn'd from his pennon, under which,
In one straight line along the ditch,
They counted thirty heads.

                              So then,
While Robert turn'd round to his men,
She saw at once the wretched end,
And, stooping down, tried hard to rend
Her coif the wrong way from her head,
And hid her eyes; while Robert said:

由于催马飞奔而目眩头晕；
由于天寒地冻，她那纤纤细指
握不牢湿淋淋的缰绳；是呀，　　　　　　　25
甚至她踏在马鞍上的皮靴中的脚趾
也失去知觉；这一切都只为了
在洪流中的干草堆侧
最后得到一个无吻的离别。

当他们走近陈腐潮湿的干草堆，　　　　30
他们看到对面那唯一的小道，
朱达斯、戈德玛和三名①
身着红装的猛士，面色阴沉
在旌旗下狞笑；旗帜下面
沿着水渠笔直地排成一行，　　　　　　35
他们点名报数，共有三十名士兵。

　　　　　　　于是
当罗伯特向他的士兵转过身时
她立刻明白将发生一个悲惨的结局。
她俯下身子，尽力拉下头罩，　　　　　40
好遮住自己的眼睛；罗伯特说②：
"喏，亲爱的，这差不多是二比一，
在普瓦蒂埃时，我们打得他们③

---

① 罗伯特·德·玛尔尼爵士是一位英国骑士，曾在普瓦蒂埃（1356）作过战。他和他的夫人热哈妮及 小队随从骑马通过法兰西，突然遇到了奸诈的法国骑士戈德玛。戈德玛带着人马一直守候在他的城堡附近，以便杀死罗伯特，抢走热哈妮。罗伯特的士兵拒绝战斗，反把罗伯特捆绑起来交给了戈德玛。本诗叙述的就是这个故事的其余部分。——译者
② 是一种紧套在头上（下巴下有系绳）的帽子。热哈妮想把她的帽子拉下来挡住眼睛，好看不见她的爱人被杀死的情景。——译者
③ 这句未说完，他本来是想告诉她：在普瓦蒂埃时，法国人虽五倍于英国人，可还是吃了败仗。——译者

1697

      'Nay, love, 'tis scarcely two to one,
45   At Poictiers where we made them run
      So fast — why, sweet my love, good cheer,
      The Gascon frontier is so near,
      Nought after this.'

              But, 'O,' she said,
      'My God! my God! I have to tread
50   The long way back without you; then
      The court at Paris; those six men;
      The gratings of the Chatelet;
      The swift Seine on some rainy day
      Like this, and people standing by,
55   And laughing, while my weak hands try
      To recollect how strong men swim.
      All this, or else a life with him,
      For which I should be damned at last,
      Would God that this next hour were past!'

60   He answer'd not, but cried his cry,
      'St. George for Marny!' cheerily;
      And laid his hand upon her rein.
      Alas! no man of all his train
      Gave back that cheery cry again;
65   And, while for rage his thumb beat fast
      Upon his sword-hilts, some one cast[1]

---

[1] *sword-hilts*: as late as the middle of the 18th century the plural 'hilts' was used for the singular with the same meaning.

望风披靡——哦,我亲爱的甜心,
请振作精神,加斯科涅边境已经很近①,　　　　　　45
从此从后,什么事情也不会发生。"

　　　　　　"呵,"她说,
"我的上帝!我的上帝!我只得
独自登上漫长的归程;然后
在巴黎出庭;那六个男人;　　　　　　　　　　　50
那查特勒底监狱的窗棂②;
那雨后的塞纳河波涛翻滚,
就如眼前的情景,人们站在一旁
放声大笑,而我挥动无力的双手
尽力回想身强体壮的男人怎样游泳。　　　　　　55
这一切,或说是为了他的生命
我最后该受到诅咒,
但愿上帝保佑这个时刻很快过去!"

他不回答,只大声呼喊:
"愿圣·乔治保佑玛尔尼!"　　　　　　　　　　60
于是他用手拉住她的缰绳。
唉!再也没有像他这样有教养的男人
会再发出这种激励人心的呼声。
他气愤得用大姆指频频拍打刀柄,
于是有人用一根长围巾,　　　　　　　　　　　65
勒住他的脖子将他捆紧。

---

① 爱德华三世执政期间,纪龙德省和加斯科涅属于英国领土。——译者
② "那六个男人"系指将把她当作一个女巫来审判,然后下令把她关进巴黎最可怕的监狱格兰德·查特勒监狱的法官们。查特勒监狱的位置就是现在的查特勒宫。这个监狱于一八〇二年被毁。一旦热哈妮被带到那儿,就会被抛进塞纳河以验证她是否有罪。她如能游泳的话,她就被判有罪,从而处以死刑,如果她淹死了,就证明她是无罪的。——译者

About his neck a kerchief long,
And bound him.

              Then they went along
To Godmar; who said: 'Now, Jehane,
Your lover's life is on the wane
So fast, that, if this very hour
You yield not as my paramour,
He will not see the rain leave off —
Nay, keep your tongue from gibe and scoff,
Sir Robert, or I slay you now.'

She laid her hand upon her brow,
Then gazed upon the palm, as though
She thought her forehead bled, and — 'No,'
She said, and turn'd her head away,
As there were nothing else to say,
And everything were settled: red
Grew Godmar's face from chin to head:
  'Jehane, on yonder hill there stands
My castle, guarding well my lands:
What hinders me from taking you,
And doing that I list to do
To your fair wilful body, while
Your knight lies dead?'

              A wicked smile
Wrinkled her face, her lips grew thin,
A long way out she thrust her chin:
  'You know that I should strangle you
While you were sleeping; or bite through

　　　　　　随后，他们走过去，
来到戈德玛跟前；戈德玛说："喏，热哈妮，
你爱人的生命危在旦夕，
在这千钧一发的时刻，　　　　　　　　　　70
你如不肯顺从作我的情妇，
他就再也看不到雨何时停——
嗨，你休得满嘴胡言乱语，
罗伯特爵士，否则我立刻将你杀死。"

她把一只手放在前额上，　　　　　　　　75
然后凝视着手掌，好像
在思索自己的额头是否出血——"不，"
她说，把头扭向一旁，
似乎再也无话可讲。
一切都已经决定：热血　　　　　　　　　80
使戈德玛满脸红得发紫：
"热哈妮，我的城堡
就在山的那边，坚守我的土地，
什么能阻止我将你带走，
并对你这可爱而任性的肉体　　　　　　　85
为所欲为，当你的骑士已一命归西？"

　　　　　　她脸上
浮起一个狡黠的微笑，双唇变薄；
她高扬起她的下巴说：
"你知道我会扼住你的咽喉，　　　　　　90
当你熟睡的时候；我会咬穿
你的喉咙，啊——愿上帝帮助，

  Your throat, by God's help — ah! 'she said,
  'Lord Jesus, pity your poor maid!
95 For in such wise they hem me in,
  I cannot choose but sin and sin,
  Whatever happens: yet I think
  They could not make me eat or drink,
  And so should I just reach my rest.'

100 'Nay, if you do not my behest,
  O Jehane! though I love you well,'
  Said Godmar, 'would I fail to tell
  All that I know?' 'Foul lies,' she said.
  'Eh? lies, my Jehane? by God's head,
105 At Paris folks would deem them true!
  Do you know, Jehane, they cry for you,
  "Jehane the brown! Jehane the brown!
  Give us Jehane to burn or drown!" —
  Eh — gag me Robert! — sweet my friend,
110 This were indeed a piteous end
  For those long fingers, and long feet,
  And long neck, and smooth shoulders sweet;
  An end that few men would forget
  That saw it — So, an hour yet:
115 Consider, Jehane, which to take
  Of life or death!'

  So, scarce awake,
  Dismounting, did she leave that place,
  And totter some yards: with her face

愿你对你可怜的使女大发慈悲,我主耶稣!"
他们会这样聪明地把我严加禁锢
我除了不断犯罪外别无他途, 95
不管发生什么事情:不过我想,
他们总不能逼我吃下饭喝下水,
于是我就正好一命归西。"

"不,如果你不从我所欲,
啊,热哈妮!尽管我这样爱你," 100
戈德玛说,"难道我会不告诉你
我所知道的一切?""可耻的谎言,"她说。
"呃?谎言?我的热哈妮,上帝作证!
在巴黎,人人都会把这些看作实情!
热哈妮,你知道他们为你而叫嚷, 105
'棕色姑娘热哈妮!热哈妮棕色姑娘!
快把热哈妮给我们烧死或淹死!'——
住嘴,罗伯特!——我亲爱的人①,
这真是叫人悲惨的结局。
对你这修长的双脚,纤细的手指, 110
光洁柔滑的两肩和长长的脖子,
凡目睹过这场面的人
都不会忘记——瞧,还有一小时,
想想吧,热哈妮,你究竟选择
生存还是毁灭?" 115

　　　　　她宛如在梦境,
下了马,她才离开了原地,
向前踉跄了几步:于是

---

① 一听到戈德玛提到热哈妮的死亡问题,罗伯特不禁再次愤然出声,于是招来戈德玛的这一句呵斥。——译者

          Turn'd upward to the sky she lay,
          Her had on a wet heap of hay,
          And fell asleep: and while she slept,
          And did not dream, the minutes crept
          Round to the twelve again; but she,
          Being waked at last, sigh'd quietly,
          And strangely childlike came, and said:
            'I will not.' Straightway Godmar's head,
          As though it hung on strong wires, turn'd
          Most sharply round, and his face burn'd.

          For Robert — both his eyes were dry,
          He could not weep, but gloomily
          He seem'd to watch the rain; yea, too,
          His lips were firm; he tried once more
          To touch her lips; she reach'd out, sore
          And vain desire so tortured them,
          The poor grey lips, and now the hem
          Of his sleeve brush'd them.

                        With a start
          Up Godmar rose, thrust them apart;
          From Robert's throat he loosed the bands
          Of silk and mail; with empty hands
          Held out, she stood and gazed, and saw
          The long bright blade without a flaw
          Glide out from Godmar's sheath, his hand
          In Robert's hair; she saw him bend
          Back Robert's head; she saw him send
          The thin steel down; the blow told well,
          Right backward the knight Robert fell,

面对长空,头枕着潮湿的干草堆,
沉沉入睡。当她熟睡之际,   120
她未做梦,分针慢慢地走了一圈
又指向了十二点;
她终于醒了,平静地叹息,
奇怪的是她变得孩子气了,她说,
"我不愿意。"戈德玛的头   125
活像悬在一根粗铁丝上,
猛地转了过来,脸色红得发烫。

罗伯特呢——两眼干涩,
他不能哭泣,似乎只在阴沉地
观看下雨,是呀,   130
他也双唇紧闭;他想再一次
接触她的嘴唇。她伸出双手,
疼痛和虚妄的情欲折磨着他们,
这时,他的衣袖轻拂着
这可怜的灰色的双唇。   135

     猛然,
戈德玛跳了起来,强行将他们分开。
他松开罗伯特咽喉上的丝带。
她伸出空空的两手,站在那儿
凝视着戈德玛寒光闪闪的长剑   140
从剑鞘飞出,看到他的手抓住
罗伯特的头发;看到他
按住罗伯特的头;看到他往下
挥舞那犀利的剑;随着砍击的声响,
罗伯特骑士应声仰卧在地上,   145
依我看,他已经半死,

And moan'd as dogs do, being half dead,
Unwitting, as I deem: so then
Godmar turn'd grinning to his men,
Who ran, some five or six, and beat
His head to pieces at their feet.

Then Godmar turn'd again and said:
    'So, Jehane, the first fitte is read[①]!
Take note, my lady, that your way
Lies backward to the Chatelet!'
She shook her head and gazed awhile
At her cold hands with a rueful smile,
As though this thing had made her mad.

This was the parting that they had
Beside the haystack in the floods.

W. MORRIS.

[①] *fitte*: (or fytte, or fit) an obsolete word for a canto or other section of a poem.

呻吟起来像狗一样。
于是,戈德玛对着随从露齿一笑,
这些士兵有五六个立刻冲上,
将罗伯特的头踩在脚下砍成肉浆。 150

接着戈德玛又转身说道:
"喏,热哈妮,这第一章就这样收场!
我的夫人,请记住,你的归途
现在是通向查特勒监狱!"
她摇了摇头,又凝视了一下 155
冰冷的双手,露出了苦笑,
好像这件事已经使她疯狂。

他们的离别就是这样
发生在洪流中的干草堆旁。

黄新渠　辜正坤　译

390. SUMMER DAWN

Pray but one prayer for me 'twixt thy closed lips,
    Think but one thought of me up in the stars.
The summer night waneth, the morning light slips,
    Faint and grey 'twixt the leaves of the aspen, betwixt the cloud-bars,
That are patiently waiting there for the dawn:
    Patient and colourless, though Heaven's gold
Waits to float through them along with the sun.
Far out in the meadows, above the young corn,
    The heavy elms wait, and restless and cold
The uneasy wind rises; the roses are dun;
Through the long twilight they pray for the dawn,
Round the lone house in the midst of the corn.
    Speak but one word to me over the corn,
    Over the tender, bowed locks of the corn.

W. MORRIS.

390. 夏天的黎明

莫里斯

用你那紧闭的双唇为我祈祷一次,
　　在高远的星空中只把我思念一遍。
夏夜消残,晨光流逝,
　　白扬的枝叶里,层封的云峦间,游移着一片模糊灰暗——
它们在那里耐心恭候着黎明: 5
　　悠闲自若,神色不变,
尽管天庭的金光将伴随朝阳穿越它们的枝干。
在远方的草原上,在玉米的苗地里,
　　沉沉的榆树静候着;燥动的风乍起,
冷峭而不安,玫瑰也一片昏黯; 10
它们围绕着玉米地里那所孤零零的房舍,
在漫长的晨熹微明中祈求黎明的降临。
　　哦,请面对玉米地,在柔嫩低垂的玉米丛
　　那边,对我说话呀,哪怕是片语只言。

黄新渠　译

391. 'AS WE RUSH, AS WE RUSH IN THE TRAIN'

As we rush, as we rush in the train,
    The trees and the houses go wheeling back,
But the starry heavens above the plain
    Come flying on our track.

All the beautiful stars of the sky,
    The silver doves of the forest of Night,
Over the dull earth swarm and fly,
    Companions of our flight.

We will rush ever on without fear;
    Let the goal be far, the flight be fleet!
For we carry the Heavens with us, dear,
    While the Earth slips from our feet!

J. THOMSON.

391. "当我们,当我们在列车上向前冲……"

汤姆逊

当我们,当我们在列车上向前冲,
 树木和房屋在朝身后滚,
但平原上方群星灿烂的苍穹
 正沿着我们的轨道飞奔。

天空上面美丽的群星
 如黑夜森林中的银色白鸽,
成群翱翔于沉闷的大地上方,
 是我们飞奔的伙伴。

我们将无畏地永远向前冲;
 不论目标多远,飞奔多快!
因为当大地从我们脚下溜走,
 亲爱的,天堂却与我们同在。

赵澧 译

编注 詹姆斯·汤姆逊(James Thomson,1834—1882),被人称为"悲观主义的诗人",与他同名同姓的《四季》的作者(见本书卷三第136首编注)却是一个现世主义者。汤姆逊的一生同曼根(见本卷第304首编注)非常相似,两人都在青年时代有过不幸的爱情,接着陷入贫穷、悲痛与酗酒之中,本诗选自他的代表作《可怕的夜城》(*The City of Dreadful Night*,1880),比他的大多数诗要欢快些。

392. ITYLUS

    Swallow, my sister, O sister swallow,
        How can thine heart be full of the spring?
            A thousand summers are over and dead.
    What hast thou found in the spring to follow?
        What hast thou found in thine heart to sing?
            What wilt thou do when the summer is shed?

    O swallow, sister, O fair swift swallow,
        Why wilt thou fly after spring to the south,
            The soft south whither thine heart is set?
    Shall not the grief of the old time follow?
        Shall not the song thereof cleave to thy mouth?
            Hast thou forgotten ere I forget?

    Sister, my sister, O fleet sweet swallow,
        Thy way is long to the sun and the south;
            But I, fulfilled of my heart's desire,
    Shedding my song upon height, upon hollow,
        From tawny body and sweet small mouth
            Feed the heart of the night with fire.

    I the nightingale all spring through,
        O swallow, sister, O changing swallow,
            All spring through till the spring be done,
    Clothed with the light of the night on the dew,

392. 伊第拉斯

斯温伯恩

燕子啊,我的姐姐,啊,燕子姐姐,
　　你的心里怎么会充满了春天?
　　　一千个夏天已经飞逝。
春天里有什么让你追赶?
　　什么在你心中激荡着歌声? 　　　　　　　5
　　　夏天过去你将怎么办?

啊,燕子姐姐,啊,美丽飞翔的燕子,
　　你为什么要到南方去寻找春天,
　　　难道温暖的南方使你留恋?
旧日的悲伤就不把你羁绊? 　　　　　　　10
　　难道歌声竟会不忠于你自己的口?
　　　难道你会比我遗忘得更先?

姐姐呀,我的姐姐,轻快的燕子呀,
　　到阳光明媚的南方路途遥远,
　　　但我把歌声唱给高山与深谷, 　　　　15
这就会满足我的心愿,
　　从我黄褐色的羽毛和甜蜜的小嘴
　　　为夜晚的情意增添火焰。

找这只夜莺整个春天都在歌唱,
　　啊,燕子姐姐,你总是见异思迁, 　　　20
　　　从春光来临到春光消逝,
露珠给夜色晶莹点点①,

---

① 这里指月光反映在露珠上。——译者

    Sing, while the hours and the wild birds follow,
        Take flight and follow and find the sun.

Sister, my sister, O soft light swallow,
    Though all things feast in the spring's guest-chamber,
        How hast thou heart to be glad thereof yet?
For where thou fliest I shall not follow,
    Till life forget and death remember,
        Till thou remember and I forget.

Swallow, my sister, O singing swallow,
    I know not how thou hast heart to sing.
        Hast thou the heart? is it all past over?
Thy lord the summer is good to follow,
    And fair the feet of thy lover the spring:
        But what wilt thou say to the spring thy lover?

O swallow, sister, O fleeting swallow,
    My heart in me is a molten ember
        And over my head the waves have met.
But thou wouldst tarry or I would follow,
    Could I forget or thou remember,
        Couldst thou remember and I forget.

O sweet stray sister, O shifting swallow,
    The heart's division divideth us.
        Thy heart is light as a leaf of a tree;
But mine goes forth among sea-gulfs hollow
    To the place of the slaying of Itylus,

唱吧,时间和野雀在飞翔,
　　飞吧,追吧,去寻找太阳。

姐姐,我的姐姐,柔和光滑的小燕子,　　　　　　　　　　*25*
　　虽然万物都坐上了春天客厅里的筵席,
　　　　你的心怎能由此而欢喜?
你在哪儿飞翔,我不随去①,
　　待到我忘却了生命,记起了死亡,
　　　　待到你想起而我忘记。　　　　　　　　　　　　*30*

燕子啊,我的姐姐,呢喃的燕子,
　　我不知道你怎么会有心思唱歌。
　　　　你有这心思吗? 是否一切都成为过去?
你追随着夏天的夫君多么好哇,
　　你春天的情侣也有一双好脚:　　　　　　　　　　　*35*
　　　　但你怎么向你的爱人春天诉说?

啊,燕子姐姐,轻快的燕子,
　　我的心成了熔化的余灰,
　　　　在我头上有波涛滚滚相聚。
但可能你会停留,我会追随,　　　　　　　　　　　　　*40*
　　但愿我能忘记,你会记起,
　　　　愿你能记住,我会忘记。

啊,可爱而放浪的姐姐,啊,容易变心的燕子,
　　你朝三暮四把我们的感情离间。
　　　　你的心像树上的叶子那样轻浮;　　　　　　　　*45*
我的心却留在海底深渊,
　　那便是伊第拉斯被害的地方呀,

---

① 事实上,夜莺和燕子都到非洲北部去过冬。——译者

>   The feast of Daulis, the Thracian sea.

>   O swallow, sister, O rapid swallow,
>   I pray thee sing not a little space.
>   Are not the roofs and the lintels wet?
>   The woven web that was plain to follow,
>   The small slain body, the flowerlike face.
>   Can I remember if thou forget?

>   O sister, sister, thy first-begotten!
>   The hands that cling and the feet that follow,
>   The voice of the child's blood crying yet,
>   *Who hath remembered me? who hath of forgotten?*
>   Thou hast forgotten, O summer swallow,
>   But the world shall end when I forget

A. C. SWINBURNE.

    色雷斯海上多利斯城摆起了酒筵①。

  啊,燕子姐姐,飞翔的燕子,
    我请求你别在小小的天地歌唱。 *50*
    难道屋梁和楣石没有血染?
  蛛网可以把你领到那个地方,
    被杀害的小家伙,花儿一般的脸蛋,
    如果你已健忘,我能否把它思念?

  姐姐呀姐姐,你头胎的儿子! *55*
    紧贴的手,紧跟的脚,
    孩儿的血还在呼吁,
    "谁能把我记住?谁已把我遗忘?"
  你已经忘记了,啊,你夏天的燕子,
    但如果我忘记了,那就是世界的末日。 *60*

罗义蕴　译

  编注　阿尔加侬·查尔斯·斯温伯恩(Algernon Charles Swinburne,1837—1909),英国著名诗人,其诗作节奏明朗,技巧纯熟,色彩丰富,有些诗成为英语中最富于音乐性的作品,著名抒情诗有《日出前的歌》(*Songs before Sunrise*)及诗集《诗与谣》(*Poems and Ballads*,1866),本篇即选自《诗与谣》。

  斯温伯恩写这首诗时,混淆了希腊神话的两个情节。(1)伊登是梯伯王热修斯的妻子,他们的独生子名叫伊第拉斯(Itylus),这位母亲忌妒其嫂有十二个孩子,想把嫂嫂的长子杀死。不料错把自己的儿子杀死。伊登悲哀不已,入神宙斯对她表示同情,为了保护她免遭丈夫的报复,就把她变成了一只夜莺。(2)雅典王潘狄翁有两个女儿,长女嫁给色雷斯王忒瑞俄斯,生了一子名伊提斯(Itys),忒瑞俄斯对他的妻子厌

---

① 多利斯在爱琴海北边,色雷斯海附近,是科云斯海湾以北十英里的小镇。——译者

倦了,把她的妹妹邀进宫来,玩弄之后割掉她的舌头。妹妹编织了一件锦袍送给姐姐,把自己的遭遇和冤屈织进了锦袍,于是姐姐把亲生的儿子伊提斯杀掉,献给丈夫当肉吃。两姊妹慌忙逃命。忒瑞俄斯带着斧头追赶上去,眼看要追到时,神把三人都变成鸟,忒瑞俄斯变成一只戴胜鸟,姐姐变成一只燕子,妹妹变成一只夜莺。国王潘狄翁听了这故事含泪而死。

393. THE GARDEN OF PROSERPINE

Here, where the world is quiet;
    Here, where all trouble seems
Dead winds' and spent waves' riot[1]
    In doubtful dreams of dreams;
I watch the green field growing
    For reaping folk and sowing,
    For harvest-time and mowing,
    A sleepy world of streams.

I am tired of tears and laughter,
    And men that laugh and weep;
Of what may come hereafter
    For men that sow to reap:
I am weary of days and hours,
    Blown buds of barren flowers,
    Desires and dreams and powers
    And everything but sleep.

Here life has death for neighbour,
    And far from eye or ear

---

[1] *Dead winds' and spent waves' riot*, *etc*.: *i.e.* a mere tumult of the air and of the water which comes to nothing, and is based on no fact, nor even on anything so definte as a dream.

393. 普洛塞耳皮那的花园①

斯温伯恩

这儿世界多么平和；
　　这儿所有的烦恼好似
奄奄的风和疲惫的波动
　　在迷离的梦里；
我眼望绿色原野生长　　　　　　　　　　5
等待春播夏收的歌谣②，
等待收获把庄稼刈倒，
　　睡意的世界流着小溪。

我厌倦了泪水和笑容，
　　厌倦了人们的笑声和哭泣，　　　　10
人人都为收获而播种，
　　一切总要跟随而至；
我厌倦了流逝的时日，
不孕的花儿盛开的花芯③，
欲望，权力，还有梦境，　　　　　　　15
　　厌倦了这一切，我只想安息。

这里生以死为邻，
　　远远离开观望和聆听
弱浪和湿风兢兢业业，

---

① 普洛塞耳皮那，罗马神话中的冥后，即希腊神话中的珀耳塞福涅。——译者
② 据罗马神话，普洛塞耳皮那每年春秋两度回到人间，象征着耕种和收获。——译者
③ 普洛塞耳皮那不降临人间时，正是严冬和酷暑，大地荒芜，万物萧条，因此有"不孕"的说法。——译者

  Wan waves and wet winds labour,
    Weak ships and spirits steer;
  They drive adrift, and whither
  They wot not who make thither;
  But no such winds blow hither,
    And no such things grow here.

  No growth of moor or coppice,
    No heather-flower or vine,
  But bloomless buds of poppies,
    Green grapes of Proserpine,
  Pale beds of blowing rushes,
  Where no leaf blooms or blushes
  Save this whereout she crushes
    For dead men deadly wine.

  Pale, without name or number,
    In fruitless fields of corn,
  They bow themselves and slumber
    All night till light is born;
  And like a soul belated,
  In hell and heaven unmated,
  By cloud and mist abated
    Comes out of darkness morn.

  Though one were strong as seven,
    He too with death shall dwell,

小船凭着心灵前行； 20
　　但他们四处飘流，
　　不知为何驶往那里①，
　　但吹来的风并不相识，
　　　这里没有长着那样的生灵。

没有生长的灌木和沼泽， 25
　　没有石南或长长的藤蔓，
只有罂粟不能绽开的幼蕊②，
　　冥后的绿色葡萄在阴间，
盛开的灯芯草苍白的床笫，
没有初萌或怒放的树叶， 30
除了罂粟头，冥后用来酿制
　　死者饮用的死的酒浆③。

苍白，默默无闻，
　　在不果的玉米地，
它们整夜躬身静静安眠 35
　　直到东方露出晨曦，
如一道迟误的灵魂之光，
在分隔的地狱天国间迷惘，
在柔和了的云和雾一旁，
　　透过黎明的阴晦。 40

就算人有七倍的力量，
　　一样难逃离死的屋寮，
不会奋翅苏醒在天堂，

---

① 意即："人们成日忙碌，但却不知为了什么"，诗人叹息生活毫无价值。——译者
② 罂粟是普洛塞耳皮那的财产之一。——译者
③ 即鸦片。——译者

                    Nor wake with wings in heaven,
                        Nor weep for pains in hell;
                    Though one were fair as roses,
                    His beauty clouds and closes;
                    And well though love reposes,
                        In the end it is not well.

                    Pale, beyond porch and portal,
                        Crowned with calm leaves, she stands
                    Who gathers all things mortal
                        With cold immortal hands;
                    Her languid lips are sweeter
                    Than love's who fears to greet her
                    To men that mix and meet her
                        From many times and lands.

                    She waits for each and other,
                        She waits for all men born;
                    Forgets the earth her mother,
                        The life of fruits and corn;
                    And spring and seed and swallow
                    Take wing for her and follow
                    Where summer song rings hollow
                        And flowers are put to scorn.

                    There go the loves that wither,
                        The old loves with wearier wings;
                    And all dead years draw thither,
                        And all disastrous things;

也不会在地狱为苦痛泣悼;
尽管他有玫瑰的逸姿, 45
他的美已晦然完结,
多美好尽管爱已安息,
 可是结局并非美好。

苍白,在走廊和门厅一旁
 她伫立,头冠安详的叶枝, 50
她的手指永生而冰凉,
 采集匆匆逝去的生灵;
她倦意的嘴唇多么销魂,
妒嫉的爱不敢让人们
与她混迹相会, 55
 他们曾时时地地与她相识。

她等待众人,等待一切,
 她等待一切出生的人;
忘掉了大地她的母亲,
 忘掉了果实和谷物的生命①; 60
而春天和种籽和燕子们
带给她翅膀,她飞向
那儿,夏日的歌声在空谷回响,
 花儿只好把轻蔑担承。

那儿残存凋谢的爱情, 65
 古老的爱带着更沉重的翅膀;
逝去的岁月都去彼岸,
 剩下世间种种祸殃;
遗弃的白昼死般的梦意,

---

① 普洛塞耳皮那的母亲是色列斯(Ceres),大地谷物和果实的女神。——译者

1725

  Dead dreams of days forsaken,
  Blind buds that snows have shaken,
  Wild leaves that winds have taken,
   Red strays of ruined springs①.

  We are not sure of sorrow,
   And joy was never sure;
  To-day will die to-morrow;
   Time stoops to no man's lure;
  And love, grown faint and fretful,
  With lips but half regretful
  Sighs, and with eyes forgeful
   Weeps that no loves endure.

  From too much love of living,
   From hope and fear set free,
  We thank with brief thanksgiving
   Whatever gods may be
  That no life lives for ever;
  That dead men rise up never;
  That even the weariest river
   Winds somewhere safe to sea.

  Then star nor sun shall waken,
   Nor any change of light;
  Nor sound of waters shaken,
   Nor any sound or sight;
  Nor wintry leaves nor vernal,
  Nor days nor things diurnal;

---

① *strays*: 'straggling threads of water.'

冻僵的幼芽在雪中泯灭, 70
风儿卷走了野树的枝叶
　颓坏的春天零乱的水漾。

我们并不确信伤情,
　也绝不相信任何欢乐;
到明天今天已经死去; 75
　时间永远不受人诱惑;
而爱情更加衰微焦急,
双唇吁出半悔的
叹息,那忘却的双眼
　流出爱难以承受的痛灼。 80

脱开爱情太多的生活,
　离弃希望和焦虑,
我们颂出简短的祈祝,
　不管诸神如何临莅,
世间没有不朽之身, 85
死去的人从未再生;
即使那河的悲凉最深
　也蜿蜒流入大海怀里。

那是星而不是太阳苏醒,
　不是任何变幻的光亮; 90
不是水波拍击的声音,
　也不是别的声响和景象;
不是枝叶的凋敝或长青,
不是身边刻刻的机遇,

Only the sleep eternal
In an eternal night.

A. C. SWINBURNE.

只有睡眠才能长青,
　在那神圣不朽的晚上。

陆　蜚　译

394. A FORSAKEN GARDEN

In a coign of the cliff between lowland and highland①,
    At the sea-down's edge between windward and lee,
Walled round with rocks as an inland island,
    The ghost of a garden fronts the sea.
A girdle of brushwood and thorn encloses
    The steep square slope of the blossomless bed
Where the weeds that grew green from the graves of its roses
        Now lie dead.

The fields fall southward, abrupt and broken,
    To the low last edge of the long lone land.
If a step should sound or a word be spoken,
    Would a ghost not rise at the strange guest's hand?
So long have the grey bare walks lain guestless,
    Through branches and briers if a man make way
He shall find no life but the sea-wind's, restless
        Night and day.

The dense hard passage is blind and stifled②
    That crawls by a track none turn to climb
To the strait waste place that the years have rifled
    Of all but the thorns that are touched not of time.

---

① *coign*: 'corner,' now usually found only in the Shakespearian phrase 'coign of vantage.'
② *blind and stifled*: 'hard to find and choked with weeds.'

394. 遗弃的花园

斯温伯恩

在低洼和高原相邻的陡峭的角地，
　　在向风和背风之间的低低的海边，
一座花园的幻影似岩石环绕的岛屿，
　　在大海前面隐约地呈现。
树丛和荆棘的枝桠缠绕在 5
　　无花险峻宽阔的斜陂，
那儿，从玫瑰花的墓冢萌出的绿草
　　　　此刻已倒地枯萎。

这片土地朝南倾斜，崎岖不平，
　　跌入下面漫长孤寂土地的远方。 10
如果脚步发出声响，言辞吐出胸膛，
　　那位陌生旅人眼前怎会不升起朦胧的幻象？
那样久灰暗空寂的行程没有了人迹，
　　如果一个人立在满是枝叶与荆棘的丛林中开辟道路，
除了海风喧嚣的白昼和黑夜，他再不会 15
　　　　发现活物。

爬行在路旁密集艰难的小径
　　被丛林阻塞，难以辨别，
没有弯道攀援狭小的荒野，那被岁月
　　掠尽一切，空余荆棘无时触及的荒野。 20

    The thorns he spares when the rose is taken;
        The rocks are left when he wastes the plain.
    The wind that wanders, the weeds wind-shaken,
            These remain.

25   Not a flower to be pressed of the foot that falls not;
        As the heart of a dead man the seed-plots are dry;
    From the thicket of thorns whence the nightingale calls not,
        Could she call, there were never a rose to reply.
    Over the meadows that blossom and wither
30   Rings but the note of a sea-bird's song;
    Only the sun and the rain come hither
            All year long.

    The sun burns sere and the rain dishevels
        One gaunt bleak blossom of scentless breath.
35   Only the wind here hovers and revels
        In a round where life seems barren as death.
    Here there was laughing of old, there was weeping,
        Haply, of lovers none ever will know,
    Whose eyes went seaward a hundred sleeping
40   Years ago.

    Heart handfast in heart as they stood, 'Look thither[①],'
        Did he whisper? 'look forth from the flowers to the sea;
    For the foam-flowers endure when the roseblossoms wither,
        And men that love lightly may die — but we?'
45   And the same wind sang and the same waves whitened,
        And or ever the garden's last petals were shed,

---

    ① *handfast in*: 'bound up in.'

当玫瑰被欺,小径放过了纷乱的荆棘;
 他荒废平原,而留下成堆的石群,
如今把迷失的风,飘摇颤栗的
   杂草留存。

花儿被落下的脚蹂躏;   25
 苗圃似死者的心已经干涸;
荆棘丛中没有传出夜莺的鸣叫,
 因为决不会有玫瑰与它应呼。
除了一只海鸟的乐声萦回
 在繁盛又凋谢的草地之上;   30
只有太阳和雨水常年来到
   这个地方。

太阳燃尽,雨水揉乱
 一朵气息奄奄,憔悴而凄凉的花儿。
生机恹然如死亡的一片园地   35
 只有风在这儿徘徊,恣意沉迷。
这儿有古老的微笑,偶尔也有
 无人知晓的恋人的叹息,
他们在沉睡的百年之前曾放眼远望:
   汪洋海区。   40

他们心连结着心伫立"眺望远方",
 他低语?"从花朵看到沧溟;
玫瑰凋谢而泡状的花朵却长存,
 淡然相爱的人们也许死去——而我们?"
同样的风在唱,同样的浪汹涌出白雪, 45
 不等花园脱落下最后的花瓣,

>   In the lips that had whispered, the eyes that had lightened,
>   Love was dead.
>
>   Or they loved their life through, and then went whither?
>   And were one to the end — but what end who knows?
>   Love deep as the sea as a rose must wither,
>   As the rose-red seaweed that mocks the rose.
>   Shall the dead take thought for the dead to love them?
>   What love was ever as deep as a grave?
>   They are loveless now as the grass above them,
>   Or the wave.
>
>   All are at one now, roses and lovers,
>   Not known of the cliffs and the fields and the sea.
>   Not a breath of the time that has been hovers
>   In the air now soft with a summer to be.
>   Not a breath shall there sweeten the seasons here-after
>   Of the flowers or the lovers that laugh now or weep,
>   When as they that are free now of weeping and laughter
>   We shall sleep.
>
>   Here death may deal not again for ever;
>   Here change may come not till all change end.
>   From the graves they have made they shall rise up never,
>   Who have left nought living to ravage and rend.
>   Earth, stones, and thorns of the wild ground growing,
>   While the sun and the rain live, these shall be;
>   Till a last wind's breath upon all these blowing
>   Roll the sea.
>
>   Till the slow sea rise and the sheer cliff crumble,

在低语过的唇边,在闪烁过光亮的眼睛里,
　　　爱就长眠。

他们会始终爱着自己的生命,又去什么地方?
　　一个近终的人——谁能将归宿知晓? 50
大海般深挚的爱犹如玫瑰必然凋残,
　　如玫瑰色的海草把玫瑰嘲笑。
死者是否接受死者将爱他们的思想?
　　还有什么爱情比陵墓更幽深?
当青草或是海浪没顶,他们便 55
　　　没有了爱情。

如今万物归一,玫瑰和爱人,
　　不知道悬崖、田野和大海。
空气中飞翔的岁月的呼吸,
　　不会随着即至的夏日而变得潮湿。 60
没有一缕气息可以让以后的花季
　　或现在欢笑和叹息的恋人感觉甜蜜。
我们将合眼入睡,当他们不再
　　　欢笑和叹息。

这里也许永远是死气沉沉; 65
　　这里一切变化结束之后才有变化的可能。
他们决不会从他们构筑的墓地走出,
　　这些把乌有的生命留给荒芜和败颓的人们。
荒野上的泥土、石头和荆棘,
　　只要还有太阳和雨,它们就不会衰败; 70
直到所有鼓噪而来的最后一丝风
　　　搅动了大海。

直到缓行的海升起,险峻的峭壁崩溃,

1735

>   Till terrace and meadow the deep gulfs drink,
>   Till the strength of the waves of the high tides humble
>   The fields that lessen, the rocks that shrink;
>   Here now in his triumph where all things falter,
>   Stretched out on the spoils that his own hand spread,
>   As a god self-slain on his own strange altar,
>   Death lies dead.

A. C. SWINBURNE.

直到深深的海湾把草坪和台地醉饮，
直到高耸的潮头，巨大的海浪把 75
　　田野吞噬，使岩石变形裂皱；
此时此地，万物在海水的胜利中萎颓，
　　行进在自己的手撒开的猎物上，
像神自刎在自己陌生的祭坛，
　　　　死亡倒地死亡。 80

　　　　　　　　　　　陆　蜉　译

395. OLIVE

Addressed to Olive Miranda Watts, aged nine years

1

Who may praise her?
Eyes where midnight shames the sun,
Hair of night and sunshine spun,
Woven of dawn's or twilight's loom,
Radiant darkness, lustrous gloom,
Godlike childhood's flowerlike bloom,
None may praise aright, nor sing
Half the grace wherewith like spring
    Love arrays her.

2

    Love untold
Sings in silence, speaks in light
Shed from each fair feature, bright
Still from heaven, whence toward us, now
Nine years since, she deigned to bow
Down the brightness of her brow,
Deigned to pass through mortal birth:
Reverence calls her, here on earth,
    Nine years old.

3

    Love's deep duty,
Even when love transfigured grows
Worship, all too surely knows

395. 奥莉芙

斯温伯恩

致奥莉芙·米兰达·沃兹,时年九岁

1

谁能把她赞美?
一双眼睛,黑夜令太阳失去光辉,
满头青丝,黑夜和太阳追逐穿飞,
交织着黎明和黄昏的朦胧,
乌黑发亮,墨黑闪光。 5
圣洁的童年,鲜花盛开。
谁都不能把她赞美,也不能唱出她的半分典雅,
像春天一样,那是
　　爱装扮着她。

2

　　无言的爱从 10
俊俏的五官,每一个部位
流泄出无声的歌唱,光的语汇。
从天上下凡,降临人间,
已是寒暑九易,依然辉耀如先。
垂下光闪闪的眼眉, 15
俯声来到人间:
尊严召唤着她,这里,在人间,
　　已度九载。

3

　　爱的深深的责任,
即使当神化的爱令崇拜日增月长 20
怎样恋爱?熟谙此道者既多又广。

How, though love may cast out fear,
Yet the debt divine and dear
Due to childhood's godhead here
May by love of man be paid
Never; never song be made
    Worth its beauty.

4

    Nought is all
Sung or said or dreamed or thought
Ever, set beside it; nought
All the love that man may give —
Love whose prayer should be, 'Forgive!'
Heaven, we see, on earth may live;
Earth can thank not heaven, we know,
Save with songs that ebb and flow,
    Rise and fall.

5

    No man living,
No man dead, save haply one
Now gone homeward past the sun
Ever found such grace as might
Tune his tongue to praise aright
Children, flowers of love and light,
Whom our praise dispraises: we
Sing, in sooth, but not as he
    Sang thanksgiving.

虽然爱能驱走怯懦、弱孱，
然而，神明的巨绩，
岂能以凡夫之爱去偿还？
因为人间的童年皆具神性。 25
再美的歌儿也配不上
　　它的美①。

4

　　白费力气，
一切讴歌、言语、梦幻、思想，全都
白费力气，让它去吧；无谓 30
人类所能奉献的一切爱就是——
爱，他的祈祷应该是："宽恕！"
我们遥望苍天，我们住在人间；
我们知道，人间不能感谢苍天，
除了用歌声，歌声曼妙， 35
　　抑扬翩翩。

5

　　没人活着，
没人去死，也许除去那一个②
如今他已辞别太阳，回了故乡③。
曾几何时，无比的优雅 40
开启了他的歌喉，
他赞美孩子们：爱与光的花朵。
我们的赞颂不过是贬损：
我们是真正地歌唱，而他却是
　　感恩祈祷。 45

---

① 可能指上文的"童年的神性"。——译者
② 指英国诗人布莱克（1757—1827）。他的《天真之歌》（1789）和《经验之歌》（1794）里有些描写儿童的精彩诗句。诗人写此诗时他早已去世。——译者
③ 即他已谢世。——译者

6

    Hope that smiled,
Seeing her new-born beauty, made
Out of heaven's own light and shade,
Smiled not half so sweetly: love,
Seeing the sun, afar above,
Warm the nest that rears the dove,
Sees, more bright than moon or sun,
All the heaven of heavens in one
    Little child.

7

    Who may sing her?
Wings of angels when they stir
Make no music worthy her:
Sweeter sound her shy soft words
Here than songs of God's own birds
Whom the fire of rapture girds
Round with light from love's face lit:
Hands of angels find no fit
    Gifts to bring her.

8

    Babes at birth
Wear as raiment round them cast,
Keep as witness toward their past,
Tokens left of heaven; and each,
Ere its lips learn mortal speech,
Ere sweet heaven pass on pass reach[①],
Bears in undiverted eyes
Proof of unforgotten skies

---

① *pass on pass reach*: 'attain to summit after summit.'

6

微笑的希望,
望着她新生的美丽,
那是天上的光影合璧,
微笑,无比甜蜜:爱,
望着太阳高挂天穹,
温暖着养育了鸽子的窝巢。
看见了,在一个孩子身上
看见了天外天,比月儿明①,
　　比太阳亮。

7

　　谁能把她歌唱?
天使们鼓动双翼奏起的仙乐
也不配把她歌唱:
她那羞赧的柔语曼声,
比上帝小鸟的歌唱还要甜美。
她浸润在爱的光辉中,
脸庞煜煜生辉,照亮一片:
天使们的玉手都找不到适宜的赠礼
　　给她献上。

8

　　初生的婴儿
带着来自天上的标记,
那是她们裹身的衣被,
那是她们往昔的证据。
不等那樱樱小嘴咿呀学语,
不等可爱的天穹高飞远去,
这时你瞧,人间的每一个儿童
那一眨不眨的眼睛里,闪烁着难忘的

---

① 天外天,指神和天使居住的地方。——编注者

Here on earth.

9

Quenched as embers
Quenched with flakes of rain or snow
Till the last faint flame burns low,
All those lustrous memories lie
Dead with babyhood gone by;
Yet in her they dare not die:
Others fair as heaven is, yet,
Now they share not heaven, forget:
She remembers.

A. C. SWINBURNE

天穹的痕迹。

9

　　一堆灰烬
熄灭了,雨点或是雪花浇灭了
一切闪光的记忆, 75
最后一束微弱的火焰暗淡了。
它们消逝了,童年已远去①,
然而,在她那里,它们不致销声敛迹;
别人像天空一样美丽,但是如今
天空已不在她们心中;她们忘记了;而她 80
　　却没有忘记。

王友贵　译

---

① 此处的"它们"指记忆,下文亦同。——编注者

396. ODE

 We are the music-makers,
  And we are the dreamers of dreams,
 Wandering by lone sea-breakers,
  And sitting by desolate streams; —
 World-losers and world-forsakers,
  On whom the pale moon gleams:
 Yet we are the movers and shakers
  Of the world for ever, it seems.

 With wonderful deathless ditties
  We build up the world's great cities,
  And out of a fabulous story
  We fashion an empire's glory:
 One man with a dream, at pleasure,
  Shall go forth and conquer a crown;
 And three with a new song's measure
  Can trample a kingdom down.

 We, in the ages lying
  In the buried past of the earth,
 Built Nineveh with our sighing,
  And Babel itself in our mirth;
 And o'erthrew them with prophesying

396. 颂歌

奥香涅西

我们是音乐的制作者①,
  我们是做梦的人,
在孤独的海浪边彳亍,
  独坐在荒凉的溪流之滨;——
我们失掉了世界,世界抛弃了我们,　　　　　5
  苍白的月光照耀着我们:
可是我们似乎永远是些
  推动世界和震憾世界的人。

我们用惊人的不朽的曲子,
建造起世界上伟大的城市,　　　　　　　　10
  我们用一个神奇的故事
  编造出一个帝国的光荣:
一个带着梦想的人,随他高兴,
  将出发去征服一个王位;
三个带着新的曲调的人,　　　　　　　　　15
  就能够把一个王国摧毁。

我们,生活在被埋葬了的
  古老久远的时代,
曾唉声叹气建造过尼尼微②,
  也高高兴兴建造过巴别塔;　　　　　20
又把它们一一推倒,

---

① 我们,指诗人们。——译者
② 尼尼微,古代亚述的都城,在底格里斯河上。见《圣经·约拿书》第三章。

To the old of the new world's worth[①];
For each age is a dream that is dying,
 Or one that is coming to birth.

A breath of our inspiration
Is the life of each generation;
 A wondrous thing of our dreaming,
  Unearthly, impossible seeming —
The soldier, the king, and the peasant
 Are working together in one,
Till our dream shall become their present,
 And their work in the world be done.

They had no vision amazing
Of the goodly house they are raising;
 They had no divine foreshowing
  Of the land to which they are going:
But on one man's soul it hath broken,
 A light that doth not depart;
And his look, or a word he hath spoken,
 Wrought flame in another man's heart.

And therefore to-day is thrilling
With a past day's late fulfilling;
 And the multitudes are enlisted
  In the faith that their fathers resisted,
And, scorning the dream of to-morrow,
 Are bringing to pass, as they may,
In the world, for its joy or its sorrow,
 The dream that was scorned yesterday.

---

① *the old ... the new*: *i.e.* the Past and the Future.

向旧世界预言新世界的价值；
因为每个时代都是垂死的梦想，
　　也是即将诞生的憧憬。

我们的一点点灵感，
赋予了每一代人以生命；
　　成为梦想中可惊的事，
　　人间所无，看似不可能——
军士、国王和农民
　　结成一体，协力同心，
直到梦想成为了现实，
　　他们的工作也终于完成。

他们正在建造的高楼大厦
当年他们并没有想象得到；
　　今天他们正在前去的地方
　　也出乎当年他们神圣的预想：
但它却在一个人的心灵上，
　　爆发出永不熄灭的光芒；
他的眼光和他说的一句话，
　　在另一个人心上点燃了火花。

因而过去未及时完成的任务
今天却令人激动万分；
　　我们的父辈反对的信仰
　　今天的群众却来赞成，
明天的梦他们不屑一看，
　　为了愉快或是为了悲伤，
他们今天却似乎要去实现，
　　昨天他们还瞧不起的梦想。

But we, with our dreaming and singing,
    Ceaseless and sorrowless we!
The glory about us clinging
    Of the glorious futures we see,
Our souls with high music ringing;
    O men! it must ever be
That we dwell, in our dreaming and singing,
    A little apart from ye.

For we are afar with the dawning
    And the suns that are not yet high,
And out of the infinite morning
    Intrepid you hear us cry —
How, spite of your human scorning,
    Once more God's future draws nigh,
And already goes forth the warning
    That ye of the past must die.

Great hail! we cry to the comers
    From the dazzling unknown shore;
Bring us hither your sun and your summers,
    And renew our world as of yore;
You shall teach us your song's new numbers,
    And things that we dreamed not before:
Yea, in spite of a dreamer who slumbers,
    And a singer who sings no more.

                      A. W. E. O'SHAUGHNESSY.

可是我们，做着梦又唱着歌，
　　停也不停，无悲无哀！　　　　　　　　　　　50
光荣在四周把我们围着，
　　我们看见了光辉的未来，
我们的心中响起崇高的音乐：
　　人们呵！我们一定是
做着梦又唱着歌，　　　　　　　　　　　　　　55
　　同你们保持住一点儿距离。

因为我们离得远远，不见黎明，
　　太阳也还未在天空高悬，
从无穷无尽的清晨
　　可以听见我们无畏的呐喊——　　　　　　60
呵，尽管你们人类瞧我不起，
　　上帝的未来已再度来临，
并且早已发出警告：
　　你们属于过去的一定得死去。

欢呼呵！我们朝着来自　　　　　　　　　　　65
　　眩目的陌生海岸的人们呼唤；
把你们的太阳和夏天带来这里，
　　让我们的世界新生如往日一般；
你得教会我们新的歌曲，
　　以及那些从前梦想不到的事：　　　　　　70
对，尽管是一个酣睡的梦想者，
　　以及一个不再歌唱的歌手。

赵　澧　译

编注　阿瑟·威廉·埃德加·奥香涅西（Arthur William Edgar O'shaughnessy, 1844—1881），写过四卷诗集。这首颂歌选自一八七四年出版的诗集《音乐与月光》（*Music and Moonlight*），是他最著名的一首诗。

397. 'OUT OF THE NIGHT THAT COVERS ME'

Out of the night that covers me,
    Black as the pit from pole to pole,
I thank whatever gods may be
    For my unconquerable soul.

In the fell clutch of circumstance
    I have not winced nor cried aloud.
Under the bludgeonings of chance
    My head is blooby, but unbowed.

Beyond this place of wrath and tears
    Looms but the Horror of the shade,
And yet the menace of the years
    Finds, and shall find, me unafraid.

It matters not how strait the gate,
    How charged with punishments the scroll,
I am the master of my fate:
    I am the captain of my soul.

                      W. E. HENLEY.

397. 大无畏①

亨利

屹立在漫漫的长夜,
  和遮天盖地的乌云;
深切感谢造化赋予
  我坚贞不屈的灵魂。

艰苦的遭遇摧残着,
  未能使我退缩号叫;
厄运打得头破血流,
  也从来不俯首求饶。

这悲惨人寰的那边
  隐伏着阴间的恐怖;
尽管残年威胁着我,
  现在将来绝不畏惧。

不管天门怎样窄狭,
  生死簿上多少罪状;
我是我命运的主人,
  我是我魂灵的船长。

初大告 译

编注 威廉·埃内斯特·亨利(William Ernest Henley,1849—1903),诗人、编辑、批评家,写过五部诗集,与史蒂文森合作写过三个剧本。

---

① 标题系译者所加。——编注者

398. PIED BEAUTY

Glory be to God for dappled things —
  For skies of couple-colour as a brindled cow;
    For rose-moles all in stipple upon trout that swim[1];
Fresh-firecoal chestnut-falls; finches'wings[2];
  Landscape plotted and pieced — fold, fallow, and plough[3];
    And áll trádes, their gear and tackle and trim[4].

All things counter, original, spare, strange[5];
  Whatever is fickle, freckled(who knows how?)
    With swift, slow; sweet, sour; adazzle, dim;
He fathers-forth whose beauty is past change:
          Praise Him.

G. M. HOPKINS.

---

[1] *rose-moles all in stipple*: stippled = dotted. Trout are speckled with red.
[2] *fresh-firecoal chestnut-falls*: like glowing coal, or chestnuts newly stripped of their husk.
[3] *plotted and pieced*: divided into fields.
[4] *trim*: equipment.
[5] *counter*: unusual. *spare*: out of the ordinary.

398. 杂色的美

霍普金斯

我把上帝赞扬，为了斑驳的物象——
　为天空的双色如同母牛的花斑，
　　为水中鳟鱼玫瑰痣像幅点彩；
新裂的栗子落、火炭烫，金翅雀翅膀，
　风景分成条块田——起伏、休闲、犁翻， 5
　　还有手艺百家，齿轮、滑车，装备驳杂。

世间万物皆有不同、独特、异样，
　只要遍布着快、慢、甜、酸的雀斑，
　　只要变化多端的光和暗使人眼花；
他创造出的它们的美超越了变化—— 10
　　赞美他吧。

飞白 译

编注 杰拉德·曼利·霍普金斯（Gerard Manley Hopkins, 1844—1889），英国诗人，早年开始写诗，一八六二年以《美人鱼的梦幻》一诗获奖。由于在意境、格律和词藻上都具有独创性，在世时很少受人赏识，直到一九三〇年全集再版，他的清新活泼的仿效"日常语言的自然节奏"的独特风格和创新精神才为新一代人所接受，并成为现代欧美重要诗人之一。他的诗大多表现自然界万物的个性以及诗人对大自然的感怀，宗教色彩较浓，名诗有《风鹰》《春秋》和《星光之夜》等。

399. THE STARLIGHT NIGHT

Look at the stars! look, look up at the skies!
   O look at all the fire-folk sitting in the air!
   The bright boroughs, the circle-citadels there!
Down in dim woods the diamond delves! the elves'-eyes!
The grey lawns cold where gold, where quickgold lies!
   Wind-beat whitebeam! airy abeles set on a flare①!
   Flake-doves sent floating forth at a farmyard scare! ——
Ah well! it is all a purchase, all is a prize.

   Buy then! bid then! — What? — Prayer, patience, alms, vows.
   Look, look: a May-mess, like on orchard boughs②!
   Look! March-blown, like on mealed-with-yellow sallows③!
These are indeed the barn; withindoors house
The shocks. This piece-bright paling shuts the spouse④
   Christ home, Christ and His mother and all His hallows⑤.

G. M. HOPKINS.

---

① *abeles*: white poplars.
② *May-mess*: medley, like blossom in spring.
③ *March-blown*: as though blown by the March wind. *sallows*: smal willow trees.
④ *shocks*: sheaves. The word generally means a stack of sheaves.
   piece-bright paling: the sky, pieced by the brightness of the stars.
⑤ *hallows*: saints.

399. 星光之夜

霍普金斯

仰望天空！看那些星星！
　那些位于上天的火堆！
　那些圆形的城堡，那些明亮的市镇！
下面幽暗的树林藏有钻石，这精灵的眼睛！
黄金和金水在灰冷的草坪闪亮①！ 5
　风儿吹起了白光，轻盈的白杨着火升腾②！
　家鸽吃惊地在农庄上空纷纷飞起！
啊！太妙了！都是买来或奖赏的礼品。

买去吧！吩咐吧！——什么？——祈祷，忍耐，誓言、施舍。
瞧瞧：那五月纷纷好像繁花纷飞！ 10
　瞧！那三月的花，好像鹅黄的柳枝吐蕾！
这里的确有仓房；房舍里面有麦堆。
这明亮的区域中有夫妻一对，
　　这是耶稣的家，有基督，圣母，还有圣徒追随。

周亚熊　译

编注　霍普金斯的诗，意境奇特，好造生词，构象亦很生动，如本诗形容天上的星星是"火堆""五月纷纷""白杨着火升腾"等，可以看出一些济慈、德莱顿、多恩等人的影响痕迹。

---

① "金水"指星儿闪烁似溶金一般。——编注者
② "白光"指树上长着的银白色的枝叶。——编注者

400. FROM 'MODERN LOVE'

In our old shipwrecked days there was an hour,
When in the firelight steadily aglow,
Joined slackly, we beheld the red chasm grow
Among the clicking coals. Our library-bower
That eve was left to us: and hushed we sat
As lovers to whom Time is whispering.
From sudden-opened doors we heard them sing:
The nodding elders mixed good wine with chat.
Well knew we that Life's greatest treasure lay
With us, and of it was our talk. 'Ah, yes!
Love dies!' I said: I never thought it less.
She yearned to me that sentence to unsay.
Then when the fire domed blackening, I found
Her cheek was salt against my kiss, and swift
Up the sharp scale of sobs her breast did lift: —
Now am I haunted by that taste! that sound.

Mark where the pressing wind shoots javelin-like
Its skeleton shadow on the broad-backed wave!
Here is a fitting spot to dig Love's grave;
Here where the ponderous breakers plunge and strike,
And dart their hissing tongues high up the sand:
In hearing of the ocean, and in sight
Of those ribbed wind-streaks running into white.
If I the death of Love had deeply planned,
I never could have made it half so sure,

400. 现代爱情（节选）

梅瑞狄斯

在我们昔日的艰难岁月中有一个时辰，
正当炉火熊熊溅火星，
我们闲坐一起，看那噼啪作响的煤块燃得通明，
小小书斋那晚上属于我们。
我们静坐一起，悄然无声，　　　　　　　　　　　5
只有时光向这对恋人浅唱低吟。
洞开的门户里，老人们饮酒闲谈，颔首频频，
我们听得见人们的唱歌声。
我们深知，人生的瑰宝正为我们降临，
我俩絮絮低语，声声不停。　　　　　　　　　　10
我说："啊，对啦，爱情也会消亡！"我从来就是这样认定。
她多么希望我收回前言，一改初心。
尔后炉火黯淡夜沉沉，
亲吻中我知她苦泪盈盈，
她伤心悲泣，胸膛隆起气难平，　　　　　　　　15
那声音，那深情，至今萦绕在我心！

寒风刺骨，凛冽强劲，
在洪波大浪上投下它尸骨般的阴影。
这里，正好在这里埋葬爱情。
激浪汹涌拍打沙滩，　　　　　　　　　　　　　20
啙啙的浪尖直冲上海滨；
倾听那海浪涌涛声阵阵，
眼望着海风吹白浪层层。
如果说我已经决定结束爱情，
我却怎么也无法将此事确定。　　　　　　　　　25

        As by the unblest kisses which upbraid
        The full-waked sense; or failing that, degrade!
        'Tis morning: but no morning can restore
        What we have forfeited. I see no sin:
30   The wrong is mixed. In tragic life, God wot,
        No villain need be! Passions spin the plot:
        We are betrayed by what is false within.

        We saw the swallows gathering in the sky,
        And in the osier-isle we heard them noise①.
35   We had not to look back on summer joys,
        Or forward to a summer of bright dye:
        But in the largeness of the evening earth
        Our spirits grew as we went side by side.
        The hour became her husband and my bride.
40   Love, that had robbed us so, thus blessed our dearth!
        The pilgrims of the year waxed very loud
        In multitudinous chatterings, as the flood
        Full brown came from the West, and like pale blood
        Expanded to the upper crimson cloud.
45   Love, that had robbed us of immortal things,
        This little moment mercifully gave,
        Where I have seen across the twilight wave
        The swan sail with her young beneath her wings.

        Thus piteously Love closed what he begat:
50   The union of this ever-diverse pair!
        These two were rapid falcons in a snare,
        Condemned to do the flitting of the bat,

---

① *osier*: willow.

勉强的接吻,有负清醒的心灵,
失去了真心,成了蜕变的感情!
正当清晨,但没有清晨能够恢复
我们失去的真情。我看不出罪过,
说不清谁错。上天明白,人生悲剧, 30
不一定都遇上小人!激情酿成这事:
是内心的虚假,使我们互相负心。

我们看见翻飞的燕子在天上聚成燕阵,
柳荫丛中听得见燕子的声声欢鸣。
对往昔夏日的欢乐,何必回首缅怀, 35
对来日多彩的夏天,也无需盼望憧憬。
暮色苍茫,大地广阔无垠,
我俩并肩漫步,心潮起伏荡激情,
一时间竟成了燕尔新人①!

年年往返的旅人欢叫不停, 40
越聚越多似无尽,
像是从西天涌来洪流滚滚,
又像是淡淡血痕,正扩向那高天红云。
爱神啊,曾不让我们柔情永存, 45
而这一瞬间,却又赐福于我们,
晚霞余晖中,我看见了:
天鹅正带着翼下的幼鸰在破浪前行。

爱神终于心生怜悯,不再折磨他们,
团聚起这一对反复无常的恋人。 50
他们像关在罗网中的鹰隼,
指责那翻飞的蝙蝠来去不定。

---

① 此处指燕子。——译者

Lovers beneath the singing sky of May,
They wandered once; clear as the dew on flowers:
But they fed not on the advancing hours:
Their hearts held cravings for the buried day.
Then each applied to each that fatal knife,
Deep questioning, which probes to endless dole.
Ah, what a dusty answer gets the soul
When hot for certainties in this our life! —
In tragic hints here see what evermore
Moves dark as yonder midnight ocean's force,
Thundering like ramping hosts of warrior horse,
To throw that faint thin line upon the shore!

                                        GEORGE MEREDITH.

五月里欢唱的晴空下，
他们徘徊流连，如花露般清新。
他们并不寄希望于未来的时辰，　　　　　　　　　55
两颗心却缅怀那昔日的温情。
深深的怀疑，如匕首使人致命
他们却一度用来互相探查无尽的苦情。
啊，在我们一生，当心灵迫切希望得到肯定，
而听到的却是如此晦涩的回声！　　　　　　　60
在这悲剧般的启示中，你看那夜色深沉，
雷电轰鸣，犹如战马奔腾，
午夜大海的威力，
朝海岸上推去茫茫一线波光浪影！

　　　　　　　　　　　　　　朱　徽　译

编注　乔治·梅瑞狄斯（George Meredith，1828—1909），英国诗人、小说家，代表作《利己主义者》以心理分析深刻著称，诗歌有《现代爱情》《悲剧人生的民谣与诗》《地球的解释》《空空的钱包及其他》《献给法国历史之歌的颂歌》等。此处选自《现代爱情》，讲述一对夫妻爱情衰微的过程，第一节丈夫讲述爱情幸福的时刻，第二节里爱情已经减退，第三节描述昔日激情的复苏，第四节在悲剧结束和妻子死后，诗人以自己的话解释了这对夫妻间爱情与信任失败的原因。

401. A BALLAD TO QUEEN ELIZABETH
Of the Spanish Armada

King Philip had vaunted his claims;
    He had sworn for a year he would sack us;
With an army of heathenish names
    He was coming to fagot and stack us[1];
    Like the thieves of the sea he would track us,
And shatter our ships on the main;
    But we had bold Neptune to back us, —
And where are the galleons of Spain?

His carackes were christened of dames[2]
    To the kirtles whereof he would tack us[3];
With his saints and his gilded stern-frames,
    He had thought like an egg-shell to crack us;
    Now Howard may get to his Flaccus,
And Drake to his Devon again,
    And Hawkins bowl rubbers to Bacchus[4], —
For where are the galleons of Spain?

Let his Majesty hang to St. James

---

[1] *fagot and stack us*: burn at the stake.
[2] *carackes*: galleons.
[3] *kirtles*: skirts.
[4] *bowl rubbers to Bacchus*: play bowls for drink. A rubber is the deciding game of a series.

401. 献给伊丽莎白女王的歌谣
（关于西班牙无敌舰队）

多布森

菲利普王夸过海口①；
　　说一年内要把我们洗劫；
他将率领异教的顽寇，
　　要把我们在火刑柱上消灭；
　　像海盗一样把我们盯住，　　　　　　　　　5
想把我们海上的船只都打翻。
　　但我们有英勇海神的眷顾
西班牙的舰队呀，请问你在何方？

他的舰队以贵妇人的名字命名，
　　开往海边，向我侵犯；　　　　　　　　　10
带着他的教徒和镀金的船尾，
　　以为我们像蛋壳一样容易打碎，
　　现在霍华德可以重温贺拉斯的诗句②，
德雷克可到德文郡再度游玩，
　　霍金斯滚完木球会酣畅痛饮③，　　　　　15
西班牙的舰队呀，你在何方？

---

① 菲利普王，即西班牙王菲利普二世，一五八八年，他派舰队与英国舰队作战。——译者
② 霍华德，英国海军上将，当时参加战争。——译者
③ 德雷克与霍金斯皆为英国著名航海家，曾参加美洲航路的开发，一五八八年西班牙无敌航队与英交战时两人都参加了战争，并立下战功。——编注者

The axe that he whetted to hack us;
He must play at some lustier games
    Or at sea he can hope to out-thwack us;
To his mines of Peru he would pack us
To tug at his bullet and chain;
    Alas! that his Greatness should lack us! —
But where are the galleons of Spain?

Envoy

Gloriana! the Don may attack us
Whenever his stomach be fain;
    He must reach us before he can rack us, ...
And where are the galleons of Spain?

AUSTIN DOBSON.

让那陛下把斧头悬在詹姆斯身旁①,
　　为劈砍我们,他曾把斧头磨亮;
还是让他做些别的铺张的游戏吧,
　　否则他的野心会更加狂妄;   20
　　妄图把我们驮到秘鲁的矿上去卖命②,
把子弹和脚镣的滋味品尝;
　　哎呀!大王陛下竟少了我们!——
西班牙舰队呀,你在何方?

跋

　　女皇格雷娜呀!西班牙胃口很大时③,   25
他们会兴风作浪;
　　把舰队开来才能把我们伤害……
但是西班牙舰队呀,你在何方?

李敬亭　译

编注　亨利·奥斯汀·多布森(Henry Austin Dobson,1840—1921),英国诗人,曾在英国商务部供职多年。他写有大量诗歌,其代表作为《带韵的短文》(*Vignettes in Rhyme*,1873)。

---

① 詹姆斯,即詹姆斯大圣,西班牙的守护神。——译者
② 秘鲁,一五八八年战时被西班牙占领,成为殖民地。——译者
③ 女皇格雷娜,即伊丽莎白女王。——译者

402. GIRD ON THY SWORD

Gird on thy sword, O man, thy strength endue,
In fair desire thine earth-born joy renew.
Live thou thy life beneath the making sun
Till Beauty, Truth, and Love in thee are one.

Thro' thousand ages hath thy childhood run:
On timeless ruin hath thy glory been:
From the forgotten night of loves fordone
Thou risest in the dawn of hopes unseen.

Higher and higher shall thy thoughts aspire,
Unto the stars of heaven, and pass away,
And earth renew the buds of thy desire
In fleeting blooms of evelasting day.

Thy work with beauty crown, thy life with love;
Thy mind with truth uplift to God above:
For whom all is, from whom was all begun,
In whom all Beauty, Truth, and Love are one.

ROBERT BRIDGES.

402. 佩上你的剑

布里吉斯

佩上你的剑吧,人呵,你就会有力量,
恢复你在尘世的欢乐吧,怀着美好希望。
过你的生活吧,浴着孕育一切的太阳,
直到美、真、爱一起都集中在你身上。

你的童年已经历了千载, 5
你的光荣遭到无穷毁灭,
你从被遗忘的失恋之夜起来,
在尚未见到希望的黎明站立。

你的思想必将追逐得越来越高,
直到够着天上星辰,然后消失, 10
你的希望在地上重又含苞,
在那花开即逝的永恒时日。

给你的工作戴上美的冠冕,让你生活里
充满爱情;使你的心儿仰望上帝,真诚无欺:
一切都是为了上帝,一切从他那里肇始, 15
在他身上美、真、爱三位结成了一体。

周向勤 译

编注 罗伯特·西摩·布里吉斯(Robert Seymour Bridges,1844—1930),曾当过医生,一九一三年至一九三〇年荣膺桂冠诗人。他最著名的是抒情短诗,其《短诗集》(*Shorter Poems*,1890)被认为是登峰造极之作。布里吉斯的诗精雕细刻,力求完美,反映了他与世无争的宁静生活,但缺乏激情。

403. I HAVE LOVED FLOWERS THAT FADE

I have loved flowers that fade,
Within whose magic tents
Rich hues have marriage made
With sweet unmemoried scents:
A honeymoon delight, —
A joy of love at sight,
That ages in an hour: —
My song be like a flower!

I have loved airs, that die
Before their charm is writ
Along a liquid sky
Trembling to welcome it.
Notes, that with pulse of fire
Proclaim the spirit's desire,
Then die, and are nowhere: —
My song be like an air!

Die, song, die like a breath,
And wither as a bloom:
Fear not a flowery death,
Dread not an airy tomb!
Fly with delight, fly hence!
'Twas thine love's tender sense
To feast; now on thy bier
Beauty shall shed a tear.

ROBERT BRIDGES.

403. 我爱凋谢的花朵

布里吉斯

我爱凋谢的花朵,
在那些神奇的天幕下
丰富的色彩与记不清的香气
举行了一次婚嫁:
有蜜月的狂喜——　　　　　　　　　　　　5
一见钟情的欢悦
而瞬间就将衰老——
呵,愿我的歌儿像朵花!

我爱微风,
沿清澈的天地,它们的娇媚　　　　　　　10
还未写出,它们就消逝,
颤抖中,又去迎接新空。
带着火样跳动的音符,
热情宣告灵魂的欲望,
随风飘去,无影无踪——　　　　　　　　15
呵,愿我的歌儿像微风!

死亡,歌唱,死亡像呼吸,
花谢如花开一样
别怕花一般的凋谢,
别怕空中的坟场!　　　　　　　　　　　20
飞翔,带着欢乐,去飞翔!
它是你爱的温柔感官
去享受,现在你上了灵柩
美神也为你落泪悲伤。

陈朴　译

404. NIGHTINGALES

Beautiful must be the mountains whence ye come,
And bright in the fruitful valleys the streams, wherefrom
    Ye learn your song:
Where are those starry woods? O might I wander there,
  Among the flowers, which in that heavenly air
    Bloom the year long!

Nay, barren are those mountains and spent the streams:
Our song is the voice of desire, that haunts our dreams,
    A throe of the heart,
Whose pining visions dim, forbidden hopes profound,
No dying cadence nor long sigh can sound,
    For all our art.

Alone, aloud in the raptured ear of men
We pour our dark nocturnal secret; and then,
    As night is withdrawn
From these sweet-springing meads and bursting boughs of May,
Dream, while the innumerable choir of day
    Welcome the dawn.

                        ROBERT BRIDGES.

404. 夜莺

布里吉斯

你飞掠的那些高山一定美丽,
　阳光铺满硕果累累的峡谷和明亮的小溪,在那里
　　你学到了自己的歌曲
哦!何处是那些头顶繁星的丛林?我真想漫游其间,
　到花丛去,那儿有天堂的气息,　　　　　　　　　　*5*
　　花儿成年四季斗艳争妍!

不,那些高山无比贫瘠,溪水也流尽:
　我们的歌是欲念的叫喊,回旋在我们的梦幻,
　　全是心灵痛苦的挣扎呢,
痛苦的景象依稀,深沉的希望被囚禁,　　　　　　　*10*
　没有哀怨的丧曲,也不会长久悲诉,
　　尽管我们有一切艺术。

只有在人类狂喜的耳里,清朗地听见
　我们倾吐着夜曲的秘密,
　　伴随着黑夜　　　　　　　　　　　　　　　　　*15*
从吐着春芳的牧场和五月盛开的花枝褪去,
　我们沉睡吧!哪怕数不清的白昼乐队
　　迎接着黎明。

　　　　　　　　　　　　　　　　　　　陈朴　译

405. IN MEMORIAM F. A. S.

Yet, O stricken heart, remember, O remember
    How of human days he lived the better part.
April came to bloom and never dim December
    Breathed its killing chills upon the head or heart.

Doomed to know not Winter, only Spring, a being
    Trod the flowery April blithely for a while,
Took his fill of music, Joy of thought and seeing,
    Came and stayed and went, nor ever ceased to smile.

Came and stayed and went, and now when all is finished,
    You alone have crossed the melancholy stream,
Yours the pang, but his, O his, the undiminished
    Undecaying gladness, undeparted dream.

All that life contains of torture, toil and treason,
    Shame, dishonour, death, to him were but a name.
Here, a boy, he dwelt through all the singing season
    And ere the day of sorrow departed as he came.

                            R. L. STEVENSON.

405. 纪念 F.A.西特韦尔[①]

斯蒂文森

伤心的人呵,可你也该记起,记起
　　他在世上过了一段最好的时光,
烟花四月他降生,阴冷的十二月却无须
　　吸那寒气,无须把头脑和心儿刺伤。

命该不知冬,只知春,一个小生命　　　　　　　　　　5
　　踏着四月鲜花来人间欢乐了一阵,
满耳都是音乐声,想想看看多高兴,
　　来了,留下,又去了,从未断过笑声。

来了,留下,又去了,如今都已完,
　　你已独自蹚过忧伤的小川,　　　　　　　　　　　10
痛苦属于你,可他,他呵,却享受着
　　无穷的快乐,无边的梦幻。

人生的一切磨难,劳苦,叛逆,
　　羞惭,耻辱,死亡,对他只是个名义,
在人间他一直保持童年,度过歌唱季节,　　　　　　15
　　悲伤的日子还未到来就逝去,像他来时。

周向勤　译

编注　罗伯特·路易士·斯蒂文森(Robert Louis Stevenson,1850—1894),十九世纪末新浪漫主义的代表,著名小说《金银岛》(*Treasure Island*,1883)的作者,写过不少诗文,包括《新天方夜谭》

[①] F.A.西特韦尔是诗人朋友西特韦尔夫人的幼婴。——译者

《绑架》《卡特林娜》《巴伦特雷的少爷》《化身博士》《岛上夜谭》等。他认为艺术的任务只是向读者叙述他们从未经历过的或有趣的事件。他的文笔细腻流畅,故事新奇浪漫,能激发读者的想象力。

406. UNTO US A SON IS GIVEN

Given, not lent,
And not withdrawn — once sent,
This Infant of mankind, this One,
Is still the little welcome Son.

New every year,
New born and newly dear,
He comes with tidings and a song,
The ages long, the ages long;

Even as the cold
Keen winter grows not old,
As childhood is so fresh; foreseen,
And spring in the familiar green.

Sudden as sweet
Come the expected feet.
All joy is young, and new all art,
And He, too, whom we have by heart.

ALICE MEYNELL.

406. 我们得到一个儿子

梅内尔

得到了,而不是添加,
一经出世就不再变卦,
这孩子,人类的幼稚,
总是受欢迎的天使。

年年新岁,
新生和新的宝贝,
他总伴随喜讯和歌声,
岁岁长存,岁岁长存;

甚至严寒
严冬亦不一般,
因为童年是那么新鲜,可以看见,
熟稔的绿荫中蕴藏着春天。

如同甜蜜
倏然降至期望的脚尖。
所有的快乐是年青,所有的艺术是新鲜,
还有他,他永远占据我们心间。

陆蜉 译

编注 艾丽丝·梅内尔(Alice Meynell,1847—1922),英国女诗人,散文作家和文艺批评家,前期写有许多吟颂爱情和自然美的诗,后期诗歌宗教情绪较浓。

407. VENERATION OF IMAGES

Thou man, first-comer, whose wide arms entreat,
    Gather, clasp, welcome, bind,
Lack, or remember; whose warm pulses beat
    With love of thine own kind: —

Unlifted for a blessing on yon sea,
    Unshrined on this highway,
O flesh, O grief, thou too shalt have our knee,
    Thou rood of every day[①]!

ALICE MEYNELL.

---

① *rood*: the cross or crucifix.

407. 对形象的崇敬

梅内尔

人,你这首先来此的先驱,你张开双臂,请求,
　　聚集,搜罗,欢迎,团聚,
忍受贫困或将一切存入记忆;在你的血管中
　　跳动着你的同类的情谊:——

你不曾因造福远处的海洋受到崇拜,
　　在这人生道上也未修建你的灵塔,
啊凡人,啊悲伤,你也应受到我们的膜拜,
　　你这日常生活中的十字架!

黄雨石　译

408. IN ROMNEY MARSH

As I went down to Dymchurch Wall,
    I heard the South sing o'er the land;
I saw the yellow sunlight fall
    On knolls where Norman churches stand.

And ringing shrilly, taut and lithe,
    Within the wind a core of sound,
The wire from Romney town to Hythe
    Alone its airy journey wound.

A veil of purple vapour flowed
    And trailed its fringe along the Straits;
The upper air like sapphire glowed;
    And roses filled Heaven's central gates.

Masts in the offing wagged their tops;
    The swinging waves peal'd on the shore;
The saffron beach, all diamond drops
    And beads of surge, prolonged the roar.

As I came up from Dymchurch Wall,
    I saw above the Downs' low crest
The crimson brands of sunset fall,

408. 在罗姆尼沼泽地

戴维森

当我信步走向戴姆丘奇围墙①,
  我听见南风在这土地上吟唱;
我看见那黄灿灿的阳光照射
  在诺曼底教堂坐落的山丘上。

尖厉的鸣响,紧绷绷,软绵绵,
  在南风中变成了声音的核心,
那电线从罗姆尼镇通往希思②
  沿着它那空中旅程蜿蜒前进。

一条紫烟织的面纱随风飞舞,
  沿着那海峡飘出来它的流苏;
上面的气体如蓝宝石在闪光;
  玫瑰色把天的中心城门抹涂。

桅杆在远处的海上摇来摆去,
  汹涌的海浪把海岸隆隆冲击;
藏红的海滩,所有钻石般水滴
  和波涛的浪花,都把海啸延续。

当我抽身离开戴姆丘奇围墙,
  我看见那丘陵草原的矮山梁
一束束殷红的晚照倾泻下来,

---

① 戴姆丘奇围墙,为防止海水流入低洼地修建的堤。——译者
② 罗姆尼、希思均位于肯特郡,两地相距九英里。——译者

20   Flicker and fade from out the west.

         Night sank; like flakes of silver fire
             The stars in one great shower came down;
         Shrill blew the wind; and shrill the wire
             Rang out from Hythe to Romney town.

25   The darkly shining salt sea drops
             Streamed as the waves clashed on the shore;
         The beach, with all its organ stops
             Pealing again, prolonged the roar.

                                JONH DAVIDSON.

那山梁忽隐忽现,暮色中消亡。 20

夜沉沉,像是银色的大火焰光
  群星撒落得恰如大阵雨一场;
南风尖厉地吹,电线尖厉地叫
  从希思到罗姆尼镇一路鸣响。

那些暗中闪光的咸的海水滴 25
  随着海浪拍击海岸随散随聚;
海滩,弹起它所有的风琴音栓,
  重奏嘹亮的乐曲,把海啸延续。

苏福忠 译

编注 约翰·戴维森(John Davidson,1857—1909),剧作家、哲学家和诗人,写有许多作品,其中既有小说、戏剧,又有诗歌。常受疾病折磨,后自杀。

409. EPITAPH ON AN ARMY OF MERCENARIES

These, in the day when heaven was falling,
    The hour when earth's foundations fled,
Followed their mercenary calling
    And took their wages and are dead.

Their shoulders held the sky suspended;
    They stood, and earth's foundations stay;
What God abandoned, these defended
    And saved the sum of things for pay.

ALFRED EDWARD HOUSMAN

409. 一支雇佣军的墓志铭

豪斯曼

这些人,在天空行将坍塌之日,
  在大地的根基已经挪动之时,
干上了他们被雇用的这一行,
  领到他们的工钱,买到的是死。

他们的肩支撑着天悬而不落;
  他们站着,大地根基不再动挪;
上帝所抛弃的,这些人来保卫,
  为挣工钱挽救下万物的总和。

苏福忠　译

编注　阿尔弗雷德·爱德华·豪斯曼(Alfred Edward Housman,1859—1936),进入二十世纪后,英国现代诗承上启下的诗人,开初写诗严格遵循传统,尤受古罗马、希腊文化影响,以后逐步转向开拓英诗的现代性。其代表作有《一个希罗普郡青年》(*A Shropshire Lad*,1896)和《最后的诗》(*Last Poems*,1922)。此诗所说的雇佣军,是德国人送给一九一四年英国远征军的称号。

410. 'IN NO STRANGE LAND'

'The Kingdom of God is within you.'

O world invisible, we view thee,
O world intangible, we touch thee,
O world unknowable, we know thee
Inapprehensible, we clutch thee!

Does the fish soar to find the ocean,
The eagle plunge to find the air —
That we ask of the stars in motion
If they have rumour of thee there?

Not where the wheeling systems darken,
And our benumbed conceiving soars! —
The drift of pinions, would we hearken,
Beats at our own clay-shuttered doors.

The angels keep their ancient places; —
Turn but a stone, and start a wing!
'Tis ye, 'tis your estrangèd faces,
That miss the many-splendoured thing.

But (when so sad thou canst not sadder)
Cry; — and upon thy so sore loss

410. "并非陌生之地"
("上帝的王国在你心中"①)

汤普森

啊,看不见的世界,我们看见了你,
啊,触摸不到的世界,我们触摸到了你,
啊,不可知的世界,我们知道了你,
不可理解的,但我们理解了你。

鱼儿遨游,是寻觅海洋?
苍鹰翱翔,是寻求太空——
我们向旋转的星宿问讯
它们在那里曾否听你嘟哝?

不在那旋转的星宿暗淡下去的地方,
不在我们木然的想象奔驰之地!——
我们倾听,翅翼翻翔
拍打着我们自己的泥板门壁。

天使仍保持着他们古老的地位;——
只需转动一块石头,扇动一只翅翼!
即是你们,即是你们那疏远的脸面,
错过了那光彩绚丽的东西。

然而(在你悲伤至极时)哭泣吧;
——于是,在你如此深痛的伤失上

---

① 见《圣经·旧约·路加福音》,第十七章,第二十一节。——译者

Shall shine the traffic of Jacob's ladder
Pitched betwixt Heaven and Charing Cross.

Yea, in the night, my Soul, my daughter,
Cry, — clinging Heaven by the hems;
And lo, Christ walking on the water,
Not of Gennesareth, but Thames!

FRANCIS THOMPSON.

架在天国与查林·克罗斯之间的①
雅各的天梯,将会有天使上下,光辉照亮②。　　　　20

是的,夜里,我的灵魂,我的女儿,
哭喊着;——攀住梯缘,依恋着天堂,
于是,瞧哪,基督行走在水上③,
不是在吉纳萨里斯河上,而是在泰晤士河上!

解珉　译

编注　弗朗西斯·汤普森(Francis Thompson,1859—1907),一个一生为疾病和贫困所苦的诗人。本诗是作者死后才被人发现的,并有可能没写完。

---

① 查林·克罗斯,伦敦市中心一地区名。——译者
② 由此梯可登上天堂,典出《圣经·创世记》,第二十八章第十二节。——编注者
③ 见《圣经·新约·马太福音》,第十四章第二十五节。——译者

411. DRAKE'S DRUM[①]

Drake he's in his hammock an' a thousand mile away,
    (Capten, art tha sleepin' there below?)
Slung atween the round shot in Nombre Dios Bay,
    An' dreamin' arl the time o' Plymouth Hoe.
Yarnder lumes the Island, yarnder lie the ships,
    Wi' sailor lads a-dancin' heel-an'-toe,
An' the shore-lights flashin', an' the night-tide dashin',
    He sees et arl so plainly as he saw et long ago.

Drake he was a Devon man, an' ruled the Devonseas,
    (Capten, art tha sleepin' there below?),
Rovin' tho' his death fell, he went wi' heart at ease,
    An' dreamin' arl the time o'Plymouth Hoe.
'Take my drum to England, hang et by the shore,
    Strike et when your powder 's runnin' low;
If the Dons sight Devon, I'll quit the port o'Heaven,
    An' drum them up the Channel as we drummed them long ago. '

Drake he's in his hammock till the great Armadas come,
    (Capten, art tha sleepin' there below?)

---

① This poem is in the Devon dialect.

411. 德雷克的战鼓

纽博尔德爵士

德雷克睡在千里之外他的吊床上,
　　(船长,你在下面可睡得安详?)
两头坠着圆圆的铅球抛在诺姆布雷戴奥斯海湾①,
　　普利茅斯霍却不断浮现在他的梦乡②。
那边隐现着那个海岛,那边停泊着那些船只③, 5
　　我们水手小伙子的舞步如竞走一样,
那海岸的灯光忽明忽灭,那夜里的海潮此起彼伏,
　　他总是那样坦然地看着它,一如他很久以前看过它一样。

德雷克他是德文郡人,曾经统辖过德文郡的海域,
　　(船长,你在下面可睡得安详?) 10
虽然他在漫游中死去,但他死得心安理得,
　　普利茅斯霍仍不断浮现在他的梦乡。
"把我的战鼓带到英国,挂在海岸边,
　　当你精神低落时把它敲响;
如果那帮先生觊觎德文郡,那我将离开天堂的避风港④, 15
　　用战鼓把他们轰到英吉利海峡,一如我们很久以前轰过他们一样。"

德雷克他睡在他的吊床上等待那庞大的无敌舰队到来⑤,
　　(船长,你在下面可睡得安详?)

---

① 死于海上的水手,一般用吊床捆起来,头脚坠上铅球葬入海底。德雷克海葬时用的是铅制棺材。——编注者
② 德雷克(英国无敌舰队首领)的舰队开战前正在普利茅斯霍玩滚木球。——译者
③ 那个海岛,离普利茅斯不远的一个小岛,今天以"德雷克岛"闻名。——译者
④ 那帮先生,指西班牙人。——译者
⑤ 指十六世纪西班牙的无敌舰队。——译者

Slung atween the round shot, listenin' for the drum,
    An' dreamin' arl the time o' Plymouth Hoe.
Call him on the deep sea, call him up the Sound,
    Call him when ye sail to meet the foe;
Where the old trade 's plyin' an' the old flag flyin'
    They shall find him ware an' wakin', as they found him long ago!

                      SIR HENRY NEWBOLT.

两头坠着圆圆的铅球抛出去,倾听着战鼓,
　　普利茅斯霍仍不断浮现在他的梦乡。　　　　　　　　　　　*20*
喊着他游戈在深深的海上,喊着他开进那个海湾①,
　　喊着他你扬帆去和敌人较量;
在那旧行业重操和老旗帜飘扬的地方②
　　他们都将发现他活灵活现,一如他们很久以前发现过他一样。

苏福忠　译

编注　亨利·纽博尔德爵士(Sir Henry Newbolt,1862—1938),英国海军编年史家与《每月评论》编辑,除写诗外还写了许多散文作品,以《海军将军大全》(*Admirals All*)最受读者欢迎。

---

① 那个海湾,指离普利茅斯不远的一个锚地。——译者
② 旧行业,和英国的各种敌人作战。——译者

412. UNWELCOME

We were young, we were merry, we were very very wise,
    And the door stood open at our feast,
When there passed us a woman with the West in her eyes,
    And a man with his back to the East.

O, still grew the hearts that were beating so fast,
    The loudest voice was still.
The jest died away on our lips as they passed,
    And the rays of July struck chill.

The cups of red wine turn'd pale on the board,
    The white bread black as soot.
The hound forgot the hand of her lord,
    She fell down at his foot.

Low let me lie, where the dead dog lies,
    Ere I sit me down again at a feast,
When there passes a woman with the West in her eyes,
    And a man with his back to the East.

MARY COLERIDGE.

412. 不受欢迎的

玛丽·柯勒律治

我们曾年青,我们曾欢乐,我们曾非常非常聪明,
　　我们欢宴,门扉洞开,
一个眼望着西方的女人,和一个
　　背向东方的男人,从我们面前走开。

啊,我们那欢快跳动的心渐渐静衰,　　　　　　　　　5
　　最喧哗的声音也已停息,
他们走过,嘴边的戏谑也顿然无声,
　　七月的艳阳变得阴冷刺脸。

桌上杯杯红葡萄酒失色发白,
　　雪白的面包黑如煤烟。　　　　　　　　　　　　10
狗儿忘了主人抚摸它的手,
　　倒下死在他的脚边。

在我再坐下欢宴前,
　　让我在狗儿躺卧的地方低低躺眠,
一个眼望着西方的女人,和一个　　　　　　　　　　15
　　背向着东方的男子,走过我们面前。

解珉　译

编注　玛丽·伊丽沙白·柯勒律治(Mary Elizabeth Coleridge,1861—1907),英国著名诗人塞缪尔·泰勒·柯勒律治的侄孙女,童年即开始写诗,死后才出版其主要著作。

413. THE LAKE ISLE OF INNISFREE

I will arise and go now, and go to Innisfree,
And a small cabin build there, of clay and wattles made①;
Nine bean rows will I have there, a hive for the honey bee,
And live alone in the bee-loud glade.

And I shall have some peace there, for peace comes dropping slow,
Dropping from the veils of the morning to where the cricket sings;
There midnight 's all a-glimmer, and noon a purple glow,
And evening full of the linnet's wings.

I will arise and go now, for always night and day
I hear lake water lapping with low sounds by the shore;
While I stand on the roadway, or on the pavements gray,
I hear it in the deep heart's core.

W. B. YEATS.

---

① *wattles*: hurdles, wickerwork.

413. 茵纳斯弗利岛

叶芝

我就要动身走了,去茵纳斯弗利岛①,
搭起一个小屋子,筑起泥巴房;
支起九行云豆架,一排蜜蜂巢,
独个儿住着,荫阴下蜂群嗡嗡唱。

我就会得到宁静,它徐徐下降, 5
从早晨的面纱落到蟋蟀歌唱的地方;
午夜是一片闪亮,正午是一片紫光,
傍晚到处飞舞着红雀的翅膀。

我就要动身走了,因为我听到
那水声日日夜夜拍打着湖滨; 10
不管我站在车行道或灰暗的人行道;
都在我心灵的深处听见这声音。

袁可嘉 译

编注 威廉·巴特勒·叶芝(William Butler Yeats,1865—1939),现代爱尔兰著名抒情诗人与作家,一九二三年诺贝尔文学奖获得者,早期具有唯美主义倾向。此诗即为早期代表作,表达了"出世"隐居的思想。后期积极参加爱尔兰民族自治运动。

---

① 爱尔兰民间传说中的一个湖中小岛,叶芝把它比作为隐居的地方。此诗作于一八九〇年。——译者

414. THE FOLLY OF BEING COMFORTED

One that is ever kind said yesterday
'Your well-beloved's hair has threads of grey,
And little shadows come about her eyes;
Time can but make it easier to be wise
Though now it seem impossible, and so
Patience is all that you have need of.' No,
I have not a crumb of comfort, not a grain;
Time can but make her beauty over again:
Because of that great nobleness of hers
The fire that stirs about her, when she stirs
Burns but more clearly. O she had not these ways,
When all the wild summer was in her gaze.
O heart! O heart! if she'd but turn her head,
You'd know the folly of being comforted.

W. B. YEATS.

414. 听人安慰的愚蠢

叶芝

昨天,一个总是那么善良的人说起,
"你爱的那个人,头发中已有了银丝,
她的眼圈下,也出现了小小的阴影,
时间只能使你自然而然地变得聪明,
虽然现在还显得不可能,因此讲 5
你需要的只是耐心。"不,不是这样,
我可得不到一滴安慰,一点安慰,
时间只能再一次焕发出她的美:
因为她的风姿非凡,华贵雍容,
炉火在她身旁跳动,她一转身, 10
炉火更为熊熊。哦当疯狂的夏日的一切
在她的目光中,她也绝无这些瑕疵,
呵,心哟,心! 只要她转过她的身
你就会知道听人安慰有多么愚蠢。

裘小龙 译

编注 叶芝在一八八九年认识莫德·贡(Maud Gonne),并爱上她,她拒绝过叶芝的多次求婚,但叶芝爱心不变。此诗即为叶芝听人说到莫德·贡韶华已逝时的感觉。

415. THE COWARD

I could not look on Death, which being known,
Men led me to him, blindfold and alone.

RUDYARD KIPLING.

415. 懦汉

吉卜林

恕我未能正视死亡,尽管当时惊险备尝,
只因把我两眼蒙住,人们让我孤身前往。

绿原 译

编注 鲁德雅德·吉卜林(Rudyard Kipling,1865—1936),英国小说家、诗人,曾获一九○七年诺贝尔文学奖。其诗作大部分写英国军队在异国的征战,英帝国的责任和光荣,充满扩张精神,有"帝国诗人"之称。主要诗作有《军营歌谣》《七海》《五国》《英国的诗歌》《东与西之歌》等,韵律和谐,音节流畅,技巧娴熟。

本诗中谈到的"懦汉"是一个士兵,由于他的软弱,被枪弹击中,毙命。

416. THE LAST CHANTEY

Thus said The Lord in the Vault above the Cherubim,
    Calling to the Angels and the Souls in their degree:
        'Lo! Earth has pass'd away
        On the smoke of Judgement Day.
    That Our word may be established shall We gather up the sea?'

Loud sang the souls of the jolly, jolly mariners:
    'Plague upon the hurricane that made us furl and flee!
        But the war is done between us,
        In the deep the Lord hath seen us —
    Our bones we'll leave the barracout', and God may sink the sea!'[①]

Then said the soul of Judas that betrayèd Him:
    'Lord, hast Thou forgotten Thy covenant with me?
        How once a year I go
        To cool me on the floe?
    And Ye take my day of mercy if Ye take away the sea!'

Then said the soul of the Angel of the Off-shore Wind:
    (He that bits the thunder when the bull-mouthed breakers flee):
        'I have watch and ward to keep
        O'er Thy wonders on the deep,
    And Ye take mine honour from me if Ye take away the sea!'

---

① *barracout*: a large fierce fish, common in the seas about the West Indies.

416. 最后的起锚歌

吉卜林

小神儿头上穹窿里的主这样说着,
  把各就其位的天使们和魂灵们呼唤:
    "诸位请看!地球已经消泯
    随着末日的烟雾腾腾。
  为了证实我们的命令,是否应将海洋收揽?"   5

皇家陆战队水兵们的魂灵高声唱道:
  "该死的飓风逼使我们卷帆逃遁!
    但我们之间战争已经分晓,
    主已从深渊中把我们找到——
  我们将把自己的骸骨留给梭鱼,由上帝去将大海沉沦!"   10

接着出卖过主的犹大的魂灵说:
  "主啊,难道您已对我的圣约置之不顾?
    我怎能一年一度
    到浮冰上去乘凉避暑?
  您要是取走了海洋,岂不使我万劫不复①?"   15

接着司掌海风的天使的魂灵说:
  (当牛嘴般的海浪逃逸时他遏制了霹雳):
    "我一直负责守看
    您大海上的奇观,
  您要是取走了海洋,岂不将我的光荣取缔!"   20

---

① 据基督教传说,犹大因出卖耶稣注定永远受火刑,仅被恩准每年在浮冰山上过圣诞节。——译者

Loud sang the souls of the jolly, jolly mariners:
  'Nay, but we were angry, and a hasty folk are we!
    If we worked the ship together
    Till she foundered in foul weather,
  Are we babes that we should clamour for a vengeance on the sea?'

Then said the souls of the slaves that men threw overboard:
  'Kennelled in the picaroon a weary band were we[①];
    But Thy arm was strong to save,
    And it touched us on the wave,
  And we drowsed the long tides idle till Thy Trumpets tore the sea.'

Then cried the soul of the stout Apostle Paul to God:
  'Once we frapped a ship, and she laboured woundily.
    There were fourteen score of these,
    And they blessed Thee on their knees,
  When they learned Thy Grace and Glory under Malta by the sea!'

Loud sang the souls of the jolly, jolly mariners,
  Plucking at their harps, and they plucked unhandily:
    'Our thumbs are rough and tarred,
    And the tune is something hard —
  May we lift a Deepsea Chantey such as seamen use at sea?'

Then said the souls of the gentlemen-adventurers —
  Fettered wrist to bar all for red iniquity:
    'Ho, we revel in our chains

---

① *picaroon*: pirate ship.

皇家陆战队水兵们的灵魂高声唱道:
　"好吧,可我们发过怒,我们是急躁的民族!
　　如果我们把船只修葺
　　直到它沉没在恶劣的天气,
　　我们可要婴儿般叫嚷着对海洋进行报复?"　　　　　　　　　25

接着被扔到船外的奴隶们的魂灵说:
　"我们沮丧的一群被囚禁在海盗船上;
　　但您的巨臂能够救人
　　它在浪尖上接触到我们,
　　我们昏昏然度过漫长的潮汐直到您的法螺贝撕裂了海洋。"　　30

接着顽强的使徒保罗的魂灵向上帝哭诉:
　"我们曾经缆索捆绑船身,让它负伤。
　　我们一共二百八十个,
　　都跪了下来为您唱赞歌,
　　当我们得知您在海边米利大的恩宠和荣光①。"　　　　　　　35

皇家陆战队水兵们的魂灵们高声唱道,
　同时拨弄着他们的竖琴,拨弄得那么笨:
　"我们的拇指粗糙而肮脏,
　　因此曲调未免不够铿锵——
　　我们可否奏一曲大海起锚歌,一如海员们平日所闻?"　　　　40

接着绅士冒险家们的魂灵说——
　他们被铐紧手腕都因犯有血腥罪行:
　"嗬:我们为我们的锁链乐不可支

---

① 据《圣经·新约·使徒行传》第二十七、二十八章,保罗和别的囚犯乘船流放意大利,途中船被风浪损坏,船上共二百七十六人在米利大岛(即今马耳他岛)得救。——译者

    O'er the sorrow that was Spain's;
45   Heave or sink it, leave or drink it, we were masters of the sea!'

  Up spake the soul of a gray Gothavn 'speckshioner①—
   (He that led the flinching in the fleets of fair Dundee②):
    'Oh, the ice-blink white and near③,
    And the bowhead breaching clear④!
50   Will Ye whelm them all for wantonness that, wallow in the sea⑤?'

  Loud sang the souls of the jolly, jolly mariners,
   Crying: 'Under Heaven, here is neither lead nor lea⑥!
    Must we sing for evermore
    On the windless, glassy floor?
55   Take back your golden fiddles and we'll beat to open sea!'

  Then stooped the Lord, and He called the good sea up to Him,
   And 'stablished his borders unto all eternity,
    That such as have no pleasure
    For to praise the Lord by measure,
60   They may enter into galleons and serve Him on the sea.

  Sun, wind, and cloud shall fail not from the face of it,
   Stinging, ringing spindrift nor the fulmar flying free⑦;
    And the ships shall go abroad
    To the Glory of the Lord
65   *Who heard the silly sailor-folk and gave them back their sea!*

            RUDYARD KIPLING.

---

① *'speckshioner*: specksioneer, or harpooner, who directs the operation of flensing (see below).
② *flinching*: flensing, cutting the blubber.
③ *ice-blink*: iceberg.
④ *bowhead*: Greenland whale. *breaching*: a whale's leap out of the water.
⑤ *whelm*: overwhelm, submerge.
⑥ *lead nor lea*: there are no soundings to be made, and no shelter is to be found.
⑦ *spindrift*: spray. *fulmar*: sea bird of the petrel kind.

同时想起了西班牙的伤心往事;
不论沉与浮,不论去与留,我们曾是海洋的主人!" *45*

一个灰色哥特哈文镇捕鲸手的魂灵大声说了①——
（他曾在美丽的丹迪港船队上领导过剥鲸）②:
"啊,冰山浮过来白晃晃
格陵兰鲸出水亮光光!
您可为它们翻滚于海上的放肆行为淹没它们?" *50*

皇家陆战队水手们的魂灵高声
叫喊起来:"穹苍之下,听不见测铅也看不见草坪!
难道要我们永远歌声凄厉
在这无风的平稳如镜的海底?
拿走你金色的提琴吧,我们将向大海逆风而行!" *55*

然后主屈尊俯就,呼唤大海前来,
命令它将边界伸延到永恒,
以便没有希望的人们
崇拜主能有准则可循,
他们可以登上大帆船,到海上把主侍奉。 *60*

它前面决不能没有太阳、风和云彩,
不能没有锐利的、轰响的浪花,更不能没有飞翔的管鼻鹱;
船只一定得航向海洋
船向主的荣光,
主把大海还给了它们,他听见了愚蠢的水手摇曲! *65*

绿原 译

---

① 哥特哈文,格陵兰的迪斯科岛南端一小镇。——译者
② 丹迪港,位于英国苏格兰东部。——译者

417. RECESSIONAL

June 22, 1897

God of our fathers, known of old,
    Lord of our far-flung battle-line,
Beneath whose awful Hand we hold
    Dominion over palm and pine —
Lord God of Hosts, be with us yet,
Lest we forget — lest we forget!

The tumult and the shouting dies;
    The captains and the kings depart:
Still stands Thine ancient sacrifice,
    An humble and a contrite heart.
Lord God of Hosts, be with us yet,
Lest we forget — lest we forget!

Far-called, our navies melt away;
    On dune and headland sinks the fire:
Lo, all our pomp of yesterday
    Is one with Nineveh and Tyre!
Judge of the Nations, spare us yet,
Lest we forget — lest we forget!

417. 礼拜后的退场曲
(一八九七年六月二十二日)

吉卜林

我们自古闻名的祖先们的上帝,
 我们辽阔战线的主,
在您尊严的手下托庇,
 我们掌管着棕榈和松树①——
率领天军的主啊,愿您与我们同在,
免得我们忘怀——免得我们忘怀!

喧闹和叫嚣已经消歇;
 帝王将相寿终正寝:
您古老的祭品仍然陈列,
 一颗卑微的、一颗悔悟的心。
率领天军的主啊,愿您与我们同在,
免得我们忘怀——免得我们忘怀!

我们远征的舰队已经溶化;
 沙冈和岬角上熄灭了战火:
看吧,我们昔日所有的浮华
 全在于尼尼微和推罗②!
宽赦我们吧,万民的总裁,
免得我们忘怀——免得我们忘怀!

---

① 此句喻大英帝国广袤的疆土。——译者
② 尼尼微系古代亚述国首都。据《旧约·约拿书》,约拿奉耶和华旨意,去尼尼微告警,尼尼微人信而悔改。推罗系古代腓尼基文化中心。据《旧约·以西结书》,推罗君主骄奢淫佚,国土倾圮。此句系诗人哀叹昔日的浮华全成泡影。——译者

If, drunk with sight of power, we loose
    Wild tongues that have not Thee in awe,
Such boastings as the Gentiles use,
    Or lesser breeds without the Law —
Lord God of Hosts, be with us yet,
Lest we forget — lest we forget!

For heathen heart that puts her trust
    In reeking tube and iron shard,
All valiant dust that builds on dust,
    And guarding, calls not Thee to guard,
For frantic boast and foolish word —
Thy Mercy on Thy People, Lord!

                          RUDYARD KIPLING.

如果我们醉于权势,放纵
　　长舌对您无所敬畏, 20
那种矜夸不啻异端所惯用,
　　或者无法无天的小族类——
率领天军的主呵,愿您与我们同在,
免得我们忘怀——免得我们忘怀!

对于未开化的心,它只信任 25
　　冒烟炮筒和铁制榴弹,
所有出身于尘土的勇敢的凡人
　　自行防范而不求您来防范,
为了如此这般的狂言妄语——
愿您怜悯您的臣民,啊主! 30

　　　　　　　　　　　　绿原　译

编注　这首诗是吉卜林诗作中最为有名的一首。它是为维多利亚女王的纪念庆典而写的,但与纪念庆典的气氛并不协调。诗人在诗中认为,"昔日的浮华"都成了过眼烟云,全变泡影,从而表达了"帝国诗人"对大英帝国日益没落的哀叹。

418. CADGWITH

My windows open to the autumn night,
In vain I watched for sleep to visit me;
How should sleep dull mine ears, and dim my sight,
Who saw the stars, and listened to the sea?

Ah, how the City of our God is fair!
If, without sea, and starless though it be,
For joy of the majestic beauty there,
Men shall not miss the stars, nor mourn the sea.

LIONEL JOHNSON.

418. 卡杰维斯①

约翰森

我的小窗向着秋夜敞开,
我枉然地等候睡神来访;
遥望群星,聆听大海
如何能使睡眼模糊,听觉迟钝?

呵,上帝的城市多么美好! 5
即使没有海和星星,它也依然一样,
那里仍有宇宙神圣美的欢乐,
人们不会怀念群星,也不哀悼海洋。

金敏 译

编注 莱昂内尔·皮戈特·约翰森(Lionel Pigot Johnson,1867—1902),英国诗人,童年便开始写诗,但后来成就并不大,虽然时有冲动,写出的诗却总少激情,这首小诗算是例外。

---

① 英国康沃尔地方一村庄。——译者

419. FOR THE FALLEN

With proud thanksgiving, a mother for her children,
England mourns for her dead across the sea.
Flesh of her flesh they were, spirit of her spirit,
Fallen in the cause of the free.

Solemn the drums thrill: Death august and royal
Sings sorrow up into immortal spheres.
There is music in the midst of desolation
And a glory that shines upon our tears.

They went with songs to the battle, they were young,
Straight of limb, true of eye, steady and aglow.
They were staunch to the end against odds uncounted,
They fell with their faces to the foe.

They shall grow not old, as we that are left grow old:
Age shall not weary them, nor the years condemn.
At the going down of the sun and in the morning
We will remember them.

They mingle not with their laughing comrades again;
They sit no more at familiar tables of home;
They have no lot in our labour of the day-time;
They sleep beyond England's foam.

But where our desires are and our hopes profound,

419. 悼阵亡将士

宾雍

母亲为她的儿子有着骄傲的谢忱,
英格兰为她在海那边阵亡的士兵。
他们是她的肉的肉,她的心的心,
为捍卫自由而死于战阵。

庄严地鼓声雷鸣,死是重于泰山, 5
悲歌唱入永恒不朽的圣坛。
在肃静之中有音乐渊渊,
在我们的泪珠上有荣光灿烂。

他们唱着战歌出阵,他们还是青年,
四肢挺直,目光真挚,信心坚实而欲燃。 10
他们坚持到底,抗拒了数不清的灾难。
他们是阵亡在敌人的面前。

他们不像剩下的我们,将永远不老,
年岁不会使他们疲劳,也不会潦倒。
当到太阳西沉,当到太阳东升, 15
我们要永远记着他们。

他们不会再同战友们一道欢笑;
也不再回到家来在食桌边闲聊;
不会和我们从事日常的辛劳:
他们已在英伦海外长眠了。 20

但何处是我们远大的希望和志愿,

Felt as a well-spring that is hidden from sight,
To the innermost heart of their own land they are known
As the stars are known to the Night;

As the stars that shall be bright when we are dust,
Moving in marches upon the heavenly plain,
As the stars that are starry in the time of our darkness,
To the end, to the end, they remain.

LAURENCE BINYON.

明明如眼不能见的地下源泉。
你们永存在祖国的最深处的心底,
犹如夜空的群星人所共知。

当我们成了尘土,群星照样放光,
照样运行在穹苍之上,
群星会灿然照着我们的墓茔,
他们是永远永远地万古常青。

(1914)

郭沫若 译

编注 劳伦斯·宾雍(Laurence Binyon,1869—1943),英国诗人,著名美术家。他长期在大英博物馆工作,尤精于东方绘画,写过许多诗。《悼阵亡将士》发表于第一次世界大战开始时,是他最著名的一首诗。

420. SWEET STAY-AT-HOME

Sweet Stay-at-Home, sweet Well-content,
Thou knowest of no strange continent:
Thou hast not felt thy bosom keep
A gentle motion with the deep;
Thou hast not sailed in Indian seas,
Where scent comes forth in every breeze.
Thou hast not seen the rich grape grow
For miles, as far as eyes can go.
Thou hast not seen a summer's night
When maids could sew by a worm's light;
Nor the North Sea in spring send out
Bright hues that like birds flit about
In solid cages of white ice —
Sweet Stay-at-Home, sweet Love-one-place.
Thou hast not seen black fingers pick
White cotton when the bloom is thick,
Nor heard black throats in harmony;
Nor hast thou sat on stones that lie
Flat on the earth, that once did rise
To hide proud kings from common eyes
Thou hast not seen plains full of bloom
Where green things had such little room
They pleased the eye like fairer flowers —
Sweet Stay-at-Home, all these long hours.
Sweet Well-content, sweet Love-one-place,
Sweet, simple maid, bless thy dear face;

1820

420. 可爱的居家少女

戴维斯

可爱的居家少女,可爱的自足之心,
你毫不知那些陌生的土地:
你从未发现过自己的胸中
竟有那么多温柔深厚的情意;
你没有航行过印度洋, 5
那里阵阵微风送来芬芳;
你从未见过成群的葡萄生长,
连绵不断,一望无际。
你没有看到星汉灿烂的夏夜
少女们在萤光下穿针走线; 10
你没见过北海的春天
那放出的光彩如同千鸟齐掠。
在白雪封锁的坚固笼中呵——
恋家的、可爱的居家少女,
当棉桃丰腴,你不会见到 15
黑色的手指采摘洁白的棉桃,
不会听见黑色鸟儿哼出和谐的曲调;
没有坐过躺在地上的石宕
它们曾竖起掩护过骄傲的国王,
迷惑了多少普通人的眼睛; 20
你从未见过鲜花盛开的平原,
那绿色的枝叶只有很少的空间
赏心悦目像极美的花瓣——
可爱的居家少女,过了这许多长长的岁月,
仅仅恋家,可爱的自足, 25
可爱朴实的少女,祝福你面容美丽;

For thou hast made more homely stuff
Nurture thy gentle self enough.
I love thee for a heart that's kind —
Not for the knowledge in thy mind. —

W. H. DAVIES.

祝福你创造的更加质朴的东西
那便是培育了无比温柔的你自己
呵,我爱你那颗纯洁善良的心——
毫不在乎你心中装了多少知识。 30

金敏 译

编注 威廉·亨利·戴维斯(William Henry Davies,1871—1940),英国诗人,小说家,早年曾当过流浪者,饱历沧桑。这首诗吟颂了返朴归真的理想。

421. TREES

    Of all the trees in England,
        Her sweet three corners in,
    Only the Ash, the bonnie Ash
        Burns fierce while it is green.

    Of all the trees in England,
        From sea to sea again,
    The Willow loveliest stoops her boughs
        Beneath the driving rain.

    Of all the trees in England,
        Past frankincense and myrrh.
    There's none for smell, of bloom and smoke,
        Like Lime and Juniper.

    Of all the trees in England,
        Oak, Elder, Elm, and Thorn,
    The Yew alone burns lamps of peace
        For them that lie forlorn.

                      WALTER DE LA MARE.

421. 树

梅尔

在英格兰可爱的三个角落内,
　　在她的一切树木中间,
唯有桦树,美丽的桦树
　　怒燃着绿色的火焰。

在英格兰所有的树木中间,
　　从海岸到海岸,
最妩媚的柳树垂下了腰枝,
　　任急风暴雨摧残。

在英格兰所有的树木中
　　不管是乳香还是没药脂,
没有一种树的烟花气味的浓郁
　　比得上杜松与菩提。

在英格兰所有树木中,
　　不论是橡树,接骨木,还是榆树与荆榛,
都不像紫杉这样如一盏盏安息灯①
　　照着那些凄然长眠的人。

黄新渠　辜正坤　译

编注　沃尔特·德·拉·梅尔(Walter de la Mare,1873—1956),英国小说家和诗人,尤擅长于写儿童故事。

---

① 因为紫杉总是长在教堂的墓地中。——译者

422. ARABIA

    Far are the shades of Arabia,
        Where the Princes ride at noon,
    'Mid the verdurous vales and thickets,
        Under the ghost of the moon;
    And so dark is that vaulted purple
        Flowers in the forest rise
    And toss into blossom 'gainst the phantom stars
        Pale in the noonday skies.

    Sweet is the music of Arabia
        In my heart, when out of dreams
    I still in the thin clear mirk of dawn
        Descry her gliding streams;
    Hear her strange lutes on the green banks
        Ring loud with the grief and delight
    Of the dim-silked, dark-haired Musicians
        In the brooding silence of night.

    They haunt me — her lutes and her forests;
        No beauty on earth I see
    But shadowed with that dream recalls
        Her loveliness to me:
    Still eyes look coldly upon me,
        Cold voices whisper and say —
    'He is crazed with the spell of far Arabia,
        They have stolen his wits away.'

                      WALTER DE LA MARE.

422. 阿拉伯半岛

梅尔

远远摇曳着阿拉伯半岛的阴影,
　　正午,王子们在岛上驰马飞奔,
或是越过灌木丛和草木葱茏的山谷,
　　头上一轮冷月,惨淡凄清。　　　　　　　5
那林中呈穹窿状的紫色花簇,
　　黑沉沉难辨踪影,
它们慢慢升起,突然群花怒放,
　　衬托着午日长空中绰约如梦的群星。

阿拉伯半岛甜蜜的音乐回荡　　　　　　　10
　　在我心中,当晨曦微明的时候,
我挣脱残梦,还依旧能够
　　分辨出那蜿蜒的溪流,
听到她那铺翠的河岸上的弦琴
　　发出清响,与身着暗色丝绸的　　　　　15
黑发缪斯们的哀乐之音声声相应,
　　在这样的夜晚,苍茫、静悠。

我被迷住了——被她的弦琴和森林;
　　我虽看不见大地上的美景,
但这一个萦绕在心中的梦　　　　　　　　20
　　使人想起她爱恋我的倩影;
她那恬静的目光冷漠地投在我身上,
　　她在絮絮低语,用的是冷漠的声音——
"遥远的阿拉伯半岛已使他如痴如醉,
　　这一切已使他丧失了理性。"　　　　　25

　　　　　　　　　　黄新渠　辜正坤　译

423. BEFORE THE ROMAN CAME TO RYE

Before the Roman came to Rye or out to Severn strode,
The rolling English drunkard made the rolling English road.
A reeling road, a rolling road, that rambles round the shire,
And after him the parson ran, the sexton and the squire;
A merry road, a mazy road, and such as we did tread
The night we went to Birmingham by way of Beachy Head.

I knew no harm of Bonaparte and plenty of the Squire,
And for to fight the Frenchman I did not much desire;
But I did bash their baggonets because they came arrayed[1]
To straighten out the crooked road an English drunkard made,
Where you and I went down the lane with ale- mugs in our hands,
The night we went to Glastonbury by way of Goodwin Sands.

His sins they were forgiven him; or why do flow- ers run
Behind him; and the hedges all strengthing in the sun?
The wild thing went from left to right and knew not which was which,
But the wild rose was above him when they found him in the ditch.
God pardon us, nor harden us; we did not see so clear
The night we went to Bannockburn by way of Brighton Pier.

My friends, we will not go again or ape an ancient rage,

---

[1] *baggonets*: bayonets.

423. 罗马人来到拉伊之前

切斯特顿

罗马人来到拉伊或者出来跨过塞文河之前①,
蹒跚的英国醉汉就造着蹒跚的英国的道路。
一条摇晃的路,一条蹒跚的路,蜿蜒着在郡里绕过,
牧师跟在他后面跑,还有教堂司事和乡绅;
一条快活的路,一条曲折的路,就像我们脚下踏的 5
那晚上我们经过比奇黑德到伯明翰去的路②。

我知道波拿巴没有害处,对乡绅也了解很多,
去打法国人我并不十分愿意;
但是我击退了他们的刺刀,因为他们排着队
来纠直一个英国醉汉造的弯曲的路, 10
从那里你我手里举着啤酒杯子走下小巷
那晚上我们经过古德温沙丘到格拉斯顿伯里去的路上③。

他们原谅了他的罪;然而为什么花朵跑着
跟在他后面;而树篱却在阳光下加固?
野东西忽而往左忽而往右,晕头转向, 15
但是野玫瑰却在他的上头,人们在沟里找到他的时候。
上帝宽恕我们,不要虐待我们;我们没有看得清楚
那晚上经过布赖顿码头到巴诺克伯恩去的路④。

我的朋友们,我们不想再去了,或者模仿古老的忿怒,

---
① 拉伊,英国东南部一地。——编注者
② 比奇黑德,英国南部一地。——编注者
③ 格拉斯顿伯里,英国西南部一地。——编注者
④ 布赖顿在英国东南部,巴诺克伯恩在英格兰中部。——编注者

20 Or stretch the folly of our youth to be the shame of age,
But walk with clearer eyes and ears this path that wandereth,
And see undrugged in evening light the decent inn of death;
For there is good news yet to hear and fine things to be seen,
Before we go to Paradise by way of Kensal Green.

G. K. CHESTERTON.

或者把我们年轻时的愚蠢延长为老年的羞耻,
而是以更加明亮敏锐的眼睛耳朵走上这条彷徨的路,
于暮色中毫不单调地看着死亡的体面旅店,
因为那里还有好消息可听,好东西可看
在我们经过绿肯色到天堂里去之前。

王央乐 译

编注 吉尔伯特·基思·切斯特顿(Gilbert Keith Chesterton, 1874—1936),英国小说家、剧作家、散文作家、诗人。

424. SEA-FEVER

I must down to the seas again, to the lonely sea and the sky,
And all I ask is a tall ship and a star to steer her by,
And the wheel's kick and the wind's song and the white sail's shaking,
And a grey mist on the sea's face and a grey dawn breaking.

I must down to the seas again, for the call of the running tide
Is a wild call and a clear call that may not be denied;
And all I ask is a windy day with the white clouds flying,
And the flung spray and the blown spume, and the sea-gulls crying①.

I must down to the seas again, to the vagrant gypsy life,
To the gull's way and the whale's way where the wind 's like a whetted knife;
And all I ask is a merry yarn from a laughing fellow-rover,
And quiet sleep and a sweet dream when the long trick's over②.

JOHN MASEFIELD.

---

① *spume*: foam.
② *trick*: spell at the wheel.

424. 恋海热

梅斯菲尔德

我一定得再去海上,去那偏僻的海天;
我想要的只是一艘高耸的船,一颗星星领它向前,
还有舵轮的反转,海风的歌唱,白帆的飘摇
海面上灰濛濛的雾气和灰濛濛的破晓。

我一定得再去海上,因为那奔潮的呼唤,   5
那么狂野,那么清晰,我无法躲闪;
我想要的只是一个刮风的日子,有飞驰的白云,
还有浪花的拍击,海鸥长啸,泡沫飞溅。

我一定得再去海上,去学那吉普赛人的流浪,
去那海鸥的路上,那海鲸的路上,那狂风利如刀锋的地方,   10
而我想要的只是漂泊中伙伴们的海外奇谈与哄笑,
还有长长轮值后一场美美的睡眠,一次甜甜的梦觉。

金敏　译

编注 约翰·梅斯菲尔德(John Masefield,1878—1967),英国诗人,自幼独立谋生,到处漂泊,后在伦敦当记者。第一部诗集《盐水谣》描写水手及下层劳动者生活,把许多水手行话写进诗中;《恋海热》即是其中一首有名的歌曲。他写了不少诗和歌谣,收集在《歌谣》《歌谣和诗》等集了中。长篇叙事诗《永恒的宽恕》名扬诗坛,二战期间,又有《轰动一时的奇闻》《致水兵》等诗歌颂英国水兵和战士的勇敢精神。一九三〇年获第二十二届英国"桂冠诗人"称号。

425. ADLESTROP

Yes. I remember Adlestrop —
The name, because one afternoon
Of heat the express-train drew up there
Unwontedly. It was late June.

The steam hissed. Some one cleared his throat.
No one left and no one came
On the bare platform. What I saw
Was Adlestrop — only the name

And willows, willow-herb, and grass,
And meadowsweet, and haycocks dry,
No whit less still and lonely fair
Than the high cloudlets in the sky.

And for that minute a blackbird sang
Close by, and round him, mistier,
Farther and farther, all the birds
Of Oxfordshire and Gloucestershire.

EDWARD THOMAS.

425. 艾德稠普

爱德华·托马斯

是呵,我记得艾德稠普①——
那个地名,因为有个热天的午后
特快列车在那里停住
太不寻常——那是六月底的时候。

蒸汽嘶嘶作响。有人清着喉咙。 　　　　5
没有人进进出出
月台空空如也,我看见
只有一个站牌——艾德稠普

还有柳树,柳兰,青草,
洁白的绣线菊,草堆也干透, 　　　　10
呵,晴朗空洁的天空
正飘起高高的五彩云绸。

就在那时,一只画眉唱起歌儿,
而似乎所有牛津郡的,
格洛斯特郡的鸟儿,全都飞来 　　　　15
围绕着它,越聚越多,像一场大雾。

佘敏　译

编注 菲利浦·爱德华·托马斯(Philip Edward Thomas,1878—1917),批评家、散文作家及诗人。他的诗多写农村风景,节奏很慢,基调舒缓,往往给人以某种难言的情绪或画面。

---

① 艾德稠普,格洛斯特郡内一个小村庄,在牛津郡附近。——译者

426. MARGARET'S SONG

Too soothe and mild your lowland airs
    For one whose hope is gone:
I'm thinking of a little tarn[①],
    Brown, very lone.

Would now the tall swift mists could lay
    Their wet grasp on my hair,
And the great natures of the hills
    Round me friendly were.

In vain! — For taking hills your plains
    Have spoilt my soul, I think,
But would my feet were going down
    Towards the brown tarn's brink.

LASCELLES ABERCROMBIE.

[①] *tarn*: a small mountain lake.

426. 玛格丽特的歌

艾伯克龙比

为了安慰希望破灭的人们
　　你低地的空气多么温暖可亲:
我想起山区那个小小的湖,
　　褐色的,而且异常孤凄。

但愿高高而飘渺的雾气　　　　　　　　　　5
　　降下潮润拢住我的头鬓,
还有大自然的丛山峻岭
　　好心和蔼地将我隐庇。

枉劳呵!——将高山作为你的平地
　　我以为已经损害我的心灵,　　　　　　10
唯愿我的双腿能往下继续走去,
　　朝着那褐色的山区湖溪。

金敏　译

编注 拉塞尔斯·艾伯克龙比(Lascelles Abercrombie,1881—1938),大学英国文学教授,诗人及批评家,著有《间奏曲与诗歌》《爱的象征》《英诗韵律原则》《诗论》等。

427. A TOWN WINDOW

Beyond my window in the night
    Is but a drab inglorious street,
Yes there the frost and clean starlight
    As over Warwick woods are sweet.

Under the grey drift of the town
    The crocus works among the mould
As eagerly as those that crown
    The Warwick spring in flame and gold.

And when the tramway down the hill
    Across the cobbles moans and rings,
There is about my window-sill
    The tumult of a thousand wings.

                JOHN DRINKWATER.

427. 城市之窗

德林克沃特

黑夜,在我的窗下
　仅有条单调湮灭的街,
然而霜与明净的星光
　好似沃克森林之上的一般温漾。

城市灰濛濛的风卷下　　　　　　　　　　5
　番红花长在舒松的土壤,
热切地想给春天加冠
　好似沃克森林春光灿烂。

当电车隆隆下山
　路轨上卵石呻吟震响,　　　　　　　　10
在我的窗台近旁
　似乎有千万只鼓翼的翅膀。

金敏　译

编注 约翰·德林克沃特(John Drinkwater,1882—1937),英国诗人及戏剧家。其诗作格调轻松,好自然,素有"小曲王子"之称。

428. THE GOLDEN JOURNEY TO SAMARKAND

PROLOGUE

We who with songs beguile your pilgrimage
  And swear that Beauty lives though lilies die,
We Poets of the proud old lineage
  Who sing to find your hearts, we know not why, —

What shall we tell you? Tales, marvellous tales
  Of ships and stars and isles where good men rest,
Where nevermore the rose of sunset pales,
  And winds and shadows fall toward the West:

And there the world's first huge white-bearded kings,
  In dim glades sleeping, murmur in their sleep,
And closer round their breasts the ivy clings,
  Cutting its pathway slow and red and deep.

II

And how beguile you? Death has no repose
  Warmer and deeper than that Orient sand
Which hides the beauty and bright faith of those
  Who made the Golden Journey to Samarkand.

And now they wait and whiten peaceably,
  Those conquerors, thosd poets, those so fair:

428. 去撒马尔罕的金色行程①

弗莱克

序诗

我们用歌声使你的朝圣愉快
　我们发誓,百合花虽死,美依然存在,
我们骄傲的老一代诗人
　不知为了什么,唱着歌寻找你的心脉,——

我们要为你讲些什么? 讲些奇妙的故事　　　　5
　船只,星星和仙人隐居的海岛,
那里决不会再有落日般苍白的玫瑰,
　风与阴影也不会向西潦倒;

那边世上最大帝国的国王们留着白须,
　睡在昏暗的林中空地,说着呓语,　　　　10
他们的胸脯紧紧缠绕着常青藤,
　慢慢切断了小径,显得暗红而幽深。

II

叫我怎样骗你? 死神并未安睡,
　它不比东方的黄沙更暖更深,
那些胸怀美与光明信念的人　　　　15
　开拓了撒马尔罕的金色行程,却在黄沙下葬身。

而今他们安静地等候,让尸骨在沙漠里变白,
　那些征服者,那些诗人,他们是那样高贵,

---
① 撒马尔罕,今乌兹别克斯坦东部一城,为朝圣地。——译者

    They know time comes, not only you and I,
        But the whole world shall whiten, here or there;

    When those long caravans that cross the plain
        With dauntless feet and sound of silver bells
    Put forth no more for glory or for gain,
        Take no more solace from the palm-girt wells;

    When the great markets by the sea shut fast
        All that calm Sunday that goes on and on;
    When even lovers find their peace at last,
        And Earth is but a star, that once had shone.

                      JAMES ELROY FLECKER.

他们明白时辰已到,不仅仅是你我
　　甚至四面八方,整个世界都将变白。　　　　　　　　　　*20*

当那些长长的朝圣队伍穿过平原,
　　步履坚定,银铃回荡,
奔波不再是为了荣誉和财富
　　也不再从棕榈树围绕的井中汲取安慰。

当海边的繁华集市紧紧关闭,　　　　　　　　　　　　　　*25*
　　平静的礼拜日便川流不息来临,
甚至当情人终于找到他们的安宁,
　　地球也不过是曾经闪耀的一颗行星。

金敏　译

编注　詹姆斯·埃尔罗伊·弗莱克(James Elroy Flecker,1884—1915),深受法国唯美主义影响的英国诗人,写诗追求异国情调,追求纯美的技巧,避免牵涉个人感情。他在东方长期住过,留下的诗中,较好的正是东方诗。这首诗描写朝圣者对尘世之外的追求,反映了"整个世界都将变白""而美依然存在",诗人们却很难寻求的唯美主义观点。

429. AFTER RONSARD

When you are old and I — if that should be —
    Lying afar in undistinguished earth,
And you no more have all your will of me,
    To teach me morals, idleness, and mirth,
But, curtained from the bleak December nights,
    You sit beside the else-deserted fire
And 'neath the glow of double-polèd lights,
    Till your alert eyes and quick judgement tire,
Turn some new poet's page, and to yourself
    Praise his new satisfaction of new need,
Then pause and look a little toward the shelf
    Where my books stand which none but you shall read:
And say: 'I too was not ungently sung
When I was happy, beautiful, and young.'

CHARLES WILLIAMS.

429. 和龙沙诗《何时你已衰老》[①]

威廉斯

当你老了,而我——如果非得那样——
　远远地躺进平常的土地,
你再也不能将我支诳,
　再也不能教我有关品行、悠闲和欢娱,
但是,隔着阴冷的十二月夜晚,　　　　　　　　　　5
　你围着别人遗弃的火炉,
在高高闪烁的灯盏下,
　翻开某些新诗人的诗书,
直到你机警的眼、敏捷的判断疲乏,
　你赞扬他满足了新的需要,　　　　　　　　　　10
然后,停下来瞧瞧书架,
　那里排列着我的书——唯有你能明了:
说道:"我也曾被别人热情地讴歌,
　而那时我还美丽、年青、幸福。"

陈朴　译

编注 查尔斯·威廉斯(Charles Williams,1886—1945),英国诗人,著有《和谐之诗》(*Poems of Conformity*)、《黑夜之窗*》(Windows of Night*)、《莎士比亚神话》(*A Myth of Shakespeare*)等。

[①] 龙沙(Pierre de Ronsard,1524—1585),法国诗人。——译者

430. THE SOLDIER

If I should die, think only this of me:
   That there's some corner of a foreign field
That is for ever England. There shall be
   In that rich earth a richer dust concealed;
A dust whom England bore, shaped, made aware,
   Gave, once, her flowers to love, her ways to roam,
A body of England's, breathing English air,
   Washed by the rivers, blest by suns of home.

And think, this heart, all evil shed away,
   A pulse in the eternal mind, no less
     Gives somewhere back the thoughts by England given;
Her sights and sounds; dreams happy as her day;
   And laughter, learnt of friends; and gentleness,
     In hearts at peace, under an English heaven.

RUPERT BROOKE.

430. 士兵

布鲁克

假如我死了,只这样怀念我:
  在异国战场的某个角落
永存的是英格兰。在那肥沃的土地里
  将隐藏着更肥沃的一粒尘土;
英格兰出生,塑造,成长哺育,
  她曾献出让人喜爱的鲜花,供人漫游的道路,
英国的儿子,呼吸着英格兰的空气,
  受到家乡江河的洗浴,阳光的祝福。

就这样想,这颗心涤荡了一切罪恶,
  永恒的心中的脉搏,照样在某处
    恢复英格兰赋予我的思想;
她的风光和声音;她幸福的梦一般的盛世,
  欢声笑语,朋友的信息,还有
    在英格兰天空下,宁静的心中的亲切情意。

姚奔 译

编注 鲁珀特·布鲁克(Rupert Brooke,1887—1915),英国诗人,曾在军队服役。

431. EVERYONE SANG

Everyone suddenly burst out singing;
And I was filled with such delight
As prisoned birds must find in freedom
Winging wildly across the white
Orchards and dark-green fields; on; on; and out of sight.

Everyone's voice was suddenly lifted,
And beauty came like the setting sun.
My heart was shaken with tears; and horror
Drifted away ... O but every one
Was a bird; and the song was wordless; the singing will never be done.

SIEGFRIED SASSOON.

431. 人人歌唱

萨松

人人忽然引吭歌唱；
我满怀欢乐
就像被囚禁的鸟儿获得解放，
展翅任意飞翔，飞过
白色的果园和碧绿的田野；飞呀，飞呀；飞到看不见的地方。　　　　5

人人歌声忽然高昂，
落日一样美景出现，
我的心随泪水而震颤；恐惧
风流云散……啊！每个人
当真成了一只鸟，无言的歌将永远唱不完。　　　　10

姚奔　译

编注　西格弗里德·萨松（Siegfried Sassoon，1886—1967），英国诗人和作家，其作品以反战诗最有名。

432. ALMSWOMEN

At Quincey's moat the squandering village ends,
And there in the almshouse dwell the dearest friends
Of all the village, two old dames that cling
As close as any trueloves in the spring.
Long, long ago they passed threescore-and-ten,
And in this doll's house lived together then;
All things they have in common, being so poor,
And their one fear, Death's shadow at the door.
Each sundown makes them mournful, each sunrise
Brings back the brightness in their failing eyes.
How happy go the rich fair-weather days
When on the roadside folk stare in amaze
At such a honeycomb of fruit and flowers
As mellows round their threshold; what long hours
They gloat upon their steepling hollyhocks①,
Bee's balsams, feathery southernwood, and stocks,
Fiery dragon's-mouths, great mallow leaves
For salves, and lemon-plants in bushy sheaves,
Shagged Esau's-hands with five green finger-tips.
Such old sweet names are ever on their lips.
As pleased as little children where these grow
In cobbled pattens and worn gowns they go,
Proud of their wisdom when on gooseberry shoots

---

① *steepling*: tall, like a steeple.

432. 救济院的妇女

布兰登

稀疏的村落尽头是昆西的护城河,
救济院里住着
全村最亲爱的朋友,两个老妇人
就像春天的恋人形影不离。
很久很久以前她们度过七十大寿, 5
那时起就共同住在这所小小的房屋里;
因为很穷,她们所有东西都是共用的,
她们担心一件事,死亡的阴影来到门前。
每次日落都引起她们感伤,
每次日出都使她们昏花的老眼重燃光芒。 10
共享晴朗的富裕日子过得多么幸福
当路边的乡亲们惊奇地凝望
果实累累,鲜花簇簇
在她们家门四周洋溢着馥郁的浓香;
多么长久地啊她们满意地凝望着高大的蜀葵, 15
属于蜜蜂的凤仙花,羽状苦艾还有紫罗兰,
火红的龙口花,巨大的锦葵叶,
借此寻求慰藉,还有茂密的柠檬香灌木丛,
有五个绿色指尖的多毛的以扫的手①
她们嘴边总是离不开这些古老美好的名字。 20
在这些花木生长的地方,她们像孩子一样高兴,
穿着修补过的木鞋和破旧的长衫。
当她们把蛋壳黏附在醋栗的嫩枝上

---

① 典出《圣经·旧约》,以扫是以撒和利百加的长子,生下来时浑身是毛。——编注者

They stuck eggshells to fright from coming fruits
25   The brisk-billed rascals; pausing still to see①
Their neighbour owls saunter from tree to tree,
Or in the hushing half-light mouse the lane
Long-winged and lordly.
                    But when those hours wane,
Indoors they ponder, scared by the harsh storm
30   Whose pelting saracens on the window swarm②,
And listen for the mail to clatter past
And church clock's deep bay withering on the blast;
They feed the fire that flings a freakish light
On pictured kings and queens grotesquely bright,
35   Platters and pitchers, faded calendars
And graceful hour-glass trim with lavenders.

Many a time they kiss and cry, and pray
That both be summoned in the selfsame day,
And wiseman linnet tinkling in his cage
40   End too with them the friendship of old age,
And all together leave their treasured room
Some bell-like evening when the may's in bloom.

                              EDMUND BLUNDEN.

---

① *brisk-billed rascals*: birds.
② *saracens*: rain drops.

吓唬将来吃果实的鸟儿,她们得意于自己的聪明,
更停下来望着她们邻近的猫头鹰 25
在一株株树间游荡,
或在幽暗中神气活现地展翅
搜寻着小路。
      但当那美好的时光消逝,
她们躲在屋内沉思,狂暴的风雨使她们恐怖,
急骤的雨点密集地敲打着窗子, 30
倾听着邮车得得地驶过,
而教堂深沉的钟声在暴风雨中消失;
她们为炉火填加燃料,奇异的火光
把国王和王后的画像照得奇形怪状,
火光照射在大菜盘、水壶、褪色的日历, 35
还有镶着紫边的高雅的更漏上。

她们多次亲吻,哭泣,并祈祷
两人在同一天里被召唤,
术士的红雀在笼子里丁丁鸣叫
结束了同她们的老年友谊, 40
而撇下她们珍爱的房间,
连同钟声似的黄昏,当山楂花儿开放的时候。

姚 奔 译

编注 埃德蒙·布兰登(Edmund Blunden,1896—1974),英国小说家和诗人,曾在牛津大学任诗歌教授。

433. AFTER LONDON

London Bridge is broken dowm;
    Green is the grass on Ludgate Hill,
I know a farmer in Camden Town
    Killed a brock by Pentonville[①].

I have heard my grandam tell
    How some thousand years ago
Houses stretched from Camberwell
    Right to Highbury and Bow.

Down by Shadwell's golden meads
    Tall ships' masts would stand as thick
As the pretty tufted reeds
    That the Wapping children pick.

All the kings from end to end
    Of all the world paid tribute then,
And meekly on their knees would bend
    To the King of the Englishmen.

Thinks I while I dig my plot,
    What if your grandam's tales be true?
Thinks I, be they true or not,
    What's the odds to a fool like you?

---

① *brock*: badger.

1854

433. 伦敦遐想

佩洛

伦敦桥已坍塌；
   路德盖特山上长满青草；
我认识卡姆登镇上一个农夫
   在本顿维尔监狱旁把一只獾子杀掉。

我听祖母讲过   5
   几千年以前
从坎勃威尔直到海伯里和鲍街，
   房屋怎样绵延不断。

沿着沙德威尔的金色草地
   高高的船桅矗立   10
犹如异常高大的孩子，采摘的
   美丽茂密的丛丛芦苇。

从世界的这端到那端
   所有国王当时都来朝贡，
在英国人的国王面前   15
   屈膝跪拜毕敬毕恭。

我一边构思我的故事一边想，
   你祖母的故事就是真的又能怎样？
我想，故事的真或假，
   对你这样一个傻瓜又有什么用场？   20

Thinks I, while I smoke my pipe
  Here beside the tumbling Fleet,
Apples drop when they are ripe,
  And when they drop are they most sweet.

J. D. C. PELLOW.

我在翻滚的弗利特河畔①
一边吸我的烟斗一边想,
成熟了的苹果自会落,
而落下来的苹果才最香。

姚奔 译

编注 约翰·迪南·科尼什·佩洛(John Dynham Cornish Pellow,1890—1982),英国作家,此诗选自其诗集《父母之道及其他》(*Parentalia and other Poems*),用传统童谣变体写成。

---

① 伦敦的一条河,从前流入泰晤士河,在路德盖特山麓和现在的舰队街之间,现引入一条地下水道。——译者

图书在版编目(CIP)数据

英诗金库:修订版:全三册:汉英对照/(英)F. T. 帕尔格雷夫原编;曹明伦,罗义蕴,陈朴编注. —上海:复旦大学出版社,2021.9
书名原文:The Golden Treasury of the Best Songs and Lyrical Poems in the English Language
ISBN 978-7-309-15785-7

Ⅰ.①英… Ⅱ.①F…②曹…③罗…④陈… Ⅲ.①英语-汉语-对照读物②英语诗歌-诗集-世界 Ⅳ.①H391.4:Ⅰ

中国版本图书馆CIP数据核字(2021)第120515号

英诗金库(修订版)
(英)F. T. 帕尔格雷夫 原编
曹明伦 罗义蕴 陈朴 编注
责任编辑/宋启立 方尚芹 杜怡顺
复旦大学出版社有限公司出版发行
上海市国权路579号 邮编:200433
网址:fupnet@fudanpress.com http://www.fudanpress.com
门市零售:86-21-65102580 团体订购:86-21-65104505
出版部电话:86-21-65642845
上海盛通时代印刷有限公司

开本 890×1240 1/32 印张 59.625 字数 1774 千
2021年9月第1版第1次印刷

ISBN 978-7-309-15785-7/H·3108
定价:258.00元(全三册)

如有印装质量问题,请向复旦大学出版社有限公司出版部调换。
版权所有 侵权必究

THE GOLDEN TREASURY

F. T. PALGRAVE

英诗金库

（修订版）

［英］F.T.帕尔格雷夫　原编
曹明伦　罗义蕴　陈朴　编注

- 中 -

复旦大学出版社

卷四

1800—1850

166. ON FIRST LOOKING INTO CHAPMAN'S HOMER

Much have I travell'd in the realms of gold[①]
    And many goodly states and kingdoms seen;
    Round many western islands have I been[②]
Which bards in fealty to Apollo hold.

Oft of one wide expanse had I been told
    That deep-brow'd Homer ruled as his demesne;
    Yet did I never breathe its pure serene[③]
Till I heard Chapman speak out loud and bold:

Then felt I like some watcher of the skies
    When a new planet swims into his ken;
Or like stout Cortez, when with eagle eyes

He stared at the Pacific — and all his men
Look'd at each other with a wild surmise —
    Silent, upon a peak in Darien.

                              J. KEATS.

---

① *the realms of gold*: 'the kingdom of letters.'
② *western islands*: a reference to the poetry of Britain.
③ *serene*: 'clear air.'

166. 初读查普曼译的荷马①

济慈

我游历过很多金色的地区,
　　看过许多美好的国家和王国;
　　到过诗人们向阿波罗②
效忠的许多西方的岛屿。

有人时常告诉我眉额深邃的荷马　　　　　　　　　　5
　　作为领地统治的一片广阔的太空,
　　可是直到我听见查普曼大声说出时,
我从未体味到它的纯净和明朗:

于是我感到像一个观察天象的人
　　看到一颗新的行星映入他的眼帘;　　　　　　　10
　　或者像魁梧的科特斯用鹰眼③

瞪视着太平洋——所有他的伙计
怀着狂野的猜测,大家面面相觑——
　　在德利英的一座高峰上默然无声④。

朱维基　译

编注 约翰・济慈(John Keats,1795—1821),英国杰出的浪漫主

---

① 乔治・查普曼(George Chapman,1559?—1634),英国剧作家。——译者
② 阿波罗是希腊神话中的太阳神,也司文艺,诗的前四句意味着诗人对文艺的爱好和阅历。——编注者
③ 赫尔曼・科特斯(Herman Cortez,1485—1547),西班牙探险家,墨西哥征服者,他并不是首先发现太平洋的人。——译者
④ 德利英(Darien)原指整个巴拿马半岛,今指其东部。——编注者

义诗人。出身寒微,做过医生的学徒,生活较为困顿。一八一六年开始发表诗作,希望在一个"永恒的美的世界"找到人生的价值,写有长诗《伊莎贝拉》《圣爱尼节前夜》《海庇里安》等。最著名的颂诗有《夜莺颂》《秋颂》《希腊古瓮颂》等。济慈死时年仅二十五岁。本诗最初发表于一八一六年十二月一日的《探究者》($Examiner$)上,表达了济慈初次接触以荷马史诗为代表的古希腊文明的欣喜之情。这是一首意大利体的十四行诗,无论从运用典故到音韵都很有特色。这是青年诗人济慈受到公众注意的第一首诗,也是浪漫主义诗歌在英国兴起的一支号角。

167. ODE ON THE POETS

Bards of Passion and of Mirth
Ye have left your souls on earth!
Have ye souls in heaven too,
Double-lived in regions new?

5   Yes, and those of heaven commune
With the spheres of sun and moon;
With the noise of fountains wond'rous
And the parle of voices thund'rous[①];
With the whisper of heaven's trees
10   And one another, in soft ease[②]
Seated on Elysian lawns
Brows'd by none but Dian's fawns;
Underneath large blue-bells tented[③],
Where the daisies are rose-scented,
15   And the rose herself has got
Perfume which on earth is not;
Where the nightingale doth sing
Not a senseless, trancéd thing[④],

---

① *parle*: 'speech'; cf. 'Parliament' and 'parlour,' both places for talk.
② *And one another*: sc. 'with one another.'
③ *tented*: co-ordinate with 'seated,' and qualifies 'those [souls] of heaven,' l. 5.
④ The implication that the nightingale's song on earth is 'a senseless trancéd thing' is nobly recanted in Keats's 'Ode to a Nightingale,' see below, No. 244.

167. 诗人颂

济慈

热情与欢乐的歌手呀①,
你们把灵魂留在大地!
你们在天上也有灵魂,
是否又生活在新的领域?

是的,与上天沟通的灵魂, 5
和太阳,月亮在一起;
伴随着泉水奇妙的声响,
伴随着雷霆大声的话语;
也伴随天上飒飒作响的树林,
一个个悠闲自得, 10
在伊利泽厄恩草坪上歇息②,
只凝视狄安娜女神的颦眉③;
在风信子兰铃花的大篷帐下,
雏菊发出了玫瑰的芬芳,
而玫瑰本身所喷出的馨香, 15
超过了世上所有甜美的气息;
那儿荡漾着夜莺的歌曲,
不是木然、恍惚的东西,

---

① 此处指鲍蒙特(Beaumont,1584—1616)与弗莱彻(Fletcher,1579—1625)。参见卷二第67首编注。——编注者
② 据希腊神话传说,伊利泽厄思(Elysium)是幸福乐土,好人死后的灵魂方能去那里。——译者
③ 狄安娜(Diana)指月神,她代表纯洁与童贞。——译者

20　　　　But divine melodious truth;
　　　　　Philosophic numbers smooth;
　　　　　Tales and golden histories
　　　　　Of heaven and its mysteries.

　　　　　Thus ye live on high, and then
　　　　　On the earth ye live again;
25　　　　And the souls ye left behind you
　　　　　Teach us, here, the way to find you,
　　　　　Where your other souls are joying,
　　　　　Never slumber'd, never cloying①.
　　　　　Here, your earth-born souls still speak
30　　　　To mortals, of their little week②;
　　　　　Of their sorrows and delights;
　　　　　Of their passions and their spites;
　　　　　Of their glory and their shame;
　　　　　What doth strengthen and what maim; ——
35　　　　Thus ye teach us, every day,
　　　　　Wisdom, though fled far away.

　　　　　Bards of Passion and of Mirth
　　　　　Ye have left your souls on earth!
　　　　　Ye have souls in heaven too,
40　　　　Double-lived in regions new!

　　　　　　　　　　　　　　J. KEATS.

---

① *cloying*: for 'cloyed,' *i.e.* satiated.
② *their little week*: *i.e.* their brief span of life.

是神圣而悦耳的真理；
那么畅达而又流利，　　　　　　　　　　　20
讲述着天上神秘的故事，
还有那金色般的历史传奇。

这是你们在天上的情景，
然后你们又活在大地；
你们留下的灵魂，　　　　　　　　　　　25
在这里指点我们把你们找寻，
你们另一个灵魂何等欢乐，
从不困倦，也不厌腻，
这儿，你们尘俗的灵魂还在讲话，
对世人讲述他们短暂的经历；　　　　　　30
讲述他们的悲哀与欢乐；
讲述他们的羞愧和荣誉；
讲述他们的激情和怨恨；
什么变得强壮，什么成为残迹：——
这样每天把我们教育，　　　　　　　　　35
给我们以智慧，尽管你们已经远去。

热情与欢乐的诗人呀，
你们已经把灵魂留在大地！
天上也有你们的灵魂存在，
又生活在崭新的领域！　　　　　　　　　40

罗义蕴　译

编注 济慈将本诗写在鲍蒙特与弗莱彻的诗歌抄本扉页上，作为献给这两位诗人的颂诗。一八二〇年本诗被收入济慈生前发表的诗集第三卷。全诗寓意着优秀的诗篇能与世长存。济慈始终深信美的事物给人以永恒的欢乐，它的魅力与日俱增，决不会化为乌有。

168. LOVE

All thoughts, all passions, all delights,
    Whatever stirs this mortal frame,
All are but ministers of Love,
    And feed his sacred flame.

Oft in my waking dreams do I
    Live o'er again that happy hour,
When midway on the mount I lay
    Beside the ruin'd tower.

The moonshine stealing o'er the scene
    Had blended with the lights of eve;
And she was there, my hope, my joy,
    My own dear Genevieve!

She lean'd against the arméd man,
    The statue of the arméd knight;
She stood and listen'd to my lay,
    Amid the lingering light.

Few sorrows hath she of her own,
    My hope! my joy! my Genevieve!
She loves me best whene'er I sing
    The songs that make her grieve.

I play'd a soft and doleful air,

168. 爱情

塞·泰·柯勒律治

一切思想、一切感情、一切欢乐、
　　激动这血肉之躯的一切力量，
都受到爱情的制约，
　　　　为他神圣的火焰而奉献琼浆。

我经常在醒着的梦里，　　　　　　　　　　5
　　重温那幸福的时光，
那时我躺在半山腰上，
　　　　在那已倾覆的塔旁。

偷偷照射这景色的月光，
　　已融汇了傍晚的一切光芒；　　　　　10
她在那儿，我的希望，我的快乐，
　　　　珍尼菲芙，我亲爱的姑娘！

她紧偎着一位武士，
　　那是一个戎装骑士的雕像；
在那夜幕徐徐降临的时刻，　　　　　　15
　　　　她伫立着聆听我的歌唱。

她自己很少忧愁，
　　我的珍尼菲芙！我的欢乐！我的希望！
当我的歌曲引起了她的悲伤，
　　　　她对我的爱就更加洋溢。　　　20

我弹奏着柔和哀怨的调子，

I sang an old and moving story —
An old rude song, that suited well
That ruin wild and hoary.

She listen'd with a flitting blush,
With downcast eyes and modest grace;
For well she knew I could not choose
But gaze upon her face.

I told her of the Knight that wore
Upon his shield a burning brand;
And that for ten long years he woo'd
The Lady of the Land.

I told her how he pined; and ah!
The deep, the low, the pleading tone
With which I sang another's love
Interpreted my own.

She listen'd with a flitting blush,
With downcast eyes and modest grace;
And she forgave me, that I gazed
Too fondly on her face.

But when I told the cruel scorn①
That crazed that bold and lovely Knight,
And that he cross'd the mountain-woods,
Nor rested day nor night;

---

① *But when I told*: there is no main clause to this sentence, which continues till taken up by a new 'when' clause, l. 65. *the cruel scorn*: i.e. of the Lady.

再吟唱一支歌谣，古老粗犷——
一个动人的故事，恰好配得上
　　那废墟的荒凉。

她羞怯地凝神倾听， 25
　　眼睑低垂，谦逊端庄；
她完全懂得我什么也不在意，
　　只凝视着她那美丽的脸庞。

我对她提起那位骑士的风采，
　　骑士背着一块打上火印的盾牌； 30
他向当地的一位女郎求爱啊，
　　已经整整有十载。

我告诉她骑士怎样消瘦；哎！
　　我用那深沉的如泣如诉的音调，
其实，我是借着别的一支恋人曲， 35
　　述说着自己的一缕情怀。

她低下温柔谦和的眉眼，
　　听着，听着，红晕飞上脸来；
她原谅我，只因我太喜悦，
　　凝视着她的面庞发呆。 40

但当我说到那残酷的轻蔑，
　　曾使勇敢可爱的骑士狂热，
他飞越丛林峻岭，
　　快马奔腾，昼夜不歇。

45　　　　　That sometimes from the savage den,
　　　　　　　　And sometimes from the darksome shade,
　　　　　　　And sometimes starting up at once
　　　　　　　　In green and sunny glade

　　　　　　　There came and look'd him in the face
50　　　　　　　An angel beautiful and bright;
　　　　　　　And that he knew it was a Fiend,
　　　　　　　　This miserable Knight!

　　　　　　　And that, unknowing what he did,
　　　　　　　He leap'd amid a murderous band,
55　　　　　And saved from outrage worse than death
　　　　　　　　The Lady of the Land;

　　　　　　　And how she wept, and clasp'd his knees
　　　　　　　And how she tended him in vain;
　　　　　　　And ever strove to expiate
60　　　　　　　The scorn that crazed his brain;

　　　　　　　And that she nursed him in a cave,
　　　　　　　And how his madness went away,
　　　　　　　When on the yellow forest leaves
　　　　　　　　A dying man he lay;

65　　　　　— His dying words — but when I reach'd
　　　　　　　That tenderest strain of all the ditty,
　　　　　　　My faltering voice and pausing harp
　　　　　　　　Disturb'd her soul with pity!

　　　　　　　All impulses of soul and sense

他有时走过野兽的巢穴, 45
　有时穿过密林,浓荫如盖,
有时,他一跃而起,
　　走过绿草如茵、阳光明媚的地带。

那儿来了一个俊士,明媚的天使,
　凝视着他的容颜风采; 50
那可怜的骑士啊,
　　知道这一定是个魔怪!

他在不知不觉之中,
　竟落入了一群强盗的世界;
从那比死亡更悲惨的处境, 55
　　把那姑娘救了出来;——

她边泣边搂住他的双膝,
　献出的柔情也毫无补益;
她力图赎回曾对他的轻蔑——
　　致使他头脑这样狂热; 60

她在石洞里看护着他,
　此时他神智明白,
躺在枯枝败叶上面,
　　他已奄奄一息;

——他临终的话——但当我 65
　唱到最深情的时刻,
我的声音颤抖,竖琴声歇,
　　同情心激动得她魂魄战栗!

灵魂和感情的搏动,

Had thrill'd my guileless Genevieve;
The music and the doleful tale,
The rich and balmy eve;

And hopes, and fears that kindle hope,
An undistinguishable throng,
And gentle wishes long subdued,
Subdued and cherish'd long!

She wept with pity and delight,
She blush'd with love and virgin shame;
And, like the murmur of a dream,
I heard her breathe my name.

Her bosom heaved — she stepp'd aside,
As conscious of my look she stept —
Then suddenly, with timorous eye
She fled to me and wept.

She half enclosed me with her arms
She press'd me with a meek embrace;
And bending back her head, look'd up,
And gazed upon my face.

'Twas partly love, and partly fear,
And partly 'twas a bashful art,
That I might rather feel, than see,
The swelling of her heart.

I calm'd her fears, and she was calm,
And told her love with virgin pride;

冲击着这纯洁的女子； 70
还有这浓密馥郁的夜色，
　　这音乐和这悲哀的故事；

希望与燃烧着希望的恐惧，
　　一种辨别不清的思绪，
长期被压抑的温柔愿望， 75
　　抑制已久的满腔情意！

她因悲喜交集而哭泣，
　　她因爱情与娇羞而红云泛起；
我听见她呼唤我的名字，
　　像梦呓一样轻声低语。 80

她胸膛起伏——一旁站立，
　　她凝视着我，轻移步履——
突然，她怯怯的目光
　　投向我来，不禁悲泣。

她用双臂拥抱着我， 85
　　温柔地紧贴着我的胸膛；
后仰着头瞧着我，
　　将我脸庞看个仔细。

一部分是爱，一部分是惧，
　　一部分是羞涩的技艺， 90
我好像没有看见，只感觉
　　她酥胸的伏起。

我镇静了她的惊惧，她安祥地，
　　用少女的骄傲诉说她的情意。

95 And so I won my Genevieve,
My bright and beauteous Bride.

S. T. COLERIDGE.

我终于赢得了珍尼菲弗，
　　　　我的新娘，聪明而美丽。

罗义蕴　译

编注　塞缪尔·泰勒·柯勒律治(Samuel Taylor Coleridge，1772—1834)，英国浪漫派诗人和批评家。一七九八年与华兹华斯合作，出版了《抒情歌谣集》(*Lyrical Ballads*)，该诗集对于浪漫主义运动在英国的兴起和发展有着重要意义。他的代表诗作有《古舟子咏》《克里斯特贝尔》《忽必烈汗》等。他常以自然逼真的形象和情景来表现浪漫的超自然的神圣内容。本诗是一首充满浪漫情调的抒情诗，借一个古老的故事来表达男女之间真挚的爱情，全诗节奏明快，逻辑清晰，一幅幅扣人心弦的画景，交织着悲喜的感情，显示了作者的艺术才华。

169. ALL FOR LOVE

O talk not to me of a name great in story;
The days of our youth are the days of our glory;
And the myrtle and ivy of sweet two-and-twenty
Are worth all your laurels though ever so plenty①.

5　What are garlands and crowns to the brow that is wrinkled?
'Tis but as a dead flower with May-dew besprinkled:
Then away with all such from the head that is hoary —
What care I for the wreaths that can only give glory?

O Fame! — if I e'er took delight in thy praises,
10　'Twas less for the sake of thy high-sounding phrases,
Than to see the bright eyes of the dear one discover②
She thought that I was not unworthy to love her.

There chiefly I sought thee, there only I found thee;
Her glance was the best of the rays that surround thee;
15　When it sparkled o'er aught that was bright in my story,
I knew it was love, and I felt it was glory.

LORD BYRON.

---

① *plenty*: 'abundant.'
② *discover*: 'show.'

169. 一切为了爱情

拜伦

哦,别跟我谈论什么故事里的伟大的人名,
我们青春的岁月是我们最光辉的时辰;
甜蜜的二十二岁所得的常春藤和桃金娘
胜过你所有的桂冠,无论戴得多么辉煌。

对于满额皱纹,花冠和王冕算得了什么? 5
那不过是五月的朝露洒上枯死的花朵。
那么,不如把这一切从苍白的头上扔开!
对于只给人以荣誉的花环我又何所挂怀?

呵,美名! 如果我对你的赞扬也感到欣喜,
那并不仅仅是为了你富丽堂皇的辞句; 10
我是想看到亲爱的人儿睁大明亮的眼,
让她知道我这爱她的人也并非等闲。

主要是因此,我才追寻你,并且把你发现,
她的目光是笼罩着你的最美的光线;
如果听到我的灿烂的故事,她闪闪眼睛, 15
我就知道那是爱,我感到那才是光荣。

查良铮 译

编注 乔治·戈登·拜伦(George Gordon Byron,1788—1824),英国伟大的浪漫主义诗人。虽出身贵族,十岁承继勋爵爵位,但他反抗暴政,讽刺伪善,写过大量抒情诗、诗剧和讽刺诗。他参加了意大利与希腊的民族独立运动,在赴希腊参加独立战争的中途,于一座小岛上染疾身故。他的著名诗作有《恰尔德·哈罗德游记》《曼弗莱德》《青铜世纪》

《唐璜》等。他的诗句富于变化,充满革命激情,对世界文学极有影响。本诗诗题原为《写于佛罗伦萨至比萨途中》,《金库》原编者将标题改为《一切为了爱情》。

170. THE OUTLAW

  O Brignall banks are wild and fair,
   And Greta woods are green,
  And you may gather garlands there
   Would grace a summer queen.
5   And as I rode by Dalton Hall
   Beneath the turrets high,
  A Maiden on the castle-wall
   Was singing merrily:
  'O Brignall banks are fresh and fair,
10   And Greta woods are green;
  I'd rather rove with Edmund there[1]
   Than reign our English queen.'

  'If, Maiden, thou wouldst wend with me,
   To leave both tower and town,
15   Thou first must guess what life lead we
   That dwell by dale and down.
  And if thou canst that riddle read[2],
   As read full well you may,
  Then to the greenwood shalt thou speed
20   As blithe as Queen of May.'
  Yet sung she, 'Brignall banks are fair,

---

[1] *Edmund*: the 'I' of l. 5. The maiden apparently knew his name, but not his calling.

[2] *read*: 'make out the meaning of,' 'interpret'; this is the oldest sense of the word. So also below, l. 25.

170. 绿林好汉

司各特

啊,宾罗村坡地十分空旷清幽,
　　格瑞塔树林一片绿油油,
你可以在这儿采集花环,
　　让夏天女皇益添锦绣。
有一天我骑马从达尔登会堂走过①,
　　那旁边有一座高高的楼角,
碉堡内有一位少女,
　　正舒放快乐的歌喉:
"啊,宾罗村坡地新鲜美丽,
　　格瑞塔树林一片绿油油,
我不愿作英国女皇,
　　但愿同爱德蒙在那儿漫游。"

"姑娘,如果你肯和我一道,
　　远离这小镇城头,
你先猜在山谷下面,
　　怎样的生活会把我们等候。
假若无论你怎样冥思苦想,
　　也难把这谜语猜透,
那就快到绿林中去,
　　像快乐的五月皇后。"
可她依然唱着:"宾罗村坡地非常美丽,

---

① 宾罗村是约克郡北区的一个村落,距格瑞塔桥南一英里,距巴那城堡五英里,达尔登会堂位于宾罗村南四英里。——译者

  And Greta woods are green;
  I'd rather rove with Edmund there
  Than reign our English queen.

25   'I read you by your bugle-horn
  And by your palfrey good,
  I read you for a ranger sworn
  To keep the king's greenwood.'
  'A ranger, lady, winds his horn①,
30   And 'tis at peep of light;
  His blast is heard at merry morn,
  And mine at dead of night.'
  Yet sung she, 'Brignall banks are fair,
  And Greta woods are gay;
35   I would I were with Edmund there
  To reign his Queen of May!

  'With burnish'd brand and musketoon②
  So gallantly you come,
  I read you for a bold Dragoon
40   That lists the tuck of drum③.'
  'I list no more the tuck of drum,
  No more the trumpet hear;
  But when the beetle sounds his hum④
  My comrades take the spear.

---

① *winds*: see above, note on No. 146, l. 11.
② *musketoon*: a musket with a large bore; the word is an augmentative of 'musket.'
③ *tuck*: 'beat.'
④ *when the beetle sounds his hum*: i.e. in the evening; cf. Gray's 'Elegy' above, No. 147, l. 7.

格瑞塔树林一片绿油油，
我不愿作英国女皇，
　　但愿同爱德蒙在那儿漫游。

"我认识你由于你响亮的号角， 25
　　我认识你由于你善跑的骏骝，
我认识你由于你宣誓成为林中看守，
　　为了保卫皇上的一片绿畴。"
"姑娘，一位看守员把号角吹响，
　　那是在曙光初露的时候； 30
他的角声，在快乐的晨曦中能够听见，
　　我的声音，却穿过死沉沉的夜晚。"
但她还是唱道："宾罗村坡地十分美丽，
　　格瑞塔森林欢乐无愁；
我愿同爱德蒙呆在那儿， 35
　　那五月女皇的宝座哟，我也不愿就！"
"你带着崭新的利剑与长枪，
　　迈步走来，威武堂皇。
因为你是勇敢的骑兵，我认识你，
　　在战鼓声中，你的名字注在册上。" 40
"我并未在战鼓声中去报到，
　　也没听见号角已吹响；
但当甲壳虫嗡嗡鸣叫时，
　　我的伙伴杠起长矛亮镗镗。

<pre>
45   And O! though Brignall banks be fair
                  And Greta woods be gay,
                Yet mickle must the maiden dare
                  Would reign my Queen of May!

                'Maiden! a nameless life I lead,
50   A nameless death I'll die;
                The fiend whose lantern lights the mead[1]
                  Were better mate than I!
                And when I'm with my comrades met
                  Beneath the greenwood bough, —
55   What once we were we all forget,
                  Nor think what we are now.'
</pre>

Chorus

<pre>
                Yet Brignall banks are fresh and fair,
                  And Greta woods are green,
                And you may gather garlands there
60   Would grace a summer queen.
</pre>

SIR W. SCOTT.

---

[1] *The fiend*; called 'Jack-o'-Lantern' or 'Will-o'-the-Wisp.' See *L' Allégro* above, No. 112, l. 104.

啊！虽然宾罗村的坡地很美丽， 　　　　　　45
　　格瑞塔的森林十分欢畅，
但你要鼓起很大的勇气，
　　才能成为我的五月女皇！

"姑娘呀！我过着默默无闻的生活，
　　我也将在默默无闻中死亡； 　　　　　　50
打着灯笼照亮草地的魔鬼，
　　也许是比我更好的情郎！
当我同我的朋友相遇，
　　就在那绿树成荫的地方，——
我们过去是什么，我们完全忘怀， 　　　　　55
　　今天要成为什么，我们谁也不去思量。"

　　　　　合　　唱
宾罗村坡地依旧新鲜美丽，
　　格瑞塔树林一片绿油油，
你可以在那儿采集花环，
　　把夏天女皇打扮，打扮。 　　　　　　　60

　　　　　　　　　　　　罗义蕴　译

编注　沃尔特·司各特（Walter Scott，1771—1832），英国著名的历史小说家和诗人。他最初从事苏格兰边区民谣的搜集与校订工作。一八〇五年，他作为中世纪传奇的现代临摹作家，一举成名。他的《最后一个行吟诗人的歌》赢得了很大的声誉。随后发表的诗作有：以亨利八世时期为背景的《玛米恩》和描述苏格兰高地氏族战争的《湖上夫人》等。本诗选自《罗克比》（*Rokeby*）第三章第十六节。全诗再现了古代民谣绿林好汉罗宾汉的故事，具有英国乡间泥土的清香，歌颂大自然的美丽和民间的淳朴生活，充满了英国人民的梦幻和向往。

171. 'THERE BE NONE OF BEAUTY'S DAUGHTERS'

There be none of Beauty's daughters
   With a magic like thee;
And like music on the waters
   Is thy sweet voice to me:
When, as if its sound were causing
The charmèd ocean's pausing,
The waves lie still and gleaming,
And the lull'd winds seem dreaming:

And the midnight moon is weaving
   Her bright chain o'er the deep,
Whose breast is gently heaving
   As an infant's asleep:
So the spirit bows before thee
To listen and adore thee;
With a full but soft emotion,
Like the swell of Summer's ocean.

                        LORD BYRON.

171. "没有一个美的女儿"

拜伦

没有一个美的女儿
　　富于魅力,像你那样
对于我,你甜蜜的声音
　　有如音乐飘浮水上:
仿佛那声音扣住了
沉醉的海洋,使它暂停,
波浪在静止、闪烁,
和煦的风也像在做梦:

午夜的月光在编织
　　海波上明亮的锁链;
海的胸膛轻轻起伏,
　　恰似一个婴儿安眠:
我的心灵也正是这样
倾身向往,对你聆听,
就像夏季海洋的浪潮
充满了温柔的感情。

　　　　　　　梁真　译

编注　本诗为歌词,作于一八一五年,并于一八一六年发表在《诗歌集》中。

172. LINES TO AN INDIAN AIR

I arise from dreams of thee
  In the first sweet sleep of night,
When the winds are breathing low
  And the stars are shining bright:
I arise from dreams of thee,
  And a spirit in my feet
Has led me — who knows how?
  To thy chamber-window, sweet!

The wandering airs they faint
  On the dark, the silent stream —
The champak odours fail
  Like sweet thoughts in a dream;
The nightingale's complaint
  It dies upon her heart,
As I must die on thine,
  O belovéd as thou art!

O lift me from the grass!
  I die, I faint, I fail!
Let thy love in kisses rain
  On my lips and eyelids pale.
My cheek is cold and white, alas!
  My heart beats loud and fast;
O! press it close to thine again
  Where it will break at last.

P. B. SHELLEY.

172. 印度小夜曲

雪莱

从夜晚第一阵香甜的睡眠中，
　　从梦见你的那些睡梦中惊醒，
身边正轻轻吹拂着习习晚风
　　头顶正烁烁闪耀着满天星星。
醒来，从梦见你的那些梦中，　　　　　　　　5
　　此时附在我脚底的一个精灵
不可思议地让我的脚步移动，
　　引我到你窗下，我的心上人！

四处飘荡的歌声已渐渐飘远，
　　消逝在那条幽暗静寂的小溪；　　　　　10
黄兰浓郁的芳菲早已经消散，
　　就像我梦中那些甜蜜的思绪；
夜莺那如泣如诉的声声哀怨；
　　也终将在它自己的心底死去，
就像我必然会在你心中长眠，　　　　　　　15
　　啊，因为我是如此深深爱你！

哦，请把我从青草地上扶起！
　　我已经虚弱无力，消瘦憔悴！
让你的爱你的吻都化作细雨，
　　让细雨洒在我的嘴唇和眼眉！　　　　　20
我心儿怦怦直跳，难以抑制，
　　我的脸颊已冰凉，面如死灰；
哦，请再次把我拥进你心里，
　　我的心最终应在你心里破碎！

曹明伦　译

编注 珀西·比希·雪莱(Percy Bysshe Shelley,1792—1822),英国杰出的浪漫主义诗人。读书时因刊印小册子《无神论的必然性》而被牛津大学开除,后支持爱尔兰独立斗争,受统治者迫害离开英国。他的抒情诗有很高的成就,著名的有《给英国人民之歌》《自由颂》《西风颂》《云雀颂》《云》等。著名长篇叙事诗有《伊斯兰的起义》,诗剧有《解放了的普罗米修斯》等。他的诗饱含热情,思想性强,音乐性强,而且充满对未来的憧憬。《金库》原编者认为雪莱在英国诗人中几乎享有最高的声誉。本诗作于一八二二年。

173. 'SHE WALKS IN BEAUTY'

She walks in beauty, like the night
   Of cloudless climes and starry skies,
And all that's best of dark and bright
   Meet in her aspect and her eyes,
Thus mellow'd to that tender light
   Which heaven to gaudy day denies.

One shade the more, one ray the less,
   Had half impair'd the nameless grace
Which waves in every raven tress,
   Or softly lightens o'er her face,
Where thoughts serenely sweet express
   How pure, how dear their dwelling-place.

And on that cheek and o'er that brow
   So soft, so calm, yet eloquent,
The smiles that win, the tints that glow
   But tell of days in goodness spent,
A mind at peace with all below,
   A heart whose love is innocent.

LORD BYRON.

173. "她身披美丽而行"

拜伦

她身披美丽而行,就好像
　晴朗无云繁星闪烁的夜晚;
明暗交织成的最美的光芒
　融会于她的明眸和容颜,
就这样化为那恬淡的柔光,　　　　　　　　5
　那柔光上苍从不赋予白天。

多一缕浓阴,少一丝淡影,
　都会有损于那难言的优美,
优美波动在她乌黑的发鬓,
　使她脸上焕发柔和的光辉;　　　　　　10
她的神情从容而甜蜜地表明
　她灵魂的寓所多么高洁珍贵。

她面容多温和,眉宇多娴静,
　但却有千般柔情,万种蜜意,
那迷人的微笑、灿烂的红晕　　　　　　15
　只能证明她生性就善良仁慈,
证明她有个宽容一切的灵魂,
　证明她心中的爱情纯洁如玉。

曹明伦　译

编注　此诗写于一八一四年,于一八一五年收入《希伯莱歌曲》发表。青年拜伦在一次舞会上看见了美丽的威尔莫·霍顿夫人。当时夫人身披丧服,黑色的丧服上缀饰有许多闪烁的金箔。美人着美衣,引发了拜伦的诗兴,舞会后他便写成了这首名诗。

174. 'SHE WAS A PHANTOM OF DELIGHT'

She was a phantom of delight
When first she gleam'd upon my sight;
A lovely apparition, sent
To be a moment's ornament;
Her eyes as stars of Twilight fair;
Like Twilight's, too, her dusky hair;
But all things else about her drawn
From May-time and the cheerful dawn;
A dancing shape, an image gay,
To haunt, to startle, and waylay.

I saw her upon nearer view,
A spirit, yet a woman too!
Her household motions light and free,
And steps of virgin-liberty;
A countenance in which did meet
Sweet records, promises as sweet;
A creature not too bright or good
For human nature's daily food,
For transient sorrows, simple wiles,
Praise, blame, love, kisses, tears, and smiles.

And now I see with eye serene
The very pulse of the machine;
A being breathing thoughtful breath,
A traveller between life and death;

174. "她是快乐的精灵"

华兹华斯

她是快乐的精灵,
当她第一次闪耀在我的眼前;
一个多么可爱的尤物,
作为片刻的珠宝送来人间。
她灰暗的头发像黄昏,　　　　　　　　　　5
她的眼睛是黄昏中美丽的星星;
但她身上其余的一切,
却来自明媚的春光和欢快的黎明。
一个欢乐的幻像,一个跳舞的阴影,
她埋伏在半路,突然使人迷惑、吃惊!　　10

我走得更近一些注视她,
一个精灵,可确又是个女人!
她做家务动作利索、灵活,
她的步伐有着处女的轻盈。
甜蜜的经历与甜蜜的许诺,　　　　　　15
融合塑造了她甜美的颜容。
她是这样一个普通的人儿,
汲取人类本性的养料并不过分:
每天有短暂的忧伤,平常的打闹,
也有赞扬、责备、哭笑和亲吻!　　　　20

现在我用安详的眼睛,
凝视人类器官脉搏的跳动,
她是生命与死亡之间的客旅,
一个富有思想的呼吸的人!

25	The reason firm, the temperate will,
	Endurance, foresight, strength, and skill;
	A perfect woman, nobly plann'd
	To warn, to comfort, and command;
	And yet a Spirit still, and bright
30	With something of angelic light.

W. WORDSWORTH.

谦让忍耐,有技巧和力量, 25
深谋远虑,有天赋的聪明;
是一个神明安排的完美的女郎,
给我们安慰、告诫和命令!
有着天使般的妩媚光辉,
她,仍是一个精灵! 30

袁广达　梁葆成　译

编注　威廉·华兹华斯(William Wordsworth,1770—1850),英国浪漫主义诗歌的奠基人之一,"湖畔派"诗人的重要代表。受卢梭"唯情论"的思想影响,他向往法国革命,但雅各宾专政的政策开始后,他的思想产生倒变,走向保守,晚年被封为"桂冠诗人"。华兹华斯写过不少意境清新、形象生动、语言质朴的诗篇。他特别擅长歌颂优雅恬静的自然景物,喜爱描绘农家的辛勤劳动和朴素习惯。他有不少小诗凝练精妙,形象生动,情趣盎然。本诗作于一八〇四年,诗中的"她"是玛丽·哈钦森(Mary Hutchinson)。华兹华斯一八〇二年与她成婚。

175. 'SHE IS NOT FAIR TO OUTWARD VIEW'

She is not fair to outward view
 As many maidens be;
Her loveliness I never knew
 Until she smiled on me.
O then I saw her eye was bright,
A well of love, a spring of light.

But now her looks are coy and cold,
 To mine they ne'er reply,
And yet I cease not to behold①
 The love-light in her eye:
Her very frowns are fairer far
Than smiles of other maidens are.

H. COLERIDGE.

---

① *I cease not to behold*: i.e. in spite of her present coldness I cannot forget the light that once shone in her eyes — indeed for me it is still there.

175. "她的外貌并不令人陶醉"

哈特利·柯勒律治

她的外貌并不令人陶醉
 比不上多少姑娘娇俏；
她的迷人处我也没有体会
 直到一天她向我莞尔一笑。
啊,我这才发现她的眸子如此明亮　　　　5
像爱的深井,光的源泉一样。

但现在她的目光羞怯而冷淡,
 怎么也不回答我的注视,
虽然我仍能在她的眼里找到
 爱情的光芒在悄悄闪烁：　　　　10
她的微皱的眉头也远比
 少女们的微笑更令我着迷。

郑敏　译

编注 哈特利·柯勒律治（Hartley Coleridge，1796—1849），塞缪尔·泰勒·柯勒律治的长子。他一生从事写作、教学和编辑工作,但成就不大。他最优秀的抒情诗发表于胡德（T. Hood）所编的《宝石集》（*The Gem*）一八二九年版。

176. 'I FEAR THY KISSES, GENTLE MAIDEN'

I fear thy kisses, gentle maiden;
    Thou needest not fear mine;
My spirit is too deeply laden
    Ever to burthen thine.

I fear thy mien, thy tones, thy motion;
    Thou needest not fear mine;
Innocent is the heart's devotion
    With which I worship thine.

P. B. SHELLEY.

176. "温柔的少女,我怕你的吻"

雪莱

温柔的少女,我怕你的吻,
　　你却无须害怕我的;
我的心已负载得够阴沉,
　　不致再给你以忧郁。

我怕你的风度、举止、声音, 5
　　你却无须害怕我的;
这颗心以真诚对你的心,
　　它只纯洁地膜拜你。

查良铮　译

编注　本诗作于一八二〇年,标题为《致——》;一八二四年被编入《诗人遗著》(*Posthumous Poems*)。

177. THE LOST LOVE

She dwelt among the untrodden ways
    Beside the springs of Dove;
A maid whom there were none to praise,
    And very few to love:

A violet by a mossy stone
    Half hidden from the eye!
— Fair as a star, when only one
    Is shining in the sky.

She lived unknown, and few could know
    When Lucy ceased to be;
But she is in her grave, and oh,
    The difference to me!

W. WORDSWORTH.

177. 失去的爱

华兹华斯

她居住在白鸽泉水的旁边①,
  无人来往的路径通往四面;
一位姑娘不曾受人称赞,
  也不曾受过别人的爱怜。

苔藓石旁的一株紫罗兰,
  半藏着没有被人看见!
美丽得如同天上的星点,
  一颗唯一的星清辉闪闪。

她生无人知,死也无人唁,
  不知她何时去了人间;
但她安睡在墓中,哦可怜,
  对于我呵是个地异天变!

郭沫若 译

编注 这首诗是华兹华斯著名的爱情诗《露茜》组诗(The Lucy Poems)中的第一篇。描写的是苏格兰山地和湖区的乡村少女,文字凝练精妙,十分感人,完全符合华兹华斯自己所提倡的诗歌作法原则。本标题为《金库》原编者所加。

---

① 白鸽泉可能指德比郡(Derbyshire)一处名为鸽谷的地方,也可能指约克郡(Yorkshire)克里夫兰(Cleveland)山中一条同名小河,这两地诗人都去过。——编注者

178. 'I TRAVELL'D AMONG UNKNOWN MEN'

I travell'd among unknown men
In lands beyond the sea;
Nor, England! did I know till then
What love I bore to thee.

'Tis past, that melancholy dream!
Nor will I quit thy shore
A second time; for still I seem
To love thee more and more.

Among thy mountains did I feel
The joy of my desire;
And she I cherish'd turn'd her wheel
Beside an English fire.

Thy mornings show'd, thy nights conceal'd
The bowers where Lucy play'd;
And thine too is the last green field
That Lucy's eyes survey'd.

W. WORDSWORTH.

178. "我曾在大海那边的异乡漫游"

华兹华斯

我曾在大海那边的异乡漫游,
　　看到的都是陌生的人们;
英格兰哪!只是到那个时候,
　　我明白了自己爱你之深。

那忧郁的梦儿已经一去不回!　　　　　　　5
　　我不愿意第二次离开你——
不愿再离开你的海岸,因为,
　　我看来已变得更加爱你。

我曾感到过那种热爱的欢乐——
　　在你那崇山峻岭的中间;　　　　　　　10
而我所珍爱的她曾摇着纺车——
　　家乡的炉火就在她身边。

白天托出了,黑夜却又藏起
　　露茜在那儿玩耍的亭榭;
而露茜最后一次眺望的土地　　　　　　　15
　　也就是你那青青的田野。

黄杲炘　译

编注　本诗为一七九九年诗人在德国短期逗留时所作,诗中表现了作者对祖国和家乡的思恋之情,也再次提到露茜姑娘。

179. THE EDUCATION OF NATURE

Three years she grew in sun and shower;
Then Nature said, 'A lovelier flower
   On earth was never sown;
   This child I to myself will take;
She shall be mine, and I will make
   A lady of my own.

'Myself will to my darling be
Both law and impulse: and with me
   The girl, in rock and plain,
In earth and heaven, in glade and bower,
Shall feel an overseeing power
   To kindle or restrain.

'She shall be sportive as the fawn
That wild with glee across the lawn①
   Or up the mountain springs;
And hers shall be the breathing balm,
And hers the silence and the calm
   Of mute insensate things.

'The floating clouds their state shall lend
To her; for her the willow bend;
   Nor shall she fail to see

---

① *lawn*: see above, note to No. 62, l. 85.

179. 造物者的启迪

华兹华斯

她三年成长,一阵阳光,一阵雨;
造物者说:"一朵花真美丽,
　　大地上的珍奇:
我要把这孩子带去;
她应该属于我,我将把她变成　　　　　　　　5
　　我的爱妻。

"对于我的情人,我自己
既是法律,也是动力:
　　这姑娘和我在岩石与平原上,
在大地与天堂,在林野与闺房,　　　　　　10
她都有一种督促的力量,
　　或去点燃激情,或去抑制欲望。

"她快活得像一只幼鹿,
跨过草原,跳上山泉,
　　发出阵阵狂喜;　　　　　　　　　　　15
她吐出香膏的气息,
她又是无声无息的东西
　　表现得那么安宁、静寂。

"浮云为她环绕;
杨柳为她弯腰;　　　　　　　　　　　　20
　　她也能看到

E'en in the motions of the storm
Grace that shall mould the maiden's form
   By silent sympathy.

'The stars of midnight shall be dear
To her; and she shall lean her ear
   In many a secret place
Where rivulets dance their wayward round,
And beauty born of murmuring sound
   Shall pass into her face.

'And vital feelings of delight
Shall rear her form to stately height,
   Her virgin bosom swell;
Such thoughts to Lucy I will give
While she and I together live
   Here in this happy dell.'

Thus Nature spake — The work was done —
How soon my Lucy's race was run!
   She died, and left to me
This heath, this calm and quiet scene;
The memory of what has been,
   And never more will be.

W. WORDSWORTH.

甚至在感情激荡之中，
默默的同情心——
　　这温柔会塑造姑娘的外貌。

"对于她，夜半的星星多么亲切；　　　　　　25
她贴耳能够听到
　　许多秘密的处所，
小溪舞蹈，自由弯绕，
来自淙淙水声的美呀
　　会溶入她的眉梢。　　　　　　　　　　30

"欢乐活泼的情感
会把她变得姿态端庄，
　　她少女的酥胸频频起伏；
我将告诉露茜这些思想，
当她和我在一起生活，　　　　　　　　　　35
　　就在这快乐的溪谷上。"

于是造物者说话了——功成业就——
我的露茜迅速地跑完了旅程①！
　　她去世了，只留给我
这高冈，这平静寂寥的山川；
也留下了这些记忆，　　　　　　　　　　　40
　　永远不会再增添。

　　　　　　　　　　　　　　冯思刚　译

编注　本诗于一七九九年作于哈兹树林（Hartz Forest），一八〇〇年发表在《抒情歌谣集》第二版上。标题为《金库》原编者所加。

---

① 露茜姑娘年轻夭折，似乎是造物者把她娶作爱妻，只给诗人留下伤感的回忆。而露茜究竟指谁，历来各家说法不一，难以考证。——译者

180. 'A SLUMBER DID MY SPIRIT SEAL'

A slumber did my spirit seal;
   I had no human fears:
She seem'd a thing that could not feel
   The touch of earthly years.

No motion has she now, no force;
   She neither hears nor sees;
Roll'd round in earth's diurnal course
   With rocks, and stones, and trees.

W. WORDSWORTH.

180. "迷糊封住了我的精神"

华兹华斯

迷糊封住了我的精神；
　我没有人世的忧惶：
她似乎超然物外，不可能
　感觉到岁月的影响。

现在她无力了，也不能动弹；
　她不再耳闻目睹；
卷在地球的日程里滚转，
　混同了岩石、树木。

卞之琳　译

编注　本诗一七九九年作于德国，与本卷 177 和 179 首同属《露茜》组诗。

181. LORD ULLIN' S DAUGHTER

A Chieftain to the Highlands bound
    Cries 'Boatman, do not tarry!
And I'll give thee a silver pound
    To row us o'er the ferry!'

'Now who be ye, would cross Lochgyle
    This dark and stormy water?'
'O I'm the chief of Ulva's isle,
    And this, Lord Ullin's daughter.

'And fast before her father's men
    Three days we've fled together,
For should he find us in the glen,
    My blood would stain the heather.

'His horsemen hard behind us ride —
    Should, they our steps discover,
Then who will cheer my bonny bride
    When they have slain her lover?'

Out spoke the hardy Highland wight,
    'I'll go, my chief, I'm ready:
It is not for your silver bright,

181. 乌林爵爷的女儿

坎贝尔

一个酋长到了高原①
　　高喊:"船夫啊,别迟延!
我给你一块银币,
　　把我们渡到河那边!"

"你是谁? 要渡过罗什干　　　　　　　　　　5
　　在这样暴风雨的夜晚?"
"啊,这是乌林爵爷的闺女,
　　我是乌法岛上的主官。

"我们赶在她父亲来人之前,
　　已经逃了三天,　　　　　　　　　　　　10
如果他发现我们在这峡谷,
　　定叫我血染荒原。

"他的马队就在我们后面追赶——
　　如果发现了我们的所在,
谁能使我漂亮的新娘欢喜,　　　　　　　　15
　　当她的新郎已被杀害?"

高原的船夫把话讲,
　　"主官,好吧,我就去:
不是为了你那亮晃晃的银币

---

① 故事发生在苏格兰西海岸,乌法是苏格兰西部莫尔岛外的一个小岛。其他人名、地名从悲剧的情节发展中可以辨出。——译者

20   But for your winsome lady: —

      'And by my word! the bonny bird
       In danger shall not tarry;
      So though the waves are raging white
       I'll row you o'er the ferry.'

25   By this the storm grew loud apace,
       The water-wraith was shrieking[①];
      And in the scowl of heaven each face
       Grew dark as they were speaking.

      But still as wilder blew the wind
30   And as the night grew drearer[②],
      Adown the glen rode arméd men,
       Their trampling sounded nearer.

      'O haste thee, haste!' the lady cries,
       'Though tempests round us gather;
35   I'll meet the raging of the skies,
       But not an angry father.'

      The boat has left a stormy land,
       A stormy sea before her, —
      When, oh! too strong for human hand
40   The tempest gather'd o'er her.

[①] *water-wraith*: see above, note to No. 127, l. 23.
[②] *drearer*: though the adjective 'drear' is fairly common, its comparative is generally supplied from 'dreary.'

而是为了你那美貌的娇妻:—— 20

"听我说吧!漂亮的鸟儿,
　　身危不容迟疑;
纵使白浪滔天,波涛咆哮,
　　我也要把你渡过去。"

狂风暴雨吼声隆, 25
　　水鬼尖声叫凄凄;
说话时分天变色,
　　天公蹙额、人焦急。

风儿愈吹愈猛烈,
　　夜色愈来愈昏黑, 30
骑士策马临峡谷,
　　蹄声嘚嘚多紧迫。

"快呀快!"姑娘高喊,
　　虽然暴风把我们席卷;
我愿面对天公的雷霆, 35
　　不愿来到盛怒父亲的面前。"

小船已离开暴风雨的海岸
　　惊涛骇浪就在前面,——
啊!猛烈的风浪谁能抵抗,
　　暴风雨执意欺凌那小船。 40

And sill they row'd amidst the roar
    Of waters fast prevailing:
Lord Ullin reach'd that fatal shore, —
    His wrath was changed to wailing.

For, sore dismay'd, through storm and shade
    His child he did discover: —
One lovely hand she stretch'd for aid,
    And one was round her lover.

'Come back! come back!' he cried in grief
    'Across this stormy water:
And I'll forgive your Highland chief,
    My daughter! — O my daughter!'

'Twas vain: the loud waves lash'd the shore,
    Return or aid preventing:
The waters wild went o'er his child,
    And he was left lamenting.

T. CAMPBELL.

他们在狂涛中把舵掌,
　　水势凶猛扑过小船:
乌林爵爷来到不幸的海岸,——
　　他的愤怒哟,变成了号哭悲惨。

他找到了自己的孩子, 45
　　穿过风暴与冥府,惊魂丧胆:——
一只可爱的手伸出求援,
　　另一只放在情人身边。

"回来吧! 回来吧!"他悲伤地呼唤,
　　这声音穿过暴风雨的海面: 50
我要宽恕你的高原主官,
　　我的女儿呀! ——啊,快回转!"

徒劳哟:怒涛拍打着海岸,
　　无法回转,无法救援,
海浪卷走了他的孩子, 55
　　留给他的只是一腔伤感。

罗义蕴　译

编注　托马斯·坎贝尔(Thomas Campell,1777—1844),苏格兰诗人,二十二岁出版了长诗《希望之乐》,轰动一时。在英国诗史上,他主要以其短诗而闻名,他的抒情诗质朴有力,旋律优美,往往带有浓厚的感伤情调。他写有许多描写战争、崇尚武功、歌颂祖国的诗。主要作品有《荷恩林登之战》《波罗地海之战》《你们英格兰的水手们》。本诗构思于一七九五年,完成于一八○四年,讲述了一个古老的苏格兰故事。

182. JOCK O' HAZELDEAN

'Why weep ye by the tide, ladie?
    Why weep ye by the tide?
I'll wed ye to my youngest son,
    And ye sall be his bride;
And ye sall be his bride, ladie,
    Sac comely to be seen' —
But aye she loot the tears down fa'[①]
    For Jock o' Hazeldean.

'Now let this wilfu' grief be done,
    And dry that cheek so pale;
Young Frank is chief of Errington
    And lord of Langley-dale;
His step is first in peaceful ha',
    His sword in battle keen' —
But aye she loot the tears down fa'
    For Jock o' Hazeldean.

'A chain of gold ye sall not lack,
    Nor braid to bind your hair;
Nor mettled hound, nor managed hawk[②],

---

① *loot*: the past tense of 'lat' = let.
② *mettled*: 'spirited.' *managed*: 'trained.'

182. 哈森汀的年轻汉①

司各特

"姑娘,你为什么在海边哭泣②?
　　你为什么这样悲伤?
我把你许配给我的小儿子,
　　你将成为他的新娘:

你将成为新娘,姑娘呀!　　　　　　　　　　5
　　打扮起来多么好看"——
但是她泪流满面哟
　　想念着哈森汀的年轻汉。

"抛掉你的悲哀,
　　擦干你灰白的面颊;　　　　　　　　　10
年轻的法兰克是爱尔顿的首领,
　　朗格里河谷的公爵也是他③;
他的脚步首先落在和平的大厦,
　　他的大刀在疆场闪亮"——
但是,哎,她仍然潸潸泪下,　　　　　　　15
　　总是把哈森汀的年轻汉牵挂

"你不会缺少金银财宝,
　　扎发的绸带更是任你挑,
你有精壮的猎犬,驯服的猎鹰,

---

① 哈森汀在苏格兰境内。——译者
② 本诗第一节是民谣。——译者
③ 朗格里河是一条小溪,流入梯河(Tees),在爱格尔斯顿附近河床增高,也许就是司各特指的爱尔顿(Errington)。——译者

    Nor palfrey fresh and fair;
    And you, the foremost o' them a',
    Shall ride our forest queen' —
    But aye she loot the tears down fa'
    For Jock o' Hazeldean.

    The kirk was deck'd at morning-tide,
    The tapers glimmer'd fair;
    The priest and bridegroom wait the bride,
    And dame and knight are there.
    They sought her baith by bower and ha';
    The ladie was not seen!
    She 's o'er the Border, and awa'
    Wi' Jock o' Hazeldean.

           SIR W. SCOTT.

你的乘骑抖擞而俊俏； 20
你是他们中最高贵的人，
　　如女皇乘坐，威风凛凛"——
但是，哎，她还是泪眼涔涔，
　　为哈森汀的小年轻汉而伤心。

教堂一清早就装饰起来， 25
　　小蜡烛闪耀得亮晶晶；
教士和新郎都在等候新娘，
　　美人和骑士全都光临，
他们去大厅、闺房找寻；
　　这姑娘早已不见踪影！ 30
她已越过了边境，
　　追随着哈森汀的年轻汉。

　　　　　　　　　　　李毅　译

编注　本诗有浓郁的边疆歌谣的色彩，也有中世纪传奇风格。逃婚是一种喜闻乐见的民谣主题。

183. FREEDOM AND LOVE

How delicious is the winning
Of a kiss at love's beginning,
When two mutual hearts are sighing
For the knot there's no untying!

Yet remember, 'midst your wooing,
Love has bliss, but Love has ruing;
Other smiles may make you fickle,
Tears for other charms may trickle.

Love he comes, and Love he tarries,
Just as fate or fancy carries;
Longest stays, when sorest chidden;
Laughs and flies, when press'd and bidden.

Bind the sea to slumber stilly,
Bind its odour to the lily,
Bind the aspen ne'er to quiver,
Then bind Love to last for ever.

Love's a fire that needs renewal
Of fresh beauty for its fuel;
Love's wing moults when caged and captured,
Only free, he soars enraptured.

Can you keep the bee from ranging

183. 自由与爱情

坎贝尔

赢得爱情最初的一吻
是多么令人心醉,
当两颗痴情的心在叹息
解开这情结的能有谁!

但是记住,当你求婚时, 5
爱情是幸福,也是后悔;
别的笑脸会使你变心,
别的美貌会使你落泪。

正像命运与幻觉的赐与,
爱情,它来了;爱情,它逗留; 10
留得愈久愈受痛苦的磨折;
当拥抱之后就告别,它就大笑飞走。

捆住海浪使它永远安静,
裹起百合花的芬芳永不散流,
缠住白杨树叶叫它永不颤抖, 15
那么,抓住爱情叫它永远缚就。

爱情的火焰需要加添新枝,
新的美可作它的燃剂:
囚在笼里的爱情羽翼会融化,
只有自由才能使它翱翔狂喜。 20

谁能使蜜蜂不整齐排列,

Or the ringdove's neck from changing?
No! nor fetter'd Love from dying
In the knot there's no untying.

T. CAMPBELL.

谁能使斑鸠的颈形永不变易?
不!你无法把快要消逝的爱情锁住,
让它变成一个结,永不脱离。

罗义蕴　译

编注　本诗原标题是《歌》,现标题系《金库》原编者所加。

184. LOVE'S PHILOSOPHY

The fountains mingle with the river
    And the rivers with the ocean,
The winds of heaven mix for ever
    With a sweet emotion;
Nothing in the world is single,
    All things by a law divine
In one another's being mingle —
    Why not I with thine?

See the mountains kiss high heaven
    And the waves clasp one another;
No sister-flower would be forgiven
    If it disdain'd its brother;
And the sunlight clasps the earth,
    And the moonbeams kiss the sea —
What are all these kissings worth,
    If thou kiss not me?

P. B. SHELLEY.

184. 爱的哲学

雪莱

出山的泉水与江河汇流，
　　江河又与海洋相通，
天空里风与风互相渗透，
　　融洽于甜蜜的深情。
万物遵循同一条神圣法则，　　　　　　　　5
　　在同一精神中会合；
世界上一切都无独而有偶，
　　为什么我和你却否？

看高高的山峰亲吻蓝空，
　　波浪和波浪相抱相拥，　　　　　　　10
没有一朵姐妹花会被宽容，
　　如果竟轻视她的弟兄；
灿烂的阳光抚抱大地，
　　明丽的月华亲吻海波，
一切甜美的神工有何价值，　　　　　　　15
　　如果，你不吻我？

　　　　　　　　　　　　　江枫　译

185. ECHOES

How sweet the answer Echo makes
    To Music at night,
When, roused by lute or horn, she wakes,
And far away o'er lawns and lakes
    Goes answering light!

Yet Love hath echoes truer far
    And far more sweet
Than e'er, beneath the moonlight's star,
Of horn or lute or soft guitar
    The songs repeat.

'Tis when the sigh, — in youth sincere
    And only then —
The sigh that 's breathed for one to hear,
Is by that one, that only Dear
    Breathed back again.

T. MOORE.

185. 爱的回声

摩尔

多甜蜜啊！回声会在夜里
　　应和甜蜜的音乐，
被琉特琴和圆号从梦中唤醒，
她会迎向远方的草地湖泊①，
　　去应答晨曦黎明。 　　　　　　　　　　5

可爱的回声从来都更真，
　　也从来都更甜，
比月光下的圆号更舒扬，
比星光下的吉他更婉转，
　　比琉特琴更缠绵。 　　　　　　　　　10

只有从少年心底发出那声叹息——
　　只有在那个时辰——
那声只对一个人发出的叹息，
那声只对心上人发出的叹息，
　　才会得到回应。 　　　　　　　　　　15

曹明伦　译

编注 托马斯·摩尔（Thomas Moore，1779—1852），爱尔兰诗人，是著名的《爱尔兰歌曲集》的作者，他创作了极富才华的东方长诗《拉拉鲁克》。他的抒情诗情感真挚，富有乐感，很多是作为歌词而创作的。本诗选自《爱尔兰歌曲集》第八册。

---

① 在希腊神话中，回声是一个有声无形的女神。——译者

186. A SERENADE

Ah! County Guy, the hour is nigh[①],
    The sun has left the lea,
The orange flower perfumes the bower,
    The breeze is on the sea.
The lark, his lay who trill'd all day,
    Sits hush'd his partner nigh;
Breeze, bird, and flower confess the hour,
    But where is County Guy?

The village maid steals through the shade
    Her shepherd's suit to hear;
To beauty shy, by lattice high,
    Sings high-born Cavalier.
The star of Love, all stars above,
    Now reigns o'er earth and sky,
And high and low the influence know —
    But where is County Guy?

                      SIR W. SCOTT.

---

① *County*: a sixteenth-century form of 'Count.'

186. 小夜曲

司各特

盖伊伯爵啊！时间快到了，
　　太阳已离开了草原，
柑桔花把芬芳送进闺房，
　　微风吹拂着海面。
整天歌声缭绕的云雀此时停止了吟唱，　　　5
　　歇息在情侣的身旁；
微风，鸟儿，花儿都在向神剖白，
　　可是盖伊伯爵在何方？

乡村姑娘偷偷躲进了林荫，
　　去倾听牧羊人向她求婚；　　　10
高贵的骑士在那高高的格子窗前，
　　把歌声献给含羞的美人。
爱情的星宿高于一切星星，
　　此刻正治理下界天庭，
远远近近受到感应——　　　15
　　可是盖伊伯爵啊，何处把你找寻？

　　　　　　　　　　　　罗义蕴　译

编注　本诗出自司各特小说《昆丁·达沃德》(*Quentin Durward*)第四章，盖伊是小说中的人物。

187. TO THE EVENING STAR

Gem of the crimson-colour'd Even,
    Companion of retiring day,
Why at the closing gates of heaven,
    Belovéd Star, dost thou delay?

So fair thy pensile beauty burns①
    When soft the tear of twilight flows;
So due thy plighted love returns
    To chambers brighter than the rose;

To Peace, to Pleasure, and to Love
    So kind a star thou seem'st to be,
Sure some enamour'd orb above
    Descends and burns to meet with thee.

Thine is the breathing, blushing hour,
    When all unheavenly passions fly,
Chased by the soul-subduing power
    Of Love's delicious witchery.

O! sacred to the fall of day,
    Queen of propitious stars, appear,
And early rise, and long delay,

---

① *pensile*: 'hanging in mid-air'; the use of the word here is rather an affectation, as is the next line, to describe the falling dew. The meaning of this and the next stanza is that Venus is so fair in the evening, so punctual in her reappearance in the morning, and so generally kindly, that she must surely attract some other planet. The attraction fortunately is only such as is necessary to maintain the balance of the solar system.

187. 致傍晚的星①

坎贝尔

深红夜色的宝石,
　　白昼隐退的伴侣,
为什么天上的大门快要关闭,
　　亲爱的星,你迟迟不肯离去?

你悬挂的美燃烧得太漂亮②,　　　　　　　　　5
　　当薄暮飘洒着温柔的泪水;
你忠贞的爱情表现得这样恰当,
　　来到了比玫瑰更艳丽的深闺;

对于安宁、欢乐和爱情,
　　你这颗星好像情意绵绵,　　　　　　　　10
一定有一个迷人的天体
　　下来热情地和你相见。

你此刻呼吸面庞绯红,
　　爱情喜悦的魅力,
那征服灵魂的力量　　　　　　　　　　　　15
　　在驱赶着你的七情六欲。

啊! 神圣的夜幕笼罩了白天,
　　那慈祥星体的女皇露了面,
升起得很早,逗留得很晚,

---

① 这里指金星,又名太白星,希腊神话中的维纳斯,司爱和美的女神。——译者
② 金星受万有引力的影响好像悬挂着,日落时显得非常美。——译者

When Caroline herself is here!

Shine on her chosen green resort,
    Whose trees the sunward summit crown,
And wanton flowers, that well may court①
    An angel's feet to tread them down.

Shine on her sweetly-scented road,
    Thou star of evening's purple dome,
That lead'st the nightingale abroad,
    And guid'st the pilgrim to his home.

Shine where my charmer's sweeter breath
    Embalms the soft exhaling dew,
Where dying winds a sigh bequeath
    To kiss the cheek of rosy hue.

Where, winnow'd by the gentle air,
    Her silken tresses darkly flow,
And fall upon her brow so fair,
    Like shadows on the mountain snow.

Thus, ever thus, at day's decline
    In converse sweet to wander far —
O bring with thee my Caroline,
    And thou shalt be my Ruling Star!

                      T. CAMPBELL.

---

① *wanton*: 'luxuriant.'

  当卡洛玲亲自到此游玩！ 20

你要照耀在她选择的绿荫，
  那儿的树梢戴上向阳的王冠，
缤纷的花朵会恳求一位仙子
  步履轻盈来到它们中间。

你要照在她香气宜人的路上， 25
  你这夜晚紫色天穹下的星，
会给出游的夜莺导航，
  也会把返家的香客带领。

你照亮我爱人甜蜜的呼吸的处所
  她的呼吸使晶莹的露珠弥漫着清香， 30
那儿飞逝的风发出一声叹息，
  为了亲吻她红色的面庞。

那儿柔和的风轻轻地吹，
  她那丝一般的黑发飘起微波，
抚摩着她美丽的额角， 35
  好像影子印在冰雪的山坡。

就这样，永远这样，当白天消逝以后，
  在甜蜜的话语中，我们走过许多路程——
啊，把我的卡洛玲带上，
  那你将是永远主宰我命运的星辰！ 40

罗义蕴　译

编注　本诗创作于一七九六年，前一部分（四个诗节）名《致南风》（To the South Wind），其余（六个诗节）名《卡洛玲》（Caroline）。作者从女神维纳斯写到心爱的姑娘。她们都是爱和美的化身。全诗把天上与人间融为一体，好似幸福本身在向自己微笑。

188. TO THE NIGHT

Swiftly walk over the western wave,
     Spirit of Night!
Out of the misty eastern cave,
     Where, all the long and lone daylight,
Thou wovest dreams of joy and fear
Which make thee terrible and dear, —
     Swift be thy flight!

Wrap thy form in a mantle grey
     Star- inwrought!
Blind with thine hair the eyes of Day,
     Kiss her until she be wearied out,
Then wander o'er city, and sea, and land,
Touching all with thine opiate wand —
     Come, long-sought!

When I arose and saw the dawn,
     I sigh'd for thee;
When light rode high, and the dew was gone,
     And noon lay heavy on flower and tree,
And the weary Day turn'd to his rest,
Lingering like an unloved guest,
     I sigh'd for thee.

188. 夜

雪莱

你凌波西行,敏捷轻盈①,
　　　夜之精灵!
在那雾濛濛的东方洞穴中,
在那漫长寂寞的白昼中,
你织着欢乐的梦、恐惧的梦,　　　　　　　5
使你那样地温柔,那样地凶猛,——
　　　你多轻盈地飞行!

一件黑灰灰的披肩把你裹紧,
　　　刻上了星星!
你用头发蒙住了白天的眼睛,　　　　　　10
你用亲吻弄得她精疲力尽;
于是你越过城市越过海洋越过森林,
把你催眠的魔杖点遍了远远近近——
　　　来吧,多久的找寻!

当我起身见到那晨曦,　　　　　　　　　15
　　　我为你而叹息;
当光明高照,白露杳杳,
当正午沉重地躺上了树梢,
当倦怠的白天已气息奄奄,
像个恼人的客人,她还在留连,　　　　　20
　　　我为你而叹息。

---

① "你"是对"夜之精灵"的直呼语。——编注者

Thy brother Death came, and cried,
    'Wouldst thou me?'
Thy sweet child Sleep, the filmy-eyed,
    Murmur'd like a noontide bee,
'Shall I nestle near thy side?
Wouldst thou me?' — And I replied,
    'No, not thee!'

Death will come when thou art dead,
    Soon, too soon —
Sleep will come when thou art fled;
    Of neither would I ask the boon
I ask of thee, belovéd Night —
Swift be thine approaching flight,
    Come soon, soon!

P. B. SHELLEY.

你的兄弟"死亡"来了,他叫道:
　　"要我吧,可好?"
你甜蜜的孩儿"睡眠"把倦眼轻眨,
像正午的蜂儿咿咿哑哑, 25
　"让我在你身边安家,
要我吧,可好?"——我回答:
　　"不,你呀,不要!"

你一死去死亡就来了,哎呀,
　　快啊,太快啦! 30
当你飞逸,睡眠就来到;
他们的恩赐我全都不要,
我要的是你,心爱的夜,——
你的飞临,多轻盈敏捷,
　　来呀,快来吧! 35

陈维杭　译

编注　本诗作于一八二一年,一八二四年发表于《诗人遗著》上,原标题是《致夜》(To Night)。

189. TO A DISTANT FRIEND

Why art thou silent? Is thy love a plant
　Of such weak fibre that the treacherous air
　Of absence withers what was once so fair?
Is there no debt to pay, no boon to grant?

Yet have my thoughts for thee been vigilant,
　Bound to thy service with unceasing care —
The mind's least generous wish a mendicant①
　For nought but what thy happiness could spare.

Speak! — though this soft warm heart, once free to hold
　A thousand tender pleasures, thine and mine,
Be left more desolate, more dreary cold②
Than a forsaken bird's-nest fill'd with snow
　'Mid its own bush of leafless eglantine③—
Speak, that my torturing doubts their end may know!

W. WORDSWORTH.

---

① *The mind's least generous wish*, etc.; *i.e.* the most selfish wish I had about you was merely that you should grant me what could not lessen your own happiness, viz. a letter or a message.
② *Be left more desolate*: sc. by what you may say.
③ *eglantine*: 'sweet-brier.'

189. 致远方的朋友

华兹华斯

你为什么沉默不语?难道说你的友情
　像草木般薄弱纤细
　分离后被不适的空气损毁了原来的美?
难道你就没有尚未还清的债务,也无可施的恩惠?

但是且让我的思想激起你的警惕,
　我命定为你效力,担当无穷的思虑——
这心情并不求助于化缘和乞讨,
　只求你让我分享你的欢愉。

说话呀!——尽管这温柔的心曾拥有你我
　过去千万种欢乐的情意,
现在却比一个被抛弃积满雪的鸟巢
在它无叶的野蔷薇灌木丛里——
　落得更加荒凉、冷凄。
说话呀!请让我结束这折磨人的疑惧。

罗义蕴　译

编注　作于一八三二或一八三三年,选自诗集《重访雅罗和其他》(*Yarrow Revisited and other Poems*),这是诗人喜爱的题材,据说是诗人看见了一个被抛弃了的积满了雪的鸟巢有感。

190. 'WHEN WE TWO PARTED'

When we two parted
  In silence and tears,
Half broken-hearted,
  To sever for years,
Pale grew thy cheek and cold,
  Colder thy kiss;
Truly that hour foretold
  Sorrow to this!

The dew of the morning
  Sunk chill on my brow;
It felt like the warning
  Of what I feel now.
Thy vows are all broken,
  And light is thy fame;
I hear thy name spoken
  And share in its shame.

They name thee before me,
  A knell to mine ear;
A shudder comes o'er me —
  Why wert thou so dear?
They know not I knew thee
  Who knew thee too well[①]:

[①] *Who*: the antecedent is 'I.'

190. "想从前我们俩分手"

拜伦

想从前我们俩分手,
　　默默无言地流着泪,
预感到多年的隔离,
　　我们忍不住心碎;
你的脸冰凉,发白,　　　　　　　　　　　　5
　　你的吻更似冷冰,
呵,那一刻正预兆了
　　我今日的悲痛。

清早凝结着寒露,
　　冷彻了我的额角,　　　　　　　　　　10
那种感觉仿佛是
　　对我此刻的警告。
你的誓言全破碎了,
　　你的行为如此轻浮;
人家提起你的名字,　　　　　　　　　　　15
　　我听了也感到羞辱。

他们当着我讲到你,
　　一声声有如丧钟;
我的全身一阵颤栗——
　　为什么对你如此情重?　　　　　　　　20
没有人知道我熟识你,
　　呵,熟识得太过了——

> Long, long shall I rue thee
>   Too deeply to tell.
>
> In secret we met;
>   In silence I grieve
> That thy heart could forget,
>   Thy spirit deceive.
> If I should meet thee
>   After long years,
> How should I greet thee? —
>   With silence and tears.

LORD BYRON.

我将长久、长久地悔恨,
  这深处难以为外人知道。

你我秘密地相会, 25
  我又默默地悲伤,
你竟然把我欺骗,
  你的心终于遗忘。
如果很多年以后,
  我们又偶然会面, 30
我将要怎样招呼你?
  只有含着泪,默默无言。

查良铮　译

191. HAPPY INSENSIBILITY

In a drear-nighted December,
    Too happy, happy tree,
Thy branches ne'er remember
    Their green felicity:
The north cannot undo them①
With a sleety whistle through them,
Nor frozen thawings glue them②
    From budding at the prime.

In a drear-nighted December,
    Too happy, happy brook,
Thy bubblings ne'er remember
    Apollo's summer look;
But with a sweet forgetting
They stay their crystal fretting③,
Never, never petting④
    About the frozen time.

Ah, would 'twere so with many
    A gentle girl and boy!

---

① *undo them*: 'bring them to ruin.'
② *Nor frozen thawings*, etc.: 'nor can the freezing of the melted snow seal them up so firmly that they will not blossom in the spring.' For *prime*, see notes to No. 11, l. 7.
③ *fretting*: a stream is said to fret its banks when it eats them away.
④ *petting*: 'taking offence,' 'falling into a pet.'

191. 不敏感的快乐

济慈

呵,十二月凄凉的寒夜里,
　一棵快乐的、快乐的树,
你的枝柯从来不牵记
　曾经有过的绿色幸福:
北方的雪雨呼啸逞强,　　　　　　　　　　　5
绝不能把你的枝柯摧伤;
化雪的料峭也无法阻挡
　春天在你的枝头吐蕊。

呵,十二月凄凉的寒夜里,
　一条快活的、快活的溪涧,　　　　　　　10
你的水沫从来不牵记
　太阳神阿波罗夏日的容颜;
只是带着甜甜的忘却,
让细浪凝固成一片洁莹,
对这冰封雪冻的季节,　　　　　　　　　　15
　你决不、决不撒气,怨怼。

啊,但愿少男少女们
　都跟你们的遭际相似!

But were there ever any
    Writhed not at passéd joy?
To know the change and feel it,
When there is none to heal it
Nor numbéd sense to steel it —
    Was never said in rhyme.

                      J. KEATS.

但是他们之中有谁人
　　对欢乐消逝不心痛神驰？
世事无常，人们都感知，
这种创伤，却无法医治，
麻木也不能使变化停止——
　　这些从未表露在诗内。

屠岸　译

编注　本诗初见于一八二九年加利纳里(Galignani)编辑的济慈诗选，重印在一八三〇年的《宝石集》(*The Gem*)上，标题为《金库》原编者加。济慈的原标题是《歌》(Song)。

192. 'WHERE SHALL THE LOVER REST'

Where shall the lover rest
    Whom the fates sever
From his true maiden's breast,
    Parted for ever?
Where, through groves deep and high,
    Sounds the far billow,
Where early violets die
    Under the willow.
        Eleu loro[1]!
    Soft shall be his pillow.

There, through the summer day,
    Cool streams are laving;
There, while the tempests sway,
    Scarce are boughs waving;
There thy rest shalt thou take,
    Parted for ever,
Never again to wake,
    Never, O never!
        Eleu loro!
    Never, O never!

Where shall the traitor rest,

---

[1] *Eleu loro*: these are not Gaelic words, or indeed words in any language, but merely sounds expressive of grief.

192. "那个情人将安息在哪里"

司各特

那个情人将安息在哪里
　　命运女神已使他离去
使他离开了钟情的姑娘
　　永远各自东西?
在那儿,穿越高低树林, 5
　　远方的大海喧腾不息,
在那儿,那棵杨柳树下,
　　早开的紫罗兰已经枯死。
　　　　哎哟,哎哟!
　　他的枕头会松软舒适。 10

在那儿,在整个夏日里,
　　清凉的溪水缓慢流逝;
在那儿,当暴风雨骤然袭来,
　　树枝儿几乎不摇晃弯曲;
你将在那儿安息长眠, 15
　　永远永远躺在那里,
绝不会再醒来,
　绝不会,哦,绝不会!
　　　　哎哟,哎哟!
　　永不起,哦,永不起。 20

那不忠的情人将安息在哪里

  He, the deceiver,
  Who could win maiden's breast,
   Ruin, and leave her?
  In the lost battle,
   Borne down by the flying,
  Where mingles war's rattle
   With groans of the dying;
    Eleu loro!
  There shall he be lying.

Her wing shall the eagle flap
 O'er the falsehearted;
His warm blood the wolf shall lap
 Ere life be parted:
Shame and dishonour sit
 By his grave ever;
Blessing shall hallow it
 Never, O never!
  Eleu loro!
 Never, O never!

SIR W. SCOTT.

就是他哟,无耻的骗子
能够赢得少女的心
　　蹂躏之后再将她抛弃?
就在这一次败仗之中, 25
　　溃逃使他力竭精疲,
战场上阵阵武器的碰响
　　伴着临死的呻吟喘息;
　　　哎哟,哎哟!
　　他就将躺在那里。 30

苍鹰将振动她的双翅
　　啄食这负心汉的尸体;
豺狼将舐食他的热血
　　当他还未闭眼咽气;
就在他的坟墓之上 35
　　将永远留下耻辱的痕迹;
神恩永不会将他宽恕,
　　永不会,哦,永不会!
　　　哎哟,哎哟!
　　永不会抹去耻辱的痕迹。 40

　　　　　　　　　　　　曹明伦　译

编注　本诗选自司各特一八〇八年出版的长篇叙事诗《玛米恩》第三章第十节。长诗叙述封建主玛米恩为了娶贵族小姐克拉尔为妻,诬陷她的未婚夫,最后阴谋暴露,玛米恩死于战争,克拉尔终于与情人团聚。全诗充满忧郁、浪漫的情调。

193. LA BELLE DAME SANS MERCI

'O what can ail thee, knight-at-arms,
    Alone and palely loitering①?
The sedge has wither'd from the Lake,
    And no birds sing.

'O what can ail thee, knight-at-arms!
    So haggard and so woebegone?
The squirrel's granary is full,
    And the harvest's done.

'I see a lily on thy brow
    With anguish moist and fever dew②,
And on thy cheeks a fading rose
    Fast withereth too.'

'I met a Lady in the Meads,
    Full beautiful — a fairy's child,
Her hair was long, her foot was light,
    And her eyes were wild.

'I made a garland for her head,
    And bracelets too, and fragrant zone;
She look'd at me as she did love,

---

① *palely loitering*: 'loitering with pale looks.'
② *moist* qualifies 'brow.'

193. 美丽的无情女郎

济慈

"哦,什么使你烦懊,戴纹章的骑士,
 脸色苍白孤零零徘徊闲荡?
湖边的茅薹早已枯萎,
 鸟儿也不再歌唱。

"哦,什么使你烦恼,戴纹章的骑士, 5
 这般憔悴,又如此悲伤?
松鼠的粮洞早已装满,
 田野里的粮食已归仓。

"我看见一朵百合花在你汗涔涔的额顶
 你极度痛苦的额顶热汗流淌, 10
你脸颊上一朵凋谢的玫瑰
 也迅速地枯萎消亡。"

"我在草地上遇见位女士,
 美丽无比——犹如仙女一样;
她头发细长,她脚步轻盈, 15
 她两眼闪着热切的光芒。

"我为她编织了一顶花冠,
 编织了手镯花环替她戴上;
她对我凝目而视似乎她爱我,

   And made sweet moan.

'I set her on my pacing steed
 And nothing else saw all day long,
For sidelong would she bend, and sing
 A fairy's song.

'She found me roots of relish sweet,
 And honey wild and manna dew,
And sure in language strange she said
 "I love thee true."

'She took me to her elfin grot,
 And there she wept, and sigh'd full sore,
And there I shut her wild wild eyes
 With kisses four.

'And there she lullèd me asleep,
 And there I dream'd — Ah! woe betide!
The latest dream I ever dreamt
 On the cold hill's side.

'I saw pale Kings and Princes too,
 Pale warriors, death-pale were they all;
They cried — "La belle Dame sans Merci
 Thee hath in thrall!"

'I saw their starved lips in the gloam

一声呻吟甜蜜芳香。 20

　"我扶她骑上我的骏马，
　　　整天痴痴地把她凝望，
　因为她屈身横坐在马背，
　　　一曲仙歌婉转悠扬。

　"她为我寻来甘美的源泉， 25
　　　野地里的蜂蜜，沾露的圣粮①，
　她用奇妙的语言对我说——
　　　'我真心实意把你爱上。'

　"她领我走进她的仙洞，
　　　哭诉她无限的哀怨悲伤， 30
　在那儿，我用四个亲吻
　　　盖住了她那热切的目光。

　"在那儿，她哄我昏然入睡，
　　　在梦里——啊！灾难临降！
　最后一个梦中我竟梦见 35
　　　在这阴风凄凄的小山旁。

　"我看见苍白的国王、王子和武士，
　　　他们都脸色苍白如死人一样；
　他们高喊——'那美丽的无情女郎哟
　　　已把奴隶的锁链缠在你身上！' 40

　"朦胧中我看见他们饥饿的嘴唇，

---

① 圣粮，即吗哪（Manna），以色列人漂泊荒野时上帝所赐的食物。见《旧约·出埃及记》第十六章第十五节。——译者

With horrid warning gapéd wide.
And I awoke and found me here
On the cold hill's side.

'And this is why I sojourn here
Alone and palely loitering,
Though the sedge is wither'd from the Lake
And no birds sing.'

J. KEATS.

> 发出可怕的警告,硕硕大张,
> 我醒来发现我就在这里,
> 在这阴风凄凄的小山旁。

> "这就是我为啥留在这里,   45
> 脸色苍白孤零零徘徊闲荡,
> 虽然湖边的茅藨早已枯萎,
> 鸟儿也不再歌唱。"

曹明伦　译

编注 此诗写于一八一九年,于一八二〇年发表。法语诗名 La Belle Dame sans Merci 来自法国诗人夏尔蒂埃(Alan Chartier,1385—1435)的同名诗。英国诗人及评论家格雷夫斯(Robert Graves,1895—1985)在其《白女神》(*The White Goddess*,1948)中评说济慈诗中的"无情女郎"同时象征了爱情、诗歌和死亡。

194. THE ROVER

'A weary lot is thine, fair maid,
　　A weary lot is thine!
To pull the thorn thy brow to braid,
　　And press the rue for wine.
A lightsome eye, a soldier's mien,
　　A feather of the blue,
A doublet of the Lincoln green —
　　No more of me you knew
　　　　My Love!
No more of me you knew

'This morn is merry June, I trow,
　　The rose is budding fain;
But she shall bloom in winter snow
　　Ere we two meet again.'
He turn'd his charger as he spake
　　Upon the river shore,
He gave his bridle-reins a shake,
　　Said 'Adieu for evermore
　　　　My Love!
And adieu for evermore.'

SIR W. SCOTT.

194. 流浪者的告别

司各特

"你注定要相思,美丽的少女,
　　你注定要苦苦相思!
拔出这棘刺,再皱皱眉头,
　　为美酒加入芸香榨汁。
轻松的眼神,士兵的举止,　　　　　　　　　　5
　　头上有蓝色翎羽
身上穿林肯绿紧身上衣——
　　你不曾听人说起过我,
　　　　亲爱的人哟!
对于我,你不曾听人说起。　　　　　　　　　10

"我相信这是欢乐的六月之晨,
　　玫瑰正含苞欲绽艳丽,
可除非玫瑰花开在冰雪严冬,
　　咱俩才可能重逢相聚。"
他一边说一边掉转马头,　　　　　　　　　　15
　　纵缰沿河岸而去,
身后回荡着他告别的声音:
　　"永别了,后会无期
　　　　亲爱的人哟!
"永别了,咱俩后会无期。"　　　　　　　　　20

　　　　　　　　　　　　　　　　曹明伦　译

编注　这首诗选自长诗《罗克比》(*Rokeby*,1813)第三章第二十八节,原诗标题为《歌》。在《新牛津英诗选集》(*The New Oxford Book of English Verse*,1972)中,此诗名为《流浪者的告别》(The Rover's Farewell)。

195. THE FLIGHT OF LOVE

When the lamp is shattered,
    The light in the dust lies dead —
When the cloud is scattered,
    The rainbow's glory is shed.
When the lute is broken,
    Sweet tones are remembered not;
When the lips have spoken,
    Loved accents are soon forgot.

As music and splendour
    Survive not the lamp and the lute,
The heart's echoes render
    No song when the spirit is mute —
No song but sad dirges,
    Like the wind through a ruined cell,
Or the mournful surges
    That ring the dead seaman's knell.

When hearts have once mingled,
    Love first leaves the well-built nest;
The weak one is singled[①]
    To endure what it once possest[②].

[①] *singled*: 'separated off'; a word often used of picking out one deer from a herd in order to chase it.

[②] *To endure what it once possest*: 'to look on as a burden that which it once counted a rich possession', viz. its own love for the other.

195. 爱情的飞逝

雪莱

当灯一破碎,
　尘世的火光便熄灭——
当云一消散,
　彩虹的光辉就褪色。
当笛一破裂, 　　　　　　　　　　　　　　5
　悠扬的音调就不再记起;
当唇一说话,
　爱情的语言便很快忘记。

当灯和笛不复存在,
　音乐和光华就会消殒, 　　　　　　　　10
当灵魂已经沉默,
　心儿就不会回荡歌声——
没有歌声,只有哀乐,
　像风儿穿过倾圮的墓缝,
又似悲哀的波涛汹浦 　　　　　　　　　15
　为死去的水手鸣起丧钟。

当两颗心儿一旦融为一体,
　爱情就离开它坚实的家园,
那弱者单独去承受
　过去的欢乐,如今的苦难。 　　　　　　20

O Love! who bewailest
  The frailty of all things here,
Why choose you the frailest①
  For your cradle, your home, and your bier?

Its passions will rock thee②
  As the storms rock the ravens on high;
Bright reason will mock thee
  Like the sun from a wintry sky.
From thy nest every rafter
  Will rot, and thine eagle home
Leave thee naked to laughter,
  When leaves fall and cold winds come.

P. B. SHELLEY.

---

① *the frailest*: i.e. the human heart, where love is born, lives, and dies.
② *Its passions will rock thee*: it is a pity that the requirements of metre made Shelley address Love as 'thou' (l. 21), 'you' (l. 23), and now again 'thee.' *Its*: i.e. the heart's.

啊！爱神！你哀怜
　　这万物脆弱的本性，
为什么偏偏选择最脆弱的①
　　作为你的摇篮、家室和棺木？

爱的激情会把你震动　　　　　　　　　　　25
　　像暴风雨震撼着高处的雀鸦；
聪颖的理智会把你嘲弄，
　　像冬季的天空失去了光华。
你窝巢中的每一块木片
　　会腐烂，你这山鹰的家呀　　　　　　30
当树叶脱落，寒风扑面，
　　会把你变得空空荡荡，成为笑话。

　　　　　　　　　　　　罗义蕴　译

编注　本诗初见于《诗人遗著》，原标题是《诗行》(Lines)。

---

① 这里指人的心。——译者

196. THE MAID OF NEIDPATH

O lovers' eyes are sharp to see,
    And lovers' ears in hearing;
And love, in life's extremity,
    Can lend an hour of cheering.
Disease had been in Mary's bower
    And slow decay from mourning,
Though now she sits on Neidpath's tower
    To watch her love's returning.

All sunk and dim her eyes so bright,
    Her form decay'd by pining,
Till through her wasted hand, at night,
    You saw the taper shining.
By fits a sultry hectic hue
    Across her cheek was flying;
By fits so ashy pale she grew
    Her maidens thought her dying.

Yet keenest powers to see and hear
    Seem'd in her frame residing;
Before the watch-dog prick'd his ear
    She heard her lover's riding;

196. 纳德巴斯的少女①

司各特

恋人的眼睛哦,最最敏锐,
　　恋人的耳朵哦,最最机警;
爱情,在生命的最后一息,
　　也能给人一个希望的时辰。
病魔曾徘徊在玛丽的闺房,　　　　　　　　　5
　　悲伤曾使她憔悴不振,
虽然她此刻坐在纳德巴斯塔楼
　　等待她的心上人快快返程。

她明亮的双眼曾暗淡无光,
　　相思使她的身体衰弱多病,　　　　　　10
从她那双消瘦的纤纤细手,
　　可知她闺房夜夜孤灯长明。
她双颊浮起的阵阵潮红
　　渐渐变得无踪无影;
她脸色逐渐变得那么苍白,　　　　　　　15
　　侍女们都以为她天命将尽。

可最最敏捷的听觉和视力
　　似乎还在她病体内留存;
护家犬还未竖起耳朵,
　　她已闻情人的马蹄声声;　　　　　　　20

---

① 纳德巴斯城堡在苏格兰东南部的皮布尔斯夏郡。相传从前城堡主人的女儿与毗邻的一位青年相爱,城堡主人反对这门婚姻,结果青年出走,姑娘一病不起。最后城堡主人只好应允了这门亲事。这首诗叙述的就是那位青年从国外归来时,姑娘等待他的情景。——译者

Ere scarce a distant form was kenn'd[1]
    She knew and waved to greet him,
And o'er the battlement did bend
    As on the wing to meet him.

He came — he pass'd — an heedless gaze[2],
    As o'er some stranger glancing;
Her welcome, spoke in faltering phrase,
    Lost in his courser's prancing —
The castle-arch, whose hollow tone
    Returns each whisper spoken,
Could scarcely catch the feeble moan
    Which told her heart was broken.

SIR W. SCOTT.

---

[1] *kenn'd*: 'recognized.'
[2] *an heedless gaze*: sc. he cast on her.

天边的人影还依稀朦胧,
 她已认出是他而挥手欢迎,
她屈身匍匐在城垛上边,
 像要飞上前迎接她的情人。

他来了——又驰过——无心的一瞥,   *25*
 仿佛在看一位不相识的陌生人;
腾跃的马蹄声盖住了
 她激动的欢呼,颤栗的嗓音——
城堡那空荡荡的拱形门洞,
 能回传细微的低语悄声,   *30*
却几乎未听见那声无力的悲叹,
 悲叹声告诉她心儿碎了。

曹明伦 译

197. THE MAID OF NEIDPATH

Earl March look'd on his dying child,
    And, smit with grief to view her —
'The youth,' he cried, 'whom I exiled
    Shall be restored to woo her.'

She's at the window many an hour
    His coming to discover:
And he look'd up to Ellen's bower
    And she look'd on her lover —

But ah! so pale, he knew her not,
    Though her smile on him was dwelling —
'And am I then forgot — forgot?'
    It broke the heart of Ellen.

In vain he weeps, in vain he sighs,
    Her cheek is cold as ashes;
Nor love's own kiss shall wake those eyes
    To lift their silken lashes.

                        T. CAMPBELL.

197. 纳德巴斯的少女

坎贝尔

马琪伯爵注视着垂危的爱女,
　　心中的悲痛令他头昏——
他喊道:"那被我流放的少年
　　要找回来,向你求婚。"

她伫立窗前,久久不舍, 5
　　守候着他的来临:
他仰望着艾琳的楼阁
　　她凝视着情人的身影——

但是,啊,这样苍白,他难以想象
　　这就是她,虽然她的微笑在他身上留连—— 10
"莫非我已被遗忘——遗忘?"
这使得艾琳心碎,多么可怜!

他哭泣,他叹惜,然而不行,
　　她的脸颊凉如死灰;
就是爱的亲吻也不能将她唤醒 15
　　让那双眼睛再抬起睫毛,丝绒样黑。

郑敏　译

编注　本诗与前一首诗(196)系同一题材,但两位诗人各有特色。司各特以民谣见长,他写的诗故事性强。坎贝尔以音乐制胜,他的诗富于悲怆的情调。原标题为《歌》(Song),现标题为《金库》原编者所加。

198. 'BRIGHT STAR, WOULD I WERE STEADFAST AS THOU ART'

Bright Star, would I were steadfast as thou art —
    Not in lone splendour hung aloft the night[①],
And watching, with eternal lids apart,
    Like nature's patient sleepless Eremite,

The moving waters at their priestlike task
    Of pure ablution round earth's human shores,
Or gazing on the new soft-fallen mask
    Of snow upon the mountains and the moors —

No — yet still steadfast, still unchangeable,
    Pillow'd upon my fair love's ripening breast,
To feel for ever its soft fall and swell,
    Awake for ever in a sweet unrest;

Still, still to hear her tender-taken breath,
And so live ever, — or else swoon to death.

                      J. KEATS.

---

① *aloft*: 'above,' 'in the highest part of.'

198. "灿烂的星！我祈求像你那样坚定"

济慈

灿烂的星！我祈求像你那样坚定——
　　但我不愿意高悬夜空，独自
辉映，并且永恒地睁着眼睛，
　　像自然间耐心的、不眠的隐士，

不断望着海涛，那大地的神父，　　　　　　　　　　5
　　用圣水冲洗人所卜居的岸沿，
或者注视飘飞的白雪，像面幕，
　　灿烂、轻盈，覆盖着洼地和高山——

啊，不，——我只愿坚定不移地
　　以头枕在爱人酥软的胸脯上，　　　　　　　　10
永远感到它舒缓的降落、升起；
　　而醒来，心里充满甜蜜的激荡；

不断、不断听着她细腻的呼吸，
就这样活着——或昏迷地死去。

查良铮　译

编注　本诗是写给他的爱人范妮·勃朗的，可能是济慈所写的最后一首诗，作于自英国赴意大利的海船上，写在《莎士比亚诗选》的空页内。诗人把自己融汇在自然、永恒与爱情之中，好似梦境与安然去世同样甜蜜。

199. THE TERROR OF DEATH

When I have fears that I may cease to be
    Before my pen has glean'd my teeming brain,
Before high-pilèd books, in charact'ry①
    Hold like rich garners the full-ripen'd grain;

When I behold, upon the night's starr'd face,
    Huge cloudy symbols of a high romance,
And think that I may never live to trace
    Their shadows, with the magic hand of chance;

And when I feel, fair creature of an hour!
    That I shall never look upon thee more,
Never have relish in the fairy power
    Of unreflecting love — then on the shore

Of the wide world I stand alone, and think
Till love and fame to nothingness do sink.

J. KEATS.

---

① *charact'ry*: 'writing.'

199. 死亡的恐惧

济慈

我担心在我的笔拾完了
　　我多产的头脑的遗穗以前，
在堆得高高的书籍用文字
　　像满仓一样贮藏透熟的谷物以前，

我可以不在人世；当我在星空上
　　望到一篇崇高传奇的巨大云象，
而觉到我决不能活着用机运的魔手
　　来描绘它们的影子的时候；

当我感到，美丽一时的人儿哟！
　　我从此再也不能看到你，
再也不能享受到无思无虑的
　　爱的魔力时！——于是在茫茫世界边岸上

我独自站在那儿沉思默想，
直到爱情与名声都化成烟云。

朱维基　译

编注　本诗所写的"死亡的恐惧"恰与前一首诗(198)所写的死亡的幸福形成鲜明的对照，表现了作者的矛盾心情。这更说明作者对生活的热爱，对美的追求。标题为《金库》原编者所加。

200. DESIDERIA

Surprised by joy — impatient as the wind —
   I turn'd to share the transport — O with whom
   But Thee — deep buried in the silent tomb,
That spot which no vicissitude can find?

Love, faithful love recall'd thee to my mind —
   But how could I forget thee? Through what power
   Even for the least division of an hour
Have I been so beguiled as to be blind

To my most grievous loss? — That thought's return
   Was the worst pang that sorrow ever bore,
Save one, one only, when I stood forlorn,

   Knowing my heart's best treasure was no more;
That neither present time, nor years unborn
   Could to my sight that heavenly face restore.

W. WORDSWORTH.

200. 伤逝

华兹华斯

心头一阵惊喜——风样急切——
　我开始了人生的这一段历程——
　啊,是同你在一起,可而今
你葬入寂寥坟地永恒的墓穴。

爱,忠实的爱永远使我记着——　　　　　　　5
　可我怎将你遗忘?什么魔力
　教我这般昏聩,竟忘却心底
最沉痛的损失?纵然这不过

发生在时光极其短暂的片刻,
　都使我的悲伤载负极大痛苦;　　　　　　10
　最不堪独自凄然伫立那时节:

　知道最心爱的宝贝离开人间,
　无论是现在还是将来的岁月,
　再不能看到她天使般的小脸。

于兴基　译

编注　该诗发表于一八一五年,系诗人为悼念夭亡的幼女凯瑟琳·华兹华斯而作。凯瑟琳·华兹华斯是诗人的第四个孩子,死于一八一二年六月,年仅三岁零九个月。

201. 'AT THE MID HOUR OF NIGHT'

At the mid hour of night, when stars are weeping, I fly[1]
To the lone vale we loved, when life shone warm in thine eye;
And I think oft, if spirits can steal from the regions of air
To revisit past scenes of delight, thou wilt come to me there
And tell me our love is remember'd, even in the sky!

Then I sing the wild song it once was rapture to hear,
When our voices, commingling, breathed like one on the ear;
And as Echo far off through the vale my sad orison rolls[2],
I think, O my Love! 'tis thy voice, from the Kingdom of Souls
Faintly answering still the notes that once were so dear.

T. MOORE.

---

[1] *stars are weeping*: a poetic conceit to account for the dew.
[2] *orison*: 'prayer.'

201. "子夜时分"

摩尔

子夜时分寒星洒露,我飞向
我们热恋时的幽谷,那时你的双眸
闪烁生命之火,我常沉思,倘若
灵魂能从神宇逸出,你是会来我身旁,
重温那逝去的欢乐,倾诉永恒之爱,即使魂在天国! 5

情意绵绵,我们声息交融,
我唱起曾使我们销魂的歌;
我那哀伤的祈祷回荡着遥远的山谷,
亲爱的,那是你从灵魂之国传来的声音,
如怨如诉,应和着那首亲切的歌。 10

谢屏 译

编注 本诗最初载于一八一三年《爱尔兰歌曲集》(*Irish Melodies*)第五册,虽以悼念为主题,但不感伤,因为歌声可以沟通天上与人间的灵魂。

202. ELEGY ON THYRZA

And thou art dead, as young and fair
    As aught of mortal birth;
And form so soft and charms so rare
    Too soon return'd to Earth!
Though Earth received them in her bed,
And o'er the spot the crowd may tread
    In carelessness or mirth,
There is an eye which could not brook
A moment on that grave to look.

I will not ask where thou liest low,
    Nor gaze upon the spot;
There flowers or weeds at will may grow,
    So I behold them not:
It is enough for me to prove
That what I loved and long must love
    Like common earth can rot;
To me there needs no stone to tell
'Tis Nothing that I loved so well[①].

Yet did I love thee to the last,
    As fervently as thou,
Who didst not change through all the past
    And canst not alter now.

[①] *'Tis Nothing*, etc.: 'that what I loved so well has now passed into nothingness.'

202. 热娜挽歌

拜伦

你死了,这么年轻、美丽,
　　没有人比得上你;
你那种娇容、那种绝色,
　　这么快回到土里!
虽然泥土承受了它,　　　　　　　　　　5
而人们也将不经意地
　　在那上面践踏,
却有一个人绝不忍
对你的坟墓注视一瞬。

我不想知道是在哪里　　　　　　　　　10
　　你静静地安眠;
让花草尽情地滋生吧,
　　我只不愿意看见:
够了,够了,只要我知道
我的所爱,我心上的人　　　　　　　　15
　　竟和泥土一样烂掉;
又何必墓碑给我指出
我所爱的原来是虚无。

但我却爱你直到最后,
　　一如你爱我那般;　　　　　　　　20
你对我始终一心一意,
　　现在更不会改变。

> The love where Death has set his seal
> Nor age can chill, nor rival steal,
>   Nor falsehood disavow;
> And, what were worse, thou canst not see
> Or wrong, or change, or fault in me.
>
> The better days of life were ours;
>   The worst can be but mine:
> The sun that cheers, the storm that lours,
>   Shall never more be thine.
> The silence of that dreamless sleep
> I envy now too much to weep;
>   Nor need I to repine①
> That all those charms have pass'd away
> I might have watch'd through long decay.
>
> The flower in ripen'd bloom unmatch'd
>   Must fall the earliest prey;
> Though by no hand untimely snatch'd,
>   The leaves must drop away.
> And yet it were a greater grief
> To watch it withering, leaf by leaf,
>   Than see it pluck'd to-day;
> Since earthly eye but ill can bear
> To trace the change to foul from fair.
>
> I know not if I could have borne
>   To see thy beauties fade;
> The night that follow'd such a morn
>   Had worn a deeper shade:
> Thy day without a cloud hath past,

---

① *sqq*. In these lines and the next two stanzas the innate selfishness of Byron's affection is made painfully apparent.

死亡给爱情贴了封条,
岁月、情敌再不会偷去,
　　负心又怎样抹掉; 25
伤心的是:你不能看见
我没有错处或改变。

生命的良辰是我们的,
　　苦时只由我忍受;
欢愉的太阳,险恶的风暴, 30
　　再不会为你所有。
你那无梦之乡的静穆,
我已羡慕得不再哭泣;
　　我无须乎怨诉
你的美色都已毫无踪影, 35
我至少没见它长期凋零。

那开得最艳的花朵
　　必然是最先凋落,
而花瓣,虽然没有手攫取,
　　也会随时间萎缩; 40
然而,假如等花儿片片萎黄,
那比看它今日突然摘去,
　　岂不更令人悲伤;
因为人的眼睛怎堪忍受
一个美人儿由美变丑。 45

我不知道我是否能忍受,
　　看你的美逐渐凋残,
随着这般早曦而来的夜
　　一定会更觉得幽暗
没有云翳的白日过去了, 50

And thou wert lovely to the last,
　　Extinguish'd, not decay'd;
As stars that shoot along the sky
Shine brightest as they fall from high.

55　　As once I wept, if I could weep,
　　My tears might well be shed,
To think I was not near, to keep
　　One vigil o'er thy bed;
To gaze, how fondly! On thy face,
To fold thee in a faint embrace, 60
　　Uphold thy drooping head;
And show that love, however vain,
Nor thou nor I can feel again.

Yet how much less it were to gain,
65　　Though thou hast left me free,
The loveliest things that still remain
　　Than thus remember thee!
The all of thine that cannot die①
Through dark and dread Eternity
70　　Returns again to me,
And more thy buried love endears
Than aught except its living years.

　　　　　　　　　　　LORD BYRON.

---

① *The all of thine*, etc; *i.e.* thy immortal spirit is with me still, and makes the recollection of thee dearer to me than anything has ever been, except thy love when alive.

直到临终你都那么鲜艳,
　你熄灭了,而不是枯凋;
你仿佛天上掠过的星星,
　在沉落的时候最为光明。

如果我能哭出,像以前, 55
　我应该好好哭一场,
因为在你临危的床边
　我不曾有一次探望;
我不曾怜爱地注视你的脸,
或者把你轻轻抱在怀里, 60
　你的头靠着我永眠;
我该悲恸:无论爱情多空,
呵,你我已不再乐于其中。

可是,从你残留下的珍异,
　尽管你都由我拾取, 65
那我也仍得不了许多,
　还不如这样把你记忆!
通过幽暗而可怕的永恒,
你那不会磨灭掉的一切
　会重回到我的心中; 70
但你埋葬的爱最使你可亲
胜过一切,除了它活的时辰。

查良铮　译

编注　本诗作于一八一二年二月,与《恰尔德·哈罗德游记》第二版同年同时出版。诗中的热娜是拜伦在东方遇到的一位姑娘,拜伦诗中几次提到,并表示出对她的爱慕之情,但究竟热娜是谁,拜伦一直没有告诉过任何人,关于这位女子的诗作,都是在热娜死后写成的。本诗初版的标题为第一行诗句。

203. 'ONE WORD IS TOO OFTEN PROFANED'

One word is too often profaned
    For me to profane it,
One feeling too falsely disdain'd
    For thee to disdain it;
One hope is too like despair
    For prudence to smother,
And Pity from thee more dear
    Than that from another.

I can give not what men call love;
    But wilt thou accept not
The worship the heart lifts above
    And the Heavens reject not, —
The desire of the moth for the star,
    Of the night for the morrow,
The devotion to something afar
    From the sphere of our sorrow?

P. B. SHELLEY.

203. "有个字过分被人们玷污"

雪莱

有个字过分被人们玷污①,
　我怎能再加以亵渎;
有种感情常被假意看轻②,
　你不至于也不尊重;
有种希望太和绝望相似,
　慎重也不忍加以窒息;
从你的心上发出的怜悯
　比别人的更珍贵可亲。

我献不出常人称道的爱,
　呈上的是虔诚崇拜;
连上帝也不至于拒绝,
　难道你竟然会摈弃。
这是灯蛾对星光的向往,
　黑夜对黎明的渴望;
我们的星球充满了忧愁,
　这可是对无忧的追求?

　　　　　　　江枫　译

---

① 指"爱"(love)一词。——编注者
② 指"爱慕之情"。——编注者

204. GATHERING SONG OF DONALD THE BLACK

  Pibroch of Donuil Dhu[1],
   Pibroch of Donuil,
  Wake thy wild voice anew,
   Summon Clan Conuil,
5   Come away, come away,
   Hark to the summons!
  Come in your war-array,
   Gentles and commons.

  Come from deep glen, and
10   From mountain so rocky;
  The war-pipe and pennon
   Are at Inverlocky.
  Come every hill-plaid, and
   True heart that wears one,
15   Come every steel blade, and
   Strong hand that bears one.

  Leave untended the herd,
   The flock without shelter;
  Leave the corpse uninterr'd,
20   The bride at the altar;
  Leave the deer, leave the steer,

---

[1] A *pibroch* is a series of variations on the bag-pipes; *Dhu* is the Gaelic for 'black.'

204. 黑唐纳的出征曲

司各特

黑唐纳的风笛曲①,
　　唐纳的风笛曲,
重新奏起你激昂的音调,
　　把唐纳兄弟召集,
去吧,去吧, 5
　　听那召唤!
穿起你的战袍,
　　无论平民,贵族。

从深幽的峡谷,
　　从陡峭的山麓; 10
在英维尔诺基,
　　风笛吹响,战旗飘拂。
来吧,披着苏格兰肩巾的山民,
　　忠诚的心,大家齐奋斗,
来吧,挥舞钢刀的人, 15
　　强劲的手把大刀擎住。

别管那羊群,
　　让它们无处遮盖,
别埋葬尸体,
　　让新娘留在神台, 20
抛开麋鹿,抛开牛犊,

---

① 指苏格兰高地麦克唐纳民族一四三一年间组织反击入侵的战歌。——译者

  Leave nets and barges:
  Come with your fIghting gear,
   Broadswords and targes①.

  Come as the winds come, when
   Forests are rended;
  Come as the waves come, when
   Navies are stranded:
  Faster come, faster come,
   Faster and faster,
  Chief, vassal, page and groom,
   Tenant and master.

  Fast they come, fast they come;
   See how they gather!
  Wide waves the eagle plume,
   Blended with heather.
  Cast your plaids, draw your blades,
   Forward each man set!
  Pibroch of Donuil Dhu
   Knell for the onset!

SIR W. SCOTT.

---

① *targes*: (or 'targets') 'shields.'

  抛开鱼网和游艇:
带着你的甲胄和武器来,
  带着你的大刀和盾牌。

迅速地来吧,   25
  像风儿吹裂了森林;
迅速地来吧,
  像大浪搁浅了舰艇:
快来吧,快来吧,
  快呀快,   30
酋长,奴仆,随从,马夫,
  房客和房主。

他们来得快,他们来得快;
  看他们集合起来!
雄鹰鼓起了翅膀,   35
  羽毛混在石南竹丛。
抛掉你的肩巾,抽出你的大刀,
  大家向前冲!
黑唐纳风笛吹响了
  向来犯者敲起丧钟!   40

          宇涛 译

  编注 本诗作于一八一六年,以《黑唐纳的风笛曲》为题发表在《阿尔宾的选集》(*Albyn's Anthology*)上,这是司各特为一首古老的歌曲填写的歌词,可能涉及一四三一年大卫·巴罗克(David Balloch)的一次远征。

205. 'A WET SHEET AND A FLOWING SEA'

    A wet sheet and a flowing sea,
        A wind that follows fast
    And fills the white and rustling sail
        And bends the gallant mast;
5   And bends the gallant mast, my boys,
        While like the eagle free
    Away the good ship flies, and leaves
        Old England on the lee.

    O for a soft and gentle wind!
10   I heard a fair one cry;
    But give to me the snoring breeze
        And white waves heaving high;
    And white waves heaving high, my lads.
        The good ship tight and free①—
15   The world of waters is our home,
        And merry men are we.

    There's tempest in yon hornéd moon,
        And lightning in yon cloud;
    But hark the music, mariners!
20   The wind is piping loud;

---

① *The good ship tight and free*: this is probably an absolute clause, 'the good ship being tight and free,' and not the object of 'give' (l. 11) which would rather require 'a good ship.' *tight*: 'water-tight.'

205. "湿漉漉的帆底，大海中的狂澜"

坎宁安

湿漉漉的帆底，大海中的狂澜，
　　风儿不住地吹卷，
涨满了白色的瑟瑟作声的风帆，
　　压弯了华丽的桅杆；
压弯了华丽的桅杆呀， 5
　　我的孩子们像雄鹰一样矫健，
好样的船只飞驰过去
　　把英格兰留在岸边。

啊！风儿轻柔地吹吧！
　　我听见一位美人在呼唤； 10
但是给我轰隆的大风，
　　也给我白浪滔天；
白浪呀滔天，我的孩子们，
　　结实、自在，这样的船——
水的世界就是我们的家， 15
　　我们的生活情趣万千。

那边弯弯的月亮起了风暴，
　　那边云层里电光闪闪；
听那音乐，海员们！
　　风儿正在高声吹奏； 20

The wind is piping loud, my boys,
    The lightning flashes free —
While the hollow oak our palace is,
    Our heritage the sea.

                      A. CUNNINGHAM.

风儿正在高声吹奏呀,我的孩子们,
　　还有一道道自由的闪电——
这空心的橡树就是我们的大厦,
　　海就是我们所接受的遗产。

罗义蕴　译

编注　阿伦·坎宁安(Allan Cunningham,1784—1842),苏格兰诗人,曾编著过四卷《古今苏格兰歌谣集》(*Songs of Scotland, Ancient and Modern*),于一八二五年出版。他也写过许多故事和传记。本诗对海员生活写得非常逼真,似乎作者也有亲身经历。

208. ODE TO DUTY

Stern Daughter of the Voice of God!
O Duty! if that name thou love
Who art a light to guide, a rod
To check the erring, and reprove;
Thou, who art victory and law
When empty terrors overawe,
From vain temptations dost set free,
And calm'st the weary strife of frail humanity!

There are who ask not if thine eye
Be on them; who, in love and truth
Where no misgiving is, rely
Upon the genial sense of youth①;
Glad hearts! without reproach or blot,
Who do thy work, and know it not:
O! if through confidence misplaced
They fail, thy saving arms, dread Power! around them cast.

Serene will be our days and bright,
And happy will our nature be,
When love is an unerring light,
And joy its own security②.

---

① *rely Upon the genial sense of youth*: *i.e.* act out of the kindliness begotten of a light heart, and not from a sense of duty; the weakness of this position is that, if the light-heartedness goes, the kindliness is apt to go too.

② *security*: *i.e.* safeguard against wrong-doing.

208. 天职颂

华兹华斯

啊,责任!天神之声的严峻女儿[①]!
　　但愿你喜欢这个美名,
因为你是一盏指路明灯,又是一把戒尺
　　防止和谴责一切错行;
你战无不胜,你主宰一切,　　　　　　　　　　5
当空虚的恐吓吓唬人们时,
你把他们从虚妄的诱惑中解脱,
平息那出自脆弱人性的倾轧纷争!

有这样的人,他们从不过问
　　你的眼睛是否注视着他们;　　　　　　10
他们在爱和真理中无忧无虑,
　　行事凭着青春无邪的感情。
愉快的心灵!无可非议,毫无污损,
他们虽无意负责,却把你的工作担承:
啊!如果他们因盲目自信而遭失败,　　　　15
令人敬畏的神明!把你拯救的臂膀伸向他们。

当爱是一盏正确的明灯,
　　当欢乐而不失之谨慎,
我们的日子将充满宁静,
　　我们的性格将娱情盈盈。　　　　　　20

---

① "天神之声"指良心。——译者

  And they a blissful course may hold
  Ev'n now, who, not unwisely bold,
  Live in the spirit of this creed,
Yet seek thy firm support, according to their need.

25   I, loving freedom, and untried,
   No sport of every random gust,
  Yet being to myself a guide,
   Too blindly have reposed my trust:
  And oft, when in my heart was heard
30   Thy timely mandate, I deferr'd
  The task, in smoother walks to stray;
But thee I now would serve more strictly, if I may.

  Through no disturbance of my soul
   Or strong compunction in me wrought,
35   I supplicate for thy control,
   But in the quietness of thought:
  Me this uncharter'd freedom tires①;
  I feel the weight of chance desires:
  My hopes no more must change their name;
40   I long for a repose that ever is the same.

  Stern Lawgiver! yet thou dost wear
   The Godhead's most benignant grace;
  Nor know we anything so fair
   As is the smile upon thy face:

---

① *uncharter'd freedom*: *i. e.* liberty of action which is not limited by any bounds such as might be laid down in a charter.

甚至现在,他们会把握幸福的旅程。
他们青春无畏,并非鲁钝,
遵奉这个信条的精神①,
也按他们的需要,寻求你坚定的后盾。

我热爱自由,然而不去尝试 25
　那感情冲动的嬉戏,
但因我自己指引航程,
　太盲目地把自己信任:
我常常在心中听到
你及时的训令, 30
　我延误工作,滑入歧径,
但现在我要更听命于你,如果可能。

不是心灵忧虑纷乱,
　也不是良心内疚不安,
而是在思想平静之中, 35
　我恳求你驾驭我的情感:
那种无约束的自由令我厌烦;
我感到渴望机缘的负担:
　我希望不必再把他们的名姓更换;
我渴望一种宁静,宁静始终一般。 40

严峻的立法者!在你脸上
　有着上帝最宽厚的慈祥;
我不知什么才这样漂亮,
　如你的笑脸一样:

---

① 指上述的爱与欢乐。——译者

Flowers laugh before thee on their beds,
And fragrance in thy footing treads;
Thou dost preserve the stars from wrong;
And the most ancient heavens, through thee, are fresh and strong.

To humbler functions, awful Power!
   I call thee: I myself commend
Unto thy guidance from this hour;
   O let my weakness have an end!
Give unto me, made lowly wise,
   The spirit of self-sacrifice;
   The confidence of reason give;
And in the light of Truth thy bondman let me live.

W. WORDSWORTH.

> 花儿在花坛对你欢笑 45
> 　你足迹所至处处散发着芬芳；
> 　你使星移斗转，永不出轨，
> 有了你，最古老的天国仍然青春健壮。

> 令人敬畏的神明啊！执行屈尊的职责，
> 　我呼唤你，我委托你 50
> 从此刻起为我导航；
> 　啊，让我软弱的本性结束吧，
> 赋予我自我牺牲的精神，
> 使卑贱者变得聪明①，
> 赋予我对理智的信心， 55
> 让我——你的奴仆——在真理的光明中永生。

罗显华　译

编注　本诗作于一八〇五年。编入《金库》的这首诗与原诗有较多差异。如在第五、第六节之间，原编者删掉了一节。

---

① 此行出自弥尔顿的《失乐园》。原句是 Be lowly wise。——译者

209. ON THE CASTLE OF CHILLON

Eternal Spirit of the chainless Mind!
   Brightest in dungeons, Liberty, thou art —
   For there thy habitation is the heart —
The heart which love of Thee alone can bind;

And when thy sons to fetters are consign'd,
   To fetters, and the damp vault's dayless gloom,
   Their country conquers with their martyrdom,
And Freedom's fame finds wings on every wind.

Chillon! thy prison is a holy place
   And thy sad floor an altar, for 'twas trod,
Until his very steps have left a trace

   Worn, as if thy cold pavement were a sod,
   By Bonnivard! May none those marks efface!
For they appeal from tyranny to God.

                            LORD BYRON.

209. 咏锡庸城堡

拜伦

不受约束的心的永恒的精灵!
　自由呵!你在监狱中明亮无比——
　因为在那儿你是住在人心里——
能约束人心的只有对你的爱情;

而当你的儿子们,被脚镣扣紧, 5
　关进这潮湿的暗无天日的地牢里,
　他们的国家因他们受难而胜利,
而自由的美名也随风传遍了远近。

锡庸!你的监狱变成了圣地,
　而你悲伤的地板是祭坛,只因 10
　庞尼瓦踩过它,留下深深的印记,

　仿佛你冰冷的铺道只是片草坪!
　但愿谁也不要把这些脚印抹去!
　因为它们向上帝控诉着暴行。

邹绛　译

编注　此诗选自拜伦长诗《锡庸的囚徒》(*The Prisoner of Chillon*,1816)序言。锡庸古堡在日内瓦湖旁。十六世纪,瑞士爱国志士庞尼瓦(Francois de Bonnivard)为了推翻萨伏依的查理第三大公(Charles Dulle Of Savoy),并建立共和政体,被囚在这个古堡达六年之久(1530—1536)。其中有四年囚于地牢,他常常走来走去,以至于在地上留下一条仿佛由斧子刻出的痕迹。拜伦在这里歌颂了为自由而甘心把牢底坐穿的英雄。

210. ENGLAND AND SWITZERLAND
1802

Two Voices are there, one is of the Sea,
   One of the Mountains, each a mighty voice:
   In both from age to age thou didst rejoice,
They were thy chosen music, Liberty!

There came a tyrant, and with holy glee
   Thou fought'st against him, — but hast vainly striven:
   Thou from thy Alpine holds at length art driven,
Where not a torrent murmurs heard by thee.

Of one deep bliss thine ear hath been bereft;
Then cleave, O cleave to that which still is left;
   For, high-soul'd Maid, what sorrow would it be

   That Mountain floods should thunder as before,
   And Ocean bellow from his rocky shore,
And neither awful Voice be heard by Thee!

W. WORDSWORTH.

210. 英格兰和瑞士
（一八〇二年）①

华兹华斯

有两个声音：一个来自大海，
　一个来自高山；都豪迈而雄浑：
　你世世代代为这声音感到欢快，
自由，这是你最钟爱的乐声！

但暴君来临，你为神圣的信念②，
　奋起向他反抗；却未能成功：
　最后你被赶出了阿尔卑斯山，
从此再也听不到山泉琤琮。

你的耳朵被剥夺了以往的幸福；
那么你就固守着尚存的一切吧；
　坚贞的少女呵，那是何等痛苦——

山洪仍像从前一样奔腾咆哮，
大海仍拍击着石岸发出怒号，
但那雄壮的声音你再也听不到！

顾子欣　译

---

① 一七九八年，古老的瑞士联盟（Swiss Confederation）破裂，一八〇二年波拿巴（Bonaparte）与瑞士联盟组成政权，实际上瑞士被征服。华兹华斯以英国诗人的身份，希望唤起瑞士民族的自豪感，以反抗入侵者。——编注者
② 这里指法国军队，他们应瑞士大党的要求而来，却怀着自己的打算。——编注者

211. ON THE EXTINCTION OF THE VENETIAN REPUBLIC

Once did She hold the gorgeous East in fee[①],
    And was the safeguard of the West, the worth
    Of Venice did not fall below her birth,
Venice, the eldest child of liberty.

She was a maiden city, bright and free;
    No guile seduced, no force could violate;
    And when she took unto herself a mate,
She must espouse the everlasting Sea.

And what if she had seen those glories fade,
    Those titles vanish, and that strength decay, —
Yet shall some tribute of regret be paid.

    When her long life hath reach'd its final day:
Men are we, and must grieve when even the shade
    Of that which once was great is pass'd away.

W. WORDSWORTH.

---

① *in fee*: 'in absolute ownership.'

211. 威尼斯共和国灭亡有感①

华兹华斯

豪华的东方曾是她的领地；
　　同时她肩负着保护西方的责任：
　　她从未玷辱过自己高贵的出身，
威尼斯呵，她是自由的长女②。

她是一座处女城，明媚而自由；　　　　　　　　　　5
　　奸邪不能淫，威武不能屈；
　　当她为自己寻找一位爱侣，
她选择了永恒的大海作配偶③。

她将如何自处？当目睹那些光荣、
　　那些称号和她的强盛一起消亡；　　　　　　　10
　　她将不得不缴纳耻辱的进贡。

当她漫长的自由的生命行将埋葬：
我们是人，念往昔伟烈丰功
　　竟不留一丝遗痕，怎能不为之哀恸。

顾子欣　译

---

① 威尼斯共和国于一八〇二年为拿破仑所灭亡。诗人在这首诗中对威尼斯的民族独立运动寄予深切的同情。——译者
② 六九七年，为逃避匈奴王入侵，北意大利城镇居民逃往威尼斯定居，奠定了未来共和国的基础，故曰"自由的长女"。——编者注
③ 九九八年，威尼斯总督清除了北亚得里亚海的海盗，每年升天节总督投一枚金戒指入水中，以表示威尼斯城与亚得里亚海结为夫妻，举行婚礼，从此受到海洋的保护。大约从一一七〇年以后，投戒指之日成为很大的节庆。——编者注

212. LONDON, MDCCCII

O Friend! I know not which way I must look
   For comfort, being, as I am, opprest
   To think that now our life is only drest
For show; mean handiwork of craftsman, cook,

Or groom! — We must run glittering like a brook
   In the open sunshine, or we are unblest;
   The wealthiest man among us is the best:
No grandeur now in Nature or in book

Delights us. Rapine, avarice, expense,
   This is idolatry; and these we adore[①]:
   Plain living and high thinking are no more:

The homely beauty of the good old cause
Is gone; our peace, our fearful innocence[②],
   And pure religion breathing household laws.

                      W. WORDSWORTH.

---

① *This is idolatry*: 'these are our idols.'
② *fearful*: 'fearing to do wrong.'

212. 作于伦敦，一八〇二年九月

华兹华斯

朋友呵！我真不知道该向何方
　去寻求心灵的安适；我不禁怅然，
　想到这一生无非是装点门面，
与工匠、厨子、马夫没什么两样。

我们都得像溪水，迎着骄阳　　　　　　　　　　5
　闪耀金光，否则便遭人白眼；
　最大的财主便是最大的圣贤；
自然之美和典籍已无人赞赏。

侵吞掠夺，贪婪，挥霍无度——
　这些，便是我们崇拜的偶像；　　　　　　　　10
　再没有淡泊的生涯，高洁的思想；

　古老的淳风尽废，美德沦亡；
失去了谨慎端方，安宁和睦，
　断送了伦常准则，纯真信仰。

杨德豫　译

213. THE SAME

Milton! thou shouldst be living at this hour:
    England hath need of thee: she is a fen
    Of stagnant waters: altar, sword, and pen,
Fireside, the heroic wealth of hall and bower,

Have forfeited their ancient English dower
    Of inward happiness. We are selfish men
    O! raise us up, return to us again;
And give us manners, virtue, freedom, power[①].

Thy soul was like a Star, and dwelt apart:
    Thou hadst a voice whose sound was like the sea,
    Pure as the naked heavens, majestic, free;

    So didst thou travel on life's common way
In cheerful godliness; and yet thy heart
    The lowliest duties on herself did lay.

W. WORDSWORTH.

---

① *manners*: 'moral character,' not 'outward behaviour.'

213. 伦敦，一八〇二年①

华兹华斯

弥尔顿！今天，你应该活在世上：
　英国需要你！她成了死水污池：
　教会，弄笔的文人，仗剑的武士，
　千家万户，豪门的绣阁华堂，

断送了内心的安恬——古老的风尚；
　世风日下，我们都汲汲营私；
　哦！回来吧，快来把我们扶持，
　给我们良风，美德，自由，力量！

你的灵魂像孤光自照的星辰；
　你的声音像壮阔雄浑的大海；
　纯净如无云的天宇，雍容，自在，

　　你在人生的寻常路途上行进，
　怀着愉悦的虔诚；你的心也肯
　　把最为低下的职责引为己任。

杨德豫　译

---

① 在这首著名的十四行诗中，华兹华斯指出当时英国社会弊端百出，有如"死水污池"，希望重新出现弥尔顿那样的革命诗人和战士，来力挽颓风，涤瑕荡秽。华兹华斯对弥尔顿甚为钦仰，在他的大量作品中，所受弥尔顿的影响几乎随处可见。他似乎隐隐以当代弥尔顿自许。但是，如所周知，他终究没有成为弥尔顿那样的革命诗人。——译者

214. 'WHEN I HAVE BORNE IN MEMORY WHAT HAS TAMED'

When I have borne in memory what has tamed
   Great nations; how ennobling thoughts depart
   When men change swords for ledgers, and desert
The student's bower for gold — some fears unnamed

I had, my Country! — am I to be blamed?
   Now, when I think of thee, and what thou art,
   Verily, in the bottom of my heart
Of those unfilial fears I am ashamed.

For dearly must we prize thee; we who find
   In thee a bulwark for the cause of men;
   And I by my affection was beguiled:

What wonder if a Poet now and then,
Among the many movements of his mind,
   Felt for thee as a lover or a child!

                           W. WORDSWORTH.

214. "我记得一些大国如何衰退"

华兹华斯

我记得一些大国如何衰退；
　当武士丢开宝剑而拿起账本，
　当学者撇下书斋去觅取黄金，
　当高风美德告辞，祖国呵！我每每

为你担忧——也许我该受责备？　　　　　　　　5
　现在，想到你，想到你在我内心
　是居于何等位置，我呵，便不禁
为那些唐突的忧虑感到羞愧。

你是人类正义事业的屏障；
　我们唯有深深敬重你，爱你；　　　　　　　　10
　我的多心是出于对你的爱慕：

这又有什么稀奇——在幽思遐想里，
诗人对你常常会揣测估量，
　就像情郎对恋人，儿女对父母！

　　　　　　　　　　　　　杨德豫　译

215. HOHENLINDEN

On Linden, when the sun was low,
All bloodless lay the untrodden snow;
And dark as winter was the flow
    Of Iser, rolling rapidly.

But Linden saw another sight,
When the drum beat at dead of night,
Commanding fires of death to light
    The darkness of her scenery.

By torch and trumpet fast array'd
Each horseman drew his battle blade
And furious every charger neigh'd
    To join the dreadful revelry.

Then shook the hills with thunder riven[①],
Then rush'd the steed, to battle driven[②],
And louder than the bolts of Heaven
    Far flash'd the red artillery.

But redder yet that light shall glow
On Linden's hills of stainéd snow;

---

① *riven*: 'split.'
② *rush'd*: in the early versions this is 'flew.'

215. 荷恩林登之战[①]

坎贝尔

夕阳沉没下林登的上空，
积雪尚未被蹂躏，未被染红；
伊塞尔河的奔流滚滚，
　　暗淡得有如寒冬。

然而林登的光景突然变换，
战鼓渊渊在万籁无声的夜半，
在命令着要命的烈火，
　　把林登的夜景点燃。

火炬与喇叭顿使军阵有条，
骑马的战士各把军刀出鞘，
战马争赴可怖的宴会，
　　激昂地在大声嘶叫。

天崩地裂的雷霆使小山摇动；
战马噢赴阵头奋勇冲锋；
赛过了天上的霹雳千声，
　　远处发光的炮火通红。

炮火的红光还将愈来愈稠，
林登四周的雪丘被血染透，

[①] 荷恩林登（Hohenlinden）位于慕尼黑以东十八英里的地方，荷恩林登战役是法国拿破仑军队重挫奥地利军的一次著名夜战，发生于一八〇〇年十二月三日。奥地利军伤亡九千余人。——编注者

        And bloodier yet the torrent flow
            Of Iser, rolling rapidly.

        'Tis morn; but scarce yon level sun[1]
        Can pierce the war-clouds, rolling dun,
        Where furious Frank and fiery Hun
            Shout in their sulphurous canopy.

        The combat deepens. On, ye brave
        Who rush to glory, or the grave!
        Wave, Munich, all thy banners wave,
            And charge with all thy chivalry!

        Few, few shall part, where many meet!
        The snow shall be their winding-sheet,
        And every turf beneath their feet
            Shall be a soldier's sepulchre.

                            T. CAMPBELL.

---

[1] *level*: *i.e.* shining from the horizon.

伊塞尔河的奔流滚滚,
　　愈来愈多的血浪横流。　　　　　　　　　　20

天亮了,出现在地平线上的太阳,
无法照透这硝烟滚滚的战场,
慓悍的法军与勇猛的奥军
　　喊叫在硫磺的穹苍。

战斗愈来愈紧,哦勇士们,　　　　　　　　　25
或奔赴荣誉,或奔向坟茔!
振奋呀,奥军,万旗并举,
　　发挥出你们的骑士精神!

多数人会战,谁能希望荣归!
积雪将成为阵亡者的寿衣,　　　　　　　　30
他们脚下践踏着的青草
　　将成为阵亡者的墓地。

郭沫若　译

编注 本诗作于一八〇一年,是诗人的著名作品之一。作者托马斯·坎贝尔,亦被译者译为妥默司·康沫尔。

216. AFTER BLENHEIM

It was a summer evening,
   Old Kaspar's work was done,
And he before his cottage door
   Was sitting in the sun;
And by him sported on the green
His little grandchild Wilhelmine.

She saw her brother Peterkin
   Roll something large and round
Which he beside the rivulet
   In playing there had found;
He came to ask what he had found
That was so large and smooth and round.

Old Kaspar took it from the boy
   Who stood expectant by;
And then the old man shook his head,
   And with a natural sigh
' 'Tis some poor fellow's skull,' said he,
'Who fell in the great victory.

'I find them in the garden,

216. 布连海姆战役之后①

骚塞

那是一个夏天的傍晚,
　老卡斯帕尔已把活儿干完,
他静坐在夕阳的余晖里,
　静坐在自己屋舍的门前;
他的小孙女威勒玛茵, 5
嬉戏在草地上,在他身边。

她看见她的哥哥皮特金,
　滚动着一件东西又大又圆,
那是他在游玩时捡来的,
　在离家不远的那条小河边; 10
老人走上前来想问个仔细,
是什么东西这么又光又圆。

老人将那东西拿在手里,
　孩子站在一旁满目惊疑;
老人看后不禁摇了摇头, 15
　接着又发出深沉的叹息:
"这是一个可怜人的骷髅,
他死于那次伟大的战役。

"我在菜园里也发现过骷髅,

---

① 布连海姆是西巴伐利亚(现属德国)境内位于多瑙河上的一座村庄。一七〇四年三月十三日,由马尔勃罗和尤金亲王统帅的英国、德国、荷兰、丹麦联军在此打败了由达拉德统帅的法国和巴伐利亚联军。——译者

  For there 's many here about;
  And often when I go to plough
   The ploughshare turns them out.
  For many thousand men, 'said he,
  'Were slain in that great victory.'

  'Now tell us what 'twas all about,'
   Young Peterkin he cries;
  And little Wilhelmine looks up
   With wonder-waiting eyes;
  'Now tell us all about the war,
  And what they fought each other for.'

  'It was the English,' Kaspar cried,
   'Who put the French to rout;
  But what they fought each other for
   I could not well make out.
  But everybody said,' quoth he,
  'That 'twas a famous victory.

  'My father lived at Blenheim then,
   Yon little stream hard by;
  They burnt his dwelling to the ground,
   And he was forced to fly:
  So with his wife and child he fled,
  Nor had he where to rest his head.

  'With fire and sword the country round
   Was wasted far and wide,
  And many a childing mother then[1]

---

[1] *childing*: 'that is about to have a child.'

它们在这儿可不算希奇； 20
　当我在田里耕地的时候，
　　　犁头常把它们从土中翻起。
　因为曾有几千名战士呵，
　都死于那次伟大的胜利。"

"告诉我们那是怎么回事情， " 25
　　小皮特金忙向爷爷发问；
　威勒玛茵也仰起了小脸，
　　　瞪着一双好奇的眼睛；
　"告诉我们那次战争的事吧，
　和他们干吗要打仗的原因。" 30

"在那次战役中，英国人
　　把法国人打得溃不成军；
　但他们究竟为啥要打仗，
　　我也搞不明白说不清。
　但大家都说，"老人讲道， 35
　"那次战役真是赫赫有名。

"我父亲那时住在布连海姆，
　　在离这小河不远的地方；
　他们一把火烧了他的房子，
　　逼得他只好逃奔他乡： 40
　他携妻带子到处去漂流，
　难以找到一个安身的地方。

"火和剑蹂躏着这里的一切，
　　举目四望到处是一片荒凉；
　有多少母亲和新生的婴儿， 45

And new-born baby died;
But things like that, you know, must be
At every famous victory.

'They say it was a shocking sight
    After the field was won;
For many thousand bodies here
    Lay rotting in the sun;
But things like that, you know, must be
After a famous victory.

'Great praise the Duke of Marlbro' won
    And our good Prince Eugene;'
'Why, 'twas a very wicked thing!'
    Said little Wilhelmine;
'Nay.. nay.. my little girl,' quoth he,
'It was a famous victory.

'And everybody praised the Duke
    Who this great fight did win.'
'But what good came of it at last?'
    Quoth little Peterkin; —
'Why, that I cannot tell,' said he,
'But 'twas a famous victory.'

R. SOUTHEY.

在那次战火中悲惨地死亡:
但你们知道,在每次著名的
战役中,都会有这样的景象。

"据说当我们赢得了胜利,
　　战场的景象令人神伤;
几千具尸首满地狼藉,
　　发烂发臭暴晒着骄阳:
但你们知道,在每次著名的
战役中,都会有这样的景象。

"马尔勃罗公爵却倍受颂扬,
　　尤金亲王也赢得了荣誉;"
"但这是多么残忍的事呵!"
　　小威勒玛茵打断他的话题;
"可是,可是……我的小孙女,
那是一次著名的战役。"

"人人都对公爵大加赞扬,
　　是他赢得了这伟大的胜利。"
"但这究竟有什么好处呢?"
　　小皮特金又打断他的话题:——
"这我也说不清,"老人喃喃自语,
"但那是一次著名的战役。"

顾子欣　译

编注　罗伯特·骚塞(Robert Southey,1774—1843),英国湖畔派诗人之一。曾获"桂冠诗人"称号,诗作甚多,但佳品较少。本诗主题可用"一将功成万骨枯"概括。

217. PRO PATRIA MORI

When he who adores thee has left but the name
    Of his fault and his sorrows behind,
O! say wilt thou weep, when they darken the fame
    Of a life that for thee was resign'd?
Yes, weep, and however my foes may condemn,
    Thy tears shall efface their decree;
For, Heaven can witness, though guilty to them,
    I have been but too faithful to thee.

With thee were the dreams of my earliest love,
    Every thought of my reason was thine;
In my last humble prayer to the Spirit above
    Thy name shall be mingled with mine!
O! blest are the lovers and friends who shall live
    The days of thy glory to see;
But the next dearest blessing that Heaven can give
    Is the pride of thus dying for thee.

T. MOORE.

217. 刑前献给爱尔兰的歌

摩尔

当他,一个真诚爱慕你的人,留下的
　　只是他的过失和悲痛,
呵,你说,你会流泪么,他为你
　　牺牲了生命,别人却污蔑他的名声?
是的,流泪吧,你的泪水一定能洗褪　　　　　　5
　　敌人的判词,不管他们加以我怎样的罪名;
上天作证,就算我对他们有罪,
　　对你,我可永远忠诚。

我初恋的梦和你连在一起,
　　我每一种理性的思念属于你　　　　　　　　10
在我去世前,恭敬地祷告天神,
　　你的名字和我自己连在一起。
呵,情人们和友人们能活下去,
　　看见你光辉灿烂的日子,真是幸运;
但上天给予的另一个最可贵的祝福,　　　　　　15
　　那就是:为了你而光荣地牺牲。

　　　　　　　　　　　　　　　　　陈　逵　译

编注　本诗发表在摩尔的《爱尔兰歌曲集》第一集(1807)。一八〇三年爱尔兰民族英雄艾默特(Robert Emmet)因起义失败,被英国政府处死。诗人与他交情甚厚,艾默特的高贵品格与惨死给他留下不可磨灭的印象。诗中的"你"指爱尔兰,拉丁文标题系《金库》原编者所加。

218. THE BURIAL OF SIR JOHN MOORE AT CORUNNA

Not a drum was heard, not a funeral note,
    As his corse to the rampart we hurried;
Not a soldier discharged his farewell shot
    O'er the grave where our Hero we buried.

We buried him darkly at dead of night,
    The sods with our bayonets turning;
By the struggling moonbeam's misty light
    And the lantern dimly burning.

No useless coffin enclosed his breast,
    Not in sheet or in shroud we wound him;
But he lay like a Warrior taking his rest
    With his martial cloak around him.

Few and short were the prayers we said,
    And we spoke not a word of sorrow;
But we steadfastly gaz'd on the face that was dead,
    And we bitterly thought of the morrow.

We thought, as we hollow'd his narrow bed

218. 爵士约翰·摩尔在科龙纳的埋葬①

沃尔夫

没有打鼓,也没有哀乐,
　　当我们把他的尸骸运到城堡,
在我们的英雄埋葬着的墓上,
　　也没有一名士兵放射礼炮。

我们埋葬他在悄悄的夜半, 5
　　使用我们的刺刀在土中翻;
靠着雾中漏出的朦胧的月光,
　　还有些闪着光的灯火暗淡。

包藏他的胸坎没有无用的棺,
　　也没有寿衣寿布把他裹缠; 10
但他躺着如像一名战士,
　　穿着他的军服和衣而眠。

祈祷的话言人少而语短,
　　我们所说的没有一句哀挽;
我们坚定地凝视着死者的面, 15
　　只沉痛地在想到明天。

当我们掘着他狭窄的墓坑,

---

① 约翰·摩尔爵士是英国反拿破仑战争的重要将领。一八〇九年一月十六日,英、法、西三国会战于西班牙科龙纳附近,这是拿破仑伊比利亚半岛战争中的一个战役。其时摩尔率二万英军直取西班牙首都马德里,因遭法军猛烈狙击而退却。摩尔奋力与法军将领苏尔特交战,掩护全军撤至科龙纳,搭乘英舰转移,自己则不幸于最后一刻战死。次日凌晨,遗骸被埋葬于战场。——译者

  And smooth'd down his lonely pillow,
That the Foe and the Stranger would tread o'er his head,
  And we far away on the billow!

Lightly they'll talk of the Spirit that's gone
  And o'er his cold ashes upbraid him, —
But little he'll reck, if they let him sleep on
  In the grave where a Briton has laid him.

But half of our heavy task was done
  When the clock struck the hour for retiring;
And we heard the distant and random gun
  That the foe was sullenly firing.

Slowly and sadly we laid him down,
  From the field of his fame fresh and gory;
We carved not a line, and we raised not a stone —
  But we left him alone with his glory.

C. WOLFE.

我们把他头上的土块放平，
　我们想到未知的敌人会来蹂躏他的头，
　　而我们已在海上航行！　　　　　　　　　　20

　　敌兵会轻蔑这阵亡了的将军，
　　　会在他的尸骸上议论纵横；
　　但只要他们让他安睡在墓中，
　　　所埋葬的英国人，他会泰然不问。

　　但我们的埋葬工作只到一半，　　　　　　　25
　　　时钟已报导着退却的时间；
　　我们已听到远远的散乱炮声，
　　　敌人在无目标地乱放子弹。

　　徐徐地悲伤地让他躺下，
　　　浑身都还带着荣誉阵地的血花；　　　　　30
　　我们没刻一行字，没立一通碑，
　　　但只让他的光荣永远伴着他。

郭沫若　译

编注　查理·沃尔夫(Charles Wolfe，1791—1823)，爱尔兰的一名教士。人们之所以现在还记得他，正是因为他写了这一首不朽的诗作。

219. SIMON LEE THE OLD HUNTSMAN

In the sweet shire of Cardigan,
    Not far from pleasant Ivor Hall,
An old man dwells, a little man, —
    'Tis said he once was tall.
Full five-and-thirty years he lived
    A running huntsman merry;
And still the centre of his cheek
    Is red as a ripe cherry.

No man like him the horn could sound,
    And hill and valley rang with glee
When Echo bandied round and round
    The halloo of Simon Lee.
In those proud days he little cared
    For husbandry or tillage;
To blither tasks did Simon rouse
    The sleepers of the village.

He all the country could outrun,
    Could leave both man and horse behind;
And often, ere the chase was done,
    He reeled and was stone-blind.
And still there's something in the world
    At which his heart rejoices;

219. 猎手西蒙·李

华兹华斯

在风光秀丽的卡迪根郡①,
　离艾弗庄园不远的地方,
住着个又矮又瘦的老人——
　从前可又高又壮。
他打猎足足有三十五年, 5
　挺快活,东奔西跑;
两颊中心至今红扑扑,
　就像熟透的樱桃。

西蒙·李吹号无人能比,
　他一声吆喝,赛似雷霆, 10
只听得回声旋绕不已,
　四下里山鸣谷应。
那时,他是个神气的猎手,
　没心思耕田种地;
清早,乡亲们常被他闹醒, 15
　起来干称心的活计。

跑起来,谁也跑他不赢,
　人也好,马也好,都被他甩下;
往往,打猎还没完,他已经
　累得个头昏眼花。 20
如今,他老了,世上也还有
　叫他开心的事情:

---

① 卡迪根郡在威尔士西部,濒临卡迪根湾。——译者

>   For when the chiming hounds are out,
>   He dearly loves their voices!
>
> 25   But O the heavy change! — bereft
>   Of health, strength, friends, and kindred, see!
>   Old Simon to the world is left
>   In liveried poverty:
>   His master's dead, and no one now
> 30   Dwells in the Hall of Ivor;
>   Men, dogs, and horses, all are dead;
>   He is the sole survivor.
>
>   And he is lean and he is sick;
>   His body, dwindled and awry,
> 35   Rests upon ankles swoln and thick;
>   His legs are thin and dry.
>   One prop he has, and only one,
>   His wife, an aged woman,
>   Lives with him, near the waterfall,
> 40   Upon the village common.
>
>   Beside their moss-grown hut of clay,
>   Not twenty paces from the door,
>   A scrap of land they have, but they
>   Are poorest of the poor.
> 45   This scrap of land he from the heath
>   Enclosed when he was stronger;
>   But what to them avails the land

出猎的猎狗齐声吠叫,
　　这声音他特别爱听!

如今,景况变得好凄凉! 25
　　他又老又穷,又弱又无力,
无亲无故的,留在世上,
　　穿的是破旧的号衣。
他主人死了,艾弗庄园
　　也已经荒凉破败①; 30
人呢?狗呢?马呢?都死了,
　　只剩他一个人还在。

他病病歪歪,干枯清瘦,
　　身躯萎缩了,骨架倾斜,
脚腕子肿得又粗又厚, 35
　　腿杆子又细又瘪。
世上,他只有一个依靠——
　　他老伴,也上了年纪;
老两口住在瀑布近旁,
　　种的是村里的公地。 40

他们的土屋长满了青苔,
　　土屋门外不到二十步
是他们种的地——巴掌大一块,
　　他们是最穷的一户!
早些年,他还有劲,还能 45
　　在外边围起篱笆;
如今,他已经无力耕种,

---

① "主人"指艾弗庄园的地主。西蒙·李不是独立谋生的猎户,而是地主的雇工,为地主打猎并管理猎犬。——译者

>   Which he can till no longer?
>
>   Oft, working by her husband's side,
>   Ruth does what Simon cannot do;
>   For she, with scanty cause for pride,
>   Is stouter of the two.
>   And, though you with your utmost skill
>   From labour could not wean them,
>   'Tis little, very little, all
>   That they can do between them.
>
>   Few months of life has he in store
>   As he to you will tell,
>   For still, the more he works, the more
>   Do his weak ankles swell.
>   My gentle reader, I perceive
>   How patiently you've waited,
>   And now I fear that you expect
>   Some tale will be related.
>
>   O reader! had you in your mind
>   Such stores as silent thought can bring,
>   O gentle reader! you would find
>   A tale in every thing.
>   What more I have to say is short,
>   And you must kindly take it:
>   It is no tale; but, should you think,
>   Perhaps a tale you'll make it.
>
>   One summer-day I chanced to see
>   This old man doing all he could

有了地也是白搭!

西蒙下地,鲁思也陪同,
　　老汉做不了的活计,她做;　　　　　　　　50
说起来寒碜:两个人当中,
　　她要算硬朗的一个。
哪怕你费尽口舌,也休想
　　劝他们歇工一天;
老两口尽心尽力,出的活　　　　　　　　　　55
　　却实在少得可怜!

他会告诉你:不出几个月,
　　他就要闭眼、入土;
因为,他越是操劳不歇,
　　脚腕便越肿越粗。　　　　　　　　　　　　60
可敬可亲的读者呵!我知道
　　你还在耐心等待,
指望下文有什么故事,
　　等我把它讲出来。

读者呵!若是宁静的沉思　　　　　　　　　　65
　　为你储备了清明的神智,
你就会懂得:每一件事情里
　　都含有一篇故事。
请你读下去,好心的读者!
　　下文很短,马上完;　　　　　　　　　　　70
它不是故事;——你若肯思索,
　　变成故事也不难。

夏天,我偶然碰见这老人:
　　使出了浑身力气,他正在

To unearth the root of an old tree,
    A stump of rotten wood.
The mattock totter'd in his hand;
    So vain was his endeavour
That at the root of the old tree
    He might have work'd for ever.

'You're overtask'd, good Simon Lee,
    Give me your tool,' to him I said;
And at the word right gladly he
    Received my proffer'd aid.
I struck, and with a single blow
    The tangled root I sever'd,
At which the poor old man so long
    And vainly had endeavour'd.

The tears into his eyes were brought,
    And thanks and praises seem'd to run
So fast out of his heart, I thought
    They never would have done.
— I've heard of hearts unkind, kind deeds
    With coldness still returning;
Alas! the gratitude of men
    Hath oftener left me mourning.

                      W. WORDSWORTH.

挖一截已经朽烂的树墩, 75
  想把根子挖出来。
他手里,十字镐摇摇晃晃;
  白费劲,汗也白流;
看来,在这树墩子旁边,
  他不知要挖多久。 80

"好西蒙,你已经累得不行,
  让我来,"我说,"把家伙给我。"
听了我的话,他满脸高兴,
  忙把十字镐递过。
我挖了一下,只一下,便把 85
  缠结的树根挖断;
而这个可怜的老汉挖它,
  挖了半天也枉然。

泪水顿时涌上他双眼,
  道谢的话儿来得那么快—— 90
感激和赞美出自他心间,
  却实在出乎我意外。
我听说世人无情无义,
  以冷漠回报善心;
然而,见别人满怀感激, 95
  我却又止不住酸辛①。

杨德豫　译

---

① 对于如此微不足道的帮助,感激之情竟如此强烈,这就透露了:由于世风浇薄,连此等细小的善举也极为稀少,极为罕见。诗人的"酸辛"就是由此而来。——译者

220. THE OLD FAMILIAR FACES

I have had playmates, I have had companions
In my days of childhood, in my joyful school-days;
   All, all are gone, the old familiar faces.

I have been laughing, I have been carousing,
Drinking late, sitting late, with my bosom cronies;
   All, all are gone, the old familiar faces.

I loved a love once, fairest among women:
Closed are her doors on me, I must not see her —
   All, all are gone, the old familiar faces.

I have a friend, a kinder friend has no man
Like an ingrate, I left my friend abruptly;
   Left him, to muse on the old familiar faces.

Ghost-like I paced round the haunts of my childhood;
Earth seem'd a desert I was bound to traverse,
   Seeking to find the old familiar faces.

Friend of my bosom, thou more than a brother,
Why wert not thou born in my father's dwelling?

220. 旧时熟悉的面庞

兰姆

我有过玩伴,我有过朋友
在我童年的时候,在我学童欢乐的日子里;
　　这些,这些都消失了,旧时熟悉的面庞!

我曾经欢笑,我曾经畅饮,
直到深夜,和我的好友促膝长谈;
　　这些,这些都消失了,旧时熟悉的面庞!

我曾经恋爱,她是最美的女性①:
她的门对我紧闭,我不应再见她——
　　这些,这些都消失了,旧时熟悉的面庞!

我有一个朋友,不能比他更好的朋友②
像个负义的人,我突然离去;
　　剩下他,思念着旧时熟悉的面庞!

像鬼魂我绕着儿时的游地徘徊;
大地像沙漠,我必须横跨,
　　寻找那旧时熟悉的面庞。

我最心爱的挚友,你比兄弟还亲③,
你为什么没有生在我家?

---

① 指安·西蒙兹,兰姆在《伊利亚散文集》中称其为艾丽丝;她嫁给了当铺老板巴特拉姆先生。——编注者
② 指诗人查尔斯·罗伊德(Charles Lloyd, 1775—1839)。——编注者
③ 指诗人柯勒律治,兰姆曾与其是同学。——编注者

So might we talk of the old familiar faces,

How some they have died, and some they have left me,
20   And some are taken from me; all are departed;
All, all are gone, the old familiar faces.

C. LAMB.

那样我们就能谈论那旧日熟悉的面庞!

他们中有些死了,有些离我而去,
有些从我身边掠走,都离去了;
这些,这些都消失了,昔日熟悉的面庞!

郑敏 译

编注 查尔斯·兰姆(Charles Lamb,1775—1834),英国散文家,笔名伊利亚(Elia)。兰姆除了散文外,还写诗,也写过戏剧,他的早期重要作品有他和他姐姐合著的《莎士比亚故事集》(*Tales from Shakespeare*,1807)。他的代表作《伊利亚散文集》(*Essays of Elia*,1823)及其续集收集了兰姆优秀的散文,如《梦中儿女》(Dream Children)、《古瓷》(Old China)、《烤猪论》(A Dissertion upon Roast Pig)。本篇以怀旧为题材,感情真挚,人物栩栩如生。

221. THE JOURNEY ONWARDS

As slow our ship her foamy track
    Against the wind was cleaving,
Her trembling pennant still look'd back
    To that dear isle 'twas leaving.
So loth we part from all we love,
    From all the links that bind us;
So turn our hearts, as on we rove,
    To those we've left behind us!

When, round the bowl, of vanish'd years
    We talk with joyous seeming —
With smiles that might as well be tears,
    So faint, so sad their beaming;
While memory brings us back again
    Each early tie that twined us,
O, sweet's the cup that circles then
    To those we've left behind us!

And when in other climes we meet
    Some isle or vale enchanting,
Where all looks flowery, wild, and sweet,
    And nought but love is wanting;
We think how great had been our bliss
    If Heaven had but assign'd us
To live and die in scenes like this,

221. 远航

摩 尔

我们的船顶着海风,缓缓地
　　在海上留下白沫的航道,
她那颤抖的舰旗
　　频频回顾刚离开的小岛。
别离了,我们亲爱的人,多么惆怅,　　　　　　5
　　切断一切联系;
我们的心,当我们继续流浪,
　　总是奔向着他们,虽然已被我们遗弃。

当岁末,传饮那同一杯酒,
　　我们谈着,笑着,何等欢畅!　　　　　　　10
那微笑,还不如把眼泪来流,
　　它的闪光这样微弱,悲伤。
当记忆将每一早年的联系召回,
　　那曾紧紧缠绕着我们的维系。
啊,那杯酒多么甜美,　　　　　　　　　　　15
　　它在我们留下的人们间传递。

当我们在他乡相遇
　　迷人的岛屿或幽谷
那里一切像花,荒野而馥郁,
　　什么也不缺,只缺少爱情的泥土;　　　　20
我们想我们将是何等的幸福
　　若是上天能允诺
我们和那些被遗弃的人重逢,

With some we've left behind us!

25   As travellers oft look back at eve
         When eastward darkly going,
     To gaze upon that light they leave
         Still faint behind them glowing, —
     So, when the close of pleasure's day
30   To gloom hath near consign'd us,
     We turn to catch one fading ray
         Of joy that's left behind us.

T. MOORE.

在这里,同生共死一起生活!

  好像旅人频频回顾,当傍晚来到   *25*
   他们走向渐渐沉入灰暗的东方,
  回头看一眼离别了的夕照
   它仍然在放出微弱的亮光——
  因此,当欢乐的一天消逝
   它将我们交给了灰暗的地方,   *30*
  那欢乐的残光我们恋恋不舍
   频频回头看那告别了的微光。

郑敏 译

编注 本诗发表在《爱尔兰歌曲集》第七集上。标题为《金库》原编者所加。

222. YOUTH AND AGE

There's not a joy the world can give like that it takes away,
When the glow of early thought declines in feeling's dull decay;
'Tis not on youth's smooth cheek the blush alone which fades so fast,
But the tender bloom of heart is gone, ere youth itself be past.

5   Then the few whose spirits float above the wreck of happiness
Are driven o'er the shoals of guilt or ocean of excess:
The magnet of their course is gone, or only points in vain
The shore to which their shiver'd sail shall never stretch again.

Then the mortal coldness of the soul like death itself comes down;
10   It cannot feel for others' woes, it dare not dream its own;
That heavy chill has frozen o'er the fountain of our tears,
And though the eye may sparkle still, 'tis where the ice appears.

Though wit may flash from fluent lips, and mirth distract the breast,
Through midnight hours that yield no more their former hope of rest;
15   'Tis but as ivy-leaves around the ruin'd turret wreathe,
All green and wildly fresh without, but worn and grey beneath.

O could I feel as I have felt, or be what I have been,
Or weep as I could once have wept o'er many a vanish'd scene, —
As springs in deserts found seem sweet, all brackish though they be,
20   So midst the wither'd waste of life, those tears, would flow to me!

LORD BYRON.

222. 青春与暮年

拜伦

随着感觉的迟钝、衰退,早年情思的光华已经黯淡,
人世间再不会带给我那随往日消逝的欣欢;
转瞬隐褪的不只是少年脸颊上艳丽的红云,
青春尚未逝去哟,心花的嫩蕊却早已零落凋残。

在幸福之舟破灭的残骸上,有一些灵魂飘荡不安, 5
或是给波涛卷入纵欲的海洋,或是给激浪冲向罪孽的浅滩:
或是航行的罗盘失灵,徒然指向大海无沿,
那颤抖摇曳的破帆,也再不能扬帆驶向岸边。

灵魂致命的寒气袭来,就像死亡降临一样凄惨,
既不会感到别人的悲痛,也不敢想象自己的辛酸, 10
那凛冽刺骨的严寒冻结了我们的泪泉,
两眼虽还光芒闪烁,眼眶内却有冰凌浮现。

唇间虽还会流泻出隽言妙语,欢乐更叫人心猿意马,神慌志乱,
这更残人静的午夜呵,再不能给人以往日的安闲;
仿佛就像常春藤的枝叶,在破楼残壁上环绕盘缠, 15
外表还是无比的翠绿清新,里面却是一片衰败的灰黯。

呵,我还能像往昔一样地感受,或像我从前的生活一般?
但愿我像过去一样地哭泣,为消逝的人生而悲悼伤感;
正如沙漠中涌现的泉水,看来甜美可口,喝来却苦涩微咸;
在人生萧瑟的荒漠上,我奔涌的泪珠源源不断! 20

黄新渠 译

编注 本诗作于一八一五年,那时拜伦才二十七岁,但似乎历尽人生的辛酸,饱尝了毁誉无常的滋味,他正探索人生的旅程,也担忧着航行的罗盘失灵。他于次年愤而出走,从此离开英国到意大利定居。本诗与第169首形成鲜明的对照。作者的思想感情好似由阳光灿烂变为乌云满天。

223. A LESSON

There is a flower, the Lesser Celandine,
    That shrinks like many more from cold and rain,
And, the first moment that the sun may shine,
    Bright as the sun himself, 'tis out again!

When hailstones have been falling, swarm on swarm,
    Or blasts the green field and the trees distrest,
Oft have I seen it muffled up from harm
    In close self-shelter, like a thing at rest.

But lately, one rough day, this flower I past,
    And recognized it, though an alter'd form,
Now standing forth an offering to the blast,
    And buffeted at will by rain and storm.

I stopp'd and said, with inly-mutter'd voice,
    'It doth not love the shower, nor seek the cold;
This neither is its courage nor its choice,
    But its necessity in being old.

'The sunshine may not cheer it, nor the dew;
    It cannot help itself in its decay;
Stiff in its members, wither'd, changed of hue,'

223. 感时

华兹华斯

有一种名叫"小燕子"的花①,
　　畏寒怯雨像许多花一样,
待大地照耀太阳的光华,
　　灿烂如阳光它重又开放!

当冰雹密集从天上落下,　　　　　　　　　　5
　　蹂躏绿色的树木和原野,
常见它闭拢花免遭践踏,
　　像在自己的躯壳里安歇。

但最近一两天我经过它,
　　看到的却是另一副模样　　　　　　　　10
它任凭暴雨恣意地击打,
　　把花瓣展开向狂风献上。

我停住了脚步暗自叹道:
　　"它本来不爱暴雨和严寒;
迎风开花也非勇敢偏好,　　　　　　　　15
　　乃是因生命衰老之必然。

阳光雨露不能使它欢愉,
　　衰老的命运它无可奈何,
枝叶已枯萎粉妆已褪去,"

---

① 小燕子花,花呈黄色,又名玄参或消痔草(Pilewort),因随燕子归来开花,随燕子离去枯萎而得名。——译者

20   And, in my spleen, I smiled that it was grey.

        To be a prodigal's favourite — then, worse truth[①],
            A miser's pensioner — behold our lot!
        O Man! that from thy fair and shining youth
            Age might but take the things Youth needed not!

                                        W. WORDSWORTH.

---

① *a prodigal's favourite*, etc. : in our youth Nature is prodigal of her gifts to us; when we are old she deals out a pittance with a miser's hand.

>   我怆然哂笑它变成灰色。 20
>
>   由大自然的骄子沦落为
>   弃儿,看我们这种命运!
>   啊!但愿老年能享那绚美
>   闪光的青春不要的一份。

于兴基　译

编注　本诗作于一八〇四年,最初载于一八〇七年出版的《诗集》(*Poems*),标题是《小燕子花》(The Small Celandline)。华兹华斯为此花还写有另外两首,一并收入《诗集》。

224. PAST AND PRESENT

    I remember, I remember
        The house where I was born,
    The little window where the sun
        Came peeping in at morn;
    He never came a wink too soon
        Nor brought too long a day;
    But now, I often wish the night
        Had borne my breath away.

    I remember, I remember
        The roses, red and white,
    The violets, and the lily-cups —
        Those flowers made of light!
    The lilacs where the robin built,
        And where my brother set
    The laburnum on his birth-day, —
        The tree is living yet!

    I remember, I remember
        Where I was used to swing,
    And thought the air must rush as fresh
        To swallows on the wing;
    My spirit flew in feathers then
        That is so heavy now,
    And summer pools could hardly cool
        The fever on my brow.

224. 今昔吟

胡德

我还记省，我还记省
　　我所诞生的门庭，
墙上有小小的窗，
　　朝阳从那儿窥进，
不觉得它是匆匆一瞬，　　　　　　　　　　5
　　也不觉得日子长得闷人；
然而如今我常常怨恨，
　　长夜不使我一眠不醒。

我还记省，我还记省
　　玫瑰花红白缤纷，　　　　　　　　　　10
紫罗兰和百合花——
　　都是创造自光明！
丁香上有小鸟砌巢，
　　为了纪念我兄弟诞生
迎春花栽种在小园——　　　　　　　　　　15
　　依然在欣欣向荣！

我还记省，我还记省
　　当我在秋千架上翻腾，
我想到颉颃的春燕
　　在空中如剪刀裁锦；　　　　　　　　　20
我的心神那时多么轻盈，
　　而今却沉重得要命。
夏日的池塘游泳
　　也不能使我镇静。

I remember, I remember
　　The fir trees dark and high;
I used to think their slender tops
　　Were close against the sky:
It was a childish ignorance,
　　But now 'tis little joy
To know I'm farther off from Heaven
　　Than when I was a boy.

　　　　　　　　　　　T. HOOD.

> 我还记省,我还记省 25
> 　　枞树林浓郁森森,
> 我常想着那尖削的树顶
> 　　直撑着和天接近;
> 那自然是儿时的无知。
> 我如今只好悲悯: 30
> 我和天是愈加远隔,
> 　　不像我在童年时分。

郭沫若　译

编注 托马斯·胡德(Thomas Hood,1799—1845),以写幽默诗著称。诗歌多采用民谣体,曾与人合作出版幽默诗集《献给大人物的颂歌和贺词》;一八二七年出版《仲夏仙子的呼吁》;一八四三年他写的《衬衫之歌》对下层劳动者表达了深切的同情,开了"社会抗议文学"的先河;此外还写过《劳动者之歌》《叹息桥》等诗,对当时社会上的不合理现象表示抗议。本诗标题为《金库》原编者所加。

225. THE LIGHT OF OTHER DAYS

Oft in the stilly night,
   Ere slumber's chain has bound me,
Fond Memory brings the light
   Of other days around me;
     The smiles, the tears
     Of boyhood's years,
The words of love then spoken;
   The eyes that shone,
   Now dimm'd and gone,
     The cheerful hearts now broken!
Thus in the stilly night,
   Ere slumber's chain has bound me,
Sad Memory brings the light
   Of other days around me.

When I remember all
   The friends so link'd together
I've seen around me fall
   Like leaves in wintry weather
     I feel like one
     Who treads alone
Some banquet-hall deserted,
   Whose lights are fled
   Whose garlands dead,
     And all but he departed!
Thus in the stilly night,

225. 昔日的光辉

摩尔

每每在那夜静时分,
　　当睡魔还未用链索把我束紧,
美好的回忆常常带着
　　那昔日的光辉把我照临:
　　　童年岁月的　　　　　　　　　　5
　　　那些泪水,那些欢欣,
　　那爱的话语倾诉衷情;
　　　那闪闪发亮的眼睛,
　　　而今却也模糊、不见踪影,
　　而今破碎了,那颗颗喜悦的心!　　10
于是在夜静时分,
　　当睡魔还未用链索把我束紧,
哀伤的回忆它便带着
　　那昔日的光辉把我照临。

我一想到那些　　　　　　　　　　　15
　　亲密无间的友人,
我眼见着在我四周
　　有如木叶在严冬的气候中凋落纷纷,
　　　我感到像一个人
　　　踽踽独行在　　　　　　　　　20
　　某个荒弃的宴会大厅,
　　　它的灯火灭尽,
　　　它的花环凋零,
　　一切都逝去只他独存!
于是在这夜静时分,　　　　　　　　25

Ere slumber's chain has bound me,
Sad Memory brings the light
Of other days around me.

T. MOORE.

当睡魔还未用链索把我束紧,
哀伤的回忆它便带着
那昔日的光辉把我照临。

邹荻帆　邹海仑　译

编注　本诗最初发表在一八一五年的《民族曲调》(*National Airs*)上。和摩尔别的抒情诗一样,以音乐的美而扣人心弦。

226. INVOCATION

Rarely, rarely, comest thou,
    Spirit of Delight!
Wherefore hast thou left me now
    Many a day and night?
Many a weary night and day
'Tis since thou art fled away.

How shall ever one like me
    Win thee back again?
With the joyous and the free
    Thou wilt scoff at pain.
Spirit false! thou hast forgot
All but those who need thee not.

As a lizard with the shade
    Of a trembling leaf,
Thou with sorrow art dismay'd;
    Even the sighs of grief
Reproach thee, that thou art not near,
And reproach thou wilt not hear.

Let me set my mournful ditty
    To a merry measure;
Thou wilt never come for pity,
    Thou wilt come for pleasure[①];
Pity then will cut away

[①] *Thou wilt come for pleasure*: in other words, the best way to become cheerful is to be cheerful.

226. 召唤

雪莱

你真难得，真难得来，
　　欢乐的精灵！
为什么从我身边跑开，
　　老见不到你的踪影？
自从你离了我的身边，　　　　　　　　　　5
我是多么烦闷，度日似年。

一个人倒霉得像我，
　　怎么能把你请回？
你愿意同快乐逍遥者一伙，
　　嘲笑别人的伤悲。　　　　　　　　　10
你呀，虚枉的精灵！
只忘不了那些不需要你的人。

像草丛中的一条蜥蜴，
　　风吹草动，马上逃走；
你一见哀伤，立时躲避。　　　　　　　　15
　　人心里感到忧愁，
吹口气，责备你不来临，
但责备你，你就是不听。

让我把这悲伤的歌曲
　　谱上快乐的音调；　　　　　　　　　20
你来不是为了怜悯痛苦，
　　而是为了凑凑热闹；
怜悯会割掉你残忍的翅翼，

    Those cruel wings, and thou wilt stay.

25
    I love all that thou lovest,
     Spirit of Delight!
    The fresh Earth in new leaves drest
     And the starry night;
    Autumn evening, and the morn
30
    When the golden mists are born.

    I love snow and all the forms
     Of the radiant frost;
    I love waves, and winds, and storms,
     Everything almost
35
    Which is Nature's, and may be
    Untainted by man's misery.

    I love tranquil solitude,
     And such society
    As is quiet, wise, and good;
40
     Between thee and me
    What diff'rence? but thou dost possess
    The things I seek, not love them less①.

    I love Love — though he has wings,
     And like light can flee,
45
    But above all other things,
     Spirit, I love thee —
    Thou art love and life! O come!
    Make once more my heart thy home!

          P. B. SHELLEY.

---

 ① *not love them less*: the subject is 'I'; 'though I love all these as much as thou dost, I am without them.'

那样,你就寸步难移。

你所爱的一切我都爱,
　　欢乐的精灵!
我爱看大地披上葱绿的新装,
　　也爱夜晚的星星;
我还爱秋天的傍晚,
和那拂晓时分的金雾弥漫。

我爱雪花,我爱冰霜,
　　爱莹洁霜雪的婉丽多姿;
我爱风,我爱波浪,
　　也爱那雷鸣电掣,
我爱大自然的一切神工,
只有它们能不沾染人的苦痛。

我爱恬静的独处,
　　也爱交游和良朋,
只要聪明、善良而和睦;
　　你我究竟有何不同?
我虽爱,而追求不到手,
但你却应有尽有。

我爱爱神,虽然他长着翅膀,
　　亮光一闪就飞去;
但我爱你,驾乎一切之上,
　　精灵呵,我最爱你:
你就是爱和生命!你来,你来,
愿你再来居住在我的胸怀。

　　　　　　　　杨熙龄　译

编注 本诗最初发表在一八二四年《诗人遗著》上,标题为《歌曲》(Song),《金库》原编者在第二版改换为《召唤》(Invocation)。雪莱把真挚的爱情同高远的理想结合起来,诗中表达了扫除人间的痛苦忧伤、带来宇宙的和谐歌唱的理想。

227. STANZAS WRITTEN IN DEJECTION NEAR NAPLES

The sun is warm, the sky is clear,
    The waves are dancing fast and bright,
Blue isles and snowy mountains wear
    The purple noon's transparent might:
    The breath of the moist earth is light
Around its unexpanded buds;
    Like many a voice of one delight①—
    The winds, the birds, the ocean-floods —
The City's voice itself is soft like Solitude's.

I see the Deep's untrampled floor
    With green and purple seaweeds strown;
I see the waves upon the shore,
    Like light dissolved in star-showers thrown:
    I sit upon the sands alone;
The lightning of the noontide ocean
    Is flashing round me, and a tone
Arises from its measured motion —
How sweet! did any heart now share in my emotion.

Alas! I have nor hope nor health,
    Nor peace within nor calm around,
Nor that content, surpassing wealth,

---

① *of one delight*: *i. e.* expressing the same happiness, though in different sounds.

227. 诗数章
（在那不勒斯附近，心灰意懒时作）

雪莱

太阳温暖，天空明净，
　　波光粼粼的大海舞蹈不息，
蓝色小鸟，积雪山岭，
　　承受着庄严中午透明的威力，
　　湿润的大地，轻轻呼吸， 5
吹嘘着她含苞待放的群英；
　　仿佛万籁一声，充满欢喜，
清风，飞鸟，海流，市廛的喧哗声，
全都像世外的音响一样轻柔温馨。

我看见未经践踏的海床， 10
　　到处是绿色紫色的海藻；
我看扑岸而来的层层波浪
　　像星星的阵雨体解形消。
　　我独自在沙滩上坐着；
中午海洋的电光 15
　　在我四周闪耀，
从它有节奏的运动中升起一种乐音，
多么美啊！有谁分享过我此刻的心情。

啊！我既没有希望也没有健康，
　　内心没有安宁，周围没有平静， 20
　　没有像哲人在冥想中所发现的那样

>   The sage in meditation found,
>   And walked with inward glory crowned —
>   Nor fame, nor power, nor love, nor leisure;
>   Others I see whom these surround —
>   Smiling they live, and call life pleasure;
> To me that cup has been dealt in another measure.
>
>   Yet now despair itself is mild
>   Even as the winds and waters are;
>   I could lie down like a tired child,
>   And weep away the life of care
>   Which I have borne, and yet must bear
>   Till death like sleep might steal on me,
>   And I might feel in the warm air
>   My cheek grow cold, and hear the sea
> Breathe o'er my dying brain its last monotony.

P. B. SHELLEY.

远比财富可贵的满足心境,
　沐浴着内在的荣光行进——
没有荣誉、权力、爱情、闲逸;
　我看见拥有这一切的人们　　　　　　　25
欢度人生,把生活称作欢悦,
我的生活之杯却斟满另一种滋味。

而绝望在此刻也显得柔和,
　甚至像流水、像清风,
我可以像困倦的孩子一样躺卧,　　　　30
　把我必须承受的忧患人生
在哭泣中消磨,
直到死亡像睡眠悄悄降落,
　直到在温暖的空气里,
觉着面颊发冷,听海洋在我　　　　　　35
逐渐死去的头脑上送来它最单调的音波。

　　　　　　　　　　　　　江枫　译

编注　本诗发表于一八一八年十二月,原诗第五诗节被《金库》略去,原编者认为不如前几节的诗艺高。诗行如下:
有人会哀叹我冷却,正像我哀叹,
　当我苍老得太快的心
正在用这不适时宜的呻吟和伤感
　加以亵渎的美好一天一去无踪;
　他们会哀叹——由于我这人
不为世人爱重——却又会感到遗憾,
　和这一天不同,这一天,
当太阳在无瑕的荣光中沉落下山,
还会像享受过的欢乐,在人们记忆中盘桓。(江枫　译)

228. THE SCHOLAR

My days among the Dead are past;
    Around me I behold,
Where'er these casual eyes are cast
    The mighty minds of old;
My never-failing friends are they,
With whom I converse day by day.

With them I take delight in weal
    And seek relief in woe;
And while I understand and feel
    How much to them I owe,
My cheeks have often been bedew'd
With tears of thoughtful gratitude.

My thoughts are with the Dead; with them
    I live in long-past years,
Their virtues love, their faults condemn,
    Partake their hopes and fears,
And from their lessons seek and find
Instruction with an humble mind.

My hopes are with the Dead; anon
    My place with them will be,
And I with them shall travel on
    Through all Futurity;
Yet leaving here a name, I trust,

228. 学人

骚 塞

和故人相处的岁月已经消逝；
　　我还看到在我周际，
偶然的目光所触之处
　　那些往日的伟大心灵啊：
他们是我始终不渝的伴侣，　　　　　　　　　5
我和他们终日絮语。

我和他们在幸福中领受欣喜，
　　也在苦难中寻求开释；
而今每当我懂得和感到
　　我负欠了他们多少情谊，　　　　　　　10
我的双颊便常常染湿
被那由衷感激的泪滴。

我的思绪呵和故人在一起；和他们
　　一起生活在漫长的往昔的日子，
爱他们的美德，责他们的过失，　　　　　15
　　分担他们的希望与忧虑，
怀着谦卑的心从他们的教训中
把真谛和探求寻觅。

我的希望尽与故人在一起；不久
　　我的位置也将和他们一起，　　　　　20
我还将和他们继续旅行
　　通向一切未来的遭遇；
在这儿也留下一个姓名，我相信

That will not perish in the dust.

R. SOUTHEY.

它不会寂灭于尘世。

邹荻帆　邹海仑　译

编注　本诗作于一八一八年,标题为《金库》原编者所加。

229. THE MERMAID TAVERN

Souls of Poets dead and gone,
What Elysium have ye known,
Happy field or mossy cavern,
Choicer than the Mermaid Tavern?
Have ye tippled drink more fine
Than mine host's Canary wine?
Or are fruits of Paradise
Sweeter than those dainty pies
Of venison? O generous food!
Drest as though bold Robin Hood
Would, with his Maid Marian,
Sup and bowse from horn and can[①].

I have heard that on a day
Mine host's signboard flew away
Nobody knew whither, till
An astrologer's old quill
To a sheepskin gave the story[②]—
Said he saw you in your glory[③]—
Underneath a new-old Sign
Sipping beverage divine,
And pledging with contented smack

[①] *bowse*: (or booze) 'drink.'
[②] *quill ... sheepskin*: i.e. the pen told the parchment.
[③] *you*: the souls of the Poets.

229. 美人鱼酒店①

济慈

已逝的诗人们之英魂哟,
你们认识的有什么乐土,
快活的田野还是生苔的洞窟,
比美人鱼酒店还更精致?
你们喝过的酒是不是 5
比我店东的加那列酒更美?
还是天堂的果子
比这些精美的鹿肉馅的饼
更为甘美? 大量的食品哟!
制得仿佛大胆的罗宾汉, 10
在同他的女郎玛丽安
用牛角杯和铁罐吃喝。

我听到过说,有一天
我店东的招牌不翼而飞,
没有人知道它飞到哪里, 15
直到一个占星家的秃笔
把这故事写在羊皮纸上,——
说道他看到你光彩辉煌,
在一个新开张的老字号
慢斟细饮着那琼浆玉液, 20
一边满意地咂嘴,一边保证,

---

① 伦敦面包街一家酒店,原来是个俱乐部,据说是由英国历史家及诗人沃尔特·雷利(Walter Ralegh,1552?—1618)所创设的,经常出入其中的有本·琼森、鲍蒙特、弗莱彻,可能还有莎士比亚等。——译者

The Mermaid in the Zodiac.

Souls of Poets dead and gone,
What Elysium have ye known —
Happy field or mossy cavern —
Choicer than the Mermaid Tavern?

J. KEATS.

要在黄道带开美人鱼酒店。

已逝的诗人之英魂哟，
你们认识的有什么乐土，
快活的田野还是生苔的洞窟，
比美人鱼酒店还要精致？

朱维基　译

230. THE PRIDE OF YOUTH

Proud Maisie is in the wood①,
 Walking so early;
Sweet Robin sits on the bush
 Singing so rarely.

'Tell me, thou bonny bird,
 When shall I marry me?'
— 'When six braw gentlemen②
 Kirkward shall carry ye.'

'Who makes the bridal bed,
 Birdie, say truly?'
— 'The grey-headed sexton
 That delves the grave duly.

'The glow-worm o'er grave and stone
 Shall light thee steady;
The owl from the steeple sing
 Welcome, proud lady.'

SIR W. SCOTT.

---

① *Maisie*: 'Mary.'
② *braw*: 'fine.'

230. 青春的骄傲

司各特

骄傲的梅西在树林中
　　大清早就走来走去；
美丽的知更鸟坐在灌木中
　　唱得特别美妙。

"告诉我，可爱的小鸟，
　　什么时候我该出嫁？"——
——"等六位漂亮的先生，
　　将把你领向教堂。"

"新房的床是谁铺的？
　　小鸟，老实地告诉我。"
——"满头银发的教堂执事
　　及时地掘好坟墓。

"坟墓与石碑上的萤火虫
　　将不断地照着你；
猫头鹰在教堂尖塔上唱着，
　　欢迎您，骄傲的女士。"

王辑　任大雄　译

编注　本诗选自《密得罗西的心脏》(*The Heart of Midlothian*, 1818)，是一个不幸的疯姑娘临终前唱的骄傲的梅西之歌，颇有古代民谣中那种言简意赅、阴森可怖的味道。标题为《金库》原编者所加。

231. THE BRIDGE OF SIGHS

One more Unfortunate
　Weary of breath,
Rashly importunate,
　Gone to her death!

Take her up tenderly,
　Lift her with care;
Fashion'd so slenderly,
　Young, and so fair!

Look at her garments
Clinging like cerements①,
Whilst the wave constantly
　Drips from her clothing;
Take her up instantly,
　Loving, not loathing.

Touch her not scornfully;
Think of her mournfully,
　Gently and humanly;
Not of the stains of her —
All that remains of her

---

① *cerements*: 'grave-clothes.'

231. 叹息桥[①]

胡德

又一个不幸的女人
　　厌倦了生命,
终于迫不及待地
　　了结了她的一生!

轻轻地捞她出水,
　　小心地抬她上堤;
她身子那么纤弱,
　　又那么年轻美丽!

瞧她那身衣裙
恍若裹尸布缠身;
从她浸透的素服
　　河水还不断下滴;
赶快把她弄干,
　　要疼爱,不要厌弃!

碰她时别显轻蔑,
想到她应感伤悲,
　　应显出高贵仁慈,
不去想她的孽罪——
如今在她身上

[①] 在一八七八年之前,通过横跨泰晤士河的滑铁卢桥需交纳通行费,故该桥行人稀少,许多不幸者因此而将其选为自杀地点。胡德有感于此,借用威尼斯那座著名的叹息桥为之命名。——译者

> Now is pure womanly.

> Make no deep scrutiny
> Into her mutiny[1]
>   Rash and undutiful:
> Past all dishonour,
> Death has left on her
>   Only the beautiful.

> Still, for all slips of hers,
>   One of Eve's family —
> Wipe those poor lips of hers
>   Oozing so clammily.

> Loop up her tresses
>   Escaped from the comb,
> Her fair auburn tresses;
> Whilst wonderment guesses
>   Where was her home?

> Who was her father?
>   Who was her mother?
> Had she a sister?
>   Had she a brother?
> Or was there a dearer one
> Still, and a nearer one
>   Yet, than all other?

> Alas! for the rarity

---

[1] *mutiny*: rebellion against the law forbidding self-destruction.

只剩下女性之美。 20

无须去过分追究
　她离经叛道之罪尤；
　　死亡已经抹去
　她的耻辱和污垢；
如今在她身上 25
　　只有美依然存留。

她虽曾误入歧途，
　可仍是夏娃的姊妹——
请从她冰凉的嘴唇
　擦去渗出的河水。 30

请替她绾好头发，
　那头散乱的秀发，
那头淡褐色的秀发；
趁好奇心在猜测
　　何处曾是她家？ 35

她的父亲是谁？
　她的母亲是谁？
她是否有位兄弟？
　她是否有位姐妹？
或是否还有一人， 40
于她比谁都亲，
　于她比谁都近？

唉，基督的仁慈

Of Christian charity
    Under the sun!
O! it was pitiful!
Near a whole city full,
    Home she had none.

Sisterly, brotherly,
Fatherly, motherly
    Feelings had changed:
Love, by harsh evidence,
Thrown from its eminence,
Even God's providence
    Seeming estranged.

Where the lamps quiver
So far in the river,
    With many a light
From window and casement,
From garret to basement,
She stood, with amazement,
    Houseless by night.

The bleak wind of March
    Made her tremble and shiver;
But not the dark arch,
    Or the black flowing river:
Mad from life's history,
Glad to death's mystery
    Swift to be hurl'd —
Any where, any where
    Out of the world!

难以普济众生！
　呆呆阳光之下 45
却是一番惨景！
在一座繁华都市，
　她竟然无家栖身！

父母双亲不认，
兄弟姐妹翻脸； 50
　亲情全都消散；
凭着不贞的证据，
爱神亦被推翻；
甚至连上帝的庇护
　似乎也与她疏远。 55

在远处河面上方，
有点点灯光闪烁，
　河面上泛着光波，
高楼低屋的窗口
透出万家灯火； 60
夜静而无家可归，
　她迷茫而又困惑。

三月料峭的寒风
　使她瑟瑟发抖；
可她不惧桥洞阴森， 65
　也不怕幽暗的急流。
不幸逼得她疯狂，
她乐于跳进水中，
　去探究神秘的死亡；
只要能脱离人世， 70
不管被冲到何方！

> In she plunged boldly,
> No matter how coldly
>   The rough river ran,
> Over the brink of it, —
> Picture it, think of it,
>   Dissolute Man!
> Lave in it, drink of it
>   Then, if you can!
>
> Take her up tenderly,
>   Lift her with care;
> Fashion'd so slenderly,
>   Young, and so fair!
>
> Ere her limbs frigidly
> Stiffen too rigidly,
>   Decently, kindly,
> Smooth and compose them;
> And her eyes, close them
>   Staring so blindly!
>
> Dreadfully staring
>   Thro' muddy impurity,
> As when with the daring
> Last look of despairing
>   Fix'd on futurity
>
> Perishing gloomily,
> Spurr'd by contumely[①],

---

① *contumely*: 'insult.'

她勇敢地纵身一跃，
全不顾水冷流急——
　　岸上的男人们哟，
放荡的男人们哟，
看看吧，想想吧！
　　要是你能下水，
就下去浸上一遭，
　　尝尝那水的滋味！

轻轻地捞她出水，
　　小心地抬她上堤；
她身子那么纤弱，
　　又那么年轻美丽！

趁她冰凉的四肢
还没有完全僵硬，
　　请怀着宽容之心，
把它们摆好放平；
然后再替她合上
　　那双茫然的眼睛！

那令人生畏的眼睛，
　　眼珠上还蒙着淤泥，
仿佛在最后一瞬，
她曾用绝望的目光
　　勇敢地凝望来世。

她虽然悲观地自杀①，
　　但却是因侮辱欺凌，

---

① 基督徒认为生命乃上帝赋予，自杀是一种犯罪。——译者

Cold inhumanity,
Burning insanity,
  Into her rest.
— Cross her hands humbly,
As if praying dumbly,
  Over her breast!

Owning her weakness,
  Her evil behaviour,
And leaving, with meekness,
  Her sins to her Saviour!

T. HOOD.

因人情世故炎凉
和她错乱的神经①
　　把她逼到了绝境——
所以请让她的双手　　　　　　　　　　　100
像默默祈祷时那样
　　谦恭地交叉在胸前。

承认她有污点，
　　承认她有罪孽，
但仍应宽大为怀，　　　　　　　　　　　105
　　留她给上帝裁决！

　　　　　　　　　　曹明伦　译

---

① 法律规定精神错乱者的行为可免负法律责任。——译者

232. ELEGY

O snatch'd away in beauty's bloom!
On thee shall press no ponderous tomb;
   But on thy turf shall roses rear
   Their leaves, the earliest of the year,
And the wild cypress wave in tender gloom:

And oft by yon blue gushing stream
   Shall Sorrow lean her drooping head,
And feed deep thought with many a dream,
   And lingering pause and lightly tread;
Fond wretch! as if her step disturb'd the dead!

Away! we know that tears are vain,
   That Death nor heeds nor hears distress:
Will this unteach us to complain[①]?
   Or make one mourner weep the less?
And thou, who tell'st me to forget,
Thy looks are wan, thine eyes are wet.

LORD BYRON.

---

① *unteach*: 'teach ... not (to).'

232. 哀歌

拜伦

竟然攫去你娇艳的生命!
你岂应负载沉重的坟茔?
　　在你草茵覆盖的墓前,
　　让玫瑰绽开最早的花瓣,
野柏在幽暗中摇曳不定。　　　　　　　　　　5

往后,傍着那溪流碧绿,
　　"悲哀"会时时低垂着头颈,
用幻梦哺育深沉的思绪,
　　逡巡留伫,又缓步轻行,
仿佛怕惊扰逝者的梦境。　　　　　　　　　　10

也明知眼泪没什么用处,
　　"死亡"对悲苦不闻不问;
那我们就该停止怨诉?
　　哀哭者就该强抑酸辛?
而你——你劝我忘却悲怀,　　　　　　　　　15
你面容惨白,你泪痕宛在!

杨德豫　译

编注　本诗发表在《希伯来歌曲集》(*Hebrew Melodies*,1815)中,原标题为诗中第一行,本标题系《金库》原编者所加。

233. HESTER

When maidens such as Hester die,
Their place ye may not well supply,
Though ye among a thousand try
    With vain endeavour.
A month or more hath she been dead,
Yet cannot I by force be led
To think upon the wormy bed
    And her together.

A springy motion in her gait,
A rising step, did indicate
Of pride and joy no common rate
    That flush'd her spirit:
I know not by what name beside
I shall it call: if 'twas not pride,
It was a joy to that allied
    She did inherit.

Her parents held the Quaker rule,
Which doth the human feeling cool;
But she was train'd in Nature's school,
    Nature had blest her.
A waking eye, a prying mind[1],

---

[1] *prying*: 'inquiring,' not used here in a bad sense.

233. 海丝特

兰姆

像海丝特那样的少女们死了,
谁取代她们的位置,你都会感到不满,
即使你成千次尝试
　　　也只是白忙一番。
一两个月前她已魂归西天, 5
还是没有力量能使我
想到那虫蛀的坟床
　　　竟然与她相联。

她的步履轻盈,
每一举步都象征着 10
异乎寻常的自尊与愉欢
　　　充溢于她的神采之间:
除了我将给予的名称
我不知道它还会叫什么:如果那不是自尊,
那便是自尊又结合愉欢, 15
　　　这在她实在是天性使然。

她的双亲信守贵格派教规①,
它使人们感情冷淡;
但她是在"天性"的学校里受到训练,
　　　"天性"已经给了她祝愿。 20
智慧的眼睛、渴求的心田,

---

① 贵格派教规(the Quaker rule),教友会教规,即在生活的所有细微处都要严肃、庄重、节制。——译者

A heart that stirs, is hard to bind①;
A hawk's keen sight ye cannot blind,
    Ye could not Hester.

My sprightly neighbour! gone before
To that unknown and silent shore,
Shall we not meet, as heretofore
    Some summer morning —
When from thy cheerful eyes a ray
Hath struck a bliss upon the day,
A bliss that would not go away,
    A sweet fore-warning②?

C. LAMB.

---

① *is*: the subject is really '(one who combines) a waking eye,' etc.; hence the verb is singular.

② *fore-warning*: a foretaste of the pleasure that her company always gave.

心儿动了,再也不能捆绑束绊;
你那鹰儿似的热切目光不容遮掩,
　　　海丝特,你不容遮掩。

我活泼的邻居呵! 先离去了　　　　　　　　　　25
走向那未知的寂静海岸,
难道我们再不能像从前
　　　在夏天的早晨那样相见——
那时你愉悦的眼睛光亮闪闪
赋予那白昼以极乐狂欢,　　　　　　　　　　　30
欢乐将永远不会消散,
　　　难道那只是甜蜜的报警的预言?

　　　　　　　　　　　　邹荻帆　邹海仑　译

编注　本诗作于一八〇三年十二月,一八一八年发表在《著作》(*Works*)中。诗中寓意着青春和美是不可能被征服的,无论是古板的教义还是死神都无能为力。

234. CORONACH

He is gone on the mountain.
    He is lost to the forest,
Like a summer-dried fountain,
    When our need was the sorest.
The font reappearing[①]
    From the raindrops shall borrow,
But to us comes no cheering,
    To Duncan no morrow!

The hand of the reaper
    Takes the ears that are hoary,
But the voice of the weeper
    Wails manhood in glory.
The autumn winds rushing
    Waft the leaves that are serest,
But our flower was in flushing[②]
    When blighting was nearest.

Fleet foot on the correi[③],
    Sage counsel in cumber[④],

---

① *font*: used in poetry for 'fount.'
② *in flushing*: in process of sending out new shoots.
③ *correi*: (more commonly 'corrie') a more or less circular hollow on a mountain, surrounded by steep slopes or precipices except at its lower end (*coire*, Gael. = a kettle).
④ *cumber*: 'trouble,' 'embarrassment.'

234. 挽歌

司各特

他死在高高的山丘,
　　他死在森林的尽头,
像夏季枯竭的清泉,
　　当我们最需要的时候。
只要有雨水滋润,　　　　　　　　　　5
　　清泉水还会长流,
可邓肯没有了翌日①
　　我们会永远忧愁!

收割者苍白的手哟
　　紧紧抓住了麦穗,　　　　　　　　10
可哭泣者还在悲伤,
　　哀悼他人品高贵。
一年一度的秋风
　　吹万片枯叶飘飞,
但当枯萎将近之时,　　　　　　　　15
　　我们的花儿正绽出新蕾。

飞毛腿陷入了泥潭,
　　大智者遇到了魔难,

---

① 长诗《湖上夫人》中的人物。——译者

> Red hand in the foray,
>   How sound is thy slumber!
> Like the dew on the mountain,
>   Like the foam on the river,
> Like the bubble on the fountain,
>   Thou art gone, and for ever!

SIR W. SCOTT.

血腥的手正在掠夺，
　　你却睡得这般香甜！ 20
像那山上的露珠，
　　像那河面的青烟，
像那泉边的水泡，
　　你一去永不复返！

曹明伦　译

编注 此诗选自司各特一八一〇年出版的长诗《湖上夫人》第三章第十六节。长诗叙述了中世纪苏格兰国王和骑士的冒险事迹，描绘了苏格兰绮丽的自然风光。

235. THE DEATH-BED

We watch'd her breathing thro' the night,
   Her breathing soft and low,
As in her breast the wave of life
   Kept heaving to and fro[①].

But when the morn came dim and sad
   And chill with early showers,
Her quiet eyelids closed — she had
   Another morn than ours.

T. HOOD.

[①] Below this line, there are two stanzas which have been omitted by Palgrave:
'So silently we seem'd to speak,
   So slowly moved about,
As we had lent her half our powers
   To eke her living out.

'Our very hopes belied our fears,
   Our fears our hopes belied —
We thought her dying when she slept,
   And sleeping when she died.'

235. 临终

胡德

眼见她彻夜喘息不停,
　呻吟轻柔而低沉,
眼见她胸脯起伏急剧,
　宛如人生波浪滚滚。

凌晨到来,朦胧而悲戚,
　潇潇晨雨,令人颤栗,
她悄然合上眼帘,
　进入了另一个天地。

崔勇　刁家崇　译

编注　本诗是纪念诗人的亡妹安妮而作,一八三一年发表在《英国人杂志》上。《金库》原编者略去中间两节。这两节是:

多么寂静,我们好像轻声低语,
　多么缓慢,我们动作如此不灵,
假使我们借给她一半的活力,
　就能延续她垂危的生命。

真挚的希望蒙蔽了恐惧,
　巨大的恐惧又把希望蒙蔽——
她沉睡了,我们以为她已死去,
　她死去了,我们以为她在休息。

236. ROSABELLE

O listen, listen, ladies gay!
    No haughty feat of arms I tell;
Soft is the note, and sad the lay
    That mourns the lovely Rosabelle.

'Moor, moor the barge, ye gallant crew!
    And, gentle ladye, deign to stay!
Rest thee in Castle Ravensheuch,
    Nor tempt the stormy firth to-day.

'The blackening wave is edged with white;
    To inch and rock the sea-mews fly[①];
The fishers have heard the Water-Sprite[②],
    Whose screams forebode that wreck is nigh.

'Last night the gifted Seer did view
    A wet shroud swathed round ladye gay;
Then stay thee, Fair, in Ravensheuch;
    Why cross the gloomy firth to-day?'

''Tis not because Lord Lindesay's heir
    To-night at Roslin leads the ball,

[①] *inch*: 'islet.'
[②] *Water-Sprite*: see note to No. 127, l. 23.

236. 罗莎白娜①

司各特

哦,请听吧,听吧,快活的女士!
　　我不讲武士们骄傲的功绩;
这曲调柔和,诗行悲伤,
　　把可爱的罗莎白娜哀悼奠祭。

"停住吧,停住船儿,风流绅士! 5
　　留步吧,屈尊留步,窈窕淑女!
今宵就请在雷文斯克城堡借宿,
　　别冒险去穿越那河口的风雨。

"黑色的巨浪镶上了白边;
　　海鸥飞往那小岛与礁石; 10
渔夫们听见了水魂的尖叫,
　　尖叫声预示着灾难临逼。

"那位天禀的先知昨夜里看见
　　湿透的尸布裹住了快活的少女;
请留步吧,美人儿,留在这城堡; 15
　　为何今晚非往阴惨的河口驶去?"

"倒不是因为林德赛家的嗣子
　　今宵在罗斯林将舞会集聚②,

---

① 罗莎白娜(Rosabelle)系苏格兰一位贵族世家女子。——译者
② 爱丁堡以南七英里处的一个村庄,以美丽的城堡和十五世纪的教堂而著名。——译者

>   But that my ladye-mother there
>   Sits lonely in her castle-hall.
>
> ' 'Tis not because the ring they ride,
>   And Lindesay at the ring rides well,
> But that my sire the wine will chide
>   If 'tis not fill'd by Rosabelle. '
>
> — O'er Roslin all that dreary night
>   A wondrous blaze was seen to gleam;
> 'Twas broader than the watch-fire's light,
>   And redder than the bright moonbeam.
>
> It glared on Roslin's castled rock,
>   It ruddied all the copse-wood glen;
> 'Twas seen from Dryden's groves of oak,
>   And seen from cavern'd Hawthornden.
>
> Seem'd all on fire that chapel proud,
>   Where Roslin's chiefs uncoffin'd lie,
> Each Baron, for a sable shroud,
>   Sheath'd in his iron panoply.
>
> Seem'd all on fire within, around,
>   Deep sacristy and altar's pale[①];

[①] *sacristy*: the room in a church where vestments and sacred vessels are kept. *altar's pale*: the precincts of the altar.

而是因为我的母亲在那儿，
　　孤零零坐在城堡的大厅里。　　　　　　　　　20

"倒不是因为那跑马挑圈①
　　林德赛勋爵有非凡的跑马技艺，
而是因为我父亲会斥责美酒
　　若不是由罗莎白娜斟满酒器。"

——在罗斯林上空，那个阴沉的夜晚　　　　　　25
　　人们看见了一团奇妙的火焰；
比熊熊的营火更大更旺，
　　比皎洁的月光更艳更鲜。

火焰在罗斯林城堡上蹿腾，
　　映红了树木丛生的幽谷深涧；　　　　　　　30
从德莱顿家林荫道能遥看火光②，
　　从霍索恩顿洞府能遥望浓烟③。

那座高耸的教堂被大火包围，
　　罗斯林的贵人都倒在里面，
每个男爵都身着全副铠甲，　　　　　　　　　　35
　　铠甲尤如一张张黑色的尸单。

教堂里里外外都烈火熊熊，
　　那幽深的圣器室，神圣的祭坛；

---

① 跑马挑圈是中世纪的一种马上游戏，参加者得在策马飞奔时用长枪挑取高悬的圈环。——译者
② 德莱顿（参见本书卷二第63首编注）家园在罗斯林附近，园内有一条长达一英里的橡树林荫道。——编注者
③ 霍索恩顿是德拉蒙德（参见本书卷一第2首编注）的家乡，离罗斯林约四英里。——编注者

  Shone every pillar foliage-bound,
   And glimmer'd all the dead men's mail.

  Blazed battlement and pinnet high,
   Blazed every rose-carved buttress fair —
  So still they blaze, when fate is nigh
   The lordly line of high St. Clair.

  There are twenty of Roslin's barons bold
   Lie buried within that proud chapelle;
  Each one the holy vault doth hold,
   But the sea holds lovely Rosabelle!

  And each St. Clair was buried there
   With candle, with book, and with knell;
  But the sea-caves rung, and the wild winds sung
   The dirge of lovely Rosabelle.

SIR W. SCOTT.

雕花饰叶的圆柱映着火光,
　　死者身上的甲胄朦胧闪现。　　　　　　　　　　40

烧着了城垛和高高的塔尖,
　　烧着了刻有蔷薇花的壁沿——
厄运降临圣·克莱尔豪府,
　　一切都葬于烈火浓烟。

罗斯林二十个勇敢的爵士　　　　　　　　　　　　45
　　被葬在那座漂亮的教堂里;
他们都有神圣的拱顶墓厅,
　　可罗莎白娜却葬身在大海里!

圣·克莱尔家的死者都埋在那儿,
　　陪伴着烛光、吊钟和书籍;　　　　　　　　　50
可只有大海低吟,狂风悲唱,
　　为可爱的罗莎白娜哀歌一曲。

曹明伦　译

编注　此诗选自司各特一八〇五年出版的长诗《最末一个行吟诗人之歌》(*The Lay of the Last Minstrel*)第六章第二十三节。长诗通过苏格兰两个贵族世家的门阀之争,表现了十六世纪苏格兰封建贵族的生活。

237. ON AN INFANT DYING AS SOON AS BORN

I saw where in the shroud did lurk
A curious frame of Nature's work;
A flow'ret crushéd in the bud,
A nameless piece of Babyhood,
Was in her cradle-coffin lying;
Extinct, with scarce the sense of dying:
So soon to exchange the imprisoning womb
For darker closets of the tomb!
She did but ope an eye, and put
A clear beam forth, then straight up shut
For the long dark: ne'er more to see
Through glasses of mortality.
Riddle of destiny, who can show
What thy short visit meant, or know
What thy errand here below?
Shall we say that Nature blind
Check'd her hand, and changed her mind,
Just when she had exactly wrought
A finish'd pattern without fault?
Could she flag, or could she tire,
Or lack'd she the Promethean fire
(With her nine moons' long workings sicken'd)
That should thy little limbs have quicken'd?

237. 唱给一个出世即夭的孩子

兰姆

分明看得见尸布的遮掩下
自然造就的一个奇异的小身体,
那一朵含苞待放却遭蹂躏的花儿,
那一个未给起名便逝去的孩子。
她躺在那小小的棺椁里   5
死去了,还来不及感受死是什么滋味。
这么快呵,她刚离开母腹的囹圄,
就要走进更幽暗的坟墓。
刚睁开的一只眼才射出一线
明澈的目光,便对着无尽的黑暗。   10
紧紧闭上,永不再洞悉
人世的生、死、悲、欢。
命运之谜呵,谁能告诉我
你短暂的来访意味着什么?
谁又能知道你在冥冥中   15
担负着什么样的使命?
难道说盲目的自然刚刚完成
一项完美无瑕的作品,
便停下了手中的活计,
改变了自己的主意?   20
是她热情衰退、精疲力竭,
还是她手中的普罗米修斯之火已经熄灭①?
(抑或是她倦于九个月的惨淡经营)

---

① 普罗米修斯之火,希腊神话中普罗米修斯把天火偷到人间,此处指生命的火种。——译者

	Limbs so firm, they seem'd to assure
25	Life of health, and days mature;
	Woman's self in miniature!
	Limbs so fair, they might supply
	(Themselves now but cold imagery)
	The sculptor to make Beauty by.
30	Or did the stern-eyed Fate descry
	That babe or mother, one must die;
	So in mercy left the stock
	And cut the branch; to save the shock
	Of young years widow'd, and the pain
35	When Single State comes back again
	To the lone man who, 'reft of wife,
	Thenceforward drags a maiméd life?
	The economy of Heaven is dark①,
	And wisest clerks have miss'd the mark②,
40	Why human buds, like this, should fall
	More brief than fly ephemeral③
	That has his day; while shrivell'd crones
	Stiffen with age to stocks and stones;
	And crabbéd use the conscience sears
45	In sinners of an hundred years.
	— Mother's prattle, mother's kiss,
	Baby fond, thou ne'er wilt miss;
	Rites, which custom does impose,
	Silver bells, and baby clothes;
50	Coral redder than those lips

---

① *economy*: in its first and widest sense, 'management of a household.'
② *clerks*: 'scholars.'
③ *ephemeral*: 'living but for a day.'

才让你那小生命这般匆匆来去?
多么壮实的身体呵,它本预示 25
健康的生活,成熟的时日,
这原来是女人的雏形!
多么美的肢体! 本该是
来日雕塑家美的模特儿,
(现在却成了冰冷的死尸)。 30
难道是命运那冷峻的眼睛
看出孩子或母亲,必死一人,
慈悲地留下了树干,
剁下了幼枝? 只为的是
免除她年少居孀的不幸, 35
还有那孤独的男人的丧妻之痛,
不让他拖曳鳏旷的残生?
上天的精明意志凶险难测,
最渊博的哲人也茫然迷惑。
为什么这人类的花蕾竟然早落, 40
寿数还不及那朝生暮死的蜉蝣?
为什么留下风烛残年的老妪,
任岁月把她们变枯木朽株?
为什么尽管良心烧炙着损人的勾当,
罪人们却百岁长寿? 45
——母亲的细语、母亲的亲吻,
可爱的孩子呵,它们会将你浸润,
那习惯定下的葬礼,
那银铃,那婴儿的衬衣,
那鲜艳的红珊瑚更胜过 50

919

Which pale death did late eclipse;
Music framed for infants' glee,
Whistle never tuned for thee;
Though thou want'st not, thou shalt have them,
Loving hearts were they which gave them.
Let not one be missing; nurse,
See them laid upon the hearse
Of infant slain by doom perverse.
Why should kings and nobles have
Pictured trophies to their grave,
And we, churls, to thee deny
Thy pretty toys with thee to lie —
A more harmless vanity?

C. LAMB.

你那刚被死亡的苍白夺去光彩的朱唇,
那为孩子的欢乐而谱写的乐曲,
那从未对你吹起的风笛,
你不曾要过它们,今天却全属于你,
这是爱你的人们对你难舍依依。　　　　　　　　　55
这些东西缺一不可,奶娘,
让它们在这被乖戾的命运
扼杀了的孩子的灵车上一一安放。
王公贵族的墓前,
绘上了战利品的图案,　　　　　　　　　　　　60
为什么庶民百姓就不让你
跟你那些可爱的玩具
这更无害的虚荣一起长眠?

邓鹏　王作虹　译

编注　兰姆的第一个孩子于一八二七年五月夭折,他写了这首诗寄给胡德表达哀伤之情。一八二九年胡德将本诗发表在《宝石》(*The Gem*)上,一八三〇年收入《兰姆诗集》(*Album Verses*)。

238. THE AFFLICTION OF MARGARET

Where art thou, my beloved Son,
    Where art thou, worse to me than dead?
O find me, prosperous or undone!
    Or, if the grave be now thy bed,
Why am I ignorant of the same①
That I may rest; and neither blame
Nor sorrow may attend thy name?

Seven years, alas! to have received
    No tidings of an only child;
To have despaired, have hoped, believed,
    And been for evermore beguiled, —
Sometimes with thoughts of very bliss!
I catch at them, and then I miss;
Was ever darkness like to this?

He was among the prime in worth,
    An object beauteous to behold;
Well born, well bred; I sent him forth
    Ingenuous, innocent and bold:
If things ensued that wanted grace②,
As hath been said, they were not base;
And never blush was on my face.

---

① *of the same*: 'the same' is an equivalent of 'it,' 'they' or 'them.'
② *ensued*: 'followed.'

238. 玛格丽特的苦恼

华兹华斯

我至爱的儿子,你在哪里,
　你在哪里?生离比死别更痛苦。
啊,归来吧,不论你是富有或潦倒穷途!
　或者,倘你已长眠地下,
那我为什么竟毫无所知　　　　　　　　　5
而不能也同样得到安息
使你不致蒙受责难和悲凄?

七年了,天啊!从不曾得到
　我独生儿子的一点信息;
我绝望过,希冀过,相信过,　　　　　　10
　而一切都永远破灭了,——
有时怀着极乐的念头!
我伸手去捕捉,但没有捉住;
这黑暗的尽头竟在何处?

他曾是无价之宝,　　　　　　　　　　　15
　悦目的美的化身,
出身高贵,教养良好,
　天生勇敢又纯真.
假如日后的事不甚光彩
也正如俗话所说,它们并不劣鄙;　　　　20
我永远不会为此羞愧。

Ah! little doth the young one dream,
    When full of play and childish cares,
What power is in his wildest scream
    Heard by his mother unawares!
He knows it not, he cannot guess;
Years to a mother bring distress;
But do not make her love the less.

Neglect me! no, I suffered long
    From that ill thought; and being blind
Said, 'Pride shall help me in my wrong;
    Kind mother have I been, as kind
As ever breathed;' and that is true;
I've wet my path with tears like dew,
Weeping for him when no one knew.

My Son, if thou be humbled, poor,
    Hopeless of honour and of gain,
O! do not dread thy mother's door;
    Think not of me with grief and pain:
I now can see with better eyes;
And worldly grandeur I despise,
And fortune with her gifts and lies.

Alas! the fowls of heaven have wings,
    And blasts of heaven will aid their flight;
They mount — how short a voyage brings
    The wanderers back to their delight!
Chains tie us down by land and sea;
And wishes, vain as mine, may be
All that is left to comfort thee.

啊,这孩子很少会梦想到,
　　在他只知嬉戏的童稚之年,
他的狂热的叫声
　　对一个无意中听到的母亲有多大力量。　　　　25
他不知道,也不可能猜想得到
多年来给母亲带来的悲痛;
但这并不使她的疼爱有一丝减少。

别管我吧!不,我曾为这不祥的念头
　　受尽了苦;由于无知曾说过:　　　　　　　　30
"自尊将减轻我的委曲;
　　我曾是一个世上从未有过的
慈祥的母亲";这话千真万确;
我曾以似晨露的泪珠洒湿走过的路
在暗中为他哀哭。　　　　　　　　　　　　　　35

我的儿子,倘你是潦倒穷途,
　　无望得到尊荣和富贵,
啊,不要怕回到你母亲的家门,
　　想到我时也不要悲伤凄楚:
我现在眼睛明亮了;　　　　　　　　　　　　　　40
我鄙弃尘世的浮华,
和那浸透贿赂和谎言的财富。

啊!天堂之鸟长着翅膀,
　　天上的狂飙将为它们鼓翼;
它们飞升——只需短短路程　　　　　　　　　　45
　　就可以把流浪人送回幸福之门!
海天之链将我们锁住;
虽属徒然,但我的希冀,
可能是留给你的唯一慰藉。

  Perhaps some dungeon hears thee groan,
   Maim'd, mangled by inhuman men;
  Or thou upon a desert thrown
   Inheritest the lion's den;
  Or hast been summon'd to the deep,
  Thou, thou, and all thy mates, to keep
  An incommunicable sleep[①].

  I look for ghosts; but none will force
   Their way to me: 'tis falsely said
  That there was ever intercourse
   Between the living and the dead[②];
  For surely then I should have sight
  Of him I wait for day and night
  With love and longings infinite.

  My apprehensions come in crowds;
   I dread the rustling of the grass;
  The very shadows of the clouds
   Have power to shake me as they pass:
  I question things, and do not find
  One that will answer to my mind;
  And all the world appears unkind.

  Beyond participation lie

---

① *incommunicable*: in an active sense, 'that cannot hold any communication with' those on earth. It is commoner in its passive sense, 'that cannot be communicated.'

② *Between*: in the 1807 edition 'Betwixt'; it is noteworthy that wherever the latter word occurs in the 1807 *Poems* Wordsworth changed it later to 'Between.'

也许你正在地牢里呻吟； 50
  被丧尽天良的人折磨成残；
也许你被抛到荒漠沙丘，
  在虎狼窝里栖身；
还是已被召唤到地狱，
你，你，还有你所有的伙伴， 55
都已长眠，再也听不到我的呼唤[①]？

我期待着幽灵，但没有一个
  愿意寻路来到我身旁：
有人谎说，活人和死者
  真的可以通灵； 60
那么，我日日夜夜
怀着无限的爱和希望守候，
早就该能见到他的身影。

我的忧虑接踵而来；
  我怕听草丛的沙沙低语； 65
头上飘过的云影
  也足以使我浑身颤栗：
我向一切提出质问，但却没有一个
能给我合意的回音；
整个世界都是冷酷无情。 70

我的困苦无法由旁人分担，

[①] 此处可参考白居易《长恨歌》中句：悠悠生死别经年，魂魄不曾来入梦。——译者

My troubles, and beyond relief:
If any chance to heave a sigh,
   They pity me, and not my grief.
Then come to me, my Son, or send
Some tidings, that my woes may end;
I have no other earthly friend.

                          W. WORDSWORTH.

也无法得到解脱:
倘能有机会长叹一声,
  人们也只是怜悯,而不会理解①。
我的儿子,回到我身边来吧,
或者捎来信息使我能摆脱痛苦,
在这世上我再没有别的亲故。

陈琳　译

编注　本诗选自一八〇七年版的《诗选》,是诗人根据小镇上一个女店主的真实遭遇而写。女店主的儿子弃家出走,长久没有音讯。母亲怀念儿子,每有过往行人从店门走过,她总要追出去探听儿子的消息。

---

① 由于玛格丽特过去从未同邻人谈起过她儿子出走的事,因此邻人只知她孤单一身,不能真正理解她内心的痛楚。——译者

239. HUNTING SONG

Waken, lords and ladies gay!
On the mountain dawns the day;
All the jolly chase is here
With hawk and horse and hunting-spear;
Hounds are in their couples yelling,
Hawks are whistling, horns are knelling,
Merrily merrily mingle they,
'Waken, lords and ladies gay!'

Waken, lords and ladies gay!
The mist has left the mountain grey,
Springlets in the dawn are steaming,
Diamonds on the brake are gleaming;
And foresters have busy been
To track the buck in thicket green;
Now we come to chant our lay,
'Waken, lords and ladies gay!'

Waken, lords and ladies gay!
To the greenwood haste away;
We can show you where he lies,
Fleet of foot and tall of size;
We can show the marks he made
When 'gainst the oak his antlers fray'd;
You shall see him brought to bay;
'Waken, lords and ladies gay!'

239. 猎歌

司各特

醒来吧,欢娱的先生和女士!
山顶上已露出淡淡的晨曦;
这儿正进行快乐的追猎,
　有苍鹰、骏马和打猎的枪戟;
猎犬正成对咆哮吠咬,　　　　　　　　　　　5
　雄鹰在呼啸,号角声声急,
各种声音愉快地交织融合,
　"醒来吧,欢娱的先生和女士!"

醒来吧,欢娱的先生和女士!
山间的雾霭早已飘移,　　　　　　　　　　　10
　黎明的清泉正腾起水雾,
林中的露珠儿像闪光的宝石;
山里人此刻可忙得正欢
　在绿荫中搜寻牡鹿的踪迹;
我们来唱一曲欢快的歌,　　　　　　　　　　15
　"醒来吧,欢娱的先生和女士!"

醒来吧,欢娱的先生和女士!
快来这苍翠碧秀的树林里,
我们将让你们看到牡鹿躺的地方,
看它敏捷的快腿,高大的身躯;　　　　　　　20
我们将让你们看到那棵橡树,
还有树上它磨角留下的痕迹;
你们将看见它被追上绝路;
　"醒来吧,欢娱的先生和女士!"

Louder, louder chant the lay,
Waken, lords and ladies gay!
Tell them youth and mirth and glee
Run a course as well as we;
Time, stern huntsman! who can balk,
Stanch as hound and fleet as hawk;
Think of this, and rise with day,
Gentle lords and ladies gay!

SIR W. SCOTT.

唱吧,唱吧,把歌儿唱得更响亮, 25
唤醒那些欢娱的先生和女士!
给他们讲一讲青春与欢乐,
来和我们一道打猎游戏;
谁能阻止时间这严峻的猎手,
像阻止猎犬矫健,雄鹰敏疾; 30
想想这吧,伴黎明而早起,
高贵的先生和艳丽的女士!

曹明伦 译

编注 本诗作于一八〇八年,发表在小说《霍女皇厅》(*Queen-Hoo Hall*)中。该小说的原作者是约瑟夫·斯特拉特(Joseph Strutt),但他中途辍笔,后由司各特完成。

240. TO THE SKYLARK

Ethereal minstrel! pilgrim of the sky!
    Dost thou despise the earth where cares abound?
Or, while the wings aspire, are heart and eye
    Both with thy nest upon the dewy ground?
Thy nest which thou canst drop into at will,
Those quivering wings composed, that music still!

To the last point of vision, and beyond,
    Mount, daring warbler! — that love-prompted strain
('Twixt thee and thine a never-failing bond),
    Thrills not the less the bosom of the plain:
Yet might'st thou seem, proud privilege! to sing
All independent of the leafy spring.

Leave to the nightingale her shady wood;
    A privacy of glorious light is thine[①],
Whence thou dost pour upon the world a flood
    Of harmony, with instinct more divine[②];
Type of the wise, who soar, but never roam —
True to the kindred points of Heaven and Home.

                            W. WORDSWORTH.

---

① *A privacy of glorious light*: *i.e.* the lark, when soaring to its height, is as invisible as the nightingale on its tree.
② *more divine*: *i.e.* than that of the earth-haunting nightingale.

240. 致云雀

华兹华斯

灵妙的歌手!天空的朝圣者!
　　你是否瞧不起忧虑重重的大地?
或是,当你展翅时,心儿和眼睛
　　都与露珠点缀的地上的鸟巢连在一起,
你那泰然的羽翼,安祥的歌曲,　　　　　　　　　　5
绝不随意降落在你的鸟巢里!

飞到幻想的最高点,再往上飞,
　　升吧,亲爱的歌手——你有爱情推动的魅力,
　　(你和心爱者永远不分离)
　　你比平常的胸怀发出更多的激情:　　　　　　10
你好像充满力量,自豪无比,
为满园春色自由地高歌一曲。

让夜莺在她的树萌下歌唱;
　　明亮的光荣属于你,
当你向全世界倾吐出一串串乐音,　　　　　　　15
　　天性更显得神圣,美丽,
你是智者,不断高翔,绝不彷徨——
对于上天和你的家族,你有无限忠诚的情意。

罗义蕴　译

编注　本诗作于一八二五年,发表于一八二七年《诗集》(*Poems*)第三版上,标题是"To a Skylark",《金库》原编者改为"To the Skylark",译文均为《致云雀》。云雀为历代英国诗人所喜爱的题材,从莎士比亚、斯宾塞,到雪莱(参考第 241 首编注),都为这种边飞边唱、直冲云宵的鸟儿写过颂歌,华兹华斯把云雀比作飘逸脱尘、绝不彷徨的智者。

241. TO A SKYLARK

Hail to thee, blithe Spirit!
   Bird thou never wert,
That from heaven, or near it,
   Pourest thy full heart
In profuse strains of unpremeditated art.

Higher still and higher
   From the earth thou springest
Like a cloud of fire;
   The blue deep thou wingest,
And singing still dost soar, and soaring ever singest.

In the golden lightning
   Of the sunken sun,
O'er which clouds are brightening,
   Thou dost float and run,
Like an unbodied joy whose race is just begun.

241. 致云雀①

雪莱

你好啊,欢乐的精灵!
　　你似乎从不是飞禽,
　　从天堂或天堂的邻近,
　　以酣畅淋漓的乐音,
不事雕琢的艺术,倾吐你的衷心。　　　　　　　　　　5

向上,再向高处飞翔,
　　从地面你一跃而上,
　　像一片烈火的轻云②,
　　掠过蔚蓝的天心,
永远歌唱着飞翔,飞翔着歌唱。　　　　　　　　　　10

地平线下的太阳③,
　　放射出金色的电光,
　　晴空里霞蔚云蒸,
　　你沐浴着明光飞行,
似不具形体的喜悦刚开始迅疾的远征④。　　　　　　　15

---

① 云雀,黄褐色小鸟,构巢于地面,清晨升入高穹,入夜而还,有边飞边鸣的习性。——译者
② "像一片烈火的轻云",不是写云雀的形貌,而是按照"火向上以求日"的意思写它上升的运动态势(据《爱丁堡评论》一八七一年四月号)。——译者
③ 原文 sunken sun,为沉落的太阳,对于前一天为落日,对于新的一天则是尚未从地平线下升起的太阳。——译者
④ 有人认为原文此处的 unbodied 本来应该是 embodied(据《爱丁堡评论》一八七一年四月号)。基于此,则此处可译为"似具有形体的喜说"或"似有形的喜悦"。——译者

                The pale purple even
                    Melts around thy flight;
                Like a star of heaven
                    In the broad daylight
20   Thou art unseen, but yet I hear thy shrill delight:

                Keen as are the arrows①②
                    Of that silver sphere,
                Whose intense lamp narrows
                    In the white dawn clear
25   Until we hardly see, we feel that it is there.

                All the earth and air
                    With thy voice is loud,
                As, when night is bare,
                    From one lonely cloud
30   The moon rains out her beams, and heaven is overflow'd.

                What thou art we know not;
                    What is most like thee?
                From rainbow clouds there flow not
                    Drops so bright to see
35   As from thy presence showers a rain of melody.

                Like a poet hidden

---

① *wert*: the oldest form of the second person singular of *was* is 'were,' *wast* being a fourteenth-century formation. From *were* was formed *wert* on the analogy of *shalt*, etc.; but *wert* is now obsolete or used wrongly as subjunctive.

② *the arrows*: the rays from the 'star of heaven.'

淡淡的紫色黎明①
　　在你航程周围消融,
像昼空里的星星,
　　虽然不见形影,
却可以听得清你那欢乐的强音——　　　　　　　　　20

那犀利无比的乐音,
　　似银色星光的利箭,
它那强烈的明灯,
　　在晨曦中暗淡,
直到难以分辨,却能感觉到就在空间。　　　　　　25

整个大地和大气,
　　响彻你婉转的歌喉,
仿佛在荒凉的黑夜,
　　从一片孤云背后,
明月射出光芒,清辉洋溢宇宙。　　　　　　　　　30

我们不知,你是什么,
　　什么和你最为相似?
从霓虹似的彩霞
　　也降不下这样美的雨,
能和当你出现时降下的乐曲甘霖相比。　　　　　　35

像一位诗人,隐身

---

① 原文 even,我同意郭沫若同志的理解,实为 twilight,为白昼与黑夜之间的过渡。由于云雀鸣于昼而不鸣于夜,故译为黎明。——译者

    In the light of thought①,
   Singing hymns unbidden,
    Till the world is wrought
40 To sympathy with hopes and fears it heeded not:

   Like a high-born maiden
    In a palace tower,
   Soothing her love-laden
    Soul in secret hour
45 With music sweet as love, which overflows her bower:

   Like a glow-worm golden
    In a dell of dew,
   Scattering unbeholden②
    Its aerial hue
50 Among the flowers and grass, which screen it from the view:

   Like a rose embower'd
    In its own green leaves,
   By warm winds deflower'd③,
    Till the scent it gives
55 Makes faint with too much sweet these heavywingéd thieves④

---

① *hidden In the light of thought*: i.e. the man himself remains unknown, though his songs flash out over the world.
② *unbeholden*: 'unseen'; a unique use of the word; 'beholden,' the participle of 'behold,' usually means 'obliged.'
③ *deflower'd*: 'robbed' sc. of its scent.
④ *heavy-wingéd*: the winds move but slowly, as though their wings were laden.

在思想的明辉之中，
吟诵着即兴的诗韵，
　　直到普天下的同情
都被未曾留意过的希望和忧虑唤醒①；　　　　　　　　40

像一位高贵的少女，
　　居住在深宫的楼台，
在寂寞难言的时刻，
　　排遣她为爱所苦的情怀，
甜美有如爱情的歌曲，溢出闺阁之外②；　　　　　　45

像一只金色的萤火虫，
　　在凝露的深山幽谷，
不显露它的行踪，
　　把晶莹的流光传播，
在遮断我们视线的芳草鲜花丛中；　　　　　　　　50

像一朵让自己的绿叶
　　荫蔽着的玫瑰，
遭受到热风的摧残，
　　直到它的芳菲
以过浓的香甜使鲁莽的飞贼沉醉；　　　　　　　　55

---

① 对这一节的理解，可参看雪莱为长诗《阿多尼》所写的前言（被删节段落）。他说他的为人，畏避闻达；他所以写诗，是为了唤起和传达人与人之间的同情。而雪莱的同情首先是对于人类争取从奴役、压迫、贫困和愚昧中解放出来的事业的同情。在《赞智力的美》一诗中，他宣称他"热爱全人类"，其实"全"也不全，因为他反对人类中的暴君、教士及其奴仆。这里，他认为，诗人应该以值得关注而未被留意过的希望和忧虑去唤醒全人类的同情。——译者
② 其实这一节所写的岂止是思春的少女，也完全有理由认为是雪莱的自况。他爱一切美好的事物，美好的事业，他爱"全人类"，但是他的爱在当时甚至不被自己的同胞所理解，而使他感到寂寞和为爱所苦。诗，是他的爱不能自已的流露。——译者

    Sound of vernal showers
      On the twinkling grass,
    Rain-awaken'd flowers,
      All that ever was
60   Joyous, and clear, and fresh, thy music doth surpass.

    Teach us, sprite or bird,
      What sweet thoughts are thine:
    I have never heard
      Praise of love or wine
65   That panted forth a flood of rapture so divine.

    Chorus hymeneal[①],
      Or triumphal chant,
    Match'd with thine would be all[②]
      But an empty vaunt —
70   A thing wherein we feel there is some hidden want.

    What objects are the fountains
      Of thy happy strain?
    What fields, or waves, or mountains?
      What shapes of sky or plain?
75   What love of thine own kind? whal ignorance of pain?

    With thy clear keen joyance

---

① *Chorus hymeneal*: 'marriage song.'

② *all*: sc. all of them; not to be taken with 'but' in the phrase 'all but' (= almost).

晶莹闪烁的草地,
　　春霖洒落的声息,
雨后苏醒的花蕾,
　　称得上明朗、欢悦、
清新的一切,都不及你的音乐。 60

飞禽或是精灵,有什么
　　甜美的思绪在你心头?
我从没有听到过
　　爱情或是醇酒的颂歌
能够迸涌出这样神圣的极乐音流。 65

赞婚的合唱也罢,
　　凯旋的欢歌也罢,
和你的乐声相比,
　　不过是空洞的浮夸,
人们可以觉察,其中总有着贫乏。 70

什么样的物象或事件,
　　是你欢乐乐曲的源泉?
什么田野、波涛、山峦?
　　什么空中陆上的形态?
是你对同类的爱,还是对痛苦的绝缘①? 75

有你明澈强烈的欢快,

---

① 在以上三节中,雪莱认为没有高尚、优美的思想和情操,就不可能创造出美的艺术。因此,赞婚的合唱、凯旋的欢歌,总有着某种贫乏。而对同类的爱和对痛苦的绝缘,却是他所珍视的品质。所谓对痛苦的绝缘,是指遇挫折而不馁,处逆境而泰然,胸怀坦荡,超然于痛苦之外。——译者

    Languor cannot be.
     Shadow of annoyance
      Never came near thee:
80   Thou lovest; but ne'er knew love's sad satiety.

    Waking or asleep
     Thou of death must deem
      Things more true and deep
       Than we mortals dream,
85   Or how could thy notes flow in such a crystal stream?

    We look before and after.
     And pine for what is not:
    Our sincerest laughter
     With some pain is fraught;
90   Our sweetest songs are those that tell of saddest thought.

    Yet if we could scorn
     Hate, and pride, and fear;
    If we were things born
     Not to shed a tear,
95   I know not how thy joy we ever should come near.

    Better than all measures[①]
     Of delightful sound,

---

① *measures*: 'music.'

倦怠永不会出现,
　　　　烦恼的阴影从来
　　　　　近不得你的身边,
你爱,却从不知晓过分充满爱的悲哀①。　　　　　　　　80

　　　是醒来或是睡去②,
　　　　你对死的理解一定比
　　　　我们凡人梦想到的
　　　　　更加深刻真切,否则
你的乐曲音流,怎能像液态的水晶涌泻③?　　　　　　85

　　　我们瞻前顾后,为了
　　　　不存在的事物自扰,
　　　　我们最真挚的笑,
　　　　　也交织着某种苦恼,
我们最美的音乐是最能倾诉哀思的曲调。　　　　　　90

　　　可是,即使我们能摈弃
　　　　憎恨、傲慢和恐惧,
　　　　即使我们生来不会
　　　　　抛洒一滴眼泪,
我也不知,怎能接近于你的欢愉。　　　　　　　　　　95

　　　比一切欢乐的音律
　　　　更加甜蜜美妙,

---

① 雪莱的悲哀常常来源于对正义的事业,对受苦的人类,对他自己所确认的真理,爱得太深、太真、太强烈,而为世俗所不理解。——译者
② 这是指对死的理解,绝不是指云雀的精神状态。有人认为死是从如梦的人生醒来,有人认为死是长眠。——译者
③ 凡人认为死亡是最大的痛苦。雪莱认为,只有参透了生死的真谛,才能超然于痛苦之外,摆脱庸俗的恐惧和忧虑,上升到崇高的精神境界。——译者

>   Better than all treasures
>   That in books are found,
> 100   Thy skill to poet were, thou scorner of the ground!
>
>   Teach me half the gladness
>   That thy brain must know
>   Such harmonious madness
>   From my lips would flow
> 105   The world should listen then, as I am listening now!

P. B. SHELLEY.

$$
\begin{aligned}
&比一切书中的宝库\\
&\qquad 更加丰盛富饶,\\
&这就是鄙弃尘土的你啊,你的艺术技巧①。
\end{aligned}
$$

100

$$
\begin{aligned}
&教给我一半,你的心\\
&\qquad 必定熟知的欢欣,\\
&和谐、炽热的激情\\
&\qquad 就会流出我的双唇,\\
&全世界就会像此刻的我——侧耳倾听。
\end{aligned}
$$

105

江枫　译

编注　本诗作于一八二〇年意大利西部来航(Leghorn),与《解放了的普罗米修斯》同年发表,是雪莱的抒情三部曲之一,其余二首为《西风颂》与《云》。这首《致云雀》是雪莱传世的佳作。雪莱生动地描绘云雀的同时,也以饱满的激情写出了他自己的精神境界、美学理想和艺术抱负。语言简洁、明快、准确且富有音乐性。

---

① "鄙弃尘土",在这里语义双关,既描写云雀从地面一跃而起,升上高空,又表达了诗人对当时流行的诗歌理论、评论以及一般的庸俗反动的政治、社会观念所持的鄙弃态度。——译者

242. THE GREEN LINNET

  Beneath these fruit-tree boughs that shed
  Their snow-white blossoms on my head,
  With brightest sunshine round me spread
   Of spring's unclouded weather,
  In this sequestered nook how sweet
  To sit upon my orchard-seat!
  And birds and flowers once more to greet,
   My last year's friends together.

  One have I marked, the happiest guest
  In all this covert of the blest;
  Hail to Thee, far above the rest
   In joy of voice and pinion!
  Thou, Linnet! in thy green array,
  Presiding Spirit here to-day,
  Dost lead the revels of the May,
   And this is thy dominion.

  While birds, and butterflies, and flowers,
  Make all one band of paramours[①],
  Thou, ranging up and down the bowers,
   Art sole in thy employment;
  A Life, a Presence like the Air,
  Scattering thy gladness without care,

---

① *paramours*: 'lovers,' as in No. 53, l. 16. and No. 62, l. 36.

242. 绿羽的红雀

华兹华斯

果树枝将它雪白的花瓣
洒落在我头上,
周围灿烂的阳光
 铺出一片晴朗无云的春色。
在这宁静的角落里   5
坐在果园的休息椅上多甜蜜!
再一次同我去年的旧友
 雀儿和花朵欢聚。

在这幸福的乐园里,
我看到一个,那最欢乐的宾客: 10
我向你欢呼,
 你比其他宾客都更纵情歌舞!
你,红雀! 你身披绿色的盛装,
你今日头戴桂冠,
这里是你的领地,   15
 你指挥着五月的狂欢。

鸟儿、蝴蝶和鲜花
像一群恋人在欢聚
而你,只有你独自一处
 在林荫中恋人们的闺房里上下飞舞。 20
一个"生命",一个似"大气"的"精灵"
在传播着你的欢乐,无忧无虑,

>
> Too blest with any one to pair,
> > Thyself thy own enjoyment.
>
> Amid yon tuft of hazel trees,
> That twinkle to the gusty breeze,
> Behold him perch'd in ecstasies,
> > Yet seeming still to hover;
> There! where the flutter of his wings
> Upon his back and body flings
> Shadows and sunny glimmerings,
> > That cover him all over.
>
> My dazzled sight he oft deceives —
> A Brother of the dancing leaves[①];
> Then flits, and from the cottage-eaves
> > Pours forth his song in gushes;
> As if by that exulting strain
> He mocked and treated with disdain
> The voiceless Form he chose to feign,
> > While fluttering in the bushes.

W. WORDSWORTH.

---

① *A Brother*: sc. in colour.

谁也比不上你更有福
　　你自己就是你的乐趣。

在阵风中闪烁着的　　　　　　　　　　25
远处的榛树丛中,
看他出神地栖在枝头,
　　然而又似要纵身飞起;
看! 他那拍动着的双翅
在他的背上和身上　　　　　　　　　　30
洒上点点阳光和疏影
　　像披上了一件衣裳①。

他常常弄得我眼花缭乱——
把他也当成摇曳着的绿色叶片;
他忽而纵身飞去,从茅屋檐下　　　　　35
　　传来他阵阵歌声;
当他在树丛中展翅飞舞,
好似要用他那欢快的音韵,
来嘲弄和傲视
　　他所假扮的那无声的形影。　　　　40

　　　　　　　　　　　　　　王家湘　译

编注 本诗作于一八〇三年,发表于一八〇七年《诗集》上,首次发表时其首节与末节与原诗略有不同,原诗首句为"五月又已来临"(The May is come again)。

---

① 华兹华斯后期写了许多写景抒情诗,被誉为"自然诗人"。他的挚友诗人柯勒律治认为在本诗的第四、五节中,他表现出"对自然的最完美忠实的想象和描述"。——译者

243. TO THE CUCKOO

O blithe new-comer! I have heard,
    I hear thee and rejoice:
O Cuckoo! shall I call thee Bird,
    Or but a wandering Voice?

While I am lying on the grass
    Thy twofold shout I hear;
From hill to hill it seems to pass,
    At once far off and near.

Though babbling only to the vale
    Of sunshine and of flowers,
Thou bringest unto me a tale
    Of visionary hours.

Thrice welcome, darling of the Spring!
    Even yet thou art to me
No bird, but an invisible thing,
    A voice, a mystery;

The same whom in my school-boy days
    I listen'd to; that Cry
Which made me look a thousand ways
    In bush, and tree, and sky.

243. 致杜鹃

华兹华斯

啊,欢乐的新客人!我听到了
　　听到了你而鼓舞欢欣:
啊,杜鹃!我该叫你作"鸟儿"吗,
　　还只是一种神奇的声音?

当我躺卧于草丛　　　　　　　　　　5
　　听到你那双叠的叫声;
好像从小峰飞向小峰,
　　时而远去时而靠近。

虽然你只向着那
　　阳光与鲜花的山谷倾诉声声,　　10
你却带给我一支故事
　　那里充满梦幻的时辰①。

三倍地欢迎啊,春天的恋人!
　　你对于我甚至
不是鸟儿,而是神物无影无形,　　15
　　是一种奥秘,是一种声音;

当我在学童时期
　　就谛听过同一个声音:那叫声
曾使我千次寻觅
　　在树丛,在乔木,在天心。　　　20

---

① 这里指童年。——编注者

To seek thee did I often rove
    Through woods and on the green;
And thou wert still a hope, a love;
    Still longed for, never seen.

And I can listen to thee yet;
    Can lie upon the plain
And listen, till I do beget
    That golden time again.

O blesséd Bird! the earth we pace
    Again appears to be
An unsubstantial, fairy place,
    That is fit home for Thee!

W. WORDSWORTH.

为寻找你我曾经常漫游
　　穿过重重树林,踏过芳草青青;
而你仍然是一个希望,一缕柔情,
　　依然渴望,而从未见过的身影。

但我还是能把你谛听;　　　　　　　　　　25
　　能躺在旷野上
谛听着,直到我真的感到
　　那黄金的时光再临①。

啊赐福的"鸟儿"! 我们脚踩的大地
　　仿佛又变成一片梦境　　　　　　　30
像仙境一样神奇的家园,
　　正好让你来安身!

邹荻帆　邹海仑　译

编注《致杜鹃》写于一八〇二年三月的一个早晨。此时华兹华斯已定居湖区。诗人并不是因为有杜鹃啼声,触景生情而动笔,而是因为诗人儿时听到杜鹃鸣叫,曾四处追踪,如今仰卧在芳草地里回忆遐想,似乎又返回金色时代,随着神秘的鸟语,再度踏入幻想境界。

---

① 这里也指童年。——编注者

244. ODE TO A NIGHTINGALE

My heart aches, and a drowsy numbness pains
    My sense, as though of hemlock I had drunk,
Or emptied some dull opiate to the drains①
    One minute past, and Lethe-wards had sunk:
'Tis not through envy of thy happy lot,
    But being too happy in thine happiness, —
        That thou, light-wingéd Dryad of the trees②,
            In some melodious plot
    Of beechen green, and shadows numberless,
        Singest of summer in full-throated ease.

O for a draught of vintage! that hath been
    Cool'd a long age in the deep-delvéd earth,
Tasting of Flora and the country green,
    Dance, and Provencal song, and sunburnt mirth!
O for a beaker full of the warm South,
    Full of the true, the blushful Hippocrene,
        With beaded bubbles winking at the brim,
            And purple-stainéd mouth③;

---

① *to the drains*: 'to the dregs.'
② *That*: i.e. in the thought that. *Dryad*: 'Wood-nymph.'
③ *mouth*: the lip of the beaker.

244. 夜莺颂

济慈

我的心儿痛,瞌睡麻木折磨
　　我的感官,我仿佛饮了毒芹,
也像是刚才饮尽了沉郁的麻醉剂,
　　全身只向迷魂河下沉①:
这并非妒忌你的幸运,　　　　　　　　　　　　5
　　而是你的幸福使我太欢欣,——
　　　因你呀,轻翼的树神,
　　　　在满长绿梽,
　　音韵悦耳、无数阴影的地方,
　　　　引吭高歌,赞颂美夏。　　　　　　　　10

哦,但愿有口葡萄美酒!冷藏
　　在幽深的地窖多年,
使人领略到花香和绿野风光②,
　　领略到跳舞,歌唱,和阳光的欢乐③!
哦,但愿有一杯满溢着温暖的南方,　　　　　　15
　　满溢着真正的,殷红的灵泉④,
　　　杯沿闪烁着连珠的泡沫,
　　　　使嘴上染着紫色;

---

① 希腊神话中地府之忘川。——编注者
② 此处的"花香",原文是"福罗拉"(Flora),即罗马神话中的女花神和花园女神。——编注者
③ 此处的"歌唱"原文是"普鲁旺斯的歌曲"(Provencal song)。普鲁旺斯,十一到十三世纪间在法国南部的骑士抒情诗的发源地。——编注者
④ "灵泉"(Hippocrene),通译为"希波克瑞涅",希腊神话中的灵感之泉,喝了泉中的水,诗人能激发出写诗的灵感。——编注者

    That I might drink, and leave the world unseen,
     And with thee fade away into the forest dim:

   Fade far away, dissolve, and quite forget
    What thou among the leaves hast never known,
   The weariness, the fever, and the fret
    Here, where men sit and hear each other groan;
   Where palsy shakes a few, sad, last grey hairs,
    Where youth grows pale, and spectre-thin, and dies;
    Where but to think is to be full of sorrow
     And leaden-eyed despairs;
   Where Beauty cannot keep her lustrous eyes,
    Or new Love pine at them beyond to-morrow.

   Away! away! for I will fly to thee,
    Not charioted by Bacchus and his pards,
   But on the viewless wings of Poesy[①],
    Though the dull brain perplexes and retards:
   Already with thee! tender is the night,
    And haply the Queen-Moon is on her throne,
     Cluster'd around by all her starry Fays;
     But here there is no light,
   Save what from heaven is with the breezes blown
    Through verdurous glooms and winding mossy ways.

   I cannot see what flowers are at my feet,
    Nor what soft incense hangs upon the boughs,
   But, in embalméd darkness, guess each sweet
    Wherewith the seasonable month endows

---

① *viewless*: 'invisible.'

我饮了就可以悄然离开人世,
　　偕你归隐到阴郁的森林。　　　　　　　　　　20

远远地隐没,消散,完全忘却
　　你在树叶间从未知道的事情,
忘却疲倦,狂热,和恼恨,
　　人们坐在这里听着彼此的悲叹;
瘫痪的老人抖落几根愁切的仅存的白发,　　　　25
　　年轻人变得苍白,消瘦死亡[①];
只要一想,心中忧伤满怀,
　　眼睛疲乏,万念俱灰;
"美"不能使她眼睛永远明亮,
　　新生的"爱"过不了明天就憔悴。　　　　　30

去呀!去呀!我要飞往你处,
　　不乘酒神和他群豹所驾的仙车,
却靠诗神无形的翼翅,
　　虽然迟钝的头脑混乱而呆滞:
呀,早已和你在一起!夜无限温柔,　　　　　　35
　　月后或已登上她的宝座,
　　周围聚着她星星的妖精:
　　　　但此地并无光芒,
除了微风从苍穹吹来的弱光,
　　穿过青翠的黄昏和苔藓的曲径。　　　　　40

我看不见脚下是什么花朵,
　　也不见萦绕树枝的是什么香气,
但在馨香的昏暗里却猜得到
　　当令的月份将以什么芳香

[①] 此处指诗人的弟弟和自己。——编注者

45   The grass, the thicket, and the fruit-tree wild;
    White hawthorn, and the pastoral eglantine①;
     Fast-fading violets cover'd up in leaves;
      And mid-May's eldest child
    The coming musk-rose, full of dewy wine,
50   The murmurous haunt of flies on summer eves.

   Darkling I listen; and, for many a time②
    I have been half in love with easeful Death,
   Call'd him soft names in many a muséd rhyme③,
    To take into the air my quiet breath;
55   Now more than ever seems it rich to die,
    To cease upon the midnight with no pain,
     While thou art pouring forth thy soul abroad
      In such an ecstasy!
    Still wouldst thou sing, and I have ears in vain —
60   To thy high requiem become a sod④.

   Thou wast not born for death, immortal Bird!
    No hungry generations tread thee down;
   The voice I hear this passing night was heard
    In ancient days by emperor and clown⑤:
65   Perhaps the self-same song that found a path
    Through the sad heart of Ruth, when, sick for home,
     She stood in tears amid the alien corn;

---

① *eglantine*: 'sweet brier.'
② *Darkling*: 'in the darkness.' *for many a time*: this sentence, to the end of l. 54, is parenthetical, explaining why 'it seems rich to die' now.
③ *muséd rhyme*: 'long thought-on verse.'
④ *requiem*: properly a mass for the repose of the dead.
⑤ *clown*: 'rustic.'

给与那碧草,丛林,野果树; 45
　　那白色的山楂,牧野的蔷薇,
　　　　那盖在树叶里的易雕的紫罗兰;
　　　　　　和五月中旬的大孩子①,
那沾着露浆的将放的麝香玫瑰,
　　夏夜嗡嗡青蝇出没之所。 50

我暗中倾听;唉,有好多次
　　我差点儿爱上了安闲的死神,
我在构诗时多次轻声唤他的名字,
　　要他把我宁静的气息带进空中;
如今死亡要比以往更壮丽, 55
　　在半夜毫无痛苦地死去,
　　　　你却如此狂喜地尽情
　　　　　　倾吐你的肺腑之言!
　　　　你将唱下去,我的耳朵却不管用
听不到你的安魂曲像泥块一样。 60

你并不是为死而生的,不朽的神鸟!
　　饥馑的年代不会糟蹋你;
我在今晚听见的歌声
　　古代的君王乡民也听到过;
也许就是打动露丝悲哀的心房② 65
　　那一首歌,那会儿她怀念故乡,
　　　　站在异国的麦田中泪滴千行;

---

① 指最早盛开的花草。——编注者
② 露丝(Ruth),亦译路得,据《圣经·旧约》载,她丈夫死后,她随婆母返回迦南。——编注者

>   The same that oft-times hath
>   Charm'd magic casements, opening on the foam
>   Of perilous seas, in faery lands forlorn.

> Forlorn! the very word is like a bell
>   To toll me back from thee to my sole self!
> Adieu! the fancy cannot cheat so well
>   As she is famed to do, deceiving elf.
> Adieu! adieu! thy plaintive anthem fades
>   Past the near meadows, over the still stream,
>   Up the hill-side; and now' tis buried deep
>   In the next valley-glades:
> Was it a vision, or a waking dream?
>   Fled is that music: — do I wake or sleep?

J. KEATS.

  也许就是在那孤寂的仙境
   经常朝着危急的海浪而开的
    那个着了魔法似的窗格①。   70

  孤寂!这两字犹如一声晨钟
   把我敲回到自己立脚的地方!
  再会哟!幻想这欺人的妖精
   不能那么顺利地耍弄她那闻名的绝技。
  再会!再会!你凄切的颂歌   75
   消失在近处的草原,静寂的河川,
    飞至山旁;如今深深埋葬
     在邻谷的林地;
   这是个幻景,还是白昼的梦?
    歌声飞逝了:——我醒呢还是睡?   80

朱维基 译

编注 济慈在诗里表达出现实是无情的,人生是短暂的,但夜莺的歌声可以带来永恒的美与永恒的欢乐,艺术是可以长存的。

---

① 中世纪传记文学中常有公主、小姐被囚禁于城堡,好似窗格也着了魔法。——译者

245. UPON WESTMINSTER BRIDGE, SEPT. 3, 1802

Earth has not anything to show more fair:
  Dull would he be of soul who could pass by
  A sight so touching in its majesty:
This City now doth like a garment wear
The beauty of the morning; silent, bare,
  Ships, towers, domes, theatres, and temples lie
  Open unto the fields, and to the sky①,
All bright and glittering in the smokeless air.

Never did sun more beautifully steep②
  In his first splendour valley, rock, or hill,
Ne'er saw I, never felt, a calm so deep!

The river glideth at his own sweet will:
Dear God! the very houses seem asleep;
  And all that mighty heart is lying still!

W. WORDSWORTH.

---

① *Open unto the fields*: *i.e.* they were visible from the outskirts of the city in the yet unpolluted air of the early morning.
② *steep*: 'bathe.'

245. 在西敏寺桥上①

华兹华斯

大地不会显出更美的气象:
　　只有灵魂迟钝的人才看不见
　　这么庄严动人的伟大场面:
这座城池如今把美丽的晨光

当衣服穿上了:宁静而又开敞, 5
　　教堂,剧场,船舶,穹楼和塔尖
　　全都袒卧在大地上,面对着苍天,
沐浴在无烟的清气中,灿烂辉煌。

初阳的光辉浸润着岩谷,峰顶,
　　也决不比这更美;我也从没 10
　　看见或感到过这么深沉的安宁!

河水顺着自由意志向前推:
　　亲爱的上帝! 屋枥似都未醒;
　　这颗伟大的心脏呵,正在沉睡!

屠岸　译

---

① 这首诗据说是诗人一八〇三年九月三日赴法国时"在马车顶上"写下的。西敏寺桥是伦敦的一座大桥。第四行"这座城池"和第十四行"伟大的心脏"都是指伦敦。——译者

246. OZYMANDIAS OF EGYPT

    I met a traveller from an antique land[①]
        Who said: Two vast and trunkless legs of stone
    Stand in the desert. Near them on the sand,
        Half sunk, a shatter'd visage lies, whose frown

5   And wrinkled lip and sneer of cold command
            Tell that its sculptor well those passions read
        Which yet survive, stamp'd on these lifeless things,
            The hand that mock'd them and the heart that fed[②];

        And on the pedestal these words appear:
10   'My name is Ozymandias, king of kings;
          Look on my works, ye Mighty, and despair!'

    Nothing beside remains. Round the decay
        Of that colossal wreck, boundless and bare
    The lone and level sands stretch far away.

                              P. B. SHELLEY.

[①] *an antique land*: 'a land famous in ancient history,' here Egypt.
[②] *survive ... The hand*, etc.: 'outlive the hand of the sculptor and the heart of the king.' *mock'd*: 'copied.'

246. 奥西曼提斯[①]

雪莱

客自海外归,曾见沙漠古国
　有石像半毁,唯余巨腿
蹲立沙砾间。像头旁落,
　　半遭沙埋,但人面依然可畏,

那冷笑,那发号施令的高傲, 5
　足见雕匠看透了主人的心,
才把那石头刻得神情唯肖,
　而刻像的手和像主的心

早成灰烬。像座上大字在目:
"吾乃万王之王是也, 10
　盖世功业,敢叫天公折服!"

此外无一物,但见废墟周围,
　寂寞平沙空莽莽,
伸向荒凉的四方。

　　　　　　　　　　王佐良　译

编注　本诗由利·亨特(Leigh Hunt)发表在《探究者》(*Examiner*)一八一八年一月号。奥西曼提斯在平沙无垠的大漠之上树起了庞大的狮身人首像来纪念自己的威权和业绩。然而雪莱却描写他的所谓盖世功业早为时间所吞没,倒是迫于他的淫威不得不为他刻像的匠人的艺术传了下来。一切写得很具体,没有一句评论而评论自在,而且有对照和讽刺。本诗反暴政的主题是十分明显的。

[①] 奥西曼提斯即公元前十三世纪的埃及王雷米西斯二世。他的坟墓在底比斯地方,形如一庞大的狮身人首像。——译者

247. COMPOSED AT NEIDPATH CASTLE, THE PROPERTY OF LORD QUEENSBERRY, 1803

Degenerate Douglas! O the unworthy lord[1]!
   Whom mere despite of heart could so far please
   And love of havoc, (for with such disease
Fame taxes him,) that he could send forth word

To level with the dust a noble horde,
   A brotherhood of venerable trees,
   Leaving an ancient dome, and towers like these,
Beggar'd and outraged! — Many hearts deplored

The fate of those old trees; and oft with pain
   The traveller at this day will stop and gaze
      On wrongs, which Nature scarcely seems to heed:

For sheltered places, bosoms, nooks, and bays,
   And the pure mountains, and the gentle Tweed,
And the green silent pastures, yet remain.

                      W. WORDSWORTH.

---

[1] In a copy of the sonnet which Wordsworth sent to Scott the month after it was written the first line runs 'Now, as I live, I pity that great Lord.' Scott greatly admired the sonnet: 'few lines,' says Lockhart, 'were more frequently in his mouth.'

247. 一八〇三年作于纳德巴斯堡，该堡为昆斯伯里勋爵的领地①

华兹华斯

卑鄙的道格拉斯！啊，堕落的勋爵！
只有他才会昧着良知喜爱浩劫，
　　（他也因此声名狼藉），
居然说出这样的话语：

荡平宏伟的建筑群
　　把古树古宅化为烟尘，
　　这般凄凉，这般疮痍！
只余下断壁颓墙，凋然塔影。

多少人叹息古树的命运，
　　过往游子对这桩罪行痛心疾首
　　　造物者也难得投之一瞥。

然而幽谷、港湾和树林依然留存天地，
　　群山依然苍翠，特威德河依然款款流淌，
静谧的牧场依然芳草萋萋。

叶上威　译

编注　本诗作于一八〇三年九月十八日，发表于一八〇七年《诗集》上，标题是《作于某古堡》(Composed at — Castle)。关于纳德巴斯，参见卷四第196首《纳德巴斯的少女》脚注。

---

① 昆斯伯里勋爵，指威廉·道格拉斯(1724—1810)，昆斯伯里地方的第四代公爵（常被错唤为"勋爵"）。他积极赞助修建赛马场、拳击场，据说，还卖掉自己的领地为私生女儿置办嫁妆。——编注者

248. ADMONITION TO A TRAVELLER

Yes, there is holy pleasure in thine eye!
   The lovely cottage in the guardian nook
   Hath stirr'd thee deeply; with its own dear brook,
Its own small pasture, almost its own sky!

But covet not the abode; forbear to sigh
   As many do, repining while they look;
   Intruders who would tear from Nature's book
This precious leaf with harsh impiety:

Think what the home must be if it were thine,
   Even thine, though few thy wants! — Roof, window, door,
   The very flowers are sacred to the Poor,

The roses to the porch which they entwine:
   Yea, all that now enchants thee, from the day
On which it should be touch'd, would melt away[1]!

W. WORDSWORTH.

---

[1] This line in the original edition and the editions of 1815 and 1827 contains a foot too many, reading 'melt and melt away'; this is a remarkable anomaly to find in a sonnet.

248. 诫游子

华兹华斯

是的,你眼中闪着这般狂喜!
　那幽谧可爱的茅舍,
　　舍旁那淙淙的溪水,青青的牧草地,
那茅舍顶上的蓝天,都深深激荡着你。

可是别垂涎这里,仰住你的赞叹, 　　　　　　5
　别像庸人一看见美就羡而生忌,
　　只有盗贼才会从大自然的画册中
把精美的画页粗暴地撕去:

请想想,要是这片宝地属于你的家,
　其实你要的并不多——不过房顶、窗门, 　　10
　　门廊前有玫瑰花藤缠绕,

那玫瑰花是献给穷人的礼品,
　啊,一切现在令你神往的景物,
　　一旦伸手触及,顷刻间就会融化消隐。

叶上威　译

编注　本诗发表于一八〇七年《诗集》上,标题是《儆戒》(Admonition),重版于一八四九至一八五〇年间,第一行为"你最好停下来——张大你明亮的眼睛(Well mayst thou halt — and gaze with brightening eye!),后来的重印本进行了各种更动,除了第一行外,《金库》取最后一种版本。原编者认为华兹华斯原本最后一行音节太多,如"melt and melt away",有损于十四行诗的节奏。本诗的主题为超脱与退隐。

249. TO THE HIGHLAND GIRL OF INVERSNEYDE

Sweet Highland Girl, a very shower
Of beauty is thy earthly dower!
Twice seven consenting years have shed①
Their utmost bounty on thy head:
And these grey rocks; that household lawn②;
Those trees — a veil just half withdrawn;
This fall of water that doth make
A murmur near the silent lake;
This little bay; a quiet road
That holds in shelter thy abode;
In truth together do ye seem
Like something fashion'd in a dream;
Such forms as from their covert peep
When earthly cares are laid asleep!
But O fair Creature! in the light,
Of common day, so heavenly bright,
I bless Thee, Vision as thou art,
I bless thee with a human heart:
God shield thee to thy latest years!
Thee, neither know I, nor thy peers;
And yet my eyes are fill'd with tears.

---

① *consenting*: 'uniting together to achieve their end.'
② *And these grey rocks*: this and the following four lines are co-ordinate with 'years' (l. 3); all the girl's surroundings had conspired to make her beautiful.

249. 献给茵沃斯奈德的苏格兰高原姑娘①

华兹华斯

可爱的苏格兰高原姑娘,
您长着一副天生丽人的模样!
两个协力的七载,
把最珍贵的礼物献上:
这儿灰色怪石嶙峋,那儿是庭院草坪;   5
那些树木——像是半起半落的幕布;
瀑布给邻近静谧的湖畔
带来淙淙的响声;
小小的湖湾;恬静的道路,
庇护着你的家园;   10
你的全貌
真像梦中的情景;
当世上的忧虑正在酣睡,
这些景物悄悄地露头!
呵,美丽的人儿!在平凡的岁月,   15
您超群出众,——我祝福您
具有天仙模样,我祝愿你
具有凡人的心肠:
愿上帝永远庇护您!
我不认识你,也不认识您的伙伴;   20
然而,我眼睛里却泪水涟涟。

---

① 茵沃斯奈德(Inversneyde),位于苏格兰中西部罗蒙湖(Loch Lomond)侧。——编注者

With earnest feeling I shall pray
For thee when I am far away;
For never saw I mien or face
In which more plainly I could trace
Benignity and home-bred sense
Ripening in perfect innocence.
Here scattered like a random seed,
Remote from men, Thou dost not need
The embarrassed look of shy distress,
And maidenly shamefacedness:
Thou wear'st upon thy forehead clear
The freedom of a mountaineer:
A face with gladness overspread;
Soft smiles, by human kindness bred;
And seemliness complete, that sways
Thy courtesies, about thee plays;
With no restraint, but such as springs
From quick and eager visitings
Of thoughts that lie beyond the reach
Of thy few words of English speech:
A bondage sweetly brook'd, a strife①
That gives thy gestures grace and life!
So have I, not unmoved in mind,
Seen birds of tempest-loving kind
Thus beating up against the wind.

What hand but would a garland cull

---

① *A bondage sweetly brook'd*: *i. e.* she did not, like so many English people when travelling abroad, lose her temper because she could not express herself in a foreign language.

我即使到了遥远的地方，
也要热情地替你祈祷；
我从未见过什么风采容貌
比从你那儿更加清晰地看到 25
家乡亲切的情意，
在无邪的思念中成熟。
你像是一粒偶然撒在这儿的种子，
远离尘嚣，
用不着胆怯， 30
那是少女才有的羞涩：
你额上显示着
山里人的无拘无束；
脸庞透露出一片欢欣；
天性带来温柔的微笑， 35
无疵可击；
在游乐中
彬彬有礼；
无须谨小慎微，但聪颖的思维
连你所有的英语词汇 40
也无法表达出原有的智慧；
受局限也不生气，
努力保持身体的优美与活力。
我看到了喜爱暴风骤雨的鸟儿
在展翅飞翔，抗着逆风， 45
我不能无动于衷。

你长得这样美丽，

For thee who art so beautiful?
O happy pleasure! here to dwell
Beside thee in some heathy dell;
Adopt your homely ways and dress①,
A shepherd, thou a shepherdess!
But I could frame a wish for thee
More like a grave reality:
Thou art to me but as a wave
Of the wild sea; and I would have
Some claim upon thee, if I could,
Though but of common neighbourhood,
What joy to hear thee, and to see!
Thy elder brother I would be,
Thy father — anything to thee!

Now thanks to Heaven! that of its grace
Hath led me to this lonely place.
Joy have I had; and going hence
I bear away my recompense.
In spots like these it is we prize
Our memory, feel that she hath eyes;
Then why should I be loth to stir?
I feel this place was made for her;
To give new pleasure like the past,
Continued long as life shall last.
Nor am I loth, though pleased at heart②,
Sweet Highland Girl! from thee to part;
For I, methinks, till I grow old,

---

① *your homely ways and dress*: 'the habits and garb of your countrymen.'
② *though pleased at heart*: sc. to have seen her.

谁个不愿为你把花儿采集?
幸福啊!能和你在一起
住在这荆棘的山谷; 50
随你家乡的风俗,穿你家乡的裙衣,
做一个放牛娃,你就是牧羊女!
而我对你奉献的祝愿
更具有严肃的现实意义:
你在我心中 55
像是咆哮大海里的一朵浪花
尽管我只是你普通的邻家,
我愿能对你提出请求,
听到你、见到你就是狂喜!
我愿做你的哥哥, 60
你的父亲——做你的什么都可以!

现在得感谢上苍!它的恩赐
把我引到这个荒凉的地方。
我心里充满欢畅,纵使离去
也已得到报偿。 65
这个地方是对我们记忆的嘉奖,
感到苍天有眼:
为啥我不愿搅动这宁静?
我认为这是为她而安排的地方。
像过去那样会赐与新的欢乐, 70
直到那生命的最后一息。
虽然我喜在心里,可爱的高原姑娘呀!
我并非不愿离开你;
因为当我秋霜暮年,

>   As fair before me shall behold
>   As I do now, the cabin small,
>   The lake, the bay, the waterfall;
>   And Thee, the Spirit of them all!

W. WORDSWORTH.

在我面前出现的
将是我现在看见的姑娘,
这小屋、这湖水、这湖湾和瀑布;
还有你,正是它们一切之中的精灵!

郭继德　译

编注　一八〇三年华兹华斯游苏格兰,写了《割麦女》(The Reaper)与本首诗,倾注了他对高原纯朴的女子的真挚感情,歌颂朴实的乡里人是浪漫主义诗歌的重要题材(参见本卷第 250 首)。

250. THE REAPER

    Behold her, single in the field,
        Yon solitary Highland Lass!
    Reaping and singing by herself;
        Stop here, or gently pass!
    Alone she cuts and binds the grain
    And sings a melancholy strain;
    O listen! for the vale profound
    Is overflowing with the sound.

    No nightingale did ever chant
        More welcome notes to weary bands
    Of travellers in some shady haunt,
        Among Arabian sands:
    A voice so thrilling ne'er was heard
    In spring-time from the cuckoo-bird,
    Breaking the silence of the seas
    Among the farthest Hebrides.

    Will no one tell me what she sings?
        Perhaps the plaintive numbers flow
    For old, unhappy, far-off things,
        And battles long ago:
    Or is it some more humble lay,
    Familiar matter of to-day?

250. 割麦女

华兹华斯

看她,在田里独自一个,
　　那个苏格兰高原的少女!
独自在收割,独自在唱歌;
　　停住吧,或者悄悄走过去!
她独自割麦,又把它捆好,　　　　　　　　　　5
唱着一支忧郁的曲调;
听啊! 整个深邃的谷地
都有这一片歌声在洋溢。

从没有夜莺能够唱出
　　更美的音调来欢迎结队商,　　　　　　　10
疲倦了,到一个荫凉的去处
　　就在阿拉伯沙漠的中央:
杜鹃鸟在春天叫得多动人,
也没有这样子荡人心魂,
尽管它惊破了远海的静悄,　　　　　　　　15
响彻了赫伯里底斯群岛①。

她唱的是什么,可有谁说得清?
　　哀怨的曲调里也许在流传
古老,不幸,悠久的事情,
　　还有长远以前的征战;　　　　　　　　20
或者她唱的并不特殊,
只是今日的家常事故?

---

① 赫伯里底斯群岛(Hebrides)在苏格兰西北的大西洋中。——译者

Some natural sorrow, loss, or pain,
That has been, and may be again?

25　　Whate'er the theme, the maiden sang
　　　　As if her song could have no ending;
　　　I saw her singing at her work,
　　　　And o'er the sickle bending;
　　　I listen'd, motionless and still①;
30　　And, as I mounted up the hill,
　　　The music in my heart I bore,
　　　Long after it was heard no more.

　　　　　　　　　　　　W. WORDSWORTH.

---

① *motionless and still*: these two words mean the same things.

那些天然的衷忧、哀痛,
有过的,以后还会有的种种?

不管她唱的是什么题目, 25
　她的歌好像会没完没了;
我看见她边唱边干活,
　弯着腰,挥动她的镰刀——
我一动也不动,听了许久;
后来,当我上山的时候, 30
我把歌声还记在心上,
虽然早已听不见声响。

卞之琳　译

编注 本诗作于一八〇三至一八〇五年间,与前一诗发表在同一书上,标题为《孤独的割麦女》(The Solitary Reaper)。此诗是华兹华斯作为"湖畔派"诗人的代表作。

251. THE REVERIE OF POOR SUSAN

At the corner of Wood Street, when daylight appears,
Hangs a Thrush that sings loud, it has sung for three years:
Poor Susan has pass'd by the spot, and has heard
In the silence of morning the song of the bird.

5   'Tis a note of enchantment; what ails her? She sees
A mountain ascending, a vision of trees;
Bright volumes of vapour through Lothbury glide,
And a river flows on through the vale of Cheapside.

Green pastures she views in the midst of the dale,
10   Down which she so often has tripp'd with her pail;
And a single small cottage, a nest like a dove's,
The one only dwelling on earth that she loves.

She looks, and her heart is in heaven: but they fade,
The mist and the river, the hill and the shade;
15   The stream will not flow, and the hill will not rise,
And the colours have all pass'd away from her eyes!

                                W. WORDSWORTH.

251. 苏珊的冥想

华兹华斯

树林街拐角上挂一只画眉,天一亮①,
就放声高唱,唱过了三年的时光:
可怜的苏珊经过这一个地点,
早晨的静悄里听见了那只鸟啼啭。

这是个迷人的曲调,她为何痛苦? 5
她看见一座山高耸,隐现着许多树,
洛斯布里有团团白云雾从中间飘过,
契普赛德幽谷里流过一长条小河。

她看见谷地中央有青青的牧场,
她常常提桶下坡去,一边跑一边晃, 10
一座单独的小房子,像一个鸽子窝,
她在世界上唯一心爱的住屋。

她看得心欢:可是全不见踪影——
云雾、小河、漫山覆盖的树荫,
小溪不肯流,高山也不肯耸立, 15
什么色彩都从她眼睛里消失。

卞之琳 译

编注 本诗作于一七九一年,为一八〇一年《抒情歌谣曲集》增订版所新收的若干首之一。

---

① 树林街(Wood Street)、洛斯布里(Lothbury)、契普赛德(Cheapside)都是地名,原在伦敦闹市中心。——译者

252. TO A LADY, WITH A GUITAR

Ariel to Miranda: — Take
This slave of Music, for the sake
Of him who is the slave of thee;
And teach it all the harmony
In which thou canst, and only thou,
Make the delighted spirit glow,
Till joy denies itself again
And, too intense, is turn'd to pain.
For by permission and command
Of thine own Prince Ferdinand,
Poor Ariel sends this silent token
Of more than ever can be spoken;
Your guardian spirit, Ariel, who
From life to life must still pursue
Your happiness; for thus alone
Can Ariel ever find his own.
From Prospero's enchanted cell,
As the mighty verses tell,
To the throne of Naples he
Lit you o'er the trackless sea,
Flitting on, your prow before,
Like a living meteor.
When you die, the silent Moon
In her interlunar swoon[1]

---

[1] *interlunar swoon*: the period when the moon is invisible.

252. 致某夫人——随赠六弦琴一架

雪莱

爱丽儿致米兰达:
请把这音乐的仆人收下,
看在送它的是你的仆人;
请教它你会的全部和声,
不是任何别人,只有你 5
才能使欢乐之神奏起,
乐极了又自悲身世,
将喜歌变成了哀诗。
得到你的王子费迪南的恩准,
并奉了他亲自的命令, 10
可怜的爱丽儿献这无言的薄礼,
它代表有言也说不出的心意。
他本是你的护神,几番死生,
一直把你的快乐追寻,
只在你寻到了幸福, 15
爱丽儿也才能有福。
像大手笔的诗句所吟,
他从普洛斯披罗的仙洞出行,
引你渡过海洋的无路之路,
走向那不勒斯的王座, 20
他腾空飞在你的船前,
像一颗流星活现。
你死了,月亮顿时无光,
昏倒在阴暗的地方,

Is not sadder in her cell
Than deserted Ariel.
When you live again on earth,
Like an unseen star of birth
Ariel guides you o'er the sea
Of life from your nativity.
Many changes have been run
Since Ferdinand and you begun
Your course of love, and Ariel still
Has tracked your steps and served your will.
Now in humbler, happier lot,
This is all remember'd not;
And now, alas! the poor sprite is
Imprisoned for some fault of his
In a body like a grave; —
From you he only dares to crave,
For his service and his sorrow,
A smile to-day, a song to-morrow.

The artist who this idol wrought[①]
To echo all harmonious thought,
Felled a tree, while on the steep
The woods were in their winter sleep,
Rocked in that repose divine
On the wind-swept Apennine;
And dreaming, some of Autumn past,
And some of Spring approaching fast,
And some of April buds and showers,

---

① *idol*: *i.e.* the guitar; termed an idol as being the image wherein the spirit of music resided; see below, l. 81.

但不及爱丽儿心里凄凉, 25
由于不见了你这姑娘。
等你重新活在人世,
爱丽儿又来服侍,
像隐形的生辰之星,
引你穿越生命的海程。 30
自从你和王子相爱,
变化不断而来,
只有爱丽儿追踪你的脚步,
听你随意吩咐,
如今他卑微然而快乐, 35
往事也就全都忘却。
不幸他已不是无拘的精灵,
由于犯错而寄托肉身,
这一下犹如进了坟墓,
不得不向你求助: 40
为了报他的忠心,解他的忧郁,
能否今天赐一笑,明天歌一曲?

乐器师精心做了此琴,
弹奏一切和谐的乐音,
他为此伐了一树, 45
树在阿平宁山的风雪高处,
那里森林摇晃着进入冬眠,
众树都睡得神仙一般香甜,
有的梦见昨天的秋阳,
有的梦见快来的春光, 50
有的梦缀满四月的花朵和雨点,

And some of songs in July bowers,
And all of love; and so this tree, —
O that such our death may be! —
55   Died in sleep, and felt no pain,
To live in happier form again:
From which, beneath Heaven's fairest star①,
The artist wrought this loved Guitar;
And taught it justly to reply
60   To all who question skilfully
In language gentle as thine own;
Whispering in enamoured tone
Sweet oracles of woods and dells,
And summer winds in sylvan cells;
65   — For it had learnt all harmonies
Of the plains and of the skies,
Of the forests and the mountains;
And the many-voicéd fountains;
The clearest echoes of the hills,
70   The softest notes of falling rills,
The melodies of birds and bees,
The murmuring of summer seas,
And pattering rain, and breathing dew
And airs of evening; and it knew
75   That seldom-heard mysterious sound
Which, driven on its diurnal round,
As it floats through boundless day,
Our world enkindles on its way:
— All this it knows, but will not tell

---

① *beneath Heaven's fairest star*: *i.e.* in an hour most fortunate for itself.

有的梦唱出了七月的闺怨,
所有的梦都梦见了爱神,
这时候死去该有何等风情!
树儿梦中被伐,毫不觉痛, 55
现在以更美的形体重生。
乐器师在天堂最美的星下,
雕制了这架心爱的吉他,
教它能对所有的知音,
发出相应的歌声。 60
它能温柔如你的话语,
用多情的声调吐露:
深山老林藏智慧,
幽谷清风送安慰。
它学到了所有乐曲, 65
不论来自天空或泥土,
来自森林或山岗,
还有喷泉的流响,
山峰的轻脆回声,
溪水的柔和清音, 70
鸟和蜜蜂的旋律,
夏天海洋的低语,
雨的拍打和露水的呼吸,
以及黄昏的歌;它熟悉
那难得听到的神秘声音① 75
在做着日常的巡行,
飘过无边际的白天,
唤起我们世界处处的火焰。
这一切它懂得而不透露,

---

① 古希腊哲学家毕达哥拉斯认为,地球在运行时会发出自有和谐的声音,所谓"神秘的声音"即指此。——编注者

	To those who cannot question well
80	The Spirit that inhabits it;
	It talks according to the wit
	Of its companions; and no more
	Is heard than has been felt before
85	By those who tempt it to betray
	These secrets of an elder day.
	But, sweetly as its answers will
	Flatter hands of perfect skill,
	It keeps its highest holiest tone
90	For our belovéd friend alone.

P. B. SHELLEY.

除非来人能够以情相诉, 80
触动它身上的音乐之神,
问得好也答得灵,
感得深才奏得妙,
除非早有旧恨待表,
休想从它身上探询 85
昔日的秘密神韵!
遇有高手来弹弄,
琴儿才放声而歌颂,
但把最高最神圣的绝唱,
留给我们亲爱的琪恩独赏①。 90

王佐良　译

编注　雪莱死后十年,米德温(Medwin)将本诗发表在《雅典诗集》(*Athenœum*),标题为《致琪恩——随赠六弦琴一架》(With a Guitar, to Jane)。《金库》原编者把标题改为《致某夫人——随赠六弦琴一架》(To a Lady, with a Guitar),原诗中最后一行的宾语把琪恩换为朋友大概也作了相应改动。

---

① 此诗是雪莱写给琪恩·威廉斯的。琪恩的丈夫爱德华·威廉斯是雪莱在意大利时期的好友,后来雪莱航海遇难,爱德华同行,也葬身鱼腹。对一个朋友之妻表达爱慕之情,是颇难下笔的,雪莱乃运用了一种文学手法,即假托琪恩为莎士比亚——诗中的"大手笔"即指他——的剧本《暴风雨》中的女主角米兰达,将爱德华比作同米兰达结婚的费迪南王子,而自比为受米兰达之父普洛斯披罗差遣的小精灵爱丽儿,表明他如何长期默默地追求着米兰达,一直暗中保护着她,而今日赠琴,所求无非是她能对他"今天赐一笑,明天歌一曲"而已。由于用了上述文学手法,此诗写得风流蕴藉,吐露了爱情而又不过分,甚为得体,所以有人说雪莱这位浪漫派并不老是捧出赤裸裸的感情,而是也能写得很文明的。——译者

253. THE DAFFODILS

I wandered lonely as a cloud
   That floats on high o'er vales and hills,
When all at once I saw a crowd,
   A host, of golden daffodils,
Beside the lake, beneath the trees,
Fluttering and dancing in the breeze.

Continuous as the stars that shine
   And twinkle on the milky way,
They stretched in never-ending line
   Along the margin of a bay:
Ten thousand saw I at a glance
Tossing their heads in sprightly dance[①].

The waves beside them danced, but they
   Out-did the sparkling waves in glee:
A Poet could not but be gay
   In such a jocund company!
I gazed — and gazed — but little thought
What wealth the show to me had brought:

For oft, when on my couch I lie
   In vacant or in pensive mood,
They flash upon that inward eye

---

① The second stanza is not in the original edition.

253. 水仙

华兹华斯

我独自漫游像一朵云
　　在天空浮过谷和山，
蓦然间我见到一群、
　　一片金黄色的水仙，
依傍着湖，长在树底，　　　　　　　　　　5
在微风中起舞翩翩。

连绵有如繁星闪光
　　烁烁在银河上面，
它们展延成无尽的长行，
　　沿着一片水湾的岸边：　　　　　　　10
我一眼瞥见万把颗，
它们抬起头曼舞婆娑。

旁边的水波跳动，它们
　　却比闪耀的水波更欢：
一个诗人怎能不开心，　　　　　　　　　15
　　亲近着这些快乐的侣伴！
我凝视——又凝视——却很少考虑
这光景给了我怎样的富足：

因为常常，当我躺在榻上
　　空闲着或沉思着的时刻，　　　　　　20
它们的身影就照亮想象——

Which is the bliss of solitude;
And then my heart with pleasure fills,
And dances with the daffodils.

W. WORDSWORTH.

想象乃孤独中的至乐；
　　　于是我的心充满了欢愉，
　　　随同水仙而翩翩起舞。

鲍屡平　译

编注　本诗作于一八〇四年，发表在一八〇七年《诗集》里，标题系原编者所加。据说，华兹华斯访友人归来，在阿尔斯沃特（Ullswater）湖畔见到一大片盛开的水仙花。约两年后，他回忆当时所见，写下了这首诗。全诗意境清新，形象生动，是自然诗人华兹华斯描写自然美给予人们快感的著名抒情诗之一。

254. TO THE DAISY

With little here to do or see
Of things that in the great world be,
Daisy! again I talk to thee,
  For thou art worthy,
Thou unassuming Commonplace
Of Nature, with that homely face,
And yet with something of a grace
  Which love makes for thee!

Oft on the dappled turf at ease[①]
I sit and play with similes,
Loose types of things through all degrees,
  Thoughts of thy raising;
And many a fond and idle name
I give to thee, for praise or blame,
As is the humour of the game,
  While I am gazing.

A nun demure, of lowly port;
Or sprightly maiden, of Love's court,
In thy simplicity the sport
  Of all temptations;
A queen in crown of rubies drest;

---

① *dappled*: 'spotted with daisies.'

254. 给雏菊

华兹华斯

在这个大千世界里,既然
我无事可做,没什么可看,
雏菊啊!我又来和你闲谈,
　　你听我谈话最相宜,
你呵,大自然平凡的产儿,　　　　　　　5
心地谦逊,面容朴实,
却又带点儿优美雅致——
　　爱心给你的赠礼!

我常在缀满花朵的草地,
悠闲地坐着,用比喻做游戏,　　　　　10
用无拘无束的各类标记——
　　由你引起的联想;
我给你起了多少个亲昵、
无谓的名字,称赞你,责备你,
这是我来了兴致,老脾气——　　　　　15
　　而我正对着你凝望。

娴静的修女,举止谦卑;
活泼的侍女,在爱神的宫闱,
天真无邪的少女,因而被
　　种种诱惑所愚弄;　　　　　　　　20
头戴宝石金冠的女王,

A starveling in a scanty vest①;
Are all, as seems to suit thee best,
    Thy appellations.

A little Cyclops, with one eye
Staring to threaten and defy,
That thought comes next — and instantly
    The freak is over,
The shape will vanish, and behold!
A silver shield with boss of gold
That spreads itself, some fairy bold
    In fight to cover.

I see thee glittering from afar —
And then thou art a pretty star,
Not quite so fair as many are
    In heaven above thee!
Yet like a star, with glittering crest,
Self-poised in air thou seem'st to rest; —
May peace come never to his nest
    Who shall reprove thee!

Sweet Flower! for by that name at last
When all my reveries are past
I call thee, and to that cleave fast,
    Sweet silent creature!
That breath'st with me in sun and air,
Do thou, as thou art wont, repair

---

① *starveling*: 'a lean and hungry-looking creature.'

衣衫单薄,饿瘦的儿郎,
这些是给你的名称,好像
　　　对你全都挺适用。

小小的赛克洛,独眼圆睁①,　　　　　　　　25
正发出威胁,公然抗命——
这想法出现,只有一瞬,
　　　怪念头一闪而逝,
那形象会消失,可是,看!
一面盾,银盾的金饰鼓鼓圆,　　　　　　　30
自己张开,庇护着厮杀间
　　　无比勇敢的小仙子。

我看见你在远处亮晶晶——
你变成一颗漂亮的小星星,
虽然不如天上的一群群　　　　　　　　　35
　　　星辰那样灿烂!
仍然像颗星,羽冠在闪烁,
你亭亭玉立,安闲自若;——
谁要是呵斥你,但愿这家伙
　　　永远得不到平安!　　　　　　　40

可爱的花儿!梦幻的遐思
过去了,我终于用这个名字
呼唤你,而且要永远坚持,
　　　安静可爱的生灵!
阳光下,大气中,你跟我同呼吸,　　　　　45
请一如往常,给我的欣喜,

---

① 赛克洛(Cyclops),即库克罗普斯,希腊神话中西西里岛的独眼巨人,一只眼生在前额正中。——译者

My heart with gladness, and a share
   Of thy meek nature!

                              W. WORDSWORTH.

让我分享你温良的心地,
这样来医治我的心!

屠岸 译

编注 本诗作于一八〇二年,与前一首同时发表。诗人以拟人化的笔法与雏菊亲切交谈,感慨万千。

255. ODE TO AUTUMN

Season of mists and mellow fruitfulness,
    Close bosom-friend of the maturing sun①;
Conspiring with him how to load and bless
    With fruit the vines that round the thatch-eaves run;
5   To bend with apples the moss'd cottage-trees,
    And fill all fruit with ripeness to the core;
        To swell the gourd, and plump the hazel shells
    With a sweet kernel; to set budding more,
And still more, later flowers for the bees,
10   Until they think warm days will never cease;
        For Summer has o'erbrimm'd their clammy cells.

Who hath not seen thee oft amid thy store?
    Sometimes whoever seeks abroad may find
Thee sitting careless on a granary floor,
15   Thy hair soft-lifted by the winnowing wind;
Or on a half-reap'd furrow sound asleep,
    Drows'd with the fume of poppies, while thy hook②
        Spares the next swath and all its twinéd flowers③;
And sometimes like a gleaner thou dost keep
    Steady thy laden head across a brook④;
Or by a cider-press, with patient look,

---

① *maturing*: 'ripening.'
② *Drows'd*: 'made drowsy.'
③ *swath*: properly 'a line of cut corn,' here 'a line of corn waiting to be cut.'
④ *laden*: i.e. carrying a sheaf of corn on her head.

255. 秋赋

济慈

雾的季节,成熟和结果的季节,
　　它是那催熟一切的阳光的挚友;
共谋着怎样在农舍屋檐外层层叠叠
　　让果实挂满藤蔓,带来祝福的时候;
苔藓斑驳的农家果树被苹果压弯,　　　　　　　　5
　　每一只果实都打心里熟透;
　　　让葫芦变大,榛子丰满
　　果仁清甜;还让花蕾不断露头,
好再开花,晚花让蜂儿不失望,
直到误以为温暖的日子过不完;　　　　　　　　10
　　其实夏日早已将那湿漉漉的蜂房装满。

谁没常看见你在仓库里奔忙?
　　一出门人们就看见你
无忧无虑地坐在粮仓的地上,
　　你的头发任轻风微微飘起;　　　　　　　　15
或者躺在收割一半的田沟里鼾睡,
　　使你沉醉的是罂粟花的香郁
　　　你的镰钩放过了下一垄庄稼
　　和紧缠的花朵;有时你像在田里拾穗
　　　涉过小溪田头将谷穗托举;　　　　　　　20
　　或者几个小时守望那榨果机压取

Thou watchest the last oozings, hours by hours.

Where are the songs of Spring! Aye, where are they?
Think not of them, — thou hast thy music too,
While barréd clouds bloom the soft-dying day①
And touch the stubble-plains with rosy hue;
Then in a wailful choir the small gnats mourn
Among the river sallows, borne aloft②
Or sinking as the light wind lives or dies;
And full-grown lambs loud bleat from hilly bourn;
Hedge-crickets sing, and now with treble soft
The redbreast whistles from a garden-croft③,
And gathering swallows twitter in the skies.

J. KEATS.

---

① *bloom*: 'lend a glow to.'
② *sallows*: 'willows.'
③ *garden-croft*: 'a piece of land enclosed for a garden.'

苹果水,耐心等候那最后的果汁滴下。

春天的歌儿在哪里?啊,在哪里?
　　你有你的音乐,不要去想念它们,
当一天将结束,团团的晚霞飘起　　　　　　　　　　25
　　将割过的田地交给玫瑰色的黄昏;
尔后小虫们唱起哀歌
　　在河上这苍黄的一团,时而高,时而低
　　　　全看风势的大小;
肥壮的羊群咩咩地在山溪边解渴;　　　　　　　　30
　　篱下的蟋蟀鸣叫,红胸脯的知更唤你
用它温柔的高音吹哨,在田园里
　　　　天空上燕子集合了,在啾啾地鸣叫。

郑　敏　译

编注　本诗表现了秋收之乐,无比恬静,无比寥廓,最后一节宛如田园交响乐,给人以音乐的享受。本诗于一八二〇年以《致秋天》(To Autumn)为题,发表在《女妖》(*Lamia*)上。

256. ODE TO WINTER

Germany, December 1800

When first the fiery-mantled Sun
His heavenly race began to run,
Round the earth and ocean blue
His children four the Seasons flew: —
    First, in green apparel dancing,
The young Spring smiled with angel-grace;
    Rosy Summer, next advancing,
Rush'd into her sire's embrace —
Her bright-hair'd sire, who bade her keep
    For ever nearest to his smiles.
On Calpe's olive-shaded steep
    Or India's citron-cover'd isles.
More remote, and buxom-brown,
    The Queen of vintage bow'd before his throne;
A rich pomegranate gemm'd her crown,
    A ripe sheaf bound her zone.

But howling Winter fled afar

256. 冬颂
(德国,一八〇〇年十二月)

坎贝尔

最初,当火焰缭绕的太阳
开始了他神圣的竞跑,
围绕着地球和蓝色的海洋
他的孩子四季紧随飞跃:
  起先,身着绿色衣裳的年轻的春   5
翩翩起舞,发出天使般典雅的微笑;
  接着,玫瑰色的夏季降临,
飞奔投入她父亲的怀抱——
满头银丝的父亲忙把话语叮咛,
  要她永远不离开他的怀抱①。   10
在卡波橄榄荫蔽的陡崖绝壁上②,
  或在印度香橼覆盖的小岛③,
在那更遥远的赤褐色的地方,
  葡萄皇后在他的宝座前俯首躬腰④;
她的皇冠镶嵌着富丽的石榴花,   15
  她的腰间扎着一串熟透了的葡萄。

但怒吼的寒冬朝着远方的群山

---

① 事实上,太阳离地球最近的时候并不在夏季,而是在春分与秋分的时候。冬天是由太阳光线的斜射造成,而不是由它和地球的距离远近所造成的。——译者
② 卡波系直布罗陀海峡的旧名。——译者
③ 香橼是一种类似于柑桔树和柠檬树的果树,生长于印度北部。——译者
④ "葡萄皇后"指秋天。——译者

To hills that prop the polar star;
And loves on deer-borne car to ride
With barren darkness at his side,
Round the shore where loud Lofoden
    Whirls to death the roaring whale,
Round the hall where Runic Odin
    Howls his war-song to the gale —
Save when adown the ravaged globe
    He travels on his native storm,
Deflowering Nature's grassy robe
    And trampling on her faded form;
Till light's returning lord assume
    The shaft that drives him to his polar field,
Of power to pierce his raven plume
    And crystal-cover'd shield.

O sire of storms! whose savage ear
The Lapland drum delights to hear,
When Frenzy with her bloodshot eye
Implores thy dreadful deity —
Archangel! power of desolation!
    Fast descending as thou art,
Say, hath mortal invocation
    Spells to touch thy stony heart?

向支撑北极星的地方仓皇逃窜①
她总爱乘坐鹿群牵引的车
带上周围的荒凉与黑暗,　　　　　　　　　　20
越过那洛弗登大漩涡咆哮的海岸②
　连吼叫的鲸鱼也会在此完蛋,
围绕着神秘的欧丁神殿堂
　北欧神的战歌面对大风的呼喊③——
只留下大地褴褛的衣衫　　　　　　　　　　25
　他驾驭着固有的风暴,
将大自然的青草衣袍踩躏
　把枯萎的形体肆意作践;
啊,是返回的太阳启用了光芒的利剑④,
　剑的威力穿透了那身乌亮的羽毛　　　　　30
和那副水晶覆盖下的盔甲,
　于是,寒冬被赶回了他的北极老巢。

啊,风暴之父!你野蛮的耳朵
总爱倾听拉布兰的鼓点⑤,
连狂风暴雨也睁大布满血丝的眼睛　　　　　35
向你敬畏的神明祈求哀怜——
天使长哟!孤寂凄凉的权威!
　告诉我,当你飞速地降临人间,
那些濒近死亡的人们祈祷的咒语
　可曾触动你那冷酷的心弦?　　　　　　　40

---

① 指冬天遗弃了北极向南飞跑。——译者
② 洛弗登(Lofoden),挪威西海岸以外的群岛,据说附近的大漩涡从前可以吞没鲸鱼和船只。——译者
③ 欧丁神(Odin),斯堪的纳维亚神话中的主神。——译者
④ 指夏天的阳光。——译者
⑤ 在中世纪,拉布兰人(The Lapland),包括居住在瑞典北部、芬兰等地的人用鼓来占卜。——译者

       Then, sullen Winter! hear my prayer
       And gently rule the ruin'd year;
       Nor chill the wanderer's bosom bare,
       Nor freeze the wretch's falling tear:
45   To shuddering Want's unmantled bed
         Thy horror-breathing agues cease to lend.
       And gently on the orphan head
         Of innocence descend.

       But chiefly spare, O king of clouds!
50   The sailor on his airy shrouds,
       When wrecks and beacons strew the steep
       And spectres walk along the deep.
       Milder yet thy snowy breezes
         Pour on yonder tented shores[①],
55   Where the Rhine's broad billow freezes,
         Or the dark-brown Danube roars.
       O winds of Winter! list ye there
         To many a deep and dying groan?
       Or start, ye demons of the midnight air,
60   At shrieks and thunders louder than your own?
       Alas! e'en your unhallow'd breath
         May spare the victim fallen low;
       But man will ask no truce to death,
         No bounds to human woe.

                                      T. CAMPBELL

[①] *yonder tented shores*: the French and the Austrians were confronting each other in the campaign during which Hohenlinden was fought (see note to No. 215), and which was only terminated by the armistice of Steyer, December 25, 1800.

那末,阴沉的隆冬!听我的祈祷,
把遭到摧残的年岁轻柔地治管;
不让严寒侵袭流浪者裸露的心胸,
冻结可怜汉流下的滚滚泪泉:
你那毛骨悚然的寒颤停止了, 45
 不再把无遮盖的贫困之家的床摇撼,
只轻轻地,轻轻地降落,
 落在天真无邪的孤儿头前。

啊,众云之王哟!首先请饶恕
那悬荡在桅杆上面的水手, 50
当遇难的船只和航标盖满了陡崖,
幽灵沿着深邃的大海徘徊游走。
你带雪的寒风,再缓和些吹吧,
 当你吹向远方帐篷林立的海岸①。
那里,莱茵河浩淼的波涛结冰, 55
 深褐色的多瑙河在奔腾怒吼。
啊,冬天的寒风哟!你可听见
 那里有多少临死时深沉的悲嚎?
半夜空中的恶魔,你可感到震惊,
 当你也比不过那雷鸣般的尖叫? 60
唉!就连你亵渎神明的呼吸
 也会将沉沦的受难者恕饶;
但人却不会向死亡乞求和平,
 人间的灾祸将永无休止。

黄新渠　黄文军　译

编注　本诗以自然的四季联想到人生的欢乐与悲哀,诗人的幻想驰

---

① 法国人与奥地利人在荷恩林登战役中交战(参见本卷第215首注),该战役于一八〇〇年十二月二十五日以在斯特尔停战而告终。——译者

骋于寰宇之间,横贯于历史的长河之中,诗人几乎在向严冬祈求,希望她能给自然界和人类更多的同情与怜恤。本诗发表在一八〇一年一月三十日《晨报》(*Morning Chronicle*)上,一八〇三年再版于《希望之乐》(*The Pleasures of Hope*)上。

257. YARROW UNVISITED

1803

    From Stirling Castle we had seen
        The mazy Forth unravell'd,
    Had trod the banks of Clyde and Tay,
        And with the Tweed had travell'd;
    And when we came to Clovenford,
        Then said my 'winsome Marrow,'①
    'Whate'er betide, we'll turn aside,
        And see the Braes of Yarrow.'

    'Let Yarrow folk, frae Selkirk town
        Who have been buying, selling,
    Go back to Yarrow, 'tis their own,
        Each maiden to her dwelling!
    On Yarrow's banks let herons feed,
        Hares couch, and rabbits burrow,
    But we will downward with the Tweed,
        Nor turn aside to Yarrow.

    'There's Galla Water, Leader Haughs,
        Both lying right before us;
    And Dryburgh, where with chiming Tweed

---

① "*winsome Marrow*": from the ballad 'Busk ye, busk ye, my bonnie, bonnie bride!' by William Hamilton (1704 — 1754), to which Wordsworth calls attention in a note. For the meaning of *marrow* see above, note to No. 127, l. 42.

257. 未访雅洛河

（一八〇三年）

华兹华斯

从斯特灵城堡，我们看见①
　曲折的福斯河自由奔腾，
我们在克莱德河、台河岸漫步，
　又沿着特威德河旅行；
我们到达克洛文福的时候，　　　　　　　　　5
　我"可爱的伙伴"这样说②：
"不管怎么样，我们该转身
　去看看雅洛河斜坡。"

"让雅罗居民在赛尔柯克镇
　做完了买卖生意　　　　　　　　　　　　10
就回到自己的雅洛河边，
　姑娘们都回到家里！
让苍鹭在雅洛河岸啄食，
　让兔子掘洞，蹲卧，
我们沿特威德河道顺流下，　　　　　　　　15
　不要去访问雅洛河。

"伽拉河水，里德河滩
　就在我们的前方，
还有德莱城，红雀在城边

---

① 斯特灵城堡，以及下面提到的福斯河、克莱德河、台河、特威德河、克洛文福、雅洛河、塞尔柯克镇、伽拉河、里德河、德莱城、迭维谷、勃恩坊牧场、圣玛丽湖，都是苏格兰的城堡名、河名、域名、湖名、地名。——译者
② "可爱的伙伴"指诗人的妹妹多罗赛·华兹华斯。——译者

20   The lintwhites sing in chorus①;
          There's pleasant Tiviot-dale, a land
            Made blithe with plough and harrow;
          Why throw away a needful day
            To go in search of Yarrow?

25   'What's Yarrow but a river bare
            That glides the dark hills under?
          There are a thousand such elsewhere
            As worthy of your wonder.'
          — Strange words they seem'd of slight and scorn;
30   My True-love sigh'd for sorrow,
          And look'd me in the face, to think
            I thus could speak of Yarrow!

          'O green,' said I, 'are Yarrow's holms②,
            And sweet is Yarrow flowing!
35   Fair hangs the apple frae the rock,
            But we will leave it growing.
          O'er hilly path and open Strath③
            We'll wander Scotland thorough;
          But, though so near, we will hot turn
40   Into the dale of Yarrow.

          'Let beeves and home-bred kine partake
            The sweets of Burn-mill meadow;
          The swan on still St. Mary's Lake

---

① *lintwhiles*: another form of 'linnet,' only used in poetry.
② *holms*: low-lying stretches of land by a river.
③ *Strath*: a wide, open valley.

跟特威德河水合唱； 20
还有逊维谷，经过犁耙
　　变得生机活泼：
为什么要花有用的一天
　　前去寻访雅洛河？

"雅罗不就是条河，没树荫， 25
　　在暗的山谷间流淌？
同样的地方有千千万，
　　值得你衷心向往。"
这些话像是贬低和轻蔑，
　　我的亲人一声喟叹， 30
看着我，心想我讲雅洛河
　　竟用这样的语言！

我说："雅洛河流域绿葱葱，
　　雅洛河流得挺舒畅！
山岩上挂的圆果真正美， 35
　　也只好让它自己长。
越过山径和开阔的大谿，
　　我们要游遍苏格兰，
可是，尽管近，我们也不要
　　转身去雅洛河滩。 40

"计家养母牛和公牛共享
　　勃恩坊牧场的鲜草；
让圣玛丽湖上的天鹅

  Float double, swan and shadow!
 We will not see them; will not go
  To-day, nor yet to-morrow;
 Enough if in our hearts we know
  There's such a place as Yarrow.

 'Be Yarrow stream unseen, unknown!
  It must, or we shall rue it:
 We have a vision of our own,
  Ah! why should we undo it?
 The treasured dreams of times long past,
  We'll keep them, winsome Marrow!
 For when we're there, although 'tis fair
  'Twill be another Yarrow!

 'If Care with freezing years should come,
  And wandering seem but folly, —
 Should we be loth to stir from home,
  And yet be melancholy;
 Should life be dull, and spirits low,
  'Twill soothe us in our sorrow
 That earth has something yet to show,
  The bonny holms of Yarrow!'

W. WORDSWORTH.

和倒影双双浮飘！
我们不去看它们,今天 　　　　　　　　45
　或明天我们都不去;
只要在心中有条雅洛河,
　我们就心满意足。

"只能如此:不去看雅洛河!
　否则我们会懊悔: 　　　　　　　　　50
我们已经有自己的想象,
　为什么要把它拆毁?
可爱的伙伴呵,长期酝酿的
　珍贵的梦境要保住!
一旦去看了,尽管美,那将是 　　　　55
　另一片雅洛河谷!

"假如忧虑随冰霜到来,
　漫游被看作愚蠢,——
我们不愿到户外去活动,
　而且心情郁闷; 　　　　　　　　　60
生活单调,情绪也低落;
　这想法会缓解伤悲:
大地上还有这样的景色——
　雅洛河风光明媚!"

屠岸　译

编注　浪漫主义诗人认为诗歌的魅力不在于理性而在于丰富的幻想,华兹华斯前后两首关于雅洛河的诗篇各有特色,《未访雅洛河》写幻想中的美,《访雅洛河》写现实中的美,而美(包括自然美与艺术美)就是心灵的安慰与永久的欢乐。本诗作于一八〇三年,发表于一八〇七年《诗集》上。

258. YARROW VISITED

September 1814

And is this — Yarrow? — *This* the Stream
    Of which my fancy cherish'd
So faithfully, a waking dream,
    An image that hath perish'd?
O that some Minstrel's harp were near
    To utter notes of gladness
And chase this silence from the air,
    That fills my heart with sadness!

Yet why? — a silvery current flows
    With uncontroll'd meanderings;
Nor have these eyes by greener hills
    Been soothed, in all my wanderings.
And, through her depths, St. Mary's Lake
    Is visibly delighted;
For not a feature of those hills
    Is in the mirror slighted.

A blue sky bends o'er Yarrow Vale,
    Save where that pearly whiteness
Is round the rising sun diffused,
    A tender hazy brightness;
Mild dawn of promise! that excludes
    All profitless dejection;
Though not unwilling here to admit
    A pensive recollection.

258. 访雅洛河
（一八一四年九月）

华兹华斯

这就是雅洛河？——是这条河流，
    我的幻想所珍爱，
忠实地珍爱的？是醒时的梦境，
    消失的影象不再来？
愿吟游诗人的竖琴临近，   5
    奏出愉快的乐曲，
打破岑寂的气氛！那静默
    使我的心灵忧郁。

怎么？一条银色的河，
    自由地蜿蜒流奔，   10
过去从没有如许青山
    抚慰我这双眼睛。
看得见圣玛丽湖水深深，
    她是如此地欢欣，
周围的山峰没一座被遗漏，   15
    镜子里全都有倒影。

蓝天覆盖着雅洛河谷，
    只有朝阳的周围
辐射着珍珠一般的亮色，
    温柔而朦胧的光辉；   20
希望的黎明！这晨光排除
    一切无益的沮丧；
虽然这里也可以允许
    做些深沉的回想。

<pre>
25   Where was it that the famous Flower
            Of Yarrow Vale lay bleeding?
        His bed perchance was yon smooth mound
            On which the herd is feeding:
        And haply from this crystal pool,
30   Now peaceful as the morning,
        The Water-wraith① ascended thrice,
            And gave his doleful warning.

        Delicious is the Lay that sings
            The haunts of happy lovers,
35   The path that leads them to the grove,
            The leafy grove that covers:
        And pity sanctifies the verse
            That paints, by strength of sorrow,
        The unconquerable strength of love;
40   Bear witness, rueful Yarrow!

        But thou, that didst appear so fair
            To fond imagination,
        Dost rival in the light of day
            Her delicate creation:
45   Meek loveliness is round thee spread,
            A softness still and holy:
        The grace of forest charms decay'd,
            And pastoral melancholy.
</pre>

---

① *The Water-wraith*: see Logan's ballad above, No. 127, l. 23.

著名的雅洛河谷之花① 25
　流血的地方在哪里?
也许他就在那块有牛羊
　吃草的岗丘上安息:
这儿晶莹澄澈的水潭
　像早晨一样静悄悄, 30
怕水怪会三次从潭底登岸,
　发出阴郁的警告。

那支歌多美,歌唱恋人们
　常常去相会,相爱,
小径引他们走进树丛, 35
　树丛把他们覆盖:
爱心使诗歌变得圣洁,
　用悲哀的力量,诗歌
描绘爱情的坚强不屈;
　作证呵,可怜的雅洛河! 40

而你在亲爱的想象中显现,
　出落得如此美丽,
阳光的创造是如此精致,
　你完全可以匹敌:
你的周围是一片娇妍, 45
　一种神圣的柔媚,
森林的美和魅力在消失,
　牧歌的哀调在衰颓。

---

① 获得"雅洛河之花"称号的不是男性而是十六世纪的一个名叫玛丽·司谷脱的姑娘。华兹华斯在这里一定是想到了有的歌谣中所歌唱的那个"躺在雅洛河岸流血"的青年。参见卷三第126首。——译者

That region left, the vale unfolds
    Rich groves of lofty stature,
With Yarrow winding through the pomp
    Of cultivated nature;
And, rising from those lofty groves,
    Behold a ruin hoary,
The shatter'd front of Newark's Towers,
    Renown'd in Border story.

Fair scenes for childhood's opening bloom,
    For sportive youth to stray in,
For manhood to enjoy his strength,
    And age to wear away in!
Yon cottage seems a bower of bliss,
    A covert for protection
Of tender thoughts, that nestle there —
    The brood of chaste affection.

How sweet on this autumnal day
    The wild-wood fruits to gather,
And on my True-love's forehead plant
    A crest of blooming heather!
And what if I enwreathed my own?
    'Twere no offence to reason;
The sober hills thus deck their brows
    To meet the wintry season.

离开了这里,山谷间展现
　　茂密高大的林丛, 50
雅洛河迂回地在那耕过的
　　壮伟的山野里流动;
看哪!高大的树丛里升起
　　古堡的颓垣残壁,
那是边境故事里有名的 55
　　纽瓦克塔的遗迹①。

美景迎接着童年的新蕾,
　　嬉戏的少年来游荡,
成年人来享受健壮的乐趣,
　　老人来消磨时光! 60
那茅舍像是幸福的小屋,
　　温柔的思想在这里
受庇护,纯洁的爱的雏儿
　　在这里相互偎依。

多么美妙呵,在这秋天 65
　　来采摘山林的野果,
来给爱人的前额戴上
　　盛开的石楠花朵!
我要是给自己也编个花冠呢?
　　这并非不近人情; 70
冷静的山岭也戴上银帽
　　去迎接严冬的来临。

---

① 边境指苏格兰与英格兰分界处。纽瓦克城堡(Newark's Towers)在雅洛河边,塞尔柯克镇西面五英里处,司各特在《最后一位吟游诗人的歌》中描写的地方。——译者

  I see — but not by sight alone,
   Loved Yarrow, have I won thee,
  A ray of Fancy still survives —
   Her sunshine plays upon thee!
  Thy ever-youthful waters keep
   A course of lively pleasure;
  And gladsome notes my lips can breathe
   Accordant to the measure①.

  The vapours linger round the heights,
   They melt, and soon must vanish;
  One hour is theirs, nor more is mine —
   Sad thought! which I would banish,
  But that I know, where'er I go,
   Thy genuine image, Yarrow!
  Will dwell with me — to heighten joy,
   And cheer my mind in sorrow.

W. WORDSWORTH.

---

① *Accordant*: 'in tune.'

不只凭视觉,我见到亲爱的
　　雅洛河,我已经得到你;
想象的光芒永不灭,她的　　　　　　　　　75
　　太阳光同你游戏!
你永远年轻的水流持续着
　　活泼欢愉的旅程;
我口中能按着你的节奏
　　发出快乐的歌声。　　　　　　　　　80

雾气围绕着群山徘徊,
　　融化开,很快就消亡;
它们的时辰太短,我的日月亦不长——
　　悲哀呀! 我要驱逐这思想,
但是我知道,无论我到哪里,　　　　　85
　　雅洛河! 你真实的身形
将跟我同在,使我欢悦,
　　安慰我悲哀的心灵。

屠　岸　译

编注　本诗作于一八一四年九月,诗人与友人何格(Hogg)访雅洛河之后,于次年发表。参见前一首《未访雅洛河》编注。

259. THE INVITATION

Best and brightest, come away,
Fairer far than this fair Day,
Which, like thee to those in sorrow,
Comes to bid a sweet good-morrow
To the rough Year just awake
In its cradle on the brake.
The brightest hour of unborn Spring
Through the winter wandering,
Found, it seems, the halcyon Morn
To hoar February born;
Bending from Heaven, in azure mirth,
It kiss'd the forehead of the Earth,
And smiled upon the silent sea,
And bade the frozen streams be free,
And waked to music all their fountains,
And breathed upon the frozen mountains,
And like a prophetess of May
Strew'd flowers upon the barren way,
Making the wintry world appear
Like one on whom thou smilest, dear.

Away, away, from men and towns,
To the wild wood and the downs —
To the silent wilderness
Where the soul need not repress
Its music, lest it should not find

259. 一个邀请

雪莱

出来吧,最明媚、最秀丽的!
你远胜过这美好的天气;
和你一样,爱慰人于忧患,
她是来对这坎坷的一年
道一声早安,趁它刚才　　　　　　　　　5
在树丛底摇篮上醒来。
仿佛是未出生的春光
一直在冬之岁月里游荡,
终于看到和煦的早晨
被霜白的二月所诞生,　　　　　　　　10
于是她充满蔚蓝的欢乐,
从天上斜身吻大地的额,
又对静默的大海微笑,
使冻结的河水泛起春潮;
叫醒泉涧,让流声潺潺,　　　　　　　15
又轻轻吹过冰雪的高山;
她像是五月的预言家。
给荒凉的道旁洒满了花,
她使冬之大地看来像你
报以微笑的人,亲爱的珍妮!　　　　20

去吧,离开城市和人群,
去到草原,到清幽的树林——
在那儿,一切如此荒寂,
心灵不必为了怕难于
在别人的心中引起回音,　　　　　　25

An echo in another's mind,
While the touch of Nature's art
Harmonizes heart to heart.

Radiant Sister of the Day
Awake! arise! and come away!
To the wild woods and the plains,
And the pools where winter rains
Image all their roof of leaves,
Where the pine its garland weaves
Of sapless green and ivy dun
Round stems that never kiss the sun;
Where the lawns and pastures be
And the sandhills of the sea;
Where the melting hoar-frost wets
The daisy-star that never sets[①],

[①] *that never sets*: this does not mean 'which never closes,' for the daisy does so each evening, but 'which is in flower all the year.'

便也抑止了自己的乐音，
因为经过自然的触摸，
心和心就会交感，融合①。

呵，美好时令的光辉的姊妹，
起来吧！出来吧！别再沉睡！　　　　　　　30
去到平原和那丛林里，
那儿有水塘，有冬天的积雨
映照出它绿叶的屋顶；
那儿，松树以暗褐的野藤
和干细的叶子编织花冠，　　　　　　　　35
绕着没吻过日光的枝干；
那儿有一片草地，有牧场，
沙石的小山朝着海洋；
在那儿，融化的雪正沾湿
一片好似星星的雏菊；　　　　　　　　　40

---

① 《金库》原编者在此处以下删去十八行，见下：
我要在门前留个字条，
对每个经常的来客写道：
"我已经到田野去漫步，
享受这一刻带来的幸福；
'沉思'呵，你可在明日来访，
和'悲伤'，一起坐在炉旁。
'绝望'呵，你的账单还未付，
'忧烦'也别尽把诗歌朗读，——
我要在墓中再偿付你——
等'死亡'去聆听你的诗句，
还有'期望'，你也快走路！
'今天'对自己已经够满足；
'希望'呵，不必老是嘲笑着
'灾难'，也不必到处跟我；
我固然长久吃你的甜食，
但在长期痛苦后，我终于
找到了片刻幸福，这是你
虽然爱我，却从未提示的。"　　　　　　　（查良铮译）——编注者

  And wind-flowers and violets①,
  Which yet join not scent to hue,
  Crown the pale year weak and new;
  When the night is left behind
45 In the deep east, dun and blind,
  And the blue noon is over us,
  And the multitudinous
  Billows murmur at our feet,
  Where the earth and ocean meet,
50 And all things seem only one
  In the universal sun.

P. B. SHELLEY.

---

① *wind-flowers*: the translation of the Greek 'anemone.'

还有待风花和紫罗兰,
它们给这羸弱的一年
缀上彩色,虽然还没香味;
但是黑夜早已远远隐退
在广阔而幽暗的东方,   *45*
蔚蓝的日子正在头上;
而在陆地和海洋的交界,
波浪正在我们脚前喋喋,
在这普遍的阳光底下,
万物多像是万众一家。   *50*

查良铮　译

编注　本诗及下一首诗的一部分由雪莱夫人一八二四年发表,题目为《比萨附近的卡西恩松林》(The Pine Forest of the Cascine, near Pisa),再版时将两诗分开。本诗名《邀请·致琪恩》(To Jane: The Invitation),另一首名《回忆:致琪恩》(To Jane: The Recollection),琪恩即第252首中提到的威廉斯夫人,即雪莱友人爱德华·威廉斯的妻子,在本诗中译者亦将其译为珍妮。

260. THE RECOLLECTION

Now the last day of many days,
    All beautiful and bright as thou,
        The loveliest and the last, is dead,
Rise, Memory, and write its praise!
Up — to thy wonted work! come, trace
    The epitaph of glory fled,
For now the Earth has changed its face,
    A frown is on the Heaven's brow.

We wander'd to the Pine Forest
    That skirts the Ocean's foam;
The lightest wind was in its nest,
    The tempest in its home.
The whispering waves were half asleep,
    The clouds were gone to play,
And on the bosom of the deep
    The smile of Heaven lay;
It seem'd as if the hour were one
    Sent from beyond the skies
Which scatter'd from above the sun
    A light of Paradise.

We paused amid the pines that stood
    The giants of the waste,
Tortured by storms to shapes as rude
    As serpents interlaced,

260. 回忆

雪莱

现在,许许多多的日子,
　　都像你那样美丽而明朗,
　　　　已经以最愉快的日子结尾,
来吧,记忆,给它写赞美诗!
来吧,开始你经常的工作,　　　　　　　　　　5
　　将飞逝而去的美景描绘,
因为,大地已改变了脸色,
　　皱纹堆在天空的前额上。

我们曾漫步去到松树林,
　　它就在大海的旁边;　　　　　　　　　　10
最轻柔的风在窝里休息,
　　暴风雨在家里安眠。
絮语的波浪正半睡半醒,
　　云彩早已经飘散了,
而在碧蓝的大海胸脯上,　　　　　　　　　　15
　　映出了天空的微笑;
看起来仿佛这一刻就是
　　来自天外的时辰,
它从太阳的上空撒下了
　　天国的一片光明。　　　　　　　　　　　20

我们停留在松林中,松树
　　像巨人屹立在荒原,
受到暴风雨的折磨,变得
　　像蟒蛇互相纠缠,

25　　　　　　And soothed by every azure breath①
　　　　　　　　That under Heaven is blown
　　　　　　　To harmonies and hues beneath②,
　　　　　　　　As tender as its own:
　　　　　　　Now all the tree-tops lay asleep
30　　　　　　　Like green waves on the sea,
　　　　　　　As still as in the silent deep
　　　　　　　　The ocean woods may be③.

　　　　　　　How calm it was! — the silence there
　　　　　　　　By such a chain was bound,
35　　　　　　That even the busy woodpecker
　　　　　　　　Made stiller by her sound④
　　　　　　　The inviolable quietness;
　　　　　　　The breath of peace we drew
　　　　　　　With its soft motion made not less
40　　　　　　　The calm that round us grew.
　　　　　　　There seem'd from the remotest seat
　　　　　　　　Of the white mountain waste,
　　　　　　　To the soft flower beneath our feet
　　　　　　　　A magic circle traced, —

---

① *soothed*: co-ordinate with 'tortured' and qualifying 'pines.'

② *beneath*: sc. heaven; the harmonies and hues of the pine-trees under the sky were as tender as those in th sky.

③ *ocean woods*: the sea-weeds growing deep down in the Mediterranean are often quite visible owing to the clearness of the water. See below, No. 275, ll. 38 – 42.

④ *by*: in the second edition Palgrave adopted 'with,' the reading substituted by Mr. W. M. Rossetti, who in his edition of 1870 introduced a number of textual alterations.

也受到每阵微风的抚慰, 25
　　风儿从蓝天下头
吹向地面的声音和色彩,
　　也变得同样温柔:
现在,树顶全都睡着了,
　　就像海上的碧波, 30
又像大海深处的树林
　　那样静止和沉默。

多么地安静!——那儿的沉默
　　被这样的链条束紧,
即使那忙个不停的啄木鸟 35
　　也只能用它的声音
使不可侵犯的寂静更寂静;
　　我们平静的呼吸的
柔和的运动并没有减少
　　我们四周的静谧。 40
仿佛从白色荒凉的山上
　　那最遥远的峰峦,
到我们脚下温柔的花儿,
　　画了个神奇的圆圈——

45   A spirit interfused around①,
    A thrilling silent life;
   To momentary peace it bound
    Our mortal nature's strife; —
   And still I felt the centre of
50   The magic circle there
   Was one fair form that fill'd with love
    The lifeless atmosphere.

   We paused beside the pools that lie
    Under the forest bough;
55   Each seem'd as 'twere a little sky
    Gulf'd in a world below;
   A firmament of purple light②
    Which in the dark earth lay,
   More boundless than the depth of night,
60   And purer than the day —
   In which the lovely forests grew
    As in the upper air.
   More perfect both in shape and hue
    Than any spreading there.
65   There lay the glade and neighbouring lawn,
    And through the dark green wood
   The white sun twinkling like the dawn
    Out of a speckled cloud.
   Sweet views which in our world above
70   Can never well be seen

---

① *interfused*: here no more than 'shed'; it has a different meaning below, l. 73.
② *firmament*: 'the vault of the sky.'

一种弥漫在四周的精神,　　　　　45
　　赋予沉默的生命以激情;
它迫使我们暂时平息了
　　人类天性的斗争——
而且我还感觉到在那儿,
　　在那神奇的圆心,　　　　　　50
一个美丽的人影用爱情
　　充实了沉寂的气氛。

我们停留在森林枝桠下,
　　那些水潭的旁边;
每个水潭像小小的天空　　　　　55
　　沉没在大地下面;
一片紫红色光芒的天穹
　　映在幽暗的大地上,
比深沉的夜晚更加无边,
　　比白昼更加明亮——　　　　60
葱茏的森林在水里生长,
　　像在高高的天空,
形体和颜色都更加完美,
　　超过了空中的一切。
在水里有空地也有草地,　　　　65
　　而穿过深绿的树林,
白色的太阳闪烁着,像曙光
　　透出了一片乌云。
我们上面的世界决不能
　　清晰地看到的美景,　　　　70

Were imaged by the water's love
Of that fair forest green;
And all was interfused beneath①
With an Elysian glow,
75 An atmosphere without a breath,
A softer day below②.
Like one beloved, the scene had lent③
To the dark water's breast
Its every leaf and lineament
80 With more than truth exprest;
Until an envious wind crept by,
Like an unwelcome thought
Which from the mind's too faithful eye
Blots one dear image out.
85 Though thou art ever fair and kind,
The forests ever green,
Less oft is peace in Shelley's mind
Than calm in Waters seen.

            P. B. SHELLEY.

---

① *interfused*: 'permeated', 'saturated.'
② *below*: the reflection in the pool would present the image of something as being beneath the earth.
③ *Like*: agreeing with 'water'; the scene had lent to the water, as though it loved it, every feature of its own.

却在水里映出来,它如此
　　钟爱那碧绿的森林:
下面的一切全都洋溢着
　　一种天堂里的光辉,
一种风平浪静的气氛, 75
　　日子比上面更柔美。
这景色好像沉醉于爱情,
　　将轮廓和每片树叶
投入了幽暗的水的怀抱,
　　显示得更加真实; 80
直到忌妒的风儿吹过来,
　　像不受欢迎的思想,
从内心无比忠诚的眼睛里
　　涂抹掉可爱的形象。
虽然你永远美丽而和蔼, 85
　　森林也四季长青,
雪莱的心里却常常少有
　　水里呈现的平静。

邹绛　译

编注　参见卷四第 259 首编注。

261. BY THE SEA

It is a beauteous evening, calm and free;
   The holy time is quiet as a Nun
   Breathless with adoration; the broad sun
Is sinking down in its tranquillity;

The gentleness of heaven broods o'er the Sea:
   Listen! the mighty Being is awake,
   And doth with his eternal motion make
A sound like thunder — everlastingly.

Dear child! dear girl! that walkest with me here,
   If thou appear untouch'd by solemn thought[1]
   Thy nature is not therefore less divine:

Thou liest in Abraham's bosom all the year,
   And worshipp'st at the Temple's inner shrine,
God being with thee when we know it not.

W. WORDSWORTH.

---

[1] *appear*: in the 1807 edition Wordsworth had 'appear'st,' but happily realizing that the subjunctive would not be out of place here, he substituted the more euphonious 'appear'.

261. 在海边

华兹华斯

那是个美丽的傍晚,安静,清澈,
 神圣的时光,静如修女一样,
 屏息着在崇奉礼赞;阔大的太阳
正在一片宁谧中逐渐沉落;

苍天的安详慈悲君临着大海:
 听啊! 那伟大的生命始终清醒①,
 用他那永恒的律动发出了一阵阵
轰雷一般的声音——千古不改。

跟我同行的孩子呵,亲爱的女孩②!
 假如你仿佛还没有接触到圣念,
 你的天性不因此而不够崇高:

你整年都躺在亚伯拉罕的胸怀③,
 你在神庙的内殿里崇拜,礼赞,
 上帝在你的身边,我们却不知道。

屠岸 译

编注 本诗于一八〇二年八月作于法国加来港,收入一八〇七年《诗集》,标题为《金库》原编者所加。

---

① "伟大的生命"指大海。——译者
② "孩子"指诗人与法国女子安奈特·瓦隆恋爱所生的女儿卡洛琳。——译者
③ 亚伯拉罕:希伯莱人的始祖。"躺在亚伯拉罕的胸怀"一语出自《圣经·新约·路加福音》第十六章第二十二节,意即死去,进入天堂。——编注者

262. TO THE EVENING STAR

Star that bringest home the bee,
And sett'st the weary labourer free!
   If any star shed peace, 'tis thou,
      That send'st it from above,
         Appearing when Heaven's breath and brow
         Are sweet as hers we love.

Come to the luxuriant skies[1],
Whilst the landscape's odours rise,
   Whilst far-off lowing herds are heard,
      And songs when toil is done,
         From cottages whose smoke unstirr'd
         Curls yellow in the sun.

Star of love's soft interviews,
parted lovers on thee muse;
   Their remembrancer in Heaven
      Of thrilling vows thou art,
         Too delicious to be riven
         By absence from the heart.

                                 T. CAMPBELL.

---

[1] *luxuriant*: presumably this means 'rich in beauty.'

262. 致傍晚的星①

坎贝尔

星催蜜蜂回巢,
星为疲乏的劳动者解除操劳!
 如果说有星星会带来宁静,
  那是您在天空高照,
  您出现在上天的盛景之中,   5
   那美妙如同我心爱者的容貌。

来到绚丽的天上
当大地的芬芳升扬,
 远处牛羊哞咩叫唤,
  收工的人们放声歌唱,   10
  村舍屋顶上炊烟袅袅,
   夕阳下如黄色的卷发一样。

星目睹着恋人们的幽会,
离别的情侣见到您就会心醉;
 他们激动的誓言   15
  由您从天上唤回,
  分别也不能从心底
   抹掉这万般甜美。

郭继德 译

编注 本诗与一八七首同一作者,同一主题,咏金星(Venus)与爱情,本诗载于一八二二年《新月刊》(*New Monthy Magazine*)卷四上。坎贝尔曾做过该刊物的编辑。

---

① 傍晚的星指日落时常看到的金星(Venus)。——译者

263. DATUR HORA QUIETI[1]

The sun upon the lake is low,
    The wild birds hush their song,
The hills have evening's deepest glow,
    Yet Leonard tarries long.
Now all whom varied toil and care
    From home and love divide,
In the calm sunset may repair
    Each to the loved one's side.

The noble dame on turret high,
    Who waits her gallant knight,
Looks to the western beam to spy
    The flash of armour bright.
The village maid, with hand on brow
    The level ray to shade[2],
Upon the footpath watches now
    For Colin's darkening plaid.

Now to their mates the wild swans row,
    By day they swam apart,
And to the thicket wanders slow
    The hind beside the hart.
The woodlark at his partner's side

---

[1] *The latin heading*: *i.e.* 'It is the hour assigned to rest.'
[2] *level*: 'streaming from the setting sun.'

263. 安歇的时分

司各特

红日西沉低悬在湖边，
　　小鸟停息了歌唱鸣啭，
山岭已染上深红的晚霞，
　　可雷欧纳德还没有回还①。
所有辛劳忧虑的人们
　　白日曾告亲人离开家园，
此时可沐浴在夕阳之中，
　　静静地依偎在心上人身边。

塔楼上那位高贵的夫人
　　正盼着她勇敢的骑士回转，
眼望西天落日的余晖，
　　欲发现铠甲明光闪闪。
那个山村少女正手搭凉棚
　　遮挡最后一缕耀眼的光线，
她站在路上急切地张望，
　　张望她的科林那件黑色衣衫②。

野天鹅白日里各自东西，
　　此刻正游向失散的侣伴，
母鹿紧紧地依偎着牡鹿，
　　漫步在浓密的树丛之间。
云雀回巢紧挨着配偶

---

① 雷欧纳德（Leonard）亦译为伦纳德，一骑士姓氏。——译者
② 科林（Colin）该骑士名字，系尼古拉（Nicholas）的昵称。——译者

Twitters his closing song —
All meet whom day and care divide,
But Leonard tarries long!

SIR W. SCOTT.

唱着终了曲迎接夜晚——
白天分离的此时都相会,
　　可雷欧纳德还没有回还。

　　　　　　　　　　　　曹明伦　译

编注　本诗选自悲剧《德佛哥尔之死》(*The Doom of Devorgoil*, 1830)第一幕第一场。标题为《金库》原编者所加,主题与卷四第186首相同,写少女的期待。

264. TO THE MOON

Art thou pale for weariness
Of climbing heaven and gazing on the earth,
Wandering companionless
Among the stars that have a different birth[①], —
And ever-changing, like a joyless eye
That finds no object worth its constancy?

P. B. SHELLEY

[①] *a different birth*: each of the stars is a flaming sun, but science has not yet pronounced on their origin; the moon is supposed to be a fragment detached from the Earth.

264. 给月

雪莱

你的脸色苍白,是因为
倦于攀登天空、注视地面,
孤零零地流浪在
身世不同的群星之间——
而且不停地变化,像一只寡欢的眼,
找不到什么景物值得长久留恋?

江枫 译

编注 本诗于一八二四年由雪莱夫人发表。原诗有第二节两行,似乎是未完成的作品,《金库》原编者未收入。译文如下:

(二)

你啊,那精灵的出色的姐妹,
它注视着你,直到对你产生了怜悯……

江枫 译

265. 'A WIDOW BIRD SATE MOURNING FOR HER LOVE'

A widow bird sate mourning for her love
    Upon a wintry bough;
The frozen wind crept on above,
    The freezing stream below.

There was no leaf upon the forest bare,
    No flower upon the ground,
And little motion in the air
    Except the mill-wheel's sound.

P. B. SHELLEY.

265. "有鸟仳离枯树颠"

雪莱

有鸟仳离枯树颠,
　　哭丧其雄剧可怜;
上有冰天风入冻,
　　下有积雪之河川。

森林无叶徒杈枒,　　　　　　　　　　5
　　地上更无一朵花,
空中群动皆息灭,
　　只闻呜唈有水车。

　　　　　　　　　郭沫若　译

编注　本诗选自未完成的剧本《查理一世》(*Charles the First*),一八二四年抽出单独发表,题名为《歌》(*A Song*)。

266. TO SLEEP

A flock of sheep that leisurely pass by,
   One after one; the sound of rain, and bees
   Murmuring; the fall of rivers, winds and seas,
Smooth fields, white sheets of water, and pure sky;

I have thought of all by turns, and yet do lie
   Sleepless; and soon the small birds' melodies
   Must hear, first uttered from my orchard trees,
And the first cuckoo's melancholy cry.

Even thus last night, and two nights more, I lay,
   And could not win thee, Sleep! by any stealth:
So do not let me wear to-night away:

   Without Thee what is all the morning's wealth?
Come, blessèd barrier between day and day,
   Dear mother of fresh thoughts and joyous health!

W. WORDSWORTH.

266. 致睡眠

华兹华斯

一头头绵羊悠闲地踱过我面前;
　蜜蜂的嗡嗡嘤嘤,雨滴的声响;
　河水的流淌,微风轻拂着海洋,
平野,白茫茫水面和一片蓝天:

这些我一一想遍,却依然无眠;　　　　　　　　　　5
　不用多久,从我果园里的树上,
　该传来小鸟第一阵的啼啭歌唱,
还有那杜鹃的第一声忧郁叫唤。

昨夜这样,还加两个不眠夜晚,
　睡眠哪,我没使你降临我身上:　　　　　　　　10
今夜请千万别再使我神疲力殚。

　没有你,哪来早晨的财富宝藏?
你来吧,白天之间的赐福栅栏——
　那清新思想和神清气爽的亲娘!

　　　　　　　　　　　　黄杲炘　译

267. THE SOLDIER'S DREAM

    Our bugles sang truce, for the night-cloud had lower'd①,
        And the sentinel stars set their watch in the sky;
    And thousands had sunk on the ground overpower'd,
        The weary to sleep, and the wounded to die.

    When reposing that night on my pallet of straw
        By the wolf-scaring faggot that guarded the slain②,
    At the dead of the night a sweet vision I saw;
        And thrice ere the morning I dreamt it again.

    Methought from the battle-field's dreadful array
        Far, far I had roam'd on a desolate track;
    'Twas autumn, — and sunshine arose on the way
        To the home of my fathers, that welcomed me back.

    I flew to the pleasant fields traversed so oft
        In life's morning march, when my bosom was young;
    I heard my own mountain-goats bleating aloft,
        And knew the sweet strain that the corn-reapers sung.

    Then pledged we the wine-cup, and fondly I swore,
        From my home and my weeping friends never to part;

---

① *lower'd*: (or loured), 'begun to look threatening.'
② *wolf-scaring faggot*: i.e. fires lighted to keep the wolves from preying on the dead.

267. 士兵的梦

坎贝尔

夜云低垂,军号吹响休战的声音,
　　监视着天空的是哨兵一般的星星;
数千名精疲力竭的人们在地上躺下,
　　疲倦者睡觉休息,受伤者寿终正寝。

午夜时分,我躺在草铺上　　　　　　　　　　　5
　　烈火驱赶着狼群,保护被杀害的士兵;
深夜里,我进入甜蜜的梦乡,
　　又做了三次梦才到黎明。

那毛骨悚然的战场忽而消隐,
　　我信步漫游,走在荒凉的小径,　　　　　　10
一路上阳光熹熹,秋高无云,
　　返回家园,有长辈把我欢迎。

我飞跑到往昔常去的田野,
　　那时迎着生命的朝阳,当我还很年轻;
我听到自己山中羊群咩咩地欢叫,　　　　　　15
　　我熟悉收玉米者哼起的甜蜜歌声。

后来,我们举杯立誓,我天真地保证
　　永不离开家园和那啜泣的友人;

My little ones kiss'd me a thousand times o'er,
20   And my wife sobb'd aloud in her fullness of heart.

'Stay — stay with us! — rest! — thou art weary and worn!' —
    And fain was their war-broken soldier to stay; —
But sorrow return'd with the dawning of morn,
    And the voice in my dreaming ear melted away.

T. CAMPBELL.

我的小宝宝吻了我一千次,
 我的妻子无限悲戚、痛哭失声。   20

"留下吧——留在我们这儿!——休息!——你筋疲力尽!"
 受战争摧残的士兵多么渴望留下啊;——
但随着黎明来临,我心里又充满悲戚,
 在梦中萦绕耳际的声音又无踪无影。

郭继德 译

编注 十九世纪英国进行着全球性的掠夺,到处建立殖民地,而她的士兵实质上成了掠夺政策的牺牲品,正像英国诗人丁尼生所描写的那样,"我们不能问为什么打仗,我们只能服从而把命丧"(Ours is not to ask why. Ours is to obey and die)。本诗作者对士兵的思乡情绪寄予无限的同情,士兵的梦境与现实的矛盾只给他们留下了痛苦与悲伤。本诗一八〇三年发表在《希望之乐》(*The Pleasures of Hope*)第七版上。

268. A DREAM OF THE UNKNOWN

I dream'd that as I wander'd by the way
    Bare Winter suddenly was changed to Spring,
And gentle odours led my steps astray,
    Mix'd with a sound of waters murmuring
Along a shelving bank of turf, which lay
    Under a copse, and hardly dared to fling
Its green arms round the bosom of the stream,
But kiss'd it and then fled, as thou mightest in dream.

There grew pied wind-flowers and violets,
    Daisies, those pearl'd Arcturi of the earth,
The constellated flower that never sets[①];
    Faint oxlips; tender blue-bells, at whose birth
The sod scarce heaved; and that tall flower that wets —
    Like a child, half in tenderness and mirth —
Its mother's face with heaven's collected tears,
When the low wind, its playmate's voice, it hears.

And in the warm hedge grew lush eglantine[②],
    Green cow-bind and the moonlight-colour'd may[③],
And cherry-blossoms, and white cups, whose wine
    Was the bright dew yet drain'd not by the day;

---

① *constellatd*: put for 'star like'; *that never sets*: see note to No. 259, l. 40.
② *eglantine*: 'sweet brier.'
③ *cow-bind*: a common wild plant also known as 'white bryony.'

268. 一个未知世界的梦

雪莱

我曾经梦见,当我在路上漫游,
　　荒凉的寒冬突然变成了阳春,
温暖的香气引导着我的脚步,
　　伴随着一阵流水潺潺的声音,
走向一片泥土的斜坡,它躺在　　　　　　5
　　一片灌木林下面,不敢让丛林
绿色的手臂将河水拥抱在怀中,
只是吻吻它就走,像你在做梦。

那儿长着各种银莲花和紫罗兰,
　　雏菊,地上那些珍珠般的明星①,　　10
那永不消失的像星星似的花朵;
　　纤弱的樱草;温柔的蓝色的风信,
它悄悄钻出土;和那高高的晶莹的花儿②,
　　像一个孩子,半体贴又半高兴——
用天上的泪珠将母亲的面孔浸润③,　　15
当它听见了微风,它游伴的声音。

暖和的树篱内长着茂盛的蔷薇,
　　碧绿的瓜藤和月光色的绣线菊;
还有樱桃花,还有洁白的酒杯④,
　　盛着白天还没有喝干的露珠;　　　　20

---

① 明星(Arcturus),即大角星,是大熊星座尾部的牧夫星座中最明亮的星。诗里用的是复数。——译者
② 那高高的晶莹的花儿,可能指百合花。——译者
③ 母亲的面孔,指大地。——译者
④ 洁白的酒杯,并非任何一种花的特定称呼。——译者

And wild roses, and ivy serpentine
   With its dark buds and leaves, wandering astray,
And flowers azure, black, and streak'd with gold,
Fairer than any waken'd eyes behold.

25 And nearer to the river's trembling edge
   There grew broad flag-flowers, purple prank with white①,
And starry river buds among the sedge,
   And floating water-lilies, broad and bright,
Which lit the oak that overhung the hedge
30   With moonlight beams of their own watery light;
And bulrushes, and reeds of such deep green
As soothed the dazzled eye with sober sheen.

Methought that of these visionary flowers
   I made a nosegay, bound in such a way
35 That the same hues②, which in their natural bowers
   Were mingled or opposed, the like array
Kept these imprison'd children of the Hours
   Within my hand, — and then, elate and gay,
I hasten'd to the spot whence I had come,
40 That I might there present it — O! to Whom?

P. B. SHELLEY.

---

① *prank*: 'decked out.'
② *the same hues*: this and 'the like array' are the objects of 'kept' (l. 37), whose subject is 'children.'

还有野蔷薇,还有蜿蜒的常春藤,
　　　　带着蓓蕾和叶子,到处攀附;
　　而蓝色、黑色和洒上金斑的花卉
　　比任何醒了的眼睛看见的都更美。

　　而更加接近河流颤抖的边沿,　　　　　　　　　25
　　　　紫里镶白的巨大水菖蒲在生长,
　　还有菖蒲中星汉灿烂的花苞,
　　　　还有飘浮的睡莲,又大又明朗,
　　它们用自己晶莹闪灼的月光
　　　　将那棵荫盖着围篱的橡树照亮;　　　　30
　　还有香蒲和那么样深绿的芦苇,
　　朴素的光彩将缭乱的眼睛安慰。

　　我想我就用这些幻想的花朵
　　　　做了个花束,仔细捆在一起,
　　使得季节女神们被囚禁的孩子①　　　　　35
　　　　都将它们在天然园林中彼此
　　融合或陪衬得同样万紫千红
　　　　握在我手中——于是兴高采烈地
　　我赶忙向着我走来的那地方飞奔,
　　我好将它奉献给——哦,什么人?　　　　40
　　　　　　　　　　　　　　　　邹绛　译

编注　作为天才的预言家和理想主义者,雪莱将他的未来世界的梦形象地描绘在诗里,但是他从季节女神那里得到的花束将奉献给谁呢?这个惟妙惟肖的结束语把梦幻又带进了现实的世界。本诗由利·亨特(Leigh Hunt)发表在《文学袖珍书》(*The Literary Pock-Book*)上,雪莱的原标题为《问》。

---

① 季节女神,即阿尔丝(Hours),掌管天气、季节的女神。孩子,指各种花儿。——编注者

269. THE INNER VISION

Most sweet it is with unuplifted eyes
    To pace the ground, if path be there or none,
While a fair region round the traveller lies
    Which he forbears again to look upon;

Pleased rather with some soft ideal scene,
    The work of Fancy, or some happy tone
Of meditation, slipping in between
    The beauty coming and the beauty gone.

If Thought and Love desert us, from that day
    Let us break off all commerce with the Muse:
With Thought and Love companions of our way —

    Whate'er the senses take or may refuse, —
    The Mind's internal heaven shall shed her dews
Of inspiration on the humblest lay.

                                W. WORDSWORTH.

269. 心灵深处的幻景

华兹华斯

最适意莫过于在这茫茫的大地上
　　信步而行,不望脚下有无路径,
即便那秀丽宜人的去处就在这漫游者的身旁,
　　他也总是克制再三,无意在那儿流连、观赏。

他更喜欢一种温柔淡雅的理想情景, 5
　　那奇妙想象力的杰作;或者,他更醉心于
一种令人神往的沉思与冥想的心境,
　　那在美的显现与消逝的瞬间悄然出现的快感。

假如思想和爱情一旦将我们背离抛弃,
　　就让我们从此与缪斯断绝一切联系: 10
只要在我们的旅途上有思想和爱情的伴侣,

　　那末,无论什么东西被我们的感观选择、取舍,
我们心灵深处的上帝也会对那最谦卑的诗句,
慨然洒下她那灵感与启示的甘露。

　　　　　　　　　　　　　　　朱通伯　译

编注　华兹华斯相信,灵感是诗人的甘露,他愈来愈从现实世界踏入幻想世界,这是他中年以后的作品,作于去斯塔法岛和爱奥那岛(Staffa and Iona)的途中,发表在《重访雅洛河及其他诗歌》(*Yarrow Revisited and Other Poems*)上。华兹华斯原诗无标题,本标题为《金库》原编者所加。

270. THE REALM OF FANCY

Ever let the Fancy roam!
Pleasure never is at home①:
At a touch sweet Pleasure melteth,
Like to bubbles when rain pelteth;
Then let wingèd Fancy wander
Through the thought still spread beyond her:
Open wide the mind's cage-door,
She'll dart forth, and cloudward soar.
O sweet Fancy! let her loose;
Summer's joys are spoilt by use,
And the enjoying of the Spring
Fades as does its blossoming;
Autumn's red-lipp'd fruitage too,
Blushing through the mist and dew,
Cloys with tasting: What do then?
Sit thee by the ingle, when②
The sear faggot blazes bright,
Spirit of a winter's night;
When the soundless earth is muffled,
And the cakèd snow is shuffled
From the ploughboy's heavy shoon;

---

① *Pleasure never is at home*: this does not mean that home life has no pleasures, but that, to find pleasure, the mind must range outside itself.
② *ingle*: 'fire burning on the hearth.'

270. 幻想的王国

济慈

让幻想永远上天入地,
愉快决不耽在家里:
甜蜜的愉快一碰即化,
像雨声淅沥时的泡沫;
那末让插翅的幻想　　　　　　　　　　　5
在还在扩展的思想中徜徉:
敞开心灵的笼门,
它会冲出,飞入彩云。
甜蜜的幻想啊!把它放开;
夏天的欢乐已耗损殆尽,　　　　　　　10
而春天的享乐
像春花般凋落:
秋天的红唇的果实,
在雾与露中羞赧,
尝尝就生厌:那怎么办?　　　　　　　15
你就坐在炉边吧,这会儿
干柴烧得熊熊发光,
像寒冬腊月深夜的精灵;
无声的大地全被覆盖,
耕童的大靴一踩,　　　　　　　　　　20
雪块就散乱;

When the Night doth meet the Noon[①]
In a dark conspiracy
To banish Even from her sky.
    — Sit thee there, and send abroad,
With a mind self-overawed[②],
Fancy, high-commission'd: — send her[③]!
She has vassals to attend her;
She will bring, in spite of frost,
Beauties that the earth hath lost;
She will bring thee, all together,
All delights of summer weather;
All the buds and bells of May
From dewy sward or thorny spray;
All the heapéd Autumn's wealth,
With a still, mysterious stealth;
She will mix these pleasures up
Like three fit wines in a cup[④],
And thou shalt quaff it; — thou shalt hear
Distant harvest-carols clear;
Rustle of the reapéd corn;
Sweet birds antheming the morn:
And in the same moment — hark!
'Tis the early April lark,
Or the rooks, with busy caw,

---

① *When the Night doth meet the Noon*: *i.e.* when mid-day is speedily followed by the on-coming darkness.
② *self-overawed*: 'filled with awe at the sense of its own high purpose.'
③ *high-commission'd*: 'charged with the high task of providing thoughts for the mind.'
④ *three fit wines in a cup*: an experiment at which any one with a reasonable palate would shudder.

黑夜与中午相会,
作见不得人的同谋,
要把黄昏逐出天宇。
你坐定在那里,心平气静, 25
给幻想以崇高使命:——
派她出国,
她自有仆从侍候;
她会不管严霜,带来
大地已经丧失了的美; 30
她会全都一起带给你
夏季天气所有的美好东西;
从露湿的草地,或多刺树枝上的
五月里所有的苞蕾与花朵;
秋天堆积的所有财富, 35
她会静静、神秘而偷偷地
把这些偷快像三种旨酒般
调和在一只杯子里,
你就把它一饮而尽:——
你将听到遥远的丰收歌; 40
收割谷物的窸窣声:
欢颂清晨的悦耳鸟鸣声;
还有,这会儿——听哪!
听那四月初的云雀叫声,
那忙碌地哑哑叫的乌鸦, 45

  Foraging for sticks and straw.
  Thou shalt, at one glance, behold
  The daisy and the marigold;
  White-plumed lilies, and the first
50 Hedge-grown primrose that hath burst;
  Shaded hyacinth, alway①
  Sapphire queen of the mid-May;
  And every leaf, and every flower
  Pearlèd with the self-same shower.
55 Thou shalt see the field-mouse peep
  Meagre from its cellèd sleep;
  And the snake all winter-thin
  Cast on sunny bank its skin;
  Freckled nest-eggs thou shalt see
60 Hatching in the hawthorn-tree,
  When the hen-bird's wing doth rest
  Quiet on her mossy nest;
  Then the hurry and alarm
  When the bee-hive casts its swarm;
65 Acorns ripe down-pattering
  While the autumn breezes sing.

  O sweet Fancy! let her loose;
  Everything is spoilt by use:
  Where's the cheek that doth not fade,
70 Too much gazed at? Where's the maid
  Whose lip mature is ever new②?
  Where's the eye, however blue,
  Doth not weary? Where's the face
  One would meet in every place?
75 Where's the voice, however soft,

---

① *Shaded*: i.e. by the trees under which it grows.
② *mature*: 'ripe,' 'full.'

在抢夺树枝和柴草。
你将一眼看到
雏菊和金盏草；
白羽的百合花，第一朵
盛开在篱边的樱草花； 50
阴暗的风信子，始终是
五月中旬的青玉皇后；
每瓣叶，每朵花，
都带着同样的雨珠。
你将看到瘦瘦的田鼠 55
在洞中醒来，探首外望；
还有瘦了一冬的蛇
把皮蜕在向阳的堤岸上；
你将看到母鸟的翅膀
静静落在生苔的巢上， 60
斑驳的窝蛋
在荆棘树上孵化；
接着是蜂房抛出了群蜂
一片匆忙和惊慌；
秋风在歌唱 65
成熟的楮子急骤落下。

  哦，甜蜜的幻想！把它放开；
一切事物都耗损殆尽：
哪里有看得太多
而不消退的面颊？ 70
哪里有成熟的嘴唇永远鲜艳的女郎？
哪里有如何蔚蓝
也不令人厌倦的眼睛？
哪里有在一切地方都会遇到的面孔？
哪里有如何温柔 75

One would hear so very oft?
At a touch sweet Pleasure melteth
Like to bubbles when rain pelteth.
Let then wingéd Fancy find
Thee a mistress to thy mind:
Dulcet-eyed as Ceres' daughter,
Ere the God of Torment taught her
How to frown and how to chide;
With a waist and with a side
White as Hebe's, when her zone
Slipt its golden clasp, and down
Fell her kirtle to her feet,
While she held the goblet sweet,
And Jove grew languid. — Break the mesh[①]
Of the Fancy's silken leash;
Quickly break her prison-string,
And such joys as these she'll bring.
— Let the wingéd Fancy roam!
Pleasure never is at home.

J. KEATS.

---

① *languid*: like Alexander (see above, No. 116, l. 96), 'with love and wine at once opprest.'

也极其常常听到的声音？
甜蜜的愉快一碰即化，
像雨声淅沥时的泡沫。
那末让插翅的幻想为你
找个合你心意的情妇： *80*
眼睛像西利兹的女儿的①
一样倩美，苦痛之神
还没有教她怎样颦眉，和詈骂；
腰身与胁腹
像希比一样白②， *85*
她捧着金杯，
腰带脱落了金扣，
裙子落到了脚边。
育夫已经衰弱乏力③。——
剪断幻想的丝绦网眼； *90*
快快绞断她的囚带，
她会带来像这样的愉快。——
让插翅的幻想上天入地，
愉快决不耽在家里。

朱维基　译

编注　本诗题名《幻想的王国》，但在济慈看来美永远是与现实和真理密切联系着的。诗人非常善于把现实生活中的现象和事物提到真正美的高度，自然的景色和事物的外貌就会焕发出特殊的美的光彩，也就是本诗提到的"让插翅的幻想上天入地，愉快决不耽在家里"的真意。本诗于一八二〇发表在《女妖》(Lamia)上，原标题是《幻想》(Fancy)。

---

① 西利兹(Ceres)，罗马神话中谷类之女神。——译者
② 希比(Hebe)，希腊神话中宙斯与赫拉的女儿，青春女神。——译者
③ 育夫，即朱庇特(Jupiter)，罗马神话中的主神。——编注者

271. HYMN TO THE SPIRIT OF NATURE

Life of Life! thy lips enkindle
 With their love the breath between them;
And thy smiles before they dwindle
 Make the cold air fire; then screen them
In those looks, where whoso gazes
Faints, entangled in their mazes.

Child of Light! thy limbs are burning
 Through the vest which seems to hide them,
As the radiant lines of morning
 Through the clouds, ere they divide them;
And this atmosphere divinest
Shrouds thee wheresoe'er thou shinest.

Fair are others; none beholds thee,
 But thy voice sounds low and tender
Like the fairest, for it folds thee
 From the sight, that liquid splendour[①];
And all feel, yet see thee never[②], —
As I feel now, lost for ever!

Lamp of Earth! where'er thou movest

[①] *that liquid splendour*: this I take to refer to the beauty of the voice, not to 'sight,' for this means 'my sight,' and no one would apply the phrase to his own eyes.

[②] *feel*: sc. thee.

271. 献给大自然精灵的颂歌

雪莱

生命的生命!你的嘴唇用爱情
　　点燃了双唇之间的呼吸;
你的微笑使寒冷的空气变成火;
　　当微笑消失了,它们悄悄地
又藏在面容中,不管谁朝那儿凝视　　　　　5
都头晕目眩,陷进它们的迷宫里。

光明的孩子!你的四肢燃烧在
　　似乎掩盖着它们的衣衫里,
就像早晨辉煌的阳光还没有
　　拨开云彩前,燃烧在云彩里;　　　　　10
而这种极其神圣的气氛,不管你
照耀在哪儿,它都会笼罩着你。

美的是别的东西:没有谁看见你,
　　但你的声音低沉又柔曼,
却是最美的,因为它将你裹起来,　　　　15
　　使我看不见,像水声潺潺;
大家都感到,但永远将你看不到——
就像我现在感到的,永远消失了!

大地的明灯!不管你向哪儿移动,

20   Its dim shapes are clad with brightness①,
       And the souls of whom thou lovest②
       Walk upon the winds with lightness
       Till they fail, as I am failing,
       Dizzy, lost, yet unbewailing!

                                    P. B. SHELLEY.

---

① *Its*: sc. the Earth's.
② *souls of whom*: an awkward expression for 'souls of those whom.'
   On the whole Palgrave showed judgement in omitting this piece when he restrung his garland.

朦胧的形体都披上光明，
　　而你所热爱的那些人们的灵魂
　　都驾着风儿轻快地飞行，
　　直到他们跌下来，就像我一样，
　　昏眩，迷惘，然而却决不悲伤！

邹绛　译

编注《解放了的普罗米修斯》(*Prometheus Unbound*，1820) 是雪莱最著名的诗剧。在诗里，曾以传播火种而造福于人类的英雄，不是向暴虐的天帝妥协，而是由于天神起义，天帝被逐，得到了光荣的解放，雪莱使上古的神话重放异彩。本诗选自《解放了的普罗米修斯》第二幕第五场，是由"空中传来的歌声"。标题系《金库》原编者所加。

272. WRITTEN IN EARLY SPRING

I heard a thousand blended notes
    While in a grove I sat reclined,
In that sweet mood when pleasant thoughts
    Bring sad thoughts to the mind.

To her fair works did Nature link
    The human soul that through me ran;
And much it grieved my heart to think
    What man has made of man[①].

Through primrose tufts, in that green bower,
    The periwinkle trail'd its wreaths;
And 'tis my faith that every flower
    Enjoys the air it breathes.

The birds around me hopp'd and play'd,
    Their thoughts I cannot measure —
But the least motion which they made
    It seem'd a thrill of pleasure.

The budding twigs spread out their fan
    To catch the breezy air;

[①] *What man has made of man*: he has at least made man better than he would have been if left to Nature; without human intercourse children would grow up mere animals.

272. 早春之诗

华兹华斯

我听见了千百种曲调在交响——
  那是我斜倚在树丛里的时候;
我心情愉快,但快乐的思想
  却把悲哀的思想送上我心头。

大自然把我躯体里面的灵魂, 5
  同她自己的杰作结合了起来;
而想起这个问题真叫我心疼:
  人们拿自己的同类怎么对待?

穿过丛丛樱草,在绿荫之下,
  朵朵长春花缀出一个个花环; 10
这是我的信仰,每一朵鲜花
  对它所呼吸的空气都很喜欢。

一只只鸟在我周围雀跃嬉戏,
  它们心中的感情我没法猜测——
但是它们的动作哪怕再微细, 15
  看来也像是带着极大的欢乐。

往四下伸展的带嫩芽的枝梢
  像扇子般招引着轻柔的风儿;

And I must think, do all I can,
    That there was pleasure there.

If this belief from heaven be sent,
If such be Nature's holy plan,
Have I not reason to lament
    What man has made of man?

W. WORDSWORTH.

我虽尽己所能，但还是想道：
　　那带着嫩芽的枝梢也有欢乐。

如果这种信念是上天的旨意，
　　或者是这大自然的神圣安排，
难道我没理由为这问题叹息：
　　人们拿自己的同类怎么对待？

黄杲炘　译

编注　本诗于一七九八年作于阿福克斯登（Alfoxden），同年发表在《抒情歌谣集》（*Lyrical Ballads*）上，标题是《早春抒怀》（Lines Written in Early Spring）。这是华兹华斯歌咏自然的一首典型诗篇，他认为人可以从大自然获得美德与智慧，否则人与禽兽无异，不能成为万物之灵。

273. RUTH: OR THE INFLUENCES OF NATURE

When Ruth was left half desolate
Her father took another mate;
 And Ruth, not seven years old,
A slighted child, at her own will
Went wandering over dale and hill,
 In thoughtless freedom, bold.

And she had made a pipe of straw,
And music from that pipe could draw
 Like sounds of winds and floods;
Had built a bower upon the green,
As if she from her birth had been
 An infant of the woods.

Beneath her father's roof, alone
She seem'd to live; her thoughts her own;
 Herself her own delight:
Pleased with herself, nor sad nor gay,
And, passing thus the live-long day,
 She grew to woman's height.

There came a youth from Georgia's shore —
A military casque he wore[1]

---

[1] *casque*: 'helmet.'

273. 鲁思（或自然的影响）

华兹华斯

鲁思，她孤孤单单被撇下，
爸爸屋里来了个后妈，
　　那时，她七岁不满；
没有谁管她，她随心所欲
在高山低谷游来荡去， 5
　　自由，冒失，大胆。

她用燕麦秆做一支短笛，
一吹，便吹出笛声嘹呖，
　　好似风声或水声；
她在草地上搭了个棚子， 10
看来，她仿佛天生就是
　　山林草莽的幼婴。

在爸爸家里，她无依无靠，
心里想什么，只自己知道，
　　乐趣也只是在自身； 15
她自满自足，不喜也不悲，
就这样度过了年年岁岁，
　　直到她长大成人。

从远隔重洋的乔治亚海边[①]，
　　来了个头戴军盔的青年， 20

[①] 乔治亚，过去是英国在北美建立的十三个殖民地（十三州）之一，现在是美国东南部的一州，濒临大西洋。——译者

With splendid feathers drest;
He brought them from the Cherokees;
The feathers nodded in the breeze
   And made a gallant crest.

From Indian blood you deem him sprung:
But no! he spake the English tongue
   And bore a soldier's name;
And, when America was free
From battle and from jeopardy,
   He 'cross the ocean came.

With hues of genius on his cheek,
In finest tones the youth could speak;
   — While he was yet a boy
The moon, the glory of the sun,
And streams that murmur as they run,
   Had been his dearest joy.

He was a lovely youth! I guess
The panther in the wilderness
   Was not so fair as he;
And when he chose to sport and play,
No dolphin ever was so gay
   Upon the tropic sea.

Among the Indians he had fought;

军盔上羽翎闪闪；
从车罗基人那里,他弄来①
这一束羽翎,挺有气派,
　　在风中轻轻摇颤。

莫把他认作印第安血胤,　　　　　　　　　　25
他说话纯粹是英国口音,
　　享有军人的名位；
当北美经过几年苦战,
争得了自由,摆脱了危难,
　　他扬帆渡海东归②。　　　　　　　　　30

他的眉宇间才华闪耀,
舌端吐出迷人的音调；
　　想当年,他还是小孩,
太阳的金焰,月亮的银辉,
柔声细语的滔滔溪水,　　　　　　　　　　35
　　给了他多少愉快！

这个小伙子,真是呱呱叫！
我想,美洲荒野的山豹
　　也不及这般英爽；
在他纵情游乐的时辰,　　　　　　　　　　40
热带海面上嬉戏的海豚
　　也不曾这般欢畅。

和印第安人一道打过仗,

---

① 车罗基人,北美印地安人的一支,聚居之地即现在的美国东南部。北美独立战争期间,车罗基人曾协同英国殖民军作战。——译者
② 北美独立战争结束于一七八一年。这时英国殖民军已被北美起义部队击溃,这个在英军中服役的青年便返回英国。——译者

    And with him many tales he brought
45   Of pleasure and of fear;
    Such tales as, told to any maid
    By such a youth, in the green shade,
      Were perilous to hear.

    He told of girls, a happy rout①!
50   Who quit their fold with dance and shout,
      Their pleasant Indian town,
    To gather strawberries all day long;
    Returning with a choral song
      When daylight is gone down.

55   He spake of plants that hourly change
    Their blossoms, through a boundless range
      Of intermingling hues;
    With budding, fading, faded flowers,
    They stand the wonder of the bowers
60   From morn to evening dews.

    He told of the magnolia, spread
    High as a cloud, high over head!
      The cypress and her spire②;
    — Of flowers that with one scarlet gleam
65   Cover a hundred leagues, and seem
      To set the hills on fire.

---

① *rout*: 'band,' as in No. 66, l. 61.
② *spire*: the cypress tree is in shape something like the spire of a church.

这就有不少故事可讲：
　有的可怕，有的甜； 45
绿荫深处，漂亮小伙子
给漂亮姑娘讲这些故事，
　只怕有几分危险。

他讲印第安姑娘们，真快活，
又跳舞，又喊叫，成群搭伙， 50
　从城里跑到郊外，
一整天忙着采集草莓，
一直采集到日落天黑，
　齐声合唱着归来。

他讲那边的奇树异花， 55
颜色随着时辰而变化，
　五光十色，变不完；
从清晨直到凝露的幽夜，
含苞的含苞，开的开，谢的谢，
　那才是园林的奇观。 60

他讲玉兰树，绿叶像云霓，
高悬在半空，俯临着大地；
　讲翠柏，树顶尖尖；
讲山花万朵，一色鲜红，
绵延几百里，望去如同 65
　野火烧遍了群山。

The youth of green savannahs spake[①],
And many an endless, endless lake
   With all its fairy crowds
Of islands, that together lie
As quietly as spots of sky
   Among the evening clouds.

'How pleasant,' then he said, 'it were
A fisher or a hunter there,
   In sunshine or in shade
To wander with an easy mind,
And build a household fire, and find
   A home in every glade!

'What days and what bright years! Ah me!
Our life were life indeed, with thee
   So pass'd in quiet bliss;
And all the while,' said he, 'to know
That we were in a world of woe,
   On such an earth as this!'

And then he sometimes interwove
Fond thoughts about a father's love,
   'For there,' said he, 'are spun
Around the heart such tender ties,
That our own children to our eyes
   Are dearer than the sun.

'Sweet Ruth! and could you go with me

---

① *savannahs*: the name given to the vast plains in the south of the U.S.A..

他讲绿茸茸大片草地,
有多少湖泽一望无际,
　　湖中的星星点点
是一群岛屿,玲珑秀丽,　　　　　　　　　70
静穆有如傍晚的云霞里
　　露出的点点青天。

"在那边,当一个渔夫,"他说,
"当一个猎人,好不快活!
　　阳光下,或者树荫下,　　　　　　　75
东游西逛,又轻松又安逸;
林子里每一块空地都可以
　　搭棚子,生火,住家!

"和你在一起,日子多幸福!
那样的一生,才不算虚度:　　　　　　　80
　　只有安宁和喜悦;
同时,我们也不会忘记
周遭是一片苦难的大地,
　　是一个不幸的世界!"

有时,他还以多情的姿态　　　　　　　　85
谈到父母对儿女的疼爱,
　　他说,"人们的心中
牢系着骨肉之情的纽带;
我们会把自己的小孩
　　看得比太阳还重。　　　　　　　　90

"鲁思呵! 求求你,跟我同去,

My helpmate in the woods to be,
   Our shed at night to rear;
Or run, my own adopted bride,
   A sylvan huntress at my side,
     And drive the flying deer!

'Beloved Ruth!' — No more he said.
The wakeful Ruth at midnight shed
   A solitary tear:
She thought again — and did agree
With him to sail across the sea,
   And drive the flying deer.

'And now, as fitting is and right,
We in the church our faith will plight,
   A husband and a wife.'
Even so they did; and I may say
That to sweet Ruth that happy day
   Was more than human life.

Through dream and vision did she sink,
Delighted all the while to think
   That, on those lonesome floods
And green savannahs, she should share
His board with lawful joy, and bear
   His name in the wild woods.

But, as you have before been told,
This Stripling, sportive, gay, and bold,
   And with his dancing crest
So beautiful, through savage lands

到那森林里,做我的伴侣,
　　搭起我们的棚屋;
跟我去吧,我选定的新娘!
当个女猎人,跟在我身旁, 95
　　追赶飞奔的野鹿!

"可爱的鲁思!"——他不再多说。
半夜里,鲁思睁眼而卧,
　　流下寂寞的泪珠;
她左思右想,拿定了主张: 100
跟他去,漂洋过海,到远方
　　去追赶飞奔的野鹿。

"既然这么办合情合理,
我们就趁早结为夫妻,
　　去教堂行礼宣誓。" 105
他们俩说办就办;我猜
那个好日子,在鲁思看来
　　抵得过人生一世。

她沉入梦想,沉入幻境,
一天到晚都高高兴兴, 110
　　想象:在僻静河滩,
在葱茏草地,在蛮荒林子,
合法地,愉快地,姓他的姓氏,
　　常与他相随相伴。

可是,我先前已经说过: 115
这莽撞后生,爱玩爱乐,
　　军盔上羽翎闪闪;
这英俊儿郎,曾经远游

Had roam'd about, with vagrant bands
    Of Indians in the West.

The wind, the tempest roaring high,
The tumult of a tropic sky
    Might well be dangerous food
For him, a youth to whom was given
So much of earth — so much of heaven,
    And such impetuous blood.

Whatever in those climes he found
Irregular in sight or sound
    Did to his mind impart
A kindred impulse, seem'd allied
To his own powers, and justified
    The workings of his heart.

Nor less, to feed voluptuous thought,
The beauteous forms of Nature wrought, —
    Fair trees and gorgeous flowers;
The breezes their own languor lent;
The stars had feelings, which they sent
    Into those favour'd bowers.

Yet, in his worst pursuits, I ween
That sometimes there did intervene
    Pure hopes of high intent:
For passions, link'd to forms so fair
And stately, needs must have their share

蛮荒的土地,在大海西头①
　有一帮印第安伙伴。 *120*

厉声呼啸的暴雨狂风,
热带天宇的喧嚣骚动,
　成了他心灵的养料;
他受之于天,受之于地,
年轻轻,性子便这般乖戾, *125*
　血液便这般狂暴!

那边,怪异的形象或声音
把一种同气相求的热忱
　传送到他的心底;
与他原有的才智合流, *130*
使他内心的种种图谋
　都显得正当合理。

万象的纷华靡丽,也同样
怂恿了他的浪荡轻狂:
　娇花与亭亭芳树; *135*
熏风吹得人意懒心慵;
一天星斗把脉脉柔情
　向烂漫园林倾注。

我想:他居心不良的谋划,
有时候,其中也会掺杂 *140*
　纯正的意图和心愿;
因为,他那些激情豪兴
既然得力于奇观丽景,

---

① 大海西头,指北美,北美在欧洲的西边。——译者

Of noble sentiment.

But ill he lived, much evil saw,
With men to whom no better law
   Nor better life was known;
Deliberately and undeceived
Those wild men's vices he received,
   And gave them back his own.

His genius and his moral frame
Were thus impair'd, and he became
   The slave of low desires:
A man who without self-control
Would seek what the degraded soul
   Unworthily admires.

And yet he with no feign'd delight
Had woo'd the maiden, day and night
   Had loved her, night and morn;
What could he less than love a maid
Whose heart with so much nature play'd —
   So kind and so forlorn?

Sometimes most earnestly he said,
'O Ruth! I have been worse than dead;
   False thoughts, thoughts bold and vain
Encompass'd me on every side
When I, in confidence and pride,
   Had cross'd the Atlantic main.

'Before me shone a glorious world

就该有高雅的一面。

但他久陷于邪恶生涯,   *145*
他那帮伙伴不明礼法,
    也不知弃恶从善;
他神志清明,却甘心愿意
和那些蛮子混同一气,
    彼此以恶习相染。   *150*

他成了卑下欲望的奴隶;
禀赋与才华,品德与道义
    都渐渐火灭烟消;
一个人若是不自检束,
就会与堕落的灵魂一路,   *155*
    追求鄙俗的目标。

他曾以毫不掺假的欢快
向鲁思求婚,与鲁思相爱,
    朝朝暮暮地相守;
他怎能不爱这样的少女——   *160*
她的心灵与自然为侣,
    孤苦,和善,又温柔?

他也对鲁思说过,很真诚:
"从前,我简直恶劣透顶;
    狂妄,虚荣和欺骗   *165*
团团围裹了我的身心;
那时,我又高傲又自信,
    到了大西洋那边。

"那时,眼前是一片新天地,

170 Fresh as a banner bright, unfurl'd
         To music suddenly;
     I look'd upon those hills and plains,
     And seem'd as if let loose from chains
         To live at liberty.

175 'No more of this — for now, by thee,
     Dear Ruth! more happily set free,
         With nobler zeal I burn;
     My soul from darkness is released
     Like the whole sky when to the east
180   The morning doth return.'

     Full soon that better mind was gone;
     No hope, on wish remain'd, not one, —
         They stirr'd him now no more;
     New objects did new pleasure give,
185 And once again he wish'd to live
         As lawless as before.

     Meanwhile, as thus with him it fared,
     They for the voyage were prepared,
         And went to the sea-shore;
190 But, when they thither came, the youth
     Deserted his poor bride, and Ruth
         Could never find him more.

     God help thee, Ruth! — Such pains she had,
     That she in half a year was mad,

像一面鲜明耀眼的军旗 170
　在军乐中展开①；
我望着那边的山岭、平原，
仿佛从此挣脱了锁链，
　从此便自由自在。

"不谈这些了；如今，有了你， 175
我才算真正幸福如意，
　热情也变得高尚；
我灵魂已从黑暗中得救，
正如曙光出现在东头，
　把整个天空照亮。" 180

他这些好心思转眼就溜走，
不留下一点指望和盼头，——
　热情已化为淡漠；
新的目标有新的乐趣，
他又巴不得还像过去 185
　过无法无天的生活。

他心里正经历这番动荡，
他们的远航已准备停当，
　双双向海岸出发啦。
可是，小伙子一到港口， 190
便甩掉鲁思，独自出走，
　她再也见不到他啦。

求上帝保佑鲁思！真可怜！
有半年光景，她疯疯癫癫，

---

① 此人身份是军人，所以爱用军队生活方面的比喻。——译者

195　　　　　And in a prison housed;
　　　　　　And there, with many a doleful song
　　　　　　Made of wild words, her cup of wrong
　　　　　　　　She fearfully caroused①.

　　　　　　Yet sometimes milder hours she knew,
200　　　　　Nor wanted sun, nor rain, nor dew,
　　　　　　　　Nor pastimes of the May,
　　　　　　— They all were with her in her cell;
　　　　　　And a clear brook with cheerful knell
　　　　　　　　Did o'er the pebbles play.

205　　　　　When Ruth three seasons thus had lain,
　　　　　　There came a respite to her pain;
　　　　　　　　She from her prison fled;
　　　　　　But of the Vagrant none took thought;
　　　　　　And where it liked her best she sought
210　　　　　　　Her shelter and her bread.

　　　　　　Among the fields she breathed again;
　　　　　　The master-current of her brain
　　　　　　　　Ran permanent and free;
　　　　　　And, coming to the banks of Tone,
215　　　　　There did she rest; and dwell alone
　　　　　　　　Under the greenwood tree.

　　　　　　The engines of her pain, the tools
　　　　　　That shaped her sorrow, rocks and pools,

---

① *her cup of wrong She fearfully caroused*: to carouse (= 'drink') as a transitive verb is found in *Othello*, but is now obsolete.

被送到牢房里关押； 195
在那儿,尝够了辛酸委屈,
她唱着一支支惨痛的歌曲,
　　歌词净是些疯话。

也有些时辰,她不算太苦:
她不缺阳光,不缺雨露, 200
　　也不缺春天的娱乐;
牢房里,这些与她同在;
清亮的溪水,调子欢快,
　　在卵石沙砾上流过。

三个季度就这样度过, 205
鲁思的苦难有了些缓和:
　　她从牢房里逃出;
四处流浪,没有人怜惜,
乐意在哪里,就在哪里
　　寻找饭食和住处。 210

重新呼吸于原野田畴,
她的思绪像滚滚川流,
　　没遮拦,永不停顿;
后来,她到了托恩河畔①,
便留在那里;孤单无伴 215
　　在冬青树下栖身。

触动她愁思的阳春景致,
引起她伤感的池水、山石,

---

① 托恩河,在英格兰西南部萨默塞特郡境内。——译者

  And airs that gently stir
  The vernal leaves — she loved them still,
  Nor ever tax'd them with the ill
    Which had been done to her.

  A barn her winter bed supplies;
  But, till the warmth of summer skies
    And summer days is gone,
  (And all do in this tale agree)
  She sleeps beneath the greenwood tree,
    And other home hath none.

  An innocent life, yet far astray!
  And Ruth will, long before her day,
    Be broken down and old.
  Sore aches she needs must have! but less
  Of mind, than body's wretchedness,
    From damp, and rain, and cold.

  If she is prest by want of food
  She from her dwelling in the wood
    Repairs to a road-side;
  And there she begs at one steep place,
  Where up and down with easy pace
    The horsemen-travellers ride.

  That oaten pipe of hers is mute
  Or thrown away; but with a flute
    Her loneliness she cheers;
  This flute, made of a hemlock stalk,

绿叶间,清风和畅;
这些,她依旧深情眷爱,　　　　　　　　　　*220*
生怕对它们有什么伤害——
　　像别人伤害她那样。

冬天,她在谷仓里过夜;
在此之前,当温暖季节
　　还不曾随风远遁,　　　　　　　　　　*225*
(人人都承认这话不假)
她一直栖宿在冬青树下,
　　再没有别处安身。

清白的生灵,走错了方向!
鲁思,过不了多久时光,　　　　　　　　　　*230*
　　就会老,就会凋残;
她必得熬受钻心的痛楚;
心灵够苦了,皮肉却更苦——
　　风雨,潮湿,严寒。

要是没吃的,饿得受不住,　　　　　　　　　*235*
她便离开林间的住处,
　　到一条大路旁边,
站在山坡上向路人乞讨——
骑马的路人见山坡陡峭,
　　慢悠悠上山下山。　　　　　　　　　　*240*

她的燕麦秆短笛已丢弃,
又用茵陈蒿做一支长笛,
　　把郁闷心情排解;
每天傍晚,匡托克山下①,

---

① 匡托克山,即匡托克丘陵,在英格兰西南部萨摩塞特郡。——译者

245   At evening in his homeward walk
        The Quantock woodman hears.

    I, too, have pass'd her on the hills
    Setting her little water-mills
        By spouts and fountains wild —
250   Such small machinery as she turn'd
    Ere she had wept, ere she had mourn'd
        A young and happy child!

    Farewell! and when thy days are told,
    Ill-fated Ruth! in hallow'd mould
225   Thy corpse shall buried be;
    For thee a funeral bell shall ring,
    And all the congregation sing
        A Christian psalm for thee,

                      W. WORDSWORTH.

疲乏的樵夫缓步回家,   *245*
 听到这笛声幽咽。

我也曾从她身旁走过——
山上,有她的小小水磨
 在荒凉泉眼旁边;
这种磨,她早年也曾推动,   *250*
那时,她不哭,也不悲痛,
 那是她快乐的童年!

别了!等到你此生结束,
苦命的鲁思呵!神圣的泥土
 会把你躯体埋藏;   *255*
送葬的钟声将为你敲动,
全村的教徒,都在教堂中
 为你把圣歌高唱。

杨德豫　译

274. WRITTEN IN THE EUGANEAN HILLS, NORTH ITALY

Many a green isle needs must be
In the deep wide sea of misery,
Or the mariner, worn and wan,
Never thus could voyage on
5   Day and night, and night and day,
Drifting on his dreary way,
With the solid darkness black
Closing round his vessel's track;
Whilst above, the sunless sky,
10   Big with clouds, hangs heavily,
And behind, the tempest fleet
Hurries on with lightning feet,
Riving sail, and cord, and plank,
Till the ship has almost drank①
15   Death from the o'er-brimming deep;
And sinks down, down, like that sleep
When the dreamer seems to be
Weltering through eternity②;

---

① *has almost drank*: the past participle of *drink* is 'drunk,' but from the 17th to the 19th century *drank* was extended from the past tense to the past participle.

② *Weltering*: to welter is properly to roll helplessly in water or some other fluid; here it is nearly equivalent to 'drifting.' The images crowd so thickly here that the sense is obscured; the picture is a ship driven by the tempest, which has almost overwhelmed it and sent it to the bottom, as it flies ever farther from the land and the sailors sit motionless, longing and yet not daring to turn the ship's head.

274. 写在意大利北部欧加宁群山中

雪莱

一定有许多绿色的岛屿
在又深又广的痛苦的大海里,
否则疲倦而憔悴的水手
决不会这样不断地追求,
白昼又黑夜,黑夜又白昼,   *5*
老是在沉闷的旅途上漂流,
同时伸手不见掌的黑暗
包围着他那帆船的航线;
头上,没有太阳的天空,
罩满了乌云,是那么沉重,   *10*
后面,快速的暴风骤雨
跨着闪电的脚步在急驰
撕裂着风帆、缆索和木板,
直到那汹涌的大海差一点
让这只帆船将死亡痛饮,   *15*
然后就不断地下沉,下沉,
仿佛一个人正在做着梦,
不断地飘荡在永恒之中;

And the dim low line before
Of a dark and distant shore
Still recedes, as ever still①
Longing with divided will.
But no power to seek or shun,
He is ever drifted on
O'er the unreposing wave,
To the haven of the grave.

Aye, many flowering islands lie
In the waters of wide Agony:
To such a one this morn was led
My bark, by soft winds piloted.
— 'Mid the mountains Euganean
I stood listening to the paean
With which the legion'd rooks did hail
The sun's uprise majestical:
Gathering round with wings all hoar,
Through the dewy mist they soar
Like gray shades, till the eastern heaven
Bursts, and then, — as clouds of even,
Fleck'd with fire and azure, lie
In the unfathomable sky, —
So their plumes of purple grain
Starr'd with drops of golden rain
Gleam above the sunlight woods,

---

① *recedes*: as he sails down the coast the farthest visible point of land ahead is always changing and so, as it were, retiring as he advances.

前面,黑暗而遥远的海岸
隐隐约约地露出的地平线, 20
老是在后退,像从前老是
渴望着挨近,心怀二意。
但没有寻求和避开命运,
越过翻腾的波浪滚滚,
他老是不断地向前漂流, 25
漂向那葬身之处的港口①。

当然,许多开花的岛屿
分布在痛苦的广阔水域里:
我的小船儿被和风引导,
今早上来到了这样的海岛。 30
——这儿,在这欧加宁群山中,
我站着倾听白嘴鸦一大群
高唱着颂歌,正在欢迎②
红红的太阳庄严地上升:
聚集着全是灰白的翅膀③, 35
它们在带露的雾气中飞翔,
像灰色的阴影,直到东方的
天空亮开了,然后像黄昏的
云彩,点缀着蔚蓝和火红,
躺在那深不可测的天空中—— 40
同样,它们那紫色的羽翼,
也洒上一滴滴金色的细雨,
闪耀在阳光璀灿的树林上,

---

① 第二十六行之后被原编者删去三十九行,第一○二行之后亦被原编者删去一四三行。——编注者
② 颂歌,是指对阿波罗的颂歌。阿波罗是太阳神,也是治疗之神。——译者
③ 灰白的翅膀,白嘴鸦的羽毛是带着一层淡紫的黑色,但在晨光熹微中,它可能现出灰白的颜色。——译者

As in silent multitudes
On the morning's fitful gale
Through the broken mist they sail;
And the vapours cloven and gleaming
Follow down the dark steep streaming,
Till all is bright, and clear, and still
Round the solitary hill.

Beneath is spread like a green sea
The waveless plain of Lombardy,
Bounded by the vaporous air,
Islanded by cities fair;
Underneath Day's azure eyes,
Ocean's nursling, Venice lies, —
A peopled labyrinth of walls,
Amphitrite's destined halls,
Which her hoary sire now paves
With his blue and beaming waves.
Lo! the sun upsprings behind,
Broad, red, radiant, half-reclined
On the level quivering line
Of the waters crystalline;
And before that chasm of light,
As within a furnace bright,
Column, tower, and dome, and spire,
Shine like obelisks of fire,
Pointing with inconstant motion

当它们这一群默默地飞翔,
乘着早晨一阵阵的大风, 45
航行在已经破碎的雾气中;
而这些消散的闪光的雾气
就纷纷流下黑暗的峭壁,
直到这孤零零的小山附近,
一切都明亮、清彻和安静。 50

伦巴第的没有波浪的平原①
像碧绿的大海展开在下面,
四周是一片白茫茫的雾气,
岛屿般散布着美丽的城市;
就在白昼的蔚蓝色眼底, 55
躺着威尼斯,海洋的骄子②——
人烟稠密的城墙的迷宫,
安菲特里特命定的宫廷③,
道路是她那白发的父亲
用碧蓝而闪光的波浪铺成。 60
看哪!后面升起了太阳,
巨大、鲜红、灿烂而辉煌,
半倚在动荡着的水平线上,
那海水像水晶一样明亮;
而在那光明的空隙面前, 65
就像在明亮的熔炉中间,
柱头、高塔、圆顶、塔尖,
闪耀得像火的方尖碑一般,
从那黑暗的海洋的祭坛上

---

① 伦巴第,意大利北部主要在波河以北的地区。——译者
② 威尼斯距离欧加宁群山不到二十英里。——译者
③ 安菲特里特(Amphitrite),海洋女神。威尼斯的土地大部分是从大海里开拓出来的。——译者

70	From the altar of dark ocean
	To the sapphire-tinted skies;
	As the flames of sacrifice
	From the marble shrines did rise,
	As to pierce the dome of gold①
75	Where Apollo spoke of old.
	Sun-girt City! thou hast been
	Ocean's child, and then his queen;
	Now is come a darker day,
	And thou soon must be his prey,
80	If the power that raised thee here
	Hallow so thy watery bier②.
	A less drear ruin then than now,
	With thy conquest-branded brow
	Stooping to the slave of slaves
85	From thy throne, among the waves
	Wilt thou be, — when the sea-mew
	Flies, as once before it flew,
	O'er thine isles depopulate,
	And all is in its ancient state,
90	Save where many a palace gate,

---

① *As*: 'as if.'
② 80, 81. *I.e.* if Fate, which had raised Venice from obscurity, give her so noble an end as to be drowned in the sea.

用不断变化的动作指向 70
兰玉一般的天空
有如祭祀的火焰熊熊,
从大理石神龛不断上升,
仿佛要穿过从前太阳神
在那儿讲话的黄金圆屋顶①。 75

阳光环绕的城市!本来就
诞生于海岸,又是他的皇后②;
黑暗的日子现在已临头,
你不久一定会作他的俘虏③,
如果命运在此使你升腾 80
她也要使你在水中葬身④。
比起现在从你的宝座上,
将战败的烙印留在额头上⑤,
屈伏于那个奴隶们的奴隶⑥,
那时你将会变成浪涛里 85
一座不那么阴沉的废墟——
海鸥会飞翔着像从前一样,
飞过你没有人烟的岛上,
一切都保存着古老的风景,
就是没有那宫殿的许多扇大门 90

---

① 从前太阳神讲话的地方,即特尔斐的阿波罗神殿。——译者
② 参看第211首编注。——编注者
③ 一八一四年威尼斯被奥地利人并吞,直到一八六六年才归还意大利。——译者
④ 原编者认为一个世纪以前威尼斯并未受海水浸蚀,而雪莱指这个城市被奥地利人摧毁后,居民从此离开这里,把她留在海浪的浸蚀之中。——译者
⑤ 雪莱很可能想到一七九七年拿破仑的占领,这次占领导致了《坎波福米奥和约》的签订。——译者
⑥ 在一切事物中,雪莱最恨的是君主政体,因此他把在欧洲到处建立君主政体的拿破仑可能要索取"国王们的国王"的称号改成为"奴隶们的奴隶"。——译者

With green sea-flowers overgrown
Like a rock of ocean's own,
Topples o'er the abandon'd sea
As the tides change sullenly.
The fisher on his watery way
Wandering at the close of day,
Will spread his sail and seize his oar
Till he pass the gloomy shore,
Lest thy dead should, from their sleep
Bursting o'er the starlight deep,
Lead a rapid masque of death①
O'er the waters of his path.

Noon descends around me now;
'Tis the noon of autumn's glow,
When a soft and purple mist
Like a vaporous amethyst②,
Or an air-dissolvéd star③
Mingling light and fragrance, far
From the curved horizon's bound
To the point of Heaven's profound④,
Fills the overflowing sky;

---

① *masque*: originally a dramatic entertainment consisting of dancing and acting in dumb show.
② *amethyst*: a precious stone of a clear purple or bluish-violet colour.
③ *air-dissolvéd*: on the analogy of 'air-borne,' 'air-bred,' etc., this can only mean 'dissolved by the. air,' but Shelley probably meant 'dissolved into air.'
④ *the point of Heaven's profound*: 'the zenith,' i. e. the point in the sky exactly over the beholder; *profound* is used as a substantive in poetry for the depths of the sky or the sea.

上面有碧绿的海葵长满,
像海洋本身的岩石一般,
轰然倒在被人抛弃的大海,
就像潮水愠怒地改变了模样。
当天色已晚的时候, 95
渔夫沿着自己的航道飘着小船,
划着桨,张着帆,
直到他绕过那阴郁的海岸,
否则你的死者从梦里边
会跃出星光灿烂的海面, 100
在渔夫经过的地方
领跳起死亡的假面舞会。

在我的四周现在是中午:
这是充满了秋光的中午,
像一块变成蒸气的紫水晶, 105
像一颗溶化在空中的星星,
一片轻柔的紫色的雾气
将光明和芳香混合在一起,
远远地从那弧形的地平线
直到深邃的蓝空的顶点, 110
充溢着整个天宇;

  And the plains that silent lie①
  Underneath; the leaves unsodden
  Where the infant Frost has trodden
115 With his morning-wingéd feet
  Whose bright print is gleaming yet;
  And the red and golden vines
  Piercing with their trellised lines
  The rough, dark-skirted wilderness②;
120 The dun and bladed grass no less,
  Pointing from this hoary tower
  In the windless air; the flower
  Glimmering at my feet; the line
  Of the olive-sandall'd Apennine③
125 In the south dimly islanded;
  And the Alps, whose snows are spread
  High between the clouds and sun;
  And of living things each one;
  And my spirit, which so long
130 Darken'd this swift stream of song, —
  Interpenetrated lie
  By the glory of the sky;
  Be it love, light, harmony④,
  Odour, or the soul of all

---

① *the plains*: this and all that follows between this line and line 130 are the subject of 'lie' in line 131.

② *dark-skirted*: the rough countryside is looked on as a dark-coloured garment with red and gold trimming.

③ *olive-sandall'd*: i.e. with olive trees at the foot of the mountain.

④ *it*: sc. 'the glory'; whether this glory proceed from external sources or from the poet's own mind which creates spiritual inhabitants for a universe without life in itself.

而草原,在下面一声不响地
躺着;那没有湿透的树叶,
初降的寒霜已经用自己
早晨飞快的步履踩过, 115
那明亮的脚印还闪闪灼灼;
那些红色和金色的藤蔓,
它们用交错的线条刺穿
披上了黑衣的崎岖的原野;
同样还有暗褐色的草叶, 120
从这灰白的高楼指向那
平静无风的天空;而鲜花,
就在我脚下闪光;在南部,
亚平宁的山麓长满橄榄树①,
隐约地勾画出半岛的身影; 125
而阿尔卑斯山,积雪的峰顶
在太阳和云彩间巍然屹立;
还有每一个活着的东西;
和我的精灵,它为此长久
遮暗了我这歌声的激流—— 130
它们现在都展现在大地上,
全身渗透着天空的辉煌;
不管它是爱,是和谐,是光,
是芳香,还是万有的灵魂,

---

① 亚平宁,纵贯意大利半岛的山脉。——译者

135	Which from Heaven like dew doth fall,
	Or the mind which feeds this verse
	Peopling the lone universe.
	Noon descends, and after noon
	Autumn's evening meets me soon,
140	Leading the infantine moon
	And that one star, which to her[①]
	Almost seems to minister
	Half the crimson light she brings
	From the sunset's radiant springs:
145	And the soft dreams of the morn
	(Which like wingéd winds had borne
	To that silent isle, which lies[②]
	'Mid remember'd agonies,
	The frail bark of this lone being),
150	Pass, to other sufferers fleeing,
	And its ancient pilot, Pain,
	Sits beside the helm again.
	Other flowering isles must be
	In the sea of Life and Agony:
155	Other spirits float and flee
	O'er that gulf: even now, perhaps,
	On some rock the wild wave wraps[③],
	With folding wings they waiting sit
	For my bark, to pilot it

---

① *to her*: sc. to evening.
② *that silent isle*: cf. ll.1,2, and 27 - 30, above.
③ *the wild wave*: i.e. which the wild wave.

它像露水样从天上降临，　　　　　　　　　　　135
或许是那哺育这首诗的心灵，
它在这荒凉的宇宙里栖身。

中午降临了，中午过后
秋夜又很快把我欢迎，
是它引来了那新月一钩　　　　　　　　　　　140
和那一颗星呀，它几乎将它从
落日辉煌灿烂的源泉中
带来一半鲜红的落霞
都像要送给那新生的月亮：
而早晨那些柔和的美梦　　　　　　　　　　　145
（它们像长上了翅膀的风
将这孤独者脆弱的小船
已经带到那静静的小岛边，
小岛座落在难忘的痛苦中）
消失了，飞向另外的受苦人，　　　　　　　　150
而那古老的舵手，痛苦之神，
又坐在船上将舵柄把稳。

在那生命和痛苦的大海里
一定有其他开花的岛屿：
其他的精灵飘浮着，飞快地　　　　　　　　　155
掠过那海湾；也许此刻在海浪
汹涌地包围着的一块岩石上，
他们收拢了翅膀，现在还
坐着，在等待我的小船，

	To some calm and blooming cove,
160	To some calm and blooming cove,
	Where for me, and those I love,
	May a windless bower be built,
	Far from passion, pain, and guilt,
	In a dell 'mid lawny hills
165	Which the wild sea-murmur fills,
	And soft sunshine, and the sound
	Of old forests echoing round,
	And the light and smell divine,
	Of all flowers that breathe and shine.
170	— We may live so happy there,
	That the Spirits of the Air
	Envying us, may even entice
	To our healing Paradise
	The polluting multitude;
175	But their rage would be subdued
	By that clime divine and calm,
	And the winds whose wings rain balm
	On the uplifted soul, and leaves
	Under which the bright sea heaves[①];
180	While each breathless interval[②]
	In their whisperings musical
	The inspired soul supplies
	With its own deep melodies;
	And the love which heals all strife
185	Circling, like the breath of life[③],

---

① *Under which*: the picture is of one standing on a hill and looking down through the tree-tops on to the sea.
② 180 – 7. The soul fills the intervals with its own music, and Love fills all round with the sense of brother-hood.
③ *Circling*: 'embracing.'

引它到平静而开花的海湾中,　　　　　　　　　160
但愿给我和我爱的人们
在那儿修一座避风的房屋,
远离开激情、罪过和痛苦,
在青山环抱着的一个山谷里,
充满山谷的是大海的絮语、　　　　　　　　　165
柔和的阳光、古老的森林、
在四面八方回响着的声音
和一切呼吸与闪光的花卉
吐出的清淡而神圣的香味。
——我们会生活得那么欢欣,　　　　　　　　170
以致天空中的那些精灵
嫉妒着我们,甚至将人们,
那些污染着一切的人群,
引诱到我们疗养的乐园中;
但是那神圣而安静的环境,　　　　　　　　　175
那些微风,它们的翅膀
将香油洒落在振奋的灵魂上,
和下面有大海升腾的叶簇,
都会制服那些人的愤怒;
而同时,那被鼓舞的灵魂　　　　　　　　　　180
会用它深沉的旋律来供应
没有了风声的每一个间歇,
旋律里充满悦耳的絮语;
而博爱,将一切纷争治疗,
像生命的呼吸一样,会拥抱　　　　　　　　　185

All things in that sweet abode
With its own mild brotherhood.
They, not it, would change; and soon①
Every sprite beneath the moon
Would repent its envy vain,
And the earth grow young again.

P. B. SHELLEY.

---

① *They, not it*: sc. the 'polluting multitude,' not the 'healing paradise.'

那可爱的地方的一切东西，
用自己温和的兄弟情谊。
是人们，不是这地方，会发生变化；
而每个精灵很快在月光下
都会将徒劳的嫉妒悔恨，
而大地又将会变得年轻。

邹绛 译

编注 本诗写于一八一八年十月，和《罗莎琳与海伦》(Rosalind and Helen)一道发表于一八一九年，标题是《写于欧加宁群山中的诗行》。欧加宁群山(Euganean Hills)，不到两千英尺高，位于意大利帕多瓦西南约十英里处。

275. ODE TO THE WEST WIND

(1)

O wild West Wind, thou breath of Autumn's being,
    Thou, from whose unseen presence the leaves dead
Are driven, like ghosts from an enchanter fleeing,

Yellow, and black, and pale, and hectic red,
    Pestilence-stricken multitudes: O thou
Who chariotest to their dark wintry bed

The wingèd seeds, where they lie cold and low,
    Each like a corpse within its grave, until
Thine azure sister of the Spring shall blow①

Her clarion o'er the dreaming earth, and fill
    (Driving sweet buds like flocks to feed in air)
With living hues and odours plain and hill:

Wild Spirit, which art moving everywhere;
Destroyer and Preserver; hear oh, hear!

(2)

Thou on whose stream, mid the steep sky's commotion,
    Loose clouds like earth's decaying leaves are shed,

---

① *Thine azure sister of the Spring*: the east wind blowing in the spring and bringing blue skies.

275. 西风颂

雪莱

一

哦,狂荡的西风,你这秋天之生命,
　　陨萚枯叶为你无形的来临而凋谢,
　　就像魑魅魍魉在驱魔术士面前逃遁,

黄的叶、黑的叶、灰的叶、红的叶,
　　逃去了瘟疫摧残的一群:哦,你,
　　又送带翅的种籽去黑暗的冬床安歇,

一粒粒种籽犹如一具具僵卧的尸体,
　　将在冰凉低矮的坟墓里越冬沉睡,
　　直到春天你蓝色的妹妹来临之时①,

向梦中的大地把她嘹亮的号角劲吹,
　　驱动欢乐的蓓蕾如羊群把空气啜饮,
　　让山岭原野充满生命的色彩和芳菲:

狂荡的精灵哟,你行遍渺渺乾坤;
你这破坏者、保护者,你听哟,你听!

二

在你的疾流之上,在天的骚动之中,
　　松散的乱云犹如地上的枯叶被摇落,

---

① 西风之妹妹即东风。春天来临,东风吹拂,天空碧蓝,故称蓝色的妹妹。——译者

　　　　　Shook from the tangled boughs of Heaven and Ocean①,

　　　　　Angels of rain and lightning: there are spread②
　　　　　　On the blue surface of thine airy surge,
20　　　　Like the bright hair uplifted from the head

　　　　　Of some fierce Maenad, even from the dim verge③
　　　　　　Of the horizon to the zenith's height,
　　　　　The locks of the approaching storm. Thou dirge

　　　　　Of the dying year, to which this closing night④
25　　　　　Will be the dome of a vast sepulchre,
　　　　　Vaulted with all thy congregated might

　　　　　Of vapours, from whose solid atmosphere
　　　　　Black rain, and fire, and hail, will burst: oh, hear!

　　　　　　　　　　　(3)

　　　　　Thou who didst waken from his summer dreams
30　　　　　The blue Mediterranean, where he lay,
　　　　　Lull'd by the coil of his crystalline streams⑤,

---

① *Shook*: used for *shaken* in Shakespeare (see No. 14,1,4) and by Milton, *Par. Lost*, vi.218,'All Earth Had to her centre shook.'
② *Angels of rain*: the original meaning of angel is 'messenger.'
③ *Maenad*: the Maenads, also called Bacchantes, were female votaries of Dionysus (Bacchus); they got their name, which means 'the frenzied women,' from their strange dress and wild dances.
④ *closing*: i.e. closing in; it does not mean that it was the last day of the year.
⑤ *crystalline*: the accent here is on the penultimate. In l.64 of the preceding poem the word has its more usual accent.

脱离天空与海洋纠缠纷乱的枝丛,

云是雨和电的信使:铺展散播
　　那即将来临的暴风雨的发丝缕缕,
铺散于你那蓝色的缥缈的巨波, 20

就像酒神的狂女扬起的灿灿发丝①,
　　甚至从茫茫地平线那昏暗的边缘
一直铺展散播到高高的九重天宇。

你这曲挽歌,对这将死的残年,
　　四合的夜幕将成为它巨墓的穹顶, 25
用你聚集的云雾的力量作为支点,

从云雾坚实稠密的浩气中将飞迸
黑雨、雷电、冰雹:你听哟,你听!

三

你把蓝色的地中海从梦中摇醒,
　　整整一个夏天,它一直在沉睡, 30
清澈晶莹的潮汐环流使它安宁,

---

① 酒神的狂女,即酒神巴克科斯(又名狄俄尼索斯)的一群女伴,因衣着怪异,形态放荡而得名,又称"酒神巴克科斯的狂女"或"酒神的狂女迈那得斯"。——译者

  Beside a pumice isle in Baiae's bay①,
    And saw in sleep old palaces and towers
  Quivering within the wave's intenser day,

35   All overgrown with azure moss and flowers
    So sweet, the sense faints picturing them! Thou
  For whose path the Atlantic's level powers

  Cleave themselves into chasms, while far below
    The sea-blooms and the oozy woods which wear
40   The sapless foliage of the ocean, know

  Thy voice, and suddenly grow grey with fear,
  And tremble and despoil themselves: oh, hear!

(4)

  If I were a dead leaf thou mightest bear②;
    If I were a swift cloud to fly with thee;
45   A wave to pant beneath thy power, and share

  The impulse of thy strength, only less free
    Than thou, O uncontrollable! If even
  I were as in my boyhood, and could be

  The comrade of thy wanderings over Heaven③,
50   As then, when to outstrip thy skyey speed

---

① *pumice*: a kind of lava; the whole of the district near Naples is volcanic.
② *If I were*: the sentence is completed by 'I would ne'er have striven,' etc. (l. 51). The relative is omitted in this line.
③ *be The comrade of thy wanderings*: i.e. run with the wind and race the clouds.

它在巴延湾的浮石岛之旁静寐①,
　　睡梦中看见了昔日的塔楼宫殿
在波涛中更浓的日光下颤颤巍巍②,

塔楼宫殿长满蓝色的花卉苔藓,　　　　　　　　35
　　幽香如此醉人,令人难以描述!
为了给你让路,大西洋也裂陷,

而在那海烟波浩渺的水浪深处,
　　海花和被枯叶覆盖的淤泥藻林
听见你的声音,顿时心惊胆怵,　　　　　　　　40

纷纷变色,哆嗦发抖,自行凋零③;
　　哦,犷荡的西风哟,你听哟,你听!

四

假若我是一片能被你卷起的枯叶,
　　假若我是一朵能随你飘飞的流云。
假若我是浪花能在你威力下喘息,　　　　　　　45

能分受你那如千钧雷霆的强劲,
　　能几乎同不可控制的你一样自由!
甚至假若我还能回到童年的时辰,

能作为你的伴侣随你在天国遨游,
　　因为那时候,即使超越你的神速　　　　　　50

---

① 巴延湾,意大利坎帕尼亚区沿海一小海湾,在那不勒斯湾之西。浮石岛,由维苏威火山喷发之熔岩积成的一座小岛。——译者
② 水中的日光浓于水面上的日光,故曰"更浓的日光"。——译者
③ 博物学家熟悉这种现象。江河湖海水底的植物与陆地上的植物一样,对季候的变化有反应,因而也受宣告季候变化的风的影响。——雪莱自注

Scarce seemed a vision, I would ne'er have striven

As thus with thee in prayer in my sore need.
    Oh, lift me as a wave, a leaf, a cloud!
I fall upon the thorns of life! I bleed!

55   A heavy weight of hours has chained and bowed
One too like thee: tameless, and swift, and proud.

(5)

Make me thy lyre, even as the forest is①:
    What if my leaves are falling like its own!
The tumult of thy mighty harmonies

60   Will take from both a deep, autumnal tone,
    Sweet though in sadness. Be thou, Spirit fierce,
My spirit! Be thou me, impetuous one②!

Drive my dead thoughts over the universe
    Like withered leaves to quicken a new birth③!
65   And, by the incantation of this verse,

Scatter, as from an unextinguished hearth
    Ashes and sparks, my words among mankind!

---

① *Make me thy lyre*: i.e. use me as thy instrument to sound fresh notes of life and high thoughts over the world.

② *Be thou me*: this may be ungrammatical, but it is better to be ungrammatical than intolerable, as 'be thou I' would have been.

③ *quicken*: 'bring to life.' Like all great souls, Shelley was looking for a new earth where freedom, justice, and truth should be more apparent than they are in the present world; he wanted too to feel that he himself was being made use of to bring about this great end.

也不算是异想天开的梦幻悠悠;

我就不会这般急切地向你求诉:
　　飐起我吧,像飐起枯叶流云波涛,
我跌落于人生的荆丛! 血流如注!

岁月的重负把我压迫,把我锁牢, 　　　　　　55
我太像你哟,像你不羁、敏捷、骄傲。

五

用我作你的琴吧,就像你用森林,
　　我纵然像森林叶败枝残又有何妨!
你那雄浑有力且又和谐的激情

将从我和森林奏出深沉的秋之乐章, 　　　60
　　悲郁但却美妙。犷荡的精灵哟,
让我们灵肉合一,让我像你一样!

请你把我枯萎的思想吹遍寰宇,
　　像吹枯萎的树叶去催沃一番新生!
请你用我这些诗行写成的咒语, 　　　　　65

像从未灭的炉中吹起热灰余烬,
　　把我心中的话语传播到人间!

Be through my lips to unawakened earth

The trumpet of a prophecy! O Wind,
If Winter comes, can Spring be far behind?

P. B. SHELLEY.

请你哟,请你通过我的嘴唇

让预言的号角响彻尘寰!西风哟,
如果冬天来临,春天还会远么?

曹明伦　译

编注　《西风颂》是雪莱最负盛名的代表作,于一八一九年秋天构思并草写于意大利佛罗伦萨附近阿诺河畔的一片树林里,于一八二〇年与《解放了的普罗米修斯》同时发表。雪莱曾追述过当时构思的情景:"当日天气温和、清爽,而携风挟雨的西风正聚集起能倾泻秋雨的乌云。如我所料,雨从黄昏下起,狂风暴雨挟带着冰雹,并伴有阿尔卑斯山南坡特有的那种壮观的雷电。"正是大自然这美丽而雄伟的景象触发了诗人蓄积已久的激情,使他写出了《西风颂》这首气势磅礴、寓意深远的诗篇,抒发了诗人对大自然的热爱,歌颂了西风摧枯拉朽、孕育新生命的精神。全诗分为五节,用意大利三行连环体写成,格律严谨,音调高昂,感情细腻,风格典雅。最末那句"如果冬天来临,春天还会远么?"可谓画龙点睛的神来之笔,使一曲西风颂曲尽其妙,声成金石,而这行诗本身也成了不朽的名句,千古之绝唱。

276. NATURE AND THE POET

*Suggested by a Picture of Peele Castle in a Storm, painted by Sir George Beaumont*①

I was thy neighbour once, thou rugged Pile!
 Four summer weeks I dwelt in sight of thee
I saw thee every day; and all the while
 Thy Form was sleeping on a glassy sea.

So pure the sky, so quiet was the air!
 So like, so very like, was day to day!
Whene'er I look'd, thy image still was there;
 It trembled, but it never pass'd away.

How perfect was the calm! It seem'd no sleep,
 No mood, which season takes away, or brings:
I could have fancied that the mighty Deep
 Was even the gentlest of all gentle things.

Ah! then if mine had been the Painter's hand
 To express what then I saw; and add the gleam,
The light that never was on sea or land,
 The consecration, and the Poet's dream②, —

I would have planted thee, thou hoary Pile,

---

① *Peele Castle*: this should be 'Piel'; it is on Piel Island off the coast of Furness in north Lancashire.
② *The consecration*: the touch which makes sacred, by suffusing the picture with imagination.

276. 大自然与诗人

(因乔治·贝欧芒爵士①所画
《暴风雨中的皮厄尔城堡②》有感而作)

华兹华斯

啊,这嶙峋的建筑物,我曾是你的近邻,
  在能望见你的地方度过了四个星期的夏季良辰。
那时候,我每天都看见你;无论是白天还是黑夜,
  那明镜似的海面上总荡漾着你倒卧的身影。

天空是那样的纯净,四周是那样的安宁! 5
  每一天都是那样的相似,多么明丽而恬静!
当我每次凝望海面,总看见你的形影;
  摇曳、抖动,却从来不曾消隐。

多么完美的宁静!既不像睡眠
  也不像季节变换而改变了的心情, 10
我幻想这浩瀚深邃的大海
  竟是一切温柔中最温柔的心。

哎!假如我也有一双画家的手,
  能绘出我所见到的一切,再加上光泽,
这光泽不属于大地也不属于海洋③, 15
  是圣洁的奉献,诗人的梦幻,——

我把你置放在另一个天地,

---

① 贝欧芒爵士曾任英国下院议员,擅长作风景画。——译者
② 皮厄尔城堡位于英国兰开夏郡北部,座落在弗内斯海上的皮厄尔岛上。——译者
③ 即只存在于人的心中。——编注者

  Amid a world how different from this!
   Beside a sea that could not cease to smile;
20   On tranquil land, beneath a sky of bliss①.

  A picture had it been of lasting ease,
   Elysian quiet, without toil or strife;
  No motion but the moving tide, a breeze,
   Or merely silent Nature's breathing life.

25   Such, in the fond illusion of my heart,
   Such picture would I at that time have made;
  And seen the soul of truth in every part,
   A steadfast peace that might not be betray'd.

  So once it would have been, — 'tis so no more;
30   I have submitted to a new control;
  A power is gone, which nothing can restore;
   A deep distress hath humanized my soul②.

  Not for a moment could I now behold
   A smiling sea, and be what I have been;
35   The feeling of my loss will ne'er be old;
   This, which I know, I speak with mind serene.

  Then, Beaumont, Friend! who would have been the Friend

---

① After this line there follows, both in the original and in the final version, the following stanza: —
'Thou shouldst have seemed a treasure-house divine
 Of peaceful years; a chronicle of heaven; —
Of all the sunbeams that did ever shine
 The very sweetest had to thee been given.'
Palgrave replaced the stanza in his second edition.

② *A deep distress*: Wordsworth's brother John had been drowned in the wreck of the *Abergavenny* on February 5, 1805.

你这古老的城堡!
放在宁静的大地上,极乐的苍穹下,
　　海在你身旁不停地欢笑。　　　　　　　　　　20

一幅永恒的、悠然自得的图画,
　　没有劳苦,没有斗争,如伊利斯安的恬静①。
只有海浪轻轻摇荡,微风徐徐吹拂,
　　或只有大自然轻柔而有生机的呼吸声。

在我心灵所渴求的梦里,　　　　　　　　　　　25
　　这就是我本要着意描绘的画景,
到处都见到真理的灵魂,
　　一种不容背叛的恒久的和平。

啊,这美好的一切——都已消逝;
　　我陷入了新的被束缚的窘境　　　　　　　　30
那力量一去不能再恢复;
　　深深的悲戚熔化了我的心灵。

而今我眼前能看见的,再也不是那
　　微笑着的大海,似昔日所识;
这损失带给我的痛苦永远不会陈旧,　　　　　　35
　　虽然我知道我心情平静,在那说话时。

可是朋友!你也会成为他的挚交②,

---

① 伊利斯安(Elysium),荷马描绘过的善人安息之地,此处指乐土。——译者
② 朋友,此处指贝欧芒爵士。——译者

If he had lived, of him whom I deplore,
This work of thine I blame not, but commend;
　　This sea in anger, and that dismal shore.

O 'tis a passionate work! — yet wise and well,
　　Well chosen is the spirit that is here;
That hulk which labours in the deadly swell,
　　This rueful sky, this pageantry of fear!

And this huge Castle, standing here sublime,
　　I love to see the look with which it braves,
— Cased in the unfeeling armour of old time —
　　The lightning, the fierce wind, and trampling waves.

Farewell, farewell the heart that lives alone,
　　Housed in a dream, at distance from the Kind[①]!
Such happiness, wherever it be known,
　　Is to be pitied; for 'tis surely blind.

But welcome fortitude, and patient cheer,
　　And frequent sights of what is to be borne!
Such sights, or worse, as are before me here: —
　　Not without hope we suffer and we mourn.

W. WORDSWORTH.

---

① *the Kind*: 'the human race.'

假如我悼念的人仍活在人间，
你的作品我不非难，反到颂赞；
看，那狂怒的大海和那阴沉的海岸。 40

啊，这热情的作品！——充满智慧，构思美妙，
大自然的活力此刻表现得何等精到，
那忧郁的天空和那弥漫着恐怖的景色，
还有那在凶涛恶浪中拼搏的古堡。

啊，这宏伟的城堡，庄严、崇高， 45
周身披挂着古老岁月铸就的战袍
我最爱看它敢于拼搏的风貌，
蔑视那雷霆、闪电、狂风和浪涛。

别了，永别了！孤独的心
在梦幻里栖身，对人类难于亲近！ 50
这样的欢乐，总是盲目，
无论何处都引起人们的怜悯。

然而我要欢迎那坚忍的精神、沉着的喜悦，
欢迎那必然出现的、通常的景象！
就像此刻见到的或更坏的遭遇：—— 55
我们受苦，我们哀叹，但并不失望。

朱通伯　译

编注　一八〇五年二月，华兹华斯的弟弟约翰在"阿勃格文号"沉船事故中遇难，给诗人以巨大的精神打击。本诗表现了诗人当时的心情，标题为《挽诗几节，有感》(Elegiac Stanzas，Suggested)，现在的标题为《金库》原编者所加。

277. THE POET'S DREAM

On a poet's lips I slept
Dreaming like a love-adept①
In the sound his breathing kept;
Nor seeks nor finds he mortal blisses,
But feeds on the aerial kisses
Of shapes that haunt thought's wildernesses.
He will watch from dawn to gloom
The lake-reflected sun illume
The yellow bees in the ivy-bloom,
　　Nor heed nor see what things they be;
But from these create he can
Forms more real than living man,
　　Nurslings of immortality!

P. B. SHELLEY.

---

① *like a love-adept*: one who is well versed in the wisdom of love may be supposed to have beautiful visions in his sleep.

277. 诗人的梦

雪莱

我睡在一个诗人的嘴唇上,
在他那轻匀的吸呼声音中,
像爱情能手一样做着梦;
他并不追求人间的幸福,
而只是饱餐空灵的亲吻, 5
亲吻幻想中出没的精灵。
从黎明到黄昏他都会观望
湖水中倒映的阳光
常春藤花上金色的蜜蜂;
　它们究竟是什么他并不在意, 10
但他却能够用它们创造出
比活着的人更真实的万物,
　精心培育的永恒的东西。

邹绛　译

编注　本诗选自《解放了的普罗米修斯》第一幕,是第四个精灵唱的歌,本标题为《金库》原编者所加。参见第271首注。

278. 'THE WORLD IS TOO MUCH WITH US'

The world is too much with us; late and soon,
  Getting and spending, we lay waste our powers
  Little we see in Nature that is ours[①];
We have given our hearts away, a sordid boon!

This Sea that bares her bosom to the moon,
  The winds that will be howling at all hours[②]
  And are up-gather'd now like sleeping flowers[③],
For this, for everything, we are out of tune;

It moves us not. — Great God! I'd rather be
  A Pagan suckled in a creed outworn[④],
So might I, standing on this pleasant lea,

Have glimpses that would make me less forlorn;
Have sight of Proteus rising from the sea;
Or hear old Triton blow his wreathéd horn.

W. WORDSWORTH.

---

① *that is ours*: 'that appeals to us.'
② *will be howling*: 'are eager to howl'; *will* is here a notional verb.
③ *up-gather'd*: 'held in restraint.'
④ *outworn*: 'obsolete.'

278. "这世界,对于我们,实在够受"

华兹华斯

这世界,对于我们,实在够受。我们从早到晚
　　不停地攫取着,消耗着,白费了许多力气。
　　而自然中投合我们心意的东西却寥寥无几。
我们献出了整个的心啊,一份廉价卑微的赠予!

这大海,面对明月倾诉着她满怀的心事与情愫,　　　　　5
　　这风儿,整日不停地呼啸怒号的风儿呀,
　　此刻也屏住了声息,宛如一朵朵睡着的花儿,
然而,对于这些,和别的一切,我们总感格格不入;

它打动不了我们——全能的上帝呀!
　　我宁愿是一个旧教哺育下的异教徒,　　　　　　　　10
　　站在快活的绿野上,才能领略到

大自然的奥秘真谛,使我不致孤寂、凄凉,
　　才能看见那普罗透斯海神从海上升起①,
　　才能聆听那特里同海神把带花螺号吹响②。

朱通伯　译

编注　本诗为华兹华斯青年时期的作品,已经孕育着一种退隐思想。原诗无题,收入一八○七年《诗集》中。

---

① 普罗透斯(Proteus),希腊神话中变化无常的海神,能知未来。——译者
② 特里同(Triton),希腊神话中半人半鱼的海神,常用螺号声使海浪平息。——译者

279. WITHIN KING'S COLLEGE CHAPEL, CAMBRIDGE

Tax not the royal Saint with vain expense[1],
With ill-match'd aims the Architect who plann'd
(Albeit labouring for a scanty band
Of white-robed Scholars only) this immense

5   And glorious work of fine intelligence!
Give all thou canst; high Heaven rejects the lore[2]
Of nicely-calculated less or more:
So deem'd the man who fashion'd for the sense[3]

These lofty pillars, spread that branching roof
10   Self-poised, and scoop'd into ten thousand cells[4],
Where light and shade repose, where music dwells

Lingering — and wandering on as loth to die;
Like thoughts whose very sweetness yieldeth proof
That they were born for immortality.

W. WORDSWORTH.

---

[1] *Tax ... with*: 'charge ... with,' *i.e.* accuse ... of.
[2] *lore*: properly 'learning'; here used for 'prudence,' 'worldly wisdom.'
[3] *for the sense*: 'to appeal to the eye.'
[4] *Self-poised*: *i.e.* with no centre pillars. *scoop'd*: a participle, co-ordinate with 'self-poised.'

279. 在剑桥王家学院教堂

华兹华斯

别指责那皇室圣徒挥霍浪费①,
　别指责那建筑师的设计与用途相悖,
　　为寥寥几位白袍学士②
建造这宏伟壮丽的殿堂。

这人类美妙智慧的丰碑!　　　　　　　　　　5
　把你所有的一切奉献出来吧,
　　上帝不赞成斤斤计较的谨小慎微;
为观瞻建成了这圣殿巍巍,

雕梁画柱支撑着铺展的拱顶,
　大殿空廓四壁内神龛千千万,　　　　　　　10
　　光和影在那里憩息,音乐声在那里萦回,

　　　留连——徘徊,好似难去难舍;
有如思想之所以可爱甜美,
　　就因为它来到世上就是为了万古不废。

薛诗绮　译

编注　本诗大概是诗人去看望弟弟克里斯朵夫(Christopher)有感而作,一八二二年以《教士素描》(Ecclesiastical Sketches)为题发表,一八三七年又改名为《教士十四行诗》(Ecclesiastical Sonnets)。《金库》原编者改为《在剑桥王家学院教堂》是很有道理的。

---

① 皇室圣徒,指教堂创建人英王亨利六世。——译者
② 白袍学士,牛津大学及剑桥大学校务会成员可穿白袍进入学校教堂,而其他人则是穿黑袍,不能进教堂。——译者

280. YOUTH AND AGE

Verse, a breeze 'mid blossoms straying,
Where Hope clung feeding, like a bee —
Both were mine! Life went a-maying
    With Nature, Hope, and Poesy,
        When I was young!

When I was young? — Ah, woeful When!
Ah! for the change 'twixt Now and Then!
This breathing house not built with hands,
    This body that does me grievous wrong,
    O'er aery cliffs and glittering sands
        How lightly then it flash'd along:
Like those trim skiffs, unknown of yore,
    On winding lakes and rivers wide,
That ask no aid of sail or oar,
    That fear no spite of wind or tide!
Nought cared this body for wind or weather
When Youth and I lived in't together.

Flowers are lovely; Love is flower-like;
    Friendship is a sheltering tree;
O! the joys, that came down shower-like,
    Of Friendship, Love, and Liberty,
        Ere I was old!

280. 青春和老年

塞·泰·柯勒律治

诗,它在花丛中飘流,
  那里,"希望"正吸吮着甜汁,像蜜蜂——
我拥有他们二者,生命正在春游
  和希望、自然、诗神相逢,
    当我还年轻的时候!   5

当我还年轻的时候?——啊,这可恨的"当"!
哀叹吧,"现在"和"当时"之间多少沧桑!
这呼吸着的屋宇不是用手建成,
  这肉躯带给我多少痛苦①,
那时,高耸的山崖,沙滩的黄澄澄   10
  都曾见过它轻快的脚步:
像这些轻盈的小艇,不知约束,
  在弯曲的湖泊,广阔的河上,
不要风帆和木桨的援助,
  不怕风暴和猛浪!   15
这肉身不怕风雨和气候的折磨
那时青春和我一起生活。

花儿可爱;爱情像花;
  友谊是遮荫的大树忧忧幽幽,
啊,欢乐像骤雨样阵阵降下,   20
  来自友谊、爱情、自由,
    在我衰老以前!

---

① 柯勒律治多年嗜用鸦片,严重损害了身体。——编注者

  Ere I was old? Ah woeful Ere,
  Which tells me, Youth 's no longer here!
25   O Youth! for years so many and sweet
   'Tis known that Thou and I were one,
  I'll think it but a fond conceit①—
  It cannot be that thou art gone!
  Thy vesper bell hath not yet toll'd: —
30   And thou wert ay a masker bold!
  What strange disguise hast now put on
  To make believe that thou art gone?
  I see these locks in silvery slips,
   This drooping gait, this alter'd size:
35   But Springtide blossoms on thy lips,
   And tears take sunshine from thine eyes②!
  Life is but thought: so think I will
  That Youth and I are housemates still.

  Dew-drops are the gems of morning,
40   But the tears of mournful eve!
  Where no hope is, life 's a warning
   That only serves to make us grieve,
    When we are old:

  — That only serves to make us grieve
45   With oft and tedious taking-leave,
  Like some poor nigh-related guest
  That may not rudely be dismist,

---

① *a fond conceit*: 'a foolish fancy.'
② *tears take sunshine from thine eyes*: not 'rob your eyes of their brightness,' but 'are lit with the brightness of your eyes.'

衰老以前？啊,可恨的"以前",
它告诉我青春已经不能再现!
啊,青春,丰盛的岁月何等甜蜜芳香 25
  人人都知道你和我合成一体,
我只把它当成一个痴想——
  已经消失了？那怎能是真的!
在你的晚祷钟声敲响之前:
你还在一个面具舞会上勇敢地留连! 30
现在你披上什么服饰
想使人们相信你已消逝？
这些发卷确已悄悄转灰,
  步履缓缓,形体蠢胖:
但你的双唇仍吐出春风的沉醉, 35
  眼泪从你的眼睛里摄取阳光!
生命不过是思想:所以我祝愿
我和青春仍住在一起,永远。

露水是清晨的明珠,
  却成为眼泪,在悲伤的夜晚。 40
那时不再有希望,生命带来悲诉
  只能使我们哀叹,
     当我们进入暮年:

——那只能使我们哀叹
拖沓的告别一再不断, 45
好像一个穷苦的近亲来访
不能急于送走,那太鲁莽,

Yet hath outstay'd his welcome while①,
And tells the jest without the smile②.

S. T. COLERIDGE.

---

① *while*: 'time'; the word is now used as a substantive only in certain phrases, 'a long while,' 'worth while,' etc.
② *without the smile*: i.e. without winning a smile.

但他早已超过受欢迎的瞬间,
还在说笑,可没人露出笑脸。

郑敏　译

编注 本诗是诗人的代表作。他用对比的手法给人以强烈的感受,"露水是清晨的明珠,却成为眼泪,在悲伤的夜晚"象征着青春与老迈,这已成为名句。本诗的前三十八行于一八二八年发表在《文学纪念品》(The Literary Souvenir)上,其余部分一八三二年发表在《黑树林》(Blackwood)上,一八三四年以本篇的形式发表在《诗作》(Poetical Works)上。

281. THE TWO APRIL MORNINGS

We walk'd along, while bright and red
    Uprose the morning sun;
And Matthew stopp'd, he look'd, and said,
    'The will of God be done!'

5   A village schoolmaster was he,
    With hair of glittering grey;
As blithe a man as you could see
    On a spring holiday.

And on that morning, through the grass
10   And by the steaming rills
We travell'd merrily, to pass
    A day among the hills.

'Our work,' said I, 'was well begun;
    Then, from thy breast what thought,
15 Beneath so beautiful a sun,
    So sad a sigh has brought?'

A second time did Matthew stop;
    And fixing still his eye
Upon the eastern mountain-top,
20   To me he made reply:

'Yon cloud with that long purple cleft

281. 两个四月的早晨

华兹华斯

我们漫步走去,
　　红彤彤的朝阳冉冉升起;
马修止步望了望说:
　　"主宰一切的是上帝旨意!"

他是个乡村教师,　　　　　　　　　　　　　5
　　灰白的头发闪闪如银;
但见他兴致勃勃,
　　看得出是个度假游春的人。

那天清晨我们穿过草地,
　　在冒着蒸气的小溪边　　　　　　　　　10
愉快地信步遨游,
　　打算在山林间度过那一天。

我问道:"我们的事儿已经开了个好头;
　　可您心中有什么芥蒂,
使您在这么美好的阳光下,　　　　　　　15
　　发出了如此哀伤的叹息?"

马修再一次停止脚步;
　　抬起眼一动不动
凝望着东方的山巅,
　　就这样他对我倾诉了心中隐痛:　　　20

"那远处带紫色细长隙缝的云彩,

　　　　　Brings fresh into my mind
　　　　A day like this, which I have left
　　　　Full thirty years behind.

25　　　　'And just above yon slope of corn
　　　　　　Such colours, and no other,
　　　　Were in the sky, that April morn,
　　　　　　Of this the very brother.

　　　　'With rod and line I sued the sport
30　　　　　Which that sweet season gave,
　　　　And, to the churchyard come, stopp'd short
　　　　　　Beside my daughter's grave.

　　　　'Nine summers had she scarcely seen,
　　　　　　The pride of all the vale;
35　　　　And then she sang; — she would have been
　　　　　　A very nightingale.

　　　　'Six feet in earth my Emma lay;
　　　　　　And yet I loved her more —
　　　　For so it seem'd, — than till that day
40　　　　　I e'er had loved before.

　　　　'And turning from her grave, I met
　　　　　　Beside the churchyard yew
　　　　A blooming Girl, whose hair was wet
　　　　　　With points of morning dew.

45　　　　'A basket on her head she bare;
　　　　　　Her brow was smooth and white;

使我想起一个日子很像今天,
虽然记忆犹新,
  那一天已经过去了整整三十年。

"就在那片麦坡的上方,   25
  跟这一样的云彩挂在天空,
那个四月的早晨,
  和今天早晨好似孪生弟兄。

"手持钓具我走向田野,
  春光明媚正是钓鱼季节,   30
不觉间来到教堂墓地,
  在女儿坟边我蓦然驻脚。

"她只不过见过九个寒暑,
  却已是整个溪谷的明星;
这孩子能歌善舞——   35
  若在世定是只讨人喜欢的夜莺。

"我的爱玛已躺在九泉之下;
  可我对她的爱与日俱增——
看来就是如此啊——
  比她死前更增加十分。   40

"离开她坟墓我满心惆怅,
  就在那墓地的紫杉下,
我遇见了一位美丽活泼的姑娘,
  清晨的露珠弄湿了她一头秀发。

"她头上顶一只篮子,   45
  额头光洁而白皙;

>   To see a child so very fair,
>   It was a pure delight!
>
>   'No fountain from its rocky cave
> 50   E'er tripp'd with foot so free;
>   She seem'd as happy as a wave
>   That dances on the sea.
>
>   'There came from me a sigh of pain
>   Which I could ill confine;
> 55   I looked at her, and looked again:
>   And did not wish her mine①!'
>
>   — Matthew is in his grave, yet now
>   Methinks I see him stand
>   As at that moment, with a bough
> 60   Of wilding in his hand②.

W. WORDSWORTH.

---

① *And did not wish her mine*: the recollection of his dead daughter was dearer to him than the companionship of any other child could be.
② *wilding*: the crab-apple tree.

看到这孩子长得如此可爱，
　　　　怎能不叫人心里欢喜！

　　"岩洞里流出的泉水，
　　　　比不上她步履轻盈；
　　她欢快得像一个海浪，
　　　　在大海里跳跳蹦蹦。

　　"我禁不住长叹一声，
　　　　心中的痛苦难以克制；
　　我把她看了又看：
　　　　却并不希望她是我孩子！"

　　——而今马修已长眠地下，
　　　　可我似乎还看见他站立的丰姿，
　　就像当年我见到的一样，
　　　　手里擎一根酸苹果树枝。

薛诗绮　译

编注　本诗表现了日常生活的事件和情节。诗人竭力采用人们真正使用的语言来叙述和描写，加上一种想象的光采，自然地呈现在读者的心灵面前。本诗的主题是惆怅哀婉的，好似中国古诗"去年今日此门中，人面桃花相映红，人面不知何处去，桃花依旧笑春风"。

282. THE FOUNTAIN

A Conversation

    We talk'd with open heart, and tongue
        Affectionate and true,
    A pair of friends, though I was young,
        And Matthew seventy-two.

5   We lay beneath a spreading oak,
        Beside a mossy seat;
    And from the turf a fountain broke
        And gurgled at our feet.

    'Now, Matthew!' said I, 'let us match
10   This water's pleasant tune
    With some old border-song, or catch[1]
        That suits a summer's noon;

    'Or of the church-clock and the chimes
        Sing here beneath the shade
15   That half-mad thing of witty rhymes
        Which you last April made!'

    In silence Matthew lay, and eyed
        The spring beneath the tree;

---

[1] *catch*: this is properly a short song for three or more persons, who all sing the same words and the same air, but begin at different times. It is also called a 'round.'

282. 泉
（一次谈话）

华兹华斯

我们敞怀谈心，
　　言语亲切率真，
这对朋友中我年纪还轻，
　　可马修是七十二岁老人。

我们躺在绿荫如盖的栎树下，　　　　　　　　　5
　　身旁有一条苔痕斑斑的石凳；
一股清泉从草地里迸发，
　　在我们脚边潺潺作声。

"喂，马修！"我说，"让我们
　　找一支古老的边区民歌，　　　　　　　　10
配上这泉水悦耳的声音，
　　这音乐对夏日的晌午最为适合；

"要不就和着那教堂报时钟乐，
　　在这儿树荫下悠然偃卧，
哼哼您去年四月写的诙谐小曲，　　　　　　　15
　　那都是超凡脱俗的杰作！"

马修静躺着没有作声，
　　望一眼流过树下的泉水；

20   And thus the dear old man replied,
         The grey-hair'd man of glee:

      'No check, no stay, this Streamlet fears,
         How merrily it goes!
      'Twill murmur on a thousand years
         And flow as now it flows.

25   'And here, on this delightful day,
         I cannot choose but think
      How oft, a vigorous man, I lay
         Beside this fountain's brink.

      'My eyes are dim with childish tears,
30   My heart is idly stirr'd,
      For the same sound is in my ears
         Which in those days I heard.

      'Thus fares it still in our decay:
         And yet the wiser mind
35   Mourns less for what age takes away,
         Than what it leaves behind①.

      'The blackbird amid leafy trees,
         The lark above the hill,
      Let loose their carols when they please,
40   Are quiet when they will.

      'With Nature never do they wage

---

① *what it leaves behind*: *i.e.* the habits acquired in youth and manhood.

然后这白发苍苍的吟游诗人
　　这可爱的老汉才把话回： 20

"这小溪流得多欢快，
　　通畅无阻它不需担忧！
淙淙汩汩一千载，
　　到那时还和现在一样流。

"在今天这快乐的日子， 25
　　我禁不住浮想联翩，
想当初我也是个精力充沛的男子，
　　多少次曾经来这儿躺在泉边。

"眼里含着稚气的泪花，
　　我的心徒然伤悲， 30
因为我又听到了泉水咿哑，
　　这声音当年曾叫我心醉。

"人们在衰亡泉水照常流：
　　可智者们看法不一般，
他们并不因年华消逝哀愁， 35
　　倒是为岁月留下的印迹悲叹。

"茂林中的乌鸫，
　　山头上的云雀，
高兴时放歌争哼，
　　不想唱也随心所欲。 40

"鸟儿们生活自在，

>   A foolish strife; they see
>   A happy youth, and their old age
>   Is beautiful and free:
>
> 45   'But we are press'd by heavy laws;
>   And often, glad no more,
>   We wear a face of joy, because
>   We have been glad of yore.
>
>   'If there be one who need bemoan
> 50   His kindred laid in earth,
>   The household hearts that were his own, —
>   It is the man of mirth.
>
>   'My days, my friend, are almost gone,
>   My life has been approved①,
> 55   And many love me; but by none
>   Am I enough beloved.'
>
>   'Now both himself and me he wrongs,
>   The man who thus complains!
>   I live and sing my idle songs
> 60   Upon these happy plains;
>
>   'And, Matthew, for thy children dead
>   I'll be a son to thee!'
>   At this he grasp'd my hand and said,
>   'Alas! that cannot be.'

---

① *approved*: sc. by his neighbours.

决不跟大自然无谓争斗，
年少时过得幸福愉快，
　　到老来依然美好自由。
　　"我们受自然规律压迫， 45
　　往往脸上强颜欢笑，
心里难以快活，
　　因为那昔日的欢乐怎能忘了。

　　"若有人独自伤心悲痛，
　　为的是亲人皆逝唯他幸存， 50
只要他跟他家人的心息息相通——
　　那么他就是个快乐的人。

　　"朋友啊我这辈子去日苦多，
　　尽管乡邻们称誉交口，
许多人都很爱我， 55
　　可我总觉得还没有被谁爱够。"

　　"这样的抱怨不应当，
　　您委曲了自己也委曲了我！
在这欢乐的原野上，
　　我活着唱我疏懒的歌： 60

　　"孩子已死难复活，
　　可马修啊，您可把我当儿子！"
他紧握我手回答说：
　　"天哪！这是办不到的事。"

65   We rose up from the fountain-side;
    And down the smooth descent
   Of the green sheep-track did we glide;
    And through the wood we went;

   And, ere we came to Leonard's rock,
70   He sang those witty rhymes
   About the crazy old church-clock
    And the bewilder'd chimes.

W. WORDSWORTH.

我们从泉边站起身,　　　　　　　　　65
　羊道斜坡绿如茵,
从那里我们往下滑行,
　接着又穿过一片树林。

在我们到达利昂那德岩之前,
　他唱起了那些诙谐小调,　　　　　70
说的是教堂的旧钟疯疯癫癫,
　乱敲一通叫人莫明其妙。

　　　　　　　　薛诗绮　译

283. THE RIVER OF LIFE

The more we live, more brief appear
  Our life's succeeding stages:
A day to childhood seems a year,
  And years like passing ages.

The gladsome current of our youth,
  Ere passion yet disorders,
Steals lingering like a river smooth
  Along its grassy borders.

But as the careworn cheek grows wan,
  And sorrow's shafts fly thicker,
Ye stars, that measure life to man,
  Why seem your courses quicker?

When joys have lost their bloom and breath,
  And life itself is vapid,
Why, as we reach the Falls of death,
  Feel we its tide more rapid?

It may be strange — yet who would change
  Time's course to slower speeding,
When one by one our friends have gone
  And left our bosoms bleeding?

283. 生命之川

康沫尔①

人生越老,岁月越短,
　　生命的历程似在飞换,
儿时的一天如同一载,
　　一载如同几个朝代。

青春的热情尚未衰逝,　　　　　　　　　　5
　　愉悦的流泉但觉迟迟,
有如一道草原中的绿溪,
　　静悄悄地蜿蜒着流泻。

但待颊上的红霞褪尽,
　　忧愁的征箭愈飞愈频,　　　　　　　10
星星哟星星,你们大小司命,
　　你们的运行为何愈来愈迅?

当快感失去了花时和吸引,
　　生命本身有如一个空瓶,
当我快要临到死境,　　　　　　　　　15
　　为什么退潮更加猛进?

怪诞呀,可能是怪诞——
　　谁也不想把日程放慢,
友人的谢世接二连三,
　　胸中的伤痛如荼如炭。　　　　　　20

---

① 即托马斯·坎贝尔(Thomas Campell, 1777—1844)。——编注者

Heaven gives our years of fading strength
   Indemnifying fleetness;
And those of youth, a seeming length,
   Proportion'd to their sweetness.

T. CAMPBELL.

是天,使我们日渐衰竭的暮年
　　得到迅速消逝的补偿,
是天,使青年时代的快乐,
　　得到相应的貌似的延长。

　　　　　　　　　　郭沫若　译

284. THE HUMAN SEASONS

Four seasons fill the measure of the year;
There are four seasons is the mind of man:
He has his lusty Spring, when fancy clear
Takes in all beauty with an easy span①:

5   He has his Summer, when luxuriously
Spring's honey'd cud of youthful thought he loves
To ruminate, and by such dreaming nigh②
His nearest unto heaven: quiet coves

His soul has in its Autumn, when his wings
10   He furleth close; contented so to look
On mists in idleness — to let fair things
Pass by unheeded as a threshold brook:

He has his Winter too of pale misfeature,
Or else he would forgo his mortal nature.

J. KEATS.

---

① *span*: 'grasp'; properly the distance from the tip of the thumb to the tip of the little finger when the hand is spread out; as a measure it is nine inches.
② *ruminate*: 'ponder on.'

284. 人的四季

济慈

一年有四季:
　一颗心灵有春夏秋冬:
他的春天情稠意浓,幻想清晰
　想用手掌轻松地把一切"美"来包容:

他有他的兴盛的夏天,当他将　　　　　　　　　　5
　早春蜜饯了的反刍草仔细品尝
青春的情思愉快地默想
　在梦里比任何时更接近天堂:

秋天里他的心灵有静静的海湾
　折起翅膀:满意于凝视　　　　　　　　　　　10
那迷雾,悠闲里,让美好的万般
　事物没受到注意就像溪水流逝:

他也有苍白而不俏俊的冬季,
要不,他就会将人性抛弃。

郑敏　译

285. A LAMENT

O World! O Life! O Time!
On whose last steps I climb,
  Trembling at that where I had stood before[①];
When will return the glory of your prime?
  No more — Oh, never more!

Out of the day and night
A joy has taken flight:
  Fresh spring, and summer, and winter hoar
Move my faint heart with grief, but with delight
  No more — Oh, never more!

P. B. SHELLEY.

---

① *Trembling at that where* ... : *i. e.* trembling to think of the position in which ... It is hopeless to guess at the idea to which he refers.

285. 悲歌

雪莱

呵,世界! 呵,人生! 呵,时间!
登上了岁月最后一重山①!
　　回顾来路心已碎,
　　昔日荣光几时还?
　　　　呵,难追——永难追! 　　　　　　　　　　5

日夜流逝中,
有种欢情去无踪。
　　阳春隆冬一样悲,
　　心头乐事不再逢。
　　　　呵,难追——永难追! 　　　　　　　　　　10

王佐良　译

---

① 雪莱大概预感他的生命短促,在本诗写就一年之后他便逝世。——编注者

286. 'MY HEART LEAPS UP WHEN I BEHOLD'

My heart leaps up when I behold
   A rainbow in the sky:
So was it when my life began,
So is it now I am a man,
So be it when I shall grow old,
   Or let me die!
The Child is father of the Man:
And I could wish my days to be
Bound each to each by natural piety①.

W. WORDSWORTH.

---

① *natural piety*: he is carrying on the idea of fatherhood; in this sense every to-day is the child of yesterday and should show filial piety towards it.

286. "我心儿激动"

华兹华斯

我心儿激动,当我一见
　彩虹出现在天空:
我童稚时期便如此;
现在成人了亦复如是;
将来年老时还当这般,　　　　5
　否则宁不寿而终!
儿童乃是成人的根子;
我但愿我一日日的生活
总由自然的虔敬来连结。

鲍屡平　译

287. ODE ON INTIMATIONS OF IMMORTALITY

From Recollections of Early Childhood

There was a time when meadow, grove, and stream
    The earth, and every common sight,
        To me did seem
    Apparell'd in celestial light,
The glory and the freshness of a dream.
It is not now as it hath been of yore; —
    Turn wheresoe'er I may,
        By night or day,
The things which I have seen I now can see no more.

    The rainbow comes and goes,
    And lovely is the rose;
    The moon doth with delight
Look round her when the heavens are bare;
    Waters on a starry night
        Are beautiful and fair;
The sunshine is a glorious birth;
But yet I know, where'er I go,
That there hath pass'd away a glory from the earth.

Now, while the birds thus sing a joyous song,
    And while the young lambs bound
        As to the tabor's sound[①],

[①] *the tabor's sound*: a tabor was a small drum often used in former times to accompany the pipe.

287. 永生颂
(幼年忆事抒怀)

华兹华斯

忆往昔，牧场、丛林、溪流、大地
  和一切寻常景致，
   在我心中
仿佛披戴着日月辰光织成的锦绣，
  好一派灿烂明媚的梦境。   5
   而今事过境迁，
  无论我处身何地，
   黑夜还是白昼，
昔日的景象已不复存在。

   彩虹时隐时显，   10
   玫瑰争妍斗艳，
  待到晴空无云时，
   皓月欣然撒辉，
    星夜流水，
    清丽晶莹；   15
   朝阳灿烂绚丽；
但我了然，无论我辗转何地，
  光辉已从大地消逝。

如今，尽管鸟儿啾啾鸣叫，
尽管羊羔像随着鼓点似地   20
  纵情欢跳，

> To me alone there came a thought of grief:
> A timely utterance gave that thought relief,
> 　　And I again am strong.
25　　The cataracts blow their trumpets from the steep, —
> 　　No more shall grief of mine the season wrong;
> 　　I hear the echoes through the mountains throng,
> The winds come to me from the fields of sleep①,
> 　　And all the earth is gay;
30　　　　　　Land and sea
> 　　Give themselves up to jollity,
> 　　And with the heart of May
> 　　Doth every beast keep holiday; —
> 　　　　　Thou child of joy,
35　　Shout round me, let me hear thy shouts, thou happy Shepherd-boy!

> Ye blessèd Creatures, I have heard the call
> 　　Ye to each other make; I see
> The heavens laugh with you in your jubilee②;
> 　　My heart is at your festival,
40　　My head hath its coronal,
> The fulness of your bliss, I feel — I feel it all.
> 　　O evil day! if I were sullen③
> 　　While Earth herself is adorning
> 　　　This sweet May-morning;
45　　　And the children are culling
> 　　　　On every side
> 　　In a thousand valleys far and wide

---

① *the fields of sleep*: i.e. 'the fields where they had slept all night.'
② *jubilee*: 'general rejoicing.'
③ *O evil day! if I were sullen*: i.e. it would be an evil day for me, if, etc.

我却独自感到萧然惆怅：
适时结束,了却这绵绵哀伤,
　　今日里我又坚毅刚强。
绝壁之间,瀑布似喇叭轰响, 25
心头伤感,顿时化作烟云散：
我听到群山中回声荡漾,
清风从露宿的田野中徐徐拂来,
　　大地一片欢畅；
　　　　无论陆地与海洋, 30
　　陶然若醉,欢庆一堂,
　　　　怀着五月的心情,
万物都像在过节一样；——
　　　　你这快活的孩子,
让我倾听那声声欢叫,在我身旁喧嚷,你这幸福的牧童啊! 35

　　得福的众生啊,我听到
　　你们彼此呼唤,我瞧见
　　天公伴随你们捧腹狂欢；
我的心啊陶醉在你们节日的喜庆中,
　　头上戴着节日的花环, 40
我感觉到了——完全感觉到了你们的无上幸福。
　　大地在亲手装点
　　这馨香甘甜的五月清晨；
　　　　倘若我锁眉蹙额,
　　　　岂不是大煞风景! 45
　　煦阳当空,春光融融,
　　　　漫山遍野,远远近近,

Fresh flowers; while the sun shines warm,
And the babe leaps up on his mother's arm: —
        I hear, I hear, with joy I hear!
    — But there's a tree, of many, one,
A single field which I have look'd upon,
Both of them speak of something that is gone;
        The pansy at my feet
        Doth the same tale repeat:
Whither is fled the visionary gleam?
Where is it now, the glory and the dream?

Our birth is but a sleep and a forgetting;
The Soul that rises with us, our life's Star,
        Hath had elsewhere its setting,
        And cometh from afar;
        Not in entire forgetfulness,
        And not in utter nakedness,
But trailing clouds of glory do we come
        From God, who is our home:
Heaven lies about us in our infancy!
Shades of the prison-house begin to close
        Upon the growing Boy,
But he beholds the light, and whence it flows,
        He sees it in his joy;

　　　　无数孩童喜撷鲜花。
　　母亲怀中的婴儿一跃而起：——
　　听见了，听见了，我高兴地听见了！
　　——我看到万树丛中独有一棵树
　　　　兀立在一块孤零零的地里，
　　　　双双在倾诉那逝去的往事①；
　　　　我足下的紫罗兰
　　亦在重温那同样的经历：
　　　　幻想之光逝向了何处？
　　　　好景美梦今又在哪里②？

　　人身降世不过是一场昏睡，逐日淡忘；
　　伴随肉体的灵魂，我们的司命星，
　　　　一度沉落他地，
　　　　现又升腾而起，迢迢飘来；
　　　　既未全然忘却前事，
　　　　亦非空空一无所赐，
　　　　我们驾着荣耀的云彩③，
　　　　辞别上苍，我们的归宿：
　　幼年时代无处不是人间天堂！
　　　　随着年岁增长，
　　囚牢的阴影渐渐攫住了孩子的心灵④。
　　他却看到了光明，看到了光明所在，
　　　　他欣喜地看到了！

---

① 双双，指"孤零零的地"与"一棵树"。——编注者
② 指本诗第一节谈到的梦境。——编注者
③ 本段前七行宣扬了佛教和婆罗门教的"灵魂存在于肉体之前，并和肉体结合"的教义。这种教义在古希腊文学中多有反映。例如柏拉图就有这样一句论断："知识即回忆。"但作者后来否认自己在灌输这种教义，并对外界给他所下的这一断论提出了抗议。——译者
④ 意指人世间势不可免的幻灭和悲苦的焦虑。——译者

                The Youth, who daily farther from the east
                    Must travel, still is Nature's priest
                    And by the vision splendid
                    Is on his way attended;
75   At legnth the Man perceives it die away,
                And fade into the light of common day.

                Earth fills her lap with pleasures of her own;
                Yearnings she hath in her own natural kind①,
                And, even with something of a mother's mind
80   And no unworthy aim,
                    The homely nurse doth all she can
                To make her foster-child, her inmate, Man,
                        Forget the glories he hath known,
                And that imperial palace whence he came.

85   Behold the Child among his new-born blisses,
                    A six years' darling of a pigmy size!
                See, where 'mid work of his own hand he lies,
                Fretted by sallies of his mother's kisses,
                    With light upon him from his father's eyes!
90   See, at his feet, some little plan or chart,
                Some fragment from his dream of human life,
                Shaped by himself with newly-learnéd art;

---

① *in her own natural kind*: 'of the sort natural to her.'

青年时代,势必逐日西去,
　却依旧是大自然的祭司①,
　　在征途中伴随着
　　美妙的幻象;
一朝成年,遂发觉幻象渐趋消失,　　　　　　　75
最终逝尽,融入寻常目光之中。

　　大地自得其乐,
　　自有天生独具的向往,
　　甚而怀着慈母般的苦心
　　和高尚的志向,　　　　　　　　　　　　80
这位和善的保姆悉心照料,竭尽全力
　让她的养子,她的宝贝——世人
　　忘却他熟悉的荣耀,
　　连同他辞别的天堂。

喜看这孩子处身于新生的极乐之中吧,　　　　85
　一个年仅六载的幼童②!
瞧,他躺在亲笔耕耘的作品中,
　　母亲疼爱地狂吻着他,
　　父亲投来了自豪的目光!
瞧,他的脚下,一份小小的计划或蓝图,　　　90
　　人生理想的片断,
正由自己用日益长进的技艺精心绘制;

---

① 指能够尽祭司之职,向众人传达他所见到大自然荣耀的人。——译者
② 作者此处系指其好友塞缪尔·泰勒·柯勒律治(Samuel Taylor Coleridge)的长子哈特利·柯勒律治(Hartley Coleridge,1796—1849)。该诗始作于一八〇二年,其时哈特利年方六岁。——译者

    A wedding or a festival,
    A mourning or a funeral;
95   And this hath now his heart,
    And unto this he frames his song:
    Then will he fit his tongue
To dialogues of business, love, or strife;
    But it will not be long
100   Ere this be thrown aside,
    And with new joy and pride
The little actor cons another part;
Filling from time to time his 'humorous stage'
With all the Persons, down to palsied Age①,
105 That life brings with her in her equipage;
    As if his whole vocation
    Were endless imitation.

Thou, whose exterior semblance doth belie②
    Thy soul's immensity;
110 Thou best Philosopher, who yet dost keep
Thy heritage, thou Eye among the blind,
That, deaf and silent, read'st the eternal deep,
Haunted for ever by the eternal Mind, —
    Mighty Prophet! Seer blest!
115   On whom those truths do rest
Which we are toiling all our lives to find,
In darkness lost, the darkness of the grave;
Thou, over whom thy Immortality

---

① *Persons*: in its Latin sense of 'characters in a play.'
② *Thou*: the child.

婚礼或者喜庆，
　　　葬礼或者哀伤，
　　——踏入他的心灵，　　　　　　　　　　95
他为此谱写了自己的诗章。
这样，他自后方能伶牙俐齿，
面对事务、爱情或者争纷应付从容。
　　　然而无须多久，
　　这一切将被弃之一旁。　　　　　　　　100
　　满怀新的欢乐和豪情，
这位小演员默诵起又一段台词，
在其"幽默舞台"上轮次扮演着①
人生的马车载乘的全部角色，
　　直至风烛残年；　　　　　　　　　　　105
　　仿佛他一生的职业，
就是无休无止的仿效模拟。

　　你那宏大的气魄②，
　　　岂是你的外表所配！
你是出类拔萃的哲人，承继了　　　　　　　110
前人的传统；你独具慧眼，
声色不露，却能看懂永恒的深邃，
无时无刻不在施展不朽的才智——
　　非凡的预言家！得福的先知！
　　　在他身上存在着　　　　　　　　　115
我们终生苦斗以求、一度在黑暗中
——墓穴般的黑暗中消失的真理；
　　你的永垂不朽之神驾驭着你，

---

① 作者此处系指沙翁喜剧《皆大欢喜》中的台词："整个世界是一座大舞台"，但"幽默"一词原文中未见。——译者
② 你，指那孩子。——编注者

	Broods like the Day, a Master o'er a Slave,
120	A Presence which is not to be put by;
	Thou little Child, yet glorious in the might
	Of heaven-born freedom on thy being's height,
	Why with such earnest pains dost thou provoke①
	The years to bring the inevitable yoke,
125	Thus blindly with thy blessedness at strife?
	Full soon thy Soul shall have her earthly freight,
	And custom lie upon thee with a weight
	Heavy as frost, and deep almost as life!

	O joy! that in our embers
130	Is something that doth live,
	That Nature yet remembers
	What was so fugitive!
	The thought of our past years in me doth breed
	Perpetual benediction: not indeed
135	For that which is most worthy to be blest,
	Delight and liberty, the simple creed
	Of Childhood, whether busy or at rest,
	With new-fledged hope still fluttering in his breast:
	— Not for these I raise
140	The song of thanks and praise;
	But for those obstinate questionings
	Of sense and outward things,
	Fallings from us, vanishings②,
	Blank misgivings of a creature

---

① *provoke*: 'challenge,' 'call upon.'
② *Fallings from us*: *i.e.* the disappearance for a time of the material world around us.

犹如主人驾驭着奴仆；
　你的存在是天意所定，必不可免。　　　　　　　120
　你这小小幼童，尚荣耀地生活在
　天赋的自由王国，
　何苦催逼年华
带来禁锢人生的枷锁——诚然它势不可免，
　盲目地使这得福之身陷入争纷?!　　　　　　　125
　你的灵魂倏忽将背上人世的重负，
　习俗似万仞高山压在你的身上，
　　重似枝头霜，深几贯终生！

欢呼啊！在我们的余烬中
　　　　存在着永生不灭；　　　　　　　　　　130
　　那转瞬即逝的往事，
　　大自然依旧记忆犹新！
　　缅怀逝去的岁月，
　在我心中孕育着永恒的祝福。
　　诚非为那最值得之物而祝——　　　　　　　135
诸如欢乐与自由，
儿时天真的信念，
闲忙与否，这些时刻在心中激荡的新生希望：
　　——亦非为它们谱写
　　感恩和颂扬的诗章；　　　　　　　　　　　140
　　而是为感觉上久难解决的问题、
　　周围的物质世界，
　　它的短暂消失和终结、
　　在尚未实现的诸世界里

145	Moving about in worlds not realized,
	High instincts, before which our mortal nature
	Did tremble like a guilty thing surprised:
	But for those first affections[①],
	Those shadowy recollections,
150	Which, be they what they may,
	Are yet the fountain-light of all our day,
	Are yet a master-light of all our seeing;
	Uphold us, cherish, and have power to make
	Our noisy years seem moments in the being
155	Of the eternal silence: truths that wake,
	To perish never;
	Which neither listlessness, nor mad endeavour,
	Nor man nor boy
	Nor all that is at enmity with joy,
160	Can utterly abolish or destroy!
	Hence in a season of calm weather
	Though inland far we be,
	Our souls have sight of that immortal sea
	Which brought us hither;
165	Can in a moment travel thither —
	And see the children sport upon the shore,
	And hear the mighty waters rolling evermore.
	Then, sing ye birds, sing, sing a joyous song!
	And let the young lambs bound
170	As to the tabor's sound!
	We, in thought, will join your throng
	Ye that pipe and ye that play,

---

① *But for*: sc. 'I raise the song of thanks for.'

> 游荡的生灵 145
> 所具的莫名恐惧、

使人性像受惊的罪人却而发颤的高尚天性;
> 而是为那纯洁无邪的情感
> 和依稀记得的往事。
> 它们——但愿如此—— 150
> 依然是我们时代的源光,
> 依然是我们视觉的主光;
> 支撑我们,赋与希望,而且能够

把我们闹嚷的人世岁月变成仿佛是
> 人生永恒静寂中的瞬间片刻: 155
> 觉醒的真理永世不会消亡。
> 懒怠也罢,疯狂的努力也罢,
> 成人也罢,孩子也罢,
> 一切与欢乐作对者也罢,

谁也无法把它们消除、毁灭! 160
> 因此,在这风平浪静的时节,
> 诚然我们远在内地,
> 我们的灵魂却能看到

曾经载渡我们来此的永存的大海,
> 倏忽便可飘抵那里, 165

观看孩子在海滨尽兴地嬉戏作乐,
倾听惊涛骇浪永不停息地奔腾远去。

> 唱吧,鸟儿,唱上一支欢乐的歌!
> 让羊羔像随着鼓点似地
> 纵情欢跳! 170
> 我们的心将加入你们的行列。
> 你们吹奏吧,你们嬉戏吧,

      Ye that through your hearts to-day
      Feel the gladness of the May!
175   What though the radiance which was once so bright
    Be now for ever taken from my sights,
      Though nothing can bring back the hour
    Of splendour in the grass, of glory in the flower;
      We will grieve not, rather find
180   Strength in what remains behind;
      In the primal sympathy
      Which having been must ever be;
      In the soothing thoughts that spring
      Out of human suffering;
185   In the faith that looks through death,
    In years that bring the philosophic mind.

    And O, ye Fountains, Meadows, Hills, and Groves,
    Forbode not any severing of our loves[①]!
    Yet in my heart of hearts I feel your might;
190   I only have relinquish'd one delight
    To live beneath your more habitual sway;
    I love the brooks which down their channels fret[②],
    Even more than when I tripp'd lightly as they;
    The innocent brightness of a new-born day
195   Is lovely yet;
    The clouds that gather round the setting sun
    Do take a sober colouring from an eye
    That hath kept watch o'er man's mortality;
    Another race hath been, and other palms are won.

---

① *our loves*: *i.e.* the love I feel for you.
② *fret*: see note to No. 191, l. 14.

五月的欢乐今日里渗入了你们的心髓。
　　　一度灿烂夺目的光辉，
　　　　　已永远从眼前消失，
　　　　这又有何妨?!
没有任何办法能让那在芳草香花中
度过的美好时光逝而复返！
　　　但我们不会为此伤感，
　　　　　而是从中寻求力量。
这力量存在于残存的事物中，
存在于经久长存的纯真同情中，
存在于解脱了人类痛苦的安宁思绪中，
存在于孕育恬静之心的未来岁月中。
　　　存在于识破了死亡的信仰中，
也存在于孕育哲理心灵的岁月中。

　　　啊！泉水、牧场、山峦、丛林，
别割断我们的一片倾慕之情！
　　　我心灵深处感觉到了你的力量，
　　　　　独自放弃心中的乐事，
借助你那永世长存的力量消度年华。
　　　我爱那辟道远去的小溪，
每当我似溪流轻快徜徉，爱恋之情更添。
　　　纯洁无瑕的曙光
　　　　依然妩媚可爱，
　　　　　聚集在夕阳周围的云彩，
　　　在密切注视人类生死的眼目中
　　　　却已呈显出一片黯淡的灰白色
又一段征程结束了，新的胜利已经赢得[①]。

[①] 西方习俗认为，人的一生是一系列路程组成的，在每一段路程中都可以赢得一件奖品。参见《圣经·新约·希伯来书》第十二章第一节："存心忍耐，奔那摆在我们前头的路程。"——译者

200 Thanks to the human heart by which we live,
Thanks to its tenderness, its joys, and fears,
To me the meanest flower that blows can give
Thoughts that do often lie too deep for tears.

W. WORDSWORTH.

多亏我们赖以生存的人类之心,
多亏人类之心的温柔、欢乐与忧愁,
即便最贱的花朵绽放,也能给我带来无限幽思,
它常常深埋在心底,令我时时黯然流泪。

张明　译

编注　这是一首极为著名的长诗,作于一八〇二至一八〇六年间,一八〇七年发表在《诗集》上,题名《颂》(Ode),现在的标题系后来补上的。诗人在诗中探索人生的真谛,重申了莎士比亚把人生看作舞台,每个演员将扮演七个场景的典故,但他又强调了觉醒的真理永世不会消亡。全诗的最后两行是常被摘引的名句,体现了华兹华斯所主张的"诗是强烈情感的自然流露。它起源于在平静中回忆起来的情感"。

288. 'MUSIC, WHEN SOFT VOICES DIE'

Music, when soft voices die,
Vibrates in the memory —
Odours, when sweet violets sicken①,
Live within the sense they quicken.

5   Rose leaves, when the rose is dead,
Are heaped for the beloved's bed;
And so thy thoughts, when thou art gone②,
Love itself shall slumber on.

P. B. SHELLEY.

---

① *sicken*: i.e. lose their scent.
② *thy thoughts*: 'the thought of thee,' like the Greek 'ἐς τὴν ἐμὴν ἀνάμνησιν.' Love shall find rest in thinking of thee, when thou art gone.

288. "音乐,虽然消失了柔声"

雪莱

音乐,虽然消失了柔声,
却仍旧在记忆里颤动——
芬芳,虽然早谢了紫罗兰,
却留存在它所刺激的感官。

玫瑰叶子,虽然花儿死去,   5
还能在爱人的床头堆积;
同样的,等你去了,你的思想
和爱情,会依然睡在世上。

查良铮 译

THE GOLDEN TREASURY

F. T. PALGRAVE

英诗金库

（修订版）

［英］F.T.帕尔格雷夫　原编

曹明伦　罗义蕴　陈朴　编注

- 上 -

复旦大学出版社

修订版说明

翻译《英诗金库》(以下简称《金库》)的念头最初萌动于一九八三年深秋。那年十一月的一天,日近中午,细雨霏霏,在成都外文书店购书后,我骑着自行车回学校,经指挥街和盐道街相汇路口,遇正下班回家的四川人民出版社编辑李陈先生。两人骑车并肩而行,他注意到我车兜里放着刚买的一册袖珍影印版 *The Golden Treasury of the Best Songs and Lyrical Poems in the English Language*。经他一番"尽快出书"的劝诱和鼓动,我翻译《英诗金库》的念头变成了组织翻译《英诗金库》的计划。那时还没有复印这个概念,想到邀约译者得提供原文,于是我俩调头,返回外文书店,将店里另外四部 *The Golden Treasury* 全部买下。

为了上报出版选题,我抓紧时间做出了《金库》入选诗篇中文目录,翻译了《金库》原编者帕尔格雷夫写的序言,草拟了出版选题计划。然后我和李陈分头扎进图书馆,翻阅"文革"前出版的文学书刊,查找与《金库》选诗对应的中文译诗,同时寻找适合的译者。经过一段时间的努力,我们找到了郭沫若、朱生豪、梁宗岱、李霁野等三十六位前辈译家翻译的一百四十七首诗,其余二百八十六首则准备以四川人民出版社译文编辑室的名义邀约国内专家学者翻译。

译文编辑室于当年岁末上报出版计划。上级认为,如此庞大的项目需要具有高级职称的人员参加。我当时只是名普通的高校教师,于是由出版社出面邀请了与我合作的罗义蕴副教授以及主要负责外联工作的陈朴先生。鉴于我早已开始了先期工作,所以编注者的分工为:我负责第一、二、三卷,罗义蕴负责第四卷,陈朴负责第五卷。我们通力合作,加之全国一百余位译者共同努力,全书的翻译和编注工作只进行了一年,于一九八四年十二月完成,一九八五年年初发稿,但因出现了一些意外情况,《英诗金库》(中英对照版)于一九八七年十月才正式出版发行,后来于一九八九年二月又出版了《英诗金库》纯中译文版。

《英诗金库》出版三十三年来,一直受到学界和读者的好评,大家都认为这是一部有价值的好书。但遗憾的是,这部书当年总共只印了二千五百九十册(其中英汉对照本一千五百五十册,纯中译文本一千零四十册),今天的英诗爱好者只能以高价从网络上邮购旧书。在此情况下,复旦大学出版社计划推出《英诗金库》修订版,这实乃学界和读者之幸事。由于罗义蕴教授年事已高,陈朴先生则已去世多年,所以这次修订工作由我一人主持。经过与复旦大学出版社反复商讨,考虑到当年参加《金库》翻译的译者大多都已去世,故决定修订版中的译诗大部分保持原貌,以存其真。这次修订除必要的字词勘误之外,只进行了以下替换和变更:替换了一九八七年版中的三十六首译诗。替换大致分三种情况:一、让同一位诗人的诗作之译文风格相对统一(如莎士比亚的十四行诗和罗伯特·赫里克的三首《衣裙之歌》等);二、选用更为当代中国读者接受的译文(如第173、231、289、325和329首等);三、分别用屠岸、杨德豫、顾子欣和曹明伦的译文替换了当年第四卷中由"虚拟译者"署名的十一首译诗(如第185、191、194、210、212、216、214、273首等)。

另外,修订版编注者的署名依照分卷顺序和贡献大小排列。

最后我要特别感谢复旦大学出版社人文编辑室的宋启立、方尚芩、杜怡顺团队。没有他们的极力敦促、精心策划和认真编校,《英诗金库》的修订版也许还遥遥无期。

曹明伦
2020年4月于成都华西坝

编注者说明

一、我国译介英国诗歌,大约始于"五四"前后。大半个世纪以来,我国的诗歌译者走过了漫长的路程,向中国人民介绍了大量的英国诗歌,在译诗实践中积累了十分宝贵的经验。另一方面,随着整个中华民族文化水平的提高,广大读者渴望有一本较大规模的英诗选本,以满足学习和欣赏英诗的需要。为此,在四川人民出版社的提议和组织下,我们编注了《英语最佳歌谣及抒情诗之金库》(简称《英诗金库》)的英汉对照本和汉译本。

二、《英诗金库》,首版于一八六一年,辑录十六世纪至十九世纪上半叶的名家诗作288首,我们主要依据的一九二九年版本又加进了十九世纪下半叶至二十世纪初的145首,共计433首,包括一百四十五位知名诗人和九名佚名诗人的颂歌、民歌、十四行诗及其他抒情形式的诗作。由于这部诗选的编者着眼于方便读者欣赏,在排列顺序上,把所选诗按情感和题材归类,在选收范围上,只收选抒情诗,因而受到欧美读者的欢迎,一百多年来,几至家喻户晓,人手一册。在我国,由于这部诗选津逮初学,大多数诗歌都是有定评的名词佳句,具有代表性,且字梳句栉,注释详尽,因而也受到中国读者的欢迎。几十年来,文学学生和各界读者一直将此书作为学习英语诗歌、培养诗歌情趣的首选读本,其中许多著名诗篇得到广为传诵,很多诗选、教材均以此书为蓝本。

三、本书编注的诗歌中,约有一百余首是录自国内诗选、杂志、报端,其余为国内专家、学者、诗人和翻译工作者近百人应约而译的新作。在处理旧译时,我们力求反映原译的历史面貌,除一般印刷错误外,原译基本不动。至于新约译诗,我们曾提出三点:(一)译诗最好能保持原作的风格,在神似的基础上争取最大限度的形似,原则上保持原诗的段落和行数,以便有利读者对读原文;(二)译文形式最好是新诗体;(三)译文应适应我国读者的需要编写必要的注释。在编注译稿的过程中,我们尽量坚持上述原则,然而由于历来"诗无达诂",有时译者和编注者对同一首诗乃至同一个字的理解也相去甚远，我们只好以尊重译者为重，可不改就不改。另外，书中还保留了少数不完全符合上述原则的译作，这是由于译诗是一个严肃而复杂的问题，为了比较对照，不便一刀切齐，人为地厘定一个标准要大家遵守，以免把多样化的译文风格变成单一化的译文风格。

四、为了帮助读者解决学习或欣赏上的困难，我们尽力保持《英诗金库》注释详尽的特色，将注释分为三种：（一）汉语编注，对诗人及其诗作进行一些必要的说明，但不作严格的评价。（二）汉语脚注，对诗中出现的背景、典故、言外之意作出详略适中的说明。（三）英文脚注，对一般词典及工具书难以解决的语词疑难给以说明。另外，我们还在大多数诗后注明了出版年代。

五、我们力求出全《英诗金库》，但由于极个别诗眼下暂不宜介绍（如伤害中国人民感情的《英国士兵》）或其他原因，此版删去了五首诗（122、129、206、207、336）。当然，至于《英诗金库》原版有删节或原编者改动了诗题的，我们也努力注明。

六、我们采用的《英诗金库》一九二九年原文版本中有不少诗行的排列或字句与其他版本不一致，估计有印刷错误，但鉴于手中资料有限，难以校勘，均照原书排印。

七、本书编注者责任分工为：

曹明伦负责第一、二、三卷；罗义蕴负责第四卷；陈朴为第五卷，即增补卷。

八、本书蒙卞之琳、王佐良、李赋宁、杨周翰、戴镏龄、袁可嘉、吴景荣、赵萝蕤、赵瑞蕻、郑敏、屠岸、许国璋、绿原、邹荻帆、方平、飞白、朱维之、黄宏煦、邹绛、黄新渠等百余位同志的各种形式的支持，谨以致谢。

九、从准备到发稿，本书前后花了一年多的时间。作为首版，由于时间和编注者的学力所限，本书从精选旧译到新译编注一定不乏疏漏，我们衷心希望读者不吝赐教，并给我们推荐更佳之作，待再版时修正补充，使《英诗金库》日臻完美。

编注者

一九八四年十二月于成都

汉译《英诗金库》序

像中国一样,英国也有选学,即把诗文精编在一个选本的学问。一五五七年的《托特尔集》就是一本有影响的英国抒情诗选,展示英国文艺复兴初期几位抒情诗人的作品。十九世纪中叶,一位叫作弗兰西斯·特纳·帕尔格雷夫(Francis Turner Palgrave,1824—1897)的诗人编了一部《英诗金库》,主要收集抒情诗,出版之后,受到欢迎,以后重版多次,并经后人补充,成为至今有名的选本之一。原编者收了 288 首诗,按时代先后分为四部份,第一部分到一六一六年,是十六世纪及十七世纪初叶的作品;第二部分到一七〇〇年,以十七世纪作品为主;第三部分到一八〇〇年,是古典主义及浪漫主义前期之作;第四部分则是十九世纪前半叶的作品,全是浪漫主义盛世之作。华兹华斯一人入选 41 首之多。后加的诗数目达 145 首,为原编的一半还多,创作年代直到二十世纪初年,把丁尼生、勃朗宁以至所谓乔治时期的诗人包括在内了。总起来看,这是一部包罗从文艺复兴直到二十世纪初年各时期抒情佳作的选本。

任何选本都受编写时的文学风尚的影响,《金库》也不例外。编者帕尔格雷夫本人是一个后期浪漫派诗人,他的选目呈现出后期浪漫主义的诗歌的长处和缺点。几位主要浪漫派诗人——华兹华斯、柯勒律治、雪莱、济慈——得到了较多的篇幅,重要的抒情作品几乎都收集在内,只是拜伦的作品入选较少。还有一个重大的遗漏:布莱克这么大诗人无一诗入选。十八世纪的格雷等人有机会展露才华,但十七世纪则少了玄学派的典型之作,邓恩一首也未收,马韦尔只收进入了《花园遐思》第二三首,未选至少同样出色的《致矜持的情人》。

有些选进的诗并不高明。托马斯·坎贝尔的歌颂英国武功的诗选得多了,这里透露了编者本人的政治思想,然而这也是十九世纪中叶不少英国诗人共有的思想,例如他的朋友,当时最有名的诗人丁尼生就写了《轻骑旅的冲锋》。

此外，从现代版本学的标准来看，编者对于作品本文的选择也失之任意之处。他不是力求体现作者的原意或最后的考虑，而是从他本人认为"最有诗意"（前言，第Ⅵ页）的这一点来确定版本的。

因此，不能说《金库》在今天还是本标准的甚至权威的选本。二十世纪中叶以后，陆续出现了新的英诗选本，如约翰·海华德（John Hayward）编的《企鹅版英诗选》（1956年）就获得好评。

然而《金库》还是大有可读的。这是因为就抒情诗而论，它所选的大部分是有定评的优秀之作。读了它们，对于英国诗的发展过程和每个时期的重要作品是可以比较清楚的。编者着重欣赏，这也比力图体现一家之说的选本要比较全面些，因而也就比较适合一般读者。《金库》自一八六一年初版以来，不断重印，这事实也说明它受到了若干代读者的爱好。

中国老一代的文学学生学习英诗，往往从《金库》开始。它帮助他们形成了诗歌趣味，也带来了某些局限性。现在是轮到新的一代中国学生来读它了。在这个时候，编出一个中英对照本，将十分有助于他们读懂所包含的诗篇。读懂也包含用马克思主义去分析，去区别优劣，但是首先要了解学习的意义，因此好译本仍是不可少的，特别是对于不识英语的青年读者。

然而诗却难译。这选本所收的四百三十多首诗里，有的十分难译。对照本的编注者们在收集和整理译诗上花了力气，既采用了旧译中的脍炙人口之作，又补充了大批新译，译者来自各方。这等于是开了译诗展览会，可以让读者看出我国在诗歌翻译上的成就和不足，对于推进文学翻译无疑也是有好处的。

王佐良
一九八四年六月

《英诗金库》初版前言

编者相信,这部小小的诗集与其他选本的不同之处在于它力图囊括用我们的语言写作的、业已弃世的诗人们的全部最佳抒情诗及歌谣——入选诗歌无一不是上乘之作。因此,读者将读到许多家喻户晓的和许多应该为人们所熟悉的诗篇。编者欲把诗歌之酷爱者视为本书的知音读者,故不能将那些迄今未被世人所知且又无价值的作品奉献给他们。

编者并不知晓抒情诗有何明确而精密的界说,但是随着编选工作的进行,他发现从实际上对抒情诗加以判别变得愈来愈清楚,愈来愈容易,与此同时,他心中也就形成了几条简单的原则。收入本书的抒情诗基本上具有这样一种意味,这就是每首诗都应该表现一种单一的思想、感情或场景。依照这一点,凡叙事诗、描述诗和教诲诗,除简洁明快并具有人类感情色彩者之外,概不收选;凡滑稽幽默诗,包括那些全然系个人批评,或即兴的,或宗教性的诙谐,除极少数真正通篇具有诗味的佳作之外,其余均视为与本书宗旨相悖;凡素体诗和十音节双行诗,虽则负有盛名,引人注目,但因既有别于我们所知晓的歌谣,又难以归入抒情诗的范畴,也概不纳入本书。然而,编者并不指望,而且也不可能使读者都认为本书所选诗篇均严格符合上述原则。有些诗,诸如格雷的《墓畔哀歌》、弥尔顿的《快乐的人》和《幽思的人》、华兹华斯的《露茜》组诗以及坎贝尔的《乌林爵爷的女儿》等,或许也同样适合编入一部叙事或描述诗集。至于民谣和十四行诗,编者唯一能说的就是,他并非凭自己的任性和偏好,而是费尽心机、精心挑选的。

对人们更有可能提出的一个问题——即何为"最佳"的等级标准,以下陈述亦是编者的全部解释。诗应与诗人的天才相称;诗应达到与它的目的一致的尽善尽美;我们应要求诗的结尾简洁明了;诗的感情、色彩及独创性不能弥补它在清晰、和谐和真实性方面的严重不足;只有个别优秀诗行的诗算不得好诗;公众的评价只能作为路标,而不能作为指南；尤其是要依据全诗而不是诗的部分来判定优劣；这些和诸如此类的原则是经常不断地为编者所考虑的。但编者不妨再补充一下，所有入选诗歌和大量未选作品都经过编者反复认真的斟酌权衡；在整个编选过程中，除了在本书"献辞"中所提到的那位杰出人物①，编者还一直得到两位颇有独立见解和判断力的朋友的帮助。编者希望这种帮助已使本书摆脱了那种必然影响个人判断的片面性。但对于最后的取舍，编者本人负有全部责任。

显而易见，把这部诗选的准则应用于今天还活着的诗人也许是令人不快的。即使眼下这样做不惹人动怒，但只须预料一下未来世纪的人们对我们这个时代的人的评价，这样做也似乎并非明智之举。倘若此书能流传于世，丁尼生、布莱恩特②、克莱尔③、洛威尔④及其他一些诗人的诗将毫无疑问地要在最佳诗歌之中获得它们的地位。但编者确信，这项工作将在遥远的未来由其他人来完成。

编者曾两度系统地阅读查麦兹⑤所编的那部未包括常见诗人全部作品的巨大诗选和各个时期的优秀诗选集，因此，本书中任何可能使人感到遗憾的删略，未必就是编者的疏漏。所选诗歌，除极少数被删去某个小节（详见诗后注释），其余都是全文照印。编者之所以不惜担着风险删去某些小节，其目的是为了使被删诗歌更接近抒情诗的风格，至于明显地从根本上与抒情诗风格相悖的诗，则一概不收入。关于所收诗的正文，凡有两种不同诗文并存的，本书的一贯原则是选择最有诗意的诗文。为尽可能地便利读者，编者在排列、拼写和标点等方面，对每首入选诗都做了大量考证和修订工作。

编者在此衷心感谢所参阅各书的版权所有人，正因为他们的许可，本书方得以出版，没有他们的慷慨赞助，编选本书的计划将付诸东流。

在编排上，编者尝试了一种最富诗意的体例。在过去三个世纪的

---

① 指丁尼生（参见本书卷五第 322 首编注）。——编注者
② 布莱恩特（William Cullen Bryant, 1794—1878），美国诗人。——编注者
③ 克莱尔（John Clare, 1793—1864），英国诗人。——编注者
④ 洛威尔（James Russell Lowell, 1819—1891），美国诗人。——编注者
⑤ 亚历山大·查麦兹（Alexander Chalmers, 1759—1834），苏格兰传记作家及编辑。——编注者

诗史中,英国在其思想意识和文化教养方面经历了不同阶段,这些思想意识和文化教养的阶段是如此的千变万化,相互对立,以致我们要通阅这些老的和新的诗篇就像是在飞驰中观看不断变幻的风景,而这样做往往会使人感到厌倦,有损于人们对美的欣赏。鉴于这一原因,编者将本书分成了四卷;卷一包括一六一六年以前的九十年,卷二从一六一六至一七○○年,卷三从一七○○至一八○○年,卷四则从一八○○年至刚结束的半个世纪。① 若以或多或少给予各卷以特色的诗人而论,这四卷可分别称之为莎士比亚卷、弥尔顿卷、格雷卷和华兹华斯卷。就这点而言,本书在它所允许的限度范围内准确地反映了我们诗歌的自然发展过程。

然而,严格的、编年史般的次序似乎更适合于以教学为目的的选本,而不适合于以欣赏乐趣并由此而增长知识为目的的选本,所以,各卷中所收的诗歌均按感情和主题分类逐级排列。莫扎特和贝多芬交响乐的展开进程,一直被编者视为本书编排的典范,每一首的位置无一不是编者精心考虑过的。因此,编者希望读者会发现本书所收的诗篇呈现出一种和谐一致,正如雪莱那高贵的语言所述,"对于自开天辟地以来,由一个伟大的精神支配着共同思想的全部诗人们所写成的那首伟大的诗",这些诗篇犹如和谐的"插曲"。

当结束这一冗长的概述之时,编者相信他自己可以毫不自负地说,他已经预见到公众舆论对本书模糊笼统的评价将会比那些对本书持过严批评态度的人的评价更为公正,因为这些批评者会把对诗的评价限制在"从那么多代诗人中只选出这么少的诗"这一范围内。大凡博得名声的人都在相当程度上具有与他名声相符的天赋或才华。如果那些诗句甜蜜但缺乏力度,或虽有思想却表达不当的诗人们的诗未被收入本书,读者切莫以为编者就不为此而百般犹豫,极为惋惜,更不要以为编者对这些诗作者有轻视之心。在这份长长的而又可怜的、已经沉默的歌手名单中,很少有人配得上诗人的荣誉,而又很少有人不具备语言技巧、美的感应、细腻的情感或严肃的思想,而正是由于这样的原因使他

---

① 原编者的这篇《前言》写于一八六一年,刚结束的半个世纪指一八○○——一八五○年。——编注者

们的作品尽管没有达到本书所要求的更高更精的优秀标准,但却比真正的平庸之作更值得一读,因为真正的平庸之作只是为了填充那些省下时间来自我完善,或用任何更高尚、更永恒的形式来取乐的人的时间。若是真把这些作品也算作平庸之作的话,我们真不知对"最佳"二字负下了多少债。犹如虚构的亚速尔岛之泉,但比该泉更具有千变万化的魔力,这门艺术不可思议的魔力能使生命的每个时期都得到相应的天惠:给少年以经验,给成年以沉着,给老年以青春。诗给予我们"比金子还要珍贵的宝藏",用世上最高尚、最健康的方法指引我们,并给我们解释大自然之真谛。但她最好的解释就是她自身。如果本书的编选计划已经达到它预期的目的,那读者将在这个选本里听到她的声音:——无论在什么地方,只要英国的诗人们在那里受到尊敬,只要英语在那里流行,这本诗选就有希望在那里觅到知音。

弗·特·帕尔格雷夫

The Golden Treasury
of
The Best Songs and Lyrical Poems in the English Language

Εἰς τὸν λειμῶνα καθίσας,
ἔδρεπεν ἕτερου ἐφ' ἑτέρῳ
αἰρόμενος ἄγρευμ' ἀνθέων
ἁδομένα ψυχᾷ.
    [Eurip. frag. 754.]

'He sat in the meadow and plucked with glad heart the spoil of the flowers, gathering them one by one.'

他坐在草地上,怀着愉快的心情摘花,把花儿一朵一朵地汇聚起来。

——欧里庇得斯——

Contents

Book First

1. Spring	002
2. Summons to Love	004
3. Time and Love (Ⅰ)	010
4. Time and Love (Ⅱ)	014
5. The Passionate Shepherd to His Love	016
6. A Madrigal	020
7. 'Under the greenwood tree'	022
8. 'It was a lover and his lass'	024
9. Present in Absence	026
10. Absence	028
11. 'How like a winter hath my absence been'	030
12. A Consolation	032
13. The Unchangeable	034
14. 'To me, fair friend, you never can be old'	036
15. Diaphenia	038
16. Rosalynde	040
17. Colin	046
18. To His Love	048
19. To His Love	050
20. Love's Perjuries	052
21. A Supplication	056
22. To Aurora	060

目 录

上 册

卷一（1509—1616）

1. 春　　　　　　　　　　　　　　　讷徐 / 003
2. 对爱的呼唤　　　　　　　　　　德拉蒙德 / 005
3. 时间和爱（之一）　　　　　　　　莎士比亚 / 011
4. 时间和爱（之二）　　　　　　　　莎士比亚 / 015
5. 牧羊人的恋歌　　　　　　　　　　　马洛 / 017
6. 小曲　　　　　　　　　　　　　　莎士比亚 / 021
7. "绿树高张翠幕"　　　　　　　　莎士比亚 / 023
8. "一对情人并着肩"　　　　　　　莎士比亚 / 025
9. 逢在离别中　　　　　　　　　　　无名氏 / 027
10. 别离　　　　　　　　　　　　　莎士比亚 / 029
11. 别离（之二）　　　　　　　　　莎士比亚 / 031
12. 安慰　　　　　　　　　　　　　莎士比亚 / 033
13. 永不变心　　　　　　　　　　　莎士比亚 / 035
14. "美丽的朋友，我看你永不会老"　莎士比亚 / 037
15. 黛尔菲妮娅　　　　　　　　　康斯特布尔 / 039
16. 罗莎琳诀　　　　　　　　　　　　洛吉 / 041
17. 科林　　　　　　　　　　　牧羊人托尼 / 047
18. 致爱友　　　　　　　　　　　　莎士比亚 / 049
19. 致爱友（之二）　　　　　　　　莎士比亚 / 051
20. 爱的谎言　　　　　　　　　　　莎士比亚 / 053
21. 祈求　　　　　　　　　　　　　　怀亚特 / 057
22. 致奥罗娜　　　　　　　　　　　亚历山大 / 061

23. True Love 062
24. A Ditty 066
25. Love's Omnipresence 068
26. Carpe Diem 070
27. Winter 072
28. 'That time of year thou may'st in me behold' 074
29. Remembrance 076
30. Revolutions 078
31. 'Farewell! thou art too dear for my possessing' 080
32. The Life without Passion 082
33. The Lover's Appeal 084
34. The Nightingale 088
35. 'Care-charmer sleep' 092
36. Madrigal 094
37. Love's Farewell 096
38. To His Lute 098
39. Blind Love 100
40. The Unfaithful Shepherdess 102
41. A Renunciation 106
42. 'Blow, blow, thou winter wind' 110
43. Madrigal 112
44. Dirge of Love 114
45. Fidele 116
46. A Sea Dirge 118
47. A Land Dirge 120
48. Post Mortem 122
49. The Triumph of Death 124
50. Madrigal 126
51. Cupid and Campaspe 128
52. 'Pack, clouds, away, and welcome day' 130
53. Prothalamion 132

23. 真正的爱	莎士比亚 / 063	
24. 交换	锡德尼 / 067	
25. 爱情无处不在	西尔维斯特 / 069	
26. 及时行乐	莎士比亚 / 071	
27. 冬之歌	莎士比亚 / 073	
28. "你在我身上会看到这样的时节"	莎士比亚 / 075	
29. 记忆	莎士比亚 / 077	
30. 循环	莎士比亚 / 079	
31. "别了！你高贵得让我不配拥有"	莎士比亚 / 081	
32. 无激情的人生	莎士比亚 / 083	
33. 情人的哀诉	怀亚特 / 085	
34. 夜莺	巴恩菲尔德 / 089	
35. "驱愁的睡神呵"	丹尼尔 / 093	
36. 情歌	莎士比亚 / 095	
37. 爱的告别	迈克尔·德莱顿 / 097	
38. 致琵琶	德拉蒙德 / 099	
39. 盲目的爱	莎士比亚 / 101	
40. 不忠实的牧羊女	无名氏 / 103	
41. 死心断念	维尔 / 107	
42. "不惧冬风凛冽"	莎士比亚 / 111	
43. 小曲	德拉蒙德 / 113	
44. 爱的挽歌	莎士比亚 / 115	
45. 斐苔尔	莎士比亚 / 117	
46. 海的挽歌	莎士比亚 / 119	
47. 考奈丽雅挽歌	威伯斯忒 / 121	
48. 死后	莎士比亚 / 123	
49. 死的胜利	莎士比亚 / 125	
50. 情歌	莎士比亚 / 127	
51. 爱神和康帕丝	黎里 / 129	
52. "云,散开吧,迎接白天"	海伍德 / 131	
53. 婚前曲	斯宾塞 / 133	

54. The Happy Heart 148
55. 'This life, which seems so fair' 150
56. Soul and Body 152
57. Life 154
58. The Lessons of Nature 158
59. 'Doth then the world go thus, doth all thus move?' 160
60. The World's Way 162
61. Saint John Baptist 164

Book Second
62. Ode on the Morning of Christ's Nativity 168
63. Song for Saint Cecilia's Day, 1687 194
64. On the Late Massacre in Piedmont 202
65. Horatian Ode upon Cromwell's Return from Ireland 204
66. Lycidas 218
67. On the Tombs in Westminster Abbey 238
68. The Last Conqueror 240
69. Death the Leveller 242
70. When the Assault Was Intended to the City 246
71. On His Blindness 248
72. Character of a Happy Life 250
73. The Noble Nature 254
74. The Gifts of God 256
75. The Retreat 260
76. To Mr. Lawrence 264
77. To Cyriack Skinner 266
78. Hymn to Diana 268
79. Wishes for the Supposed Mistress 270
80. The Great Adventurer 278
81. Child and Maiden 282
82. Counsel to Girls 286

54. 称心满意	德克尔	/ 149
55. "看起来这般炫丽的生命"	德拉蒙德	/ 151
56. 灵与肉	莎士比亚	/ 153
57. 人生	培根	/ 155
58. 大自然给我们上的课	德拉蒙德	/ 159
59. "难道世界就这样,一切就这样进行?"	德拉蒙德	/ 161
60. 今世众生路	莎士比亚	/ 163
61. 施洗圣约翰	德拉蒙德	/ 165

卷二(1616—1700)

62. 圣诞清晨歌	弥尔顿	/ 169
63. 一六八七年圣塞西莉亚日之歌	约翰·德莱顿	/ 195
64. 哀皮德蒙特大屠杀	弥尔顿	/ 203
65. 为克伦威尔从爱尔兰归来作贺拉斯体颂歌	马韦尔	/ 205
66. 黎西达斯	弥尔顿	/ 219
67. 写在威斯敏斯特寺墓群之前	鲍蒙特	/ 239
68. 最后的征服者	谢尔利	/ 241
69. 死亡使人人平等	谢尔利	/ 243
70. 当矛头指向这座城市的时候	弥尔顿	/ 247
71. 哀失明	弥尔顿	/ 249
72. 幸福生活的本色	沃顿	/ 251
73. 高贵的天性	琼生	/ 255
74. 上帝的赐与	赫伯特	/ 257
75. 退路	沃恩	/ 261
76. 赠劳伦斯	弥尔顿	/ 265
77. 赠西里克·斯金纳	弥尔顿	/ 267
78. 狄安娜赞	琼生	/ 269
79. 对想象中情人的希望	克拉休	/ 271
80. 伟大的冒险家	无名氏	/ 279
81. 童男与少女	塞德利	/ 283
82. 给少女们的忠告	赫里克	/ 287

83. To Lucasta, on Going to the Wars	288
84. Elizabeth of Bohemia	290
85. To the Lady Margaret Ley	294
86. The Loveliness of Love	296
87. The True Beauty	302
88. To Dianeme	304
89. 'Go, lovely rose!'	306
90. To Celia	310
91. Cherry-Ripe	312
92. The Poetry of Dress I	314
93. The Poetry of Dress II	316
94. The Poetry of Dress III	318
95. On a Girdle	320
96. To Anthea Who May Command Him Any Thing	322
97. 'Love not me for comely grace'	326
98. 'Not, Celia, that I juster am'	328
99. To Althea from Prison	330
100. To Lucasta, on Going Beyond the Seas	334
101. Encouragements to a Lover	336
102. A Supplication	338
103. The Manly Heart	342
104. Melancholy	346
105. To a Lock of Hair	350
106. The Forsaken Bride	354
107. Fair Helen	360
108. The Twa Corbies	366
109. To Blossoms	370
110. To Daffodils	372
111. Thoughts in a Garden	374
112. L'Allégro	382
113. Il Penseroso	398

83. 出阵前告别鲁加斯达	洛夫莱斯	/ 289
84. 波希米亚的伊丽莎白	沃顿	/ 291
85. 赠玛格丽特·莱伊女士	弥尔顿	/ 295
86. 爱之可爱	达利	/ 297
87. 真的美	加鲁	/ 303
88. 致黛安	赫里克	/ 305
89. "去,可爱的玫瑰"	沃勒	/ 307
90. 致西丽娅	琼生	/ 311
91. 成熟的含桃	坎皮恩	/ 313
92. 衣裙之歌(之一)	赫里克	/ 315
93. 衣裙之歌(之二)	赫里克	/ 317
94. 衣裙之歌(之三)	无名氏	/ 319
95. 咏腰带	沃勒	/ 321
96. 致主宰他一切的安西娅	赫里克	/ 323
97. "爱我别因为我潇洒英俊"	无名氏	/ 327
98. "不,西莉亚"	塞德利	/ 329
99. 狱中寄阿尔西娅	洛夫莱斯	/ 331
100. 出海前告别鲁加斯达	洛夫莱斯	/ 335
101. 致一个失恋的小伙子	萨克林	/ 337
102. 祈求	考利	/ 339
103. 情人的决心	威瑟	/ 343
104. 幽思	弗莱彻	/ 347
105. 致一绺头发	司各特	/ 351
106. 被抛弃的新娘	无名氏	/ 355
107. 美丽的海伦	无名氏	/ 361
108. 两只乌鸦	无名氏	/ 367
109. 咏花	赫里克	/ 371
110. 咏黄水仙花	赫里克	/ 373
111. 花园遐思	马韦尔	/ 375
112. 快乐的人	弥尔顿	/ 383
113. 幽思的人	弥尔顿	/ 399

114. Song of the Emigrants in Bermuda	416
115. At a Solemn Music	420
116. Alexander's Feast, or, the Power of Music	424

Book Third

117. Ode on the Pleasure Arising from Vicissitude	438
118. The Quiet Life	444
119. The Blind Boy	448
120. On a Favourite Cat, Drowned in a Tub of Goldfishes	450
121. To Charlotte Pulteney	456
123. The Bard	460
124. Ode Written in Mdccxlvi	474
125. Lament for Culloden	476
126. Lament for Flodden	480
127. The Braes of Yarrow	484
128. Willy Drowned in Yarrow	490
130. Black-eyed Susan	494
131. Sally in Our Alley	500
132. A Farewell	506
133. 'If doughty deeds my lady please'	508
134. To a Young Lady	512
135. The Sleeping Beauty	514
136. 'For ever, fortune, wilt thou prove'	516
137. 'The merchant, to secure his treasure'	518
138. 'When lovely woman stoops to folly'	520
139. 'Ye flowery banks o' bonnie doon'	522
140. The Progress of Poesy	524
141. The Passions	536
142. Ode on the Spring	548
143. The Poplar Field	554
144. To a Mouse	556

114. 百慕大移民之歌	马韦尔	/ 417
115. 闻庄严的音乐有感	弥尔顿	/ 421
116. 亚历山大的宴会或音乐的力量	约翰·德莱顿	/ 425

卷三（1700—1800）

117. 沧桑世事中的欢乐颂	格雷	/ 439
118. 平静的一生	蒲柏	/ 445
119. 盲孩	西伯	/ 449
120. 可爱的小猫淹死在金鱼盆	格雷	/ 451
121. 致夏绿蒂·普尔吞勒	菲利普斯	/ 457
123. 行吟诗人	格雷	/ 461
124. 颂歌，作于一七四六年	柯林斯	/ 475
125. 吊库洛登战场	彭斯	/ 477
126. 弗洛顿哀歌	珍·艾略特	/ 481
127. 雅罗溪畔	罗根	/ 485
128. 威利葬身雅罗溪	无名氏	/ 491
130. 黑眼睛苏珊	盖伊	/ 495
131. 我们巷里的萨莉	卡雷	/ 501
132. 告别	彭斯	/ 507
133. "假如姑娘喜爱我英勇的业绩"	格雷厄姆	/ 509
134. 给一位少女	柯珀	/ 513
135. 睡美人	罗杰斯	/ 515
136. "命运，你要永远证明"	汤姆森	/ 517
137. "为了万无一失"	普赖尔	/ 519
138. "可爱的女子甘愿作蠢事"	哥尔德斯密斯	/ 521
139. "可爱的杜河两岸鲜花开"	彭斯	/ 523
140. 诗的进程	格雷	/ 525
141. 激情	柯林斯	/ 537
142. 春日颂情	格雷	/ 549
143. 白杨林	柯珀	/ 555
144. 致鼷鼠	彭斯	/ 557

145. A Wish 562
146. To Evening 564
147. Elegy Written in a Country Church-yard 570
148. Mary Morison 584
149. Bonnie Lesley 588
150. 'O my luve's like a red, red rose' 592
151. Highland Mary 594
152. Auld Robin Gray 598
153. Duncan Gray 602
154. The Sailor's Wife 606
155. Jean 612
156. John Anderson 616
157. The Land o' the Leal 618
158. Ode on a Distant Prospect of Eton College 622
159. Hymn to Adversity 632
160. The Solitude of Alexander Selkirk 638
161. To Mary Unwin 644
162. To the Same 646
163. The Dying Man in His Garden 652
164. To-morrow 656
165. 'Life! I know not what thou art' 660

Book Fourth
166. On First Looking into Chapman's Homer 664
167. Ode on the Poets 668
168. Love 672
169. All for Love 682
170. The Outlaw 686
171. 'There be none of beauty's daughters' 692
172. Lines to an Indian Air 694

145. 一愿	罗杰斯	/ 563
146. 薄暮散歌	柯林斯	/ 565
147. 墓畔哀歌	格雷	/ 571
148. 玛丽·莫里孙	彭斯	/ 585
149. 美丽的拉丝莱	彭斯	/ 589
150. "呵,我的爱人像朵红红的玫瑰"	彭斯	/ 593
151. 高原上的玛丽	彭斯	/ 595
152. 老罗宾·格瑞	林德赛夫人	/ 599
153. 邓肯·葛雷	彭斯	/ 603
154. 水手妻	米克尔	/ 607
155. 吉恩	彭斯	/ 613
156. 约翰·安徒生	彭斯	/ 617
157. 永恒的天国	奈恩夫人	/ 619
158. 远眺伊顿公学咏怀	格雷	/ 623
159. 厄运赞	格雷	/ 633
160. 亚历山大·塞尔克的孤独	柯珀	/ 639
161. 致玛丽·昂温	柯珀	/ 645
162. 我的玛丽	柯珀	/ 647
163. 濒死的园丁	塞威尔	/ 653
164. 明天	柯林斯	/ 657
165. "生命哟,我不清楚你的奥秘"	巴勃尔德夫人	/ 661

中　册

卷四(1800—1850)

166. 初读查普曼译的荷马	济慈	/ 665
167. 诗人颂	济慈	/ 669
168. 爱情	塞·泰·柯勒律治	/ 673
169. 一切为了爱情	拜伦	/ 683
170. 绿林好汉	司各特	/ 687
171. "没有一个美的女儿"	拜伦	/ 693
172. 印度小夜曲	雪莱	/ 695

173.	'She walks in beauty'	698
174.	'She was a phantom of delight'	700
175.	'She is not fair to outward view'	704
176.	'I fear thy kisses, gentle maiden'	706
177.	The Lost Love	708
178.	'I travell'd among unknown men'	710
179.	The Education of Nature	712
180.	'A slumber did my spirit seal'	716
181.	Lord Ullin's Daughter	718
182.	Jock O' Hazeldean	724
183.	Freedom and Love	728
184.	Love's Philosophy	732
185.	Echoes	734
186.	A Serenade	736
187.	To the Evening Star	738
188.	To the Night	742
189.	To a Distant Friend	746
190.	'When we two parted'	748
191.	Happy Insensibility	752
192.	'Where shall the lover rest'	756
193.	La Belle Dame Sans Merci	760
194.	The Rover	766
195.	The Flight of Love	768
196.	The Maid of Neidpath	772
197.	The Maid of Neidpath	776
198.	'Bright Star, would I were steadfast as thou art'	778
199.	The Terror of Death	780
200.	Desideria	782
201.	'At the mid hour of night'	784
202.	Elegy on Thyrza	786
203.	'One word is too often profaned'	792

173.	"她身披美丽而行"	拜伦	/ 699
174.	"她是快乐的精灵"	华兹华斯	/ 701
175.	"她的外貌并不令人陶醉"	哈特利·柯勒律治	/ 705
176.	"温柔的少女,我怕你的吻"	雪莱	/ 707
177.	失去的爱	华兹华斯	/ 709
178.	"我曾在大海那边的异乡漫游"	华兹华斯	/ 711
179.	造物者的启迪	华兹华斯	/ 713
180.	"迷糊封住了我的精神"	华兹华斯	/ 717
181.	乌林爵爷的女儿	坎贝尔	/ 719
182.	哈森汀的年轻汉	司各特	/ 725
183.	自由与爱情	坎贝尔	/ 729
184.	爱的哲学	雪莱	/ 733
185.	爱的回声	摩尔	/ 735
186.	小夜曲	司各特	/ 737
187.	致傍晚的星	坎贝尔	/ 739
188.	夜	雪莱	/ 743
189.	致远方的朋友	华兹华斯	/ 747
190.	"想从前我们俩分手"	拜伦	/ 749
191.	不敏感的快乐	济慈	/ 753
192.	"那个情人将安息在哪里"	司各特	/ 757
193.	美丽的无情女郎	济慈	/ 761
194.	流浪者的告别	司各特	/ 767
195.	爱情的飞逝	雪莱	/ 769
196.	纳德巴斯的少女	司各特	/ 773
197.	纳德巴斯的少女	坎贝尔	/ 777
198.	"灿烂的星!我祈求像你那样坚定"	济慈	/ 779
199.	死亡的恐惧	济慈	/ 781
200.	伤逝	华兹华斯	/ 783
201.	"子夜时分"	摩尔	/ 785
202.	热娜挽歌	拜伦	/ 787
203.	"有个字过分被人们玷污"	雪莱	/ 793

204.	Gathering Song of Donald the Black	794
205.	'A wet sheet and a flowing sea'	798
208.	Ode to Duty	802
209.	On the Castle of Chillon	808
210.	England and Switzerland 1802	810
211.	On the Extinction of the Venetian Republic	812
212.	London, Mdcccii	814
213.	The Same	816
214.	'When I have borne in memory what has tamed'	818
215.	Hohenlinden	820
216.	After Blenheim	824
217.	Pro Patria Mori	830
218.	The Burial of Sir John Moore at Corunna	832
219.	Simon Lee the Old Huntsman	836
220.	The Old Familiar Faces	844
221.	The Journey Onwards	848
222.	Youth and Age	852
223.	A Lesson	856
224.	Past and Present	860
225.	The Light of Other Days	864
226.	Invocation	868
227.	Stanzas Written in Dejection near Naples	874
228.	The Scholar	878
229.	The Mermaid Tavern	882
230.	The Pride of Youth	886
231.	The Bridge of Sighs	888
232.	Elegy	898
233.	Hester	900
234.	Coronach	904
235.	The Death-Bed	908
236.	Rosabelle	910

204. 黑唐纳的出征曲	司各特	795
205. "湿漉漉的帆底,大海中的狂澜"	坎宁安	799
208. 天职颂	华兹华斯	803
209. 咏锡庸城堡	拜伦	809
210. 英格兰和瑞士	华兹华斯	811
211. 威尼斯共和国灭亡有感	华兹华斯	813
212. 作于伦敦,一八〇二年九月	华兹华斯	815
213. 伦敦,一八〇二年	华兹华斯	817
214. "我记得一些大国如何衰退"	华兹华斯	819
215. 荷恩林登之战	坎贝尔	821
216. 布连海姆战役之后	骚塞	825
217. 刑前献给爱尔兰的歌	摩尔	831
218. 爵士约翰·摩尔在科龙纳的埋葬	沃尔夫	833
219. 猎手西蒙·李	华兹华斯	837
220. 旧时熟悉的面庞	兰姆	845
221. 远航	摩尔	849
222. 青春与暮年	拜伦	853
223. 感时	华兹华斯	857
224. 今昔吟	胡德	861
225. 昔日的光辉	摩尔	865
226. 召唤	雪莱	869
227. 诗数章	雪莱	875
228. 学人	骚塞	879
229. 美人鱼酒店	济慈	883
230. 青春的骄傲	司各特	887
231. 叹息桥	胡德	889
232. 哀歌	拜伦	899
233. 海丝特	兰姆	901
234. 挽歌	司各特	905
235. 临终	胡德	909
236. 罗莎白娜	司各特	911

237.	On an Infant Dying as Soon as Born	916
238.	The Affliction of Margaret	922
239.	Hunting Song	930
240.	To the Skylark	934
241.	To a Skylark	936
242.	The Green Linnet	948
243.	To the Cuckoo	952
244.	Ode to a Nightingale	956
245.	Upon Westminster Bridge	964
246.	Ozymandias of Egypt	966
247.	Composed at Neidpath Castle, the Property of Lord Queensberry, 1803	968
248.	Admonition to a Traveller	970
249.	To the Highland Girl of Inversneyde	972
250.	The Reaper	980
251.	The Reverie of Poor Susan	984
252.	To a Lady, with a Guitar	986
253.	The Daffodils	994
254.	To the Daisy	998
255.	Ode to Autumn	1004
256.	Ode to Winter	1008
257.	Yarrow Unvisited	1016
258.	Yarrow Visited	1022
259.	The Invitation	1030
260.	The Recollection	1036
261.	By the Sea	1044
262.	To the Evening Star	1046
263.	Datur Hora Quieti	1048
264.	To the Moon	1052
265.	'A widow bird sate mourning for her love'	1054
266.	To Sleep	1056

237.	唱给一个出世即夭的孩子	兰姆 /	917
238.	玛格丽特的苦恼	华兹华斯 /	923
239.	猎歌	司各特 /	931
240.	致云雀	华兹华斯 /	935
241.	致云雀	雪莱 /	937
242.	绿羽的红雀	华兹华斯 /	949
243.	致杜鹃	华兹华斯 /	953
244.	夜莺颂	济慈 /	957
245.	在西敏寺桥上	华兹华斯 /	965
246.	奥西曼提斯	雪莱 /	967
247.	一八〇三年作于纳德巴斯堡,该堡为昆斯伯里勋爵的领地	华兹华斯 /	969
248.	诫游子	华兹华斯 /	971
249.	献给茵沃斯奈德的苏格兰高原姑娘	华兹华斯 /	973
250.	割麦女	华兹华斯 /	981
251.	苏珊的冥想	华兹华斯 /	985
252.	致某夫人——随赠六弦琴一架	雪莱 /	987
253.	水仙	华兹华斯 /	995
254.	给雏菊	华兹华斯 /	999
255.	秋赋	济慈 /	1005
256.	冬颂	坎贝尔 /	1009
257.	未访雅洛河	华兹华斯 /	1017
258.	访雅洛河	华兹华斯 /	1023
259.	一个邀请	雪莱 /	1031
260.	回忆	雪莱 /	1037
261.	在海边	华兹华斯 /	1045
262.	致傍晚的星	坎贝尔 /	1047
263.	安歇的时分	司各特 /	1049
264.	给月	雪莱 /	1053
265.	"有鸟仳离枯树颠"	雪莱 /	1055
266.	致睡眠	华兹华斯 /	1057

267. The Soldier's Dream	1058
268. A Dream of the Unknown	1062
269. The Inner Vision	1066
270. The Realm of Fancy	1068
271. Hymn to the Spirit of Nature	1076
272. Written in Early Spring	1080
273. Ruth: Or the Influences of Nature	1084
274. Written in the Euganean Hills, North Italy	1106
275. Ode to the West Wind	1124
276. Nature and the Poet	1134
277. The Poet's Dream	1140
278. 'The world is too much with us'	1142
279. Within King's College Chapel, Cambridge	1144
280. Youth and Age	1146
281. The Two April Mornings	1152
282. The Fountain	1158
283. The River of Life	1166
284. The Human Seasons	1170
285. A Lament	1172
286. 'My heart leaps up when I behold'	1174
287. Ode on Intimations of Immortality from Recollections of Early Childhood	1176
288. 'Music, when soft voices die'	1194

Additional Poems

289. 'I strove with none'	1198
290. Rose Aylmer	1200
291. The Maid's Lament	1202
292. To Robert Browning	1206
293. 'Proud word you never spoke'	1208
294. 'Well I remember how you smiled'	1210

267. 士兵的梦	坎贝尔	1059
268. 一个未知世界的梦	雪莱	1063
269. 心灵深处的幻景	华兹华斯	1067
270. 幻想的王国	济慈	1069
271. 献给大自然精灵的颂歌	雪莱	1077
272. 早春之诗	华兹华斯	1081
273. 鲁思（或自然的影响）	华兹华斯	1085
274. 写在意大利北部欧加宁群山中	雪莱	1107
275. 西风颂	雪莱	1125
276. 大自然与诗人	华兹华斯	1135
277. 诗人的梦	雪莱	1141
278. "这世界，对于我们，实在够受"	华兹华斯	1143
279. 在剑桥王家学院教堂	华兹华斯	1145
280. 青春和老年	塞·泰·柯勒律治	1147
281. 两个四月的早晨	华兹华斯	1153
282. 泉	华兹华斯	1159
283. 生命之川	康沫尔	1167
284. 人的四季	济慈	1171
285. 悲歌	雪莱	1173
286. "我心儿激动"	华兹华斯	1175
287. 永生颂	华兹华斯	1177
288. "音乐，虽然消失了柔声"	雪莱	1195

下 册

卷五（1850—1910）

289. "我从不与人斗"	兰多	1199
290. 罗斯·艾尔默	兰多	1201
291. 一个少女的悲哀	兰多	1203
292. 致罗伯特·布朗宁	兰多	1207
293. "你从不说骄傲的话"	兰多	1209
294. "我清楚记得你怎样面带微笑"	兰多	1211

295. To a Waterfowl	1212
296. Rondeau	1216
297. The War Song of Dinas Vawr	1218
298. Three Men of Gotham	1222
299. The Grave of Love	1226
300. A Jacobite's Epitaph	1228
301. The Battle of Naseby	1232
302. Blackmwore Maidens	1240
303. The Wife A-Lost	1244
304. The Nameless One	1248
305. Brahma	1254
306. To Eva	1258
307. And Shall Trelawny Die?	1260
308. The Shandon Bells	1264
309. 'I thought once how Theocritus had sung'	1270
310. 'What can I give thee back, O liberal'	1272
311. 'Yet love, mere, love, is beautiful indeed'	1274
312. 'If thou must love me'	1276
313. 'How do I love thee?'	1278
314. A Musical Instrument	1280
315. The Slave's Dream	1284
316. The Arsenal at Springfield	1290
317. Children	1296
318. 'I do not love thee!'	1300
319. Rubáiyát of Omar Khayyám of Naishápúr	1304
320. The Chambered Nautilus	1336
321. The Men of Old	1340
322. The Miller's Daughter	1346
323. St. Agnes'eve	1348
324. Sir Galahad	1352
325. Break, Break, Break	1360

295. 致水鸟	布莱恩特	1213
296. 珍妮吻了我	亨特	1217
297. 戴纳斯·弗尔的战歌	皮科克	1219
298. 戈瑟姆的三个人	皮科克	1223
299. 爱情之墓	皮科克	1227
300. 杰克拜特的墓志铭	麦考莱	1229
301. 纳什比之战	麦考莱	1233
302. 布莱克默的姑娘	巴恩斯	1241
303. 悼亡妻	巴恩斯	1245
304. 小人物	曼根	1249
305. 梵天	爱默生	1255
306. 给伊娃	爱默生	1259
307. 难道特里劳尼非死不成？	霍克	1261
308. 沙丹的钟声	马奥尼	1265
309. "我想起昔年那位希腊的诗人"	伊丽莎白·布朗宁	1271
310. "你那样慷慨豪爽的施主呀"	伊丽莎白·布朗宁	1273
311. "不过只要是爱,是爱,就够你赞美"	伊丽莎白·布朗宁	1275
312. "如果你一心要爱我"	伊丽莎白·布朗宁	1277
313. "我究竟怎样爱你？"	伊丽莎白·布朗宁	1279
314. 乐器	伊丽莎白·布朗宁	1281
315. 奴隶的梦	朗费罗	1285
316. 斯普林菲尔德的军械库	朗费罗	1291
317. 孩子们	朗费罗	1297
318. "我并不爱你"	诺顿	1301
319. 奥马尔·哈亚姆之柔巴依集	菲茨杰拉德	1305
320. 带壳的鹦鹉螺	霍姆斯	1337
321. 咏古人	霍顿勋爵	1341
322. 磨坊主的女儿	丁尼生	1347
323. 圣·安妮节的前夜	丁尼生	1349
324. 加拉海德爵士	丁尼生	1353
325. 破碎,破碎,破碎	丁尼生	1361

326.	The Brook	1362
327.	'As thro' the land at eve we went'	1368
328.	'The splendour falls on castle walls'	1370
329.	'Tears, idle tears'	1372
330.	'O Swallow, Swallow, flying, flying South'	1374
331.	'Now sleeps the crimson petal'	1378
332.	'Come down, O maid, from yonder mountain height'	1380
333.	'Ring out, wild bells'	1384
334.	'Come into the garden'	1388
335.	'In love'	1396
337.	A Christmas Hymn	1398
338.	'The year's at the spring'	1404
339.	'Give her but a least excuse to love me'	1406
340.	The Lost Leader	1408
341.	Home-Thoughts, from Abroad	1412
342.	Home-Thoughts, from the Sea	1414
343.	Misconceptions	1416
344.	A Woman's Last Word	1418
345.	Life in a Love	1422
346.	A Grammarian's Funeral Shortly after the Revival of Learning in Europe	1424
347.	Porphyria's Lover	1436
348.	Rabbi Ben Ezra	1442
349.	Prospice	1460
350.	The Execution of Montrose	1464
351.	Tubal Cain	1482
352.	Qua Cursum Ventus	1488
353.	'Say not'	1492
354.	'Where lies the land to which the ship would go?'	1494
355.	'O may I join the choir invisible'	1496
356.	Airly Beacon	1502
357.	The Sands of Dee	1504

326. 小溪	丁尼生	1363
327. "黄昏里,我们过麦地"	丁尼生	1369
328. "辉煌的夕照映着城堡"	丁尼生	1371
329. "泪哟,泪哟"	丁尼生	1373
330. "燕子呵,燕子,飞吧,飞向南方"	丁尼生	1375
331. "时而是紫色的花瓣在沉睡"	丁尼生	1379
332. "下来吧,少女啊,从那儿山巅下来"	丁尼生	1381
333. "敲吧,乱钟"	丁尼生	1385
334. "走进花园吧"	丁尼生	1389
335. "在爱情里"	丁尼生	1397
337. 圣诞赞歌	多梅特	1399
338. "一年恰逢春季"	罗伯特·布朗宁	1405
339. "就给她一丁点的借口来爱我吧!"	罗伯特·布朗宁	1407
340. 失去的领导者	罗伯特·布朗宁	1409
341. 异域乡思	罗伯特·布朗宁	1413
342. 乡思,自海上	罗伯特·布朗宁	1415
343. 误解	罗伯特·布朗宁	1417
344. 一个女人最后的话	罗伯特·布朗宁	1419
345. 终身的爱	罗伯特·布朗宁	1423
346. 一位文法家的葬礼	罗伯特·布朗宁	1425
347. 波菲里亚的情人	罗伯特·布朗宁	1437
348. 拉比本·埃兹拉	罗伯特·布朗宁	1443
349. 展望	罗伯特·布朗宁	1461
350. 蒙特罗斯之死	艾顿	1465
351. 土八该隐	麦凯	1483
352. 风吹船儿去何方	克劳	1489
353. "你可不要说"	克劳	1493
354. "这只船儿要驶向什么地方?"	克劳	1495
355. "噢!但愿我能加入那无形的合唱团"	乔治·艾略特	1497
356. 爱丽·彼耿	金斯利	1503
357. 迪河的沙丘	金斯利	1505

358.	Ode to the North-East Wind	1508
359.	Young and Old	1514
360.	O Captain! My Captain!	1516
361.	'Playing on the virginals'	1520
362.	The High Tide on the Coast of Lincolnshiire	1524
363.	The Forsaken Merman	1540
364.	The Song of Callicles on Etna	1552
365.	Shakespeare	1558
366.	A Summer Night	1560
367.	Morality	1568
368.	The Future	1572
369.	Philomela	1580
370.	Requiescat	1584
371.	The Scholar Gipsy	1586
372.	Rugby Chapel	1610
373.	Mimnermus in Church	1626
374.	Heraclitus	1630
375.	Amaturus	1632
376.	The Married Lover	1636
377.	The Toys	1640
378.	Keith of Ravelston	1644
379.	The Blessed Damozel	1650
380.	Rest	1664
381.	Song	1666
382.	Remember	1668
383.	Up-Hill	1670
384.	Song	1672
385.	A Birthday	1674
386.	Barbara	1676
387.	Old Love	1682
388.	Shameful Death	1690

358. 东北风颂	金斯利	/ 1509
359. 青年和老年	金斯利	/ 1515
360. 啊,船长,我的船长哟!	惠特曼	/ 1517
361. "我安坐在一架钢琴边轻轻弹奏"	英格洛	/ 1521
362. 林肯郡海岸边的海啸(一五七一)	英格洛	/ 1525
363. 被遗弃的人鱼	阿诺德	/ 1541
364. 喀利克勒斯的埃特纳火山歌	阿诺德	/ 1553
365. 莎士比亚	阿诺德	/ 1559
366. 夏夜	阿诺德	/ 1561
367. 德行	阿诺德	/ 1569
368. 未来	阿诺德	/ 1573
369. 夜莺	阿诺德	/ 1581
370. 安灵曲	阿诺德	/ 1585
371. 吉普赛学者	阿诺德	/ 1587
372. 拉格比公学的教堂	阿诺德	/ 1611
373. 明纳摩斯在教堂里	柯雷	/ 1627
374. 赫拉克利图斯	柯雷	/ 1631
375. 爱之歌	柯雷	/ 1633
376. 婚后的情人	帕特摩	/ 1637
377. 玩具	帕特摩	/ 1641
378. 拉弗尔斯顿的基思	多贝尔	/ 1645
379. 天上的小姐	但·加·罗塞蒂	/ 1651
380. 安息	克·乔·罗塞蒂	/ 1665
381. 歌	克·乔·罗塞蒂	/ 1667
382. 记着我	克·乔·罗塞蒂	/ 1669
383. 上山	克·乔·罗塞蒂	/ 1671
384. 歌	克·乔·罗塞蒂	/ 1673
385. 生日	克·乔·罗塞蒂	/ 1675
386. 巴巴拉	史密斯	/ 1677
387. 往日的爱情	莫里斯	/ 1683
388. 羞辱的死亡	莫里斯	/ 1691

389.	The Haystack in the Floods	1694
390.	Summer Dawn	1708
391.	'As we rush, as we rush in the train'	1710
392.	Itylus	1712
393.	The Garden of Proserpine	1720
394.	A Forsaken Garden	1730
395.	Olive	1738
396.	Ode	1746
397.	'Out of the night that covers me'	1752
398.	Pied Beauty	1754
399.	The Starlight Night	1756
400.	From 'Modern Love'	1758
401.	A Ballad to Queen Elizabeth	1764
402.	Gird on thy Sword	1768
403.	I Have Loved Flowers That Fade	1770
404.	Nightingales	1772
405.	In Memoriam F. A. S.	1774
406.	Unto Us a Son is Given	1778
407.	Veneration of Images	1780
408.	In Romney Marsh	1782
409.	Epitaph on an Army of Mercenaries	1786
410.	'In no strange land'	1788
411.	Drake's Drum	1792
412.	Unwelcome	1796
413.	The Lake Isle of Innisfree	1798
414.	The Folly of Being Comforted	1800
415.	The Coward	1802
416.	The Last Chantey	1804
417.	Recessional	1810
418.	Cadgwith	1814
419.	For the Fallen	1816

389. 洪流中的干草堆	莫里斯	1695
390. 夏天的黎明	莫里斯	1709
391. "当我们,当我们在列车上向前冲……"	汤姆逊	1711
392. 伊第拉斯	斯温伯恩	1713
393. 普洛塞耳皮那的花园	斯温伯恩	1721
394. 遗弃的花园	斯温伯恩	1731
395. 奥莉芙	斯温伯恩	1739
396. 颂歌	奥香涅西	1747
397. 大无畏	亨利	1753
398. 杂色的美	霍普金斯	1755
399. 星光之夜	霍普金斯	1757
400. 现代爱情(节选)	梅瑞狄斯	1759
401. 献给伊丽莎白女王的歌谣	多布森	1765
402. 佩上你的剑	布里吉斯	1769
403. 我爱凋谢的花朵	布里吉斯	1771
404. 夜莺	布里吉斯	1773
405. 纪念 F. A. 西特韦尔	斯蒂文森	1775
406. 我们得到一个儿子	梅内尔	1779
407. 对形象的崇敬	梅内尔	1781
408. 在罗姆尼沼泽地	戴维森	1783
409. 一支雇佣军的墓志铭	豪斯曼	1787
410. "并非陌生之地"	汤普森	1789
411. 德雷克的战鼓	纽博尔德爵士	1793
412. 不受欢迎的	玛丽·柯勒律治	1797
413. 茵纳斯弗利岛	叶芝	1799
414. 听人安慰的愚蠢	叶芝	1801
415. 懦汉	吉卜林	1803
416. 最后的起锚歌	吉卜林	1805
417. 礼拜后的退场曲	吉卜林	1811
418. 卡杰维斯	约翰森	1815
419. 悼阵亡将士	宾雍	1817

420.	Sweet Stay-at-Home	1820
421.	Trees	1824
422.	Arabia	1826
423.	Before the Roman Came to Rye	1828
424.	Sea-Fever	1832
425.	Adlestrop	1834
426.	Margaret's Song	1836
427.	A Town Window	1838
428.	The Golden Journey to Samarkand	1840
429.	After Ronsard	1844
430.	The Soldier	1846
431.	Everyone Sang	1848
432.	Almswomen	1850
433.	After London	1854

420. 可爱的居家少女	戴维斯	1821
421. 树	梅尔	1825
422. 阿拉伯半岛	梅尔	1827
423. 罗马人来到拉伊之前	切斯特顿	1829
424. 恋海热	梅斯菲尔德	1833
425. 艾德稠普	托马斯	1835
426. 玛格丽特的歌	艾伯克龙比	1837
427. 城市之窗	德林克沃特	1839
428. 去撒马尔罕的金色行程	弗莱克	1841
429. 和龙沙诗《何时你已衰老》	威廉斯	1845
430. 士兵	布鲁克	1847
431. 人人歌唱	萨松	1849
432. 救济院的妇女	布兰登	1851
433. 伦敦遐想	佩洛	1855

卷一

1509—1616

1. SPRING

    Spring, the sweet Spring, is the year's pleasant king;
    Then blooms each thing, then maids dance in a ring,
    Cold doth not sting, the pretty birds do sing,
        Cuckoo, jug-jug, pu-we, to-witta-woo[1]!

5   The palm and may make country houses gay,
    Lambs frisk and play, the shepherds pipe all day,
    And we hear ay birds tune this merry lay,
        Cuckoo jug-jug, pu-we, to-witta-woo!

    The fields breathe sweet, the daisies kiss our feet,
10   Young lovers meet, old wives a-sunning sit,
    In every street these tunes our ears do greet,
        Cuckoo jug-jug, pu-we, to-witta-woo!
        Spring! the sweet Spring!

T. NASH.

---

[1] *jug-jug*: the conventional representation of the nightingale's song; *pu-we* is perhaps intended for the cry of the peewit or plover; *to-witta-woo*, more commonly 'to-wit-to-woo,' is supposed to represent the hoot of the owl. cf. No. 27, l. 7.

1. 春

讷徐

春,甘美之春,一年之中的尧舜,
处处都有花树,都有女儿环舞,
微寒但觉清和,佳禽争着唱歌,
　　嗵嗵,啾啾,哥哥、割麦、插一禾!

榆柳呀山楂,打扮着田舍人家,
羊羔嬉游,牧笛儿整日价吹奏,
百鸟总在和鸣,一片悠扬声韵,
　　嗵嗵,啾啾,哥哥、割麦、插一禾!

郊原荡漾香风,雏菊吻人脚踵,
情侣作对成双,老妪坐晒阳光,
走向任何通衢,都有歌声悦耳,
　　嗵嗵,啾啾,哥哥、割麦、插一禾!
春!甘美之春!

郭沫若　译

编注　妥默斯·讷徐(Thomas Nash, 1567—1601)现通译为托马斯·纳什,英国剧作家及诗人。《春》选自他一五九三年创作的喜剧《夏天的最后的遗嘱》(*Summer's Last will and Testament*)。

2. SUMMONS TO LOVE

        Phoebus, arise!
     And paint the sable skies
    With azure, white, and red:
Rouse Memnon's mother from her Tithon's bed
That she thy càreer may with roses spread:
The nightingales thy coming cach-where sing:
      Make an eternal spring,
Give life to this dark world which lieth dead;
     Spread forth thy golden hair
In larger locks than thou wast wont before,
      And emperor-like decore[①]
With diadem of pearl thy temples fair:
     Chase hence the ugly night
Which serves but to make dear thy glorious light.

      — This is that happy morn,
      That day, long-wished day
       Of all my life so dark,
(If cruel stars have not my ruin sworn
      And fates[②] my hopes betray),
      Which, purely white, deserves
An everlasting diamond should it mark.

---

① *decore*: 'decorate'.
② *And fates my hopes betray*: the 'not' must be understood from the previous line.

2. 对爱的呼唤

德拉蒙德

> 太阳哟,升起来吧!
> 用碧蓝、雪白和鲜红
> 涂抹这黑暗的天空:
> 将门农之母从提托诺斯卧榻上唤醒①
> 让她用玫瑰花铺开你一天的行程:
> 处处夜莺啼,歌唱你的来临:
> 　　　创造出一个永恒之春,
> 为这僵死的黑暗世界带来生命;
> 　　　撒开你的一绺绺金发,
> 撒得更宽更广,浩渺无垠;
> 　　　用那珍珠镶成的王冠
> 来装饰你那美丽的额顶:
> 　　　然后再去驱赶那丑陋的黑夜
> 它只能使你的金光更珍贵十分。

> ——哦,这就是那个快乐的黎明,
> 　　那一天哟,是我黑暗生涯中
> 　　渴望已久的时分,
> （假如无情的星宿还未断言我的灭亡,
> 　　倘若命运女神还未出卖我的希望),
> 　　这纯洁的一天就理所当然
> 值得用一颗不朽的钻石来将它标明。

---

① 门农（Memnon）之母即黎明女神厄俄斯（Eos），提托诺斯（Tithonus）是门农之父,埃塞俄比亚王。——译者

This is the morn should bring unto this grove
My Love, to hear and recompense my love.
      Fair King, who all preserves①,
         But show thy blushing beams,
         And thou two sweeter eyes
Shalt see than those which by Peneüs' streams
         Did once thy heart surprise.
Now, Flora, deck thyself in fairest guise:
         If that ye, winds, would hear
A voice surpassing far Amphion's lyre,
         Your furious chiding stay;
         Let Zephyr only breathe,
         And with her tresses play②.
      —— The winds all silent are,
         And Phoebus in his chair③
         Ensaffroning sea and air
         Makes vanish every star;
         Night like a drunkard reels
Beyond the hills, to shun his flaming wheels:
The fields with flowers are deck'd in every hue,
The clouds with orient gold spangle their blue;
         Here is the pleasant place ——

---

① *preserves*: in modern grammar this would be 'preservest.' But in 14th-century Englishs -*s* was the regular ending of the second person singular.

② After this line Palgrave has omitted the line, 'Kissing sometimes those purple ports of death,' which apparently means her lips, from which issue words that slay her lovers.

③ *Phoebus in his choir*: *i.e.* the Sun-god's chariot.

在此良晨应当携我的情侣到这林中来
倾听,来酬答我的爱情。
  哦,保护万物的太阳神哟,
  你就放射出通红的光芒吧,   25
  你将看见一双甜蜜的眸子
胜过你在珀涅俄斯溪畔见过的眼睛,
  而那双眼睛曾惊扰你的心灵①。
哦,弗罗拉,用最美的衣裳将你打扮②:
  那么,风儿哟,你们会听见一个声音 30
远远胜过安菲翁的竖琴③,
  停息你们狂暴的怒号;
  只让微风儿吹拂飘萦,
  轻轻地拨弄她的头发,
  温柔地亲吻她的红唇④。   35
  ——所有的风儿都屏住了声息,
  福波斯驾驶着他的马车⑤
  用金辉染饰天空与海洋,
  使每一颗星星都失去踪影:
  黑夜像蹒跚的醉汉躲到山那边, 40
远远地避开他那喷火的车轮;
鲜花点缀的原野五彩缤纷,
蓝天上布满金光灿烂的彩云;
  这儿就是那快乐的地方——

---

① 太阳神阿波罗曾在珀涅俄斯溪畔遇见并爱上女神达佛涅(Daphne)。古罗马诗人奥维德(Ovid,公元前43年—公元17年)曾写诗赞颂达佛涅美丽的眼睛。——译者
② 弗罗拉(Flora),罗马神话中传说的花神。——译者
③ 安菲翁(Amphion)系主神宙斯之子。以竖琴的魔力筑成忒拜城。——译者
④ 《金库》原编者删去了这行原诗,为译文节奏和谐起见,故将这句译出。——译者
⑤ 在希腊神话中,太阳神既称阿波罗(Apollo),又称福玻斯(Phoebus),他每天驾三匹马拉的载着太阳的金马车由东向西驶过天空。——译者

And nothing wanting is, save She, alas[①]!

        W. DRUMMOND OF HAWTHORNDEN.

[①] *save She*: the nominative of the pronoun is normally used after 'save,' a relic of the time when the phrase was a nominative absolute, 'She being safe.'

一切都有了,唉,就是她没来临!

曹明伦　译

编注 威廉·德拉蒙德(William Drummond,1585—1649),苏格兰诗人,他在文学上的最高造诣是他那些精妙绝伦的十四行诗,这些诗为他赢得了一个光荣称号——苏格兰的彼特拉克(Francesco de Petrarch,1304—1374,意大利诗人,首创十四行诗)。德拉蒙德的主要作品有诗集《天国之花》、散文集《柏树林》等。他还撰写了《苏格兰史》。

3. TIME AND LOVE (I)

When I have seen by Time's fell hand defaced①
　　The rich proud cost of out-worn buried age②;
When sometime lofty towers I see down-razed③,
　　And brass eternal slave to mortal rage④;

When I have seen the hungry ocean gain
　　Advantage on the kingdom of the shore,
And the firm soil win of the watery main⑤,
　　Increasing store with loss, and loss with store;

When I have seen such interchange of state,
　　Or state itself confounded to decay⑥,
Ruin hath taught me thus to ruminate —
　　That Time will come and take my Love away:

— This thought is as a death, which cannot choose
But weep to have that which it fears to lose.

　　　　　　　　　　　　　　W. SHAKESPEARE.

---

① *fell*: 'cruel.'
② *cost*: 'costly object'; an obsolete use found in 2 *Hen.* IV, I. iii, 60, 'leaves his part-created cost A naked subject to the weeping clouds.'
③ *sometime lofty*: i.e. which once were lofty.
④ *eternal* as the epithet of 'brass' is often found in the Roman poets.
⑤ *the firm soil win of the watery main*: 'the land encroaching on the sea.' In some parts of the coast the sea is gaining on the land, in others the land is gaining on the sea; thus the 'store' is balanced by the 'loss.'
⑥ *state itself confounded to decay*: i.e. not merely gained by another element, but wholly disappearing.

3. 时间和爱(之一)

莎士比亚

当我眼见前代的富丽和豪华
　　被时光的手毫不留情地磨灭;
当巍峨的塔我眼见沦为碎瓦,
　　连不朽的铜也不免一场浩劫;

当我眼见那欲壑难填的大海 　　　　　　　　　　5
　　一步一步把岸上的疆土侵蚀,
汪洋的水又渐渐被陆地覆盖,
　　失既变成了得,得又变成了失;

当我看见这一切扰攘和废兴,
　　或者连废兴一旦也化为乌有; 　　　　　　　10
毁灭便教我再三这样地反省:
　　时光终要跑来把我的爱带走。

哦,多么致命的思想! 它只能够
哭着去把那刻刻怕失去的占有。

梁宗岱　译

编注 威廉·莎士比亚(William Shakespeare,1564—1616),英国著名剧作家及诗人。除三十七部剧作外,他还写有长诗《维纳斯与阿多尼》(*Venus and Adonis*,1593)、长诗《鲁克丽丝受辱记》(*The Rape of Lucrece*,1594)、《十四行诗集》(*Sonnets*,1609),以及短诗《让声音最亮的鸟儿歌唱》和《女王颂》。他的《十四行诗集》共集诗一百五十四首,前部分(1—126首)歌颂了他与一位俊男之间炽热的友情,后部分(127—152首)审视了他对一位美女(黑肤女郎)的迷恋之情,最后两首则是对

一首写爱火被冷泉浇灭的希腊讽刺短诗的模仿。莎翁的十四行诗只有序号,没有标题。这首《时间与爱》系莎翁十四行诗的第64首,《时间与爱》与本书中其他莎翁十四行诗前的标题一样,均为《金库》原编者所加。

4. TIME AND LOVE (II)

Since brass, nor stone, nor earth, nor boundless sea①,
   But sad mortality o'ersways their power,
How with this rage shall beauty hold a plea②,
   Whose action is no stronger than a flower?

O how shall summer's honey breath hold out
   Against the wreckful siege of battering days,
When rocks impregnable are not so stout
   Nor gates of steel so strong, but time decays?

O fearful meditation! where, alack!
   Shall Time's best jewel from Time's chest lie hid③?
Or what strong hand can hold his swift foot back,
   Or who his spoil of beauty can forbid?

O! none, unless this miracle have might④,
That in black ink my love may still shine bright.

W. SHAKESPEARE.

---

① *Since brass, nor stone*, etc.: 'Since there is neither brass, nor stone,' etc.
② *hold a plea*: 'plead.' The usual meaning of the phrase is to try an action.
③ *Time's best jewel*: the poet's mistress, whom Time will one day gather to the chest where he stores his spoils.
④ *none, unless*, etc.: his lady's reign will not be over when she is dead, but only when she is forgotten, and that she will not be so long as her poet's verses are read.

4. 时间和爱（之二）

莎士比亚

既然青铜砖石陆地和沧海之水，
　　其力量都不能抗拒阴森的死亡，
那么力量并不比娇花更强的美
　　又怎么能与死亡的狂怒相对抗？

哦，夏日那些甜蜜芬芳的生命　　　　　　　　　　5
　　怎么能经受时日毁灭性的攻击，
既然坚韧的巉岩和牢固的铁门
　　面对岁月的侵蚀也非坚如磐石？

哦，可怕的思绪！哦，在何处
　　时间的瑰宝能躲过时间的橱柜？　　　　　　10
有什么巨手能够阻拦走兔飞鸟？
　　又有谁能禁止时光把美艳损毁？

哦，没有，除非这奇迹有力量，
使我爱友在这墨迹中永放光芒。

曹明伦　译

编注 此诗系莎氏十四行诗第 65 首。诗人在诗中表达了这样一种思想：时间能摧毁一切，柔脆的美却能与它对抗，文学是永恒的。

5. THE PASSIONATE SHEPHERD TO HIS LOVE[①]

Come live with me and be my Love,
And we will all the pleasures prove
That hills and valleys, dale and field,
And all the craggy mountains yield.

There will we sit upon the rocks
And see the shepherds feed their flocks,
By shallow rivers, to whose falls
Melodious birds sing madrigals[②].

There will I make thee beds of roses
And a thousand fragrant posies,
A cap of flowers, and a kirtle[③]
Embroider'd all with leaves of myrtle.

A gown made of the finest wool,
Which from our pretty lambs we pull,
Fair lined slippers for the cold,
With buckles of the purest gold.

A belt of straw and ivy buds
With coral clasps and amber studs:

---

① *Passionate*: 'in love', which state is sometimes called 'the tender passion.'
② *madrigals*: here used loosely for 'songs.' A madrigal is strictly a five- or six-part song written according to elaborate rules.
③ *kirtle*: 'petticoat.'

5. 牧羊人的恋歌

马洛

来吧,和我生活在一起,做我的爱人,
在这里将使我们快乐无边:
这里有峻峭秀丽的山峦,
还有风光明媚的山谷田园。

在那边,我俩坐在山岩上, 5
看牧羊人喂养可爱的羔羊;
在浅浅的小溪旁,
鸟儿随着潺潺流水把爱情歌唱。

在那边,我将用玫瑰编一顶花冠,
用成千的花束做床, 10
用爱神木的叶子织成长裙;
一切都献给你,绚丽与芬芳!

从羔羊身上剪下最好的羊毛,
为你做防寒的鞋衬和长袍;
用纯金为你制作鞋扣, 15
该是多么珍贵,多么荣耀!

常春藤和芳草做的腰带,
珊瑚带扣点缀着琥珀水晶。

And if these pleasures may thee move,
Come live with me and be my Love.

Thy silver dishes for thy meat
As precious as the gods do eat,
Shall on an ivory table be
Prepared each day for thee and me.

The shepherd swains shall dance and sing
For thy delight each May-morning:
If these delights thy mind may move,
Then live with me and be my Love,

C. MARLOWE.

假如这些享受能打动你的心，
来吧，和我生活在一起，做我的爱人！　　　　　　　*20*

银碟里盛着你吃的美味儿，
如同天上众神所用的一样，
丰盛的佳肴将为我俩
摆在象牙制的桌面上。

牧羊少年们在每个五月的早晨，　　　　　　　　　*25*
将为你纵情舞蹈，高歌入云；
假如这些欢乐能打动你的心，
来吧，和我生活在一起，做我的爱人！

袁广达　梁葆成　译

编注　克里斯托弗·马洛（Christopher Marlowe，1564—1593）英国戏剧家、诗人。他从事文学创作的时间只有短促的五年，却留下了极为可观的戏剧创作的遗产。他最出名的剧作是《浮士德博士的悲剧》。短诗《牧羊人的恋歌》歌颂理想的爱情，是一首有代表性的优秀抒情诗。

6. A MADRIGAL

    Crabbed Age and Youth
    Cannot live together:
      Youth is full of pleasance①,
    Age is full of care;
      Youth like summer morn,
    Age like winter weather,
      Youth like summer brave②,
    Age like winter bare:
      Youth is full of sport,
      Age's breath is short,
    Youth is nimble, Age is lame:
    Youth is hot and bold,
    Age is weak and cold,
    Youth is wild, and Age is tame: —
      Age, I do abhor thee,
      Youth, I do adore thee;
    O! my Love, my Love is young!
    Age, I do defy thee —
    O sweet shepherd, hie thee③,
    For methinks thou stay'st too long④.

                        W. SHAKESPEARE.

---

① *Pleasance*: 'enjoyment.'
② *brave*: 'fair to see,' generally referring to clothes.
③ *hie thee*: 'hasten.'
④ *stay'st*: 'delayest.'

6. 小曲

莎士比亚

  乖戾的老年与青春
不能在一起生存:
  青春充满了欢乐,
老年却充满忧心。
  青春似夏日朝霞,   5
老年像严寒冬令;
  青春如夏天华美,
老年像冬日凋零:
  青春生机勃勃,
  老年气喘不匀,   10
青春敏捷,老年跛行:
  青春热情无畏,
  老年虚弱惧冷,
青春激昂,老年恭顺:——
  我憎恨你,老年,   15
  我崇拜你,青春;
爱人哟,我的爱人正年轻!
  老年哟,我定要与你抗争——
  哦,心爱的牧羊人,快去吧,
我看你呆了太多时辰。   20

            曹明伦 译

编注 此诗选自一五九九年出版的诗集《爱的礼赞》(*The Passionate Pilgrim*),据说是莎氏在该诗集中唯一的诗作。

7. 'UNDER THE GREENWOOD TREE'

Under the greenwood tree
Who loves to lie with me,
And turn his merry note
Unto the sweet bird's throat —
Come hither, come hither, come hither!
    Here shall he see
    No enemy
But winter and rough weather.

Who doth ambition shun
And loves to live i' the sun,
Seeking the food he eats
And pleased with what he gets —
Come hither, come hither, come hither!
    Here shall he see
    No enemy
But winter and rough weather.

W. SHAKESPEARE.

7. "绿树高张翠幕"

莎士比亚

绿树高张翠幕,
谁来偕我偃卧,
翻将欢乐心声,
学唱枝头鸟鸣:
盍来此?盍来此?盍来此? 5
　目之所接,
　精神契一,
唯忧雨雪之将至。

孰能敝屣尊荣,
来沐丽日光风, 10
觅食自求果腹,
一饱欣然意足:
盍来此?盍来此?盍来此?
　目之所接,
　精神契一, 15
唯忧雨雪之将至。

朱生豪　译

编注 此诗选自《皆大欢喜》(*As You Like It*)第二幕第五场。

8. 'IT WAS A LOVER AND HIS LASS'

It was a lover and his lass
   With a hey and a ho, and a hey nonino!
That o'er the green cornfield did pass
In the spring time, the only pretty ring time①,
When birds do sing hey ding a ding, ding:
   Sweet lovers love the Spring.

Between the acres of the rye
These pretty country folks would lie:

This carol they began that hour,
How that a life was but a flower:

And therefore take the present time
   With a hey and a ho, and a hey nonino!
For love is crownèd with the prime
In spring time, the only pretty ring time,
When birds do sing hey ding a ding, ding:
   Sweet lovers love the Spring.

                      W. SHAKESPEARE.

---

① *ring time*: *i.e.* the season for giving a wedding-ring.

8. "一对情人并着肩"

莎士比亚

一对情人并着肩,
　嗳唷嗳唷嗳嗳唷,
走过了青青稻麦田,
春天是最好的结婚天,
听嘤嘤歌唱枝头鸟,　　　　　　　　　　　　5
　姐郎们最爱春光好。

小麦青青大麦鲜,
乡女村男交颈儿眠,

新歌一曲意缠绵,
人生美满像好花妍,　　　　　　　　　　　　10

劝君莫负艳阳天,
　嗳唷嗳唷嗳嗳唷,
恩爱欢娱要趁少年,
春天是最好的结婚天,
听嘤嘤歌唱枝头鸟,　　　　　　　　　　　　15
　姐郎们最爱春光好。

朱生豪　译

编注 此诗选自《皆大欢喜》第五幕第三场。

9. PRESENT IN ABSENCE

Absence, hear thou my protestation
  Against thy strength①,
   Distance, and length;
Do what thou canst for alteration②:
  For hearts of truest mettle
  Absence doth join, and Time doth settle.

Who loves a mistress of such quality,
  He soon hath found
   Affection's ground
Beyond time, place, and all mortality.
  To hearts that cannot vary
  Absence is Present, Time doth tarry.

By absence this good means I gain,
  That I can catch her,
   Where none can watch her,
In some close corner of my brain:
  There I embrace and kiss her;
  And so I both enjoy and miss her.

            ANON.

---

① *strength*: 'completeness.'
② *thou canst*: 'you can,' in *Poet. Rhap. for alteration*: 'to make me change.'

9. 逢在离别中

无名氏

呵,离别,听我在抗议
　　抗议你的完全,
　　时间和距离;
尽你所能来将我改变吧:
　　面对真诚坚强的心灵,　　　　　　　　5
　　离别犹相逢,时光也停息。

谁爱上这种品格的情侣,
　　他不久就会发现
　　爱的天地
超越了时间、空间和生死。　　　　　　　　10
　　对于忠贞不渝的心灵,
　　离别乃相逢,时光也停滞。

正是用离别这种美妙的方式,
　　在谁也看不见她的地方
　　我能与她相遇,　　　　　　　　　　　15
在我隐秘的心灵深处:
　　我和她拥抱亲吻;
　　把她赞赏,将她铭记。

黄新渠　译

10. ABSENCE

Being your slave, what should I do but tend[①]
    Upon the hours and times of your desire?
I have no precious time at all to spend
    Nor services to do, till you require;

Nor dare I chide the world-without-end hour
    Whilst I, my sovereign, watch the clock for you,
Nor think the bitterness of absence sour
    When you have bid your servant once adieu;

Nor dare I question with my jealous thought
    Where you may be, or your affairs suppose[②],
But like a sad slave, stay and think of nought
    Save, where you are, how happy you make those; —

So true a fool is Love, that in your will,
Though you do anything, he thinks no ill[③].

                          W. SHAKESPEARE.

---

① *tend*: 'attend.'
② *your affairs suppose*: 'conjecture what is your business.'
③ *in your will ... he thinks no ill*: 'he believes that your intentions are always good.'

10. 别离

莎士比亚

既然是你奴隶,我有什么可做,
　　除了时时刻刻伺候你的心愿?
我毫无宝贵的时间可消磨,
　　也无事可做,直到你有所驱遣。

我不敢骂那绵绵无尽的时刻,
　　当我为你,主人,把时辰来看守;
也不敢埋怨别离是多么残酷,
　　在你已经把你的仆人辞退后;

　　也不敢用妒忌的念头去探索
你究竟在哪里,或者为什么忙碌,
　　只是,像个可怜的奴隶,呆想着
你所在的地方,人们会多幸福。

爱这呆子是那么无救药的呆
凭你为所欲为,他都不觉得坏。

梁宗岱　译

编注　此诗系莎氏十四行诗第57首。诗人在此宣称他心甘情愿做他爱友的奴仆。

11. 'HOW LIKE A WINTER HATH MY ABSENCE BEEN'

How like a winter hath my absence been
From Thee, the pleasure of the fleeting year!
What freezings have I felt, what dark days seen,
What old December's bareness everywhere!

And yet this time removed was summer's time[①];
The teeming autumn, big with rich increase[②],
Bearing the wanton burden of the prime[③]
Like widow'd wombs after their lords' decease:

Yet this abundant issue seem'd to me
But hope of orphans, and unfather'd fruit[④];
For summer and his pleasures wait on thee,
And, thou away, the very birds are mute;

Or if they sing,'tis with so dull a cheer[⑤],
That leaves look pale, dreading the winter's near.

W. SHAKESPEARE.

---

① *this time removed*: 'time of separation.'
② *The teeming autumn*, etc.: an absolute clause equivalent to, 'while the teeming autumn was bearing.' *big*: 'pregnant.'
③ *wanton burden*: 'luxuriant produce'; a *burden* is that which is borne in the womb; *prime*: 'spring,' as being the first season of the year.
④ *But hope of orphans*, etc.: Autumn is the mother and Spring the father; but Spring has vanished, so that the children when born will be fatherless.
⑤ *cheer*: 'face,' 'expression of countenance'; this, the original meaning, is now obsolete. The second meaning 'mood,' 'State of mind,' hardly survives except in the phrases 'of good cheer,' 'what cheer?' — and perhaps the latter is now only slang. The word is used in the sense of 'cheerfulness' from the 14th century onwards. Cf, note on No. 163, l. 3.

11. 别离(之二)

莎士比亚

你是飞驰流年中之欢娱时辰,
　　离别你之后这日子多像冬天!
我觉得天多冷,天色多阴沉,
　　满目皆是十二月的萧瑟凄惨!

然而我俩这次分离是在夏末, 5
　　当丰饶的初秋正孕育着万物,
孕育着春天种下的风流硕果,
　　就像怀胎十月而丧夫的寡妇。

可是这丰饶的秋实在我眼中
　　不过意味着没有父亲的孤幼, 10
因夏天及其欢娱总把你侍奉,
　　你一离去连小鸟也不再啁啾;

即或它们啼鸣其声也那么悲哀,
树叶闻声失色,生怕严冬到来。

曹明伦　译

编注 此诗系莎氏十四行诗第97首,表现了诗人别离爱友后的悲哀心情。

12. A CONSOLATION

When in disgrace with fortune and men's eyes
    I all alone beweep my outcast state,
And trouble deaf heaven with my bootless cries,
    And look upon myself, and curse my fate;

Wishing me like to one more rich in hope,
    Featured like him, like him with friends possest①,
Desiring this man's art, and that man's scope②,
    With what I most enjoy contented least;

Yet in these thoughts myself almost despising,
    Haply I think on Thee — and then my state,
Like to the lark at break of day arising
    From sullen earth, sings hymns at heaven's gate;

For thy sweet love remember'd such wealth brings,
That then I scorn to change my state with kings.

                             W. SHAKESPEARE.

---

① *Featured*: 'formed,' 'shaped,' with reference to life rather than the face.
② *I. e.* those occupations which generally give him pleasure are least able to satisfy him now.

12. 安慰

莎士比亚

逢时运不济,又遭世人白眼,
　　我独自向隅而泣恨无枝可依,
忽而枉对聋聩苍昊祈哀告怜,
　　忽而反躬自省咒诅命运乖戾;

总指望自己像人家前程似锦,　　　　　　　　　　5
　　梦此君美貌,慕斯宾朋满座,
叹彼君艺高,馋夫机遇缘分,
　　却偏偏看轻自家的至福极乐;

可正当我妄自菲薄自惭形秽,
　　我忽然想到了你,于是我心　　　　　　　　10
便像云雀在黎明时振翮高飞,
　　离开阴沉的大地歌唱在天门;

因想到你甜蜜的爱价值千金,
我不屑与帝王交换我的处境。

曹明伦　译

编注 此诗系莎氏十四行诗第29首,歌颂了爱的伟大力量。诗人一想到他所爱的人,满腹的愤懑和怀旧的哀思都消失了。

13. THE UNCHANGEABLE

O never say that I was false of heart,
    Though absence seem'd my flame to qualify:
As easy might I from myself depart
    As from my soul, which in thy breast doth lie;

That is my home of love; if I have ranged,
    Like him that travels, I return again,
Just to the time, not with the time exchanged[①],
    So that myself bring water for my stain.

Never believe, though in my nature reign'd
    All frailties that besiege all kinds of blood[②],
That it could so preposterously be stain'd
    To leave for nothing all thy sum of good[③]:

For nothing this wide universe I call,
Save thou, my rose: in it thou art my all.

W. SHAKESPEARE.

---

① *Just*: 'punctually'; *exchanged*: 'changed,' 'altered' — an obsolete sense.
② *all kinds of blood*: 'people of different temperaments.'
③ *so ... stain'd To leave*, etc.: *i.e.* 'as to leave.'

13. 永不变心

莎士比亚

哦,千万别说我曾虚情假意,
  虽分离似乎平缓了我的激情。
我的灵魂就寄寓在你的心里,
  而我宁抛肉体也不愿弃灵魂。

那是我爱之家;若我曾流浪,
  现在就像旅行者又重返家园,
准时归来,没因久别而变样,
  所以我自己带水来洗涤污点①。

虽然在我的性情和气质之中
  存在着人类天性易有的疵颣,
但别以为我愚蠢得荒唐昏庸,
  竟为虚无而抛弃你全部的美:

因为我把这茫茫宇宙视为虚无,
除了你这玫瑰;你是我的万物。

曹明伦　译

编注　此诗系莎氏十四行诗第 109 首,表现了诗人对他的爱友忠贞不渝的爱。

---

① "带水来洗涤污点",此处的"水"喻眼泪。——译者

14. 'TO ME, FAIR FRIEND, YOU NEVER CAN BE OLD'

  To me, fair Friend, you never can be old,
   For as you were when first your eye I eyed
  Such seems your beauty still. Three winters cold
   Have from the forests shook three summers' pride①;

5   Three beauteous springs to yellow autumn turn'd
   In process of the seasons have I seen,
  Three April perfumes in three hot Junes burn'd,
   Since first I saw you fresh, which yet are green②.

  Ah! yet doth beauty, like a dial-hand,
10   Steal from his figure, and no pace perceived③;
  So your sweet hue, which methinks still doth stand④,
   Hath motion, and mine eye may be deceived:

  For fear of which, hear this, thou age unbred, —
  Ere you were born, was beauty's summer dead⑤.

W. SHAKESPEARE.

---

① *shook* for 'shaken' is not uncommon in the 17th century, which often used the past tense of strong verbs in place of the past participle.

② *which* for 'who' is often found in Shakespeare and his contemporaries; it occurs frequently in the Authorised Version of the Bible (1611), notably in the Lord's Prayer.

③ *Steal* I take to be intransitive, and *his* to be put for 'its,' *i.e.* beauty's; beauty slowly vanishes from the figure it adorns, as the hand steals imperceptibly round the clock.

④ *still* is the adjective, going with 'stand.'

⑤ Posterity is addressed collectively in the former line, individually in the latter, where 'you' = 'any of you.'

14. "美丽的朋友,我看你永不会老"

莎士比亚

美丽的朋友,我看你永不会老,
　　因为自从我第一眼看见你以来,
你似乎依然保持着当初的美貌。
　　严冬三度从森林摇落盛夏风采,

阳春也已三度化为暮秋的枯黄,
　　在四季的轮回之中我三度看见
炎炎六月三次烧焦四月的芬芳,
　　我当初见你年轻,如今仍当年。

唉,可是美就像钟面上的指针,
　　会不为人所察觉而悄悄地移动;
所以我以为能永驻的你的青春
　　也许在流逝而我的眼睛被欺哄。

唯恐如此,我告诉未来的后世:
你们尚未出生,美的夏天已消失。

曹明伦　译

编注 此诗系莎氏十四行诗第104首,诗中的情调不同于他的其他一些诗。诗人在有些诗中想用诗来使他所爱的人的美永生,但在这首诗中却哀叹美终将会消逝。

15. DIAPHENIA

Diaphenia like the daffadowndilly,
White as the sun, fair as the lily,
Heigh ho, how I do love thee!
    I do love thee as my lambs
    Are belovéd of their dams;
How blest were I if thou would'st prove me.

Diaphenia like the spreading roses.
That in thy sweets all sweets encloses,
Fair sweet, how I do love thee!
    I do love thee as each flower
    Loves the sun's life-giving power;
For dead, thy breath to life might move me[①].

Diaphenia like to all things blesséd
When all thy praises are expresséd,
Dear joy, how I do love thee!
    As the birds do love the spring,
    Or the bees their careful king;
Then in requite, sweet virgin, love me!

HENRY. CONSTABLE.

---

① *For dead*: *i.e.* For. Were I dead.

15. 黛尔菲妮娅

康斯特布尔

  黛尔菲妮娅像朵水仙花,
   如骄阳般纯洁,似百合般光华,
哎呀呀,我多么地爱您啊!
   我真诚地爱您,就像小羊
    亲昵可爱的妈妈;   5
我该何等地幸运,倘您把我嘉纳。

  黛尔菲妮娅像盛开的玫瑰花,
   您的馨香凝聚了所有的芳华,
心爱的人儿,我多么地爱您啊!
   我真心地爱您,就像每一朵鲜花   10
    倾慕太阳生机的强大;
假如我离别人世,您唤春的气息也使我精神焕发。

  黛尔菲妮娅如万物洪福广大,
   当您全部的赞语已尽情表达,
亲爱的娇娃,我多么地爱您啊!   15
   就像百鸟喜爱三月阳春,
    或如蜜蜂崇拜蜂王豁达:
那末,倾心相许,可爱的人儿,爱我吧!

付勇林 译

编注 亨利·康斯特布尔(Henry Constable,1562—1613),英国诗人。作品不多。主要作品有诗集《狄安娜》(1592)等。

16. ROSALYNDE

Like to the clear in highest sphere①
    Where all imperial glory shines,
Of selfsame colour is her hair
    Whether unfolded, or in twines:
        Heigh ho, fair Rosalynde!
Her eyes are sapphires set in snow,
    Resembling heaven by every wink;
The Gods do fear whenas they glow②,
    And I do tremble when I think
        Heigh ho, would she were mine!

Her cheeks are like the blushing cloud
    That beautifies Aurora's face,
Or like the silver crimson shroud③
    That Phoebus' smiling looks doth grace;
        Heigh ho, fair Rosalynde!
Her lips are like two budded roses
    Whom ranks of lilies neighbour nigh④,
Within which bounds she balm encloses
    Apt to entice a deity:
        Heigh ho, would she were mine!

---

① *the clear*: 'the brightness.'
② *whenas they glow*: 'when her eyes sparkle.'
③ *shroud*: 'covering'; in this sense it is obsolete, though we still use the expression 'shrouded in mystery.'
④ *Whom*: 'who' in the sixteenth century was not restricted to persons.

16. 罗莎琳达

洛吉

晶莹透亮,似在那高高的天上
　　那里金光灿烂,壮丽辉煌,
她的秀发闪着纯净的光泽
　　不论是飘曳婆娑,还是挽髻摇荡:
　　　　多美啊,罗莎琳达! 5
那双明眸犹如宝石湛蓝,嵌在雪地之上,
　　眨巴着眼睛,与天空辉映闪光;
它们光芒四射,众神也汗颜、恐慌,
　　当我春心萌动,不免战栗摇晃
　　　　多美啊,但愿她是我的娇娘! 10

她双颊红晕,犹如绚丽的云霞
　　映得奥罗娜也娇艳非常①,
那双颊又像深红色的盖布
　　是太阳神的笑颜使它更为荣光;
　　　　多美啊,罗莎琳达! 15
她双唇鲜嫩,有如玫瑰初放
　　就开在那行行百合的近旁,
在这片天地里,她饱蕴芳香
　　诱使神灵也心花怒放:
　　　　多美啊,但愿她是我的娇娘! 20

---

① 奥罗娜(Aurora),罗马神话中的曙光女神。——译者

  Her neck is like a stately tower
    Where Love himself imprison'd lies,
  To watch for glances every hour
    From her divine and sacred eyes:
25   Heigh ho, for Rosalynde!
  Her paps are centres of delight,
    Her breasts are orbs of heavenly frame,
  Where Nature moulds the dew of light①
    To feed perfection with the same:
30   Heigh ho, would she were mine!

  With orient pearl, with ruby red②,
    With marble white, with sapphire blue
  Her body every way is fed,
    Yet soft in touch and sweet in view:
35   Heigh ho, fair Rosalynde!
  Nature herself her shape admires;
    The Gods are wounded in her sight;
  And Love forsakes his heavenly fires
    And at her eyes his brand doth light:
40   Heigh ho, would she were mine!

  Then muse not, Nymphs, though I bemoan
    The absence of fair Rosalynde,
  Since for a fair there's fairer none,

---

① *Nature moulds the dew of light*, etc.: Rosalynde's breast is conceived as giving out a soft radiance ('the dew of light'), which goes to complete the sum of her perfections.

② *orient*, from meaning 'eastern,' came, as applied to pearls, to mean 'brilliant,' the pearls of the Indian seas being superior to those of the mussels of Europe.

她的脖颈与庄严的塔楼一样
　　囚住了爱神,他就此安躺,
希冀她非凡圣明的慧眼
　　时时投来深情的目光
　　　　多美啊,罗莎琳达!　　　　　　　　　　25
她的乳房是快乐的中央,
　　她的酥胸是苍穹的太阳,
造物主在那儿造就晶莹的光亮
　　又用它把完美哺养:
　　　　多美啊,但愿她是我的娇娘!　　　　30

珍珠的色彩,红宝石的透亮
　　大理石的洁白,蓝宝石的幽光
她的身体处处都是这样,
　　那么丰姿柔美,甜润芬芳:
　　　　多美啊,罗莎琳达!　　　　　　　　　35
造物主艳羡她的身段;
　　她秀目流盼使众神遍体鳞伤;
爱神也丢弃神圣的火炬
　　因为她的眼里,爱火在升腾向上:
　　　　多美啊,但愿她是我的娇娘!　　　　40

别惊讶,仙女们,虽然我哀伤①
　　美丽的罗莎琳达不在我的身旁,
因为美人难再有美人的媲美,

---

① 此处原文作 Nymphs,指希腊神话中属于山林水泽的仙女。——译者

               Nor for her virtues so divine[①]:
45   Heigh ho, fair Rosalynde;
      Heigh ho, my heart! would God that she were mine!

T. LODGE.

[①] *so divine*: i.e. is there any one so divine.

也再没人有她那样贞洁、高尚:
　　多美啊,罗莎琳达;
多美,我的心肝!上帝,但愿她是我的娇娘!

付勇林　译

编注　托马斯·洛吉(Thomas Lodge,1558?—1625),英国诗人、小说家及戏剧家。《罗莎琳达》选自他一五九〇年写成的传奇故事《罗莎琳达、尤菲绮斯黄金遗产》(*Rosalynde*,*Euphues Golden Legacy*)。这个故事为莎士比亚的戏剧《皆大欢喜》提供了基本情节和大量细节。

17. COLIN

Beauty sat bathing by a spring
    Where fairest shades did hide her;
The winds blew calm, the birds did sing,
    The cool streams ran beside her.
My wanton thoughts enticed mine eye
    To see what was forbidden:
But better memory said, fie!
    So vain desire was chidden: —
        Hey nonny nonny O!
        Hey nonny nonny!

Into a slumber then I fell,
    When fond imagination[①]
Seem'd to see, but could not tell
    Her feature or her fashion[②].
But ev'n as babes in dreams do smile,
    And sometimes fall a-weeping,
So I awaked, as wise this while[③]
    As when I fell a-sleeping: —
        Hey nonny nonny O!
        Hey nonny nonny!

                THE SHEPHERD TONY.

---

① *fond*: from 'foolish,' its original meaning, this word came to mean 'foolishly affectionate,' and then — its only modern meaning — 'tender,' 'loving,' without any idea of disparagement.
② *her fashion*: 'her shape.'
③ *this while*: 'this time,'

17. 科林

牧羊人托尼

丽人沐浴在清泉的近旁
　　葱郁的树荫把她的倩影掩藏；
微风轻拂，百鸟儿欢唱，
　　冰凉的小溪淌过她身旁。
轻飘的思绪怂恿我　　　　　　　　　　　　　　5
　　把她的玉体探望、观赏：
可美好的记忆说，不要脸！
　　应该唾弃这般虚浮的欲望：——
　　　　　嗨，啰哩啰哩哦！
　　　　　嗨，啰哩啰哩！　　　　　　　　　10

于是我渐渐地沉入梦乡，
　　这时痴情的想象
恍惚中看见，却描绘不清
　　那美人的花容，袅娜的体状。
就像熟睡的婴儿时而酣笑，　　　　　　　　15
　　时而又泪水流淌，
我不觉醒来，这时神清气爽
　　就和梦中一样：——
　　　　　嗨，啰哩啰哩哦！
　　　　　嗨，啰哩啰哩！　　　　　　　　20
　　　　　　　　　　　　付勇林　译

编注　牧羊人托尼（The Shepherd Tony），生平不详，也许就是安东尼·马迪（Anthony Munday，1553—1633）。

18. TO HIS LOVE

Shall I compare thee to a summer's day?
    Thou art more lovely and more temperate:
Rough winds do shake the darling buds of May,
    And summer's lease hath all too short a date;

Sometime too hot the eye of heaven shines,
    And often is his gold complexion dimm'd;
And every fair from fair sometime declines[①],
    By chance, or nature's changing course, untrimm'd[②].

But thy eternal summer shall not fade
    Nor lose possession of that fair thou owest[③];
Nor shall death brag thou wanderest in his shade,
    When in eternal lines to time thou growest[④]:

So long as men can breathe, or eyes can see,
So long lives this, and this gives life to thee.

W. SHAKESPEARE.

---

① *from fair*: 'from fairness.'
② *untrimm'd*: the prefix un- is either negative, as in 'unmoved,' or privative, signifying the reversal of an action, as in 'unfold.' Here it has the latter force; to trim is to make neat, so to untrim is to disarrange.
③ *owest*: this was originally the same word as to 'own' and meant to 'have'.
④ *to time*: *i.e.* to all time.

18. 致爱友

莎士比亚

我是否可以把你比喻成夏天?
　　虽然你比夏天更可爱更温和;
狂风会使五月娇蕾红消香断,
　　夏天拥有的时日也转瞬即过;

有时天空之巨眼目光太炽热,　　　　　　　　　　5
　　它金灿灿的面色也常被遮暗;
而千芳万艳都终将凋零飘落,
　　被时运天道之更替剥尽红颜;

但你永恒的夏天将没有止尽,
　　你所拥有的美貌也不会消失,　　　　　　　10
死神终难夸口你游荡于死荫①,
　　当你在不朽的诗中永葆盛时:

只要有人类生存,或人有眼睛,
我的诗就会流传并赋予你生命。

　　　　　　　　　　　　　　曹明伦　译

编注　此诗系莎氏十四行诗第18首,诗人在这首诗中表达了"唯有文学可以同时间抗衡"的思想。

---

① 此行语出《圣经·旧约·诗篇》第二十三篇第四节:"虽然我穿行于死荫之幽谷,但我不怕罹祸,因为你与我同在,你会用牧杖引我,用权杖护我。"——译者

19. TO HIS LOVE

When in the chronicle of wasted time①
    I see descriptions of the fairest wights②,
And beauty making beautiful old rhyme
    In praise of ladies dead, and lovely knights;

Then in the blazon of sweet beauty's best③
    Of hand, of foot, of lip, of eye, of brow,
I see their antique pen would have, exprest
    Ev'n such a beauty as you master now④.

So all their praises are but prophecies
    Of this our time, all you prefiguring;
And, for they look'd but with divining eyes⑤,
    They had not skill enough your worth to sing:

For we, which now behold these present days,
Have eyes to wonder, but lack tongues to praise.

                            W. SHAKESPEARE.

---

① *wasted*: not 'misused,' but simply 'spent,' 'past.'
② *wights*: 'persons,' almost obsolete except in a few phrases like 'luckless wight.'
③ *blazon*: 'description,' properly a description of armorial bearings.
④ *you master*: 'have as your own.'
⑤ *but with divining eyes*: i.e. not haying seen you, they could but guess at your beauty.

19. 致爱友（之二）

莎士比亚

当我从那湮远的古代的纪年，
　　发见那绝代风流人物的写真，
艳色使得古老的歌咏也香艳，
　　颂赞着多情骑士和绝命佳人，

于是，从那些国色天姿的描画， 5
　　无论手脚、嘴唇，或眼睛或眉额，
我发觉那些古拙的笔所表达
　　恰好是你现在所占领的姿色。

所以他们的赞美无非是预言
　　我们这时代，一切都预告着你； 10
不过他们观察只用想象的眼，
　　还不够才华把你歌颂得尽致：

而我们，幸而得亲眼看见今天，
只有眼惊羡，却没有舌头咏叹。

梁宗岱　译

编注 此诗系莎氏十四行诗第 106 首。

20. LOVE'S PERJURIES

On a day, alack the day!
Love, whose month is ever May,
Spied a blossom passing fair①
Playing in the wanton air②;
Through the velvet leaves the wind,
All unseen, 'gan passage find③;
That the lover, sick to death,
Wish'd himself the heaven's breath.
Air, quoth he, thy cheeks may blow④;
Air, would I might triumph so!
But, alack, my hand is sworn
Ne'er to pluck thee from thy thorn;
Vow, alack, for youth unmeet;
Youth so apt to pluck a sweet.
Do not call it sin in me
That I am forsworn for thee⑤;
Thou for whom Jove would swear
Juno but an Ethiope were⑥,
And deny himself for Jove⑦,

---

① *passing fair*: 'surpassingly beautiful.'
② *wanton*: 'sportive.'
③ *'gan*: *i.e.* began.
④ He addresses his lady: — 'The air may touch thy cheeks—would that I might do the same'!
⑤ To be *forsworn* is to break an oath.
⑥ *Ethiope*: 'a blackamoor.'
⑦ *deny himself for Jove*: 'assert that he was Jove no longer.'

20. 爱的谎言

莎士比亚

有一天,唉,那一天!
爱永远是五月天,
见一朵好花娇媚,
在款款风前游戏;
穿过柔嫩的叶网,　　　　　　　5
风儿悄悄地来往。
憔悴将死的恋人,
羡慕天风的轻灵:
风能吹上你面颊,
我只能对花掩泣!　　　　　　　10
我已向神前许愿,
不攀折鲜花嫩瓣;
少年谁不爱春红?
这种誓情理难通。
今日我为你叛誓,　　　　　　　15
请不要把我讥刺;
你曾经迷惑乔武①,
使朱诺变成黑人②,
放弃天上的威尊,

---

① 乔武(Jove),通译作约芙,即罗马神话中的主神朱庇特(Jupiter)。——编注者
② 朱诺(Juno),天后,主神朱庇特之妻。——编注者

20   Turning mortal for thy love.

                                    W. SHAKESPEARE.

来作尘世的凡人。 20

朱生豪　译

编注　此诗选自《爱的徒劳》(*Love's Labour's Lost*)第四幕第三场。

21. A SUPPLICATION

    Forget not yet the tried intent①
    Of such a truth as I have meant;
    My great travail so gladly spent②,
        Forget not yet!

    Forget not yet when first began
    The weary life ye know, since whan③
    The suit, the service none tell can④;
        Forget not yet

    Forget not yet the great assays⑤,
    The cruel wrong, the scornful ways,
    The painful patience in delays,
        Forget not yet

    Forget not! O, forget not this,
    How long ago hath been, and is
    The mind that never meant amiss⑥—
        Forget not yet!

---

① *the tried intent*, etc.: 'the proved purpose of the devotion which I have endeavoured to show.'
② *travaill*: 'toil.'
③ *since whan The suit*: 'for how long I have been your suitor.' *whan* is an earlier form of 'when.'
④ *the service*: i.e. [and] the service [which] none can tell.
⑤ *assays*: 'trials,' to which you have subjected me.
⑥ *I.e.* Remember how long I have been wishing you well, as I do now.

21. 祈求

怀亚特

可别忘记我所表示的
如此一片忠诚的真切意愿；
我莫大的痛苦已那么愉快地完成，
　　　　　　可别忘记！

可别忘记当初开始　　　　　　　　　　　5
你知道的那厌倦的生活，从此
那种乞求，那种服务真是难以述说；
　　　　　　可别忘记！

可别忘记那些严重的考验，
那残酷的屈辱，藐视的方式，　　　　　10
几次拖延了的痛苦的忍耐，
　　　　　　可别忘记！

别忘记！咳，不要把这忘记，
多久以前已经是，现在也是
这决不能被误解的心意——　　　　　　15
　　　　　　可别忘记！

> Forget not then thine own approved[①]
> The which so long hath thee so loved,
> Whose steadfast faith yet never moved —
>   Forget not this!

SIR THOMAS. WYATT.

---

① *thine own approved*: 'one whom you have tested.'

别忘记还有你自己赞许的
那个你曾如此长久这样爱过的人,
他的坚贞信念可永不动摇——
　　　不要把这忘记!　　　　　　　　20

林天斗　译

编注　托马斯·怀亚特(Thomas Wyatt,1503?—1542),亦译为魏阿特或华埃特,英国文艺复兴时期新诗歌的第一位代表。主要作品有与萨里等人合作的《托特尔杂集》(*Tottel's Miscellancy*)和用三韵体写成的讽刺诗《论贫穷与富有》。他曾与宫廷女官安娜·波琳相恋,后来波琳做了亨利八世的继室。他为此写了许多以爱情为题材的诗歌,《祈求》便是其中一首。

22. TO AURORA

O if thou knew'st how thou thyself dost harm,
    And dost prejudge thy bliss, and spoil my rest[①];
    Then thou would'st melt the ice out of thy breast
And thy relenting heart would kindly warm.

O if thy pride did not our joys controul,
    What world of loving wonders should'st thou see!
    For if I saw thee once transform'd in me[②],
Then in thy bosom I would pour my soul;

Then all my thoughts should in thy visage shine,
    And if that aught mischanced thou should'st not moan[③]
    Nor bear the burthen of thy griefs alone;
No, I would have my share in what were thine[④]:

And whilst we thus should make our sorrows one,
This happy harmony would make them none.

                W. ALEXANDER, EARL OF STERLINE.

---

① *prejudge thy bliss*: 'decide what will make for your happiness without having tried it.'
② *transform'd in me*: 'assuming a different form by entering my body'; i.e. handing over thy heart and soul to me.
③ *if that*: archaic for 'if'.
④ *were*: subjunctive, 'would be.'

22. 致奥罗娜

亚历山大

哦,倘若你知道怎样把自己伤害,
　竟预知你的幸福,扰乱我的平静:
　那末你胸中的冰块将消融殆尽
你温柔的心肠就会春光一派。

哦,倘若你的清高未把欢乐阻碍,　　　　　　　　　　　5
　世上什么爱的奇迹你不收获!
　如果你把全部身心交付与我,
我将把灵魂倾注于你的心怀;

于是我一腔思恋将闪在你脸上,
　如果你遭受不幸,不要自艾自怨　　　　　　　　　　10
　也不要独自把忧伤的重负承担;
不,我愿与你一起把甘苦分享:

当我们这样把痛苦融为一体,
幸福的和声将把它全然荡涤。

付勇林　译

编注　威廉·亚历山大(William Alexander,1567?—1640),英国诗人。《致奥罗娜》系他的十四行诗集《奥罗娜》(*Aurora*,1604)第33首。

23. TRUE LOVE

Let me not to the marriage of true minds
    Admit impediments. Love is not love[1]
Which alters when it alteration finds,
    Or bends with the remover to remove[2]: —

O no! it is an ever-fixed mark
    That looks on tempests, and is never shaken;
It is the star to every wandering bark,
    Whose worth's unknown, although his height be taken[3].

Love's not Time's fool, though rosy lips and cheeks[4]
    Within his bending sickle's compass come[5];
Love alters not with his brief hours and weeks,
    But bears it out ev'n to the edge of doom[6]: —

If this be error, and upon me proved,

---

[1] *Let me not ... Admit*: 'May I never own that there are.'
[2] *bends with the remover*, etc.: 'is disposed to draw back from one who is himself drawing back.'
[3] *although his height be taken*: the position of the star in the sky when accurately taken may serve as a guide to the mariner, who however knows nothing of the astrological significance of the star.
[4] *Time's fool*: 'The dupe of Time.'
[5] *bending sickle*: Time is generally represented as a mower with a curved scythe.
[6] *bears it out*: 'endures without giving way.'

23. 真正的爱

莎士比亚

我不承认两颗真诚相爱的心
　　会有什么阻止其结合的障碍①。
那种见变就变的情不是真情,
　　那种顺风转舵的爱不是真爱②。

哦!爱情是恒定的灯塔塔楼,　　　　　　　　　　　　5
　　它面对狂风暴雨而岿然屹立;
爱情是指引迷航船只的星斗,
　　其方位可测但价值鲜为人知。

真正的爱并不是时间的玩物,
　　虽红唇朱颜难逃时间的镰刀;　　　　　　　　　10
爱并不因时辰短暂而有变故,
　　而是持之以恒直至天荒地老。

　　倘若有人证明我这是异端邪说,

---

① 在西方的结婚仪式上,主持仪式的牧师会分别对新郎新娘和参加婚礼的宾客说两段话。一曰(对新郎新娘):"最后审判日到来之时,世人心中的秘密都将暴露,所以,若你俩任何一方知晓有任何使你俩不能合法结合的障碍(impediment),请现在就承认。"二曰(对来宾):"我将宣布这对新人结为夫妻。若你们中有人知晓,按上帝的戒律或人间的法律,有任何使这对新人不能缔结神圣婚姻的障碍(impediment),请此刻就说出,不然就永远保持沉默。"此处的"障碍"(impediments)专指"合法婚姻的障碍"(如未达结婚年龄或重婚等等)。——译者
② 这两行诗的原文通常能让西方读者联想到《圣经·新约·哥林多前书》第十三章保罗对爱的论述。——译者

I never writ, nor no man ever loved[①].

                                    W. SHAKESPEARE.

---

① *nor no man*: in 16th and 17th century English the double negative did not produce an affirmative.

那我未曾写过诗,也没人爱过。

曹明伦　译

编注 此诗系莎氏十四行诗第116首,诗人宣称真正的爱可以征服时间。

24. A DITTY

My true-love hath my heart, and I have his,
    By just exchange one for another given:
I hold his dear, and mine he cannot miss,
    There never was a better bargain driven:
        My true-love hath my heart, and I have his,

His heart in me keeps him and me in one,
    My heart in him his thoughts and senses guides:
He loves my heart, for once it was his own,
    I cherish his because in me it bides:
        My true-love hath my heart, and I have his.

SIR P. SIDNEY.

24. 交换

锡德尼

我的真实情人占有我的心,我也占有他的心,
　我们两人公公平平,彼此以你心换我心,
我和他的心亲密无间,他不会因失去我的心
　再没有比这更好的交换:
　　我的真实情人占有我的心我也占有他的心。　　　　5

他的心在我体内使他和我成为一体,
　我的心在他体内引导他的思想感官,
他爱我的心,因为以前原是他的,
　我爱他的心,因为它在我体内安眠;
　　我的真实情人占有我的心,我也占有他的心。　　　10

李霁野　译

编注　菲利普·锡德尼(Philip Sidney,1554—1586),英国诗人、学者。他曾在伊丽莎白女王宫廷任朝臣,后触怒女王,退隐乡间。他的主要作品有《诗辩》、牧歌传奇《阿卡迪亚》(*The Countess of Pembroke's Arcadia*)和十四行组诗《爱星者和星星》。

25. LOVE'S OMNIPRESENCE

Were I as base as is the lowly plain,
    And you, my Love, as high as heaven above,
Yet should the thoughts of me your humble swain
    Ascend to heaven, in honour of my Love.

Were I as high as heaven above the plain,
    And you, my Love, as humble and as low
As are the deepest bottoms of the main,
    Whereso'er you were, with you my love should go.

Were you the earth, dear Love, and I the skies,
    My love should shine on you like to the sun,
And look upon you with ten thousand eyes
    Till heaven wax'd blind, and till the world were done.

Whereso'er I am, below, or else above you,
Whereso'er you are, my heart shall truly love you.

                         J. SYLVESTER.

25. 爱情无处不在

西尔维斯特

假如我像低低的平原一样卑下,
　　而你,我的爱人,像天空一样高悬,
你的卑微仆人为尊崇你的身价,
　　他的思念也会高升上天。

假如我像平原上的天空一样高, 5
　　而你,我的爱人,像最深的海底
一样的卑下,一样的渺渺,
　　我的爱也追随你,无论你在哪里。

假如你是大地,我是天空,亲爱的,
　　我的爱像太阳一般对你照耀, 10
并用万只眼睛看望着你,
　　直到天变浑噩,世界云散烟消。
无论我在你之下,在你之上,
　　无论你在哪,我都爱你赤胆忠肠。

李霁野　译

编注 乔舒亚·西尔维斯特(Joshua Sylvester, 1563—1618),是一个不很出名的英国诗人。作为诗歌翻译家,他翻译了法国诗人杜巴尔塔斯的《创世记》;作为诗人,这首十四行诗是他留传后世不多的作品之一。

26. CARPE DIEM

O Mistress mine, where are you roaming?
O stay and hear! your true-love's coming
    That can sing both high and low;
Trip no further, pretty sweeting①,
Journeys end in lovers' meeting —
    Every wise man's son doth know.

What is love? 'tis not hereafter;
Present mirth hath present laughter;
    What's to come is still unsure:
In delay there lies no plenty, —
Then come kiss me, Sweet-and-twenty,
    Youth's a stuff will not endure.

W. SHAKESPEARE.

---

① *sweeting*: properly a sweet apple, and hence a term of affection.

26. 及时行乐

莎士比亚

你到哪儿去,啊我的姑娘?
听呀,那边来了你的情郎,
　　嘴里吟着抑扬的曲调。
不要再走了,美貌的亲亲;
恋人的相遇终结了行程,　　　　　　　　　5
　　每个聪明人全都知晓。

什么是爱情?它不在明天;
欢笑嬉游莫放过了眼前,
　　将来的事有谁能猜料?
不要蹉跎了大好的年华;　　　　　　　　10
来吻着我吧,你双十娇娃,
　　转眼青春早化成衰老。

朱生豪　译

编注　此诗选自《第十二夜》(*Twelfth Night*)第二幕第三场。标题系《金库》原编者所加。

27. WINTER

When icicles hang by the wall
    And Dick the shepherd blows his nail①,
And Tom bears logs into the hall,
    And milk comes frozen home in pail;
When blood is nipt, and ways be foul,
Then nightly sings the staring owl
        Tuwhoo!
Tuwhit! tuwhoo! A merry note!
While greasy Joan doth keel the pot②.

When all aloud the wind doth blow,
    And coughing drowns the parson's saw③,
And birds sit brooding in the snow④,
    And Marian's nose looks red and raw:
When roasted crabs hiss in the bowl⑤—
Then nightly sings the staring owl
        Tuwhoo!
Tuwhi! tuwhoo! A merry note!
While greasy Joan doth keel the pot.

W. SHAKESPEARE.

---

① *blows his nail*: breathes on his finger-tips to warm them.
② *keel the pot*: 'cool the contents of the pot by stirring.'
③ *saw*: 'trite maxim.'
④ *brooding*: the first meaning is to sit on eggs, and so to sit still as if one were trying to hatch out a scheme.
⑤ *crabs*: heated ale with spice or sugar and a roast crab-apple or a slice of toast added was a favourite drink for winter evenings.

27. 冬之歌

莎士比亚

当一条条冰柱檐前悬吊,
　　汤姆把木块向屋内搬送,
牧童狄克呵着他的指爪,
　　挤来的牛乳凝结了一桶,
刺骨的寒气,泥泞的路途, 5
大眼睛的鸱鸮夜夜高呼:
　　　　哆呵!
哆喂,哆呵! 它歌唱着欢喜,
当油垢的琼转她的锅子。

当怒号的北风漫天吹响, 10
　　咳嗽打断了牧师的箴言,
鸟雀们在雪里缩住颈项,
　　玛利恩冻得红肿了鼻尖,
炙烤的螃蟹在锅内吱喳,
大眼睛的鸱鸮夜夜喧哗: 15
　　　　哆呵!
哆喂,哆呵! 它歌唱着欢喜,
当油垢的琼转她的锅子。

朱生豪　译

编注 此诗选自《爱的徒劳》第五幕第二场。

28. 'THAT TIME OF YEAR THOU MAY'ST IN ME BEHOLD'

That time of year thou may'st in me behold
    When yellow leaves, or none, or few, do hang
Upon those boughs which shake against the cold,
    Bare ruin'd choirs, where late the sweet birds sang.

In me thou see'st the twilight of such day
    As after sunset fadeth in the west,
Which by and by black night doth take away,
    Death's second self, that seals up all in rest.

In me thou see'st the glowing of such fire,
    That on the ashes of his youth doth lie[1]
As the death-bed whereon it must expire,
    Consumed with that which it was nourish'd by[2]:

— This thou perceiv'st, which makes thy love more strong,
To love that well which thou must leave ere long.

W. SHAKESPEARE.

---

[1] *such fire That*, etc.: in strict grammar 'that' should be 'as.' his = its, referring to 'fire.'

[2] *Consumed with*: *i.e.* 'together with', fire and fuel disappear together.

28. "你在我身上会看到这样的时节"

莎士比亚

你在我身上会看到这样的时节,
　　那时黄叶飘尽,或余残叶几片
依随枯枝在萧瑟的冷风中摇曳,
　　昔日百鸟齐鸣的歌坛颓败不堪。

你在我身上会看到这样的黄昏, 5
　　夕阳西坠后渐渐隐去西天薄暮,
沉沉黑夜一点一点将暮色吞尽,
　　像死亡之化身遮盖安息的万物。

你在我身上会看到这样的炉火,
　　躺在其青春的灰烬中朝不保夕, 10
仿佛是在临终床上等待着殒落,
　　等待喂养过它的燃料把它窒息。

待看到这些,你的爱意会更浓,
对即将离去的生命会更加珍重。

曹明伦　译

编注　此诗系莎氏十四行诗第73首。

29. REMEMBRANCE

When to the sessions of sweet silent thought
    I summon up remembrance of things past[1],
I sigh the lack of many a thing I sought,
    And with old woes new wail my dear time's waste[2];

Then can I drown an eye, unused to flow,
    For precious friends hid in death's dateless night[3],
And weep afresh love's long-since-cancell'd woe,
    And moan the expense of many a vanish'd sight[4].

Then can I grieve at grievances foregone[5],
    And heavily from woe to woe tell o'er
The sad account of fore-bemoanèd moan,
    Which I new pay as if not paid before:

— But if the while I think on thee, dear friend[6],
All losses are restored, and sorrows end.

W. SHAKESPEARE.

---

[1] *sessions ... summon*: he calls memory to bear witness as in a court of law.
[2] *with old woes*, etc.: 'and utter afresh my old lamentations for the waste of my past life.'
[3] *dateless*: 'marked by no fixed limits.'
[4] *expense*: 'loss.'
[5] *foregone*: 'gone-before,' 'past.' The verb to forgo (= go without) is often spelt 'forego,' and its past participle then is identical in form with this word.
[6] *the while*: 'at such a time.'

29. 记忆

莎士比亚

每当我把对前尘往事的回忆
　传唤到审理冥想幽思之公堂，
便会为残缺许多旧梦而叹息，
　昔年伤悲又令我悲蹉跎时光；

于是我不轻弹的眼泪会奔涌，　　　　　　　　　　　　　　　　5
　哭被死亡之长夜掩埋的故友，
又伤早已被注销的爱之伤痛，
　又哀许多早已经支付的哀愁；

于是我会为昔日冤情而悲叹，
　重述一段段不堪回首的痛苦，　　　　　　　　　　　　　　　10
仿佛那伤心的旧债未曾偿还，
　而今我又伤伤心心重新支付。

但我此时若想到你，我的爱友，
一切便失而复得，顿消许多忧。

曹明伦　译

编注 此诗系莎氏十四行诗第30首，主题与第29首（参见本卷第12首）大致相同。

30. REVOLUTIONS

Like as the waves make towards the pebbled shore,
   So do our minutes hasten to their end;
Each changing place with that which goes before,
   In sequent toil all forwards do contend①.

Nativity, once in the main of light,
   Crawls to maturity, wherewith being crown'd,
Crooked eclipses 'gainst his glory fight,
And Time that gave doth now his gift confound.

Time doth transfix the flourish set on youth②,
   And delves the parallels in beauty's brow;
Feeds on the rarities of nature's truth,
   And nothing stands but for his scythe to mow:

And yet, to times in hope, my verse shall stand③
Praising thy worth, despite his cruel hand.

W. SHAKESPEARE.

---

① *sequent*: 'following one another.'
② *transfix the flourish*: 'pierce through the gloss.'
③ times in hope: 'ages yet to come.'

30. 循环

莎士比亚

像波涛涌向铺满沙石的海岸,
 我们的时辰也匆匆奔向尽头;
后浪前浪周而复始交替循环,
 时辰波涛之迁流都争先恐后。

生命一旦沐浴其命星的吉光,　　　　　　5
 并爬向成熟,由成熟到极顶,
不祥的晦食便来争夺其辉煌①,
 时间便来捣毁它送出的赠品。

光阴会刺穿青春华丽的铠甲,
 岁月会在美额上挖掘出战壕,　　　　10
流年会吞噬自然创造的精华,
 芸芸众生都难逃时间的镰刀。

可我的诗篇将傲视时间的毒手,
永远把你赞美,直至万古千秋。

曹明伦　译

编注 此诗系莎氏十四行诗第 60 首。

---

① "晦食"指上文的命星被遮掩,而非指日食。——译者

31. 'FAREWELL! THOU ART TOO DEAR FOR MY POSSESSING'

Farewell! thou art too dear for my possessing,
  And like enough thou know'st thy estimate:
The charter of thy worth gives thee releasing①;
  My bonds in thee are all determinate.

For how do I hold thee but by thy granting?
  And for that riches where is my deserving?
The cause of this fair gift in me is wanting,
  And so my patent back again is swerving②.

Thyself thou gav'st, thy own worth then not knowing,
  Or me, to whom thou gav'st it, else mistaking;
So thy great gift, upon misprision growing③,
  Comes home again, on better judgement making.

Thus have I had thee as a dream doth flatter;
In sleep, a king; but waking, no such matter.

W. SHAKESPEARE.

---

① *charter*: properly a written grant of rights by the Sovereign; here his lady's worth had given her such rights.
② *patent*: a right similarly granted to the exclusive enjoyment of some privilege.
③ *upon misprision growing*: 'being based upon a misconception of your own value.' The word is derived from the verb to misprize, and must not be confounded with the legal term misprision (akin to the French méprendre), meaning a wrongful act or omission.

31. "别了！你高贵得让我不配拥有"

莎士比亚

别了！你高贵得让我不配拥有，
　而且你多半也清楚自己的身价。
你的身价给你免除义务的自由；
　我与你之间的盟约就到此作罢。

因我拥有你怎能只凭你的应诺？　　　　　　　5
　我凭什么值得拥有这一诺千金？
我没有理由消受你的恩光渥泽，
　所以请收回你给我的特许凭证。

你应诺我时尚未认清你的价值，
　不然就是挑受惠人时有所疏忽，　　　　　　10
因此你这份送错人的厚赆重礼，
　经重新斟酌之后应该物归原主。

于是我曾拥有你，像拥有一个梦，
　我在梦里是君王，可醒来一场空。

曹明伦　译

编注　此诗系莎氏十四行诗第87首。

32. THE LIFE WITHOUT PASSION

They that have power to hurt, and will do none,
That do not do the thing they most do show①,
Who, moving others, are themselves as stone,
Unmoved, cold, and to temptation slow, —

They rightly do inherit Heaven's graces②,
And husband nature's riches from expense③;
They are the lords and owners of their faces,
Others, but stewards of their excellence.

The summer's flower is to the summer sweet,
Though to itself it only live and die④;
But if that flower with base infection meet⑤,
The basest weed outbraves his dignity:

For sweetest things turn sourest by their deeds;
Lilies that fester smell far worse than weeds.

W. SHAKESPEARE.

---

① *do the thing they most do show*: i.e. devote themselves to the service of love, for which their appearance has so amply qualified them.
② *rightly do inherit*, etc.: 'it is right that they should be endowed with supreme beauty.'
③ *from expense*: 'from being expended.'
④ *Though to itself*, etc.: i.e. that which is self-contained and self-centred will yet give pleasure if it be beautiful. The 'only' is misplaced, as so often in English; it goes with 'to itself.'
⑤ *with base infection meet*: 'become tainted with decay.'

32. 无激情的人生

莎士比亚

有戕贼之力而并不为非作歹，
　　有美艳之貌而不行风流之事，
能使人动情自己却超乎情外，
　　对诱惑能持重如石漠然置之——

这样的人才无愧于承受天恩，
　　才没有挥霍浪费自然之精华；
他们才真是自身美貌的主人，
　　而别人只是自己姿色的管家。

夏日娇花虽然只有一荣一枯，
　　但却为夏日奉出鲜艳与芳菲，
可娇花若容卑鄙的霉菌侵入，
　　连最贱的荒草也会比它高贵；

因为高洁者纳污则最脏最丑，
　　百合花一旦腐烂比衰草还臭。

曹明伦　译

编注　此诗系莎氏十四行诗第94首。诗人说，只有忠贞不渝，能抗拒诱惑的人才配得上天赐的美貌。

33. THE LOVER'S APPEAL

  And wilt thou leave me thus?
   Say nay! say nay! for shame!
   To save thee from the blame①
   Of all my grief and grame②.
5   And wilt thou leave me thus?
   Say nay! say nay!

  And wilt thou leave me thus,
   That hath loved thee so long③
   In wealth and woe among④?
10   And is thy heart so strong
  As for to leave me thus?
   Say nay! say nay!

  And wilt thou leave me thus,
   That hath given thee my heart
15   Never for to depart
   Neither for pain nor smart?
  And wilt thou leave me thus?

---

① *To save thee*, etc.; *i.e.* promise not to leave me, and so save thyself from the charge of causing me pain.
② *grame*: 'sorrow.'
③ *That hath*: should be 'have,' the antecedent being 'me.'
④ *In wealth and woe among*: 'wealth' is used in its original sense of 'prosperity.' 'Among' is rarely found with a singular noun which is not a noun of multitude.

33. 情人的哀诉

怀亚特

你真要把我抛离？
　不要！不要！那可羞愧！
　别让人把你责怪，
　给我带来忧伤和悲哀。
你真要把我抛离？　　　　　　　　　　5
　不要！不要！

你真要把我抛离？
　我爱你那么久长，
　曾经共度欢乐和苦难。
　难道你的心似铁石一般？　　　　　　10
你真要把我抛离？
　不要！不要！

你真要把我抛离？
　我把心儿奉献
　决不是为了离异，　　　　　　　　　15
　更不是为了痛苦和悲戚。
你真要把我抛离？

Say nay! say nay!

And wilt thou leave me thus,
And have no more pity
Of him that loveth thee?
Alas! thy cruelty!
And wilt thou leave me thus?
Say nay! say nay!

SIR T. WYATT.

不要！不要！

　你真要把我抛离？
　　连同我对你的深爱，
　　没有更多的哀怜， 20
　　啊,残酷的人啊！
　你真要把我抛离？
　　　不要！不要！

　　　　　　　　　　　　谢屏　译

编注　参见本卷第 21 首编注。

34. THE NIGHTINGALE

  As it fell upon a day
  In the merry month of May,
  Sitting in a pleasant shade①
  Which a grove of myrtles made②,
5   Beasts did leap and birds did sing,
  Trees did grow and plants did spring,
  Every thing did banish moan
  Save the Nightingale alone.
  She, poor bird, as all forlorn,
10   Lean'd her breast up-till a thorn③,
  And there sung the dolefull'st ditty
  That to hear it was great pity④,
  Fie, fie, fie, now would she cry;
  Tereu, tereu, by and by:
15   That to hear her so complain
  Scarce I could from tears refrain;
  For her griefs so lively shown⑤
  Made me think upon mine own.
  — Ah, thought I, thou mourn'st in vain,
20   None takes pity on thy pain:

---

① *Sitting*: 'as I was sitting.'
② *grove*: so in the original and in the *Passionate Pilgrim*; *England's Helicon* has 'group.'
③ *up-till*: 'up to.'
④ *That* is the conjunction, = 'so that.'
⑤ *lively*: 'vividly.'

34. 夜莺

巴恩菲尔德

在欢乐的五月里
恰逢有一天,
我坐在舒适的荫凉处
头顶上有一丛长春藤攀援,
处处野兽奔逐,鸟儿啼啭, 5
万木葱茏,百草吐艳,
世间的万物都已忘掉了忧愁
唯独那只夜莺郁郁寡欢。
她呀,可怜的鸟儿,神色凄苦,
胸脯靠着蒺藜, 10
低吟着一支小曲悲楚哀怨
让人听着实在可怜。
啾、啾、啾,这时她在哭诉;
嘟噜、嘟噜,一会儿又愁肠欲断:
听着她满腹冤屈 15
我止不住泪流满面;
她的痛苦是这样历历在目,
让我也想起自己的苦难。
——唉,我思量,你忧伤也是枉然,
谁也不会把你可怜; 20

Senseless trees, they cannot hear thee,
Ruthless beasts, they will not cheer thee;
King Pandion, he is dead,
All thy friends are lapp'd in lead[①];
All thy fellow birds do sing
Careless of thy sorrowing:
Even so, poor bird, like thee
None alive will pity me.

R. BARNFIELD.

[①] *lapp'd in lead*: 'enclosed in leaden coffins.'

没心肝的树啊，它们充耳不闻，
残忍的野兽，也不把你鼓舞、慰勉；
潘狄翁国王已魂归九天①，
你的挚友也都进了铅造的墓棺：
所有的小鸟还在婉转歌唱，
毫不理睬你正遭受着苦难：
正是这样，可怜的鸟儿，我像你
活着的谁也不把我可怜。

付勇林　译

25

编注 理查德·巴恩菲尔德（Richard Barnfield，1574—1627），英国学者及诗人，主要作品有《钟情的牧羊人》(*Passionate Pilgrim*)等。

---

① 潘狄翁（Pandion）是古希腊雅典王。传说他的大女婿忒瑞俄斯奸污他的次女菲罗墨拉后割去了她的舌头，但菲罗墨拉将受辱之事织进一件绣袍示以其姊普罗克涅。普罗克涅杀子飨其夫，携菲罗墨拉逃走，忒瑞俄斯持斧追赶，众神把他们三人都变为鸟。菲罗墨拉被变成了一只夜莺。——编注者

35. 'CARE-CHARMER SLEEP'

Care-charmer Sleep, son of the sable Night,
    Brother to Death, in silent darkness born,
Relieve my languish, and restore the light;
    With dark forgetting of my care return.

And let the day be time enough to mourn①
The shipwreck of my ill-adventured youth;
    Let waking eyes suffice to wail their scorn②,
Without the torment of the night's untruth.

Cease, dreams, the images of day-desires,
    To model forth the passions of the morrow③;
Never let rising Sun approve you liars④
    To add more grief to aggravate my sorrow;

Still let me sleep, embracing clouds⑤ in vain,
And never wake to feel the day's disdain.

                                S. DANIEL.

---

① *let the day be time enough*, etc.; *i.e.* let not my sleep be but a continuation of my waking sorrows with all the added exaggerations of dreamland.
② *their scorn*: 'the scorn in which they see I am held.'
③ 'And you dreams, which do but re-echo my waking thoughts, come not to anticipate the suffering that I shall encounter next day.'
④ *Never let rising Sun approve you liars*: 'do not paint things worse than they will prove to be when the next day comes.'
⑤ *embracing clouds*: 'dreaming in a world of pure fancy.'

35. "驱愁的睡神呵"

丹尼尔

驱愁的睡神呵,漆黑的夜神之子,
　你,死神的胞弟,在幽暗中诞生,
祛除我的愁思吧,让光明复归故里①;
　复归故里,与忧虑悄然辞行。

悠悠白日已足以让我哀吟　　　　　　　　　　　　5
人生沉浮,青春时荒谬的冒险:
　睁着眼已够去泣诉世人的薄情,
　就别让夜的虚伪来将我磨难。

梦啊,你这白日欲望的幻像,
　请别再把来日的痛苦产生,　　　　　　　　　　10
别让东升的朝阳赞赏你说谎
　使我旧伤未除又添上了新恨:

还让我睡吧,徒劳地拥抱幻云,
别让我醒来去领受白日的欺凌。

付勇林　译

编注　塞缪尔·丹尼尔(Samuel Daniel,1562—1619),英国宫廷诗人。这首诗系他的十四行诗集《迪莉娅》(*Delia*,1592)第51首。

---

① 诗人感到清醒的世界太黑暗,故把睡眠称为"光明复归"。——编注者

36. MADRIGAL

Take, O take those lips away
    That so sweetly were forsworn,
And those eyes, the break of day,
    Lights that do mislead the morn[①]:
But my kisses bring again,
        Bring again —
Seals of love, but seal'd in vain.
        Seal'd in vain!

                      W. SHAKESPEARE.

[①] *Lights that do mislead the morn*: i.e. her eyes are so bright that the morn takes them for the Sun — a common conceit of the period.

36. 情歌

莎士比亚

莫以负心唇,
　婉转弄辞巧:
莫以薄幸眼,
　颠倒迷昏晓;
定情密吻乞君还,
当日深盟今已寒!

朱生豪　译

编注　此诗选自《一报还一报》(*Measure for Measure*)第四幕第一场,表达了玛利安娜被她的未婚夫安哲鲁遗弃后的凄凉心情。标题《情歌》系《金库》原编者所加。

37. LOVE'S FAREWELL

Since there's no help, come let us kiss and part, —
    Nay I have done, you get no more of me;
And I am glad, yea, glad with all my heart,
    That thus so cleanly I myself can free[①];

Shake hands for ever, cancel all our vows,
    And when we meet at any time again,
Be it not seen in either of our brows
    That we one jot of former love retain.

Now at the last gasp of love's latest breath,
    When, his pulse failing, passion speechless lies,
When faith is kneeling, by his bed of death,
    And innocence is closing up his eyes,

— Now if thou would'st, when all have given him over,
From death to life thou might'st him yet recover!

M. DRAYTON.

---

① *cleanly*: 'entirely.'

37. 爱的告别

迈克尔·德莱顿

既然没有办法了,让我们亲吻分离,
    我为你做过的,你再也不能从我得去;
我欢喜,是呀,我满心欢喜,
    我这样完全摆脱了自己。

握手永别,取消我们所有的誓言,
    而且无论何时再见,
不要显在我们各自的眉间
    我们保存了我们前恋的一星一点。

现在爱的临终呼吸发出最后喘息,
    他的脉搏衰微,热情安卧无语,
信仰跪在他的死榻一隅,
    无辜在将他的双眼合起,——

假如你愿,在一切抛弃他的瞬间,
    你仍然可以使他从死里生还!

李霁野 译

编注 迈克尔·德莱顿(Michael Drayton,1563—1631),英国诗人。这首十四行诗系他一五九三年出版的诗集《意念,牧人之歌》(*Idea, the Shepherd's Garland*)第61首。

38. TO HIS LUTE

My lute, be as thou wert when thou didst grow
    With thy green mother in some shady grove,
    When immelodious winds but made thee move,
And birds their ramage did on thee bestow[①].

    Since that dear Voice which did thy sounds approve,
Which wont in such harmonious strains to flow[②],
    Is reft from Earth to tune those spheres above,
What art thou but a harbinger of woe?

Thy pleasing notes be pleasing notes no more,
    But orphans' wailings to the fainting ear;
    Each stroke a sigh, each sound draws forth a tear[③];
For which be silent as in woods before:

Or if that any hand to touch thee deign,
Like widow'd turtle still her loss complain[④].

                              W. DRUMMOND.

---

① *ramage*: 'the song of birds,' from the French *ramage*, with the same meaning.
② *wont*, now used only as an adjective, was formerly the past tense of won, or wone, meaning to dwell, to be accustomed.
③ *Each stroke a sigh*: 'each touch of the strings ⟨draws forth⟩ a sigh.'
④ *turtle*: 'turtle-dove.' *still*: 'continually.' *her loss*: 'the loss of her,' i.e. the owner of the 'dear Voice.'

38. 致琵琶

德拉蒙德

我的琵琶,还去到矮丛下面,
  同你绿色母亲在原来地方,
  那时噪声的风使你摇晃,
鸟儿将狂野的歌落在你的身边。

  那亲爱的声音曾经将你的声调赞赏, 5
那声音一贯是和谐流利,
  你除了传送哀愁,还能做什么呢,
现在它已经离开大地,到了天上?

使人喜悦的音调已不再使人喜悦,
  听力衰微的耳朵听来只是孤儿哀泣; 10
  每一声响只使人流泪叹气;
因此像以前在林间一样保持沉默:

假如有人要用手抚摸你,
像失偶的鸽子,永远悲叹她逝去。

李霁野　译

39. BLIND LOVE

O me! what eyes hath love put in my head
    Which have no correspondence with true sight;
Or if they have, where is my judgement fled
    That censures falsely what they see aright[①]?

If that be fair whereon my false eyes dote,
    What means the world to say it is not so?
If it be not, then love doth well denote
    Love's eye is not so true as all men's; No,

How can it? O how can love's eye be true,
    That is so vex'd with watching and with tears?
No marvel then though I mistake my view;
    The sun itself sees not till heaven clears.

O cunning Love! with tears thou keep'st me blind,
Lest eyes well-seeing thy foul faults should find!

W. SHAKESPEARE.

---

① *censures*: 'estimates' — without the modern idea of blaming.

39. 盲目的爱

莎士比亚

天哪,爱赐给我的是什么眼力,
 它们所见与真情实景大不一样!
如果说所见是真,理智在哪里,
 它竟然把眼中的真实判为虚妄?

若我昏花的眼睛迷恋的是真美,
 那世人都说并非如此又是何由?
若所见不美,那爱就明确意味
 情人的眼睛不如常人的看得透。

何以至此?哦,爱眼怎会明晰,
 它既要望眼欲穿又要泪眼汪汪?
所以我即便看花眼也不足为奇,
 因太阳也须晴日方可明鉴八方。

狡猾的爱哟,你用泪弄花我眼,
 唯恐明眼会发现你丑陋的缺陷。

曹明伦 译

编注 此诗系莎氏十四行诗第 148 首。

40. THE UNFAITHFUL SHEPHERDESS

While that the sun with his beams hot
    Scorchéd the fruits in vale and mountain,
Philon the shepherd, late forgot[①],
    Sitting beside a crystal fountain,
        In shadow of a green oak tree
    Upon his pipe this song play'd he:
Adieu Love, adieu Love, untrue Love,
Untrue Love, untrue Love, adieu Love;
Your mind is light, soon lost for new love.

So long as I was in your sight
    I was your heart, your soul, and treasure;
And evermore you sobb'd and sigh'd
    Burning in flames beyond all measure:
        — Three days endured your love to me,
    And it was lost in other three!
Adieu Love, adieu Love, untrue Love,
Untrue Love, untrue Love, adieu Love;
Your mind is light, soon lost for new love.

Another Shepherd yon did see
    To whom your heart was soon enchainéd;
Full soon your love was leapt from me,
    Full soon my place he had obtainéd.

---

① *late forgot*: lately deserted by his mistress.

40. 不忠实的牧羊女

无名氏

太阳炽烤着幽谷和山岗,
  使果实枯萎,草木焦黄,
新近失恋的牧羊人菲朗,
  坐在一条清彻晶莹的溪旁,
   在一棵橡树的阴影之中   5
   他吹出的笛声婉转悠扬:
告别了,姑娘,不忠实的姑娘;
你的心儿是那样轻飘,
新欢使你顷刻将旧情淡忘。

当我在你身边的那些时光,   10
  我是你的爱人、灵魂和宝藏,
你常常是这样叹息、泣诉,
  你的情焰曾发射过度的光芒:
   可你对我的爱情只延续了三天,
   另外三天爱情的火焰就死亡! 15
告别了,姑娘,不忠实的姑娘;
你的心儿是那样轻飘,
新欢使你顷刻将旧情淡忘。

你看见了另一位牧羊少年,
  你的心儿立刻把他迷上,   20
你的爱情倏然离我而去,
  他代替我做了你的情郎。

>   Soon came a third, your love to win,
>   And we were out and he was in.
> 25   Adieu Love, adieu Love, untrue Love,
>   Untrue Love, untrue Love, adieu Love;
>   Your mind is light, soon lost for new love.
>
>   Sure you have made me passing glad①
>   That you your mind so soon removéd,
> 30   Before that I the leisure had
>   To choose you for my best belovéd:
>   For all your love was past and done
>   Two days before it was begun: —
>   Adieu Love, adieu Love, untrue Love,
> 35   Untrue Love, untrue Love, adieu Love;
>   Your mind is light, soon lost for new love.

ANON.

---

① *passing glad*: 'surpassingly glad.'

很快第三位少年赢得了你的爱。
  你俩双双而去,把我们丢在一旁。
告别了,姑娘,不忠实的姑娘,   *25*
你的心儿是那样轻飘,
新欢使你顷刻将旧情淡忘。

你的确使我心花怒放,
  高兴你这么快就改弦易张,
当我还来不及有空暇考虑   *30*
  选择你做我未来的新娘:
    尽管你三天前才开始的爱情
    现在已飘然而去,不知何方:——
告别了,姑娘,不忠实的姑娘,
你的心儿是那样轻飘,   *35*
新欢使你顷刻将旧情淡忘。

          曹明伦 译

41. A RENUNCIATION

If women could be fair, and yet not fond①,
    Or that their love were firm, not fickle still②,
I would not marvel that they make men bond③
    By service long to purchase their good will;
But when I see how frail those creatures are,
I muse that men forget themselves so far.

To mark the choice they make, and how they change,
    How oft from Phoebus they do flee to Pan;
Unsettled still, like haggards wild they range④,
    These gentle birds that fly from man to man;
Who would not scorn and shake them from the fist⑤.
And let them fly, fair fools, which way they list?

Yet for disport we fawn and flatter both⑥,
    To pass the time when nothing else can please,
And train them to our lure with subtle oath⑦,

---

① *fond*: 'foolish.' See note to No. 17, l. 12.
② *Or that*: 'if that' is often found for 'if'. If the subordinate sentence contains two clauses, the second is often introduced by 'that' alone.
③ *bond*: 'whether we be bond or free.'
④ *haggards*: 'wild hawks.'
⑤ *from the fist*: where the hawk was carried in the mediaeval sport of hawking.
⑥ *disport*: 'sport.'
⑦ *lure*: anther hawking metaphor; a lure was a bunch of feathers used to recall the bird to the falconer.

41. 死心断念

维尔

假如女人漂亮而不愚蠢,
　或是爱情专一而又坚定,
毫不奇怪,这会使得男人
　对她们效忠,买她们的心;
当我发见她们意志不坚,　　　　　　　　　　5
我慨叹男人也行为失检。

她们选定对象,却又变更,
　从漂亮张三,到丑怪李四①;
永远无常,野鹰一般飞腾,
　是驯顺的鸟,却逢人追驰;　　　　　　　10
谁瞧得起她们,留在手上,
不让漂亮蠢货任意飘荡?

为了取乐,我们奉承低头,
　不妨消磨时间,趁此排遣,
并用诡誓引诱她们上钩,　　　　　　　　15

---

① 此行原诗分别用希腊神话中的太阳神(Phoebus)和潘神(Pan)比喻美男子和相貌丑陋的男人。——译者

Till, weary of their wiles, ourselves we ease①;
And then we say when we their fancy try②,
To play with fools, O what a fool was I!

        E. VERE, EARL OF OXFORD.

---

① *ourselves we ease*: 'we relieve ourselves of them.'
② *when we their fancy try*: 'when we make trial of their love.'

到厌腻她们诡诈,给摔开;
试过她们的风情,我们说,
玩弄傻货,自己何等傻货!

戴镏龄　译

编注　爱德华·维尔(Edward Vere,1550—1604),英国贵族诗人,世袭牛津伯爵。

42. 'BLOW, BLOW, THOU WINTER WIND'

            Blow, blow, thou winter wind,
            Thou art not so unkind[1]
                As man's ingratitude;
            Thy tooth is not so keen
5   Because thou art not seen,
                Although thy breath be rude.
    Heigh ho! sing heigh ho! unto the green holly:
    Most friendship is feigning, most loving mere folly:
           Then, heigh ho! the holly!
10   This life is most jolly.

            Freeze, freeze, thou bitter sky,
            That dost not bite so nigh[2]
                As benefits forgot:
            Though thou the waters warp[3],
15   Thy sting is not so sharp
                As friend remember'd not[4].
    Heigh ho! sing heigh ho! unto the green holly:
    Most friendship is feigning, most loving mere folly:
           Then, heigh ho! the holly!
20   This life is most jolly.

                                    W. SHAKESPEARE.

---

[1] *unkind*: 'unnatural.'
[2] *bite so nigh*: 'so deeply.'
[3] *warp*: now meaning to bend, had originally the idea of changing or turning; the effect of the wind is to change the appearance of the water either by ruffling its surface or by freezing it.
[4] *friend remember'd not*: 'the forgetting of one friend by another.'

42. "不惧冬风凛冽"

莎士比亚

> 不惧冬风凛冽,
> 　风威远难邋及
> 　　人世之寡情;
> 　其为气也虽厉,
> 　其牙尚非甚锐, 　　　　　　　　　5
> 　　风体本无形。
> 噫嘻乎!且向冬青歌一曲:
> 友交皆虚妄,恩爱痴人逐。
> 　噫嘻乎冬青!
> 　可乐唯此生。 　　　　　　　　10

> 不愁亘天冰雪,
> 　其寒尚难邋及
> 　　受施而忘恩;
> 　风皱满池碧水,
> 　利刺尚难邋比 　　　　　　　　15
> 　　捐旧之友人。
> 噫嘻乎!且向冬青歌一曲:
> 友交皆虚妄,恩爱痴人逐。
> 　噫嘻乎冬青!
> 　可乐唯此生。

朱生豪　译

编注 此诗选自《皆大欢喜》第二幕第七场,诗中将大自然的善与人类的恶进行了对照。

43. MADRIGAL

My thoughts hold mortal strife
I do detest my life,
And with lamenting cries,
Peace to my soul to bring①,
Oft call that prince which here doth monarchize②:
— But he, grim grinning King,
Who caitiffs scorns, and doth the blest surprise③,
Late having deck'd with beauty's rose his tomb,
Disdains to crop a weed and will not come.

                                              W. DRUMMOND.

---

① *to bring*: 'in order that I may bring.'
② *monarchize*: the only entirely independent sovereign in the world is Death.
③ *blest*: 'fortunate, happy.'

43. 小曲

德拉蒙德

我的心进行着殊死的战争，
我实在憎恶我的生命，
为使我的灵魂得到安息，
我发出阵阵悲哀的呼声，
我时常呼唤那位君主，那位至高无上的死神： 5
——可他，冷酷狰狞的君王哟，
他鄙视懦夫弱汉，给人意外之幸运，
他只用美人的蔷薇去装点他的墓碑，
不屑为刈一株小草而屈尊光临。

曹明伦　译

44. DIRGE OF LOVE

    Come away, come away, Death,
    And in sad cypres let me be laid;
        Fly away, fly away, breath;
    I am slain by a fair cruel maid.
    My shroud of white, stuck all with yew,
            O prepare it!
    My part of death, no one so true
            Did share it.

    Not a flower, not a flower sweet
    On my black coffin let there be strown[1];
        Not a friend, not a friend greet
    My poor corpse, where my bones shall be thrown:
    A thousand thousand sighs to save,
            Lay me, O where
    Sad true lover never find my grave[2],
            To weep there.

                          W. SHAKESPEARE.

---

[1] *black*: *i.e.* covered with a black pall.
[2] *never find*: this is subjunctive, = 'may never find.'

44. 爱的挽歌

莎士比亚

过来吧,过来吧,死神!
　　让我横陈在凄凉的柏棺的中央①;
飞去吧,飞去吧,浮生!
　　我被害于一个狠心的美貌姑娘。
为我罩上白色的殓衾铺满紫杉;　　　　　　　　　　　5
没有一个真心的人为我而悲哀。

莫让一朵花儿甜柔,
　　撒上了我那黑色的、黑色的棺材;
没有一个朋友迓候
　　我尸身,不久我的骨骸将会散开。　　　　　　10
免得多情的人们千万次的感伤,
请把我埋葬在无从凭吊的荒场。

朱生豪　译

编注　此诗选自《第十二夜》第二幕第四场。

---

① 此处"柏棺"原文为cypres,自来注家均肯定应作crape(丧礼用之黑色皱纱)解释;按字面解cypres为一种杉柏之属,径译"柏棺",在语调上似乎更为适当,故仍将错就错,据字臆译。——译者

45. FIDELE

Fear no more the heat o'the sun
    Nor the furious winter's rages;
Thou thy worldly task hast done,
    Home art gone and ta'en thy wages:
Golden lads and girls all must[①],
As chimney-sweepers, come to dust.

Fear no more the frown o'the great,
    Thou art past the tyrant's stroke;
Care no more to clothe and eat;
    To thee the reed is as the oak[②]:
The sceptre, learning, physic, must
All follow this, and come to dust.

Fear no more the lightning-flash
    Nor the all-dreaded thunder-stone[③];
Fear not slander, censure rash;
    Thou hast finish'd joy and moan:
All lovers young, all lovers must
Consign to thee, and come to dust[④].

W. SHAKESPEARE.

---

① *Golden*: 'resembling gold, either in beauty or value.' Cf. the Golden Age, the Golden Legend, the Golden Treasury, etc.
② *the reed is as the oak*: i.e. all earthly things, whether strong or weak, are equally unimportant.
③ *thunder-stone*: 'thunderbolt.'
④ *Consign to thee*: 'seal the same contract with thee.'

45. 斐苔尔

莎士比亚

不用再怕骄阳晒蒸,
　　不用再怕寒风凛冽;
世间工作你已完成,
　　领了工资回家安息。
才子娇娃同归泉壤,　　　　　　　　　5
正像扫烟囱人一样。

不用再怕贵人嗔怒,
　　你已超脱暴君威力;
无须再为衣食忧虑,
　　芦苇橡树了无区别。　　　　　　10
健儿身手,学士心灵,
帝王蝼蚁同化埃尘。

不用再怕闪电光亮,
　　不用再怕雷霆暴作;
何须畏惧谗人诽谤,　　　　　　　　15
　　你已阅尽世间忧乐。
无限尘寰痴男怨女,
人天一别,埋愁黄土。

　　　　　　　　　朱生豪　译

编注　此诗选自《辛白林》(*Cymbeline*)第四幕第二场。原诗共四节,《金库》原编者删去了最末一节并加标题《斐苔尔》。

46. A SEA DIRGE

Full fathom five thy father lies;
    Of his bones are coral made;
Those are pearls that were his eyes;
    Nothing of him that doth fade
But doth suffer a sea-change①
Into something rich and strange.
Sea-nymphs hourly ring his knell;
Hark! now I hear them, —
    Ding, dong, bell.

W. SHAKESPEARE.

---

① *Nothing of him that doth fade*, etc.; *i. e.* every perishable part of him is undergoing a change. *But doth*: 'which does not.'

46. 海的挽歌

莎士比亚

五㖊的水深处躺着你的父亲，
　　他的骨骼已化成珊瑚；
他眼睛是耀眼的明珠；
　　他消失的全身没有一处不曾
受到海水神奇的变幻，　　　　　　　　　　5
化成瑰宝，富丽而珍怪。
海的女神时时摇起他的丧钟，
　　叮！咚！
听！我现在听到了叮咚的丧钟。

朱生豪　译

编注　此诗选自《暴风雨》(*The Tempest*)第一幕第二场。标题《海的挽歌》系《金库》原编者所加。

47. A LAND DIRGE

Call for the robin-redbreast and the wren,
    Since o'er shady groves they hover
    And with leaves and flowers do cover
The friendless bodies of unburied men.
    Call unto his funeral dole①
    The ant, the field-mouse, and the mole,
To rear him hillocks that shall keep him warm
And (when gay tombs are robb'd) sustain no harm;
But keep the wolf far thence, that's foe to men,
For with his nails he'll dig them up again②.

                                  J. WEBSTER.

---

① *dole*: 'lament,' from the Lat. *dolor*.
② *them*: the 'men' of the previous line.

47. 考奈丽雅挽歌①

威伯斯特

招唤知更雀和鹪鹩一齐来帮一手，
它们在树丛里跳去跳来，
唤来用树叶和花朵去掩盖
无亲无故的没有人掩埋的尸首。
唤来参加他的丧礼—— 5
野地的耗子、土拨鼠、蚂蚁，
给他翻上些土堆让他温暖，
逢陵墓盗挖的时候，不至于遭难；
要赶走豺狼，那是人类的仇敌， 10
它们会用爪子挖掘得一片狼藉。

卞之琳　译

编注　约翰·威伯斯特（John Webster，1580？—1625），英国诗剧作家，著名作品有《白魔》（*The White Devil*，1612）和《马尔菲公爵夫人》（*The Duchess of Malfi*，1623）。这两部都是悲剧，诗风峭拔，颇见功力，有人说他仅次于莎士比亚。

---

① 这首挽歌是威伯斯特一六一二年发表的悲剧《白魔》中考奈丽雅（Cornelia）的歌词。查尔斯·兰姆在《英国戏剧诗人范例》一书中说："我从未见过什么能比得上这首挽歌的，除了（莎士比亚的）《暴风雨》里那首使斐迪南想起他父亲淹死的小曲。正如那首是关于水的，轻盈似水；这首是关于土的，泥土气重。两者都感觉那么强烈，似乎融进了所思考的元素。"——译者

48. POST MORTEM

    If thou survive my well-contented day①
    When that churl Death my bones with dust shall cover②,
    And shalt by fortune once more re-survey
        These poor rude lines of thy deceasèd lover③;

5   Compare them with the bettering of the time,
        And though they be outstripp'd by every pen,
    Reserve them for my love, not for their rhyme④
    Exceeded by the height of happier men.

    O then vouchsafe me but this loving thought —
10   'Had my friend's muse grown with this growing age,
    A dearer birth than this his love had brought
        To march in ranks of better equipage⑤;

    But since he died, and poets better prove,
    Theirs for their style I'll read, his for his love.'

W. SHAKESPEARE.

---

① *well-contented*: the epithet is transferred from the poet, who is quite content to die, to the day of his death.
② *churl*: a word used from early times as the opposite of noble or gentle. Death is no gentleman, for he is quite regardless of people's feelings.
③ *lover*: in the seventeenth century this word had not its present narrow meaning, but was applied to any one who loved another.
④ *Reserve them*: 'keep them in your possession.' *rhyme*: in the wide sense, 'verses.'
⑤ *ranks of better equipage*: 'better equipped ranks,' i.e. making a fairer show of poetic ability.

48. 死后

莎士比亚

假如我寿终正寝后你尚在世,
　假如死神早早将我埋入黄土,
那时你若偶然翻开我的遗诗,
　重读你亡友这些粗陋的词赋;

当你把拙笔与后世华章比较, 5
　发现每一新篇都远胜过它们,
请你为了我的爱而保存拙稿,
　虽它们不及幸运天才的妙文。

哦,那时请赐我这一份爱意:
　"吾友之缪斯若能生在今朝, 10
他的爱能写出更华美的诗句,
　能与盛世诗豪词杰共领风骚;

但他已去,而时人更富文采,
那我品今贤才藻,读他的爱。"

曹明伦　译

编注　此诗系莎氏十四行诗第 32 首。诗人希望他的爱友保存他的诗,因为他的诗充满了真实的感情。

49. THE TRIUMPH OF DEATH

No longer mourn for me when I am dead
    Than you shall hear the surly sullen bell①
Give warning to the world, that I am fled
    From this vile world, with vilest worms to dwell;

Nay, if you read this line, remember not
    The hand that writ it; for I love you so,
That I in your sweet thoughts would be forgot
    If thinking on me then should make you woe②.

O if, I say, you look upon this verse
    When I perhaps compounded am with clay③,
Do not so much as my poor name rehearse,
    But let your love even with my life decay;

Lest the wise world should look into your moan④,
And mock you with me after I am gone.

W. SHAKESPEARE.

---

① *No longer ... Than you shall hear*: 'only so long as you hear.'
② *woe*: 'sorrowful.' Its use as an adjective, though now obsolete, is common in Spenser.
③ *compounded*: 'united.'
④ *wise world*: too wise, that is, to grieve over what is gone.

49. 死的胜利

莎士比亚

我死去的时候请别为我哀戚,
　　那时你会听见阴沉沉的丧钟
向世人宣告我已经脱身而去,
　　已离开这浊世去伴蠢豕蛆虫。

若读此诗也别去想写它的手, 5
　　因为我对你的情意山高水长,
以致我宁愿被你遗忘在脑后,
　　也不愿你因为想到我而悲伤。

哦,我是说如果你读到此诗,
　　而那时我也许已经化为尘土, 10
你千万别念叨我卑微的名字,
　　让你的爱与我一道朽于棺木;

以免聪明人看出我死后你伤心,
像嘲笑我一样把你也当作笑柄。

　　　　　　　　　　　曹明伦　译

编注 此诗系莎氏十四行诗第 71 首。

50. MADRIGAL

Tell me where is Fancy bred[①],
Or in the heart, or in the head?
How begot, how nourishéd?
    Reply, reply.
It is engender'd in the eyes,
With gazing fed; and Fancy dies[②]
In the cradle where it lies:
    Let us all ring Fancy's knell;
    I'll begin it, — Ding, dong, bell,
        — Ding, dong, bell.

W. SHAKESPEARE.

---

① *Fancy*: 'love.'

② *Fancy dies*, etc.: love, which is born in the eyes, may die there before coming to maturity; which means no more than that the eyes can show the birth and speedy death of love.

50. 情歌

莎士比亚

告诉我爱情生长在何方?
还是在脑海?还是在心房?
它怎样发生?它怎样成长?
　　回答我,回答我。
爱情的火在眼睛里点亮, 5
凝视是爱情生活的滋养,
　它的摇篮便是它的坟堂。
　让我们把爱的丧钟鸣响。
　　叮珰!叮珰!
　　叮珰!叮珰! 10

朱生豪　译

编注　此诗选自《威尼斯商人》(*The Merchant of Venice*)第三幕第二场。标题《情歌》系《金库》原编者所加。

51. CUPID AND CAMPASPE

Cupid and my Campaspe play'd
At cards for kisses; Cupid paid:
He stakes his quiver, bow, and arrows,
His mother's doves, and team of sparrows;
Loses them too; then down he throws
The coral of his lip, the rose
Growing on 's cheek (but none knows how)[①];
With these, the crystal of his brow[②],
And then the dimple of his chin;
All these did my Campaspe win;
At last he set her both his eyes[③]—
She won, and Cupid blind did rise.
  O Love! has she done this to thee?
  What shall, alas! become of me?

J. LYLY.

---

① *on 's*: 'on his.'
② *crystal*: 'transparent clearness.'
③ *set*: 'staked.'

51. 爱神和康帕丝

黎里

爱神和康帕丝斗牌①
赌接吻,爱神被击败;
他又赌箭筒,弓和矢,
母亲的麻雀和鸽子②;
输了,摔下嘴唇珊瑚,　　　　　　　　　　5
两颊上的玫瑰花株,
泛起的那无名面红;
加上眉宇晶亮玲珑,
还有下巴上的酒涡,
通通被康帕丝赢走。　　　　　　　　　　10
最后,他拿两眼去赌,
又输了,他变成矇瞽,
　　爱神,她待你是这样?
　　哎,什么是我的下场?

戴镏龄　译

编注 约翰·黎里(John Lyly, 1554？—1606),英国文艺复兴时代的剧作家,他第一个用散文体代替诗体创作喜剧。本诗选自喜剧《康帕丝》(Campaspe)第三幕第五场,诗中形象而活泼地描绘了美和爱的魅力,这种魅力甚至支配了爱神。

---

① 爱神指维纳斯之子丘比特(Cupid);康帕丝(Campaspe,又译作坎巴斯帕)传说是古希腊亚历山大皇帝的爱妃,以美貌著称。——译者
② 麻雀和鸽子等是献给维纳斯的鸟,为她拉车,此外,还有燕子和天鹅。——译者

52. 'PACK, CLOUDS, AWAY, AND WELCOME DAY'

Pack, clouds, away, and welcome day,
With night we banish sorrow;
Sweet air blow soft, mount lark aloft
To give my Love good-morrow[1]!
Wings from the wind to please her mind
Notes from the lark I'll borrow;
Bird prune thy wing, nightingale sing,
To give my Love good-morrow;
    To give my Love good-morrow
    Notes from them all I'll borrow.

Wake from thy nest, Robin-red-breast,
Sing birds in every furrow;
And from each bill, let music shrill
Give my fair Love good-morrow!
Blackbird and thrush in every bush,
Stare, linnet, and cock-sparrow[2],
You pretty elves, amongst yourselves
Sing my fair Love good-morrow!
    To give my Love good-morrow
    Sing birds in every furrow!

T. HEYWOOD.

---

[1] *good-morrow*: 'good morning.'
[2] *Stare*: 'starling,' which is a diminutive of the former.

52. "云，散开吧，迎接白天"

海伍德

云，散开吧，迎接白天，
　　夜尽了，驱走忧伤；
朝气轻吹，云雀升起，
　　给我爱早安送上！
我要借云雀的歌声，　　　　　　　　　　5
　　趁风娱她的心肠；
鸟儿整翅，流莺清啭，
　　给我爱早安送上！
　　　要借大家的歌声，
　　　给我爱早安送上。　　　　　　　10

知更鸟从窠里醒起，
　　田沟上鸟语响亮；
每张鸟喙鸣声清新，
　　给我爱早安送上！
枝头的乌鸦和画眉，　　　　　　　　　15
　　八哥、红鸟、麻雀郎，
可爱的小精灵们，大家
　　给我爱早安送上！
　　　田沟上鸟语响亮，
　　　给我爱早安送上。　　　　　　　20

戴镏龄　译

编注　托马斯·海伍德（Thomas Heywood，1570?—1641?），英国剧作家，本诗选自他以罗马神话为题材写成的戏剧《鲁克丽丝受辱记》（*Rape of Lucrece*，1608）第四幕第六场。

53. PROTHALAMION

Calm was the day, and through the trembling air
    Sweet-breathing Zephyrus did softly play①—
A gentle spirit, that lightly did delay
Hot Titan's beams, which then did glister fair;
    When I (whom sullen care,
Through discontent of my long fruitless stay
    In princes' court, and expectation vain
Of idle hopes, which still do fly away
    Like empty shadows, did afflict my brain)
    Walk'd forth to ease my pain
Along the shore of silver-streaming Thames;
Whose rutty bank, the which his river hems②,
    Was painted all with variable flowers,
And all the meads adorn'd with dainty gems
    Fit to deck maidens' bowers,
    And crown their paramours③
Against the bridal day, which is not long④:
Sweet Thames! run softly, till I end my song.

There in a meadow by the river's side
    A flock of nymphs I chancéd to espy,

---

① *Zephyrus*: 'the west wind.'
② *rutty*: 'abounding in ruts.'
③ *paramours*: 'lovers.'
④ *is not long*: 'is close at hand.'

53. 婚前曲

斯宾塞

宁静的日子呀,阵阵清风
　　轻微地吹拂,在空中飘荡,
　　大气柔和,使晴空的骄阳①
明媚温煦,不致烧灼碧空;
　　　我正感不受用, 5
由于淹留王廷常是失意,
　　期望终成梦想,无从实现②,
冀求的东西都徒然飞逝,
　　无影无踪,心情苦不堪言,
　　　于是散步排遣, 10
沿着清凌凌的泰晤士河,
两岸上发出稠密的枝柯,
　　各种奇卉,无不鲜花怒放,
青草地上珠光宝气繁多,
　　　宜于装饰闺房, 15
　　　插在情人头上,
迎接佳期,屈指就在目下,
可爱的河,轻轻流到歌罢。

河边上呈现出一块草坪,
　　那儿我瞥见仙女一大群, 20

---

① 此处"骄阳",原文作 Hot Titan's beam,即希腊神话中的"提坦",天神乌拉诺斯和地神该亚的十二个子女,其中之一是太阳神赫利俄斯的父亲,此处喻太阳。——编注者
② 斯宾塞曾经屡次想要晋升伊丽莎白宫廷,均未成功。——编注者

All lovely daughters of the flood thereby①,
With goodly greenish locks all loose untied
    As each had been a bride;
And each one had a little wicker basket
    Made of fine twigs, entrailéd curiously②,
In which they gather'd flowers to fill their flasket③,
And with fine fingers cropt full featéously④
    The tender stalks on high.
Of every sort which in that meadow grew
They gather'd some; the violet, pallid blue,
    The little daisy that at evening closes,
The virgin lily and the primrose true,
    With store of vermeil roses⑤,
    To deck their bridegrooms' posies
Against the bridal day, which was not long:
Sweet Thames! run softly, till I end my song.

With that I saw two swans of goodly hue
    Come softly swimming down along the lee⑥;
    Two fairer birds I yet did never see;
The snow which doth the top of Pindus strow
    Did never whiter show,
Nor Jove himself, when he a swan would be

---

① *the flood thereby*: 'the stream which ran beside them.'
② *entrailéd*: 'entwined.'
③ *flasket*: 'a long shallow basket' (Johnson); the word is a diminutive of 'flask.'
④ *full featéously*: 'very skilfully or elegantly.'
⑤ *vermeil*: a poetic form of 'vermilion.'
⑥ *the lee*: here and in l. 115 below, Spenser uses this word for 'stream' or 'current.'

好姑娘,在邻近川泽成长,
　　头上飘散着美丽的青鬓,
　　好像新人出聘。
她们都携着一只小柳筐,
　　细条做料子,精工编织成,　　　　　　　　　25
用来采集花枝,满满盛装,
　　纤纤手指,摘取巧妙认真,
　　顶部嫩的花梗。
草原上这样那样花灿烂,
每样采一些,紫罗兰淡蓝,　　　　　　　　　　30
　　黄昏时合上眼睛的雏菊,
以及百合纯洁,樱草烂漫,
　　嫣红玫瑰成束,
　　献作新郎礼物,
迎接佳期,屈指就在目下,　　　　　　　　　　35
可爱的河,轻轻流到歌罢。

接着有漂亮的天鹅一双①,
　　飘飘然在水上顺流下游,
　　平生初见,最美的鸟两头,
雪洒在坪达山的高峰上②,　　　　　　　　　　40
　　输掉白的光芒;
宙父变做天鹅追求妮黛③,

---

① "天鹅一双"象征去参加婚礼的两位贵族新娘。——译者
② 坪达山在希腊北部,山势雄伟,林木茂盛,山顶常为白雪覆盖。——译者
③ 宙父即希腊神话中的主神宙斯,妮黛(又译作"勒达")是斯巴达王后。传说当妮黛在河中洗浴之时,宙父化为一只白天鹅与她亲近,生美人海伦。——编注者

   For love of Leda, whiter did appear;
  Yet Leda was (they say) as white as he,
45   Yet not so white as these, nor nothing near;
    So purely white they were,
  That even the gentle stream, the which them bare,
  Seem'd foul to them, and bade his billows spare
   To wet their silken feathers, lest they might
50   Soil their fair plumes with water not so fair,
    And mar their beauties bright,
    That shone as Heaven's light
  Against their bridal day, which was not long;
  Sweet Thames! run softly, till I end my song.

55   Eftsoons the nymphs, which now had flowers their fill[①],
   Ran all in haste to see that silver brood
   As they came floating on the crystal flood;
  Whom when they saw, they stood amazèd still
    Their wondering eyes to fill;
60   Them seem'd they never saw a sight so fair[②]
   Of fowls, so lovely, that they sure did deem
  Them heavenly born, or to be that same pair
   Which through the sky draw Venus' silver team;
    For sure they did not seem
65   To be begot of any earthly seed,
  But rather angels, or of angels' breed;
   Yet were they bred of summer's heat, they say,
  In sweetest season, when each flower and weed

---

① *Eftsoons*: 'soon after.' *had flowers their fill*: 'flowers, as many as they wanted.'
② *Them seem'd*: 'it seemed to them.'

也比不上这对赛粉欺银；
论白,宙父、妮黛难分好坏,
　但是都难和这一双接近, 45
　　她们异常白净。
轻柔的流水,负载着她们,
似嫌形秽,戒浪花莫溅喷
　她们的洁羽,那样就必然
使浑水给她们带来污痕, 50
　让太阳般美颜
　　因此添上缺陷,
临近佳期,屈指就在目下,
可爱的河,轻轻流到歌罢。

仙女采花不久,收获丰满, 55
　奔去看这对洁白的俦侣,
　　正泛泛而来,清水上飘浮,
姑娘见了,无不感到茫然,
　　惊得直瞪两眼；
这样的美禽,似从未见过, 60
　多可爱呀,一定生在天堂,
或是给爱神挽车的双鹅①,
　挽她的车穿过云霄之上；
　　她们绝对不像
我们这个尘世间的产物, 65
而是天使,或是同一种族。
　据说她们是在夏季出生,
　和煦时节,花草枝叶扶疏,

---

① 此处爱神指维纳斯,她的车由鸟拖曳,参见本卷第51首注②。——编注者

                    The earth did fresh array;
70   So fresh they seem'd as day,
            Even as their bridal day, which was not long:
            Sweet Thames! run softly, till I end my song.

            Then forth they all out of their baskets drew
                    Great store of flowers, the honour of the field,
75   That to the sense did fragrant odours yield,
            All which upon those goodly birds they threw
                    And all the waves did strew,
            That like old Peneus' waters they did seem
                    When down along by pleasant Temper's shore
80   Scatter'd with flowers, through Thessaly they stream,
                    That they appear, through lilies' plenteous store,
                    Like a bride's chamber-floor.
            Two of those nymphs meanwhile two garlands bound
            Of freshest flowers which in that mead they found,
85   The which presenting all in trim array,
            Their snowy foreheads therewithal they crown'd;
                    Whilst one did sing this lay
                    Prepared against that day,
            Against their bridal day, which was not long:
90   Sweet Thames! run softly, till I end my song.

            'Ye gentle birds! the world's fair ornament,
                    And Heaven's glory, whom this happy hour
                    Doth lead unto your lovers' blissful bower,

大地新装披身，
　　好似旭日东升，　　　　　　　　　　　　　70
恰似佳日，屈指就在目下，
可爱的河，轻轻流到歌罢。

仙女从筐里取出许多花，
　　这些都是田野上的光辉，
　　发散出扑鼻的阵阵香味；　　　　　　　75
她们把花撒向好鸟身上，
　　水波吐秀流芳，
像泌罗斯江水流声活活，
　　沿着丹丕的可喜山谷间，
满载花枝，从帖撒利流过①；　　　　　　80
　　有数不尽的百合花，乍看，
　　像香闺的铺板。
这时其中两位仙女挑选
最鲜的花做成两顶花冠，
　　装饰得异常精致而整齐，　　　　　　　85
加在她们的洁白的额端，
　　一位唱着歌词，
　　用于那个日子，
频祝佳期，屈指就在目下，
可爱的河，轻轻流到歌罢。　　　　　　　90

　　"温柔的鸟儿，是人间光采，
　　　　天上荣华，当这幸福时光，
　　　将导入你们情人的新房，

---

① 泌罗斯河，习惯译为珀涅俄斯河（Peneus），发源于希腊北部，流经丹丕的可嘉峪，穿过帖撒利平原，注入东北部的萨罗尼加海湾。传说每隔八年在此河上举行太阳神阿波罗的庆典，届时河面上撒满鲜花。——编注者

Joy may you have, and gentle heart's content
        Of your love's couplement;
And let fair Venus, that is queen of love,
    With her heart-quelling son upon you smile,
Whose smile, they say, hath virtue to remove①
    All love's dislike, and friendship's faulty guile
        For ever to assoil②.
Let endless peace your steadfast hearts accord③,
And blessed plenty wait upon your board;
    And let your bed with pleasures chaste abound,
That fruitful issue may to you afford④
        Which may your foes confound,
        And make your joys redound⑤
Upon your bridal day, which is not long:
Sweet Thames! run softly, till I end my song.'

So ended she; and all the rest around
    To her redoubled that her undersong⑥,
    Which said their bridal day should not be long:
And gentle Echo from the neighbour ground
        Their accents did resound⑦.
So forth those joyous birds did pass along

---

① *virtue to remove*, etc.: 'power to put an end to any distaste which a lover may feel, and once for all to dispel any treachery in the mind of a friend.'

② *assoil*: 'to absolve, forgive,' and so 'get rid of.'

③ *accord*: 'bring into agreement.'

④ *That fruitful issue*, etc.: 'which may give you abundant offspring to uphold you against your enemies.' The succession of the two relatives 'That' and 'Which' is awkward.

⑤ *redound*: lit. 'to overflow,' Lat. *redundare*.

⑥ *undersong*: 'chorus or burden.'

⑦ *resound*: 'repeat'; not often found as a transitive verb.

愿你们高高兴兴,称心开怀,
　　彼此成亲互爱。　　　　　　　　　　95
爱神和戳人心肠的儿子①,
　　请一齐对你们发出微笑,
人们说,他们的笑能够使
　　爱情的厌恶,友谊的花招
　　永排除或取消。　　　　　　　　　　100
祝你们忠贞而永远和睦,
你们每顿餐都饱享口福,
　　你们合欢双栖,鱼水深情,
多男多女,后嗣绵绵相续,
　　仇家为此吃惊,　　　　　　　　　　105
　　你们无限欢欣,
吉日良辰,屈指就在目下,
可爱的河,轻轻流到歌罢。"

她唱完诗行,周围一切人
　　都应声和她,发出了帮腔,　　　　　110
　　说她们的佳期指日在望,
附近响起了悠扬的回声,
　　发出余音铿铿。
欢乐的鸟群来展翅飞舞,

---

① 维纳斯之子丘比特是一位有双翅,手持弓箭的裸体美少年。他的箭射中谁的心,谁便坠入情网。——编注者

	Adown the lee that to them murmur'd low,
115	
	As he would speak but that he lack'd a tongue,
	Yet did by signs his glad affection show,
	Making his stream run slow.
	And all the fowl which in his flood did dwell
120	'Gan flock about these twain, that did excel
	The rest, so far as Cynthia doth shend[①]
	The lesser stars. So they, enrangéd well,
	Did on those two attend,
	And their best service lend
125	Against their wedding day, which was not long:
	Sweet Thames! run softly, till I end my song.

  At length they all to merry London came,
  To merry London, my most kindly nurse,
  That to me gave this life's first native source,
130   Though from another place I take my name,
    An house of ancient fame:
  There when they came whereas those bricky towers[②]
  The which on Thames' broad aged back do ride,
  Where now the studious lawyers have their bowers,
135   There whilome wont the Templar-knights to bide[③],
    Till they decay'd through pride:
  Next whereunto there stands a stately place,
  Where oft I gainéd gifts and goodly grace
    Of that great lord, which therein wont to dwell,

---

① *Cynthia*: 'the Moon.'
② *whereas*: 'where.' Cf. 'whenas,' No. 16, l. 8.
③ *whilome*: 'formerly.'

顺沿着窃窃私语的河川,   115
水虽无舌,却似有话要吐,
　　终于用信号表明其喜欢,
　　　　吩咐河流放缓。
水面上聚集的全部飞禽
都齐来环绕这一对千金,   120
　　她们两位真是举世无俦,
像明月的光辉胜过众星;
　　在二人的左右,
　　　　大家齐整伺候,
迎接佳期,屈指就在目下,   125
可爱的河,轻轻流到歌罢。

大伙终来到欢乐的京城①,
　　这京城是我最亲的奶娘,
　　我从小是由她抚育成长,
虽然我的姓从别处生根,   130
　　出身世阀名门;
他们抵达了砖砌的高楼,
　　俯瞰浩渺的古泰晤士河,
好学的律师们在此居留,
　　圣堂武士当初也是住客②,   135
　　　　因骄傲而摧折;
挨次是一座庄严的院邸,
这儿我常得到宠爱赏赐,
　　我的大恩主曾里面居住③,

---

① "欢乐的京城"指伦敦。——编注者
② "圣堂武士"指一一一八年左右参加东征十字军的武士团成员。——译者
③ "大恩主"指莱斯特伯爵(Earl of Leicester,1532?—1588),是斯宾塞在文学方面的第一个提携人。——译者

140   Whose want too well now feels my friendless case①;
             But ah! here fits not well
             Old woes, but joys, to tell②
         Against the bridal day, which is not long:
         Sweet Thames! run softly, till I end my song.

145   Yet therein now doth lodge a noble peer,
             Great England's glory and the world's wide wonder,
         Whose dreadful name late through all Spain did thunder,
         And Hercules' two pillars standing near
             Did make to quake and fear:
150   Fair branch of honour, flower of chivalry!
             That fillest England with thy triumphs' fame,
         Joy have thou of thy noble victory,
             And endless happiness of thine own name
             That promiseth the same;
155   That through thy prowess and victorious arms
         Thy country may be freed from foreign harms,
             And great Eliza's glorious name may ring
         Through all the world, fill'd with thy wide alarms
             Which some brave Muse may sing
160   To ages following,
         Upon the bridal day, which is not long:
         Sweet Thames! run softly, till I end my song.

         From those high towers this noble lord issúing
             Like radiant Hesper, when his golden hair

---

① *Whose want*: this is the object of 'feels'; 'my friendless state feels, all too deeply, the loss of him.'
② *Old woes*: object of 'to tell.'

我今天因孤寂不胜伤逝； 140
　　啊，不宜诉旧苦，
　　开心事该吐露，
预祝佳期，屈指就在目下，
可爱的河，轻轻流到歌罢。

于今的宅主是一位贵人， 145
　　他使英国增光，举世震惊，
　　全西班牙响彻他的大名①；
地中海的两条岩柱狭门②
　　为之哆嗦丧魂；
荣誉的花枝，骑士的花朵， 150
　　英国到处谈论你的胜利，
你为你的丰功感到快活；
　　你的姓永和幸福相联系，
　　它有幸福含义③。
由于你的勇敢，你的战功， 155
外患的侵入将成为无从，
　　女王英名远扬世界各方，
到处有你所引起的惶恐，
　　付与诗人歌唱，
　　后代永记不忘， 160
吉日良辰，屈指就在目下，
可爱的河，轻轻流到歌罢。

那位大贵人走出了高楼，
　　像亮晶晶的长庚星，头上

---

① "贵人"指埃塞克斯伯爵(Earl of Essex，1567—1601)，他曾率海军占领西班牙的加的斯港。——译者
② 指直布罗陀海峡南北两岸对峙的巨岬。——译者
③ 埃塞克斯伯爵的姓 Devereux 与法文 heureux(幸福)音近。——译者

In th' ocean billows he hath bathéd fair,
Descended to the river's open viewing
    With a great train ensuing.
Above the rest were goodly to seen
    Two gentle knights of lovely face and feature,
Beseeming well the bower of any queen,
    With gifts of wit and ornaments of nature,
        Fit for so goodly stature,
That like the twins of Jove they seem'd in sight
Which deck the baldric of the Heavens bright;
    They two, forth pacing to the river's side,
Received those two fair brides, their lovers delight;
    Which, at th' appointed tide,
    Each one did make his bride
Against their bridal day, which is not long:
Sweet Thames! run softly, till I end my song.

E. SPENSER.

金发在海浪中洗涤发亮；   *165*
他光临景色广阔的河流，
 大批扈从随后。
就中颇为仪表不俗的是，
 两位骑士，俊秀而又温文，
堪和任何佳丽结成伉俪，   *170*
 聪明的资质，天然的锦文，
  恰好身材相称，
看来像天帝生的双胞胎，
黄道带上成对焕发光采；
 他们二位向前走到河旁，   *175*
迎候两新娘，他们的心爱；
 按照预定时光，
  结成夫妻两双，
迎接佳期，屈指就在目下，
可爱的河，轻轻流到歌罢。   *180*

戴镏龄　译

编注 埃德蒙·斯宾塞(Edmund Spenser，1552？—1599)，英国文艺复兴时期最伟大的诗人。他的主要作品有长诗《仙国女王》(*The Faerie Queene*)、十四行诗组《爱情小诗》和两首婚姻颂歌——《婚后曲》和这里介绍的《婚前曲》。《婚前曲》是诗人一五九六年为两位贵族小姐出嫁而写的一首贺诗，诗中把她们比作两只洁白的天鹅在泰晤士河上顺流而下直到新郎府邸。此诗与《婚后曲》一样，以语言优美脍炙人口。

54. THE HAPPY HEART

Art thou poor, yet hast thou golden slumbers①?
    O sweet content!
Art thou rich, yet is thy mind perplexed?
    O punishment!
Dost thou laugh to see how fools are vexed
To add to golden numbers, golden numbers②?
O sweet content! O sweet, O sweet content!
    Work apace, apace, apace, apace;
    Honest labour bears a lovely face;
Then hey nonny nonny, hey nonny nonny!

Canst drink the waters of the crispéd spring③?
    O sweet content!
Swimm'st thou in wealth, yet sink'st in thine own tears?
    O punishment!
Then he that patiently want's burden bears
No burden bears, but is a king, a king!
O sweet content! O sweet, O sweet content!
    Work apace, apace, apace, apace;
    Honest labour bears a lovely face;
Then hey nonny nonny, hey nonny nonny!

T. DEKKER.

---

① *thou*, i.e. the reader; the second and fourth lines are exclamations, not addresses.
② *golden numbers*: 'large sums of gold.'
③ *crispéd*: lit. 'curled,' so 'ruffled.'

54. 称心满意

德克尔

你没有钱,却睡得甜丝丝?
　　　　哦,知足常乐!
你富裕,莫非却惶惑不安?
　　　　哦,惩罚谴责!
愚人为钱上堆钱而忧烦,　　　　　　　　　5
你看见不是觉得这可笑?
哦,知足常乐,知足常常乐!
　加快工作呀,加快,加快,
　认真干活,就面容可爱;
嘟哩,咳,嘟哩,咳,嘟哩啊嘟哩!　　　　10

泉水涟漪,将它酌来品尝?
　　　　哦,知足常乐!
钱里翻滚,又泪水中浸泡?
　　　　哦,惩罚谴责!
贫穷的担子咬紧牙根挑,　　　　　　　　15
这种人没负担,是南面王!
哦,知足常乐,知足常常乐!
　加快工作呀,加快,加快,
　认真干活,就面容可爱;
嘟哩,咳,嘟哩,咳,嘟哩啊嘟哩!　　　　20

戴镏龄　译

编注 托马斯·德克尔(Thomas Dekker,1570?—1632),英国剧作家及散文家。这首诗选自他的喜剧《能忍受考验的格里丝尔》(*The Pleasant Comodie of Patient Grissill*,1603)。

55. 'THIS LIFE, WHICH SEEMS SO FAIR'

This Life, which seems so fair,
Is like a bubble blown up in the air
By sporting children's breath,
Who chase it everywhere
And strive who can most motion it bequeath.
And though it sometime seem of its own might,

Like to an eye of gold, to be fix'd there,
And firm to hover in that empty height,
That only is because it is so light.
— But in that pomp it doth not long appear;
For, when 'tis most admired, in a thought[①],
Because it erst was nought, it turns to nought[②].

W. DRUMMOND.

[①] *in a thought*: 'swift as a thought,' or, as we shuld say, 'in a flash.'
[②] *erst*: 'at first'; it is the superlative of ere = 'before.'

55. "看起来这般炫丽的生命"

德拉蒙德

  看起来这般炫丽的生命
倒像是肥皂泡飘浮在空中,
  由嬉戏的孩子们把它吹胀,
  把它追逐到整个世尘,
努力使它不停息地飘荡。
虽然它有时也显得庄重,

  像纯粹的黄金,凝固不变,
稳稳地翱翔在茫茫太空,
可这正是因为它过分轻飘。
  ——不能长久地保持它浮华的幻影;
因为哟,虽然它得到片刻的赞美,
可它本原就是虚无,定在虚无中消溶。

曹明伦 译

56. SOUL AND BODY

Poor Soul, the centre of my sinful earth,
    [Fool'd by] those rebel powers that thee array①,
Why dost thou pine within, and suffer dearth,
    Painting thy outward walls so costly gay②?

Why so large cost, having so short a lease,
    Dost thou upon thy fading mansion spend③?
Shall worms, inheritors of this excess,
    Eat up thy charge? is this thy body's end?

Then, Soul, live thou upon thy servant's loss,
    And let that pine to aggravate thy store④;
Buy terms divine in selling hours of dross⑤;
    Within be fed, without be rich no more: —

So shalt thou feed on death, that feeds on men⑥,
And death once dead, there's no more dying then.

W. SHAKESPEARE.

---

① *array*: 'deck out,' 'adorn.'
② *costly* is here an adverb, 'in a costly manner.'
③ *mansion* in the 17th century had no implied idea of splendour; it meant simply 'an abiding place,' 'dwelling.'
④ *aggravate*: 'increase,' literally 'make heavier.'
⑤ *terms*: 'periods of time.'
⑥ *feed on death*: i.e. get food for the soul from the destruction of worldly interests.

56. 灵与肉

莎士比亚

可怜的灵魂,我罪恶肉体之中央,
　　被你装饰的叛逆之躯束缚的奴隶,
你为何在里面忍饥挨饿饥瘦面黄,
　　却把这外壳粉饰得这般华美艳丽?

这寓所租期太短,而且摇摇欲坠①,
　　那你干吗要为这破房子挥金如土?
难道你的租金不将由蛆虫来消费?
　　难道被蛆虫吞食不是肉体的归宿?

所以哟,用你肉体的损耗来度日,
　　让它消瘦憔悴,以增加你的给养;
用短促的时辰去换取永恒的租期②,
　　让内心充实,别再虚有一副皮囊。

这样你就能吞噬吞食世人的死神,
而死神一死,死亡就再不会发生③。

曹明伦　译

编注　此诗系莎氏十四行诗第 146 首。

---

① 肉体乃灵魂之寓所,反之灵魂则为肉体的房客。——译者
② 喻牺牲现世的肉体享乐以求灵魂被拯救。——译者
③ 《圣经·旧约·以赛亚书》第二十五章第八节云:"上帝将吞噬死亡,直至永远。"《圣经·新约·哥林多前书》第十五章第二十六节曰:"上帝要毁灭的最后敌人就是死亡。"《圣经·新约·启示录》第二十一章第四节说:"死亡将不复存在。"——译者

57. LIFE

  The World's a bubble, and the Life of Man
    Less than a span①;
  In his conception wretched, from the womb
    So to the tomb;
5   Curst from the cradle, and brought up to years
    With cares and fears.
  Who then to frail mortality shall trust,
  But limns the water, or but writes in dust②.

  Yet since with sorrow here we live opprest,
10   What life is best?
  Courts are but only superficial schools
    To dandle fools③:
  The rural parts are turn'd into a den
    Of savage men:
15   And where's a city from all vice so free,
  But may be term'd the worst of all the three④?

  Domestic cares afflict the husband's bed,

---

① *span*: properly the distance from the tip of the thumb to the tip of the little finger at their widest stretch, taken arithmetically to be nine inches; it is often used vaguely for a short space.
② *limns*: 'paints.' To 'limn the water' is equivalent to 'ploughing the sand.'
③ *To dandle fools*: i.e. to keep them occupied and prevent their becoming a nuisance.
④ *the three*: i.e. the Court, the Country, and the City.

57. 人生

培根

尘世是泡沫,人生世上,
　　　　短促不长;
成胎多苦难,从母怀里,
　　　　一直到死;
幼小不幸,长大成人后, 5
　　　　多忧多愁。
脆弱的众生怎堪信赖?
是水面涂绘,沙上题写。

既然人世充满了忧郁,
　　　　乐土何处? 10
宫廷是表面学堂,
　　　　专供玩弄优孟;
乡村成了这样的地区,
　　　　蛮荒所居;
有哪个城市,百弊缺少, 15
不比宫廷、乡村更加糟?

家累使丈夫睡梦不稳,

> Or pains his head:
> Those that live single, take it for a curse,
> Or do things worse:
> Some would have children: those that have them moan
> Or wish them gone:
> What is it, then, to have, or have no wife,
> But single thraldom, ro a double strife①?
>
> Our own affections still at home to please②
> Is a disease:
> To cross the sea to any foreign soil,
> Perils and toil:
> Wars with their noise affright us; when they cease,
> We are worse in peace; —
> What then remains, but that we still should cry
> Not to be born, or, being born, to die?

LORD BACON.

---

① *single thraldom*: this is the state of having no wife; for there a man is still in subjection to his possessions, his servants, his employment or his needs. This sentence is an instance of the figure called Chiasmus, where of four terms the first and fourth go together, as do the second and third. Perhaps the best known instance in English occurs in Matthew vii. 6, 'Give not that which is holy unto the dogs, neither cast ye your pearls before swine, lest they trample them under their feet and turn again and rend you'; where the 'trample' refers to the swine and the 'turn' to the dogs.

② *still*: 'continually.'

　　　　或是头疼；
　　独身汉把独身当灾难，
　　　　或更难堪；　　　　　　　　　　　*20*
　　想有儿女，有了又悲叹，
　　　　自添麻烦；
　　究竟讨老婆，还是不讨，
　　是鳏居还是一对争吵？

　　闭门不出，以身娱为务，　　　　　　*25*
　　　　不免谬误；
　　跨海飘洋到他国国土，
　　　　既险又苦；
　　战争喧嚣可怖，逢太平
　　　　更欠安宁；　　　　　　　　　　*30*
　　对于生，既生又要死亡，
　　到头来有谁难免悲伤？

　　　　　　　　　　　　戴镏龄　译

编注　弗朗西斯·培根（Francis Bacon, 1561—1626），英国文艺复兴时期最重要的散文作家及政治家、哲学家。马克思、恩格斯称他为"英国唯物主义和整个现代实验科学的真正始祖"（《马克思恩格斯全集》第二卷，人民出版社一九五七年版，第一六三页）。本诗是作者据古希腊的一首警句诗衍译而成的。

58. THE LESSONS OF NATURE

Of this fair volume which we World do name
    If we the sheets and leaves could turn with care,
Of Him who it corrects, and did it frame①,
    We clear might read the art and wisdom rare:

Find out His power which wildest powers doth tame,
    His providence extending everywhere,
His justice which proud rebels doth not spare,
    In every page, no period of the same②.

But silly we, like foolish children, rest
    Well pleased with colour'd vellum, leaves of gold,
Fair dangling ribbands, leaving what is best③,
    On the great Writer's sense ne'er taking hold;

Or if by chance we stay our minds on aught,
It is some picture on the margin wrought④.

W. DRUMMOND.

---

① *Of Him* depends on 'art and wisdom.'
② *period of*: 'limit to.'
③ *ribbands*: i.e. the bookmarkers.
④ *some picture*: i.e. some incident which illustrates the working of divine laws; but we do not investigate the laws themselves.

58. 大自然给我们上的课

德拉蒙德

我们把这美丽的书叫做"世界",
　如果我们能仔细翻阅每一页,
　就会看清创造世界、改造大地
　　的神真是才艺无双、智慧无比:

他的神力能驯服狂暴的力量,   5
　他仁慈的恩泽普照四面八方,
　骄傲的叛逆也难逃他的法网,
　每一页记载的时期都不一样。

但我们愚蠢得像无知的孩子,
　只爱金碧辉煌、五彩的羊皮纸   10
和飘扬的美丽丝带,却没抓住
　书的精华,这伟大作者的意图;

偶尔有什么使心灵停留一下,
那只不过是每页边上的图画。

　　　　　　　　　　　许渊冲　译

编注　此诗和本卷第61首均选自德拉蒙德于一六二三年出版的诗集《天国之花》(*Flowers of Sion*,参见本卷第2首编注)。

59. 'DOTH THEN THE WORLD GO THUS, DOTH ALL THUS MOVE?'

Doth then the world go thus, doth all thus move?
   Is this the justice which on Earth we find?
   Is this that firm decree which all both bind?
Are these your influences, Powers above?

Those souls which vice's moody mists most blind,
Blind Fortune, blindly, most their friend doth prove;
And they who thee, poor idol, Virtue! love,
   Ply like a feather toss'd by storm and wind[1].

Ah! if a Providence doth sway this all,
   Why should best minds groan under most distress?
Or why should pride humility make thrall,
   And injuries the innocent oppress?

Heavens! hinder, stop this fate; or grant a time
When good may have, as well as bad, their prime.

W. DRUMMOND.

---

[1] *Ply*: 'go to and fro.'

59. "难道世界就这样,一切就这样进行?"

德拉蒙德

难道世界就这样,一切就这样进行?
    难道这就是在地球上找到的公平?
      这就是约束一切、不可改变的天命?
    这就是你们的影响吗,天上的神明?

    被罪恶的迷雾蒙住了眼睛的人们,   5
盲目的命运是他们盲目的保护神;
美德呵!热爱你的人把你当成偶像,
    他们自己却像鹅毛在风雨中飘荡。

啊!如果天上有一个神明主宰一切,
    为什么让好人在苦难中悲痛欲绝?   10
为什么谦逊反倒成了傲慢的奴隶,
    而清白无辜的人却反被践踏在地?

天呀!别让命运滥发不公平的报酬,
    小人得志,好人也该有得意的时候。

许渊冲 译

编注 此诗收在一六五六年出版的诗人的《诗遗作》内。

60. THE WORLD'S WAY

Tired with all these, for restful death I cry[1]—
    As, to behold desert a beggar born[2],
And needy nothing trimm'd in jollity[3],
    And purest faith unhappily forsworn[4],

And gilded honour shamefully misplaced[5],
    And maiden virtue rudely strumpeted[6],
And right perfection wrongfully disgraced,
    And strength by limping sway disabled,

And art made tongue-tied by authority[7],
    And folly, doctor-like, controlling skill,
And simple truth miscall'd simplicity[8],
    And captive Good attending captain Ill: —

— Tired with all these, from these would I be gone,
Save that, to die, I leave my Love alone.

                                        W. SHAKESPERAE.

---

[1] *all these*: sc. the following.
[2] *As*: 'for example.'
[3] *needy nothing*, etc.: 'some empty non-entity decked out in fine array.'
[4] *unhappily forsworn*: 'compelled by unkind fate to break its word.'
[5] *gilded honour*, etc.: 'riches and honours heaped upon unworthy persons.'
[6] *strumpeted*: 'prostituted,' compelled to marry without love.
[7] *I.e.* a strong man prevented from acting by a weakling who has authority over him.
[8] *simplicity*: 'want of intelligence.'

60. 今世众生路

莎士比亚

对这一切都厌了,我渴求安息,
 譬如我眼见英才俊杰生为乞丐,
平庸之辈却用锦裘华衣来装饰,
 纯洁的誓约被令人遗憾地破坏,

显赫的头衔被可耻地胡乱封赏,   5
 少女的贞操常蒙受粗暴的玷污,
正义之完美总遭到恶意的诽谤,
 健全的民众被跛足的权贵束缚,

文化与艺术被当局捆住了舌头,
 俨如博学之士的白痴控制智者,   10
坦率与真诚被错唤为无知愚陋,
 被俘的善良得听从掌权的邪恶:

 对这一切都厌了,我真想离去,
 只是我死后我爱友会形单影只。

曹明伦 译

编注 此诗系莎氏十四行诗第66首。

61. SAINT JOHN BAPTIST

The last and greatest Herald of Heaven's King
    Girt with rough skins, hies to the deserts wild[①],
Among that savage brood the woods forth bring,
    Which he more harmless found than man, and mild.

His food was locusts, and what there doth spring[②],
    With honey that from virgin hives distill'd[③];
Parch'd body, hollow eyes, some uncouth thing
    Made him appear, long since from earth exiled.

There burst he forth: 'All ye whose hopes rely
    On God, with me amidst these deserts mourn,
Repent, repent, and from old errors turn!'
    — Who listen'd to his voice, obey'd his cry?

Only the echoes, which he made relent[④],
Rung from their flinty caves, Repent! Repent!

W. DRUMMOND.

---

① *Girt with rough skins*: see Matthew iii. 4, 'And the same John had his raiment of camel's hair, and a leathern girdle about his loins; and his meat was locusts and wild honey.'

② *His food was locusts*: locusts, beetles, and grasshoppers were the only 'flying creeping things which have four feet' allowed as food by the Mosaic Law (Lev. xi. 21 – 23).

③ *virgin hives*: natural hives which had never been pillaged before.

④ *relent*: 'the echoes alone showed signs of grace by repeating the Baptist's message.'

61. 施洗圣约翰[①]

德拉蒙德

天主最后一个,也是最伟大的使徒
　　束着粗皮腰带,来到最荒凉的国土,
来到在树上筑巢为生的野人群中,
　　发现他们比文明人更善良,更谦恭。

他吃的是昆虫和当地生长的东西, 　　　　　　　　5
　　还有他从原始蜂窝里采来的蜂蜜,
远离尘世之后,长时间的流浪生活
　　使他皮肤发裂,眼睛陷得像个深窝。

他忽然放声大喊:"你们把希望寄托
　　在上帝身上的人,快同我来到沙漠, 　　　　　10
　　忏悔吧,忏悔吧,改过自新,回头是岸!"
——有谁听他的话?有谁照他说的去干?

只有他那慈悲为怀的回声在萦回,
从无情的石洞里喊道,"忏悔吧!忏悔!"

许渊冲　译

[①] 圣约翰,犹太先知,祭司撒迦利亚和以利沙伯之子,耶稣之表哥。相传他早年隐居于死海之滨,后为迎接救世主的降临在旷野传道,并在约旦为包括耶稣在内的信徒施洗礼。——编注者

卷二

1616—1700

62. ODE ON THE MORNING OF CHRIST'S NATIVITY

    This is the month, and this the happy morn
        Wherein the Son of Heaven's Eternal King
    Of wedded maid and virgin mother born,
        Our great redemption from above did bring;
5   For so the holy sages once did sing
    That He our deadly forfeit should release,
And with His Father work us a perpetual peace.

    That glorious Form, that Light unsufferable,
        And that far-beaming blaze of Majesty
10   Wherewith He wont at Heaven's high council-table
        To sit the midst of Trinal Unity[1],
    He laid aside; and, here with us to be,
        Forsook the courts of everlasting day,
And chose with us a darksome house of mortal clay.

15   Say, heavenly Muse, shall not thy sacred vein
        Afford a present to the Infant God?
    Hast thou no verse, no hymn, or solemn strain
        To welcome Him to this His new abode,
    Now while the heaven, by the sun's team untrod[2],
20   Hath took no print of the approaching light[3],

---

[1] *Trinal*: 'Threefold.'
[2] *Now while the heaven*, etc.; *i.e.* before sunrise
[3] *took*: for 'taken'; cf. note to No. 14, l. 4.

62. 圣诞清晨歌

弥尔顿

序歌

就在这一月,这幸福的黎明,
　　天上永生王的儿子降诞尘境,
为初嫁的处女,童贞的母亲所生,
　　给我们从天上带来伟大的救拯;
　　神圣的先哲们曾经这样歌咏,　　　　　　5
说他必将我们救出可怕的深渊,
同他父亲为我们创造持久的和平。

他容光焕发,灿烂辉煌,
　　光轮放射的火焰,万丈光芒,
他本来在高天上的议案之旁,　　　　　　　10
　　坐在一体而三位的中央①;
如今舍去,来和我们同住一个地方,
离弃那长明不夜的殿堂,
甘以必朽的肉体作为在人间的篷帐。

天上的诗神呀,你那神妙的天才,　　　　　15
　　何不献上贡品给这神圣的婴孩?
难道没有诗歌、颂辞,或庄严的天籁,
　　用以欢迎他初次到这新居里来?
　　现在正当高空澄碧,未经日轮的践踹,
不见阳光扫射,留痕迹于九陔,　　　　　　20

---

① "一体而三位"指视圣父上帝、圣子耶稣及圣灵为一体的宗教学说。——编注者

And all the spangled host keep watch in squadrons bright?

See how from far, upon the eastern road,
The star-led wizards haste with odours sweet①:
O run, prevent them with thy humble ode②
25And lay it lowly at His blessed feet;
Have thou the honour first thy Lord to greet,
And join thy voice unto the angel quire
From out His secret altar touch'd with hallow'd fire③.

THE HYMN

It was the winter wild④
30While the heaven-born Child
All meanly wrapt in the rude mangel lies;
Nature in awe to Him
Had doff'd her gaudy trim,
With her great Master so to sympathize:
35It was no season then for her
To wanton with the sun, her lusty paramour.

Only with speeches fair
She woos the gentle air

---

① *star-led wizards*: the Magi; see Matt. ii. 1.
② *prevent*: in its literal sense 'come before.'
③ A reference to Isaiah vi. 6, 7, 'Then flew one of the seraphims unto me, having a live coal in his hand, which he had taken with the tongs from off the altar; And he laid it upon my mouth.'
④ *It was the winter*: historically, of course, the birth of Christ cannot have taken place in the winter. The winter solstice (Dec. 25th) was fixed on as the date commemorating his birth because in early pagan cults there was a festival of the Sun on that day.

单见闪烁的群星分队瞭望,警戒。

看哪,从东方遥远的路途上,
　　明星引领的术士,赶来贡献馨香!
快些,要尽先把你卑微的歌辞献上,
　　谦虚地在他的脚下安放, 　　　　　　25
　　你要抢先,争取最初迎主的荣光,
　　放开你的歌喉,加入天使的合唱,
接触神坛的圣火发为热烈的篇章。

颂歌

　　荒芜而零落的冬天,
　　天生的婴儿降诞人间, 　　　　　　30
全身裹上粗布,躺在粗糙的马槽中间;
　　大自然对他分外恭敬,
　　把浓妆艳服脱落干净,
　　为了对她伟大的主宰表示同情;
　　这时节,不是她跟日头—— 　　　　35
她强健的情夫,放肆逸乐的季候。

　　她只能用委婉的语言,
　　请求温厚的高天,

                To hide her guilty front with innocent snow;
40   And on her naked shame,
                    Pollute with sinful blame①,
            The saintly veil of maiden white to throw;
                Confounded, that her Maker's eyes
        Should look so near upon her foul deformities.

45   But He, her fears to cease②,
                    Sent down the meek-eyed Peace;
            She, crown'd with olive green, came softly sliding
                Down through the turning sphere③,
                      His ready harbinger④,
50   With turtle wing the amorous clouds dividing⑤;
                  And waving wide her myrtle wand⑥,
        She strikes a universal peace through sea and land.

                    No war, or battle's sound
                    Was heard the world around:
55   The idle spear and shield were high uphung;

---

① *blame*: 'wrong-doing.'
② *cease*: its transitive sense, 'put a stop to,' dates, like the intransitive, 'come to an end,' from the 14th century.
③ *the turning sphere*: according to the Ptolemaic system of astronomy the Earth was a fixed body at the centre of eight globes or spheres which revolved round it and formed the paths of the Sun, the Moon, and the planets.
④ *His ready harbinger*: harbinger (connected with 'harbour') is here used in its original sense of one sent on before to provide lodging for a royal personage. *His* = Christ's.
⑤ *turtle wing*: the turtle-dove has always been deemed the symbol of love.
⑥ *myrtle wand*: the myrtle being sacred to Venus was considered the emblem of love.

  撒下纯洁的雪片,来遮盖她的丑脸;
   在她赤裸的羞耻上面,   40
   在她可诅咒的罪污上面,
  抛撒洁白如处女的罗纱,把她遮掩;
   因为创造者的眼光逼近,
使她自惭形秽,觉得恐惧惶惑万分。

   但创造者不愿使她惧怕,   45
   先派下和平之神的法驾;
  她头戴橄榄叶的翠冠,轻轻飞下①;
   飞过转动着的群星,
   负着先驱者的使命,
  插了鸠鸽的羽翼,拨开缤纷的云层②;   50
   她挥动桃金的短梃③,
遍击山海陆地,击出普世的和平。

   普天之下不见战云,
   杀声消弭,金革不闻:
  高高地挂起无聊的长矛和巨盾;   55

---

① 橄榄枝叶是和平的象征。——译者
② 鸠鸽也象征和平。——译者
③ 桃金的短梃是和平女神手中所拿的棒,上端有一颗明星。——译者

   The hookéd chariot stood①
   Unstain'd with hostile blood;
  The trumpet spake not to the arméd throng;
   And kings sat still with awful eye②,
60   As if they surely knew their sovran Lord was by③.

   But peaceful was the night
   Wherein the Prince of Light
  His reign of peace upon the earth began;
   The winds, with wonder whist④,
65   Smoothly the waters kist,
  Whispering new joys to the mild oceán —
   Who now hath quite forgot to rave⑤,
While birds of calm sit brooding on the charméd wave⑥.

   The stars, with deep amaze,
70   Stand fix'd in steadfast gaze⑦,
  Bending one way their precious influence⑧;

---

① *hookéd chariot*: hooks and scythe were fixed to the wheels or the frames of war chariots to catch the enemy in a charge.
② *awful*: 'full of awe, or wonder' — not as usually, 'inspiring awe.'
③ *sovran*: this is the correct spelling — from the late Lat. *superanus*—of 'sovereign'; the modern form is due to a confusion with 'reign.'
④ *whist*: 'silent,' an adjective derived from the interjection.
⑤ *forgot*: cf. l. 20, 'took.'
⑥ *birds of calm*: it was fabled of the halcyon or kingfisher that it bred at the winter solstice in a nest floating on the waves, during which time perfect calm prevailed in Nature.
⑦ *The stars ... Stand fix'd*: under the Ptolemaic system, as under the Copernican, the 'fix'd stars,' as they are now called, would usually appear to revolve round the Earth.
⑧ *one way*: sc. towards Bethlehem. *influence*: an ethereal fluid was supposed to stream from the stars and affect human destinies.

驾就的车马停住不跑,
　仇恨的鲜血不染战袍,
　　喇叭,军角,也不向武装的群众呼号。
　　各国君王们危坐怅望,
觉得他们威严的主就在身旁。 60

　　寒夜深沉,万籁静止,
　　　这时候光明的王子,
　　开始在地上作和平的统治。
　　风儿带着异样的静寂,
　　　频向众水接吻细细, 65
　　向温厚的海洋私语快乐的消息;
　　海洋也忘记了怒号,
和平的鸟翼孵复着驯服的波涛。

　　群星们都深深惊奇,
　　　凝眸注视,长时伫立, 70
　　他们的眼光都向一个目标看齐;

     And will not take their flight
     For all the morning light,
   Or Lucifer that often warn'd them thence①;
75   But in their glimmering orbs did glow②
   Until their Lord Himself bespake, and bid them go③.

     And though the shady gloom
     Had given day her room④,
   The sun himself withheld his wonted speed,
80   And hid his head for shame
     As his inferior flame⑤
   The new-enlighten'd world no more should need;
     He saw a greater Sun appear
   Than his bright throne or burning axletree could bear.

85   The shepherds on the lawn⑥
     Or ere the point of dawn⑦
   Sate simply chatting in a rustic row;
     Full little thought they than⑧
     That the mighty Pan
90   Was kindly come to live with them below;

---

① *Lucifer*: [= Light-bringer] 'the Morning Star.'
② *orbs*: may mean the stars themselves.
③ *bespake*: now only used as a transitive verb. In its intransitive sense it means go more than 'spake.'
④ *her room*: 'the space she — i. e. day — required.' Day being put for Aurora, the dawn, is feminine.
⑤ *As*: 'As though.'
⑥ *lawn*: any stretch of grass-covered land is rightly, though not commonly, so termed.
⑦ *Or ere*: 'before.'
⑧ *than*: 'then.'

虽然清晨全部的光辉
　和太白晨星，都命令他们引退，
他们仍徘徊依恋，不忍离弃岗位；
　依然循着轨道，放出光明，　　　　　　　　75
直等救主亲来指示，下了散队的命令。

黑夜的荫翳已开，
　让路给白昼进来，
太阳自己却姗姗地不敢冒昧上台；
　他为羞惭而遮面，　　　　　　　　　　　80
　因他较弱的火焰，
不如这世界新点着的光辉那样鲜艳；
　这是个更大的太阳，
不是他原来的光座和火轴所能承当。

　东方还未见晨曦，　　　　　　　　　　　85
　　牧羊人在草地里，
三五成群，并坐着谈天说地；
　他们连做梦都未曾梦见过：
　　大能的牧神会惠然降落①
到他们中间跟他们同过牧羊的生活；　　　　90

---

① "牧神"原为异教的潘神（Pan），头生两角，下肢作羊脚形。据史家普鲁塔克（Plutarch）说，当罗马皇帝提庇留在位时，有一个船夫路经巴克西群岛，听见有人大声喊道："潘神死了。"皇帝问了许多卜者，都不知所答。耶稣正在那时诞生，他是好牧人；所以人们传说他是代替潘神而出世的。——译者

> Perhaps their loves, or else their sheep
> Was all that did their silly thoughts so busy keep①.
>
> When such music sweet
> Their hearts and ears did greet
95 As never was by mortal finger strook②—
> Divinely-warbled voice
> Answering the stringéd noise,
> As all their souls in blissful rapture took③:
> The air, such pleasure loth to lose,
100 With thousand echoes still prolongs each heavenly close.
>
> Nature that heard such sound
> Beneath the hollow round
> Of Cynthia's seat the airy region thrilling④,
> Now was almost won
105 To think her part was done,
> And that her reign had here its last fulfilling⑤;
> She knew such harmony alone
> Could hold all heaven and earth in happier union.
>
> At last surrounds their sight⑥
110 A globe of circular light,

---

① *silly*: 'simple,' 'homely.'
② *strook*: for 'struck'; an obsolete past part. of 'strike.'
③ *As*: 'in such a way as.'
④ *I.e.* thrilling the airy region [which lies] beneath the hollow round [= sphere] of the Moon's orbit. The sphere of the Moon (see note to l. 48) was the globe next outside the earth. *Cynthia*: see note on No. 53, l. 121.
⑤ *its*: this is one of the three places in Milton where this word occurs; the others being *Pat. Lost*, I. 254, and IV. 813 (Masson).
⑥ *surrounds their sight*: 'was visible all round them.'

他们简单的脑筋，
所忙碌思索的只是爱人和羊群。

　　　他们受于耳，感于心：
　　　　这样酣美的乐音，
　　绝不像人手所能奏弹的鸣琴； 95
　　　　神奇婉转的歌吟，
　　　　伴着弦乐的高音，
　　使他们的灵魂，深觉幸福、欢欣；
　　　　天空愿这欢欣长保，
使万千山谷鸣应，响彻云霄。 100

　　　大自然听了这悠扬的音韵，
　　　　仰见一轮皓月，流光如银，
　　在玉兔银座之下的空界，莫不振奋；
　　　　她于是完全承认，
　　　　自己的责任已尽， 105
　　她的统治任务从此已告完成；
　　　　只有这样和谐的乐音，
才能使天和地团结更紧，契合更深。

　　　蓦地里火光出现，
　　　　环绕牧人的视线， 110

>
> That with long beams the shamefaced night array'd;
> The helméd Cherubim
> And sworded Seraphim
> Are seen in glittering ranks with wings display'd,
> 115　　　　Harping in loud and solemn quire①
> With unexpressive notes, to Heaven's new-born Heir②.
>
> Such music (as 'tis said)
> Before was never made
> But when of old the sons of morning sung,
> 120　　　　While the Creator great
> His constellations set
> And the well-balanced world on hinges hung;
> And cast the dark foundations deep,
> And bid the weltering waves their oozy channel keep③.
>
> 125　　Ring out, ye crystal spheres!
> Once bless our human ears,
> If ye have power to touch our senses so;
> And let your silver chime
> Move in melodious time;
> 130　　And let the bass of heaven's deep organ blow;
> And with your ninefold harmony
> Make up full consort to the angelic symphony④.
>
> For if such holy song,

---

① *quire*: the original spelling of 'choir.'
② *unexpressive*: 'inexpressible.' *Heir*: the riming of this word to 'quire' is note-worthy.
③ *weltering*: 'rolling.'
④ *consort*: for 'concert.'

照彻黝黑的深夜,灿烂而明艳。
　　嗻嚕啪头盔遮掩①,
　　撒拉弗腰佩火剑②,
　　都张开翅膀在辉煌的队伍中显现。
　　弦琴上谱出嘹亮、庄严的调子,　　　　　　115
不可言传的妙音,祝颂新生的神嗣。

　　　据说这样的乐歌,
　　　　从未有人演唱过,
　　只在远昔,清晨之子曾一度放歌,
　　　　创造者就在那时节,　　　　　　　　120
　　　　把众星在太空罗列,
　　把地球装上枢纽,平衡而妥帖;
　　　　布置黑暗的渊底在深处,
　　吩咐蜿蜒的河流,依从软泥的水路。

　　　晶莹的天体呀,请响起箫鼓③,　　　　125
　　　好使我们人类也一享耳福,
　　如果你有法子叫我们领悟;
　　　　演奏你白银般的新声,
　　　　节拍铿锵,透彻太清,
　　鼓动霄汉间的风琴,形成中天的和鸣。　130
　　　让你回环九叠的乐歌,
　　与天使们所弹唱的交响曲相调和。

　　　如果这神圣的大籁,
　　　　永远包围我们想象的心怀,

---

① 嗻嚕啪为第二等天使,最初见于《圣经·创世记》第三章第二四节。——译者
② 撒拉弗为第一等天使,见《圣经·以赛亚书》第六章第二节。——译者
③ 古希腊哲学家毕达哥拉斯认为,地球在运行时会发出特有的和谐声音。——编注者

	Enwrap our fancy long,
135	Time will run back, and fetch the age of gold①;
	And speckled vanity
	Will sicken soon and die,
	And leprous sin will melt from earthly mould②;
	And Hell itself will pass away,
140	And leave her dolorous mansions to the peering day.
	Yea, Truth and Justice then
	Will down return to men,
	Orb'd in a rainbow; and, like glories wearing,
	Mercy will sit between
145	Throned in celestial sheen,
	With radiant feet the tissued clouds down steering③;
	And Heaven, as at some festival,
	Will open wide the gates of her high palace hall.
	But wisest Fate says No;
150	This must not yet be so;
	The Babe yet lies in smiling infancy
	That on the bitter cross
	Must redeem our loss;
	So both Himself and us to glorify:
155	Yet first, to those ychain'd in sleep④

---

① *the age of gold*: Hesiod, a Greek poet of the 8th century B.C., divided the history of the world into five ages, the first of which, when Saturn ruled, was termed the Golden Age; it was the period of universal happiness, peace, and prosperity.

② *earthly mould*: i.e. man, formed from the dust of the earth.

③ *clouds down steering*: 'directing the clouds in their course beneath her.'

④ *ychain'd*: y- (corresponding to the German ge-) was a common prefix to past participles in Middle English. It still survives in a few archaic words, 'yclept,' 'yclad.'

时间便能倒溯,回到原始快乐的时代。 135
　　尘世间污秽的豪奢,
　　马上就枯萎,死绝,
　　丑陋的罪恶也将从尘土中消灭;
　　地狱也会自行取消,
把悲哀的邸宅,留交光天化日的明朝。 140

　　从此真理和正义比肩
　　飘然下来,回到人间,
　　全身披上虹彩;让"慈爱"坐在中间,
　　衣锦还乡,丰姿翩翩,
　　敷座于夺目的光辉里面, 145
驾着薄纱似的云霞,策天马而凯旋。
　　帝乡如遇佳节良辰,
巍峨的殿堂,将广开重重的天门。

　　但最智慧的命运之神却说,不,
　　现在时机还未成熟, 150
神圣的婴孩还在天真的微笑中哺乳;
　　他必须在痛苦的十字架上,
　　拯救我们的丧亡,
这样才能使他自己和我们同得荣光;
　　先要唤起沉睡中的死人, 155

>
> The wakeful trump of doom must thunder through the deep,
>
>> With such a horrid clang
>> As on mount Sinai rang
>> While the red fire and smouldering clouds outbrake:
>> The aged Earth aghast
>> With terror of that blast
>> Shall from the surface to the centre shake,
>>> when, at the world's last sessión,
>> The dreadful Judge in middle air shall spread His throne.
>
>> And then at last our bliss
>> Full and perfect is,
>> But now begins; for from this happy day①
>> The old Dragon under ground,
>> In straiter limits bound,
>> Not half so far casts his usurpéd sway;
>> And, wroth to see his kingdom fail,
>> Swinges the scaly horror of his folded tail②.
>
>> The oracles are dumb;
>> No voice or hideous hum
>> Runs through the archéd roof in words deceiving③:
>> Apollo from his shrine
>> Can no more divine,

160
165
170
175

---

① *But now begins*: the 'perfect bliss,' which will follow the Day of Judgement ('then'), has its beginning with the birth of Christ ('now').
② *swinges*: 'strikes,' 'lashes.'
③ *archéd roof*: many of the ancient oracles were in natural caves.

让审判的号筒,像霹雳震撼死寂的地狱之门。

  这样可怕的响声,
  好比西乃山上的雷鸣①,
那时血红的火焰,和浓黑的烟雾喷迸。
  恐惧侵袭了年老的地球,   *160*
  它经不起这号筒的怒吼。
从地面直到地心,它将浑身发抖。
  那时最后的审判到来②,
威严的审判者要在半空把座位展开。

  到那时,我们的幸福,   *165*
  可以开始得到满足,
可以得到完全;那时我们开始舒服,
  但地下的老龙却要吃苦③,
  他必须受种种的束缚,
他所僭取的权力,只能截断于中途;   *170*
  他含恨看他的帝国垮台,
竖起战栗的鳞甲,把蜷曲的尾巴乱摔。

  一切占卜巫术哑了口,
  半句清楚的话都没有,
苍穹之下,一切含糊的谎言都得罢休: *175*
  阿波罗在他的庙里④,
  顿失说预言的神力,

---

① 摩西上西乃山,耶和华从火焰浓烟中授诫给他。——译者
② "末日审判":《圣经·启示录》第二〇章,说天地的末日有一个大审判,总清算人间的善恶。——译者
③ 老龙就是撒旦。——译者
④ 阿波罗是希腊神话中的日神,俊美而善说预言。——译者

>   With hollow shriek the steep of Delphos leavings:
>   No nightly trance or breathéd spell[1]
>   Inspires the pale-eyed priest from the prophetic cell[2].
>
>   The lonely mountains o'er
>   And the resounding shore
>   A voice of weeping heard, and loud lament;
>   From haunted spring and dale
>   Edged with poplar pale
>   The parting Genius is with sighing sent;
>   With flower-inwoven tresses torn
>   The nymphs in twilight shade of tangled thickets mourn.
>
>   In consecrated earth
>   And on the holy hearth
>   The Lars and Lemures moan with midnight plaint[3];
>   In urns, and altars round
>   A drear and dying sound
>   Affrights the Flamens at their service quaint;
>   And the chill marble seems to sweat[4],
>   While each peculiar Power forgoes his wonted seat.

---

[1] *nightly*: 'in the night,' not 'happening each night.'

[2] *pale-eyed*: 'dim-eyed,' through long seclusion from the light of day.

[3] *Lars*, or Lares, were the protecting deities of a house, the spirits of departed ancestors to whom honour was paid in the home. *Lemures* were hostile spirits of the dead who roamed the earth as spectres. The word is here a dissyllable, being pronounced as English(Masson). It is to be noticed that 'hearth' goes with 'Lars' and 'consecrated earth' with 'Lemures,' an instance of Chiasmus, for which see above, note on No. 57, l. 24.

[4] The sweating of statues is a portent often mentioned, *e.g.* by Cicero, Virgil, and Lucan, as heralding some event of national importance.

只带凄凉的悲鸣,长辞特尔斐的绝壁①;
不再有托梦或灵谶,
祭司们黯然神伤,不能再从斗室发出预言。 *180*

越过几重寂寞的峰峦,
在怒潮澎湃的海滩,
可以听见低声的啜泣和高声的哭喊②;
从他住惯了的泉边谷里,
四周满是白杨萧萧的墓地, *185*
守护神叹息着作临去的依依;
山鬼搔着满织花朵的鬈发③,
在繁枝密叶的丛林荫中,心如刀扎。

在他们圣地的里面,
在神秘的炉灶上边, *190*
冤魂和灶神在半夜里泣诉,呜咽;
在墓地和祭坛四近,
有阴森的临死呻吟,
惊动那些举行古怪仪式的祭司们;
寒冷的大理石也汗流浃背, *195*
因为特权者一个个离开原来的地位。

---

① 特尔斐山崖上有日神庙,以预言灵验而著名。——译者
② 哭喊声是:"潘神死了。"——译者
③ 山鬼是希腊山林的女神,以花织发,居无定处,犹如我国传说中的巫山女,或《楚辞》中的山鬼。——译者

          Peor and Baalim[1]
          Forsake their temples dim,
     With that twice-batter'd god of Palestine:
200   And moonéd Ashtaroth[2]
          Heaven's queen and mother both,
     Now sits not girt with tapers' holy shine;
          The Lybic Hammon shrinks his horn[3],
     In vain the Tyrian maids their wounded Thammuz mourn.

205   And sullen Moloch, fled,
          Hath left in shadows dread
     His burning idol all of blackest hue;
          In vain with cymbals' ring
          They call the grisly king[4],
210   In dismal dance about the furnace blue[5];
          The brutish gods of Nile as fast,
     Isis, and Orus, and the dog Anubis, haste.

          Nor is Osiris seen

---

[1] *Peor*, properly the name of a mountain, is used, as in Numbers XXV. 18. for Baal-peor, a god of the Moabites and Midianites. *Baalim*: the Hebrew Plural of Baal, the chief male divinity of the people of Canaan; the plural form is due to the fact that he was worshipped under many different modifications.

[2] *Ashtaroth*: the Hebrew plural of Ashtoreth or Astarte, the principal goddess of the Phœnicians.

[3] *The Lybic Hammon*: Amun, an Egyptian deity (hence 'Lybic,' i.e. African), was represented as a ram or a man with a ram's head. *shrinks*: 'draws back.'

[4] *grisly*: 'horrible, grim.'

[5] *furnace blue*: burning with a blue flame.

匹欧和巴力他们①
　　出了暗淡的殿门,
　　带走了两次被打倒的巴勒斯坦之神②;
　　戴月的亚斯他录③,　　　　　　　　　　　　　200
　　兼为天界之后与母,
　　再也不能在烛光环绕之中端坐如故;
　　里比克哈蒙的尖角也收缩④,
　　推罗的处女徒然痛哭她们受伤的塔牧⑤。

　　忧郁的摩洛也逃奔⑥,　　　　　　　　　　　205
　　在可怕、阴森的地窖,
　　丢下他可憎的偶像,面目漆黑而狰狞。
　　他们鸣锣响钹像发狂,
　　徒然喊叫那可怕的王,
　　恐怖的舞蹈,演在纯青的炉火之旁。　　　　210
　　尼罗河畔的野神也这样,
　　爱西,阿罗和神犬阿努比都赶快逃亡⑦。

　　在孟非安林中或草原里的

---

① 匹欧、巴力为迦南之主神。——译者
② 两次被打倒的巴勒斯坦之神是大衮,他两次扑倒在耶和华的约柜前,见《圣经·撒母耳记上》第五章第三、四节。——译者
③ 亚斯他录是腓尼基的女神,头有两角作新月形。——译者
④ 哈蒙是利比亚和卜埃及的大神,形状如山羊,有大而曲的角:有时可以像人一样站起来,坐在座位上。——译者
⑤ 塔牧是叙利亚神话中的美男子,曾与一只野猪斗争而受伤身死,他的血开出秋牡丹花。后来叙利亚女子一年一度礼拜他。——译者
⑥ 摩洛是迦南偶像,祭祀仪式最可怕,要把儿童活活烧死。见《圣经·利未记》第一八章第二一节,《圣经·列王纪下》第二三章第十节。——译者
⑦ 爱西是埃及女神,奥西里之妻,阿罗之母。阿罗为晨曦之神。阿努比是埃及管死亡的神,其形象似豺狼,罗马人却以为像狗。——译者

	In Memphian grove, or green,
215	Trampling the unshower'd grass with lowings loud;
	Nor can he be at rest
	Within his sacred chest;
	Nought but profoundest hell can be his shroud;
	In vain with timbrell'd anthems dark①
220	The sable-stoléd sorcerers bear his worshipt ark②.

	He feels from Juda's land
	The dreaded infant's hand;
	The rays of Bethlehem blind his dusky eyn③;
	Nor all the gods beside
225	Longer dare abide,
	Not Typhon huge ending in snaky twine;
	Our Babe, to show his Godhead true,
	Can in His swaddling bands control the damnéd crew.

	So, when the sun in bed
230	Curtain'd with cloudy red
	Pillows his chin upon an orient wave,
	The flocking shadows pale
	Troop to the infernal jail,
	Each fetter'd ghost slips to his several grave;
235	And the yellow-skirted fays
	Fly after the night-steeds, leaving their moon-loved maze④.

---

① *anthems dark*: as the timbrel, or tambourine, is a cheerful instrument, a transferred epithet describing time or place.

② *sable-stoléd*: the stole was properly the outer garment of Roman matrons, a long tunic reaching to the feet with short sleeves.

③ *eyn*: the common plural of 'eye' from the 14th to the 16th century.

④ *maze*: 'winding tracks on the grass.'

奥西里也赶快逃避①,
　牛鸣声嚣,践踏着久旱的枯干草地; *215*
　　　　他神秘的心境,
　　　　不得些儿安静,
　除了地狱深渊,他简直无处遁形。
　　　徒有用手鼓配合的颂赞,
　使那穿丧服、抬神舆的魔术师更形惨淡。 *220*

　　　　他觉得犹太地方
　　　　有可畏的婴儿巨掌,
　伯利恒的曙光逼人,使他眯眼成盲。
　　　　此外所有的各种神祇,
　　　　也都不敢再事栖迟, *225*
　台封巨人也不能系住缱绻的发丝②。
　　　　我们的圣婴大显神性,
　能用褓裸的衣带,控制地狱的精灵。

　　　　太阳还未起床洗脸,
　　　　云霞帐子,红如火焰, *230*
　他的脸颊枕在东海的波涛上面。
　　　　阵阵夜影,脸色发青,
　　　　成队开入地狱的牢门,
　每一个戴足镣的幽魂都躲进坟茔。
　　　　身穿黄裳的嫦娥仙侣, *235*
　追随夜马,辞去月宫,高处的琼楼玉宇。

---

① 奥西里是埃及光明神,被弟弟黑暗神台封所杀,爱西、阿罗母子为他复仇。奥西里是太阳,爱西是月亮,阿罗是朝阳。奥西里形状像公牛,爱西像母牛。以色列人出埃及后,仍念念不忘这两个埃及的神祇,亚伦作金牛,也是为这缘故。——译者
② 台封(Typhon)是神话中的巨人,鼻喷火焰,有一百个头,长发缱绻,飘荡如水草。——译者

>   But see, the Virgin blest
>   Hath laid her Babe to rest;
>   Time is, our tedious song should here have ending:
>   Heaven's youngest-teeméd star
>   Hath fix'd her polish'd car,
>   Her sleeping Lord with hand-maid lamp attending:
>   And all about the courtly stable①
>   Bright-harness'd angels sit in order serviceable②.

J. MILTON.

---

① *courtly*: 'serving as a court' to the new-born King.
② *Bright-harness*' d: ' clad in shining armour.' *serviceable*: ' ready for service.'

看哪,圣母的胸前,
圣婴在躺着安眠;
现在我们必须结束这冗长的诗篇。
天上最年轻的星族, *240*
已准备雪亮的辇毂,
有如使女擎灯,护侍睡眠中的救主;
高贵的马厩四周,
坐着盛装的天使们——轮流侍候。

朱维之 译

编注 约翰·弥尔顿(John Milton,1608—1674),十七世纪最杰出的诗人。他早年接受文艺复兴时期的人文主义思想,积极参加资产阶级领导的反对封建政权的斗争。他的生活和创作都与英国资产阶级革命联系在一起。弥尔顿的诗内容进步,题材革新,风格明朗,有庄严宏伟的气势。他的主要作品有《失乐园》(*Paradise Lost*,1667)、《复乐园》(*Paradise Regained*,1671)和《力士参孙》(*Samson Agonistes*,1671)等。《圣诞清晨歌》展示了弥尔顿精湛的诗技,是英语文字中最美丽的作品之一,但也表现出了他诗歌中的清教徒特征。

63. SONG FOR SAINT CECILIA'S DAY, 1687

    From Harmony, from heavenly Harmony
        This universal frame began[1];
    When Nature underneath a heap
        Of jarring atoms lay[2]
    And could not heave her head,
    The tuneful voice was heard from high
        Arise, ye more than dead[3]!
    Then cold, and hot, and moist, and dry
    In order to their stations leap,
        And Music's power obey.
    From harmony, from heavenly harmony
        This universal frame began:
    From harmony to harmony
    Through all the compass of the notes it ran,
    The diapason closing full in Man[4].

    What passion cannot Music raise and quell?
    When Jubal struck the chorded shell[5]

---

[1] *universal frame*: 'structure of the Universe.'

[2] *jarring atoms*, etc.; cf. Genesis i. 2, 3, 'And the earth was without form, and void; and darkness was upon the face of the deep ... And God said, Let there be light; and there was light.'

[3] *more than dead*; i.e. worse than dead, for the dead have at least lived once.

[4] *diapason*: 'the whole range of notes.'

[5] *the chorded shell*: 'the lyre,' which, according to the Greeks, was invented by Hermes from the chance finding of the shell of a tortoise across which the sinews of the animal remained stretched tight.

63. 一六八七年圣塞西莉亚日之歌①

约翰·德莱顿

  这个宇宙结构
    从音乐,从天上的音乐起首。
   当自然还在一堆
    散乱的原素下面②
    抬不起头,   5
  就从天外传来了悦耳的声音
    起来,你们这些连死都不如的东西!
  一霎时冷、热、干、湿,
   各就各位,
    都服从了音乐的威力。   10
  这个宇宙结构
    从音乐,从天上的音乐起奏。
    它从和谐到和谐,
  通过全部音符的领域,
    把整个音域归结成人。   15

  什么热情,音乐不能引它起落?
    当犹八演奏起七弦琴③,

---

① 圣塞西莉亚(St. Cecilia),基督教圣女,公元二三〇年在罗马殉难,后被尊为音乐保护圣徒,其殉难日被定为"圣塞西莉亚日"。——编注者
② "散乱的原素"指宇宙无形体时的状态。——编注者
③ 犹八(Jubal),弦琴之父,见《圣经·创世记》第四章第二一节。——编注者

	His listening brethren stood around,
	And, wondering, on their faces fell
20	To worship that celestial sound.
	Less than a god they thought there could not dwell
	Within the hollow of that shell
	That spoke so sweetly and so well.
	What passion cannot Music raise and quell?
25	The trumpet's loud clangor
	Excites us to arms,
	With shrill notes of anger
	And mortal alarms[①].
	The double double double beat
30	Of the thundering drum
	Cries 'Hark! the foes come;
	Charge, charge, 'tis too late to retreat!'
	The soft complaining flute[②]
	In dying notes discovers
35	The woes of hopeless lovers,
	Whose dirge is whisper'd by the warbling lute.
	Sharp violins proclaim[③]
	Their jealous pangs and desperation,
	Fury, frantic indignation,
40	Depth of pains, and height of passion
	For the fair disdainful dame.

---

① *alarms*: in the literal sense 'calls to arms.'
② *complaining*: 'plaintive.'
③ *Sharp*: 'high-pitched.' A violin has notes which can be reached by no other instrument.

他的兄弟们站在周围倾听，
　　他们赞叹不已，俯伏在地，
　　显露出对天上的音声的崇敬。　　　　　　　20
在那弦琴的音箱中，
　　他们相信住着神一样的精灵
　　才能倾诉得这样甜美，动听。
什么热情，音乐不能引它起落？

　喇叭高声响着　　　　　　　　　　　　　　25
　　用忿怒和致命的警号
　尖锐的音调
　　激励我们去斗争。
　鼓声隆隆雷鸣
　　咚咚、咚咚、咚咚，　　　　　　　　　　30
　　高喊："听，敌人逼近；
后退已迟，前进、前进！"

轻柔、哀诉的笛声
　　以微弱的旋律透露
　　绝望的爱人的悲苦，　　　　　　　　　　35
他的哀歌以啭鸣的琵琶低诉。

　尖声的提琴
抒发他们那嫉妒的失望和苦痛
忿怒，忿怒得发狂，
深深的苦痛，激烈的热情　　　　　　　　　　40
　　为了那个美丽高傲的女郎。

>   But oh! what art can teach,
>   What human voice can reach
>   The sacred organs praise?
> 45   Notes inspiring holy love,
>   Notes that wing their heavenly ways
>   To mend the choirs above.
>
>   Orpheus could lead the savage race,
>   And trees unrooted left their place
> 50   Sequacious of the lyre;
>   But bright Cecilia raised the wonder higher;
>   When to her Organ vocal breath was given,
>   An Angel heard, and straight appear'd —
>   Mistaking Earth for Heaven!
>
>   *Grand Chorus*
> 55   As from the power of sacred lays
>   The spheres began to move,
>   And sung the great Creator's praise
>   To all the blest above;
>
>   So when the last and dreadful hour
> 60   This crumbling pageant shall devour
>   The trumpet shall be heard on high,
>   The dead shall live, the living die,
>   And Music shall untune the sky[1].

J. DRYDEN.

---

[1] *Music shall untune the sky*; as Music had at first 'tuned,' *i.e.* brought into harmony, the several discordant atoms of which the Universe is composed, so at the last day it will 'untune' the Cosmos, that is, reduce it again to 'jarring atoms.'

可是呵！什么艺术能够教导，
什么人间声音能比得上
  这种神圣的风琴的赞扬？
这曲调激起神圣的爱，   45
  这曲调向天上高高飞扬，
增美了天上天使的合唱。

俄耳甫斯能领着野兽，
树木连根离开它们的地方   50
  跟着竖琴走①，
可是辉煌的塞西莉亚创造了更妙的奇迹：
当她把人唱歌的气息赋予了风琴
一个天使听见了，立刻出现——
  把地上当成了天堂！   55

〔大合唱〕
  由于神圣歌曲的威力
    天体就开始移动，
  对天上一切圣灵
    唱出对伟大救世主的赞颂；

当最后那个可怕的时间   60
把这分崩离析的世界吞没
喇叭会在天空响起，
死的将活，活的要死，
音乐将使天宇分解而还原。

张君川 译

---

① 俄耳甫斯是希腊神话传说中的歌手，善弹竖琴，传说他奏的音乐可感动鸟兽木石。参见本卷第66首注释。——编注者

编注 约翰·德莱顿(John Dryden,1631—1700),诗人、剧作家、批评家。生于清教徒家庭,毕业于剑桥大学并获文学士学位,一六七〇年受封为桂冠诗人,并在宫廷任职。他写过许多政论诗、讽刺诗和颂诗,颂诗中最著名的是他为庆祝圣塞西莉亚日而写的两首短诗(即本卷的第63首和116首),诗中把音乐颂扬为最美妙的艺术,生动地再现各种乐器的力量。

64. ON THE LATE MASSACRE IN PIEDMONT

Avenge, O Lord! Thy slaughter'd Saints, whose bones
    Lie scatter'd on the Alpine mountains cold;
    Even them who kept Thy truth so pure of old,
When all our fathers worshipt stocks and stones[①],

Forget not: in Thy book record their groans
    Who were Thy sheep, and in their ancient fold
    Slain by the bloody Piemontese, that roll'd
Mother with infant down the rocks. Their moans

The vales redoubled to the hills, and they
    To Heaven. Their martyr'd blood and ashes sow
O'er all the Italian fields, where still doth sway

The triple tyrant: that from these may grow
A hundred-fold, who, having learnt Thy way,
    Early may fly the Babylonian woe.

J. MILTON.

---

① *stocks*: 'blocks of wood.'

64. 哀皮德蒙特大屠杀①

弥尔顿

主呵,替你的被屠杀的圣徒复仇吧!
　看他们尸骨在阿尔卑斯山遗弃;
　别忘记这些人,因他们在我们祖先
还崇拜木石时,就信守纯正的古教义;

请你把他们的呻吟记在簿子上, 5
　因他们是你的羔羊,却在古栅里,
　被那些血腥的皮德蒙特人杀害,
连抱着婴儿的母亲都推下峭壁。

山谷的哭声震山头,山头的回声
　冲云霄。请你把殉难者们的血与灰, 10
　播种在三重冠暴君统治底下的②

意大利国土内,使圣徒蕃殖千百倍,
待他们晓得了你的报仇的意旨,
　便及早躲避巴比伦大劫的连累③。

殷宝书　译

---

① 这是一六五五年写的一首诗;因天主教徒皮德蒙特干在该年春季屠杀国内非天主教徒而作。这些教徒所信奉的宗教是很原始的一种教派,但其教义颇接近宗教改革后的新教,所以天主教徒时时在迫害他们。这一年,此教派的许多居民被屠杀,连奶着孩子的母亲,都被推到岩下摔死。悲惨的消息传来后。英国人愤怒异常,提出抗议,克伦威尔都几乎出兵远征。——译者
② 教皇戴的冠,有三层帽沿。——译者
③ 弥尔顿把天主教的罗马看作罪孽深重的地方,好像《圣径·新约》中"启示录"里所说的罪孽深重的巴比伦一样,因而他相信罗马有一天也要像巴比伦一样受神谴而遭到毁灭。——译者

65. HORATIAN ODE UPON CROMWELL'S RETURN FROM IRELAND

The forward youth that would appear①,
Must now forsake his Muses dear,
    Nor in the shadows sing
    His numbers languishing.

'Tis time to leave the books in dust,
And oil th' unuséd armour's rust,
    Removing from the wall
    The corslet of the hall.

So restless Cromwell could not cease②
In the inglorious arts of peace,
    But through adventurous war
    Urgéd his active star③:

And like the three-fork'd lightning, first,
Breaking the clouds where it was nurst,
    Did thorough his own side
    His fiery way divide:

---

① *forward*: 'eager,' 'spirited.' *appear*: sc. before the world. The road to fame now, says Marvell, is through action not letters.
② *cease*: in the obsolete sense of 'rest.'
③ *Urgéd his ... stars*: 'directed his destiny.' The stars were commonly supposed to regulate the lives of men, cf. note to No. 62, l. 71; but Cromwell forced his star to do his bidding.

65. 为克伦威尔从爱尔兰归来作贺拉斯体颂歌[①]

马韦尔

将要成名的热血青年,
现在应抛弃缪斯神仙;
　　也别在阴影中吟哦
　　含情脉脉的诗歌。

这是让书本尘封的时候, 5
该把生锈的甲胄上油;
　　并且从墙上拿下
　　厅堂里挂的紧身甲。

如此繁忙的克伦威尔不能
在不光彩的和平艺术中安宁, 10
　　便通过冒险的战争,
　　驱动他活跃的司命星。

并且像三叉状的闪电开始
冲破乌云的包围圈子,
　　他火爆地彻底分裂 15
　　自己这边的势力。

[①] 克伦威尔(Oliver Cromwell,1599—1658),十七世纪英国资产阶级革命领袖,曾统帅国会军与王军作战。共和国成立之后,克伦威尔掌握了政权,其后他曾率军镇压爱尔兰民族起义。贺拉斯体是以古罗马诗人贺拉斯(Horatius,公元前65—公元8)命名的一种四行诗体。——译者

(For 'tis all one to courage high
The emulous, or enemy;
  And with such, to enclose
  Is more than to oppose;)

Then burning through the air he went
And palaces and temples rent;
  And Caesar's head at last
  Did through his laurels blasts.

'Tis madness to resist or blame
The face of angry heaven's flame[①];
  And if we would speak true,
  Much to the man is due.

Who, from his private gardens, where
He lived reserved and austere
  (As if his highest plot
  To plant the bergamot),

Could by industrious valour climb
To ruin the great work of Time,
  And cast the Kingdoms old
  Into another mould;

Though Justice against Fate complain,

---

① *blame The face of angry heaven's flame*: a rather confused expression for 'reprove the lightning to its face.'

（因为不论竞争或对敌，
同样都激发高度的勇气；
  用这种勇气去包揽，
  胜过用它去对抗。）   20

接着他燃烧着从空中穿过，
轰破宫殿和神殿一座座。
  最后是猛击恺撒①
  把他头上的桂冠打。

对天上的烈焰的怒颜相抗   25
或者责难都属疯狂；
  假如我们愿讲真话，
  不少事应归功于他，

他沉默寡言而又简朴地
生活在他的私人庭园里②   30
  （仿佛他最大的打算
  只不过是种植佛手柑），

从那里，他勤劳勇敢地攀登，
能毁灭"时间"的伟大工程③，
  并且把古老的王国   35
  铸造成另一种样式。

  虽然"正义"对"命运"控诉，

---

① "恺撒"在此喻英王。——编注者
② 克伦威尔在四十一岁前赋闲在家，直到长期国会选举时才脱颖而出。——译者
③ 指"英国宪法"。"英国宪法"是由许多不同年代的"成文法""习惯法"和"惯例"所构成，即所谓"不成文宪法"，故有"时间"的伟大工程之说。——译者

And plead the ancient Rights in vain —
But those do hold or break
As men are strong or weak.

Nature, that hateth emptiness,
Allows of penetration less①,
And therefore must make room
Where greater spirits come.

What field of all the Civil War
Where his were not the deepest scar?
And Hampton shows what part
He had of wiser art;

Where, twining subtle fears with hope,
He wove a net of such a scope
That Charles himself might chase
To Carisbrook's narrow case;

That thence the Royal actor borne
The tragic scaffold might adorn:
While round the arméd bands
Did clap their bloody hands;

---

① *Allows of penetration less*: 'can still less admit the interpenetration of matter,' *i. e.* that where one body already is another can be put without removing the first.

并且枉然为旧法权辩护——
　　但这些或保住或完蛋，
　　　像人们或衰弱或健康①。　　　　　　　40

大自然对于空无不喜欢，
不用说容许有物来塞填，
　　故必须留虚位以待
　　　更伟大的精灵到来。

在整个内战的哪一处战场　　　　　　　　45
他不曾留下最深的创伤？
　　然而在汉普顿却显出②
　　　他在哪方面有更高的艺术；

在那儿，把恐惧和希望交缠，
他织成如此规模的一张网，　　　　　　　50
　　连查理都慌忙奔到
　　　卡里斯布鲁克的小笼牢。

因此那皇家的演员天才，
就可能装饰悲惨的断头台③，
　　而四周武装的一帮　　　　　　　　　55
　　　用血淋淋的手鼓掌。

---

① 即：旧法权只有在掌权者掌握住政权，有力量支持它们时，才会有效。反之，则完蛋。——译者
② 查理一世兵败后逃到苏格兰，国会用四十万英镑将他买回，囚于纳斯比附近的汉普顿堡。一六四七年底，国王趁革命派军队内讧之机出逃，逃至怀特岛时被岛上军官拘留于卡里斯布鲁克城堡。有人认为国王出逃是克伦威尔精心设下的圈套。——译者
③ 指一六四九年一月三十日查理一世被送上白厅前的断头台处死。——译者

	He nothing common did or mean
	Upon that memorable scene,
	But with his keener eye
60	The axe's edge did try;

　　　Nor call'd the Gods, with vulgar spite,
　　　To vindicate his helpless right;
　　　　But bow'd his comely head
　　　　Down, as upon a bed.

65　　　— This was that memorable hour
　　　Which first assured the forcéd power①
　　　　So when they did design
　　　　The Capitol's first line,

　　　A Bleeding Head, where they begun,
70　　　Did fright the architects to run;
　　　　And yet in that the State
　　　　Foresaw its happy fate!

　　　And now the Irish are ashamed
　　　To see themselves in one year tamed:
75　　　　So much one man can do
　　　　That does both act and know.

　　　They can affirm his praises best,
　　　And have, though overcome, confest
　　　　How good he is, how just

---

① *assured the forcéd power*: 'secured the power which had been seized by force.'

在那难忘的场面他没有
做什么事情平常或下流，
　　而是用更犀利的目光
　　去试斧刃的锋芒。　　　　　　　　　　　　60

也不带卑下的恶意呼叫老天，
为维护他失效的权利申辩；
　　却把优雅的头低垂，
　　好像在床上安睡。

——这就是那令人难忘的时刻，　　　　　　65
首先保证了权力的夺得，
　　于是他们才描画，
　　设计国会大厦，

在开始的时候，血淋淋的人头
把建筑师们吓得都逃走；　　　　　　　　70
　　然而这国家从其中
　　预见到国运昌隆！

可现在爱尔兰却感到羞辱，
见到自己在一年内被驯服：
　　一个人竟能干这么多，　　　　　　　　75
　　既行动又知道如何做。

对他最好的赞扬他们能作证，
并且虽然被征服，也承认
　　他多么善良和公正，

     And fit for highest trust;

  Nor yet grown stiffer with command,
  But still in the Republic's hand —
    How fit he is to sway
    That can so well obey! —

  He to the Commons' feet presents
  A Kingdom for his first year's rents,
    And (what he may) forbears①
    His fame, to make it theirs:

  And has his sword and spoils ungirt
  To lay them at the Public's skirt.
    So when the falcon high
    Falls heavy from the sky,

  She, having kill'd, no more does search
  But on the next green bough to perch,
    Where, when he first does lure,
    The falconer has her sure.

  — what may not then our Isle presume②
  While victory his crest does plume③?
    What may not others fear
    If thus he crowns each year?

---

① *what he may*: 'so far as he can.'
② *presume*: 'expect.'
③ *his crest does plume*: 'sets a plume on the top of his helmet.'

值得最大地信任。 80

他没有因掌权而变得更严厉，
却仍然在共和国的手掌里——
　　他服从命令听指挥，
　　因而多适合去支配！——

他把一个共和国献在人民脚前， 85
作为他头一年所付的租钱，
　　而且（也许是）避免用
　　他的名，使国家属公众。

还解开带子，把他的战利品
和剑放入共和国的衣裙①。 90
　　因此当鹰隼飞翔，
　　从高空猛然下降，

这时候，它捕杀完毕后就不再干，
而是栖息在第二根绿枝上。
　　养鹰者一开始呼唤它， 95
　　就能够使它听话。

——他盔顶插上了胜利的羽毛，
有什么不会降临我们的海岛？
　　如果他每年都得荣耀，
　　那些人对什么不吓倒？ 100

不久前他到高卢去像恺撒，

---

① 暗喻克伦威尔凌驾于国会之上。——译者

As Caesar he, ere long, to Gaul,
To Italy an Hannibal,
   And to all states not free
   Shall climacteric be.

The Pict no shelter now shall find
Within his parti-colour'd mind[①],
   But from this valour sad[②],
   Shrink underneath the plaid —

Happy, if In the tufted brake[③]
The English hunter him mistake[④],
   Nor lay his hounds in near
   The Caledonian deer.

But thou, the War's and Fortune's son,
March indefatigably on;
   And for the last effect
   Still keep the sword erect:

Besides the force it has to fright
The spirits of the shady night,
   The same arts that did gain
   A power, must it maintain.

A. MARVELL.

---

① *parti-colour'd*: 'variegated,' and so 'variable, unreliable.'
② *valour sad*: i.e. Cromwell's.
③ *tufted brake*: 'thicket growing in clumps.'
④ *mistake*, etc.: 'take him for something else than what he is, and so refrain from setting on his hounds to chase him as a deer.'

又前往意大利,像个汉尼拔①,
　　不自由的国家便都得
　　来到关键的时刻。

在他的五色斑斓的心里,　　　　　　　　105
苏格兰人现在将找不到荫蔽②,
　　只能从冷静的勇士前,
　　蜷缩在方格呢的下边——

幸运啊,如果在莽莽的林薮,
英格兰的猎人把他认错,　　　　　　　　110
　　所以不放猎狗去追逐
　　这头苏格兰的鹿。

然而你,战争和命运的骄子,
不屈不挠地向前直驰;
　　而为了最后的结果,　　　　　　　　115
　　仍然把利剑直握:

这把剑除了有力量去吓退
昏昏暗夜中的魑魅,
　　它还具有同样的艺术
　　把获得的政权紧紧维护。　　　　　　120

吴钧陶　译

编注　安德鲁·马韦尔(Andrew Marvell,1621—1678),玄学派诗

---

① 汉尼拔:迦太基军事统帅(公元前247—前183年),曾率军横扫意大利。——译者
② 克伦威尔于一六五〇年春节进占苏格兰,征服该地拥戴查理一世之子作国王的动乱,"五色斑斓"暗指苏格兰的格子花呢。——译者

人,毕业于剑桥大学,大革命后曾被任命为共和国拉丁文秘书弥尔顿的助手,后任议员。马韦尔写有哲理诗、抒情诗、赞美诗及讽刺诗共五十余首,其中最有名的是《致羞涩的情人》(1650)。他的许多诗篇有玄学派的激情,说理的风格,夸张奇妙的意象,"在轻松的抒情诗的优雅之下蕴藏着坚强的理智"。这首颂歌一方面歌颂了克伦威尔,另一方面也赞扬了查理一世。诗写得明白流畅,一扫玄学派诗人的晦涩风格。

66. LYCIDAS

Elegy on a Firend drowned in the Irish Channel

     Yet once more, O ye laurels, and once more①
     Ye myrtles brown, with ivy never sere,
     I come to pluck your berries harsh and crude,
     And with forced fingers rude
5   Shatter your leaves before the mellowing year②.
     Bitter constraint, and sad occasion dear③
     Compels me to disturb your season due④:
     For Lycidas is dead, dead ere his prime,
     Young Lycidas, and hath not left his peer:
10   Who would not sing for Lycidas? he knew
     Himself to sing, and build the lofty rhyme⑤.
     He must not float upon his watery bier
     Unwept, and welter to the parching wind,
     Without the meed of some melodious tear⑥.

---

① *Yet once more*: it was the second death in Milton's circle within the year; King vas drowned in August, and Milton's mother, who lived with him at Horton, had died the previous April.
② *before the mellowing year*: 'ere Autumn comes to ripen them.'
③ *dear*: not the common word meaning 'beloved' or 'costly,' but a different word now only found in poetry, meaning 'grievous.'
④ *Compels*: the singular is used because the two subjects express but one idea.
⑤ *to sing*: sc. 'how to sing.'
⑥ *meed*: 'due tribute.' *melodious tear*: put for 'tearful melody' or 'sad song,' by a kind of Hypallage or reversal of terms.

66. 黎西达斯①
(悼友人溺于爱尔兰海峡)

弥尔顿

我再一次来,月桂树啊②,
棕色的番石榴和常春藤的绿条啊③,
在你们成熟之前,来强摘你的果子,
我不得已伸出我这粗鲁的手指,
来振落你们这些嫩黄的叶子④。 5
因为亲友的惨遇,痛苦的重压,
迫使我前来扰乱你正茂的年华;
黎西达斯死了,死于峥嵘岁月,他,
年轻的黎西达斯,从未离开过爹妈。
谁能不为黎西达斯哀声歌唱? 10
他自己也善于吟咏,气韵高昂。
他以波涛为灵床,漂浮在水上,
不该没人为他哀哭,他在寒风中翻腾,
该有一份感伤的泪珠儿为他滚滚⑤。

---

① 在这首独唱的悲歌里,作者哀悼自己亲爱的朋友爱德华·金;他不幸于一六三七年在从切斯特渡海去爱尔兰的途中溺水而死。黎西达斯(Lycidas)是希腊、罗马神话中的牧羊美少年,人人称羡;弥尔顿借这古典牧歌的形象来体现同学少年的形象。——译者
② 月桂树象征诗歌的灵感,与诗歌女神缪司(Muse)相联系。月桂、番石榴和常春藤三者都象征诗歌;桂冠由此三者编成。——译者
③ 古代希腊人宴会时,歌人手执番石榴枝,象征司美女神的美,常春藤象征永生。——译者
④ 诗人说自己的诗艺还未成熟。——译者
⑤ "感伤的泪珠儿"指哀歌。斯宾塞(Spencer)曾以《缪司的泪珠》为哀歌的题目。——译者

	Begin then, Sisters of the sacred well
15	
	That from beneath the seat of Jove doth spring,
	Begin, and somewhat loudly sweep the string.
	Hence with denial vain and coy excuse;
	So may some gentle Muse
20	With lucky words favour my destined urn;
	And as he passes, turn①
	And bid fair peace be to my sable shroud.

    For we were nursed upon the self-same hill,
    Fed the same flock by fountain, shade, and rill
25   Together both, ere the high lawns appear'd
    Under the opening eye-lids of the morn,
    We drove a-field, and both together heard②
    What time the gray-fly winds her sultry horn③,
    Battening our flocks with the fresh dews of night④,
30   Oft till the star, that rose at evening bright,
    Toward heaven's descent had sloped his westering wheel⑤.
    Meanwhile the rural ditties were not mute,
    Temper'd to the oaten flute⑥;
    Rough Satyrs danced, and Fauns with cloven heel
35   From the glad sound would not be absent long;
    And old Damoetas loved to hear our song.

---

① *as he passes*: 'Muse,' being put for poet, is here masculine.
② *drove*: sc. 'our flocks.'
③ *the gray-fly*: 'perhaps a dor-beetle.' *winds her sultry horn*: 'drones at noon-tide.'
④ *Battening*: 'feeding full.'
⑤ 'Till the Evening-star (Venus) had begun to sink in the west.'
⑥ *Temper'd*: 'attuned,' 'sung in tune.' *oaten*: 'made of the straw of oats'; though reeds would be more suitable for a shepherd's pipe.

开始唱吧,你们从育芙的宝座下① 15
喷浦的圣泉中出来的缪司姊妹们啊;
开始弹吧,高拂弦琴的天风啊。
不用推辞,不用做忸怩的神情。
祈愿温柔的缪司诗神,
也把祝福的言词赐给我的骨灰瓶②, 20
当哀歌轮到我的时辰,
请祝福我的卧尸,使得安宁!

  因为我们俩,在同一小山上长大,
放牧同一羊群,在泉边、荫下
和泽畔;当高原的草场还在朦胧里, 25
晨曦熹微的时候,我们就在一起。
我们一同在田野上看管羊群,
一同谛听中午闷热时蝇蚋的声音。
早起喂养羊群,草上的鲜露晶莹,
直到夜晚的明星出现,晶光熠熠, 30
经行中天,直到西斜而低垂。
同时,少不了唱唱农家小调;
跟牧笛和谐,清音缥缈;
粗野的撒蒂尔们闻声起舞③,
偶蹄的芬恩们闻声就快快赶上④, 35
连老达摩塔斯也爱听我们的歌唱⑤。

---

① 九个缪司女神是天神朱庇特(Jupiter,即育芙)的女儿,从圣泉中出生,圣泉名沛涟,是九缪司的神祠,在奥林匹斯神山脚下,育芙的宝座在奥林匹斯山上。——译者
② 诗人为爱友写哀歌时,想到自己有朝一日也同样有人为他写哀歌。——译者
③ 撒蒂尔(Satyr)是森林之神,喜欢吹笛和跳舞。——译者
④ 芬恩(Faun)和撒蒂尔在罗马神话中是一对快乐的牧神,芬恩的形象是偶蹄、有尾、有角,半人半山羊,略似希腊的潘(Pan)。——译者
⑤ 达摩塔斯(Damoetas)是神话中的老牧神。——译者

>   But O the heavy change, now thou art gone,
>   Now thou art gone, and never must return!
>   Thee, Shepherd, thee the woods, and desert caves,
> 40 With wild thyme and the gadding vine o'ergrown①
>   And all their echoes, mourn:
>   The willows and the hazel copses green
>   Shall now no more be seen
>   Fanning their joyous leaves to thy soft lays.
> 45 As killing as the canker to the rose②,
>   Or taint-worm to the weanling herds that graze③,
>   Or frost to flowers, that their gay wardrobe wear④
>   When first the white-thorn blows;
>   Such, Lycidas, thy loss to shepherd's ear.
>
> 50   Where were ye, Nymphs, when the remorseless deep
>   Closed o'er the head of your loved Lycidas?
>   For neither were ye playing on the steep
>   Where your old bards, the famous Druids, lie,
>   Nor on the shaggy top of Mona high,
> 55 Nor yet where Deva spreads her wizard stream:
>   Ay me! I fondly dream —
>   Had ye been there — for what could that have done?
>   What could the Muse herself that Orpheus bore,
>   The Muse herself, for her enchanting son⑤,

---

① *gadding*: 'straggling.'
② *canker*: 'caterpillar'; more often called 'cankerworm.'
③ *taint-worm*: a crawling insect supposed to infect cattle. *weanling*: 'newly weaned.'
④ *that their gay wardrobe*, etc.: *i.e.* which have bloomed in the early spring.
⑤ *enchanting*: *i.e.* able to charm beasts and trees by his song.

但是,啊! 来了个严峻的变化!
你去了,而且永远不再回来啦!
你,牧神,你,树林和旷野的各洞窟,
为野生的麝香花和柔藤所覆盖的洞窟, 40
以及各洞窟的回声,都在哭泣。
杨柳的依依,榛树丛的青青,
如今不再映入你的眼睛,
吹拂叶子的乐曲,不再供你清听。
黎西达斯死去的消息传到牧人耳里, 45
好像锈病残暴地摧毁着蔷薇,
传染病摧残新断奶的羊羔,倒在草地,
或严霜摧残披着鲜艳华服的花卉
正当这样的芳时,五月花初吐蓓蕾。

  山林女仙宁芙们啊,无情的深渊① 50
把你们心爱的黎西达斯没顶时,你们在哪里?
你们既不在峭壁巉岩上嬉戏,
那是你们特鲁德老诗人们的长眠地②,
也不在莫拿高山那树木毵毵的顶上③,
又不在狄洼展开神奇河流的地方④。 55
唉,我愚妄地梦见"你们好像在那里"
——可是你们在那儿为他做了什么呢?
亲自生下俄耳甫斯的缪司,她自己⑤
又为自己俊美的儿子做了什么呢?

---

① 宁芙(Nymph),希腊神话中的山林仙女。——译者
② 特鲁德们(The Druids)是英国古代的哲人、僧侣和诗人特鲁德所创的教派,以威尔士西北安格勒塞岛为中心。——译者
③ 莫拿(Mona),安格勒塞岛的高山,山上多长林木。——译者
④ 狄洼(Deva),河名,在切斯特,爱德华·金出帆处。——译者
⑤ 俄耳甫斯(Orpheus),希腊神话中的音乐家,他的琴音能感动草木鸟兽。他的母亲是缪司卡里俄珀(Calliope),司叙事诗的。——译者

    Whom universal nature did lament,
    When by the rout that made the hideous roar①
    His gory visage down the stream was sent,
    Down the swift Hebrus to the Lesbian shore?

    Alas! what boots it with uncessant care
    To tend the homely, slighted, shepherd's trade
    And strictly meditate the thankless Muse②?
    Were it not better done, as others use,
    To sport with Amaryllis in the shade③,
    Or with the tangles of Neæra's hair?
    Fame is the spur that the clear spirit doth raise
    (That last infirmity of noble mind)
    To scorn delights, and live laborious days;
    But the fair guerdon when we hope to find,
    And think to burst out into sudden blaze,
    Comes the blind Fury with the abhorréd shears
    And slits the thin-spun life. 'But not the praise'
    Phoebus replied, and touch'd my trembling ears;
    'Fame is no plant that grows on mortal soil,
    Nor in the glistering foil④
    Set off to the world, nor in broad rumour lies;
    But lives and spreads aloft by those pure eyes⑤
    And perfect witness of all-judging Jove;

---

① *rout*: 'disorderly crowd.'
② *I.e.* to devote oneself to serious poetry.
③ *To sport with Amaryllis*, etc.; *i.e.* to write love songs. Amaryllis and Neæra are two shepherdesses in the *Eclogues* of Virgil.
④ *foil*: a thin metal plate put under a jewel to show it off.
⑤ *by those pure eyes*: 'according to the light in which Jove sees it.'

全宇宙的万物都为他的孩子哀悼,　　　　　　　　60
他在混乱中发出可怕的喊叫,
他那血淋淋的头颅被抛入河中,
从奔流的希布鲁斯河漂流到列斯博岛①。

啊! 那有什么好处,不断熟虑
这些平常的,受轻视的牧人歌曲,　　　　　　　65
深思冥想,苦吟无报酬的诗句?
和阿玛莱利斯在树荫下做做游戏,
或者揪着尼艾拉的鬓发相嬉②,
像其他的牧童一样,岂不更惬意?
荣誉是鞭策,把纯洁的精神提起,　　　　　　　70
(使高贵的心灵把最后的弱点抛弃)
藐视逸乐,甘心过劳苦的日子;
但当我们希望能得到酬劳,
想要爆发突然的火光时,
来了瞎眼的复戾,带着可厌的镰刀③,　　　　　75
割断曼妙如锦的生活。福玻斯宣告④,
振动我们颤栗的耳朵般地说道:
"不用称赞;荣誉不是生长于尘世的花草,
也不是尘世土银箔镜子的倒影,反照,
也不靠传播广远的流言、风谣,　　　　　　　　80
而是由判断万事的育芙大神的全智,
由他那双明察秋毫的慧眼使你升高;

---

① 俄耳甫斯侮辱了赛果斯的女子,她们为了复仇而把他撕成碎片,他的头颅被抛入希布鲁斯河(Hebrus),漂流到爱琴海的列斯博岛。——译者
② 阿玛莱利斯(Amaryllis)、尼艾拉(Neæra),维吉尔《牧歌》中的农家少女。——译者
③ 复戾(Fury),罗马神话中的三个复仇女神,司恶运。弥尔顿在这里借用为残酷的命运。——译者
④ 福玻斯(Phoebus)是诗歌之神,即阿波罗,太阳神。——译者

  As he pronounces lastly on each deed,
  Of so much fame in heaven expect thy meed.'

85   O fountain Arethuse, and thou honour'd flood
  Smooth-sliding Mincius, crown'd with vocal reeds,
  That strain I heard was of a higher mood①:
  But now my oat proceeds②,
  And listens to the herald of the sea
90   That came in Neptune's plea③;
  He ask'd the waves, and ask'd the felon winds④,
  What hard mishap hath doom'd this gentle swain?
  And question'd every gust of rugged wings
  That blows from off each beakéd promontory:
95   They knew not of his story;
  And sage Hippotades their answer brings,
  That not a blast was from his dungeon stray'd;
  The air was calm, and on the level brine
  Sleek Panope with all her sisters play'd.
100   It was that fatal and perfidious bark
  Built in the eclipse, and rigg'd with curses dark⑤,
  That sunk so low that sacred head of thine.

---

① *That strain*: i.e. ll. 76-84; after which the shepherd strain begins again.
② *my oat*: 'oaten pipe.'
③ *in Neptune's plea*: 'to speak in defence of Neptune,' the sea-god, who protested his innocence in the matter.
④ *felon*: 'savage,' 'cruel.'
⑤ *Built in the eclipse*: there has always been a superstition that eclipses, especially eclipses of the sun, portend disaster.

他最后将宣布每个人的每一行为,
在天上有你盼望的荣誉,作为酬劳。"

  啊,阿瑞土斯泉,光荣的流水①,   85
明洲斯柔滑的河边,生长能歌的芦荻,
所唱的曲子,表现更高的情意。
但现在,我的牧歌仍在开展,
并倾听大海的传令官歌唱,
他传达的是海神尼普顿的愿望②。   90
他责问浪涛,责问凶恶的风波,
为什么给这山乡少年这么大的灾祸?
他责问一阵阵飞过的暴风,
它们正从钩形的岬角吹过。
风和浪并不知黎西达斯的来历;   95
贤明的希玻达德斯代为说明心意③:
那一天他并没有从风的地牢放出大气④;
那时天空平稳,海上静谧,
漂亮的帕诺佩和姊妹们在海上游戏⑤。
那是因为命运和靠不住的船只,   100
制造紊乱,装载了可诅咒的阴翳,
使虔诚的头颅沉入深深的海底。

---

① 阿瑞土斯(Arethuse)本是神话中的山林女仙,曾为河神阿尔斐俄斯所追求,终于变成河流。明洲斯河在诗人维吉尔生长的地方。——译者
② 尼普顿(Neptune),罗马神话中的海神。——译者
③ 希玻达德斯(Hippotades),风的管理者。——译者
④ 这里把风拟人化了。古罗马维吉尔在《伊尼德》第一卷,描写风怎样被关在地牢里,有时把它们放出来。——译者
⑤ 帕诺佩(Panope)姊妹是海上的精灵,晴天出来游戏。说明爱德华·金溺水时并无风暴,海上平静,是船只本身出毛病,或命运作祟。——译者

Next Camus, reverend sire, went footing slow①,
His mantle hairy, and his bonnet sedge②.
105　Inwrought with figures dim, and on the edge
Like to that sanguine flower inscribed with woe:
'Ah! who hath reft,' quoth he, 'my dearest pledge③?'
Last came, and last did go
The pilot of the Galilean lake;
110　Two massy keys he bore of metals twain
(The golden opes, the iron shuts amain④);
He shook his mitred locks, and stern bespake;
'How well could I have spared for thee, young swain,
Enow of such as for their bellies' sake
115　Creep and intrude and climb into the fold!
Of other care they little reckoning make
Than how to scramble at the shearers' feast⑤,
And shove away the worth bidden guest.
Blind mouths! that scarce themselves know how to hold
120　A sheep-hook, or have learn'd aught else the least
That to the faithful herdman's art belongs!
What recks it them? What need they? They are sped⑥;

---

① *Camus*: god of the Cam, or Granta, the river on which Cambridge stands.
② *sedge*: 'flags,' growing on the banks of rivers; the lines mean 'His mantle [was] hairy, and his bonnet [was made of] sedge [and] inwrought, etc.'
③ *reft*: the past participle of a verb, now obsolete except in poetry, to 'reave,' meaning to seize by force. *pledge*: like the Latin *pignus*, used for 'child,' children being pledges of love between the parents.
④ *amain*: 'forcibly.'
⑤ *scramble at the shearers' feast*: i.e. struggle for preferment and other church emoluments.
⑥ *What recks it them*? 'What does it concern them?' *They are sped*: 'they have got what they wanted.' Cf. 'God speed you.'

228

剑河之神,可敬的祖先,行动缓慢①,
　　他的斗篷毛氄氄,他的帽子是茅秆,
　　缀上惨淡的花边,他的帽缘　　　　　　　　105
　　像是猩红色的花,象征灾难。
　　他说,"啊！谁夺去我最亲爱的孩子?"
　　最后来,而最后去的,
　　是加利利湖上的舟子②;
　　他带着两把不同的金属大钥匙　　　　　　110
　　(金的管开,铁的管闭,十分结实)。
　　他抖动主教的发卷严厉地说道:
　　"小伙子啊,我免了你该有多好③?
　　我看得够了,那些贪婪的贼,
　　偷偷地,连挤带爬地进了教会!　　　　　　115
　　对于关心人的事,他们极少关怀,
　　却热衷于争夺剪羊毛宴会的席位,
　　那些值得邀请的客人却被挤开。
　　他们不懂怎样使用牧杖,瞎指挥!
　　起码的牧羊知识也没有学会!　　　　　　120
　　该关心什么？它们缺少什么？全不理会。
　　他们自己吃饱了,爱听听邪曲的歪诗,

---

① 剑河之神(Camus)或剑桥大学先辈之灵来哀悼黎西达斯。——译者
② 加利利湖的舟子指耶稣的门徒彼得,他原先是加利利的渔夫,是初期基督教创始人之一。传说他管天堂的门,有两把钥匙,是第一任主教。——译者
③ "免了你",指免进腐朽的教会之门,去做牧师。弥尔顿和金都是剑桥大学培养,预备做牧师的。弥尔顿拒绝了,金溺死了,都免了。——译者

	And when they list, their lean and flashy songs①
	Grate on their scrannel pipes of wretched straw②;
125	The hungry sheep look up, and are not fed,
	But swoln with wind and the rank mist they draw③
	Rot inwardly, and foul contagion spread:
	Besides what the grim wolf with privy paw
	Daily devours apace, and nothing said:
130	— But that two-handed engine at the door
	Stands ready to smite once, and smite no more.'

	Return, Alpheus, the dread voice is past
	That shrunk thy streams; return, Sicilian Muse,
	And call the vales, and bid them hither cast
135	Their bells and flowerets of a thousand hues.
	Ye valleys low, where the mild whispers use④
	Of shades, and wanton winds, and gushing brooks,
	On whose fresh lap the swart star sparely looks,
	Throw hither all your quaint enamell'd eyes
140	That on the green turf suck the honey'd showers
	And purple all the ground with vernal flowers⑤.
	Bring the rathe primrose that forsaken dies⑥,

---

① *their lean and flashy songs*: an allusion to the dreary and unsatisfying preachments of the hireling clergy. *flashy*: 'watery,' 'insipid.'
② *scrannel*: 'thin, meagre.'
③ *draw*: 'breathe in.' The 'wind' is spiritual pride, and the 'mists' are false doctrines.
④ *use*: 'dwell.' *the whispers Of shades*: a compressed expression for 'the whispers of trees that cast a shade.'
⑤ *purple*: a very vague colour, comprising any shade from crimson to violet. *vernal*: 'of spring.'
⑥ *rathe*: 'early.'

在劣等的芦笛上吹吹刺耳的曲子；
饥饿的羊群仰头求食，没有人喂，
只让它们喝西北风，吸收迷雾尘埃，　　　　　125
让它们内脏枯萎，瘟疫蔓延开来；
特别是那些残酷的狼，魔爪伸得长长，
每天吞食羊群，他们却一声不响①。
但那站在门口的，双手拿武器，
准备一劳永逸地把它彻底摧毁②！　　　　　130

阿尔斐俄斯啊，回来吧③；
那威吓河流的可怕声音过去啦④；
西西里的缪司啊，请回来吧⑤，
呼召山谷们，快把花种撒下，
种出钟形花和万紫千红的小花。　　　　　135
溪谷深深，在那儿常有温柔的对话，
谈到树荫、轻盈的风和洋溢的河注。
连黑星也要向这鲜艳的溪谷瞟一眼⑥，
睁开你们英俊闪光的两眼，看一看
这绿色草地吸收甜蜜的阵雨，　　　　　140
三春的花朵染红大地，文采郁郁。
有早春开放，不见阳光便死的樱草花，

---

① 残酷的狼指罗马天主教会。他们剥削西欧各国的教民。——译者
② 这两行预言英国教会将要被改革。"武器"，有人解释为斧子，如《圣经·马太福音》第三章第十节所说："现在斧子已经放在树根上，凡不结好果子的树，就砍下来，丢在火里。"——译者
③ 阿尔斐俄斯（Alpheus）是阿尔斐俄斯河的神，他曾追求山林女仙阿瑞士斯（Arethuse），她逃到西西里时，月神把她变成河流；他便带他的河流穿过地下和海底赶到西西里和她合流。——译者
④ 威吓河流的声音，典出《圣经·旧约·诗篇》第一〇四篇第九节："你的斥责一发，水便奔逃；他的雷声一发，水便奔流。"——译者
⑤ 西西里的缪司（Sicilian Muse）是司牧歌的女神。——译者
⑥ 黑星指天狼星。——译者

        The tufted crow-toe, and pale jessamine①,
        The white pink, and the pansy freak'd with jet,
145   The glowing violet②,
        The musk-rose, and the well-attired woodbine③,
        With cowslips wan that hang the pensive head,
        And every flower that sad embroidery wears:
        Bid amarantus all his beauty shed,
150   And daffadillies fill their cups with tears
        To strew the laureat hearse where Lycid lies④.
        For, so to interpose a little ease,
        Let our frail thoughts dally with false surmise⑤;
        Ay me! whilst thee the shores and sounding seas⑥
155   Wash far away, — where'er thy bones are hurl'd,
        Whether beyond the stormy Hebrides
        Where thou perhaps, under the whelming tide,
        Visitest the bottom of the monstrous world⑦;
        Or whether thou, to our moist vows denied⑧,
160   Sleep'st by the fable of Bellerus old,
        Where the great Vision of the guarded mount
        Looks toward Namancos and Bayona's hold,
        — Look homeward, Angel, now, and melt with ruth:

---

① *tufted*: 'growing in clusters.'
② *freak'd*: 'streaked.'
③ *woodbine*: 'honeysuckle.'
④ *laureat*: 'crowned with laurel.' *hearse*: besides its modern meaning, this word means a coffin, or a bier, or a framework used to cover either of them.
⑤ *I.e.* Let us, to ease our aching hearts, pretend that we have found his body.
⑥ *the shores*: some such verb as 'hold' must be supplied; for 'wash far away,' though appropriate to 'seas,' cannot with equal propriety be applied to 'shores.' This figure of speech is called Zeugma.
⑦ *monstrous*: 'teeming with monsters.'
⑧ *our moist vows*: 'our tearful prayers.'

丛生的百脉根花,淡黄色的茉莉花,
纯白的石竹,三色堇装饰着点点划划,
生长着紫罗兰和麝香蔷薇花, 145
还有浓妆淡抹的忍冬花,
青白的西樱草挂在沉思的额头,
每一朵花都带愁容,蹙额凝眸。
叫不凋花倾注全部的美,
水仙花用眼泪盛满它们的玉杯 150
洒向黎西达斯长眠的诗人茔垒。
因此,我们暂且不必紧张,
让我们的意马心猿放开推想:
啊,浅水的海滩和深水的海洋
把你的骸骨远远冲去,卷向何方! 155
可能在西海多风暴的岛外洪荒①,
在那儿你沉在浪潮的下边,
到了怪物世界的底面;
或者是你不依我们含泪的祈愿,
去睡在古传奇所说的倍莱鲁斯的近旁, 160
那儿仿佛有伟大的守望者的岗哨山上②
可以监视拿曼柯斯和巴约那的哨岗③。
天使长啊,请多照顾故乡,慈悲为怀④;

---

① 西海的群岛名希珀莱特群岛(Hebrides),约二百小岛散布在苏格兰港外。爱德华·金是在爱尔兰海溺死的,可能被漂到北方去。——译者
② 倍莱鲁斯(Bellerus)是传说中英国南部蒙特湾地极区的巨人,地极区海上有个高耸的巉岩,其上仿佛有把椅子,传说是天使长弥迦勒坐在那上面瞭望的椅子。他从那巉岩上一直望到西班牙的拿曼柯斯和巴约那。因此那岩被称为岗哨山。——译者
③ 拿曼柯斯(Namancos)和巴约那(Bayona)都是西班牙沿岸的地名。——译者
④ 天使长弥迦勒瞭望时看得极远处,请他特别看顾近处周围,救救黎西达斯。——译者

— And, O ye dolphins, waft the hapless youth!

165　　　　　Weep no more, woeful shepherds, weep no more,
　　　　　　For Lycidas, your sorrow, is not dead,
　　　　　　Sunk though he be beneath the watery floor;
　　　　　　So sinks the day-star in the ocean-bed①,
　　　　　　And yet anon repairs his drooping head
170　　　　　And tricks his beams, and with new-spangled ore②
　　　　　　Flames in the forehead of the morning sky:
　　　　　　So Lycidas sunk low, but mounted high
　　　　　　Through the dear might of Him that walk'd the waves;
　　　　　　Where, other groves and other streams along,
175　　　　　With nectar pure his oozy locks he laves③,
　　　　　　And hears the unexpressive nuptial song
　　　　　　In the blest kingdoms meek of joy and love.
　　　　　　There entetain him all the saints above
　　　　　　In solemn troops, and sweet societies,
180　　　　　That sing, and singing in their glory move,
　　　　　　And wipe the tears for ever from his eyes.
　　　　　　Now, Lycidas, the shepherds weep no more;
　　　　　　Henceforth thou art the Genins of the shore
　　　　　　In thy large recompense, and shalt be good④
185　　　　　To all that wander in that perilous flood.

---

① *the day-star*: 'the Sun.'
② *tricks*: 'sets off,' 'adorns.' *new-spangled ore*: 'gold glittering with renewed brightness.'
③ *oozy*: i.e. defiled with sand and mud from the sea-bottom.
④ *In thy large recompense*: 'by way of full compensation to thee.'

你，海豚啊，请飘送这不幸的少年回来①!

　　　　别再哭泣,悲伤的牧人,别再哭泣, 165
　　　　因为你们所悲悼的黎西达斯没有死②,
　　　　虽然他现在可能沉在碧波之下,
　　　　好像太阳沉落在海洋的眠床上,
　　　　不久又把那低垂的头颅高昂,
　　　　闪动着他的眼光,重新大放光芒, 170
　　　　从他那晨空样的前额射出金光:
　　　　黎西达斯已经升得高,虽曾沉得低,
　　　　通过那走在水波上的救主的大力③,
　　　　沿着高处别有的丛林和清溪,
　　　　有琼浆玉液洗净他鬈发上的污泥, 175
　　　　听聆意想不到的祝婚歌词,
　　　　享受那温柔国土的爱和欢喜④。
　　　　上界的圣者全部都接待他,
　　　　有美妙的各级天使,庄严的队队天军,
　　　　他们歌唱,用光辉的姿态歌唱, 180
　　　　永远擦干他双眼的泪痕。
　　　　现在,黎西达斯啊,牧人们不再哭泣;
　　　　从今以后,你是海岸上的神人⑤,
　　　　你的巨大酬报,将要恩及
　　　　一切在大海风波中颠簸的人们。 185

---

① 古代希腊的弹唱诗人阿利昂(Arion)乘船往哥林多去的途中,被舟子抛入海中,有海豚背负他,获救。他的音乐使海豚入迷。——译者
② 说他活在天国。他的死像太阳沉落而又上升。——译者
③ 《圣经·马太福音》第十四章第二十五节:"夜里四更天,耶稣在海面上行走。"——译者
④ 《圣经·新约·启示录》第十九章第九节:"被请赴羔羊之婚筵的有福了。"预言末日审判后坏人灭亡而好人得赴羔羊的婚礼,一同享乐。——译者
⑤ 罗马传说:溺水而死的人将变为该地区保护航行者的精灵。——译者

Thus sang the uncouth swain to the oaks and rills[①],
While the still morn went out with sandals grey[②];
He touch'd ahe tender stops of various quills[③],
With eager thought warbling his Doric lay:
And now the sun had stretch'd out all the hills[④],
And now was dropt into the western bay:
At last he rose, and twitch'd his mantle blue[⑤]:
To-morrow to fresh woods, and pastures new[⑥].

J. MILTON.

[①] *Thus sang*: here the pastoral poem ends and Milton speaks of the singer as of some one outside himself.

[②] *morn went out*: the grey morning 'goes out' as full day comes in.

[③] *quills*: i.e. the pipes on which he played.

[④] *all the hills*: i.e. the shadows of all the hills.

[⑤] *twitch'd*: 'hitched it up round him.'

[⑥] *fresh woods*: his sorrow for his dead comrade drove him from the haunts where they had lived together. There may be an allusion here to the fact that a few months after writing *Lycidas* Milton went to Italy for fifteen months.

静谧的黎明时分,白茫茫一片,
　　他出去和粗野的牧童向橡树、小溪唱和,
　　在各种的芦笛上试吹温柔的曲调,
　　吹出热烈的情思,谱出多利安的牧歌①;
　　直到夕阳西下,把群山的影子拉长,
　　射进西边深山中的凹地。
　　他终于起来了,披上蓝色的斗篷②:
　　明天将奔向清鲜的树林,新的草地。

朱维之　译

---

① 古希腊牧歌的名作者多是用多利安方言写的。——译者
② 蓝色的斗篷是牧人的装束。——译者

67. ON THE TOMBS IN WESTMINSTER ABBEY

Mortality, behold and fear,
What a change of flesh is here!
Think how many royal bones
Sleep within these heaps of stones;
5   Here they lie, had realms and lands①,
Who now want strength to stir their hands,
Where from their pulpits seal'd with dust
They preach, 'In greatness is no trust.'
Here's an acre sown indeed
10 With the richest royallest seed
That the earth did e'er suck in
Since the first man died for sin:
Here the bones of birth have cried②
'Though gods they were, as men they died!'
15 Here are sands, ignoble things,
Dropt from the ruin'd sides of kings:
Here's a world of pomp and state
Buried in dust, once dead by fate③.

F. BEAUMONT.

---

① *Here they lie, had realms*: sc. who had realms.
② *bones of birth*: sc. of noble birth.
③ *once dead*: i.e. when it is once dead.

67. 写在威斯敏斯特寺墓群之前①

鲍蒙特

望而生畏吧！命定死亡的人们，
看血肉之躯在此变得谁能辨认！
想一想古今多少帝王的骸骨，
只落得与累累石堆同眠为伍。
他们曾拥有王国领地，如今沉睡不起，　　　　　5
连挥动一下自己的手臂也无能为力。
从他们那些尘埃密封的讲台，
传来的说教是："伟大不可信赖。"
撒在这弹丸之地内的一行一陇
尽都是最豪富、最高贵的龙种；　　　　　　　10
而大地不断地把他们吮吸吞灭，
自从他们中间第一人死于罪孽。
出身显贵的尸骨在这里一直叫喊：
"别看在世犹神，死去也和凡人一般。"
这里有的是沙粒，微不足道的沙粒——　　　　15
从化为灰烬的王公们身上洒落的遗迹。
这里有说不尽富丽堂皇、威武庄严的排场，
一旦命运注定死亡，只能在尘埃中埋葬。

编注 弗朗西斯·鲍蒙特（Francis Beaumont，1584—1616），英国文学史上与约翰·弗莱彻（参见本卷第104首编注）齐名的剧作家和诗人，两人合写了十多部剧本，如《菲拉斯特》（1609，又名《流血的爱情》）、《少女的悲剧》（1611）等。鲍蒙特还写了《厌恶女人者》（1606）、《燃杵骑士》（1607）等名剧。

---

① 威斯敏斯特寺（The Westminste Abbey，又译为西敏寺），英国历代君主及著名将相国葬之地。——译者

68. THE LAST CONQUEROR

Victorious men of earth, no more
    Proclaim how wide your empires are;
Though you bind-in every shore,
    And your triumphs reach as far
        As night or day,
Yet you, proud monarchs, must obey
And mingle with forgotten ashes, when
Death calls ye to the crowd of common men.

Devouring Famine, Plague, and War,
    Each able to undo mankind,
Death's servile emissaries are[①];
    Nor to thse alone confined,
        He hath at will
More quaint and subtle ways to kill[②];
A smile or kiss, as he will use the art[③],
Shall have the cunning skill to break a heart.

                                        J. SHIRLEY.

[①] *servile emissaries*: 'slaves sent out do his bidding.'
[②] *quaint*: 'ingenious.'
[③] *A smile or kiss*: i.e. when given to another.

68. 最后的征服者

谢尔利

世间的胜利者哟！莫再扬言
　你们的帝国如何辽阔；
尽管你们囊括了远近的海岸，
　尽管你们的战功赫赫，
　　如日夜广被人寰。　　　　　　　　　5
但高傲的君主们！当死神一声召唤，
你们也必须听从，置身芸芸众生的行列
同他们的灰烬掺合在一起，被人忘却。

那吞噬一切的饥荒、瘟疫和战火，
　每一桩都能使人类濒于毁灭。　　　　10
它们都是死神派出的卑顺的使者，
　但人间的灾难绝不限于这些，
　　因为死神还专擅
更机智、更高明的杀人手段。
一笑一吻，只要运用得十分巧妙①，　　15
那狡黠的伎俩都将令人心碎魂销。

　　　　　　　　　　　　　　黄宏勋　译

编注　詹姆斯·谢尔利（James Shirley，1596—1666），剧作家和诗人，著有三十五部剧本，多数是悲喜剧。本诗选自他一六五三年写成并上演的假面剧《爱神与死神》(Cupid and Death)。

---

① 一笑一吻，指致人于死地的虚情假意。——译者

69. DEATH THE LEVELLER

    The glories of our blood and state①
        Are shadows, not substantial things;
    There is no armour against fate;
        Death lays his icy hand on kings;
            Sceptre and Crown
            Must tumble down,
    And in the dust be equal made
    With the poor crooked scythe and spade.

    Some men with swords may reap the field,
        And plant fresh laurels where they kill;
    But their strong nerves at last must yield;
        They tame but one another still②;
            Early or late
            They stoop to fate,
    And must give up their murmuring breath③
    When they, pale captives, creep to death.

    The garlands wither on your brow;
        Then boast no more your mighty deeds;
    Upon Death's purple altar now④
        See where the victor-victim bleeds;

---

① *blood and state*: 'birth and position.'
② *tame but one another*: i.e. they cannot vanquish death.
③ *murmuring*: i.e. complaining of the shortness of life.
④ *purple*: 'royal.'

69. 死亡使人人平等

谢尔利

我们的血统和权势带来的荣华,
  不是什么实体,而只是幻影;
从来没有能抵挡住命运的盔甲;
  当死神冰冷的手放在国王们头顶:
    权杖与王冠   5
     终久要倒翻,
它们将同卑微的长曲镰和和铁锹,
不分高低,同样在尘土中长眠。

有些人或许能用利剑刈割田中作物,
  在杀戮众生之地种植新的月桂①;   10
可是他们坚强的神圣最后也要屈服;
  他们绝不可能把死亡征服击退:
    他们或早或迟
     也得向命运屈膝,
纵然抱怨人生苦短,最终也得吞声咽气,   15
像一群苍白无力的俘虏,爬进死亡之域。

重重的花环在你的额头凋残,
  再不要夸耀你的什么丰功伟业!
请看,在死神紫黑色的祭坛②
  胜利者——受害者此刻都在流血。   20

---

① 月桂在此喻荣誉、功勋。——译者
② 紫色本是象征皇家王者的颜色,西方各国古帝王均着紫袍。此处转用于死神,
以示其至高无上的权威。——译者

>   Your heads must come
>   To the cold tomb;
> Only the actions of the just
> Smell sweet, and blossom in their dust.

J. SHIRLEY.

你们高贵的头颅
　　也要钻入冰冷的坟墓；
唯有正真的人们的正义行为，
　　在尘埃中蓓蕾盛开，永葆芳菲。

黄宏勋　译

编注 此诗选自谢尔利一六五九年发表的诗剧《埃阿斯与尤利西斯之争》(*The Contention of Ajax and Ulysses*)第三场，是谢尔利诗歌中之佳作。

70. WHEN THE ASSAULT WAS INTENDED TO THE CITY

Captain, or Colonel, or Knight in arms,
   Whose chance on these defenceless doors may seize,
   If deed of honour did thee ever please,
Guard them, and him within protect from harms.

He can requite thee; for he knows the charms[1]
   That call fame on such gentle acts as these,
   And he can spread thy name o'er lands and seas,
Whatever clime the sun's bright circle warms[2].

Lift not thy spear against the Muses' bower:
   The great Emathian conqueror bid spare
The house of Pindarus, when temple and tower

   Went to the ground: and the repeated air
Of sad Electra's poet had the power
   To save the Athenian walls from ruin bare.

J. MILTON.

---

[1] *charms*: 'spells,' *i.e.* his verse.
[2] *Whatever clime*: in apposition to 'lands and seas.'

70. 当矛头指向这座城市的时候

弥尔顿

上尉、上校、贯甲执戈的武士,
 快来保卫手无寸铁的居民,良机勿失,
 你们要是向往那丰功伟绩的荣耀,
就来把城中的居民和诗人加意护持①。

他会报答你们,因为他素来深知   5
 为这样的义举召唤声誉的方式,
 他还能够将你们的英名传播四海,
传到阳光普照下的任何乡村与城池。

不要把矛头挥向这缪司的园林:
 显赫的艾玛西亚征服者也曾下令②,   10
 把神庙、高塔连城镇一齐荡平,

 却不许损害品达的故居一厘一分;
 高吟悲怆的伊莱克屈的行吟诗人,
 还挽救了雅典的墙垣免遭毁损③。

谭建华 译

---

① 一八四二年十月,埃吉山之战失利,王军进逼伦敦。——译者
② 指亚历山大大帝,他诞生于艾玛西亚的佩拉。公元前三三六年,亚历山大攻入希腊,陷底比斯城。该城劫后幸存的居民都沦为奴隶,所有房屋一律夷为平地。但诞生于该城的著名诗人品达,虽已去世一百多年,他的英名仍使他的后代和故居得到赦免,幸免于难。——译者
③ 斯巴达人于公元前四○四年攻陷雅典,本拟摧毁全城,幸得一位乐师奏起欧里庇得斯的悲剧《伊莱克屈拉》感动了征服者,只拆毁了雅典通往庇拉乌斯港之间的路墙,保存了雅典。——译者

71. ON HIS BLINDNESS

When I consider how my light is spent
   Ere half my days, in this dark world and wide,
   And that one talent which is death to hide
Lodged with me useless, though my soul more bent

5   To serve therewith my Maker, and present
      My true account, lest He returning chide, —
      Doth God exact day-labour, light denied?
   I fondly ask: — But Patience, to prevent[1]

   That murmur, soon replies; God doth not need
10   Either man's work, or His own gifts; who best
      Bear His mild yoke, they serve Him best: His state

Is kingly; thousands at His bidding speed
   And post o'er land and ocean without rest: —
   They also serve who only stand and wait.

                        J. MILTON.

---

[1] *fondly*: 'foolishly.'

71. 哀失明

弥尔顿

想到了在这茫茫黑暗的世界里,
 还未到半生这两眼就已失明①,
 想到了我这个泰伦特,要是埋起来②,
会招致死亡,却放在我手里无用,

虽然我一心想用它服务造物主,
 免得报账时,得不到他的宽容;
 想到这里,我就愚蠢地自问,
"神不给我光明,还要我做日工?"

但"忍耐"看我在抱怨,立刻止住我:
"神并不要你工作,或还他礼物。
 谁最能服从他,谁就是忠于职守,

他君临万方,只要他一声吩咐,
 万千个天使就赶忙在海陆奔驰,
 但侍立左右的,也还是为他服务。"

殷宝书 译

---

① 一六五一年,弥尔顿一目失明;一六五二年,因写《替人民声辩》操劳过度,双目失明,时年四十四岁——编注者
② 泰伦特是古时算银子的单位。《圣经·诗篇》中的泰伦特喻诗人的才能。——编注者

72. CHARACTER OF A HAPPY LIFE

How happy is he born or taught
    That serveth not another's will;
Whose armour is his honest thought,
    And silly truth his highest skill[1]!

Whose passions not his masters are,
    Whose soul is still prepared for death;
Untied unto the world with care
    Of princely love or vulgar breath;

Who hath his life from rumours freed[2],
    Whose conscience is his strong retreat;
Whose state can neither flatterers feed,
    Nor ruin make accusers great;

Who envieth none whom chance doth raise
    Or vice; who never understood[3]
How deepest wounds are given with praise;
    Nor rules of state, but rules of good[4]:

---

[1] *silly*: 'simple.'
[2] *hath his life from rumours freed*: i.e. never listens to gossip, nor retails it.
[3] *who never vnderstood*: i.e. has never learnt by receiving praise to which he knew he was not entitled.
[4] I.e. in his management of people is not guided by politic considerations but by a simple love of justice.

72. 幸福生活的本色

沃顿

多么幸福啊！不管是天生还是学会
　　他从不亦步亦趋,屈从别人的旨意;
正直的思想是他赖以护身的甲铠,
　　他最高超的技艺就是单纯的真理。

他不愿让情欲充当自己的主人, 5
　　他的灵魂总是做好死去的准备。
他不希罕贵人的眷爱,也不担心
　　俗人的议论。他在世上全无牵累。

他使自己一生摆脱流言蜚语,
　　良知是他坚实而可靠的归宿。 10
他的地位既不会招致奉承阿谀,
　　他的垮台也不会使告发者有利可图①。

他从不妒羡谁走了运而青云直上,
　　谁因作恶而升迁。他也从不曾体验
非分的赞颂可能造成多么深刻的创伤; 15
　　他不懂治国之术,只知道为善的规范。

---

① 罗马帝国时期,告密者对有钱有势的人提出控告若能获胜,可分得受控人的一笔财产。——译者

> Who God doth late and early pray
>   More of his grace than gifts to lend[1];
> Who entertains the harmless day
>   With a well-chosen book or friend;
>
> — This man is free from servile bands[2]
>   Of hope to rise, or fear to fall;
> Lord of himself, though not of lands;
>   And having nothing, he hath all.

SIR H. WOTTON.

---

[1] *I.e.* to grant him spiritual rather than material benefits.
[2] *servile bands*: 'enslaving chains.'

他从早到晚祈祷上帝的仁慈宽宥,
　远胜于从上帝那里乞求赏赐;
他伴同一本精选的书、一位良友,
　度过那有益无害的骎骎佳日。 20

——这样的人摆脱了卑躬屈膝的桎梏:
　他不希冀荣升,也不惧怕贬谪;
他是自己的主宰,虽然不是什么领主;
　他空无所有,却又拥有世间一切。

黄宏勋　译

编注　亨利·沃顿(Henry Wotten,1568—1639),十六世纪末、十七世纪初的政治活动家、旅行家,曾出任詹姆士一世驻威尼斯大使,伊顿公学院长。其书信、论文、杂诗于一六五一年汇集出版,题名为《沃顿遗迹集》(*Reliquiae Wottonianae*)。

73. THE NOBLE NATURE

It is not growing like a tree
In bulk, doth make Man better be;
Or standing long an oak, three hundred year①,
To fall a log at last, dry, bald, and sere:
    A lily of a day
    Is fairer far in May②,
Although it fall and die that night;
It was the plant and flower of Light.
In small proportions we just beauties see;
And in short measures life may perfect be.

B. JONSON.

---

① Nor [is it] standing long [that doth make] an oak [better be].
② *fairer far*: sc. than the oak.

73. 高贵的天性

琼生

并不是长得像一棵树干,
使一个人超俗出凡;
也不是像棵橡树挺立三百年,
最后倒下来落个叶枯枝干:
　只开一天的百合花 5
　在五月里更为鲜艳,
　尽管它枯死就在当晚——
　这植物花朵光彩灿烂。
在小小的范围中我们看到全美;
在短短的尺度内生命可以精粹。 10

李霁野　译

编注　本·琼生(Ben Jonson,1573? —1637),英国剧作家、诗人、评论家,一生著有戏剧十八部。他是英国第一位桂冠诗人,死后葬在威斯敏斯特教堂,墓碑上的铭文是"罕见的本·琼生"。琼生的抒情短诗淳朴,富有旋律美。这首小诗是诗人一首题为《为高贵的卡里爵士和莫里森爵士的友谊及永恒的记念而作颂歌》的诗中的第七小节,收在诗人死后出版的诗集《丛林》(*Underwoods*)里。

74. THE GIFTS OF GOD

When God at first made Man,
Having a glass of blessings standing by;
Let us (said He) pour on him all we can:
Let the world's riches, which dispersèd lie,
    Contract into a span.

So strength first made a way①;
Then beauty flow'd, then wisdom honour, pleasure:
When almost all was out, God made a stay,
Perceiving that alone, of all His treasure,
    Rest in the bottom lay.

For if I should (said He)
Bestow this jewel also on my creature,
He would adore my gifts instead of me,
And rest in Nature, not the God of Nature:
    So both should losers be②.

Yet let him keep the rest③,
But keep them with repining restlessness:
Let him be rich and weary, that at least,
If goodness lead him not, yet weariness

---

① *made a way*: 'entered into the composition of man.'
② *both*: *i.e.* both God and man.
③ *keep the rest*: 'all the other qualities.'

74. 上帝的赐与

赫伯特

上帝造人之初,
身边放着一盏祝福之浆①。
上帝说:让我们尽情向他倾注,
让世上分散各处的宝藏
    紧缩成一生的跨度。　　　　　　　　　　5

于是力量首先进入人身,
接着流进了美;智慧、荣誉和欢娱。
眼看一切即将齐备,上帝蓦然停顿,
他觉察到:在他拥有的全部宝库里,
    唯独安息留在底层。　　　　　　　　　10

倘若我把这颗明珠,
上帝说,也赐给我所创造的人子,
他就不会崇拜我,而只崇拜我的礼物;
他将在自然,而非自然的神性中安息②。
    那样,上帝和人都将失误。　　　　　　15

还是让他保有其余珍宝,
但在保持时永不安宁地焦虑埋怨。
让他富足,让他厌倦!总有一朝,
假如善行不能引他前来,至少厌倦

---

① 据《圣经·创世记》所载,太初上帝用泥土造人,常掺之以水。这里的"一盏祝福之浆"是用来喻指上帝赐给人类的各种福祉。——译者
② 自然即客观世界;自然的神性,根据基督教教义,即创造世界之神,也就是上帝。——译者

20   May toss him to my breast.

G. HERBERT.

会把他投向我的怀抱。 *20*

黄宏勋　译

编注　乔治·赫伯特(George Herbert,1593—1633),著名的玄学派诗人。出身贵族。剑桥大学毕业后曾留校任"公共演说员"。最后放弃出仕之念,当了牧师。他的主要作品有诗集《寺庙》(1633),共收短诗一百六十首;散文集《寺庙的牧师》(1652)。他的诗富于音乐性、戏剧性,十分口语化,但具有浓郁的宗教色彩。

75. THE RETREAT

Happy those early days, when I
Shined in my Angel-infancy!
Before I understood this place
Appointed for my second race,
Or taught my soul to fancy aught
But a white, celestial thought;
When yet I had not walk'd above
A mile or two from my first Love,
And looking back, at that short space
Could see a glimpse of His bright face;
When on some gilded cloud or flower
My gazing soul would dwell an hour,
And in those weaker glories spy
Some shadows of eternity;
Before I taught my tongue to wound
My conscience with a sinful sound,
Or had the black art to dispense[1]
A several sin to every sense[2],
But felt through all this fleshly dress
Bright shoots of everlastingness.

O how I long to travel back,

---

[1] *I.e.* learnt, at the instigation of the Devil, to indulge each of my senses in its own peculiar pleasures.

[2] *several*: 'separate.'

75. 退路

沃恩

早年的日子多么欢乐！当我还是婴孩，
在襁褓中闪闪发亮，似天使一样洁白。
那时我还不理解,我被派到这块土地
为的是在这里开始第二次生命的经历①。
那时除了纯洁的、天国的思想，　　　　　　　　5
我的灵魂还没有学会作非分妄想；
那时我离开太初纯真之爱
还没有走出一两哩路以外；
侧身回顾，隔着那短短的空间，
尚能瞥见上帝光辉灿烂的容颜；　　　　　　　10
面对那些泛着金光的云彩花朵，
我凝视一切的灵魂常恋恋不舍；
在那些不太强烈的荣光中，
我窥见了永恒的形影朦胧。
那时我还没有教会舌头发音，　　　　　　　　15
用有罪的声音刺伤我的良心；
而且我也不懂那种阴暗的法术，
把种种罪恶向不同的感官注入②；
可是我透过肉体的层层衣饰，
常感到永恒的光焰喷涌不息。　　　　　　　　20

啊！我是多么渴望走一段回头路，

---

① 据宗教传说，人降生人间之前都有过"前世"，故有第二次生命之说。——译者
② 据基督教义和传说，幼儿生性纯洁，犹如天使；成年后通过感官的享受，沾染上种种恶习，陷入各种罪恶之中。——译者

And tread again that ancient track!
That I might once more reach that plain,
Where first I left my glorious train①;
From whence th' enlighten'd spirit sees
That shady City of Palm trees!
But ah! my soul with too much stay
Is drunk, and staggers in the way: —
Some men a forward motion love,
But I by backward steps would move;
And when this dust falls to the urn,
In that state I came, return.

         H. VAUGHAN.

---

① *my glorious train*: *i.e.* the company of the saints.

踏着往昔留下的足迹重新漫步。
那样我或许再度到达那片原野,
那里我初次离开我的光荣行列①。
受到启示的精灵将从此看清   25
密布着棕榈树荫的那座圣城②。
唉!可惜我的灵魂在世间逗留太久,
它醉了,像醉汉在路上晃晃悠悠。
多少人喜爱向前运动,从不反顾,
可我却宁愿转过身来,挪动脚步。   30
当骨灰坛中落满了我的骨灰,
来自尘土的我又在尘中复归③。

黄宏勋　译

编注　亨利·沃恩(Henry Vaughan,1622—1695),威尔士出生的抒情诗人。曾先后在牛津大学学诗,在伦敦学法律,以后又回乡行医。沃恩早年属玄学派诗人,晚年专写宗教诗。他的诗反映了他对大自然所抱的神秘主义观点,对十九世纪诗人华兹华斯有较大的影响。

---

① 即圣者使徒的行列。——译者
② 据《圣经》所载,棕榈城(又称杰列科城)系以色列人最初到达圣地时占有的第一座圣城。——译者
③ 《圣经》云:"从尘土中来,到尘土中去。"意为人本由泥土造成,死后又回到泥土中去。——译者

76. TO MR. LAWRENCE

Lawrence, of virtuous father virtuous son,
   Now that the fields are dank and ways are mire,
   Where shall we sometimes meet, and by the fire
Help waste a sullen day, what may be won

From the hard season gaining? Time will run
   On smoother, till Favonius re-inspire[1]
   The frozen earth, and clothe in fresh attire
The lily and rose, that neither sow'd nor spun.

What neat repast shall feast us, light and choice,
   Of Attic taste, with wine, whence we may rise[2]
To hear the lute well touch'd, or artful voice

   Warble immortal notes and Tuscan air?
   He who of those delights can judge, and spare
To interpose them oft, is not unwise[3].

                          J. MILTON.

---

[1] *Favonius*: the West wind.
[2] *Attic taste*: 'refined elegance.'
[3] *spare To interpose them oft*: 'avoid indulging in them too often.'

76. 赠劳伦斯①

弥尔顿

劳伦斯,你父子贤孝,我十分钦敬!
  如今道途泥泞,四野湿寒,
  我们可有机会在一起聚会,
围炉闲坐,消磨一个阴天?

在严峻季节里可还能找点安适?   5
  能这样,日子会更好过,直到地面
  被春风融解,而那些不识耕织的
蔷薇与百合也穿上崭新的衣衫。

我们要有清淡精致的食品,
  富有雅典滋味,也要有美酒,   10
然后起身去听听琵琶弹奏,

  或美妙歌喉唱出的托斯卡纳调子②。
  谁能够欣赏这样的逸致闲情,
  要偶一为之,可也不算不聪明!

殷宝书　译

---

① 劳伦斯是弥尔顿失明后常来拜访的青年人,他父亲是个政治家兼神学家。——译者
② 指意大利音乐。当时意大利音乐被认为是欧洲最美好的音乐。——编注者

77. TO CYRIACK SKINNER

Cyriack, whose grandsire, on the royal bench
  Of British Themis, with no mean applause
  Pronounced, and in his volumes taught, our laws,
Which others at their bar so often wrench[1];

To-day deep thoughts resolve with me to drench[2]
  In mirth, that after no repenting draws[3];
  Let Euclid rest, and Archimedes pause,
And what the Swede intend, and what the French.

To measure life learn thou betimes, and know
  Toward solid good what leads the nearest way;
  For other things mild Heaven a time ordains[4],

And disapproves that care, though wise in show,
  That with superfluous burden loads the day[5],
  And, when God sends a cheerful hour, refrains[6].

J. MILTON.

---

[1] *wrench*: 'distort.'
[2] *resolve*: 'make up your mind.'
[3] *that after*, etc.: 'which is followed by no repentance.'
[4] *other things*: i.e. other than the pursuit of 'solid good.'
[5] *that care ... That*: the former 'that' is a demonstrative and the latter a relative; a modern poet would probably have written 'the care ... which.'
[6] *refrains*: i.e. from enjoying it.

77. 赠西里克·斯金纳

弥尔顿

西里克，他的祖先是不列颠的忒弥斯①，
　　从来不用花言巧语的溢美之词，
　　用的是宏文巨著来把法律阐释，
不像别的讼棍歪曲条文钻空子。

而今，深思的他决定和我纵情欢笑，　　　　　　　　　　5
　　我们都不会因此而懊丧烦恼；
　　欧几里德、阿基米德都别打扰，
瑞典、法国想干什么也不在乎了②。

你有时要对生活追根究底来探讨，
　　也深知修身为善哪条是近道；　　　　　　　　　　　10
　　　其他事儿老天到时自然会指教。

只要举止得体，这些思前虑后不必要，
　　过分的操心把一天的时间占完了，
　　　天赐的欢乐时光只得白白浪费掉。

谭建华　译

---

① 西里克·斯金纳是弥尔顿的青年朋友。其外祖父爱德华·柯克男爵是著名的法官，曾为王室特权与英王詹姆斯对抗，还编辑出版李特尔顿论《地权》的著作。忒弥斯(Themis)是希腊神话中法律与正义女神。——译者
② 意为："不必过问数学和国际政治风云"。——译者

78. HYMN TO DIANA

Queen and Huntress, chaste and fair,
   Now the sun is laid to sleep,
Seated in thy silver chair
     State in wonted manner keep:
        Hesperus entreats thy light,
     Goddess excellently bright.

Earth, let not thy envious shade
   Dare itself to interpose;
Cynthia's shining orb was made
     Heaven to clear when day did close:
        Bless us then with wishèd sight,
     Goddess excellently bright

Lay thy bow of pearl apart
   And thy crystal-shining quiver
Give unto the flying hart
     Space to breathe, how short soever;
        Thou that mak'st a day of night,
     Goddess excellently bright!

                              B. JONSON.

78. 狄安娜赞[①]

琼生

贞洁而美丽的皇后兼猎手,
  如今太阳已沉沉入梦,
你在银光闪灼的宝座内,
  保持着往昔的端庄仪容:
    无比光明的女神哟,   5
    金星祈求你撒下清辉重重。

地球呵,别让你的嫉妒的阴影,
  遮蔽那皎洁的真容;
当白昼的运行终于完结,
  赛西娅的闪光球体照耀着清澈明朗的苍穹[②]: 10
    无比光明的女神哟,
    请赏赐我们如意的姿容。

扔掉你那晶莹透明的箭囊,
  放下你那珠光宝气的神弓;
给疾驰飞奔的牡鹿   15
  留下喘息的间隙,不管这瞬间多么短促:
    无比光明的女神哟,
    你把黑夜变成通明的白昼!

            黄新渠 译

[①] 狄安娜(Diana),罗马神话中的月亮和狩猎女神。——编注者
[②] 赛西娅(Cynthia),狄安娜的别名。——编注者

79. WISHES FOR THE SUPPOSED MISTRESS

Whoe'er she be,
That not impossible She
That shall command my heart and me;

Where'er she lie,
Lock'd up from mortal eye
In shady leaves of destiny:

Till that ripe birth
Of studied Fate stand forth①,
And teach her fair steps tread our earth;

Till that divine
Idea take a shrine
Of crystal fleshy through which to shine:

— Meet you her, my Wishes,
Bespeak her to my blisses,
And be ye call'd, my absent kisses.

I wish her beauty
That owes not all its duty

---

① *Till that ripe birth Of studied Fate*: 'Till She, the matured product which Fate has ordained, appear; *studied* is used in an active sense, 'working with deliberate intent.'

79. 对想象中情人的希望

克拉休

不管她是何人，
她将来都绝不可能
主宰支配我和我的心灵；

无论她在何处，
现在都避开世人的眼目 5
幽藏于生命之树繁茂的叶簇；

直到命运注定的
那成熟的生命出世，
并教她优雅的脚步踏上大地；

直到神性的意念 10
依附于肌肤的圣殿，
透过水晶般躯体放射光焰；

——我的希望哟，迎接她吧，
告诉她我要说的心里话，
我授权与你替我吻吻她。 15

我希望她美丽
那美丽要天生丽质，

  To gaudy tire, or glist'ring shoe-tie①;

   Something more than②
20   Taffata or tissue can③,
  Or rampant feather, or rich fan.

   A face that's best
   By its own beauty drest,
  And can alone commend the rest:

25   A face made up
   Out of no other shop
  Than what Nature's white hand sets ope.

   Sidneian showers
   Of sweet discourse, whose powers
30   Can crown old Winter's head with flowers.

   Whate'er delight
   Can make day's forehead bright
  Or give down to the wings of night.

   Soft silken hours,
35   Open suns, shady bowers;
  'Bove all, nothing within that lowers.

---

① *tire*: 'head-dress.'
② *Something more*: *i.e.* in the way of beauty I wish her something more, etc.
③ *Taffata*: (or taffeta) a thin glossy silk. *tissue*: cloth interwoven with gold or silver. *can*: used absolutely for 'can accomplish.'

不要华美的衣裙鞋袜装饰；

 我对美的要求
  胜过薄纱丝绸，   20
鲜艳的羽毛绣扇也还不够。

 那张脸最好
  是它天生的美貌，
能说明那玉体娉婷窈窕；

 那张脸的妆扮   25
  不需要化妆品商店
胜过自然的素手打扮的容颜。

 锡德尼式的言辞①
  动听又甜蜜，
语言之魅力令寒冬也鲜花遍地。   30

 无论怎样的欢畅
  能使白昼焕发容光，
或把绒毛赋予夜的翅膀。

 温馨柔软的时辰，
  旭日和幽凉的树荫；   35
尤其是不要沾惹卑贱的下层。

---

① 锡德尼（参见卷一第 24 首编注）在当时被推崇为最有教养、最有才艺、最善言辞的绅士典范。——译者

>
> Days, that need borrow
> No part of their good morrow
> From a fore-spent night of sorrow①;
>
> 40
> Days, that in spite
> Of darkness, by the light
> Of a clear mind are day all night.
>
> Life, that dares send
> A challenge to his end,
> 45
> And when it comes, say, 'Welcome, friend.'
>
> I wish her store
> Of worth may leave her poor
> Of wishes; and I wish —— no more②.
>
> — Now, if Time knows
> 50
> That Her, whose radiant brows
> Weave them a garland of my vows;
>
> Her that dares be
> What these lines wish to see:
> I seek no further, it is She.
>
> 55
> 'Tis She, and here
> Lo! I unclothe and clear③

---

① 'Days which owe none of their happiness to their contrast with the sorrows of the previous night.'
② 'I wish that the blessings she has may be so many that she has none left to wish for.'
③ *here Lo! I unclothe*: 'in these verses I reveal my thoughts.'

日子哟，那日子毋须
　　　从前一天夜晚的忧伤里
才得到它们欢乐的翌日；

　　日子哟，尽管 40
　　　充满阴沉黑暗
可心灵之光使黑夜也是白天。

　　生命哟，它胆敢
　　　与它的末日挑战，
"欢迎，朋友，"当末日来临，高喊。 45

　　我希望她洪福无量
　　　使她再无任何奢想；
而我也没有——别的希望。

　　——现在，若"时间"知晓
　　　她，她辉煌的容貌 50
本身就编织成我的誓言诗稿；

　　她敢于变成
　　　这诗行所希冀的佳人；
我再也不寻求了，她就是我的情人。

　　这就是她，这里 55
　　　瞧哟！我已完全揭示

275

My wishes' cloudy character.

Such worth as this is
Shall fix my flying wishes①,
And determine them to kisses②.

Let her full glory,
My fancies, fly before ye③;
Be ye my fictions: — but her story④.

R. CRASHAW.

---

① *fix*: 'render constant.'
② *determine*: 'direct.'
③ *fly before ye*: 'outstrip you'; i.e. may she be more than I have even fancied.
④ *her story*: i.e. a truthful account of her.

  我所希望的被笼罩的品质。

   如此这般的价值
   将使我的希望固定
   并支配它们前去接吻。 60

   我的想象哟,让她大放光华,
   也许她比我的想象更佳;
   想象就归想象吧——但她还是她。

曹明伦　译

编注　理查德·克拉休(Richard Crashaw,1613?—1649),英国诗人,以牧师为职业,但他除了写宗教诗外也写了大量非宗教的现世诗篇。《对想象中情人的希望》选自他一六四六年出版的诗集《缪司之乐》(*Delights of the Muses*),原诗共有四十二小节,《金库》原编者删去了二十一小节并对保留的二十一小节做了适当的顺序调整。

80. THE GREAT ADVENTURER

Over the mountains
    And over the waves,
Under the fountains
    And under the graves;
Under floods that are deepest,
    Which Neptune obey;
Over rocks that are steepest
    Love will find out the way.

Where there is no place
    For the glow-worm to lie;
Where there is no space
    For receipt of a fly;
Where the midge dares not venture
    Lest herself fast she lay[①];
If love come, he will enter;
    And soon find out his way.

You may esteem him
    A child for his might;
Or you may deem him
    A coward from his flight;
But if she whom love doth honour
    Be conceal'd from the day,

---

① *Lest herself fast she lay*: 'lest she entangle herself.'

80. 伟大的冒险家

无名氏

越巍峨高山，
　　跨茫茫大海，
在每一条溪流中，
　　在每一座坟墓里，
在海神也得止步的　　　　　　　　　　　5
　　最深的水下，
在最陡最峭的悬崖绝壁，
　　爱情总会自由地来去。

在萤火虫也不能
　　容身的地方，　　　　　　　　　　10
在苍蝇也无法
　　飞进的天地，
连蚊虫也不敢冒险闯入，
　　生怕被紧紧地缠在那里；
但如果爱情来临，他会进入，　　　　　15
　　并很快寻路而自由来去。

因为他非凡异常，
　　你可以视他为孩子；
由于他飘浮不定，
　　可视他为胆小的东西；　　　　　　20
但假若爱情所垂青的她
　　在命定之日被人藏匿，

    Set a thousand guards upon her①,
      Love will find out the way.

    Some think to lose him
      By having him confined;
    And some do suppose him,
      poor thing, to be blind;
    But if ne'er so close ye wall him,
      Do the best that you may,
    Blind love, if so ye call him,
      Will find out his way.

    You may train the eagle
      To stoop to your fist②;
    Or you may inveigle
      The phoenix of the east;
    The lioness, ye may move her
      To give o'er her prey;
    But you'll ne'er stop a lover:
      He will find out his way.

              ANON.

---

① *Set*: sc. Though you set.
② *To stoop to your fist*: to come at your call like a hawk in the mediaeval sport of fowling.

纵然你派上一千名卫兵，
　　爱情也会前去与她相遇。

有人想避开爱情， 25
　　将他幽禁限制；
有人认为爱情
　　是盲目的可怜东西；
可是,若你因他不紧,
　　不用尽你全部力气， 30
盲目的爱哟,如果你这样称他,
　　仍然会寻路而自由来去。

你可以训练出猎鹰
　　驯服地站在你手臂；
或许你可以捕获 35
　　东方的不死神鸟①
你甚至可让母狮
　　将她的猎物放弃；
但你绝不能阻止爱情，
　　他总会寻路而自由来去。 40

曹明伦　译

编注　此诗选自英国诗人珀西（Thomas Percy，1729—1811）编辑的《英诗辑古》（*Reliques*，1765），标题系《金库》原编者所加。

---

① 据埃及神话传说,此鸟每五百年自焚而死,然后由灰中再生,又名长生鸟。据说此鸟十分稀少,生活在阿拉伯荒漠,要想捕获是非常难的事。——译者

81. CHILD AND MAIDEN

Ah, Chloris! that I now could sit
    As unconcern'd as when
Your infant beauty could beget
    No pleasure, nor no pain!
When I the dawn used to admire,
    And praised the coming day,
I little thought the growing fire
    Must take my rest away.

Your charms in harmless childhood lay
    Like metals in the mine;
Age from no face took more away
    Than youth conceal'd in thine.
But as your charms insensibly
    To their perfection prest,
Fond love as unperceived did fly,
    And in my bosom rest.

My passion with your beauty grew,
    And Cupid at my heart,
Still as his mother favour'd you,
    Threw a new flaming dart:
Each gloried in their wanton part;
    To make a lover, he

81. 童男与少女

塞德利

呵,克罗瑞斯!
　　假如我能坐下,像你那样
在襁褓中无忧无虑,安详甜美,
　　这不会带给我欢乐而是忧伤!
我羡慕过黎明的瑰丽朝霞,　　　　　　　　　　5
　　我羡美过白昼的明媚阳光;
但我未曾想到日益增长的爱火
　　竟使平静离开了我的心房。

你童年时代天真无邪的魅力
　　像金属蕴藏在矿山;　　　　　　　　　　10
岁月依旧会从你的脸上带去
　　你那青春焕发的容颜。
然而,你的妩媚在无声无息地
　　日臻完美、动人、娇艳;
我对你的爱恋也在不知不觉地　　　　　　　15
　　升华,腾跃,嵌入心田。

我的爱情伴随你的美丽而剧增,
　　丘比特占据了我的心房,
而他的母亲对你则倍加宠爱[①],
　　又一支炽热利箭射入你的胸膛:　　　　　20
母子俩为他们的嬉戏而洋洋自得;
　　为了造就一个情郎,

[①] 丘比特的母亲指维纳斯。——编注者

Employ'd the utmost of his art —
To make a beauty, she.

SIR C. SEDLEY.

为了铸成一个美女，
　　他们各自施展出平生的伎俩。

黄新渠　黄文军　译

编注　查尔斯·塞德利(Charles Sedley，1639？—1701)，英国诗人及剧作家。这首诗是他的喜剧《桑园》(*The Mulberry Garden*，1668)第三幕第二场中女主人公维多利亚唱给剧中人克罗瑞斯的一支歌，诗名为《金库》原编者所加。

82. COUNSEL TO GIRLS

Gather ye rose-buds while ye may,
    Old Time is still a-flying[①];
And this same flower that smiles to-day,
    To-morrow will be dying.

The glorious Lamp of Heaven, the Sun,
    The higher he's a-getting
The sooner will his race be run,
    And nearer he's to setting.

That age is best which is the first,
    When youth and blood are warmer;
But being spent, the worse, and worst[②]
    Times, still succeed the former.

Then be not coy, but use your time;
    And while ye may, go marry:
For having lost but once your prime[③],
    You may for ever tarry.

R. HERRICK.

---

① *still*: 'always.'
② *being spent*: *i.e.* it (the first age) being spent.
③ *prime*: 'period of perfection.'

82. 给少女们的忠告

赫里克

可以采花的时机,别错过,
　　时光老人在飞驰:
今天还在微笑的花朵
　　明天就会枯死。

太阳,那盏天上的华灯,
　　向上攀登得越高,
路程的终点就会越临近,
　　剩余的时光也越少。

青春的年华是最最美好的,
　　血气方刚,多热情;
过了青年,那越来越不妙的
　　年月会陆续来临。

那么,别怕羞,抓住机缘,
　　你们该及时结婚:
你一旦错过了少年,
　　会成千古恨。

屠岸　译

编注　罗伯特·赫里克(Robert Herrick,1591—1674),英国资产阶级革命时期和复辟时期的所谓"骑士派"诗人之一。他一生写了不少以淳朴的农村生活为题材的抒情诗,以田园抒情诗和爱情抒情诗著称,主要诗集有《雅歌》(1647)和《西方乐土》(1648)。

83. TO LUCASTA, ON GOING TO THE WARS

Tell me not, Sweet, I am unkind
    That from the nunnery
Of thy chaste breast and quiet mind
    To war and arms I fly.

True, a new mistress now I chase,
    The first foe in the field;
And with a stronger faith embrace[1]
    A sword, a horse, a shield.

Yet this inconstancy is such
    As you too shall adore;
I could not love thee, Dear, so much,
    Loved I not Honour more.

R. LOVELACE.

---

[1] *stronger faith*: *i.e.* than he had shown in pursuit of love.

83. 出阵前告别鲁加斯达

洛夫莱斯

爱,请不要说我无情,
　我离开了你的胸心,
像修道院般的纯洁和平,
　而要飞向战阵。

是的,我在追求新的女主,　　　　　　　　　5
　是战场上首遇的敌人;
要拥抱得加紧认真,
　用剑,用马,用盾。

然而这一下的不志诚,
　你也会加以崇敬;　　　　　　　　　　　10
亲爱的,我就不配真爱你了,
　如果我不更爱我的荣名。

郭沫若　译

编注 理查德·洛夫莱斯(Richard Lovelace,1618—1658,即洛夫莱斯上校),英国骑士诗人。生于伦敦名门望族,毕业于牛津大学,内战时曾随军出征。诗人所称的鲁加斯达(Lucasta),据说出于他的未婚妻Lucy Sachevell 的名字。这首诗和本卷 99 首、100 首均选自他于狱中辑成的诗集《鲁加斯达》(*Lucasta*,1649)。

84. ELIZABETH OF BOHEMIA

 You meaner beauties of the night,
  That poorly satisfy our eyes
 More by your number than your light,
  You common people of the skies,
 What are you, when the Moon shall rise?

 You curious chanters of the wood①
  That warble forth dame Nature's lays,
 Thinking your passions understood
  By your weak accents; what's your praise
 When Philomel her voice shall raises?

 You violets that first appear,
  By your pure purple mantles known
 Like the proud virgins of the year②,
  As if the spring were all your own, —
 What are you, when the Rose is blown?

 So when my Mistress shall be seen
  In form and beauty of her mind,
 By virtue first, then choice, a Queen③,

---

① *curious*: this may mean either 'finely wrought' or 'skilful'; both meanings are now obsolete.
② *proud virgins*: purple being the mark of noble birth.
③ *By virtue first, then choice*: i.e. first by her innate goodness, then by her marriage to Frederick.

84. 波希米亚的伊丽莎白①

沃顿

夜空平庸的美人②,
　　难以使我销魂,
你是苍穹的凡人,
　　我赞赏你的众多而非你的光晕,
你算得了什么哟,当月亮一旦升起? 　　　　5

林中灵巧的歌手,
　　吟唱着自然之歌,
自诩你微弱的声音
　　扣人心弦,美妙动听,
你算得了什么哟,当夜莺轻啭歌喉? 　　　10

初放的紫罗兰哟,
　　身披紫色的花瓣,
像当年骄傲的花卉,
　　似乎春光都在你们身上聚汇,——
你算得了什么哟,若是玫瑰盛开? 　　　　15

当皇后的风姿和美丽的心灵
　　被众人赏识,
先因端正品德,后有良缘缔结③。

---

① 波希米亚,古代中欧一小国,现为捷克一地区。伊丽莎白系波希米亚王后。——译者
② "平庸的美人"喻指星星。——译者
③ 伊丽莎白于一六一三年嫁给后来成为波希米亚王的弗雷德里克伯爵。——译者

                    Tell me, if she were not design'd
20   Th' eclipse and glory of her kind?

                                                SIR H. WOTTON.

告诉我,难道不是造化要她
使淑女们黯然失色,或大放光彩?

谢屏　译

85. TO THE LADY MARGARET LEY

Daughter to that good Earl, once President
   Of England's Council and her Treasury,
     Who lived in both, unstain'd with gold or fee,
And left them both, more in himself content,

Till the sad breaking of that Parliament
   Broke him, as that dishonest victory
     At Chaeronea, fatal to liberty,
Kill'd with report that old man eloquent; —

Though later born than to have known the days
   Wherein your father flourish'd yet by you,
     Madam, methinks I see him living yet;

So well your words his noble virtues praise,
   That all both judge you to relate them true,
     And to possess them, honour'd Margaret.

                             J. MILTON.

85. 赠玛格丽特·莱伊女士

弥尔顿

令尊曾经就任英国议院议长、财政大臣,
 两度显贵,都出污泥而不染,
 两度去职,却无愧于扪心自问①,
您就是这位好伯爵的骨肉千金。

在那议院横遭摧残的可悲时辰,   5
 他五内迸裂,有如那雄辩的长者,
 当凯罗尼亚传来可耻的胜利音讯,
葬送了自由,也破碎了老人的身心②。

恨我生也晚,不逢辰,未曾耳闻目睹
 令尊大人咤叱风云的盛时光景,   10
  从您身上,我看到他依然栩栩如生;

您赞誉他的高尚品德的珠玑之言,
 印证了您言之真诚,您之真诚,
  您也有他一样的品质,玛格丽特夫人。

谭建华 译

---

① 莱伊女士的父亲詹姆斯·莱伊爵士,一六二四年任财政大臣,一六二八年任议院议长,颇有声誉。英王查尔斯一世于一六二九年独断专横,解散议院。解散后第四天,莱伊爵士就忧愤而逝。——译者
② 希腊九十八岁的著名演说家伊索克拉底获悉马其顿国王菲利浦于公元前三八八年以卑鄙手段大败雅典人,使其降为一个省的地位,便引颈自尽了。——译者

86. THE LOVELINESS OF LOVE

It is not Beauty I demand,
   A crystal brow, the moon's despair,
Nor the snow's daughter, a white hand,
   Nor mermaid's yellow pride of hair:

Tell me not of your starry eyes,
   Your lips that seem on roses fed,
Your breasts, where Cupid trembling lies
   Nor sleeps for kissing of his bed: —

A bloomy pair of vermeil cheeks
   Like Hebe's in her ruddiest hours,
A breath that softer music speaks
   Than summer winds a-wooing flowers,

These are but gauds: nay, what are lips[①]?
   Coral beneath the ocean-stream,
Whose brink when your adventurer sips
   Full oft he perisheth on them.

And what are cheeks, but ensigns oft
   That wave hot youth to fields of blood?
Did Helen's breast, though ne'er so soft,

---

① *gauds*: 'idle adornments.'

86. 爱之可爱

达利

我不要花容月貌、绝色佳人,
　　那皎洁的容颜令月亮也灰心,
我不要雪的女儿,纤纤白手,
　　也不要美人鱼金黄的发鬟。

别对我讲你那星星般的眼睛, 5
　　你那看起来玫瑰般丰满的嘴唇,
你的酥胸,丘比特躺在那里颤抖
　　忘了睡眠,只顾把温床亲吻。

那红润美丽的粉颊桃腮
　　恰如赫柏正值她青春妙龄①, 10
那比音乐还柔和的馨香呼吸
　　胜似仲夏微风向花儿求婚,

这些只是妆饰:哦,红唇算什么?
　　不过是珊瑚长在大海底层,
当冒险者冒险去把它们啜吮, 15
　　往往就在大海的边沿葬身。

红颜又算什么? 不过是旗帜
　　蛊惑热血青年投入血的战争;
海伦的酥胸(虽从未这般柔软)

---

① 赫柏(Hebe),希腊神话中在奥林匹斯山为众神斟酒的青春女神。——译者

20   Do Greece or Ilium any good[1]?

Eyes can with baleful ardour burn;
   Poison can breath, that erst perfumed;
There's many a white hand holds an urn
   With lovers' hearts to dust consumed.

25 For crystal brows — there's nought within[2];
   They are but empty cells for pride;
He who the Syren's hair would win
   Is mostly strangled in the tide.

Give me, instead of Beauty's bust,
30   A tender heart, a loyal mind
Which with temptation I could trust,
   Yet never link'd with error find, —

One in whose gentle bosom I
   Could pour my secret heart of woes,
35 Like the care-burthen'd honey-fly
   That hides his murmurs in the rose, —

My earthly Comforter! whose love
   So indefeasible might be[3]

---

[1] *Ilium*: 'Troy.'
[2] *For*: 'As for.'
[3] *indefeasible*: literally 'that cannot be defeated, or done away with,' so 'indestructible.'

　　　　给希腊和特洛伊带去了什么幸运①?　　　　　　20

　　　明眸中可燃起有害的情焰；
　　　　　馨香的气息也可能是毒品；
　　　有多少纤纤白手捧着灰甏
　　　　　把情郎的心儿化为粉尘。

　　　至于那两弯蛾眉——更不值一提；　　　　　　25
　　　　　它们只是为骄傲备下的空陵；
　　　谁若想去赢得塞壬的秀发②，
　　　　　他十有八九会在波涛中丧命。

　　　那就别再给我美人的胸房，
　　　　　请给我一颗忠实温柔的心，　　　　　　　　30
　　　这颗心儿我能够迷恋、信赖，
　　　　　而绝不会发现过失与不贞，——

　　　往那颗温柔纯洁的心里
　　　　　我能倾述胸中的悲哀与隐情，
　　　就像那忧心忡忡的蜜蜂　　　　　　　　　　　35
　　　　　把它的怨诉藏在玫瑰花心，——

　　　我人世间的安慰哟！她的爱情
　　　　　应该是这般地不渝忠贞，

---

① 海伦,希腊神话中的美女,斯巴达国王墨涅拉俄斯之妻。后来她被特洛伊王子帕里斯拐走,引起特洛伊战争。这场战争给希腊人和特洛伊人都带来了不幸。——译者
② 塞壬希腊神话中半人半鸟的女妖。她们栖身海岛,用美妙的歌声诱惑航海者。——译者

    That, when my spirit won above[①],
40   Hers could not stay, for sympathy.

              G. DARLEY.

---

① *won above*: 'succeeded in reaching heaven.'

当我的灵魂到达极乐天堂，
　她的心也因同感而不复生存。 *40*

曹明伦　译

编注　乔治·达利（George Darley，1795—1846），英国诗人和剧作家，著有诗剧《西尔维娅》（*Sylvia*）和《懒惰的劳动者》（*The Labours of Idleness*）。按他的生活年代，这首诗应该编在卷四。《金库》初版时标明此诗系无名氏作，故收编于此。现用的诗名系《金库》原编者所加。

87. THE TRUE BEAUTY

He that loves a rosy cheek①
    Or a coral lip admires,
Or from star-like eyes doth seek
    Fuel to maintain his fires;
As old Time makes these decay,
So his flames must waste away.

But a smooth and steadfast mind,
    Gentle thoughts, and calm desires,
Hearts with equal love combined②,
    Kindle never-dying fires: —
Where these are not, I despise
Lovely cheeks or lips or eyes.

T. CAREW.

---

① *He*: this word has no grammatical connexion with anything in the sentence, being picked up by *his flames* (l. 6), *i.e.* the love of one who admires a rosy cheek, etc.

② *equal love*: according to the French proverb there is no such thing; *il y a toujours un qui aime et un qui tend la joue*.

87. 真的美

加鲁

颊如玫瑰红，
唇如珊瑚赤，
星眼殊耀燃，
有人为之热；
迟暮俱凋谢， 5
热情亦衰竭。

心平气亦和，
宁静而谦抑，
一视能同仁，
爱之永不灭：—— 10
世若无斯人，
颊唇眼何益？

郭沫若　译

编注　托马斯·加鲁（1598?—1639?），英国宫廷派诗人。出身贵族，受业于牛津大学，是位学者诗人。加鲁擅长于爱情诗、墓志铭体诗、挽歌等。他受古典主义诗歌和玄学派诗歌影响很大。此诗原名《回归的倨傲》，共有三个小节；珀西的《英诗辑古》将诗名改为《不消褪的美》；《金库》原编者删去了第三小节并改诗名为《真的美》。

88. TO DIANEME

Sweet, be not proud of those two eyes
Which starlike sparkle in their skies;
Nor be you proud, that you can see
All hearts your captives; yours yet free:
Be you not proud of that rich hair
Which wantons with the lovesick air[①];
Whenas that ruby which you wear[②],
Sunk from the tip of your soft ear,
Will last to be a precious stone
When all your world of beauty's gone.

R. HERRICK.

---

① *wantons*: 'sports.'
② *Whenas*: a variant of 'when.'

88. 致黛安

赫里克

心爱的,不要骄傲:你的双眼
像星星似的在天空中闪耀;
你也不要骄傲:你能看见
别的心都作你的俘虏,你自己的心仍还自由;
你那和害相思的空气调情的丰满头发,   5
你也不要骄傲它;
一旦你所戴的那块红宝石
从你柔软的耳边落掉,
它还是一块宝石,
你的美却完全消失了。   10

        李霁野 译

89. 'GO, LOVELY ROSE!'

    Go, lovely Rose!
Tell her, that wastes her time and me[1],
    That now she knows,
When I resemble her to thee[2],
How sweet and fair she seems to be.

    Tell her that's young
And shuns to have her graces spied,
    That hadst thou sprung
In deserts, where no men abide,
Thou must have uncommended died.

    Small is the worth
Of beauty from the light retired[3]:
    Bid her come forth
Suffer herself to be desired,
And not blush so to be admired.

    Then die! that she
The common fate of all things rare
    May read in thee:
How small a part of time they share
That are so wondrous sweet and fair!

                              E. WALLER.

---

[1] *wastes her time and me*: this is an instance of the figure of speech called Zeugma, the verb 'wastes' being used in a different sense with its two objects.

[2] *resemble*: 'compare,' an archaic use.

[3] *retired*: 'withdrawn'; this transitive sense is now used only in military phrases.

89. "去,可爱的玫瑰"

沃勒

去,可爱的玫瑰!
告诉她别浪费青春,使我憔悴,
　　叫她现在要领会:
我正是把她同你来比配,
她看来是多么可爱,多么美! 5

　　告诉那年轻的姑娘家,
不要把自己的美貌隐藏,
　　说,如果你这朵花
在没有人迹的沙漠里生长,
你必定会到死也没人赞赏。 10

　　如果从亮光下躲开,
美又有什么价值?没有;
　　叫她从暗地里走出来,
允许人家来向她追求,
有人爱慕,用不着害羞。 15

　　然后你死去!她由此
会知道一切希罕的东西
　　都有共同的遭际:
那些可爱的、美丽的珍奇
只能活一个短促的瞬息! 20

屠岸　译

编注　埃德蒙·沃勒(Edmund Waller, 1606—1687),英国诗人,曾

出任"长期国会"议员,一六四三年因卷入一起王室阴谋而被开除国会并被驱逐出国,七年后重返英国时写过一首歌颂克伦威尔的赞词,但查理二世复辟后他又写诗庆贺。

90. TO CELIA

Drink to me only with thine eyes①,
    And I will pledge with mine;
Or leave a kiss but in the cup②
    And I'll not look for wine.
The thirst that from the soul doth rise
    Doth ask a drink divine;
But might I of Jove's nectar sup,
    I would not change for thine③.

I sent thee late a rosy wreath④,
    Not so much honouring thee
As giving it a hope that there
    It could not wither'd be;
But thou thereon didst only breathe
    And sent'st it back to me;
Since when it grows, and smells, I swear,
    Not of itself but thee⑤!

                              B. JONSON.

---

① *Drink to me*: *i.e.* show your goodwill to me by your looks rather than by drinking my health.
② *but*—as so often in verse—is misplaced; it goes with 'leave,' 'only leave a kiss.'
③ *change*: 'take it in exchange.'
④ *late* for 'lately' is now found only in poetry.
⑤ The latter line goes with both verbs in the former line; the growth of the flowers and their scent are both derived from Celia.

90. 致西丽娅

琼生

请用你的眼神为我祝酒,
　　我也用我的眼睛为你干杯!
愿你把一个热吻留在杯中,
　　天下的醇醪算它最美;
我灵魂渴望着这一杯啊,　　　　　　　　　　5
　　啜饮一口心也醉。
即使众神仙献出他们的美酒,
　　我也不愿交换这神圣的一杯!

我曾经赠你一环玫瑰,
　　不是为了荣耀和献媚,　　　　　　　　10
只为花环祈福,
　　愿它永不枯萎。
蒙你对它亲吻呼吸,
　　又把花环给我送回;
从此它永久鲜艳、芳香,　　　　　　　　15
　　只因你赐给它无比光辉!

　　　　　　　　　　　袁广达　梁葆成　译

91. CHERRY-RIPE

There is a garden in her face
    Where roses and white lilies grow;
A heavenly paradise is that place,
    Wherein all pleasant fruits do flow①;
There cherries grow which none may buy,
Till 'Cherry-Ripe' themselves do cry.

Those cherries fairly do enclose
    Of orient pearl a double row②,
Which when her lovely laughter shows,
    They look like rose-buds fill'd with snow③:
Yet them nor peer nor prince can buy,
Till 'Cherry-Ripe' themselves do cry.

Her eyes like angels watch them still;
    Her brows like bended bows do stand④,
Threat'ning with piercing frowns to kill
    All that attempt with eye or hand⑤
Those sacred cherries to come nigh,
— Till 'Cherry-Ripe' themselves do cry!

THOMAS CAMPION.

---

① *flow*: 'spring in profusion.'
② *orient pearl*: see above, note to No. 16, l. 31.
③ The pronouns are a little vague: 'which' is the object of 'shows' and refers to rows of pearl; 'they' refers to 'cherries.' 'And when her laughter displays her teeth, her lips look like a rose with snow in its midst.'
④ *like bended bows*: this is a very happy simile, an arched eyebrow being regarded as a great beauty.
⑤ *with eye or hand*: her admirers may not even look at the lips of this very imperious lady; they would hardly wish to touch them — with their hands.

91. 成熟的含桃

坎皮恩

她的脸上有一个花苑，
　　那里玫瑰和百合怒放；
那地方是个天上的乐园，
　　各种美味鲜果在园中生长。
那里的含桃无人能购采，　　　　　　　　　　5
直到"成熟的含桃"欢呼前来①。

两排灿烂的珠宝，
　　被含桃紧紧包围
每当她嫣然一笑，
　　它们像雪中的玫瑰蓓蕾，　　　　　　　10
但是贵族王孙都不能购采，
直到"成熟的含桃"欢呼前来。

她的眼睛像守卫含桃的天使，
　　她的双眉像待发的弯弓，
她蹙着眉头示警要处死　　　　　　　　　　15
　　任何人胆敢向仙果靠拢
企图用眼贪看，用手强采，
直到"成熟的含桃"欢呼前来。

李霁野　译

编注 托马斯·坎皮恩（Thomas Campion，1567？—1619），英国诗人及音乐家，著有剧本多部，剧中音乐均由他自己创作。

---

① "成熟的含桃"是街上叫卖樱桃的农人的喊声。——编注者

92. THE POETRY OF DRESS

I

A sweet disorder in the dress
Kindles in clothes a wantonness[1]; —
A lawn about the shoulders thrown[2]
Into a fine distractión[3], —
An erring lace, which here and there[4]
Enthrals the crimson stomacher —
A cuff neglectful, and thereby[5]
Ribbands to flow confusedly, —
A winning wave, deserving note,
In the tempestuous petticoat, —
A careless shoe-string, in whose tie
I see a wild civility[6], —
Do more bewitch me, than when art[7]
Is too precise in every part.

R. HERRICK.

---

[1] *Kindles in clothes a wantonness*: 'produces a sportive appearance in one's clothing.'
[2] *lawn*: properly a kind of very fine linen, and so anything made of such material; here a lawn scarf.
[3] *Into a fine distractión*: 'so as to produce a dainty disorder.'
[4] *erring*: in its literal sense, 'wandering.'
[5] *neglectful*: 'showing marks of its owner's neglect.' *thereby*: 'beside it,' i.e. close to the cuff.
[6] *a wild civility*: 'an untaught refinement'; but 'wild' implies more than 'untaught,' and 'civility' more than 'refinement'; wild and civil are at opposite poles, so that this expression is an Oxymoron or contradiction in terms.
[7] *Do*: the subject extends from l. 3 to l. 12.

92. 衣裙之歌（之一）

赫里克

礼服上一道美妙的紊迹
为衣饰平添情趣一丝：——
披搭双肩的亚麻围巾儿
东飘西荡优雅无比，——
歪斜的花边胡乱飞舞　　　　　　　　5
竭力去迷惑绯红的胸衣——
漫不经心的袖口儿旁边
丝带儿根根惶然飘逸，——
可爱的波纹，迷人的旋律，
都来自�作响的裙裾，——　　　　10
从随心着意的鞋带儿结上
我看见了一种不羁的闺仪，——
哦，假若艺术处处拘泥于精确，
衣裙之自然倒更令我着迷。

曹明伦　译

93. THE POETRY OF DRESS

II

Whenas in silks my Julia goes
Then, then (methinks) how sweetly flows
That liquefaction of her clothes①.

Next, when I cast mine eyes and see
That brave vibration each way free②;
O how that glittering taketh me!

R. HERRICK.

---

① *liquefaction*: properly 'melting.' The folds of a fabric have been so often compared to fluids that we now speak of 'flowing robes,' etc. without any idea that we are wing a metaphor.
② *brave vibration each way free*: i.e. the beautiful play of the light as it darts freely in all directions over the silk.

93. 衣裙之歌（之二）

赫里克

我的朱丽娅披丝裙飘然而过，
我觉得她那般轻盈，那般婀娜，
飘拂的衣裙宛若流动的水波。

我随即投去目光，蓦然发现，
那华美的飘动向四面八方闪烁；　　　　5
啊，那绚丽的光芒迷住了我！

　　　　　　　　　　　　曹明伦　译

94. THE POETRY OF DRESS

III

My Love in her attire doth shew her wit,
    It doth so well become her;
For every season she hath dressings fit,
    For Winter, Spring, and Summer.
    No beauty she doth miss
        When all her robes are on;
    But Beauty's self she is
        When all her robes are gone.

ANON.

94. 衣裙之歌(之三)

无名氏

我爱人对衣裙颇有鉴赏能力,
　　衣裙与她真是天生就相宜;
她有四季更换的裙袍衣衫,
　　无论寒冬、春秋和炎炎夏日。
当她的玉体裹进一身盛装,　　　5
　　她绝不会失去丝毫美丽;
而当她脱下所有的衣裙,
　　美哟,即是她的天生丽质。

曹明伦　译

95. ON A GIRDLE

That which her slender waist confined
Shall now my joyful temples bind;
No monarch but would give his crown
His arms might do what this has done.

It was my Heaven's extremest sphere[①],
The pale which held that lovely deer;
My joy, my grief, my hope, my love
Did all within this circle move.

A narrow compass! and yet there
Dwelt all that's good, and all that's fair:
Give me but what this ribband bound,
Take all the rest the Sun goes round.

E. WALLER.

[①] *my Heaven's extremest sphere*: 'the orbit which bounded my Heaven.'

95. 咏腰带

沃勒

愿围绕她的细腰的腰带
把我的快乐的太阳筋束缚:
能双臂像这样把她拥抱在怀,
任何君主都愿放弃他的王国。

腰带围绕可爱小鹿的地方,   5
是我的王国最广的范围:
我的快乐,我的悲伤,我的爱情,我的希望,
都在那一个框框内旋转迂回。

是一个狭窄的范围!可是
那里包括一切善,一切美: 10
只要把这条带所束缚的恩赐给我,
可以将太阳普照的一切收回。

李霁野 译

96. TO ANTHEA WHO MAY COMMAND HIM ANY THING

Bid me to live, and I will live
    Thy Protestant to be①;
Or bid me love, and I will give
    A loving heart to thee.

A heart as soft, a heart as kind,
    A heart as sound and free②
As in the whole world thou canst find,
    That heart I'll give to thee.

Bid that heart stay, and it will stay,
    To honour thy decree;
Or bid it languish quite away,
    And 't shall do so for thee.

Bid me to weep, and I will weep
    While I have eyes to see;
And, having none, yet I will keep
    A heart to weep for thee.

Bid me despair, and I'll despair

---

① *Protestant*: 'one who makes a protestation (*i.e.* a solemn declaration)' — HERE of his devotion.
② *sound and free*: here these words mean the same, 'untouched by love.' Cf. the word 'heart-whole.'

96. 致主宰他一切的安西娅

赫里克

叫我活,我就活
　　做你忠实的信徒:
叫我爱恋,我就会,
　　把一片痴心献给汝。

一颗温柔的心,一颗仁慈的心,　　　　　　　　　　　　*5*
　　一颗天真烂漫的心
寻遍天地才能找到的这颗心,
　　我愿意献给您的这颗心。

叫这颗心留在你身边,它就会留着
　　听从你的使唤,　　　　　　　　　　　　　　　　　*10*
或者叫它憔悴,
　　它会为你而憔悴。

叫我流泪,我就流泪
　　只要我有眼睛可以看见:
若是没有眼睛流泪,　　　　　　　　　　　　　　　　　*15*
　　可我仍有一颗为你流泪的心。

叫我绝望,我就会

　　　　　Under that cypress tree[①];
　　　　Or bid me die, and I will dare
　　　　　　E'en Death, to die for thee.

　　　　Thou art my life, my love, my heart,
　　　　　　The very eyes of me,
　　　　And hast command of every part,
　　　　　　To live and die for thee.

　　　　　　　　　　　　R. HERRICK.

---

① *cypress tree*: the cypress is the emblem of mourning.

在那棵柏树下哀伤：
或叫我死亡,我就会
　视死如归,为你早殇。　　　　　　　　　　　*20*

你是我的生命,我的爱,我的心
　我最最珍爱的眼睛,
你主宰着我的每一部分,
　为你而生,为你而死。

蒋炳贤　译

97. 'LOVE NOT ME FOR COMELY GRACE'

Love not me for comely grace,
For my pleasing eye or face,
Nor for any outward part,
No, nor for my constant heart, —
    For those may fail, or turn to ill,
    So thou and I shall sever:
Keep therefore a true woman's eye,
And love me still, but know not why —
    So hast thou the same reason still
    To doat upon me ever!

ANON.

97. "爱我别因为我潇洒英俊"

无名氏

爱我别因为我潇洒英俊,
别因为我漂亮的脸庞或眼睛,
别因为我美丽的外表,
也不要因为我的一片忠诚,——
    这一切都会衰老,消失,   *5*
      于是你我将各奔前程;
保持一个女人真正的眼力,
仍然爱我吧,但不知道为何原因——
    于是你就有了一个不变的理由,
      你对我的爱情就会永恒。   *10*

曹明伦 译

98. 'NOT, CELIA, THAT I JUSTER AM'

Not, Celia, that I juster am[①]
    Or better than the rest;
For I would change each hour, like them,
    Were not my heart at rest.

But I am tied to very thee[②]
    By every thought I have;
Thy face I only care to see,
    Thy heart I only crave.

All that in woman is adored
    In thy dear self I find —
For the whole sex can but afford[③]
    The handsome and the kind.

Why then should I seek further store,
    And still make love anew?
When change itself can give no more,
    'Tis easy to be true.

SIR C. SEDLEY.

---

① *Not ... that*: *i.e.* the reason of my constancy is not that ...
② *to very thee*: 'to thy very self.'
③ *afford*: 'supply, produce.'

98. "不,西莉亚"

塞德利

不,西莉亚,我并不比别人
　　更为正直或忠诚;
像别人一样,我随时会变心,
　　如果我的心不安宁。

然而我的每一个思想　　　　　　　　　　5
　　把我和你本人捆紧①;
只有你的脸庞我要望,
　　只有你的心我要亲。

女性的一切值得称赞的,
　　我发现全在你一身——　　　　　　10
全部女性只产生了一个
　　美丽而温柔的人。

为什么我还要追求别的;
　　去探索新的爱情?
变心本身给不了我什么,　　　　　　15
　　我就易于忠贞。

屠岸　译

---

① 你本人,即不是你的身份、地位、财产等等。——译者

99. TO ALTHEA FROM PRISON

When Love with unconfinéd wings
    Hovers within my gates,
And my divine Althea brings
    To whisper at the grates;
When I lie tangled in her hair
    And fetter'd to her eye,
The Gods that wanton in the air
    Know no such liberty.

When flowing cups run swiftly round
    With no allaying Thames,
Our careless heads with roses crown'd,
    Our hearts with loyal flames;
When thirsty grief in wine we steep,
    When healths and draughts go free —
Fishes that tipple in the deep
    Know no such liberty.

When, like committed linnets, I[1]
    With shriller throat shall sing[2]
The sweetness, mercy, majesty
    And glories of my King;
When I shall voice aloud how good

---

[1] *committed*: 'imprisoned'; the full phrase is 'committed to prison.'
[2] *shriller*: *i.e.* than the linnets; hardly a fortunate adjective.

99. 狱中寄阿尔西娅①

洛夫莱斯

爱情张开自由的翅膀
  在我的牢房飞翔,
把我高洁的阿尔西娅
  带到铁窗旁与我低语;
她的一缕青丝缠结了我   5
  她的一双明眸吸住了我,
天上的神灵飘逸飞驰
  不知道有这种自由。

斟满的酒杯过数巡
  美酒香甜味醇厚②,   10
我们无忧无愁地头戴玫瑰花冠,
  忠贞的爱情燃炽着我们的胸膛;
开怀畅饮共消万年愁,
  恣情祝饮堪酣畅——
深渊中唼喋不休的游鱼   15
  也不知道有这种自由。

像幽禁笼中的红雀
  我提高嗓子歌唱
欢乐、仁慈、威严
  与君王的丰功伟业;   20
我要放声歌唱

---

① 参见本卷第83首编注。——编注者
② 即酒中没有掺水之意。——译者

>   He is, how great should be,
>   Enlargéd winds, that curl the flood①,
>   Know no such liberty.
>
>   Stone walls do not a prison make,
>   Nor iron bars a cage;
>   Minds innocent and quiet take
>   That for an hermitage:
>   If I have freedom in my love②
>   And in my soul am free③,
>   Angels alone, that soar above,
>   Enjoy such liberty.

R. LOVELACE.

---

① *curl the flood*: break the surface of the water into waves.
② *freedom in my love*: *i.e.* freedom to love Althea.
③ *in my soul* here means no more than 'in my thoughts.'

他多么善良,该多么伟大,
掀起波涛汹涌的暴风狂飙
　　也不知道有这种自由。

石墙关不住一个囚犯,　　　　　　　　　　　　　25
　　铁栅也难锁住笼鸟;
清白无罪、宁静恬逸的心灵
　　把这儿权充隐居之所:
只要我有自由爱我心爱的人儿,
　　心里就万分泰然自若。　　　　　　　　　　30
只有逍遥云霄的安琪儿
　　才能享受这种自由。

　　　　　　　　　　　　　蒋炳贤　译

100. TO LUCASTA, ON GOING BEYOND THE SEAS

If to be absent were to be
    Away from thee;
  Or that when I am gone
    You or I were alone;
      Then, my Lucasta, might I crave
Pity from blustering wind, or swallowing wave.

Though seas and land betwixt us both,
    Our faith and troth,
  Like separated souls,
    All time and space controls[①]:
Above the highest sphere we meet
Unseen, unknown, and greet as Angels greet[②].

So then we do anticipate
    Our after-fate,
  And are alive i' the skies,
    If thus our lips and eyes
Can speak like spirits unconfined
In Heaven, their earthy bodies left behind.

                            R. LOVELACE.

---

① *controls*: the verb is singular because 'faith and troth,' the subject, are looked on as one idea. 'Twin souls' may be separated, but they rise superior to all considerations of time and space; and so do Lovelace and Lucasta through the faith they have in each other.

② *Unseen, unknown*: *i.e.* unrecognized by the outside world.

100. 出海前告别鲁加斯达

洛夫莱斯

如果我不在，
　　那就远离了您；
　如果我外出，
　你我都孤单；
那时,我的鲁加斯达,我是不是可以恳求　　　　　5
呼啸的狂风,或奔腾的怒潮发发慈悲。

纵然我们相隔千山万水,
　　我们的海誓山盟,
　把两相分离的心灵,
　天长地久永相连：　　　　　　　　　　　　10
我们在飘渺的苍穹相会
人寰不知不觉,像天使一样相迎。

就这样我们瞻望
　　未来的命运,
　我们生活在苍穹,　　　　　　　　　　　　15
　若是这样,我们的嘴巴和眼睛
都会像天堂里自由的天使一样说话,
把自己的臭皮囊丢在身后。

蒋炳贤　译

编注　这首诗是《鲁加斯达》(参见本卷第83首编注)的第一首,原诗共四节,《金库》原编者删去了第二节。

101. ENCOURAGEMENTS TO A LOVER

Why so pale and wan, fond lover?
    Prythee, why so pale?
Will, when looking well can't move her,
    Looking ill prevail?
    Prythee, why so pale?

Why so dull and mute, young sinner?
    Prythee, why so mute?
Will, when speaking well can't win her,
    Saying nothing do't?
    Prythee, why so mute?

Quit, quit, for shame! this will not move[①],
    This cannot take her;
If of herself she will not love,
    Nothing can make her;
    The devil take her!

SIR J. SUCKLING.

---

① *Quit*: 'cease to act so.'

101. 致一个失恋的小伙子

萨克林

为什么这样子苍白、憔悴,痴心汉?
　　请问,为什么这样子苍白?
红光满面既不能叫她心转,
　　难道哭丧脸就换得回来?
　　为什么这样子苍白? 5

为什么这样子发呆、发愣,小伙子?
　　请问,为什么这样子发愣?
漂亮话尚且嵌不进她的心模子,
　　难道装哑巴反而会成?
　　为什么这样子发愣? 10

算了,算了,争点气? 这样子不行,
　　这样子你一点也降不了她;
如果她自己一点也并不动情,
　　随你怎样也勉强不了她:
　　魔鬼准保放不了她! 15

　　　　　　　　　卞之琳　译

编注　约翰·萨克林(John Suckling,1609—1642),英国保皇派骑士诗人,曾冒过险,打过仗,也写过一些剧本。《致一个失恋的小伙子》是他一六四六年发表的剧本《阿格劳拉》(*Aglaura*)中的一段插曲。

102. A SUPPLICATION

Awake, awake, my Lyre!
And tell thy silent master's humble tale
    In sounds that may prevail;
    Sounds that gentle thoughts inspire:
        Though so exalted she
        And I so lowly be,
Tell her, such different notes make all thy harmony.

    Hark! how the strings awake:
And, though the moving hand approach not near,
        Themselves with awful fear
    A kind of numerous trembling make[①].
    Now all thy forces try;
    Now all thy charms apply;
Revenge upon her ear the conquests of her eye[②].

        Weak Lyre! thy virtue sure[③]
Is useless here since thou art only found
        To cure, but not to wound,
        And she to wound, but not to cure.

---

① *numerous*: 'rhythmic,' 'musical'; 'number' is often used in the sense of rhythm or verse.

② *I.e.* As she has vanquished me with her eyes, do you in turn vanquish her through her ears.

③ *virtue*: 'power.'

102. 祈求

考利

醒来吧,醒来吧,我的竖琴!
把你沉默主人微不足道的故事,
　　用动听的声音诉说给她听,
　　引起她的温存的情思:
　　她虽然那样高超,　　　　　　　　　　5
　　我虽然这样渺小,
告诉她,音调不同使你的音律协调。

　　听哪,琴弦现在醒了!
而且,虽然没有人动手去接近,
　　它们自己怀着敬畏的情调,　　　　　10
　　发出一种颤巍巍的声音。
　　现在用尽你们的全部力气;
　　现在运用你们的全部魅力;
在她的耳朵里报复她眼睛征服的东西。

　　无力的竖琴!你对此丝毫无用,　　　15
因为你没有力量伤害,只有力量治疗,
　　她却和你完完全全不同,
　　她只会伤害,却治疗不了。

>   Too weak too wilt thou prove[1]
>   My passion to remove;
>   Physic to other ills, thou'rt nourishment to love.
>
>
>   Sleep, sleep again, my Lyre
>   For thou canst never fell my humble tale
>   In sounds that will prevail,
>   Nor gentle thoughts in her inspire;
>   All thy vain mirth lay by,
>   Bid thy strings silent lie,
>   Sleep, sleep again, my Lyre, and let thy master die.
>
>   A. COWLEY.

---

[1] the second *too* = moreover; music can relieve pain and grief, but my passion is too deep-seated to be so cured.

> 要治好我的激情,
>   将证明你太不行, 20
> 你是爱情的营养,你只能治别的疾病。
>
> 再睡吧,再睡吧,我的竖琴!
> 因为你诉说不了我的卑微故事,
>   用动听的声音,
>   也不能在她心里引起情思; 25
>   把你的枉然的欢乐都放在一旁,
>   使你的琴弦别再发响,
> 再睡吧,再睡吧,我的竖琴,让你的主人死亡。

李霁野 译

编注 亚伯拉罕·考利(Abraham Cowley,1618—1667),英国保皇派诗人。《祈求》一首选自考利的四卷长篇圣诗《大卫》(*Davideis*,1668)的第三卷。

103. THE MANLY HEART

Shall I, wasting in despair,
Die because a woman's fair?
Or make pale my cheeks with care
'Cause another's rosy are?
Be she fairer than the day
Or the flowery meads in May —
    If she think not well of me,
    What care I how fair she be?

Shall my silly heart be pined①
'Cause I see a woman kind;
Or a well disposéd nature
Joinéd with a lovely feature?
Be she meeker, kinder, than
Turtle-dove or pelican,
    If she be not so to me,
    What care I how kind she de?

Shall a woman's virtues move
Me to perish for her love?
Or her well-deservings known
Make me quite forget mine own?
Be she with that goodness blest
Which may merit name of Best;

---

① *pined*: 'distressed.'

103. 情人的决心

威瑟

为了一个美丽的妇人，
我就消瘦憔悴丧生？
或者焦心使自己面颊苍白，
因为她的面颊是玫瑰颜色？
即使她比白日更为美丽，　　　　　　　5
或美过五月开花的草地，
　　假如她对我并不怀好感，
　　我何必关怀她美貌娇颜？

我的糊涂的心可会
因为一个妇人和蔼就憔悴？　　　　　10
或因为她脾气很好，
她的容貌又极窈窕？
即使她比鸽子和企鹅
更为柔顺，更为温和①，
　　假如她对我并不这样，　　　　　15
　　我管她什么和爱心肠？

妇女的美德会使我感动，
对她钟情，把自己消灭无踪？
她的优点理应声名外扬，
我自己的优点就应全忘？　　　　　　20
即使她有善良的福分，
应该得到最好的名声，

---

① 鸽子象征爱；据埃及传说，企鹅以自己的血饲子女。——编注者

>   If she be not such to me,
>   What care I how good she be?
>
> 'Cause her fortune seems too high,
> Shall I play the fool and die?
> She that bears a noble mind
> If not outward helps she find,
> Thinks what with them he would do
> That without them dares her woo;
>   And unless that mind I see,
>   What care I how great she be?
>
> Great or good, or kind or fair①,
> I will ne'er the more despair②;
> If she love me, this believe,
> I will die ere she shall grieve;
> If she slight me when I woo,
> I can scorn and let her go;
>   For if she be not for me,
>   What care I for whom she be?

G. WITHER.

---

① *Great or good, or kind or fair*: a summary of the qualities given in the four previous stanzas, but in the reverse order.

② *the more*: i.e. more on account of her possessing those qualities.

假如她对我并不这样，
　　　我何必管她多么善良？

　　　因为命运似乎使她地位太高，　　　　　　　25
　　　我就呆头傻脑为她死掉？
　　　假如她有崇高的心灵，
　　　不在外表条件上计较斤斤，
　　　心想他没有条件竟敢向她求欢，
　　　有条件他岂不更为大胆？　　　　　　　　30
　　　　除非我看到那样心灵，
　　　　她多么伟大我何必关心？

　　　伟大，和蔼，美丽，善良，
　　　我都不会更为绝望；
　　　假如她爱我，可以相信：　　　　　　　　35
　　　我宁愿死，也不使她伤心；
　　　假如我求爱她看我不起，
　　　我会轻视她并让她走去；
　　　　因为假如她不向我倾心，
　　　　我何必管她对谁钟情？　　　　　　　　40

　　　　　　　　　　　　　　　　李霁野　译

编注 乔治·威瑟（George Wither，1588—1667），英国诗人，毕业于牛津大学，一六三九年曾任保皇军上尉，三年后又任国会军少校，后升为克伦威尔手下的少将，王政复辟后遭到三年监禁。

104. MELANCHOLY

Hence, all you vain delights,
As short as are the nights
   Wherein you spend your folly:
There's nought in this life sweet,
If man were wise to see't,
   But only melancholy,
   O sweetest melancholy!
Welcome, folded arms, and fixéd eyes,
A sigh that piercing mortifies①,
A look that's fasten'd to the ground,
A tongue chain'd up without a sound!
Fountain heads and pathless groves②,
Places which pale passion loves③!
Moonlight walks, when all the fowls
Are warmly housed, save bats and owls!
   A midnight bell, a parting groan④—
   These are the sounds we feed upon;
Then stretch our bones in a still gloomy valley⑤;
Nothing's so dainty sweet as lovely melancholy.

J. FLETCHER.

---

① *that piercing mortifies*: 'that penetrates the hearer and renders him dead to the world.'
② *Fountain heads*: the springs where the water issues from the earth.
③ *pale passion*: i.e. the lover grown pale with longing.
④ *a parting groan*: 'the groan of one on the point of death.'
⑤ *still*: in its usual 17th-century sense, 'always.'

104. 幽思

弗莱彻

而今,所有你无益的欢乐,
像夜晚一样短暂,
　　你在那里任岁月在愚行中蹉跎:
而人生原没有什么欢欣,
只有聪明人才能自知,　　　　　　　　　　5
　　唯独幽思,
　　嗬!最最甜蜜的幽思!
欢欢喜喜地迎着交臂与凝眸,
一声震耳欲聋的长叹,
一副盯住地面的神色,　　　　　　　　　　10
一只缄口无言的结舌!
源泉与无径的丛林,
斯人独憔悴的去处!
月夜漫步,这时除了蝙蝠和猫头鹰以外,
野禽都暖洋洋地在窝里栖息!　　　　　　15
　　一阵夜半钟声,一声临终的呻吟——
　　这些都是我们听得见的声息;
在长年阴郁的幽谷里我们舒展身心;
没有什么比美好的幽思更沁人心脾。

蒋炳贤　译

编注 约翰·弗莱彻(John Fletcher, 1579—1625),英国诗人及剧作家,在英国文学史上与弗朗西斯·鲍蒙特(见本卷第67首编注)是一对著名的文学创作合作者。据传,弗莱彻一六一三年还同莎士比亚合

写了《亨利八世》和《两位高贵的亲戚》。《幽思》选自他与鲍蒙特合著的剧本《优秀的勇士》(*The Nice Valour*，1647)第三幕第三场。评论家认为弥尔顿的《幽思的人》一诗(参见本卷第113首)曾受到《幽思》的影响。

105. TO A LOCK OF HAIR

Thy hue, dear pledge, is pure and bright
As in that well-remember'd night
When first thy mystic braid was wove①,
And first my Agnes whisper'd love.

5   Since then how often hast thou prest
The torrid zone of this wild breast,
Whose wrath and hate have sworn to dwell
With the first sin that peopled hell②;
A breast whose blood's a troubled ocean,
10 Each throb the earthquake's wild commotion!
O if such clime thou canst endure
Yet keep thy hue unstain'd and pure,
What conquest o'er each erring thought
Of that fierce realm had Agnes wrought!
15 I had not wander'd far and wide
With such an angel for my guide;
Nor heaven nor earth could then reprove me
If she had lived, and lived to love me.

Not then this world's wild joys had been
20 To me one savage hunting scene,

---

① *braid* is especially used of a plait of woman's hair; he terms it 'mystic' as being connected with the mysteries of love.
② *sworn to dwell With the first sin*: 'allied themselves with murder.'

105. 致一绺头发

司各特

你的容颜,亲爱的人,还是这样皎洁,
就像在那难忘的夜晚一样,
那时你第一次梳起神秘的辫子,
我的爱格妮,第一次悄声说出了爱。

  从那时起,你常常紧贴着   *5*
我这狂放的胸上最炙热的地方,
蕴藏其中的忿恨曾经发誓,
要和地狱里头等罪恶相厮混。
这胸中的血液是个汹涌的海洋,
每一次跳动都是一次猛烈的地震!   *10*
啊,如果这样的震荡你都忍受过来,
还保持着你的洁白的容颜不染上污垢,
那么,爱格妮不知降服了多少
藏在那激烈的胸怀中的错误念头!
有这样一个天使为我引导,   *15*
我决不至浪迹四海,到处漂流;
如果她还活在人间,活着爱我,
天地都不能对我加以谴责。

  那时候人间的狂欢,在我看来,
已不是野蛮的狩猎,   *20*

My sole delight the headlong race
And frantic hurry of the chase;
To start, pursue, and bring to bay,
Rush in, drag down, and rend my prey,
Then — from the carcass turn away!
Mine ireful mood had sweetness tamed①,
And soothed each wound which pride inflamed; —
Yes, God and man might now approve me
If thou hadst lived, and lived to love me!

                                                SIR W. SCOTT.

---

① *sweetness*: *i.e.* thy sweetness would have tamed my angry moods.

我唯一的爱好已不是穷追,
和猎物的狂跑;
已不是出发、紧追、逼得它走投无路、
冲上去、拖倒在地、撕开我的猎物,
然后又舍弃那具尸骸,掉头不顾。
甜蜜的情意会驯服我这暴躁的脾气,
骄傲引起的创伤也可以得到慰藉;——
是的,如果你还活在人间,活着爱我,
上帝和世人现在都会对我赞美!

王培德　译

编注 瓦尔特·司各特(Sir Walter Scott, 1771—1832),英国浪漫主义时期著名诗人及小说家。这首诗选自他的小说《修墓老人》(*Old Mortality*,又译作《清教徒》)第二十三章,按年代应该编在卷四(参见本书卷四第170首编注)。

106. THE FORSAKEN BRIDE

O waly waly up the bank,
    And waly waly down the brae[1],
And waly waly yon burn-side
    Where I and my Love wont to gae[2]!
I leant my back unto an aik[3],
    I thought it was a trusty tree;
But first it bow'd, and syne it brak[4],
    Sae my true Love did lichtly me[5].

O waly waly, but love be bonny
    A little time while it is new;
But when 'tis auld, it waxeth cauld
    And fades awa' like morning dew.
O wherefore should I busk my head[6]?
    Or wherefore should I kame my hair[7]?
For my true Love has me forsook,
    And says he'll never loe me mair.

---

[1] *waly*: (pronounced 'wawly') an exclamation of grief. *bank* and *brae* in northern dialect have the same meaning, 'slope' or 'hill.'

[2] *wont*: see note to No. 38, l. 6.

[3] *aik*: 'oak.'

[4] *syne*: a Scottish form of *since*, the earliest meaning of which is 'then,' 'thereupon.'

[5] *did lichtly me*: 'treated me with disdain.' To *lightly* is a transitive verb, chiefly found in its Scottish form, meaning 'to treat lightly.'

[6] *busk*: 'attire.'

[7] *kame*: 'comb.'

106. 被抛弃的新娘

无名氏

伤伤心心挨上这山头,
　　凄凄切切步下这山丘,
愁肠欲断寻到这溪边,
　　我与我爱人曾在这儿戏游!
轻轻地倚上一棵橡树,　　　　　　　　　　　　5
　　我想这树儿是可靠的朋友;
可它先点头弯腰,随即猝然断折,
　　就像我忠实的爱人对我轻侮反眸。

哎哟,哎哟,如果说爱情美好,
　　唯有初恋时它才美好香甜;　　　　　　　10
但待新欢之后,它就渐渐冷却
　　像清晨的露珠儿一去不复返。
哦,我干吗还梳理我的发鬓?
　　哦,我干吗还妆饰我的容颜?
我忠实的爱人已将我抛弃,　　　　　　　　15
　　他说他不再把我喜欢。

>Now Arthur-seat sall be my bed;
>   The sheets shall ne'er be 'fil'd by me;
> Saint Anton's well sall be my drink,
>   Since my true Love has forsaken me.
> Marti'mas wind, when wilt thou blaw
>   And shake the green leaves aff the tree?
> O gentle Death, when wilt thou come?
>   For of my life I am wearíe.
>
> 'Tis not the frost, that freezes fell[①]
>   Nor blawing snaw's inclemencie;
> 'Tis not sic cauld that makes me cry,
>   But my Love's heart grown cauld to me.
> When we came in by Glasgow town
>   We were a comely sight to see;
> My Love was clad in the black velvét,
>   And I myself in cramasie[②].
>
> But had I wist, before I kist,
>   That love had been sae ill to win;
> I had lockt my heart in a case of gowd
>   And pinn'd it with a siller pin.
> And, O! if my young babe were born,
>   And set upon the nurse's knee,
> And I mysell were dead and gane,

---

① *fell*: 'cruelly.'
② *cramasie*: or cramoisy, 'crimson cloth.'

亚瑟山将是我的安身之地①,
　　此身再不会挨上衾褥枕席;
我将啜饮圣安东井中的清水②,
　　因为我的爱人已将我抛弃。　　　　　　　20
圣马丁节的风啊,你何时吹来③,
　　将树上的片片绿叶儿吹离?
好心的死神哟,你何日光顾?
　　我对我的生命早已厌腻。

最冷的不是凛冽的风霜,　　　　　　　　　　25
　　不是那无情的大雪飞扬,
也不是冻得我哀号的寒冰,
　　而是我爱人冷酷的心肠。
当我俩来到格拉斯哥城旁④,
　　那时我们憧憬美好的时光;　　　　　　30
我爱人兴高采烈,身着天鹅绒黑衫,
　　我红妆艳抹,也分外漂亮。

假若在接吻之前我就知晓
　　获得爱情历来就如此艰辛;
我会把我的心儿锁入金袋,　　　　　　　　35
　　再用一颗金针将袋儿缝紧。
哦!假若我的孩子已经降生,
　　能够在保姆的膝盖上站稳,
那我将离开这个世界,

---

① 亚瑟山是爱丁堡东面一座小山,高八百英尺。——译者
② 圣安东山是亚瑟山北邻小山。山上有井。山和井均由山脚下的圣安东尼教堂而得名。此句意为她要入教堂作修女。——译者
③ 圣马丁节(Marti'mas)是西方宗教节日,为每年的十一月十一日。——译者
④ 格拉斯哥是苏格兰中南部主要港口城市。——译者

40 For a maid again I'll never be.

               ANON.

因为我已失去少女的童贞。　　　　　　　　　　　　40

曹明伦　译

编注　此诗最早见于一七三三年出版的《茶桌杂集》(*Tea-table Miscellany*)。但有人认为它在一六七〇年之前就已在民间流传。

107. FAIR HELEN

I wish I were where Helen lies;
Night and day on me she cries;
O that I were where Helen lies
    On fair Kirconnell lea①!

Curst be the heart that thought the thought,
And curst the hand that fired the shot,
When in my arms burd Helen dropt②,
    And died to succour me!

O think na but my heart was sair③
When my Love dropt down and spak nae mair!
I laid her down wi' meikle care④
    On fair Kirconnell lea.

As I went down the water-side,
None but my foe to be my guide,
None but my foe to be my guide⑤,

---

① *lea*: 'a grassy field.'
② *burd*: a poetic word, used chiefly in northern dialects, for 'lady.' Its origin is uncertain.
③ *think na but*: in Scott 'think na ye.' This requires a note of interrogation at the end of the next line.
④ *I laid her down*: in Scott, 'There did she swoon'; with which reading *wi' meiklc care* must mean 'to my great grief.'
⑤ The repetition of this line admirably marks the intentness with which Adam followed Helen's murderer; he had but one idea in his mind, to avenge her.

107. 美丽的海伦

无名氏

但愿我躺在海伦躺下的地方,
她日日夜夜为我哭泣哀伤,
哦,我多想躺在海伦躺下的地方,
　　躺在美丽的克尔科勒草地上!

该诅咒那副滋生邪念的心肠,　　　　　　　5
诅咒那罪恶之手开了罪恶的一枪,
美丽的海伦倒进我的怀抱,
　　为救我的性命她却殒玉消香!

哦,谁知道我心儿有多么痛苦
当我的爱人倒下,她欲言口难张,　　　　10
我悲痛欲绝将她轻轻放下,
　　放在美丽的克尔科勒草地上。

当我愤怒地冲过那条小溪,
我只看见仇人在我前方,
我只看见仇人在我前方,　　　　　　　　15

On fair Kirconnell lea;

I lighted down my sword to draw,
I hackéd him in pieces sma',
I hackéd him in pieces sma①',
  For her sake that died for me,

O Helen fair, beyond compare!
I'll make a garland of thy hair
Shall bind my heart for evermair
  Until the day I die.

O that I were where Helen lies.
Night and day on me she cries;
Out of my bed she bids me rise,
  Says, 'Haste and come to me!'

O Helen fair! O Helen chaste!
If I were with thee, I were blest,
Where thou lies low and takes thy rest
  On fair Kirconnell lea.

I wish my grave were growing green,
A winding-sheet drawn ower my een,
And I in Helen's arms lying,
  On fair Kirconnell lea.

I wish I were where Helen lies;

---

① Here the repetition seems to depict the gloating joy which Adam took in the mutilation.

就在美丽的克尔科勒草地上。

当啷啷我抽出雪亮的宝剑,
把他劈成肉泥,剁成肉酱,
把他劈成肉泥,剁成肉酱,
  为了替我献身的美丽姑娘。   20

哦,海伦,你的美貌天下无双!
我要用你的秀发编一个花冠戴上,
这花冠将永远系住我的心,
  直到有朝一日我也死亡。

哦。我多愿躺在海伦躺下的地方, 25
她日日夜夜为我哭泣哀伤;
她唤我快快从床上爬起,
  唤我快快去到她的身旁!

哦,美丽的海伦,纯洁的海伦!
我能与你同在,那真是天恩浩荡, 30
同你一起躺在你的安息之地,
  在那美丽的克尔科勒草地上。

但愿我的坟上长满青草,
但愿一张裹尸布将我盖上,
但愿我躺在海伦的怀里, 35
  在那美丽的克尔科勒草地上。

我多愿躺在海伦躺下的地方,

Night and day on me she cries;
And I am weary of the skies,
      Since my Love died for me.

ANON.

她日日夜夜为我哭泣哀伤；
我已经厌倦了这蓝天白云，
　　因为我的爱人为我而夭亡。 40

曹明伦　译

编注　此首选自司各特编纂的《苏格兰边区歌谣》(*Minstrelsy of the Scottish Border*, 1802)。诗中的海伦生活在詹姆士五世时代，是苏格兰西部邓弗里斯郡一位乡绅的女儿。一天，海伦与她的爱人亚当·福莱明正沿着小溪散步。海伦的另一个追求者从对岸举枪向福莱明射击，海伦用身体掩护福莱明，自己却饮弹而亡。

108. THE TWA CORBIES[1]

As I was walking all alane
I heard twa corbies making a mane;
The tane unto the t'other say[2],
'Where sall we gang and dine to-day?'

'— In behint yon auld fail dyke[3],
I wot there lies a new-slain Knight;
And naebody kens that he lies there,
But his hawk, his hound, and lady fair.

'His hound is to the hunting gane,
His hawk to fetch the wild-fowl hame,
His lady's ta'en another mate,
So we may make our dinner sweet.

'Ye'll sit on his white hause-bane[4],
And I'll pick out his bonny blue een;
Wi' ae lock o' his gowden hair
We'll theek our nest when it grows bare[5].

---

[1] *Corbies*: 'carrion crows.'
[2] *The tane ... the t'other*: the 'the's' are of course redundant, being contained in 'tane' and 't'other.'
[3] *fail dyke*: 'wall of turf.'
[4] *hause-bane*: 'neck-bone,' i.e. collar-bone; *house* is also spelt 'halse.'
[5] *theek*: 'roof or thatch.'

108. 两只乌鸦

无名氏

我独个儿漫步时,
听到两只乌鸦在商谈;
一只对另一只说,
"今天我们上哪儿去吃饭?"

"在那边古老的泥草墙脚下, 5
我见到躺着一位刚殒命的骑士;
谁都不知道他躺在那里,
除了他的鹰、他的猎狗,和他的美人儿。

"他的猎狗去狩猎,
他的鹰把野禽送回家, 10
他的美人儿另有所欢,
因此我们可以好好吃一顿。

"你可坐在他白皙的颈骨上,
我可啄食他俊秀的碧眼:
把他一绺金黄头发 15
当作茅草覆盖我们快剥落的巢。

'Mony a one for him makes mane,
But nane sall ken where he is gane;
O'er his white banes, when they are bare,
The wind sall blaw for evermair.'

ANON.

"不少人都会谈论他,
但谁都不知道他到哪里去;
在他嶙嶙的白骨上
吹着永不停息的风。" *20*

蒋炳贤　译

编注 此诗选自司各特编纂的《苏格兰边区歌谣》。诗人在诗中用生动、简朴,又带有冷嘲的风格,表达了对死者的哀悼之情。

109. TO BLOSSOMS

Fair pledges of a fruitful tree①,
    Why do ye fall so fast?
Your date is not so past②,
But you may stay yet here awhile
    To blush and gently smile,
        And go at last.

What, were ye born to be
    An hour or half's delight,
    And so to bid good-night?
'Twas pity Nature brought ye forth
    Merely to show your worth,
        And lose you quite.

But you are lovely leaves, where we
    May read how soon things have
    Their end, though ne'er so brave③:
And after they have shown their pride
    Like you awhile, they glide
        Into the grave.

R. HERRICK.

---

① *pledges*: 'offspring.' See above, note on No. 66, l. 107.
② *date*: 'term of existence.'
③ *brave*: 'handsome.'

109. 咏花

赫里克

结实累累果树的美丽保证,
  为什么你们落得这样迅速?
  你们的日子不能这样飞度;
你们可以在这里停留一会,
  羞羞答答,轻笑微微,   5
    最后才走自己的道路。

什么!难道你们生来只为
  一点钟或半点钟享乐,
  于是说声晚安走脱?
可惜大自然使你们来到人世,   10
  只是为显示显示你们的价值,
    然后你们就完全没有下落。

但是你们是可爱的书页,
  在那里可以读到,美丽的事物
  怎样很快就会到了终途: 15
同你们完全一模一样,
  它们闪耀过片刻荣光,
    它们就滑进坟墓。

            李霁野 译

110. TO DAFFODILS

Fair Daffodils, we weep to see
    You haste away so soon;
As yet the early-rising Sun
    Has not attain'd his noon.
        Stay, stay,
Until the hasting day
    Has run
But to the even-song;
And, having pray'd together, we
    Will go with you along.

We have short time to stay, as you,
    We have as short a Spring;
As quick a growth to meet decay
    As you, or any thing.
        We die,
As your hours do and dry
    Away
Like to the Summer's rain;
Or as the pears of morning's dew,
    Ne'er to be found again.

                                        R. HERRICK.

110. 咏黄水仙花

赫里克

美的黄水仙,凋谢得太快,
　　我们感觉着悲哀;
连早晨出来的太阳
　　都还没有上升到天盖。
　　　　停下来,停下来, 5
　　等匆忙的日脚
　　　　跑进
　　黄昏的暮霭;
在那时共同祈祷着,
　　在回家的路上徘徊。 10

我们也只有短暂的停留,
　　青春的易逝堪忧;
我们方生也就方死,
　　和你们一样,
　　　　一切都要罢休。 15
　　你们谢了,
　　　　我们也要去了,
　　如同夏雨之骤,
或如早晨的露珠,
　　永无痕迹可求。 20

　　　　　　　　　郭沫若　译

111. THOUGHTS IN A GARDEN

  How vainly men themselves amaze①
  To win the palm, the oak, or bays,
  And their uncessant labours see
  Crown'd from some single herb or tree,
5   Whose short and narrow-vergéd shade②
  Does prudently their toils upbraid;
  While all the flowers and trees do close③
  To weave the garlands of repose.

  Fair Quiet, have I found thee here,
10   And Innocence thy sister dear!
  Mistaken long, I sought you then
  In busy companies of men:
  Your sacred plants, if here below,
  Only among the plants will grow:
15   Society is all but rude④
  To this delicious solitude.

  No white nor red was ever seen
  So amorous as this lovely green⑤.
  Fond lovers, cruel as their flame,

---

① *amaze*: 'bewilder.'
② *narrow-vergéd*: 'making but a small margin round their heads.'
③ *close*: 'combine.'
④ *all but rude*: 'almost barbarous.'
⑤ *amorous*: in the obsolete sense of 'lovely'.

111. 花园遐思

马韦尔

多么傻,人们把自己弄糊涂,
要赢得棕榈、月桂或栎树①!
他们无休止的劳作只得到
一种香草或一棵树来荣耀。
这些短短的、窄窄的遮蔽物② 5
正该责备他们的辛苦,
而此时所有的鲜花和树木
为编织恬静的花环在合作。

美好的安宁啊,原来你在此处,
还有你亲爱的妹妹"天趣"! 10
我好久都弄错,在忙碌的人群
交往中寻找你的踪影;
而你的神圣的草木只是在
这些草木之中才郁郁葱葱;
同这里美妙的孤寂相比, 15
社会几乎是粗野而已。

从未曾见过粉白与脂红
像这可爱的碧绿使人心动③。
多情的恋人们像情焰般残忍,

---

① 棕榈、月桂和栎树的枝叶做成的冠冕在西方均被作为胜利与荣誉的象征。——译者
② 指桂冠。——译者
③ 这里是说,男女性爱远不如对大自然之爱。——编注者

    Cut in these trees their mistress' name:
    Little, alas, they know or heed
    How far these beauties hers exceed!
    Fair trees! wheres'e'er your barks I wound,
    No name shall but your own be found[①].

    When we have run our passions' heat
    Love hither makes his best retreat:
    The gods, that mortal beauty chase,
    Still in a tree did end their race[②]:
    Apollo hunted Daphne so,
    Only that she might laurel grow;
    And Pan did after Syrinx speed
    Not as a nymph, but for a reed.

    What wondrous life in this I lead!
    Ripe apples drop about my head;
    The luscious clusters of the vine
    Upon my mouth do crush their wine;
    The nectarine and curious peach[③]
    Into my hands themselves do reach;
    Stumbling on melons, as I pass,
    Ensnared with flowers, I fall on grass.

    Meanwhile the mind, from pleasure less[④],

---

① 'If I carve any name upon you, it will be your own.'
② *Still*: 'always.'
③ *curious*: 'rare.'
④ *from pleasure less*: 'withdraws from smaller outside enjoyment into its own internal happiness.'

在树上刻下了情人的芳名。 20
呜呼,他们不注意,不知道
自然美胜过她们有多少!
美丽的树木啊! 要是我来损伤,
我只把你们的大名刻上。

一旦我们燃旺了情火, 25
爱情就向这里完满地退却。
世间的美人所寻求的众神,
总是在树上终止其追奔。
阿波罗把达佛涅死劲儿盯住
竟然使她要化作月桂树①。 30
潘神把西冷克丝神追赶,
爱山水的仙女便变成芦杆②。

在这里生活我过得多美妙!
我身旁成熟的苹果往下掉。
甘美的葡萄累累悬垂, 35
酒般的蜜汁滋润了我的嘴。
油桃和珍贵的桃子鲜红,
它们来到了我的双手中。
我走过,甜瓜把我绊倒,
而鲜花又诱惑我扑卧青草。 40

我的心这时从较少的欢乐

---

① 达佛涅是希腊神话中的河神珀涅俄斯的女儿,她被太阳神阿波罗苦苦追求,但是她只爱山林田野,便一直逃避。最后,在险些被追上的时候,她向主神宙斯祈祷求助,使她变成了一株月桂树。——译者
② 西冷克丝是希腊神话中居于阿卡狄亚群山的山林水泽间的仙女。她喜欢畋猎,坚守贞洁的处女身。她被人身羊足的畜牧潘神追求,逃到拉东河边,向水中仙女们求救,使自己变成了一株芦苇。潘神便用芦杆制成箫。——译者

  Withdraws into its happiness;
  The mind, that ocean where each kind
  Does straight its own resemblance find;
45 Yet it creates, transcending these①,
  Far other worlds, and other seas②;
  Annihilating all that's made
  To a green thought in a green shade.

  Here at the fountain's sliding foot
50 Or at some fruit-tree's mossy root,
  Casting the body's vest aside,
  My soul into the boughs does glide;
  There, like a bird, it sits and sings,
  Then whets and combs its silver wings③,
55 And, till prepared for longer flight,
  Waves in its plumes the various light④.

  Such was that happy Garden-state
  While man there walk'd without a mate;
  After a place so pure and sweet,
60 What other help could yet be meet!
  But 'twas beyond a mortal's share
  To wander solitary there;

---

① *these*: the objects of the material universe.
② *where each kind*, etc; *i.e.* there is nothing in nature which the human mind cannot picture to itself; it can indeed go beyond this and create other worlds for its own enjoyment.
③ *whets*: 'trims,' 'dresses.'
④ *Waves in its plumes the various light*: 'causes the changing light to flicker in its plumage.'

缩回,而享受它自己的幸福①。
这颗心似海洋,自然界每一样
都立刻能找到自己的肖像。
然而它超越这些物质外, 45
创造遥远的世界和大海。
它使所有的现实都幻灭成
绿色的阴影中绿色的思忖②。

在这泉水的变动的本源,
或者在果树生苔的根前, 50
把躯体的外衣扔在一旁,
我的灵魂溜上了枝干。
像小鸟坐在那儿歌唱,
然后梳理着银色的翅膀。
把羽毛扇出彩色的光辉, 55
然后准备向更远处高飞③。

当男人还没有伴侣同行,
那乐园就是如此情形。
有了这样安恬的去处,
还要什么配偶帮助④! 60
但是在那儿孤寂地漫游,
是太大的幸福那能让凡人消受。

---

① 这里是指,心灵通过感官享受到的乐趣,远远比不上它独有的快乐,因而心灵转而内向。——编注者
② 诗人的意思是说,无邪的思想比污染的尘世更可爱。来到无尘的环境,人也就变得无邪了。——编注者
③ 新柏拉图主义认为,人的灵魂只有暂时摆脱肉体才能与神相交,从而窥见真理(向更远处高飞)。——编注者
④《圣经·旧约·创世记》第二章第十八节载:"耶和华说,那人独居不好,我要为他造一个配偶帮助他。"这节诗涉及了上帝要在伊甸园造夏娃以帮助亚当的故事。——译者

Two paradises 'twere in one,
To live in Paradise alone.

65 How well the skilful gardener drew
Of flowers and herbs this dial new!
Where, from above, the milder sun
Does through a fragrant zodiac run;
And, as it works, th' industrious bee
70 Computes its time as well as we.
How could such sweet and wholesome hours
Be reckon'd, but with herbs and flowers!

A. MARVELL.

独个儿生活在伊甸乐园里,
是两个天堂合并在一起。

灵巧的园丁把这香草 65
和花卉的日晷规划得多么好①!
柔和的阳光从天上穿过
芬芳的黄道带闪闪射落,
这时候,勤劳的蜜蜂正忙,
像我们一样计算着时光。 70
如果不用花草怎能算清
如此甜蜜的、有益的光阴!

吴钧陶 译

编注 这是一首著名的玄学诗,身处百花争艳、草木茂盛的花园中,诗人浮想联翩,思考着人生和自然的许多问题。

---

① 各种花卉在一年四季中按时序开放和凋谢。"花卉的日晷"指用不同的花卉表明时节。——译者

112. L'ALLÉGRO

    Hence, loathéd Melancholy,
Of Cerberus and blackest Midnight born
    In Stygian cave forlorn
'Mongst horrid shapes, and shrieks, and sights unholy!
    Find out some uncouth cell,
Where brooding Darkness spreads his jealous wings①
    And the night-raven sings;
There, under ebon shades and low-brow'd rocks②
    As ragged as thy locks③,
In dark Cimmerian desert ever dwell.

    But come, thou Goddess fair and free,
    In heaven yclep'd Euphrosyne,
And by men, heart-easing Mirth,
Whom lovely Venus at a birth
With two sister Graces more
To ivy-crownéd Bacchus bore:
Or whether (as some sager sing)
The frolic wind that breathes the spring,

---

① *jealous wings*: as grudging that the light shall enter.
② *ebon*, from ebony, a hard black wood, is often used in poetry for 'black.'
③ *ragged*: 'rough,' 'irregular.'

112. 快乐的人

弥尔顿

躲开吧,可憎的惆怅,
你原是塞比拉斯与午夜所生①,
 在冥河孤零的岩洞,
周围是可怖的情景、声音与形象。
 去找个荒凉地窟,   5
在那里黑煞神展开了周密的翅膀,
 乌鸦在彻夜歌唱
那里的黑影像乌檀,岩石崚嶒
 像你的乱发蓬松,
就永远到这样西木里荒漠里居住②! 10

 优美的女神呵,我们欢迎你,
  你在天上叫攸夫洛斯妮③,
在人间却叫开心的欢喜;
爱神维纳斯,一胎生了你
和你那两个姊姊格莱斯,   15
给带着藤萝花冠的白卡斯④。
有些人还做了更好的解说:
说那位满怀春意的载佛⑤,

---

① 塞比拉斯(Cerberus)是守卫地狱入口的有三个头的怪狗。——译者
② 据荷马说,西木里人(Cimmeriaus)住在世界的西端;这是一块完全昏暗的地方。——译者
③ 维纳斯(Venus)有三个侍女,总名格莱斯(Grace),攸夫洛斯妮(Euphrosyne)是格莱斯之一;此词含有欢喜的意思。——译者
④ 白卡斯(Bacchus),酒神。——译者
⑤ 载佛(Zephyr),西风神。——译者

20	Zephyr, with Aurora playing[1],
	As he met her Once a-Maying —
	There on beds of violets blue
	And fresh-blown roses wash'd in dew
	Fill'd her with thee, a daughter fair[2],
	So buxom, blithe, and debonair[3].
25	Haste thee, Nymph, and bring with thee
	Jest, and youthful jollity,
	Quips, and cranks, and wanton wiles[4],
	Nods, and becks, and wreathéd smiles[5],
	Such as hang on Hebe's cheek,
30	And love to live in dimple sleek;
	Sport that wrinkled Care derides,
	And Laughter holding both his sides.
	Come, and trip it as you go
	On the light fantastic toe;
35	And in thy right hand lead with thee
	The mountain nymph, sweet Liberty;
	And if I give thee honour due,
	Mirth, admit me of thy crew,
	To live with her, and live with thee
40	In unreprovéd pleasures free;
	To hear the lark begin his flight

---

[1] *Zephyr ... Aurora*: 'the West wind and the Dawn.'

[2] *Fill'd her with thee*: 'made her pregnant,' 'made her thy mother.'

[3] *buxom* and *blithe* had much the same meaning in the 17th century, viz. 'merry,' 'lively.' The former word is now used rather in the sense of 'plump,' 'comfortable-looking.' *debonair*: 'genial.' [French, *de bonne aire*, of good disposition.']

[4] *cranks*: 'verbal conceits.' *wanton wiles*: 'sportive tricks.'

[5] *becks*: 'bows.' *wreathéd*: properly 'twisted,' *wreathe* being cognate with 'writhe.' The act of smiling makes curved lines in the face.

有一天遇到游春的奥罗拉①,
就和她在一起厮混玩耍, 20
并在滴露的初放玫瑰
和蓝色紫萝兰花床上婚配,
于是生下你这小姑娘,
活泼快乐,美妙无双。

 女神呵,快来吧,还请你携带 25
好玩的嬉谑和年轻的愉快,
俏皮话,双关语,逗人的把戏,
点头,招手,常挂在何碧②
脸上的嫣然巧笑,爱钻进
小圆酒涡里面的微哂; 30
还有那乐以忘忧的爱打闹,
以及双手捧腹的哄堂笑。
你来吧,还请你来时跷脚走,
单踩着轻盈的小脚趾头;
而且你还要用你的右手, 35
牵着山林神——愉快的自由;
你要不嫌我礼貌不周,
欢喜神,请答应我的请求,
让我跟你们在一起生活,
共享着不越礼数的欢乐: 40
让我们静听飞鸣的云雀,

---

① 奥罗拉(Aurora),黎明女神。——译者
② 何碧(Hebe),诸神的侍女,是青春的象征。——译者

  And singing startle the dull night
  From his watch-tower in the skies,
  Till the dappled dawn doth rise;
45 Then to come, in spite of sorrow,
  And at my window bid good-morrow
  Through the sweetbriar, or the vine,
  Or the twisted eglantine;
  While the cock with lively din
50 Scatters the rear of darkness thin,
  And to the stack, or the barn-door,
  Stoutly struts his dames before;
  Oft listening bow the hounds and horn
  Cheerly rouse the slumbering morn,
55 From the side of some hoar hill,
  Through the high wood echoing shrill.
  Sometime walking, not unseen,
  By hedge-row elms, on hillocks green,
  Right against the eastern gate
60 Where the great Sun begins his state
  Robed in flames and amber light,
  The clouds in thousand liveries dight[1];
  While the ploughman, near at hand,
  Whistles o'er the furrow'd land,
65 And the milkmaid singeth blithe,
  And the mower whets his scythe,
  And every shepherd tells his tale[2]

---

[1] *dight*: 'arrayed.'

[2] *tells his tale*: probably 'relates his story,' a sense in which the phrase has been used since the 13th century; rather than 'counts up the sum' [of his sheep], which sense of the phrase is not found before the 19th, though the separate words are used in such senses earlier.

它的歌声在惊破残霄，
直待五彩的朝霞升起，
在高空里飞鸣不已，
让我移身走向窗前， 45
隔着野蔷薇或葡萄引蔓，
或是蟠曲纠缠的藤萝，
向晨光问好，尽情快活；
同时，高声报晓的雄鸡，
已驱散漫漫黑夜的残余， 50
它雄视阔步地在雌鸡前面走，
直到草垛或谷仓门口；
听，号角齐鸣，猎犬狂吠，
愉快地唤醒了清晨的酣睡，
那荒山之坡，高林之丛， 55
都在回荡着尖锐的响声；
有时我们沿榆墙散走，
或在山坡的绿草深处，
直接走向东方的大门，
欢迎那宏伟的朝阳光临， 60
它身披火焰，灿烂辉煌，
使天际云霭，也披上霓裳：
同时农夫在左近扶犁，
吹着口哨，耕着田地；
挤奶女郎正唱得高兴， 65
刈草工人在磨刀不停，
溪谷下面的每一牧羊人，

  Under the hawthorn in the dale.
   Straight mine eye hath caught new pleasures
  Whilst the landscape round it measures;
  Russet lawns, and fallows grey①,
  Where the nibbling flocks do stray;
  Mountains, on whose barren breast
  The labouring clouds do often rest②;
  Meadows trim with daisies pied③,
  Shallow brooks, and rivers wide;
  Towers and battlements it sees
  Bosom'd high in tufted trees④,
  Where perhaps some Beauty lies,
  The Cynosure of neighbouring eyes⑤,
   Hard by, a cottage chimney smokes
  From betwixt two aged oaks,
  Where Corydon and Thytsis, met,
  Are at their savoury dinner set
  Or herbs, and other country messes
  Which the neat-handed Phillis dresses;
  And then in haste her bower she leaves
  With Thestylis to bind the sheaves;
  Or, if the earlier season lead⑥,
  To the tann'd haycock in the mead.

---

① *Russet*: 'reddish-brown.' A *lawn* is any open space in the middle of trees. *fallows*: 'fields which have been ploughed and harrowed, but not sown.'
② *labouring*: 'teeming, heavy with rain.'
③ *pied*: 'variegated,' qualifying 'meadows.'
④ *Bosom'd*: either (1) 'standing out like a bosom,' or (2) 'enclosed as in a bosom'; 'high' suggests the former.
⑤ *Cynosure*: 'the centre of attraction.'
⑥ *if the earlier season lead*: 'if it is earlier in the year, so that she is summoned to the hay, rather than the corn.'

在山楂树下正查点羊群。
　　这时我巡视周围的景色,
马上感到多样的愉快: 70
褐色的草原,灰色的荒地,
吃草的羊群聚散在东西;
在那光秃的山腰深处,
经常停着孕雨的云雾;
草原整洁有雏菊杂生, 75
浅溪潺湲,大河奔腾;
青楼巍峨,雉堞迤逦,
出没在林木繁茂之际,
那里也许有美人居住,
牵惹着邻村少年的眼目。 80
在两株古老的橡树中间,
有一所茅屋飘着炊烟,
克里顿、哲西斯从田里回来,
因午餐就在这里安排,
虽说吃的是粗茶淡饭, 85
却都是斐力斯纤手所备办;
然后她匆匆离开草舍,
和塞斯蒂里斯同去收割①;
但如果一年的季节还早,
她要往草地去堆积干草。 90

---

① 克里顿、哲西斯、斐力斯、塞斯蒂里斯,这些都是希腊诗人塞奥克利塔(Theocritus)的牧歌诗里常见的牧羊人男女的名字。——译者

    Sometimes with secure delight①
    The upland hamlets will invite②,
    When the merry bells ring round③,
    And the jocund rebecks sound④
95   To many a youth and many a maid,
    Dancing in the chequer'd shade;
    And young and old come forth to play
    On a sunshine holy-day⑤,
    Till the live-long day light fail:
100   Then to the spicy nut-brown ale,
    With stories told of many a feat,
    How Faery Mab the junkets eat;
    She was pinch'd, and pull'd, she said;
    And he, by Friar's lantern led⑥;
105   Tells how the drudging Goblin sweat⑦
    To earn his cream-bowl duly set,
    When in one night, ere glimpse of morn,
    His shadowy flail hath thresh'd the corn⑧
    That ten day-labourers could not end;

---

① *secure*: 'free from care'; the Latin *securus*.
② *invite*: 'appeal to our fancy.'
③ *ring round*: 'ring in succession.'
④ *rebecks*: a kind of old-fashioned fiddle.
⑤ *holy-day* and holiday were originally the same word; the meaning here is that of the latter.
⑥ *Friai's lantern*: 'the will-o'-the wisp.'
⑦ *Sweat*: the past tense; in modern English, 'sweated.'
⑧ *shadowy*: the flail is so called presumably because it was plied in the darkness.

山村居民,足食丰衣,
有时把客人请到村里,
于是铃声响遍各处,
提琴奏出快乐的乐曲,
看呵,男女青年无数, 95
在斑驳树影下,载歌载舞;
在一个风和日丽的假期,
老的、少的也同来游戏,
直到大家消遣了长昼,
才共赏加料的栗色啤酒, 100
人人讲起荒唐的故事,
说起麦布仙如何最贪吃①。
女的说,仙女掐过她一把,
男的说,鬼火有一回迷住他;
又讲起不辞辛苦的妖魔, 105
流着大汗,为挣碗奶酪,
在一个夜晚天还未曙,
他挥动连枷,紧忙打谷,
打得十个工人不抵他;
然后这笨妖便歇在地下, 110

---

① 麦布(Mab),小妖的皇后。——译者

	Then lies him down the lubber fiend①,
110	
	And, stretch'd out all the chimney's length②,
	Basks at the fire his hairy strength③;
	And crop-full out of doors he flings④,
	Ere the first cock his matin rings⑤.
115	Thus done the tales, to bed they creep,
	By whispering winds soon lull'd asleep.
	Tower'd cities please us then⑥
	And the busy hum of men,
	Where throngs of knights and barons bold,
120	In weeds of peace high triumphs hold⑦,
	With store of ladies, whose bright eyes
	Rain influence, and judge the prize⑧
	Of wit or arms, while both contend⑨
	To win her grace, whom all commend⑩.

---

① *lies him down*: this use of 'lie' with a reflexive pronoun is possibly due to a confusion, by no means obsolete to-day, with the transitive verb 'to lay.' *lubber*: defined by Phillips in 1706 as 'a mean Servant that does all base Services in a house; a Drudge.' There is no idea of clumsiness about this use of the word.

② *all the chimney's length*: the old-style hearth was six or eight feet from side to side, or often more, with projecting walls forming the 'chimney corner.'

③ *Basks*: in the transitive sense of 'to expose to the warmth' this word does not appear to have been used since Pope.

④ *crop-full*: 'having eaten his fill.' The crop is properly the enlarged part of a bird's gullet.

⑤ *his matin*: 'his morning call.'

⑥ *please us them*: i.e. when the rustics have gone to bed the poet loves to sit and read of the doings in great cities.

⑦ *weeds*: 'garments.'

⑧ *Rain influence*: sc. on the competitors.

⑨ *both*: i.e. both wit and arms.

⑩ *her grace, whom all commend*: 'the favour of the Queen of Beauty.'

靠着炉火旁边取暖,
壁炉都被他占去大半边;
吃饱了肚子,他急忙往外跑,
深怕人家鸡公报了晓。
讲完故事大家爬上床,   *115*
微风阵阵送人入睡乡。

 然后我们来逛逛城市,
人声在鼎沸,从无休止;
在这里聚集着武士英雄,
衣饰华丽,歌舞升平,   *120*
美人的明眸脉脉含情,
谁智谁勇,要她们来判定,
为争取大家属望的青睐,
才子英雄便展开竞赛。
司婚之神在这里常出入,   *125*
黄袍披身,高举火炬;
还有游行,宴会,与联欢,
化装舞蹈与盛装表演:

125   There let Hymen oft appear①
    In saffron robe, with taper clear,
    And pomp, and feast, and revelry,
    With mask②, and antique pageantry;
    Such sights as youthful poets dream
130   On summer eves by haunted stream.
    Then to the well-trod stage anon,
    If Jonson's learned sock be on③,
    Or sweetest Shakespeare, Fancy's child,
    Warble his native wood-notes wild④.
135   And ever against eating cares⑤
    Lap me in soft Lydian airs⑥
    Married to immortal verse,
    Such as the meeting soul may pierce⑦
    In notes, with many a winding bout⑧
140   Of linkèd sweetness long drawn out,
    With wanton heed and giddy cunning⑨,
    The melting voice through mazes running,

---

① *Hymen*: the god of Marriage, who was represented in a yellow robe and carrying a torch.

② *mask*, in the sense of a dramatic entertainment, is now spelt 'masque.'

③ *Jonson's learned sock*: The sock was the light shoe worn by the ancient comic actor, as the buskin was the high boot of the tragedian. 'Sock and buskin' is often used for Comedy and Tragedy.

④ *his native wood-notes wild*: the contrast is between the learning of Jonson and the untaught natural style of Shakespeare, who had 'little Latin and less Greek.'

⑤ *against eating cares*: 'to shield me from cares that eat the heart,' Horace's 'curas edaces,' *Od*. II. xi. 18.

⑥ *Lap*: 'enfold.'

⑦ *the meeting soul*: 'the soul which lends itself to the music.'

⑧ *bout*: a 'phrase' in music.

⑨ *I.e.* performed playfully, yet carefully, with bewildering rapidity, and yet with technical skill.

这都是青年诗人,在夏夜
　　河畔上,独自梦想的情节。　　　　　　　　　　　　130
　　然后就到最好的剧院,
　　看琼生渊博的喜剧在上演①;
　　或莎士比亚,清新而美妙,
　　在歌唱村野自然的曲调。
　　　为了防止恼人的忧虑,　　　　　　　　　　　135
　　再让我听利地亚乐曲②,
　　最好要谱以不朽的诗文,
　　以便深深地打动灵魂;
　　要腔调富有回旋转折,
　　借以吐出连绵的和谐;　　　　　　　　　　　　140
　　要信口歌唱,技巧惊人,
　　那声音才能绕过迷津,
　　打开封闭着和谐的大门,
　　放出和谐里藏着的灵魂;
　　即使奥夫斯自己听到③,　　　　　　　　　　　145

---

① 琼生(Ben Jonson)是当时的桂冠诗人,以喜剧著称,他在作品里爱卖弄笔墨。——译者
② 希腊音乐有三种曲调,利地亚曲调的特征是温柔。——译者
③ 奥夫斯(Orpheus)是传说中的音乐家,善鸣琴,百兽闻声率舞。在结婚那一天,他的爱人,由黎迪斯(Eurydice),突然死了,被拖到地狱去。奥夫斯跟到地狱,用琴音软化了地狱诸神;于是他们答应他领回他的爱人,但还有一个条件:就是在回到人间的路上,他不能回过头来看她。但因他在途中急于看她一眼,一回头,地狱诸神便把他的爱人又抢回地狱去。——译者

Untwisting all the chains that tie
The hidden soul of harmony①;
145　　　That Orpheus' self may heave his head②
From golden slumber, on a bed③
Of heap'd Elysian flowers, and hear④
Such strains as would have won the ear
Of Pluto, to have quite set free
150　　　His half-regain'd Eurydice.

These delights if thou canst give,
Mirth, with thee I mean to live.

J. MILTON.

---

① The harmony in a man's soul is looked on as being bound by the chains of the external world and only set free by the influence of music.
② *That*: i.e. [so beautiful a strain] that ...
③ *golden*: see note on No. 45, l. 5.
④ *El*ysian: Elysium was the abode of good men after death in classical mythology; Homer depicts it as a far from comfortable locality, but English writers have always used the term to denote a place of perfect happiness.

也会从黄金梦中惊觉，
丢开那布满鲜花的床铺，
来倾听这歌曲；因它会迷住
坡劳图的耳音，会使他放释①
他释到半途的由黎迪斯。 *150*

你要能给我这些样欢喜，
欢喜神，我愿意永远跟着你。

殷宝书　译

编注　此诗和它的姊妹篇《幽思的人》(参见本卷 113 首)是弥尔顿早期作品中最成熟的两首诗，这两首诗大约写于一六三二年，于一六四五年初次付印。诗人当时对意大利诗歌感兴趣，给这两首诗都按上了意大利文的题目。在《快乐的人》一诗中，诗人说"快乐"是大自然的骄子；在《幽思的人》中，诗人则称"幽郁"为不幸和天性的女儿。

---

① 坡劳图(Pluto)是地狱的首神。——译者

113. IL PENSEROSO

Hence, vain deluding Joys,
The brood of Folly without father bred①!
How little you bestead②
Or fill the fixéd mind with all your toys!
    Dwell in some idle brain,
And fancies fond with gaudy shapes possess③
    As thick and numberless
As the gay motes that people the sunbeams④,
    Or likest hovering dreams
The fickle pensioners of Morpheus' train.

    But hail, thou goddess sage and holy,
    Hail divinest Melancholy!
Whose saintly visage is too bright
To hit the sense of human sight,
And therefore to our weaker view
O'erlaid with black, staid Wisdom's hue;
Black, but such as in esteem
Prince Memnon's sister might beseem⑤,

---

① *without father bred*: they had no double parentage, but sprang from Folly only.
② *bestead*: 'avail.'
③ *fancies fond with gaudy shapes possess*: 'fill foolish imaginations with showy ideas.'
④ *motes*: 'the minute specks of dust that are seen when a sunbeam enters a room.'
⑤ *beseem*: 'become,' 'suit.'

113. 幽思的人

弥尔顿

躲开吧,骗人的欢乐,
你原是愚蠢所生,没有父亲!
　对一颗沉着的心,
　你那些把戏能起的作用不多!
　　住到空洞的脑子里,　　　　　　　　　5
去给那荒唐的幻想以五光十色
　千变万化的形态,
像阳光里面大量纤尘的飞腾,
　或更像飘忽的春梦——
那班跟随着莫非斯的轻浮伴侣①。　　　　10

　但是呵,无比神圣的忧郁,
　我欢迎你这聪明的圣女!
你怕自己的容颜太光明,
照得人们睁不开眼睛,
才带上智慧光,沉静而黑暗,　　　　　　15
使脆弱的肉眼能把你看见;
但这样黑暗,大家却认为
能媲美麦木楠太子的妹妹②,

---

① 莫非斯是睡神。——译者
② 据荷马说,麦木楠是埃塞俄比亚太子,最美;他的妹妹海梅拉也同样姣
　美。——译者

  Or that starr'd Ethiop queen that strove
  To set her beauty's praise above
  The sea-nymphs, and their powers offended:
  Yet thou art higher far descended:
  Thee bright-hair'd Vesta, long of yore,
  To solitary Saturn bore;
  His daughter she; in Saturn's reign
  Such mixture was not held a stain:
  Oft in glimmering bowers and glades
  He met her, and in secret shades
  Of woody Ida's inmost grove[①],
  Whilst yet there was no fear of Jove.
   Come, pensive nun, devout and pure,
  Sober, steadfast, and demure,
  All in a robe of darkest grain[②]
  Flowing with majestic train,
  And sable stole of cypres lawn[③]
  Over thy decent shoulders drawn[④]
  Come, but keep thy wonted state,
  With even step, and musing gait,
  And looks commercing with the skies[⑤],
  Thy rapt soul sitting in thine eyes[⑥]:

[①] *Ida's inmost grove*: it was in a woody cavern on Mount Ida in Crete that the infant Zeus (Jove) was hidden from his father; here Milton follows the Greek legend of Cronos.

[②] *grain*: 'hue.' 'Grain' was originally a scarlet dye, then used of any fast colour produced by dyeing, and so came to mean simply 'colour.'

[③] *sable stole*: 'black robe.'

[④] *decent*: 'shapely.'

[⑤] *commercing*: 'holding intercourse.'

[⑥] rapt: 'absorbed.'

或变了星宿的埃国的后妃①
（她自夸比海上仙人更俊美， 20
因而把这些仙人得罪）。
然而你的出身更高贵：
金发的维斯特原在古昔②
给塞屯生的女儿就是你③；
她虽然也是塞屯所出， 25
但那时这结合还不算耻辱；
幽邃的花荫，林中的隙地，
或埃达茂林哪里最隐僻
（那时他还不必怕岳夫）④，
便常是他们两人的幽会处。 30

　来吧，沉思的女尼，虔敬，
纯洁，肃穆，端庄，而安定，
你身穿颜色暗淡的长衫，
身后的衣襟飘舞蹁跹；
一条漆黑的细纱披巾 35
遮住了你的双肩圆润。
来吧，请维持你平日尊严，
要步履整齐，举动安娴，
仰面常与云天交接，
眼睛确是神能守舍； 40

---

① 加西欧匹亚（Cassiopea）（即仙后座），是埃塞俄比亚王塞夫斯（Cepheus）的太太，自称比海中女神还美丽。——译者
② 维斯特是司家庭的女神，象征着贞节，传说是塞屯的女儿。——译者
③ 塞屯是黄金时代的统治者，后被岳夫神打倒。——译者
④ 岳夫（Jove），即约芙（宙斯）。——编注者

There, held in holy passion still①,
Forget thyself to marble, till②
With a sad leaden downward cast
Thou fix them on the earth as fast③;
45 And join with thee calm Peace, and Quiet,
Spare Fast, that oft with gods doth diet④,
And hears the Muses in a ring
Ay round about Jove's altar sing⑤;
And add to these retired Leisure⑥
50 That in trim gardens takes his pleasure; —
But first, and chiefest, with thee bring
Him that yon soars on golden wing
Guiding the fiery-wheeléd throne,
The cherub Contemplatión;
55 And the mute Silence hist along⑦,
'Less Philomel will deign a song⑧
In her sweetest saddest plight⑨,
Smoothing the rugged brow of Night,
While Cynthia checks her dragon yoke
60 Gently o'er the accustom'd oak⑩,
— Sweet bird, that shunn'st the noise of folly,

―――――――

① *held in holy passion still*: 'kept motionless through religious feeling.'
② *to marble*: 'till thou turn (to all appearances) to marble.'
③ *as fast*: sc. as they were before fixed on the heavens.
④ *Spare Fast, that oft with gods doth diet*: *i. e.* fasting often brings a fuller realization of the dlvine presence.
⑤ *Ay*: (rimes with 'day') 'ever.' Not the same word as 'Aye' — riming with 'die,' and meaning 'yes.'
⑥ *retired*: 'secluded'; not in the sense of 'retired from business.'
⑦ *hist*: 'summon without noise.'
⑧ *'Less*: 'unless.'
⑨ *plight*: 'state of mind,' 'mood' — an obsolete sense.
⑩ *the accustom'd oak*: 'the oak over which I am accustomed to see her.'

要这样怀着圣洁的情意，
你才能木石般忘掉了自己，
直到你悲伤地收回眼光，
把它紧紧地注视到地上。
你要带来安静与和平，　　　　　　　　　　45
还有斋戒，因它和神灵
常共享香火并倾听缪斯①
围绕着岳夫神坛咏圣诗；
此外还带来退隐的闲散，
因他最欣赏修整的林园；　　　　　　　　50
最要紧是带来那位天使，
他的大名叫作沉思，
都是他张着黄金翅膀，
领导着火轮一样的太阳；
还要带来悄然的寂静，　　　　　　　　　55
除非夜莺赏我们歌声，
它是那样悲哀而温柔，
恰能舒展深夜的眉头，
月姊同时也慢御龙车，
从那熟识的橡树上经过；　　　　　　　　60
甜蜜的鸟儿呵，你最怕嘈嚷，

---

① 缪斯，诗神。——译者

  Most musical, most melancholy!
  Thee, chauntress, oft, the woods among
  I woo, to hear thy even-song;
65 And missing thee, I walk unseen
  On the dry smooth-shaven green,
  To behold the wandering Moon,
  Riding near her highest noon①
  Like one that had been led astray②
70 Through the heaven's wide pathless way,
  And oft, as if her head she bow'd,
  Stooping through a fleecy cloud.
   Oft, on a plat of rising ground③
  I hear the far-off curfeu sound④
75 Over some wide-water'd shore,
  Swinging slow with sullen roar;
  Or, if the air will not permit⑤,
  Some still removéd place will fit⑥,
  Where glowing embers through the room
80 Teach light to counterfeit a gloom⑦;
  Far from all resort of mirth,
  Save the cricket on the hearth,

---

① *her highest noon*: 'the highest point she attains in the sky.'
② *one that had been led astray*: this is only an expansion of 'wandering'(1.67), an epithet applied to the Moon from the apparent irregularity of its movements.
③ *plat* = plot.
④ *curfeu*: this is a 19th century spelling and not apparently used by MIlton, who wrote 'curfew.'
⑤ *the air*: 'the weather.'
⑥ *still removéd place*: 'quiet, secluded spot.'
⑦ *Teach light to counterfeit a gloom*: i.e. the light is so dim that it takes the appearance of darkness; this is, of course, a strong hyperbole.

你的歌声最和谐,最悲伤!
我们的歌手呵,我常到树林去
寻找你,欢喜听你的夜曲。
我找不到你,就只好单独　　　　　　　　65
在干爽平坦的草地上散步;
抬头瞻望着徘徊的淡月,
她正在天空绝顶处驱车,
仿佛在一片茫茫烟海里,
迷失了方向,辨不出东西,　　　　　　70
有时还从白云深处,
探出头来寻找去路。

　我时常站在高坡之上,
倾听远处晚钟的声响,
它回旋荡漾,凄凉悲惋,　　　　　　　75
在那广阔的河水两岸;
如果天时并不相宜,
我便找个幽静的屋里;
炉中的余火还在发光,
把一层阴影给全屋罩上,　　　　　　80
一切欢笑都不到这里来,
只有炉边叫着的蟋蟀,

　　　　　Or the bellman's drowsy charm①
　　　　　To bless the doors from nightly harm.
85　　　　　Or let my lamp at midnight hour
　　　　　Be seen in some high lonely tower,
　　　　　Where I may oft out-watch the Bear②
　　　　　With thrice-great Hermes, or unsphere
　　　　　The spirit of Plato, to unfold
90　　　　　What worlds or what vast regions hold
　　　　　The immortal mind, that hath forsook③
　　　　　Her mansion in this fleshly nook④:
　　　　　And of those demons that are found
　　　　　In fire, air, flood, or under ground,
95　　　　　Whose power hath a true consent⑤
　　　　　With planet, or with element.
　　　　　Sometime let gorgeous Tragedy
　　　　　In scepter'd pall come sweeping by⑥,
　　　　　Presenting Thebes, or Pelops' line,
100　　　　　Or the tale of Troy divine;
　　　　　Or what (though rare) of later age

---

① *the bellman's drowsy charm*: the night watchman who patrolled the streets, crying the hours (for few had clocks), and muttering charms to keep off evil spirits.
② *out-watch the Bear*: 'sit up till the constellation of the Great Bear has vanished'—which, as in Northern latitudes it never sets, means sitting up till sunrise.
③ *forsook*: for 'forsaken.'
④ *mansion*: 'abiding place.'
⑤ *consent*: 'agreement, harmony.'
⑥ *In scepter'd pall*: 'wearing the royal robe and carrying the sceptre.'

再就是令人困倦的更鼓,
在驱逐鬼祟,给家门祝福。
　　让我的灯火,直到夜半,　　　　　　　85
还在孤独的高楼里燃点,
或有时熊星虽已倾落,
我还在钻研赫密斯的巨作①,
或唤醒柏拉图,听他解说②
是什么辽阔的宇宙或境界　　　　　　　90
容纳着那永生不死的精神,
那辞去今生皮囊的灵魂;
并让他讲解地、水、火、风③
都藏有什么样子的精灵,
以及精灵或四行行星　　　　　　　　　95
都是怎样气运相通。
有时我阅读堂皇的悲剧,
于是王袍在眼前飘举,
那里讲塞布斯,或皮劳坡斯④,
或关于神圣特洛亚的故事⑤,　　　　　100
甚或我要偶尔有情趣,

---

① 相传赫密斯是魔术、炼金术、天文学的专家。——译者
② 柏拉图在《对话录》里说,神创造的灵魂和天上星辰一样多,每一个灵魂都是顶着一颗星托生的。——译者
③ 在柏拉图时代,有一种传说,说地、水、火、风这四大因素,都有一个魔照管着。——译者
④ 塞布斯是希腊悲剧的故事所发生的最集中的地点。皮劳坡斯是阿加门农（Agamemnon）、奥莱斯蒂斯（Orestes）等人的先人;这些人常被写为悲剧的主人公。——译者
⑤ 欧里庇得斯、索福克勒斯等,常以特洛亚的战争故事为悲剧主题。——译者

Ennobled hath the buskin'd stage①.

But, O sad Virgin, that thy power
Might raise Musaeus from his bower,
105 Or bid the soul of Orpheus sing
Such notes as, warbled to the string,
Drew iron tears down Pluto's cheek②
And made Hell grant what Love did seek!
Or call up him that left half-told
110 The story of Cambuscan bold,
Of Camball, and of Algarsife,
And who had Canacé to wife③,
That own'd the virtuous ring and glass④;
And of the wondrous horse of brass
115 On which the Tartar king did ride:
And if aught else great bards beside
In sage and solemn tunes have sung⑤
Of turneys, and of trophies hung⑥,
Of forests, and enchantments drear,
120 Where more is meant than meets the ear.

Thus, Night, oft see me in thy pale career,
Till civil-suited Morn appear,

---

① *I.e.* or the tragic plays of more modern times, though few of these are excellent. In *L'Allégro* (l. 133) Milton ignored Shakespeare's tragedies, and here he shows that he found little to admire in the post-Hellenic tragedians generally. For *buskin'd* see note on No. 112, l. 132.

② *iron tears*: 'unyielding,' 'stern'; the epithet is transferred from Pluto's character to his tears.

③ *And who had*: sc. 'And of him who had.' The tale does not go far enough to tell us who became Canace's husband.

④ *virtuous*: 'containing hidden virtues, or magic properties.'

⑤ *tunes*: 'verses.'

⑥ *turneys*: or tourneys, 'tournaments.' *hung*: sc. on trees or posts.

也读读现代舞台的悲剧。
　　但是,忧郁的贞女呵,我愿你
能把缪夏斯从卧房唤起①,
或让奥佛斯,随琴声起伏,　　　　　　　　　105
唱出来令人神往的歌曲,
(他曾使坡劳图涕泗横流,
使地狱答应爱情的请求);
或唤起那个人,他虽未讲完,
却已讲到勇敢的康巴汗,　　　　　　　　　110
康贝尔以及阿尔吉塞夫,
讲到谁娶了加纳西做媳妇
(她有神戒和宝镜各一),
以及谁给的青铜的神驹
(那是鞑靼国王的御骑)②;　　　　　　　　115
你还要把其他大诗人唤起③,
因他们运用圣洁的曲调,
也唱过比武,猎获的枪刀,
和令人可怖的妖怪与山林
(要注意故事的弦外之音)④。　　　　　　　120
夜呵,就让我这样勤谨,
直到素服的黎明来临⑤,

---

① 缪夏斯据说是奥佛斯的儿子,也善于音乐。——译者
② 乔叟的《坎特伯雷故事集》里的"武士侍从的故事",讲的是关于鞑靼国王康巴汗,他两个儿子阿尔吉塞夫、康贝尔和他的女儿加纳西的故事。有一天来了一个生客,给加纳西一只魔术指环,人带上便能懂鸟语;一只宝镜,人一照便能见未来;又给国王一只铜马,人骑上便能飞到任何地方去。但乔叟并没有把这个故事写完。——译者
③ 指意大利诗人塔索(Tasso)、阿里渥斯妥(Ariosto)和英国诗人斯宾塞(Spenser);他们都写过传奇史诗。——译者
④ 故事里暗藏着教训的用意。——译者
⑤ 雅典王的孙子塞夫斯,出去打猎,黎明女神见而爱之。——译者

        Not trick'd and frounced as she was wont①
        With the Attic Boy to hunt,
125   But kercheft in a comely cloud②
        While rocking winds are piping loud,
        Or usher'd with a shower still,
        When the gust hath blown his fill,
        Ending on the rustling leaves
130   With minute drops from off the eaves③.
        And when the sun begins to fling
        His flaring beams, me, goddess, bring
        To archéd walks of twilight groves,
        And shadows brown, that Sylvan loves④,
135   Of pine, or monumental oak,
        Where the rude axe, with heavéd stroke,
        Was never heard the nymphs to daunt
        Or fright them from their hallow'd haunt.
        There in close covert by some brook
140   Where no profaner eye may look,
        Hide me from day's garish eye⑤,
        While the bee with honey'd thigh,
        That at her flowery work doth sing,
        And the waters murmuring,
145   With such consort as they keep⑥
        Entice the dewy-feather'd Sleep;

---

① *trick'd and frounced*: 'decked out and curled.'
② *kercheft*: 'covered with a kerchief, or couvre-chef(= head-cover).'
③ *minute drops*: 'falling at intervals of a minute.' Cf. 'minute gun,' 'minute bell.'
④ *Sylvan* or Silvanus, was the Latin god of the woods and fields.
⑤ *garish*: 'glaring.'
⑥ *consort*: 'company,' 'society.'

她没有梳装打扮,像往常
跟着塞夫斯打猎时那样,
看她头上乌云遮面, 125
狂风正在兴波助澜,
待狂风吹得心满意足,
也许落一阵细雨簌簌;
将停的雨点打着树叶,
像房檐滴水一声声滴落。 130
女神呵,在太阳开始投射
耀眼的光芒时,请你把我
带到阴森的林径中间,
或山神所爱的巨橡参天
古柏蔽日的幽静所在, 135
在那里听不到樵夫砍柴,
因而山林女神不受惊,
不会离弃这圣洁的环境。
请把我藏在浓荫下,小河旁,
不让闲杂人往这里窥望, 140
也不让太阳往这里眨眼睛;
同时,那两腿传粉的蜜蜂,
边忙边唱,在花木之间,
小河流水,水声潺潺,
这些和其他安静的声音, 145
会引来轻盈似羽的睡神。

  And let some strange mysterious dream
  Wave at his wings in airy stream①
  Of lively portraiture display'd,
150 Softly on my eyelids laid;
  And, as I wake, sweet music breathe
  Above, about, or underneath,
  Sent by some Spirit to mortals good②,
  Or the unseen Genius of the wood③.
155   But let my due feet never fail
  To walk the studious cloister's pale④,
  And love the high-embowéd roof⑤,
  With antique pillars massy-proof⑥,
  And storied windows richly dight⑦
160 Casting a dim religious light;
  There let the pealing organ blow
  To the full-voiced quire below⑧
  In service high and anthems clear⑨,
  As may with sweetness, through mine ear⑩,
165 Dissolve me into ecstasies⑪,
  And bring all Heaven before mine eyes.
   And may at last my weary age

---

① *Wave at his wings*: 'Hover at the wings of Sleep.'
② *good* qualifies 'Spirit,' — 'kindly affected to mortals.'
③ *Genius*: 'spirit of the place.'
④ *pale*: 'enclosure.'
⑤ *high-embowéd*: 'with high arches.'
⑥ *massy-proof*: 'able to bear the weight of the mass resting on them.'
⑦ *storied*: 'depicting a story.' *dight*: see above, note to No. 112, l. 62.
⑧ *quire*: see above, note to No. 62, l. 115.
⑨ *service high*: 'full, musical service'; cf. 'High Mass.'
⑩ *As*: sc. 'Such as.'
⑪ *Dissolve me into ecstacies*: 'melt me into transports,' sc. of religious fervour.

让睡神把神秘的梦带来，
让栩栩如生的画面展开，
要连绵像小河流水一样，
轻轻地在我睡眼里映放。 150
待我醒觉时要叫我听到
天地四方送来的仙乐，
因山林无形的好精气，善幽灵，
常这样奏给凡人倾听。

　但我不该吝惜脚步， 155
应到教堂的走廊里散步，
我爱那崇高的圆形顶盖，
也爱那梁柱，坚实而古怪，
还有那画着故事的门窗，
会放进宗教的幽暗辉光。 160
伴奏的风琴要发音响亮，
下面的歌队要齐声合唱，
完整的乐曲，嘹亮的圣歌，
要在我耳里回旋转折，
于是我在极乐中溶解， 165
在我眼前会出现天国。

　我愿我的衰老的余年，

	Find out the peaceful hermitage,
	The hairy gown and mossy cell
170	where I may sit and rightly spell①
	Of every star that heaven doth show,
	And every herb that sips the dew;
	Till old experience do attain
	To something like prophetic strain②.

| 175 | These pleasures, Melancholy, give, |
| | And I with thee will choose to live. |

J. MILTON.

---

① *spell*: 'tell out the import.' 'spell' is intransitive, the 'of' meaning 'about.'

② *prophetic*: a prophet is an inspired teacher, one who claims to be 'the mouthpiece of God'; he does not necessarily make predictions. Milton expresses here the idea that if we had a full understanding of any one part of creation, we should understand the whole meaning of the Universe.

能找到一个安静的寺院，
在那里我身披麻衣，住暗室，
安定地坐着，来仔细辨识 *170*
万千颗星星在天空罗布，
和雨露滋润的每一种草木；
直到我老时，凭着经验，
能有未卜先知的预见。

你要能给我这些欢喜， *175*
忧郁呵，我愿意和你在一起。

殷宝书　译

编注 请参见本卷第62和112首编注。

114. SONG OF THE EMIGRANTS IN BERMUDA

Where the remote Bermudas ride
In the ocean's bosom unespied,
From a small boat that row'd along
The listening winds received this song:
   'What should we do but sing His praise
That led us through the watery maze①
Unto an isle so long unknown,
And yet far kinder than our own?
Where He the huge sea-monsters wracks②,
That lift the deep upon their backs,
He lands us on a grassy stage,
Safe from the storms and prelate's rage:
He gave us this eternal spring
Which here enamels everything,
And sends the fowls to us in care
On daily visits through the air;
He hangs in shades the orange bright
Like golden lamps in a green night,
And does in the pomegranates close
Jewels more rich than Ormus shows③;

---

① *His praise That*: 'the praise of Him who.'
② *wracks*: another form of 'wrecks.'
③ *Jewels*: i.e. its seeds.

114. 百慕大移民之歌①

马韦尔

遥远的百慕大群岛浸泡
在海洋的难以窥见的怀抱。
有一条小船划着正颠簸,
而倾听的海风听到了这首歌:
　"我们该做什么,除了赞美 　　　　　5
上帝把我们带出这一片水,
去登上久无人烟的海岛,
那儿比家乡的大岛更好?
上帝在那儿毁灭了巨海妖,
它们曾用背脊掀起了波涛。 　　　　10
上帝把我们送到草丛里,
避开了暴风雨和主教的怒气②。
上帝给我们这永恒的春天,
这里的一切都渲染得鲜艳;
又送飞禽给我们照看, 　　　　　　15
从空中上帝每天来拜访;
还在树荫里挂上甜橙,
像绿色的夜里金色的小灯。
石榴中藏着的宝石一颗颗,
比霍尔木兹所见的更其多③。 　　　20

---

① 百慕大是大西洋中一群岛,一六二二年由西班牙人发现,一六八四年成为英国殖民地。在英王查理一世与议会战争时期,许多英国人曾逃到该岛避难。本诗描写了一批难民到达百慕大的激动心情。——编注者
② 此行暗示出这批移民是因主张宗教改革而在国内受到迫害的清教徒。——译者
③ 霍尔木兹,波斯湾霍尔木兹海峡北侧一海岛,以富庶闻名。——译者

He makes the figs our mouths to meet,
And throws the melons at our feet;
But apples plants of such a price[1],
No tree could ever bear them twice.
With cedars chosen by His hand
From Lebanon He stores the land;
And makes the hollow seas that roar
Proclaim the ambergris on shore.
He cast (of which we rather boast)
The Gospel's pearl upon our coast;
And in these rocks for us did frame
A temple where to sound His name.
Oh! let our voice His praise exalt
Till it arrive at Heaven's vault,
Which thence (perhaps) rebounding may
Echo beyond the Mexique bay!'
Thus sung they in the English boat
An holy and a cheerful note;
And all the way, to guide their chime,
With falling oars they kept the time.

A. MARVELL.

---

[1] *apples*: 'pine-apples'; each plant bears only one fruit. *plants* is a verb.

上帝要无花果长出给我们尝，
把甜瓜扔在我们的脚旁。
然而是那样的代价种菠萝，
没有一株能长得出两个①。
雪松则是上帝亲手选，　　　　　　　　　　25
到这里是从黎巴嫩那么远；
还使轰隆咆哮的海浪
宣告龙涎香冲到了岸上②。
上帝在我们的海岸上抛出
（我们夸口说）福音的珍珠；　　　　　　　30
而这些岩石为我们构造
一座呼唤他圣名的神庙。
哦！让我们高声赞美他，
声音直响彻上天的苍穹下，
从那里（也许）能够反弹，　　　　　　　　35
墨西哥湾的那一边也回响！"
他们在英国的小船上这样唱
这首歌，神圣而又欢畅，
一路上，为了能协调一致，
往下划的船桨便用来打拍子。　　　　　　40

　　　　　　　　　　　　吴钧陶　译

---

① 菠萝，多年生常绿草本植物。每株只长出一个球状果实。——译者
② 龙涎香，抹香鲸肠胃中的一种分泌物，从鲸体内排出后呈蜡状漂浮于海面或被冲上海岸。具有持久的香气，是十分名贵的香料。——译者

115. AT A SOLEMN MUSIC

Blest pair of Sirens, pledges of Heaven's joy,
    Sphere-born harmonious Sisters, Voice and Verse!
Wed your divine sounds, and mixt power employ
    Dead things with inbreathed sense able to pierce[1];
And to our high-raised phantasy present[2]
That undisturbéd Song of pure concent[3]
Ay sung before the sapphire-colour'd throne
    To Him that sits thereon,
With saintly shout and solemn jubilee[4];
Where the bright Seraphim in burning row
Their loud uplifted angel-trumpets blow;
And the Cherubic host in thousand quires
Touch their immortal harps of golden wires,
With those just Spirits that wear victorious palms,
    Hymns devout and holy psalms
    Singing everlastingly;
That we on earth, with undiscording voice[5]
May rightly answer that melodious noise[6];

---

[1] 'Able to penetrate inanimate things with the feeling which you breathe into them.'
[2] *high-raised phantasy*: 'exalted imagination.'
[3] *concent*: 'harmony.'
[4] *jubilee*: 'shouts of joy.'
[5] *That*: sc. 'So that.'
[6] *noise*: the word originally contained no unpleasant idea. Cf. the Biblical phrase 'to make a joyful noise' for 'to sing psalms.'

115. 闻庄严的音乐有感

弥尔顿

天赋的两位赛壬,天上欢乐的见证①,
　　是和睦的天仙女神,是诗句和歌声!
圣洁的歌喉有着神妙的魅力,
　　顽石为之点头,草木随之生情,
也使我们神魂颠倒。　　　　　　　　　　5
沉醉于那无忧而谐和的悦耳之音。
在闪耀着蔚蓝宝石光辉的王座之前,
　　为高踞其上的天帝不停地讴吟,
唱和的是圣徒们不禁迸发的忘情共鸣。
爽朗的撒拉弗吹响号角掀起了轻雾,　　　10
雾霭中响彻了天使们高昂的号角声;
噱嚧啪带头发起了磅礴的大合唱②,
拨弹起永恒的金色丝弦的大竖琴。
正直的灵魂高擎起胜利的棕榈叶,
　　把圣诗和虔诚的赞歌　　　　　　　15
　　不住口地高声吟咏:
于是,世间凡人也来协调地齐声同唱,
满可以和悠扬动听的天乐相呼应。

---

① 该诗颂赞歌手及其所唱诗篇,故"赛壬"非指用迷人的歌声引诱水手,致人死命的女妖,而指柏拉图所谓坐在八重天上运行着的星座上,引吭高歌"简单旋律的赞美诗"的赛壬。——译者
② 撒拉弗和噱嚧啪分别为第一等天使和第二等天使。参见第 62 首《颂歌》第 112、113 行注。——编注者

>
> As once we did, till disproportion'd sin[①]
> Jarr'd against nature's chime, and with harsh din
> Broke the fair music that all creatures made
> To their great Lord, whose love their motion sway'd
> In perfect diapason[②], whilst they stood
> In first obedience, and their state of good.
>   O may we soon again renew that Song,
>   And keep in tune with Heaven, till God ere long
>   To His celestial consort us unite[③],
> To live with Him and sing in endless morn of light!

J. MILTON.

[①] *disproportion'd*: 'wanting in harmony.'
[②] *diapason*: see above, note on No. 63, l. 18.
[③] *consort*: 'company.'

可惜好景不长,过分的罪过
冲搅了天籁,刺耳的喧哗 　　　　　　　　　　　*20*
破坏了天下生灵
善心热肠,毕恭毕敬,
伴随音乐,山呼舞蹈,
答谢天主的爱而献上的心弦之声。
　啊,但愿不久又能把歌儿更新, 　　　　　　　*25*
　再和天籁齐鸣,
　上帝就会让天人合一,随侍左右,
同在不灭的晨曦之下齐声讴咏。

谭建华　译

116. ALEXANDER'S FEAST, OR, THE POWER OF MUSIC

'Twas at the royal feast for Persia won
    By Philip's warlike son —
    Aloft in awful state
    The godlike hero sate
    On his imperial throne;
His valiant peers were placed around[①],
Their brows with roses and with myrtles bound
    (So should desert in arms be crown'd);
    The lovely Thais by his side
    Sate like a blooming eastern bride
    In flower of youth and beauty's pride; —
    Happy, happy, happy pair!
      None but the brave
      None but the brave
    None but the brave deserves the fair!

    Timotheus placed on high
    Amid the tuneful quire
With flying fingers touch'd the lyre;

---

① *peers*: 'nobles,' not 'equals.'

116. 亚历山大的宴会或音乐的力量

约翰·德莱顿

是菲力普尚武的儿子①
　　在战胜了波斯后的御宴上——
　　神一样的英雄
　　以威严的英姿
　　坐在他的宝座之上；　　　　　　　　　　5
他的英勇的贵族排列两旁,
额发上别着玫瑰,桃金娘②
　　（这是按战功加冕的）；
　　可爱的泰绮丝坐在他身旁③
　　像朵花似的东方新娘　　　　　　　　　　10
　　正青春年华,美的骄傲：——
　　　　多么幸福,幸福,幸福的一双！
　　　　　　只有英雄
　　　　　　只有英雄
　　　　只有英雄才配美丽的娇娘！　　　　　15

蒂莫修斯在悦耳的唱诗班中间④
　　高高坐在上边,
　　以飞快的指头拨动琴弦：

---

① 指马其顿国王菲力普二世(Philip Ⅱ,公元前 382—336)之子亚历山大大帝 (Alexander the Great,公元前 356—323)。亚历山大在征服埃及之后于公元前三三一年在阿贝拉再次大败波斯国王大流士三世,继而征服全波斯。——编注者
② 桃金娘是爱神维纳斯之圣花,象征爱情。——编注者
③ 泰绮丝是古代雅典的名妓,曾伴随亚历山大出征。——编注者
④ 蒂莫修斯是亚历山大时代的著名演奏家。——编注者

        The trembling notes ascend the sky
20   And heavenly joys inspire.
        The song began from Jove
    Who left his blissful seats above —
    Such is the power of mighty love!
    A dragon's fiery form belied the god[①];
25   Sublime on radiant spires he rode[②]
    When he to fair Olympia prest,
    And while he sought her snowy breast,
        Then round her slender waist he curl'd,
    And stamp'd an image of himself, a sovereign of the world.
30   — The listening crowd admire the lofty sound;
        A present deity! they shout around:
    A present deity! the vaulted roofs rebound[③]:
            With ravish'd ears
            The monarch hears,
35   Assumes the god,
            Affects to nod
    And seems to shake the spheres.

    The praise of Bacchus then the sweet musician sung,
        Of Bacchus ever fair and ever young:
40   The jolly god in triumph comes!
        Sound the trumpets, beat the drums!
            Flush'd with a purple grace
            He shows his honest face:

---

① *belied*: 'disguised.'
② *spires*: 'spiral coils.'
③ *rebound*: 're-echo.'

颤动的旋律升上青天
  激起了天庭的喜悦。 20
    这支歌首先歌唱朱庇特①
在天上都离开他幸福的宝座,——
瞧,爱情有多么强大的力量!
朱庇特装扮成一条火龙,
昂头扭身,光芒四射, 25
走近美貌的奥林匹亚女神②,
寻求她雪白的酥胸,
  再缠绕她修长的腰身,
印上他自己的形象——世界的至尊。
  ——倾听的人群仰慕这崇高的声音; 30
  他们高呼,当今的神明!
    穹隆回响:当今的神明!
    君王不禁狂喜地来
    倾听,
    装出一副神祇的威仪, 35
    装模作样地颔首,
  有如震动苍穹。

然后乐师甜蜜地歌唱,对酒神赞颂,
歌颂酒神永远美好,永远年轻;
  这欢乐的神明欢喜若狂了! 40
  吹起喇叭,敲起鼓!
    紫红的酒韵上了他的面庞,
    他现出了他真诚的面孔。

---

① 朱庇特,罗马神话之主神。亚历山大曾自称是朱庇特之神子,并编造了朱庇特变作巨蟒与他母亲奥林匹亚丝相会的故事。下文的火龙即巨蟒。——编注者
② 指亚力山大的生母奥林匹亚丝(Olympias)。——编注者

    Now give the hautboys breath; he comes, he comes[①]!
45   Bacchus, ever fair and young,
      Drinking joys did first ordain;
      Bacchus' blessings are a treasure,
      Drinking is the soldier's pleasure;
        Rich the treasure,
50   Sweet the pleasure,
      Sweet is pleasure after pain.

    Soothed with the sound, the king grew vain;
    Fought all his battles o'er again,
   And thrice he routed all his foes, and thrice he slew the slain.
55   The master saw the madness rise,
      His glowing cheeks, his ardent eyes;
      And while he Heaven and Earth defied
      Changed his hand and check'd his pride[②].
      He chose a mournful Muse
60   Soft pity to infuse;
      He sung Darius great and good,
        By too severe a fate
      Fallen, fallen, fallen, fallen[③],
        Fallen from his high estate,
65   And weltering in his blood;
      Deserted, at his utmost need,
      By those his former bounty fed;

---

① *hautboys*, now commonly spelt 'oboes,' are wood-wind instruments about two feet long and having a compass of about two and a half octaves.
② The pronouns are rather confused; 'he' and the second 'his' refer to Alexander, the first 'his' to Timotheus.
③ *Fallen*: the repetition of this word is intended to mark the greatness of the fall.

让双簧管吹奏吧,他到了,他到了!
　　酒神,永远美好,永远年轻。　　　　　　　　　45
　　他首次指令饮酒作乐;
　　酒神的赐与是一件至宝,
　　饮酒是军人的欢乐:
　　　　酣畅淋漓
　　　　欢乐甜蜜,　　　　　　　　　　　　　　50
　　苦后的欢乐有不尽的甘美。

　　国王受这种声音抚慰,变得虚狂,
　　回想起他打胜的所有战争,
他三次击溃敌人,三次杀死敌兵①。
　　乐师看到他头脑发狂,　　　　　　　　　　　55
　　他发光的双颊,他炽热的眼;
　　向天地挑战,
　　就换了手法,遏止了他的傲气。
　　　改选了一个悲哀的缪斯,
　　　倾注了温柔的怜悯情思;　　　　　　　　60
　　他歌唱伟大而善良的大流士,
　　　命运太严酷,
　　而殒落了,殒落了,殒落了,殒落了,
　　　从他高高地位殒落了,
　　　他浸染在他的血泊里;　　　　　　　　　　65
　　在最需要帮助的时际,
　　却被他以前恩宠的人捐弃;

---

① 指亚历山大于公元前三三三年一败大流士三世,公元前三三二年征服埃及和公元前三三一年再败大流士三世。——编注者

>
> On the bare earth exposed he lies
> With not a friend to close his eyes.
> 70   — With downcast looks the Joyless victor sate,
> Revolving in his alter'd soul
>   The various turns of Chance below;
> And now and then a sigh he stole①,
>   And tears began to flow.
>
> 75   The mighty master smiled to see
> That love was in the next degree②;
> 'Twas but a kindred-sound to move,
> For pity melts the mind to love.
> Softly sweet, in Lydian measures
> 80   Soon he soothed his soul to pleasures.
> War, he sung, is toil and trouble,
> Honour but an empty bubble;
> Never ending, still beginning③,
>   Fighting still, and still destroying;
> 85   If the world be worth thy winning,
>   Think, O think; it worth enjoying;
> Lovely Thais sits beside thee
> Take the good the gods provide thee!
>   — The many rend the skies with loud applause④;
> 90   So Love was crown'd, but Music won the cause.
> The prince, unable to conceal his pain,
>   Gazed on the fair

---

① *a sigh he* stole: *i.e.* he softly sighed.
② *in the next degree*: 'the next stage.' It needed but a little change in the music to carry the king from pity to love.
③ *still*: 'continually.' Its general meaning at that time.
④ *many*: 'meiny.'

他暴尸于光秃的地面,
都没有一个朋友给他合上眼。
　　——胜利者落落寡欢地坐着, 70
在他情绪变了的灵魂中考虑到
　　人世的遭遇难以逆料;
他时而偷偷发出一声叹息,
　　泪开始流了。

　　伟大的大师微笑地看见 75
紧接下面的是爱情;
只要再拨动相邻的琴弦,
怜惜又把心儿化成怜爱
轻柔的甘美,以吕底亚的音乐旋律①
抚慰他的灵魂,使他很快就变得欢愉。 80
他歌唱,战争是辛劳,战争是烦恼,
荣誉只是空幻的泡沫;
永不熄止,还总在开始,
　　继续战斗,继续破坏;
如果世界值得你去征服, 85
　　你想啊,想,更值得享乐:
可爱的泰绮丝就坐在你身旁,
有上帝赐给你财富供你享用!
　　——随从们高声欢呼震破长空:
爱神就这样加冕了,可是音乐占了上风。 90
这位王公,难以掩饰他的苦痛
　　　注视着美人

---

① 吕底亚,古代小亚细亚一个奴隶制国家。吕底亚音乐以其柔婉而著称。——编注者

               Who caused his care,
               And sigh'd and look'd, sigh'd and look'd,
95   Sigh'd and look'd, and sigh'd again:
               At length with love and wine at once opprest①
               The vanquish'd victor sunk upon her breast.

               Now strike the golden lyre again:
               A louder yet, and yet a louder strain!
100   Break his bands of sleep asunder
               And rouse him like a rattling peal of thunder.
               Hark, hark! the horrid sound
                  Has raised up his head:
                  As awaked from the dead
105   And amazed he stares around.
               Revenge, revenge, Timotheus cries,
               See the Furies arise!
                  See the snakes that they rear②
                  How they hiss in their hair,
110   And the sparkles that flash from their eyes!
                     Behold a ghastly band,
                     Each a torch in his hand!
               Those are Grecian ghosts, that in battle were slain
                     And unburied remain
115   Inglorious on the plain:
                     Give the vengeance due
                     To the valiant crew!
               Behold how they toss their torches on high,
               How they point to the Persian abodes

---

① *at once*: 'at the same time.'
② *they rear*: 'lift erect.'

是她引起了他的幽怨,
他又叹息又看,边看边叹,
　叹息了又看,还再叹息:　　　　　　　　　　95
结果为爱又为酒所压抑,
被征服的胜利者把头垂在她的胸前。

　　那就再奏起金色的竖琴;
再高些,还要高些的旋律!
把他睡眠的束缚撕破　　　　　　　　　　　100
震醒他像一阵霹雳
听呵,听! 那可怕的声音
　已经震得他抬起了头:
　他仿佛从死里醒来
惊奇地注视着四周。　　　　　　　　　　　105
蒂莫修斯喊:报仇! 报仇!
看复仇女神起来了!
　瞧她们竖起的头上的蛇
　蛇在她们发丝中嘶鸣,
蛇眼里闪出火星①!　　　　　　　　　　　110
　　瞧这灰秃秃的一帮,
　　每人手中一只火把!
那是希腊鬼魂死在战场
　　还没得到埋葬
　　在原野上就丧失荣光:　　　　　　　　115
　　英勇的战士啊
　　应该去报仇!
瞧他们怎样把火把猛然高高举起,
他们怎样指向波斯海岸

---

① 传说中的三个复仇女神以蛇为发,眼中滴血。——编注者

120 And glittering temples of their hostile gods①.

  — The princes applaud with a furious joy;

  And the King seized a flambeau with zeal to destroy;

   Thais led the way

   To light him to his prey,

125 And like another Helen, fired another Troy!

   — Thus, long ago,

  Ere heaving bellows learn'd to blow②,

   While organs yet were mute,

   Timotheus, to his breathing flute

130   And sounding lyre,

  Could swell the soul to rage, or kindle soft desire.

   At last divine Cecilia came,

   Inventress of the vocal frame;

  The sweet enthusiast from her sacred store

135   Enlarged the former narrow bounds,

   And added length to solemn sounds

  With Nature's mother-wit, and arts unknown before.

  — Let old Timotheus yield the prize

   Or both divide the crown;

140 He raised a mortal to the skies;

   She drew an angel down!

             J. DRYDEN.

---

① *of their hostile gods*: *i.e.* of the gods of the Persians, who were hostile to the Greeks.

② *learn'd to blow*: *i.e.* for musical purposes. Bellows had been used for ages to kindle fires.

指向与他们为敌的神祇闪光的庙宇。 *120*
——王公们带着愤怒的狂热欢呼：
国王怀着毁灭的激情抓起一支火炬；
  泰绮丝领着路
   照着他去捕获牺牲品，
活像另一个海伦，烧毁另一座特洛伊①！ *125*

  就这些，久久以前，
在风箱还未用于吹奏乐章，
  在风琴还没发出声响，
   蒂莫修斯拿起他呜咽的笛
   和响亮的竖琴， *130*
能吹奏得灵魂发怒，或者点燃起温柔的爱欲。
  最后神圣的塞西莉亚来了②，
   是她创造了音乐乐器；
这位甜美的信徒从她神圣的宝藏
  以自然天赋的才智和前所未有的艺术 *135*
   把以往狭窄的音域扩张，
还赋予庄严的声响以长度，
  ——使老蒂莫修斯放弃了奖赏，
   或者两人平分桂冠；
他把一个凡人举到天上； *140*
  她把一个天使引到地上！

张君川　译

编注 此诗与本卷第63首是德莱顿为庆祝圣塞西莉亚日而写的两首著名颂歌（参见本卷第63首正文及编注）。

---

① 其实海伦并未烧毁特洛伊，但由于她与帕里斯私奔到该城，导致了该城的毁灭。——编注者
② 参见本卷第63首。——编注者

卷三

1700—1800

117. ODE ON THE PLEASURE ARISING FROM VICISSITUDE

  Now the golden Morn aloft
    Waves her dew-bespangled wing,
  With vermeil cheek and whisper soft[1]
    She woos the tardy Spring:
5   Till April starts, and calls around
  The sleeping fragrance from the ground,
  And lightly o'er the living scene
  Scatters his freshest, tenderest green.

  New-born flocks, in rustic dance,
10   Frisking ply their feeble feet;
  Forgetful of their wintry trance[2]
    The birds his presence greet[3]:
  But chief, the sky-lark warbles high
  His trembling thrilling ecstasy;
15   And lessening from the dazzled sight,
  Melts into air and liquid light.

  Yesterday the sullen year
    Saw the snowy whirlwind fly;
  Mute was the music of the air,

---

[1] *vermeil*: see note on No. 53, l. 33.
[2] *their wintry trance*: before the habits of birds had been sufficiently studied for their migrations to be known, it was generally supposed that they slept through the winter.
[3] *his*: i.e. April's.

117. 沧桑世事中的欢乐颂

格雷

金色的晨姑,在上空翱翔,
　闪着她露珠般璀灿的翅膀,
双颊泛红,轻声细语,
　她爱上这姗姗来迟的春郎:
"四月"使者一启程就唤醒了　　　　　　　　　　5
沉睡在大地上的芬芳,
并徐徐走过生机盎然的景物,
把最鲜最嫩的绿色撒上。

新生羊羔跳着朴实的舞蹈,
　欢乐地动弹着稚嫩的脚掌;　　　　　　　　10
鸟儿竟忘却了冬日的睡眠①
　而去欢迎春天四月的出场:
天空的骄子——云雀——高声颂唱
一阵颤栗激动的喜狂;
然后又逐渐消失在绚丽的景物里,　　　　　　15
融入大气与清彻的流光。

昨天,那个沉郁的岁月,
　满目都是冰雪的旋风飞扬;
沉寂,就是空中的音乐,

---

① 鸟类冬天迁徙的习惯,还未被人们充分了解时,一般人认为它们在冬眠。——译者

20　　　　　　　　The herd stood drooping by;
　　　　　　　　　Their raptures now that wildly flow
　　　　　　　　　No yesterday nor morrow know;
　　　　　　　　　'Tis Man alone that joy descries
　　　　　　　　　With forward and reverted eyes.

25　　　　　　　　Smiles on past Misfortune's brow
　　　　　　　　　　　Soft Reflection's hand can trace,
　　　　　　　　　And o'er the cheek of Sorrow throw
　　　　　　　　　　　A melancholy grace;
　　　　　　　　　While Hope prolongs our happier hour,
30　　　　　　　　Or deepest shades, that dimly lour①
　　　　　　　　　And blacken round our weary way,
　　　　　　　　　Gilds with a gleam of distant day.

　　　　　　　　　Still, where rosy Pleasure leads②,
　　　　　　　　　　　See a kindred Grief pursue;
35　　　　　　　　Behind the steps that Misery treads
　　　　　　　　　　　Approaching Comfort view;
　　　　　　　　　The hues of bliss more brightly glow
　　　　　　　　　Chastised by sabler tints of woe,
　　　　　　　　　And blended form, with artful strife③,
40　　　　　　　　The strength and harmony of life.

　　　　　　　　　See the wretch that long has tost
　　　　　　　　　　　On the thorny bed of pain,
　　　　　　　　　At length repair his vigour lost

---

① *deepest shades*: the object of 'Gilds' (l. 32).
② *Still*: 'constantly.'
③ *blended*: 'being blended together.'

牛羊伫立,垂头彷徨: 20
它们现在又欢呼雀跃
忘了昨日寒冷和来日冰霜:
唯独人类见欢乐之时
才用展望和回顾的目光。

温和的回忆之手,能够悄悄 25
　　在过去的愁蹙眉间追溯微笑①,
并且透过悲哀的两颊,
　　投射一股忧郁的恩宠光耀。
"希望"延长了我们幸福的时辰,
当最深的阴影,朦胧笼罩, 30
并变黑了疲乏的旅程时,
遥远的黎明就为它涂上金光一道。

常在玫瑰色的欢乐之中,
　　会看见一种忧愁追踪;
但在悲伤的脚印后面, 35
　　又邻接一片舒适开阔的天空:
幸福的色调多么绚丽光彩,
可也会被哀伤的阴霾消融,
通过混合与巧妙的拼搏,
力量与生命的和谐又能相通。 40

看那不幸的人,
　　长久被抛进荆棘丛,
最后却追回他失去的活力,

---

① 即沉思回忆使我们不禁对过去的苦难有了微笑。——编注者

>   And breathe and walk again;
> 45 The meanest floweret of the vale,
>   The simplest note that swells the gale,
>   The common sun, the air, the skies,
>   To him are opening Paradise.

T. GRAY.

他再度奋起,重向前冲:
那山谷里最卑微的花朵,
那搅动微风的最简单的丝桐①,
那普通的大气、天空和日光,
对他,都是敞开的天宫。

45

黄绍鑫　译

编注　托马斯·格雷(Thomas Gray,1716—1771),英国十八世纪后半期诗人。他一生只写过十余首诗,但都广为流传,其中最负盛名的是《墓畔哀歌》(见本卷第 147 首)。他的诗优雅但少雕琢,流畅而不松散,明晰却有余味,虽缺乏浪漫主义的奔放热情,但也没有缥缈、暧昧等缺点。诗人不务声名,一生大部分时间在剑桥大学从事教读研究,曾拒绝封给他的桂冠诗人称号。

---

① 丝桐:指音乐。——译者

118. THE QUIET LIFE

Happy the man, whose wish and care
    A few paternal acres bound,
Content to breathe his native air
        In his own ground.

Whose herds with milk, whose fields with bread
    Whose flocks supply him with attire;
Whose trees in summer yield him shade,
        In winter fire.

Blest, who can unconcern'dly find
    Hours, days, and years slide soft away
In health of body, peace of mind,
        Quiet by day,

Sound sleep by night; study and ease
    Together mix'd; sweet recreation,
And innocence, which most does please
        With meditation.

Thus let me live, unseen, unknown;
    Thus unlamented let me die;
Steal from the world, and not a stone
        Tell where I lie.

A. POPE.

118. 平静的一生

蒲柏

他真快乐,把关注和希望
　　放在几亩祖传的田里,
满足于在他自己的土地上
　　　　　　吸故乡的空气。

牛给他奶,羊给他衣裳,　　　　　　　　　　5
　　田地给他提供面包;
林木在夏天给他遮太阳,
　　　　　　到冬天给燃料。

真幸福,他漫不经意地让
　　一刻刻,一天天,一年年溜走,　　　　10
心灵平和,身体也健康,
　　　　　　白天没忧愁,

夜晚是酣眠;读书和休息
　　相互交替;愉快的消遣,
以及天真,那天真带沉思　　　　　　　　15
　　　　　　最使人喜欢。

让我这样默默地生活,
　　死的时候也没人哀伤;
悄悄地离去,没墓碑道破
　　　　　　我长眠的地方。　　　　　　20

屠岸　译

编注 亚力山大·蒲柏(Alexander Pope，1688—1744)，英国诗人，文名盛于十八世纪。他的诗精心雕琢，技巧圆熟，在英国诗歌史上有一定地位。主要作品有《批评论》、《奇发记》、《人论》等等。这首短诗原题是《孤独颂》，据他自称，写于十二岁时。

119. THE BLIND BOY

O say what is that thing call'd Light,
    Which I must ne'er enjoy;
What are the blessings of the sight,
    O tell your poor blind boy!

You talk of wondrous things you see,
    You say the sun shines bright;
I feel him warm, but how can he
    Or make it day or night?

My day or night myself I make
    Whene'er I sleep or play;
And could I ever keep awake
    With me 'twere always day.

With heavy sighs I often hear[1]
    You mourn my hapless woe;
But sure with patience I can bear
    A loss I ne'er can know.

Then let not what I cannot have
    My cheer of mind destroy;
Whilst thus I sing, I am a king,
    Although a poor blind boy.

C. CIBBER.

---

[1] *With heavy sighs*: qualifies 'mourn,' not 'hear.'

119. 盲孩

西伯

你们说的"光",是什么东西?
　　我永远不可能感觉出来;
你们能够"看",是什么运气?
　　请告诉我这个可怜的盲孩!

你们讲到了种种奇景,
　　你们说太阳光辉灿烂;
我感到它温暖,可它怎么能
　　把世界分出黑夜和白天?

这会儿我玩耍,待会儿我睡觉,
　　这样分我的白天和夜晚;
假如我老是醒着,睡不着,
　　我觉得那就是白天没完。

我听见你们一次又一次
　　为我的不幸而叹息"唉……"
可我完全能忍受这损失——
　　损失是什么我并不明白。

别让我永远得不到的东西
　　把我愉快的心情破坏;
我歌唱,我就是快乐的君王,
　　尽管我是个可怜的盲孩。

屠岸　译

编注　科利·西伯(Colley Cibber,1671—1757),英国演员、剧作家及诗人,一七三〇年被授封为桂冠诗人。

120. ON A FAVOURITE CAT, DROWNED IN A TUB OF GOLDFISHES

'Twas on a lofty vase's side,
Where China's gayest art had dyed
    The azure flowers that blow,
Demurest of the tabby kind,
The pensive Selima, reclined,
    Gazed on the lake below.

Her conscious tail her joy declared;
The fair round face, the snowy beard,
    The velvet of her paws,
Her coat that with the tortoise vies,
Her ears of jet, and emerald eyes[1],
    She saw; and purr'd applause.

Still had she gazed, but 'midst the tide
Two angel forms were seen to glide,
    The Genii of the stream[2]:
Their scaly armour's Tyrian hue
Through richest purple to the view
    Betray'd a golden gleam.

The hapless Nymph with wonder saw;

---

[1] These nouns are the objects of 'saw' (l. 12); *i.e.* she saw them reflected in the water.

[2] *Genii*: 'presiding spirits.'

120. 可爱的小猫淹死在金鱼盆

格雷

在一个巍立着的花瓶之边,
最惬意的中国艺术曾经绘染,
　　碧兰的花朵正在开放,
来了一只沉思的小猫——类似虎斑①
她端庄地横卧着　　　　　　　　　　　　　5
　　凝视下边的湖面。

她自觉的尾巴表明她的愉快:
她看见自己漂亮的圆脸,雪白的胡须,
　　还有那天鹅绒似的脚掌,
可与龟甲媲美的外衣,　　　　　　　　　　10
她黑玉样的双耳,翡翠般的眼珠,
　　她瞧见这一切便喝彩:咪!咪!咪!

她静静注视,注视,在涟漪处,
有两个天使影像,游来游去,
　　这是河川的精灵:　　　　　　　　　　15
它们披着鳞状的泰雅甲胄②,
透过浓重的红紫色调,
　　显露出的金色,光怪陆离。

那个倒霉的"女神"惊奇地探看:

---

① 虎斑是一种普通的杂色猫。——译者
② 泰雅,古代腓尼基国一城池,以染料和染织品而著称。——编注者

                    A whisker first, and then a claw
                        With many an ardent wish
                    She stretch'd, in vain, to reach the prize —
                    What female Heart can gold despise?
                        What Cat's averse to Fish?

                    Presumptuous maid! with looks intent
                    Again she stretch'd, again she bent,
                        Nor knew the gulf between —
                    Malignant Fate sat by and smiled —
                    The slippery verge her feet beguiled;
                        She tumbled headlong in!

                    Eight times emerging from the flood
                    She mew'd to every watery God
                        Some speedy aid to send. —
                    No Dolphin came, no Nereid stirr'd,
                    Nor cruel Tom nor Susan heard —
                        A favourite has no friend!

                    From hence, ye Beauties, undeceived,
                    Know one false step is ne'er retrieved,
                        And be with caution bold.
                    Not all that tempts your wandering eyes
                    And heedless hearts, is lawful prize,
                        Nor all that glisters, gold[1]!

                                                T. GRAY

---

① *glisters*: 'glitters.'

她首先伸出胡须,然后才用爪子, 20
　一种多么迫切的渴望啊!
她伸展肢身,但无法夺取那个奖励——
什么样的女人心灵才蔑视金子?
　什么样的小猫不喜爱鱼?

好个大胆妄为的姑娘!多么急躁, 25
她一再伸爪,一再弯腰,
　全不顾那里边的深渊——
命运恶神坐在一旁微笑——
她双脚误从边缘一滑;
　可怜就一头栽进水里了 30

她八次从洪流奋起①,
咪咪嘶叫,向水神求饶,
　多么盼望有人救援:——
海豚并不会来,涅瑞伊得也不会到②,
汤姆和苏珊都没一人听见: 35
　一个可爱的小宝贝竟没个朋友相照!

因此,你们这些未受欺骗的美貌姑娘,
一失足就千古难返,
　一定要有慎重的勇敢:
那些取悦于目,诱惑你心灵的物件, 40
并不都是有合法的奖赏,
　一切发光东西,并非全是金子的灿烂!

黄绍鑫　译

---

① 有句谚语说:"猫有九次生命",这可能是说:九次落险,都能得救,这里用"八次"与此意相同。——译者
② 古希腊歌手阿利昂被抛入海中,海豚迷恋他的音乐而救他上岸(参见卷二第66首脚注);涅瑞伊得是希腊神话中的海之女神。——编注者

编注 格雷的好友霍拉斯·威帕尔(Horace Walpole)养有两只爱猫,莎娜和塞莉玛。一七四七年,塞莉玛不幸溺死于金鱼盆中,格雷致函威帕尔表示惋惜,信中附有此诗。此诗后来于一七四八年匿名发表。

121. TO CHARLOTTE PULTENEY

Timely blossom, Infant fair①,
Fondling of a happy pair②,
Every morn and every night
Their solicitous delight③,
Sleeping, waking, still at ease,
Pleasing, without skill to please④;
Little gossip, blithe and hale,
Tattling many a broken tale,
Singing many a tuneless song,
Lavish of a heedless tongue;
Simple maiden, void of art,
Babbling out the very heart,
Yet abandon'd to thy will⑤,
Yet imagining no ill,
Yet too innocent to blush;
Like the linnet in the bush
To the mother-linnet's note
Moduling her slender throat⑥;
Chirping forth thy petty joys,

---

① *Timely*: 'born just when the parents wished for it.'
② *Fondling*: 'one fondly loved,' 'a pet.'
③ *solicitous delight*: *i.e.* the source both of their anxiety and of their pleasure.
④ *without skill*: her charm was not the outcome of art, but entirely natural.
⑤ *Yet*: 'as yet.'
⑥ *Moduling*: 'modelling,' *i.e.* adapting.

121. 致夏绿蒂·普尔吞勒

菲利普斯

适时的花朵,漂亮的女孩,
爸爸妈妈的小乖乖,
每天早晨,每个夜晚,
是他们的安慰和愉快,
无论安睡、觉醒,样样自在,   5
但并不故意讨人喜爱:
说些不成句的话语,
编造些断断续续的故事,
唱一些走了调的歌曲,
喋喋不休,没完没止;   10
天真少女,毫不骄矜,
总想把心里歌声吐倾,
你陶然自得,
你无邪天真;
你纯雅大方,   15
像红雀栖在树林,
听见母亲的歌唱,
就模仿着那纤细的声音;
喳喳吱吱唱出欣喜,

20　　　　　　　　Wanton in the change of toys[①],
　　　　　　　　　Like the linnet green, in May
　　　　　　　　　Flitting to each bloomy spray;
　　　　　　　　　Wearied then and glad of rest,
　　　　　　　　　Like the linnet in the nest: —
25　　　　　　　　This thy present happy lot,
　　　　　　　　　This, in time will be forgot:
　　　　　　　　　Other pleasures, other cares,
　　　　　　　　　Ever-busy Time prepares;
　　　　　　　　　And thou shalt in thy daughter see,
30　　　　　　　　This picture, once, resembled thee.

A. PHILIPS.

[①] *Wanton*: 'capricious.'

>   调皮地变换着玩具, *20*
>   又好似五月的翡翠,
>   轻快地飞翔在香花丛里,
>   疲倦时就快乐地歇息,
>   恰似巢中的小鸟儿;——
>   这就是你今天的好运气, *25*
>   这一幕幕终究会被忘记:
>   别的欢乐与别的焦虑,
>   匆忙的时间之神又为你准备;
> 你将来在你女儿身上,
> 会看见她多么像你自己。 *30*

黄绍鑫　译

编注　安布罗斯·菲利普斯(Ambrose Philips, 1675？—1749), 英国诗人, 其代表作是《田园诗集》(*Pastorals*)。

123. THE BARD

A *Pindaric Ode*

'Ruin seize thee, ruthless King!
 Confusion on thy banners wait!
Tho' fann'd by Conquest's crimson wing
 They mock the air with idle state.
Helm, nor hauberk's twisted mail,
Nor e'en thy virtues, tyrant, shall avail
To save thy secret soul from nightly fears,
From Cambria's curse, from Cambria's tears[1]!'
— Such were the sounds that o'er the crested pride[2]
 Of the first Edward scatter'd wild dismay,
As down the steep of Snowdon's shaggy side
 He wound with toilsome march his long array: —
Stout Glo'ster stood aghast in speechless trance;
'To arms!' cried Mortimer, and couch'd his quivering lance.

 On a rock, whose haughty brow
Frowns o'er old Conway's foaming flood,
 Robed in the sable garb of woe,
With haggard eyes the Poet stood;

---

[1] *Cambria's*: a Latinized form of Cymru, the Welsh name for Wales.
[2] *crested pride*: the crest is properly the badge worn on the top of the helmet.

123. 行吟诗人

(品达体)①

格雷

'毁灭吧,残暴的王②!
　　快纷乱了,你的战旗!
尽管为你征服者的血翅所鼓荡,
　　它们仍在舞弄微风,悠然得意。
暴君,不论是你的铠甲层层,　　　　　　　　　　　　5
抑或你的所谓德行,
都挡不住威尔士人的恨,威尔士人的憎
他们在黑夜把恐惧注入你的心灵!'
——当爱德华一世率领疲惫之师,
　　长长地从斯诺登的峭壁纡徐而下时③,　　　　10
这些声音不啻投下惊惶的暗影,
　　笼罩在他矜夸战伐的头盔之顶:——
魁梧的格洛斯达惊呆地站着,失神不语④;
'拿起武器!'莫蒂默喊着把抖颤的长矛高举。

　　一块巨岩,眉宇峥嵘,　　　　　　　　　　　　15
俯视着古老的康韦河波涛汹涌⑤。
　　诗人站在岩石上,
穿着丧服,憔悴颜容;

---

① "品达体"是以古希腊诗人品达(Pindar,公元前518?—438?)命名的一种颂歌体。英国许多诗人把不规则的诗体称为品达诗。——编注者
② "残暴的王"指爱德华一世。——译者
③ 斯诺登山在威尔士境内。——译者
④ 格洛斯达(Gloucester)和下一行中的莫蒂默(Mortimer)均为随爱德华一世远征的王公贵族。——译者
⑤ 康韦河为威尔士卡那旺郡的边界。——译者

	(Loose his beard and hoary hair
20	Stream'd like a meteor to the troubled air;)

And with a master's hand and prophet's fire
Struck the deep sorrows of his lyre:
    'Hark, how each giant oak and desert cave
        Sighs to the torrent's awful voice beneath!
25   O'er thee, O King! their hundred arms they wave
        Revenge on thee in hoarser murmurs breathe[①];
Vocal no more, since Cambria's fatal day[②],
To high-born Hoel's harp, or soft Llewellyn's lay[③].

'Cold is Cadwallo's tongue,
30   That hush'd the stormy main;
Brave Urien sleeps upon his craggy bed:
    Mountains, ye mourn in vain
    Modred, whose magic song
Made huge Plinlimmon bow his cloud-topt head.
35   On dreary Arvon's shore they lie
Smear'd with gore and ghastly pale:
Far, far aloof the affrighted ravens sail;
    The famish'd eagle screams, and passes by.
Dear lost companions of my tuneful art,
40   Dear as the light that visits these sad eyes,
Dear as the ruddy drops that warm my heart,

---

① *hoarser*: 'ever growing hoarser'; it can hardly mean 'hoarser than those of the torrent.'
② *Vocal no more*: i.e. since the defeat of the Welsh the woods and caves had not re-echoed the songs of the people.
③ *soft*, or gentle, says Palgrave, is the epithet commonly used of Llewelyn in contemporary poetry. Welsh historians depict him as a mild ruler, a patron of letters, and — despite his warlike life — a lover of peace.

(长髯和银发蓬松,
像流星的曳光穿过天空;) 20
大师的手啊,预言者的火,
他挥动七弦琴,响起深沉的哀歌:
"听,巨大的橡树和空穴都在哀鸣,
　　与下面急湍的怒吼相呼应!
在你头上,暴君,千万巨臂在挥舞, 25
　　嘶哑的低语宣泄着复仇的怨怒。
自从威尔士灭亡,诗国一片寂寥,
没有高贵的霍尔的竖琴,卢埃林的柔和曲调①。

"能叫怒涛平息的卡德瓦罗
　　不再引吭高歌; 30
勇敢的尤里安长眠在岩石之间②;
　　莫迪里特,曾以神奇的歌感动高山③,
　　令普林利蒙大山为之俯下云巅;
群山啊,现在你们哀伤他们也徒然。
　　他们都躺在阿冯河荒凉之岸, 35
染着污血,一副苍白的颜面。
高高地惊恐的乌鸦在盘旋,
　　尖叫着的秃鹰也来回打转。
多可贵啊,我的逝去的歌朋诗侣,
　　可贵如照拂愁容的阳光煦煦; 40
可贵如醇醪温暖我的心房;

---

① 霍尔(Hoel),威尔士古代诗人和武士。卢埃林(Llewellyn)是威尔士最后一位独立君主。——译者
② 卡德瓦罗(Cadwallo)和尤里安(Urien)均为古代不列颠王。——译者
③ 莫迪里特(Modred),古代威尔士诗人。——译者

  Ye died amidst your dying country's cries —
No more I weep. They do not sleep;
  On yonder cliffs, a griesly band①,
45   I see them sit; they linger yet,
    Avengers of their native land:
With me in dreadful harmony they join②,
And weave with bloody hands the tissue of thy line.'

  "Weave the warp and weave the woof③,
50   The winding-sheet of Edward's race:
Give ample room and verge enough④
  The characters of hell to trace.
Mark the year and mark the night
When Severn shall re-echo with affright
55 The shrieks of death thro' Berkley's roofs that ring,
Shrieks of an agonizing king!
  She-wolf of France, with unrelenting fangs
That tear'st the bowels of thy mangled mate
  From thee be born, who o'er thy country hangs
60 The scourge of Heaven! What terrors round him wait!
Amazement in his van, with Flight combined,
And Sorrow's faded form, and Solitude behind.
"Mighty victor, mighty lord,
  Low on his funeral couch he lies!
65 No pitying heart, no eye, afford

---

① *griesly*: or grisly, 'grim,' 'horrible.'
② *join*: in the 17th and 18th centuries this word was pronounced as 'jine' — riming with 'line.'
③ *the warp*: the threads running lengthwise in a loom; *the woof* is that which is woven on to the warp.
④ *verge*: 'edging,' where the pattern would come.

但你们都在国破时的哀号中死亡——
我不再啜泣,他们也并非沉睡;
　　在那边岸上,晦冥中我看见一群相知,
他们俯仰徘徊,盘桓不退,　　　　　　　　　　45
　　这群要为故国雪耻的壮士:
他们与我心会神交,以杀伐之手,
共同把复仇的命运之网织就。"

"织经织纬,织横织竖,
　　织成爱德华王族的裹尸布:　　　　　　　　50
幅要够宽,长应合度,
　　裹上所有恶贯满盈的狂徒。
牢记某年,认清那夜,
　　塞弗恩宫将有可怖的叫声响彻①;
死亡的尖叫穿越伯克利房顶,　　　　　　　　55
　　那是垂死的王凄厉的哀鸣!
　　狐媚狼心的法兰西王后,以吮血獠牙②
切碎她夫王的六腑五脏;
　　她的儿郎也给国家招来天谴神罚,
围绕着他,只有各种惨剧在酝酿!　　　　　　60
先是'惊恐',接着是'逃遁'如风,
后面'悲伤'的枯形和'孤独'的孑影与共。
"强大的征服者,强大的王,
　　如今委身于下葬的灵床。
没有怜惜的心,悼亡的泪,　　　　　　　　　65

---

① 爱德华二世于一三二七年被妻子谋杀于塞弗恩宫毗邻的伯克利堡。——译者
② 法兰西王后指爱德华二世之王后伊莎贝拉,其子即爱德华三世。——译者

    A tear to grace his obsequies.
Is the sable warrior fled?
Thy son is gone. He rests among the dead.
The swarm that in thy noon-tide beam were born?
    — Gone to salute the rising morn.
Fair laughs the Morn, and soft the zephyr blows,
    While proudly riding o'er the azure realm
In gallant trim the gilded Vessel goes;
    Youth on the prow, and Pleasure at the helm;
Regardless of the sweeping Whirlwind's sway,
That, hush'd in grim repose, expects his evening prey.

"Fill high the sparkling bowl,
The rich repast prepare;
    Reft of a crown, he yet may share the feast:
Close by the regal chair
    Fell Thirst and Famine scowl
    A baleful smile upon their baffled guest.
Heard ye the din of battle bray,
    Lance to lance, and horse to horse?
    Long years of havoc urge their destined course,
And thro' the kindred squadrons mow their way.
    Ye towers of Julius, London's lasting shame,
With many a foul and midnight murder fed,
    Revere his Consort's faith, his Father's fame,

去点染葬仪的悲哀。
是否黑王子已逃去①？
你们的儿子已逝,正与别的亡灵相聚。
那一群,凭着你的炎炎之焰滋长?
——消失了,迎来冉冉上升的朝阳。　　　　　　70
拂拂和风,灿灿晨光,
　　赫赫然在蓝天之上,
镀金的船英武地起航:
　　'青春'屹立船首,'欢乐'把尾舵执掌;
不怕'旋风'在阴暗中潜藏,　　　　　　　　75
妄图攫取牺牲,待黄昏时作浪。

"斟满那闪光的酒杯,
把丰盛的筵席准备,
　　失去王冠,他还可以享受佳肴美味:
紧挨着君王的座位,　　　　　　　　　　　80
　　可怕的'饥'和'渴'联袂而来,
　　投给遭罢黜的王不吉的青睐②。
你们可听见厮杀的喧嚣,
　　马对马,矛对矛?
　　连年的战祸,无了的烽火;　　　　　　85
族亲队队从征,辗转于血泊③。
　　伦敦的永恒耻辱——朱利叶斯众塔④,
你们内中多少奸计和深夜的谋杀,
　　但慑于他妻子的刚愎和父亲的声名

---

① "黑王子"指爱德华三世之长子,死于一三七六年。——译者
② 传说理查德二世被废黜后死于饥饿。——译者
③ 此四行说的是"玫瑰战争"。——编注者
④ 朱利叶斯众塔即著名的伦敦塔,有人认力此塔为朱利叶斯·恺撒所建。英国宫庭许多谋杀、阴谋都发生在该塔内。——译者

90　　　And spare the meek usurper's holy head!
　　　Above, below, the rose of snow,
　　　　　Twined with her blushing foe, we spread
　　　The bristled boar in infant-gore
　　　　　Wallows beneath the thorny shade.
95　　　Now, brothers, bending o'er the accursèd loom,
　　　Stamp we our vengeance deep, and ratify his doom.

　　　"Edward, lo! to sudden fate
　　　　　(Weave we the woof; The thread is spun;)
　　　Half of thy heart we consecrate
100　　　　(The web is wove; The work is done.)"
　　　'Stay, O stay! nor thus forlorn
　　　Leave me unbless'd, unpitied, here to mourn:
　　　In yon bright track that fires the western skies
　　　They melt, they vanish from my eyes.
105　　　But O! what solemn scenes on Snowdon's height
　　　　　Descending slow their glittering skirts unroll[①]?
　　　Visions of glory, spare my aching sight,
　　　　　Ye unborn ages, crowd not on my soul!
　　　No more our long-lost Arthur we bewail: —

---

① *skirts*: 'borders.'

饶了荏弱的僭位者的命①！ 90
上和下，织成一种玫瑰白如雪，
　　和他纠缠的仇敌红如血②。
襁褓中的野猪，鬃毛竖起③，
　　在荆棘丛荫下乱滚一气。
好，兄弟们，让我们俯身被诅咒的织机上， 95
深深织下我们的仇恨，宣告独夫的灭亡。

"爱德华，你瞧！（我们织纬，我们织经）
　　我们把你的妻子作为供品④，
向突然降临的命运之神供奉。
　　（网已织就，事已告成。）" 100
'等等啊，别把我留下孤独无依，
无人悲悯地一个人在这儿哀泣。
在那边，光明之路照得西天火赤，
他们融化了，从我的视野消失。
啊，斯诺登顶峰是什么壮景奇观？ 105
　　徐徐而下，飘飘的衣袂闪闪。
光辉的景象啊，令我应接不暇了，
　　未来的时代啊，我的灵魂装不下了！
我们不再为失去很久的阿瑟王悲哭⑤，

---

① 亨利四世从理查二世手中夺得王位。其子亨利五世后成为英国人民爱戴的国王。亨利六世虽生性荏弱，但由于王后玛格莱特的铁腕以及其父亨利五世的好名声而在一段时间内维护了兰开斯顿家族（参见下条注释）的王权，但最后仍被理查三世刺杀于伦敦塔内。——译者
② 红白玫瑰分别代表爱德华三世后裔中的兰开斯特家族和约克家族。这两个王室家族为争夺英国王权而进行了英国历史上有名的"玫瑰战争"（1455—1485）。——译者
③ 野猪是理查二世的族徽图案。——译者
④ 爱德华一世的王后埃利诺死于格兰彻姆。爱德华一世在其遗体运往伦敦途中停歇过的地方都竖了十字架。——译者
⑤ 威尔士人把传说中的阿瑟王（又译亚瑟王）视为自己的不列颠王。——译者

110   All hail, ye genuine kings! Britannia's issue, hail!

         'Girt with many a baron bold
        Sublime their starry fronts they rear;
          And gorgeous dames, and statesmen old
        In bearded majesty, appear.
115   In the midst a form divine①!
        Her eye proclaims her of the Briton-Line;
        Her lion-port, her awe-commanding face②
        Attemper'd sweet to virgin-grace③.
        What strings symphonious tremble in the air,
120   What strains of vocal transport round her play?
        Hear from the grave, great Taliessin, hear;
          They breathe a soul to animate thy clay.
        Bright Rapture calls, and soaring as she sings,
        Waves in the eye of Heaven her many-colour'd wings.

125   'The verse adorn again④
        Fierce War, and faithful Love,
        And Truth severe, by fairy Fiction drest.
          In buskin'd measures move⑤
        Pale Grief, and pleasing Pain,
130   With Horror, tyrant of the throbbing breast.
        A voice as of the cherub-choir

---

① *a form divine*: Queen Elizabeth, granddaughter of Henry VII.
② *lion-port*: 'proud carriage,' like that of a lion.
③ *Attemper'd ... to*: 'qualified by.'
④ *The verse* is the object of 'adorn,' whose subjects follow in the next two lines.
⑤ *In buskin'd measures*: i.e. in tragic verse. The buskin was the high boot worn in tragedy on the Greek and Roman stage. Cf. above, No. 112, l. 132.

都欢呼啊,真正的王,不列颠的后裔,欢呼①,　　　　　110

　　'俊武的王侯环绕,奕奕精神,
组成堂堂正正的前沿星阵。
　　富艳的仕女如云;还有元老名臣,
银须给盛典增添庄严成分。
中央是一位至尊女性②,　　　　　　　　　　　　　115
真正不列颠血统,眉目是证明:
有狮子的英伟,威仪令人敬畏;
更有青春的柔妩匀入圣洁的秀美。
围绕她,多少竞奏的繁弦急管③,
　　妙曲清歌啊,令人意畅心欢。　　　　　　　120
伟大的塔里亚辛,从你的坟茔,你听④,
　　他们要赋予你的遗骨以新的生命。
光明的"狂欢"在呼唤,边飞翔,边歌唱,
在天国的灵境中,鼓动她色彩缤纷的翅膀。

　　'酷烈的战争,忠贞的爱情,　　　　　　　125
　　严峻的真理,经想象的装整,
使诗篇异彩纷呈。
　　伴着悲剧诗的韵律⑤,
出现苍白的"悲伤",醉人的"痛苦",
还有悸动心灵的"暴君"——"恐怖"。　　　　　130
从烂漫的伊甸吹来阵阵清风,
　　依稀带着天使们的歌诵。

---

① "真正的王"指亨利七世,他是威尔士人的后裔。——编注者
② 至尊女性指女王伊丽莎白一世。——译者
③ 指伊丽莎白时代的诗人和戏剧家。——译者
④ 塔里亚辛(Taliessin)是六世纪威尔士行吟诗人。——译者
⑤ 此行诗及下两行暗喻莎士比亚的出现;其后两行指弥尔顿的崛起;再后两行指弥尔顿以后的英国诗人。——译者

>   Gales from blooming Eden bear,
>   And distant warblings lessen on my ear①,
>   That lost in long futurity expire.
> 135   Fond impious man, think'st thou yon sanguine cloud
>   Raised bythy breath, has quench'd the orb of day?
>   To-morrow he repairs the golden flood
>   And warms the nations with redoubled ray.
>   Enough for me: with joy I see
> 140   The different doom our fates assign:
>   Be thine Despair and sceptred Care;
>   To triumph and to die are mine.'
>   — He spoke, and headlong from the mountain's height
>   Deep in the roaring tide he plunged to endless night

T. GRAY.

---

① *lessen*: 'sound fainter,' as coming from a greater distance.

我还听见远方隐隐的吟咏,
他们要遗响在久远的时空。
执迷不悟的人,你以为你翻起的血云,   *135*
　　已经淹没了太阳?
明天他就恢复金色的洪流滚滚,
　　用双倍的光线温暖万国千邦。
我已经心满意足,怀着欢欣,
　　我看到我们的不同命运: *140*
主宰着你的是失望和忧伤,
　　而我则在胜利中死亡。'
——诗人说完,从高山顶上
俯冲入怒吼的急流,消失在黑夜茫茫。

谢耀文　译

编注《行吟诗人》(又译作《歌手》)作于一七五四至一七五七年。相传英王爱德华一世于一二八二年征服威尔士后曾屠杀威尔士的诗人和歌手。格雷据此传说写成此诗。诗中歌颂了威尔士人反对侵略的壮举,对吞并威尔士的爱德华一世进行了诅咒。诗中单引号内的诗行(一行以上的)为行吟诗人的独诵,双引号内的诗行为合诵,没有引号的是作者本人的宣叙和描述。

124. ODE WRITTEN IN MDCCXLVI

How sleep the Brave who sink to rest
By all their Country' wishes blest!
When Spring, with dewy fingers cold,
Returns to deck their hallow'd mould,
She there shall dress a sweeter sod
Than Fancy's feet have ever trod①.

By fairy hands their knell is rung,
By forms unseen their dirge is sung;
There Honour comes, a pilgrim grey,
To bless the turf that wraps their clay;
And Freedom shall awhile repair
To dwell, a weeping hermit, there!

W. COLLINS.

---

① *Than Fancy's feet*, etc.; 'than has ever been trodden in imagination.'

124. 颂歌，作于一七四六年

柯林斯

勇士们睡着了，沉入了安眠，
带着全国人祝福的心愿！
春神以冰凉的手指沾着露，
回来装饰这神圣的泥土，
她就要布置起一片草地， 5
比幻想踏过的更加美丽。

仙子的手把丧钟敲响，
无形的精灵把挽歌低唱；
荣誉来到了，白发的旅人，
来祝福这覆盖他们的草坪； 10
自由将立刻赶到此地，
做哀哭的隐士，住在这里！

屠岸　译

编注　威廉·柯林斯（William Collins，1721—1759），英国诗人，所著《颂歌集》流传至今。这首颂歌歌颂了一七四五年法国军队击败英、荷、奥等国联军的一系列战斗中的阵亡将士。

125. LAMENT FOR CULLODEN

The lovely lass o' Inverness,
    Nae joy nor pleasure can she see;
For e'en and morn she cries, Alas!
    And ay the saut tear blin's her ee[1];
5 Drumossie moor — Drumossie day —
    A waefu' day it was to me!
For there I lost my father dear,
    My father dear, and brethren three.

Their winding-sheet the bluidy clay,
10   Their graves are growing green to see;
And by them lies the dearest lad
    That ever blest a woman's ee!
Now wae to thee, thou cruel lord,
    A bluidy man I trow thou be;
15 For mony a heart thou hast made sair
    That ne'er did wrang to thine or thee.

R. BURNS.

---

[1] *saut*: 'salt.' *blin's*: 'blinds.'

125. 吊库洛登战场①

彭斯

因弗内斯的可爱女郎,
　看不见愉快与欢畅;
唉! 朝朝暮暮她都在涕哭,
　盐的泪水浸瞎了她的目光:
德腊莫西的原野——德腊莫西的天日——②　　　　5
　多么哀伤的日子哟,留在我的心上!
在那里,我失去了亲爱的父亲,
　还有三个兄弟也死在战场。

他们的尸布裹着血染的躯干,
　他们的墓园芳草青青可见,　　　　10
他们身旁还躺着最亲爱的少年!
　他的祝福曾使一位妇女心欢!
残酷的暴君呀! 如今悲哀会落到你头上③,
　你是个嗜血成性的恶汉;
你叫多少人伤心落泪,　　　　15
　他们对你同你的一伙无仇无冤。

黄绍鑫　译

编注　罗伯特・彭斯（Robert Burns，1759—1796），苏格兰大诗人。他写了许多诗来表达苏格兰农村青年的日常生活和他所追求的

---

① 库洛登(Culloden)在下文提到的因弗内斯附近。一七四六年,觊觎英国王位的查理・爱德华在此战败。——编注者
② 德腊莫西(Drumossie)是库洛登原野的另一名称。——译者
③ "残酷的暴君"指乔治二世之次子康伯兰德公爵威廉・奥古斯都(William Augustus),他因在战争中残暴成性而被称为"康伯兰德屠夫"。——译者

自由平等思想,诗中充满了对生活的热爱。主要作品有《苏格兰方言诗歌》和大量优秀的短诗,如《我的心呀在高原》《昔日的时光》《红红的玫瑰》等。

126. LAMENT FOR FLODDEN

I've heard them lilting at the ewe-milking①,
    Lasses a' lilting before dawn of day②;
But now they are moaning on ilka green loaning —③
    The Flowers of the Forest are a' wede away④.

At bughts, in the morning, nae blythe lads are scorning⑤,
    Lasses are lonely and dowie and wae⑥;
Nae daffing, nae gabbing, but sighing and sabbing⑦,
    Ilk ane lifts her leglin and hies her away⑧.

In har'st, at the shearing, nae youths now are jeering⑨,
    Bandsters are runkled, and lyart, or grey⑩;
At fair or at preaching, nae wooing, nae fleeching⑪—
    The Flowers of the Forest are a' wede away.

---

① *lilting*: 'singing.'
② *a'*: 'all.'
③ *ilka*: 'every.' *loaning*: an open uncultivated piece of ground, near a farmhouse or village, on which the cows are milked.
④ *The Flowers of the Forest*: i.e. the young men of Ettrick Forest. *wede away*: 'weeded out.'
⑤ *bughts*: or boughts, 'sheepfolds.' *scorning*: i.e. jeering at each other.
⑥ *dowie*: 'dull and lonely.'
⑦ *daffing*: 'playing the fool.' *gabbing*: 'scoffing.'
⑧ *leglin*: 'milk-pail.'
⑨ *shearing*: 'reaping.'
⑩ *Bandsters*: 'sheaf-binders.' *runkled*: 'wrinkled.' *lyart*: 'grizzled.'
⑪ *fleeching*: 'wheedling.'

126. 弗洛顿哀歌①

珍·艾略特

我曾听见姑娘们挤羊奶时的歌唱,
　　她们的歌声迎来一日的黎明;
如今她们的悲吟声在茵绿的奶场回荡,
　　——原来啊,埃特里克森林之花均已凋零②。

羊圈旁,清晨里,再也听不见小孩们的戏语, 5
　　姑娘则悲伤、忧郁,孤苦伶仃;
没有了欢娱和嬉笑,只有叹息与哀吟,
　　个个都手提奶桶匆匆行。

谷熟日,收割时,再也听不见小伙们的笑声,
　　捆草的人都是皱纹满脸,灰发银鬓; 10
集市上,教堂前,再也看不见小伙们求爱谈情
　　——原来啊,埃特里克森林之花均已凋零。

---

① 弗洛顿(Flodden),苏格兰地名。一五一三年瑟雷侯爵率英格兰军在这里击败苏格兰军,并杀死了苏格兰王詹姆士四世。——译者
② 森林之花,指青年男子。——译者

> At e'en, in the gloaming, nae younkers are roaming
>   'Bout stacks with the lasses at bogle to play[①];
> But ilk maid sits dreary, lamenting her dearie —
>   The Flowers of the Forest are weded away.
>
> Dool and wae for the order, sent our lads to the Border[②]!
>   The English, for ance, by guile wan the day:
> The Flowers of the Forest that fought aye the foremost,
>   The prime of our land, are cauld in the clay.
>
> We'll hear nae mair lilting at the ewe-milking;
>   Women and bairns are heartless and wae[③];
> Sighing and moaning on ilka green loaning —
>   The Flowers of the Forest are a' wede away.

J. ELLIOT.

---

① *bogle*: 'bogy,' 'goblin.'
② *Dool*: 'grief.'
③ *heartless*: 'dejected.'

夜晚里,黄昏时,再也看不见小伙们,
　　在草堆旁与姑娘们嬉戏,装扮小妖精;
只看见姑娘们个个伤心而坐,悲悼心上人　　　　　　15
　　——原来啊,埃特里克森林之花均已凋零。

最可恨是那征召令,遣我儿男去边境!
　　那英格兰巧施毒计,一战胜我兵;
埃特里克森林之花,一直奋战在前线,
　　我苏格兰精英今已长埋黄土尸成冰。　　　　　　20

再也听不见了姑娘们挤羊奶时的歌唱;
　　妇女儿童无不肝肠寸断,悲痛填膺,
声声哀叹与悲吟在每个茵绿的奶场回荡
　　——原来啊!埃特里克森林之花均已凋零。

周式中　译

编注　珍·艾略特(Jean Elliot,1727—1805),苏格兰一贵族女子。这首诗是她所作并流传于世的唯一作品,原题名《森林之花》,于一七五六年匿名发表,后被司各特收入《苏格兰边区歌谣》第二卷。

127. THE BRAES OF YARROW

'Thy braes were bonny, Yarrow stream,
    when first on them I met my lover;
Thy braes how dreary, Yarrow stream,
    When now thy waves his body cover!
For ever now, O Yarrow stream,
    Thou art to me a stream of sorrow;
For never on thy banks shall I
    Behold my love, the flower of Yarrow.

'He promised me a milk-white steed
    To bear me to his father's bowers;
He promised me a little page
    To squire me to his father's towers;
He promised me a wedding-ring, —
    The wedding-day was fix'd to-morrow; —
Now he is wedded to his grave,
    Alas, his watery grave, in Yarrow!

'Sweet were his words when last we met;
    My passion I as freely told him;
Clasp'd in his arms, I little thought
    That I should never more behold him!
Scarce was he gone, I saw his ghost;

127. 雅罗溪畔

罗根

"昔日我与恋人初会此地,
　　你的两岸一派好风光,雅罗溪①;
如今你的波涛吞没了他的躯体,
　　你的两岸满目凄凉,雅罗溪!
从今往后,雅罗溪啊,　　　　　　　　　　　　5
　　你成了我悲伤的溪,
在你岸边我永远看不见了
　　我心上的人儿,这雅罗的花枝。

"他曾许诺,送我一匹乳白的骏马,
　　接我到他父亲的别墅;　　　　　　　　　10
他曾许诺,送我一个年少的仆从,
　　接我到他父亲的楼屋;
他曾许诺,赠我订婚的戒指,
　　定明天两情成眷属,——
他如今竟把坟墓作洞房,　　　　　　　　　15
　　雅罗溪哟,成了他水的坟墓!

"当我俩最后相会,他吐露一腔蜜意;
　　我倾听他缕缕情衷,
我偎身在他的怀抱,怎料此番一别,
　　就不能再度相逢!　　　　　　　　　　　20
他人方离去,魂即入眼帘;

---

① 雅罗溪(Yarrow,又译雅洛河),苏格兰塞尔扣克郡境内埃特里克河(Ettrick)的支流。——编注者

>   It vanish'd with a shriek of sorrow;
>   Thrice did the water-wraith ascend①,
>   And gave a doleful groan thro' Yarrow.
>
> 'His mother from the window look'd
>   With all the longing of a mother;
> His little sister weeping walk'd
>   The green-wood path to meet her brother;
> They sought him east, they sought him west
>   They sought him all the forest thorough;
> They only saw the cloud of night,
>   They only heard the roar of Yarrow.
>
> 'No longer from thy window look —
>   Thou hast no son, thou tender mother!
> No longer walk, thou lovely maid;
>   Alas, thou hast no more a brother!
> No longer seek him east or west
>   And search no more the forest thorough;
> For, wandering in the night so dark,
>   He fell a lifeless corpse in Yarrow.
>
> 'The tear shall never leave my cheek,
>   No other youth shall be my marrow②—
> I'll seek thy body in the stream,
>   And then with thee I'll sleep in Yarrow.'
> — The tear did never leave her cheek,

---

① *water-wraith*: 'spirit of the stream'; a wraith is properly the apparition of a person just dead or on the point of death.
② *my marrow*: 'mate.'

忽听一声凄厉,不见了他的影踪;
幽灵复显现,三度出清涟,
　　但闻一片哀吟,回荡在雅罗上空。

"他母亲倚窗眺望,　　　　　　　　　　25
　　心底里充满母亲的愁怀;
他小妹一路哭泣,
　　去林中迎接哥哥的归来;
他们东寻西觅,
　　他们找遍了茫茫的林海;　　　　　30
看见的,只有夜空中飘浮的云朵,
　　听见的,只有雅罗溪水咆哮澎湃。

"你慈爱的母亲!别再倚窗眺望——
　　你的儿子,已经永远离去!
你可爱的姑娘,别再去林中迎候;　　　35
　　唉!你再没有哥哥可寻觅!
别再东寻西找,
　　别再踏遍这茫茫的林地;
他已迷途于沉沉的黑夜,
　　葬身在雅罗溪底。　　　　　　　　40

"我满颊泪水流不尽,
　　今生今世不再有心爱的青年——
我将寻你入溪水,
　　伴你在雅罗溪底长眠。"
——她满颊的泪水流不尽,　　　　　　45

No other youth became her marrow;
She found his body in the stream,
And now with him she sleeps in Yarrow.

JOHN. LOGAN.

今生今世不再有心爱的青年；
她与恋人在溪底相会，
伴他在雅罗溪底长眠。

周式中　译

编注　约翰·罗根（John Logan，1748—1788），以牧师为职业的苏格兰诗人，著有《罗根诗集》(*Poems by the Rev. Mr. Logan, One of the Ministers of Leith*)。

128. WILLY DROWNED IN YARROW

Down in yon garden sweet and gay
    Where bonnie grows the lily,
I heard a fair maid sighing say,
    'My wish be wi' sweet Willie!

'Willie's rare, and Willie's fair,
    And Willie's wondrous bonny;
And Willie hecht to marry me[1]
    Gin e'er he married ony[2].

'O gentle wind, that bloweth south
    From where my Love repaireth,
Convey a kiss frae his dear mouth
    And tell me how he fareth!

'O tell sweet Willie to come doun
    And hear the mavis singing[3],
And see the birds on ilka bush
    And leaves around them hinging[4].

'The lav'rock there, wi' her white breast[5]
    And gentle throat sae narrow;
There's sport eneuch for gentlemen

---

[1] *hecht*: a Scotch form of 'hight,' 'promised.'
[2] *Gin*: 'if.'
[3] *mavis*: 'song-thrush.'
[4] *hinging*: 'hanging.'
[5] *lav'rock*: 'lark.'

128. 威利葬身雅罗溪

无名氏

在那芬芳明媚的花园中,
　　百合盛开,多么艳丽,
我听见一位美貌的姑娘在叹息,
　　"我的心永远属于你,亲爱的威利!

"威利是稀世的青年,威利是俊美的儿郎, 　　　　5
　　威利是人中精英,拔萃出类;
威利对我信誓旦旦诉衷肠,
　　今世若联姻,唯与我作配。

"啊! 轻柔的风,南拂的风,
　　我恋人从你那儿呼吸。 　　　　10
请传给我他的亲吻,
　　请告诉我:他可安适!

"啊,请叫亲爱的威利快来到,
　　听听那画眉的歌声,
看看那枝头的小鸟, 　　　　15
　　个个在翠叶间藏隐。

"那里的云雀,露出洁白的胸脯,
　　她那柔美的歌喉,多么细亮;
那边的男子正纵情游乐,

491

On Leader haughs and Yarrow[1].

'O Leader haughs are wide and braid[2]
    And Yarrow haughs are bonny;
There Willie hecht to marry me
    If e'er he married ony.

'But Willie's gone, whom I thought on,
    And does not hear me weeping;
Draws many a tear frae 's true love's e'e
    When other maids are sleeping.

'Yestreen I made my bed fu' braid,
    The night I'll mak' it narrow,
For a' the live-lang winter night
    I lie twined o' my marrow[3].

'O came ye by yon water-side?
    Pou'd you the rose or lily[4]?
Or came you by yon meadow green,
    Or saw you my sweet Willie?'

She sought him up, she sought him down,
    She sought him braid and narrow;
Syne, in the cleaving of a craig[5],
    She found him drown'd in Yarrow!

                          ANON.

---

[1] *haughs*: the level strips of land running along a valley beside a river.
[2] *braid*: 'broad.'
[3] *twined o'*: 'parted from.'
[4] *Pou'd*: 'pulled.'
[5] *Syne*: 'afterwards.' Cf. No. 106, l. 7.

　　　　在那里德河滨,雅罗岸上①。 20

"啊,里德河滨广又宽,
　　雅罗溪畔风光美;
威利在此信誓旦旦诉衷肠,
　　今世若联姻,唯与我作配。

"我思念的恋人,今已离去, 25
　　听不见我的悲泣声声;
他忠贞的情侣,泪流如注,
　　别的姑娘尚在酣眠沉沉。

"昨夜我铺开宽宽的床,
　　今宵我裹起窄窄的被, 30
长长冬夜无尽头,
　　孤身失伴难成寐。

"啊! 你们从那溪畔来,
　　可曾采枝玫瑰花? 可曾摘朵百合花?
啊! 你们从那绿草如茵的地方来, 35
　　可曾见我心上人? 可曾看到威利他?"

她寻他寻遍各地,
　　她找他找遍东西;
终于来岸边,巨石中开处,
　　竟发现,他已葬身雅罗溪! 40

　　　　　　　　　　　周式中　译

---

① 里德河(Leader):位于贝里克郡内。——译者

130. BLACK-EYED SUSAN

All in the Downs the fleet was moor'd,
    The streamers waving in the wind,
When black-eyed Susan came aboard;
    'O! where shall I my true-love find?
Tell me, ye jovial sailors, tell me true
If my sweet William sails among the crew.'

William, who high upon the yard
    Rock'd with the billow to and fro,
Soon as her well-known voice he heard,
    He sigh'd, and cast his eyes below:
The cord slides swiftly through his glowing hands,
And quick as lightning on the deck he stands.

So the sweet lark, high poised in air,
    Shuts close his pinions to his breast
If chance his mate's shrill call he hear①,
    And drops at once into her nest: —
The noblest captain in the British fleet
Might envy William's lips those kisses sweet.

'O Susan, Susan, lovely dear,
    My vows shall ever true remain;
Let me kiss off that falling tear;
    We only part to meet again.

---

① *chance*: for 'perchance.'

130. 黑眼睛苏珊

盖伊

船队泊碇在海湾,
  风中飘扬着旗幡,
黑眼睛苏珊登上甲板
  "啊!何处找到我心爱的威廉?
告诉我,快乐的水手们,实实告诉我,   5
我亲爱的威廉是否在你们中间?"

威廉正高高地站在
  巨浪拍打的船坞边,
他一听到她的熟悉声音,
  他叹息,然后垂下眼睑: 10
船索轻轻滑过他赤热的手,
闪电般地落在他伫立的甲板。

像泰然高翔在空中的云雀,
  紧紧敛起双翼在胸前,
只要一听到他的伴侣呼唤,   15
  就会立刻扑到她的身边:——
不列颠船队里最高贵的船长,
也要嫉妒威廉的吻哟,那样蜜甜。

"啊!苏珊,苏珊,我的爱,
  我的誓言永远不会改变;   20
让我吻去你的泪滴;
  我们分别,只是为了再见。

Change as ye list, ye winds; my heart shall be
The faithful compass that still points to thee.

'Believe not what the landmen say
   Who tempt with doubts thy constant mind;
They'll tell thee, sailors, when away,
   In every port a mistress find;
Yes, yes, believe them when they tell thee so,
For Thou art present wheresoe'er I go.

'If to far India's coast we sail,
   Thy eyes are seen in diamonds bright,
Thy breath is Afric's spicy gale,
   Thy skin is ivory so white.
Thus every beauteous object that I view
Wakes in my soul some charm of lovely Sue.

'Though battle call me from thy arms
   Let not my pretty Susan mourn;
Though cannons roar, yet safe from harms
   William shall to his Dear return.
Love turns aside the balls that round me fly,
Lest precious tears should drop from Susan's eye.'

The boatswain gave the dreadful word,
   The sails their swelling bosom spread;
No longer must she stay aboard;
   They kiss'd, she sigh'd, he hung his head.
Her lessening boat unwilling rows to land;
'Adieu!' she cries; and waved her lily hand.

J. GAY.

任凭服役的名册和风向变换,
我的心依然指向你的忠实罗盘。

"不要相信陆上的人传言, 25
  他们要来试探你忠贞的心田;
他们会告诉你,飘海的水手,
  会在每个港口找到他们的情伴;
对啊!对啊!相信他们这些话吧,
因为我不管走到哪里,你都会出现。 30

"如果我们航行到印度海岸,
  会看到你的眼珠那样光闪,
你的呼吸像非洲吹来的香风,
  你的皮肤似象牙白皙一般。
我所瞧见的每一个秀丽影像, 35
都叫我想起可爱苏珊的容颜。

"虽然战斗要我离开你的怀抱,
  但是,美丽的苏珊呀,你切莫心酸;
虽然炮声隆隆,但我平安无恙,
  威廉会再次回到他的情人跟前。 40
爱情会把环绕我的子弹抛开,
以免苏珊的珍贵泪水流淌不干。"

水手长发出了可怕的命令,
  霎时就要起锚张帆;
她不能再留在甲板上; 45
  他俩吻别,他垂下了头,她长吁短叹。
她的轻舟不愿驶回海岸;
"再见吧!"她呼喊,挥动玉手纤纤。

黄绍鑫 译

编注 约翰·盖伊（John Gay，1685—1732），英国剧作家及诗人，主要剧作有《乞丐的歌剧》（*Beggar's Opera*），主要诗作有《牧人的星期》（*The Shepherd's Week*）、《乡村的游戏》等。

131. SALLY IN OUR ALLEY

Of all the girls that are so smart
    There's none like pretty Sally;
She is the darling of my heart,
    And she lives in our alley.
There is no lady in the land
    Is half so sweet as Sally;
She is the darling of my heart,
    And she lives in our alley.

Her father he makes cabbage-nets①
    And through the streets does cry 'em;
Her mother she sells laces long
    To such as please to buy 'em:
But sure such folks could ne'er beget
    So sweet a girl as Sally!
She is the darling of my heart,
    And she lives in our alley.

When she is by, I leave my work,
    I love her so sincerely;
My master comes like any Turk,
    And bangs me most severely —
But let him bang his bellyful,
    I'll bear it all for Sally;

---

① *cabbage-nets*: nets to boil cabbages in.

131. 我们巷里的萨莉

卡雷

在所有漂亮的姑娘中,
　　可没一个像美丽的萨莉;
她是我心中的情人,
　　就住在我们巷里。
这地方没有一个女郎　　　　　　　　　　5
　　比得上萨莉一半美丽;
她是我心中的情人,
　　就住在我们巷里。

她父亲编织了许多笊篱,
　　大街小巷叫卖不止;　　　　　　　　10
她的母亲贩卖花边带,
　　谁喜欢就来买几尺;
但是啊!这些人中定找不到
　　这么娴美的萨莉!
她是我心中的情人,　　　　　　　　　　15
　　她就住在我们巷里。

当她从我身旁走过,我立即放下工作,
　　我爱她这么诚挚;
我的主人真像一个暴君,
　　笞责我呀!十分严厉——　　　　　　20
但任凭他怎样顿足怒骂,
　　我忍受一切无非为了萨莉;

>   She is the darling of my heart,
>   And she lives in our alley.
>
> Of all the days that's in the week
>   I dearly love but one day —
> And that's the day that comes betwixt
>   A Saturday and Monday;
> For then I'm drest all in my best
>   To walk abroad with Sally;
> She is the darling of my heart,
>   And she lives in our alley.
>
> My master carries me to church,
>   And often am I blamed
> Because I leave him in the lurch
>   As soon as text is named;
> I leave the church in sermon-time
>   And slink away to Sally;
> She is the darling of my heart,
>   And she lives in our alley.
>
> When Christmas comes about again
>   O then I shall have money;
> I'll hoard it up, and box it all,
>   I'll give it to my honey:
> I would it were ten thousand pound,
>   I'd give it all to Sally;
> She is the darling of my heart,
>   And she lives in our alley.
>
> My master and the neighbours all

她是我心中的情人，
　　她住在我们巷里。

一周中的七天时辰，　　　　　　　　　　25
　　我只特爱一个日子——
那一天就是介于
　　星期六与星期一间的日子；
那时哟！我得穿上最好的衣服，
　　同萨莉一道出外游憩，　　　　　　30
她是我心中的情人，
　　她就住在我们巷里。

主人有时带我到教堂，
　　但我常常被他责备，
因为我一听到念诵经文，　　　　　　　35
　　就置他不顾，悄悄离去，
布道时，我就溜出教堂，
　　偷偷去会我的萨莉；
她是我心中的情人，
　　她就住在我巷里。　　　　　　　　40

圣诞节又要来临，
　　那时我会得到银币；
我把钱通通储存起来，
　　献给我亲爱的伴侣：
但愿我有一万镑，　　　　　　　　　　45
　　将一齐送给萨莉；
她是我心中的情人，
　　就住在我们巷里。

我的主人和邻居，

503

50   Make game of me and Sally,
And, but for her, I'd better be
A slave and row a galley;
But when my seven long years are out[1]
O then I'll marry Sally, —
55   O then we'll wed, and then we'll bed,
But not in our alley!

H. CAREY.

---

[1] *my seven long years*: *i.e.* his period of apprentliceship.

>   无不戏谑我和萨莉,　　　　　　　　　　　　　　50
>   如果不是为了她,
>   我宁肯做个划船的奴隶;
>   当我七年学徒期满,
>   啊!那时我一定要娶萨莉,——
>   哦!那时要举行婚礼,要共枕席,　　　　　　　55
>   但是不在我们巷里!

黄绍鑫　译

编注 亨利·卡雷(Henry Carey,1693?—1743),英国剧作家及诗人。相传他就是著名颂歌《国王万岁》(*God Save the King*)的作者。

132. A FAREWELL

Go fetch to me a pint o' wine,
    An' fill it in a silver tassie[①];
That I may drink before I go
    A service to my bonnie lassie;
The boat rocks at the pier o' Leith,
    Fu' loud the wind blaws frae the Ferry,
The ship rides by the Berwick-law,
    And I maun leave my bonnie Mary.

The trumpets sound, the banners fly,
    The glittering spears are rankéd ready;
The shouts o' war are heard afar,
    The battle closes thick and bloody;
But it's not the roar o' sea or shore
    Wad make me langer wish to tarry;
Nor shout o' war that's heard afar —
    It's leaving thee, my bonnie Mary.

R. BURNS.

[①] *tassie*: 'cup.'

132. 告别

彭斯

给我捎一品脱酒来,
　　注入那银色的酒杯;
好让我在出征之前,
　　和那好姑娘干一杯。
船儿在拉斯码头摇晃, 5
　　风儿在渡头狂吹,
舟儿从贝里克劳驶过,
　　我得离开好玛莱。

号角齐鸣,旗帜招展,
　　闪亮的戈矛已排开, 10
战争逼临,血腥又阴森,
　　厮杀之声自远来。
不是海啸或岸边的浪涛
　　使我想再逗留一会;
也不是远处的厮杀之声, 15
　　而是离开你,好玛莱。

袁可嘉　译

编注 此诗原题为《我美丽的玛莱》,《告别》系《金库》原编者所换。

133. 'IF DOUGHTY DEEDS MY LADY PLEASE'

If doughty deeds my lady please
    Right soon I'll mount my steed;
And strong his arm, and fast his seat,
    That bears frae me the meed.
I'll wear thy colours in my cap,
    Thy picture in my heart;
And he that bends not to thine eye
    Shall rue it to his smart[1].
        Then tell me how to woo thee, love;
            O tell me how to woo thee!
        For thy dear sake, nae care I'll take,
            Tho' ne'er another trow me[2].

If gay attire delight thine eye
    I'll dight me in array[3];
I'll tend thy chamber door all night,
    And squire thee all the day.
If sweetest sounds can win thine ear,
    These sounds I'll strive to catch;
Thy voice I'll steal to woo thysell,
    That voice that nane can match.

---

[1] *Shall rue it to his smart*: this seems a combination of 'Shall rue it' and 'Shall do so to his smart,' which are the same in meaning; their union in one phrase really gives another sense, 'Shall suffer for it, and shall pay for so suffering.'
[2] *trow*: 'believe.'
[3] *dight*: 'clothe.'

133. "假如姑娘喜爱我英勇的业绩"

格雷厄姆

假如姑娘喜爱我英勇的业绩,
　　我愿意立刻跨上我的骅骝;
坚强的臂膀,结牢的坐骑,
　　会使我赢得奖励。
我的帽沿将载有你的彩色标志, 5
　　你的影像将印在我的心里;
没有屈从你明眸的那个人哟!
　　他定会自作自受,懊悔莫及。
　　　姑娘呀!请告诉我怎样才能求得你的爱;
　　　请告诉我,怎样才能讨得你欢喜! 10
　　　纵使别人不相信我,
　　　为了亲爱的你,我什么也不介意。

假如漂亮衣服,能够使你悦目,
　　我定要把衣着穿得华丽整齐;
我愿意通夜照看你的房门, 15
　　整天服侍着你。
假如甜美声音能够使你悦耳,
　　我就愿学会这些歌曲;
我要悄悄来掬取你的欢心,
　　你的歌声无人可以比拟。 20

But if fond love thy heart can gain,
   I never broke a vow;
Nae maiden lays her skaith to me[①],
   I never loved but you.
For you alone I ride the ring,
   For you I wear the blue,
For you alone I strive to sing,
   O tell me how to woo!
      Then tell me how to woo thee, love;
         O tell me how to woo thee!
      For thy dear sake, nae care I'll take,
         Tho' ne'er another trow me.

                    R. GRAHAM OF GARTMORE.

---

① *skaith*: or scathe, 'harm.'

假如你接受我这片痴情,
　　我永远也不会背弃我的盟誓;
没有一个姑娘会把我伤害,
　　但是,除了你,我绝不会把别人念记。
只因为你,我才跑马夺环①,
　　只因为你,我才穿着蓝色服饰②;
又因为你,我才努力歌唱,
　　哦!告诉我,怎样才牵住你这缕情丝!
　　姑娘啊,告诉我!怎样才得到你的爱;
　　怎样才能获得你的欢喜!
纵使别人不相信我,
　　为了亲爱的你,我什么也不介意。

黄绍鑫　译

编注　罗伯特·格雷厄姆(Robert Graham, 1735?—1797),英国诗人、学者,写有各种抒情诗。

---

① "跑马夺环"是中古时期的一种游戏。竞技者在纵马急驶中,设法用长矛挑走高悬的环圈,非技艺高超者不能为。——译者
② "蓝色"系英国保守党员或有学问的妇女的一种标志,也常是律师、顾问等专业服饰颜色。故公务员常被称为"蓝衣",这里的意思是:"除掉你,我就不愿为任何人服役。"——译者

134. TO A YOUNG LADY

Sweet stream, that winds through yonder glade①,
Apt emblem of a virtuous maid —
Silent and chaste she steals along,
Far from the world's gay busy throng:
5   With gentle yet prevailing force,
Intent upon her destined course;
Graceful and useful all she does,
Blessing and blest where'er she goes②;
Pure-bosom'd as that watery glass,
10   And Heaven reflected in her face.

W. COWPER.

---

① *Sweet stream*: if, as appears, this is intended as an address to the stream, 'winds' should be in the second person (*i.e.* either 'windest' or 'wind').
② *Blessing and blest*: 'conferring favours and receiving gratitude.'

134. 给一位少女

柯珀

蜿蜒地流过林地的小溪，
是贞洁少女的适当标记——
沉静而圣洁，她悄悄前行，
远离这世上嚣嚷的人群：
她以温和却饱满的力量， 5
专心地朝着决定的方向；
她做的一切挺优雅，有用处，
到哪儿总替人又被人祝福；
她胸怀纯洁，溪水般透明，
她脸上反映着天国的宁静。 10

屠岸 译

编注 威廉·柯珀（William Cowper，1731—1800），英国诗人。他的诗力求朴素率真，接近日常口语，主要诗作有《阿尼颂诗》《任务》和《收到我母亲的画像之后》等。

135. THE SLEEPING BEAUTY

Sleep on, and dream of Heaven awhile —
    Tho' shut so close thy laughing eyes,
Thy rosy lips still wear a smile
    And move, and breathe delicious sighs!

Ah, now soft blushes tinge her cheeks
    And mantle o'er her neck of snow;
Ah, now she murmurs, now she speaks
    What most I wish — and fear to know!

She starts, she trembles, and she weeps!
    Her fair hands folded on her breast:
— And now, how like a saint she sleeps!
    A seraph in the realms of rest!

Sleep on secure! Above control
    Thy thoughts belong to Heaven and thee:
And may the secret of thy soul[1]
    Remain within its sanctuary!

S. ROGERS.

---

[1] *may the secret*, etc. : the fears the poet expressed in l. 8 have triumphed over his wishes.

135. 睡美人

罗杰斯

睡下去吧,一时梦想天国——
  虽然你的笑眼紧紧闭着,
你的玫瑰嘴唇仍然现出微笑,
  活动,并发出叹气声十分轻妙!

她的面颊染着轻微羞红, 5
  她的雪白颈子着色异曲同工;
一时她喃喃低语,一时说话,
  说的我最愿知道——可是又害怕!

她惊动,她颤抖,她啜泣!
  她的美丽双手在胸上摺起: 10
——现在她睡得多像一个圣者!
  像一个天使在安息的境界!

安安稳稳地睡下去!
  你的思想和你向上天皈依:
愿你的灵魂秘密 15
  停留在神圣的境地!

李霁野　译

编注 塞缪尔·罗杰斯(Samuel Rogers,1763—1855),英国银行家、诗人。他一生最著名的诗篇是《记忆的欢乐》(*Pleasures of Memory*)。

136. 'FOR EVER, FORTUNE, WILT THOU PROVE'

For ever, Fortune, wilt thou prove
An unrelenting foe to Love,
And when we meet a mutual heart
Come in between, and bid us part?

Bid us sigh on from day to day,
And wish and wish the soul away;
Till youth and genial years are flown,
And all the life of life is gone?

But busy, busy, still art thou,
To bind the loveless joyless vow[①],
The heart from pleasure to delude[②],
And join the gentle to the rude.

For once, O Fortune, hear my prayer,
And I absolve thy future care;
All other blessings I resign,
Make but the dear Amanda mine.

J. THOMSON.

[①] *To bind the loveless joyless vow*: *i.e.* to bring about marriages where there is neither love nor happiness.

[②] *The heart from pleasure to delude*: 'to entice the heart away from its true happiness.'

136. "命运,你要永远证明"

汤姆森

命运,你要永远证明
你是爱情的无情敌人,
当我们遇到一颗互爱的心,
你总来到中间,让我们离分?

让我们一天一天地叹气, 5
总愿,总愿我们的灵魂脱体;
直到生命中的生命消逝,
青春和大好年华飞驰?

但是你总还是忙去忙来,
使无爱无欢的誓约不能解开, 10
使心灵得不到欢乐,
使温存的和粗暴的一同过活。

命运呵,请听从我一次祈祷,
将来我不再使你操劳;
对其他一切幸福我都罢休, 15
只要你使亲爱的阿曼达为我所有。

李霁野 译

编注 詹姆斯·汤姆森(James Thomson,1700—1748),十八世纪苏格兰诗歌新潮流的代表,主要作品有《四季》(由《春》《夏》《秋》《冬》四首诗构成)、《自由》和《惰巫堡》等。他也喜欢描写乡村景象和农民的生活。

137. 'THE MERCHANT, TO SECURE HIS TREASURE'

The merchant, to secure his treasure,
    Conveys it in a borrow'd name①:
Euphelia serves to grace my measure,
    But Cloe is my real flame.

My softest verse, my darling lyre
    Upon Euphelia's toilet lay②—
When Cloe noted her desire③
    That I should sing, that I should play.

My lyre I tune, my voice I raise,
    But with my numbers mix my sighs;
And whilst I sing Euphelia's praise,
    I fix my soul on Cloe's eyes.

Fair Cloe blush'd: Euphelia frown'd:
    I sung, and gazed; I play'd, and trembled:
And Venus to the Loves around
    Remark'd how ill we all dissembled.

                          M. PRIOR.

---

① *a borrow'd name*: under a label which misdescribes either the goods or the sender. By sending valuable articles as being of little value he would think to run less risk of having them stolen; by representing the goods as belonging to some neutral he would hope to save them from being captured in war.
② *toilet*: now more commonly 'toilet-table.'
③ *noted*: 'expressed.'

137. "为了万无一失"

普赖尔

为了万无一失,商人故弄玄虚,
　　让他珍宝上的标记名不副实:
尤菲丽娅确实于我相宜,
　　但克洛娅才真正令我倾心。

尤菲丽娅的梳妆台上
　　放着我可爱的七弦琴和柔美的诗文,
可只要克洛娅向我示意
　　我就将为她歌唱,为她弹琴。

我调整琴弦,提高嗓门,
　　但旋律中混杂着叹息的声音;
当我把尤菲丽娅赞美,
　　克洛娅的秋波却勾住我的灵魂。

克洛娅满面羞红;尤菲丽娅紧锁眉心:
　　我唱歌,我凝视;我弹琴,我颤栗:
而与恋中人同在的维纳斯
　　注意到我们如何把邪念掩饰。

文楚安　译

编注 马修·普赖尔(Matthew Prior, 1664—1721),英国诗人,擅长写短诗。这首短诗以幽默的笔调讽刺了虚伪的爱情。

138. 'WHEN LOVELY WOMAN STOOPS TO FOLLY'

When lovely woman stoops to folly
    And finds too late that men betray, —
What charm can soothe her melancholy,
    What art can wash her guilt away?

The only art her guilt to cover,
    To hide her shame from every eye,
To give repentance to her lover
    And wring his bosom, is — to die.

O. GOLDSMITH.

138. "可爱的女子甘愿作蠢事"

哥尔德斯密斯

可爱的女子甘愿作蠢事,
　发觉受了骗,已经太晚,——
什么妙方能缓解愁思,
　什么良策能洗去罪愆?

若是要遮盖她的罪名,
　让她的羞耻避开众人,
使她的情人悔恨,痛心,
　只有一个方法——去自尽。

屠岸　译

编注　奥利弗·哥尔德斯密斯(Oliver Goldsmith,1728?—1774),英国诗人、剧作家、小说家,主要作品有小说《威克菲尔德的牧师》(*The Vicar of Wakefield*)、喜剧《委曲求全》(*She Stoops to Conquer*)和诗作《荒村》(*The Deserfed Village*)、《报复》等。

139. 'YE FLOWERY BANKS O' BONNIE DOON'

Ye flowery banks o' bonnie Doon[1],
    How can ye bloom sae fair!
How can ye chant, ye little birds,
    And I sae fu' o' care!

Thou'll break my heart, thou bonnie bird
    That sings upon the bough;
Thou minds me o' the happy days
    When my fause Luve was true.

Thou'll break my heart, thou bonnie bird
    That sings beside thy mate;
For sae I sat, and sae I sang,
    And wist na o' my fate.

Aft hae I roved by bonnie Doon
    To see the woodbine twine;
And ilka bird sang o' its love,
    And sae did I o' mine.

Wi' lightsome heart I pu'd a rose,
    Frae aff its thorny tree;
And my fause luver staw the rose[2],
    But left the thorn wi' me.

R. BURNS.

---

[1] *Doon*: a river in Ayrshire, running into the Firth of Clyde.
[2] *staw*: 'stole.'

139. "可爱的杜河两岸鲜花开"

彭斯

可爱的杜河两岸鲜花开,
 怎开得那么美丽?
小鸟啊,你们怎么能歌唱,
 而我是满怀的忧虑。

可爱的小鸟在枝头歌唱,   5
 你真是叫我心碎;
你叫我想起快活的往日,
 当假情还是真爱。

小鸟在伴侣之旁歌唱,
 你真是叫我伤心;   10
我曾经那样坐着歌唱,
 不知自己的命运。

为了看忍冬的盘绕,我常在
 美丽的杜河边游荡;
鸟儿都唱着自己的爱情,   15
 我也为爱情歌唱。

轻快地我从多刺的树上,
 摘下一朵玫瑰;
但我那假情人留下了刺,
 却偷走了玫瑰。   20

袁可嘉　译

140. THE PROGRESS OF POESY

A Pindaric Ode

    Awake, Aeolian lyre, awake,
    And give to rapture all thy trembling strings.
    From Helicon's harmonious springs
        A thousand rills their mazy progress take:
5   The laughing flowers that round them blow
    Drink life and fragrance as they flow.
    Now the rich stream of Music winds along
    Deep, majestic, smooth, and strong,
    Through verdant vales and Ceres' golden reign[1];
10   Now rolling down the steep amain,
    Headlong, impetuous, see it pour:
    The rocks and nodding groves rebellow to the roar.

        O Sovereign of the willing soul,
    Parent of sweet and solemn-breathing airs,
15   Enchanting shell! the sullen Cares[2]
        And frantic Passions hear thy soft control.
    On Thracia's hills the Lord of War
    Has curb'd the fury of his car
    And dropt his thirsty lance at thy command.
20   Perching on the sceptred hand[3]

---

[1] *Ceres' golden reign*: 'the ripe cornfields.' Ceres was the goddess of corn.

[2] *Enchanting shell*: see note on No. 63, l. 17. The lyre is called the 'Sovereign of the willing soul,' as having supreme power over those who lend themselves to its influence.

[3] *Perching*: this refers to 'the feather'd king.'

140. 诗的进程
（品达体）

格雷

醒来吧,诗圣们的弦琴,醒来①,
让你震颤的琴弦激荡欢乐的情怀!
从赫利孔山谐响淙淙的灵泉发源②,
  千百条溪流萦回宛转。
欢笑的花卉在溪边竞放,   5
从流泉汲取生命和芬芳。
"音乐"的不竭之泉盘曲流行,
深湛、庄严、顺畅、强劲。
通过翠谷和金黄玉米地,
突然泻落高峻的陡壁。   10
看那直下的飞流,发着吼声,
使岩石丛林都回荡着轰鸣。

啊,谛听的灵魂的至上权威,
你孕育美妙庄严的歌曲;
迷人的琴啊!阴沉的忧虑,   15
  狂热的激情,都听你的柔和驾驭。
思雷舍山的战神,服从你的意旨③,
遏制住发狂的战车的奔驰;
他嗜血的长矛也因此委地。
旋律的魅力控住了羽翼之王④,   20

---

① 诗圣们,指古希腊早期的抒情诗人。——译者
② 赫利孔山是文艺九女神缪斯居住的地方。——译者
③ 指希腊神话中的战神阿瑞斯(Ares),其庙宇在希腊境内的思雷舍山上。——编注者
④ 羽翼之王指主神朱庇特(Jupiter)的神鹰。——译者

  Of Jove, thy magic lulls the feather'd king
  With ruffled plumes, and flagging wing:
  Quench'd in dark clouds of slumber lie
  The terror of his beak, and lightnings of his eye.

25 Thee the voice, the dance, obey
  Temper'd to thy warbled lay①.
   O'er Idalia's velvet green
   The rosy-crownéd Loves are seen
  On Cytherea's day,
30   With antic Sports, and blue-eyed Pleasures②,
   Frisking light in frolic measures;
  Now pursuing, now retreating,
   Now in circling troops they meet:
  To brisk notes in cadence beating
35   Glance their many-twinkling feet③.
  Slow melting strains their Queen's approach declare:
   Where'er she turns the Graces homage pay:
  With arms sublime that float upon the air
  In gliding state she wins her easy way:
40 O'er her warm cheek and rising bosom move
  The bloom of young Desire and purple light of Love.

  Man's feeble race what ills await!
  Labour, and Penury, the racks of Pain④,
  Disease, and Sorrow's weeping train,
45   And Death, sad refuge from the storms of Fate!

---

① *Temper'd*: cf. above, note on No. 66, l. 33.
② *antic*: 'uncouth,' 'grotesque.' It is the same word as 'antique.'
③ *many-twinkling*: 'quickly tripping.'
④ *racks*: 'tortures.'

歇息在朱庇特执掌神笏的手上，
他羽毛松乱，垂下翅膀；
在黑沉沉的睡云的裹绕中，
把恐怖的尖喙和眼睛的电火收藏。

歌咏与舞蹈以你为基准， 25
宛转与婆娑全依你的抑扬妙韵。
 在爱达利亚的如茵碧草上①，
 戴着玫瑰花冠的爱侣来来往往，
呈现维纳斯节的空前盛况
 古怪的"娱乐"，蓝眼的"欢喜"②， 30
 踏着谐谑的节奏轻快地嬉戏；
时而追赶，时而后退，
 或以回环的队形相会；
合着活泼的旋律，
 快速的碎步好像清风拂水。 35
袅袅歌声宣布美中之后的莅临③：
 她每一顾盼都流露端庄优雅的情性，
玉臂仿佛乘风飘举，
 姗姗行进中最是袅娜娉婷。
她的温暖面颊和丰满胸脯正显现， 40
青春的希望之花和爱的红紫光焰。

 喑弱之民何等多灾多祸！
辛劳、贫困、痛苦的折磨；
疾病迁延，悲愁的涕泪涟涟，
 最后死亡凄惨地结束命运风暴的摧残！ 45

---

① 爱达利亚是女神维纳斯的圣地。——译者
② 诗人常喜欢把表达感情的抽象词语作拟人化的描述。——译者
③ 这一节指以表达崇高的古典美为主题的古希腊抒情诗的兴盛。——译者

>   The fond complaint, my song, disprove①,
>   And justify the laws of Jove.
>   Say, has he given in vain the heavenly Muse?
>   Night, and all her sickly dews,
> 50 Her spectres wan, and birds of boding cry②
>   He gives to range the dreary sky:
>   Till down the eastern cliffs afar
>   Hyperion's march they spy, and glittering shafts of war③.
>
>   In climes beyond the solar road,
> 55   Where shaggy forms o'er ice-built mountains roam,
>   The Muse has broke the twilight gloom
>   To cheer the shivering native's dull abode.
>   And oft, beneath the odorous shade
>   Of Chili's boundless forests laid,
> 60   She deigns to hear the savage youth repeat④
>   In loose numbers wildly sweet
>   Their feather-cinctured chiefs, and dusky loves.
>   Her track, where'er the Goddess roves,
>   Glory pursue, and generous Shame,
> 65   Th' unconquerable Mind, and Freedom's holy flame.
>
>   Woods, that wave o'er Delphi's steep⑤,

---

① *fond*: 'foolish.'
② *Night*, etc.: these two lines are the indirect objects of 'He gives,' 'He gives to Night, etc. [power or leave] to range.'
③ *Hyperion's march*: 'Sunrise.' The Titan Hyperion was the father of Helios (the Sun) who is often called by the name of his father.
④ *repeat*: 'tell of.'
⑤ *Delphi*: a town at the foot of Mount Parnassus in Greece, six miles north of the Gulf of Corinth. Here was the famous oracle of Apollo, the god of divination and also of poetry.

但我的诗不要无谓的哀诉,
只要证明上苍的必然规律①;
不然他岂不白白把神圣的缪斯造就?
黑夜和它的凋伤百草的凝露,
惨淡的阴魂,不祥之鸟的啼呼,   50
这些他也任其占据阴郁的天宇;
直到它们从东边远远的高崖下方,
窥见初升旭日的缕缕闪光。

 就在远离太阳之路的极区,
那里有蓬头乱鬓的人影在冰峰徘徊,   55
缪斯冲破晨昏的阴霾,
 把欢乐带进瑟缩着的土民的幽居②。
她也常寝卧在智利无边的密林,
在那散发着芬芳的浓荫,
倾听那些粗犷的年轻人,   60
用狂放不羁的动人音韵,反复歌咏
他们系着羽毛的首领和幽昧的爱情。
凡是女神漫游的地方,她都探索不停,
容易蒙受的耻辱,不朽的荣名,
自由的神圣火焰,不可征服的心灵。   65

阿波罗神殿山上起伏的层层林木③,

---

① 以下六行,诗人用日出作比喻:正如日出结束了黑夜,诗歌也会使悲惨的生活结束。——编注者
② 指北欧的极区,那里一年有六个月不见太阳。作者意即:这些偏远的地域也有激起人们欢乐的诗歌,可能是指北欧的神话传说和史诗。——译者
③ 诗人在这一节中回溯了诗歌从希腊,中经意大利,发展到英国的进程。——编注者

>   Isles, that crown th' Aegean deep,
>   Fields that cool Ilissus laves,
>   Or where Maeander's amber waves
> 70   In lingering lab'rinths creep,
>   How do your tuneful echoes languish,
>   Mute, but to the voice of anguish!
>   Where each old poetic mountain
>   Inspiration breath'd around;
> 75   Every shade and hallow'd fountain
>   Murmur'd deep a solemn sound:
>   Till the sad Nine, in Greece's evil hour,
>   Left their Parnassus for the Latian plains.
>   Alike they scorn the pomp of tyrant Power,
> 80   And coward Vice, that revels in her chains.
>   When Latium had her lofty spirit lost,
>   They sought, O Albion, next thy sea-encircled coast.
>
>   Far from the sun and summer-gale
>   In thy green lap was Nature's Darling laid,
> 85   What time, where lucid Avon stray'd,

爱琴海上皇冠似的岛屿①，
　　凉爽的伊利萨斯河流经的田野②，
　　或者琥珀色的梅安达江水③，
百折千回地绕过的城池村舍，　　　　　　　　　　　70
　　啊，你们回响四方的歌声已哑然消歇，
　　现在只有痛苦的呻吟和呜咽④！
原来骚人墨客徜徉的名山，
　　曾经怎样触发他们的灵感；
每一处林荫胜地和名泉，　　　　　　　　　　　　75
　　有怎样崇高的吟哦，雄浑而深湛！
直至希腊的凄苦岁月，悲哀的缪斯
　　告别帕那萨斯山，移向拉丁平原⑤。
她们蔑视暴君的穷极奢侈，
　　也鄙弃懦夫的败行：拖着锁链寻欢⑥。　　　　80
一旦拉丁文化的崇高精神也消失，
她们便奔向啊，英格兰，你的波涛环抱的海岸。

　　于是远离地中海风日流丽之地，
在绿色怀抱中诞生了自然的骄子⑦，
　　那里有清沥的埃文河盘绕逶迤。　　　　　　　85

---

① 此处是古希腊著名抒情诗人萨福和阿尔修斯的诞生地。——译者
② 伊利萨斯河流过雅典城外。——译者
③ 梅安达江是荷马史诗中绕特洛伊城蜿蜒的一条江。——译者
④ 希腊于十五世纪为土耳其人征服，此后经历了漫长的异族统治压迫。——译者
⑤ 帕那萨斯山是文艺女神原来居住的地方，作者在这里是指诗神从希腊徙向罗马。——译者
⑥ 希腊于公元前一四七年为罗马所征服。公元前三世纪罗马便开始汲取希腊的思想、语言和艺术，这种汲取直至基督纪元一直有增无已。拉丁文学的黄金时代是随着奥古斯都于公元一四年的死亡而开始走向终结的。从此罗马开始了专制的暴政，而希腊部分国民中也逐渐产生一种不思反抗的怯懦精神。——译者
⑦ 指莎士比亚。——译者

    To him the mighty Mother did unveil
    Her awful face: the dauntless Child
    Stretch'd forth his little arms, and smiled.
    This pencil take(she said), whose colours clear
90   Richly paint the vernal year①:
    Thine, too, these golden keys, immortal Boy!
    This can unlock the gates of Joy;
    Of Horror that, and thrilling Fears,
    Or ope the sacred source of sympathetic Tears.

95   Nor second He, that rode sublime
    Upon the seraph-wings of Ecstasy,
    The secrets of the Abyss to spy:
     He pass'd the flaming bounds of Place and Time:
    The living Throne, the sapphire-blaze,
100   Where Angels tremble while they gaze,
    He saw; but blasted with excess of light,
    Closed his eyes in endless night.
    Behold where Dryden's less presumptuous car
    Wide o'er the fields of Glory bear
105   Two coursers of ethereal race
    With necks in thunder clothed, and long-resounding pace.

    Hark, his hands the lyre explore!
    Bright-eyed Fancy, hovering o'er,
     Scatters from her pictur'd urn
110   Thoughts that breathe, and words that burn.
    But ah! 'tis heard no more ——

---

  ① *the vernal year*: 'the springtime of the year.'

当强有力的"母亲"向他展示
不加铅黛的脸庞时,这无畏的孩子
微笑着伸出他小小的双臂。
她说:拿去吧,这支生花彩笔,
富丽地绘出春日的旖旎; 90
这些金色钥匙也属于你,永生的孩儿!
这把用来把欢乐之门打开;
那把管令人悚然的惨祸和恐惧,
或者将同情的神圣泪泉引来。
  还有一位不让他人的诗国骄子①, 95
他乘着兴会淋漓的天使的羽翼
去窥探渊薮的隐秘,
  超越"时间"和"空间"火焰升腾的界限;
看见气象万千的王座和宝石般蓝焰,
那里天使群一边颤栗,一边凝望。 100
但为极度的光芒所伤,他从此失明②,
在不尽长夜中闭上眼睛。
请看德莱顿车骑的雍容,
两匹骏马真是天厩龙种③;
驰驱在广袤的光荣之野, 105
鬃毛闪着雷电,蹄声响入长风。

听,他的手正发挥弦琴的妙用!
目光炯炯的"想象",高高翱翔,
  从她装饰着图案的诗瓮,
  倾泻出燃烧的诗句,充满活力的思想。 110
但,咳!这些已经沉寂无闻④——

---

① 指弥尔顿。——译者
② 拟喻弥尔顿因极度劳累而失明(参见卷二第71首《哀失明》)。——译者
③ 意指德莱顿用英雄双行体写诗。——编注者
④ 德莱顿死于一七〇〇年。——编注者

                    O! Lyre divine, what daring Spirit①
                    Wakes thee now? Tho' he inherit
                    Nor the pride, nor ample pinion,
115   That the Theban Eagle bear,
                    Sailing with supreme dominion
                        Thro' the azure deep of air:
                    Yet oft before his infant eyes would run
                        Such forms as glitter in the Muse's ray
120   With orient hues, unborrow'd of the sun②:
                    Yet shall he mount, and keep his distant way
                    Beyond the limits of a vulgar fate:
                    Beneath the Good how far — but far above the Great.

                                                    T. GRAY.

---

① *what daring Spirit*: *i.e.* 'how presumptuous am I to dare to follow such great names!'

② *orient*: see above, note on No. 16, l. 31. *unborrow'd of the sun*: the hues flashed from the poet's inspiration, they were not material but mental.

啊,神圣的琴,什么自告奋勇的精神,
今天又把你唤醒?他虽没有继承①
品达的才情,像这只底比斯山鹰②,
  宽宽健翮,凛凛雄姿,
  自去自来,不受约束,
飞翔在蓝天高处;
但在他孩提的眼前常常呈现,
  缪斯的光辉所照耀的纷纷妙象,
带着东方色彩,又非借自太阳。
  他将攀登向上,远远离开
卑琐庸俗的市侩氛围,
即使未入佳境——却高出"伟大"的名位。

谢耀文 译

编注 《诗的进程》同本卷第 123 首《行吟诗人》,是格雷同一时期所作的两首品达体颂歌。《诗的进程》把诗歌与溪流相比,时而庄严平缓,时而狂放奔腾,追溯了诗歌从希腊到英国的发展变化,歌颂莎士比亚、弥尔顿、德莱顿等伟大诗人。

---

① "他"指诗人自己。——译者
② 品达(参见本卷第 123 首注)曾把自己比喻为"宙斯的神鹰"。——编注者

141. THE PASSIONS

An Ode for Music

When Music, heavenly maid, was young,
While yet in early Greece she sung,
The Passions oft, to hear her shell,
Throng'd around her magic cell
Exulting, trembling, raging, fainting,
Possest beyond the Muse's painting;
By turns they felt the glowing mind
Disturb'd, delighted, rais'd, refin'd;
Till once, 'tis said, when all were fir'd,
Fill'd with fury, rapt, inspir'd,
From the supporting myrtles round
They snatch'd her instruments of sound,
And, as they oft had heard apart
Sweet lessons of her forceful art,
Each, for Madness ruled the hour,
Would prove his own expressive power.

First Fear his hand, its skill to try,
   Amid the chords bewilder'd laid,
And back recoil'd, he knew not why,
   E'en at the sound himself had made.

141. 激情
（音乐颂）

柯林斯

远在古希腊时期,"音乐"仙女
正值妙龄,弹唱一曲曲妙乐;
为聆听她的里拉琴音,"激情"①
常常向她神奇的琴室涌进,
他们欢欣而激动,颤栗而眩晕, 5
入迷到"缪斯"也难加以形容;
各种"激情"感到那炽热的心
既不安又高兴,在升华,变精纯;
直到喜怒哀乐在胸中一下充盈,
着魔般地狂烈而富有灵性。 10
据说"激情"当即从爱神木架②
把"音乐"仙女的乐器取下;
　"疯狂"既然暂时左右了一切,
　"激情"都想证实自己的才学:
因为每一种"激情"多次聆听过 15
仙女高超技艺所弹奏的妙乐。

"恐惧"想头一个显露才情,
　却在拨弄琴弦时惶惑不安;
一听到自己奏出的乐音
　就不知怎的不敢往下弹。 20

---

① 里拉,古希腊的一种七弦竖琴。——译者
② 爱神木架指悬挂"音乐"仙女乐器的桃金娘树。——译者

Next Anger rush'd, his eyes on fire,
    In lightnings own'd his secret stings[①];
In one rude clash he struck the lyre
    And swept with hurried hand the strings.

25 With woeful measures wan Despair,
    Low sullen sounds, his grief beguiled,
A solemn, strange, and mingled air,
    'Twas sad by fits, by starts 'twas wild.

But thou, O Hope, with eyes so fair,
30   What was thy delightful measure?
Still it whisper'd promised pleasure
    And bade the lovely scenes at distance hail!
Still would her touch the strain prolong;
    And from the rocks, the woods, the vale,
35 She call'd on Echo still through all the song;
    And, where her sweetest theme she chose,
    A soft responsive voice was heard at every close;
And Hope enchanted smiled, and waved her golden hair.

And longer had she sung, — but with a frown
40   Revenge impatient rose:
He threw his blood-stain'd sword in thunder down;
    And with a withering look
    The war-denouncing trumpet took[②],
And blew a blast so loud and dread,

---

① *In lightnings own'd his secret stings*: i.e. betrayed by the lightning which flashed from him the rage that was consuming him within.
② *war-denouncing*: 'war-proclaiming.'

接着"愤怒"眼冒火光冲上前,
　　电闪般地泄露了隐秘的创伤;
他的手指急骤地拨弄琴弦,
　　使里拉发出一阵阵嘈响。

为排遣悲痛,"失望"的乐声　　　　　　　　　　25
　　低沉而抑郁,节奏哀婉凄凉,
这是一曲庄严而奇特的集锦,
　　一时粗犷,一时显得悲伤。

啊你,生就一双明眸的"希望",
　　你愉悦的旋律是什么?　　　　　　　　　　30
它低低倾吐可指望的欢乐,
　　要我们迎接那美妙的远景!
她总想更久些拨弄这调子;
　　她总想让"回音"将她的歌声
在树林、溪谷、巉岩间响彻;　　　　　　　　　35
　　她想她所唱的动听的曲子,
　　总听得见柔音在结尾时低回;
"希望"飘动着金发,笑得使人心醉。

她还想往下歌唱——然而"复仇"
　　皱着眉头忿然起身,　　　　　　　　　　　40
将带血污的剑猛然扔掉;
　　他脸上一副肃杀的神情,
拿起宣战的号角,
吹出一阵十分响亮、可怕的号音,

45　　　　Were ne'er prophetic sounds so full of woe.
　　　　　　　And ever and anon he beat
　　　　　　　The doubling drum with furious heat①;
　　　　And, though sometimes, each dreary pause between,
　　　　　　　Dejected Pity at his side
50　　　　　　Her soul-subduing voice applied,
　　　　　　Yet still he kept his wild unalter'd mien,
　　　　While each strain'd ball of sight seem'd bursting from his head.

　　　　Thy numbers, Jealousy, to nought were fix'd②;
　　　　　　Sad proof of thy distressful state!
55　　　　Of differing themes the veering song was mix'd;
　　　　　　And now it courted Love, now raving call'd on Hate.

　　　　With eyes up-rais'd, as one inspir'd,
　　　　Pale Melancholy sat retir'd;
　　　　And from her wild sequester'd seat,
60　　　　In notes by distance made more sweet,
　　　　Pour'd through the mellow horn her pensive soul;
　　　　　　And dashing soft from rocks around
　　　　　　Bubbling runnels join'd the sound③;
　　　　Through glades and glooms the mingled measure stole,
65　　　　　Or, o'er some haunted stream, with fond delay,
　　　　　　Round an holy calm diffusing,

---

① *The doubling drum*: 'echoing.'
② *Thy numbers ... to nought were fix'd*: 'thy song was not constant to one theme.'
③ *runnels*: 'streams.'

那调子孕含着深深的伤痛。 45
　　他时时敲击着回音鼓,
　　鼓声咚咚充满狂怒;
虽然他身旁面容沮丧的"怜悯"
　　在每一阴郁沉闷的间隙
　　　插入她灵魂压抑的嗓音, 50
　　但他无动于衷,神色一样暴戾,
眼眦到眼眶都快要迸裂。

"嫉妒"啊,你的旋律一点不固定:
　　表明你痛苦的处境可怜!
你多变的曲子包含的主题各异; 55
　　时而求"爱情"垂青,时而疯狂地召唤"仇恨"。

呆在荒芜一隅的"忧郁"与世隔绝,
她仰望上天,受到神灵的启迪;
她吹起音色圆润的号角,
将胸中萦绕的情素倾倒; 60
号角声传自远方显得更动听:
　　涧水自岩缝汩汩流泻,
　　　潺潺声与号角声融为一体;
悄悄穿过浓荫和开阔地上空,
　　交融的旋律轻轻飘越小溪, 65
　　　在神圣的静谧中散布

  Love of peace and lonely musing①,
  In hollow murmurs died away.

  But O! how alter'd was its sprightlier tone,
70 When Cheerfulness, a nymph of healthiest hue,
   Her bow across her shoulder flung,
   Her buskins gemm'd with morning dew②,
  Blew an inspiring air, that dale and thicket rung③,
  The hunter's call to Faun and Dryad known④!
75 The oak-crown'd Sisters and their chaste-eyed Queen⑤,
   Satyrs and Sylvan Boys, were seen⑥
  Peeping from forth their alleys green:
  Brown Exercise rejoic'd to hear⑦;
  And Sport leap'd up, and seiz'd his beechen spear.

80 Last came Joy's ecstatic trial⑧:
  He, with viny crown advancing,
   First to the lively pipe his hand addrest⑨;

---

① *Love of peace and lonely musing* : (sc. of lonely musing) these words, together with 'an holy calm,' are the object of 'diffusing,' which qualifies 'measure.'
② *buskins*: 'high boots.' For another use cf. note on No. 112, l. 132.
③ *that*: 'so that.'
④ *Faun*: a rural deity, with the horns and feet of a goat. *Dryad*: a wood nymph.
⑤ *The oak-crown'd Sisters*, etc.: the oak was sacred to Jupiter, rather than to Diana, whose special tree — though not in her aspect as huntress — was the laurel. She is termed 'chaste-eyed' as being ever a virgin; the 'Sisters' are her attendant nymphs.
⑥ *Satyrs*: woodland gods, companions of Bacchus.
⑦ *Brown*: 'tanned by the sun.'
⑧ *ecstatic trial*: 'rapturous efforts,' sc. to make music.
⑨ *addrest*: 'directed.'

  对和平和孤独沉思的情愫,
 低吟着缓缓地悠然远逝。

当无比健美的"快活"仙女
靴上沾着晨露的珍珠,   70
 肩上挎着出猎的弓弩,
 吹起了响彻林壑的动人乐曲,
那农神树仙所熟悉的猎笛声:
 啊!音调是那么生气蓬勃!
贞洁的月神和侍候她的女仙(她们头戴栎树叶冠), 75
 以及林神和"林孩子"
从绿荫往外窥视:
皮肤晒黑的"运动"高兴地倾听,
 "体育"抓住山毛榉矛枪一跃而起。

"快乐"最后做了热情的努力: 80
他头戴藤冠移步向前,
 先想取下脆音的风笛;

  But soon he saw the brisk awak'ning viol①,
   Whose sweet entrancing voice he lov'd the best:
  They would have thought who heard the strain
    They saw, in Tempe's vale, her native maids②
   Amidst the festal-sounding shades
  To some unwearied minstrel dancing;
  While, as his flying fingers kiss'd the strings,
   Love fram'd with Mirth a gay fantastic round③:
   Loose were her tresses seen, her zone unbound;
  And he, amidst his frolic play,
  As if he would the charming air repay,
Shook thousand odours from his dewy wings.

  O Music! sphere-descended maid,
  Friend of Pleasure, Wisdom's aid!
  Why, goddess, why, to us denied,
  Lay'st thou thy ancient lyre aside?
  As in that lov'd Athenian bower
  You learn'd an all-commanding power,
  Thy mimic soul, O nymph endear'd,
  Can well recall what then it heard.
  Where is thy native simple heart
  Devote to Virtue, Fancy, Art?
  Arise, as in that elder time,
  Warm, energic, chaste, sublime!
  Thy wonders in that god-like age
  Fill thy recording Sister's page; —

---

① *viol*: a generic term for all stringed instruments played with a bow.
② *her*: sc. the vale's.
③ *Mirth* is here female, as in No. 112, l. 13.

但马上看见使他动心的弦琴,
　　那甜美的琴音使他心醉:
听见其旋律的人还以为 　　　　　　　　　　85
　　　　他们目睹了泰卑谷的仙女①
　　　　在喜气洋溢的树荫里
为不知疲倦的行吟诗人跳舞。
他的指头飞快地拨弄琴弦,
　　"爱情"与"欢笑"跳起幻想的圆舞; 　　　　90
　　"欢笑"没系腰带,散着发辫;
他一面弹着快活的乐曲,
　　一面从带露的双翼将馥郁的香气抖落,
似乎以此来报答迷人的氛围。

啊音乐,你天上下凡的仙女! 　　　　　　　　95
　　"欢乐"的知交,"智慧"的助手!
仙女啊,为什么将我们拒绝,
丢开你的古里拉琴不理?
你在雅典可爱的树荫底下,
培养了征服一切的才华, 　　　　　　　　　100
仙女啊,你善于模仿的灵魂,
能将当时听到的一切记在心。
你献身给"善行"、"幻想"和"艺术",
如今这颗纯真的心在何处?
起来呀,一如在那远古时期, 　　　　　　　105
那样温馨、高洁、庄严、有活力!
你在那神圣年代创造的奇迹,
有你的史仙姐姐记录在典籍②。

---

① 泰卑谷,皮尼乌斯河流经古希腊西塞里的地区,叫泰卑谷,即泰卑流域,风景秀丽,为古代诗人所歌颂。后引申为任何风景绝美的地方。——译者
② "史仙姐姐"指司历史的缪斯克利娥(Clio)。——编注者

'Tis said, and I believe the tale,
Thy humblest reed could more prevail,
Had more of strength, diviner rage,
Than all which charms this laggard age,
E'en all at once together found,
Cecilia's mingled world of sound: —
O bid our vain endeavours cease;
Revive the just designs of Greece:
Return in all thy simple state!
Confirm the tales her sons relate!

W. COLLINS.

人们相信，我也不疑这样的传说：
　　你手中最寒伦的芦笛也更优越，　　　　　　　　　*110*
　　有更强的力，表达的忿怒更圣洁，
　　超过使这个慵懒时代着迷的一切，
　　齐声合鸣时的庞大旋律，
　　甚至超过塞西利亚的音乐世界①：
　　啊，停止我们追名逐利的努力；　　　　　　　　　*115*
　　再现古希腊人心目中的格局：
　　让你全部的朴素真诚复苏！
　　来证实她的子孙所述不谬②！

　　　　　　　　　　　　　　　　　陈兆林　译

---

① 塞西莉亚(Cecilia)，罗马的音乐守护神，公元二三〇年殉难。参见第二卷第 63 首注——译者
② 她的子孙所述，意为以你所创造的奇迹来证明关于建造底比斯城的古老传说是确实的。根据这一古希腊传说，底比斯国王安菲翁从众神的信使、发明里拉琴的赫耳墨斯手中得到了那把琴，他用琴的魔力筑成底比斯城。——译者

142. ODE ON THE SPRING

    Lo! where the rosy-bosom'd Hours,
        Fair Venus' train, appear,
    Disclose the long-expecting flowers
        And wake the purple year!
5   The Attic warbler pours her throat[1]
    Responsive to the cuckoo's note,
    The untaught harmony of Spring:
        While, whispering pleasure as they fly,
        Cool Zephyrs through the clear blue sky
10   Their gather'd fragrance fling.

    Where'er the oak's thick branches stretch
        A broader, browner shade,
    Where'er the rude and moss-grown beech
        O'er-canopies the glade,
15   Beside some water's rushy brink
    With me the Muse shall sit, and think
    (At ease reclined in rustic state)
        How vain the ardour of the Crowd,
        How low, how little are the Proud,
20   How indigent the Great!

    Still is the toiling hand of Care;

---

[1] *The Attic warbler:* 'the nightingale.'

142. 春日颂情

格雷

看呀！哪里有袒胸的阿尔丝女神①，——
　　美丽的维纳斯的随从——降临
哪里的花蕾就急待绽放，
　　并唤醒了这玫瑰色的青春！
小夜莺倾吐着她的歌声，　　　　　　　　　　　5
回答杜鹃唱出的律音，
这就是春神的自然协韵：
　　凉爽的微风女郎絮语着她们的欢欣，
　　当她们飘过清彻的蓝空时，
散发出她们凝聚着的芳芬。　　　　　　　　　10

那儿有橡树的浓密枝叶
　　伸展出宽阔、棕黑的荫影，
那儿有粗壮苔生的毛榉
　　帐幕般地遮盖着空坪，
在那条急流的水边　　　　　　　　　　　　15
我和缪斯坐着度忖，
（舒坦而纯朴地依依靠靠）
　　世人的追求多么虚荣，
　　骄傲者是多么低贱、渺小，
权势者又是多么困窘！　　　　　　　　　　20

焦虑者的操劳，这时，双手变得安闲；

---

① 阿尔丝（Hours），指掌管天气、季节的女神。在雅典殿堂出现的是年轻姑娘的形象。——译者

>   The panting herds repose:
>   Yet hark, how through the peopled air
>   The busy murmur glows!
> 25 The insect youth are on the wing,
>   Eager to taste the honied spring
>   And float amid the liquid noon①:
>   Some lightly o'er the current skim,
>   Some show their gaily-gilded trim
> 30 Quick-glancing to the sun.
>
>   To Contemplation's sober eye
>   Such is the race of Man:
>   And they that creep, and they that fly,
>   Shall end where they began②.
> 35 Alike the busy and the gay
>   But flutter through life's little day,
>   In Fortune's varying colours drest:
>   Brush'd by the hand of rough Mischance,
>   Or chill'd by Age, their airy dance
> 40 They leave, in dust to rest.
>
>   Methinks I hear in accents low
>   The sportive kind reply③:
>   Poor moralist! and what art thou?
>   A solitary fly!
> 45 Thy joys no glittering female meets,
>   No hive hast thou of hoarded sweets,

---

① *the liquid noon*: 'the clear, bright air of noon.'
② *I.e.* Men are but insects, and whether they creep or fly they soon return to dust.
③ *The sportive kind*: 'the dancing insect-tribe.'

喘息的牛羊变得恬静:
但是,听啊! 通过稠密的空间,
　　繁忙的低语又在闪荡回萦!
幼小的虫儿翩翩飞翔, 25
急切去品尝这甜蜜的春。
它们在晶莹的正午浮游:
　　有的轻轻掠过水面波纹,
　　有的显示它们的光彩衣服,
在阳光下耀眼炫神。 30

对于哲士的清醒目光,
　　这就是人类的生活旅程:
它们有的爬,有的飞,
　　却都要归宿到当初的途径。
忙碌与快乐的人们哟! 35
无非是烦扰度过短促的一生,
时而穿上幸福之神的各色衣服:
　　时而会被不幸的命运碰损,
　　或因衰老变得僵硬,
抛却了他们快活的舞蹈,走进坟茔。 40

我想,我听见了一种低沉的声音,
　　乐天派在答应:
可怜的说教者呀! 你是什么?
　　只不过像一只孤独的飞蝇①!
在你的欢乐中总遇不着闪光的女性, 45
你也没有贮蜜的金瓶,

---

① 格雷是一个单身汉,也是一个退隐者,这句"孤独"二字即自指。——译者

>   No painted plumage to display:
>   On hasty wings thy youth is flown;
>   Thy sun is set, thy spring is gone —
>   We frolic while 'tis May.

T. GRAY.

你没有绘绣过的羽毛值得夸耀:
　　你的青春就蓦然飞腾;
　　日已落,春已去——
我们欢乐趁年轻。　　　　　　　　　　　　　50

　　　　　　　　　　　　　　　黄绍鑫　译

143. THE POPLAR FIELD

The poplars are fell'd; farewell to the shade
And the whispering sound of the cool colonnade;
The winds play no longer and sing in the leaves,
Nor Ouse on his bosom their image receives.

Twelve years have elapsed since I first took a view
Of my favourite field, and the bank where they grew;
And now in the grass behold they are laid,
And the tree is my seat that once lent me a shade.

The blackbird has fled to another retreat,
Where the hazels afford him a screen from the heat;
And the scene where his melody charm'd me defore
Resounds with his sweet-flowing ditty no more.

My fugitive years are all hasting away,
And I must ere long lie as lowly as they,
With a turf on my breast and a stone at my head,
Ere another such grove shall arise in its stead.

'Tis a sight to engage me, if anything can,
To muse on the perishing pleasures of man;
Though his life be a dream, his enjoyments, I see,
Have a being less durable even than he.

W. COWPER.

143. 白杨林

柯珀

白杨已伐尽；簌簌的叶声，
树荫的清凉，全都不留踪影；
枝头的和风不再嬉戏啸吟，
乌思河不再映照它袅娜的身形。

光阴荏苒！记得十二年前　　　　　　　5
我首次眺望白杨葱茏的河岸：
如今一株株却委身草丛间，
遮阳的树成了我就坐的地方。

八哥飞远，去寻觅它的栖息处，
那里有榛树作帘幕抵御暑热；　　　　10
我迷恋过这儿鸟雀啁啾的景色，
如今再听不到它甜美的小曲。

我一生的岁月流逝匆匆，
我行将如白杨委身草丛，
身上覆盖草根土，墓石立头边，　　　15
直到白杨林再次成长的那天。

这幅景象使我浮想联翩：
欢娱易散；纵然人生似梦，
不过一霎那，但乐事称心
原比人生甚至更短暂。　　　　　　　20

陈兆林　译

144. TO A MOUSE

On Turning Her Up in Her Nest with the Plough, November 1785

    Wee, sleekit, cow'rin', tim'rous beastic,
    O what a panic's in thy breastie!
    Thou need na start awa sae hasty,
        Wi' bickering brattle①!
5   I wad be laith to rin an' chase thee
        Wi' murd'ring pattle②!

    I'm truly sorry man's dominion,
    Has broken nature's social union,
    An' justifies that ill opinion
10   Which makes thee startle
    At me, thy poor earth-born companion,
        An' fellow-mortal!

    I doubt na, whiles, but thou may thieve③;
    What then? poor beastie, thou maun live!
15   A daimen-icker in a thrave④
        'S a sma' request:
    I'll get a blessin' wi' the lave⑤,

---

① *bickering brattle*: 'hurrying scamper.'
② *pattle*: a small spade-like implement.
③ *whiles*: 'at times.'
④ *A daimen-icker in a thrave*: 'an occasional ear of corn in a bundle of sheaves.' Strictly a thrave or threave consists of 24 or 28 sheaves, eack measuring thirty inches round.
⑤ *the lave*: what is left.

144. 致鼹鼠

（一七八五年十一月用犁头掘起鼹鼠巢，有感而作）

彭斯

光滑、畏缩，胆怯的小东西，
啊，你心里是多么恐惧！
你不用慌慌张张逸去，
　　突然向前猛冲，
我不想拿着凶残的犁，　　　　　　　　　　5
　　跟在背后追踪。

人的统治，真叫我遗憾，
中断了自然界的交往相连，
证明了那么一种偏见，
　　使你见了我这个人——　　　　　　　10
你可怜的朋友，又同是生物，
　　便会大吃一惊！

你有时要偷窃，我毫不怀疑；
那又算什么？你得活，可怜的东西！
一把麦子上的零星儿穗，　　　　　　　　15
　　这要求并不算多；
留下来的尽够我享用呢，

And never miss't!

Thy wee bit housie, too, in ruin!
Its silly wa's the win's are strewin':
And naething, now, to big a new ane[①],
 O' foggage green[②]!
An' bleak December's winds ensuin'
 Baith snell an' keen[③]!

Thou saw the fields laid bare and waste
An' weary winter comin' fast,
An' cozie here, beneath the blast,
 Thou thought to dwell,
Till, crash! the cruel coulter past[④]
 Out thro' thy cell.

That wee bit heap o' leaves an' stibble
Has cost thee mony a weary nibble!
Now thou's turn'd out, for a' thy trouble,
 But house or hald[⑤],
To thole the winter's sleety dribble[⑥]
 An' cranreuch cauld[⑦]!

But, Mousie, thou art no thy lane[⑧]

---

① *to big*: 'to build.'
② *foggage*: 'moss.'
③ *snell*: 'biting.'
④ *coulter*: the iron blade in front of the ploughshare.
⑤ *But*: 'without.' *hald*: 'abiding-place.'
⑥ *thole*: 'endure.'
⑦ *cranreuch*: 'hoar-frost.'
⑧ *thy lane*: 'alone.'

我也不会错过!

你那小巢也成了废墟!
大风呼呼向破壁吹去,　　　　　　　　20
如今你要再筑新居,
　　也找不到青草;
惨淡的冬风又刺骨,又尖利,
　　眼看就要来到。

你看见田地荒芜而空净,　　　　　　　25
沉闷的冬天飞快来临,
你原来打算在这儿住定,
　　这避风的安乐窝——
哗啦一声!犁刀够残忍,
　　打你的巢里穿过。　　　　　　　30

那一小堆断梗残叶,
你辛苦拖来,一点一滴,
费了大劲,你终被赶出;
　　如今你无屋无房,
借以躲避冬天的雨雪　　　　　　　　35
　　和那冰冷的白霜!

但是也不止你一个,鼹鼠,

In proving foresight may be vain;
The best laid schemes o' mice an' men
    Gang aft a-gley①,
An' lea'e us nought but grief an' pain,
    For promised joy.

Still thou art blest, compared wi' me!
The present only toucheth thee;
But, och! I backward cast my e'e
    On prospects drear!
An' forward, tho' I canna see,
    I guess an' fear!

R. BURNS.

---

① *Gang aft a-gley*: 'go often awry.'

证明预见也许没用处；
最妙的策划，不管人和鼠，
  都会常常落空，   40
留下的不是预期的乐趣，
  而是愁闷苦痛！

和我相比，你还算有福气，
只是眼前影响了你：
但是噢，我眼睛回顾过去，   45
  多么惨淡的光景！
往前探望，我猜疑，我恐惧，
  虽然我还看不清！

袁可嘉 译

145. A WISH

Mine be a cot beside the hill;
    A bee-hive's hum shall soothe my ear;
A willowy brook that turns a mill,
    With many a fall shall linger near.

The swallow, oft, beneath my thatch
    Shall twitter from her clay-built nest[①];
Oft shall the pilgrim lift the latch,
    And share my meal, a welcome guest.

Around my ivied porch shall spring
    Each fragrant flower that drinks the dew;
And Lucy, at her wheel, shall sing
    In russet gown and apron blue[②].

The village-church among the trees,
    Where first our marriage-vows were given,
With merry peals shall swell the breeze
    And point with taper spire to Heaven.

S. ROGERS.

---

① *clay-built nest*: the swallow's nest is built of clay and straw.
② *russet*: 'reddish-brown.'

145. 一愿

罗杰斯

在小山旁边有小屋一座；
　　蜜蜂的嗡嗡声安慰我的耳朵；
岸上有垂柳的小溪转动水磨，
　　有许多处溪水在附近垂落。

在我的茅屋檐下，从泥巢里　　　　　　　　　　5
　　时常有燕语呢呢；
时常有香客拉开门栓，
　　受欢迎的客人，同我共进一餐。

在我的攀满藤萝的门廊下，
　　有各种各样饮露的香花；　　　　　　　　10
露晞在纺车跟前歌唱，
　　穿着蓝色围裙和褐色衣裳。

树林中农村的教堂
　　首先我们在那里宣布结婚誓言，
欢快的钟声在风里高扬，　　　　　　　　　　15
　　高高地上升指向苍天。

　　　　　　　　　　　　　李霁野　译

146. TO EVENING

If aught of oaten stop or pastoral song[1]
May hope, O pensive Eve, to soothe thine ear,
    Like thy own brawling springs,
    Thy springs, and dying gales;

O Nymph reserved, — while now the bright-hair'd sun
Sits in yon western tent, whose cloudy skirts
    With brede ethereal wove[2]
    O'erhang his wavy bed;

Now air is hush'd, save where the weak-ey'd bat[3]
With short shrill shriek flits by on leathern wing,
    Or where the beetle winds[4]
    His small but sullen horn,

As oft he rises 'midst the twilight path,
Against the pilgrim borne in heedless hum, —
    Now teach me, maid composed,
    To breathe some soften'd strain,

Whose numbers, stealing through thy dark'ning vale,
May not unseemly with its stillness suit;

---

[1] *aught of*: a Latin idiom for any.
[2] *brede*: 'embroidery.'
[3] *Now*: i.e. 'Now that', we are still in the sub-ordinate sentence.
[4] *winds*: 'blows.'

146. 薄暮散歌

柯林斯

如果响起了什么笛管和牧歌,
幽思的夜啊!愿它能娱悦你的听觉,
  像那淙淙的泉水,
   你的泉水和那春风的柔波;

啊!缄默的女神,——现在灿烂的太阳,   5
坐在西方的营帐,云裙婆娑,
  横挂在他的闪动的床帏上,
   是一片天工织成的锦罗;

此刻,太空寂静,只有瞎眼的蝙蝠
尖叫一声,展翅飞掠而过,   10
  还有那些甲虫
   吹着低细与沉闷的号角,

它们常常飞旋在黄昏道上干扰香客,
他们也并不留心这些小虫低声吟哦,——
  你泰然自若的女郎呀!请教我   15
   唱一支柔和的歌,

音响会悄悄透过幽黑的小山谷,
同它的寂静,十分调和;

                    As musing slow I hail
20   Thy genial loved return.

            For when thy folding-star arising shows
            His paly circlet, at his warning lamp
                    The fragrant Hours, and Elves
                    Who slept in buds the day,

25   And many a Nymph wreathes her brows with sedge
            And sheds the freshening dew, and lovelier still
                    The pensive Pleasures sweet,
                    Prepare thy shadowy car.

            Then let me rove some wild and heathy scene;
30   Or find some ruin midst its dreary dells,
                    Whose walls more awful nod
                    By thy religious gleams.

            Or if chill blustering winds or driving rain
            Prevent my willing feet, be mine the hut
35   That, from the mountain's side,
                    Views wilds and swelling floods,

            And hamlets brown, and dim-discover'd spires;
            And hears their simple bell; and marks o'er all[1]
40   Thy dewy fingers draw

---

[1] *o'er all* qualifies 'draw.'

我慢慢寻思，欢呼
　　你真正的爱人所得到报赏的快乐。　　　　　　　20

因为当你的羊栏星升在天边①
显露出它苍白的饰环，
　　它的警灯照耀着这芬芳的阿尔丝②，
　　照耀着白日沉睡在花苞中的小神仙，

许多女神用苇环把她们的眉梢装点，　　　　　25
吐出点点露滴，甜蜜新鲜，
　　独自沉思的快乐仙子，
　　正为你准备了荫凉的车骖。

让我在荒野的石楠丛景中漫游，
或去幽谷中寻觅那废墟遗馆，　　　　　　　　30
　　凭着你虔诚的光辉，会看见
　　那些敬畏地点头的城垣。

假如寒冷的急风骤雨
使我的步履维艰，
　　只好在山旁我的那间小屋里，　　　　　　35
　　凭览荒野与澎湃的狂澜，

也可远眺棕色的村落，隐约的塔尖；
还可谛听悠扬的钟声，细看
　　你的晶莹手指
　　徐徐拉下昏暗的帷幔。　　　　　　　　　40

---

① 羊栏星晚上出现，提醒牧羊人把羊群驱回羊栏。——译者
② 阿尔丝，指掌管天气和季节的女神。——编注者

　　　　　　The gradual dusky veil.

　　　　　While Spring shall pour his showers, as oft he wont[①],
　　　　　And bathe thy breathing tresses, meekest Eve!
　　　　　　　While Summer loves to sport
　　　　　　　Beneath thy lingering light;

45　　　　While sallow Autumn fills thy lap with leaves;
　　　　　Or Winter, yelling through the troublous air,
　　　　　　　Affrights thy shrinking train
　　　　　　　And rudely rends thy robes;

　　　　　So long, regardful of thy quiet rule,
50　　　　Shall Fancy, Friendship, Science, smiling Peace,
　　　　　　　Thy gentlest influence own,
　　　　　　　And love thy favourite name!

　　　　　　　　　　　　　　　W. COLLINS.

---

① *he wont*: see above, note to No. 38, l. 6.

春神习惯地飘洒他的阵雨,
温柔的夜啊!可以沐浴你蓬松的发卷!
　　夏女纵情地欣喜游玩
　　在你迟迟不愿离开的夕阳下面;

苍黄的秋姑把枯叶装满你的衣兜,　　　　　　　　　　45
冬神,呼啸寒风,动荡不安,
　　惊吓着枯死的万物,
　　并粗暴地撕碎了你的袍纶;

再见吧!留心你的静穆的王国,
想象、友谊、知识、微笑的和平,　　　　　　　　　　50
　　这世上的最温和的感化力都会属于你,
　　并赞美你这令人喜爱的声名!

　　　　　　　　　　　　　　黄绍鑫　译

147. ELEGY
WRITTEN IN A COUNTRY CHURCH-YARD

    The curfew tolls the knell of parting day,
        The lowing herd wind slowly o'er the lea①,
    The ploughman homeward plods his weary way,
        And leaves the world to darkness, and to me.

5   Now fades the glimmering landscape on the sight,
        And all the air a solemn stillness holds②,
    Save where the beetle wheels his droning flight,
        And drowsy tinklings lull the distant folds.

    Save that from yonder ivy-mantled tower
10   The moping owl does to the moon complain
    Of such as, wandering near her secret bower,
        Molest her ancient solitary reign③.

    Beneath those rugged elms, that yew-tree's shade,
        Where heaves the turf in many a mouldering heap,
15   Each in his narrow cell for ever laid,
        The rude Forefathers of the hamlet sleep④.

    The breezy call of incense-breathing morn,
        The swallow twittering from the straw-built shed,

---

① *lea*: 'pasture-land.'
② *all the air* is the object of 'holds.'
③ *reign*: 'realm.' Cf. 'Ceres' golden reign,' No. 140, l. 9.
④ *rude*: 'unlearned.'

147. 墓畔哀歌[①]

格雷

晚钟响起来一阵阵给白昼报丧,
　　牛群在草原上迂回,吼声起落,
耕地人累了,回家走,脚步踉跄,
　　把整个世界留给了黄昏与我。

苍茫的景色逐渐从眼前消退,　　　　　　　　　　5
　　一片肃穆的寂静盖遍了尘寰,
只听见嗡嗡的甲虫转圈子纷飞,
　　昏沉的铃声催眠着远处的羊栏。

只听见常春藤披裹的塔顶底下,
　　一只阴郁的鸱枭向月亮诉苦,　　　　　　　　10
怪人家无端走近它秘密的住家,
　　搅扰它这片悠久而僻静的领土。

峥嵘的榆树底下,扁柏的荫里,
　　草皮鼓起了许多零落的荒堆,
各自在洞窟里永远放下了身体,　　　　　　　　15
　　小村里粗鄙的父老在那里安睡。

香气四溢的晨风轻松的呼召,
　　燕子从茅草棚子里吐出的呢喃,

[①] 沿用郭沫若旧译名;原题为"哀歌,作于某乡村墓园"。原诗最初不署名,于一七五一年印成小册子发行。一般认为开始写作于一七四二年,是年格雷失去了他的挚友理查·威斯特,也有人相信作于一七四六年和一七五〇年之间。诗一发表即受读者热烈欢迎,至今仍为任何英国诗选所必收的作品。——译者

    The cock's shrill clarion, or the echoing horn,
20   No more shall rouse them from their lowly bed.

    For them no more the blazing hearth shall burn,
      Or busy housewife ply her evening care;
    No children run to lisp their sire's return[①],
      Or climb his knees the envied kiss to share.

25   Oft did the harvest to their sickle yield,
      Their furrow oft the stubborn glebe has broke[②];
    How jocund did they drive their team afield!
      How bow'd the woods beneath their sturdy stroke!

    Let not Ambition mock their useful toil,
30   Their homely joys, and destiny obscure;
    Nor Grandeur hear with a disdainful smile
      The short and simple annals of the Poor.

    The boast of heraldry, the pomp of power,
      And all that beauty, all that wealth e'er gave,
35   Awaits alike th' inevitable hour; —
      The paths of glory lead but to the grave.

    Nor you, ye Proud, impute to these the fault
      If Memory o'er their tomb no trophies raise,
    Where through the long-drawn aisle and fretted vault[③]
40   The pealing anthem swells the note of praise.

---

① *to lisp*: 'to announce in childish speech.'
② *glebe*: 'sods.'
③ *long-drawn* means no more than 'long.' *fretted vault*: 'carved roof.'

公鸡的尖喇叭,使山鸣谷应的猎号
　　再不能唤醒他们在地下的长眠①。　　　　　　　　　20

在他们,熊熊的炉火不再会燃烧,
　　忙碌的管家妇不再会赶她的夜活;
孩子们不再会"牙牙"地报父亲来到,
　　为一个亲吻爬到他膝上去争夺。

往常是:他们一开镰就所向披靡,　　　　　　　　　　25
　　顽梗的泥板让他们犁出了垄沟;
他们多么欢欣地赶牲口下地!
　　他们一猛砍,树木就一棵棵低头!

"雄心"别嘲讽他们实用的操劳,
　　家常的欢乐、默默无闻的运命;　　　　　　　　　30
"豪华"也不用带着轻蔑的冷笑
　　来听讲穷人的又短又简的生平。

门第的炫耀,有权有势的煊赫,
　　凡是美和财富所能赋予的好处,
前头都等待着不可避免的时刻:　　　　　　　　　　35
　　光荣的道路无非是引导到坟墓。

骄傲人,你也不要怪这些人不行,
　　"怀念"没有给这些坟建立纪念堂,
没有让悠长的廊道、雕花的拱顶
　　洋溢着宏亮的赞美歌,进行颂扬。　　　　　　　　40

---

① 此行按字面译是:"再不能把他们从低矮的床铺上唤醒。"一说"低铺"既指穷人家矮铺,也指坟墓。——译者

Can storied urn or animated bust①
　　Back to its mansion call the fleeting breath?
Can Honour's voice provoke the silent dust②,
　　Or Flattery soothe the dull cold ear of Death?

45　Perhaps in this neglected spot is laid
　　Some heart once pregnant with celestial fire;
Hands, that the rod of empire might have sway'd,
　　Or waked to ecstasy the living lyre:

But Knowledge to their eyes her ample page
50　　Rich with the spoils of time, did ne'er unroll;
Chill Penury repress'd their noble rage③,
　　And froze the genial current of the soul④.

Full many a gem of purest ray serene
　　The dark unfathom'd caves of ocean bear:
55　Full many a flower is born to blush unseen,
　　And waste its sweetness on the desert air.

Some village-Hampden, that with dauntless breast
　　The little tyrant of his fields withstood,
Some mute inglorious Milton here may rest,
60　　Some Cromwell, guiltless of his country's blood.

---

① *storied urn*: the urn inscribed with the history of the dead man.
② *provoke*: 'call forth.'
③ *rage*: 'fervour,' 'enthusiasm.'
④ *genial*: 'natural.'

栩栩的半身像，铭刻了事略的瓮碑，
　　难道能恢复断气，促使还魂？
"荣誉"的声音能激发沉默的死灰？
　　"谄媚"能叫死神听软了耳根？

也许这一块地方，尽管荒芜，　　　　　　　　　　45
　　就埋着曾经充满过灵焰的一颗心；
一双手，本可以执掌到帝国的王笏
　　或者出神入化地拨响了七弦琴。

可是"知识"从不曾对他们展开
　　它世代积累而琳琅满目的书卷；　　　　　　50
"贫寒"压制了他们高贵的襟怀，
　　冻结了他们从灵府涌出的流泉。

世界上多少晶莹皎洁的珠宝
　　埋在幽暗而深不可测的海底；
世界上多少花吐艳而无人知晓，　　　　　　　　55
　　把芳香白白地散发给荒凉的空气。

也许有乡村汉普敦在这里埋身，
　　反抗过当地的小霸王，胆大，坚决；
也许有缄口的弥尔顿，从没有名声。
　　有一位克伦威尔，并不曾害国家流血①。　　60

---

① 汉普敦(Hampden，1595—1647)，在国会曾为反对查理王一世的领袖，后在内战中阵亡。他和克伦威尔(1599—1658)是表亲，常在乡居接受后者的来访。弥尔顿(1608—1674)早年住过他处英格兰中部离"哀歌的墓园"斯托克·坡吉斯(Stoke Poges)不远的乡村，写过他早期几篇名诗，晚年又从伦敦退居近旁另一处，格雷实际上也只是由家乡墓园启发而写这首诗，并非专写这特定坟园；而随便提到的几位名人都和邻近地方有关，则更出于巧合。克伦威尔在十八世纪英国名声不好，文人都加以谴责。——译者

>   Th' applause of list'ning senates to command,
>   The threats of pain and ruin to despise,
>   To scatter plenty o'er a smiling land,
>   And read their history in a nation's eyes①,
>
> 65   Their lot forbad: nor circumscribed alone
>   Their growing virtues, but their crimes confined;
>   Forbad to wade through slaughter to a throne,
>   And shut the gates of mercy on mankind②,
>
>   The struggling pangs of conscious truth to hide,
> 70   To quench the blushes of ingenuous shame③,
>   Or heap the shrine of Luxury and Pride
>   With incense kindled at the Muse's flame④.
>
>   Far from the madding crowd's ignoble strife,
>   Their sober wishes never learn'd to stray;
> 75   Along the cool sequester'd vale of life
>   They kept the noiseless tenour of their way⑤.
>
>   Yet e'en these bones from insult to protect
>   Some frail memorial still erected nigh,

---

① *read their history*, etc.: 'to see throughout the country the results of their government.'
② *shut the gates of mercy*: i. e. by pronouncing excommunications and anathemas.
③ *The struggling pangs*, etc.: 'to conceal from the world the appeals which truth made to them in their own hearts, and to learn brazen effrontery in their dealings with the world.'
④ *I. e.* to prostitute their talents by fulsome adulation of the rich and powerful. See the Dedications of many eighteenth-century writers.
⑤ *tenour*: 'course.'

要博得满场的元老雷动的鼓掌,
　　无视威胁,全不管存亡生死,
把富庶、丰饶遍播到四处八方,
　　打从全国的笑眼里读自己的历史。

他们的命运可不许:既不许罪过 65
　　有所放纵,也不许发挥德行;
不许从杀戮中间涉登宝座
　　从此对人类关上仁慈的大门;

不许掩饰天良在内心的发作,
　　隐瞒天真的羞愧,恬不红脸; 70
不许用诗神的金焰点燃了香火
　　锦上添花去塞满"骄""奢"的神龛。

远离了纷纭人世的钩心斗角,
　　他们有清醒的愿望,从不学糊涂,
顺着生活的清凉僻静的山坳, 75
　　他们坚持了不声不响的正路。

可是叫这些尸骨免受到糟蹋,
　　还是有脆弱的碑牌树立在近边,

  with uncouth rhymes and shapeless sculpture deck'd.
80   Implores the passing tribute of a sigh.

  Their name, their years, spelt by th' unletter'd Muse,
    The place of fame and elegy supply:
  And many a holy text around she strews,
    That teach the rustic moralist to die.

85   For who, to dumb forgetfulness a prey,
    This pleasing anxious being e'er resign'd,
  Left the warm precincts of the cheerful day①,
    Nor cast one longing lingering look behind?

  On some fond breast the parting soul relies,
90   Some pious drops the closing eye requires;
  E'en from the tomb the voice of Nature cries,
    E'en in our ashes live their wonted fires②.

  For thee, who, mindful of th' unhonour'd dead③,
    Dost in these lines their artless tale relate;
95   If chance, by lonely contemplation led④,
    Some kindred spirit shall inquire thy fate,

  Haply some hoary-headed swain may say,
    'Oft have we seen him at the peep of dawn
  Brushing with hasty steps the dews away,

---

① *precincts*: properly 'an enclosed space.'
② The first two lines express the need felt by the dying for human care and sympathy; the second two the influence the dead exercise over the living.
③ *For thee*: 'as for thee,' i.e. the poet.
④ *chance*: used as an adverb, 'perchance.'

点缀了拙劣的韵语、凌乱的刻划,
　　请求过往人就便献一声惋叹。　　　　　　　　　　80

无文的野诗神注上了姓名、年份,
　　另外再加上地址和一篇诔词;
她在周围撒播了一些经文,
　　教训乡土道德家怎样去死。

要知道谁甘愿舍身喂哑口的"遗忘",　　　　　　　　85
　　坦然撇下了忧喜交织的此生,
谁离开风和日暖的明媚现场
　　而能不依依地回头来顾盼一阵?

辞世的灵魂还依傍钟情的怀抱,
　　临闭的眼睛需要尽哀的珠泪,　　　　　　　　　　90
即使坟冢里也有"自然"的呼号
　　他们的旧火还点燃我们的新灰①。

至于你,你关心这些陈死人,
　　用这些诗句讲他们质朴的故事,
假如在幽思的引领下,偶然有缘份,　　　　　　　　95
　　一位同道来问起你的身世——

也许会有白头的乡下人对他说,
　　"我们常常看见他,天还刚亮,
就用匆忙的脚步把露水碰落,

---

① 灰(或尘),按基督教说法,就是肉体。——译者

100   To meet the sun upon the upland lawn;

    'There at the foot of yonder nodding beech
     That wreathes its old fantastic roots so high,
    His listless length at noontide would he stretch,
     And pore upon the brook that babbles by.

105   'Hard by yon wood, now smiling as in scorn,
     Muttering his wayward fancies he would rove;
    Now drooping, woeful wan, like one forlorn,
     Or crazed with care, or cross'd in hopeless love.

    'One morn I miss'd him on the custom'd hill,
110   Along the heath, and near his favourite tree;
    Another came; nor yet beside the rill,
     Nor up the lawn, nor at the wood was he;

    'The next with dirges due in sad array
     Slow through the church-way path we saw him borne, —
115   Approach and read (for thou canst read) the lay
     Graved on the stone beneath yon aged thorn.'

THE EPITAPH

    Here rests his head upon the lap of Earth
     A Youth, to Fortune and to Fame unknown;
    Fair Science frown'd not on his humble birth[①],
120   And Melancholy mark'd him for her own.

---

① *Science*: in the general sense of knowledge. *frown'd not on*: 'did not disdain.'

上那边高处的草地去会晤朝阳;

"那边有一棵婆娑的山毛榉老树,
　　树底下隆起的老根盘错在一起,
他常常在那里懒躺过一个中午,
　　悉心看旁边一道涓涓的小溪。

"他转游到林边,有时候笑里带嘲,
　　念念有词,发他的奇谈怪议,
有时候垂头丧气,像无依无靠,
　　像忧心忡忡或者像情场失意。

"有一天早上,在他惯去的山头,
　　灌木丛、他那棵爱树下,我不见他出现;
第二天早上,尽管我走下溪流,
　　上草地,穿过树林,他还是不见。

"第三天我们见到了送葬的行列,
　　唱着挽歌,抬着他向坟场走去——
请上前看那丛老荆棘底下的碑碣,
　　(你是识字的)请念念这些诗句。"

墓铭

这里边,高枕地膝,是一位青年,
　　生平从不曾受知于"富贵"和"名声";
"知识"可没有轻视他生身的微贱,
　　"清愁"把他标出来认作宠幸。

>Large was his bounty, and his soul sincere;
>>Heaven did a recompense as largely send:
>He gave to Misery all he had, a tear,
>>He gain'd from Heaven, 'twas all he wish'd, a friend.

>125 No farther seek his merits to disclose,
>>or draw his frailties from their dread abode,
>(There they alike in trembling hope repose,)
>>The bosom of his Father and his God.

T. GRAY.

他生性真挚,最乐于慷慨施惠,
　　上苍也给了他同样慷慨的报酬:
他给了"坎坷"全部的所有,一滴泪;
　　从上苍全得了所求,一位朋友。

别再想法子表彰他的功绩,
　　也别再把他的弱点翻出了暗窖
(它们同样在颤抖的希望中休息)①,
　　那就是他的天父和上帝的怀抱。

卞之琳　译

编注　这首诗是托马斯·格雷诗作中最主要的作品,对后世影响很大。诗人在诗中表达了对农民的同情。全诗结构匀称、步伐整齐,表现出很高的艺术技巧。由于诗人在一定程度上解决了革新旧传统的问题,这首诗不但是古典主义诗歌的杰作,也是浪漫主义诗歌的先声。

---

① "颤抖的希望",是因为基督教义认为世界末日即最后审判日,届时死人都得从坟墓里起来接受审判。——译者

148. MARY MORISON

O Mary, at thy window be,
    It is the wish'd, the trysted hour[①]!
Those smiles and glances let me see
    That make the miser's treasure poor:
    How blythely wad I bide the stoure[②],
A weary slave frae sun to sun,
    Could I the rich reward secure,
The lovely Mary Morison.

Yestreen, when to the trembling string
    The dance gaed thro' the lighted ha',
To thee my fancy took its wing, —
    I sat, but neither heard nor saw:
    Tho' this was fair, and that was braw[③],
And yon the toast of a' the town,
    I sigh'd, and said amang them a'
'Ye arena Mary Morison.'

O Mary, canst thou wreck his peace
    Wha for thy sake wad gladly dee?
Or canst thou break that heart of his,
    Whase only faut is loving thee?

[①] *trysted*: 'appointed for meeting.'
[②] *bide the stoure*: 'endure the dust.'
[③] *braw*: 'handsome.'

148. 玛丽·莫里孙

彭斯

玛丽啊,请你在窗边站好,
　　这是盼望中约会的良辰,
让我瞧你的眼神和微笑,
　　它们使守财奴的珠宝失灵;
　　我甘心情愿忍受苦恼, 5
一天又一天做疲倦的奴臣,
　　只要能得到这丰厚的酬劳,
可爱的玛丽·莫里孙。

昨晚上,伴着微颤的琴弦
　　人们舞遍明亮的大厅; 10
我的心飞向你的跟前,
　　我坐着,眼不看来耳不听:
　　虽然这个俊来那个俏,
那边还有全城大美人,
　　我当着众人叹口气说道: 15
"你们可不是玛丽·莫里孙。"

玛丽啊,你岂能断送他的安宁,
　　他乐于为你而舍身?
你岂能粉碎他那颗心,
　　它错只错在对你有情? 20

If love for love thou wiltna gie,
At least be pity to me shown;
A thought ungentle canna be
The thought o' Mary Morison.

R. BURNS.

万一你不愿以爱还爱,
至少也对我有点怜悯!
玛丽·莫里孙的心意
决不会冷漠无情。

袁可嘉　译

149. BONNIE LESLEY

O saw ye bonnie Lesley
    As she gaed o'er the border?
She's gane, like Alexander,
    To spread her conquests farther.

To see her is to love her,
    And love but her for ever;
For nature made her what she is,
    And never made anither!

Thou art a queen, fair Lesley,
    Thy subjects we, before thee;
Thou art divine, fair Lesley,
    The hearts o' men adore thee.

The deil he couldna scaith thee[1],
    Or aught that wad belang thee;
He'd look into thy bonnie face,
    And say 'I canna wrang thee!'

The Powers aboon will tent thee[2];
    Misfortune sha'na steer thee[3];

---

[1] *scaith*: 'harm.'
[2] *tent*: 'protect.'
[3] *steer*: 'molest.'

149. 美丽的拉丝莱

彭斯

啊,你瞧见美丽的拉丝莱,
  当她翻越过边境?
她走了,就像亚历山大①
  去征服更多的人。

一见她你就生了爱心,
  爱她个无穷无尽;
造化使她成这个模样,
  没再造第二个这样的人。

你是皇后,美丽的拉丝莱,
  我们都是你的子民;
你是神明,美丽的拉丝莱,
  人们衷心向你致敬。

连魔鬼也不能把其欺凌,
  损害你或你的一星半丁;
他瞧瞧你那美丽的脸儿,
  说:"我可不敢欺侮您。"

天上的神明会照顾你,
  不会给你带来恶运;

---

① 亚历山大,希腊的著名国王。——译者

>   Thou'rt like themselves sae lovely,
>   That ill they'll ne'er let near thee.
>
>   Return again, fair Lesley,
>   Return to Caledonie!
>   That we may brag we hae a lass
>   There's nane again sae bonnie.
>
>   R. BURNS.

你像天使一般可爱,
　　他们不会让恶事挨近。 20

回来吧,美丽的拉丝莱,
　　快回到凯尔杜纳来①!
我们好夸嘴有一个姑娘,
　　谁也没有她那样美。

袁可嘉　译

---

① 凯尔杜纳,苏格兰之古时或诗中的别名。

150. 'O MY LUVE'S LIKE A RED, RED ROSE'

O my Luve's like a red, red rose
    That's newly sprung in June:
O my Luve's like the melodie
    That's sweetly play'd in tune.

As fair art thou, my bonnie lass,
    So deep in luve am I:
And I will luve thee still, my dear,
    Till a' the seas gang dry:

Till a' the seas gang dry, my dear,
    And the rocks melt wi' the sun;
I will luve thee still, my dear,
    While the sands o' life shall run.

And fare thee weel, my only Luve!
    And fare thee weel a while!
And I will come again, my Luve,
    Tho' it were ten thousand mile.

R. BURNS.

150. "呵,我的爱人像朵红红的玫瑰"

彭斯

呵,我的爱人像朵红红的玫瑰,
 六月里迎风初开;
呵,我的爱人像支甜甜的曲子,
 奏得合拍又和谐。

我的好姑娘,多么美丽的人儿!   5
 请看我,多么深挚的爱情!
亲爱的,我永远爱你,
 纵使大海干涸水流尽。

纵使大海干涸水流尽,
 太阳将岩石烧作灰尘,   10
亲爱的,我永远爱你,
 只要我一息犹存。

珍重吧,我唯一的爱人,
 珍重吧,让我们暂时别离,
但我定要回来,   15
 哪怕千里万里!

王佐良 译

151. HIGHLAND MARY

Ye banks and braes and streams around
    The castle o' Montgomery,
Green be your woods, and fair your flowers,
    Your waters never drumlie①!
There simmer first unfauld her robes,
    And there the langest tarry②;
For there I took the last fareweel
    O' my sweet Highland Mary.

How sweetly bloom'd the gay green birk③,
    How rich the hawthorn's blossom,
As underneath their fragrant shade
    I clasp'd her to my bosom!
The golden hours on angel wings
    Flew o'er me and my dearie;
For dear to me as light and life
    Was my sweet Highland Mary.

Wi' mony a vow and lock'd embrace
    Our parting was fu' tender;
And pledging aft to meet again,
    We tore oursels asunder;

---

① *drumlie*: 'muddy.'
② The verbs are subjunctive, expressing a wish; in prose it would be 'May summer unfold, etc.'
③ *birk*: 'birch.'

151. 高原上的玛丽

彭斯

你们啊,河岸、山坡和溪水,
　　环绕着蒙哥马利的寨楼,
愿你们林木苍翠花儿美,
　　愿你们的清水长流!
夏天在哪儿初露面目,　　　　　　　　5
　　那儿它返留最久;
我和亲爱的高原玛丽
　　最后在那儿分手。

快活的青桦树开得多美,
　　好一片山楂花盛开;　　　　　　　10
在那芬芳的树荫底下,
　　我把她紧搂在胸怀!
宝贵的时刻展开仙翼,
　　飞过我俩的头顶,
因为亲爱的高原玛丽　　　　　　　　15
　　可贵如光和生命!

山盟海誓紧紧相抱,
　　侬侬是我们的别离;
约定日后再常来相会,
　　我们俩就忍痛别去;　　　　　　　20

But, oh! fell Death's untimely frost,
    That nipt my flower sae early!
Now green's the sod, and cauld's the clay,
    That wraps my Highland Mary!

O pale, pale now, those rosy lips,
    I aft hae kiss'd sae fondly!
And closed for ay the sparkling glance
    That dwelt on me sae kindly;
And mouldering now in silent dust
    That heart that lo'ed me dearly!
But still within my bosom's core
    Shall live my Highland Mary.

R. BURNS.

但是啊,死亡像过早的霜冻
　　使我的花儿早夭!
如今裹着高原的玛丽
　　是冷冷的土,青青的草!

如今苍白是那双朱唇, 25
　　我曾热烈地接吻!
永闭了是那明亮的眼睛,
　　它们曾温柔地向我盯!
如今消蚀于无声的尘土
　　是她那爱我的心! 30
但是在我心灵的深处,
　　玛丽将永远长存!

　　　　　　　　袁可嘉　译

152. AULD ROBIN GRAY

When the sheep are in the fauld, and the kye at hame①,
And a' the warld to rest are gane,
The waes o' my heart fa' in showers frae my e'e,
While my gudeman lies sound by me.

5 Young Jamie lo'ed me weel, and sought me for his bride;
But saving a croun he had naething else beside;
To make the croun a pund, young Jamie gaed to sea;
And the croun and the pund were baith for me.

He hadna been awa' a week but only twa②,
10 When my father brak his arm, and the cow was stown awa'③;
My mother she fell sick, and my Jamie at the sea —
And auld Robin Gray came a-courtin' me.

My father couldna work, and my mother couldna spin;
I toil'd day and night, but their bread I couldna win;
15 Auld Rob maintain'd them baith, and wi' tears in his e'e
Said, Jennie, for their sakes, O, marry me!

My heart it said nay; I look'd for Jamie back;

---

① *the kye*: (or ky) the old plural of cow; kine is a double plural, being ky + the plural suffix -en, seen in 'oxen.'
② *He hadna been awa' a week but only twa*: 'he had been away for only two weeks.'
③ *stown*: 'stolen.'

152. 老罗宾·格瑞

林德赛夫人

羊群入了栏,牛群也回了家,
整个世界进入了安静的夜晚,
我心中的悲哀呀,就变成一阵阵泪雨,
而我的丈夫正熟睡在我身边。

年轻的吉米爱我,要我做他的新娘; 5
他只有一个克朗,此外什么也没有:
为了把克朗变成金镑,吉米航海去了;
那克朗和金镑全是为了我的缘由。

他走了不过两个星期光景,
我爹折断了胳膊,有人偷了我们家的牛; 10
我妈生了病,而我的吉米在海上——
老罗宾·格瑞来向我求婚了,在这时候。

爹不能干活了,妈不能纺纱了;
我日夜劳动,也养不活父母;
老罗宾·格瑞供养了他们,含着泪说, 15
珍妮,嫁给我吧,为了你爹妈的缘故!

我心里说不,我巴望着吉米回来;

        But the wind it blew high, and the ship it was a wrack;
        His ship it was a wrack — why didna Jamie dee?
20   Or why do I live to cry, Wae's me?

        My father urgit sair; my mother didna speak;
        But she look'd in my face till my heart was like to break;
        They gi'ed him my hand, but my heart was at the sea
        Sae auld Robin Gray he was gudeman to me.

25   I hadna been a wife a week but only four,
        When mournfu' as I sat on the stane at the door,
        I saw my Jamie's wraith, for I couldna think it he —
        Till he said, I'm come hame to marry thee.

        O sair, sair did we greet, and muckle did we say[①];
30   We took but ae kiss, and I bad him gang away;
        I wish that I were dead, but I'm no like to dee;
        And why was I born to say, Wae's me!

        I gang like a ghaist, and I carena to spin;
        I daurna think on Jamie, for that wad be a sin;
35   But I'll do my best a gude wife ay to be,
        For auld Robin Gray he is kind unto me.

                                        LADY A. LINDSAY.

---

① *greet*: 'weep.'

可是风刮得猛啊,船已经遇难;
他的船破了——吉米怎么会不死呢?
我为什么还活着哭呢? 天哪,天!   20

爹竭力劝我,妈虽然不说什么,
却注视着我,使我的心呀,快要破碎:
爹妈把我许给了他,尽管我的心在海上;
他就成了我的丈夫——那老罗宾·格瑞。

我做了他的妻子不过四个星期光景,   25
有一天我悲伤地坐在门口的石头上,
我看见了吉米的水魂,我本来不信是他——
可是他说,我回家娶你来了,姑娘!

呵,我们俩哭成了泪人儿,还说了许多话;
我们只吻了一次,我就央求他离开: 30
我啊,真不如死了好,可我又不像要死;
为什么我说这种话呢? 天哪,唉!

我活着像个幽灵,也不想织布;
我不敢想念吉米,那将是一种罪过;
唉! 让我努力做一个好妻子吧,   35
因为老罗宾·格瑞待我不错。

屠 岸 译

编注 安妮·林德赛夫人(Lady Anne Lindsay,1750—1825),她最初匿名发表此诗,直到一八二三年才承认自己的作者权。

153. DUNCAN GRAY

Duncan Gray cam here to woo,
    Ha, ha, the wooing o't[1],
On blythe Yule night when we were fou[2],
    Ha, ha, the wooing o't:
Maggie coost her head fu' high[3],
Look'd asklent and unco skeigh[4],
Gart poor Duncan stand abeigh[5];
    Ha, ha, the wooing o't!

Duncan fleech'd, and Duncan pray'd[6];
Meg was deaf as Ailsa Craig;
Duncan sigh'd baith out and in,
Grat his een baith bleer't and blin'[7],
Spak o' lowpin ower a linn[8]!

Time and chance are but a tide,
Slighted love is sair to bide;
Shall I, like a fool, quoth he,

---

[1] This refrain is repeated after the first, second, and last lines of each stanza as here printed.
[2] *fou*: 'full,' *i.e.* of drink.
[3] *coost*: 'cast,' *i.e.* tossed.
[4] *asklent*: 'aslant.' *skeigh*: 'saucy.'
[5] *Gart*: 'made.' *abeigh*: 'at a distance.'
[6] *fleech'd*: 'entreated.'
[7] *Grat*: the past tense of 'greet'; see l. 29 of the previous poem.
[8] *lowpin ower a linn*: 'jumping down a waterfall.'

153. 邓肯·葛雷

彭斯

邓肯·葛雷来这儿求爱,
　　哈,哈,他那求婚,
快乐的圣诞夜,我们喝了个醉,
　　哈,哈,他那求婚。
梅吉头翘得天样高, 5
斜眼横扫,十分骄傲,
可怜邓肯进不好,退不妙,
　　哈,哈,他那求婚!

邓肯哄她,邓肯求她,
梅吉像阿尔赛岛装聋作哑①, 10
邓肯叹着气,一口出,一口进,
眼睛哭得又花又湿润,
说要跳下瀑布自尽!

时间和机缘不过像潮水,
难熬是遭人漠视的情爱, 15
难道我得像傻瓜,他说,

---

① 阿尔赛岛是苏格兰和爱尔兰之间的一个海岛。——译者

> For a haughty hizzie dee①?
> She may gae to — France for me!
>
> How it comes let doctors tell,
> Meg grew sick — as he grew heal②;
> Something in her bosom wrings,
> For relief a sigh she brings;
> And O, her een, they spak sic things!
>
> Duncan was a lad o' grace;
>   Ha, ha, the wooing o't!
> Maggie's was a piteous case;
>   Ha, ha, the wooing o't!
> Duncan couldna be her death,
> Swelling pity smoor'd his wrath③;
> Now they're crouse and canty baith④:
>   Ha, ha, the wooing o't!

R. BURNS.

---

① *hizzie*: 'hussy.'
② *heal*: a northern dialect form of 'hale.'
③ *smoor'd*: 'smothered.'
④ *crouse and canty*: 'cheerful and merry.'

为骄傲的姑娘丧命,
她给我滚到法国①!

怎么回事,让大夫来说,
梅吉得病,邓肯有福; 20
她心里隐隐作痛,
她叹口气,松一松,
啊,她眼睛道出这种种!

邓肯是个厚道少年,
  哈,哈,他那求婚! 25
梅吉也委实可怜,
  哈,哈,他那求婚!
邓肯不会要她送命,
怜悯消了他的气愤;
如今他们俩又矫健又开心! 30
  哈,哈,他那求婚!

袁可嘉 译

---

① 即"滚蛋"之意。——译者

154. THE SAILOR'S WIFE

And are ye sure the news is true?
    And are ye sure he's weel?
Is this a time to think o' wark?
    Ye jades, lay by your wheel;
Is this the time to spin a thread,
    When Colin's at the door?
Reach down my cloak, I'll to the quay,
    And see him come ashore.
For there's nae luck about the house,
    There's nae luck at a';
There's little pleasure in the house
    When our gudeman's awa'.

And gie to me my bigonet[1],
    My bishop's satin gown;
For I maun tell the baillie's wife
    That Colin's in the town.
My Turkey slippers maun gae on,
    My stockins pearly blue;
It's a' to pleasure our gudeman,
    For he's baith leal and true[2].

Rise, lass, and mak a clean fireside,

---

[1] *bigonet*: 'cap or head-dress'; usually spelt with two g's.
[2] *leal*: 'loyal.'

154. 水手妻

米克尔

你们肯定说消息没错?
  你们肯定他平安无事?
那还用得着再干什么活?
  姑娘们,放下手中的纺车!
科林已到了大门口,   5
  那何必还在织线纺纱?
递斗篷给我,我要去码头,
  亲自去接他登岸回家。
家中的主子一出门在外,
  屋里就没一件事儿如意;   10
谁都显得无精打采,
  谁也碰不上好运气。

递给我那件上等袍,
  递给我那顶上等帽;
我要去看望郡长妻,   15
  告诉她科林回来了。
我要穿上这双软便鞋,
  还有这双浅蓝色的袜;
我要使夫君感到欣慰,
  他是那样的情真意挚。   20

姑娘快去把炉火生旺,

                    Put on the muckle pot;
                Gie little Kate her button gown
                    And Jock his Sunday coat;
25   And mak their shoon as black as slaes,
                    Their hose as white as snaw;
                It's a' to please my ain gudeman,
                    For he's been long awa'.

                There's twa fat hens upo' the coop
30   Been fed this month and mair;
                Mak haste and thraw their necks about①
                    That Colin weel may fare;
                And spread the table neat and clean,
                    Gar ilka thing look braw②,
35   For wha can tell how Colin fared
                    When he was far awa'?

                Sae true his heart, sae smooth his speech,
                    His breath like caller air③;
                His very foot has musie in't
40   As he comes up the stair —
                And will I see his face again?
                    And will I hear him speak?
                I'm downright dizzy wi' the thought,
                    In troth I'm like to greet!

45   If Colin's weel, and weel content,

---

① *thraw*: 'twist.'
② *Gar*: 'make.'
③ *caller*: 'fresh.'

把那口大锅摆上;
去叫小凯蒂换上长袍,
叫杰克穿起外套;
将黑皮鞋擦得亮闪闪,
袜子要雪白雪白;
这都是为我夫君快活——
他离家已经很久。

鸡笼里两只母鸡已肥,
养了怕有两来月;
快快捉了来快快宰,
好把科林来款待。
清清爽爽地摆好饭桌,
样样收拾得顺眼;
科林一个人长期在外,
怎么过日子难说?

他为人忠厚,说话和蔼,
生命充满了朝气;
他走上楼轻巧随便,
脚步声使人惬意——
但能不能同他再相见?
再听到他的言语?
这念头真使我昏昏然,
真巴不得实实在在见他一面!

我只要科林如意、平安,

I hae nae mair to crave;
And gin I live to keep him sae,
 I'm blest aboon the lave[①];
And will I see his face again,
50 And will I hear him speak?
I'm downright dizzy wi' the thought,
 In troth I'm like to greet.
For there's nae luck about the house,
 There's nae luck at a';
55 There's little pleasure in the house
 When our gudeman's awa'.

W. J. MICKLE.

---

① *aboon the lave*: 'above the rest.'

> 　　就没有别的打算：
> 　我若一辈子使他喜欢，
> 　　就感到幸福无边。
> 　但能不能同他再相见？
> 　　再听到他的语言？　　　　　　　　　　*50*
> 　这念头真使我昏昏然，
> 　　巴不得实实在在见他一面。
> 　一家的主子出门在外，
> 　　事情就不会顺遂；
> 　家里谁都愁眉展不开，　　　　　　　　　*55*
> 　　好运气一去不回。

陈兆林　译

编注　威廉·米克尔(William Mickle，1735—1788)，苏格兰诗人，著有诗集多部，但《水手妻》未曾收入他出版的诗集。

155. JEAN

Of a' the airts the wind can blaw①
　　I dearly like the West,
For there the bonnie lassie lives,
　　The lassie I lo'e best:
There's wild woods grow, and rivers row,
　　And mony a hill between;
But day and night my fancy's flight
　　Is ever wi' my Jean.

I see her in the dewy flowers,
　　I see her sweet and fair:
I hear her in the tunefu' birds,
　　I hear her charm the air:
There's not a bonnie flower that springs
　　By fountain, shaw, or green②,
There's not a bonnie bird that sings
　　But minds me o' my Jean.

O blaw ye westlin winds, blaw saft
　　Amang the leafy trees;
Wi' balmy gale, frae hill and dale
　　Bring hame the laden bees;
And bring the lassie back to me

---

① *airts*: 'quarters of the heaven.' *blaw*: *i.e.* blow from.
② *shaw*: 'a small wood.'

155. 吉恩

彭斯

风儿吹自四面八方,
　　我最眷恋西方。
那里有位美丽的女郎,
　　是我最爱的姑娘。
虽然丛林莽莽,河水流淌,
　　隔有连绵山岭,
我的心儿却日夜驰飞,
　　总向着我的吉恩。

在滴翠的花丛间我看到丽人,
　　看见她娉婷又温存;
在小鸟的鸣啭中我听到丽人,
　　听见她使空气消魂。
只要清泉、丛林和绿茵草坪,
　　有活泼的鸟儿在歌吟,
有娇艳的鲜花在吐蕊,
　　不禁让我思念吉恩。

哦,吹吧,西风你轻柔地吹吧,
　　吹过葳蕤的树林;
馨香的和风,吹出山冈、峡谷,
　　把满载的蜜蜂送回院庭;
也将那心爱的姑娘带到我身旁,

> That's ay sae neat and clean;
> > Ae smile o' her wad banish care;
> > Sae charming is my Jean.

> What sighs and vows amang the knowes[1]
> > Hae pass'd atween us twa!
> How fond to meet, how wae to part
> > That night she gaed awa!
> The Powers aboon can only ken
> > To whom the heart is seen,
> That nane can be sae dear to me
> > As my sweet lovely Jean!

R. BURNS.

---

[1] *knowes*: 'small round hillocks.'

她永远那么纯洁匀称；
嫣然一笑便驱散千般忧虑，
　　那般迷人我的吉恩。

在那山间我们俩曾有过　　　　　　　　　　　25
　　多少蹉叹又多少山盟海誓！
相逢多快活，离别多忧愁，
　　那夜当她（别我）而去！
只有上帝呵才能明悉，
　　我心属意何人？　　　　　　　　　　　30
我再没有更为亲近的人，
　　除了我温柔可爱的吉恩！

三畏　译

编注 此诗前两节为彭斯与吉恩（Jean Armour）新婚之后作；后两节则为一位名叫约翰·汉密尔顿（John Hamilton）的爱丁堡音乐商所作。

156. JOHN ANDERSON

John Anderson my jo, John[1],
    When we were first acquent
Your locks were like the raven,
    Your bonnie brow was brent[2];
But now your brow is beld, John[3],
    Your locks are like the snow;
But blessings on your frosty pow[4],
    John Anderson my jo.

John Anderson my jo, John,
    We clamb the hill thegither[5],
And mony a canty day, John[6],
    We've had wi' ane anither:
Now we maun totter down, John,
    But hand in hand we'll go,
And sleep thegither at the foot,
    John Anderson my jo.

R. BURNS.

---

[1] *jo*: 'sweetheart'; it is a corruption of 'joy.'
[2] *brent*: 'clear,' *i.e.* without lines.
[3] *beld*: 'bald.'
[4] *pow*: 'head.'
[5] *thegither*: 'together.'
[6] *canty*: 'merry.'

156. 约翰·安徒生①

彭斯

约翰·安徒生,我爱,
　　想我们当初结识,
你的剑眉挺拔,
　　你的头发乌黑;
如今你眉毛脱尽,约翰,
　　你的头发雪白;
约翰·安徒生,我爱,
　　祝福你那一头白发!

约翰·安徒生,我爱,
　　我们曾同登山丘;
多少个快活日子,约翰,
　　我们曾一同享有;
如今得蹒跚下坡,约翰,
　　我们走,手携着手;
约翰·安徒生,我爱,
　　山脚下长眠相守。

袁可嘉　译

---

① 本诗系根据一首旧歌词改编,旧作极滑稽轻佻,原刊一七六八年伦敦出版的《假面具》歌集。——译者

157. THE LAND O' THE LEAL

I'm wearing awa', Jean,
Like snaw when it's thaw, Jean,
I'm wearing awa'
   To the land o' the leal[①].
There's nae sorrow there, Jean,
There's neither cauld nor care, Jean,
The day is ay fair
   In the land o' the leal.

Ye were ay leal and true, Jean,
Your task 's ended noo, Jean,
And I'll welcome you
   To the land o' the leal.
Our bonnie bairn 's there, Jean,
She was baith guid and fair, Jean[②];
O we grudged her right sair
   To the land o' the leal!

Then dry that tearfu' e'e, Jean,
My soul langs to be free, Jean,
And angels wait on me
   To the land o' the leal.

---

① *leal*: 'loyal.'
② *guid*: 'good.'

157. 永恒的天国

奈恩夫人

我已在渐渐离去,琼,
就如消融的冰雪,琼,
我已在渐渐离去
　　前往永恒的天国。
那里无悲伤忧虑,琼,　　　　　　　　　　5
也无严寒和盛暑,琼,
啊,一切都那么美好
　　在那永恒的天国。

你那样忠贞不渝,琼,
你已尽自己责任,琼,　　　　　　　　　　10
我将等待迎接你
　　前往永恒的天国。
我们爱女在那里,琼,
她生前乖巧伶俐,琼;
啊,咱曾不愿她永别　　　　　　　　　　15
　　前往永恒的天国。

拭干你的眼泪吧,琼,
我灵魂渴望自由,琼,
天使们已来接我
　　前往永恒的天国。　　　　　　　　　20

Now fare ye weel, my ain Jean①,
This warld's care is vain, Jean;
We'll meet and ay be fain②
   In the land o' the leal.

LADY NAIRNE.

---

① *ain*: 'own.'
② *fain*: 'glad.'

祝福你，我亲爱的琼，
尘世之虑皆是虚，琼；
啊，我们将幸福团聚
在那永恒的天国。

于兴基　译

编注 奈恩夫人（Lady Nairen，1766—1845），苏格兰诗人，著有短诗共八十七首。

158. ODE ON A DISTANT PROSPECT OF ETON COLLEGE

Ye distant spires, ye antique towers
   That crown the watery glade,
Where grateful Science still adores[1]
   Her Henry's holy shade;
And ye, that from the stately brow[2]
Of Windsor's heights th' expanse below
   Of grove, of lawn, of mead survey,
Whose turf, whose shade, whose flowers among[3]
Wanders the hoary Thames along
   His silver-winding way:

Ah happy hills! ah pleasing shade!
   Ah fields beloved in vain[4]!
Where once my careless childhood stray'd,
   A stranger yet to pain!
I feel the gales that from ye blow
A momentary bliss bestow,
   As waving fresh their gladsome wing
My weary soul they seem to soothe,

---

[1] *Science*: 'knowledge.'

[2] *And ye*: sc. spires and towers. This long vocative case — the first fourteen lines of the Ode — leads up to the 'I feel,' etc. in l. 15.

[3] *Whose turf, whose shade, whose flowers*: referring respectively to the lawn, the grove, and the mead of the previous line; but the change of order is remarkable.

[4] *beloved in vain*: because his love could not keep him near them.

158. 远眺伊顿公学咏怀

格雷

你远处的尖顶,你古老的塔楼,
　　像王冠戴在泽地之上,
你那里的学府,犹在感念
　　亨利王的圣恩浩荡①;
你耸立温莎高地巍峨的边缘, 5
俯瞰着一片辽阔的平川,
　　森林、绿地、草原,
在那芬芳、绿荫、鲜花之间,
古老的泰晤士河潺潺流淌,
　　银光闪烁,曲曲弯弯: 10

啊,明媚的群山!啊,迷人的绿荫!
　　啊,可爱的田野,我向往的地方!
回想快活的童年,我曾在此漫游,
　　不知道什么是人生的忧伤!
习习清风从那边吹来, 15
吹拂着我的身体,激起我一阵欢狂,
　　风儿振动起快乐的羽翼,
似抚慰我忧郁的心房,

---

① 亨利王,亨利四世,伊顿公学的创始人。——译者

  And, redolent of joy and youth,
20   To breathe a second spring.

  Say, Father Thames, for thou hast seen
   Full many a sprightly race
  Disporting on thy margent green
   The paths of pleasure trace;
25   Who foremost now delight to cleave
  With pliant arm, thy glassy wave?
   The captive linnet which enthral?
  What idle progeny succeed[①]
  To chase the rolling circle's speed
30   Or urge the flying ball?

  While some on earnest business bent
   Their murmuring labours ply
  'Gainst graver hours, that bring constraint[②]
   To sweeten liberty:
35   Some bold adventurers disdain
  The limits of their little reign[③]
   And unknown regions dare descry:
  Still as they run they look behind[④],
  They hear a voice in every wind,
40   And snatch a fearful joy[⑤].

[①] *succeed*: 'are my successors.'
[②] *'Gainst*: 'to be ready for.'
[③] *reign*: 'realm.'
[④] *Still*: 'continually.'
[⑤] L. 31—40: While some are preparing their lessons, others are breaking bounds.

风儿吹送来欢乐与青春的气息,
　　犹如带给我第二度春光。   20

啊,泰晤士河——我的父亲,你曾看见
　　多少次欢愉的追逐嬉戏,
在你绿流的岸边留下了
　　一道道快乐的行踪径迹:
请告诉我:如今是谁最先快活地   25
轻舒他温柔的手臂,分开你草绿的波澜?
　　是谁在把捕获的红雀戏玩:
谁个年轻贪闲
继承了滚环的游戏,
　　或是教圆球飞旋在运动场间?   30

一些人埋头于学业,
　　朗朗诵读,刻苦而勤勉,
准备学好功课,迎接更为严峻的时刻,
　　可爱的自由,却受到羁绊:
一些人大胆而冒险,   35
藐视他们小天地的局限,
　　敢于发现那未知的境界;
他们在奔跑时仍不断回首探看,
但当听见风声的召唤,
　　便觉一阵强烈的喜悦涌到心田。   40

  Gay hope is theirs by fancy fed,
   Less pleasing when possest;
  The tear forgot as soon as shed,
   The sunshine of the breast:
45 Theirs buxom health, of rosy hue,
  Wild wit, invention ever new,
   And lively cheer, of vigour born;
  The thoughtless day, the easy night,
  The spirits pure, the slumbers light
50   That fly th' approach of morn.

  Alas! regardless of their doom
   The little victims play!
  No sense have they of ills to come
   Nor care beyond to-day:
55 Yet see how all around them wait
  The Ministers of human fate
   And black Misfortune's baleful train!
  Ah show them where in ambush stand
  To seize their prey, the murderous band!
60   Ah, tell them they are men[①]!

  These shall the fury Passions tear[②],
   The vultures of the mind,
  Disdainful Anger, pallid Fear,
   And Shame that skulks behind;
65 Or pining Love shall waste their youth,

---

① *tell them they are men*: i.e. warn them of the evils that prey upon humanity.

② *These*: he apportions the calamities among the children; *this* (l. 71) and *those* (l. 75) denote others of them.

他们的想象丰富了美妙的憧憬,
　　他们的收获并非那样甘甜!
洒落的泪水,瞬即干涸,
　　心中的太阳,光辉耀眼:
他们健美的身躯,闪烁着玫瑰色的光焰,　　　　45
他们焕发出智慧,涌出崭新的创造波澜,
　　他们蓬勃的朝气,吹开了快乐的笑脸:
无忧无虑的白昼,舒舒服服的夜间,
天真纯洁的心灵,轻轻软软的睡眠
　　一宵就飞越到明天。　　　　　　　　　　50

啊! 不管那人生末日何时到来,
　　年少时只须游玩!
不管命运的灾难何日降临,
　　今日里只顾尽欢:
可是请看:就在他们的周围　　　　　　　　　55
那人类命运的主宰官,
　　和种种可怕灾难,正向他们虎视眈眈!
啊,请告诉他们,深壕暗堑,
潜伏着伺机捕捉他们的杀人匪帮!
　　啊,请告诉他们,他们却是人,太平凡!　　60

这种种灾难将刺伤他们激烈的情感,
　　贪婪的品质,
傲慢的愤怒,苍白的恐惧,
　　隐匿的羞耻!
或者,那苦恼的爱情将耗尽他们的韶光,　　　　65

  Or Jealousy with rankling tooth
   That inly gnaws the secret heart,
  And Envy wan, and faded Care,
  Grim-visaged comfortless Despair,
70   And Sorrow's piercing dart.

  Ambition this shall tempt to rise,
   Then whirl the wretch from high,
  To bitter Scorn a sacrifice
   And grinning Infamy①.
75 The stings of Falsehood those shall try,
  And hard Unkindness' alter'd eye,
   That mocks the tear it forced to flow;
  And keen Remorse with blood defiled,
  And moody Madness laughing wild
80   Amid severest woe.

  Lo, in the vale of years beneath
   A griesly troop are seen②,
  The painful family of Death,
   More hideous than their Queen:
85 This racks the joints, this fires the veins,
  That every labouring sinew strains,
   Those in the deeper vitals rage:
  Lo, Poverty, to fill the band,
  That numbs the soul with icy hand,
90   And slow-consuming Age.

---

 ① *grinning Infamy*: to *grin* is to draw back the lips and show the teeth; this is more often a mark of pain or rage than of mirth.
 ② *griesly*: 'horrible.'

或者,那嫉妒的利齿,
　　将咬碎他们秘密的心房,
终于,嫉妒渐渐消退,忧虑淡忘,
冷酷无情的一片绝望,
　　悲伤的利剑刺透胸膛。　　　　　　　　　　　　70

于是,这种不幸将诱发起勃勃野心,
　　可怜的人又被抛入高空,
遭到无情的耻笑,
　　招来冷酷的讥讽。
虚伪的利刺会来折磨心灵　　　　　　　　　　　75
残酷地目露狰狞,
　　嘲笑受害者悲痛的眼泪;
玷污了的血液触动着深深的悔恨,
在极度的悲伤之中,
　　阴郁的愤怒发出疯狂的笑声。　　　　　　　80

啊,在那岁月之河的深谷,
　　发现了一支可怕的队伍,
那痛苦的死神家族,
　　比他们的女王更令人恐怖:
这个人折断了周身关节,这个人烧着全身血液,　85
那个人抽痛了每一根活动的筋腱,
　　那些人五脏六腑都被撕裂:
啊,贫困,你也去加入杀人者的行列,
用你冰冰的手扼杀了人的灵魂,
　　还有,你渐渐耗尽人生的岁月。　　　　　　90

>   To each his sufferings: all are men,
>   Condemn'd alike to groan;
>   The tender for another's pain,
>   Th' unfeeling for his own.
> 95 Yet, ah! why should they know their fate,
>   Since sorrow never comes too late,
>   And happiness too swiftly flies?
>   Thought would destroy their paradise.
>   No more; — where ignorance is bliss,
> 100   'Tis folly to be wise.

T. GRAY.

人人都有自己的苦:大家都是平凡的人,
　　一样会在痛苦中呻吟,
对他人的苦却心生恻隐,
　　对自身的苦却麻木不仁。
可是啊! 他们又何必知道自己的命运, 95
因为悲伤从不姗姗来临,
　　幸福总是一瞬就飞逝?
思考将毁灭他们的天庭。
啊,够了;——既然无知就是欢乐,
　　明智便是愚氓。 100

周式中　译

159. HYMN TO ADVERSITY

  Daughter of Jove, relentless power,
  Thou tamer of the human breast,
  Whose iron scourge and torturing hour
  The bad affright, afflict the best!
5   Bound in thy adamantine chain
  The proud are taught to taste of pain,
  And purple tyrants vainly groan
With pangs unfelt before, unpitied and alone.

  When first thy Sire to send on earth
10   Virtue, his darling child, design'd,
  To thee he gave the heavenly birth[①]
  And bade to form her infant mind.
  Stern, rugged Nurse! thy rigid lore
  With patience many a year she bore:
15   What sorrow was, thou bad'st her know,
And from her own she learn'd to melt at others' woe.

  Scared at thy frown terrific, fly
  Self-pleasing Folly's idle brood,
  Wild Laughter, Noise, and thoughtless Joy,
20   And leave us leisure to be good.
  Light they disperse, and with them go

---

① *birth*: 'infant.'

159. 厄运赞

格雷

你主神之女,无情的力量①,
　　你训诫着人的心灵,
在你铁的鞭笞、血的酷刑下
　　恶徒胆战,英杰心惊!
在你铮铮铁链的拴锁下,　　　　　　　　　　5
不可一世的骄横者也要尝这苦酒一樽,
　身着紫袍的暴君发出了无用的呻吟,
感受到从未有过的痛楚,孤苦伶仃,无人同情。

当你的父神做出安排,
　　将爱女"美德"降送世上,　　　　　　10
他献给你天神的婴儿,
　　嘱你培植她方始萌芽的思想。
你这严峻的保姆! 一副铁石心肠
她年复一年,耐心接受你严厉的教育,
　你要她懂得什么是悲伤,　　　　　　　15
她备尝痛楚,懂得了同情他人的凄苦。

你皱起可畏的双眉,惊散了
　　那自满愚蠢的懒惰儿郎
那疯狂的笑声和喧嚣,那无聊的快乐,
　　给了我们欢欣却少了端庄。　　　　　20
那不共患难的朋友,那逢迎阿谀的敌人,

---

① 厄运是由主神朱庇特(Jupiter)的意志所决定,故此诗人称"厄运"为主神之女。——译者

           The summer Friend, the flattering Foe①;
             By vain Prosperity received,
         To her they vow their truth, and are again believed②.

25   Wisdom in sable garb array'd
                Immersed in rapturous thought profound,
             And Melancholy, silent maid,
                With leaden eye, that loves the ground,
             Still on thy solemn steps attend:
30   Warm Charity, the general friend,
             With Justice, to herself severe,
         And Pity dropping soft the sadly-pleasing tear③.

             O, gently on thy suppliant's head
                Dread Goddess, lay thy chastening hand!
35   Not in thy Gorgon terrors clad,
                Nor circled with the vengeful band
                (As by the impious thou art seen)
             With thundering voice, and threatening mien,
             With screaming Horror's funeral cry,
40   Despair, and fell Disease, and ghastly Poverty:

             Thy form benign, O Goddess, wear,
              Thy milder influence impart,
              Thy philosophic train be there

---

① *The summer Friend*: the modern phrase is a 'fair-weather friend.' *the flattering Foe*: i.e. our flatterers, who are really our enemies.

② I.e. it is only in our prosperity that such people come to us and delude us by their pretence of devotion.

③ *the sadly-pleasing tear*: sad, but yet giving pleasure to the one for whom it is shed.

也都随之逃遁；
　　但当幸运到来,他们便又接踵临门,
表白他们的忠诚,一再骗取信任。

　　智慧,穿着貂皮的外衣, 25
　　　　沉溺于兴奋的思想,
　　忧郁,像个无言的女仆,
　　　　她阴沉的目光只俯视着地上,
　　依然伴随着你严肃的脚步。
　　温暖的慈善之神,她给大众带来友情, 30
　　　　还有公正,她严于律己,
还有怜悯,她洒落悲伤的泪水,安慰痛苦的心灵。

　　啊,你可畏的女神,请将那训诫之手,
　　　　轻轻搁在祈求者的头部!
　　不要穿上那戈耳工的服装①, 35
　　　　不要与复仇一帮为伍,
　　不要对渎圣者那样冷酷,
　　不要发出雷霆般的怒吼,不要显露威吓的面目。
　　不要发出恐惧的凄厉哀嚎,
不要带来绝望,致命的疾病,可怕的贫苦: 40

　　啊,女神,请现出你仁慈的形象,
　　　　请变得温和善良,
　　请用你的条条哲理

---

① 戈耳工(Gorgon),希腊神话中的三个蛇发女怪。——译者

To soften, not to wound my heart.
The generous spark extinct revive,
Teach me to love and to forgive,
Exact my own defects to scan,
What others are to feel, and know myself a Man.

T. GRAY.

抚慰我的心灵,而莫将它刺伤;
请重新点燃那熄灭了的仁爱之火,
教育我去爱,去原谅,
让我洞察自身的弱点,
了解他人的情感,深知自己与凡人一样。

周式中　译

160. THE SOLITUDE OF ALEXANDER SELKIRK

I am monarch of all I survey,
  My right there is none to dispute;
From the centre all round to the sea
  I am lord of the fowl and the brute.
O solitude! where are the charms
  That sages have seen in thy face?
Better dwell in the midst of alarms
  Than reign in this horrible place.

I am out of humanity's reach,
  I must finish my journey alone,
Never hear the sweet music of speech;
  I start at the sound of my own.
The beasts that roam over the plain
  My form with indifference see;
They are so unacquainted with man,
  Their tameness is shocking to me.

Society, friendship, and love
  Divinely bestow'd upon man,
O had I the wings of a dove

160. 亚历山大·塞尔克的孤独①

柯珀

极目所望皆是我的领土,
  我的权利无人来争夺;
以此为圆心,极目海域,
  在动物世界我称王道孤。
孤独啊,哲人曾将你称赞, 5
  可现在你的魅力哪里存身?
我宁愿在忧伤中辗转,
  也胜似在此唯我独尊。

我陷入与世隔绝的境地,
  必须只身捱尽人生旅程, 10
听不到尘世间声律甜蜜,
  对自己的声音也感到吃惊。
平川里徜徉着野畜异兽,
  对我的身形它满眼冷漠;
它们对人类如此生疏, 15
  但它们的驯服使我十分惶惑。

相互的交往,友谊,爱情,
  都是上天赐予人们;
我若肩生鸽子的快翼②,

---

① 亚历山大·塞尔克是一名苏格兰水手,曾被抛弃在一座荒岛上度过了四年多孤独的生活。英国著名作家笛福以他的真实故事为根据写成了《鲁滨逊漂流记》。——译者
② 《圣经·旧约·诗篇》第五五篇云:"但愿我有翅膀像鸽子,我就飞去,得享安息。"——译者

How soon would I taste you again!
My sorrows I then might assuage
 In the ways of religion and truth,
Might learn from the wisdom of age,
 And be cheer'd by the sallies of youth.

Ye winds that have made me your sport,
 Convey to this desolate shore
Some cordial endearing report①
 Of a land I shall visit no more:
My friends, do they now and then send
 A wish or a thought after me?
O tell me I yet have a friend,
 Though a friend I am never to see.

How fleet is a glance of the mind!
 Compared with the speed of its flight,
The tempest itself lags behind,
 And the swift-wingéd arrows of light.
When I think of my own native land
 In a moment I seem to be there;
But, alas! recollection at hand
 Soon hurries me back to despair.

But the seafowl is gone to her nest,
 The beast is laid down in his lair;
Even here is a season of rest,
 And I to my cabin repair.

---

① *some cordial endearing report*: 'some heart-felt affectionate message.'

就立刻飞去重温欢欣！
那时沿宗教与真理的正轨，
　　我将会减轻我的不幸，
生活的哲理将予我以启迪，
　　勃发朝气会使我精神振奋。

我已无缘归去，啊，清风，
　　请将那里真挚的音讯
往这荒凉的海滨吹送，
　　虽然我一直受你摆弄：
故旧是否还把我惦记，
　　还探询我存殁的消息？
纵然我们已相会无期，
　　请说一声：还有一个知己。

任凭风暴多么迅急！
　　无论电闪有如箭离弦，
比起快捷的刹那思绪，
　　电掣风驰也竟然迟缓。
对故园我深情向往，
　　一回想它就像在眼前，
怎奈摆不开此时景况，
　　我随即感到惆怅无限。

但海鸟都一一归巢，
　　兽类各自返回穴窟，
此地一样有安息时刻，
　　我也转向自己的小屋。

45   There is mercy in every place①,
             And mercy, encouraging thought!
             Gives even affliction a grace
             And reconciles man to his lot.

                                    W. COWPER.

---

① *mercy*: *i.e.* the mercy of God which gives a silver lining to every cloud.

无处没有上天的恩惠,
　　仁惠实在激励人心!
它使人乐天命,度逆境,
　　调谐人类的命运。

　　　　　　　　　　　　陈兆林　译

编注　柯珀原诗是七节,原编者在将其收入《金库》时删掉了第四节。

161. TO MARY UNWIN

Mary! I want a lyre with other strings①,
Such aid from heaven as some have feign'd they drew②,
An eloquence scarce given to mortals, new
And undebased by praise of meaner things,

That ere through age or woe I shed my wings③
I may record thy worth with honour bue,
In verse as musical as thou art true,
Verse that immortalizes whom it sings: —

But thou hast little need. There is a Book
By seraphs writ with beams of heavenly light,
On which the eyes of God not rarely look,
A chronicle of actions just and bright —

There all thy deeds, my faithful Mary, shine;
And since thou own'st that praise, I spare thee mine.

W. COWPER.

---

① *a lyre with other strings*: i.e. diviner powers of song.
② *have feign'd they drew*: if poetic inspiration does not come from heaven, one would like to know what is its source; but a mind like Cowper's regards no writing as inspired except the Bible.
③ *ere ... I shed my wings*: i.e. ere I cease to sing.

161. 致玛丽·昂温①

柯珀

玛丽！我要一把竖琴有着奇异的琴弦②，
　　恰似有人自诩，得自天国的襄助，
　　仙声妙曲，鲜为人间所有，
新奇且不因赞颂凡俗而被低贬。

敛翼而度过漫漫岁月和重重苦难之前③，
　　我不胜荣幸能够记下您的盛誉，
　　用韵文配上和您一样真诚的旋律，
它会使诗行称颂的您永世留传。

可您却不需要这一切。自有那书④
　　由六翼天使借圣灵天光写就，
　　字字句句无一不为上帝所关注，
是正直且光辉灿烂的德行簿。

您的全部言行熠熠闪烁，我忠实的玛丽，
赞颂于您是当之无愧，我将一切奉予您。

三畏　译

---

① 玛丽比柯珀大七岁，曾无微不至地关怀诗人，诗人称她为第二个母亲。——译者
② 此处"琴弦"指写诗的灵感。——译者
③ "敛翼"指死去，亦引申为停止歌唱。——译者
④ "那书"即《圣经·启示录》第二十章，第一二节所载的"生命册"，上帝据此记载人们的善行，末日审判也以此为据。——译者

162. TO THE SAME

The twentieth year is well-nigh past
Since first our sky was overcast;
Ah, would that this might be the last!
    My Mary!

Thy spirits have a fainter flow,
I see thee daily weaker grow —
'Twas my distress that brought thee low,
    My Mary!

Thy needles, once a shining store,
For my sake restless heretofore,
Now rust disused, and shine no more;
    My Mary!

For though thou gladly wouldst fulfil
The same kind office for me still,
Thy sight now seconds not thy will,
    My Mary!

But well thou play'dst the housewife's part,
And all thy threads with magic art
Have wound themselves about this heart,
    My Mary!

Thy indistinct expressions seem

162. 我的玛丽

柯珀

我们的天空初起乌云，
第二十个年头已经将尽，
唉，但愿这是最后的不幸！
　　　我的玛丽！

你的精神越来越低落，　　　　　　　　　5
我看你一天天越来越弱；
使你衰下去的是我的苦楚，
　　　我的玛丽！

你的针一时亮光闪闪，
在此以前为我从不安闲，　　　　　　　10
现在不再闪光，生锈放在一边；
　　　我的玛丽！

虽然你会欢欢乐乐，
同样仁慈地为我做活，
你的视力不能同心愿合作！　　　　　　15
　　　我的玛丽！

但是家庭主妇任务，你完成得好，
你的全部线索用魔术的技巧，
把我的心一重一重围绕，
　　　我的玛丽！　　　　　　　　　　20

你的并不清楚的表现，

Like language utter'd in a dream;
Yet me they charm, whate'er the theme,
    My Mary!

Thy silver locks, once auburn bright,
Are still more lovely in my sight
Than golden beams of orient light,
    My Mary!

For could I view nor them nor thee,
What sight worth seeing could I see?
The sun would rise in vain for me,
    My Mary!

Partakers of thy sad decline
Thy hands their little force resign;
Yet, gently press'd, press gently mine,
    My Mary!

Such feebleness of limbs thou prov'st
That now at every step thou mov'st
Upheld by two; yet still thou lov'st,
    My Mary!

And still to love, though press'd with ill,
In wintry age to feel no chill,
With me is to be lovely still,
    My Mary!

But ah! by constant heed I know
How oft the sadness that I show

好像是梦中的语言;
无论表示什么,仍然使我喜欢,
　　　我的玛丽!

你的银发,一度乌黑发亮,
现在比东方初晓的金光,
更为我的眼睛所欣赏,
　　　我的玛丽!

因为,看不见它们,看不见你,
还有什么值得看的东西?
太阳为我也是白白升起,
　　　我的玛丽!

可怜和你同枯同朽,
同样无力的是你的双手,
可是我你握手,同样轻柔,
　　　我的玛丽!

你的四肢这样软弱无力,
每走一步就要两人扶起,
可是你仍然把人爱惜,
　　　我的玛丽!

虽然抱病,你仍然爱人,
冬季年龄并不觉得凄冷,
对于我依然是可爱可亲,
　　　我的玛丽!

但是,我凭经常留心深懂;
我每每显出忧心忡忡,

Transforms thy smiles to looks of woe,
My Mary!

And should my future lot be cast
With much resemblance of the past,
Thy worn-out heart will break at last —
My Mary!

W. COWPER.

总把你的微笑变为愁容,
　　　我的玛丽!

假如我将来的命运
和过去很相似相近,　　　　　　　　　　　50
终于会粉碎你疲累的心——
　　　我的玛丽!

　　　　　　　　　　　李霁野　译

163. THE DYING MAN IN HIS GARDEN

Why, Damon, with the forward day①
Dost thou thy little spot survey,
From tree to tree, with doubtful cheer②,
Observe the progress of the year,
What winds arise, what rains descend,
When thou before that year shalt end?

What do thy noonday walks avail,
To clear the leaf, and pick the snail③
Then wantonly to death decree
An insect usefuller than thee?
Thou and the worm are brother-kind④,
As low, as earthy, and as blind.

Vain wretch! canst thou expect to see
The downy peach make court to thee⑤?
Or that thy sense shall ever meet

---

① *with the forward day*: 'as the day advances.'
② *with doubtful cheer*, etc.; *i.e.* watch the coming on of the trees and plants with pleasure or disappointment; *cheer* meant originally the face, and then the expression of the face — in which sense it is used once by Tennyson ('your cruel cheer') — and so the mood of the person which lies behind that expression. Cf. No. 11, l. 13.
③ *To clear*: sc. undertaken in order to clear; so with 'pick' and 'decree.'
④ *brother-kind*: 'akin by brotherhood'; cf. mankind.
⑤ *make court to thee*: 'attract thee.'

163. 濒死的园丁

塞威尔

是呀！园丁，时光如箭飞去，
你不是又在巡视你的小块土地，
一棵树，一棵树，神情不定①
观察着岁月的流逝，
当你的生命快要结束时，　　　　　　　　　　　5
会吹什么风？会降什么雨？

正午，你在园中徒劳，
扫除落叶，将蜗牛拾起，
然后随意宣判虫类的死罪，
但你是否比飞虫更有裨益？　　　　　　　　　　10
你同小虫是亲兄弟，
都是那样卑贱，粗俗，无知。

勤劳的可怜人！你是否希望看见
那毛茸茸的蜜桃，会向你致意？
或者，希望你能感到　　　　　　　　　　　　　15

---

① "神情不定"指注意着树木的生长，有时使人高兴，有时令人失望。——译者

The bean-flower's deep-embosom'd sweet[1]
Exhaling with an evening's blast[2]?
Thy evenings then will all past!

Thy narrow pride, thy fancied green[3]
(For vanity's in little seen[4]),
All must be left when Death appears,
In spite of wishes, groans, and tears;
Nor one of all thy plants that grow
But Rosemary will with thee go.

G. SEWELL.

---

[1] *sweet*: for 'sweetness,' sc. of scent.
[2] *Exhaling*: 'pouring out,' lit. breathing [itself] out.
[3] *Thy narrow pride*: the 'little spot' of which the owner felt so proud. *thy fancied green*: the plants and grass which so captivated his fancy.
[4] *vanity's in little seen*: 'is shown in little things.'

那豆花的酥胸的甜密,
随着晚间柔风而呼吸?
你所有的傍晚都会过去!

你狭隘的骄傲,幻想中的绿意
(虚荣是看不见的东西), 20
当死神来到时,全部要撇下,
谁管你的希冀、嗟叹和哭泣;
你的花木更无一株会成长,
只有一枝迷迭香将与你同栖①。

黄绍鑫 译

编注 乔治·塞威尔(George Sewell,? —1726),英国贫民作家,曾写过一幕悲剧和一些小册子。

---

① 迷迭香是一种芳香的常青灌木,旧时葬礼上常在灵柩前插上这种树枝。——译者

164. TO-MORROW

    In the downhill of life, when I find I'm declining,
        May my lot no less fortunate be
    Than a snug elbow-chair can afford for reclining,
        And a cot that o'erlooks the wide sea;
5   With an ambling pad-pony to pace o'er the lawn①,
        While I carol away idle sorrow,
    And blithe as the lark that each day hails the dawn
        Look forward with hope for to-morrow.

    With a porch at my door, both for shelter and shade too,
10   As the sunshine or rain may prevail;
    And a small spot of ground for the use of the spade too,
        With a barn for the use of the flail:
    A cow for my dairy, a dog for my game,
        And a purse when a friend wants to borrow;
15   I'll envy no nabob his riches or fame②,
        Nor what honours await him to-morrow.

    From the bleak northern blast may my cot be completely
        Secured by a neighbouring hill;
    And at night may repose steal upon me more sweetly
20   By the sound of a murmuring rill:

---

① *pad-pony*: 'an easy-paced pony.' A pad is (1) a road or path, (2) a horse for riding thereon.

② *nabob*: originally a Mohammedan official under the Mogul empire; afterwards used for a wealthy person who had made his fortune in India.

164. 明天

柯林斯

我发现我正在衰老,正在生活的下坡路上,
　　但愿我的命运像安乐椅那样舒畅,
它让人们安稳地倚躺,
　　或像一间能够俯瞰大海的小房;
我骑着小马在草坪漫步, 5
　　唱罢了心中悠悠的哀伤,
每天,我像快活的云雀欢迎黎明,
　　等到明天,满怀希望。

如果太阳或风雨肆虐,
　　我门口的走廊,既可避雨,又能乘凉; 10
有一小块土地可使用银锄,
　　还有一个可挥舞连枷的谷仓:
奶场有母羊,打猎有神犬,
　　钱包可以充实朋友的空囊,
我不羡慕富豪的财产和名声, 15
　　更不羡慕他所期待的荣光。

愿我的小屋凭峙邻近的小山
　　挡住北风呼啸,安然无恙,
愿小河潺潺的水声,
　　夜间传来,送我入梦乡; 20

And while peace and plenty I find at my board,
     With a heart free from sickness and sorrow,
With my friends may I share what to-day may afford,
     And let them spread the table to-morrow.

25   And when I at last must throw off this frail covering
     Which I've worn for three-score years and ten,
On the brink of the grave I'll not seek to keep hovering,
     Nor my thread wish to spin o'er again:
But my face in the glass I'll serenely survy,
30   And with smiles count each wrinkle and furrow;
As this old worn-out stuff, which is threadbare to-day,
     May become everlasting to-morrow.

J. COLLINS.

一颗心灵消除了疾病愁苦,
　　餐桌上也就能健饭安康,
但愿和友人分享我今天的供应,
　　让他们好为明天的饭桌另作铺张。

最后,我还须抛却这件 25
　　穿了七十年的破旧衣裳,
在坟墓边缘我不会继续盘桓,
　　我希望之线也不会再次织纺;
但我要静静地审视我镜中的容颜,
　　微笑地数数它每条皱纹的深长; 30
因为这件已经绽线的破旧衣衫,
　　也许会变成明天的永久希望。

黄绍鑫　译

编注　约翰·柯林斯(John Collins,1742?—1808),演员,于一八〇四年出版了他唯一的一部诗歌集。

165. 'LIFE! I KNOW NOT WHAT THOU ART'

Life! I know not what thou art,
But know that thou and I must part;
And when, or how, or where we met
I own to me 's a secret yet.

Life! we've been long together
Through pleasant and through cloudy weather;
'Tis hard to part when friends are dear —
Perhaps 'twill cost a sigh, a tear;
— Then steal away, give little warning,
Choose thine own time;
Say not Good Night, — but in some brighter clime
Bid me Good Morning.

A. L. BARBAULD.

165. "生命哟,我不清楚你的奥秘"

巴勃尔德夫人

生命哟,我不清楚你的奥秘,
但知道你我必将分离;
何时何地我俩怎样相逢,
这秘密依然在我心中。

生命哟,你与我长久相依, 5
同赏明媚春光,共沐凄风苦雨;
挚友分别,离情难断——
也许要付出眼泪和悲叹
——那就悄然而去吧,无须多言,
由你自己选择时机; 10
不用说再见,——但在更光明的境地
向我道一声早安。

陈凡 译

编注 安娜·利蒂希亚·巴勃尔德夫人(Anna Letitia Barbauld,1743—1825),英国女诗人。此诗是她一首题为《生命》的短诗的首尾两节,其余部分被《金库》原编者删去.